ABOUT TIME

THE UNAUTHORIZED GUIDE TO
DOCTOR WHO
EXPANDED 2ND EDITION

1970–1974

SEASONS 7 TO 11

TAT WOOD
with additional material by LAWRENCE MILES

Out Now from Mad Norwegian Press...

Time, Unincorporated 1: The Doctor Who Fanzine Archives (Lance Parkin)

More Digressions: A New Collection of "But I Digress" Columns
by Peter David, with an introduction by Harlan Ellison

Wanting to Believe: A Critical Guide to The X-Files, Millennium and The Lone Gunmen
by Robert Shearman

Coming Soon from Mad Norwegian Press...

Time, Unincorporated 2: The Doctor Who Fanzine Archives (Classic Series Cornucopia)
Time, Unincorporated 3: The Doctor Who Fanzine Archives (New Series Cornucopia)

Chicks Dig Time Lords

Fluid Links: The Unauthorized Guide to the Doctor Who Eighth Doctor Adventures
by Lars Pearson, Robert Smith?, Michael D. Thomas and Anthony Wilson

ANGELINK NOVEL SERIES
By Lyda Morehouse, winner of Philip K. Dick Award, Shamus Award,
and the Barnes and Noble "Maiden Voyage" Award.

Resurrection Code (all-new prequel)

Also Available from Mad Norwegian Press...

AHistory: An Unauthorized History of the Doctor Who Universe [Second Edition]
Doctor Who: The Completely Unofficial Encyclopedia
Dusted: The Unauthorized Guide to Buffy the Vampire Slayer
Now You Know: The Unauthorized Guide to G.I. Joe

THE ABOUT TIME SERIES
by Lawrence Miles and Tat Wood

About Time 1: The Unauthorized Guide to Doctor Who (Seasons 1 to 3)
About Time 2: The Unauthorized Guide to Doctor Who (Seasons 4 to 6)
About Time 4: The Unauthorized Guide to Doctor Who (Seasons 12 to 17)
About Time 5: The Unauthorized Guide to Doctor Who (Seasons 18 to 21)
About Time 6: The Unauthorized Guide to Doctor Who (Seasons 22 to 26, TVM)
About Time 7 (forthcoming)

Copyright © 2009 Mad Norwegian Press (www.madnorwegian.com)

Cover art by Steve Johnson; Jacket & interior design by Christa Dickson

ISBN: 978-0-9759446-7-7
Printed in Illinois. Second Edition: May 2009

table of contents

table of contents

Essays

how does this book work  ?

About Time prides itself on being the most comprehensive, wide-ranging and at times almost *shockingly* detailed handbook to *Doctor Who* that you might ever conceivably need, so great pains have been taken to make sure there's a place for everything and everything's in its place. Here are the "rules"…

Every *Doctor Who* story gets its own entry, and every entry is divided up into four major sections. The first, which includes the headings **Which One is This?**, **Firsts and Lasts** and **X Things to Notice**, is designed to provide an overview of the story for newcomers to the series (and we trust there are more of you, owing to the success of the Welsh series) or relatively "lightweight" fans who aren't too clued-up on a particular era of the programme's history. We might like to *pretend* that all *Doctor Who* viewers know all parts of the series equally well, but there are an awful lot of people who - for example - know the 70s episodes by heart and don't have a clue about the 60s. This section also acts as an overall Spotters' Guide to the series, pointing out most of the memorable bits.

After that comes the **Continuity** section, which is where you'll find all the pedantic detail. Here there are notes on the Doctor (personality, props and cryptic mentions of his past), the supporting cast, the TARDIS and any major Time Lords who might happen to wander into the story. Following these are the **Non-Humans** and **Planet Notes** sections, which can best be described as "high geekery"… we're old enough to remember the *Doctor Who Monster Book*, but not too old to want a more grown-up version of our own, so expect full-length monster profiles. Next comes **History**, which includes all available data about the time in which the story's supposed to be set.

Of crucial importance: note that throughout the **Continuity** section, *everything* you read is "true" - i.e. based on what's said or seen on-screen - except for sentences in square brackets [like this], where we cross-reference the data to other stories and make some suggestions as to how all of this is supposed to fit together. You can trust us absolutely on the non-bracketed material, but the bracketed sentences are often just speculation.

The only exception to this rule is the **Additional Sources** heading, which features any off-screen information from novelisations, writer interviews, etc that might shed light on the way the story's supposed to work. (Another thing to notice here: anything written in single inverted commas - 'like this' - is a word-for-word quote from the script or something printed on screen, whereas anything in double-quote marks "like this" isn't.)

The third major section is **Analysis**. It opens with **Where Does This Come From?**, and this may need explaining. For years there's been a tendency in fandom to assume that *Doctor Who* was an "escapist" series which very rarely tackled anything particularly topical, but with hindsight this is bunk. Throughout its history, the programme reflected, reacted to and sometimes openly *discussed* the trends and talking-points of the era, although it isn't always immediately obvious to the modern eye. (Everybody knows that "The Sun Makers" was supposed to be satirical, but how many people got the subtext of "Destiny of the Daleks"?). It's our job here to put each story into the context of the time in which it was made, to explain *why* the production team thought it might have been a good idea.

Up next is **Things That Don't Make Sense**, basically a run-down of the glitches and logical flaws in the story, some of them merely curious and some entirely ridiculous. Unlike a lot of TV guidebooks, here we don't dwell on minor details like shaky camera angles and actors treading on each others' cues - at least unless they're *chronically* noticeable - since these are trivial even by our standards. We're much more concerned with whacking great story loopholes or particularly grotesque breaches of the laws of physics.

Analysis ends with **Critique**; though no consensus will ever be found on *any* story, we've not only tried to provide a balanced (or at least not-too-irrational) view but also attempted to judge each story by its own standards, *not just* the standards of the post-CGI generation.

The last of the four sections is **The Facts**, which covers ordinary, straightforward details like cast lists and viewing figures. We've also provided a run-down of the story's cliffhangers, since a lot of *Doctor Who* fans grew up thinking of the cliffhangers as the programme's defining points.

how does this book work?

This gives you a much better sense of a story's structure than a long and involved plot breakdown (which we're fairly sure would interest nobody at this stage, barring perhaps those stories presently missing from the BBC archives).

The Lore is an addendum to the Facts section, which covers the off-screen anecdotes and factettes attached to the story. The word "Lore" seems fitting, since long-term fans will already know much of this material, but it needs to be included here (a) for new initiates and (b) because this is supposed to be a one-stop guide to the history of *Doctor Who*.

A lot of "issues" relating to the series are so big that they need forums all to themselves, which is why most story entries are followed by mini-essays. Here we've tried to answer all the questions that seem to demand answers, although the logic of these essays changes from case to case. Some of them are actually trying to find *definitive* answers, unravelling what's said in the TV stories and making sense of what the programme-makers had in mind. Some have more to do with the real world than the *Doctor Who* universe, and aim to explain why certain things about the series were so important at the time. Some are purely speculative, some delve into scientific theory and some are just whims, but they're *good* whims and they all seem to have a place here. Occasionally we've included footnotes on the names and events we've cited, for those who aren't old enough or British enough to follow all the references.

We should also mention the idea of "canon" here. Anybody who knows *Doctor Who* well, who's been exposed to the TV series, the novels, the comic-strips, the audio adventures and the trading-cards you used to get with Sky Ray ice-lollies, will know that there's always been some doubt about how much of *Doctor Who* counts as "real", as if the TV stories are in some way less made-up than the books or the short stories. We'll discuss this in shattering detail later on, but for now it's enough to say that *About Time* has its own specific rules about what's canonical and what isn't. In this book, we accept everything that's shown in the TV series to be the "truth" about the *Doctor Who* universe (although obviously we have to gloss over the parts where the actors fluff their

lines). Those non-TV stories which have made a serious attempt to become part of the canon, from Virgin Publishing's New Adventures to the recent audio adventures from Big Finish, aren't considered to be 100 percent "true" but do count as supporting evidence. Here they're treated as what historians call "secondary sources", not definitive enough to make us change our whole view of the way the *Doctor Who* universe works but helpful pointers if we're trying to solve any particularly fiddly continuity problems.

It's worth remembering that unlike (say) the stories written for the old *Dalek* annuals, the early Virgin novels were an honest attempt to carry on the *Doctor Who* tradition in the absence of the TV series, so it seems fair to use them to fill the gaps in the programme's folklore even if they're not exactly - so to speak - "fact".

You'll also notice that we've divided up this work according to "era", not according to Doctor. Since we're trying to tell the *story* of the series, both on- and off-screen, this makes sense. The actor playing the Main Man might be the only thing we care about when we're too young to know better, but anyone who's watched the episodes with hindsight will know that there's a vastly bigger stylistic leap between "The Horns of Nimon" and "The Leisure Hive" than there is between "Logopolis" and "Castrovalva". Volume IV covers the producerships of Philip Hinchcliffe and Graham Williams, two very distinct stories in themselves, and everything changes again - when Williams leaves the series, not when Tom Baker does - at the start of the 1980s.

There's a kind of logic here, just as there's a kind of logic to everything in this book. There's so much to *Doctor Who*, so much material to cover and so many ways to approach it, that there's a risk of our methods irritating our audience even if all the information's in the right places. So we need to be consistent, and we have been. As a result, we're confident that this is as solid a reference guide / critical study / monster book as you'll ever find. In the end, we hope you'll agree that the only realistic criticism is: "Haven't you told us *too* much here?"

And once we're finished, we can watch the *new* series and start the game all over again.

7.1: "Spearhead from Space"

(Serial AAA. Four Episodes, 3rd January - 24th January 1970.)

Which One is This? And Now In Colour! Shop dummies come to life and blow people up in bus queues; killer replicas lurk in Madame Tussauds. And, if *that* lot didn't send you behind the sofa, there's Jon Pertwee's nude scene.

Firsts and Lasts The first story of the 1970s, the beginning of the Doctor's exile on Earth (not to mention a whole slew of assaults on the Home Counties, usually at monthly intervals), the start of what's commonly referred to as "the UNIT era" and the debut of Jon Pertwee as the Third Doctor. Pertwee was considerably more famous (especially among the series' target audience) than his two predecessors, so for the first time, small children had proof that the series was "just pretending". (Indeed, unlike Hartnell and Troughton, Pertwee appeared as himself in public rather than in character - sometimes driving Chitty Chitty Bang Bang.[1])

In tone, "Spearhead from Space" is more markedly different from anything seen before - as close to a complete reboot as you can get. UNIT are rethought (after 6.3, "The Invasion"), and the Brigadier is deployed as a permanent "boss" for the Doctor, as signing him missions like various other acronymic agencies in ITC adventure series of the time. As a result, the Doctor finally makes the jump from "wandering scholar" to "adventure hero". Even the programme's change of format - from a series about an old man who travels through space and time, to a series about an alien who defends the Earth from less benign aliens - fits the action-serial format. (Soon enough, Our Hero will be dressing like Jason King[2], and using martial arts on various henchmen.) There's a more overt love of gadgetry, so the Third Doctor spontaneously acquires a Bond-style homing beacon wristwatch.

Manifestly, this is the first story made in colour, although this transition mattered less to the viewers than it did to the BBC's overseas marketing department (although not in the ways you'd expect - see **The Lore**). Henceforth, the technical opportunities that colour opens up will be

Season 7 Cast/Crew

- Jon Pertwee (the Doctor)
- Caroline John (Liz Shaw)
- Nicholas Courtney (Brigadier Lethbridge-Stewart)
- John Levene (Sergeant Benton)

- Barry Letts (Producer)
- Terrance Dicks (Script Editor)

explored enthusiastically, if not always wisely (see 7.2, "Doctor Who and the Silurians"). Making the shift seem even greater, "Spearhead from Space" is the *only* story in the classic (sorry) series to be shot completely on film, instead of video with occasional filmed inserts, giving it the look of an ITC adventure show, albeit one with a lot less beige. (Film, with its different texture, has a way of making you think that Roger Moore or Tony Curtis are going to turn up at any moment. Despite this risk, the BBC Wales series is processed in post-production to give it a uniform film-like sheen but the result is noticeably different from real film. See **Did *Doctor Who* Really End in 1969?** under 6.7, "The War Games" and **Which Is Better: Film or Video?** under 12.3, "The Sontaran Experiment".)

Capping off this transition, the episode's begin and end with a new lurid Op art sequence. The credits are delivered as a series of slides rather than a scroll (whereas the 60s *opening* titles were like nothing else on television, the black and white end-graphics had been a legacy of the 1950s) - although even here, the emphasis on colour means that the credit-text is occasionally yellow rather than white, and has its own typeface. The title "Spearhead from Space" zooms in toward the viewer - this experiment isn't repeated, but it's characteristic of the title-tinkering that goes on in Season Seven (see especially 7.3, "The Ambassadors of Death"). We get our first colour monster in Episode Four - and to nobody's great surprise, it's green.

On a more prosaic level, this story also sees the first appearance of Liz Shaw (who instigates the tradition of the Doctor having a single female companion or "assistant", as they start calling them) and the Autons. First appearances of two guest actors we're going to see a lot in the years to come: John Woodnutt (see 10.3, "Frontier in Space", etc.) and Prentis Hancock (see 10.4, "Planet of the Daleks", etc.). Turning up surprisingly late in the series' history, this is the first time we're told that the Doctor has two hearts (see **When Did The Doctor Get A Second Heart?** under 6.1, "The Dominators"). It's the first use of the words "dimensionally transcendental" and "dematerialisation code", and the first time the Doctor himself selects the name "Dr John Smith" [see 4.9, "The Evil of the Daleks" and 5.7, "The Wheel in Space"].

When "Spearhead from Space" was repeated it on Friday evenings eighteen months after its initial broadcast, it became the first story *not* to be shown on Saturdays. And...(sob)... it's the very last sighting of the Freezer Machine prop from "The Space Museum", which (as you'll doubtless recall from Volumes I and II) was the BBC's all-purpose "space" prop for the 1960s. Appropriately, it's here seen in the Doctor's new lab, and takes its curtain-call four and a half minutes into episode three.

Four Things to Notice
About "Spearhead from Space"

1. The moment when the shop window dummies come to life in episode four and begin the mass slaughter of bystanders in an English suburban high street is one of the most famously scary sequences in the entire run of *Doctor Who*. Everybody who grew up in the 60s or 70s remembers seeing this, although curiously not everybody can remember *where* they saw it, and often misremember it as *The Avengers* or something else on the other channel.

Look out, though, for the moment when the Autons smash their way through the shop window - that's right, they don't show the actual window-breaking but instead cut away to a bobby's reaction upon his being confronted by menacing mannequins. (Curiously, PC Plod seems to be on a tea-break with a GPO engineer, rather than on patrol as he ought to be.) One might almost surmise that the wholesale plundering of this story's iconography for the big relaunch with X1.1, "Rose", in 2005 was merely a pretext for gloating that BBC Wales could afford fake glass.

2. After an all-action debut in "The Invasion", complete with a base inside a Hercules transporter plane, UNIT settles down to be the rather low-rent World Army we're going to see from now on. Accordingly, Liz Shaw is escorted to a secret base

under St Pancras station, but the lab she and the Doctor use is apparently part of the same car park, only screened off and filled with bottles of frothy stuff. (Perhaps they have to crack the secret formula of Diet Pepsi as a money-spinning sideline?) The comparison with the BBC Wales UNIT or even the preposterously well-funded Torchwood from Series Two is heartbreaking. Still, at least the Brig himself has an office - even though he hardly uses it and spends most of his time hanging around in the Doctor's lab. As offices of Top Secret military agencies go, the Brig's office is rather cosy (he even has a box file behind his head with a big red X on it - surely not *the* X-Files?), but it's at the end of a corridor made of breeze-blocks and lined with drainage pipes. Did it used to be the toilets?

3. Sam Seeley - the poacher who comes across a Nestene energy unit, and squirrels it away in his truck - is the first of a new kind of character we'll see a lot in the Pertwee stories: the comedy yokel. This being a Bob Holmes script, the comedy - such as it is - comes from a crafty man on the make, and his distrustful wife assuming the worst when he acts secretively. Couple this with the fact that Seeley's accent is very wrong indeed (for a story that's supposedly happening in Essex) and he instigates a long and dishonourable sequence of what we'll be calling "Pigbin" figures (as Pigbin Josh, from 8.3, "The Claws of Axos" is by far the most egregious example). Seeley, at least, speaks something recognisably like real people - using consonants and everything - but it sets an unfortunate precedent. Of course, he's not the *only* crafty man on the make, as Mullins the Porter (who phones the tabloids to blab about the Doctor's weird blood) also makes trouble, but technically isn't a comedy yokel. He's a comedy Welshman, which is a different thing entirely (see **Why Didn't Plaid Cymru Lynch Barry Letts?** under 10.5, "The Green Death").

4. Observe Jon Pertwee's shameless gurning as he's strangled by the rubber Nestene tentacle, as if he's already realised what a strange way this is to make a living. What's more, this was a remount because the first attempt looked worse. Five more years of this ahead, people.

The Continuity

The Doctor The Doctor collapses as soon as he reaches Earth [immediately after his regeneration, it seems], and for the first few hours his behav-

When are the UNIT Stories set?

In "The Sontaran Stratagem" (X4.4), they try to make a joke of this topic, with the Tennant Doctor seemingly unsure if his former self worked for UNIT in the 70s or 80s. And it's *still* a touchy subject: in the whole of *Doctor Who* fandom, there's no single question as contentious as this. The reason's simple. To answer it, you have to make a choice between the intentions of the production team in the late 60s and the actual statements made by the series in the early 80s, a choice which comes with a built-in generation gap.

Nobody doubts that when Derrick Sherwin and Kit Pedler first conceived UNIT, the plan was for the new Earth-bound stories to take place in the near-future rather than the present. The *Radio Times* write-ups and BBC continuity announcements for 1968's "The Invasion", acting on information received from the production office, state that the story takes place in 1975 (although it's important to remember that the actual story never states this[5]). The Target novelisation of "Invasion of the Dinosaurs" - re-titled, with usual Target panache, *Doctor Who and the Dinosaur Invasion* - baldly states that it's 1977, meaning that the Doctor's had a remarkably busy two years.

But 1977 is also the date for the unimpeachably canonical "Mawdryn Undead" (20.3), made in 1983, in which the Brigadier has been retired from UNIT for at least a year. This is a fact. There's no ambiguity, no room for manoeuvre. When Sarah Jane claims that she comes from '1980' in "Pyramids of Mars" (13.3), she *might* at least be approximating. Moreover, Sarah may have told a gobsmacked Laurence Scarman she was 'from 1980', but when Christmas 1981 came around, it turned out that she'd been back in her own time for at least three years. (Here we're thinking of 18.7A, "K9 And Company" - sorry, we can't wish that one away, as there's a whole spin-off series now.)

But in "Mawdryn Undead" the date is used, clearly and explicitly, over and over and over again. The story's even set against the backdrop of the Queen's Silver Jubilee, and thus the UNIT episodes are finally tied to a proper calendar. (It's not hard to see how the 80s production team ended up doing this. By the time "Mawdryn Undead" was made, the UNIT stories were seen as a distinctly early-70s phenomenon, and the fact that they were originally meant to be a little more futuristic was no longer remotely relevant. The 80s programme-makers just assumed the stories were always supposed to be contemporary.)

It's worth remembering that in the eyes of many of the public, the closest thing to *Doctor Who* was *Doomwatch*. The series existed to scare the viewers about what was happening behind closed doors, and the publicity for it made a lot of play about the factual basis of all the scripts. *Doomwatch* was supposedly right out of the scientific journals, but had scripts about stolen atomic bombs, British astronauts and (oh, yes) cross-bred human-chicken monsters. The "not-too-far-into-the-future" aspects of this were offset by topical material in the dialogue, and characters wearing achingly fashionable clothes. It was a game, as was the relationship between *Doctor Who*'s fantasy touches and matter-of-fact normality.

At the time of broadcast, only the really rabidly attentive regular *Doctor Who* viewer (remember: no "fans" as such existed yet) would log all the "futuristic" touches and try to work out how far in the future the UNIT stories were set. Casual viewers would see them as throwaway touches of storytelling contrivance, much in the way that Columbo's wife is always a fan of the murderer. That is, provided they noticed them at all. It comes down to whether you assume that the world in which the stories happen is some fantasy-land (what American fans like to call "The Whoniverse") or, like the viewers in 70s Britain, that it happens in our world but with a few names changed and some details altered.

The fact is, Season Seven is no more "futuristic" than any of the ITC action serials of the time. In fact, you could reasonably argue that of the classic series' entire run, only "The Invasion", "The Ambassadors of Death" "The Android Invasion" and "Battlefield" were deliberately conceived of as near-future stories, and that by 1970, the writers were already starting to forget these stories *weren't* supposed to be in the present day. "The Invasion" entails a world where computers (programmed in ALGOL) can answer the phone, but in "Terror of the Autons", it's rare for people to sit close enough to a transistor radio for the signal to unexpectedly activate killer plastic flowers.

For that matter, Season Eight capitalises on the immediacy of the setting and the topical nature of the scripts. Other than the British space programme - and the blatantly absurd technology which seems to be an inevitable part of any family SF series (e.g. the Mad Professor with Pet Monster in "Robot" or the colour videoscreens in

continued on page 11...

iour's erratic, with selective amnesia. The extent of his memory-block is unclear - he seems to have a deliberate "firewall" around matters connected to the TARDIS later on, but he immediately recognises the Brigadier and he's never much in doubt about his own identity. [Almost all subsequent stories have his memory back almost unaffected, save for his ability to recall the formula for time travel (8.3, "The Claws of Axos"; 10.1, "The Three Doctors"). He is, for instance, able to recount his trial to Jo in "Frontier in Space".] He's hazy on events after arriving on Earth and collapses in a field - understandably, as he's comatose for most of it.

What is a surprise, not least to the Doctor himself, is that he remembers details about the planet Delphon. [This is usually interpreted as the Doctor finding a chink in the "barriers" on his memory, but in the light of his later conduct, it's potentially the first sign that he can "download" information about places and species that he hasn't encountered. A cut scene in 8.5, "The Daemons", at least, indicates that the production team thought it was the latter. For more, see 2.5, "The Web Planet"; X1.5, "World War Three"; **Did Doctor Who End in 1969?** and - for a possible explanation - 15.2, "The Invisible Enemy".] He's initially not happy with his new face and hair, then thinks it looks distinctive.

It's established that the Doctor has two hearts, and his blood - when analysed - doesn't seem to be human [cf. *The TV Movie*, in which his blood doesn't appear to be real blood of any kind]. He can apparently put himself in a coma, during which an EEG scan shows no brain activity. [This follows his being shot in the head from very close range - Dr Henderson claims this only caused 'a slight burn on the scalp', but perhaps the coma is a function of the "first fifteen hours after a regeneration" get-out-of-jail card played in X2.0, "The Christmas Invasion". If that story's *deus ex machina* is to be believed, the Doctor could have been beheaded and recovered soon after.] The Doctor's pulse, when awake but in bed, is ten a minute. [Compare this with it being '170' in 7.4, "Inferno."] Dr Henderson never gets to take his blood pressure.

When the new Doctor arrives on Earth, he's dressed in clothes that look a lot like his predecessor's - even though the jacket nearly fits, and the Second Doctor was obviously less broad in the shoulder. [It's probably the same costume, as the

knee is cut, as it was in "The War Games".] Somehow, his shoes have become the obvious hiding place for the TARDIS key [see also 12.1,"Robot"].

The Third Doctor's personality is already fully-formed within hours of emerging from TARDIS, and he presents himself as an over-extravagant scientist / adventurer, calling the Brigadier 'my dear fellow' as soon as he regains consciousness. [Here, as in later regeneration stories, there's the implication that the Doctor's new personality is shaped by the first things he sees and hears once he starts to recover. The Third Doctor's "dandy" look is established when he steals some clothing from a hospital visitor, and he's so enamoured by the car he "borrows" that he eventually gets his own, Bessie ("Doctor Who and the Silurians"). Indeed, this seems to explain why the Third Doctor was so inclined towards vehicles in general. Neither of his previous incarnations seemed passionate about them. (Season Five sees him constantly trying to learn to pilot a helicopter, but more out of curiosity than anything else.)]

He has a stylised cobra tattooed on his right forearm. [This is sometimes mistaken for a mermaid, and is seen just once more, in "Doctor Who and the Silurians". *The Discontinuity Guide* suggested this is a Time Lord criminal brand, something that's exploited in *The New Adventures* but nowhere on screen.] He's a competent driver.

• *Ethics*. The Third Doctor is happy to lie, to steal and to manipulate Liz Shaw in order to get the TARDIS key. Right from the start he makes his freedom in the TARDIS of prime importance, so much so that he's willing to leave Earth even when he knows there's a potential alien threat on the planet. [It could be argued that he's just testing to see if the Ship really *has* been disabled, although it was said at his trial in "The War Games" that 'The secret (of the TARDIS)... will be taken from you'. So he can't be in doubt that the rest of the sentence was carried out; see also "Inferno"]

• *Inventory*: The Doctor wears a wrist watch which homes in on the TARDIS. [It's never seen before or since (although clunkier homing devices turn up in 18.3, "Full Circle", etc.). The Second Doctor apparently didn't own the wrist watch, and it's perhaps evidence that a series of unseen adventures occurred between Seasons Six and Seven: see "The War Games" and **Is There A Season 6B?** under 22.4, "The Two Doctors".] He carries firecrackers for lock-picking, wears a gold

When are the UNIT Stories set?

...continued from page 9

all the public buildings) - there's little to suggest that the writers thought of themselves as churning out anything but contemporary adventure stories. At least one achingly modish and fashion-conscious show of the same period was using CSO to fake TV screens. (We're going to mention *The Goodies* a lot, so if you don't know about it, just accept that from 1970 to 1979, the BBC Visual Effects team was flat-out on two high-profile family shows. *The Goodies* had a bigger budget per episode, as a comparison between *Kitten Kong* and 11.2, "Invasion of the Dinosaurs" makes amply clear.)

Granted, Sarah's 'I'm from 1980' line caused a lot of viewers in 1975 Britain to shout 'Uh?' at the screen, but as much as anything else, this was because the public, by Tom Baker's second year, had pretty much bought the idea of UNIT as almost exactly contemporary. Tales like "The Daemons" (8.5) had been set in a present day that was fast receding. We all forgot about the mention of BBC3, and only remembered the trousers and haircuts. (We have to stress yet again, for overseas readers and those born too late: in a small island with a lot of people, and national broadcasters making sure we all knew the latest trends, fashions changed a lot faster and are more rigorously documented. Any film or TV episode made in Britain between 1956 and 1995 can be dated to within three months by the trained eye; from the twenty years after 1964, you can do it to almost the week.) Even without hindsight, these things made UNIT stories appear contemporary.

Cumulatively, the constant stream of such details outweighs any effort at futurism. There's a fictitious BBC3 in "The Daemons", but it shows 1971 rugby matches with Bill McLaren commentating, and it uses the same stock music as BBC1 and 2 when transmission is interrupted. The various regional police forces changed their cars twice in this period, going from the Jags with bells (or sirens in cities) to so-called "panda-cars" (see 11.5, "Planet of the Spiders") and then the "jam sandwich" vehicles with the reflective orange stripes (25.3, "Silver Nemesis"). These changes were around 1971-2 and then 1975-6, and were announced ahead of time in the media. Ambulances had similar make-overs, so "The Hand of Fear" is easily datable as pre-1978, even without those dungarees or the tax-disc in Dr Carter's Austin.

The point is this: had Sarah *really* been from 1980 in Season Thirteen, she would never have worn the denim outfit with the cork wedgies she donned in the previous story (13.2, "Planet of Evil"). And if she was expecting to return to London five minutes before leaving Loch Ness in "Terror of the Zygons," she would have hidden that terribly-trendy-for-1975 watchstrap, unless she was expecting to be home around the time Lord Toffingham ice-lollies came out (an eighteen-month period with that story's transmission date slap in the centre). Thanks to "K9 and Company," we know how she dressed in 1981 - meaning exactly right for that year and that job - so she can't have lost her dress-sense when hanging around with a wide-eyed bohemian alien. This might all seem trivial, but casual viewers would have commented upon trivia such as this, and it would've stuck in the memory. Indeed, some of those casual viewers actually wrote the later episodes; the rest (twelve million of them, as opposed to a few thousand paid-up fans) would need a very good reason to adjust their memories of old stories and accept weird dates like 1979 for "The Invasion" and 1983 for "The Time Monster".

And even if you *were* paying attention, there's a huge anomaly: "The Ambassadors of Death" causes headaches partly by being completely out of keeping with everything around it, and also in having a sort-of sequel, "The Android Invasion", that reinforces the awkwardly-advanced British Space Programme that the adventures after "Ambassadors" seemed to contradict. Worse, the Space Programme is said to involve Sarah Jane. That's the same Sarah Jane who, in her own series - "Warriors of Kudlak" episode two - says that the first manned Mars landing on Mars still hasn't happened by 2008. Similarly, the diligent attempts in "The Android Invasion" to make Devesham seem present-day outweigh the Space Centre's attempted futurism. (The most advanced piece of which is the sliding doors - the circuit the Doctor draws is pretty simplistic even for 1975.)

This is all our way of saying: though the space-age Britain seen in Season Seven is clearly ahead of the "real" Britain in the early 70s, it's massively ahead of Britain in the *late* 70s as well. That being the case, trying to match that the rocket programme seen in "Ambassadors" against real-world history - and thereby claim that it *must* be the future - is something of an act of futility. It's just

continued on page 13...

ring on his right little finger and has a bracelet on that wrist.

The Doctor says that he has no use for money. [Some have interpreted this to mean that he's independently wealthy, or that the TARDIS has an unlimited cash ATM, although as stated it just means that it's not important to him. Either way, even the disabled TARDIS - presumably - can provide his material needs.]

• *Background.* Here he describes himself as a doctor of 'practically everything'. [cf. 5.4, "Enemy Of The World"; 6.5, "Seeds of Death"; 3.6, "The Ark"; et al.] Rather pleasingly, he doesn't break the habit of two lifetimes and start talking about his home planet, his people or how old he really is just yet. [This comes as a surprise to those of us raised on the novelisation of this story - "Doctor Who and the Auton Invasion" - but in fact, the words "Time Lord" aren't used during Pertwee's whole first year.]

The Supporting Cast

• *Liz Shaw.* Here introduced as a wry, intelligent, rather relaxed woman in her twenties - self-confident without being aggressive, and having no time for UNIT's cloak-and-dagger methods. [She is, in fact, much closer to being a true "feminist" companion than any of the later ones who actually declare themselves as such.]

TThe Brigadier says that Liz had degrees in 'medicine, physics and a dozen other subjects'. [We can't take this at face value, and have to presume that he's just generalizing to acknowledge that Liz is clever. Even if she were a child prodigy, and allowing for maximum overlap of study, she's just not old enough to have completed that many courses (the medical degree alone would take five years). Besides, it's bizarre to think that she's achieved fourteen courses to degree / Masters level, yet doesn't have a PhD.

[Working from the Brigadier's comments, it's possible to salvage two hypothetical career paths for Liz. As she was at Cambridge in the 1960s, it's possible she had a combined honours course in Natural Sciences (which would encompass physics and chemistry), then transferred to a medical degree with the honours course counting as a part of it. If her intended field of research was something like NMR scanners or advanced prosthesis - in other words, something combining electronics and biology - then most of what she does in her on-screen tenure would have been

covered.

[Despite Liz's proficiency with a hypodermic, however, she doesn't seem to have actually *practiced* medicine. So this hypothetical postgraduate course might have allowed her to be a known face around colleges, and thus familiar to Professor Lennox (7.3, "The Ambassadors of Death"), without her actually completing a research fellowship. If she began her degree at eighteen, she might've only been twenty-six on completion of this triple-decker course, allowing for a year-long detour into military support for a number of high-profile Government research programmes. The question still remains as to why the Brigadier selected her over anyone more experienced with extra-terrestial threats or exotic biohazards, but if he's only got the one position open, he might've opted for an all-rounder.

[Alternatively, the fact that Liz is addressed as 'Miss Shaw' might indicate that she became a consultant surgeon very young. As "surgery" was originally something done by the local barber between haircuts, "proper" doctors sought to differentiate between themselves and bonecutters. Thus, it's a quirk of the British medical system that surgeons are called "mister" rather than "doctor"; it's a promotion rather than an insult. The only snag is that you need to spend several years as a junior surgeon (a mere "doctor") to become a consultant. Liz could have done five years of med school and another three training in surgery, then three more on top of that to get back to being 'Miss Shaw' — but alas, this doesn't really allow her time to (forgive the phrase) bone up on all the other fields in which she's proficient. Basically, this scenario would make her a vital part of some hospital's staff, not the kind of person who is whisked away at short notice to run spectrographic analyses on bits of plastic. And it would again force us to ask: why should a young consultant surgeon be the kind of person the Brigadier wants to help him defend Earth from the scum of the galaxy?]

Liz is also an expert on meteorites and has a research programme of some description at Cambridge. UNIT originally hires her as a form of scientific adviser, much like the Doctor himself; it's not a job she particularly wants, although she doesn't seem to mind the Doctor commandeering her as his assistant.

Her suit has a jacket with plastic panels that look like giant-sized bubble-wrap. [This may have been designed to look "futuristic", but these days,

When are the UNIT Stories set?

...continued from page 11

not going to fit, so there's no real point in trying. And please, let's not evoke any piffle about the Time War changing everything, while (it would seem) leaving Dickens' biographical details unaltered (X1.3, "The Unquiet Dead").

For that matter, it's obvious that adventures made in 1975 and 2005 are, unless otherwise stated, part of the same chronology. The 2006 episode 'School Reunion' and the spin-off *Sarah Jane Adventures* serve to reinforce this. Amongst other things, Sarah reminisces with the Tenth Doctor about events thirty-odd years before Christmas 2007. Nevertheless, show "Ambassadors" to a newcomer today, and that person will probably note Liz's s boots, skirt and hat and the cars, and then the music. Only if you *prompt* them will anyone comment on the fact that the story supposes Britain has been landing men on Mars for years in what is obviously, screamingly, 1970.

Bigger events help date these stories, two of which need more discussion. One gets a whole essay later in this book (**Was 1973 The *Annus Mirabilis?*** under 10.2, "Carnival of Monsters" elaborates on the full impact of the Yom Kippur War, but note the sudden topicality of "Terror of the Zygons" and the idea that a Scots laird might be a major player in Europe's energy plans). The other can genuinely be described as epoch-making: decimalisation is a key event in British culture and 15th of February, 1971, marks a *latest* possible date for any stories that mention old money. All prices were in both systems for at least eighteen months beforehand, with the one in bigger lettering being the Roman-derived "LSD" (pounds, shilling and pence - we'd been using the same system for nearly two thousand years, so it really *was* a wrench to change) until the 71 event (labelled, inevitably, "D-Day"). Harold Wilson's government announced the change in 1968, and if anything you'd expect that the regime that staged manned Mars probes and sanctioned BBC3 might have done it a bit earlier. In "An Unearthly Child" (1.1), Susan thinks it's going to happen sooner - this *might* be significant, but not as much as Barbara and the rest of the class finding the idea ridiculous. Note that pre-decimal price-tags are still used in the shops in "Spearhead", suggesting 1970 at the latest. Similarly, Mao Tse-Tung's death in 1976 came rather later than many in the West expected, so the projected date of "The Mind of Evil" (8.2) - which cites him as alive - can't have been much

later than the broadcast one.

So, we have a timetable. The first UNIT-age story (5.5, "The Web of Fear") takes place in 1968, the same year it was broadcast. "The Invasion" takes place a bit later and the stories from "Spearhead from Space" to "Terror of the Zygons" take us from late 1970 to 1976. (This assumes, on the evidence on screen, that the Brigadier was rounding up when he described "The Invasion" as taking place four years after "The Web of Fear" - but that's as much leeway as you've got.)

And yet, sometimes even the most exacting and obsessive *Doctor Who* fans are unwilling to swallow this early-70s version of UNIT. Why? Perhaps because so many of them grew up thinking of the UNIT era as representing a shiny new near-future Britain that with hindsight, they can't think of it any other way, even though the near-future in question is now several decades in the past. Certainly, it's interesting that there don't seem to be many "late-70s UNIT" supporters among fans born after 1970. *The New Adventures* writers, many of whom roughly belonged to this camp, by and large treated the UNIT stories as being set at time of broadcast. (The UNIT-related novel *No Future* doesn't make any sense unless you stick with the early-70s dating; arguably, not even then.) Or to pick another example, in the foreword to his novel *The Face of the Enemy*, David A. McIntee refutes the blatant "Mawdryn Undead" dating and claims that it doesn't count because the Doctor was in the middle of a warp ellipse at the time (well, that explains everything).

Attempts to resolve this quickly turn into rather territorial conflicts as Fan A and Fan B's pet theories. Some fans will ignore even the biggest and most obvious facts - if we can legitimately use the word "facts" here - simply to back up their own "golden age" view of the programme's history. It is, if you will, like the *Doctor Who* version of creationism. Attempts to justify any systematised account on logic alone are perhaps a bit disingenuous; it's more about aesthetics.

We should ask a simple question here, and leave it at that. Given what we know about the *Doctor Who* universe, is there any real reason that the UNIT stories *shouldn't* be set in the early '70s? Is there any real reason that the "hard" evidence should be ignored, just to make a point about the intentions of the production team in the late '60s? Is there anything in the televised UNIT stories

continued on page 15...

it simply suggests she has a friend who's a fashion designer. This is somewhat in character, especially as every other woman (except Mrs Seeley) is dressed as if it's 1969.]

• *UNIT.* The Brigadier believes it's UNIT's mandate to investigate 'the odd, the unexplained'. [As opposed to just alien activity. This is a bit of an open-ended mandate, and one wonders if there's a UNIT file on *every* mystery or weird item, such as what the lyrics of "American Pie" actually mean, Jimmy Hoffa's disappearance, why Steve Martin is still allowed to make films and why one can only ever find odd socks.]

The official line seems to be that Earth is more likely to be attacked now that humanity's sending probes out into space and drawing attention to itself. [In fact, of all the alien crises during the UNIT era, only "Spearhead from Space", "The Ambassadors of Death", and "The Android Invasion" (13.4) could feasibly have been directly caused by space missions. However, X3.13, "Last of the Time Lords" indicates that Earth's technological and social status is monitored, with passing spaceships being given traffic reports. Perhaps pre-spaceflight societies are under an embargo: this could simply mean that the moon landing got humanity marked up a grade on the cosmic social network and Earth is now no longer off-limits to hostile takeover bids. How the Brigadier could *know* all of this, however, is another matter.]

The Brigadier tells Liz that two alien attacks have occurred on Earth since UNIT was formed. [As far as we know, UNIT wasn't in existence during the Yeti incident in "The Web of Fear" (5.5) - although the dates we have for that story make the 1968 treaty (X3.12, "The Sound of Drums") plausibly just ahead of the fungal assault on the Tube - but the group was definitely around during "The Invasion". Most likely, the Brigadier is just simplifying for Liz's benefit, since he says that the Doctor was involved in both.

[Then again, he immediately makes the connection between the Doctor and the mysteriously-appearing police box even though he's never seen the TARDIS before. Perhaps he's heard about it from second-hand sources, *or* there's a "missing" UNIT story / a similarly hushed-up alien incursion that UNIT didn't have anything to do with, but knows about. It's tempting to invoke Torchwood at this juncture (see the essay with 9.3, "The Sea Devils"). Oddly, Pertwee seems to have re-dubbed the offending line - the Brigadier

is shot from behind, the pitch of his voice goes up and he lisps slightly. Perhaps the production team was correcting something which, technically speaking, wasn't a mistake.]

UNIT has its own tracking station, and its commanding officer is female. She's addressed as 'Ma'am' [unlike Brigadier Bambera in 26.1,"Battlefield"]. She has a skirt in the regulation colour (taupe, a sort of mushroomy beige) and the UNIT badge on her tie, upside down. The blokes present have red detailing on the jackets and gold ties. This story's "Sector Five" is designated as the area that the Nestene meteorites land, being somewhere that includes Epping Forest (the woodland around and partially inside East London and South Essex). The Brigadier takes orders from Major-General Scobie (who's regular army rather than UNIT), and can usually call on support platoons as well as his headquarters staff.

The Brig has no qualms about facing the press, so UNIT is a well-known organisation by this stage. [See also 8.1, "Terror of the Autons"; 10.1, "The Three Doctors" and a lot of other stories that debunk the idea of UNIT as a "covert" organization.] The reporter Wagstaffe knows the Brig by name and on sight.

UNIT HQ seems to have a vending machine rather than a canteen.

• *The Brigadier.* When trying to convince Liz Shaw that there's a possible threat from outer space, it's the Brigadier who's the open-minded one. [He's something of a Mulder to her Scully - this is a severe contrast to his behaviour in some later stories.] He finds it remarkably easy to accept that the new Doctor *is* the Doctor.

The Brig's second-in-command is Captain Jimmy Munro [he seems to have been written as the same character as Captain Jimmy Turner in "The Invasion"], who is on attachment from the regular army. A "Hawkins" is given charge of the meteorite fragments [see the next story for why people's ears prick up upon hearing this]. The Brig has a black Rover staff car with diplomatic markings and a pennant.

The TARDIS The Ship arrives on Earth in the same area as the Nestene meteorites. [This is either another remarkable coincidence, or the Time Lords deliberately set the Doctor down close to the first Earth-bound crisis of the era. Given the Time Lord President's knowledge of UNIT (10.1, "The Three Doctors"), the Doctor might have been

When are the UNIT Stories set?

...continued from page 13

which makes it impossible, or even difficult, to accept that those stories might be set as early as 1970?

Other than Sarah Jane's comment in "Pyramids of Mars", the answer would seem to be "no". Despite the best efforts of many fan-writers, it really isn't worth trying to exactly match political events in the UNIT world to our own. Yes, the Prime Minister is female in "Terror of the Zygons", but it's silly to assume that it must be Margaret Thatcher, when the previous Prime Minister in "The Green Death" clearly isn't James Callaghan. Paul Cornell's suggestion in *No Future*, that it's actually Shirley Williams, is at least a lot more entertaining. Since the PM in "The Green Death" is called "Jeremy", and seems inspired by that other great B-list 70s politician Jeremy Thorpe, this makes a kind of sense (see **Who's Running the Country?** under 10.5, "The Green Death"). And if you need further proof,

when Barry Letts wrote his UNIT-era novel *The Ghosts of N-Space* (1996), he chose to set it in 1975 rather than 1980. Since Letts is the man who had his hands on the steering-wheel throughout the UNIT era, who are we to argue? Even if you don't consider *Ghosts* as 100% canonical, it tells you a lot about the attitudes of the people who were there at the time.

The hardcore UNIT stories are, on the whole, quite at home in the years 1970 - 76. There's simply no reason to move them, again. A lot of people are (or were) sentimentally attached to the idea of UNIT as being in "the future", even though we're now a long time after that supposed period. For them, the fact that Mondas didn't appear in December 1986 is a big worry (4.2, "The Tenth Planet"), just as they'll now have to deal with the lack of any 'Vote Saxon' signs on our streets.

For a more detailed chronology, see **What's the UNIT Timeline?** under "The Daemons" (8.5).

---

dropped somewhere that has the Brigadier's boys nearby to avoid Torchwood complications: see the essay with "The Sea Devils"]. The Doctor describes the TARDIS as being "dimensionally transcendental".

The Ship is currently incapable of dematerialising, as the Time Lords have changed the dematerialisation code [q.v. "Terror of the Autons" but see also "The Three Doctors"]. The TARDIS key only works for the Doctor, not the Brigadier, as it has a metabolism detector [something that's evidently been turned off by 11.3, "Death to the Daleks", when the Doctor can lend his key to anyone he likes]. The Doctor says his Ship contains an 'entire laboratory'.

The Non-Humans

• *The Nestenes*. A collective consciousness, moving from world to world as a form of energy and creating a suitable physical shell for itself on arrival, the Nestene intelligence acts as a single "brain" even though Channing - its mouthpiece - refers to himself as 'the Nestenes'. It first comes to Earth in 'five or six' hollow plastic meteorites. Six months later, around fifty more enter the atmosphere through a funnel of thin superheated air, including an all-important 'swarm leader'. The energy units then send out a signal, enabling the Autons to detect them for collection [presumably the energy from the original five or six meteorites

controlled the minds of the humans who found them, in order to set up the Auton construction process].

The 'meteorites' are bulbous, translucent, not quite spherical, have a pinkish glow and emit a vibrato chiming sound. [This is muffled when the energy unit is placed inside something else, so we assume that it's not dramatic license and people can actually hear it.] The meteorite energy is stored inside an environment tank, where it begins to take shape as a squiddy thing with green tentacles [the original cover for the novelisation renders this as an octopus], something that's ideal for Earth even though it's not the Nestenes' natural form. The spheres go blue when "downloading" into this environment tank, or when the Doctor analyses one. The Nestenes seem to believe that all energy is a form of life, and they have 'no individual identity'.

Curiously, when Hibbert asks what the Nestenes' final form will look like, Channing replies, 'I cannot tell you, yet'. He also says he, 'merely provided an environment tank in which the energy units can create the ultimate life form'. [Does Channing *seriously* not know what the final form of the Nestenes - the being of whose collective intelligence he partakes - will look like? It's possible that the Nestenes manifest differently according to each target planet (by comparison, see X1.01, "Rose"). "Terror of the Autons" begins the widely-held notion that the Nestene are some form of octopi.]

Nestenes seem able to control human beings' thoughts, apparently through telepathy. Compared to most disembodied psychic entities, the Nestenes seem very reluctant to manipulate anyone's minds - Channing can control the factory's managing director, Hibbert [although this seems to require line-of-sight contact to maintain its potency], but brute force is required to deal with obstacles such as the Doctor, Ransome and Mrs Seeley.

Channing claims they've been colonising other planets for a thousand million years, and there are other Nestene groups apart from those assembling on Earth. It seems that they can detect the 'brain-prints' of specific humans - and the Doctor - and use these to identify individuals. [This might explain why the weak-minded Hibbert was selected out of all of the plastics manufacturers on the planet.]

• *Autons*. Plastic creations of the Nestenes, the implication being that the Nestene intelligence can animate anything made from the alien plastic. [NB: The script and novelisation of "Terror of the Autons" claim that the plastic developed for these and other Nestene nasties (identified by the Master as 'Polynestene') is unique, but we never get on-screen confirmation of this. However, the fact that they make their own dummies rather than "possessing" ready-made ones seems like probable confirmation. That, or they build their own dummies because they want ones with gun-hands.

[One line in "Terror of the Autons" suggests that the Nestenes can control *any* plastic, but the same episode has plastic daffodils with complex instructions encoded in their very cellular structure. Then again, the Master might have tinkered and enhanced their make-up and abilities. Both interpretations are open here, although either one makes the end of "Rose" contradict something.]

An Auton mannequin is tremendously strong and immune to gunfire. The right hand can swing open, via a hinge where the knuckle of the little finger [the "pinky", if you're American] would be, revealing a weapon which makes a rocket-like "whoosh" when fired. [This may be a treatment of the same sound effect used for the X-Ray Laser in 5.1, "The Tomb of the Cybermen"; it's a standard Radiophonic effect, used a lot in *Zokko!* And *Bleep & Booster* around then.] This weapon normally

just kills, but can completely vapourise a body on the command 'total destruct'.

Auton facsimiles are perfect replicas of human beings, even retaining the memories of the original, although there's a waxy sheen to the skin. When a facsimile is destroyed, its face reverts to a blank plastic mask and the original human being regains consciousness. [So the facsimile-making process must induce a trance-state, for some reason. Nestenes are telepathic, so does the facsimile "tap into" the mind of the subject? The survival of the originals - all people in authority - might help explain why the obvious disruption to the nation is so quickly healed.] The Doctor believes that the Nestenes are telepathic to such a degree, they'll know about their defeat on Earth.

Autons can track individual human beings by their brain-patterns, albeit over a limited range. Not wholly autonomous [ironically], the Autons seem to shut down completely when the Nestene consciousness is destroyed.

Planet Notes The Institute of Space Studies in Baltimore believes that Earth's section of the galaxy contains over five-hundred planets capable of supporting life. [This is odd: Project Ozma, the first attempt to contact extraterrestrials by checking for signals on the 21cm hydrogen waveband - see 8.1, "Terror of the Autons" - was launched in 1961. The project leader, Frank Drake, explained his now-famous "Green Bank" formula for calculating the potential "audience" of ETs capable of sending such signals. Using the best available data for number of planet-bearing stars, fractions of those likely to have intelligent life, the length of any kind of civilisation and so on (all basically guesses), he arrived at five hundred for the entire galaxy.

[Others, notably *The New York Times* Science Editor Walter Sullivan (the unsung hero of Season Seven, as his books and articles announced Plate Techtonics and the Moho Gap) tweaked the numbers based on their own assumptions of what "life", "intelligence" and "civilization" might also mean, and thus derived much bigger numbers. Sullivan claimed in 1964 that the potential ET planets could, with a sufficiently long-lasting average culture, be as high as 50,000. Carl Sagan did his sums two radically different ways (depending on whether he intended his calculations to scare world leaders about nuclear winter or sell his novel about SETI - although the figure Jodie

When Did the Doctor Get His Driving Licence?

The Doctor's lack of formal ID has long been a problem, so we can conclude that if there *is* a driver's licence, he never carries it. He's seen to carry UK currency for various ages, including pre- and post-Decimal coins, but never any paperwork until he joins UNIT. Even this has him down as "Dr. John Smith", so anything from his first two incarnations is going to be inconsistent (see 5.7, "The Wheel In Space" for the first use of this name, and it's Jamie who decides on it). If he decided to get formal "proof" of his existence in the two weeks between destroying WOTAN and leaving Earth, the chances are that the name "Who" would be on the documents (see **Is His Name Really Who?** under 3.10, "The War Machines").

There is, of course, a problem straight away. Under current UK law, no-one can drive over the age of seventy without regular testing. Assuming the UNIT era to be almost the dates of first broadcast, this wouldn't have been compulsory for anyone *already* in possession of a licence, but someone taking the test or being issued with a provisional licence for the first time may have had more difficulty. In applying to the DVLC (Driver Vehicle Licensing Centre; now the DVLA, "A" standing for "Authority"), he'd need to give a date of birth, a permanent address and so on. A medical might be required (he's over sixty, after all), and certainly a rudimentary eye-test forms part of the basic driving exam. The First Doctor might not have submitted to such humiliation, and almost definitely wouldn't lie about his age – assuming he was sure what it was. (There's his casual mention of 'every time I come back to London' at the start of "The War Machines", so it's possible that other visits occurred before we even met him, but this is shaky ground.) What we have to worry about, chiefly, is how he learned to drive in the first place.

The first time we see the Doctor drive anything one might normally drive is in "The Invasion" (6.3), when he uses a UNIT jeep that's somehow kept inside a Hercules transporter plane. However, up to this point we've seen him fly a helicopter in "Fury From The Deep" (5.6). He learned this by watching Astrid Ferrier in "Enemy of the World" (5.4), so it's entirely possible that the Doctor's driving skills were similarly acquired. The only other time we see contemporary transport with the early Doctor as a passenger is the taxi in "The War Machines". There may not have been any formal lessons, and the idea that the Doctor learned everything he knows about driving from a London cabbie might at least explain some of the Third Doctor's behaviour behind the wheel.

However, the Austin Metropolitan FX3 – the classic 1950s "black cab" – is diesel-powered and has totally different gearing to most vehicles. Had he tried to drive a jeep like a taxi-driver, he would've broken down. (Fortunately the Automobile Association has a call-out service, and in those days there were roadside boxes to ring for assistance. They look remarkably like police boxes, so the Doctor may have joined for a laugh.) Thus, the Doctor is breaking several laws when he's driving around London. Then, of course, there's photo ID. The Driving Licence has only recently added this, and despite recent developments it's still optional. So if we assume that the rest of Britain stayed much the same when Jeremy Thorpe's government was sending men to Mars and funding time-travel experiments, it may not have mattered that the person driving Bessie in "Robot" (12.1) didn't in any way resemble her owner.

The assumption has always been that the licence came as part of the process of being formally "identified" for UNIT purposes. He must have had a licence to buy Bessie, unless the Brigadier did it for him. However, this isn't as certain as one might think. Chinn, in "The Claws of Axos" (8.3), indicates that the Doctor's file is empty and that no official record of his existence can be traced (and if there is a year's gap between "Terror of the Autons" and "The Mind of Evil", then this is very remiss). Whenever asked for ID he provides a UNIT pass, which Jo carries for him on most occasions. When arrested in "Invasion of the Dinosaurs" (11.2), he has nothing to prove his identity. Perhaps Jo took his pass to Peru with her. (Assuming it isn't the one that turns up inside a straw hat worn by a much later Doctor – 26.1, "Battlefield".)

And there's a lot more to consider here than just this Doctor's love of cars. Although he seems puzzled by the offer of a salary, the Doctor isn't always short of the readies. If the country acknowledges his existence, then he pays tax, pays National Insurance and must legally be defined as either a British Subject or not. If not, his access to naval bases and all the government research facilities in Season Seven must be a matter for diplomatic staff. If he's been granted citizenship, he technically would have had to undergo the same checks as immigrants and all UN personnel. As the Brigadier often points out, the Doctor is "attached" to UNIT, not a full member. Outside UK territory, he has no more legal status than he did when the TARDIS dumped him in Oxley Wood at the start of his

continued on page 19...

Foster gives in *Contact* is way off both of these). The highest estimate in wide circulation was 53,000, boldly proclaimed by Isaac Asimov in his (ostensibly) non-fiction book *Extraterrestrial Civilisations*, the one Philip Martin read when writing "Vengeance on Varos" (22.2). This was Sullivan's estimate amended, as biologists found more ways life on Earth was flourishing in hitherto-overlooked environments.]

According to the Doctor, the people of the planet Delphon communicate using their eyebrows. [See A2, "The Curse of Fatal Death", for a similarly odd mode of communication.]

History

• *Dating*. [Probably 1970, or at the latest early 1971. See **When are the UNIT Stories Set?**. "Planet of the Spiders" (11.5) claims that the Third Doctor arrived on Earth 'months' after "The Invasion".]

The clothes in the shop window are still priced in pounds, shillings and pence rather than decimal currency [Britain went decimal in February 1971]. Mullins the Porter uses a phone that still has 'Button B' [the pre STD-dialling system for GPO public call-boxes, phased out with decimalisation] and three coin-slots. In the production line scene, we hear a record in the charts during the week of broadcast: "Oh, Well" by Fleetwood Mac. [This was stricken from the BBC video and DVD releases; the clearances for TV transmission are different.] The UNIT staff car has an 'O' registration number consistent with a 1969 model. The fictional newspapers *seem* to be based on those of the era, with Wagstaffe's *Daily Post* apparently an analogue of the real but soon-to-be-defunct *Daily Sketch*. John Sanders in Ealing Broadway has a 'New' confectionary department. The Doctor's anti-Nestene gadget has valves rather than transistors and little Mary Quant flowers on the buttons. Et cetera.

[We can, maybe, perhaps, be more precise with the months involved, as the two meteor showers are six months apart and unexpected. The two annual big showers are the Leonids and Perseids, in January and August, so "unexpected" arrivals would be at other times. As it looks like early autumn, we might suppose April for the first wave. This is admittedly guesswork, though.]

The Analysis

Where Does This Come From? At a surface level, this seems to be trading on a basic fascination with objects coming to life. The memorable scene of the Autons twitching in shop windows does indeed have this at its core, but here it mainly remains in the foreground - the sequel ("Terror of the Autons") is the place where objects actually run riot. Iconic though the Ealing Massacre sequence is, it seems almost like an afterthought.

What's *more* curious about the Nestenes and their evil scheme, though, is that it's actually two variations on a time-honoured theme. In the nineteenth century, when Romanticism was remodelling the idea of a unified and valuable "self", older stories about stealing souls and sending images of friends to trick you (of the sort diligently collected by those antiquarians who went around pickling folk-tales) got a whole new lease of undeath. German author ETA Hoffmann, the usual name to bring up here, popularised the word *Doppelgänger* for this. Then throughout the nineteenth century, stories of mesmerism and drugs made people act on the volition of others. Images or doubles of loved ones, such as "fetches" (see 15.3, "Image of the Fendahl"), were a lingering gothic cliché. (Shelley met himself, or so he said, a week before he died.)

Finally, the twentieth century brings us two distinct versions: the brainwashing / mind control variant and the android / alien replica. The latter taps into a general mistrust of things that look human but aren't (such as waxworks and those clockwork automata about which Hoffmann wrote), as well as the deep-rooted fear that you could be fooled into thinking someone was your friend, then betrayed.

Once this idea is introduced, it becomes dizzying and scary to think how far your life is determined by the ability (or otherwise) to read tiny clues and construct a general idea of what someone is like. If these can be misled - say, by a double-agent or con-man - that's one thing, but something *not even human* is quite another. Gerry Anderson knew this, and his late 60s serial *Captain Scarlet and the Mysterons* (in which aliens threaten Earth by creating perfect "intelligent" duplicates of any object or human) took this to wonderfully morbid extremes. This was an era, after all, in which English gentlemen could hold any sort of alarming secrets, and sugarlumps

When Did the Doctor Get His Driving Licence?

...continued from page 17

exile. Officially, then, he might not exist. As we'll see, this might have put him in great peril (see **All Right, Then... Where Were Torchwood?** under 9.3, "The Sea Devils").

Surprisingly, there is a way out of all this, in amid the military bureaucracy that otherwise causes the Doctor so much hassle. The British Army has often had provisions for employing non-UK citizens. This isn't always straightforward: the Gurkha regiments have been embroiled in a protracted and high-profile legal case (publicised by Joanna Lumley) for equality of pension rights. It's claimed that as Commonwealth citizens, this ought to have been automatic - especially after so much service.

By contrast, West Germany in the aftermath of World War II had a large number of stateless persons, many of whom were employed as drivers, dog-handlers or interpreters. To get any one of these onto the books was a matter of getting a junior minister to draft what's known as a Statutory Instrument. These are like one-off Parliamentary by-laws; thousands are passed every year and only lightly scrutinised. If someone in a position of authority requests a legal statement - such as making a non-existent man scientific advisor to an international military organization - it can be arranged, as could letting him drive such vehicles as he needs to. Season Seven provides a number of ministerial types who know about the Doctor without having met him, two of whom (Masters and Quinlan) conveniently die before any awkward questions arise.

However, it's a bit more complicated as his sponsor, the Brigadier, is himself in an ambiguous legal situation - he's simultaneously in the British Army and outside its jurisdiction. He is, however, a brigadier and so is as established a figure as a lawyer, doctor or vicar - the kind of person you get to vouch for you when applying for a passport or somesuch. This, though, re-opens the issue of photo ID; someone whose driving licence is issued under such special circumstances would need to have it authorised for his personal use, so the photograph / regeneration issue remains. He's all right, though, so long as nobody looks too closely into his records.

But being the Doctor, he can't even stay out of trouble even just going to work. Bessie's "super-drive" and inertial damping brake enable him to break all accepted speed limits in the UK, especially since those limits were considerably lowered during the fuel crisis (see **Who's Running the Country?** under 10.5, "The Green Death"). At certain points in "Day of the Daleks" (9.1) and at the end of "The Green Death", he also would have risked prosecution for driving under the influence of alcohol; maybe that super-charged alien metabolism saves him from failing breathalyser tests. By "Planet of the Spiders" (11.5), he's happily stealing hovercraft, so not having a valid licence for either of his improbable cars is a minor infraction. There doesn't seem to be any protection under law for UNIT personnel, any more than for policemen who injure the public in the course of their duties. (Although, as has been noted before, UNIT troops appear to be licensed to kill and don't need to caution suspects before opening fire.)

The Doctor is also capable of piloting more complex vehicles, including spaceships (10.3, "Frontier In Space"; 6.5, "The Seeds of Death"; 7.3, "The Ambassadors of Death"; 1.7, "The Sensorites"; 21.6, "The Caves of Androzani" and so on). Did he qualify for these? He claims to be a fully accredited pilot for the Mars-Venus run (which is more complicated than it sounds[6]) and can repair a spaceship in mid-flight, so he probably passed the practical exam if not the theory. Most cogently, does he – as is hinted in "Robot" – carry all of these documents around but not his UK Driving Licence?

could be bugging devices in disguise (see **Is Doctor Who Camp?** under 6.5, "The Seeds of Death"). There's an awful lot of *Scarlet* in "Spearhead".

There's also a real-life neurological condition, Capgras Syndrome (also known as "Capgras delusion"), in which the subject becomes convinced that a loved one has been replaced with a fake, then becomes distressed that nobody else can see it. Those afflicted invent increasingly elaborate accounts of who else has been "got at", all to keep the subterfuge secret. Note that Capgras victims only revise their perception of close friends or relatives - the more familiar the "duplicated" person was before the onset of the illness, the greater the effect and the distress. It's a rare syndrome, but it gets to the core of who we think we are. The notion pushes so many of our buttons, paranoid thrillers have used it again and again. See *Invasion of the Body-Snatchers* (1956) and *I Married A Monster From Outer Space* (1958), to name but two of the post-McCarthy flicks to equate this with subversion of a more routine kind. Throw in an overall early-70s disquiet about identity-theft (see *The Stepford Wives*) and it's hard to see why - other than 4.8, "The Faceless Ones" - they didn't do this one more often.

Ahh, but they had. We're talking about television, so bear in mind that the budget usually requires that aliens be played by the same actors we've just seen in another role. All through the 1960s, brainwashing and duplication were the two most cost-effective means of suggesting extraterrestrial conspiracy. Actors liked it too - apart from the chance to get more work, they liked playing two versions of the same character. These days, giving actors different versions of their routine characters is usually done with the cliché of parallel universes - as we'll see in three stories' time ("Inferno" and of course, X2.5, "The Rise of the Cybermen" et al), but it was planned right from the word go as a staple of *Doctor Who*. If you read Volume I, the whole scenario of a world like Earth - only on the other side of the Sun from us - is being pitched from every writer they approach, usually with Barbara having an evil twin. Only a year later, William Hartnell is hoping to play his own double (see **What Other Spin-Offs Were Planned?** under 18.7-A, "K9 and Company") and the fiendish Daleks have a robot duplicate who looks a bit like the Doctor if you squint very, *very* hard (2.8, "The Chase"). Then there's Hartnell pulling double-duty as the Abbot of Amboise (3.5, "The Massacre"). Conspirators who look like friends - *Prisoner of Zenda* lookey-likeys (that's the preferred British spelling, for reasons we won't go into here) and impostors of all kinds - were Troughton-era standbys, now given a new twist for the seventies.

The *other* big variation on a time-honoured theme is mind-control. This isn't exactly a novel idea (1.5, "The Keys of Marinus" is the first "classic" example, but we could stretch a point and say 1.3, "The Edge of Destruction"). The waxy Channing can overpower his stooge Hibbert with such ease, and in a way so familiar to *Doctor Who* viewers, that it's never actually commented upon. After all, nasty alien conspirators *do* this sort of thing, don't they? Then again, the Nestenes have the remarkable ability to control minds but they almost always resort to violence instead, as if in deliberate defiance of a cliché.

Another angle worth addressing: the opening scene and the premise of things disguised as meteorites coming to take over a factory could charitably be called a "reference" to *Quatermass II*. In fact,

the way it's handled is closer to the film version, although the conspiracy element of the original will be touched on here and (to a greater or lesser extent) in the whole UNIT / Pertwee cycle. Other 1960s series riffed on this with varying degrees of success. Robert Holmes had the thankless task of wrapping up what was intended as a long-running conspiracy thriller, *Undermind* (1965, and made by ABC, makers of *The Avengers*), and had ventured into flying-saucer territory (another go at following *Quatermass II*'s mining of this seam of paranoia). The space-alien gimmick hid the fact that this was apparently intended as a satire. Five years after "Spearhead", Robert Banks Stewart - the creator of *Undermind* - would also try duplication within the *Who* format (see 13.1, "Terror of the Zygons").

More alarmingly, the BBC had just been showing a drama serial called *Counterstrike* (1969). *Adam Adamant Lives!* creator Tony Williamson devised this in 1966, but it was put on ice for three years. It entailed Bad Aliens disguised as humans coming here, in a bid to destroy all life on Earth and grab the planet for themselves. Fortunately, a worldwide scientific / military organisation had a Nice Alien advising them. Does this sound familiar? Of course there were differences: the Nice Alien was young and dishy (with black contact-lenses so you knew he wasn't a local boy), used a less obvious pseudonym ("Simon King") and drove a sports-car in the *Prisoner*-lite titles. Plus, the series was made in black and white. That was the problem - it was not only the last drama series the BBC made in monochrome, but the transmission of episode six (of ten) was pre-empted by the in-depth investigation into the breaking story of the conviction of those notorious crime leaders, the Kray Twins (see 4.7, "The Macra Terror"). Notoriously, this episode was wiped before anyone could actually get a chance to see it. We'll pick this up under 8.2, "The Mind of Evil".

Essentially, if you want to sell a new format for present-day adventures, *and* introduce a new Doctor, then you need a plot that everyone at home can sing along with. Many fans think of "Spearhead" as an innovative device that retools *Doctor Who* from top to bottom, but much of it had been done before - including a lot in recent *Doctor Who*, and also a lot by the same author. Holmes had written the bulk of this script before in his 1965 film treatment *Invasion* (the final script of which was by *Avengers* stalwart, Roger Marshall), in which Japanese actors play aliens - the male one is injured and on the run, with his two female pursuers passing themselves off as nurses. Notably, all the material about Broca's Area (a more substantial plot-point in the movie: see also 13.5, "The Brain of Morbius") is reproduced verbatim. The notion of using a glorified ECT system as the defence against telepathically-linked foes is one in the proposed script "Aliens in the Blood" from a year earlier, and looks like a legacy from Holmes' involvement in the task of ending *Undermind* in the space of two episodes. The same missile footage from "The Invasion" (the *Doctor Who* one) crops up in the similarly-named film, made apparently on less than the budget of a four-part *Doctor Who*. The scene in which Scobie comes face-to-face with his own double, however, is seemingly lifted straight out of the 1965 Bond movie *Thunderball*.

And finally: the Autons are inanimate beings activated by "souls" contained in spheres, with a disembodied animating spirit behind it all - the the same premise behind the Yeti. (They were originally to have been the last Troughton adversaries; see Volume II.) The climax of "Spearhead" was shot in the same factory that doubled for IE about a year earlier (see "The Invasion"). It's also interesting to note that the Brigadier takes the time to re-introduce UNIT to the viewers, as if he's talking to a new audience, and that - rather than the full-on military outfit of "The Invasion" - UNIT has become a general bureau of sorting-out-strange-events. Much like UNCLE, or SHADO, or Department S, or... you get the idea. (Actually, the *best* analogue for this original "World Army" is the World Intelligence Network in Gerry Anderson's 1968 series *Joe 90*. The rest of this volume will reveal a lot more about links between Anderson and UNIT-era *Who*.)

Things That Don't Make Sense Not for the last time (see especially "Planet of the Daleks"), the villains' strategy has a problem of scale. Fair enough that the Nestenes want to dominate Earth, but their plan for doing so entails them replacing various key personnel, giving conflicting orders and then... bursting out of shop windows and shooting cyclists. This would be fairly ineffectual even if they only wanted to conquer Ealing Broadway, but they're after the whole world. The fact that the plastics factory makes the sort of dolls that the majority of British households would have owned

offers a far more subversive strategy - maybe they needed the Master's help to refine this idea (see "Terror of the Autons"), although even his best shot is a bit haphazard. Still, even handing out flowers and hoping people will keep them close to radios is better than randomly zapping old ladies at bus stops.

Ranged against this alien menace, however, we have UNIT - a crack international military intelligence organization that holes up in a car park. And not for the last time (but so obviously in this story, we'll ask it here), what were the international UNIT agencies doing while this global catastrophe took place in one shopping precinct? Did it not occur to the Nestenes that if the Autons *did* take over the entire UK, the rest of the world would probably nuke the British Isles and hope for an east wind? The set for the Brig's office includes a wooden partition with a door and a gap where it *doesn't* meet the ceiling [so the door's obviously not for security - something of a liability in UNIT's line of work].

As for Channing, the Nestenes' mouthpiece and coordinator... how, precisely, did the energy from the first fall of energy units manifest as a Hugh Burden replica to put the whammy on Hibbert and start production of the Autons and Facsimiles? Channing would need to take over the plastics factory to get made, but need to be made to take over the plastics factory. [Does the spearhead force have a handy method of stealing the identity of the first passing intelligent being? Perhaps the units themselves have hypnotic abilities, but the Swarm Leader never uses any on Seeley or his wife.] If the Channing model was developed as the sort of person a downtrodden dollmaker might trust with his company, did the Nestenes' investigations into what humans consider trustworthy not deduce that the inability to smile and the greasy face were potential liabilities? [Basically, this is one of those "invasion of Earth" stories that require the aggressors to have undertaken detailed negotiations with bank-managers and shop-stewards some months before: see also "The Faceless Ones" and X3.4, "Daleks in Manhattan".]

It's said that the plastics factory is 'fully automated', but the doll-head sequence in episode two uses footage from a human-staffed factory, apparently listening to Radio One as they work. Anyway, if they'd sacked the entire workforce one afternoon, just before Scobie came, there would be pickets outside. And how can a successful plastics factory - taking delivery and distributing Autons and dolls all around the country by lorry, as it would - be so close to where a poacher can make a decent living? Do they have special stealth-juggernauts that rabbits can't hear?

Despite being stated as being in Essex, the area around Ashbridge Cottage Hospital seems populated by the Welsh to an odd extent. How, exactly, do the journalists that besiege the Brigadier know about the mysterious meteorites? After all, the porter who phoned in the story only knew about someone (the Doctor) not having human blood. [He might well have overheard more, but this isn't shown on screen.]

As late as episode four, Channing doesn't have much of an inkling that the Doctor isn't local (see below), so why abduct him? They could have just waited until he awoke and offered him money, hypnotised him or simply asked "Mister, can we have our ball back?" It's like they looked at the clock and thought: "it's been twenty-three minutes since the start of the episode, let's draw attention to ourselves."

A few questions arise concerning Major-General Scobie and his doppelgänger. First, the UNIT switchboard fails to spot anything odd about "Scobie" calling from the factory mere moments after the Brigadier called him at home. Second, the Brig himself doesn't connect the dots between this anomaly, the fact that Auto Plastics makes replicas of people and the fact that Scobie had one done. More glaringly, even if we presume that Autons need to keep Scobie alive so the Scobie-facsimile can tap his brainwave patterns (or whatever), why not just stuff the original in a cupboard at the factory, rather than "waxifying" him and putting him on display at Madame Tussauds? As matters stand, they do this for no good reason other than giving Our Heroes a chance to notice. [To be fair, a good reason for this plot-twist existed, but they cut it: see **The Lore**.]

Anyway, consider what it would take to get Madame Tussauds to replace their (unconvincing) celebrity effigies of Georgie Best or Faye Dunaway with those of civil servants and obscure generals. Was the Tussauds head of marketing replaced with a Nestene and, if so, what are the odds that people working all day with wax dummies wouldn't have noticed? For that matter, the Doctor deduces that the Scobie "mannequin" is the genuine article because the man's watch is set to the correct time, *not* because the "dummy" is visibly

wobbling about. (On a similar note, look to the left when Liz says, 'There are no astronauts, famous personalities' - a female "dummy", dressed in blue, flickers her eyes *very* visibly.) And besides, by what technique can the Nestene process the human body so that it can go a whole day without breathing or blinking, yet not develop any peristalsis, and which allows the victim to recover instantly when the Nestene octopus dies?

[A side note about Tussauds: even if you've never seen the unconvincing dummies at this pointless attraction, the alleged likenesses of the US presidents here should alert you to how dodgy their imitation celebrities were back then. So not only is Britain under threat from duplicates who look *vaguely* like people in positions of authority, a bit, in the dark, but it's hard to suppress a giggle when the Doctor asks Liz, 'Do you recognise any of these people?' The scene starts off with a shot of a waxwork figure that's probably supposed to be Richard Nixon, then the most powerful man on the planet.]

Channing's "spidey-sense" is haphazard - he can identify Ransome's brain-print from a few miles away, but needs to be told that it's his mind-slave Hibbert at the door. He also fails to detect that the Doctor's mind is different from any other visitor's - notably at Tussauds, when Channing convinces himself that the waxified Scobie is the 'alien' presence he sensed. He also entirely fails to spot or mentally detect the Doctor and Liz - his two primary troublemakers - when they're standing around pretending to be dummies.

Yes, he's a bit confused after his regeneration, but notice how the Doctor leaves his watch on in the shower and even momentarily thinks that Dr Beavis' hat will fit. On the other hand, even if we assume that the Brig has somehow heard about the TARDIS off-screen, it's strange that he's quite prepared for the mysterious stranger to be the Doctor, even when it's plainly visible that the man in the hospital bed is taller and has different hair and sideys. [Not even the Season 6B theory can explain this one.]

Liz Shaw, stealing the TARDIS key from the Brigadier's office, doesn't react to the fact that the Brigadier is interviewing a man who's babbling about being attacked by plastic monsters with ray-guns in their arms. [Given her cynicism about all of this, she might have been expected to take the piss.] Moments later the Brigadier (rightly) expects the Doctor to try to leave in the TARDIS as soon as possible, even though it's completely out of character for the Doctor he knows; the Second Doctor never had any visible urge to leave in the middle of a crisis. And moments after *that*, Liz is ready to acknowledge that the Doctor was trying to escape, even though she still doesn't believe in aliens, and certainly doesn't believe in a time-travelling police box.

Prentis Hancock's character, another reporter, is called "Jimmy". [This isn't a problem in and of itself, but what with Captain Munro also having that name, and with both this story and "The War Games" having a character called "Ransome", you wonder if anyone's paying attention.] The Auton looking for the Swarm-Leader seems awfully conspicuous, walking about as he does without a face-mask. It also feels the strange need to smash Mrs Seeley's plates, as if the football-sized Swarm Leader might be hidden in a drying-rack. For an encore, it's also seen trying to look behind the piano. One of the corpses in the bus-queue posthumously picks at his fingernails and sleeve. When the Scobie-facsimile gets zapped, none of Scobie's troops shoot the Doctor for what *looks* like a fatal attack on their commanding officer.

Oh, and when the Doctor tries to flee Earth, you can see the knee of the smoke-machine operator behind the TARDIS.

Critique With most *Doctor Who* stories pre-1980 (as we'll discuss further in the next story's critique), you have to make accommodation for the programme's serialized nature, and the way in which the series was meant to be watched on a week-to-week basis. "Spearhead from Space" is an interesting exception: if anything, it's vastly improved by watching it all in one sitting. The 1988 BBC video release did this story's reputation no end of good by removing the cliffhangers and making it a ninety-minute movie, because it's paced like one.

As is often the case with Robert Holmes scripts, it's a string of set-pieces, intended to set up the ones to follow. They seem to have been devised more as a checklist of things to include in an alien insurrection story, as opposed to the logical consequences of the initial premise. Holmes'. other scripts routinely find him indulging at least one element of wish-fulfilment, but this is almost all expediency - it introduces the new set-up, the aliens, the new Doctor and the threat, and then ends it.

This might explain why it's also very bottom-

heavy, with all the "good" bits stuffed into the last episode. The other three adventures of this season all set up a situation and a location, then see how much they can derive from it (something that unsympathetic modern viewers might see as time-wasting digressions into moorland, Marylebone Station, an alien spaceship and a parallel universe), but "Spearhead" even makes a location-shoot in Madame Tussauds vital for plot-exposition. Compare this to a routine Pertwee romp (say, 9.5, "The Time Monster"), and what comes across most is its no-nonsense approach: it's no-frills, but cheese-free. (Well, calling *anything* with Pertwee in "no frills" is a bit daft, but you know what we mean.)

But we have to take the climax - with the Autons coming to life on Ealing Broadway - out of the equation when evaluating this as a four-part story. That *one* scene has come to represent an entire method of making *Doctor Who* - indeed, there will be times in future where it's held up as the *only* way of making it. For a large chunk of fandom, this scene was untouchable before 1989, and by the time *Doctor Who* gained a new audience who didn't remember it well enough to make unfavourable comparisons, the series' whole emphasis had changed. Yet no other Pertwee story attempts anything like this. For that matter, the slaughter of pedestrians isn't even in keeping with the story's pace and mood. Subsequent attempts to recapture the impact of that scene have been better-executed (X2.10, "Love and Monsters" is the least flawed) but somehow blander. Cardiff-pretending-to-be-London has cosmetically removeed all the accidental incursions of reality; even the graffiti and posters are for fake things that only exist in *Who*. It's now lit like a movie and done on frame-removed VT that isn't anything like the news footage we'd see were it really happening. Spooky music aside, the use of an untouched location and the same film-stock as used for riots, strikes or bombings on that night's bulletins makes "Spearhead from Space" the one attempt at Yeti-in-the-Loo-*Who* that came off, unless you saw the first minute of "Invasion of the Dinosaurs" (11.2) in colour. Unlike every subsequent Pertwee story's attempt to scare us this way, the script and directing show rather than tell, so we're spared embarrassing *faux* news reporters and just given almost unmediated coverage of events.

Without this one scene, it's doubtful that "Spearhead from Space" would be so well-remembered. Perhaps significantly, the story's attempts to spin out a mood of mystery and brooding menace didn't play well with audiences during a repeat showing on BBC2 in 1999. (Still, that's what happens when you put something that requires imagination and concentration in the slot usually filled by *Star Trek: Voyager*.) The main story puts its emphasis on making us curious about the new Doctor, which was fun at the time but...

We know how things turned out, so none of us can see Season Seven quite straight any more. This year has UNIT and Pertwee, but there's no Venusian Aikido, no Mike Yates, no Master, no Jo and we don't actually see the sonic screwdriver. As an era-opener, "Spearhead from Space" is even more odd - there's no CSO, no synthesizers, no Bessie and not much Pertwee, really. It's got a different texture to anything before or since, not just all shot on film but edited differently to any other story. (Only those entirely made on VT come close in terms of how it affects the acting, but the pacing and shot-composition of something like 12.3, "The Sontaran Experiment" or 24.3, "Delta and the Bannermen" is unlike this one too.) To get a measure of what viewers expected in terms of pace, style, setting, music and performance, the best way is to steel yourself and watch a cleaned-up bit of "The Space Pirates" (6.6) on DVD. As a whole, Season Seven is a series of experiments in seeing how far away from *that* the programme-makers can get, and still justifiably call the result *Doctor Who*.

Visually, of course, this is a whole different series. Once we get back into Television Centre, those stainless steel sets will return for twenty-one consecutive episodes, but here we have oak-panelled corridors, factories, a cottage, a garage and a lab that's apparently set up in a school gym. Straightforward things like people picking up phones happen in dynamic new ways, either shot from overhead or right down low. This could have been irritating (modish touches usually date really fast - see, for instance, X2.9, "the Satan Pit" for at least one piece of fast-editing that's already a museum-piece), yet somehow this story's camera-work still looks "clever" rather than "period".

The music is also a lurch away from Season Six, in which Brian Hodgson gave stories "atmospheres" that blurred the boundaries between music and sound-effects, or in which Dudley Simpson had a small band whose instruments were subtly (or otherwise) distorted and "flanged"

like so many records of that year. (The big exception is "The War Games", in which Simpson has a church-organ and a military band, and even then he puts a cymbal through the wringer for the War Lords' base theme.) Here, Simpson's got the biggest combo since "The Evil of the Daleks" (4.9), and makes the basic sound of this story very contemporary. There's an electric guitar, a muted cornet and a jazz flute. (Not hummed into - which was *so* last year by the time this was written - but a style of cool associated with British performers who graduated from saxophone to flute, eg Tubby Hayes.)

If it seems strange that we're putting such emphasis on surface features, it's because that's what casual viewers in January 1970 would have noticed first. Unless they recognised a logo or Lethbridge-Stewart - who last appeared a year before - the only thing that connects this adventure serial with *Doctor Who* is the theme-tune and an incapacitated police box. For better or worse, this story's peculiar filming makes it stand out. No bad performances have been allowed (as might have been, and usually was, the case with VT). As director, Derek Martinus keeps finding things to make shots interesting. Occasionally Holmes lets in flashes of what will become his trademark character-humour, but the script is mainly notable for a shark-like simplicity and purity of purpose.

That said, one could easily argue that the story gets so "lean", it threatens to tip over into "skeletal". Alas, the main victim of this approach is Jon Pertwee. By story's end, we still haven't much idea who this new Doctor is. Pertwee begins by playing Troughton, then proceeds to remove anything from his performance that isn't comfortable - as opposed to starting with an idea of who his character *is* and then adding to it. Only during in the climactic scene with Channing does he seem to relax, and even *that* probably owes to it being a reshoot, done after the end of the next story had been filmed. Still, it's an interesting idea to make us wait for the new Doctor to emerge halfway through episode two. And as with his previous script, Holmes tells us how much trouble the Doctor's in before he actually participates in the action.

But if nothing else, this is the first time since 1963 that we've come to a story entirely fresh. Amidst the new Doctor showing up and the series' entire *raison d'etre* changing, Liz asks questions on our behalf (even though she's the alleged expert) and the Brigadier answers most of them (even though he's the alleged investigator). Back in 1966, Ben and Polly were embedded in the TARDIS well enough for the lead actor's alarming change to be a jolt; this time it's *all* new, and the level of surprise seems uniform. This would be a major flaw with less talented performers, and it's *still* a decently big job, with Courtney and John trying to sell us this new series before the star gets out of bed. "The Christmas Invasion" tried something similar, but was an hour-long episode with no week-long breaks between plot twists, and had the benefit of established regular characters. Pertwee, Courtney and John here rise to the thankless task of jump-starting the series from scratch, but they don't flourish until the next story. Strangely enough, the *real* beneficiary is Hugh Burden as Channing - but he would've become annoying had this been any longer or slower.

As a reboot of the entire series, "Spearhead from Space" does a job efficiently if not imaginatively. Nevertheless, this relaunch got *another* relaunch a year later, meaning that rather than declaring "welcome to the 1970s" as planned, this story now looks like it's saying "Welcome to 1970". As with a lot of the pop culture of its year of broadcast, Season Seven is oddly amorphous. Like the new Doctor, it's waiting for an identity to form, and it begins by deciding what it's not as opposed to what it *is*.

The Facts

Written by Robert Holmes. Directed by Derek Martinus. Viewing figures: 8.4 million, 8.1 million, 8.3 million, 8.1 million. Audience Appreciation was 57% for the last episode. However, as we'll see in **The Lore**, we have reason to believe that the repeat showing gained an entirely new audience with virtually no overlap from the original transmission, so we *might* be justified in giving figures of 11.3 million, 11.1 million, 11.7 million and 12.0 million. Certainly, more people remember this than things that were ostensibly seen by far more people.

Supporting Cast George Lee (Corporal Forbes), Tessa Shaw (UNIT Officer), Hugh Burden (Channing), Neil Wilson (Seeley), Talfryn Thomas (Mullins), Antony Webb (Dr Henderson), Helen Dorward (Nurse), Alan Mitchell (Wagstaffe), Prentis Hancock (2nd Reporter), John Breslin (Captain Munro), John Woodnutt (Hibbert), Derek Smee (Ransome), Hamilton Dyce (Major General Scobie), Henry McCarthy (Dr Beavis).

Working Titles "Facsimile".

Cliffhangers UNIT soldiers shoot the new Doctor as he runs through the woods towards the guarded TARDIS; one of the mannequins at the plastics factory comes to life, and menaces the former employee who's snooping around there; Major-General Scobie opens his front door, only to come face-to-face with his Auton replica.

What Was In The Charts? "(Call Me) Number One", The Tremeloes; "Two Little Boys", Rolf Harris; "Liquidator", Harry J All-Stars; "Melting Pot", Blue Mink. Plus we should mention "Oh, Well (Part One)" by Fleetwood Mac, just dipping out of the Top 20 that week.

The Lore

• To reiterate, if you haven't read Volume II... Jon Pertwee's friend Tenniel Evans suggested that it might be worth his applying for the role of the Doctor. (Pertwee later returned the favour in 10.2, "Carnival of Monsters", where Evans plays Major Daly.) Pertwee had hitherto been a comedy actor, specialising in funny voices for radio shows like *Waterlogged Spa* and *The Navy Lark*[3]. His film roles included his playing several doddery old men in the *Carry On* series - *Carry On Screaming* (1966), in fact, has him playing Scotland Yard's scientific advisor (the Doc), who's killed by a werewolf / ape-man with uncertain anthropological origins (cf. "Inferno"). Entertainingly, the DVD chapter-selection for the film has a picture of Pertwee gurning and the caption "Regeneration". (The scene has been given a fresh interest for *Doctor Who* viewers, as the ape-man's severed finger grows into a second copy, 'Oddbod Junior', when the Doc applies an electrical charge. If the significance eludes you, see X4.13, "Journey's End.")

Anyway, Pertwee's agent had been in talks with producers Peter Bryant and Derrick Sherwin since February. You might recall from Volume II that the production team had a fairly high rate of turnover right about now, but Bryant - the nominal producer at this stage - had drawn up a wish-list of potential Third Doctors, and Pertwee was in the top three. Ron Moody was apparently the first choice, whereas younger viewers had nominated

Dad's Army star John le Mesurier, whose usual performance isn't too far off how Pertwee might have been *expected* to approach the part. Pertwee could adapt to playing almost any role - that is, assuming he was told what the character actually was. It took a while before the simple idea of playing the Doctor *as* Jon Pertwee occurred to anyone, so the courtship-dance of agent and producer dragged on until the putative star felt comfortable with the idea. They formally signed in late May, and the decision to cast Pertwee was kept secret until Troughton's departure had been recorded.

• Prior to this, Pertwee had made records of children's songs, and played guitar in light entertainment shows (he even claimed to have "discovered" singer Adam Faith when he was a regular on *Six-Five Special*). Even as late as 1969, radio comedy was so massively popular, his role as the imaginatively-named "Chief Petty Officer Pertwee" in *The Navy Lark* made him instantly familiar as Jon Pertwee, Star of Film and Radio. (Even so, he tended to avoid too much TV acting. His reputation as a comedian got in the way of him being considered for straight roles, but he was a frequent guest on panel games.)

• Pertwee came from a famous family: his father and uncle had been pre-war celebrities, and his cousin Bill was frequently on TV (notably in *Dad's Army*) and on radio (notably in *Round the Horne* - these shows will become significant later in this volume). Before and during his stint as the Doctor, Pertwee appeared as himself on quiz-programmes and chat-shows - something Troughton would never have done, and Hartnell was seldom asked to do even while playing TV's biggest hero.

• The series was re-tooled, partly because of a cost-cutting idea Sherwin had formally proposed on the last day of 1968 (use UNIT and not-entirely-futuristic Britain as the main source of stories, immobilize the TARDIS and have a grown-up scientist as the female co-star), but also because BBC1 was introducing colour. Indeed, the first recording done for the new series was an experimental studio session playing with Colour Separation Overlay (CSO) in August. As you probably know, this exciting new technique is going to dominate 1970s *Doctor Who*, embolden the writers (even if it didn't always come off), and become the ancestor of all the blue-screen and green-screen stuff routinely done today. American technicians had been trying it since 1965, but with the British 625-line PAL system, it took a lot

of fine-tuning.

Around the time that ABC (makers of *The Avengers*, not the US network) was forcibly merged with Rediffusion in 1968 to make Thames Television, the ABC technical team at Teddington Lock had ironed out a lot of the snags - but they weren't going to tell their rivals at the BBC how they'd done it. So there's an effects arms-race going on all through the Pertwee era, and the "defections" of director Paul Bernard and visual effects man Ian Scoones to *Doctor Who* will prove significant.

• With the whole of BBC1 gearing up for the advent of colour transmissions in late November 1969, recording for *Doctor Who* would have to begin at least four months after the last session for "The War Games". Even though the scripts were coming in rather more efficiently than had been the case for Season Six, it seemed sensible to delay transmission until January, thus getting material in the can ahead of time. Ironically, then, almost all of Troughton's objections about the production schedule had now been met (see Volume II, specifically "The Invasion" and 5.4, "The Enemy of the World") now that he wasn't around. Starting a twenty-five episode season in January meant that the new stories would finally go out of synch with the school year - but on the plus side, more people would have received colour tellies for Christmas.

• Pertwee was presented to the world as the new Doctor on 7th of June, at a press-conference at his house where a Yeti accosted him. The Yeti were originally slated as the returning monsters to launch the new Doctor (see 6.1, "The Dominators" et seq for the full story on this), hence their appearance here and in Season Seven's publicity shots alongside Silurians and spacesuited Ambassadors of Death. As the Yeti are inanimate objects activated by "souls" in spheres, it's at least possible that the Nestene energy-units predate everything else in the story. Plus, the script meetings for "Facsimile" (as "Spearhead from Space" was then called) were conducted back when the plug was being pulled on plans for "The Laird of McCrimmon" storyline, which was originally envisaged as the Third Doctor's debut and Jamie's departure.

• Contrary to the impression often given in telescoped accounts, Pertwee did *not* wear the cape and frills at this photo-shoot but instead had on a fairly ordinary business suit - see the photo of him reading that week's *Radio Times* whilst the Yeti is lunging at him. (If you get a big enough print, the date is clearly legible.) When asked how the Doctor should dress, Pertwee at first thought a Nehru-suit would be the way to go, but it soon became obvious that this was the basic wardrobe requirement for villains. The improvised look for the next meeting with the *Radio Times* - combining the fashionable frilly shirts of the time with his grandfather's opera-cape and a velvet jacket - seemed nearer to what this more "grounded" Doctor would wear, and gave the scriptwriters something of a handle on this new version of the character. Christine Rawlins, who supervised costumes for this and the rest of Season Seven's stories, had similar ideas and the script was revised to account for the rather theatrical-looking bricolage. (This may have been the *Radio Times* shoot that provided the cover for the 3rd of January, 1970 issue, which proudly announced the new season but omitted any article to accompany the shot.)

• Sherwin's idea for UNIT was to have a central authority-figure (the Brigadier) and a fresh set of underlings for each story to suggest the size of the agency. It's not unreasonable to assume that a global organisation would have more than one Captain, possibly a number on secondment from overseas (especially if the export-drive behind the series took off), but the idea didn't last very long. Neither, as it turned out, did the concept of a grown-up assistant. Liz Shaw was conceived when characters like her were thin on the ground, but by the time "Spearhead" aired, there were rather a lot of positive role-models in mini-skirts. (We also get rather a lot of them in this season, notably Petra Williams in "Inferno".) That said, anyone who thinks Liz's introduction owes a little to *The Man from UNCLE* should ponder earlier drafts of "Spearhead", in which UNIT HQ is hidden in a dingy shop and / or a kiosk at a railway station.

• Caroline John was cast as Liz, much to her surprise. Her previous work had been in the theatre. She had been in the first National Theatre productions of *The Royal Hunt of the Sun* (see 1.6, "The Aztecs") and *Rosencrantz & Gildenstern are Dead* (see 18.5, "Warriors' Gate"), but was seeking to branch out. In between National Theatre engagements, she worked in a Repertory company[4]. More in hope than expectation, she had some bikini shots taken and distributed, whereupon Bryant and Sherwin gave her agent a call. She had been based in Ipswich (and had thus worked with

Anthony Webb - here paying Dr Henderson - when he was in Rep with her) and had a long commute by train every morning. Stop us if you've heard this before, but she bought a big scientific dictionary in case the terminology she had to speak actually made sense, but the book contained very little of it.

• The new series needed new titles. Oddly, the 625-line colour monitors were less conducive to Howlround than had been hoped, so Bernard Lodge sourced the patterns generated by a photo of Pertwee in monochrome, and placed coloured gels underneath. One plan included the Doctor's cape being flung over the camera to start the sequence and another had him holding it up like Dracula. Instead, just the face-shot and a diamond pattern were used. These were dubbed with various versions of the signature tune over the next few years, and the titles standardised from "Terror of the Autons" onwards. The trial shots for Pertwee's titles were made in early August, just after the CSO experiment.

• The more-or-less finalised script for "Facsimile" was now ready, having been commissioned in January and discussed since the latter stages of Robert Holmes' previous story, "The Space Pirates" (6.6). By this time, Derek Martinus was being courted to direct. The programme's limitations had long frustrated him (we direct you to Volume I and 5.3, "The Ice Warriors" for more), but the prospect of making the first colour story was too good to miss. However...

• This being the first story of the 1970s, it's perhaps appropriate that a scene-shifters' strike disrupted it. The move of all drama and comedy from Lime Grove to Television Centre meant more work for the same pay, what with bigger studios and lengthier construction-times. Colour cameras were also less forgiving on hastily-built sets, and the BBC took its sweet time agreeing to take on more staff. Negotiations dragged on over the summer, during which the reallocation of resources proceeded almost as planned. (The Alexandra Palace studio used for News bulletins closed - see X2.6, "The Idiot's Lantern" - whilst Riverside was turned over almost exclusively for music recording, including this story's score.)

When it came, the strike itself was brief but the knock-on effects were still being felt throughout October. The practical consequence was that in the rush to get the various Christmas specials ready, all other pre-recorded series being made in TVC were rationed. Obviously, the BBC gave *The*

Black and White Minstrel Show and *It's Lulu!* top priority. So Sherwin had a dilemma... whether to delay the recording of this story and possibly miss the new Doctor's January debut, or try and make it somewhere else. He pressed on and sought to retain the cast he and Martinus had put together, although some (like the original Dr Lomax) were unavailable for the rescheduled production.

Nonetheless, it seems that this story *always* had a pretty high film-to-studio ratio for a four-parter. The increased cost of colour filming (more a matter of lighting than anything else) made the location-work more affordable if the costs of bigger sets were defrayed across more episodes, hence the string of seven-part stories this year. However, the new Doctor's debut involved a cottage hospital, a factory and a patch of woodland - to say nothing of a high-street that turns into a battleground. The Ealing unit were gearing up for this story when the plans were revised.

• Despite planning to wear glasses, Caroline John was deemed to look better with vast sixties-style eyelashes (added every day in make-up). John met her new co-star in the make-up tests, and recalls that he was nervous about playing it straight. Many people have confirmed this: Pertwee would often begin to put on a show when confronted with any newcomers, even if (according to Derek Ware) there was just one other person in the room. Although he was the star, he was now working with Courtney (who'd been in the series before) and John (who'd worked with Olivier). Nevertheless, Pertwee had a clear idea how his Doctor would be different from his predecessors, and determined to put his stamp on the part from day one. As it turned out, his first scene as the Doctor had him gagged and in a wheelchair, but characteristically he opted to do all his own stunts. Simply being himself in front of a camera, it seems, was the most daunting thing he'd ever attempted.

• The gears of Dr. Beavis' 1920s car caused difficulty even for a petrol-head like Pertwee. One out-take has him very nearly reversing it through a hedge. Perhaps not surprisingly, they opted not to show the Doctor and Liz going to places like Madame Tussaud's in it.

• The factory exterior may seem familiar: it's the TCC Condenser complex at Acton, which includes the Guinness Factory used in "The Invasion" for International Electromatics. Appropriately, this was the first major scene with

the Brigadier to be filmed. Courtney had just become a father, and welcomed regular work. In between parts, he had been working in a shop in Shepherd's Market, West London, specialising in model soldiers.

• The new scheme had the story entirely filmed on 16mm at various locations; the bits that had been planned for studio were to be filmed during the time that rehearsals for the studio recording would have taken place. This caused another snag, as Pertwee was on holiday in Ibiza (an astonishingly exotic and jet-set thing to do, in those days) so he couldn't get back much before the second shoot was to start. Sherwin briefly entertained notions of doing *all* of *Doctor Who* like this and flogging it overseas. After the fight he'd had getting permission to try an all-film story, Sherwin could be forgiven for pitching potential new markets to the BBC hierarchy. And as we've noted, the look of this story puts *Doctor Who* firmly into the same bracket as Lew Grade's hit exports like *The Champions* and *Strange Report*. (If you think the BBC weren't interested in that sort of thing, check out the titles for *Counterstrike* or the doomed *Paul Temple*, about which we'll hear a lot more in the next story.)

• In those days the BBC owned a great many out-of-the-way facilities (like the former Ealing Films studios), and so had access to alternative sites. One was the Engineering Training facility at Wood Norton, in Oxfordshire. It was bought from a French nobleman before the War and kept in readiness for emergencies - not just the odd strike, but nuclear war. (We're not joking here... observe how, in episode four, Liz finally grasps the enormity of the situation when she finds that the BBC isn't broadcasting any radio at all. It's still part of the crisis contingency plan that submarine commanders listen out for Radio 4, and if it's *not* on the air, they're at liberty to open their sealed orders.) We'll see the complex again, in 12.1, "Robot", doubling as Think Tank. (13.4, "The Android Invasion" also uses it and disguises the nearest sizeable town, Evesham, as 'Devesham'. Clever, eh?)

The emergency bunker is used as the tracking station in the first scene, although by "Robot" the official line was apparently that no such place existed. Other parts of the complex became the hospital interiors, the patio outside where the Brigadier examines the shard of plastic, the UNIT lab and the Brigadier's office. The discovery of a

Victorian shower-stall led Pertwee to suggest the shower scene. (The tattoo visible on Pertwee's arm is a legacy of a rowdy birthday on HMS *Hood* during World War II.)

• Sherwin, looking like he hasn't slept for a month, plays the dumbfounded doorkeeper with whom the Doctor argues in episode two. He was a last-minute replacement for someone called Geoff Brighty. (We've absolutely no idea why he was replaced - how you can give a substandard performance when your part has no lines, and just stands there when someone else shouts at you, is a mystery.) In one version of the script, this character was revealed to be an Auton as well.

• To explain an apparent Scobie anomaly mentioned in **Things That Don't Make Sense**, the Scobie-facsimile is having to risk detection, so the original is kept alive to mask the signal. But that scene, like a lot of other expository material, was cut. Scobie's cottage was actually the hotel where the cast and crew were staying, and the cottage where Meg Seeley shoots an Auton was nearby (it's the curiously-named Wheelbarrow Cottage, owned by a Mrs Bragg).

• Madame Tussauds was only available at certain times (i.e. the small hours). Pertwee, John, Burdon, Hamilton Dyce (Scobie), John Woodnutt (Hibbert) and - oddly, as he's not in the scene - Courtney were accompanied there by some extraordinarily patient extras playing dummies.

• Hugh Burden (Channing) was the star of peculiar period detective show *The Mind of JG Reeder*. Based upon a series of books by Edgar Wallace, this was about a shabby public prosector who investigated crimes. Burden also wrote a couple of the scripts. At the time, this show was about the most popular drama Thames were making, so *Doctor Who* grabbing Burden between series was a bit of a coup. Hamilton Dyce (Scobie) usually played priests or magistrates (he'd just been in the *Doomwatch* episode with the rats, but had been in the notorious *Big Breadwinner Hog* as a crimelord). He died shortly after this, just before the release of *The Pied Piper* (the one with Donovan and Donald Pleasence), which he'd been in.

• Filming would have concluded (or near enough), save that Martinus was unhappy with the climactic scene of the Nestene succumbing to the Doctor's jamming device. The whole thing was restaged at Ealing a fortnight after the rest of the story was shot (just after the moor chase scenes of the next story were concluded). Burden had other things on, so one of the chief Auton actors - the

suspiciously-named Ivan Orton (maybe he never worked again on anything, ever, or more likely it's someone else trying not to admit to slumming as a *Doctor Who* monster - does anyone know what John Gielgud was up to that month?) doubled as his "corpse". The sound of the dying Nestene Consciousness was recycled from "Fury from the Deep" (5.6), and was made by multi-tracking the squeak of a rubber-soled shoe on lino.

• Although the US bought the rest of Seasons Seven, Eight and Nine as a job-lot - and Australia, Hong Kong Dubai et al bought all 14 stories - the Yanks, contrary to Martinus' ambitions, weren't offered "Spearhead". Still, this story was repeated during the following summer, on Fridays from 9th to 30th of July. The official ratings weren't much (under three million for the first episode) and the experiment wasn't repeated until 1992. Anecdotally, on the other hand, the general public seems to recall the repeats better than the original transmission. Maybe it helped that this was the slot usually reserved for *Nationwide*, and the repeats got the Frank Bellamy illustration treatment in the *Radio Times*.

All subsequent repeats in the Pertwee era are one-episode compilations rather than serials. The repeats in late 1999 on BBC 2 on Tuesdays (in the slot usually reserved for imported "cult" drivel) did far worse, and compounded the damage done by a dreadfully misconceived "Theme Night". We pick *that* story up in Volume VII.

7.2: "Doctor Who and the Silurians"

(Serial BBB. Seven Episodes, 31st January - 14th March 1970.)

Which One is This? There are three-eyed Lizard-Men in caves under a nuclear reactor in Surrey-pretending-to-be-the-North. They have dinosaurs as watchdogs, and use Geoffrey Palmer to spread a plague about in London, hoping to get humans off "their" world. All this, and Fulton Mackay.

Firsts and Lasts The start of the "classic" look for 70s Doctor Who, not only because it's the first story to use colour video, but also because it sees the first use of CSO: the all-purpose special-effect of 70s television. As we'll see, this was a process which delighted a generation by ensuring that all giant monsters, miniature people or inserted pictures had little yellow lines around them. (In fact, most other television programmes put *blue* lines around their monsters, but after 9.1, "Day of the Daleks", *Doctor Who* avoided blue in case it accidentally made the TARDIS vanish.)

Crucially, it's the first story produced by Barry Letts, CSO's biggest fan, who's in charge of the series for the rest of the Pertwee run. It's also Malcolm Hulke's first solo script for the series (he collaborated on 4.8, "The Faceless Ones" and 6.7, "The War Games"), and his input to this phase of the programme will be massively influential.

Here we see the first appearance of the Doctor's car, Bessie; of the Silurians; and of fully-fledged dinosaurs. This is also the only *Doctor Who* story to have "Doctor Who and..." in its title, something that was always a feature of the early Target novelisations (and many of the scripts for Hartnell and Troughton adventures), although in this case there's no particular reason for it to be there (but see **The Lore**). And when the Doctor stops the nuclear reactor going critical by 'fusing the control of the neutron flow', it's the first hint of this era's most shameless and memorialised technobabble (see 9.3, "The Sea Devils").

Behold, the first of three appearances by sitcom stalwart and National Treasure Geoffrey Palmer - in each of these he plays an authority figure who dies stoically before meeting the Doctor (see also 9.4, "The Mutants" and X4.0, "Voyage of the Damned"). As he's not yet famous, Palmer's first death scene is slightly undignified, but it allows us to marvel at his stiff upper lip and the sheer 1970-ness of this near-future setting.

This is the first *Doctor Who* story that doesn't even mention the TARDIS. (Well, 3.2, "Mission to the Unknown" didn't either, but that's a special case.) And episode seven is the first and only occasion when the Doctor is seen in a t-shirt and jeans.

Seven Things to Notice About "The Silurians":

1. The first of Season Seven's monumental seven-part stories, "The Silurians" is also the first colour story to be made "properly" in a television studio. The set-designers, lighting teams and cameramen are thinking it's like black and white drama only with added tinting, and everyone is obviously figuring out what else they can do. So this story - visually and as a script - has to walk the line between fast-paced 70s action TV and old-fashioned, slow-paced SF thriller, and in many ways this is *Doctor Who* at its most

Quatermass-y. Alert viewers might want to tick off the *Quatermass* left-overs as they appear, including the ancient hi-tech civilisation; the prehistoric race-memories; the British scientific institute in crisis; the alien disease; the psychic force that makes people go mad and the post-war paranoia of an invisible threat right in the middle of London.

2. That said, as a seven-part story "Doctor Who and the Silurians" goes down a few detours. On the plus side, this means that nobody seeing it an episode per week could honestly have predicted where the story was going. It looks like it's *Godzilla*, then an alien invasion, then... who knows? We get a manhunt across the moors, a plague in London, and finally a doomsday device. With hindsight it looks like a very leisurely *Doctor Who* yarn (or three somehow jumbled up), but imagine how it looked to anyone who'd been away for a while, and last saw the series when Ice Warriors were chasing Troughton about the moon (6.5, "The Seeds of Death"). However, the flip-side to this mutability lies in episode six, when we see nearly two minutes' worth of the Doctor sitting in his laboratory and looking at microscope slides. Again, these days it's regarded as a liability, but seen one episode a week, it gives the impression of a story unfolding in real-time. Well, a bit.

3. By now you'll be familiar with the idea that until about 1975, a large part of the programme's appeal was that nothing else on television sounded like *Doctor Who*. This was true of the sound effects and also the music. Here, without using synthesizers, Carey Blyton delivers a score that is quite, quite unique. That's a *good* thing, right? Well, until somebody tried using a gamelan, an ophicleide and a crumhorn in the same ensemble, nobody would have known if it could be made to work.

4. Jon Pertwee gets the chance to gurn horribly again, when he's knocked out by the Silurian's eye-weapons at the end of episode six. He's still trying to play the role straight, but one of the series' great understatements occurs when the Doctor inspects one of the Silurians' victims and says, 'She was found in the barn, paralysed with fear... she may have seen something.' An honourable mention, though happens when the Doctor first confronts the hitherto-unseen monster, and asks 'Hello, are you a Silurian?', as if he were Prince Charles visiting a primary school.

5. As we'll see in **Additional Sources**, the nov-

What's the Origin of the Silurians?

We began the first attempt at this by saying that people should concentrate on what's said on screen and what the real palaeontology says. However, even our own essay missed a few obvious clues, so to start again...

The first thing to reiterate is that we shouldn't get hung-up on the name "Silurian". They use the name themselves when announcing their presence to the Sea Devils (who are called "Sea Devils" in the same story, 21.1, "Warriors of the Deep"). If we disregard any connection with the Silurian era - the bit where hefty armoured fish and trilobites did their stuff 430 million years ago - and just treat it as a *name* (like, oh, "the Sontarans"), we can save ourselves a lot of trouble. So let's not worry about whether we should call them "Eocenes" or "Earth Reptiles". They call *themselves* "Silurians", and for all we're told, it might be their word for "far and distant things". Then again, as we'll see, the term "Eocenes" - for all the Doctor advocates use of it in 9.3, "The Sea Devils" - is equally wrong.

The next thing to ponder is Quinn's globe from 200 million years ago, which has Pangea on it. That's still pre-dinosaur, but it's rather earlier than is useful. Bear in mind that for most of the public until the 1980s, the standard account of prehistoric life was typified by the sequence from Disney's *Fantasia*, where a hacked-about version of Stravinsky's *The Rite of Spring* was accompanied by a lurid and severely truncated pageant of volcanoes, eclipses and dinosaurs, all in the space of twenty minutes. The Silurian Era is represented by one fish morphing into several species, then suddenly we have Dimetrodons (a process that skips the Carboniferous Era completely and leaps into a strangely swampy Devonian).

The earlier scenes from this were echoed in "Edge of Destruction" (1.3), when a solar system condenses out of dust in a few minutes. Even in the mid-1970s, few would have questioned the basics of this Technicolor extravaganza.

These days we're less certain that dinosaurs were cold-blooded or sluggish, and the idea that reptiles died out en masse because of overheating is completely discredited. One thing that was grudgingly accepted then - but is now pretty certain - is that the break-up of the original unitary land-mass we call "Pangea" began 195 million years ago, and caused different chunks to have different local species. Why should Quinn have a globe of this, you might ask? He's interested in geology, and his chum the Silurian scientist is interested in everything. Quinn admits that the Scientist hasn't told him much, so maybe part of that "not-much" was proof of the then-theory that Pangea split into Godwanaland and Laurasia. (As we've seen, this wasn't universally accepted when the story was made.)

Red herrings aside (save for the watchdog pet dinosaur in 7.2, "Doctor Who and the Silurians", to which we'll return), we can get on with looking at the facts. The reptile-men foresaw that a small planet would render Earth uninhabitable, and opted to sleep through the consequences. They awoke to find apes were running Earth. That small planet wasn't what killed the dinosaurs - whatever did that arrived with no warning (see 19.6, "Earthshock" for the *Doctor Who* account of this event). So if we're going with a scenario wherein the Silurians are post-dinosaur, we have to explain why they aren't terribly well-adapted to all the Cenozoic Era innovations, such as grass and fruit.

(How do we know the Silurians don't eat fruit, you might ask? Their eyesight. Having one eye seeing everything red-tinted is a liability if you're using colour to determine what's poisonous. Colour vision prevents you eating poisonous berries, or even fruit that isn't ripe, and only fructivorous and omnivorous animals are found to have it. Unless the Silurians have an undisclosed ability to change their skin-colour to attract mates or scare off rivals - something that might have made the bickering in episode five more entertaining - colour vision of any kind is rather redundant for reptile people. This might indicate that it's a vestigial leftover from before the third eye developed. Or it's possible that they harvest only fruit they *know* they can eat and have technological ways of determining edibility. However, the scant evidence we have makes at least a good case for them just sticking to meat. Anyway, look at those mouths.)

One of the helpful things about intelligence, culture and communication is that individuals who would be less viable as parents under normal circumstances live long enough to have offspring. But an intelligent species is actually *less* likely, upon reaching a certain plateau, to undergo rapid biological change. If the Silurians can stare a hole in a wall, they've pretty much peaked. A little thing such as an Ice Age isn't going to worry beings who can centrally-heat caves. And intelligence is a *definite* plus if you're hoping to withstand a global catastrophe. Communication skill is better at han-

continued on page 33...

elisation is a thing of wonder. However, as a side effect, it convinced everyone that this story is Derbyshire's only contribution to the otherwise Home Counties orientated invasion-of-the-month club. In fact, Wenley Moor is never specifically located in the broadcast story (it took "The Sea Devils" to give on-air confirmation of it being in Derbyshire), and thus the story might as well take place in Yorkshire or Devon, even if the location work was done rather closer to home. (See **The Lore** for the full anti-climactic truth.) Attempts to locate the story by means of minor characters' speech are hindered by the farmer and his wife sounding German. The Reptile-men themselves sound Cornish, but that's probably not deliberate.

But wherever this adventure actually occurs, observe how it takes full advantage of its singular-looking locations and spends the best part of an episode doing a "man-hunt" with helicopter shots. (You may sob quietly, however, when the dramatic impact of this is undercut by today's audiences hearing the sound of the signalling device and then saying "Po cootah" like on *Teletubbies*.) In short, even though doing a whole year of Earth-based stories was a cost-cutting strategy, they're splashing out on using more location filming per episode than ever before, even if "Spearhead From Space" is removed from the equation.

6. The amusingly-named Doctor Quinn (Fulton Mackay), seems to be on happy-pills as he explains about the constant threat of meltdown, the emotional disturbance at the facility and the savage deaths of two close friends, grinning from ear to ear throughout. As Liz hears the Doctor overtly suggest that they address the plague by trying 'every drug in existence', one wonders what goes on at the taxpayers' expense down these caves. Non-British, non-old-enough readers should consider that after Mackay's stint at Slade Prison in *Porridge*, he was the original custodian of the British version of *Fraggle Rock*.

7. The final scene - in which the Brigadier follows government orders and (apparently) wipes out the entire Silurian race, while the Doctor can only look on, appalled - is one of the series' key moments. As a story in which the Doctor attempts to act as peacemaker between the human and the "other" (the word "alien" is inappropriate here), "The Silurians" says a lot more about the ethics of *Doctor Who* than any straightforward invasion-from-outer-space story. We'd like to think the series was always like this.

The Continuity

The Doctor The Doctor's feud with UNIT is obviously underway even before the Brigadier blows up the Silurians. He's happy to refer to the Silurian civilisation as 'alien' even after it's revealed to be native to Earth, and claims that his life 'covers several thousand years'. [He's not several thousand years old. See **The Obvious Question: How Old Is He?** under 16.5, "The Power of Kroll" but also 8.2, "The Mind of Evil". It's notable that he claims his life 'covers' several thousand years, and he might be referring to the span of history he's witnessed. However, he's witnessed rather more than that, so it's odd either way.]

Here the Doctor takes broad-spectrum antibiotics with no difficulty [compare with the "aspirin" debate in "The Mind of Evil"].

• *Ethics*. The Doctor values Silurian lives as highly as human ones, and has no problem with the idea of helping the two species live together even though he must realise that a human / Silurian world might contradict known history. The Doctor acts as though the future he sketches is possible and worth trying to achieve, and judges individual humans and Silurians on how far they're prepared to countenance the idea. [He seems much less concerned with changes to the timeline than the First Doctor; see 1.6, "The Aztecs". The Third Doctor's memories are a bit hazy in this period, but it seems safe to assume that he *does* remember the "correct" timeline, and is altogether aware that such a massive change in history would warrant immediate intervention from the Time Lords. That said, he seems unfamiliar with the Silurians' presence in the 1970s, yet will show no surprise that Silurians and Sea Devils are back in 2084 (21.1, "Warriors of the Deep"), nor that the Silurians are noticeably different from the Sea Devils ("The Sea Devils"). Perhaps he studies the Silurians after the Wenley Moor incident; this might explain why he's more conciliatory towards the Brigadier as the next story starts, but even this acquired knowledge doesn't discourage him, somehow, from recommending a historically dubious peace accord in "The Sea Devils". Perhaps, given the relatively small number of Silurians activated, he might think he can manage an accord without the official history "knowing" about it. The other alternative, of course, is that his frustration with the Time Lords, and with UNIT, may have given him a

What's the Origin of the Silurians?

...continued from page 31

dling short-term problems, and the Silurians have both.

This does, however, raise some interesting options when we assess their history, as does the fact that they aren't mammals. They have much longer lifespans, lay eggs (according to Hulke's novelisation) and have opposable thumbs. From an evolutionary standpoint these guys are winners, and even their shortcomings might be helpful. Being reptilian, they aren't really built for sustained running, so they'd have to be nimble - both physically and mentally - to avoid being prey. In some ways, the combination of natural smarts and reptilian DNA should have provided a more elegant solution to that inconvenient impending doom than just hiding in caves. As opposed to trying to carry their old life wholesale into the new dawn, they could easily have left eggs and some pre-recorded messages - letting a new generation rebuild from scratch, adapt to the new environment and take what they need from the previous civilization.

But the thing is, fandom's become fixated on the idea that the catastrophe they're avoiding is the same one that wiped out the dinosaurs. We've got ourselves tangled up trying to make their culture and their biology fit together. The Silurians *as a species* might have withstood the late-Cretaceous apocalypse, but the individual members of the race we encounter were evidently born much *much* later. We know that from the dialogue: they use the word "apes" to describe mankind. Not "mammals" or "primates", but "apes". They recognise humans as being developments of creatures they knew as vermin. *One* throwaway comment could be discarded as the result of a translation glitch or whatever, but they use the term repeatedly for the best part of four episodes. So if the Silurians know about apes *and* can make the distinction between them and monkeys or lemurs, we're looking at an earliest age of 34 million years ago - the start of the Oligocene Epoch. That presumes, however, that they're using "ape" in the widest possible meaning of the word. If they're being specific (and the fact that they have file photos of Orang Utans suggests they are), then it's a whole Epoch nearer our time: the Miocene.

Superficially, this is attractive as a time for them to hide. The early phase of this, about 23 million years ago, has a rapid burgeoning of different types of mammal, including far more ape species than we have at the moment. Nobody at the time could point to any one ape variety and say, "that one will evolve into beings who will one day split the atom and invent Country and Western", or "those orange ones will co-star with Clint Eastwood and appear in *Dunston Checks In*". The very early Miocene even has a sudden spike in average temperatures, causing the recently-formed Antarctic ice-cap to melt again, which is ideal for any cold-blooded reptile-men seeking to build cities.

The question becomes, then, how any Silurians around in the Miocene survived the chilly end to the Oligocene. The obvious answer is that even if they didn't have cities at first, intelligent reptiles have more to gain from discovering fire than mammals did. The final phase of the Oligocene was nowhere near as bad as the Ice Ages. Most of the big reptiles are aquatic. The Sea Devils could have lasted for all of this time, and only required hibernation units when the climate looked like getting drastically worse.

Errr... yes, the Sea Devils. They're intelligent turtles - intelligent, *tool-using* turtles - which makes us stop to wonder. Surely, the advantages of tool-use for aquatic survival are outweighed by the ability to out-swim a shark. Yet these guys are bipedal and have opposable thumbs, neither conditions being exactly optimal for the life aquatic. And there's another thing: that team-up with the Silurians in 2084 ("Warriors of the Deep"). It might *seem* entirely natural that two races of intelligent reptiles would go together, but in fact it's suspiciously cozy. To observe what happens on screen, we have two very diverse species of reptile men who act like the accounts and IT departments of the same company, meeting up before a bowling tournament against another firm.

So perhaps one of these races created the other, unless someone else created both of them. After all, that third eye's a bit handy, isn't it? A built-in remote-control / power-drill is unprecedented in the reptile world. So, come to think of it, is a summoning device that works across such a range. On balance, it's easier to imagine the Silurians creating the Sea Devils than vice versa (those Sea Devil gills, if they *are* gills, are like feathers on a cat), but it's also worth noting that the Sea Devils have much more machinery to play with (they lack built-in weapons, and therefore have hand-guns). We could envisage a sequence of

continued on page 35...

sense of "to hell with it".]

His chief motivation in wanting to revive the Silurians: 'There's a wealth of scientific knowledge down here, Brigadier. And I can't wait to get started on it.' [It's a clear-cut sign of his "greed" for knowledge, which comes to a head in 11.5, "Planet of the Spiders".]

• *Inventory*. He's still carrying his sonic screwdriver, somewhere. He also carries a vial of liquid that can percolate through Bessie's fuel system and jumpstart her.

• *Background*. He hasn't been potholing "in some time". He's seen dinosaurs before, in the flesh, but doesn't know enough about Earth prehistory to recognise the Silurians. However, he seems to think that the moon is a relatively new arrival in the solar system. [Not something that's acknowledged by human research, although it was a theory at the time. As the Silurians were poisoning 'apes' and not shrew-like mammals, the planetary disaster they feared might conceivably, just, perhaps, have involved the Fifth planet of the Fendahl, 12 million years ago (see 15.3, "Image of the Fendahl"). It may even have involved Mondas.]

• *Bessie*. As anyone who grew up with Target novelisations will know, the Doctor's car is 'a sprightly yellow roadster' [this makes it sound like a botched version of *Little Red Rooster*]. The Doctor has evidently only acquired "her" recently, and is already making modifications. Her licence-plate reads WHO 1. [Has this been officially registered? If he deliberately chose the number, it's the first sign that he's trying to generate a deliberate air of mystery around himself, as befits a more showman-like Doctor. Either that, or it's just his surname. See 3.10, "The War Machines".]

The Supporting Cast

• *Liz Shaw*. She's literally and figuratively let her hair down. By now she's accepted that the Doctor isn't human, and she's formally a member of UNIT rather than just a consultant. Her grasp of medicine is good enough for her to suggest treatments the Doctor hasn't thought of. She can give injections without the patient noticing.

• *UNIT*. There's nothing about the Doctor in the files at Central Intelligence Records [see also 8.3, "The Claws of Axos"], and the Brigadier sees him as a personal responsibility. UNIT is called in to investigate scientific and personnel problems at the Wenley Moor nuclear research centre, which

seems a little outside its usual mandate [suggesting that the British government likes to use the organisation to troubleshoot important national projects; we'll see a lot more of this in the next few years]. The Brigadier needs ministerial approval to get reinforcements from the regular army. It's suggested that the Permanent Under-Secretary, Masters, has the authority to recall UNIT from Wenley Moor.

• *The Brigadier*. Much more cynical than during previous crises, refusing to take the Doctor's word that there's a prehistoric monster in the caves even after everything he's seen. [Either he's under pressure from the powers-that-be, or he's skeptical that *every* strange happening has to involve monsters.] He waits for the Doctor to leave before detonating the explosives that either kill the Silurians or, at the very least, seal their vaults. The Brig declares that he wants the base 'sealed', and it's only the Doctor's supposition that genocide is taking place. [The existence of the Silurians isn't in the Brigadier's report to Masters; despite Liz's belief that the Brigadier was acting under orders from above, it's possible the government didn't even know about the Silurians until much later. Jo Grant and Mr Walker, however, have read about them by "The Sea Devils".] Whatever the truth, the Brigadier does his "duty" here.

The Non-Humans

• *The Silurians*. Upright-walking sentient reptiles, with clawed hands, triceratops-like crests and third eyes in their foreheads. Silurians can apparently see through these extra eyes: at will, Silurians can use them to cause pain, unconsciousness or death in living beings. More impressively, the eyes can burn through walls and seal up the holes with a solid ash-like substance afterwards, or even act as remote-controls for Silurian technology.

Silurians don't wear clothes, but have curious "ruffs" of reptilian skin around their necks [their ancestors probably had defensive frills, like Australian frill-necked lizards]. Silurians are stronger and tougher than humans, and being cold-blooded [as dinosaurs were thought to be, back when this was written], they're comfortable in great heat.

The Silurians originally occupied Earth millions of years ago, before the development of humanity. Dr Quinn, who makes the first contact with them, believes they were native to the Silurian era –

What's the Origin of the Silurians?

...continued from page 33

events where the Silurians bred the Sea Devils to farm the oceans, then an unexpected mass extinction event caused the end of the Cretaceous but had less effect on the sea-going reptiles. The surviving Sea Devils rounded up all the Silurian eggs they could, and taught a new generation.

It might also be worth mentioning that just a couple of years before "Warriors of the Deep" was broadcast, Dr Dale Russell of the Natural Museum of Canada has gained considerable publicity for his idea that the dinosaur stenonychosaurus - a scavenger with a hefty brain capacity - could have evolved into something anthropomorphic. (His hypothetical "lizard man" mock-up has no third eye, but the Silurians' extra orbs *do* appear artificial, and some adaptation of the pineal gland would be useful for reptiles in any case.) Russell's humanoid dinosaurs even have the right number of fingers for our purposes, and an opposable thumb and binocular vision. The intriguing thing about Russell's Troodontid is that it comes at a period of the Cretaceous Era when a lot of novel developments are happening. Flowers appear for the first time. If a new niche develops, adaptation speeds up. Most of the older species of dinosaurs were pretty much standardized, with very little variation, and so had less room to manoeuvre when a new situation arose (such as a spaceship or meteor crashing and causing a few years of cold weather and lousy crops). However, the assumption that any biped with a big brain-to-body-mass ratio would land up looking like us is iffy: what about parrots?

Even if the mass extinction *hadn't* happened in a single event, the days of this particular category of dinosaurs were numbered. A new breed, with a greater brain / body-mass ratio and at least the capacity to wield tools and see in 3D (with all the consequent changes in brain-architecture) could have withstood a lot more than the hadrosaurs. Well, maybe. Brain / body-mass ratios aren't the whole story (lots of animals have proportionately large brains but can't do much with them; our brains are convoluted, which is a different story) and this thing's eyes look like they are more used

for night-vision - probably picking on our small mammal ancestors. (Not our *actual* ancestors but their siblings: our ancestors would be the ones who didn't get eaten and lived to breed.) The fact remains, though, that the 60 million years of the Cretaceous Era weren't all alike. There were significant developments, both environmentally and geographically (continental drift kept happening), so if there's a good time to look for the ancestors of the Silurians, this is it.

Enough about how they got started... what happened to make it end? We can pretty much rule out the moon's arrival (unless it was drawn down by crystals - very New Age radfem - in some psychic attempt to free the Xylox as in *The Sarah Jane Adventures*). The very existence of life on Earth suggests the moon was here right from the start (no tidal movement, no stirring up of that amino "soup" we hear so much about - see 26.2, "Ghost Light"; 17.2, "The City of Death"), but it may have taken an excursion. If Mondas came close, the moon's orbit might have done a figure eight and the Cybermen's future home could have wandered off with *our* satellite, returning it on the next close encounter.

However, as mentioned before, there's been a theory that we can observe a cycle of abrupt mass extinctions roughly every 26 million years. Physicist Richard Muller suggests that our sun has a twin, a darker remnant star he calls "Nemesis", that pulls comets out of whack and sends them crashing to Earth every so often (on his "Nemesis hypothesis", see - obviously - 25.3, "Silver Nemesis"). Few people are altogether convinced, but the extinction cycle is more or less there (mass extinction events seem to be getting more spaced-out). So is this the period of Mondas' orbit? Maybe, but the last major wipe-out of species before we started doing it ourselves was 12 to 13 million years ago. We invite readers to look at "Image of the Fendahl" (15.3), and devise whichever scenario seems most apt. We should also note that even if Adric's death actually caused the K/T Event (as it's known, because the German spelling "Kretaceous" makes a more useful acronym), something else more predictable might have been on its way to do slightly less damage.

roughly 430 million years ago - yet has a globe among his effects which depicts the world as it was 200 million years ago. [Either date is clearly wrong, as the Doctor establishes in "The Sea Devils". There was no life anywhere on land dur-

ing the Silurian era, and 200 million BC is still some way wide of the "large reptile" era. See **What's the Origin of the Silurians?**] Both the Doctor and Dr Quinn / Miss Dawson seem to come up with the name "Silurians" independently of each other.

The Silurians are familiar with apes, but not with humans until now. Their leader states that millions of years ago, they detected a 'small planet' approaching the Earth, and calculated that it would draw off the atmosphere. They built a shelter in the Wenley Moor caves [plus other shelters in other places, judging by later events] and went into hibernation, waiting for life to return, but the approaching planet was drawn into Earth's orbit and became the moon. The hibernation mechanism was faulty [see the audio *Bloodtide* for how this came about], and didn't begin to revive them until the nuclear research station was put into operation.

Silurian technology is much more advanced than human technology, with mechanical hibernation chambers [that's 'hibernation' rather than "suspended animation", suggesting that Silurians hibernate naturally but need machinery to do it for such long periods]. They seem to possess a scanning / hypnosis device that numbs Quinn's mind to the point that he walks around as commanded. [Maybe this only works on the willing, as they're never seen trying to hypnotize the prisoners into submission or revealing secrets.] They can also move the walls of their caves so quietly, the trapped UNIT men don't hear the passage closing behind them.

The Silurians can speak and understand English [possibly built-in technology, like the eye]. The ones in the caves have their own personal agendas instead of a racial master plan, frequently threatening to kill each other [these must be quite high-ranking Silurians if they possess a weapon as powerful as the molecular disperser].

[NB: "Warriors of the Deep" implicitly contradicts a lot of the above, showing 'Sea Devil warriors' who have been in hibernation for 'hundreds of years'. Upon revival, some kind of 'orientation' briefs them on the changed situation in minutes - the dialogue suggests either a mental "download" or possibly telepathy. By this point, Silurians' third eyes have no function beyond letting us know who's speaking, and - just to confuse us further - they call *themselves* 'Silurians', even when speaking in private to their Sea Devil allies. See also the accompanying essay, and **Things That Don't Make Sense**.]

When one of the men who encountered the Silurians' pet dinosaur loses his mind, he ends up drawing Palaeolithic-style pictures on the wall, including the outline of a Silurian even though he's apparently never seen one. The Doctor believes this is a 'race memory'. [The man draws mammals as well as reptile-men, suggesting a time when Silurians and large mammals co-existed. If the dinosaur triggered this state, then some kind of dinosaur life was presumably around as well.] Humans facing the Silurians for the first time tend to suffer absolute atavistic terror, with headaches and feelings of oppression being common among susceptible people working closest to the caves. [This is never fully explained. It may be part of the same race memory process (with the humans subconsciously sensing the Silurians' presence), or it may be a side effect of the buried Silurian technology. Probably the latter, as the effect gets worse whenever the Silurians drain power from the station.]

Apes once raided the Silurians' crops, and the Silurians used a bacterium especially engineered to kill them off. The bacterium is highly contagious and kills humans within hours. The Silurians also have a microwave-based molecular disperser, which they intend to use to destroy the 'protective belt' around the Earth [see **Things That Don't Make Sense**].

The Silurians think of Earth as their planet, but here it's never explicitly stated that they evolved on it. [The Doctor's reference to them as 'alien' could arguably indicate that they colonised the world, although this isn't the view taken by later writers - see 4.2, "The Tenth Planet" for a possible sidelight on this].

• *Dinosaurs*. The Silurians at Wenley Moor apparently only have one dinosaur to act as a guard dog. It's clearly related to large carnivores like the tyrannosaurus, although its arms and teeth are noticeably different. [The Doctor identifies a tyrannosaurus on sight in "Invasion of the Dinosaurs", but says the Silurians' creature is like nothing he's seen before.]

History

• *Dating*. [Early 1971.] Again, Britain is still using pre-decimal currency, and the police drive Mk II Jaguars with bells. The UK has an advanced nuclear research project by this stage, attempting to find a safe, reliable form of energy [obviously this project is shut down, which may explain the government's great interest in new forms of power in 7.4, "Inferno"]. In London, there's a Ministry of Science so well-known that taxi drivers don't have to ask for its address [as befits a Britain which has its own space programme]. Cost of the cyclotron at Wenley Moor: £15 million.

Additional Sources The Target novelisation of the story, *Doctor Who and the Cave-Monsters* (1974), is one of the most fondly-remembered of the early novels and, as they did back then, fleshes out much of the background to the plot.

All three of the speaking-part reptile people get names (Okdel for the Old Silurian, Morka - a name later used in Jim Mortimore's novel *Blood Heat* - for the Young Silurian, K'to for the scientist). We get a diagram showing the layout of the research station. There's a prologue set millions of years in the past, which sees the species go into hibernation and establishes that their shelter is one of many across the world. As usual with Hulke's novels, there's more of a "morality play" feel to the human characters, with Quinn dying because he's a bad person (he's planning to wipe out the reptile people once he's got their science, something which doesn't seem at all true of him on TV). Major Barker (as "Major Baker" is called in the book) believes that Britain is under siege from communists, bankers and trade unionists. We're also told that he had to resign from the army after shooting a surrendering IRA sniper. The Doctor and Liz discuss Jung (in a children's book!) during their conversation about race memory. Weirdly, the password when the Doctor and Liz try to get into Wenley Moor is "Silurians". (It was "Cloudburst" in the unused scene on TV.) It's established that Morka himself kills Quinn. Miss Dawson gets a chance to redeem herself in the closing crisis - a more sensible and less sweaty solution is found involving an 'off' switch, and the Doctor doesn't need to remove any clothing.

Crucially, the Brigadier only seals up the caves in the final chapter instead of killing the occupants. (Apart from the Doctor's sour asides at the start of the next story, the main on-screen evidence that contradicts this is Walker's comment in "The Sea Devils". Hulke must have written this book almost immediately after the latter script, as it came out just before Letts' *Doctor Who and the Daemons*[7]. So the traditional fan-revisionist stance, with the Brigadier merely sealing off one of thousands of shelters instead of committing genocide, is one Hulke himself instigated. We'll pick this up when considering the novel *Doctor Who and the Sea Devils*.)

But most notably, the word "Silurians" is never used as a name for the creatures anywhere in the text of the novel. It's only on the back cover; by 1973, Hulke had figured out that his palaeontology was wonky. The book opts to call them "reptile people" (whereas *The New Adventures* - especially with regards stories set in the future - repeatedly refer to them as 'Earth Reptiles'). K'to's death is told with him having a flashback to hatching from an egg.

Better yet, the novelisation has a cover which neatly sums up most of the great childhood obsessions of the 1970s: *Doctor Who*, an alien monster, a dinosaur and - for some reason - a volcano erupting. Unfortunately, the back cover blurb describes the Doctor's encounter with a "40 ft. high *Tyrannosaurus Rex*, the biggest, most savage mammal which ever trod the earth!" (The book is now out on CD read by Caroline John, who has a great time impersonating Pertwee.)

The Analysis

Where Does This Come From? As we're going to see, UNIT gets called in to secure a lot of energy-generating schemes. The mid-1950s had seen Britain take a lead in the use of nuclear power, with the Queen opening the facility at Calder Hall, and for one brief moment it looked like we'd cracked fusion. (Here we're referring to the now-notorious ZETA, which might be said to have started the widespread press scepticism about any such claims later on - see the essay with the next story for a classic example.)

By 1970, we'd shifted from automatically assuming that British engineers would make the next great leap forward to fervently hoping that the newest bit of Big Science would put us back on top. It was still possible, although the culture shock of needing to co-operate with France over Concorde was just sinking in. The big hope of the early 70s was the Linear Motor (these days called "maglev"; it was designed by the telegenic Professor Eric Laithwaite), and the way the incoming government let this get squandered was, for many, the last straw.

Note, though, that all of the projects are government-funded and run by administrators with scientific credentials (apparently in a totally different field), but who are clueless about management. To nobody's surprise, Dr Lawrence has friends in high places. Professors (which in Britain means scholars attached to a specific university) run such projects, not lords. The advent of the private sector in government-funded Big Science is, axiomatically, a bad thing (see 10.5, "The Green Death"). So the "normality" that the Silurians subvert was consistently in the news at the time of broadcast.

In other ways, we're also on familiar ground. The connections to *Quatermass* are obvious (especially *Quatermass and the Pit* this time, which also deals with the alien influence on Earth's pre-history), but note that "Doctor Who and the Silurians" turned up just two years after Kubrick's *2001: A Space Odyssey* - and every other writer had his or her own theory about the relationship between Atlantis and the Missing Link. We ought to warn you now that the 70s was a golden age for bonkers theories that caught the public's imagination, and we're going to have to explain these - or remind you if you'd subsequently buried the memory of Romark, Pyramid-power or Est. *Life on Mars* and pop-nostalgia shows fail to convey the true strangeness of this period. Frankly, it seemed weird enough at the time. So proceed through the rest of this book on your guard against half-forgotten garbage, and keep an eye out (your third if possible) for the likes of ley-line hunting, *Chariots of the Gods* (more on this under 8.5, "The Daemons") and Israeli showman Uri Geller (he bent spoons with his "psychic abilities", and used to claim that his powers came from extra-terrestrials before it got too embarrassing).

Anyway... if you've read Volume II, you'll know how we got to this state. People would earnestly pontificate about what a thoroughly bad lot "Man" was. (They talked about their own species in the abstract like that, "Man does this, Man does that", as if to exonerate themselves.) There were plenty of children's TV shows like this (many of them by Bob Baker and Dave Martin, of whom more later) over the following years, all fitted out with ancient civilisations, Neolithic stone circles and buried psychic powers. So "The Silurians" is a good lead-in. However, we're going to have to reach further back for where this story *really* comes from...

It's perhaps too obvious to need saying, but for all the 70s flavouring[8], this story's roots are Victorian. First, there's geologist Charles Lyell's once-shocking discovery that the Earth has been around for a lot longer than humans have. The feeling of awe that most eight year olds gain upon understanding of the age of the Earth is something an entire culture came to terms with in the mid-nineteenth century. Then there's the idea that the

deep past, and the depths of the Earth, contain power that civilised society could not possibly comprehend (we'll pick up the Krakatoa theme in two stories' time). And one of the many themes in late-Victorian literature is the "How would we like it?" idea, with other races treating *us* as we were treating other parts of the planet. (Obvious examples would include Conrad's *Heart of Darkness*, with the Romans using the Thames as the Belgians were using the Congo; Rider-Haggard's *She*, with a Queen Empress who knew Jesus and patronises the British for their culture's immaturity the way we did to America; and of course Wells' *The War of the Worlds*, with heavily-armed Imperialists trashing Woking but falling victim to tropical diseases.)

All told, it's hardly a stretch to see the Silurians as both parodic little-Englanders complaining about these smelly new residents *and* the coming of the White Man threatening all-purpose indigenous peoples (see 8.4, "Colony in Space", also by Hulke, and "The Mutants"). It's that satirical tendency overall, rather than specific "sources", that bears most heavily on this story: the ability to look at ourselves from outside, and find ourselves wanting.

Then again, it would be churlish to ignore Lord Lytton's *The Coming Race* (1871), a massive bestseller telling of subterranean troglodytes / *Ubermenschen* with different technology threatening to rise and engulf us. The underground-dwellers of this book lived on "Vril", a liquid electricity that was some kind of life-essence, and the word caught on enough for a beef extract drink to be called "Bovril" and promoted with extraordinarily lurid ads. The origin of the word is in the Jain faith, as explained to the West by the French Consul to India - one Francois Jacolliot (1837-1890) - and which reached Lytton. Supposedly, he then inspired a German "Vril Society" (a real-life Nazi version of Torchwood who - according to science writer / space advocate Willy Ley and others - found a crashed Atlantean flying saucer and got it to work).

The Coming Race seems to have inspired the Theosophical Society, who are sort-of responsible for many of the sillier things found in Volume II. Versions of Vril are to be found in the writings of Himmler and George Lucas (the latter, if you couldn't guess, calls it "The Force"). Sir Edward Bulwer-Lytton (as the book's author had been) also gave us the classic opening line, "It was a dark and stormy night..." and the first Roman-set melo-drama (a toga-ripper, if you will), called *The Last Days of Pompeii*. It just begged to be adapted as soon as someone got around to inventing cinema. Basically, Lytton is the Terry Nation of Victorian literature, picking up on ideas that touch the national psyche so well as to overcome any lack of finesse in the writing.

But as with "Inferno", the *main* specific influence on "The Silurians" is Arthur Conan-Doyle's second-best-known hero, Professor Challenger. In this case, we're specifically talking about *The Lost World*. Speculating on the idea of places where time has stood still, and invites the primordial to come and visit us, shatter our pretensions towards control (cf *Godzilla, The Beast from 20 000 Fathoms* et al). HP Lovecraft wove some of this into his Cthulu stories, a fact that caused *Doctor Who* tie-in writers to co-opt the Sea Devils into their efforts at a consistent cosmology (see **Are All These Gods Related?** under 26.3, "The Curse of Fenric").

For many people, though, the fact that humanity is not coeval with the planet chafed on the notion that we were special enough to have an elevated relationship with a creator. So some people, seeking to harmonise both world-views, proposed the idea of a civilised race before Man. Examples of this covered elsewhere in *About Time* include the bizarre Teutonic mythos of the *Werlteislehre* (see 16.1, "The Ribos Operation") and Immanuel Velikovsky's *Worlds In Collision* (see 11.3, "Death to the Daleks"). This last chimed with one theory about the moon's creation (a hot topic in the early 1970s, as we thought we'd get answers live on TV) and can be seen lurking behind the obvious silliness of "The Tenth Planet".

We'll pick this up when discussing "The Daemons", "Death to the Daleks" and "The Time Monster" (9.5), but suffice to say that school textbooks solemnly informed us that the gravity of a passing planet pulled the moon from the Earth's molten crust (and was all the really heavy stuff, which is why it formed a sphere so quickly before cooling). Others said we "borrowed" the moon from the orbit of a really big passing planet. There was no doubt at the time that planets used to wobble about a lot in the pre-Cambrian era, before settling down and doing what Kepler said they should.

One then-novel idea, which has become so mainstream that it's hard to think of it as a dismissible new theory along the lines of Atlanteans inventing cricket, is plate tectonics. It was only in the 1960s that geologists took the idea of continental drift seriously, and the news filtered into the public domain via those earnest educational weekly mags like *Look and Learn* or *World of Wonder*. Schools were still not entirely convinced as late as 1975, which is why the Doctor explains to Liz that Quinn's globe reflects how the continents were arranged millions of years ago. (See 19.6, "Earthshock" for how long it took BBC Special Effects...)

Then there's the Silurian disease, with its bacterium sub-plot that brings something nasty-but-feasible into the heart of modern Britain. (We were congratulating ourselves about wiping out smallpox, so schools' TV was full of stuff about cholera epidemics in Victorian London.) The lab scenes of episode six - and the dissolves in particular - echo dramas about plagues like *80,000 Suspects* (set in early 60s Bath), the biopics of great scientists (generally played by Paul Muni or Edward G Robinson), and, indeed, Hartnell curing the Sensorites of their 'plague' (1.7, "The Sensorites"). At that time, Marius Goring (he was Maxtible in 4.9, "The Evil of the Daleks"; see also 22.3, "The Mark of the Rani") was regularly doing this sort of thing in *The Expert*, usually in scenes directed in the same manner. (If you get to see any BBC drama from the 60s that isn't *Doctor Who*, you'll greet this style of interlude like' an old friend; it's almost the equivalent of the channel-zapping from News 24 to US / global news stations to the kids' shows you get in a Russell T Davies two-parter.)

Biological warfare was a low-budget form of Yellow Peril / Red Menace that B-movies could do: it was cheap, insidious and made people turn on one another - just the sort of low down, dirty trick them rooskies would try. More to the point, though, plague at the time was the most favoured explanation for the extinction of the dinosaurs. It seemed appealing to a lot of people that something so tiny could fell these mighty brutes. (This chimed with the ironic end of *The War of the Worlds*, for anyone who missed the Malaria parallel.) Besides, alien infiltrators always got associated with disease because they're foreigners.

Director Timothy Combe suggests that the Silurian POV shot at the end of episode two is inspired by Magwitch's first appearance in David Lean's film of *Great Expectations* (1946). To be honest it doesn't look much like that, but the split-screen triple-vision with one eye tinted red does look a lot like (guess what) the Martian POV in George Pal's *The War of the Worlds* (1953). That film was responsible for all notions of contact with "otherness" to be interpreted as Cold War parables. Wells and Hulke, though, were far more subtle and set their sights on satirising the very audiences who lapped it all up.

Things That Don't Make Sense Let's just get this out of the way... if Liz wants to be taken seriously, she really should rethink her wardrobe. We're sure the nation's dads loved it but, as a young woman working in a predominantly male environment, it must have dawned on Liz that those minis and boots only serve to distract from her academic credentials. Still, at least she isn't running up and down ladders (wait until the next story for that one, when even the Doctor seems to be sneaking glances). But when talking about Liz's wardrobe, we should perhaps ask whether that little suitcase she pops on Bessie's back seat is dimensionally transcendental: in the course of the story, Liz seems to have lots of short skirts and about a dozen tops (not including her spelunking gear).

Human beings suffer uncontrollable terror, and even amnesia, when faced with the Silurians. At least until episode four, when the Silurians show themselves in full and characters keep forgetting to be scared. Liz, who recoils with primal horror the first time she sees one (an incident that requires UNIT to negligently let her work alone, unguarded, in a local barn even though there's a potential hostile in the area), doesn't even flinch the second time. And when a Silurian hunting-party finally overruns the base in the last episode, not one single member of staff has the expected nervous breakdown. It's said that only 'certain' humans fall under the influence, but why would that be the case? Don't all humans have the same ancestry?

Furthermore, the whole notion of the guard-osaurus falls into *Scooby Doo* territory: it's presumably there to scare off / kill interlopers, but draws more attention to the caves than it deflects.

The Brigadier spots Silurian footprints and asks the Doctor if they're the same as the "tyrannosaurus" ones from the cave, to which the Doctor replies, 'No, these are the footprints of a biped.' So, um, how many legs did the guard dinosaur have? Later in the caves, the Doctor and Liz stumble upon the Silurians' guard-dino; we can safely presume that it's "leashed" by one of the

Silurians' invisible barriers, but this is never said. For all the two of them know, the dino might charge out and bite their heads off while they're trading a bit of exposition, yet they don't step back or leg it at all. They might as well be looking at a patch of blue paint.

At times, the Doctor's memory lapses go well beyond blocks on dematerialisation theory. 'Never could stand that man', he says about Dr Lawrence in episode two, as if they know each other of old - when actually, they meet for the first time here. Episode one also features the Doctor asking Dr Quinn, 'You have your own nuclear reactor, do you?' even though they've discussed just that in a previous scene. (Even Quinn seems to be a little taken aback by this, his perma-grin briefly faltering.) But for his part, Quinn has an extremely curious notion of the phrase "acting with discretion". He's trying to prevent the authorities from learning about the Silurians, but then he blathers to the Doctor - a member of UNIT - about the two junior techs who were injured while pot-holing, *and then he proposes that a cover-up is taking place.* Granted, as he suggests to Ms Dawson, Quinn is probably just 'acting normally', but he's practically begging for an official investigation.

Farmer Squire and his wife sound German. Meanwhile, the Silurians seem to be from Yeovil. For someone who hasn't actually met the Silurians, the Doctor draws a diagram of one for Doris Squire - with scant regard for her mental health - not only very quickly but surprisingly accurately. (And no, he's not copying the wall drawings from episode one, because they were in profile and his sketch is full-face.) Nobody seems to have told the director that the second cliffhanger looks like a botched attempt at 3D, and sounds like Liz and the Silurian playing at being a steam-train.

More bizarre behaviour from Quinn: what does he hope to accomplish by blundering onto Squire's farm looking for the lost Silurian? He *knows* that the police and UNIT are present, and he can't do anything if they've already found the creature. Going there only serves to cast suspicion upon himself; surely, it'd be far better to just search the outlying area. And when Quinn does so, his signal device must be *toothrattlingly* loud, if the Doctor and Brigadier can hear it from so far away and over Bessie's engine noise. Later, when the Doctor and Liz are riffling through Quinn's office papers, why does the Brigadier enter the room as if he fully expected to find the Doctor there?

So, the Permanent Under-Secretary and the head of a top-secret research station are briefed on the existence of troglodyte reptile men. Within moments, not only does Masters seem surprisingly comfortable with the idea, but Miss Dawson bursts in and announces Dr Quinn's death. Somehow, she's intuited that the people around the table will comprehend her use of the term 'Silurians'. (The Doctor and Liz have already used the word to describe the era which Quinn's globe seems to represent, but Dawson doesn't know that.) Later on, Major Baker's miraculously using the name too. [A possible explanation is that the Silurians *do* call themselves just that, and Quinn and the imprisoned Baker hear them using it. That said, it's worth noting that the name "Silurian" doesn't just apply to a time-period. The rocks that gave their name to the era were so-called because they were characteristic of an area of Wales once inhabited by a tribe called "Siluri". Indeed, the Mid-Wales region still occasionally uses the name, hence the Silurian Male Voice Choir. Yes, really! See **Why Didn't Plaid Cymru Lynch Barry Letts?** under 10.5, "The Green Death". In which case, our only worry is why ancient Celts picked such a similar name.]

Dr Lawrence is a project leader who's so obtuse that the alarming confirmation of all the Doctor's theories and the news that Dr Quinn has been murdered fails to make him face facts. Neither is Major Baker's equally dramatic entrance - in which he accuses the Doctor of selling out humanity to the reptile men, then falling ill - enough to make Lawrence come to terms with reality. So how did Lawrence land up running a project this big? Even the Permanent Under-Secretary, who knows him well and seems to have got him the gig, can only *attempt* to exonerate the man.

But then, despite Major Baker contracting what's obviously a virulent disease, Masters thinks it's a good idea to head back to London, even though he's feeling a little faint. And once the plague breaks out, why does the Doctor research the cure at the Wenley Moor base? Another facility would provide more security against the Silurian assault that he should *know* is coming, and as most of the equipment and samples are shipped in, it's not like he'd lose much if any time.

In episode six, there's a strange misunderstanding of how medicine works. When Liz goes a bit woozy, the Doctor suggests it's because her antibiotics have worn off, and that she should go and get another jab. Antibiotics aren't like caffeine, you know. Basically, this scenario would only make sense if the bacterial infection was waiting for a certain kind of antibiotic to somehow lose effectiveness against it (which could only happen if the bacterium mutated in the space of half an hour), or if Liz's blood cells were being replaced at something like six times normal speed. Anyway, if Liz is feeling woozy because of the disease's effects, then shouldn't she fall ill and die like everyone else? Later, disaster strikes again as the first reported instance of an overseas death occurs in Paris. Yet no strange deaths are reported en route from Derbyshire to London, or London to Paris, meaning that someone abruptly dropped dead in gay Paree without infecting anyone on the way. [They must have got T-Mat working.]

The Silurian third eye - all very Theosophical and what have you - has some alarming and inconsistent features. We can swallow the idea of it being used to knock out the Doctor, open doors in the cave-base, operate machinery with just a head-wobble and even (up to a point) that it can melt through rock and brick. What we *don't* buy is that in episode seven (as the Silurian raiders make their exit with the unconscious Doctor), it not only makes rock grow back, it can re-plaster a wall. True, we've observed the sonic screwdriver "healing" barbed wire (X1.10, "The Doctor Dances"), but this still seems like having a magic upholstery beam. ("Set phasers to linoleum"...)

The Doctor's powers of concentration are amazing: he seems utterly oblivious to the wall-charring, whining noise and burning smell going on behind him while he's focussed on writing on a bit of paper. And while it perhaps makes sense that he'd crumple the paper he's writing on - to stop the Silurians from realising it's the formula for the plague-cure - does he really have time to do so? And why does the Doctor take the time to write out the entire formula for Liz? They've been working with a vast array of indexed drugs, so why not just tell her the sample number (or numbers, if it's a couple of drugs in combination)?

The Van Allen Belt is named as the protective area around the Earth that filters out a lot of the sun's radiation. Whereas *in fact* the Van Allen Belt is just a layer of radiation (the thing that filters radiation is the ozone layer). [But it's only Liz who explicitly mentions the Van Allen Belt, and she's under a lot of stress. Who knows? Given the way she's accessorised - including getting her skirt snagged on her belt in the first episode - and the fact that the chain-store "Van Allen" was briefly fashionable back then, her mind may be wandering due to the Doctor's bold fashion-statement in that scene.] However, using microwaves to disperse either of these is like using sonic hypno-signals in space. Hulke is following Whitaker in more than one way. [That said, the idea of diminishing the Van Allen Belt isn't entirely relegated to fiction - physicist Robert Hoyt and the late Robert Forward seriously proposed HiVOLT, a means of using high-voltage tethers to weaken the Belt and further space exploration.]

A logic flaw that only becomes clear after "The Ambassadors of Death" (7.3): a few weeks after this story, the honour of a successful "First Contact" is enough for Sir James Quinlan to justify murders, conspiracies and sabotage, yet Whitehall sanctions whatever action it is the Brigadier takes expressly to prevent this happening in Wenley Moor. Clearly, some aliens are more equal than others.

Finally, the Silurians seem *awfully* confident that they can wait out the impending "nuclear disaster" and awaken in fifty years time, considering a faulty alarm clock was what caused humanity to inherit the planet, and got them all into this mess in the first place.

Critique   Received wisdom would have one believe that "Doctor Who and the Silurians" is great, but also that it's two, maybe three episodes too long. What nonsense. If the 2000 repeat of this story in the *Star Trek* slot did nothing else, it proved that week by week (as this was *meant* to be seen, not all in one go on DVD), this unfolds very methodically. Given the ground it covers, it's actually one of the *leanest* stories ever made (and certainly one of the most comprehensible adventures not to have long, slow info-dumps). Every episode pushes us into a new state of play, with a few concessions to anyone who missed a week. So actually, the only thing wrong with this story (apart from the music and one or two flawed performances, to which we'll return) is that if anything, it's not long *enough*.

If anything, "The Silurians" is best thought of as the first seven episodes of a series that only, er, well, lasted seven episodes. Once you accept that the Silurians are here and want their planet back, they could've unleashed a different plan to remove

the apes every week or every month. Ideally, we'd have all experienced *The Silurians* as a good little independent series, *or* as a four-part *Doctor Who*, followed by a sequel about a plague a while later. Call Jon Pertwee's character "Dr John Smith" and craft a different military set-up, and you've got separate show. And evaluating *that* as vintage *Doctor Who* would then be as pointless as judging it by other things shown on BBC1 at teatime circa 1970 (like *The Monkees*, *The Rolf Harris Show* or *Star Trek*).

Any flaws result from its being made as a *Doctor Who* adventure: in such a state, it requires a dramatic and definite ending (hence the contrived business of the overloaded reactor and the Brigadier's orders), and monster costumes made in a hurry, funded from a budget that needs to last a whole year. It has to sketch an entire society with four costumes and three speaking aliens. It needs one big control-room set and a lot of caves. And it makes viewers think the bits with the Doctor and Liz pouring over test tubes in episode six is "filler material". (If you resist thinking of this "fluff" as occurring in the sixth episode out of seven, the objection starts to drop away. Series like *Battlestar Galactica* or *Heroes* routinely have bigger *longueurs*, by virtue of having 22 hours per year to tell their story.) Only Nicholas Courtney's presence, the UNIT uniforms and a throwaway line about the sonic screwdriver give any connection with *Doctor Who* as it was understood until January, just five weeks earlier.

The worst side effect of this is that, as with the next two stories, the reset button isn't so much pressed as it's cudgelled. By story's end, the Doctor finds himself in league with people who act against his every instinct: the UNIT seen here, for all the support they give the Doctor when he's useful to them, is only a step above Torchwood as far as his moral parameters stretch. Had the Brigadier's apparently blowing up the Silurian caves elicited more consequences - had it warranted more than a couple of mentions in future, one of those mumbled in the next story - we could have watched a different (and possibly better) series. But, from now on, grumbles about 'the military mind' are more just kneejerk one-liners than a chance for Pertwee to express any genuine outrage. It takes alternate timelines before he lets rip ("Inferno", "Day of the Daleks"), but at least we know from these that he's electrifying when given the opportunity. This Doctor isn't the superman he starts to become from the next story onwards, and his only real advantages are an open mind and a willingness to listen.

But we need to look at the even bigger picture here - because as you've hopefully guessed, 1970 was a curious time in British television. The two big networks had switched to colour, yet most of the viewers hadn't. BBC2 (the supposedly avant-garde channel) had shown the majority of video-taped drama made in colour so far, so directors with experience in the basic differences of floor-management, lighting and costume requirements were at a premium, and were unlikely to have made much bread-and-butter telly in 625-format. And the void isn't confined to BBC series - you can see the very same problems in ATV / ITC's *Timeslip* (their very own low-budget, live-action Sunday evening children's adventure show).

The point is that at this juncture, practically everyone was making it up as they went along. The result is a series of shows that make wild experiments and bold dashes in some directions, whilst playing safe in others. And if nothing else, "Doctor Who and the Silurians" fits into this pattern by attempting, awkwardly, to use colour for storytelling purposes. The Silurians' subterranean base gets a more earthy look than the sterile human variety but, unfortunately, even with colour sets (and the splendid restoration for DVD), this causes an odd problem. Watch the first few minutes of episode five, and you'll see that Lawrence's office is all one colour. Liz's dress blends in with the curtain so well, she almost looks camouflaged. The Silurians are the same colour as their base, and the beige UNIT uniform blend into the rocks. All of this is lit for mono-chrome, with no attempt to use lighting for dra-matic purposes, and all these different environ-ments are lit from above in exactly the same way. Everything seems to pull back from trying to make television more like film; there's something of a retreat into a cautious, theatrical approach. It's only temporary, but once you notice this, there's no mistaking it. The first cliffhanger unveils CSO to the BBC1 viewership, albeit after a lot of stalling. In just a few weeks, "The Ambassadors of Death" will begin with a pre-credit scene that - in amongst setting up a mystery and trying to make the show look more 70s - proudly announces, "Look! We can do *this!*", when showing the vast blue screen turning into a huge telly. All the CSO work in "The Silurians" is low-key, for storytelling purposes only, and embedded in scenes that are

almost routine for TV drama of the era.

Yes, Season Seven seems a bit painstaking by BBC Wales standards, but few of *their* stories would pass muster if measured by the criteria that are appropriate here. Neither should we catego-rize this as a later-era Pertwee / UNIT story "gone wrong". This is emphatically *not* a trial-run for "Invasion of the Dinosaurs", nor a warm-up for "The Sea Devils". It is what it is, and if later stories aren't like it, that's their hard luck. This is first story made since John Wiles was booted as pro-ducer in 1966 that's pitched toward grown-ups, with the assumption that *some* of them will be in the audience. This isn't "adult" in the sense of dirty movies or *Torchwood*, it's "mature".

As director, Timothy Combe isn't trying to wow us with shock tactics, he's making the story (which is the novelty here) clear. Everything else has to be made as matter-of-fact (and as much like mainstream television) as possible for the Silurians to be a disruption. The montage of UNIT coping with the plague is another example of this dichotomy: that style of sequence is very familiar to anyone who's seen 1960s BBC drama (other than *Doctor Who* or soaps, that is), but it's *colour* that inhibits even the most seasoned modern viewer from donning those mental rose-tinted glasses sometimes required to watch old televi-sion. The three seven-parters this year all have that problem, but "The Silurians" has fewer flam-boyant distractions. Besides, why *would* you watch this all in a single sitting? It's not a race.

As for the Silurians themselves... well, sure, obviously they don't quite match the standards of prostheses and masks we expect these days. They occasionally look and sound ludicrous, with West Country accents and wobbling heads. We're expected to buy their technological skill but we're made to witness them having difficulty holding beakers and tripping over their own feet. They're still a lot better than they needed to be, though. Even today, three animatronic masks is beyond the series' resources, which is why the new series has a single talking Ood or Judoon, and a lot of goons in the background. Here, even though it's the indefatigable Peter Halliday doing all the voic-es, we have up to four talking Silurians in some scenes, and some genuine conflict between them. A child who expects this will be like, say, "Daleks in Manhattan" (X3.4) might be bemused by the slow pace and silly music, but would be rewarded with a plot they can follow and aliens with com-prehensible motives - whose disputes never get as silly as the Cult of Skaro gossiping in corners.

This adventure is a transitional work in another way too: the music. Everyone has an opinion on this, but few seem to notice that it's schismatic. Some of it is scored with familiar instruments in major keys for very small children, like a *Jackanory* or *Play School* story about soldiers chasing monsters. It's more enigmatic and minor key when dealing with the Silurians themselves. The percussion arpeggio theme for the lost civilisation would have been the starting-point for most stories, but here it's sandwiched between clarinet and piano music worthy of a school play. If this seems petty, consider what it tells us about the production team's approach: namely, that nobody seems to know who watches *Doctor Who* any more. (Pay particular attention to the way the very next story seems made for an entirely different audience.) For better or worse, we've swapped producer in mid-stream, and the research shows they've been making it for the wrong demographic. Occasionally we see glimpses of a version of a better version of *Doctor Who* that wouldn't have lasted as long, as well as a more infantile version that didn't deserve to.

Similarly, the cast all pitch their performances differently but not consistently. We can't correlate the seriousness of any actor's performance to whether he / she gets to share a scene with a man in flippers and a wobbly reptile head. Geoffrey Palmer (Masters) gives pretty much the same performance no matter what he's in, but Thomasine Heiner (Miss Dawson) seems to be in a children's show and Peter Miles (Dr Lawrence) is in a sitcom - a terrible, ITV early seventies sitcom of the kind nobody would be allowed to see these days, except in clips on documentaries on how standards have changed. Knowing how the character ends up, he could have modulated the paranoia to make each new setback push him further, but instead he begins with borderline hysteria and then ramps it up. Miles cornered the market in sarcastic, whiney petulance and prima-donnaism, but here he went too far; we're left wondering how Lawrence was put in charge of such a complex and sensitive undertaking.

Which brings us to another curious feature of this story: a child viewer today, and to some extent in 1970, is waiting for the moment when these hysterical non-believers are confronted with Silurians in their base. It never comes. Dr Lawrence freaks out and dies because of them, but

he's never shown gibbering when he realises it's all true. The story doesn't go down the predicted route at any turn. Only when the reactor is set up to overload does it look like they're deploying a conventional *Doctor Who* plot-ruse, and even *then* the Doctor really doesn't know how to switch it off. This is a story with two - count 'em - two manhunts, one across moorland and one in London. Combe is relying on the story-concept to hold the viewers' attention, something that today would require an almost reckless amount of faith in the youth of the nation. Or whoever he thought was watching.

The Facts

Written by Malcolm Hulke. Directed by Timothy Combe. Viewing figures: 8.8 million, 7.3 million, 7.5 million, 8.2 million, 7.5 million, 7.2 million, 7.5 million. Audience appreciation fluctuated between 57 and 58%, except for a spike of 60% for episode four.

Supporting Cast Fulton Mackay (Dr Quinn), Norman Jones (Major Baker), Peter Miles (Dr Lawrence), Thomasine Heiner (Miss Dawson), Ian Cunningham (Dr Meredith), Paul Darrow (Captain Hawkins), Peter Halliday (Silurian voices), Geoffrey Palmer (Masters), Richard Steele (Sergeant Hart), Dave Carter (Old Silurian), Nigel Johns (Young Silurian), Harry Swift (Private Robins), Pat Gorman (Silurian Scientist), Alan Mason (Corporal Nutting).

Working Titles "The Monsters" (as in "Doctor Who and the..."; one suspects it was intended as a clever double-meaning).

Cliffhangers The Doctor descends into the caves, and finds himself menaced by a dinosaur; alone in a barn, Liz Shaw finds something inhuman bearing down on her and breathing heavily; the Doctor (along with the audience) comes face-to-face with a Silurian for the first time in Dr Quinn's cottage; in the Silurian base, the Young Silurian uses his third eye to try to kill the captive Doctor; Major Baker dies of the horribly disfiguring bacteria outside the hospital, and the Doctor announces that he's just the first; the Silurians burn their way into the lab where the Doctor's working on the cure for the disease, and use their eye-weapons to bring him down.

What Was In The Charts? "Witches Promise", Jethro Tull; "Let's Work Together", Canned Heat; "Come and Get It", Badfinger; "Ruby (Don't Take Your Love To Town)", Kenny Rogers; "Love Grows (Where My Rosemary Goes)", Edison Lighthouse; "I Want You Back", The Jackson Five; "Wandrin' Star", Lee Marvin.

The Lore

• To quickly recap the production team musical chairs... Peter Bryant and Derrick Sherwin had been taking turns as credited producer, but in fact had been sharing duties since 6.4, "The Krotons". Both were planning to leave soon, but events forced their hand. Sherwin had been at work with actor Jon Rollason (the "forgotten" sidekick to Steed in *The Avengers*; he's also the oily journalist Harold Chorley in 5.5, "The Web of Fear"), and they had devised a series called *Special Project Air* that looked like a winner. Sherwin and Bryant had set up a lavish pilot film with overseas location, and had bagged Peter Barkworth (see 5.3, "The Ice Warriors"), no less, as the star. The plan was to film in Singapore before starting work on the new season of *Doctor Who*, then get cracking on Pertwee's debut in October. They hoped that Bryant would take over as nominal producer of *Who* from "The Silurians" on, and if the new show took off, they'd look after the older series - assuming the BBC still wanted to make it after the end of Pertwee's first year - whilst launching the new one.

Naturally, it didn't pan out like that. Two episodes of *Secret Project Air* got made and were shown to widespread indifference in November. This was 1969, when German TV companies started getting the bright idea that if British companies made programmes their viewers liked, it was cost-effective to shove large sums of money into Anglo-German co-productions. So whilst ITC gave Jason King his own show at the request of der Bundesrepublik, the BBC got to work on adapting *Paul Temple* for television. The radio version of the Francis Durbridge thrillers had been a fondly-remembered hit (some people in the UK still get moderately emotional on hearing the tune *Coronation Scot* but, as with *The Devil's Galop* - see 24.3, "Delta and the Bannermen" - it's more for the era than for any specifics of the plot), but the TV adaptation was going horribly wrong. So Bryant and Sherwin were called in to advise; of course, by "called in", we mean "taken from whatever they

were doing" and by "advise", we mean "produce this turkey or get fired".

The BBC bosses had a Plan B. They hoped to rope in someone who'd directed *Doctor Who*, plus had shown great initiative and the ability to rewrite scripts to suit contingencies. Someone with immense logistical savvy, and intense enthusiasm for the series. That man was - wait for it - Douglas Camfield, who was then directing episodes of *Paul Temple*. He would probably have accepted this field-commission, had it not been for medical problems that only came to light during the recording of "Inferno". Fortunately, the BBC had someone else with pretty much the same qualifications, even if he'd only directed one *Who* adventure to date. And that person was...

• Barry Letts, who by this time was a jack-of-all-trades. He'd begun as a child actor, been in work in the early days of live TV drama (co-starring with Patrick Troughton) and had gone on to write and direct. He also did the script for a curious episode of short-lived soap *The Newcomers*. It's one of four episodes that exist in the archives, none of them looking like they're from the same series as their fellows. Letts' episode is like *Who's Afraid of Virginia Woolf?* intercut with *Last of the Summer Wine*, and it went out six months before he directed 5.4, "The Enemy of the World". When making that story, Letts heard Troughton list complaints about the remorseless timetable of making 42 episodes a year, and he'd proposed to the BBC drama heads a series of revisions based on Troughton's suggestions and some of his own. Letts took the gig on condition that he could use it as a shop window for his directing, perhaps thinking that the series wouldn't last long enough for him to get bored or pigeon-holed.

• As we'll see, the next three stories were an exercise in crisis-management (it wouldn't be *Doctor Who* if things ran smoothly, would it?). As soon as Letts took over full control of commissioning stories and casting the regulars, the measures he proposed became standard practice and made everyone's lives a lot easier, but he didn't get to implement them *just* yet. He was contractually obliged to stay with his current project: a soap called *The Doctors*. While this state of affairs lasted, Letts was officially producer of *Doctor Who*, but Trevor Ray (officially credited as "associate script editor", sometimes) did a lot of the day-to-day running. Letts was brought onto the team on 20th of October, while the team were in Wood Norton filming what was still called "Facsimile" (see last story). The first production meeting for the new story seems to have entailed Letts being introduced to Terrance Dicks by Bryant and Sherwin, who then left the series for all practical purposes. Ray joined them soon after, with Robin Squire taking the bulk of the deputy script editor duties. (Ray had other things on his plate, as we'll see in the next story.)

Whilst discharging his other duties, Letts boned up on his new job and found that something like 58% of viewers were over 21. He made a few notes for things to change, like the UNIT uniforms (he felt they were a bit "comic opera", although the design was supposedly authentic; see 8.1, "Terror of the Autons") and the "Jimmy of the month" change of personnel under the Brigadier. Publicity for this story emphasised the car and the family-appeal, not the increasingly "adult" elements of the drama this year. Letts also made one significant change to the script, shifting the emphasis of the last episode of "The Siluirians" from the Doctor's curiosity about this alien science to simple outrage that intelligent beings could be treated as disposable because they were deemed a "threat". Over the coming years, this will become the programme's stock-in-trade. The rest of the episode was unchanged, making the Doctor's conclusion that the Brigadier has been ordered to commit genocide something of a non-sequitur.

• On being told Bryant and Sherwin's bold new concept for *Doctor Who*, Malcolm Hulke was contemptuous, stating it left just two ideas - mad scientists in labs or invaders from space - open out of a formerly unlimited range. (This is a bit rich, given that Hulke's previous contributions had been "The Faceless Ones", i.e. the first real invaders-from-space-in-contemporary-Britain story; and "The War Games", which has aliens abducting humans *and* a lot of stuff in a lab with an amoral scientist. Nevertheless, as we saw in Volume I, he'd submitted a lot of unused ideas.) Dicks now claims that he simply replied "dinosaur-men want their planet back" as a counter-example. Whatever the case, it seems that the cave setting came before any other element.

• While the first draft was being planned, it became apparent that Brian Wright's "The Mists of Madness" was probably not going to get made, and that David Whitaker's "The Carriers of Death" needed a lot more work. Thus, the Hulke story was brought forward to be the new Doctor's second adventure. As with Hulke's previous efforts

since the very start of the series, his scripts worked on the premise that the character was called "Doctor Who" and had people address him as such. He also followed the 60s custom of calling stories "Doctor Who and the...", and nobody corrected this when the captions were being prepared. Hulke's novelisation reintroduces some ideas from the first script, like Quinn's father (a noted physicist) coercing his son into following his field rather than geology as a career. As anyone who's seen Honor Blackman-era *Avengers* will know, Hulke tended to bone up on obscure aspects of science, then give viewers the selected highlights and a lot of "did you know" facts. This gave actors a sense of the script being solidly plausible, but on the downside, Hulke was occasionally prone to jumping onto the first bit that took his fancy and not following through. When this story was broadcast, schoolchildren wrote in to point out the error inherent in the name "Silurian" and the goof with the Van Allen Belt.

• One of Sherwin's last acts as producer was to hire Timothy Combe to direct this story. As a production assistant, Combe had helped out when the director of 1.8, "The Reign of Terror" (Henric Hirsch) fell ill. He'd also supervised the model Dalek battle at the end of "The Evil of the Daleks", and had worked on *The Newcomers*.

• The nearest we get to the setting being acknowledged as Derbyshire is Liz telling the Doctor that 'that part of the country' is famous for caves. (Derbyshire has many remarkable caves, and if it helps the local economy to let non-UK folks think there's a connection with *Doctor Who*, we won't spoil it here. In fact, one Derbyshire cave, Treak Cliff Cavern, was used as a CSO slide in 12.5, "Revenge of the Cybermen".) However, although Combe looked into the possibility of a shoot at Wookey Hole (again, see "Revenge of the Cybermen"), the entire story is made in reasonable proximity to Television Centre.

The first sequence to be filmed was the Marylebone Station sequence, with Geoffrey Palmer arriving for real from his Buckinghamshire home. Contrary to popular belief, the ticket-collector is Trevor Ray, not Terrance Dicks. Terrance is there, though, as are many of the production team in a cost-cutting exercise. Letts took a dim view of this and it would be a long time before production staff would appear in front of the camera (see 13.5, "The Brain of Morbius" for the next prominent example of it happening). The Wenley

Moor scenes were executed in the Guildford area, and that rustic street-scene in episode one is Godalming High Street (it's changed a bit since).

• Bessie is based on a not-too-elderly Ford Popular chassis with a glass-fibre shell. Ray, it seems, first suggested that this kit-car could be a permanent vehicle for the Doctor, after the experiment with the Vauxhall in the previous story. Pertwee had seen a television programme that featured the company making these conversions, Siva / Neville Tickett (Design), so the idea was almost bound to be explored. Subsequent stories made play with Bessie's "unexpected turn of speed" by undercranking the camera, but here she's merely transport. The abortive Gerry Anderson project *Secret Service* has a remarkably similar vehicle, "Gabriel", which can be seen in most *UFO*[9] episodes. Steve McQueen drives a markedly similar car - identified as a 1905 Winton Flyer - in the film adaptation of *The Reivers* (1969). Bessie's registration number wasn't actually WHO1 (as someone else already owned it), but rather MTR5. Any time you see the car with WHO1 plates, it's filmed on private property.

• Production manager Christopher D'Oyly-John recalls that Combe's location filming was slightly shambolic. Film cameraman "Fascist Fred" Cameron is said to have mocked the director behind his back, and apparently knew in advance that the Marylebone shoot would need to be remounted. (D'Oyly-John may be embroidering this tale for comic effect, but this is the only adventure he worked on between "The Invasion" and "Inferno". To be fair, almost any director would seem slovenly compared to the downright scary pace of Douggie Camfield's shoots. Certainly, nobody else recalls Combe as being particularly inept or amateurish, and Letts hired him again for 8.2, "The Mind of Evil".) On location in Godalming, the crew shared a hotel with a conference for Olivetti, and the two parties tried to out-drink one another. Thus, when the shoot over-ran and no-one else was available, it was, apparently, a hung-over production manager who donned Silurian head and gloves and menaced Caroline John in a hay-barn for the second cliffhanger. (Again, we have to approach this anecdote with caution.)

• During filming of the last scene, the explosion ignited the grass. The fire brigade was called, and Ray copped the flak. John seems only to have been needed for one location day. She didn't like location work much, especially the lack of suitable toilet facilities, and improvised with three large umbrellas to preserve her modesty. If you look closely in the scenes in episodes two and six - shot at the Milford Chest Hospital - you'll see that one of the nurses, the one who doesn't get close-ups, is Bella Emberg. Overseas readers will have to take it on trust that by the time of her guest cameo in X2.10, "Love and Monsters" (where Elton shows her a photograph of Rose), and the famous cut scene on the bus in X3.0, "The Runaway Bride", she'd been a household name and then a "where are they now?" case. She also pops up again later in the Pertwee era, so keep a look out for her. You'll also see the taxi-driver twice more (well, "see" is pushing it; Mostyn Evans is wearing an Exxilon mask and a big shroud on one of those occasions, but look at 10.5, "The Green Death").

• The Brigadier's rapid turnover of Captains results in future *Blake's 7* star Paul Darrow making an appearance (we don't know if Hawkins is called "Jimmy" but it's a safe bet). Also in the cast is Fulton Mackay, fresh from his first long-term TV role in the Derren Nesbitt vehicle *Special Branch* (now remembered, if at all, for the horrid floral shirts with matching ties that made the star's chest resemble flock wallpaper). A couple of years later, Mackay become a household name for his role in *Porridge*, and would be considered as Pertwee's possible replacement as the Doctor. As you may recall, he shares with Hannah Gordon (she's Kirsty in 4.4, "The Highlanders") the rare distinction among *Doctor Who* guest-cast of having a rose named after him.

Former Guards officer Geoffrey Palmer was already a regular guest-artist on all the usual shows you could cite here (his TV debut was in *The Army Game*), but he would be instantly recognisable from 1976 after playing Uncle Jimmy in *The Fall and Rise of Reginald Perrin* and a great many similar parts thereafter. Like Palmer, Peter Miles (as Dr Lawrence) will also make return visits, notably as Nyder in 12.4, "Genesis of the Daleks".

• During rehearsals, as John remembers it, Pertwee was a little put out that nobody was paying attention to Apollo 12 (the second mission to land on the moon). Pertwee got his Nehru-collar when he and John were given futuristic lab-coats (John's had been used in episode two). In one of his first acts as producer, Letts had words with the *Radio Times* about their coverage of the previous story, "Spearhead from Space" - a source of contention was how they'd picked up General

Scobie's habit of referring to the Brigadier as "Stewart" (an old public-school insult, getting people's names slightly wrong - think of how Churchill pronounced "Nazi"), and some spoilers that appeared in the pre-season publicity. They had also accompanied the first colour episode with a still of the Doctor and the Brigadier in caving gear from this story.

• Only after a day spent shooting a man in a dinosaur suit against a CSO backdrop did the production team realise they could have just used a puppet. Ironically, this is why this dinosaur looks halfway decent (cf "Invasion of the Dinosaurs"; 10.2, "Carnival of Monsters"). An assistant in the Visual Effects team - Bertram Collacott - toiled in the suit, with oxygen fed to him through a tube by Anna Braybrook, who built the costume. (In the cast list attached to the script, Collacott's "character" is listed thus: *Bertram the Friendly Monster - Himself.*)

• One of Letts' bright ideas, first attempted here, was recording scenes according to set-order. The decision was more or less forced on them - designer Barry Newbery found that the cave-wall sets, contracted out to a nearby company, were shoddily made and would not stay up, so the cave sequences were attempted on the second week. During recording of these, Pertwee ridiculed the scripted suggestion that Liz would go caving in a mini-skirt, so John was fitted out with a boiler-suit, tin hat and boots. Because of the hassle of keeping the set vertical, they opted to get two recording days in a week, and leave the cave standing in the studio overnight. Letts would more diligently follow this precedent later. The rest of the story was recorded in episode order as per usual, except for the beginning of episode four (to avoid rebuilding the set for Quinn's Cottage for the reprise, about thirty seconds' worth of new material).

• The Silurians had small electric bulbs, operated by twelve-volt batteries, built-in to the head pieces. The actors' tongues would push plastic pegs, and thereby work their mouthpieces timed to pre-recorded dialogue by Peter Halliday (see 6.3, "The Invasion"; "Carnival of Monsters" and others). A trial version of the voice-effect was tried with Sheila Grant (she's the Quark voices in 6.1, "The Dominators"). Gerry Abouaf made the heads and James Ward made the bodies; they were both members of the effects department (such things would hitherto have been part of Costume rather than Effects, but the lines become blurred from now on).

• Carey Blyton, composer of this story's (shall we say) *distinctive* soundtrack, had a curious but formidable background in music. While writing this score, he divided his time between doing advertising jingles and his post as Professor of Harmony, Counterpoint and Orchestration at Trinity College. His last major television work had been adding a clarinet part to the *Andy Pandy* theme when they remade a few episodes in colour.

He scored "The Silurians" with what he felt were appropriately old instruments, such as ophicleides, crumhorns and Serpents. (The last was a sort of leather clarinet in a zig-zag formation, looking more like plumbing than a musical instrument. An ophicleide - since you ask - was a bass version of this, used by Mendelssohn and Berlioz in their compositions, but these days replaced by tubas.) Blyton had the luxury of picking projects that interested him, as he had royalties coming in from a few long-running ads and his best-known work, *Bananas in Pyjamas*. He rang Combe to play him the crumhorn, the sound he wanted for the Silurians. Contrary to what's been stated elsewhere, it was a genuine wind instrument (a mediaeval oboe) and not a synthesiser effect. According to Combe, it sounded even worse over the phone. Blyton would soon bring his exotic tone-colours to "Death to the Daleks" and "Revenge of the Cybermen". Oh, and his aunt wrote *Noddy*.

7.3: "The Ambassadors of Death"

(Serial CCC. Seven Episodes, 21st March - 2nd May 1970.)

Which One is This? British astronauts are swapped for radioactive aliens; UNIT get a half-episode shootout in a warehouse a la *The Ipcress File* and John Abineri gatecrashes a different ambassador's reception from the one he's more famous for today. The term 'moral duty' gets a right pummelling and Liz wears an amazing hat, in a space paranoid conspiracy thriller *not* about viruses or faking the moon-landings.

Firsts and Lasts The TARDIS console is removed from the Ship for the first time, allowing the

Doctor to work on it in his UNIT HQ lab. As such, this is the last mention of the Time Vector Generator (a central element in David Whitaker's previous story, 5.7, "The Wheel in Space"). Benton, veteran of "The Invasion" (6.3), returns to the programme to make his colour debut and is promoted to Sergeant. (In fact, a generation of British schoolkids could be forgiven for thinking "Sergeant" was his first name.) Here Benton's just an average UNIT member, not the all-purpose odd-job man for the Brigadier he becomes later. He only appears in two episodes and doesn't even get to speak to the Doctor.

First time the cliffhanger is announced with the "sting" beginning the end theme, as becomes standard for the next two decades (see the accompanying essay), although the rest of the title-sequence is messed up royally. We get our first sight of actor Michael Wisher, who will return to the series many times (see, in particular, 10.2, "Carnival of Monsters" and 12.4, "Genesis of the Daleks"). Behind the scenes, Ian Scoones has arrived and brought his spaceship-model expertise with him. Also on hand for the first time: the Havoc stunt team (more on this in **Things to Notice**).

Most importantly, for anyone who's been reading *About Time* from the start, this is the last story written by David Whitaker. Even though the finished version differs greatly from what he wrote, it has his stamp on it, and nowadays there's a real sense of the torch being handed on. (Malcolm Hulke - in many ways Whitaker's heir as the "conscience" of the series - is mainly responsible for getting this story to the screen.)

First sight of the "Pertwee Death Pose": supine with one knee aloft. It happens here when he returns from space and gets gassed by Reegan, but he gets to do it *twice* in the next story alone. There'll be many, many more...

Seven Things to Notice
About "The Ambassadors of Death":

1. Since "The Seeds of Death" (6.5), which was directed by - ooh, look! - Michael Ferguson, they've been monkeying with the opening captions. Soon they'll settle on the format most people associate with Pertwee stories, but here, the story title doesn't appear all at once. Instead, the words "The Ambassadors" arrive first, in a slow zoom, followed by the sudden and pleasantly over-dramatic addition of "OF DEATH", complete with sinister electronic sound-effect (the now-famous "sting" that ends every episode from now on, albeit clumsily edited). This is also the only story to sandwich the cliffhanger reprise halfway through the opening credits, another attempt to make the series look more dynamic. The result is either kitsch or "gritty", depending on whether you were seven at the time.

2. The magic breadvan. You'll know it when you see it. They're shooting for a James Bond approach with this, a vehicle driven by sinister government conspirators that can change its appearance at the flip of a switch, but the result is more *Rentaghost* than *Thunderball*. The programme-makers wasted a lot of time on this "Special effect" that might have been better spent checking that Liz Shaw's hair is the same length from scene to scene.

3. The sight of the spacesuit-clad "ambassadors" walking towards the space centre, faceless and framed against the sun, is one of those scenes that nobody who saw the programme as a child has ever been able to comfortably forget. It's actually one that the director has used before and since (in "The Seeds of Death" and "The Claws of Axos"), but here the pacing of it - and the spaced-out Debussy-style music - make it altogether more eerie. In the other two scenes like it, the monsters were menacing despite being a bit slow; here they're alien, and it's precisely *because* they move at their own pace that they're uncanny.

4. This being a Whitaker story (at least to begin with), "radiation" behaves exactly like static electricity except that it's conducted by wood as well. In a more innocent age, when we were writing Volume II, we thought things like this were either charmingly dated or some kind of folk-memory of an older tradition of storytelling (see **What Planet Was David Whitaker On?** under 5.7, "The Wheel In Space"). These days, we cling to such items in a desperate bid to make it appear that the climax of "Evolution of the Daleks" (X3.5) actually makes sense, somehow.

5. Experienced *Doctor Who* fans will greet the credit 'Action By Havoc' - denoting the team who will perform all manner of stunts in the Pertwee era - with a huge, nostalgic rush of affection. Indeed, the warehouse fight in episode one - a full-on Action moment like you'd get in *The Sweeney* a few years later - is almost as if Derek Ware's butch lads are setting out their stall. "Meet the gang 'cos the boys are here / boys to entertain you". Get a good look at each of the faces, because you'll be spotting them in fights and falls for the

next few years. Especially keep an eye on the blond UNIT trooper who seems to get killed three times, and seems baffled when a rifle is shot from his hands. That's Terry Walsh, and from now until - ooh, seven years hence in "The Deadly Assassin" (14.3) at least - he'll be popping up all over the shop. (Sometimes even when you aren't supposed to notice him; see especially 11.4, "The Monster of Peladon".)

6. Cyril Shaps is back (see 5.1, "The Tomb of the Cybermen"), which means we get a Cyril Shaps Death Scene. In fact we get *two*, as there's a moment when the radioactive spacemen seem ready to zap Dr Lennox but spare him at the last moment. However, the hurried re-writing of this story means that Lennox's *real* death - a nasty incident where he's locked in protective custody and someone brings him a meal that's a radioactive isotope in disguise - looks very odd now. As we'll see in **Things That Don't Make Sense**, we've got a whodunnit. However, the messed-up editing of the multiple versions of the script and last-minute decision to bring back John Levene makes it seem like the lovely Sergeant Benton is in on the conspiracy and bumps off Lennox himself.

7. For the first time since his last seven-part story (4.9, "The Evil of the Daleks"), Dudley Simpson has gone to town on a lush score, albeit one where the music cues are occasionally at odds with what we see. Whilst the main "alien" music uses a whiny synth sound with a processed flute arpeggio effectively, and the battle scenes use a UNIT theme we'll hear done electronically in "The Mind of Evil" (8.2), there's moments where the score veers from jazzy stuff seemingly from a French *nouvelle vague* thriller to a smoochy saxophone more suitable for Soho strip-clubs in the 50s.

Most noticeably is a piece of ersatz Bach for the docking scene in episode one. Some commentators think it sounds like *A Whiter Shade of Pale*[10], but it's much more like Jacques Loussier's nightclub jazz arrangements of Bach - especially the version of *Air on a G String* used for the ads for *Hamlet* cigars. As these ads used to show losers consoling themselves after mishaps, this is perhaps unfortunate.

The Continuity

The Doctor Still brooding about the Brigadier's slaughter of the Silurians, although he's at least still prepared to work with UNIT. It's implied that the Doctor still doesn't have all of his memories: concerning what he knows about the alien signal, he says, '... in my mind, the information's here, but I can't reach it.' [Throughout Season Seven it's implied that large chunks of his memory are missing, although it's not *yet* suggested that he can't remember how the TARDIS is supposed to work. Later stories suggest the latter is what's keeping him on Earth, and he here works on the console as if the fault's purely technical. It's as if the alien signal, like the name 'Devil's End', somehow fills in his head with dematerialisation codes.] He can withstand considerably more g-force than humans.

The Doctor is capable of making an object in his hand vanish without trace, then reappear again moments later. He calls this 'transmigration of object' and says there's a great deal of difference between that and pure science. [This isn't time travel, and nor can it be simple sleight-of-hand. The Doctor never demonstrates this ability again, ever. Or does he?[11]]

Even the Third Doctor, fond as he is of machinery, doesn't trust computers.

• *Ethics*. On this occasion, he doesn't actively try to make peace between humans and aliens, but considers his work done as soon as he's sure they won't kill each other. [Getting off the planet is still his priority, and he only does what's necessary rather than seeing himself as a full-time peacemaker.]

• *Inventory*. There's a jeweller's eyeglass in his pocket.

• *Background*. He recognises the sound of the aliens' communication, but can't remember where from. [We're clearly meant to think that he's had prior experience of this species, and that his amnesia is blotting out, but the end of the story calls this into question.]

• *Bessie*. A switch on the dashboard activates an anti-theft device, so anyone touching the car gets stuck to it by a 'force-field'. Victims of this can soon escape, as the device isn't strong enough 'yet'. Bessie has a canvas roof, yet seems to be bullet-proof. [The Doctor is concerned, though, about the Brigadier's men damaging her with gunfire in 8.5, "The Daemons".] Liz isn't able to out-

How Believable is the British Space Programme?

If you had asked anyone in 1950s Britain which nation would be first to the Moon and when, most people would have said "us" and "around 1980". In the era of *Dan Dare*, the conquest of Everest and the Festival of Britain (see **What Kind of Future Did We Expect?** under 2.2, "The Dalek Invasion of Earth"), British aerospace companies were busily trying to harness jet power for commercial use and beat the sound barrier. Both of these were immediate goals of the de Havilland company, based in Hatfield, Herts. Their "Comet" airliner ushered in the Jet Set and, until the death of dashing test pilot (and son of the founder) Geoffrey de Havilland, Mach 1 - the speed of sound - was an attainable goal. America's Chuck Yaeger got there first in the Bell X1, in 1947... or at least, he was the first credited for it. (Some Spitfire pilots managed it by accident in tight dives, but few were conscious at the time.) *The Quatermass Experiment* (1953) and the earlier radio serial *Journey Into Space*[16] (in which the first episode contains a priceless line about how a rough take-off had shattered every valve in the radio - see also 6.5, "The Seeds of Death") simply stated that it would be British (or Commonwealth) astronauts up there first. David Lean's film *The Sound Barrier* makes the unspoken connection between jet power and the moon, repeatedly.

The shift in emphasis from aircraft to rockets is less obvious than it seems now, however. Whilst ICBM programmes necessitated the development of missiles capable of the thrust required for escape velocity, the process developed for the X1's successors - dropping a small rocket-plane from a high-altitude jet like a B52 - continued well into the 1970s for the Shuttle tests. This resulted in Neil Armstrong getting *close* to being the first astronaut in 1960 in the X15. In Britain, the various aircraft companies had advanced testbed models of such craft up until 1962-3. The BAC / English Electric "Mustard" (an acronym for Multi-Unit Space Transport And Recovery Device - look, it was the sixties) was, in effect, the space shuttle two decades early[17]. A prototype in wind-tunnels was shown to visitors from US rivals Lockheed and Bell, who promptly made their own (the X20, or "Dyna-Soar" - look, it was the sixties). This was a shuttle on top of a missile, and nearly ready when Alan Shepard was first sent up in a Mercury.

Arthur C Clarke, a member of the British Interplanetary Society and one of the developers of the first plans, wrote *A Prelude to Space* (1948), which describes how this approach might have got a British astronaut up by 1965. The Nazis had been helpful there too, with their Messerschmidt 163 Komet - a rocket-powered fighter that was simply too fast for any test pilot to control. The technology behind this was something the Americans and Soviets ignored, so the British grabbed it. In 1952, Clarke had received a visit from the Americans' secret weapon: Alexander Satin, Chief Engineer of the Office of Naval Research and (incidentally) nephew of the composer Rachmaninoff. America, Satin realised, almost had the thrust but not the navigation. Clarke's paper on "Geostationary Satellites", from 1945, was all that was missing.

However, pure rocketry wasn't the British way. Apart from the recent memories of Werner von Braun sending V2s to trash London, the Ministry of Defence (formerly the War Office) had been caught up in the romance of Spitfires and Lancaster bombers. Rockets don't have on-board pilots with handlebar moustaches. "Piggy-back" would have been the obvious route into space, using a bomber as launcher for a smaller ship (in the post-Suez era this would have "sold" the retention of the Vulcan and Victor to a sceptical nation). Bristol Siddely developed an air-breathing engine, the Thor (used in the Bloodhound missiles you can see in the "medley" in 6.3, "The Invasion"), and with refinements it could have propelled an aircraft to Mach 7, i.e. seven times the speed of sound. That's easily within reach of escape velocity had a smaller ship been launched piggy-back.

The most effective air-breathing engine is a ramjet, which uses the speed of the air intake to compress the air with the injected fuel, usually self-igniting. It's low-maintenance and fuel-efficient. Ramjet research in the US was left to one side, but British companies continued to investigate the problems of supersonic combustion and openly speculated on materials needed to withstand Mach 14. The size of payload as a percentage of the launch mass goes up from 4% (the best any rocket ever managed) to 35%. Southampton University had something on the drawing board in 1962. If you've experienced the feature film *Thunderbirds Are Go!*, you'll have seen a refinement of this idea with the Zero X mission to Mars taking off from an airport (with cars driving remarkably close to the runway), aided by radio-controlled "Lifting Bodies". Amazingly, in a film with a pink Rolls Royce pursuing a helicopter gunboat and

continued on page 53...

race her pursuers, suggesting that Bessie isn't yet souped up any more than is street-legal. [See 9.4, "The Mutants" for the Doctor's decision to exceed the laws of the UK and Physics, and 9.5, "The Time Monster" for a first use of this.]

The Supporting Cast

• *Liz Shaw*. Either she has fewer reservations than the Doctor about UNIT's treatment of the Silurians, or she doesn't seem to want to rock the boat. She met Dr Lennox once, while she was doing research at Cambridge, prior to his being somehow being disgraced in such a fashion that his degree was revoked. She also recognizes General Carrington as a member of Mars Probe 6 and knows at least a smattering of French.

• *The Brigadier*. As in the Silurian crisis, the Brigadier is wary of aliens and doesn't wholly disagree with Carrington's assessment that they're a threat. Yet, once Carrington has revealed his plan and silenced all other protesting voices, the Brig is forthright in his opposition. He's prepared to use force (and is plainly seen gunning down opponents in the notorious warehouse shoot-out), but only once he knows the facts. He has the authority to hold people on security charges for 'a very long time', can find Araçibo and Algonquin on a map and isn't averse to appearing on TV.

• *Benton*. Promoted to Sergeant. He's able to do basic forensic checks and handle distraught scientists. [He has to be likeable straight off, so his "doppelgänger" in the next story can seem "bad".] He's already demonstrating an ability to have ideas too simple for the Brigadier to think of, such as using Bessie as a troop-transporter.

• *UNIT*. They have land rovers with the logo on the sides, and drive these through populated areas with impunity [as with the Mystery Machine from *Torchwood*]. UNIT's base is close to the National Space Complex, which is in turn 'seven miles' from the warehouse. [Even if we assume that this isn't the same complex as the one in 13.4, "The Android Invasion", i.e. Devesham, it gives a bit more support for the idea that UNIT is based in the West of England, even though the script seems to assume London. In the last episode, Benton shows Carrington's bunker to be somewhere between off the M4 motorway, around Reading. Depending on the Doctor's definition of 'not far from here' and Benton's of 'quite near the Space Centre', we're looking at Berkshire and Gloucestershire as the most likely sites of the orig-

inal UNIT building. See **Where Is UNIT HQ?** under 8.3, "The Claws of Axos", for more.]

UNIT have apparently got the right to open fire on human combatants without giving warnings. In some ways they're subordinate to the national military - a General can pull rank on the Brigadier and replace all UNIT troops, placing them under guard. [The same was implied in 7.1, "Spearhead from Space". We'll see a lot of this later, in "The Claws of Axos" for example.] The basic uniform has changed, with most ranks getting a white rollneck under a V-neck tunic with a zip, although the Brigadier's outfit remains the same.

The TARDIS The console has been removed from the Ship and set up in the lab at UNIT HQ, where the Doctor is trying to reactivate the console's time vector generator. [That's 'reactivate', not "repair". See **Why Doesn't the TARDIS Work?** under "The Time Monster".] The reactivated generator is capable of projecting someone several seconds into the future, with a miniature version of the usual TARDIS wheezing, groaning noise. [It's fair to assume that the console can make short hops in space as well, since it wouldn't have squeezed through the TARDIS doors otherwise. The end of 6.2, "The Mind Robber" episode one seems to imply this, although it's debateable whether that actually happened. Alternatively, it's possible the Doctor just took it apart, somehow, and reassembled it outside the Ship.

[In "The Edge of Destruction" (1.3), it's suggested that the power of an entire star lies under the TARDIS time rotor, and it's doubtful that the displaced console has access to this energy. This has since become the default explanation of how the Ship works and why the Time Rotor goes up and down, especially since X1.11, "Boom Town". We note that the console was powered down but not shifted in 17.5, "The Horns of Nimon", so there must be some kind of "plug" for all that energy. As seen in 22.2, "Vengeance on Varos", the console has some residual power of its own, and see also 7.4, "Inferno".]

The Non-Humans

• *The Aliens*. Never named, the aliens encountered by the Mars Probe mission aren't native Martians. Carrington notes that they were 'on Mars' before humans, and believes them to come from a different galaxy. The aliens require exposure to radiation to survive, the radiation emitted

How Believable is the British Space Programme?

...continued from page 51

"Cliff Richard Junior" performing on a giant rocket-powered guitar, this one detail is almost entirely accurate.

Rocketry, though, was more of a fringe interest until 1953. The development of a guidance system looked like too tough a nut to crack; von Braun hadn't got this sorted, and *he'd* had first the entire Nazi war-effort, and then the US military, at his disposal. When it seemed like a good idea for Britain to get the Bomb, an efficient delivery system seemed entirely sensible too. Sure, we had Vulcan bombers, but they flew too low and slow to evade these new MiG fighters developed by the Soviets (still the most likely recipients of such weaponry). De Havilland got the gig, and the "Blue Streak" ballistic missile went into production. Based in the Isle of Wight, Sanders-Roe went solo and produced the "Black Knight" rocket, with which they got to 400 miles high in 1961; the US gave them money to test the various re-entry shield materials. Their launches were remarkably Heath Robinson (see 26.3, "The Curse of Fenric" for an example of why this illustrator's name became an adjective) but were, until Gagarin's launch, ahead of anything in the world.

After a few early tests at Spadeadam in the Lake District[18], Woomera in Australia became the principal site for Blue Streak test-launches. What the Americans had in industrial muscle, British technicians made up for in skilled detailed work. If you were making rockets one at a time, then the Rolls Royce company's traditions - good enough for US companies to use its aero-engines - would have sufficed. Well, that's sort of the case... the government were already tightening the purse strings, so the plan was to get hold of Rocketdyne's best engine and adapt it a bit. Rolls Royce's engineers "adapted" the S3D beyond all recognition. British-designed engines were notable mainly for the development of using hydrogen peroxide as an oxidant (indeed, the Rocket Propulsion Establishment at Westcott, Buckinghamshire, conducted tests on the hydrogen peroxide use into the 1970s), but passed through a heated silver mesh - well in advance of anything in Baikonur or White Sands. Nevertheless, for political reasons the American model was adopted as standard.

Several fuel / oxidant combinations were tried, most of them ingenious self-igniting combos like nitric acid / aniline or hydrazine and hydrogen peroxide. The last works by breaking down into superheated steam and very hot oxygen; this combination has all the properties of the fictional "M3 Variant" mentioned in "The Ambassadors of Death", but is rather safer. It's also comparatively cheap, especially set against the costs per foot-pound (as they measured it then) of the Rocketdyne F1 used in the Saturn V[19].

However, being based on the imported American design, Blue Streak's motors used kerosene and liquid oxygen and took ages to fuel-up. In the event of a war, critics said, the missiles would still be getting the volatile materials slowly and very gently pumped into their tanks even as Soviet / Chinese / Welsh missiles fell on London. For this reason, Blue Streak was eventually abandoned as a military programme. (It also had the recurrent problem that as the fuel was used up, the remaining fuel sloshed about in the tanks, affecting the guidance.) Although de Havilland had drawn up proposals for purpose-built depots (what we'd now call "silos") the proposal was not considered by the MoD, although - mysteriously - when the US Dept of Defense hired RAND's Herman Kahn to devise a raid-response system, he came up with something almost identical.

Other countries found ways around this, but hadn't got as good an engine. In the spirit of the age, with Science *sans Frontieres* being both idealistic and affordable, the European Launcher Development Organisation (ELDO) pooled expertise from Britain, France, Germany, Italy, Holland and, um, Belgium. For these purposes, Australia became part of Europe. In 1962, Blue Streak was agreed upon as the missile to be used as the first stage of the ELDO rocket Europa 1. Stage Two was the French Coralie (the weak link of earlier test-launches), and the Third Stage was a German missile called Astris. By 1970, on the tenth launch, they had all three stages working perfectly and launched it from Woomera - during "Inferno", actually.

But as with the TSR 2 fighter, just because a project is streets ahead of anyone else's, that doesn't always mean it's going to get propped up with taxpayer money. Defence Secretary Duncan Sandys' spending review in 1962 cut funding for Blue Streak and Mustard. Roy Jenkins (Sandys' replacement when Labour got into power in 1964) later nixed TSR2, and Technology Minister Anthony Wedgewood-Benn finally pulled the plug on Blue Streak in 1968. This, more than any

continued on page 55...

by their ambassadors being measured at over 2,100,000 rads. One touch from an alien - even through clothing - can kill or cause small explosions, and when one of them touches a metal beam, the soldier at the other end of it instantly collapses. [He's probably only stunned, since he seems back on duty later in the story. A guard also survives direct contact with one of the ambassadors in episode seven.] This death-touch appears to be a controlled, conscious act, as it doesn't happen every time they touch something [though they killed one of the Mars Probe 6 astronauts by accident, so among their own kind it might just be a handshake]. The aliens aren't damaged by bullets [probably due to some sort of 'force-field', as the Doctor says, or possibly because they're radiating enough energy to melt bullets - see also X1.6, "Dalek"], and they're not susceptible to g-force.

The alien on board the spacecraft - though never seen in full - is roughly humanoid but covered in a featureless blue-grey substance which sparkles. On the other hand, the ambassadors on Earth are similar to human beings, though their skin is pale blue and their facial features are covered in hideous disfiguring lumps. [It's fairly obvious that the alien on the ship is the same species but clothed, wearing a kind of shroud and connected to machinery by organic-looking tendrils. Their skin may suggest that they evolved on an Earth-like planet, but damaged themselves with radiation and eventually became dependent on it - much like the original Daleks, oddly enough. Did we mention that this is a David Whitaker story?] The aliens have a means of conditioning the Earth astronauts into believing they're on Earth watching football [an international as it happens, as it's said that 'we' are losing, although England equalised whilst the Doctor was talking to the alien]. They do this benevolently to protect the astronauts' sanity - and yet threaten to destroy Earth [somehow] if their ambassadors aren't returned.

The alien spacecraft is an ovoid mass of glowing matter which looks almost organic, is about half a mile in diameter and is very manoeuvrable for its mass. It can stop in space after approaching Earth very rapidly [and would need some kind of stealth technology that can be switched off, for the plot to make any sense at this point]. The aliens initially sought to establish diplomatic relations with Earth but seem to be running to a deadline.

They have very little patience, and are prepared to destroy the entire planet if betrayed. [It's fair to assume that they don't open talks with Earth after this encounter.] They "speak" through radio impulses.

History

• *Dating.* [Early 1971. It's not long after the events of "Doctor Who and the Silurians", as the Doctor's still brooding.] The police cars, white now, are still pre-panda. They use sirens, not bells, suggesting proximity to a city [the change was gradual, as was the shift to panda-cars by 1972 and then "Jam Sandwich" vehicles from 1976].

By this point Britain has its own extraordinarily advanced space programme, Mars Probe 7 being the latest to put astronauts on the Martian surface. [Mankind has already visited Mars when "The Ambassadors of Death" opens, and it's not unreasonable to think that the first manned flight there took place in the late 60s. However, some evidence suggests that the first moon landing - which occurred in real life on 20th of July, 1969 - took place as scheduled: in 4.2, "The Tenth Planet," Ben (who's from 1966) doesn't know that man has walked on the moon, and the Doctor and Martha, when trapped in 1969 in X3.10, "Blink," mention that the moon landing hasn't happened yet. This does, however, raise the very odd possibility that mankind landed on Mars *before* the moon.

[General Carrington was an astronaut on Mars Probe 6 and is now established as head of the new Space Security section, suggesting that the last mission was perhaps around a year before "Ambassadors". But we're not told which of the Mars Probes was the first to actually put people on the planet's surface; the early missions could have been unmanned. In a world where the authorities have some inkling of the potential alien threat to Earth, it makes sense for more resources to be put into space exploration. The fact that Carrington isn't *specified* as the first man on Mars, however, suggests that others went there before him. (Incidentally, this being a Whitaker script, we might wonder if Carrington's 'Space Security' section is a pre-cursor to the 'Space Security Service' in 3.2, "Mission to the Unknown" and 3.4, "The Daleks' Master Plan". Whitaker had drifted away from the series by then, but as these were Dalek stories, he may have taken a proprietorial interest.)]

Video and computer technology are surprising-

How Believable is the British Space Programme?

...continued from page 53

technical matter, explains why the Space Race became a two-horse one.

Just to make the point clearer and more poignant, the second Black Arrow flight - a two-stage launch with no payload - was successfully run on 4th of March 1970, a fortnight before "The Ambassadors of Death" episode one. The programme (Black Arrow, that is, not *Doctor Who*) was curtailed in early 1971, but they already had all the components. As the pre-flight checks were so advanced for the fourth launch, it was actually deemed more cost-effective to proceed rather than cancel it and fire everyone. The final Black Arrow launched Britain's first orbital satellite - Prospero - which is still up there in polar orbit, bleeping for anyone who cares to tune in. (The solar panel was designed to last for a year. It's still going and is expected to last another century.) Built by Marconi and launched on a rocket developed from leftovers (Blue Streaks converted into Black Arrows by adding Black Knight engine components), Prospero made Britain the sixth country to send a satellite of its own into space.

Because of the decision some years earlier to expand the Universities (see various comments in Volume I), and a new government making what it tended to call "realistic" decisions, the entire British space presence and membership of ELDO (the European team-effort launcher that became the ESA scheme, and pretty much de facto a French prestige project) were "proxmired". (This is why almost all subsequent launches are with their co-designed First Stage, which became the French Ariane rocket and why "Ariane" is the only new girl's name in France for a generation. Germany and France were the only big players left, and now almost all ESA launches *not* farmed out to Canaveral or Baikonur are from Equatorial French Guiana.)

We should here point out that (as was commented upon by a number of people who read the First Edition of this book) that the British rocket programme for sub-orbital flights carried on very successfully from 1957 to 2005. The Skylark rockets were designed in 1955, and at one stage had two hundred technicians working on them. Government funding was cut to even *this* in the late 70s (on the assumption that Shuttle flights would be rather more frequent than they are), but it carried on with industrial and University funding, conducting experiments of anything up to

1000 km above sea level. Despite ownership of the project being handed around like a bag of jelly babies, 441 of these rockets were launched, and this had economic benefits. British expertise in space hardware, especially satellite construction, is eminently exportable. Devices that outlast their projected working life are so much more remunerative. Patents for things everyone else sends up are also a nice little earner. Nevertheless, we need overseas buyers for most of these.

But if we're looking at what went wrong with the British space programme, the apocryphal version is that Concorde netted the government support that aerospace research needed, chiefly because Tony Benn's parliamentary constituency was Bristol South, home of the construction plant that built the Anglo-French jet. The *real* trouble began earlier: with wartime memories still fresh, ministers in the late 1950s thought of the nation's defence as being run from radar stations and big bomber-planes, as opposed to holes in the ground. (De Havilland had devised a system of - as mentioned - what we'd now call "Silos", a proposal that was released after the cancellation but shortly before Herman Kahn at RAND came up with almost identical proposals.) The remaining projects specialised in making things work with scant resources and no long-term security. Even today, Beagle II was, until the last few minutes, streets ahead of everyone else. (With the success-rate of *all* unmanned Mars probes being about 25%, we've no reason to be too upset - at least we didn't lose it because half the team used metric and the other lot inches, like NASA did in 1999.)

Essentially, there was no political will behind space. Government advisors said it wasn't economic - but in fact, at present space is earning the UK more per person involved in doing it than oil, let alone rock music. As we've seen, a small shift of emphasis around the time of the Suez Crisis could have put us on the moon ahead of America or Russia. The set-up presented in "The Ambassadors of Death" and "The Android Invasion" posits a space department more akin to the BBC than NASA, which is far more plausible. Had such a nationalised body existed and pooled various projects from University departments and various aerospace companies - as opposed to setting them competing for a contract which they would overspend and result in their getting cancelled - the trajectory envisaged for British aerospace in

continued on page 57...

ly advanced [not just for the early 70s, but the late 70s too]. Similarly, Athens has a facility that can detect impending solar flares. As head of Space Security, Carrington liases with a security council in Geneva. [It's presumably the same body that oversees UNIT's activities, but compare all of this with "The Invasion" (6.3), in which Britain doesn't seem to have any rocket capability at all.] Carrington says he has a plane to catch as, 'The Security Council has an emergency meeting in an hour'. [So not only is air-travel very fast, but Heathrow's security and baggage-handling have improved immeasurably.] Mars Probe 7 has solar batteries. The American space agency can prepare space missions at short notice.

Mars Probe 6 was the first mission to encounter the aliens, who inadvertently killed General Carrington's fellow astronaut. [Carrington didn't tell the authorities about the aliens, but set his own agenda to destroy them as head of Space Security; see **Things That Don't Make Sense**, though.] Mars Probe 7 took off from Mars nearly eight months ago, and is now only a few hours' rocket-travel from Earth; Recovery 7 and Recovery 8 take off here, although the latter wasn't scheduled to go into space for another three months. [If Recovery units are sent out to meet returning capsules which can't get back to Earth on their own, there's at least one other mission going on at this point.]

On the whole, the general public doesn't know about the existence of aliens despite the Yeti, Cyberman and Auton incidents. [But since Wakefield makes a worldwide live broadcast about the alien UFO, which is interrupted by gunfire and the sound of Carrington shouting 'we're being invaded', a lot of people must be getting suspicious. Maybe the authorities pass it off as an Orson-Welles-style hoax - assuming the broadcast even went out.] There's no indication that humans have found any trace of the Ice Warriors on Mars [although UNIT seem to know what 'Martians' look like in "The Christmas Invasion"].

The SOS signal was done away with 'years ago'. [In real-life, this happened in 1985.]

The Analysis

Where Does This Come From? Lurking in this story is an implicit rebuke at what Doctor Who had become since Verity Lambert's day - namely, that the advent of advanced and incomprehensible

beings is instinctively reacted to as a threat. This attitude has been developing for some time; with the Doctor's notorious speech in "The Moonbase" (4.6) about "there are some corners of the Universe which have bred the most terrible things", the series took on a rigorously xenophobic tone. From a show about seeing the marvels of the cosmos and shedding parochial expectations, it's become rather obsessed with defining "otherness" as "inferiority", "pollution" or "invasion".

Admittedly, they can be fairly charming when doing this, unlike the rabidly paranoid UFO or its current avatar Torchwood, but it's a noticeable shift away from the programme's original spirit, and one that Whitaker is here keen to bring into the open. To that end, "The Ambassadors of Death" relies on the audience making the same mistake - even the Doctor is investigating this as an intellectual puzzle, rather than as a stand against General Carrington's pettiness. However, Whitaker's premise - whilst still more or less intact - was handed to another writer with something to say on the matter, and that changes the equation a bit.

Since the last time Malcolm Hulke wrote about an influx of aliens (4.8, "The Faceless Ones"), MP Enoch Powell had delivered his notorious 1968 "Rivers of Blood" speech - a means of whipping up hysteria against immigration, even though Powell himself invited health workers from India and the Caribbean to fill vacancies in the NHS. Outright invasions were one thing, but this slow, voluntary surrender of what he cited as the national character was altogether more terrifying. He touched a nerve, and even dock workers whose politics in every other respect were diametrically opposed to his marched in support. It was thinly-veiled racism, of course. Statistically, the biggest influxes of immigration were from Australia (and, in recent years, Poland), but nobody seemed to mind *them*. As you might recall, Hulke is rather more cosmopolitan in his perspective on this: the Chameleons in "The Faceless Ones" were chastised for their methods, not their ambition, and the ordinary soldiers caught up in the auditions for the galaxy's greatest army (6.7, "The War Games") were each treated as people rather than ethnic stereotypes.

For Hulke and his generation of post-war optimists, the key was to keep talking to one another. Both the UN and the EEC were seen as first and foremost conversations, then world heritage supervisors and international peacekeepers. The idea that trade is the key to all things was a sim-

How Believable is the British Space Programme?

...continued from page 55

the guidebook to the 1951 Festival, with the moons of Saturn in our grasp by 2001, is feasible.

Moreover, as a member of both the European organisations such as ELDO and ESA and the Commonwealth, Britain would be in a unique position to pool expertise and resources from about half the planet. (This is, of course, without recourse to any "borrowed" techniques from all the crashed spaceships and thwarted invasions that seem part of *Doctor Who*'s version of British science these days.) A semi-independent space quango coordinating smaller projects, with clear objectives, seems to have been all that was missing. As Blue Streak and Black Arrow became embroiled in red tape, resulting in protracted discussions of who got to see which bit of the blueprint, the bills mounted and defence priorities over-rode prestige or employment ones. Yet as Concorde showed, national pride and a set task can achieve wonders. Look at how many British engineers are involved in the various teams competing in Formula One racing. An entire generation could have worked for our space programme, not just in engineering but in medicine and food technology.

That said, the "Ambassadors of Death" / "Android Invasion" version is completely unlike how a *real* British Space Programme would have gone in some ways. The most obvious difference is the big TV screens in the Mission Control place(s) - here we're assuming that Devesham in "Android" and the one where Ralph Cornish worked in "Ambassadors" are different places. The Black Arrow launches were supervised from within concrete sheds with lots of meters and lights, but with only a teleprinter to relay information about how it looked or what was happening. John Wakefield, broadcasting from mission control, would have been surplus to requirements - unlike the US version, this wasn't a made-for-TV extravaganza.

Moreover, many of the facilities seen in *Doctor Who* wouldn't have been available to the Commonwealth Astronauts. Specifically, the TV Mars programme seems to have benefited from another key 70s discovery in *Doctor Who*: some kind of effective anti-radiation treatment. Bob Baker and Dave Martin's works provide ample evidence of this being developed. (Indeed, all it needs is for Ian Chesterton to have a spare phial left over from Alydon's gift-box; see 1.2, "The Daleks".) And somehow, the prolonged microgravity and detrimental effect on bones and muscles has been circumvented. Soviet biologists devoted careers to this, so the end of the Cold War apparently had a peace dividend long before such things happened in our world.

But as with "Inferno", the *main* implausibility of this set-up is the odds of it happening in Southern England. Aside from Woomera, the logical place for launch and landing is as close to the Equator as possible - perhaps Guadalupe, British Guiana or Uganda. After 1949's "Groundnut Scheme", many Foreign Office field stations in such locations were kept "on ice" and would have been highly suitable. Of course, we're assuming that geopolitical events happened more or less as planned in this otherwise rather unfamiliar timeline. The partition of India and Pakistan seems to have occurred (although it's never mentioned in *Doctor Who*) and so the shift of emphasis to Africa - which led to a strange and almost forgotten attempt to harvest groundnuts (basically peanuts) for oil and cultivate huge chunks where nothing much had grown - would go as the history books (at least, those that bother to mention it) say it did.

So the key factor in this hypothesising is that it only needs small shifts of emphasis during the Atlee and Eden Governments for it all to come to pass. In essence, it requires a few things not to go wrong that did in our timeline. And as we've seen in Volumes I and II, the feeling in Britain is that we've more or less allowed Russia and America to "borrow" space for a few decades, and will one day reclaim it for good.

plistic nineteenth-century leftover like cholera, witchcraft and slavery. Countries that didn't want to participate - like China and the USSR - were mainly bad because they kept themselves out of the world-wide exchange of ideas and culture. (Here the two political streams converge: the Soviet system's collapse and the erosion of China's hardline Maoist state are both as much to do with telecommunications between ordinary members of the public as the rhetorical postures of various heads of state.)

So in Hulke's version of "Ambassadors", it's the refusal to allow anything other than pre-set commands to pass between the humans and the abducted aliens that causes the crisis. Here again, the general pattern is applicable in the microcosmic scale to the bigots who sided with Enoch, although that doesn't necessarily make this a parable "about" racism. For those who weren't in Enoch's camp, the question was how far one could expect immigrants to become "just like us" - and were we damaging something important by expecting or forcing this? Again, this was a universal theme made into a practical concern, especially if you were at school in Britain at the time.

It's hard to convey just how excitingly "other" the newly-arrived Indians, Pakistanis, Bangladeshis (they weren't called that for another year, though), Sri Lankans (similarly rebranded), Jamaicans, Trinidadians, Nigerians, Greek Cypriots and others seemed at first. In particular, when they started banding together in large enough numbers to set aside the need to always talk or write in English, and how excitingly alien everything about them looked. We've mentioned before (start with **What Are The Dodgiest Accents In The Series?** under 4.1, "The Smugglers") how the forty or so ethnic groups from the Indian Subcontinent were bracketed together in one thirty-minute show on Wednesday mornings called *Nai Zindagi Naya Jeevan*. (It was on BBC2, so hardly anyone could see it, and those who did probably saw it in colour and were *really* freaked.) The title translates as "New Way, New Life" or "Asian Programme", depending on whether you worked for the *Radio Times* or not.

What a generation's-worth of familiarity removes is how startling this show looked and sounded if you'd tuned in too early for *Play School*. The clothes were gaudy even by early 70s standards, and the soundtrack had "unearthly" music and speech that everyone white and over thirty said sounded like a tape playing backwards. Why did the Yanks bother sending men to the moon when we'd already made contact with alien intelligences in Leicester and Solihull? Teachers tried to cope with having one non-English-speaking pupil in a class of thirty by making that pupil almost a visual aid. Of course, the better teachers attempted to make the other students conceive of how well *they* would cope if the situation were reversed.

This is, naturally, one of the hallmarks of the early years of *Doctor Who*. Both here and in "Doctor Who and the Silurians", Hulke has tried to place the viewer closer to the aliens than the humans, but this story has Whitaker's old concern of how humans abuse anything new they get their hands on (see, for instance, 4.3, "The Power of the

Daleks" or 2.3, "The Rescue") at its heart. The 1970s would see *Doctor Who* cope with the human / alien (or British / foreign) interface in far more intriguing and grown-up ways, once the initial thrill of space monsters coming here to insult famous landmarks / steal our women / rape our minerals wore off. But note that here, unlike any subsequent story, the fundamental problem is figuring out what the other lot are *saying*. A scene cut from episode two - where it emerges that the signal sent twice in episode one is a pictogram showing how to build the translator - is therefore mightily significant. Is there a point where communication becomes impossible?

Here is the nub of it: as with Miss Dawson in Hulke's last script, the broadcast version of Carrington isn't so much a racist as a reductivist. His thought process is that people were killed, ergo the perpetrators must be inhuman killers, therefore they must be wiped out for our safety. Asking their side of the story never occurs to anyone. (This will be repeated, less sensibly, in the revelation of how General Williams almost caused mutual genocide in 10.3, "Frontier in Space".) The Draconians and (less plausibly) the Silurians all speak English and can give an account of themselves, but *really* alien aliens might not have any common ground with which to establish contact. This is a rare instance of *Doctor Who* ignoring SF cop-outs and looking at what the scientists are doing.

As for all the technical stuff, it comes from Project SETI as much as Apollo. Starting in 1960, there were undertakings to listen for signs of alien life, and send signals using pictograms - as happens here with the aliens' radio signals. The accurate names of the radio telescopes show that someone did some homework on First Contact scenarides (cf 18.7, "Logopolis" and 8.1, "Terror of the Autons"). This, and the factoid in "Spearhead from Space" about the number of planets hereabouts capable of supporting intelligent life, show the programme-makers had a better-read audience in mind than they did with, say, "The Seeds of Death" (with its rather haphazard, children's TV approach to Yuri Gagarin and Leonardo da Vinci).

Here we have to remind everyone that there was an entire sub-genre of science-thrillers, where the accuracy of the technical background was a major selling-point. People had seen the real thing and were in no mood to swallow excuses of "artis-

Why Did the "Sting" Matter?

Time, and familiarity, have made the world forget just how remarkable, how bizarre and how *important* the theme music of *Doctor Who* really was. So much so that when the 1996 TV Movie re-recorded the theme tune in the *Star Trek: The Next Generation* style (big orchestra, bombastic military sound, absolutely no hint of anything futuristic or experimental whatsoever) it was accepted as a perfectly normal part of a modern science-fiction series.

Rather than as, say, an abomination.

It wasn't always that way. Viewers were a lot more open-minded about what "belonged" in TV science fiction, and where the boundaries between experiment and storytelling lay. Part of the deal, when a film or TV show took you somewhere else, was that you were made to *hear* another world. If George Martin or Joe Meek could do it, you'd think that aliens could. We've got a lot more to say about this, in **What's Going On With This Music?** under "The Mutants" (9.4), but here we're going to restrict ourselves the first three renditions of the theme tune. That's all of them pre-1980, with the 1972 versions as a counter-example.

Listen to the original 1963 theme again, bearing in mind the time in which it was made, and one thing has to strike you. *This was like nothing else on Earth.* The BBC's Radiophonic Workshop had been producing electronic music since 1958, not only composing scores for TV and radio but devising their own instruments out of spare parts. Yet until that point the tendency had been to produce pieces which were so avant-garde as to be almost incomprehensible to the general public (e.g. the Workshop's theme for the BBC afternoon news, not so much a tune as a series of skittering, lurching atmosphere-effects which many listeners found quite disturbing).

The *Doctor Who* theme was a genuine landmark, an alliance between the very best of the Workshop's "experimental" material and the kind of dramatic, approachable soundtrack that befitted a contemporary adventure serial. We're used to it now (see **When Was *Doctor Who* Scary?** under 15.1, "Horror of Fang Rock"), but the children of the early 60s have frequently called it "bloody terrifying", and that's hardly a surprise. It pre-empts the psychedelia of the late 60s by some years. Every episode of the programme bears the credit "Title Music by Ron Grainer", but it's Delia Derbyshire's radiophonic arrangement and production (a "realisation" which Grainer himself had

nothing to do with, and found utterly bewildering), that really makes it. Derbyshire created a kind of electronic music that had more texture than anything recorded *anywhere* else before 1963, and what's more she made it truly populist.

What all the documentaries and dramas about Derbyshire (a small industry around the time Volume III first appeared) omit is how far her work ran in parallel with avant garde composers of the time, but skipped the slow process of critical acceptance and went straight for people's front rooms. While Karlheinz Stockhausen and Pierre Schaeffer were getting all theoretical, and Leon Theremin's baby was made a novelty item, films like *Forbidden Planet* had happily made valve-modulators and "electronic tonalities" the standard vocabulary of space. However, every time someone did something like this it was treated as a one-off. In 1951, the Ealing comedy *The Man in the White Suit* used what we'd call "samples" of a bassoon and a tuba making gurgles, and manipulated these into what became known as "The White Suit Samba" (Anyone who was a kid in 70s Britain knows that all science sounds like this, as did Rolf Harris - TV host and *so* much more - teaching kids to swim.)

The press made a big thing of this, but it was forgotten until the Radiophonic Workshop teamed up with George Martin to foist "Timebeat" onto the record-buying public a decade later. We have to look at the "Workshop" bit of the name: the people doing the funny noises and catchy tunes were producing these one-offs to order on an industrial scale. The arrival of tape made sound a physical, manipulable object. Anyone with time, patience and talent could make music out of speech, or sounds. The Radiophonic Workshop was always pushed for time, but had a knack of finding people with the talent - rather odd, when you consider that nobody really did this sort of thing as a hobby.

So in early 1967, they were ordered / given permission to go back and fix all the things they didn't like about the 1963 theme realisation. ("They" in this case being Derbyshire and Dick Mills, of whom much more for the rest of these books.) They'd already done this once, as the pilot episode used thunderclaps rather maladroitly, but this time the sibilant hissing under the bass and melody tracks was replaced with what's often described as "bubbling" but is rather percussive.

continued on page 61...

tic license" or "appealing to the mainstream audience" when confronted with howlers or infelicities. The *mainstream* audience wanted things realistic and solidly-based in what was known in those days; the fad for using a circular mask on the camera to suggest a view through binoculars (see also "Terror of the Autons") is one result, and the use of music for space-based adventures because everyone knew that sound doesn't travel in a vacuum were manifestations of this. *Doomwatch* was perhaps the most inevitable programme of 1970. Pseudo-documentary films - in an era when documentaries were showing ever-more extraordinary and alarming things - were the new basic model of science-fiction films. (One odd feature of this: so much of the iconography of "Ambassadors" is similar to the film *The Andromeda Strain*, it's a surprise to many that the *Doctor Who* one came first. Mind you, if we're talking about the visual motifs we ought to acknowledge Roger Marshall's *Avengers* story "The Positive-Negative Man", with a chap in wellies destroying safes and killing people by touching them after walking up to them very slowly.)

Along those lines, John Wakefield (Michael Wisher's journalist character) is a recognisable pastiche of a BBC science reporter. The two with the most relevance for the Apollo coverage are Michael Charlton (the man on the spot at Cape Kennedy) and James Burke (the *Tomorrow's World* presenter, who not only explained the technical terms on the live feed from Houston, but filmed behind-the-scenes items on what it's like to wear a spacesuit, become weightless, use the emergency exits from the capsule, etc.). Burke will be significant in later background pieces. What's important to note *now* is why Wakefield is present at all. He's the story's Sir Basil Exposition, of course, but his account of events are entirely couched in how the British Mars missions of the story's present-day differ from the old-fashioned American moon-shots, which *Doctor Who* viewers would be very familiar with. *Quatermass* was never this tele-centric - it had Fleet Street types like Conrad and Fullalove filing stories for their papers and a radio reporter covering the spaceship crashing in a street in Croydon. That, however, emphasised the impact of this momentous event on Joe Public, whereas Wakefield's account assumes viewers are well-used to what ought to be happening. The age-old problem with media SF - the infodump - has a new solution, and one that only works with the "near future" format.

For that matter, numerous tiny details of the US space missions have seeped into this story. There's the fact that some of the space-capsules have the number Seven (as with the Mercury missions) and the entire docking procedure and the crawling through the hatches. (See this story's essay for why any British space missions in the pipeline were radically different, and at the time were pretty well-known.)

The biggest allusion is, of course, the spooky look of a space-helmet with the visors down. It was rammed home to us that the gold layer was to filter the hard UV rays and that - contrary to what Hollywood had shown us up until now (except, of course *2001: A Space Odyssey*) - the astronaut's faces wouldn't be visible. They weren't movie stars, they were pilots.

This is, of course, part of our national project to feel good about not doing it the American way. We compensated for being pipped to a "first" (that we'd been raised to assume was ours) by telling ourselves that the Yanks had achieved it by sacrificing anything that seemed like individuality or character. Quite naturally, this wasn't true, and we suspected that the strain would tell. While most people in Britain aren't sure if Neil Armstrong's even still alive, Buzz Aldrin has proven rather endearing by admitting that he had problems adjusting.

British viewers - especially after consuming several mainstream dramas about war veterans and explorers - could get a handle on the difficulty of adjusting to life after something extraordinary. Therefore, a character such as General Carrington is easier to comprehend, although not condone, than a man so highly-trained as to have no life outside his job. It had become a commonplace that spaceflight created a paradox in which those who went to the moon and safely returned had their sense of wonder surgically removed. David Bowie had become a one-hit wonder with *Space Oddity*, a song about precisely that: Major Tom and his controller are faced with something unimaginable, so they talk about shirts. Cynics in the UK noted that Armstrong and Aldrin were sent 240,000 miles to give Richard Nixon a photo-op. It seemed as though nobody at NASA had any sense of proportion. The people being sent into space were the people *least* suited to contact with genuinely strange beings. Most of them seemed ill-at-ease talking to other humans.

Why Did the "Sting" Matter?

...continued from page 59

The fact that we can't find a vocabulary for it even now, forty-odd years later, is impressive.

An interesting factor in the perception of the pre-1980 versions is that the human ear has real difficulty locating the source of the sorts of sounds used for the melody. Frequencies above 4000Hz are easier to place spatially by intensity (louder in one ear than the other means they're more in one direction than another), frequencies below 1000Hz because of the phase difference (the time it takes to hit one ear compared to the other). The nearly-pure tones used for the main tune are around 3000Hz, and there's no "attack" (a sound of striking, plucking or rubbing) to help us figure out what instrument's being played. This melody is apparently coming from somewhere outside the speakers on the television and just "happening" without any material objects being used. For 1963 audiences, this was really unsettling. As with the Daleks not being obviously men in rubber suits, the fact that parents didn't have a ready answer for the questions "What is it?" and "How did they do that?" was crucial. Up until the mid-1970s, the theme tune and bizarre graphics were the single scariest thing in *Doctor Who* and therefore in all of television before the 9.00pm watershed.

The main theme is variations on this until 1980. What happens in 1970, when they have to fit it to a new title-sequence, is a slight addition of echo but a more considered approach to matching it to the time allowed. We all know that every story from "The Seeds of Death" (6.5) onward has a more-or-less unique opening procedure, but the music has been tailored to this simply by fading it in earlier or later. Now, as well as the "judder" start - most obvious in "Spearhead from Space" (7.1) - they're trying to make the end-theme finish the way the single version they released always had. With cast-lists varying and only the main staff credited (except on the last episode of each story), it was usually easier to fade that too. So there was a specially-crafted end sequence, although "Doctor Who and the Silurians" (7.2) needed even this extended. Sometimes they needed to go back to an earlier edit of the music when the credits got lengthy (the last broadcast occasion of this is 15.6, "The Invasion of Time"). When watching whole stories, it's noticeable, sometimes, that the end theme is in a slightly different key to the titles. What we're driving at is that even though the visuals settled down after 8.1, "Terror of the Autons"

(then *again* after 11.1, "The Time Warrior" *and* 12.3, "The Sontaran Experiment" *and* 14.1, "The Masque of Mandragora"), the music is still not entirely formularised.

Characteristically, 1970s stories begin with a theme-version that runs through the main refrain once, then ends on a slow fade of the two-note pattern. This does the same job that the previous opening sequences did, ushering us into a place where the normal rules of television drama don't quite work. (This was sometimes replaced by just the usual fade into the "middle-eight", as in "Terror of the Autons", but it seems to have been down to individual directors.)

From "The Ambassadors of Death" onward, the end music begins with what is usually called "the Sting": it's how everyone thinks of the cliffhangers, to the perplexity of anyone watching black and white episodes. It's been used in the BBC Wales version, and the Peter Howell and Keff McCulloch renderings of the end-music had approximations of it. It's so familiar that its debut in the *opening* credits of "Ambassadors" is often neglected, sadly, as a key moment in the theme's evolution. Watch that story now, and there's a sense that they've "finally" reached where they were "obviously" going, *not* that this is the latest in a long line of recent innovations trying to refresh an apparently moribund series.

Almost by accident, though, the sting made cliffhangers more emphatic. It was part of Letts and Dicks' attempt to move in the direction of both Saturday-Morning serials and social-comment drama. This seems odd until you think that hitherto, *Doctor Who* had been a brand-identity for odd places and times, but now had to look like it belonged in the present day. Whereas the titles and incidental music were often at odds in the past, now the titles had to seem at least as cutting-edge as anything else on telly.

Moreover, since 1963 the other programmes on the box had sharpened up their act. *Doctor Who* had to be cutting-edge and unique, but not *too* far out of synch with the hit shows. Those opening titles were an attempt (like much else in that story) to make *Doctor Who* look like it belonged in a television landscape that included *Mission: Impossible* and *The Champions* without actually being like them. The end titles and revised music were an attempt to match this, to close off each episode with an appropriate iconography rather

continued on page 63...

Things That Don't Make Sense [This could take a while, so take your protein pills and put your helmet on.]

Everyone comments on the fact that Wakefield *seems* to announce to the world the existence of killers from space, yet nobody reacts at all, ever. But if we're being fair, this isn't unprecedented. In real life in 1977, people watching ITV's *Early Evening News* in the Southern region had their transmissions interrupted, untraceably, *for six minutes,* by someone or something called Vrillon. He claimed to represent the Ashtar Galactic Command, and proceeded to order the peoples of Earth to abandon all weapons, give up money, grow daffodils, etc. At around the same time, something similar happened on German TV. Nobody's ever claimed credit for the Vrillon incident, and nobody has satisfactorily proven that it's a hoax, yet you never hear anyone talk about it, even as a joke at the pub. [We defy anyone to watch it on YouTube, however, without giggling and then dozing off.]

So to quickly summarize... The Thing That Doesn't Make Sense here (beyond the questionable policy of letting Wakefield broadcast direct from Mission Control at all, thus allowing the public to witness any cock-ups first-hand) *isn't* that nobody in *Doctor Who* ever remembers invasions or evacuations of London, but that people who make snarky comments about this in fanzines or online expect them to when nobody in *our* world ever does. In March 1980, we came close to a nuclear war because of a flock of migrating swans; in 1984, a throwaway joke by Ronald Reagan during a mike-check led the Soviet High Command to expect an invasion and activate plans for a pre-emptive mobilisation into West Berlin (we thought this was an urban myth, then the Soviet documents were declassified - yikes!); Britain had a drug-addicted Prime Minister within living memory... all real, all forgotten. [All of that said, the *level* of denial on the new series and *Torchwood* - given events in numerous stories like "The Christmas Invasion" and *Torchwood* 1.13, "End of Days" - has gone beyond a joke. We now return you to "The Ambassadors of Death".]

The TARDIS console has a special panel that squirts anyone standing next to it into the future [was this designed as an ejector seat or something]? Worse, it's the one panel we always see the Pertwee Doctor using for launching the Ship. So if it had ever worked before, Jamie or Vicki might have been stranded in flight with no pilot. (See "The Time Monster" for an apparent use of this same facility - but if we're using *that* story to make sense of something, we're in trouble.) And when Liz disappears, the Doctor dashes across to where she was standing and fiddles with the console. Lucky for him that she just happened to move to the other side of the console upon reappearing in the middle of the jumps, otherwise they would have materialised inside each other. [Or maybe the TARDIS respects their personal space.] Also, you can hear an awful lot of footsteps, even while they're both "travelling to the future" and absent from the room. [The editing crew, one presumes, neglected to strip out the audio for these bits.]

So if Britain had Mars probes *this* advanced at its disposal for as long as we're meant to believe, then why, in "The Invasion", did UNIT need to go to Moscow to get a launcher set up? Then there's the matter of Recovery 7's return; we're told that unlike the comparatively primitive American space vessels of the 1970s, British technology ensures Van Lyten's ship will land with pinpoint accuracy, under perfectly normal circumstances, back at the launch-site. So basically, they want Recovery 7 to hurtle down right onto the building where the people directing them are trying to remain very, very calm. Never mind that if Recovery 7 misses by a few yards, it'll crash into a huge refinery full of M3, conventional fuel and liquid oxygen. [Ah, you might counter, the refinery is obviously located some distance away... well, if *that's* true, then at the slow rate they're said to pump in the M3 variant, Reegan's sabotage in episode five would take hours to have any effect, not than the few seconds we're shown. In either case, having the pipes and their controls out in the open air like that is just silly.]

In episode two, the Doctor halts the hijacked lorry by making it look as if Bessie has stalled in the middle of the road. Fine, but this gambit only works because Sergeant Collinson, amazingly, fails to recognize the Doctor as the strange man in the frilly shirt who interrogated him earlier in the episode, only now acting all doddery and feeble. [Collinson's amnesia *almost* becomes plausible if we presume he had some UNIT tea during his incarceration. Much in this volume, in fact, only makes sense if there's a Torchwood agent going around posing as a char-lady, and doping everyone in UNIT with Retcon.] Conversely, the Doctor fails to remember Carrington's face - and identify

Why Did the "Sting" Matter?

...continued from page 61

than just list the actors, film cameramen and who-ever. That screaming noise isn't just arresting, it is a release of tension. It gives the audience permission to gasp or yell (and in some ways sounds like the television can't believe it either). Then, with that little cathartic outburst, we're returned to normal television for 167 1/2 hours.

Once Dudley Simpson and the others heard it, they began scoring the ends of episodes in upward scales leading to the start-note of the sting[20]. In some ways this marks the point at which individual stories cease to have such distinct identities, reversing the trend since "The War Machines" (3.10). More than at any time since Dalekmania, Doctor Who is brand-identity but now was about subversion of normality. Again, it had to look and sound different from anything else, but not too different.

That is a crucial point when considering the next refit, the 1972 "Delaware" version. Where adding the sting had made the series regain a contemporary edge by being just ahead of the pack with regard to electronic noises, the Delaware rendition was dated even before they finished making it. Compared to what Stevie Wonder or even - heaven help us - Chicory Tip were getting into the charts earlier that year, it was cumbersome. Worse, it sounded identifiably like some kind of keyboard instrument. We will enlarge on this later, but the wider point is that the Radiophonic Workshop had to sound better than anything Geoff Love could produce[21]. This one didn't.

Here in the twenty-first century, music in television (and fantasy television especially) is even more standardised, even more banal than it was in the worst 60s adventure serials. Modern SF isn't supposed to sound peculiar, or alien, or alarming. It's supposed to sound like Jerry Goldsmith or John Williams, and that's about all. "The TV Movie" theme is a truly terrible piece of work, not because it isn't "like" the original - this is, after all, a series which thrives on change - but because it's "like" everything else you hear these days, and that simply defeats the whole point of the programme. And this isn't the place to discuss the entire output of Murray Gold, whose scores seem to absorb every trend going. (Compare his "Chancellor Flavia" theme to the titles for the new Battlestar Galactica - and don't get us started on the supposedly heartbreaking telepathic singing in X4.3,

"Planet of the Ood".) Never mind that the BBC's website obituary for Tristram Cary, calling him "the Murray Gold of his day", is misguided to the point of being insulting. The Murray Gold of that era of television was Tony Hatch.

The point is that relaunched Doctor Who had to overcome its former reputation for cheapness by sounding cinematic, whereas in the 70s the possession of synthesizers and scoring suites for individual episodes had been more costly and slick than hiring an orchestra for a few reusable underscores such as Star Trek or The Baron. Whatever you thought of a Dudley Simpson score, you appreciated the effort that had gone in. Every episode in the 1970s was an event, and the opening and closing titles were part of the ritual of special-ness, of Saturday-ness, of the rules being bent for twenty-five minutes. Anyone who heard the Derbyshire version(s) of the theme on first transmission now, upon hearing it again, has a curious craving to eat sausage and chips or beans on toast[22].

Once the series' reputation was so badly damaged by the worst mistakes of the 80s, and since the programme's nature was completely mis-remembered by the media of the 90s, even the programme's fans forgot how startlingly creative so much of it was. There was a time when Doctor Who was considered the most technically sophisticated programme on television - not because of the plastic spaceships or wobbly monster costumes, but because of the little things that nobody chooses to recall. Documentaries on the making of 2001: A Space Odyssey somehow skip the fact that the film's effects team consulted with director Douglas Camfield after seeing "The Daleks' Master Plan" (3.4).

These days, the images are the subject of behind-the-scenes programmes that fill as much airtime as the episodes, but nobody knows who does the "special sound". This element of the series' original success has been ignored. Doctor Who began life as a series about a moody, eccentric technocrat with a talent for building improbable machines out of futuristic spare parts. And the people who defined its atmosphere better than anyone else - the BBC Radiophonics team - were themselves mainly moody, eccentric technocrats with a talent for building improbable machines out of futuristic spare parts. The "cult of the amateur", a cornerstone of British culture and a particularly vital ingredient in the success of Doctor Who, comes across in its early electronic soundtracks more than it does anywhere else.

ABOUT TIME 1970-1974

him as one of the baddies - when next they meet, just because Carrington is wearing sunglasses when he pushes Bessie off the road.

But then, the Doctor and Liz suffer more than one lapse of judgment in this adventure. The two of them happily accept help from Taltalian's assistant Dobson, entirely failing to consider that he might working for same conspiracy as his treacherous boss - which he is. When the baddies force Liz off the road by simply driving in front of Bessie, she brashly flees on foot as opposed to just popping a 180 and zooming back the way she came. And observe episode six, in which the ambassadors freak Liz out to the point that she goes to the containment chamber window and screams, 'Let me out!' - when, er, the chamber door is unlocked.

The warehouse shoot-out clearly sees Derek Ware (credited as 'UNIT Sergeant') stumbling back against some crates in a, "Dear me, I've just been fatally shot" manner. Yet he's back on duty in episode two, and he *might* be the soldier who hurriedly dashes into Quinlan's office and gets blasted by an ambassador at the start of episode five. Granted, there's a precedent for someone surviving the ambassadors' touch (episode seven sees their "death touch" merely stunning a policeman), but either way, Ware's character demonstrates remarkable stamina when he's *also* part of the raid on the villains' base in episode seven. (The gig is up in "Inferno", though, when Ware is credited as 'Private Wyatt' and plunges to his doom.)

Taltalian's demand, at gunpoint, that the Doctor turn over the tape of the alien broadcast seems a bit rash - does the Doctor have the only copy, or has Taltalian somehow rounded up all the spares? When Cornish summons Taltalian to account for his actions, Taltalian appears on a visi-screen. Not only is this fairly amusing for fans of *The Goodies* (see 9.3, "The Sea Devils"), but it later becomes obvious that to appear on said screen, Taltalian must stand right behind the door. So, er, the cameras in this base are aligned so that people have to stand right behind doors when taking a call. In which case, why is Liz so surprised when Taltalian pops up from behind that door? Never mind that there's a bloody phone right next to it, and that it's somehow secure enough for Dobson to use when contacting his mysterious superiors. (By the way, the first *Mission Impossible* movie - and in particular the scene where Tom Cruise hides a computer disc from a gun-totin' Jean Reno with legerdemain

- will never seem the same once you've experienced the Doctor's 'transmigration of object' with the missing tape and Taltalian, done twenty-five years earlier.)

Taltalian's accent seems to vanish on film. He also does everything short of wearing a T-shirt saying, "This briefcase I'm fiddling with is booby-trapped", yet the Doctor never gets the hint. And considering that it's designed to kill *both* the Doctor and Taltalian, the time-bomb really is a shockingly weak piece of ordnance: it doesn't even destroy the table it's sitting on, and the Doctor only requires a small forehead bandage afterward. Between the cliffhanger of episode four and the reprise in episode five, the Doctor's cloak itself falls victim to 'transmigration of object'. This scene also has the Brigadier struggle with a locked door in such a way that makes you wonder why he doesn't just walk through the flimsy wall.

Concerning Reegan's sabotage ploy in episode five... he has a plausible story and a fake pass, but when he shows these to Private Goober, he blows his cover by impatiently knocking the Private out, just so he can raise the alarm a few moments later. As luck would have it, this coincides with the Brigadier ignoring a message from Benton to come and see Lennox ASAP, just because he just feels like visiting the refinery on the off-chance that there's some malfeasance for him to discover a little too late. Or rather, it's too late to stop the sabotaged lift-off by rushing into Mission Control and yelling "Stop the countdown!", but it's *probably* in enough time for him to whip out his radio or press a conveniently-placed alarm-switch that places like this always seem to have by law.

Van Lyden and the boys are up in space watching the footie. Perhaps the aliens have caused a consensual hallucination of England losing one-nil and then equalising at the eleventh hour, but as they're *surprised* at this outcome, it's not something that came from their own minds. The issue here is that brainwashing tends to make people see what they expect (see 19.7, "Time-Flight" and the essay with 8.1, "Terror of the Autons"), so they *should* have dreamed a humiliating defeat after it went to penalties, as invariably happens. But the astronauts seem confused at this late development, which happened whilst the telly was off and they were in a trance so the Doctor could talk to the Michelin Man; ergo it really happened, independently of their imaginations. If you're following all of this, it means either that the aliens have been allowing BBC coverage of major sporting events but *not* John Wakefield's reports about the astronauts going AWOL (which you'd think they'd be more keen to see, what with them being on telly) or superintelligent extra-terrestrials crossed cosmic gulfs to learn the Offside Rule and witness terrible haircuts, *and then* used this knowledge to run match-simulations, complete with commentators unable to use adverbs properly[12]. As David Coleman would say, "quite remarkable".

And now it's time, boys and girls, to guess who killed Lennox. It can't be Carrington's thug Reegan, who's displaying an unlikely knowledge of rocket-science at the same moment. It might be Carrington himself - he somehow (we think) frees Collinson from UNIT custody, and indeed, the assassin's voice *sounds* a bit like him - but we have the problem that Lennox would have recognized him and doesn't. Anyway, Carrington would have been spotted wandering around in a UNIT uniform. Even if he'd faked credentials, surely *someone* would have told the Brigadier had Carrington arrived as himself and visited Lennox's cell prior to his murder, no matter how much he pulled rank.

All right, so maybe Carrington has an inside man at the base... who has a handy supply of radioactive isotopes... and the right keys to Lennox's cell... and was fortuitously rostered on that afternoon... but who was of *no* other use to Carrington in delaying UNIT's investigations, or supplying him with helpful information (such as - say - the fact that the Doctor's an alien, and should therefore be locked up under the Emergency Powers Act). One obvious suspect is Dobson, Taltalian's right-hand man and who's known to be feeding Carrington information from inside the complex, but we'd *still* have to deal with how someone so well-known in the place could pass unnoticed in a stolen UNIT uniform. And, er, omitted to tell Carrington anything more helpful. As we mentioned in **Things To Notice**, we can't entirely dismiss Benton as a suspect, and his declaration to Lennox that, 'Yes, sir, I'll lock the door', becomes a lot more creepy with that in mind.

More worrying still, *where* have they locked Lennox? In a holding-cell of the variety that Collinson was liberated from, meaning that UNIT must know their security has been compromised and done nothing about it. Then they use the same cell *again* for the Doctor's post-spaceflight decontamination and abduction, never mind that

the Doctor takes his clothes off in a room he knows to be only bolted from outside. Trusting of him, no?

The British spaceships are remarkably (which is to say: implausibly) fast. Fair enough, they would *need* to be speedy if you're intent on sending a two-man astronauts to Mars, in a cabin that most truckers would baulk at sleeping in for more than three nights, with the expectation that the men involved won't kill one another after months on end. But even allowing that space exploration in the *Doctor Who* universe is vastly in advance of the real world (albeit only for this one story), and even given the presence of the mysteriously powerful "M3 variant" rocket-fuel, the rockets of the 1970s are *so* fast that a mission from Earth can somehow go into a terminal orbit of the sun within fifteen minutes. (Compare with 4.6, "The Moonbase".) Actually, though, this is only weird if you know less about launch-windows than Kit Pedler - meaning the *really* odd thing is that the Doctor and Cornish can decide when to launch to suit their own agenda, and not in accordance with the orbital period of Mars Probe 7.

But look at the mission schedule: Mars Probe 7 spends seven months going to Mars, then 'nearly eight months' coming back, ignoring the fact that Earth and Mars have different-length orbits (so even if you get one leg of the round-trip down to six months, the other would take at least nine). More to the point, there's no evident concern about the fact that one of the Mars Probe 6 crew died in extremely mysterious circumstances. The current astronauts - Frank Michaels and Joe Lefee - don't seem as if they're going to Mars to investigate, nor do they seem to have any extra precautions in case of ambush. Isn't it negligent of the authorities to let their men blithely wander into a potentially hostile situation?

And we can't rationalize this away by saying that Carrington and his allied covered up events pertaining to Mars Probe 6... after all, Michaels and Lefee are here given *such* a media blitz for popping to Mars for what seems like a few groceries, it's hard to see how the absence of Jim Daniels - Carrington's fellow astronaut, accidentally killed by the aliens - upon Carrington's return would fail to warrant massive speculation and concern in the media. Had the authorities just said "Jim's ill", it would have raised all manner of red flags in the months to come, so the cover-story must have been *astonishing* to allow Carrington to come back and do all the interviews solo, then become head of a new Space Security body without someone like Liz knowing anything about the details. Besides, Carrington seems to have received no psychiatric evaluation, grief counselling or whatever - you know, the sort of thing that might have ferreted out his xenophobic, revenge-fueled intentions. Even in a world where a commissioner for the International Arabian Horse Association was picked to head FEMA, would *you* hire Carrington to run the new security division?

Nor does Ralph Cornish, as the head of Mission Control, seem to know information pertaining to the previous Mars mission. So either he's new to the job (in which case, his briefing omitted this vital information), or he's remarkably incurious about what his astronauts might encounter on Mars. Similarly, when Michaels and Lefee go missing for seven months, Cornish entirely fails to consider that maybe, just maybe, there's a connection to the loss of the previous Mars Probe astronaut. (Van Lyden, at least, has presence of mind to speculate on whether the Mars Probe 7 occupants are the original crew.)

And we *might* take issue with the mechanics of the swap of the ambassadors for Michaels and Lefee. It's perhaps sensible that the aliens send their ambassadors to Earth in the comparatively primitive Mars Probe capsule (either for reasons of diplomacy, or because they're cautious about first contact with Earth), but it's odd that they don't find it remotely suspicious, in all that time, that Michaels and Lefee have no knowledge of the *real* purpose of their mission and must be hypnotized into watching the footie. The end of episode five suggests the aliens' ship has a cloaking device, and they surely could've overtaken the Mars Probe and got their ambassadors back in that time but - nope, they just hang out on Mars for more than half a year, twiddling whatever passes for their thumbs.

Then there's the second swap, when the ambassadors are taken from inside the capsule under the noses of everyone in Space Control. It's not impossible, but we must ask how the Magic Breadvan got in through that narrow gangway and down stairs - and out again the same way - without anyone noticing. Because unless the lead-lined vehicle was actually brought into the room, the radiation trail would be a dead giveaway.

Anyway, why *do* the aliens only broadcast instructions on how to build the translation device the day before the ambassadors arrive, and not - say - in the nearly eight months beforehand that it takes the ambassadors to reach Earth? For that matter, it's established that Reegan can only give the ambassadors simple commands such as "move forward", so how does he describe which parts they're meant to steal, and where precisely they're located? And do the aliens only provide a short list of terms for bossing their ambassadors around, and not more cordial stuff such as, "We're pleased to receive you, visitors from another world", or "Hello, are you an ambassador OF DEATH?" The translation is, after all, derived from abstract mathematics and pictograms, so either Carrington figured out an entire alien communication system in a day and filtered out all but the imperative tense, *or* he received, in with the instructions for building the translation device (which themselves needed translating) an inflammatory alien phrasebook from which he cherry-picked what - fortunately for him - turned out to have been basic commands. But how did he know that the burbles meant "touch that object and make radiation run along it like static electricity" and not 'M'sieur, with these isotopes you are spoiling us"[13]? Anyway, how much diplomacy do the aliens expect the ambassadors to undertake, if they've only got simple dialogue such as this at their disposal?

In episode two, Carrington's accomplices suddenly manifest a pair of futuristic-looking stun guns. But from whence did they procure such handy weaponry, why didn't UNIT and the Doctor find their use more of a clue, and why doesn't Carrington hand them out to his men sooner, if he's is *so* concerned about Collinson only killing during the warehouse fight if it's 'absolutely necessary'? [Never mind that Collinson does so with relish, clearly enjoying his work. We might imagine that the stun guns are government prototypes - but again, that should immediately raise questions about a conspiracy at work in the government. Clearly, the stun guns are only used so the Brigadier can "get shot" and live, but they're at odds with the rest of the story, and are conspicuously never seen again. Mind you, UNIT could have used them in a number of forthcoming stories where they open fire on civilians without warning.]

Also in episode two, other than sheer plot contrivance, what takes Bessie *so* long to do a three-point turn in an open field? In episode three, Dr

Lennox puts on a protective radiation suit but doesn't don a helmet, evidently unconcerned if radiation eats away at his brain.

Mars Probe 7 can be locked off 'manually', a feature purely designed - it seems, weirdly - to stop Mission Control from piloting the craft by remote if the astronauts get into a pickle. In the pre-credit sequence, Van Lyden ominously says '...*something* took off from Mars', as if he knows he's in the teaser for a kids' melodrama. Five minutes later, the Brig asks the astronaut if what he's docking with really is Mars Probe 7 and Cornish snorts derisively, as if the question were totally out of left field. Upon realising that he's being gassed, the Doctor exclaims 'Fish!' and falls on his front; a few seconds later, he's on his back in the Pertwee Death Pose. (Note that this happens a few seconds before he emerges from the shower to get dressed and his clothes are all on hangers - but there's no underwear, not even socks.)

In episode six, even Carrington refers to the guys in spacesuits as 'aliens', although he's supposed to be keeping up the pretence that they're the astronauts, and nobody picks him up on this. A problem with hindsight: the Doctor has the perfect opportunity to incapacitate Reegan with Venusian karate at the end of episode six (Reegan isn't even holding a gun!) yet refrains from doing so. And the key to Reegan's radiation chamber is the same one needed to escape from the bunker... this is a security hazard, surely?

In the final episode, Carrington replaces UNIT with his own hand-picked men. These aren't the brightest lads - if you hear gunshots resonating down a long tunnel, then see someone in a different uniform from yours (the head of an organisation you've been told to relieve of guard duties and lock up) driving from that tunnel towards a checkpoint, would *you* wait until the siren sounded before stopping him and asking a few questions? Thought not. Mind you, UNIT's lads made exactly the same mistake when the Magic Breadvan left with the unconscious Doctor, and the UNIT troopers in episode seven - the ones that allow Reegan's goons to briefly overpower them, after they've been defeated and disarmed - aren't models of military efficiency either.

According to the map Benton uses, the launch-site is right next to Heathrow Airport. In fact he points to Windsor Castle, which is even more alarming.

Critique We said in the critique for "Doctor Who and the Silurians" that in any given scene, uncertainty seems to exist concerning who the story was aimed at. There's no such ambiguity here: from the start, this was intended for small boys. Possibly with their dads (hence all the lab technicians in short skirts), but primarily boys under twelve.

It's got the lot. In the episode one alone, we cut between a mystery on board a spaceship and a warehouse shoot-out. Fortunately (and unlike, say, 13.6, "The Seeds of Doom"), this story's ambition isn't limited to spinning a thrilling action yarn. Despite - or maybe because of - its juvenile intentions, it's acted with commitment across the board. On top of that we get well-executed car-chases, stunts, fights and a nicely creepy body-disposal scene. And overlaid on *that* is the entire element of strangeness: the aliens slowly moving towards people and zapping them with a single touch; the abruptly non-literal camera-work when one of them removes its helmet; and the downright psychedelic spaceship, with a distorted voice telling the Doctor to 'move towards the light'. They *must* have known what they were doing - this story ticks all the boxes for a conspiracy thriller with action set-pieces, and then turns around and criticizes the whole genre in the last two episodes.

So what, if anything, is wrong with it? Let's rephrase that - apart from the scene with the tape vanishing and reappearing and everything else that involves Taltalian, what's wrong with it?

Well, in a lot of ways, the problem is its unremitting urgency. The programme-makers are committed to seeing how far down this road they can go without becoming a totally different series, but there's very little light and shade along the way. In some ways this is welcome but, by and large, the entire seven-part story is one-note. When Liz tells a hulking guard 'I won't hurt you', it's a rare moment of wit in an adventure with only a few laboured comedy moments - almost all of them stemming from the Doctor (unless Robert Cawdron was *deliberately* playing Taltalian for laughs). If the series had diligently followed this model for four or five stories in a row, it would probably have expired after 1972, but they made "Ambassadors" without knowing if they'd still have a show in three months' time.

Making topical stories is always going to date things - just imagine how incomprehensible Derek Acorah's cameo in X2.12, "Army of Ghosts" will be years after the fact. Manned flights to Mars (as launched from somewhere in Berkshire) weren't on the news agenda in 1970, but Apollo 13 ran into difficulty between episodes four and five of "Ambassadors". As a result, viewers would have seen the Doctor's jaunt into orbit as the point of this adventure, not as filler in the middle of a straightforward thriller.

But if *Doctor Who* is doing the same as every *other* show, why make it? The school of thought that deems the space-launch as a pointless digression wants all *Doctor Who* stories to be reducible to simple soundbite "messages". If you're one of those people, then the rest of the Pertwee era will suit you right down to the ground. In many ways, the Doctor dressed up in a spacesuit - bristling against the mangled English of astronautese and telling Mission Control he doesn't want to talk to them any more - is a form of wish-fulfillment for anyone dismayed at NASA's way of going about things. The same applies to the abducted astronauts, who amidst all their space missions are more concerned about whether England can come back from a goal down. It's not played outright for laughs, but everyone watching would have thought that this is perhaps how it *should* be.

Essentially, "Ambassadors" was made as entertainment, with its own uniquely *Who*-ish mix of action-thriller and pop-art gimmickry, as a concerted effort to try to keep up with the competition. Unfortunately, that makes it seem like a museum-piece now. They gambled a lot on a mix of the dayglo futuristic and the grimly everyday. Similarly, the entire conspiracy plot relies upon there being a known world to disrupt and make distrustful, so this is the very earliest they could have done anything of that kind. It's also pretty much the *latest* they could have got away with it. The obvious proof is the horrible failure of "The Android Invasion"(13.4), an attempted pastiche of this story and "Spearhead from Space". To nick a NASA metaphor, there's only a limited launch window for a space-conspiracy story based around British Mars missions, and this is it.

What the Doctor's spell as Major Tom does is put the concerns of Carrington and Reegan into a much bigger context in which national (even human) concerns seem pretty small fry. If anything, it should have come earlier in the story. Even today, it's a welcome change of pace between Reegan's repetitive thuggery and Carrington blathering about his 'moral duty'. Alas, the actual

launch looks like *Button Moon* or *The Clangers*. At least they were trying to treat spaceflight seriously, with efforts towards depicting G-force and weightlessness that audiences would have demanded and which *Star Trek* never bothered with. Some of it looks silly now, or at the very least pathetically obvious as to how it was made. There are moments, though, that are as competent and mysterious as anything in the entire series. Moreover they carefully arranged for no two episodes to be quite the same. It's very similar, in that one regard, to the previous story.

As with "Doctor Who and the Silurians", "Ambassadors" keeps the authority figures and the monsters at arms' length, and only the Doctor and Liz get to interact with both before the seventh episode. However, the futuristic is embedded in the story's "everyday" in ways that "Silurians" never attempted. The spacesuited aliens are "blanks", but carry with them the promise of a different world in the near future; they're characteristically seen slowly advancing on security guards or in the backs of vans in muddy fields, not a NASA-like sterile white space in Florida. As we said, a gamble. It could easily have looked ridiculous. (And in one regard, as we keep saying, it does - Reegan, however, as a character able to slip from one "world" in the story to the other, is a genuine threat the way Dr Quinn never was.) Once again, the lack of any continuity between the worlds of each story is a flaw, so one week we're blithely sending Englishmen to Mars and the next everyone is amazed at an electronic door opener.

Meanwhile, Pertwee is finding that his new-found confidence to just *be* the Doctor is running aground when the script has other ideas. Fortunately, the decision to sell this version of the near-future via calm authority-figures and methodical professionals totally at home with the technology makes the Doctor stand out in other ways too - the disjunction between the Hartnell / Troughton hybrid of the dialogue and Pertwee's delivery is just one aspect of a deeper isolation. Ronald Allen (as Cornish) nimbly switches from distrust of the Doctor and respect for Carrington to the reverse, almost invisibly. He's not the only actor getting his teeth into a better role than he had in the Troughton era (in 6.1, "The Dominators", only eighteen months earlier but seemingly from another century) as John Abineri is trying very hard to make Carrington plausible, and seems to relish being in almost as many scenes as the regulars. (See 5.6, "Fury from the Deep" for his thankless role there.)

Ultimately, this story is a fashion-victim. The jazzy score, pre-credit sequences, modish set-piece fights and Whitehall cover-up storyline all belong to a sub-genre of television drama that was already on its way out when this was made. It has one foot in ITC's *Department S* and another in shows like *Undermind* and the hapless *Counterstrike*. (Indeed, in a lot of ways it resembles the almost-forgotten *Object Z* from 1965, a series about how ministry officials try to stop the public from panicking when a huge asteroid is discovered approaching very fast. A promising premise, but the surviving first episode is just people in jumpers explaining astronomy to people in suits.)

Admittedly, nobody else making stuff on video-tape had quite the "look at me" panache that director Michael Ferguson brings to this project, and nobody making a filmed series for export dared show the grubby bits of Britain so honestly (and thus so thrillingly - recognisable school play-ing-fields were such a change after labs and caves). But even as a unique mix of ingredients from elsewhere, this story has the same shelf life as those ingredients. In a couple of years, the Conspiracy Thriller will turn around and Hollywood will find a new twist by making the protagonist the *only* person who knows the truth and everyone - even friends - turn against him. Malcolm Hulke will have a pop at that himself (in "Invasion of the Dinosaurs") with, shall we say, mixed results. Here, though, in Spring 1970, we're looking at a mid-sixties leftover. It's stylish but sadly dated, like Liz's hat and boots.

The Facts

Written by David Whitaker (and an uncredited Malcolm Hulke, and maybe, possibly Trevor Ray - see **The Lore**). Directed by Michael Ferguson. Viewing figures: 7.1 million, 7.6 million, 8.0 million, 9.3 million, 7.1 million, 6.9 million, 5.4 million. It's been four years since any episode hit the nine million mark, and the Audience Appreciation figures are mainly around 60%. (As is often the case, the one with the lowest ratings got the highest AIs: 62% for the last episode. We'd love to see the feedback about episode five, shown during the Apollo 13 mission, but there doesn't seem to be any.)

Only episode one survives in full colour,

though the 2002 BBC video release also features recovered and re-colourised clips from the remaining episodes.

Supporting Cast Ronald Allen (Ralph Cornish), Robert Cawdron (Taltalian), John Abineri (General Carrington), Ric Felgate (Van Lyden), Michael Wisher (John Wakefield), Dallas Cavell (Quinlan), James Haswell (Corporal Champion), Derek Ware (Unit Sergeant), William Dysart (Reegan), Cyril Shaps (Lennox), John Lord (Masters), James Clayton (Private Parker), Peter Noel Cook (Alien Space Captain), Peter Halliday (Aliens' Voices), Geoffrey Beevers (Private Johnson).

Working Titles "Carriers of Death", "Invaders From Mars".

Cliffhangers In the space centre's computer room, Dr. Taltalian unexpectedly pulls a gun on the Doctor and Liz; the Doctor orders the Recovery 7 capsule to be cut open, even though the villains have promised a "surprise" inside; Liz Shaw, chased by General Carrington's men, tries to escape over a bridge and ends up toppling over the railing towards the water; the Doctor finds the body of Sir James in the man's office, unaware that one of the alien astronauts is moving in on him from behind; the Doctor's Recovery craft links up with Mars Probe 7, just as the half-mile-long alien ship appears and heads straight for him; General Carrington, finally revealed as the villain, puts a gun to the captive Doctor's head and apologises for having to do his 'moral duty'.

What Was In The Charts? "Bridge Over Troubled Water", Simon & Garfunkel; "Spirit In The Sky", Norman Greenbaum; "Venus", Shocking Blue; "Question", The Moody Blues; "Gimme Dat Ding", The Pipkins; "All Kinds of Everything", Dana; "Young Gifted and Black", Bob and Marcia.

The Lore

• The idea to do a definitive First Contact story dated back to the creator rotation on "The Web of Fear" (5.5), when Derrick Sherwin became script editor and Peter Bryant took over as producer. They'd both been involved in the previous David Whitaker story (5.4, "The Enemy of the World"). The First Contact idea interested Whitaker, but every time he came up with a proposal, the series' format had changed. Terrance Dicks, taking over as Sherwin's assistant and then replacement, kept channels open and the first proper "Invaders from Mars" treatment arrived in May, with Jamie and Zoe removed and a vague sketch of the Doctor. About eight weeks later, a more UNIT-friendly and conceptually smart version (called "The Carriers of Death") was submitted. In this, a gangster takes advantage of some gullible-but-invulnerable alien ambassadors who were sent to Earth as a swap for humans who went to Mars.

By August, the story was in danger of being abandoned altogether, as Whitaker's conception of the series had become out of key with Sherwin's. (To be fair to Whitaker, he had only a few hints as to who this new Doctor was, and was mainly given a list of things to avoid as opposed to a strong brief of what the story should be like. So hardly anyone could have delivered a workable script on the first go.) There's reason to believe that Dicks' assistant Trevor Ray was assigned the job of tactfully reworking the first episode, just to show how it should go (Ray was paid £150 over the odds, apparently for *something* to do with this story), although Dicks claims that Ray had nothing to do with it. Come October, and the first three episodes of what had become a seven-parter were submitted. Neither the author nor the *third* producer to work on this story, Barry Letts, had any enthusiasm for it.

• After the script for "Doctor Who and the Silurians" was done and dusted, Malcolm Hulke was asked to perform CPR on this project. He found the confused mash-up of three separate conceptions of the story horrifying. (He reserved comment until later, eventually suggesting that lack of guidance from the top that was the root cause of the trouble. This seems to back up Dicks' assertion that no-one person was in charge of this project.) Whitaker's attempts to keep pace were further complicated by his moving to Australia in mid-draft. By November, it was agreed that Whitaker would be paid for the first three episodes and Hulke would assume uncredited writing duties *in toto* for episodes four to seven, later reworking the first three (again) to match his idea of where the story should go after this. At the very least, Hulke had the advantage that he'd seen Pertwee's Doctor in action, and added the conjuring trick with the tape to suit the new boy's performance.

• To jump ahead a little bit, Dicks thanked Whitaker for all his work and later pointed out that episode one had been shown 'to great acclaim' at an international drama conference. (Presumably, this explains why a decent copy of that episode survived the cull.) After nearly a decade writing and lecturing in Australia, Whitaker returned to Blighty and began work on "The Enemy of the World" novelisation, but died aged 51 in 1980. It was only some time later that the full extent of Hulke's work on this story became known.

• Incoming director Michael Ferguson was already well-versed in doing science-fiction in colour: eighteen months earlier, he directed an *Out of the Unknown* episode ("The Yellow Pill", recorded 28th of June, 1968), then another in October (Brian Hayles' "1+1+1.5"). These were both near-future stories: one a paranoid thriller, the other a satire about the population explosion, with some striking design work. (At the time, BBC2 had all the coolest stuff.) Ferguson obtained permission to add new scenes - all the better to use every resource available. In just the first episode, we have an entire sequence using videotape editing to make Liz and the Doctor pop in and out of existence. For that matter, he also got to play with a helicopter that wasn't scripted.

Meanwhile, Letts was like a kid in a sweetshop with CSO, and booked a session on 3rd of January (the day Pertwee made his screen debut as the Doctor) just to see what he could do with blue cloth and a doll's house. (You can see this on the DVD of "Carnival of Monsters". Note that the examples Letts uses are from "Ambassadors": a space-station the size of TC1, the main studio, and a rocket research base. His little chum who walks in and out of the model is assistant floor manager Margot Heyhoe, after whom the laundry on Reegan's magic breadvan was named.)

• Havoc had two days' preparation for the warehouse fight, which was consciously modelled on a 1930s Warner Brothers gangster-movie shoot-out. This and other stunt-heavy scenes had been shot by end of January, allowing production to start while the regulars were still making "The Silurians" episode seven. In fact, the *first* scene filmed was the isotope-theft in the final episode.

• Costume designer Christine Rawlins devised a spacesuit that was a more streamlined model of those used by NASA. (This became the BBC's basic spacesuit for much of the early seventies, with *Monty Python's Flying Circus*; 8.4, "Colony in

Space" and 10.4, "Planet of the Daleks" using them.) The helmets were salvaged from the curious 1968 Hammer Films space-western *Moon Zero Two* (see 5.3, "The Ice Warriors"). Derek Ware got his Havoc lads to fall over spectacularly when the implacable aliens confronted them, but kept his high-falls specialist, Roy Scammell, for the scene at the fuel supply. (It was Southall Gas Works, one yet to be decommissioned after the change to North Sea Gas; see comments on "Fury from the Deep" and "Doctor Who and the Silurians".) Scammell also doubled for Liz a few days later, as they needed someone to take the fall over the weir *and* Caroline John couldn't drive on public roads until after she'd passed her test.

• The Gas Works shoot was Nicholas Courtney's first work on this story, but his big moment came in the shootout. The BBC had use of the place, formerly a Condenser factory. (Note the presence of those big ceramic things, looking like stacked earthenware dishes, including one conveniently suspended from the ceiling for a UNIT trooper to swing at Sergeant Collinson.) They filmed UNIT's arrival first, while equipping the location with charges to simulate ricochets and sugar-glass for messrs Chuntz and Ware to break. Ware recalls this as the first time Courtney felt comfortable shooting even a prop pistol (so maybe "The Web of Fear" having episodes missing is a blessing after all).

The next day, Pertwee, Caroline John and John Abineri (then called General "Cunningham" - why they re-named him at such short notice is unclear; possibly the real military had someone with that name) joined the production. Then came the weir stuff, in Marlowe, Buckinghamshire, for which Havoc's Billy Horrigan donned a wetsuit in case of emergencies. (The wood was very slippery at the best of times and a fine drizzle meant John had to wear a wig to prevent it looking like Liz had an afro; you'll now know why they gave her that hat. Bear this in mind - well, maybe not the hat bit - when we get to "Inferno".)

• Next came the hijack scenes for episode two, and Ferguson really went to town on explosions, motorcycle stunts (the speciality of Havoc's Marc Boyle) and a helicopter. Derek Ware did the stunt of hanging from a helicopter, which took three goes. (He claims it cost £72 a go just to start up the chopper's engines.) The first time was perfect, but the camera missed it; the second time he slipped and straddled the landing-strut, pulling the helicopter off course; and the last time he

landed on his feet - safely but not *looking* dangerous, which is a professional no-no.

Then a real accident happened out of shot, when one of the bike-riders (Stan Hollingsworth) let the bike get loose and effectively fired it towards the camera. Director's assistant Pauline Silcock (the other person name-checked on the Magic Van - see how we're trying to be a full-service reference guide?) received a nasty gash to her leg and was replaced. All of this pushed costs up. Letts, still finding his feet as a producer, consulted with Ferguson about this and was told, "It's your job to stop me!" As we'll see, Letts took this to heart.

• The scenes at the entrance to the Space Research Centre were filmed in Kent. The building was, in fact, the Blue Circle Cement Works, and they cancelled a strike to let *Doctor Who* film there. Filming ended on Wednesday, 4th of February, and the following Monday saw the start of rehearsals leaving up to studio recording on Friday. You will note that they had reverted to the Hartnell era schedule, meaning one episode per week.

• Ferguson found that the videodisc unit was great fun, and did amusing and exciting things if you hit it when it was playing. For the results of this, watch what happens when we get our first glimpse of a helmet-less Ambassador. Ferguson probably had this happy accident when working on the BBC2 series, and found ways to make it happen to order without the unions jumping on him for a) risking a valuable and delicate piece of BBC property and b) thumping it himself instead of letting a paid-up member of EETPU doing this clearly demarcated task.

• As for the business with the titles and the way "OF DEATH" launches itself straight into the viewer's lap... Ferguson had already decided to pep up with the inserted cliffhanger reprise to episode two, and opted for the two-stage titles. With the radiophonic "sting" being used, it cannot - as is sometimes said - have been a snap decision. The full title "The Ambassadors of Death" was only decided upon after the start of rehearsals, so perhaps the two-stage version was influenced by the uncertainty of whether it was going to be "The Ambassadors", "The Carriers of Death" or some combination thereof, possibly once again using the "Doctor Who and the" prefix.

• Episode one had the new scene with the Doctor and Liz popping through time. Dicks had a hand in this, and it makes the use of the isolated console in the next story less of an unprecedented move (another "warm-up" for "Inferno" happens in episode five). The state of the console was of great concern, and in Ferguson's next story ("The Claws of Axos"), they'll have built a new one.

• As you'll recall from "The Space Pirates" (6.6), the BBC had set up a Space Unit for coverage of the Apollo moonshots. A large part of this was studio simulations of what the various capsules and modules were doing out of shot. (This had a big flashing sign saying "simulation", just in case anyone was dumb enough to mistake a model in clear 625-line colour for a grubby NTSC shot with ghosting, the best we could expect from space until the film as developed.

As part of this expansion, Ian Scoones, late of Century 21 Productions (Gerry Anderson's puppets and spaceships) came to the BBC. It fell to him, as assistant to visual effects man Peter Day, to make and film the Mars Probe 7 and Recovery 7 models. Another assistant, Rhys Jones, made the more aetherial alien ship interior from glass fibre and fake cobwebs. This involved Pertwee against a CSO blue backdrop, with a platform for him to seemingly "float" on in the same colour.

• Before this, the sequence of the Doctor experiencing excessive G-forces was achieved by the technical marvel of a very powerful blast of warm air. Ferguson recalls that Pertwee was game for anything that made it look "real" and would reflect well on the Doctor's endurance or bravery.

• The videotape editors incurred a lot of hassle trying to make everything fit and the session for the first episode overran, whereupon it decided that Doctor Who should be allotted more time than mainstream dramas.

• By the time episode five was being rehearsed, it was obvious that Douglas Camfield wanted to use John Levene as the UNIT sergeant in "Inferno", so Corporal Benton (from "The Invasion") was reintroduced and promoted for this adventure. You will note that while he's prominent in the studio scenes in episode seven, he's mysteriously absent from the pre-filmed attack on the Bunker - despite his being the one to locate it and suggest the use of Bessie. There was a sergeant in episode five - possibly Derek Ware's character, who holds the Doctor's translation machine in episode seven, or possibly Dr Lennox's killer (noted in some accounts as "Sgt West"). The last episode was recorded the day before episode

two aired, and included Caroline John's husband Geoffrey Beevers (see 18.6, "The Keeper of Traken") in the last scenes recorded, the UNIT base sequences.

• Ronald Allen (Ralph Cornish) had appeared in the series before (see, if you dare, "The Dominators"), and since then he'd taken on the role that defined his career: the suave motel manager David Hunter in Crossroads[14]. Michael Wisher here made his debut (on screen, at any rate; he'd been a voice performer in 6.5, "The Seeds of Death") as Wakefield, the anxious, bearded, bespectacled TV presenter at space control. Wisher will shortly return (in "Terror of the Autons"), and five years later he'll be the first Davros, after doing a lot of Dalek voices in this era.

Robert Cawdron (Taltalian) was given zat outrrragious fronsh accent in rehearsals (they redubbed the one line he gets on film, but forgot to change the delivery). John Abineri (General Carrington) had been Van Lutyens in "Fury from the Deep".

And of special note... Ric Felgate (the astronaut Van Lyden) had been in Ferguson's two earlier stories (3.10, "The War Machines"; 6.5, "The Seeds of Death") - and was the director's brother-in-law. Like the other kidnapped astronauts, he doubled as one of the spacesuited aliens. His scenes took place in a set where the makers of Doomwatch had a stake; they had need of a space-capsule for the episode "Re-Entry Forbidden", and liased with the Who crew to go halves on the costs. The capsule was big enough to contain a hand-held camera, so they did upside-down shooting in the hopes that it would look like weightlessness. A feed from this was CSOed on to a gauze screen that was tinted the right saturated blue by coloured lights. (Like we said, kids in a toyshop.)

• The Head of Drama, Shaun Sutton, wasn't entirely certain about re-commissioning Doctor Who and asked Letts for ideas. Letts had a plan for a Barry-McKenzie-for-kids called Snowy Black, and had even cast the lead (imagine if the BBC had pre-empted Crocodile Dundee by fifteen years[15]). Dicks was working on a sitcom idea called Better Late (this might explain why A Man's Life was forwarded to the Doctor Who office; see "The Claws of Axos"). Hulke had an idea for a drama about Gilbert and Sullivan.

• That we have any colour footage of "Ambassadors" other than episode one owes to

Ian Levine, a rather extreme fan of whom we'll hear more in Volumes IV, V and VI. He asked a friend, Tom Lundie, to make off-air Betamax recordings of the 525-line NTSC transmissions of this adventure and a few other Pertwee stories. Unfortunately, Lundie's tape of this story didn't copy so well; the recording was made from WNED 17 Buffalo, but Lundie was over the border in Toronto and his system was slightly incompatible with the signal. The only way Levine could convert them into a useable format for British machines was to copy them to Sony U-matic tapes.

When it later transpired that even the American companies had wiped their copies of these stories, Levine's tapes became the only known colour versions of "Doctor Who and the Silurians", "The Ambassadors of Death", "Terror of the Autons" and "The Daemons". Unless anyone else in America made off-air copies in the late 70s (if so, please email the publishers of this book straightaway), this is probably as good as we will get. It's also the source of the colour clips of "The Mind of Evil" episode six. (Lundie couldn't afford the then-exorbitant cost of blank tape, so he crammed what he could onto the end of other stories.)

7.4: "Inferno"

(Serial DDD. Seven Episodes, 9th May - 20th June 1970.)

Which One is This? Doctor Who in an Exciting Adventure with the British Union of Fascists. A drilling project to the centre of the Earth releases green werewolf-producing goo and destroys the world (yes, really!). The Doctor gets to explain the plot in two separate dimensions to two different Brigadiers, but only beats up one Sergeant Benton.

Firsts and Lasts Last appearance of Liz Shaw (save for a cameo in 21.7, "The Five Doctors"), who vanishes between seasons and never even gets a proper goodbye scene. Final appearance of the original TARDIS console, which has served the programme faithfully since 1963 but which disappears in the great TARDIS re-fit of Season Eight. This is also the last ever seven-part *Doctor Who* story. And it's the first use of Swarfega as a mutagenic slime - that's the seventies equivalent of the Foam Machine for the Troughton stories or Orange Sparkly Pixie Dust for BBC Wales.

The Doctor uses bizarre martial arts, specifically Venusian karate, for the first time. This means it's also the first time he gets to shout 'hai!'. And of course, it's the first time Terry Walsh doubles for Pertwee in a fight-scene (wearing an asbestos suit).

This story marks the end of the Innes Lloyd formula of one big main set for a whole story. In fact, it's the start of out-of-sequence recording as a routine part of the production. It's also the last time an entire story has music from stock. With the title "Inferno" being projected over some nice stock footage of erupting volcanoes, it's the last time a story gets its own title-sequence (unless you count the whole of Season Twenty-Three as one story - which nobody really does - or the McGann movie). Off-screen, another change is that it's the last time they use the church-hall in Kensington for rehearsals; from now on they get custom-made facilities at the "Acton Hilton".

Seven Things to Notice About "Inferno":
1. You read that right: Earth is destroyed in the penultimate episode. Understandably but sadly, this is a tough act to follow and most of episode seven is taken up with everyone waiting for the Doctor to wake up. Beforehand, the tension has successfully ratcheted up concerning the impending disaster in both the normal UNIT set-up and an Evil Parallel Universe(tm), although the latter is pretty much the same. It's an alternate history where fascists have been running Britain as a republic since the 1940s - and yet, despite this massive historical revision, all the same people are present and the 1969 Ford Cortina comes in the same colour-scheme.

2. The "fascist" version of the drilling project has, predictably, an all-white staff. In "our" world, there's a pleasingly "futuristic" ethnic mix of ancillary staff, but nobody seems to have told them that they're playing technicians. Observe the climax of episode seven, when one of the techies mills around in shot as if trying to see himself on the monitor. Nonetheless, the fascists - who are running to a strict timetable maintained by slave labour and judicious firing-squads - have only got their drilling-to-the-centre-of-the-Earth-and-unleashing-powers-Man-was-not-meant-to-tamper-with scheme six hours ahead of the ramshackle UNIT-world version.

3. Unusually, for much of this story the central characters aren't the Doctor and his companion, but drilling expert Greg Sutton and project assistant Petra Williams, who play out a kind of love

story against the backdrop of the world/s ending. (Greg, in particular, speaks for the audience in the first few episodes. He's the newcomer around here, while the Doctor's already a permanent fixture at the Inferno project and doesn't need things explained to him. It's the first time the series has tried this approach since 1.1, "An Unearthly Child", which is apt, as the actor playing Greg also appeared in that story as one of the cavemen. He's evolved a bit since then, but he's still oozing testosterone.)

4. In many ways, the intensity of the plot and acting is underlined by the constant noise of drilling, in the huge great set that dominates this story. In episode one it's merely loud and intrusive; by the climax, it's relentless and even more shrill, so everyone has to shout. This is fine for most of the adventure, with tempers running high and a permanent state of crisis surrounding the impending end of the world - twice - but makes the scenes where the Doctor yells things like 'Good morning, professor' a bit silly. It also means that the burgeoning romance(s) between Greg and Petra is conducted at the tops of their voices whilst dripping sweat.

5. As a direct opposite to the *Star Trek* notion, this story's villain has a goatee in "our" dimension and is clean-shaven in the Evil Parallel Universe. (Although technically, Spock wasn't "evil" in the Mirror Universe.) He also wears a white Nehru-suit, white gloves and cool shades when working for the Evil Parallel Government. White is definitely this season's colour as far as government installations are concerned, and silver lamé belts are a must-have accessory if you're drilling into the Earth or sending people off it in rockets. Taking the three seven-parters as a whole, it looks as if some civil servant ordered in thousands upon thousands of white cotton safari-suits, accessorised with those kinky-boots of wellies, and then the Government sponsored any projects where these could be used up. Even the Doctor wears the boots in "Silurians", although he's trying for the Marlon Brando look at the time.

Also notice how, when this story's singular omission - a nasty bearded version of the Doctor - became the programme's principle villain starting in the *next* story, he comes equipped with a black Nehru-suit and black gloves. By the same token, the Evil Parallel Brigadier has no moustache (but bears a spectacular scar and an eye-patch). Is it, we wonder, a coincidence that Terrance Dicks

removed his own Jason King-style moustache and director Douglas Camfield grew a beard at almost *exactly* the time this was made?

6. There's a lot of shooting at people, with occasional lapses into cowboy sound-effects, but the main action concerns people falling off things. Because the Doctor visits an Evil Parallel Universe where GPO trimphones are exactly like ours, some characters get to fall off the same absurdly high gangways *twice* in different episodes. Yet somehow, even if you're watching the whole thing in one go, seeing members of Havoc going 'WAAAAAAAAA!!!' never gets old.

What's *really* remarkable, though, is that there's only one major injury. It happens in a stunt so low-key, only those looking for it would think anything was wrong. In the interest of maintaining some suspense about this, you have until **The Lore** to figure out what we're referring to.

7. "megga-volts". The set-designers went to art-school, not technical college.

The Continuity

The Doctor He initially sees nothing wrong with the idea of tapping the Earth's core for energy, even though he must at least suspect that nothing in recorded history entails human beings using this sort of power source at this time. He even helped get the project started. He *certainly* doesn't have any idea what's really down there, despite remembering similar incidents at volcanic eruptions. Nor is he aware of the existence of parallel universes before now, though he surmises that the alternative Earth he visits is a 'parallel space-time continuum' and a 'twin world'. [The existence of parallel universes is such a massively significant piece of information, it's impossible to believe the Time Lords are ignorant of it, especially as it only takes a little tinkering with the TARDIS console to move the Doctor between dimensions (admittedly aided by the flukey timing of Stahman's switch-off of power). Do the Time Lords suppress this sort of knowledge, or have the Doctor's memory lapses blocked off or wiped out the relevant data? As the TARDIS console *can* journey to such realms, it's possible the Time Lords wanted to eliminate even the small possibility of the Doctor escaping there, and locked off the information in his mind.]

The Doctor insists that he can't take people from the doomed world back to the one he

What's Wrong with the Centre of the Earth?

Since we last tackled this question, fresh information has come to light and made everything a lot more confusing. To go by X3.0, "The Runaway Bride", it now appears that the Earth was congealed around a spaceship containing subatomic particles with very odd properties. It might initially sound as though this explains the peculiarities surrounding Stahlman's Gas, but actually it makes the properties of the green ooze and much of the rest of the "Inferno" downright baffling, as opposed to it all just being weird and unexplained.

We should clarify what the problem is: we're treating everything below our feet as one undifferentiated lump. "Inferno" handles matters a mere 30km down, still more or less at crust-level. At sea, Stahlman and his staff could possibly have penetrated the upper mantle (you've only got only about 10 km of crust to chew through), but they're on land in, um, East Mercia or somewhere. On land, we're looking at a minimum of 35 km of drilling before we hit Moho (see **The Lore**). The deepest drilling to date managed about 12 km, out of a radius of 6300 km, so the core is out of our depth in almost every sense.

To refresh everyone's school memories of this sort of thing: the four layers are inner core, outer core, mantle and crust. We must now, distressingly, discuss horrible snacks on sale in motorway service stations and school canteens. It's a sad fact, but the best visual aid for geophysics is something called a "Scotch Egg". (It's mysteriously unknown in Scotland, the same way nobody in the UK has ever seen the things Americans call "English Muffins".) Due to advances in fast-food technology and several petitions, these grotesque objects are almost extinct but provide an exact analogy.

So... think about something the size of a cricketball. It has a hard-boiled egg in the centre, surrounded by sausage-meat (usually the cheapest kind available), then breadcrumbs on the outside. When deep-fried for an indeterminate amount of time and left until someone is so hungry they'd eat anything, it's *still* utterly disgusting. But the proportions of the four layers - breadcrumbs, sausage, egg-white and yolk - are *exactly* right as a cross-section of the planet's composition.

As you might expect, the crust is the lightest and is mainly alumino-silicates. Mantle is solid rock that, under the immense forces at work, behaves as a liquid. Then you've got both liquid and solid iron, each mixed with nickel. That's pretty much the standard account textbooks gave when "Inferno" was written, and a lot has been done to confirm it since. It's actually a bit more complicated than that - the mantle isn't one layer, it's three and a half. The so-called "D" layer right at the bottom is *thought* to be chemically different, a sort of "grit" that's too dense to get into the core, but too heavy to remain part of the lower mantle. They can't get a ladle and test it, but the analogy with the composition of meteorites holds good for everything else that *can* be tested.

By the same process, there's a transition layer between the upper and lower mantle. We know a lot about the upper mantle because it keeps popping out to see us - this is the cue for all *Austin Powers* fans to put on a silly voice and say "magma". That transition layer (400-650 km down) is full of dense things such as garnet, that sink when basalt rises. And on top of the mantle is the Moho Discontinuity, probably.

And at the centre of it all, according to "The Runaway Bride", is a Racnoss spaceship fuelled by Huon particles. These are sparkly orange glowing things (just for a change) but have not existed naturally for thousands of millions of years. There's 'a remnant in the heart of a TARDIS' and in a spaceship left over from these 'Dark Times' - and, um, inside Donna. The particles 'unravel the atomic structure', can be extracted from water and catalysed by anxious brides with endorphin overloads. Sometimes they're a form of energy, sometimes they're particles and sometimes they're a chemical compound. Oh, and they attract anything else that contains them. So once you've got a critical mass, you can pull other Huon-heavy things across space and time.

This sounds like *exactly* the sort of thing that could make people turn into werewolf-like primords. After all, nothing about either of these phenomena makes any sense whatsoever, so why shouldn't they be connected? Besides, if we assume that Stahlman's Gas and the un-named green goo are the result of something predating the laws of physics as we currently understand them, we're on familiar ground. *The New Adventures* suggested this on a pretty regular basis (see **Are All These "Gods" Related?** under 26.3, "The Curse of Fenric"). Matter from either a previous Universe, or a phase when the Great Vampires were created (18.4, "State of Decay") and all *sorts* of peculiar things (of a variety that the Time Lords resolved when fixing various design

continued on page 77...

knows, as it would create a 'dimensional paradox' and endanger all the universes. [But how does he know this, if he hasn't heard about parallel universes before? Does he have experience of other dimensions which aren't parallel universes, but something even stranger? And why doesn't his *own* presence in the other universe cause a dimensional paradox? Are Time Lords protected from this sort of thing? It was tempting to consign much of the aforementioned to **Things That Don't Make Sense**, but it's *possible* this stems from the Doctor's blocked-off memories seeping through. Compare what's known here about parallel realms with X2.5, "Rise of the Cybermen", in which the Tenth Doctor says travel between parallel worlds happened more easily while the Time Lords were around to monitor it - possibly suggesting that significant developments occur after this adventure, if not as a direct result of it. See 26.1, "Battlefield", where this is discussed as though it's routine for the Doctor, and **Is Pete's World the Empire of the Wolf?** in Volume VII.]

He suggests that the other dimension is 'sideways' in time [much as in "Battlefield"], and concludes that there's an 'infinity' of universes, defined by the conscious choices of their inhabitants. [By 13.3, "Pyramids of Mars" this is demonstrable fact.]

The Doctor can use Venusian karate to briefly paralyse or knock out humans, with just a couple of fingers near the victim's throat. Prolonged pressure can leave the victim permanently paralysed. [Odd that a martial art invented by another species is so good at finding weak spots in the human body. Maybe Venusian martial arts have a Zen element, and the Doctor's just applying the same philosophy on Earth.] His normal pulse is 170 [85 per heart?] and his hearts can go at different rates. He usually works out epsilon coordinates in his head.

It appears, from his influence at ministerial level, that the Doctor has already joined the various gentlemen's clubs he claims to belong to later [eg 8.1, "Terror of the Autons"] and scientific peer-review boards. [His reputation has reached the ears of people such as Masters as early as 7.2, "Doctor Who and the Silurians", but doors were opened to him in 3.10, "The War Machines" as if he were well-established. For someone who told the Time Lords in "The War Games" (6.7) that he was worried about being recognised, he's making himself very conspicuous.]

• *Ethics*. Fixing the TARDIS is still the Doctor's main concern. So much so that when nobody at the Inferno project listens to him, he gets stroppy and goes back to his experiments even though there's a lethal menace threatening the centre. [Or perhaps *because* of the threat. Even if we excuse it as an attempt to find out if he can leave before committing himself to trying to stop the experiment, the fact that the Doctor's first act on being barred from the drilling is to trick Liz and switch through power to make a hasty exit looks a bit shabby. It's the last time we see him so unwilling to help out in an avoidable catastrophe; even in one that's part of recorded history (X4.2, "The Fires of Pompeii"), he's persuaded to intervene. After seeing one Earth destroyed, he becomes noticeably more concerned about the fates of individuals on the "orthodox" planet. By "The Mind of Evil" (8.2), the events in "Inferno" constitute his worst nightmare.]

Observing the deviation in events between the two Earths, the Doctor concludes that 'free will is not an illusion after all'. [In subsequent stories on Earth, he's hazy on what the "scripted" future is, so perhaps his very presence places history into a state of flux. See the essay with 9.1, "Day of the Daleks".]

The Doctor muses on motiveless murder as being somehow worse than any other kind. Whatever his later gripes, he seems to trust the Brigadier to conduct a thorough investigation without his help. He personally persuaded the Brigadier and Sir Keith to allow UNIT and specifically himself to 'observe' this project.

Sir Keith says that the Doctor's 'calculations on initial stresses' were 'invaluable' with regards the preparations for the Inferno project, and that the Doctor came to his answers in 10 minutes, whereas Stahlman had a team of mathematicians working for a month. [It's one thing for the Third Doctor to take an interest in the scientific discoveries of the era (see, just for a start, 11.1, "The Time Warrior"), but it's quite another for him to goose such endeavours along. Or maybe it's just a matter of his applying good maths rather than alien science.

[We might surmise that the Doctor's work on the Inferno project was a form of cupboard-love - a means of getting his hands on a nuclear reactor - but chances are that UNIT could have provided another reactor suitable for his console tinkering. This leads us to suspect that there is some special

What's Wrong with the Centre of the Earth?

...continued from page 75

flaws in Creation) were possible, is often posited.

Even in unimpeachably canonical stories such as "Planet of Evil" (13.2), biological changes follow ingestion of contra-terrene matter[24], including a regression to a bestial state and the consumption of "life force". Many of the novels suggested a set-up by which Earth was agglomerated around a shell protecting the outside universe from the baleful influence of this weird matter and / or patches of nonsensical space from the Dark Times. This was supposedly why the Time Lords took such an interest in this otherwise insignificant planet. In other *About Time* volumes, we've speculated on the influence of Omega and his chums on slowing down the expansion of the cosmos, so the notion that the Time Lords removed an entire category of subatomic particles from the whole of creation, without unbalancing the rest of it and making the universe contract to the size of Wembley Stadium or whatever, isn't quite as preposterous as it seems.

There are two snags with this as an explanation for the green goo and its effects. The Huon mass within the buried Web-Star is inactive (it has to be, otherwise there's no point in doing nasty things to Donna at all, and every TARDIS ever made would have been pulled to the Earth's molten core). The other returns us to the problem of the planet's structure. Stahlman's gas is right at the top of the magma, in the gap between mantle and crust. We would have to explain why the influence of Huon particles can permeate the dense layers of nickle-iron, garnet and olivine - to say nothing of those concentrated layers of thick metallic silt at each boundary - and yet is somehow prevented from affecting us by a few kilometres of relatively flimsy alumino-silicates. It's like a bullet going through steel and brick, but being stopped by wallpaper on the other side of the brick. Admittedly, this would be easier to explain than how catalysis can generate subatomic particles, but it's still massively unsatisfying as a solution to our first problem: the green goo 30 km beneath our feet that causes people to defy the Second Law of Thermodynamics whilst devolving into something utterly unlike our evolutionary ancestry, but the same in all instances.

Worse, it rules out all the other solutions we came up with in the First Edition of this book. While in some ways this is a relief, it nonetheless brings us to the original issue. Something about this green goo makes hot things stay hot far longer than is plausible *and* rearranges the DNA of anyone who touches it. Moreover, it's accompanied by a gas that's a prodigious supply of energy but will - if released - blow the Earth apart, gathering force as it's released instead of dispersing it. In short, it reverses Entropy in some ways, gaining energy from somewhere and getting more as time passes.

Stated this way, something left implicit in the script is made obvious - the fact that the Doctor is near to a release of this stuff and then visits a parallel universe (where, despite all other historical changes, they're also drilling for it) can't be a coincidence. Whatever else this goo is, it's some kind of tap into a weird space-time event - perhaps in the same way as the Crystal of Kronos from "The Time Monster" (9.5). And here we recall that in that adventure and "Inferno", the Doctor is hurled from the safety of the TARDIS into the space-time vortex, the second time definitely owing to the crystal's effect. So we have to account for the presence of *two* curious substances: the green goo and this odd quartz trident that's a manifestation of something outside time, on the same planet. Or maybe we don't...

Let's take a step back. The Crystal of Kronos disappeared 3,500 years ago and re-appeared in the 1970s. Volcanoes marked both events. Maybe exposing magma to the crystal's properties produces the goo and the gas. Compared to positing that Rassilon put a Band-Aid on the Universe and everyone mistakes it for a planet, this sounds relatively sensible but still causes problems. Does every planet have such a crystal and, if not, what's special about this one? (Well, there's a big spaceship with semi-inert Huon particles at the centre, for starters.) The fact remains that when a volcano erupted on the site of Atlantis in "The Time Monster", suddenly the Master gained access to a unique crystal lost for millennia. (He has a TARDIS and some oven-gloves, so he could probably spot it when no-one else would have done, even if this meant moving to Athens for a while but failing to pick up the local accent.) We could *even*, if we chose, connect the crystal's re-emergence with either Stahlman's antics or those of Professor Zaroff (4.5, "The Underwater Menace"), but there seems little point now that Craig Hinton isn't around to write a novel about it.

This seems to cover everything except the pri-

continued on page 79...

property of the stuff being produced at the drilling site that the Doctor needs; see the accompanying essay for more speculation.]

• *Background.* The Doctor was present during the eruption at Krakatoa in 1883, and recognises the sound made by the primords even though he apparently doesn't recognise the primords themselves. He regards the royal family as 'charming', and knew the Queen's grandfather in Paris. [Given the Doctor's liking for big social events, he probably met the future Edward VII at the International Exhibition of 1889, the year Edward opened the Eiffel Tower. It may also have been the 1904 meeting that led to the Entente Cordiale, although this was less fun, so not really the Doctor's style.]

The Supporting Cast

• *Liz Shaw.* She's now helping the Doctor to work on the TARDIS console, and seems to understand the process (enough to let her replace bypass wires, certainly) rather than just handing the Doctor his tools. [This makes her comments about her just passing the Doctor test tubes - as quoted by the Brigadier in the next story - even more improbable, as she's clearly getting a thorough tutorial that's worth a dozen years' study in any ivory tower.]

• *Brigadier Lethbridge-Stewart.* Surprisingly, he wasn't born with a moustache. He puts a fair amount of effort into turning his temporary base of operations into a home-from-home (or rather, gets Benton to do it for him). By episode four, he's calling Miss Shaw 'Liz'. [She's on his staff, but perhaps not subordinate to him in a strictly military sense. We'll confine speculation to the fact that she returns to Cambridge rather abruptly... it's never officially acknowledged on screen that the Brigadier is married, but the production team assumed as much - see 8.5, "The Daemons" - so we doubt their relationship got unprofessional. The only time the Brig seems to have a relationship with a woman that's less than courteous is with Doris (11.5, "Planet of the Spiders"; "Battlefield"), and he's embarrassed at admitting this.]

• *Sergeant Benton.* Now acting as the Brigadier's right-hand man, and here becomes a regular member of the Doctor's circle [although it's doubtful he has an "official" position as the messenger between the Brigadier and the rest of UNIT, since traditionally a higher-ranking officer would fill that role - as Captain Yates does in Season Eight].

The Supporting Cast (Alternate)

• *Section-Leader Elizabeth Shaw.* She read Physics at University and considered becoming a scientist. She rapidly loses patience with the Brigade-Leader's attempts to impose his will on a situation beyond his or anyone's control. Nevertheless, she's a loyal officer of the Republic and considers free-speech movements to be 'crackpot'. She's a stickler for procedure, delaying the Doctor's execution until the correct forms have been filled in.

• *Brigade-Leader Lethbridge-Stewart.* He's a bully. He has what appears to be a duelling-scar on his left cheek and up to his brow, over which an eye-patch is always worn. He's less good in a fist fight than his counterpart. He can be as sardonic as "our" Brigadier, but cracks under the pressure and resorts to infantile name-calling and sarcasm [see also 5.5, "The Web of Fear"].

• *Platoon Under-Leader Benton.* He's surly and by-the-book. His only solution to a crisis is to insist on more parade-ground drill.

The TARDIS The Doctor can use nuclear power from the Inferno project to fuel the TARDIS console, but states that its storage units always have some energy left [demonstrating that the console is no longer "in touch" with the Ship's power source]. An overload of energy sends the console across dimensions [the Doctor's amnesiac tinkering with the controls is at least partly responsible]. After further work the Doctor believes the TARDIS console to be fully operational, and he seriously seems to think that it can get him off the planet [after returning to the TARDIS first, presumably], but in fact it just shifts him a few seconds forward in time and a short distance in space.

Operating the TARDIS console involves epsilon co-ordinates, a principle which Liz seems to understand. The Time Rotor has taken a real beating, and seems barely to be holding together. As with the last story, there is a section of the console, nearest the Time-Vector Generator, that affects people or objects nearest it. [See 7.3, "The Ambassadors of Death"; 5.7, "The Wheel in Space". A cut line has Liz explain that this is how Bessie went to Nazi-Bizarro-World.] The console uses 'tri-gamma circuits'.

The Non-Humans

• *Primords.* The mutagenic substance which somehow makes its way up the pipes of the

What's Wrong with the Centre of the Earth?

...continued from page 77

mords. After all, if the goo is making people regress through evolution, why should they look like Oddbod from *Carry On Screaming*? We might tentatively suggest that the goo's apparent ability to step outside our spacetime is at work here - maybe this is how we *would* have developed but for some outside intervention. There's enough candidates to choose from in *Doctor Who*'s version of the Ascent of Man but, just for the sake of argument, suppose the primords are what humanity would have become had the Fendahl not shown up (15.3, "Image of the Fendahl"). This *wouldn't* explain the primords' need for heat, nor the ability to generate it in such quantities (without scorching their clothing). However, the counter-entropic business we mentioned earlier might just cover this. (Perhaps they're not snarling, but instead are saying, in reverse, "Why is everyone moving backwards?")

This is, however, overlaying two highly unlikely side effects of a temporal anomaly on top of one another. A simpler solution, for some readers at least, might be that like all other green goo, it does odd things to DNA involving fusion with other lifeforms. (See 10.5, "The Green Death"; 12.2, "The Ark in Space"; and 12.4, "Genesis of the Daleks".) Exactly *which* other lifeform the unfortunate Harry Slocum and others at Project Inferno might be merging with is unclear (the Pyroviles can do it unaided; see X4.2, "The Fires of Pompeii") but we had to say it. If the similarity between Kontron crystals and the Crystal of Kronos inspires any of you to write stories about Were-Bandrils (22.5, "Timelash"), please keep it to yourselves.

We're now left with just two lingering details: why didn't the Daleks encounter this when they drilled to remove the inner core (2.2, "The Dalek Invasion of Earth") and how come there isn't a volcano under the Thames Barrier, considering Torchwood drilled right the way through, for some reason, allowing the Empress of the Racnoss free access to her lost ship ("The Runaway Bride")? For the first problem, we simply say "The Slyther": there's no evidence (beyond the novel *War of the Daleks*) that the Black Dalek's pet is a Skaro native, so it might well be a Kaled mutant further mutated by the green goo. We'll get back to you on the second problem in a later volume.

Inferno project - boiling green slime, basically - has an instant effect on human tissue [cf 10.5, "The Green Death"; 12.2, "The Ark In Space"]. The Doctor describes this as a 'retrogression of the body cells': the skin is stained green-blue, and within minutes the victim begins behaving in a primal, murderously violent manner. Before long the full transition from human to primord takes place, although it can take longer if only a small amount of the substance was touched. Heat seems to accelerate the process, and the slime never cools. [The name "primord" is never spoken, only appearing in the end credits, whereas the novelisation just refers to them as mutants. Since these mutants are a previously-unknown race, the word "primord" looks more like scriptwriter's shorthand than an attempt to give them a proper designation.]

Primords are recognisably human, but with ape-like swathes of hair around the face and body. They're so abnormally strong and tough, they can survive for minutes after being shot, although they thrive on heat and can be killed by cold. Objects they touch can remain hot for more than a day. They seem to want to carry on the primord line by exposing more people to the green goo, but even people touched by primords are "infected". [No explanation is ever given for the origin of the slime. See **What's Wrong with the Centre of the Earth?**.]

Planet Notes

• *Earth*. The green mutagenic slime is found twenty miles below the surface, just at the crust, and the Doctor implies that some of it may have been released at Krakatoa. If the crust is penetrated, then the energy of the Earth's core will be released. Magma will flood the world, and the Doctor believes that within weeks or even days, the planet will disintegrate into a ball of gases. There's a high-pitched whine just before penetration, which the Doctor describes as 'the sound of this planet screaming out its rage' [as people are pointing guns at him, this is excusable rhetoric - see **Where Does This Come From?**]. The primords hear a similar noise in their heads.

• *Parallel Earth*. The alternative Britain is a republic and obviously a fascist state, policed by the Republican Security Forces and employing forced labour at the Inferno project. The Brigade-Leader refers to the Defence of the Republic Act, 1943, so Britain has been in this state for some time. [Assuming that such an act would have been passed shortly after the Republic's creation, this suggests that fascism took root in the country in response to the events of World War Two - or more probably *instead* of it. Perhaps significantly, the script (and the character's prop badge) refers to "Stahlman" as "Stahlmann" in the parallel universe.]

This Britain evidently has a single leader, a serious-looking gentleman whose photograph appears on propaganda posters. The royal family has been executed. Contrary to popular belief the Nazis are nowhere to be seen, but the Republic was established around a leader like Oswald Moseley [if not Moseley himself]. Sutton is at the project under duress; Sir Keith Gold is hinted as being Jewish [the first draft called him 'Mulvaney'], but nonetheless runs a Government-led investigation in fascist Britain.

[What's striking about this universe is that so many little things are similar. Liz Shaw made the decision to join the military rather than become a scientist, yet the implication is that up until this point, her history was more or less the same, even though this flies in the face of logic. A Britain run by fascists should have so many millions of life-changing differences, the odds against *exactly the same* Inferno staff and UNIT personnel ending up together in both universes are astronomical. There are two likely explanations and a wild card. One: there's a "proper" timeline, and all parallel universes tend to automatically veer towards it (up to and including some characters using the same phraseology as their duplicates - note Stahlman's 'cautious old women' in both universes, for instance). Two: this universe was deliberately engineered. This is certainly the view taken by the novel *Timewyrm: Revelation*, which suggests that the Timewyrm designed the whole thing just to get on the Doctor's nerves. Three (and to date the least popular): out of all the possible alternatives the TARDIS chose this universe as the nearest fit, possibly because of the green goo's presence. See the essay for our reasoning on this.]

History

• *Dating.* [1971.] According to the Brigade-Leader's desktop calendar, it's the 23rd of July by end of the crisis. [Some have suggested that this adventure actually takes place before "Ambassadors", making Liz's exit smoother. At the end of the Carrington business, the Doctor as

good as says goodbye to Liz, and she opts to stay and help Cornish and his team. It certainly makes the start of "Ambassadors" make more sense if Liz has seen the Doctor vanish before. The main hint that "Ambassadors" follows straight after "Silurians", though, is that the Doctor is grumbling about the Brigadier's blowing up the Silurian caves. It would admittedly be something of a surprise if the Doctor didn't bear this particular grudge for years, although why we're experiencing the stories out of order is another matter - see **Who's Narrating This Series?** under 23.1, "The Mysterious Planet". See also 8.3, "The Claws of Axos" and 8.4, "Colony in Space" for another theory regarding swapped story-order.]

The project nicknamed "the Inferno" is the British government's latest plan to generate energy, with Professor Stahlman believing that pockets of "Stahlman's gas" beneath the Earth's crust can be tapped and harnessed. [The Earth's crust hasn't been penetrated before (although a private attempt was made in 4.5, "The Underwater Menace"), so its existence may only have been demonstrated theoretically, hence Stahlman's insistence that his 'theories' will soon be proved correct. But there's no indication here that such a gas actually exists, and it's certainly not the green slime, which is at crust-level.] Stahlman has been working on the project [in various stages] for eleven years. It uses a robot drill fed by cables.

The drilling project is in Eastchester, England. [Don't look for it on the map, it's another made-up town. We humbly propose at least one town in Northamptonshire that could plausibly be a toxic hole populated by creatures who've de-evolved - see "Battlefield" - although if you'd rather retain continuity with "The Dalek Invasion of Earth" (2.2) and have such vast earthworks near to the Bedfordshire Levels, then how about Milton Keynes? We are certainly some distance from either UNIT HQ or London. Of course, there is a real "Westchester" but that's in New York state.]

Additional Sources Since Liz's disappearance is never satisfactorily explained on screen, unless you buy the swapped running-order theory, Liz-Shaw-departure stories are always popular among fan-writers. The novel *The Scales of Injustice* (by Gary Russell, 1996), when not playing Hob with Silurian chronology, gives us an exit scene, although other tie-in works such as *The Devil Goblins of Neptune* (Martin Day and Keith

Topping, 1997), *The Wages of Sin* (David A. McIntee, 1999) and "Prisoners of the Sun" (Tim Robins' short story in *Decalog*, 1994) establish that she keeps getting drawn back into events with UNIT and the Doctor in one way or another. Jim Mortimore gave Liz a horrible death almost in passing in *Eternity Weeps* (1996), but that took place on a moonbase in 2003, and her assistant was a friendly Silurian. (Maybe back then, an attempt to combine *Moonbase 3* and *The Scales of Injustice* seemed like a good idea.) Liz also got her own spin-off video series, *P.R.O.B.E.*, written by Mark Gatiss, and which BBV proclaimed as "The British *X-Files*". (Well, if Mulder and Scully were middle-aged women who smoked pipes, maybe...)

David A. McIntee's *The Face of the Enemy* (1998), in which the Master and Ian Chesterton visit the ashen remains of Parallel Earth, presents itself as a sequel to "Inferno", although the fate of the Fascist Continuum related there is hard to credit against what's seen on screen. Oh, and Paul Cornell's novel *Timewyrm: Revelation* (1991) had the Doctor realise that the face he saw on the posters in the parallel world - the face of the republic's totalitarian leader - was one of the faces the Time Lords offered him at his trial ("The War Games"). The face wasn't actually seen on screen, but never mind.

The Analysis

Where Does This Come From? In some ways, our story begins in 1957. This was, as you'll doubtless recall with exact detail, International Geophysical Year - meaning that the nations of the world all did big prestigious projects connected with Earth Science. Britain sent Dr Vivian Fuchs off on his polar jaunts[23], America drilled into the depths and the Soviets upstaged everyone with Sputnik.

Walter Munk, a contributor to the field of oceanography and geophysics, had suggested the American endeavour, and it was later dubbed Project Mohole (see where this is going?).

Effectively, Mohole was geology's very own space programme. It was intended to probe a hypothetical gap between the crust and the mantle. (Andrija Mohorovicic, a Croatian geologist and meteorologist, had theorized the existence of such about a century ago, and thus it was called the Mohorovicic Discontinuity or "Moho".) In this period, not only was the Earth's age still up for debate, but the new and controversial theory of

"Continental Drift" was short of evidence to substantiate it (see "Doctor Who and the Silurians").

Now things start to get odd. Project Mohole was backed by Munk's friends, the American Miscellaneous Society (AMSOC), which was set up to cover projects that didn't fit into other categories for funding. AMSOC got government money and official affiliation from the National Research Council (NRC), for a while. They decided that undersea fissures were less likely to be contaminated, and they made good progress on the test samples off California and set up a semi-permanent mooring off Guadalupe, Mexico. They had a boat called CUSS 1 and 13,500 feet of drill-pipe. It went much better than anyone expected, but this is where the trouble starts. The NRC took over completely and, as a state-funded body, they had to justify every cost-increase to Congress. Bean counters axed the project before Phase II could start, in late 1966. At least, this is what we're told now... (We'll pick this up in **The Lore**, so for now let's leave matters on a cliffhanger.)

Stories about drilling into the Earth's core weren't new, of course. Many have taken the line where the Doctor shouts out, 'Listen to that! It's the sound of this planet screaming out its rage!' as a reference to the most obvious and famous: Sir Arthur Conan-Doyle's *When The World Screamed* (1928). In this, it's Professor Challenger, the arrogant science-hero (and more of an author-surrogate than Sherlock Holmes) whose scheme pricks the skin of a living planet. Stahlman has some of Challenger's ego, but none of his redeeming charm or tendency to be right about everything.

We've already had one Challenger-style story this year (*The Lost World* feeds directly into "Doctor Who and the Silurians", and we'll be back this way in Season Eleven). The Doctor here shows a few of the Professor's character-traits, and his relationship with the two Greg Suttons is possibly similar to that between Challenger and the reporter Ned, but the story's overall style is closer to *Doomwatch*. Creators Kit Pedler and Gerry Davis (see Volume II) and producer Terence Dudley (see Volume V) took topical concerns and turned them into jeremiads about politicians and big business abusing science and creating horrible new threats. Raymond Williams (Cambridge Don and so much more), upon reviewing this story and *Doomwatch* in *The Listener*, comments on how far the men in lab-coats have replaced the Russians as the "enemy within", since no-one knows enough to question them. At least not in

Whitehall, where the ability to translate Catullus from memory (thus eliminating the need to be told that he was a Roman poet) is an asset, and ignorance of how your car works is proof of your being "the right sort of chap". CP Snow wrote a series of books about exactly this (and it seems that Pip and Jane Baker read them - see 24.1 "Time and the Rani"). Then again, after Calder Hall, Zeta and Concorde, the "Big Science" stories on the news were generally about domesticating frontiers-of-science research, such as new power sources.

Unless the quest for cold fusion gets sexy again, it's doubtful that many writers these days would start a script with a rather excessively driven scientist trying to develop a new power source. In the late 60s, the oil industry was a source of dramas such as *The Troubleshooters*, where rugged men (e.g. Ray Barrett of 2.3, "The Rescue") did rugged things in hot and dangerous places while people in three-piece suits sat in boardrooms making deals. The nearest anyone got to this in America was *Dallas* and *Dynasty*, where oil was an off-screen source of money motivating stupid plots. Even in Douglas Sirk melodramas, oil production was a plot convenience, not a subject in and of itself. These days the whole emphasis is on not using as much, so in all probability, the story would have the power companies trying to *sabotage* benign scientists who've found ways to avoid using energy. (We refer the curious reader to the 1990s attempt to relaunch *Doomwatch*, with its use of a cyclotron with a miniature black hole as both plot maguffin and murder-weapon. There's also the 1985 landmark drama *Edge of Darkness*, where what happens to the "missing" plutonium is the cause of a strange eco-parable.)

However, in 1970 news programmes were full of thrilling, dynamic helicopter-shots of the new British oil fields. The Queen had been making speeches about the fact that the UK had cracked nuclear power long before the Americans or the Russians. North Sea gas was still being installed in homes nationwide. On top of that, the environmental movement was also picking up (as it were) steam, putting ideas like solar power into the world's mass-consciousness on a rather charmingly amateurish basis (see "The Green Death"; 12.1, "Robot"). In the same vein, the Stahlman project comes across as a freakish hybrid of every power-dream and power-nightmare of the era: a cheap, natural energy source that involves the same kind of drilling you'd find on the latest hi-tech oil rigs, yet releases forces even worse than a nuclear meltdown (see **The Lore**). As we'll see throughout this volume, energy availability became a daily concern for many people.

We should also discuss the parallel universe storyline. Alternative-world stories have a history that goes back hundreds of years - it's been variously suggested that "Inferno" deliberately rips off the *Star Trek* episode "Mirror, Mirror", but that was unbroadcast in Britain at that time. American writers tend to treat fascist takeover as a remote hypothetical matter, since few of them grew up with a real threat of invasion. It's not like anyone of that generation didn't wonder what Britain would be like if the Nazis won; enough books on this theme were published even in wartime. Kevin Brownlow and Andrew Mollo's award-winning 1963 film *It Happened Here* was shot in ersatz documentary style. Earlier treatments include the 1952 bestseller *The Sound of His Horn* by "Sarban" and of course Philip K. Dick's *The Man In The High Castle* (1962). Terrance Dicks, who admits to reading *Astounding Science Fiction* in the 1940s, must have read dozens of "counterfactuals" before Roddenberry got hold of it from the same source. And if we want to get *really* picky, the first of these was published in 1937: as "Murray Constantin", Katherine Burdekin wrote *Swastika Night* around the time GK Chesterton and Winston Churchill were contributing to *If: or History Rewritten*.

Then again, "evil double" episodes were already a staple of TV adventure serials, and the scar-faced Brigadier owes as much to ITC as to space opera. It's notable, though, that whereas *Star Trek*'s "evil" universe is run by an empire instead of a federation, *Doctor Who*'s "evil" universe is a Britain is run by Fascists, in which hardly anyone seems to be bothered. With its "Unity is Strength" posters, the fascist Britain is straight out of *1984* - or at the very least, it's straight out of Nigel Kneale's BBC TV adaptation of it (see **The Lore**). Of course, the *most* famous instance before this was John Wyndham's short story, "Random Quest", adapted for *Out of the Unknown* and directed by Christopher Barry (1.2, "The Daleks"; "The Daemons" and lots else) with an all-star cast. This was shown on 11th of February, 1969. The film *Quest for Love*, which retained a lot of the TV version's changes and a great many less good ones besides, opened in 1971 and confirmed Joan Collins' reputation as box-office poison.

However, anyone who's read Volume II and this season's notes will have guessed that this is visually a pastiche of the *Quatermass* serials, specifically the oil-refinery location work from *Quatermass II*. The shots of Bromley (Ian Fairburn) staggering down the staircase on the outside of a gasometer look so much like the hapless PR man Ward in episode three of the 1955 serial, we suspect Douglas Camfield sneaked into the archives.

Things That Don't Make Sense Let's start with the big one: if this stuff causes horrible mutations, melts any receptacle into which it is poured and will blow up the planet if released, then it can't have been physically encountered yet. So how does Stahlman know for sure that it's there at all, let alone that it's a power source of any kind? For all anyone knows, it might just be a whole lot of nitrogen. Sure, he can hypothesise, but this wouldn't get him control of such a big operation; without conclusive evidence, the best he could hope is to be consulted and occasionally interviewed on telly. Anyway, how is an un-used gas guaranteed to outperform North Sea Gas if nobody knows its composition? How does Stahlman get a huge government project like this up and running with precisely zero proof? It seems that the British Government are so impressed with their space programme's unexpected success, they're at the point where any professor with a foreign-sounding name will get backing, no questions asked (at least until 9.5, "The Time Monster").

But as it turns out, Stahlman's Gas is accompanied by a substance that makes things and people really, really hot. Luckily everyone who's affected is wearing some form of cotton that resists scorching. (If they had nylon clothes like everyone else in the early 70s, they'd be naked in seconds, plus everyone would know where they were from the smell.) Neither to they leave smouldering footprints, possibly because Stahlman (or more likely Sir Keith) has wisely invested in insulated white wellies.

Upon finding a bubbling, *steaming* green goo that he's never seen before, Harry Slocum just decides to touch it. After this turns him into a furious furry fireball, he then feels an uncontrollable urge to kill and, um, 'step up the reactor power *three more points*'. Because that's what primordial beast-men do, isn't it? Isolate the controls for a nuclear reactor and push it to eleven whilst sating their blood-lust. [We might presume that Slocum

is driven by an irrational desire to make things hotter, but as he had nothing to do with that aspect of the drill's operation, he seems to have received an intelligence upgrade that lets him figure out the controls at a glance while ignoring the possible consequences - such as making the place go "boom".] It's also curious that Slocom seems to lose strength and die from a gunshot wound in the exact moment that the reactor is powered down - if the temperature in a control room quite a way from the reactor rose enough for the heat to sustain Slocum, why didn't the entire complex go up in flames or the reactor explode?

Sir Keith *has* to know about Stahlman's general disposition, yet he somehow fails to predict that Stahlman will act insulted upon being introduced to Greg Sutton, and makes no effort to warn Sutton about this in advance. It takes the Doctor no time at all to figure out that anyone who touches a primord turns into a monster, but when Stahlman touches the mutant slime, the Doctor responds with a casual, 'I wouldn't have done that if I were you' instead of the more sensible "everybody get away from him right now" or "quick, amputate that hand!". The only reason for the Doctor's reaction would be if he doubts a link exists between this mysterious goo and the red-hot fuzzies - this *is* the same Doctor we're talking about, right? Never mind why, precisely, Stahlman feels the urge to personally place the goo-filled cracked jar back into its carrying case, instead of just ordering a tech - the one who's standing right there, wearing insulated gloves - to do so.

Later on, when the Doctor hopes to prove to the Brigadier that Stahlman is carrying a stolen microcircuit, he allows Stahlman to leave the room and thus ditch the incriminating evidence. What, it didn't occur to him that Stahlman would do so? Anyway, the circuit is so small that simply letting Stahlman pull out his wallet and keys isn't really sufficient. You'd have to give him a good padding down to figure out if he's carrying it, provided it's advised to get that close to someone with the primord taint.

In episode two, Liz asks the Doctor to use his 'door handle' gadget to let her out of the hut - yet upon racing back there, she's got one of her own. [Was it buried in her purse?] Why is Bessie turned 180 degrees upon arrival in the parallel universe? [But then, the Doctor also seems to arrive on a different side of the console from where he started.] It's also somewhat odd that Bessie gets transported, but the bookshelves in the Doctor's hut -

which if anything seem closer to the console - don't. [Maybe the books knew that they'd get burnt if they went to a fascist state. No? Please yourselves.] And upon arrival in the fascist world, the Doctor takes Bessie out for a drive. Presumably, he's headed back to the drilling site, even though everyone else seems to traverse the distance on foot easily enough. Is he just knackered from the inter-dimensional journey or does he somehow intuit that he's going to be in a chase soon? Running between the Doctor's hut and the reactor room does seem to take a fair amount of time, except for when we approach the cliffhanger to episode six, when it's so dramatically important that Petra and Greg do it in seconds.

Precisely why is Evil Parallel Liz's hair that colour? Wouldn't she be trying to flaunt her Aryan / Celtic gingerness? Why does the Inferno control room in the Evil Parallel Universe have a bolt-on gadget exactly like the one the Doctor has fitted to supply power to the TARDIS console? And despite World War II not having happened, not only are computers are at exactly the same stage of development here as in our world (see 26.3, "The Curse of Fenric"; "The War Machines"), but Evil Parallel BBC1 - to judge by the Doctor's comment to Greg in episode six - improbably shows *Batman*.

The primords are strong enough to bend metal bars, yet the Doctor can overpower the infected Bromley just flinging a mattress on top of him [maybe it's really really cold]. Anyway, if Bromley were strong enough to bend the bars of his cell, then why didn't he do just that, and escape? In episode five, Evil Liz reveals that the Evil UNIT troops found the console in the Doctor's hut, yet she and the Brigade-Leader are never heard to ask about it during the Doctor's interrogation. For that matter, they seem to think the Doctor is a spy / saboteur, yet they've not detailed anyone to take the strange device apart and see what the hell it's supposed to do.

As events whip into a frenzy in episode six, the Brigade-Leader deems the Doctor's console as his best means of escape. Yet he opts to wait around in the reactor room as Petra rewires the circuitry, when he *must* know that if the power gets flowing, the Doctor will probably leave without him. The primords' resistance to bullets has been shown to increase as it gets hot, yet it's hotter than ever when the Brigade-Leader successfully guns down Stahlman in the reactor room. Then Petra fails,

and the Doctor seems to give up entirely rather than - y'know - racing back to the reactor room to see if he can do the job himself.

Back in "our" world, the Brigadier knows that Sir Keith went to London in an attempt to get the minister to halt the project. But when Sir Keith goes missing, the Brigadier is left in the dark as to the minister's decision, as he 'isn't available'. Obviously, this being Britain, nobody will admit to knowing what the minister decided until cleared to do so, but wouldn't the abrupt vanishing of a top-level bureaucrat at such a sensitive juncture alert the security services? And wouldn't Sir Keith's disappearance prompt the minister's staff to ask him about the verdict (which *must* have been for immediate closure)? In episode seven, Sutton says he 'heard' the Doctor has returned, even though the only people to know - Liz, the Brigadier and Sir Keith - have only just left the lab.

And the climax... well, the most efficient way for the Doctor to halt the proceedings would be to quietly stress to the Brigadier that Stahlman is turning into a primord and must be detained immediately. Instead he opts for counterproductively raving like a lunatic and hitting machinery with a wrench. But then, Sir Keith doesn't fare any better. With a preponderance of evidence that the project is headed for disaster, with Stahlman having locked himself in the drilling room, *and* with the minister having consented that the project should be halted, Sir Keith baulks at closing down operations, insisting that 'the order to close down must come from [Stahlman].' Never mind oafish public servants such as Walker (9.3, "The Sea Devils"), the nice ones are in danger of killing us all as well.

Like Wenley Moor, this project has been going for years, with full Government backing. But if energy is at such a premium, why did they proceed with a Mars programme? And now that the Doctor has shut down both projects, it seems that all of Britain's power being produced at the Nuton Power Complex [so let's hope nothing bad happens there, eh?].

Critique Hooray! Another big government science project with metal walls and a staff in white boots, overalls and silver belts. Another location with lots of pipes and big gas containers, and people falling off them whenever the plot sags. Another instance of something under the ground causing staff difficulties. And *another* neurotic boss who resents the Doctor. A casual viewer of Season Seven might have every reason to switch over, thinking that the "new" direction for *Doctor Who* had run out of steam in under six months.

Of course that isn't the case, but that joyous thrill that 60s *Who* had of not knowing where or when we would be next week, and creating whole new worlds *once a month* has never seemed more remote. Yet if we're being honest with one another, the science bases with booted and suited technicians have been exactly that: bases. Each seven-part story has set up a premise, and then been the place to which the Doctor, the Brigadier and Liz have experienced another jaunt into a different aspect of that premise.

As we've said, each story looks like the start of a totally different series. "Inferno" could easily have spent a year exploring different parallel realities with different Brigadiers and Lizes. (And why not? Change was in the air... they even talked about having the console as the means of transport from now on and losing the police box. This was, after all, the year the Metropolitan Police ditched the real ones.) Over on ITV, *Timeslip* had shown the annoying brats meeting two mutually-exclusive versions of their future selves, so it's not as if audiences weren't ready for a series of this kind. But *Doctor Who* never turned into *Sliders*, so this became yet another so-called blind alley in Season Seven.

The point is that, whatever this story's merits, this need for a reliable yardstick is where the rot sets in for the UNIT era. To demonstrate how bad the Fascist Inferno staff are, the "originals" are sketched in with broad strokes. Nicholas Courtney ceases to play "Lethbridge-Stewart" and starts doing his turn as "the Brig". The excruciating epilogue sets the seal on this. Similar worries arise with the discovery that Sergeant Benton has become the audience identification character. On the plus side, however, after the Yeti-in-a-loo stuff we've had, this is our first glimpse of the Doctor adrift in an alien world where nobody knows him. Pertwee really comes into his own here as a thoroughly new kind of Doctor.

Just in passing: it's interesting that Don Houghton is the first new writer to be commissioned since Pertwee was cast. Until now, the Doctor has done a lot of variations on Hartnell or Troughton tropes, and we start getting sequences that play to Pertwee's strengths, such as the car-chases and fights. One might say that "Inferno" is

the first story conceived of as a star vehicle. The Venusian Aikido stuff will become routine and almost self-parodic later on, but here it's a rabbit pulled out of a hat, and the first recognizably Doctor-ish thing we've seen that neither of the first two versions would have done. However much the later stories allow indulgences like the Whomobile, it's hard to imagine any of the other actors lined up to replace Troughton seeming so comfortable adding Spock, Steed and Bond riffs to the Doctor's repertoire.

By contrast, note that the other two seven-parters this year take a concept, hold it up to the light and examine it from every angle. However, this story (and "story" is a troublesome word here) is three or four separate ideas that crop up in a few days of the Doctor's life. In the essay we'll suggest a means by which the parallel Earth thing is a consequence of the werewolf thing, but it took a bit of doing. The sequence of events here is puzzling, even without it all happening *again* with the same people in different uniforms.

And there's no getting away from it: the starting-point - Stahlman drilling and snapping at people - gets repetitive even at an episode per week. ('There's never been a bore like this one', as Sir Keith warns us in episode one.) Once again, the trouble comes from trying to do it *all* in seven weeks: potentially we've got two four-part stories (the primords and the drilling causing a catastrophe), and a whole new series being premiered. The drilling becomes less interesting as the Doctor and Greg know right from the outset that it's going to cause trouble. Meanwhile, the primords just look silly, even if the consequences of their presence are visually arresting and well-handled.

The problem is that this story's Unique Selling Point *is* unique. If we could judge it against other parallel Earth stories, we'd know whether the apparent squandering of a whole new world - and its intriguingly altered history - on four episodes of chases, werewolves and regulars parodying their normal characters was the best way to do this. Yet the fact remains, no matter how highly fandom regards this story, no matter how many Top Ten polls it ranks on, no matter how much people anticipated the DVD release, many people evaluate "Inferno" for the premise's potential, not what we actually get. Selling the very concept of alternate universes takes *so much* of the available time, the Nazi-world isn't explored or given any subtlety. One could argue that seven episodes (or twenty-six) about this and *only* this would have been a better start idea: set up the concept and *then* introduce the primords. But we can't really say whether it's good of its kind, because it's the only time that twentieth-century *Doctor Who* does such a thing. What we *can* say is that if you're going to do car chases and shoot-outs, plus a set-piece stunt fall in each episode, you could do far worse than having Douglas Camfield in charge.

British viewers tend to be patient where adventures and series about complex social nuances are concerned. Ratings are never the whole story (and in the seventies they're even more unreliable than usual), but the steep decline at the end of Season Seven might indicate viewer-fatigue as much as a memorably hot summer getting under way. It's probably no coincidence that the best Alternate Universe pieces have been fake documentaries like *Confederate States of America* or *It Happened Here*. The ideas are definitely intriguing, but as drama they're often redundant unless alternate versions of the same person meet one another - and that's explicitly precluded in this story. Significantly, the only other instance of a parallel universe story in "orthodox" *Who*, "Battlefield" (26.1), involved visitors from a realm too expensive to show on screen coming here and leaving us hints of how this world might work. This was treated as a breakthrough as late as 1989, so seeing them get it pretty much right in 1970 is doubly impressive.

It's also become customary in fandom to praise the early UNIT stories for their "gritty realism"; it's one of those *DWM* terms that fans have picked up, such as "continuity", "era" or "fitting", then altered to suit their needs. On most occasions, it's used to praise stories like "Inferno" over supposedly "silly" pieces like (picking at random) 15.4, "The Sun Makers" or 25.2, "The Happiness Patrol". But if nothing else, those two "silly" stories permit the characters a bit of emotional range and reflection on how they got into this mess. Cordo from "The Sun Makers" and Susan Q from "The Happiness Patrol" seem to come from a recognisable place, but in "Inferno", Petra comes from other television programmes and Stahlman is pure B-movie.

We're going to have a go at the notion that surface mimesis is the be-all and end-all of television drama in a whole essay in Volume V, but just look at "Inferno" in the light of what the BBC Wales series has taught us to expect from a *Doctor Who* adventure. Look at the way the Fascist Britain is

shown to be threatening by making a known and liked character suffer a sea-change. Benton's transformation into a werewolf is simply there as an obstacle for the Doctor's party. But when Jackie is upgraded into a Cyberman in "The Age of Steel" (X2.6), the emphasis is on Pete and Rose and how they react to this news. Even in the scowling earnestness of the last cliffhanger of "Inferno", we're at a remove from what people we know would do in these circumstances. Nobody cries, nobody swears, nobody prays, nobody steps out of the character-notes and *everyone* waits for the last speaker to finish his or her line. There's never any thought for the families of the people caught up in this. Yes, absolutely "Inferno" has a heck of a lot going for it - but to praise it for "realism" (gritty, smooth or extra-spreadable) is just misguided.

Given that *nothing* of this kind had been shown when the story was made, the lack of laboured explanation is commendable. But less welcome is the blunt instrument of the "alternate" characterisation. Short of having the bearded Stahlman renamed "Hitler Von Scientist", they couldn't have made it any plainer. This is a story with a geologist called 'Petra', after all. The fundamental problem with parallel universes - especially the cop-out ones where the same actors play slightly different versions of the same characters - is that there's a tendency for writers and directors to assume that they're intrinsically interesting. As abstract notions they certainly are, and for actors it can be a welcome change of pace. But in and of themselves, they're a lazy conceit and rely on skilled directors to make them work dramatically.

Even for viewers who care about Liz Shaw, it's hard work coming to feel anything for Section Leader Shaw just because she looks like Liz in a wig. Even if you do, her fate doesn't matter much if the real Liz is relatively safe. (It's a common mistake: look at how X4.5, "The Poison Sky" practically forces you at gunpoint to shed a tear when Martha's Evil Clone dies.) It doesn't help that nobody in the last two stories really knew what Liz was supposed to be like. Nazi-Liz is basically "our" Liz without a sense of humour - but for most of the previous sixteen weeks, that had pretty much been "our" Liz too. Playing Evil Fascist Wig-Wearing Liz doesn't even allow John to arch her eyebrows or turn an innocuous line into a put-down. Camfield (or Letts) should be credited with making this story-element work as well as possible, but it's an uphill battle.

All of that said, "Inferno" *does* pay off in spades when the world really ends in front of our eyes. Episode six has to be the tensest twenty-five minutes in the programme's history, and everyone involved keeps from spilling over into hamminess. (We try not to condemn individual actors, but it's interesting that Olaf Pooley, as Stahlman, has been sidelined by this stage.) But once you've done that, where do you go next? Episode seven is about the Doctor either being unconscious or renouncing Schopenhauer, and it ties up with a massively disappointing climax and a tag scene apparently pasted in from an altogether different and inferior show.

Conceptually and technically, each story this year has broken new ground, then effectively said "this far and no more". "Inferno" sets the boundaries for how mature the series will get in its portrayal of interrogation, its attempts to make a political drama out of a fantasy notion and its depiction of the Doctor as a fish out of water. It nudges at the boundaries of acceptable violence for the time. The flaw with this as a procedure is that it makes the children's adventure-serial elements of the story - especially the sound effects of gunfire - seem more obvious and out-of-place than even the Magic Breadvan was in the last story. The rag-bag of stock-music doesn't help dispel this impression. Apart from Pooley and the primord make-up, it's hard to point to anything here that's actually *bad* about any of this, but it's harder to see why this story has such a reputation. People seem enamoured with the *idea* of "Inferno", as opposed to the three hours of television actually in existence.

The Facts

Written by Don Houghton. Directed by Douglas Camfield (sort of; see **The Lore**). Viewing figures: 5.7 million, 5.9 million, 4.8 million, 6.0 million, 5.4 million, 5.7 million, 5.5 million. For June this is fairly good, but not that big an improvement on what Troughton was getting at the same time of year. Audience Appreciation steady at 60-61%, except for episode six dipping to 58%, and there being an unknown score for episode five.

Supporting Cast Olaf Pooley (Professor Stahlman / Director Stahlman), Christopher Benjamin (Sir Keith Gold), Derek Newark (Greg Sutton), Sheila Dunn (Petra Williams / Dr Petra Williams), David Simeon (Private Latimer), Derek Ware (Private Wyatt), Walter Randall (Harry Slocum), Ian Fairbairn (Bromley).

Working Titles "Project Inferno", "Operation Mole-Bore", "The Mo-Hole Project".

Cliffhangers Harry Slocum, formerly a project technician and now the first of the primords, bursts in on the Doctor and company inside the Inferno power room; Liz and the Brigadier enter the Doctor's hut, in time to see him vanish along with the TARDIS console; as the Doctor tries to fix the warning computer on "evil" Earth, Benton puts a gun to his head and asks whether he's going to go to the firing squad quietly or get shot here and now; while the Inferno project counts down to zero, the Doctor attempts to sabotage it but just finds himself at the end of Stahlman's pistol; trapped in the Inferno station on a disintegrating world, the Doctor is just about to suggest a way out when a primord starts to smash its way through the door; an immense wall of lava bears down on the hut where the Doctor and party are trying to re-activate the TARDIS console (and this time, you know that most of them aren't going to escape in the next episode).

What Was In The Charts? "The Seeker", The Who; "Groovin' With Mr Bloe", Mr Bloe; "Do The Funky Chicken", Rufus Thomas; "I Don't Believe in If Anymore", Roger Whittaker; "Yellow River", Christie; "In the Summertime", Mungo Jerry; "Up Around the Bend", Creedence Clearwater Revival.

The Lore

• Barry Letts had taken over *Doctor Who* at short notice, and had thus far been supervising other people's leftover projects. Terrance Dicks had likewise been working with people who'd done *Doctor Who* before he started (with the notable exception of his "find", Robert Holmes). Now, as the various other options for a final story for Season Seven ran into trouble, Dicks called in a favour from his former boss...

When script-editing *Crossroads*, Don Houghton had put work Dicks' way. He'd also written *Emergency Ward 10* episodes that Letts had either directed or followed with a script of his own. Houghton was now freelance, trying to get work writing horror movies; he provided Dicks with an idea based upon what he'd read about the Mohole project and the abrupt lack of any information about it after 1966. He'd been interested enough to ask the US Embassy (who must have been pleased, at the time, that someone other than an anti-Vietnam protester was calling), but they said it was classified. Likewise, the Science Museum was told nothing useful.

This looked enough like a conspiracy to intrigue Houghton, but not enough like a seven-part story to please Dicks. Effectively, he added the Alternate Universe plot as a piece of blatant padding. Meanwhile, Letts thought it ought to have lots of stock footage of volcanoes. He knew from experience that plenty existed, and that it looked good in colour (even though he settled for monochrome while using such stuff in "The Enemy of the World").

• The seven scripts were in just before Christmas 1969, although significant changes were made before filming began four months later. The threat to Earth was mainly atmospheric, with Stahlman's Gas causing the planet to over-heat. Far more time was spent with the Doctor watching history repeat in the original Earth (including UNIT chasing him); Sir Keith Mulvaney (as he's named here) is removed early on and - significantly - there were no primords. Bear in mind that when the story was commissioned, the series' long-term future was in the balance, and the production team were still cobbling together possible replacement series for the Saturday Teatime slot. It's been proposed that the plan was to show Earth being destroyed as a cliffhanger to what was potentially the final end for Doctor Who - but frankly, it's hard to imagine Letts and Dicks doing anything so downbeat.

• While the rewrites were coming in, it was confirmed that Douglas Camfield - now a free-lancer after years at the BBC, and who worked on the troubled Paul Temple with Bryant and Sherwin - would direct the last story of this block. Letts knew Camfield from his time as an actor and admired him. As we've seen, one of Camfield's earliest decisions was to use John Levene as Benton (as in Camfield's last story as director, 6.3, "The Invasion") and, to set this up, Benton appeared in the previous story, "The Ambassadors of Death". (For that matter, Camfield had used Levene in Paul Temple, where he appeared in the title sequence.)

As was often the case, Camfield cast people whom he trusted and who were familiar with his briskly militaristic style of directing. Thus Ian Fairbairn (the reactor tech Bromley), Walter Randall (the infected Harry Slocum - he was Tonilla, Autoc's assistant, in 1.6, "The Aztecs"), Derek Newark (Greg Sutton) and the Havoc team led by Derek Ware were involved. Rising star Kate O'Mara (of whom much more in Volume VI) was initially on tap for Petra Williams, but a lucrative Hammer horror came up at the wrong time. Olaf Pooley (Stahlman) hadn't worked for Camfield before, but had at least played tennis with him. Pooley had recently been the star of a TH White adaptation by Southern, The Master, which was produced by John Braybon (see **Where Does All Of This Come From?** under 1.1, "An Unearthly Child"). This was about a hypnotic super-villain imprisoned on an island in the Channel (sounds like a daft idea - see "The Sea Devils")

• [Here we need to stop and borrow the script's time-saving terminology: they designate the alter-nate Earth as "Warp 2", with "Warp 1" being the reality that Doctor Who stories are normally set in.] As the revised scripts came in, some elements needed refining. The spelling for the Warp 2 material was phonetic ('Pryvat Kep Owt! Newkleer Reaktor' and so on) - quite why this was introduced after 1943 is a mystery, as the fad for phonetic spelling was about forty years earlier. The folks in Warp 2 had weird months.

As we've mentioned, the original story was monsterless by request, but the production team later asked for a more visible threat for children, as well as providing a more urgent if abstract men-ace. So the 'Primeords' (as it's spelled here) were described as being ape-like, with the clear impli-cation that they were evolutionary regressions. Another change: Stahlman is killed when the coolant gas causes him to freeze and turn to pow-der. At Dicks' request, the Doctor acquired a novel form of self-defence: Feltian Karate. In part this owed to Terry Walsh being asked for pointers on how to do camera-friendly martial arts that wouldn't cause harm if kids copied it at home. Eventually this became Venusian Karate / Aikido. At this stage, the Man from the Ministry was Sir Keith Rose.

• On his way to another location, production assistant Christopher D'oyly-John had passed the Berry Wiggins bitumen plant in Kent. This looked exactly right for the Inferno base, but had a small problem - a lot of oil processing was going on, so smoking was strictly forbidden. The cast and crew were provided with fruit, crisps and chewing gum, and it's reckoned that most people put on a stone during the filming. Amid problems with yet another wig, Caroline John found the toilet facilities to be a problem - namely, there weren't any. She was three months pregnant at the time (now you see why the stuff at the weir in the last story worried her), and had by now resolved to leave the series. Her main problem was how to break this news to the producer...

• Just for a change, the story's first shot was actually the first filmed (although a planned scene where Bessie overtakes Greg's car was scrapped). As usual, Camfield proceeded methodically and rapidly, with over 50 set-ups per day - almost twice the average. (Even so, there wasn't time to film Private Collins getting strangled and UNIT searching for Slocum. This was covered by the Brigadier telling the Doctor 'Another murder, this time one of my men' in the penultimate scene of episode one.)

Camfield, characteristically, insisted on precise military details, so only the Brigadier wore the now-familiar "Men In Beige" UNIT suit, and the rest were fitted with regular army combat drag. For Warp 2, the uniforms had a European feel, with Soviet-issue SKS rifles and hefty lace-up Gestapo-style boots (without studs - *that's* how cautious they were about fire). Unlike the usual UNIT guns, the rifles were real and fired blanks - the stage-hands had to catch the dropped guns in blankets to prevent accidental discharge. (Apart from anything else, they were dropped into haystacks with obvious fire-risk.) Camfield also decided to make the primords more like werewolves than ape-men (a converse switch from dog to anthropoid happens in "Day of the Daleks").

• The soldiers' boots caused a problem when Pertwee drove at the RSF troops in episode three. Alan Chuntz couldn't jump as far as he thought, and the car's mud-guard gashed his shin. He continued before they finally whisked him to hospital. He needed 18 stitches (ironically, the boots prevented much worse injuries), then insisted on returning to the set to avoid upsetting Pertwee.

• Havoc were used extensively, and not always in obvious ways. Many of the cast were wary of filming so high up, especially on the 150-foot storage tank used a lot in both Warps. Pertwee had the worst vertigo - Derek Ware and Alan Chuntz had to walk him slowly around the rim for over ten minutes before filming the Warp 2

chase. The bitter wind made matters worse, as well as making later episodes' scenes of the world overheating a bit more uncomfortable to film. Ware, as the head Havoc honcho, was cast at short notice as Private Wyatt and coaxed the star into looking directly at him (and his primord make-up) rather than down, joking between takes and generally reassuring Pertwee. Paradoxically, as Wyatt was officially an acting role and fell to Ware after another actor had been considered, Havoc high-fall specialist Roy Scammell had already been assigned to double for the falling Wyatt. So basically, one stuntman stood in for another (Scammell also plays the RSF trooper who shoots Wyatt down). Despite 007's best efforts, this fall - over seventy feet - held the UK record for many years.

Similar height anxieties affected Ian Fairbairn, who had to walk on a slightly lower gantry and have freezing carbon-dioxide shot at him from a fire-extinguisher. This being April Fool's Day, Havoc member and future *EastEnders* star Derek Martin (see also 15.3, "Image of the Fendahl") was the victim of a prank where his Jag was alleged to have been hit by a lorry. Many of the Havoc team were ex-army (and one was still in the TA), so they helped John Levene to look convincing as a Sergeant. Despite the gruelling schedule, Camfield was up late entertaining his "troops" with his guitar and anecdotes.

• To the annoyance of the studio planners, after the dispute that had disrupted "Spearhead from Space", *Doctor Who* took full advantage of the bigger studios in Television Centre. However, the recording was planned for a new working practice, as developed from the experiment of "Doctor Who and the Silurians": namely, recording two episodes simultaneously. *Doctor Who* was one of two productions to try this format, the idea being that striking the sets every day of recording was likely to cause delays and wear-and-tear. Some of the sets were duplicated at the Ealing film studio for ease of editing (notably the Doctor's flip between realities in episodes one and three, with Bessie needing to be wheeled on and off between takes: a lot less hassle at Ealing than in Studio 3, TVC.) Ian Scoones, the new model expert, filmed the complex with help from outside contractors (this will cause trouble in later stories). The model was made mainly from saucepans.

• Wally Randall's practical jokes abounded, with him donning Liz's wig and lab-coat while still in primord make-up, then standing in for John without anyone telling Pertwee. He also rigged a half-crown coin on an invisible wire and took to leading Pertwee around the studio with it, later offering John a "sweet" that contained mustard. Things got a bit less good-natured, though, when the complex scene of Slocum in the reactor power room was rehearsed. A lot of remounts were needed, but the crunch came when the Doctor answered Stahlman's phone call (at the start of episode two). Camfield had the camera aligned so Pertwee could only do this whilst staying in shot, but the star didn't see the logic of it and became grumpy. Camfield stormed down from the gallery.

• It helped matters that Camfield had resorted to casting his wife, Sheila Dunn, as Petra (see 3.4, "The Daleks' Master Plan"). She had been reluctant to let him direct another stressful *Doctor Who*, but - fearful that letting on about his heart-murmur would stop him getting any directing work ever again - they had agreed to keep his condition secret. (Bear this in mind as this story unfolds.) Dunn helped to defuse this particular row, but the problem wasn't going to go away. Camfield was also rushing between rehearsals and editing, as the time between recording and broadcast was narrowing rapidly.

• Now matters with Camfield's health grew worse, and he collapsed during rehearsals. (This was apparently tachycardia rather than a full-blown heart attack, but certainly a heart condition of some sort.) Hardly anyone on the studio floor knew about this, and it was kept secret whilst Camfield was alive. Most of the cast, in fact, didn't even realise it. Letts agreed to take over as director. He became frustrated, though, at having to step into someone else's shoes, and resolved to direct a story from scratch as soon as possible (see the very next story, "Terror of the Autons").

• As part of the "Nazi Britain" theme, it was decided that the radio announcer should sound like Lord Haw-Haw (an Irish Fascist who broadcast propaganda from France during wartime). Pertwee volunteered to do the voice, but Letts opted to lose this scene during editing, figuring that everyone in Britain would recognise Pertwee straightaway. (Foreigners were another matter: the scene was retained in exports, and it's also in the video release. The DVD has it as an extra.)

• The lighting plan for the Warp 2 sequences was changed. Camfield wanted a much darker set but Letts, wearing his producer's hat, knew that he'd have to field all the complaints from the technical bods. As an in-joke, the "Big Brother" photo is of Visual Effects boss Jack Kine, which echoes his predecessor's face being that of the "real" Big Brother in Rudolph Cartier's *Nineteen Eighty-Four*. The main difficulty in rehearsals (perhaps surprisingly, given everything that was going on) was making the Fascist counterparts of Benton and Liz sufficiently brutal. Caroline John was put-out that the Brigade-Leader was given more of the interrogation sequences than scripted; it seems to have confirmed her feeling that the directors thought of Liz as mainly window-dressing, reinforcing her decision to leave and get on with motherhood before typecasting set in. The final climactic scene in episode six caused a lot of trouble (note that Liz isn't actually seen to shoot the gun - John was wary of firearms, but still hadn't told anyone why). Courtney based a lot of the Brigade-Leader's bluster on memories of Benito Mussolini. There was something about an eyepatch that we're obliged under British law to mention, but life really is too short.

• So, about this story's odd jumble of stock-music... due to a misunderstanding later resolved, Camfield refused to work with Dudley Simpson. This story's music is taken from stock, notably Delia Derbyshire's compositions "Blue Veils and Golden Sands" and "The Delian Mode". These were both on the 1967 album *BBC Radiophonic Workshop* (known as *The Pink Swirly Album* after the cover-design - listen for the crackles). A lot of the other music came from related sources: an album called *Selection* features electronic tonalities by "Nikki St George" (AKA Brian Hodgson) and pieces by Dave Vorhaus. His advent in the *Doctor Who* soundtrack can hardly be called unexpected, as by this stage he'd worked with Hodgson and Derbyshire for over three years in the bands Unit Delta Plus and White Noise.

Vorhaus, a physicist and classical cellist who "discovered" electronic music after hearing a talk by Hodgson and Derbyshire in 1966, formed a company with them called Kaleidophon. Its habit of making unlikely sounds in grubby North London bedsits seems, with hindsight, like a logical continuation of "Telstar" producer Joe Meek's more famous sonic alchemy. After a brief collaboration with Paul McCartney, the three formed White Noise, with various session drummers and singers. Their album *An Electric Storm*, which was largely made after hours at the Radiophonic Workshop (it's all right - the BBC know about it now), was first released in 1969 and has just been remastered and reissued. (Everyone is now claiming they always loved it, really.) The dozen or so people who bought it on vinyl all formed hugely successful prog-rock bands - such as Emerson, Lake and Palmer (see 8.4, "Colony in Space"). The sound-effect / background music for the TARDIS console transferring between dimensions was Vorhaus's "Build Up To...", which utilises elements of "The Visitation" by White Noise, and which we'll hear again in "Colony in Space". (The full story of how the Radiophonic Workshop put the "Delia" in "psychedelia" will be explored in **What's Going On With This Music?** under 9.4, "The Mutants".)

• It was becoming increasingly apparent that the series' new format was a hit with the public and BBC bigwigs. Ronnie Marsh, Head of Serials at BBC TV was prepared to commission a new series with shorter adventures. As "Inferno" (the last seven-part story) was being discussed, Letts and Dicks found themselves having to conjure a year's worth of story ideas out of thin air, with five story-slots to fill. Nonetheless, at least one back-up plan was still in play: Terry Nation's *The Incredible Robert Baldick* (see 9.1, "Day of the Daleks")

Here it becomes relevant that Letts was having tangential thoughts about "Inferno". For a start, if everyone in Warp 2 had a Fascist counterpart, where was the Doctor's evil twin? Could this make an exciting long-running story for the (now guaranteed) next series? Why was a Brigadier talking to a Sergeant - why not a permanent Captain in the team? Most of all, how do you avoid scenes with the Doctor and Liz either telling each other things they ought to know already, or talking completely over the heads of the viewers, or being patronising while explaining everything to the Brigadier, thus making his leadership look ineffective?

The solution now seems obvious: make Sergeant Benton a regular character who asks all the questions, and give the Doctor and Liz equal opportunities explaining everything to him and the viewers. However, this was 1970, and Terrance Dicks wanted to ditch the bluestocking and wheel on a dim dolly-bird to get captured and need rescuing. So Liz had to go. If only Letts could find a way to break it to Carrie John...

season 8

8.1: "Terror of the Autons"

(Serial EEE. Four Episodes, 2nd January - 23rd January 1971.)

Which One is This? An Evil Time Lord! Explosions! Killer toys! Explosions! Killer Daffodils! Explosions! Killer inflatable armchairs! Explosions! Auton policemen! Explosions! People falling off extremely tall radio telescopes! Explosions! Sinister GPO engineers... (you get the basic idea).

Firsts and Lasts This story sets up the recurring cast and recurring themes for the rest of the UNIT era, now that the various scientific installations of Season Seven are out of the way. Here we see the first appearance of Jo Grant, the archetypal ask-lots-of-questions-and-get-captured companion; the first time UNIT's people wear regular army uniforms; the first appearance of Captain Yates, the Brigadier's new regular right-hand man; the first time we hear 'Greyhound' and 'Trap One' as UNIT radio call-signs; and the first appearance of the "classic"-style UNIT lab, the Third Doctor's natural environment.

Behind the scenes, it's the first story where the Radiophonic Workshop (generally Dick Mills) performs the entire soundtrack from Dudley Simpson's score and post-synchs it to existing footage. (Hitherto, the music was composed and recorded in advance, then played back during recording. There's near-precedents for this, such as 4.7, "The Macra Terror" and 6.4, "The Krotons", but we'll go into the details of why this is different later.) It's also the first full story not to have a director credited (see **The Lore**, and 3.8, "The Gunfighters").

We get the first use of the 'your hearts are in the right places' thigh-slapper.

But above all else: it's the first appearance of the Master.

Four Things to Notice
About "Terror of the Autons"...

1. Obviously happy with the way the new CSO technique had turned out in Season Seven (see 7.2, "Doctor Who and the Silurians"), here Barry Letts - as producer *and* director on this story - recklessly tries to make it do absolutely everything. You need a museum for one shot? Have Dave Carter (dressed as a museum attendant) stand in front of a blue screen and add a postcard. You can make a factory to build Autons (with a strangely sloping floor) with a caption slide of some computers. And why build a complicated fully-working "death doll", when you can put an actor in a full-size "death doll" suit? As a result, CSO is here used to depict everything from a shrunken corpse in a lunchbox to the views out of various car windows. (The original colour version of "Terror of the Autons" has long been lost, and the 1993 VHS version was electronically reconstituted. This is, perhaps, a mercy as the little blue lines are so much less noticeable.) The deployment of CSO also explains why Mrs Farrell's kitchen is, apparently, the size of an aircraft hanger.

2. Robert Holmes is spreading his wings as a dialogue writer. The Magritte-like image of the bowler-hatted Time Lord in mid-air is odd enough, without his nonchalant description of the Master's nuclear-plus-a-bit-more-clout Volatiser as 'such an amusing idea'. Not to mention the Master's sanitised account of McDermott's death, after an Auton plastic seat suffocates the troublesome manager: 'He sat down in this chair here, and... just slipped away.' (Note also that for once the henchman, Rex Farrell, gets a brilliantly dry punchline to the scene of McDermott's surreal murder.) Goodge's complaint about the effect of hard-boiled eggs on his digestion is countered by his associate Phillips asking about 'the hydrogen line'. (It wouldn't be a Holmes script without a

Season 8 Cast/Crew

- Jon Pertwee (the Doctor)
- Katy Manning (Jo Grant)
- Roger Delgado (the Master)
- Nicholas Courtney (Brigadier Lethbridge-Stewart)
- Richard Franklin (Captain Yates)
- John Levene (Sergeant Benton)

- Barry Letts (Producer)
- Terrance Dicks (Script Editor)

How Does Hypnosis Work?

For the purposes of this essay, we'll stick to discussing hypnosis as the temporary over-riding of an individual's personality. There are, in fact, many longer-term changes made to individuals or groups affected by brainwashing, possession or "conversion" (as we're going to discuss in 8.2, "The Mind of Evil"). We also need to differentiate between the mechanical hypnosis used by the Cybermen and others via "hypnotic signals", and the processing and subversions of individuals (as in, just for example, 5.7, "The Wheel in Space").

The word "hypnosis" is from the Greek for "sleep". The patient / victim is in an altered state of consciousness. The most basic form we see in *Doctor Who* is simply to wait for the subject to doze off, then electronically influence their mind. The Morpho Brain Creatures (1.5, "The Keys of Marinus") and the Macra (4.7, "The Macra Terror") exploit this simple but generally fallible technique. Conversely, the Cybermen's hypnotic signals in 6.3, "The Invasion" are merely a means of making everyone fall asleep at once.

The *other* main idea of hypnosis is a charismatic individual exerting some "influence" over the patient. The figure most associated with this was Franz Anton Mesmer, whose researches into an invisible "force" were directed to instilling universal harmony (see "The Keys of Marinus", and 18.5, "The Keeper of Traken"). Mesmer's belief was that there was a soul-fluid, akin to the notion of the aether doing the rounds about then. This fluid had properties like electricity. (Indeed, the early versions of Mesmer's performance / experiments involved electrically charged vessels - *baquets* - being filled with water and iron filings. Amazingly, no casualties are recorded.) The soul (or in Latin, "Animus" - as in "Animation", "Animosity" or "Animal") is affected by electrical activity and, by analogy, should be influenced by something with the same properties as a magnet but for the different field of the aether.

He called this process "Animal Magnetism" (again, using "Animal" as the adjectival form of "Animus"). Other people simply called it "Mesmerism". It became associated with Radical politics in France, as well as the fear of *somnambules*, spreading subversion in England and elsewhere. (This is the earliest *Manchurian Candidate* paranoia, but not too far from the witch-craze of the seventeenth century - see 25.3, "Silver Nemesis".)

But in *Doctor Who* terms, we have this ill-defined "psychic energy", which may well be manipulated on the physical plane (as seen in 19.7, "Time-Flight", but also stories as diverse as 19.3, "Kinda"; 8.5, "The Daemons"; 26.1, "Battlefield" and 2.5, "The Web Planet" - note the name of the *primum mobile* on Vortis). Of course, the oddest version in the programme's canon is the closest to the source. In "The Evil of the Daleks" (4.9), the statically-charged Daleks have 'processed' Arthur Terrell. As hypnosis is a form of "Animal Magnetism", and as magnets affect static electricity, so Terrell's being hypnotised by Daleks causes metal objects to stick to him. In the "gothic" mode (and "gothic" we remind ourselves, is about taking the forms of stories which are grounded in a world-view that's been discarded but using them anyway), Mesmer looms large. (See **Why Is That Portrait in Maxtible's Parlour?** under "The Evil of the Daleks".)

But more recent theories are allowed equal footing. The Master is demonstrably a most formidable mesmerist, yet "The Mark of the Rani" (22.3) has him resorting to neuro-chemistry to make his victims obey him. For the most part, however, a simple stare and a few well-chosen words is enough for his "pigeons". This is evidently a form of telepathy. If such a force were to exist, and the stronger mind *could* dominate the weaker, it would most likely be through the visual cortex - the part of the human brain most connected to other parts. After all, about 1/6th of the brain's energy is given over to seeing, and about 30% of the available space is somehow connected with visual perception in one way or another, but the cortex is only *one* part of the brain involved in seeing and interpreting what's seen. It would make sense for the hippocampus' memory / emotion nexus to be involved in the sort of hypnosis we see the Master (the Delgado one in particular) do.

If people care about fulfilling their instructions on a deeper emotional level, and if these subsume all previous memories, it doesn't need micro-managed control from a hypnotist giving instructions moment-by-moment. The subject's priorities will be realigned around the instructions, and he / she will improvise accordingly and in-character. A useful comparison would be an addict, whose entire motivation has been chemically changed even as he / she retains the same knowledge and intelligence. Indeed, it might not be an analogy, but a genuine connection between the fulfilment of the hypnotist's instructions and an endorphin release.

continued on page 95...

fart-gag.) But best of all... when Jo ruins his experiment, the Doctor - believing her to be UNIT's charlady - delivers the oddest insult in television history: 'You ham-fisted bun-vendor!'

3. Episode three sees a confrontation between UNIT and the Autons in a quarry, a somewhat rare instance a quarry appearing *as* a quarry rather than (say) an alien planet. (See also 2.2, "The Dalek Invasion of Earth"; 13.1, "Terror of the Zygons"; and 14.2, "The Hand of Fear". We also refer you to **The Lore**.) An episode later, it turns out it's the *same* quarry where the amazing bus-driving Auton holes up while waiting for a UNIT assault. Conveniently, it's right next to the radio telescope that's in episodes one and four. Typical of *Doctor Who*, this all dovetails into a final battle in which efforts to save Earth from alien invasion come down to a heroic bunch of soldiers shooting at a bus in a field. Count the number of somersaults executed as things explode.

4. More cost-cutting is apparent with the music. Instead of a full combo such as he had with "The Ambassadors of Death" (7.3), Dudley Simpson is packed off to the BBC Radiophonic Workshop and left to play with their toys. (As it turned out, it wasn't *much* cheaper and took way too long for comfort.) At the time, this ensured that *Doctor Who* sounded like no other programme on television. Later, when everyone was used to synthesizers, it sounded like frogs and wasps having a fight in a biscuit tin. These days, with Old Skool electronica back in vogue, the music during this phase of the show is being reappraised. Season Eight's music is entirely by Simpson, allowing him to re-use bits (the "Master" theme will get a lot of air-time; apologies if that's a spoiler), but it's fair to say this is the least excruciating soundtrack of this year's batch. The reason? He's letting the synth *be* a synth, rather than trying to fake up an orchestra.

The Continuity

The Doctor Right from the start there's an obvious rivalry between the Doctor and the Master, and it's felt on both sides. The Doctor describes his opponent as an 'unimaginative plodder', even though the Master's degree in cosmic science was of a higher class than his, while the Master believes curiosity to be the Doctor's weakness. [The Doctor admits as much later in this life and at least one other - see 21.6, "The Caves of Androzani", also

by Holmes.] The Doctor thinks that whatever the Master is up to, he's hardly likely to advertise. [It happens that he's wrong, and such a statement sounds very bizarre these days, now that we've seen the Master become Prime Minister, and his almost public goading of the Doctor in X3.12, "The Sound of Drums".] The two Time Lords clearly enjoy playing games with each other at this stage - the Master's already devising over-complicated death-traps and the Doctor admits to 'looking forward' to the coming duels between them.

However much flak he might give the Brigadier himself, the Doctor refutes the suggestion that he's not solving enough problems. Benton calls the Doctor 'sir'; the Brigadier describes him as a scientific consultant to UNIT. The Doctor claims to belong to the same club as Lord "Tubby" Rowlands, the man in charge of a ministry department with some bureaucratic influence over UNIT. [He might be bluffing, but this is the first time any Doctor could have plausibly made such a claim.] He opens Farrell Jr.'s safe by just listening to the tumblers.

Only the tea-lady[25] and the Brigadier's personal staff are allowed access to the Doctor's lab. It's furnished [by the Doctor, it seems] with odds and ends and memorabilia, including photos of pre-War aircraft, a puffer-fish suspended from the ceiling and an Art Nouveau dressing table and mirror. There's a hatstand with a blacksmith's apron on it [cf 18.2, "Meglos"] and what appears to be a Singer sewing machine on top of the solvents cabinet. A pair of canoe-paddles are mounted on the wall, and some abstract paintings `are dotted around. A spiral staircase leads to somewhere even more personal, apparently. [Every six-year-old wants to know whether the Doctor ever needs the toilet; this is our best clue yet.] The Master uses this entrance rather than the green church-like doors. Fortunately for the Doctor's touchy experiments, there are fire-extinguishers around.

[This whitewashed lab is clearly part of a reclaimed Victorian warehouse, apparently near docks, with wooden floorboards and government-issue benches among the more Doctorish chairs and bookcases. It's also up at least one flight of stairs from the Brigadier's office. We've checked, and the lab in 9.5, "The Time Monster" (and possibly thereafter) *isn't* the same place, despite the obvious similarities. One of the lab chairs seen here pops up in the TARDIS in the Atlantis yarn - and appears to be the same one that's sporadically

How Does Hypnosis Work?

...continued from page 93

Perhaps - and this is more to do with the effects used on screen than anything else - the optic nerve is the weak point. This would explain the Master's disguises in "The King's Demons" (20.6) and "Castrovalva" (19.1), if not excuse them. Recently, the Welsh series (and *Torchwood*, a little) has suggested that that the TARDIS itself performs some variant this, using 'perception filters' to disguise its true form. (More on this in a bit.) Connect the dots, and it appears that the Master uses the same basic techniques to make everyone trust him. This seems, however, like using a sledgehammer to crack a nut.

On the face of it, the issue of trust is entirely unconnected with visual perception. For the sake of internal consistency, we can assume that the "fear centres" of the human (and Draconian, to judge by 10.3, "Frontier in Space") brain that can be stimulated by ultrasonics can also be suppressed by similar means, and a blind trust in a specific person or group of people *could* be instilled. After all, this technology was available to humans in the 1960s ("The Invasion"). On screen, the visual side effects of this are remarkably consistent: in "Frontier in Space", Draconians see humans and humans see Draconians; in "The Mind of Evil", Professor Kettering sees water, everyone in the room *with* Senator Alcott sees a big pink Chinese dragon, and the tied-up, tormented Doctor sees stock publicity stills of a cross-section of 1960s monster-costumes. The Master has merely refined the ability to make people see what they expect to see (as in "Time-Flight") and used it instead of rubber masks.

We should take this opportunity to address a recurring theme in *Doctor Who* from a psychological perspective. We're constantly shown examples of selective memory "wiping", which is neurologically impossible. The Time Lords do it a great deal, as happens with Jamie and Zoe in 6.7, "The War Games". These days Torchwood uses little pills that erase whole days - why they don't come clean and use pens that make bright flashes is another matter.

The key thing to bear in mind (sorry) is that human recall doesn't act like a tape that's running in your head. It's more like (to use an analogy that's only slightly less misleading) a story we tell ourselves to account for sensory impressions. Experiments with eye-witness accounts show that the questions you ask can cause someone, if you're not extremely careful, to "rewrite" the experience. Everything that happens rewires neural connections and causes an irreversible change. (Sorry to drop this on you *now*, but even reading this book has irrevocably altered your brain.) The importance given in retrospect to apparently insignificant details makes their nature appear to change, and it's disturbingly easy to persuade someone to assign more importance to something and thus distort the subject's recollections.

There's an everyday example you've all doubtless encountered. If you're in a room with a lot of small, regular noises (say, the fridge humming, a clock ticking, rain on the roof and a car alarm in the next street) and one of them abruptly stops, you convince yourself within a fraction of a second that the one that suddenly isn't there was the one you were listening to just before it stopped. This owes to the way we distinguish between all sorts of sensory input we're getting simultaneously - if we couldn't grade these in order of novelty and filter the less useful ones, we'd go mad constantly thinking "this shirt's warm","that light's a bit more orange than the one in my room","I hate the sound of this computer's fan" and so forth whilst trying to remember things and make conversation.

Memory is thus intimately connected with the emotional "strength" attached to any fact or moment. It's also linked with how many other things it can be tied to. Barring extreme head-trauma or ECT treatment, it's hard to make someone forget everything as we don't assign brain-space to facts, personal memories and the "To Do" list in separate compartments. (In fact, the "brain-space" concept is another fallacy, and our recall is theoretically unlimited by anything such as the death of neurons or the size of cranium. There isn't one bit of the brain dedicated to memory.) The "routes" of associations by which we arrive at a required memory are multiply redundant.

Once again, the key is how much you care about one of the items in any route. So if someone could adjust the level of emotional involvement you have about (say) a sister's birthday in 1978 when you missed episode two of "The Pirate Planet", they could unpick the way that you get from this to what was number one that week, which subject you were studying in school on the last lesson before, where you were when so and so did such and such, and how you learned the for-

continued on page 97...

been in the console room ever since 1.1, "An Unearthly Child".]

We get confirmation that the Doctor exhales carbon dioxide like anyone else. He knows stuff about the alien Lamadines, fission grenades and the Master, so his memory's not a complete blank. He tells Rossini he can 'get money quite easily'.

• *Ethics.* The Doctor didn't destroy the Nestene energy unit that survived the last invasion attempt [7.1, "Spearhead from Space"] because it would have felt like murder, even though its essence [provided it still had any] presumably died when the Nestene octopus expired, and even though he *did* kill the rest of the Nestene presence on Earth without compunction. [Then again, did he? The implication is that he cut the connection between the Nestene Consciousness and Earth, removing the animating psychic force from the plastic people and big rubber squid. The Doctor himself says that the Autons were 'never really alive in the first place'. But if *that's* true, why all the ethical qualms about destroying it? See **Things That Don't Make Sense**.]

• *Inventory.* The Doctor seems to instinctively home in on the Master's TARDIS when he sees it, despite the fact that it's disguised as a horse-box, but he carries a small box-shaped listening device and uses it to check the machine's true nature. He has a wallet, but no money. He's now wearing a red velvet jacket, a purple-lined cape and no tie or cravat. The shirt's still got a bit of frill.

The Supporting Cast

• *Josephine Grant.* The Doctor's new assistant, provided by UNIT, is introduced as a cute, vaguely hapless and more-than-enthusiastic girl [the emphasis is on "girl", whereas Liz Shaw was firmly depicted as a "woman"] who's just there to pass the Doctor his equipment and ask lots of questions. She's also presented as a hip young thing who probably knows all the fashionable boutiques. [Suffice to say, a pictorial dictionary of early 70s terms such as "Kooky" and "Dolly-bird" would probably have a photo of her.]

Jo failed general science at A-Level and got the UNIT job thanks to relatives in high places. [10.3, "Frontier in Space" specifies her uncle as part of a semi-improvised spiel, but 10.5, "The Green Death" confirms it.] The Brigadier offloads her onto the Doctor, calculating (correctly) that the Doctor won't bring himself to look her in the eye and tell her she's unsuitable for the job. She refers

to the Brigadier as 'sir', for now. The Doctor warms to her remarkably quickly [she seems to appeal to his paternal side], tweaking her chin and calling her 'Jo' without being invited.

Listing Jo's positive qualities [because it's quicker]: she claims to be trained in escapology, cryptology and explosives [although we never especially see her using the latter two - unless you count her *maybe* deducing the meaning of 'Thascales' in "The Time Monster"]; she's eager and good at fire-fighting; she's weak-willed enough to get hypnotized [by Season Ten, she's a lot more resilient], but she's tough enough to bounce back afterward; she can sweet-talk the apparently dour Campbell into rushing through the Doctor's supplies; and she doesn't take up much space. She usually has a big bunch of skeleton keys on her. [This will save a lot of time later on; see, for instance, 10.2, "Carnival of Monsters", by Holmes.]

The most characteristic Jo moment in this story: when she knocks over a whole pile of crates while spying on the Master and Rex. Instead of running or hiding, she stands up, looks straight at them, gives a goofy smile and says 'Oh... hello'.

[Something to mention that's almost never commented upon: whereas the Doctor probably holds a fairly high rank in UNIT - he gets saluted by lower ranks and called 'sir' when Benton remembers (usually when Douglas Camfield is directing) and much later warrants a salute from a Colonel in X4.04, "The Sontaran Stratagem" - Jo's status within this organisation is very odd. She's always 'Miss' to Benton but 'Jo' to Yates, and the Doctor refers to the Brigadier as her 'superior officer' in 8.5, "The Daemons". So if she's assigned a rank, it's likely to be Lieutenant, probably as a courtesy for intelligence staff (and more a matter of her pay-scale than actual ability to order corporals about; Benton treats her as one of the lads, for the most part). This uncle of hers must have considerable clout to get a kid practically straight out of school, with bad A-levels, into an elite and semi-secret organisation as a commissioned officer. "The Green Death" suggests he's with the UN, which makes sense of his influence over UNIT, but that story's novelisation also says he's a Cabinet Minister. Anyway, if Jo has a position within the chain of command, then Yates' "hands off" approach is entirely a matter of military protocol rather than simply not fancying her - note that he seems to think he's in with a chance with

How Does Hypnosis Work?

...continued from page 95

mula for the volume of a sphere[29]. However much the mind (or at least the frontal-lobe functions) might split these into "facts" and "experiences" and "things to do", the current research indicates that brain has them all circulating, waiting to be selected and used according to one of these criteria.

An ability such as *that* allows not only control over people's memories and allegiances, but what they perceive as important now. It recently emerged (X3.12, "The Sound of Drums") that the TARDIS chameleon circuit is at least partially connected with the perceptions of observers. This makes all that chameleon circuit business in 18.7, "Logopolis" really pointless, but if nothing else it's allowed Torchwood to install an invisibility shield around their lift (not even *slightly* like *The Tomorrow People*, then). By making some memories painful and others addictively attractive, the hypnotist can also persuade people not to see what is in front of them but what they've been *told* to see. Any discrepancies between actual sense-data and expected ones become the subject of Cognitive Dissonance (see "The Macra Terror") until the stress becomes too much. In "Terror of the Autons", Rex Farrell displays a lot of the classic symptoms.

So what's happening? The most obvious idea is that *Doctor Who* uses the version employed by real qualified hypnotists today, which is technically a form of fascination. This involves "distracting" the frontal-lobe "I" and placing the patient into a sleep-like brain-state. Within this "Alpha" state of brain-wave activity, information and suggestion can be "slid" into the mind without the conscious self necessarily knowing. This involves a willingness on the patient's part - note how stage hypnosis is legally and practically a voluntary act by the participants. The Doctor seems able to do this, even on apparently surly guards (16.1, "The Ribos Operation"; 15.4, "The Sun Makers"), but mainly only resorts to it when it's a friend or a recently-hypnotised subject. (See 5.2, "The Abominable Snowmen"; 14.2, "The Hand of Fear"; 14.6, "The Talons of Weng-Chiang" and most memorably 13.1, "Terror of the Zygons".) Only in "Battlefield" is there any noticeable attempt to coerce virtual strangers into doing as he wants. Regardless, the fact that *any* humans can withstand the Master's power indicates that he's not using any "superhuman" force (except, that is, in the case of "Time-Flight") to coerce his subjects.

Captain Chin Lee in the next story. What rank the mysterious tea-lady might hold is another matter.]

• *The Brigadier*. Just when we were thinking the Brig has become the Doctor's ideal boss, he seems to have endured some kind of memory-lapse concerning the Nestenes. [Regrettably, we'll see a lot of this in future. Like Agent Scully in *The X-Files*, the Brig seems to make occasional visits to some kind of memory-wiping facility, purely so he can ask exactly the right questions that a casual viewer would ask. Maybe that's why the location of UNIT HQ keeps changing - he simply walks into some official-looking building assuming that it's where he works, and nobody dares to tell him it's a bowls club or children's hospital. Whatever the case, the collective memory of Lethbridge-Stewart is of a pompous prig straight out of *Monty Python*, who spends six weeks shooting at aliens and then needs persuading that there's life on other planets at the start of the next adventure. See **Things That Don't Make Sense** for more.]

When Captain Yates volunteers to go on a dangerous mission with the Doctor, the Brig immediately replies 'I'm not entirely desk-bound yet' and goes himself. He carries hand-grenades, just on the off chance he'll need to use some. He's finally started wearing "proper" army gear, a standard uniform and combat fatigues.

• *Captain Yates*. The young, fresh-faced, slightly upper-class officer now working on the Brigadier's personal staff already knows the Doctor. He apparently cleaned up after the last Nestene incident ["Spearhead from Space"]. Jo calls him 'Mike' by episode three; the Doctor and Benton take a great deal longer.

• *Liz Shaw*. She's gone back to Cambridge. Apparently, she's the one who told the Brig that what the Doctor needs is someone who can 'hand you a test-tube and tell you how brilliant you are'. [See 7.4, "Inferno" and - indeed - most of Season Seven for why this is a dubious thing to say.]

• *UNIT*. The Doctor orders his equipment from the scientific supply section of UNIT, run by a 'dolly Scotsman' called Mr. Campbell.

The Brigadier's interest in the Master's volatiser suggests that he's not opposed to capturing alien technology for use in human weapons projects. He here uses a blue non-military Austin 1100 as transport, like the one your uncle had. [Or maybe not, if you're a non-British reader.] The radio call-sign 'Greyhound' is reserved for the Brigadier, and the other officers are 'Trap One', 'Trap Two' and so on. [The reference is to greyhound racing, where the dogs are in enclosures called "traps" - like the ones for race horses but smaller - and released simultaneously to chase fake rabbits on a glorified model railway. Anyone who views UNIT as class-bound should note that dog racing is stereotypically a working-man's sport, associated mainly with East London and Yorkshire.]

There's a river [possibly a port; in the first Lab scene we hear foghorns and see cranes] outside the Doctor's lab window, handy for throwing bombs into, although Benton says they're likely to get complaints about this. [See **Where is UNIT HQ?** under 8.3, "The Claws of Axos".]

The Supporting Cast (Evil)

• *The Master.* Even before he gives his name [all right, *title*], it's clear that he's a control freak: the economy of his movements, the precision of his speech and his first action after stepping down from the horse-box that has materialised at a circus (shooting his cuffs and smoothing out his jacket) bespeak attention to detail. With Rossini and Farrell, he's clearly selected his victims with care. His first line: 'I am usually referred to as the Master... Universally.'

Despite his apparent light build and short stature, the Master is physically very strong. He has dark, deep-set eyes, a van-dyke beard, a Nehru suit and a ring with a large(ish) black jewel on his left hand. [In short, he looks like a Bond Villain or Svengali right from the outset - the obvious references within *Doctor Who* are the two Stahlmans from "Inferno" and the nasty aliens from 6.7, "The War Games". Indeed, the War Lord as played by Philip Madoc is the nearest visual and narrative equivalent. The War Chief - a fallen Time Lord from the same story, and who offers the Doctor a share - is also something of a precedent, although there's no (repeat: *no*) evidence that he's the Master in a previous incarnation. Certainly, Terrance Dicks established they weren't the same Time Lord in his novel *Timewyrm: Exodus*; as Dicks co-created both characters, one presumes he ought to know.]

Here the Master's presented as a fallen Time Lord who revels in power, displaying a casual cruelty towards the "weak" human species. The Master knows the Doctor of old; the Time Lord messenger says that after 'what happened last time', the Master will want to kill the Doctor. There's a hint that he only picks Earth as his target to annoy the Doctor [although the novelisation suggests that the Nestenes helped him escape custody, so this scheme may be part of a payback plan for all concerned; see **The Lore**]. However, he at least acknowledges the Doctor to be an interesting adversary. Though obviously intelligent and usually quite rational, the Master's anger often seems to cloud his judgement, whereas the Doctor believes vanity is his weakness. Here he's mostly po-faced as he goes about his work, showing only occasional moments of sly humour.

The Master is an accomplished hypnotist, able to mesmerise human beings without saying a word, or give them suicidal or homicidal instructions moments after meeting them. [A learned skill, not a Time Lord trait. The Doctor doesn't display anything similar until 26.1, "Battlefield", although as so many people end up trusting the Doctor for no good reason, he may have *some* knowledge in this field. Certainly, the Fourth Doctor not only does it to security guards and Sarah Jane (in 13.1, "Terror of the Zygons") but also one of his own people (in 15.6, "The Invasion of Time"), and claims to have hypnotic powers in 16.5, "The Power of Kroll". And of course, there's always Aggedor (9.2 "The Curse of Peladon").] Away from the Master's influence, the hypnotised mind constantly attempts to free itself, and strong-willed subjects can resist him altogether. He knows all about Rossini, the circus owner [through research, not telepathy].

Weapons the Master here employs include a rod-like device [not referred to as a "tissue compression eliminator" until 19.7, "Time-Flight"] which can kill someone by shrinking them to just a few inches in height; and a volatiser, a small canister with roughly the same power as a fifteen-megaton bomb. He can disguise himself with realistic masks of other human beings, and can turn one of his victims into a decoy with a mask of his own face. [In a story obsessed with plastic, we might conclude that the masks must be Nestene in origin, but the Master doesn't seem like the kind of person who'd trust his face with a potentially lethal covering. The masks continue to function in later stories after he's betrayed the Nestenes, so he probably had a job-lot from an earlier scam.] These masks appear to disguise his height as well [see also "The Claws of Axos"; 9.3, "The Sea Devils"].

The Master says he has 'so few worthy opponents', and always misses them when they're gone.

The TARDIS(es) The Doctor is trying to repair the TARDIS' dematerialisation circuit, hoping to get the Ship working again. [In "Spearhead from Space", the TARDIS doesn't work because the Time Lords have changed the dematerialisation *code*; see "The Claws of Axos".] Steady-state micro-welding is involved in this work.

The Master's TARDIS is referred to *as* a TARDIS [q.v. 2.9, "The Time Meddler"]. It's evidently in full working order, at least until the Doctor steals its dematerialisation circuit, although the circuit isn't compatible with the Doctor's own vehicle as it needs a Mark One circuit and the Master's is a Mark Two. [The Doctor seems to imply the Master can't use his Mark One circuit because the Time Lords put a limitation on it, not because it's the wrong type, which might make sense if TARDISes are backward compatible and the Master's Ship is a bit newer. For more on this, see **Why Doesn't the TARDIS Work?** under "The Sea Devils".]

The Time Lords The main baddy in this story claims he's 'usually referred to' as 'the Master'. Both the Doctor and the Time Lords [or at the very least, Bowler-Hat Man] know him by that title. [Nearly all the Time Lords who resigned / reneged / legged it seem to have titles rather than names. We later discover that the Time Lords / Ladies who toed the line and kept to their vows are all blessed with really silly names like 'Zorac', 'Gomer' and 'Romanadvoratrelunda', so maybe the renegades aren't *allowed* names any more. Well, maybe. If that were the case, they could perhaps say something like "I used to be called _____".

[Given the Time Lords' tendency to make people forget things that might cause trouble, it's *possible* that the Doctor's renunciation of his Prydonian vows (mentioned a lot in future, but see 14.3, "The Deadly Assassin" for a start) involved his name being unpicked from everybody's memory. If so, it suggests that all the memories he has of his past, and the Master playing tricks on people at the Academy ("The Time Monster" gives us a really outstanding example - not *good*, you understand, but outstanding) hail from a time before he had a name beyond $\Theta^3 \Sigma X^2$.

(For where that one started, see "The Sea Devils".) It might also explain why even the Doctor seems confused about his past at times, like how old he is and stuff like that.

[We might also conclude that a newly-invested Time Lord picks a name upon the swearing of these vows. This matches the British system of investing a peer of the realm as well as various other rituals, such as entering a monastery or submitting work for the Eisteddfod. It may also be significant that the Doctor remembers what the Oath *was* (see 14.2, "The Hand of Fear" for his recital when denying Eldrad a lift back to Kastria in the Jurassic era) and the details of his life as a full-blown Time Lord (eg 10.2, "Carnival of Monsters"; 20.1, "Arc of Infinity"). Even his mentor, the K'anpo Rinpoche (11.5, "Planet of the Spiders"), seems unaware that either he or his pupil had names.

[The BBC Wales series has picked up on this and had various telepathic entities failing to find any name when they rummage around in the Doctor's head (see, for instance, X2.4, "The Girl in the Fireplace"). It's clearly stated that both renegades chose their new names ("The Sound of Drums"). X4.09, "Forest of the Dead" establishes that the Doctor's real name is so secret, he will only reveal it under highly unusual circumstances. (Even if we don't find out what those circumstances are, as only someone from his future knows it. Of course, that might not even be a name he has yet...)]

The Time Lord tribunal that tried the Doctor ["The War Games"] still exists [see also 8.4, "Colony in Space"], and here sends a messenger who's acquainted with the Doctor - sporting a bowler hat and umbrella to blend in with the locale - to warn him about the Master. The messenger appears out of nowhere with a TARDIS-style groaning noise, hovers in mid-air and knows that the Doctor is about to trigger one of the Master's death-traps. [If the Time Lords can transport people to and from specific points in space and time, and are so all-seeing that they know where the Master's laid traps, then why on Earth can't they just find the Master and transport him into prison? There are clearly "rules" here, governing the amount of intervention the Time Lords can make in the outside universe, but it's impossible to guess what those rules are. The messenger, for example, refuses to help the Doctor deal with the volatiser. For all we can tell, he may only be a hologram, but his umbrella is real enough to grab the Doctor's wrist. See 12.4, "Genesis of the Daleks", for more of this sort of thing.]

The Doctor knows the messenger personally, recognising him on sight [mind you, who *else* would be re-enacting Rene Magritte paintings at a crime-scene?] and commenting on his weakness for sarcasm. The messenger claims to have come 29,000 light years to Earth. [If he comes straight from the Time Lord planet, this suggests it's either near the centre of Earth's galaxy (which doesn't contradict anything else we're ever told) or elsewhere in Mutter's Spiral. No other galaxy is that close, and Gallifrey is near to at least one other star-system (13.5, "The Brain of Morbius"), so it can't be just out in the middle of nowhere. *The New Adventures* somewhat lazily take it as read that the Doctor's homeworld is close to the galactic core. However, this is not what the Time Lord says; he merely states that his co-ordinates have shifted, 'not bad after 29,000 light-years'. With a Holmes script, it could be a unit of time. All we can conclusively say is that this distance is the last time he took his bearings. See **When (And Where) Is Gallifrey?** under 13.3, "Pyramids of Mars".] Once the messenger's arrived on Earth, he can vanish and re-appear again with a simple "pop" instead of all that wheezing and groaning.

According to the Master, Time Lords are expected to die with dignity.

The Non-Humans

• *Nestenes*. A disembodied, mutually telepathic intelligence, according to the Doctor. He also suspects that their form [on a planet like Earth] is 'analogous to a cephalopod'. [Terrance Dicks' novelisation ramps up the stakes on this, and describes the manifesting creature as, 'a many-tentacled monster, something between spider, crab, and octopus' (p120).]

Nestenes can channel their energy to Earth and into one of their plastic meteorite-pods through a radio telescope. As before, their spherical container glows initially glows blue, then reverts to red after "downloading" a fresh batch of Auton energy [so presumably the blue tint was for "input"].

The Nestenes change the molecular structure of plastic, energising it to turn it into quasi-organic matter, but it remains inert for most of the time. The Doctor suggests they can put life into *anything* plastic [i.e. after they've changed its structure, so they can't animate any plastic item at will by remote, else they wouldn't *need* to distribute plas-

tic flowers - far easier to suffocate Britain's housewives with the clingwrap already in their homes, etc.]. Given the right equipment, the Doctor can "hack" the Autons' cellular programs and convert the programming into a pictorial code.

• *Autons*. Apart from the standard Auton mannequins (which here wear carnival-style headpieces in order to mask their appearance), new Autons used by the Master include a child's toy in the form of a hideous troll, which comes to life when exposed to heat and smothers anyone in the vicinity; a telephone cord which attempts to strangle its victim on receiving a specific signal; a selfinflating plastic chair, which folds up to suffocate the person sitting in it; and Master-designed "autojets", plastic daffodils which are activated by short-wave radio and programmed on a cellular level to home in on the nearest human face. The Master plans to activate the flowers simultaneously, each one spraying a fast-setting plastic over the victim's nose and mouth. Carbon dioxide can dissolve this plastic after two minutes. [Unlike the Autons in "Spearhead from Space", most of these new Autons aren't controlled by the Nestene collective but require specific signals from outside sources. This might result from the limited Nestene presence on Earth this time.] The daffodils are so like real ones as to have cells, rather than being one long polymer over and over again.

There are no Auton facsimiles here, although Auton mannequins can wear imperfect facemasks - not as good as the Master's - to disguise themselves as human beings. One Auton has the power of speech, apparently channelling the Nestenes directly. Unlike many an alien invader, this one can actually use contractions (such as 'It's too late').

• *Lamadines*. According to the Doctor, Lamadines have nine opposable digits and pioneered the advanced engineering technique of steady-state micro-welding. [Well, someone had to.] It tends to involve more smoke than fire.

History

• *Dating*. [Late 1971, probably around October. The Doctor's been working on the dematerialisation circuit for at least three months, and he was busy with the TARDIS console in "Inferno", so some time has passed.] Liz left some time ago; the Doctor's been 'agitating for a new assistant' ever since.

There's a National Space Museum in Britain

[we didn't get one until 1999, and it's in Leicester], and the Brigadier signed the permission slips for the Nestene energy unit to be displayed there. [Apart from the obvious breach of security, it's interesting that UNIT has no problem with museums displaying obviously alien artefacts, when it keeps the existence of aliens under wraps most of the time. Possibly there's an "official" story to go with the energy unit, in an attempt to counter public rumour about the Auton menace.]

The circus where the Master arrives is near Tarminster. [Yet another made-up English town; Tarminster is a large enough to have its own County police and HQ. We'll look at England's fictitious towns later, but this sounds a bit like the invented places in the West of England used by Thomas Hardy in his "Wessex" novels. In these, a place like Dorchester would be renamed "Casterbridge", Cerne Abbas would be "Abbot's Cernal" and so on. It would make sense if the makers of *Doctor Who* changed the names to protect the innocent. If we pretend that "Tarminster" is the real town of Warminster - long known as the UK's flying saucer sighting capital - the proximity of a radio telescope and the location of new UNIT HQ suddenly makes sense. See **Where Is UNIT HQ?** under "The Claws of Axos".

[A cut scene lists other non-existent stops on the Auton tour: Oxeter, Billington and Dryfield. The broadcast dialogue says this promotion is restricted to the Home Counties - the rather parochial term for those counties directly abutting Greater London - but that phrase is commonly used to mean anywhere within commuting distance, and so could stretch to Southend, Reading, Crawley or Luton. Basically, it's anywhere that would suffer if someone nuked London, and where people don't talk like Pigbin Josh or any more identifiable regional accent.]

The telescope base is called "Beacon Hill" [dozens of places across the UK are called that, mainly with Iron Age forts on them] and according to a sign, it's run by the "Ministry of Technology". [Not the equally fictitious "Ministry of Science" from "Doctor Who and the Silurians", so maybe there's been an election or a major reshuffle after all the prestige projects that went wrong in Season Seven.]

Additional Sources The 1975 Target novelisation of "Terror of the Autons" (another favourite of the pre-video age) is notable for its cover illustration

by Peter Brookes. In an amazingly lurid montage of zig-zaggedly framed images (one showing the Doctor in the doorway of the Radio telescope apparently doing a Dusty Springfield impression, flailing his arms around), we see an enormous one-eyed Nestene octopus, with a single huge claw, reaching out over the radio-telescope station. Some younger *Doctor Who* fans imagined that a Nestene really looked this, even though no such octopus appears anywhere in the actual story. (Too bad - it would've been preferable to the CGI cowpat seen in X1.01, "Rose".)

Indeed, the Bane in the pilot episode of *The Sarah Jane Adventures* looks like a deliberate reference to this illustration. The novel also sees Professor Phillips disguised as a clown, a nice GK Chesterton-ish idea (i.e. he's so obvious that nobody sees him), and Terrance Dicks - who wrote the novelisation - makes much play of this as a sign of the Master's perverse sense of humour. Similarly, there's a graphic account of the Master telling Farrell that he relishes the Doctor's continual ingenuity in escaping from certain death - and then, as soon as he's alone, splitting the oak table with his fist in frustration. Best of all, it makes use of that most existential horror of all 70s *Doctor Who* (but first mentioned in "The War Games"): the idea that if the Master is caught, the Time Lords will reverse his life-stream, so that (all together now) *it would be as though he had never existed.*

The Analysis

Where Does This Come From? British Social History 101: Pop Culture.

The reasons cited as to why Glam Rock happened (*our* Glam Rock, not what some Americans think it means) include the invention of colour television, the move away from acid back to amphetamines, and the advent of a new generation of teenage girls who were bored with "meaningful" singer-songwriters and "heavy" hairy hippies. With hindsight the ingredients were all around by the end of 1970 (when Marc Bolan swapped denim for satin and Tolkien for Chuck Berry), but the *true* beginning of this gloriously gaudy period of fashion, music and adventures in gender-identity was the arrival of Jo Grant in TV's *Doctor Who*. (This will explain a lot of what's to come, so please pay attention.)

Throughout the sixties, *Doctor Who* and *Top of the Pops* had kept their eyes on one another, but now they seemed interchangeable. The bands whose performances fit best with the new BBC house-style made out big time. Long noodling solos and supposedly profound lyrics were a lot less fun than three-minute blasts of straightforward rock 'n' roll with football-chant choruses, often performed by men in make-up and cartoonish colour-scheme costumes. They gave a working-class British spin to rock and roll and Pop Art[26]. Certainly, that's what *Top of the Pops* audiences found, and the sets and electronic effects made the frequent appearances by Bolan's band T-Rex (and The Sweet, Roxy Music, Slade, Wizzard and David Bowie) look, as everyone's dad would grumble, "like something off *Doctor Who*".

As we'll see, many of the special effects were tried in *Doctor Who* and then used on *ToTP* if they worked. And like *Doctor Who*, the Glam that's lasted best is the work of people who know how to be sophisticated and grown-up, but made a conscious decision to do something simple and fun. (We'll develop the Bolan theme under "The Daemons". If you're using the **What Was In The Charts?** selections as background, listen carefully to *Ride A White Swan*. Better yet, see the acts perform in clips from the time.) *Doctor Who* from now until "The Time Warrior" (11.1) at least will either inspire or *be* inspired by this movement. The UK charts (like *Doctor Who*) interspersed this gleeful excess with beardie folk-singer types and Californian singer-songwriters in cheesecloth shirts. Most of these demanded that we go back to nature and realign our chakras (weirdly, Bolan and Bowie had a foot in each camp) the way many of the beardie folks in *Doctor Who* would be doing. We'll pick up this debate as we go along.

As *Doctor Who* stories moved in an ever more *Doomwatch*-y direction, it was perhaps inevitable that the whole issue of plastic would be revisited. The first episode of *Doomwatch*, a supposedly "grown-up" series, had been about a virus designed to digest waste plastic getting loose and making planes crash. Stuff that made people uncomfortable about the extent of plastic in domestic use was always popular with the British public. As we saw in the first Auton story, the possibility of non-living objects being invested with some animating force has a long pedigree as a thing to scare children. But the strictly linear nature of "Spearhead from Space" didn't allow time for elaboration on the basic idea of killer shop-dummies, so here *anything* plastic is deemed

a potential threat. (Here we pause to re-mention that there really *were* inflatable armchairs on sale in 1970.) "Plastic" was now no longer just an adjective for things being remouldable; it was a synonym for artifice, insincerity and tawdriness. The other routine image for this level of fakery and tackiness was the circus, and - oh, look! - this story starts there.

Let's look at this more closely. What is the main thing that plastic dolls and circuses have in common? It's the sense of jadedness and disillusionment children experience when rosy memories of these things are re-examined in the light of maturity. 1960s *Doctor Who* was all about the headrush of the first time: whether it's seeing a new planet, being there when a big moment in history happens or simply seeing something that's unlike anything attempted on television. By contrast, 1970s *Who* is about going backstage and seeing people doing their jobs as well as they can under trying circumstances. Notice how Season Seven, a transition year in almost every way, had Autons infiltrating through a plastics factory that was a market-leader. Season Eight begins with the Master taking advantage of a company whose dogged following of long-established business practices had left it almost bankrupt. It's run by a son, Rex Farrell, who's too afraid of the man who wrecked the family firm to do anything about it.

Once Holmes finds his feet as a writer, he'll distort the series to the extent that it will almost *always* focus on losers such as Rex Farrell, and the Doctor will either give them their lives back or be unable to stop them getting killed. This is just good practice: heroic, dynamic figures have no need for salvation or hope, and little reason to be tempted by sinister manipulators. It catches the national mood of things sliding out of our control, personally or culturally. It's also, for that matter, easier to do on a BBC budget.

Even before Holmes becomes script editor in Season Twelve, this is a trend that the Earthbound stories will follow, although not as *noticeably* just yet. All the Dicks / Letts stable of writers will handle it in different ways, but the change towards what we regard as Holmes' style is very abrupt. (That's chiefly because he made the big breakthrough in 6.6, "The Space Pirates", where he shifted the focus from dashing space-captains to washed-up miner Milo Clancey. He'll cement the trend further in 10.2, "Carnival of Monsters".) In "Doctor Who and the Silurians", the human characters are motivated by noble-sounding ideals of scientific breakthroughs, defending the nation and saving the planet. But by "The Green Death" (10.5), we're in a world of multinationals giving cabinet ministers kickbacks and humanity being brainwashed to increase company profits. Almost without anyone noticing, the series has made cynicism part of the normality that alien invasions not only interrupt but rely upon.

It would be silly, however, to say that "Terror of the Autons" changed everything overnight. The "plucked from today's headlines" nature of the Farrell family's drama, as a microcosm of the decline of manufacturing industry, happens in the context of a story that does everything short of tie Jo to a railway line. It's a surprise that the Master's Volatiser isn't a big black sphere with a fizzing fuse and the word BOMB painted on it. Remember that every era of *Doctor Who* has another current or recent series it *really* wants to be, whether it's Innes Lloyd's obsession with *The Power Game* or Russell T Davies' attempts to make *Billie the Dalek-Slayer*. So by introducing a Time Lord who's behind absolutely everything that goes wrong in the entire word (and a couple of others), the BBC seems to be looking over its shoulders at ITV's big children's adventure hit...

We're talking, regretfully, about sodding *Freewheelers*. It was like an update of Enid Blyton's *Famous Five*, but with three kids, a boat and a Nazi war criminal. Southern TV, whose main source of income was kids' adventure shows, made this from spring 1968 and really only stopped because Thames made *The Tomorrow People* (which was *Freewheelers* with psi-powers). During what has to be the most packed school holiday ever, the original threesome (two geeky lads and a posh girl they never noticed was female until it was time to cook) repeatedly ran into sinister schemes hatched by Von Gelb (Geoffrey Toone - he went on to play the high priest Hepesh in 9.2, "The Curse of Peladon"). They thwarted these with the assistance of Colonel Buchan (Ronald Leigh-Hunt, who was Commander Radnor in 6.5, "The Seeds of Death").

Eventually the original cast left to sign on the dole or something, and Wendy Padbury did the cooking whilst Eric Flynn (the dashing Leo Ryan in 5.7, "The Wheel in Space") did the "Now see here, you young idiots..." authority-figure duties. The schemes always ended with Von Gelb escaping to play Wagner records and 3D chess again. If you're following this line of thought, then consid-

er that stories such as "The Mind of Evil" (8.2) and "The Sea Devils" could easily be *Freewheelers* six-parters that acquired monsters somehow. Other UNIT adventures have more in common with this show than fans feel comfortable admitting. Even UNIT's first outing (6.3, "The Invasion") mimicked the almost-contemporary *Freewheelers* yarn "Doomsday". (Drugs in the water supply lead to thousands - well, dozens of extras - falling unconscious in Trafalgar Square as a private army who dress very like IE troops march around. Buchan even infiltrated a lighthouse-cum-enemy-base dressed as a works inspector, very like the Brig's disguise in "The Mind of Evil".)

All this diet-Bond, child-friendly stuff with helicopters and speedboats was fairly routine children's television fare - we merely single out *Freewheelers* as the most successful, and the one made under the same constraints as *Doctor Who* (as opposed to being made on film and imported). It found solutions to the logistical and script problems that *Doctor Who* was forced to follow. Inevitably all adventures were filmed in refineries, with large numbers of extras in fascistic uniforms start to look alike. Pinning all the malfeasance on a single recurring villain simply completes the process, but it's worth noticing how far the first two stories of this season move the ostensible alien invasion down in the mix.

As with maggots in Wales, "Terror of the Autons" is the classic example of something everyday turned against us. The cheery costume-wearing chaps and chicks (literally chicks: women dressed as fluffy hatchlings, as well as men in Viking drag and a host of other uses for "resting" actors) who came door-to-door and checked if you were using their products were a familiar sight in the 1960s. Plastic daffodils were usually to promote something else - detergent most commonly, rather than simply the "Look! It's plastic!" approach seen on screen here.

That said, fake flowers have a long pedigree. The Royal British Legion sold paper poppies in the streets or in newsagents, for benefit of widows and orphans of ex-service personnel, or to pay for those soldiers, sailors or others who were injured on duty and needed special facilities. These days MacMillan, a charity for cancer hospices and specially trained nurses, give out smaller daffs in brooch form. Similarly, after the 1960s had given us Gonks as the standard gift from fairgrounds and the usual lucky mascot for schoolkids sitting exams or entering *Top of the Form*[27], the early 70s saw various European nations trying to inflict their idea of "cute" or "crazy" toys on us. The German fad for troll-dolls was one of a number of really shoddy plastic novelties blighting Christmases of the era.

If that sounds a bit xenophobic, consider the Master at this stage of the game. He's every sinister foreign manipulator rolled into one. He can pass for one of us, in character, but as himself his diction's slightly *too* good, his skin slightly too dark, and his claim to all the titles he uses slightly too reliant on overseas validation. It's been a frequent response in times of national unease to pin trouble on a malign force who can hypnotise the weak-minded and control hidden armies. Victorian London had Moriarty, Fu Manchu and Dracula. France had Fantomas. Weimar Germany had Dr Mabuse. Post-War America had Commies and Aliens roughly interchangeably brainwashing the nation's youth with mind-control rays, horror-comics and rock music. In Elizabethan London, Christopher Marlowe made a career out of identifying these villains and showing them getting their comeuppance (see 3.5, "The Massacre"). Bond-villains and Nazi war criminals were just the most recent manifestations of the archetypal Hypnotic Sexy Foreigner, single-handedly causing every single bad thing.

The Master is, if anything, a purer form of this than even the Daleks. In fact, with his hypnosis, impenetrable rubber masks and devious schemes to infiltrate big scientific establishments, he's International Rescue's arch-nemesis The Hood all over again. (Although if the *Thunderbirds* analogy were complete, he'd be Benton's half-brother and have the ability to cast a spell over the loyal retainer.) Let's go down the kitsch TV food-chain: were it not for the lack of tilted cameras and captions saying "POW!!" or "JEHOSEPHAT!!!", the Master's reign of terror with joke-shop novelties would be exactly the sort of thing Cesar Romero would inflict on Gotham City and Adam West would sort out. Thus, Benton becomes Chief O'Hara.

Things That Don't Make Sense We have to start with an overarching problem that applies to a *lot* of Master stories: his goal, it seems, is to conquer / destroy-then-conquer / conquer-then-destroy Earth. All right, but what if he succeeded? Surely, such a deviation of established history would attract the Time Lords' notice and warrant their direct intervention. Has this possibility not

dawned on the Master and his alien allies, and are they genuinely prepared for the full might of the most powerful beings in the cosmos coming to bear on them? [The "get-out clause" presented in the new series in "The Sound of Drums" - that the Master hears 'drumming' that compels him to wreak destruction, no matter how sloppily - papers over a surprising amount of his extraordinarily thin motivations. At least the new series had the good grace to delay the Master miraculously becoming Prime Minister until after the Time Lords had been exterminated.]

Once the Master steals the remaining Nestene sphere, UNIT discerns there's a real risk that the Autons might return. But how long does it take for the Brigadier to think about checking on plastics factories? Three whole scenes. The last incursion was only four stories ago. Why did he authorise such a dangerous item as the sphere to go on display in a museum anyway? [A smaller glitch is that no spheres are actually seen to survive events of "Spearhead from Space", although Terrance Dicks' novelisation says that UNIT found one that had 'never been collected [by the Autons] or activated' just lying about the factory afterward. The book also says the Doctor kept the last sphere as a sort of 'barometer' (p15) to check periodically on whether or not the Autons were coming back - but if so, it's even more reckless to lend it out.]

The Master starts off his campaign of terror with the volatiser, a pocket-sized device as powerful as a nuclear warhead, but then tries to kill the Doctor with an enormous bomb in a large box, which barely ripples the water after it's thrown in the river. If he's got 'volatisers' and what the novelisation identifies as 'A Sontaran Fragmentation Grenade' (aah, childhood lore), why is he mucking about with killer dolls, inflatable chairs, daffodils, dribble-glasses, fake-doggy-doo, etc?

Consider also that Master sets up the trap so that the volatiser will hit the floor and explode if anyone enters the radio-telescope installation. The Doctor deals with it by hurling himself through the door and catching the device in mid-fall rather than, say, climbing into the room through the great big window (or just breaking it) and picking it up at leisure. At the very least, wouldn't it have been polite to evacuate his friends from the area before taking the risk?

How did the Master set the locked-room snare up without getting himself, um, "volatised"? Did he do something complicated with his TARDIS?

Let's be honest, it's a pretty crummy booby-trap - had the Doctor had been carrying some nail-scissors, he could have thwarted it without the need to show off his potential as a cricketer.

But the main problem with the volatiser is that if it goes off as the Master intends - or if someone other than the Doctor is unlucky enough to open the door - it would destroy the very radio-telescope that the Master needs to make his (excuse the phrasing) master plan work. Even by *his* standards, this is counter-productive fiendishness.

More worryingly, if the research station head knows that Goodge and Phillips have gone AWOL, he presumably checked the cabin before calling in UNIT. So the Master arrived, killed Goodge, hid him in the lunch-box, hypnotised Phillips, took him away, waited for the director to case the joint, went back and *then* set up the booby-trap. That's vaguely plausible, although it requires more forethought than the Master typically displays.

The Brigadier has his own staff car, yet he goes off go to meet a distinguished astrophysicist in Bessie. Jo goes from making out lists of plastics factories to personally creeping around Farrell's factory within seconds of screen-time. We might imagine that several days pass between scenes, and that she's just especially lucky to happen upon the plastics factory the Master's using, but the awkward editing and the fact that she's wearing the same clothes seems to suggest otherwise. [It's also been brought to our attention that the Master has one UNIT ammo-box in the lab where he's brewing Autons and - apparently - a *different* one for Jo's gift-package. This isn't necessarily a mistake, but making the plot-logic work with just one box involves a far longer gap between the two scenes than we're shown. Perhaps the hypnotized Jo went off and had a long lunch, then did some clothes shopping, and then returned to UNIT after the "discovery" of the car with the Master's bomb. If so, did he hypnotise her twice, or feed a "time-delay" into his instructions that she return to the lab by a certain time?]

And when they chuck the Master's box-bomb out the window and scare a few seagulls, Benton says, 'We'll get complaints'. Okay, so why is a top-secret military-intelligence body worried about the neighbours? Besides, who is there likely to complain, and what do they *think* is happening in this fashionable penthouse laboratory with all the soldiers and frequent deliveries of Scanning Molecular Structural Analysers? Apparently, UNIT also has a SWAT team of glaziers who can fix the broken window in less time than it takes for Jo to sit down, even though the Doctor's lab is evidently located fifty feet up and right over the water's edge. Sorry to keep on about her, but how does the tea-lady get her trolley up such a narrow staircase? [Right, now for episode two...]

The Master deliberately lures the Doctor to the circus in the hopes that his stooge, Professor Phillips, will blow the Caped Crusader up, but he fails to stash his TARDIS elsewhere in case the plan [as he somewhat expects, even] fails. As matters stand, the Master only has himself to blame when the Doctor finds his Ship and lifts its dematerialisation circuit. Oh, and the explosion in question sounds like a "crack!", followed by the curious noise of a toilet flushing.

Soon after, the Brigadier and Yates need the Doctor to holler that the faceless policeman shooting at them with a gun-hand is, in fact, an Auton. Only then does Yates stop shooting and drive into one. Afterward, the Brig has an absolutely pointless briefing session in the Doctor's lab - it's probably just an info dump to bring viewers back up to speed, but it means that (as the Doctor himself says) the Brig is just explaining what everyone in the already knows. Maybe we shouldn't be so quick to judge, however, as Yates - who apparently cleaned up after the first Auton incursion - routinely forgets what he should know about them. And why is it happening in the Lab anyway?

Mr Brownrose from the Ministry comes calling to debrief UNIT on dozens of "strange deaths" that occur across the Home Countries. These owe to people accidentally triggering the killer daffodils early, but the authorities seem utterly perplexed as to the cause of death. So did *all* of these deaths happen in seclusion, to the point that no family member or friend witnessed the lethal flower spew? Did *none* of the victims, in the Doctor-estimated 'two minutes' of consciousness available to them, have time to race out and summon a neighbour, or flag down someone in the street, or write something down, thus tipping the authorities off to the nature of the problem? And were *none* of the auto-jets accidentally triggered by stray short-wave radio signals while the victims were out walking in public? (If the mixture only becomes soluble in carbon-dioxide after two minutes, it probably gives off fairly distinctive vapours, aldehydes or somesuch, that someone would have noticed on finding the bodies.)

In episode four, the Master spares the Doctor

and Jo so he can use them as hostages - a means of stopping UNIT from bombing his coach. But, er, why bother? He need only reach the radio-telescope and summon the Nestene to put his endgame into action, so if UNIT obliterates the coach, he'll just lose some expendable Autons and Farrell. If he'd just said, "to hell with the coach" and continued threatening Jo as planned, he could've retrieved his dematerialisation circuit from the Doctor and killed him (and Jo too, just to keep his trigger finger supple), then sauntered off to the radio-telescope at his own speed. (Remember: without the Doctor's help, UNIT wouldn't know to guard the facility.) But *oh* no... he has to get cute and keep the story going for no good reason.

The Doctor seems awfully eager to leave the TARDIS door open for most of the story - it's even standing open while he's away from the lab in episode three. Although this volume isn't usually concerned with actors fluffing their lines, we have to mention the painfully obvious botched dialogue in episode three, since most viewers do. Mike Yates: 'I'd just gone out to fetch some cocoa.' The Doctor: 'Fetch a tin of what?'

Yates seems awfully trigger-happy in the finale, attempting to shoot someone in response to Jo yelling nothing more than, 'Look!' (It happens that he's firing at the Master, but it happens too quick for him to establish this.) It's also a bit optimistic for Yates to declare, 'We've got him now', when the Master boards the coach, failing to consider that he might, just might, try to drive the damn thing away. [Then again, the Doctor may have briefed him not to expect the Master to think of anything that isn't stupidly overcomplicated, and reliant on a lot of flukey coincidences.]

The one everyone seems to notice: at the end, the Master switches sides upon realising that the Nestene will undoubtedly turn upon him. What, it didn't occur to him before now? (Besides, when the Nestene are expelled, what exactly is happening when the glittery effect arrives and everyone starts flailing around slowly, like Brian Cant on *Play School* being a deep-sea diver?) But then, the Doctor's last line is quite gobsmackingly wrong too: we've seen six deaths and heard about dozens more, yet the bastard says he's 'quite looking forward' to the Master having another pop at Total World Domination next week.

Critique In case you missed it, we'll say it again: "Terror of the Autons" is the first truly Glam Rock *Doctor Who*. When Barry Letts and Robert Holmes unite, the result is something with one foot in the prosaic and mildly sardonic, and another in the lurid and fantastic. This happens with other writer / director combos (notably Michael Briant and Malcolm Hulke), but with less of the giddy thrill that "Terror of the Autons" and "Carnival of Monsters" (10.2) provide. Here's an adventure where even someone's packed-lunch is turned into something funny, scary and (the phrase is unavoidable, if inappropriate for the egg-beset Arnold Goodge) larger-than-life.

Along those lines, remember that Pop Art used collage as one of its principle weapons, along with redoing photographs as paintings with the colour cranked up. "Carnival of Monsters" comments on the nature of collage, but "Terror of the Autons" just gets on and does it. Past stories have contained moments of Pop Art brilliance (mainly in Seasons Two and Six, but see **Did Sergeant Pepper Know the Doctor?** under 5.1, "The Tomb of the Cybermen"), but here we see the first of an entirely new, completely 1970s batch of deliberate and emphatic assaults on the everyday. Fascinating and intense though the experiments of the last year were, this is a show and a writer finding their groove. In fact, what's *really* interesting is what the director / producer has done with the raw material.

Because it's a lot easier to do television drama that's worthy and dull than one that resembles a comic book. Even now, just hiring good writers and actors and pointing a camera at the result is not enough. What most critics miss about "Terror of the Autons" is how far in advance it was of the usual TV practice for late 1970 / early 1971. Not just all the (ahem) "courageous" CSO work, but in the pacing and the demands it makes of the casual viewer. It's shot and edited in ways that evoke a sense of a different world made from bits of our own. The script permits this, but it could easily have made in the *verite* style of "Spearhead from Space". Letts has chosen to emphasise the elements that another director would try to cover up.

Back when the only people with copies of old stories crammed two four-parters onto a three-hour tape by editing out the cliffhangers, many people with nth-generation copies made a game from trying to guess where episodes ended. "Terror of the Autons" caused a lot of confusion, looking as though it was made in seven-minute instalments. (The *real* cliffhangers, in fact, were by far the least satisfying candidates.) Even when given an official VHS release in recoloured skuzzorama, it seemed oddly edited. The music is dubbed in such a way that jolting jumps between scenes are brandished as being natural and planned. We're straight into a new scene with no lead-in, establishing shots or pauses between lines of dialogue. When Mrs Farrell finds her dead husband, her scream covers the beginning of the next scene, on film.

For almost the first time, it's hard to follow a *Doctor Who* story half-heartedly - because if you turn away from the screen and rely on your ears, you're unaware that the story has moved on to a different place, sometimes with different people. It may seem like a minor point *now,* but this rapid form of montage - familiar to film buffs by 1970 - was unknown in mainstream TV drama made either on film or electronically recorded. (This is clearly deliberate, and more noticeable in the video sequences than on film. Much of the filmed work is edited more conventionally, with two seconds of establishing-shot before the dialogue or action begins, and occasional shots of cars going from A to B instead of just arriving at B a split-second after deciding to leave A.)

The latter half of episode three provides a wealth of good examples. In the space of a heartbeat, we go from the Doctor and Jo picking up on a mention of the name "Farrell" to Mrs Farrell being asked about her husband's death. We know that the lengthy phone cord is significant somehow, so whilst the Brig and the Doc argue, we follow Jo over to the desk and watch as she chats on the phone in question to Mr Campbell. Like many of the scenes in the Doctor's lab, we have a high-angle camera (look at the way she's introduced, shot from eight feet up *through* the metal frame, alternating with low-angle shots of the Doctor). The Doctor and the Brigadier go to Farrell's factory, with the spooky music running as we cut back and forth from this and a troll doll menacing Jo. There's longer-than-necessary shots of people looking at a plastic daffodil. The music and pictures tell us something that the dialogue and acting carefully ignore.

As if to reinforce the point, when you might expect the usual TV grammar of alternating between one-shot and two-shot (a medium close-up of one actor, then a shot of that actor and whoever's listening from slightly further back), Letts

stays with Pertwee as he dissects the doll, even as the dialogue continues around him. This is partly to avoid freaking out kids who think their teddies are real (as if the sight of this thing strangling someone wouldn't do that), but it's mainly to place the Doctor's reactions - as more information comes to him - at the heart of things.

You don't need much analysis to see that Letts is consciously doing something completely at odds with the much-hyped "gritty realism" of Season Seven. Simply watching any other television from the period, even other *Doctor Who* stories, will illustrate the point. The number of shots-per-minute here is well ahead of that for a comparable prime-time drama of 1971. (We counted, and our ad hoc sample was an episode of *Columbo* and one of *Upstairs, Downstairs*.)

So Letts sat and took notes when watching *The Birds* and *A Bout de Souffle*. Hooray! That alone wouldn't make a memorable story, but he's working with a template for a different kind of *Doctor Who* altogether - one with the present-day-with-a-twist elements from Season Seven infused with Saturday Morning serials. The script has ordinary people doing their jobs, but like a sitcom, not in the toecurling "matey" way of "Inferno" (7.4). They grumble about eggs or the cost of meat, try to cover up their company's recent failures, try to stick it to the boss (and here, if anywhere, Mike Yates makes sense as a secondary male lead character - ganging up with Jo to have some fun while the Brig's away) and complain about change.

Even the GPO engineer (before we discover his real identity) is a vivid and quickly sketched-in character. We come to know Mr Campbell, who's just someone that Jo flirts with by phone to speed up delivery of supplies, better than we knew Bruno Taltalian in "The Ambassadors of Death". In a curious way, this makes ordinary criteria of "good" and "bad" acting irrelevant here - the characters are primarily archetypes and get detail by contradicting the clichés: the usual white-coated scientist gets to talk formulae and make sententious statements about the Future of Mankind, whereas Goodge and Philips discuss packed lunches and indigestion. These little nuggets of everyday life help ground the hyper-real production. It sounds like an easy trick, but even Letts failed to pull it off when making "Planet of the Spiders" (11.5).

And, to be honest, it's not *entirely* successful here, either. While this was good enough as a weekly half-hour dip into a strange world where joining a circus was a safer career option than running a plastics factory, watched as a ninety-minute story it's top-heavy, with exciting set pieces and thin plot-logic to string them together. (We'll see this a lot when the Master's in town.) This is the visual equivalent of four packets of Skittles - it's an adventure which gives the viewer a tartrazine and saccharine buzz. Superficially lurid and exciting it may be, but afterwards you miss having something more substantial. A lot of it seems written on the "Scenes We Would Love To See" principle, dreaming up stunts and sight-gags and making everything else subordinate to these.

Granted, there's a lot to be said for "Do You Remember...?" moments as the biggest legacy of 70s *Doctor Who*, and nobody did them better than Holmes. But while this story *ju-u-ust* gets away with it through sheer momentum, it sets a dangerous precedent. Pertwee has made this a star-vehicle, and even undercuts his new male co-star by co-opting his dialogue (see the scene where Yates feeds a line about the Master's hypnotic abilities at the start of episode two). Rather than being an outsider, on the periphery of other people's stories and coming in to disrupt them, this story is *all* about the Doctor. Those other characters, well-crafted though they may be, orbit him and come to see him in his lab. From now on, UNIT works for him and not vice-versa.

Remember, this is a story in which the Brigadier admits that the aliens in question have devoted their entire efforts to giving UNIT a hard time, where Jo brazenly tells the viewers that she's the Doctor's new assistant and where a Time Lord intervenes simply to introduce a new arch-villain. We're drifting from *Doctor Who* being a fantasy adventure series that kids can enjoy to one made specifically and exclusively *for* kids, especially boys. We've wandered down this path before, almost by accident, but it's going to be systematically explored for the next five years. If all the stories had been as entertaining as this one, however, it wouldn't have been so much of a problem.

The Facts

Written by Robert Holmes. Directed by Barry Letts. Viewing figures: 7.3 million, 8.0 million, 8.1 million, 8.4 million.

Supporting Cast John Baskcomb (Rossini), David Garth (Time Lord), Christopher Burgess (Professor Philips), Andrew Staines (Goodge), Michael Wisher (Rex Farrell), Harry Towb (McDermott), Stephen Jack (Farrell Senior), Barbara Leake (Mrs Farrell), Terry Walsh (Auton Policeman), Pat Gorman (Auton Leader), Haydn Jones (Auton Voice), Dermot Tuohy (Brownrose), Norman Stanley (Telephone Man).

Working Titles "The Spray of Death".

Cliffhangers Jo, under hypnosis, tries to open the Master's bomb-box at UNIT HQ; in the back of the police car that's apparently rescued himself and Jo from Rossini's circus, the Doctor pulls away the face of one of the policemen to reveal the blank expression of Auton mannequin; the Doctor receives a telephone call from the Master in his lab, at which point the flex on the phone tries to throttle him (leading to some vintage Pertwee gurning).

What Was in the Charts? "Ride A White Swan," T. Rex; "Voodoo Chile (Slight Return)", The Jimi Hendrix Experience; "Grandad", Clive Dunn; "Ape Man", The Kinks.

The Lore

• As we touched upon with "Inferno", Barry Letts had requested that he be allowed to direct a few stories whilst producing, although it was no longer BBC practice. (In the 1950s, the distinction between "producer" and "director" was notional - the majority of television drama had the same person putting the project together and telling the cameras where to look during the broadcast. Later, it become standard BBC policy to strictly demark responsibilities. This also extended to writing, as the Writers Guild was vigilant in preventing too many writer-producers from self-commissioning. Bear this in mind for this volume and beyond.) Directing had been part of the deal when Letts was asked to become the series' caretaker (see "Doctor Who and the Silurians"), as he hoped to use the high-profile series as a shop window for his directing, then move on after his second year.

Once the immediate shock of inheriting *Doctor Who* resolved itself into mere crisis-management, Letts and Terrance Dicks decided on a shift of emphasis towards thrills-and-spills in the tradition of Saturday Morning serials. One aspect of "Inferno" that hadn't been explored was the

Doctor's alternate-universe self, if he existed at all. Maybe an evil Doctor existed somewhere? The idea, and thus the plans for the 1971 series as a whole, began to form. Better still, with the Daleks removed, the post of "regular arch-nemesis" had a vacancy. During his involvement in the initial planning for 6.7, "The War Games" (as you'll have seen, this was rather less organised than BBC Wales' strategic planning sessions), Robert Holmes had speculated that the Time Lords might not all be saints. And as soon as the idea of a bad Time Lord as a regular villain occurred, Dicks said that this guy had to have a title (ideally "The Master"), and Letts knew immediately who should play the part...

• When he was an actor, Letts had literally crossed swords with Roger Delgado, another veteran of the Alexandra Palace era of live TV drama. For hopefully obvious reasons, little of Delgado's early work remains in the archive. (His part as Conrad, the journalist in *Quatermass II* who gives his life to get the story out, is a rare exception - the film version replaces him with Sid James.) He had been Porthos in Rex Tucker's production of *The Three Musketeers* (see 3.8, "The Gunfighters; 4.1, "The Smugglers" and 9.5, "The Mutants") and any number of sinister Spaniards, wily Orientals and nefarious Arabs.

Delgado was born in Whitechapel, in the heart of the East End of London, with a Spanish father and a Belgian mother - so he could be as English as any part required. This was a two-edged sword, as typecasting kept him in work but proved frustrating. Radio was one way around this, and both prestigious dramas and factual programming (schools and religious readings being his particular fortes) used him a great deal[28]. In one series from 1966, *The Slide*, he played a scientist called Gomez. His role is fairly like Bernard Quatermass (and when the author, Victor Pemberton, used a similar premise for 5.6, "Fury from the Deep", it took very little work to make the Doctor perform the same plot-function). In the same year, Delgado was one of Charlton Heston's antagonists in *Khartoum*.

This isn't the place to go into Delgado's entire film career, so instead we'll return to television, especially ITC. Their early phase entailed making men in tights ride horses around Surrey, creating a constant need for sinister foreigners - certainly more than Warren Mitchell and Leo McKern could meet unaided. In 1962, the comparatively highbrow *Sir Francis Drake* came along (see 3.9,

"The Savages"), with a semi-regular part for Delgado as Mendoza, the Spanish Ambassador. He alternately schemed against Elizabeth I and frantically engaged on damage-limitation when others make botched attempts to stop Drake. (See "Colony In Space" later this year.) He took parts in almost all of the later spy-caper series made by Lew Grade's company, and in 1969 played a casino manager in an episode of spooky comedy-thriller *Randall and Hopkirk (Deceased)*. (In the same story, "The Ghost Who Broke the Bank at Monte Carlo", Nicholas Courtney played one of villain Brian Blessed's henchmen. It's perplexing if you watch it now.)

• It seems the plan was to revert to the more traditional male-female "kids" hanging around with the Doctor, with the Brigadier made more of a "boss". To this end, two new characters were devised to ask the Doctor stupid questions and get captured. One was a regular Captain for the Brig to liaise with, order around and have as a foil; the other was a less-educated girl sidekick, intended as a secret-agent-cum-secretary (just like the one in *Doomwatch*). Dicks has been known to suggest that girls are just in dramas to get tied to railway tracks, but he might be kidding. (We can at least hope.)

The auditions used two pieces of script. One was a mildly flirtatious banter scene with added info-dump (at least, this is how Richard Franklin recalled it later) and the other was a mood-piece about ghosts in a crypt; unsuitable to *Doctor Who*, but thought to be very effective. Mike had to protect Jo from a poltergeist that destroys anything that gets close - a fact demonstrated with a book thrown at it (see 8.5, "The Daemons"). Derrick Sherwin had previously tried to minimise the "clutter" by restricting the regular cast to just the Doctor, Liz and the Brigadier, but Letts wanted to establish a wider circle of UNIT personnel. Partly this was to add variety to the exposition and investigation scenes, but mainly it would make non-regular viewers feel more familiar with the people under threat in any given scene.

• Richard Franklin was actually the second choice to play Mike Yates. Ian Marter was front-runner, but didn't realise that it was a recurring character. He had a prior commitment, so declined. Letts nevertheless kept his contact details (see "Carnival of Monsters"; 12.1 "Robot"). Franklin, who had served in the army before university (and joined the TA afterwards), had let his hair grow (at the audition, Letts asked if he in fact had ears) and adopted a compromise hair-length shortly before filming started. It still looked longer than the regular army men who filled out big scenes, but they had the excuse that these stories were set in the future. (As it turned out, the army regulations *were* relaxed a little, in the mid-seventies.) Franklin rode a Honda 250, so Yates wound up using motorbikes a lot.

• Dozens of actresses were auditioned for the role of Jo; the two names of alternates that keep cropping up in interviews are Anouska Hemple and Shakira Baksh. This should tell you what Jo was originally intended to be like (whenever Hemple and Baksh were mentioned in the press - which was frequently back then - words like "sultry" and "sophisticated" cropped up). You may also wish to ponder how Rula Lenska (21.4, "Resurrection of the Daleks") would have handled the role had she got it.

After sitting through fifty or so fair-to-middling Diana Rigg impressions, Letts found his Jo. Katy Manning got the part after attending the wrong audition and turning up late. Although completely wrong for the character they had in mind, they rewrote Jo to suit her. Without her glasses, Manning had to vamp around what she thought the script *might* have said if she could actually read it. (Pertwee - who requested someone sufficiently short for the Doctor to be a "mother hen" to in shot - had bumped into Manning once before and thought she had the "right stuff", so her arrival suited him fine. He may even have suggested that she audition, but the memories on this point get a little hazy.) Manning kept her extreme myopia a secret until the first day of location shooting, when she ran into a tree. Subsequently, Pertwee always held her hand in chase sequences (note how much faster this story's chase is than, say, "The Sea Devils").

• Robert Holmes' starting point was a Christmas gift of a Troll doll, either German or Danish depending on who you ask. It was so hideous, he deemed it something you'd only give your worst enemy (and yet, he never said who gave it to him...). His original storyline has some intriguing differences. The Master uses a mind-control ray (he'd obviously not been cast yet) and has - get this - a "curiously ornate pocket watch" (see X3.11, "Utopia"). The circus was more prominent, being the means of dispensing the plastic flowers around the country. The trigger for their eponymous "Spray of Death" was a rise to

65° F. Dicks vetoed this, on the grounds that it was a risky limitation if the Nestene plan was solely concerned with invading Britain - "Why not just go to Morocco?", he asked. (As it turns out, Pertwee really *had* gone there, one of the perks of the new format being three months' holiday. He was astonished when a French-speaking policeman recognised "Docteur Who".) Dicks, himself off on holiday (a more traditional seaside bucket-and-spade affair) urged Holmes to deliver on time and up to the required word-count.

• Bearing in mind the change in script layout (BBC format TV scripts have the left-hand side of the page open for camera-directions), Dicks stipulated fifty pages per episode. Even today, the assumption is that a page of dialogue is about thirty seconds of screen time when produced on the standard BBC-issue typewriters (and even today, the guidelines have strict font requirements). We mention this because Holmes put in a lot of visual material that took less space to describe - episode one of "The Space Pirates" isn't much to look at on paper. Dicks had to tidy up the draft considerably, mostly to find reasons to link all the set pieces and make the action sequences distinctive. The end result is undeniably Holmes, but we have to acknowledge Dicks' hand in the storyline.

• A few final changes were made just prior to - or during - filming. (Partly this was to cover unforeseen events, and partly because Letts wasn't sure they could get regular Army back-up - an airstrike using stock footage was a better threat all round and, as we'll see, helped out with another problem.) The title "The Spray of Death" alluded to the daffodils, which now didn't arrive until episode three, and omitted the "star" monsters returning. Retitling it "Terror of the Autons" meant that episode one needed at least a cameo by the plastic men. This late addition seems to have come after the set designs were submitted (and may be the cause of the apparent continuity mess with the UNIT ammo-box). It was recorded with episode three.

• During the break, Pertwee had made an appearance in the portmanteau horror *The House That Dripped Blood* with Ingrid Pitt (see "The Time Monster") and submitted a storyline co-written with Reed de Rouen (who was Pa Clanton in 3.8, "The Gunfighters"; see also **What Else Didn't Get Made?** under 17.6, "Shada"). The filming began with the Autons handing out flowers to shoppers in Chalfont St Peter, then nearby driving scenes at

Chalfont St Giles (both in Buckinghamshire, just outside the M25 now). Curiously, the quarry used wasn't the Gerrards Cross one that traditionally doubled for alien planets, which is only two miles away. Pertwee's first day of filming was at Robert Brothers' Circus, pitched then on a patch of ground at Lea Bridge Road, Leyton. (Don't look for it now, it's a building-site and will be the Olympic stadium soon.) Pertwee knew some of the staff and got them on-screen appearances. Here the publicity photos introducing Jo and the Master were shot (so the TARDIS prop was brought along). Courtney was introduced to Manning (apparently, this is how he found out that John had left).

• In a quarry in Dunstable, Bedfordshire, Terry Walsh - appearing as the fake policeman (his first on-screen credit) - missed his footing in the fall where the UNIT car nudges an Auton over a cliff. He insisted on finishing the take before being taken to hospital. Also rushed off for X-rays was Katy Manning, who sprained her ankle (method acting?) on one of the day's first scenes. The production manager joked that she could still be replaced, which appears to have been the point when Pertwee really became protective of her. (The production manager's sister had just spent a year playing Liz Shaw, by the way.) Some rewrites explained Jo's limp (even though the studio work to accompany it came weeks later, when Manning was on her feet again). The new UNIT uniforms should, as UN military outfits, have had blue berets, but Letts was concerned about CSO sequences. These days, the real UN takes a less forgiving line and so we have the red berets of the *Unified* Intelligence Taskforce.

• Nicholas Courtney was reportedly suffering from depression at the time and needed, or so it is said, a good deal of persuading to return to the series. He'd had other acting work and some casual labour just to keep the money coming (a three-month lay-off wasn't always such a blessing as Pertwee thought). He spent much of the main day of filming at the radio telescope inside the trailer, supposedly shaking. After some frantic rewrites, the Brigadier's involvement for that day was reduced to one line, and much of the location work used Havoc's Marc Boyle as a body-double. Later on the Brigadier's dialogue was simplified, losing an explanation that the Autons, being telepathic, have to be taught how Earth's defences will deal with them, plus an argument with the Doctor about killing the Master.

• The Radio telescope was a GPO relay station near Dunstable (hence the use of the local quarry - there was a plastics factory nearby that they used later). The story's climax - the shoot-out between the newly-remodelled UNIT troops and Autons with big heads - had its share of logistical problems. The Havoc team had issues with doing falls whilst unbalanced by the Auton heads, and one solution was to use small trampolines, then time the explosions to seem as though they had sent the killer dummies somersaulting (and so that they could fall onto safety mats more precisely). This effect proved popular with kids and directors, and became the Havoc trademark stunt for *Doctor Who* (see "The Sea Devils", "Battlefield" and many others). The first attempt, apparently, caused stuntman Terry Walsh to overshoot a bit.

Havoc used a dozen men that day, a record for *Doctor Who* at the time. Letts was very concerned that the star wanted to do all of his own stunts; Pertwee was persuaded that some of the more challenging and risky ventures could cause problems if the whole shoot had to stop, drop and rush the lead actor to hospital. (Presumably the delays when Manning had been whisked off were on Letts' mind.) Pertwee accepted use of a good enough double where absolutely necessary, and so Walsh donned the cape and a wig for the scene where the Master tries to drive a bus into the Doctor. Or, at least, he did for the rear shots - Pertwee got his own way and one take *did* have the bus coming towards him at 15mph, but it was shot with a lens that foreshortened the image to make it seem a lot closer than it was. Nevertheless, Walsh henceforth became Pertwee's regular double - and by Season Eleven, the whole country knew it.

• By now, you'll have guessed that it was a lab coat-wearing Roy Scammell who fell in episode four's other big stunt (when a technican, struck by the Master, plunges to his death). Michael Wisher, returning after a shave, wore the latex mask and played possum as the dead Farrell (rather too well for comfort in one take). The radio telescope was a model taken on location for forced-perspective shots.

• 8th of October saw the first studio day. This was the start of a more concerted effort to use the studios efficiently, so it was two episodes a fortnight, on consecutive days, where possible from now on. Day one was devoted to the complex set-ups, such as McDermott's death-by-furniture (deflating was slower than inflating, so this was shot in reverse and played backwards and faster), death-by-doll (the doll costume was late and the glue was still drying - not nice under studio lights), abduction by fake police and the discovery of Goodge's body. (The latter took two hours to set up and almost another to record, and they had to try again in the second block.)

• Assorted titbits worth mentioning at this juncture... the last scene had been rewritten after comments that the first ending, where the Doctor muses that either he or the Master will be destroyed one day, was too bleak. The filmed Nestene materialisation was thought not good enough, so something similar was tried in the studio electronically. The scene of the Master's arrest caused problems, as Franklin's delivery of the line 'We've got him now' was so over the top as to cause laughter in the studio. He was granted a rare chance to redub it when the filmed scene was played onto the videotape.

• Letts availed himself of new editing facilities and began the traditional Sunday sessions during rehearsals for the second block. Many lines in the script never made it to the screen (and even if they *had* been recorded, it's unlikely they'll pop up on a DVD - the original of "Terror of the Autons" was wiped, so even the televised version will need reconstituting from other sources). In fact, Letts wound up doing a fair amount of trimming for timing purposes: the most significant cuts made include the Master's listing the itinerary, the Bowler-wearing Time Lord explaining that an alien energy field prevented attempts to imprison the Master, a scene where a policeman is killed when investigating the coach (which is why Bill McGuirk is credited for episode three - the location work for this was apparently filmed but dropped, and the matching studio sequence also went, evidently after the credit-caption had been made), the Nestene leader admonishing the Master for wasting time on his feud with the Doctor, and Benton being detailed to watch the car with the ammo-box in just in case the Master returns for it. The set-up for how the Doctor knows that the box contains a bomb was also removed.

Other cuts included: more on Goodge's hatred of eggs; the Master watching the hypnotised Jo leave and calling her '... a pretty little thing. A pity I couldn't keep her' (so his tendency to keep blondes as pets seems to go back a long way - see "The Time Monster"; "The Sound of Drums" and,

stretching a point, 19.1, "Castrovalva"). We also get a name for the plastic used in the chair ("Polynestene", of course) and the solvent used to save Jo (dimethylsulphoxide - it's a real one, look it up), plus more on Rex Farrell's skittish behaviour once he's no longer afraid of his father.

• The new system of dubbing the music on *after* final video-editing was introduced here, along with the wholly-electronically-realised scores. Doing either for the first time would be tricky, but from now until Season Eleven there will be several last-minute sprints to finish the dubbing before transmission. Monophonic synthesizers required each "instrument" to be added in turn, rather than all playing at once. Dudley Simpson opted to leave "gaps" in the score for sound-effects.

• Public reaction was mixed. Some critics thought it was getting a bit tired, the police queried the use of Auton bobbies and Labour Peer Baroness Bacon - a Home Office minister until the election months earlier - griped in a debate about Mass Communication that children "must have gone to bed and had nightmares". (She gave absolutely no proof of this - her comments came in February 1971, but her use of "recent" may mean the Pertwee era so far, not just this story.) Nevertheless, plans to bring back the Autons were laid in the 1980s (see Volumes V and VI).

8.2: "The Mind of Evil"

(Serial FFF. Six Episodes, 30th January - 6th March 1971.)

Which One is This? *Thunderball* meets *Porridge*. The Master smoothly graduates from Batman baddie to Bond villain, as the Fate of the World is determined by panto dragons and the Doctor speaks in tongues. But for *Doctor Who* fans now, "The Mind of Evil" is best remembered as "the Pertwee that's now in black and white".

Firsts and Lasts First appearance of UNIT's Corporal Bell, who's the first uniformed woman in the Brigadier's inner circle and therefore has the job of answering the telephones. First (and until eighteen years later in 26.3, "The Curse of Fenric", the only) instance of non-English dialogue translated with subtitles. And a small detail but a significant one: Harry Mailer, the arch-criminal, often begins sentences "What the hell...", "Why the hell..." and so on. (Even six months earlier, they were changing a scripted "damn" to "darned".)

At last, the Doctor is actually *called* UNIT's "scientific advisor" on screen. (The phrase will become so well-established in the novelisations that nearly five years after its last use, they can still play with it in "City of Death" (17.2). However, its absence makes Season Seven seem odd when you watch it again.)

First use of an overt on-screen "flashback" sequence (as would happen once a year in Pertwee's remaining stories, and again in the early 1980s), as the Doctor is apparently tormented by cardboard cutouts of old adversaries.

Six Things to Notice About "The Mind of Evil"...

1. As the Master's second story, and the first in which he doesn't have to share the limelight with a large number of monsters, "The Mind of Evil" gives the new Public Enemy Number One a chance to develop a proper sense of humour, letting Roger Delgado pull out all the stops in his performance. Not only does the Master get to sneer, gloat, ooze charm and poke fun at UNIT whenever possible, he also tries major-league villainy the human way, so he's even seen with a fat cigar in the back of a chauffeur-driven car and while he's deactivating the missile's fail-safe. Between this, his forged credentials and his unconvincing rubber mask, you half-expect him to say, "I love it when a plan comes together."

2. Only a few minutes of the final episode exists in a colour 525-line format, and most people seem to agree after seeing this that it's far more effective in *cine-verite* monochrome. If nothing else, the lack of colour covers a lot of potentially wonky effects. We've got what looks like a few pictures from the *Radio Times* Tenth Anniversary special being flushed down a toilet, a shed exploding and more fun with CSO as the UNIT soldiers stand in front of a photograph of a nuclear-powered missile and point at it urgently.

3. The Doctor is confronted with all of his worst fears, allegedly. These include a Zarbi (2.5, "The Web Planet"), a War Machine (3.10, "The War Machines"), Koquillion (2.3, "The Rescue") and a Silurian (7.2, "Doctor Who and the Silurians"). Perhaps his embarrassment at having been given such a hard time by such a lame array of antagonists is what gives him a coronary. It isn't until episode five that we actually witness him seeing a Dalek, although we hear someone shout-

ing 'Exterminate annihilate destroy' into a Ring Modulator on the wrong setting.

4. Three of the five cliffhangers are basically the same, with someone about to die while the Keller Machine goes a bit mental and attacks someone by making the picture go all wavy. The only real variety comes at the end of episode two, when the Keller process manifests itself as a big pink dragon (looking not unlike Big Bird), attacking a hammy American Senator in what looks like a brothel. Curiously, all of the Pertwee seasons have a clumsy rubber lizard in the second story.

5. Captain Yates' description of the (female) Chinese officer Chin Lee - 'quite a dolly' - is guaranteed to make you want to punch him. The cutesy music that accompanies her arrival, however, makes you want to punch Dudley Simpson.

6. The tie-in novels have perpetrated many irksome sentimental theories about the Master's true relationship with the Doctor but nothing said in any medium matches the insight we get here, in a script that wasn't even written with him in mind. About five minutes into episode four, the Master's biggest fear is revealed as the Doctor towering over him, laughing at him. Less celebrated, but equally intriguing, is a dissolve a few minutes later between an unconscious Doctor and a weary Master.

The Continuity

The Doctor Experiencing fear-hallucinations from the Keller machine, the Doctor sees a variety of old acquaintances: a Silurian, a Zarbi, an "Ice Lord" [6.5, "The Seeds of Death"], a Dalek, a War Machine, a Cyberman, and, um, Koquillion. [Koquillion from "The Rescue" is a minor villain by anyone's standards. However, it should be remembered that his costume was originally a form of ceremonial dress on Dido, possibly linked to Dido's Hall of Judgement, and in "The Rescue" the Doctor states that he's been to Dido before. Did the Doctor once have trouble with the law there, so much so that he feared for his life? If not, then he may just hallucinate Koquillion because it reminds him of the time right after he lost his granddaughter.] These images seem to indicate that the Third Doctor's amnesia is clearing very rapidly, although the most specific horror is a world destroyed by fire [an obvious reference to 7.4, "Inferno"]. This is described as occurring 'some time ago'.

The Doctor loses to Jo at draughts, considering

the game too simple. He prefers three-dimensional chess. He states that simple human medicine could easily kill someone with his metabolism. [Fan-lore has always maintained that the lethal pill he's offered is just an aspirin, but this isn't specified either on screen or in Terrance Dicks' novelisation. Dr Summers hands Jo the medication with a bit more import than someone doling out such a commonplace drug, and one hopes he'd prescribe something a bit more potent for someone who's been psychologically and physically tortured. Be honest: does aspirin *sound* like a credible treatment? He might as well have prescribed a cup of tea and a slice of cake.

[Incidentally, the long-standing confusion might owe to an urban myth about Bruce Lee. School playground lore has it that Lee died in 1973 after ingesting a painkiller because his body was so astonishingly highly tuned - mind you, it makes Lee seem a lot less intimidating as a martial artist if he could be felled everyday pharmacy or Mars bars. The autopsy, we now know, showed cannabis in his system; hushing that up might have added to the mystique.]

• *Ethics*. He refuses to carry a gun when it's offered, but he's prepared to immobilize the Master and leave him to die when it becomes necessary [c.f. 9.5, "The Time Monster"]. The Keller process has been worrying him ever since he heard about it. [Which means that as hinted in "Inferno", he's begun to take an active interest in the human experiments of the era. He thinks there's something "evil" about the machine, so his instincts may perhaps be warning him about either the creature inside it or the Master, even though the process is self-evidently unnatural.]

The Doctor's attempts to bargain with Mailer amount to, 'Let us go, and I'll do the best I can for you.' [In the previous story he claimed to have access to a good amount of money - was that a fib or is he just loathe to offer bribes to convicts?] He chides the Brigadier for cutting it a bit close in saving him and Jo from the hardened convict Mailer, but expresses no reservation about the Brig shooting the man dead. And at story's end, when Jo laments that their actions got Barnham killed, the Doctor sharply says, 'How do you think I feel?'

• *Inventory*. Jo carries the Doctor's UNIT pass as well as her own [which is how it's going to be from now on].

• *Background*. The Doctor states that he's been a scientist for 'several thousand -' before breaking off. [See "Doctor Who and the Silurians", for more on his apparent age.]

The Doctor speaks the Chinese dialect of Hokkien, and says it's been a while since he's had the chance to use it. He claims to have shared conversations with Mao Tse Tung, and to have been given leave to use Mao's personal name [but since Chairman Mao must *surely* represent so many things that the Doctor can't stand, he could be bluffing to impress his Chinese host]. He also claims to have been in a cell in the Tower of London with Sir Walter Raleigh during the reign of Elizabeth I [in 1592], when Raleigh kept going on about potatoes.

He seems to have some prior experience of the type of mind parasite found inside the Keller Machine. It takes him a remarkably short time to deduce that people are being killed by phobias, as if he expected that this would happen. [He's also unfazed by someone drowning from water that spontaneously manifests in the victim's body - strangely, he seems to forget all of this by X3.2, "The Shakespeare Code", when it happens again and he claims never to have seen the like. (Although technically, the Third Doctor doesn't *witness* the prison drwoning.) The same story has him claiming that he hasn't met Queen Bess (even though 9.2, "The Curse of Peladon" hints that he attended her coronation), although it's possible he just means that he hasn't met her in his tenth incarnation.]

The Supporting Cast

• *Jo Grant*. She's already fiercely loyal to the Doctor, considering him a genius. She's no longer calling anyone in UNIT "sir" [so it's possibly a while since "Terror of the Autons"; see **History**]. Jo's been trained to use guns, or so the Doctor claims. As has already become a habit, she disobeys the Doctor's instructions to keep away from dangerous situations.

• *UNIT*. It's again suggested that UNIT takes its orders from Geneva. UNIT HQ / the Brigadier uses the call sign 'Jupiter'; Yates is 'Venus' [perhaps to disguise UNIT's involvement in this diplomatically-sensitive bomb-disposal]. Corporal Bell wears an RAF uniform with skirt, which is a shade of blue-grey [it's clearly the same she wears in the next story, where we can see it in colour] and totally unlike any other UNIT uniform ever seen. [We assume she's on attachment, hence her short tenure.] UNIT has a forensic team, a little more

How Does "Evil" Work?

In stories like "The Mind of Evil", we've been presented with a nice easy Mediaeval world view. There's Good, there's Evil, neither can be converted and both are states of being.

Yet as the programme veered away from reason and empiricism as its guiding principles - the Doctor's morality became less a choice we could all have made and instead became part of his being a Time Lord (and still later on, perhaps something more) - the matter became more complicated. Even so, a definite cut-off point could be found. You judged beings by whether they considered the consequences of their actions on others. (Save, of course, God-like aliens who could do pretty much what they wanted, simply because explaining them would remove some of their puissance and mystery - see 13.3, "Pyramids of Mars".)

Almost all the 60s and 70s stories took this basic line: "evil" was simply knowing what "good" was and not doing it (allowing that "good" altered a little from case to case). By the 1980s, this emphasis on ethical standards was rather passé and we got things which were bad because, well, they were bad. Eric Saward's term as script editor re-used old monsters partly to avoid explaining why they were doing such terrible things to people. In the tie-in books, this became all-out Manichaeanism. The Universe contained things left over from a previous Creation, and these affected conscious beings into doing otherwise motiveless and Laws-of-Physics-defying spectacular wickedness, even as "our" Universe created moral antibodies. This looked like a good fit, until the BBC Wales series deployed a story (see X2.08-2.09, "The Impossible Planet" / "The Satan Pit") that seemingly removed this from the table, whilst providing an incarnation of all bad things that had no other explanation. However, a later story in *The Sarah Jane Adventures* put this notion back onto the agenda ("The Secrets of the Stars").

It's worth noting in passing that the usual TV space-opera equation of having a body to being fallible breaks down in *Doctor Who* almost from the word "go" (or, if you prefer, "exterminate!"). Invisible aliens are mischievious, capricious or downright bad. Disembodied minds are corrupting influences. Even when people are "purified" and develop psi-powers, they're not above being petty or vindictive (see 9.4, "The Mutants"). Thus the Gnostic idea, that all matter is wretched and only the spirit is holy, is rejected as bosh.

In the specific case of "The Mind of Evil", most of the 'evil' impulses being removed form the Stangmoor Prison criminals seem identical to the effects of testosterone. Admittedly Jo also feels the alien's effects, but women still have some testosterone sloshing around - it just isn't out of balance with oestrogen like those of us with defective X chromosomes, causing facial hair and an interest in Airfix kits.

However, for this story to work, "evil" has to be *more* than the absence of "good". It has to have a substance, which can be extracted and fed to an alien mind-parasite in a popcorn machine. This is admittedly far easier for children to take in than a disquisition on the contingency of moral autonomy or the Kantian Categorical Imperative, but it causes problems for all subsequent stories where a character has to undergo a change of heart (or "turn good", as it's commonly known). If this substance is innate in all humans, then is it found in every conscious species? Does it, as it might perhaps seem, form a necessary part of consciousness? Is it finite, in which case a population explosion would diminish the amount of evil per capita, or is it self-replicating? How can characters undergo changes of heart, if the innate evil is unassailable within the head (or wherever) of the individual?

Compounding this issue, *Doctor Who* is often about redemption - so an idea that people are genetically "bad" seems out of keeping. (When they *are* that way, they generally cease being "people" and become forces of chaos, i.e. "monsters". We'll pick this idea up in Volume VII.) Even when entire species are shown to be irredeemable, it's because of perfectly understandable motives linked to their survival as a race. Only *one* being has ever actually proclaimed itself to be evil (Sutekh, in "Pyramids of Mars"). Heck, even the alleged Devil ("The Satan Pit") declines to actually say, "I'm doing this because I'm Ba-a-a-aad, mwah-ha-ha!". In that story, though, the previous handy explanation - different laws of physics from before time began - is explicitly discounted. So what, then, is the Keller alien eating?

The clue may lie in the way the alien develops the ability to teleport. In the early 70s, such a skill was routinely assumed to be proof of the mind's operation outside three-dimensional space. (Any number of ITV shows that state this as fact; *The Tomorrow People* and *Space: 1999* are the least unwatchable at present.) "Mind" can exist without

continued on page 117...

professional than the one in 7.3, "The Ambassadors of Death".

• *The Brigadier.* Has the power to put D-notices on the press, and he's a crack shot in a crisis. Disguised as a delivery man during UNIT's assault on the prison, he's forced to pretend to be cockney and doesn't look at all comfortable. He has the right to supervise murder investigations (giving the police a 'courtesy call' about it). He backs the Doctor to the hilt regarding his recommendation that the Keller Machine be destroyed, and yet again ["The Ambassadors of Death"] is seen shooting opponents.

• *Captain Yates.* Shot at, captured and ridiculed by the Brigadier, yet he still charms his way around logistical problems. He can ride motorbikes, but doesn't know about the Doctor's Venusian Karate. [It's interesting that he seems on the verge of dragging the Doctor to an assignment by force, instead of just telling him, "There's been a murder."]

• *Sergeant Benton*: Shot at, zapped by psychic forces, left for dead twice and yelled at by the Brig but then put in charge of Her Majesty's Prison, Stangmoor - a busy 36 hours for him. As with "The Invasion" (6.3), the Brigadier's got him on surveillance duties - until he faints under the influence of Chin Lee's whammy, after which Benton volunteers to join the assault on Stangmoor as a kind of memorial to Captain Yates (who's believed to be dead).

The Supporting Cast (Evil)

• *The Master.* Here he shows his talent for gaining the confidence of the establishment, as it's been nearly a year since he installed the Keller Machine at Stangmoor Prison. Chin Lee, a victim of his hypnosis, has a small metal implant under her ear which keeps her under his control when he's not around. The device can also transmit and amplify the power of the Keller Machine through the wearer's mind. The Master himself is still disguising himself with face-masks, and he's clearly acquired some wealth on Earth. He can out-arm-wrestle a hardened criminal without difficulty. It's not clear where the mind parasite in the Keller Machine comes from. [The Master's apparently been trapped on Earth since "Terror of the Autons", so he must have had it in his TARDIS for some time, waiting for a rainy day.]

The Master's greatest fear, exposed by the Machine, is the Doctor. The hallucination of the Doctor he sees is a mocking one, and appears larger-than-life, suggesting that the Master has a serious inferiority complex [his claim in "Terror of the Autons", that the Doctor is *almost* his equal, isn't something he really believes]. Here his motive for triggering a World War has to be a mixture of spite and megalomania.

His TARDIS has an outside phone line [does he dial "9" first?] and he uses a trimphone handset [see also X1.5, "World War Three" and X3.13, "Last of the Time Lords", the latter being the same prop John Simm used so often in *Life on Mars*].

The Non-Humans

• *The Keller Machine.* The device used to remove all traces of aggression from convicts is an alien 'mind parasite', attached to a Master-created control mechanism. It looks like a pulsating brain once it's exposed. The Doctor implies there's more than one of these creatures in the universe, and states that they're incredibly resilient, although an atomic explosion or a massive electrical discharge can kill them.

The British authorities believe the Keller Machine can suck "evil" out of people's minds, but the Doctor initially doesn't believe a word of it. However, anyone subjected to the creature under controlled conditions *does* apparently lose the ability to hate or hurt, and the Doctor concedes that the creature 'feeds on the evil of the mind'. [It's some kind of psychic energy generated by "evil", rather than an actual substance; see this story's essay.] He also describes it, with typical melodrama, as the greatest threat to humanity since the beginning of time.

The more "evil" the Machine takes, the stronger it gets, and it eventually gains the ability to teleport over short distances in search of new victims. Those it attacks experience hallucinatory terror and die of fear, but the hallucinations must in some way be corporeal, as a victim with a fear of drowning has water in his lungs and a victim with a fear of rats has scratches on his skin. [This is so much like the Carrionites' activities in "The Shakespeare Code", it would be remarkable if no connection existed. The Master must have paid more attention in history lessons at the Time Lord Academy than the Doctor, hence the events in 8.5, "The Daemons" and "The Time Monster".] Other people can witness these horrors, the Doctor describing the effect as 'collective hallucination'.

The Doctor momentarily restrains the creature

How Does "Evil" Work?

...continued from page 115

"matter" in such situations, which is why the absorption of mind-power allows the Keller Machine to break the usual laws of physics. This might also explain how people abnormally aged or youthened by temporal seepage retain their basic personality and memories (see 9.5, "The Time Monster"; 18.1, "The Leisure Hive"). The point is that despite the number of affable machines and wise computers in *Doctor Who*, no-one ever disputes the existence of the soul. (Nobody, that is, save the Master when he's disguised as a trendy vicar - see 8.5, "The Daemons"). Indeed, for possession to happen with the depressing regularity it does in mid-70s *Doctor Who*, this has to be a given.

A *bigger* clue, though, comes in the apparently contradictory phenomenon seen in the first two episodes of "The Mind of Evil", in which the Keller Machine's victims experience stigmata-like physical manifestations of psychic states. The psychic force affects the body, but not vice versa. Curiously, since we wrote the first version of this essay, we've seen an identical (or near enough) occurrence of this phenomenon: the Carrionites (X3.2, "The Shakespeare Code"), with their DNA-matching voodoo dolls and a remarkably similar drowning-on-dry-land gag, offer the notion that they were exiled from our dimension at the beginning of time, and use a conceptual version of Block Transfer Computation (see 18.7, "Logopolis"). This allows us to retain the original suggestion that "evil" is the psychic residue of a leftover prior state of matter, even though the old explanation for this has been firmly kyboshed. (See **What's Wrong with the Centre of the Earth?** under 7.4, "Inferno"

for more.)

However, this *still* lacks the idea of there being any element of choice and, as the Carrionites were inadvertently released by Shakespeare but didn't "infect" anyone else (something of a shame, since a story where Emperor Rudolph II of Prague or some similar power-mad occultist was blighted and became some kind of Sith Lord would be the logical outcome), we have to restrict ourselves to noting similarities rather than establishing a definite link. They select Shakespeare and Peter Street for their abilities, but aren't actively sought.

What's curious is that although whatever the Carrionites did belongs in the same category of things-antithetical-to-the-order-of-the-universe as Huon particles (X3.0, "The Runaway Bride") and black holes with cat-flaps, this *otherness* makes them "foreign" rather than "evil" as the term is usually understood. (Mind, in BBC Wales *Doctor Who* and its derivatives - *Torchwood* especially - these often amount to the same thing.) As we'll see (see **Does This Universe Have an Ethical Standard?** under 12.1, "Robot"), this runs counter to the rather more enlightened morality of the pre-1989 series - or, at least, the 60s and 70s adventures. "The Mind of Evil", like the Doctor's notorious speech about fighting evil in "The Moonbase" (4.6), prefigures the BBC Wales approach. In order to keep good faith with the series' overall moral tendencies (evident in stories such as 12.4, "Genesis of the Daleks"; 14.5, "The Robots of Death" and 16.2, "The Pirate Planet" to name but three clear examples), it's perhaps best to assume that the alien *did* feed on testosterone, but that censorship intervened.

---

with a loop of wire that channels electric current that alternates on much the same frequencies as the beta rhythms of the human brain. The creature is more effectively rendered harmless and immobilised when a subject who's already been drained of his "evil" is present to act as a screen. However, the prisoners at Stangmoor become more aggressive when it attacks and start to roll around in agony when things get too intense.

History

• *Dating*. [Mid-1972. The Master installed the Keller Machine at Stangmoor 'nearly a year' ago, and was posing as Emil Keller some time before that, which suggests that it's been that long since

"Terror of the Autons". Lance Parkin's *AHistory* suggests that the line about the machine being installed nearly a year prior is a leftover from an earlier draft of the script which didn't feature the Master. Careless of the script editor, you might think, but not implausible. Anyway, it's there. There's a possible way around this, but not everyone will like it - see **What's the UNIT Timeline?** under "The Daemons".]

UNIT have been entrusted [by the UN?] with the politically sensitive tasks of policing the World Peace Conference and disposing of a Thunderbolt missile. [So its original mandate to investigate 'new and unusual menaces to mankind' has been stretched, although right back in "The Invasion" it swiftly moved from investigation to armed response with no political repercussions.] The Thunderbolt is nuclear-powered [so probably recent] and contains nerve gas - something that's been illegal, the Master tells us, for many years. Evidently, the British Army can't be involved with this - even the act of disposing it, it seems - but British-trained soldiers with UNIT uniforms can.

The main flashpoint in global affairs is, apparently, between the US and China. Senator Alcott's greatest fear is a hallucination of a "Chinese dragon", as opposed to, say, "the Russian Bear" or something representing Cuba [unless the dragon is the result of a phobia about the Welsh].

Mao Tse Tung [as it was still spelled then] is still leader of China [putting this story well before his death 1976].

The Analysis

Where Does This Come From? (For our thoughts on the geopolitical tensions of this period, see 9.1, "Day of the Daleks".)

No proper analysis of "The Mind of Evil" can occur without considering how Britain had rethought prisoner rehabilitation with regard to ethics and the options opened up by science. It's a long and complicated tale... we *could* try contrived puns about consecutive sentences and strapping yourselves in, but life's too short. That's another one. Sorry.

In this period, there were a large number of people (mainly over forty) who contended that society had gone wrong with all these uncontrollable young people running around doing what they wanted. If techniques existed to make people buy drinks they hadn't hitherto wanted, what *else* could the brainwashers do? Since the advent of the Teddy-Boys (see 24.3, "Delta and the Bannermen"), the press had been periodically full of horrifying tales of each new youth cult.

Meanwhile older thugs (such as the Kray Twins) seemed to have such sway that imprisonment simply meant their organisation would pay fewer utility bills. Rumours did the rounds that more - shall we say - "pro-active" forms of rehab were being trialled in jails. Vacaville Prison, California, was the centre of stories never quite disproved - former inmates told wild tales of doping with Pemoline (AKA Cylert, an ADHD drug now withdrawn) and something with the too-good-to-be-true acronym M.I.N.D. (the Magnetic Integrated Neuron Duplicator), a gadget that supposedly altered the subject's behaviour and political opinions. Such details were given some credence, as it was known that the US government wasn't above such things. The experiments conducted in the 1950s with LSD 25 are notorious (not to mention hilarious, in the case of British soldiers dosed as part of precautionary tests here, then sent out on manoeuvres - there's footage of this), but they were only the tip of the iceberg

We'll pick up on this shortly, but one thing made British prisons a bit different. Almost all of the major prison reforms had taken place in the previous century and a half. The threat of sending people to Australia had worked, but the cost of shipping was in fact too high, so other means had to be found and applied nationally. Elizabeth Fry, a social reformer / Christian philanthropist, had campaigned to outlaw various inhumane practices against women prisoners, arguing that prison in itself was the deterrent. Another prison reformer, John Howard, had earlier (around the 1780s) managed to outlaw jailers from charging payment to inmates for food and blankets.

So the focus of carceral procedure was definitely shifting towards rehabilitation, but hardened criminals required drastic methods. It was the prevailing belief that you could tell "criminal tendencies" through physical markers; just as a woman whose big toe was more than a certain distance from her other toes would destined for prostitution or moral dereliction so - through the insights of the "science" of Phrenology - you could measure the bumps on someone's head and tell if s/he was destined to murder someone if given the chance. What, then, do you do with all these people? The obvious answer was to lock them up just in case, and stop them reproducing if they hadn't already, but this wasn't practical.

As the new Social Science movement grew in influence, the more progressive thinkers advocated a process of conditioning, rather like puppy-training. It was also, curiously, like joining a monastery. Hardened criminals, for whom the shock of imprisonment had little effect, were originally isolated. When mixing with others, they wore hoods to prevent conversation. This instigates the whole idea of haircuts and special prison uniforms, to symbolically remove the convict from his previous life and thus break bad habits such as killing people. The worst offenders were set pointless tasks to tire and bore them - they walked on giant wheels, unpicked rope (oakem) and (when the idea of prisons becoming cost-effective caught on after the 1865 and 1877 Prison Acts) sewed mail-bags.

They also had dull, high-carbohydrate, low-protein meals (like the notorious "confinement loaf" used in US prisons since the 80s) to slacken them physically and bore them into compliance. It was widely believed - but there's scant evidence to confirm this - that prison tea contained some form of bromide, a chemical to counteract testosterone and make inmates more compliant. True or not, the very *thought* that they'd been drugged did most of the work. The idea was to condition the convict by first depleting major criminals of status, then make their previous lives seem abstract and unreal. Through this thoroughly British combination of stodgy food, existential angst and strong fashion statements, the shocking rise in serious crimes committed (the first half of the nineteenth century had seen a near-doubling) was halted and eventually reversed.

After World War II, Criminal Psychology gained in influence. In this phase, this notion of self-reinvention as a "cure" for criminality was given a boost, with prisons more inclined to retrain people for careers - the assumption being that most criminals were criminals because they'd missed out on schooling. The further assumption was that convicts were sentenced to be redeemed. (See **Does The Universe Have An Ethical Standard?** under 12.1, "Robot" for more in nineteenth-century British thinking on prisons and its bearing on the Time Lords.) Of course, the *real* solution, we were told, was to find ways to make the population at-large more at ease and less prone to criminal acts. As we'll see (24.2, "Paradise Towers"), this thinking fed into urban planning just as it had earlier been part of the entire cultural project of Britain (see **Did The BBC Actually Like *Doctor Who*?** under 3.8, "The Gunfighters").

So now we reach the 1970s. A large part of the rhetoric in "The Mind of Evil" applies what we all thought was happening in America to a British context. Europe viewed crime as a social problem, but the medicalisation of crime, making it something that could be dosed away, fitted a *perceived* tendency among Americans to think that one could fix unhappiness through chemicals, or by lying on a couch and saying bad things about your parents. To European (and especially British) eyes, this looked like an attempt to "cure" people of

their souls. You might as well take a pill to stop it raining.

When applied here, the American model led to all those Valium zombies (see 4.2, "The Tenth Planet"). The links between therapy and brain-washing seemed fairly obvious, with both the Soviet use of "mental hospitals" for dissidents and the American cult EST using interrogation techniques to destroy the personality and rebuild it to the specifications of the "therapist". We heard rumours of worse to come.

We knew *some* of what follows, and the rest confirmed our worst suspicions. You'll recall from "The Macra Terror" (4.7) that the thin lines between advertising, social psychology, neurology and brainwashing theories were occasionally crossed. In recent years, we've found out how frequently CIA funding accompanied such a line-crossing, but at the time, the fear of what *might* have been possible did a lot more work for interested parties than the proven techniques, such as they were.

But the story of this story *really* starts with the Korean War, and the number of US pilots who not only confessed to doing illegal and naughty things but *stuck to the same details* when they returned home. As US pilots were self-evidently blameless (well, those were more innocent times), the public and various Pentagon types reasoned some kind of voodoo had been performed. The appearance of the head of the Hungarian Church (Cardinal Mindszenty) at the Nazi war trials - apparently while doped up to the eyeballs and zombified - confirmed to many that the evil commies had developed something that was to psychology what the atom bomb was for warfare. Following this, a survey indicated that by the standard definitions, over half of Americans had some kind of undiagnosed mental illness. (Please note, however, that the survey was weighted so that feeling a bit grumpy or frustrated was "wrong" rather than just indicating that one was grown-up, and of course necessitated treatment.) The pharmaceutical industry went into overdrive and produced wonder drugs to "cure" everyone. The result: an epidemic of numbed addicts.

After a century of well-documented head trauma cases triggering personality changes or the loss of a specific ability, the idea took hold that some bits of the brain were autonomous and dedicated. Surgery on the "afflicted" area would cure someone of being violent, oversexed, depressed or just awkward. From 1940 to 1970, this - of course -

meant prefrontal lobotomy. And we can't help but notice that the originator of this technique, Dr Sarles, is from Switzerland - the supposed home of Emil Keller. Almost all of the adverse effects we see in Barnham are those routinely associated with lobotomy patients. (The Soviet Union outlawed this practice in 1950, saying it contravened "the principles of Humanity". When Joe Stalin says something's inhumane, it's time for a rethink.)

Naturally, this all makes 1970 an interesting time for "The Mind of Evil" to have been written. Whilst the advent of thorazine slowed down the rate of surgical interventions, enough was happening for the ones that *didn't* work to become part of popular culture. However, the most spectacular failures were hushed up until long after this. Remember those CIA tests of LSD? One of the students who acted as a guinea-pig was Ken Kesey - he of the Merry Pranksters and their psychedelic schoolbus. Although the film version of *One Flew Over the Cuckoo's Nest* changed significant details and came four years after this story, the book (1962) was a bestseller and made the equation between enforced lobotomy and the US government's treatment of dissent part of the mainstream.

Of course, it would be inconceivable that any American university or hospital should conduct experiments against someone's will to alter their minds, so they paid a Canadian hospital to do it for them. Dr Ewen Cameron was well-respected enough in his field for the press to praise anything he did. It took decades before the full story of "Psychic Driving" came out, by which time many of the components were in the public domain. The use of tapes when sleeping was commonplace by 1970 (again, see "The Macra Terror"), but they were part of an entire CIA project called "MKULTRA". This sought to rebuild people's minds from scratch after "depatterning" them with various drugs and excessive ECT. (That's "excessive" according to the guidelines set out by the British psychiatrists Page and Russell, whose own use of the technique is now notorious - thirty times the present recommended strength.) So pretty much all of the ideas floating around about conditioning hardened convicts had at least a veneer of credibility.

But Dr Harold Wolff (CIA director Allen Dulles' head of research into mind-control techniques in the early 50s), was unconvinced that any Sino-Soviet technological breakthrough - say, a hypno-ray or pill - really existed. At least, he thought that privately; the official line was that the Free World had to be vigilant against subversion, infiltration and mental domination of any kind. It was becoming clear that each nation's method of altering a subject's personality was culturally specific. The Russians used police interrogation techniques known the world over, just a bit more diligently (sleep-deprivation, beatings and solitary confinement, taken to extremes in Siberia); the Chinese exerted slow, relentless social sanctions to remove the subject's self-worth and status. Logically, then, the US went down the path of psychoanalysis and pills.

And the European method of personality modification? As a rule, it's to be up-front and say, "Here is what the experts recommend... you may disagree, but the consequences are all on your own head". They issued messages about the potential benefits of compliance, such as wealth and acceptance and getting the girl / boy. Britain in particular has specialised in installing a mental Mary Poppins in everyone's head saying, "I wouldn't do that if I were you". Our advertising has traditionally been just a shade more subtle and socially-specific than anyone else's. The wartime Ministry of Information (Orwell's "Minitru") became the Central Office of Information, makers of the TV spots persuading us to cross the road safely ("Splink") and to try not to drive after drinking. And in general, it does so through the longest-established social sanction: jokes. It's entirely aimed at mass movements.

But actually "depatterning" individuals (rather than writing books and TV shows about it), never really caught on here as a concept - possibly because the Wartime legacy of telling ourselves "We won't be swayed" took decades to wear off, but *mainly* because we were too busy giving rather intensive attention to people from other countries who tried bombs and bullets instead of infiltration and subversion. Observe the effect of Barnham (whose "evil" impulses the Keller Machine extracts) on Mailer: death doesn't scare him, but being made into someone else - even someone nicer - reduces him to panic. Not being swayed by the mob is considered a good thing here, especially in countries where sheep-like conformity has previously caused bad things to happen.

It was the "eccentrics" who gave Britain the Industrial Revolution, penicillin, the Bouncing Bomb, television, steam trains blah blah, and

France can point to as many similar figures. To fully comprehend how European "The Mind of Evil" is, imagine a 1971 film version made in America: Barnham would be some kind of messiah-figure, totally mellowed-out and able to scare monsters by being so Zen. Jon Voigt would probably play him, and James Taylor would provide the music.

(Hmmm... there's a thought. The wide-eyed Barnham is named "George", and becomes a gentle giant after the Keller process mentally castrates him. His former associate Vosper is a short, crafty man called "Lenny". Has someone tried to pull a switch on Steinbeck? And isn't it about now that Norman Mailer starts writing about convicts?)

Oh, all right, let's talk about *A Clockwork Orange*. The book was written in 1962 as a rejoinder to earlier suggestions that criminal behaviour by the British youth was somehow a medical problem. Much of it is a fairly mechanical set of inversions - so instead of rock music, it's Beethoven; instead of American slang, it's a corrupted Russian argot; instead of coffee-bars, it's milk-bars and so on. One of the more interesting things about it is that Your Humble Narrator is largely doing the police's job for them. He keeps other wannabe terrors in their place, controls his own gang's activities and only becomes a public menace when a raid organised by someone else as a means of setting him up goes wrong. He only hurts his own and he's good to his mother.

British readers will know where this is going: he's a one-man Kray brothers. The thing to remember about the Krays - vain, well-connected hoodlums who had official portraits by David Bailey, and may or may not have had boyfriends in high places (*A Clockwork Orange* alludes to this rumour by having Alex live in a tenement named after Lord Boothby, Ronnie Kray's one-time lover[30]) - is that their reign of terror in East London ended with the dominant twin Ronnie getting sent to Broadmoor, a hospital for the criminally insane. Ronnie was the bisexual one, and we note that the author, Anthony Burgess, reported hearing the phrase "as queer as a clockwork orange" in Bethnal Green, home of the Krays. 1950's "treatments" for homosexuality included chemical injections supposed to remedy introspection - this was, of course, the first symptom of the condition, along with reading books, listening to slow music and pondering mortality.

Even in the early 1970s, we're still in the tail-end of the Behaviourist school of psychiatric treatment, with glorified versions of puppy-training and anything which can "correct" abnormalities such as homosexuality (still classified as an illness by the American Psychiatric Association until 1974), depression and anxiety. After the 1957 Wolfenden Committee report on the "problem" of homosexuals, attempts were made to go for testosterone treatments to remove such side effects, whilst retaining the services of the bright chaps who displayed them.

Burgess, though, seems to have thought that any attempt to alter someone, for *whatever* reason, smacked of the law playing God. Even before the film of his book came out, he was on television discussing the apparent links between criminal deviance, sexual deviance and state repression. Before Kubrick made the image of Malcolm McDowell in a bowler and mascara the standard image of "ultraviolence", those people who'd read the book assumed that the Nadsats were Mods (see 2.7, "The Space Museum"), the early 60s youth-cult whose obsession with style and staying up all hours made their rivals allege that they were all "nancy boys". The media hysteria over a fight at Brighton between Mods and Rockers kicked off the constant pressure on successive Home Secretaries to "do something" about youth and find a way to condition people into behaving themselves... which is where we came in.

Things That Don't Make Sense So we've got an action-thriller story in which the Master embarks upon not one but *two* hugely flawed dastardly plans that go beyond all realms of sense when performed simultaneously. Let's go through this slowly, shall we?

Dastardly Plan No. 1: the Keller Machine. It's got a strange backstory. The most evil person in the Universe is stuck on Earth at the moment, but apparently he's got a being which feeds on evil and which he can't control very well. Did he have it lying around in his TARDIS on the off chance that it might come in useful, despite the obvious risk to himself? If so, why doesn't it feed off *him*, making him go all Zen, and learn to hop around the world? [Perhaps it did. Compared to "Terror of the Autons", the Master comes off as a loveable loser in most of his later appearances. Watch "The Time Monster" and 10.3, "Frontier in Space" and see how cuddly and unthreatening he is. Maybe the alien siphoned off his mojo.]

It gets worse: the Master has allowed the mind-parasite to become unstable by letting it feast upon the bad vibes of major criminals in Switzerland. That's *Switzerland*, where the prisons are full of tax-dodgers and parking-offenders. Anyway, we're told that 112 prisoners have been Kellerized - are there *that* many hardened convicts in Switzerland period? [That said, it's hard to know what to make of Professor Kettering's line: 'The machine has been used very successfully in Switzerland. One-hundred and twelve cases have been processed to date.' Option A is that the 112 treatments were actually split between Switzerland and Stangmoor, partly because it's hard to believe that the Keller Machine has been pointlessly left sitting at Stangmoor for a year just gathering dust, with the alien starving. This would also mean that the Master instigated the Keller scheme more like two years ago, and then the gap between this story and "Terror of the Autons" gets even more loopy. Option B is that the details about the machine's trial runs in Switzerland are purely invented, part of the Master's faked cover story. Either way...]

We know that at worst, it only takes the combined malignancy of a mere 112 prisoners and Barnham to give the alien the power to teleport. And the Master is deluded enough to think he can control this thing? Logic would dictate that the use of the machine in the UK - and in a prison with hundreds or more violent offenders - would probably make the creature unstoppable, but the Master diligently makes sure that the Government installs it in Stangmoor anyway. Does the phrase "All You Can Eat" ring a bell?

Dastardly Plan No. 2: the Thunderbolt Missile. The Master is planning to use Thunderbolt to trigger a nuclear war, and thereby destroy the planet on which he is trapped. His TARDIS is inoperative. Unless he's carrying the Ship around on his person, it's highly unlikely that he could escape the scheduled atomic holocaust. He's not thought this one through, has he? [Maybe he's *counting* on the Time Lords spotting a major mess-up of cosmic history and sending someone to fix it, allowing him to hijack a functioning TARDIS. Or is that too sensible for him?]

Dastardly Plans in Collision: the Master uses the Keller Machine to assault the delegates at the peace conference, thus linking the attacks to Stangmoor prison for the Doctor's benefit, when he could have just given Chin Lee a gun and told her to shoot people instead. [He seems to like showing off. Just try and imagine all the more effi-

cient ways he could take over Earth or the cosmos if he refrained from trying to impress the Doctor.] Anyway, having the Machine present runs the risk that the Master's private militia will get Kellered into submission, and - when the time comes - break off from shooting at UNIT to pick flowers and sing Cat Stevens songs.

[By the by, in episode one it's said that the Keller Machine is "65%" full of evil impulses. Even if the Master installed this gauge just for show, why does nobody think to ask what will happen when the Machine gets "full"? If 112 is 65%, then plenitude is forty hoodlum-brains away, assuming that everyone "treated" is equally evil. If some of the Swiss patients were library-fine defaulters, then a couple more like Barnham would have made it a pressing concern.]

Aiding the Master we have the hypnotized Chin Lee. She taps the Keller Machine via remote and kills people by staring at them, but she *also* pointlessly steals and destroys secret plans that the Master doesn't actually want, thus risking exposure and putting the Master's goals at risk. [After all, if she's caught, she'll be unavailable for whammy-duties.] Besides, if she *must* make dire asseverations that everyone else is stealing secret documents, you'd think she *might* - even under hypnosis - avoid setting fire to those very documents in public, in a park, within sight of UNIT's current base and surrounded by kids. Even her chauffeur is watching. Conversely, for the Doctor to work out the connection between the Keller process and Chin Lee, there can only be a single Chinese girl in the whole of Britain. [Even in 1971, this was a bit of a stretch.] It's also rather curious, with Chin Lee wearing the Keller transmission device, that Fu Peng never thinks to ask his assistant, "What's that on your neck?"

A side note while we're on the topic of espionage: the Master here uses the *exact same disguise* he deployed against Captain Yates in the previous story, even though UNIT must have surely deduced how the killer phone-flex got in the Doctor's lab. [Then again, Mike would probably recognise him better from behind...] It's not even convincing this time around, actually looking like a man wearing a mask (as opposed to them bringing back Norman Stanley to play the Telephone Mechanic). Then he removes his disguise and exits a GPO tent *as himself*, in full view of UNIT's base of operations, and walks into a waiting limo right under UNIT's noses. And because he evidently hasn't provided the heroes with enough clues, he leaves his fiendishly impenetrable rubber mask behind in the tent.

Senator Alcott's "biggest fear" is revealed as the Chinese [so of course he's the best man to send to a Peace Conference], yet when Chin Lee invites him to her suite, he goes unarmed and without any of his aides. (And what's up with the flickering lights in the room, seen even before Alcott arrives? In some measure this looks like a spooky manifestation of Chin Lee's power, but watch long enough, and it's as if the Chinese delegation hasn't paid their utility bill. Or maybe they've got him a room above an all-night tattoo-parlour.) Then Alcott is psychically assaulted, and the "Chinese dragon" menacing him looks like the kind of book-end you get in novelty shops. If this represents his "greatest fear", then he must hide at the end of February when the news is full of Chinese New Year dragon malarkey, and absolutely mess himself if he ever goes to a British theatre at Christmas and sees *Mother Goose*.

UNIT are in charge of security at the conference, at which the fate of the world will be decided, yet their CO drops everything to dress up as a delivery-man while most of his staff are unconscious or in combat. So does that leave Corporal Bell to handle every *other* possible threat to mankind? It's as if invading aliens are considerate to the point of forming an orderly queue. [On the Dark Side of the Moon? Do they need to clock in?] Had the Bandrils attacked Earth this week, we'd have been stuffed. Also, the Brigadier doesn't believe an assault on Stangmoor prison would work because you'd 'need an army' to get in. And he doesn't call the army because...?

Consider that Thunderbolt is a nuclear-powered gas missile. Once it's hijacked, the goodies intend to make it self-destruct, thus spreading fallout and nerve-gas across the Home Counties, and rather conspicuously announcing its existence on the eve of a peace conference... yet Jo and the Doctor are perfectly safe, despite being in a helicopter above Ground Zero. [As we'll see, Terrance Dicks changed this ending to make more sense than the one Houghton wrote.]

A round up of lingering details: having been locked alone in a cell for at least an hour or more, Jo "suddenly remembers" that the contents of her scattered breakfast are still on the floor. Episode three ends with the Master wishing to see how long the Doctor can hold out against the Keller Machine, but in doing so, he *leaves the room*.

What's to stop the Machine from killing the Doctor while he's out? Yes, that would eliminate a mortal enemy, but he wants the Doctor to help him restrain the parasite.

Later, the Master tells the tied-up Captain Yates that he bought and paid for some 'mercenaries' to hijack Thunderbolt for him (see **The Lore** for why this happened). Is he lying just to keep Yates in the dark? Captain Yates, having successfully followed the missile-snatchers back to their lair, gets himself captured because he insists on sneaking for a closer look. What exactly about this scenario was so unclear that he needed a better viewpoint?

Episode five opens with the Keller Machine sparing the Doctor and Jo to go in hot pursuit of Mailer... so why *doesn't* it catch and kill him? Anyway, Mailer is such a hard-case that he scratches his nose and musses his hair with a loaded revolver. He also waves it around for emphasis when trying to impress the Doctor with how worldly-wise he is. Later, after freeing itself from the Doctor's electrical loop, the Keller Machine kills two prison guards - as opposed to just teleporting itself into the cells, and making its way through the far-yummier convict population.

A big one: this "top-security" prison has a secret tunnel that's cited in the building plans, and yet has never been sealed. Despite this, nobody has ever escaped. Is this a prison for Britain's thickest thugs? More distressing is the fact that after such a kerfuffle, Our Heroes don't seem to actually use the secret passage, preferring instead to send a delivery-van into the courtyard and a few squaddies over the wall with grappling-hooks.

And the *really* big one: this alien feeds on evil. It uses that evil to psychically teleport. So where do the deaths-by-phobia come into this? What does the alien gain from doing it? If its ancestors did something comparable to avoid getting eaten, it could've just mellowed out any predators so they'd go veggie. And as mentioned, if the Master's modified it to chuck out bad vibes, how is giving it a malefactor-buffet going to make it obedient? The two facets to this alien's psychic abilities just don't match up. Maybe (and this is a long-shot), the stigmata are a waste-product of whatever biological process equates to "digesting" evil. So that means that drowning in a dry room is literally a load of crap. Except, how does that make it afraid of Barnham? It's like a human being becoming petrified in close proximity to an empty dinner plate.

Critique After some fits and starts, this is the story where the various attempts to redefine *Doctor Who* come into focus. A number of items tried out over the previous years are brought back and consolidated. In many ways, this story is a synthesis of all the experiments of Season Seven: it has the action-sequences of "The Ambassadors of Death", the near-future *verité* style of "Doctor Who and the Silurians" and the small character flaws and moments of wit from "Spearhead from Space". The Brigadier is back to his sharp form from that story, but above all else, Don Houghton has brought the crispness of his writing from "Inferno" to the party. He's also restored the Venusian Karate and sense of the Doctor as literally cosmopolitan (complete with preposterous anecdotes).

In fact, this story begins *so* like Season Seven, it's a shock for first-time viewers when the pompous Prison Governor and Professor Kettering (who seem on their way to becoming the authority-figures whose bluster and defensiveness would impede the Doctor for the whole story) die. One of them perishes in the first episode, and the other... actually, can *you* remember what happened to the Governor? He just gets mixed down as soon as "Keller" is identified.

Indeed, the Brigadier having the same Captain for two stories running is a first. It's interesting for a lot of reasons, not the least of which is the way it alters the Brigadier's relationship with the Doctor and Benton. All the regulars now have fixed roles, and Richard Franklin has become the action-hero companion. (He does the job well enough here, but not *ever* very comfortably.) The Brig is now the man behind the desk giving out assignments. Benton thus becomes an extension of Jo, oddly enough (in this story, unlike most, Jo takes on the duties one might expect of Mike), and they bring in another upper-class military twit (Major Cosgrove) to make the Brig look good while Mike's away. Later on, the formulaic nature of UNIT stories will make this almost seem like a sitcom, but here we're not quite so rigid. Jo in particular looks like a more seasoned officer than she will in a year's time. (This story proves that Manning could have been *much* better if the scripts had allowed it, or if everyone had avoided playing it so safe.) Franklin gets more variety here than in most stories, but he gives essentially the same performance as always - without giving too much away, this is surprising in the light of later

developments towards the end of this book.

Added to the mix, less smoothly but hugely significantly, is the whole legacy from the black-and-white phase. The clean break made in Season Seven allowed space for this new series to establish its own identity, but here we get on-screen confirmation that this is *Doctor Who* after all: the two-hearted aristocrat helping UNIT is the same character we saw fight Daleks, Cybermen and, um, War Machines. If nothing else, this reminded casual viewers that there's more than one way to make a *Doctor Who* story, and that others had been tried in the past. Most of the "flashback" monsters seen in the Doctor's alien-induced hallucinations were one-offs and practically forgotten, meaning they're just emblematic of the Doctor's extraordinary past, not intended to make viewers remember specific old stories. As a side effect of this, it's abundantly clear that the present UNIT format is just one phase of a long-running series that's been through many such phases, and might one day end too. And to confirm this story's status as the culmination of the entire run of the series so far, the chief villain turns out to be the Master.

Here, once again, the story misdirects us. The Master's entire modus operandi has changed and he's abruptly the character we'll see from now on: charming and witty, calm and inventive, but above all completely at home inside the institutions of Britain. In this story, he goes from being the Doctor's antagonist to the Doctor's flipside. Despite his different motivations, everything he does is the way the Doctor might have done it in other incarnations. Go back and look at how the Second Doctor behaved in Season Four - he adopted fake identities and used their authority (or ability to slip past unnoticed) to overthrow regimes he didn't like. Even the Third Doctor resorts to this in "The Curse of Peladon" (9.2), by which time the Master has borrowed this Doctor's habit of doing spectacular leaps or driving off in odd vehicles. Delgado's scenes with Pertwee have yet to become formulaic or ritualized, but it's with William Marlowe as Mailer that he looks like a bigger threat than anything the Doctor's faced. The Master's ability to seemingly give people what they want - while always getting the better of the deal - became absurd in later stories, but here he has formidable back-up. He's just arrived, and already he's dominating the series. Roger Delgado *is* the Master - accept no substitute.

Watched Saturday by Saturday, the story uses

its two main focal points (the prison and UNIT's dual responsibilities) to give a sense of a wider world in which the routine *Doctor Who* stuff is happening. This is an enormous breakthrough and should have been followed up. Watched all in one go, the problems become more obvious. Why is UNIT in charge of the Peace Conference, and why does the Brig take all his staff to sort out the business with Stangmoor and Thunderbolt *at the very moment* that it becomes obvious that someone's trying to stir up trouble? How can there be *two* prison riots in rapid succession without the Home Office intervening and sending in the regular army? Why are all the cliffhangers the same? It gets repetitive if swallowed whole, but watched as a serial, it's far more successful until the rather garbled ending. UNIT are never as interesting as this again, and while the sight of the Brig bristling as Fu Peng cuts him dead is amusing, it's a worrying sign that the head of UNIT is becoming a comic stereotype. Courtney is already finding new ways to do the same old schtick, as this is the last time the Brigadier gets anything new to do.

Still, as strange as it might sound, losing the colour has been this story's salvation. Today's viewers are forced to focus on the absence of other things, like overt changes to the everyday world for the sake of a story. This being the first story since "Spearhead from Space" to have location work in visitable, known places (and places familiar from other television drama that aimed at mirroring reality), it doesn't need such a hard sell. It's got children playing in a park, which even "The Ambassadors of Death" omitted to include. And we're given to understand that the dragon looks better now than it did with colour.

And while - yes, all right - some of the characterisation is a bit scant, nobody involved is spectacularly bad. The convicts have cockney accents but they're perfectly adequate, rather than anyone trying Brummie or Scouse and failing. Bits of the music are oddly arresting in a Wendy Carlos kind of way (and as we said, this is a good year before *A Clockwork Orange*). Nobody's doing Children's Television Acting, but nothing here is unsuitable for young viewers, or too complex for them to follow. (We know: we've tried it on some.)

Six stories in, it's clear that the production team have found another way to do the UNIT / Earth format. The audience keeps growing and getting more enthusiastic for this apparently limited version of *Doctor Who*. But can they keep it up?

The Facts

Written by Don Houghton. Directed by Timothy Combe. Viewing figures: 6.7 million, 8.8 million, 7.5 million, 7.4 million, 7.6 million, 7.3 million.

Only black-and-white prints of "The Mind of Evil" exist in the BBC archive, although the VHS release contains various random clips from episode six in colour.

Supporting Cast Pik-Sen Lim (Captain Chin Lee), Michael Sheard (Dr. Summers), Simon Lack (Professor Kettering), Neil McCarthy (Barnham), Fernanda Marlowe (Corporal Bell), Roy Purcell (Chief Prison Officer Powers), Eric Mason (Senior Prison Officer Green), William Marlowe (Mailer), Haydn Jones (Vosper), Kristopher Kum (Fu Peng), Tommy Duggan (Senator Alcott), Patrick Godfrey (Major Cosworth).

Working Titles "Man Hours", "Doctor Who and Pandora's Box", "The Pandora Machine".

Cliffhangers Left alone to examine the Keller Machine, the Doctor suddenly finds himself under attack from it as (imaginary) flames start to lick his body; lured to the Chinese delegation's suite by Chin Lee, the American representative sees her change into an oriental dragon; handcuffed to a chair in the same room as the Machine, the Doctor begins to suffer monster-hallucinations as part of the Master's experiment (this week's opportunity for a champion gurning session from Pertwee); the active Machine, having learned to teleport around the prison, materialises in the same room as the Doctor, Jo and prisoner Mailer; Mailer aims his pistol at the Doctor during UNIT's assault on Stangmoor, and there's the sound of a gunshot.

What Was in the Charts? "The Resurrection Shuffle", Ashton, Gardner and Dyke; "She's A Lady", Tom Jones; "Rupert", Jackie Lee; "Stoned Love", The Supremes; "My Sweet Lord", George Harrison; "Baby Jump", Mungo Jerry.

The Lore

• After the rapid and effective script-changes for "Inferno", Don Houghton was in Terrance Dicks' good books. Houghton was at work on one of his two scripts for *Ace of Wands* - both of which are, shall we say, riffs on the same themes found in his work on *Who*[31]. His first idea for this adventure was of the so-called Pandora device (for use in prisons to curb evil vibes), and a debate about the ethics of interfering with someone's mind for even benign purposes. To stretch this to the required six episodes, the author's wife suggested that the power of this accumulated evil could be used to sabotage a peace conference. (We'll return to Mrs Houghton later.)

• Barry Letts had been impressed by Timothy Combe's handling of the complicated logistics of "Doctor Who and the Silurians", and thought that a thriller with a lot of set-piece military action suited his talents. Letts tactfully mentioned to the RAF how helpful the Army had been when making "The Invasion", and - lo! - a genuine Bloodhound surface-to-air missile and a squad of troops were laid on for the Thunderbolt sequences. Due to a misunderstanding, the troops were in uniform and not prison fatigues - but that's what script editors are for (hence the line about "mercenaries" in the studio sequence that followed). As we'll see, Letts shrewdly exploited the sibling rivalry between the armed forces again in the following year (see 9.3, "The Sea Devils"). As it turned out, the army helped with this story too, loaning marines to scale the prison walls in episode five.

• So, there's a story about the Pandora Machine (also called the Malusyphus process in some drafts), and a subplot about its inventor, Keller, trying to start a war between China and America. The US delegate is framed for killing Cheng Tiek, the original head of the Chinese delegation, by Chin Lee leaving Alcock's ID at the scene. There's also a borrowed (albeit disarmed, you'll be pleased to hear) S.A.M. Thing is, Letts and Dicks had the bright idea of introducing a new regular arch-villain. Thus, Emil(e) Keller / Dalbiac became a pseudonym for the Master.

• In practical terms, they needed a prison, a limo, helicopters and lots of stunts on motorbikes - all done on film. This is looking costly. Some trims are made to "Terror of the Autons", and a few more rewrites were needed to shift scenes to studio sets. We hope you're keeping track of all these small changes, because Houghton surely was...

• The prison was a bit of a headache. For obvious reasons a maximum-security facility was impractical, especially with fake weapons involved. The Home Office was asked if any good-looking Open prisons were available[32], but instead it was decided that Dover Castle, near to London and a decent-sized airfield, could be used. It looked (all together now) 'like Dracula's castle'. (That was another Dicks addition, to pre-empt criticism.) It had lots of steps and a nice high vantage-point to put the camera. Combe hoped to get as much of the action as possible in wide-shots, and thus film all the battle-scenes in one day. Down the road, the airfield at RAF Manston was picked as the optimum location for the climax. (This had been reworked, as 'Keller' had to escape, and Combe decided that only a helicopter could get the Doctor and Jo out of the way in time. Originally, the Doctor used the van's mirror to make the Gorgon-monster destroy itself, Yates drove it to a safe distance before it exploded and the Master hitched a lift disguised as a Pigbin-ish tramp.)

• Location filming started two days after the end of studio work on the previous story, with the prison material. Combe was in shades as one of the bad guys. One inadvertent addition was Mike Yates aiming his motorbike at a pile of boxes; Richard Franklin regretted not allowing the stunt team to double for him, but Letts and Combe liked the shot of his mistake and kept it in.

• Benton's remarkable versatility is a by-product of another actor falling ill immediately before the location filming began, and had to be covered with new dialogue in the studio work. The Embassy scenes were shot at Cornwall Gardens, South Kensington (see 3.10, "The War Machines", with which this story also shares a set designer) and Kensington Gardens, around the corner. The children playing in the park include Combe's own kids; his main casting headache was in finding suitable Chinese-looking performers. He'd gone through a specialist agency who provided a few of varying appropriateness, but Chin Lee was a problem until someone pointed out that Mrs Houghton, Pik-Sen Lim, had an Equity card. In similar vein, guest-villain William Marlowe (Mailer) suggested his then-wife for the new semi-regular part of Corporal Bell. (Due to a mix-up, some of the press got it into their heads that she was the Doctor's latest assistant.)

• A scene was filmed at the Commonwealth Institute with the various delegates arriving at the conference. It re-used Francis Williams (the Master's chauffeur) as an African delegate and various others, but mainly entailed Andy Ho as Fu Peng. Ho, a veteran oriental "heavy" (he was the hallucinated sumo wrestler in the *Out of the Unknown* episode "Lamda One", if that helps) proved to have a monotonous voice, so Combe ditched the entire scene and hired Kristopher Kum, in studio-only appearances, to play the delegate. (To jump ahead slightly, the Fu Peng material was slightly amended, and the dialogue in subtitles was supplied by Hokkien- and Cantonese-speaking Pik-Sem Lin. There would have been more, but Pertwee had difficulty mastering this part of the script.)

• After three weeks, two of which were for rehearsals (during which time, Pertwee got the cast to do breathing exercises based around the name "Tim Combe" and led the assembled parties in carol-singing), the studio work began. After Letts' experiments with out-of-sequence recording in the last two stories, Combe found that a hybrid approach - two episodes in two recording days - was most practical. Complicating matters, the big set-piece fight in episode three was a bit botched: the charges used for the gunfire went off out of sequence, and Katy Manning injured her back when an extra fell on her. This and the scene where the Master and Mailer start the riot were remounted during the following week's recording.

Another odd glitch was that the new floor-paint reacted oddly with water, making it extremely slippery. During the fight in the Governor's office, a jug fell off the desk and Delgado slipped - Letts thought it looked better than the choreographed fight, so that take was kept.

• Senator Alcott's hallucination of what the production team called "Puff the Magic Dragon" was originally explained away as a bad reaction to jellied eels (no, seriously). Another small cut was that the Doctor's hallucination of old foes would have included the Slyther (2.2, "The Dalek Invasion of Earth"), the Servo Robot (5.7, "The Wheel in Space") and a Sensorite (1.7, "The Sensories") - so yes, it could in fact have been sillier. The effect of the Keller Machine hopping about was done like the TARDIS dematerialisations, and its killing effect involved static interference and a red tint on the picture.

• In episode three, the Master is listening to prog-rockers King Crimson (another sure sign that he's evil). In fact, it's officially Crim frontman Robert Fripp's solo project *The Wake of Poseidon*, but most of the band play on it (see 23.1, "The Mysterious Planet"). In the original script, the Doctor calmed himself after hallucinating Koquillian and company with 'Andromedic (sic) yoga'. Another cut explained that the Doctor's hankie was given to him by Madame de Pompadour - see X2.4, "The Girl in the Fireplace". Also, the original ending saw the Doctor, for once, injured and confined to hospital.)

• Contrary to what's been written elsewhere, Major Cosworth was intended as a one-off character. He was played by Patrick Godfrey (who'd been Tor in 3.9, "The Savages").

• After all the changes made, Houghton was less inclined to work for the series again, but in any case he was flat out. Apart from writing for *New Scotland Yard* (a series exploiting the Metropolitan police's relocation to distance itself from old-fashioned cop-shows; see the essay with 2.1, "Planet of Giants"), he was becoming a big cheese at Hammer Films. His interest in mind-bending Chinese villains culminates in Hammer's bizarre one-off co-production with chop-sockie magnate Run Run Shaw, *The Legend of the Seven Golden Vampires*. His main legacy, though, was the damp Scots soap *Take the High Road*, the series that replaced *Crown Court* as what you watched if you were off school sick, to test whether you were really ill or faking. (Suffice to say, nobody watched either show if they could avoid it.)

• William Marlowe (Mailer) returned as the rather more benign Lester in "Revenge of the Cybermen" (12.5), and eventually married Roger Delgado's widow (see 11.5, "Planet of the Spiders"). Michael Sheard (Dr Summers) had also been a medic in "The Ark" (3.6) - we'll keep coming back to him. (Indeed, Sheard very nearly became a Doctor - see A4, "Dalek Invasion Earth: 2150AD" in Volume VI.) Neil McCarthy (Barnham) will be almost a compulsory feature of any British-made fantasy film of the early 80s and returns as base leader Thawn in "The Power of Kroll" (19.5). At the time "The Mind of Evil" was shown, he was one of the clueless adults in *Catweazle*, a series we'll discuss a lot in this book.

8.3: "The Claws of Axos"

(Serial GGG. Four Episodes, 13th March - 3rd April 1971.)

Which One is This? Bolognese-men land in their space-going bouncy castle and terrorise people who work at a nuclear power station. They offer us a magic potion to make our frogs grow and feed everyone, and although they look very nice to begin with, the wily Doctor knows better than to trust people in spandex.

But for most fanboys, it's the one where the tramp we now know as Pigbin Josh is pulled through a giant sphincter and the Doctor communicates with a very rude-looking "eye".

Firsts and Lasts First appearance of the new-look TARDIS console and console room, although the architecture will be re-done at least twice over the next couple of years. (It's in a mess the first time we see it, so there's never a great moment of unveiling. The Doctor's ripped the guts out of most of the console, and even the Master's disgusted.) First use of two key concepts in *Doctor Who* history: time loops and the High Council of Time Lords.

First time (unless you count the peculiar gizmo used on the Ice Warriors in 6.5, "The Seeds of Doom") that the Doctor is seen to fire a gun - and not at the bad guys, either, but instead to shoot a pistol out of agent Bill Filer's hand, before departing with the Master in the TARDIS. First use of the Master's laser-pistol, which provides the BBC's standard-issue laser-pistol noise for a generation (and got sampled onto a hit record).

Something that most people miss, but is very significant: they've decided to try making a model spaceship "fly" by putting it in front of a blue screen and zooming in or panning past. They'll keep attempting to make this work until the Sylvester McCoy era, with mixed results.

We have the TV debut of Tim Pigott-Smith (playing - what else? - an officer; see also 14.1, "The Masque of Mandragora") and it's Derek Ware's first official speaking role (if what Pigbin Josh does counts as speech). We also get to see Havoc's Stuart Fell for the first time in the UNIT era; he's seen guarding Axos and - guess what? - he's zapped by the Master and does a somersault.

Four Things to Notice
About "The Claws of Axos"...

1. Michael Ferguson's directing again and, as with "The Ambassadors of Death" (7.3), he's on a mission to cram in as many memorable, innovative and downright trippy shots as possible. Soldiers don't just go 'aargh' and fade out when they get zapped, they do somersaults or explode into balls of flame. Ministers don't just talk to their underlings, they teleconference via conveniently placed desktop TVs. Oh, and there's the growing and shrinking frog.

Unlike more recent attempts in shows such as *Farscape* and *Lexx*, the concept of an organic spaceship is here an excuse to combine Jefferson Airplane-style oil-pattern light-shows with undulating ceilings, groping tendrils and cameras zooming in and out wildly - often all at once, overlaid on one another and in lurid orange shades. (The cast hated the Axos set, but agree that it looked drastically better on screen. Ponder that for a moment.) The result looks as though someone has tried to recreate the look of *Barbarella* after hearing it described down the phone. As with "The Ambassadors of Death", Ferguson's guiding principle isn't so much "will the audience get the point?" as it's "what does this button do?"

2. Bill Filer, 'from Washington HQ', seems to have been brought in as an alternative love-interest for Jo, but he doesn't last. The noticeably non-American Paul Grist plays him competently but if the chemistry between Katy Manning and Richard Franklin was minimal, this goes into negative numbers. Imagine one of the older Osmond brothers playing Felix Leiter from the Bond films, and you've got the idea. The trouble is, nobody tells us anything about him, he's just *there*. Most people assume that he's from UNIT's US franchise, but even this causes problems (see **Things That Don't Make Sense** and investigate, if you dare, fan-made videos on this topic). This might have led to all sorts of stories about the Doctor and Jo going to Roswell or the Bermuda Triangle (and fan-fiction has played up to this with *Shaft* crossover stories and the like) but it was never picked up on screen.

3. Compounding the silliness of the whole Pigbin Josh sub-plot, Dudley Simpson and his magic Moog have conjured a piece of music so inane as to burn its way into the memory. It sounds like a Victorian Music-Hall song, but

Where's UNIT HQ?

And how many UNIT HQs are there?

The problem, of course, is that the Doctor's laboratory looks different almost every time we see it. Leaving aside the possibility that his constant experiments with bits of the TARDIS are doing weird things to space-time inside the building, at the very least he seems to keep moving from room to room (does he keep blowing them up?), even if UNIT doesn't uproot itself and head for a new installation every few months. Though UNIT has branches all over the world, everything we're told indicates that at any given time, it has only one UK base of operations (not including "holiday" base-camps such as the school in "Invasion of the Dinosaurs").

Let's *try* (if such a thing is humanly possible) to keep things simple. Let's assume that when the lab "changes", it's just a new lab, not a new building. The lab in Season Seven has a makeshift set-up, evidently to go with the apparently peripatetic UNIT HQ that's been stuffed into someone's garage. The only "UNIT lab" seen is at the start of "The Ambassadors of Death" (7.3), which might just, maybe, be the same as the one in "Terror of the Autons" (8.1). If so, there could well be only *two* different HQs in use throughout the Third Doctor's exile, despite the unpredictable décor. The building in "Terror of the Autons" apparently *isn't* the building seen in "The Three Doctors" (10.1), since the former has a handy river /canal running past the window (with houseboats and what might be cranes on the banks), and the latter obviously doesn't. The "Autons" lab is apparently in a warehouse conversion, which could conceivably be in London. (Trendy folks and occasional semi-official bodies lived in a few of these at time of broadcast, but more often it was witnessed in TV shows about hip young crimebusters. *Ace Of Wands*, Thames' near-miss rival for *Doctor Who*, springs to mind.) The Doctor's been there long enough to have put his own stamp on the décor (puffer-fish suspended from the ceiling, photos of biplanes) and a standing rule about the tea-lady.

But if we're counting buildings, we *can* safely assume that the HQ being used in "The Daemons" (8.5) is the same as the one in "Planet of the Spiders" (11.5), as the Doctor is using the same garage. So we have two HQ buildings, and the move has to take place somewhere in the middle of Season Eight, probably after "The Claws of Axos". In "Axos", the HQ has a nifty space-tracking room that's never seen again, but the rest of the place is in keeping with the non-lab bits in "The Three

Doctors". Just because we don't *see* the space-tracking room again, though, it doesn't follow that it's no longer there. Indeed in "Colony in Space" (8.4), the Doctor's lab looks somewhat under-furnished. To be blunt, it looks as if he's working in a corridor. This certainly suggests that he's just moved into new quarters, or rather is halfway through moving. (Once again, swapping the running order of Season Eight stories reduces the complications; see What's the UNIT Timeline? under "The Daemons". Maybe they *did* get complaints after "Terror of the Autons", were halfway through moving in when the Time Lords had a mission for the Doctor. Then they fully settled in when Axos showed up and stayed put.) Nevertheless, the oddly-shaped green doors are constant in both of the Season Eight stories using labs, so the moving may have been done in phases. Certainly, they put the Doctor in wherever he is in "Colony" for long enough to write 'Laboratory, Authorised Persons Only' on the door. The lab in 9.4, "The Mutants" isn't much better (from what little we see of it), but the following story seems to be the same room as all later tales until 12.1, "Robot", only shot from different angles.

"The Ambassadors of Death" throws up a couple of other details worth considering. One is that they definitely have at least one prison cell, with a yard outside. The other is that this place is near the Space Research Centre (which we suspect is on the site of the real-life equivalent in Westcott, Bucks), which is about seven miles from a warehouse (like the ones in Aylesbury). Both are near the spot Benton indicates on a map: somewhere around Reading, Slough or High Wycombe (not right next to each other in real life, but it's a small map and he's a bit vague). If UNIT at one point shared premises with another organisation (as is tangentially hinted in both "Axos" and "Autons"), it must have been someone very tolerant of incarcerations, explosions and unannounced visits from fugitive scientists, ministry officials and GPO repairmen. We note that the GPO man (actually the Master) says that his pass has been checked several times already when Yates accosts him. Yet wherever UNIT are based later on, they let Lupton wander in (11.5, "Planet of the Spiders") and Sarah Jane comes and goes as she pleases.

So up until shortly before "The Daemons", they were on the shore of a fairly big river /canal somewhere around Reading. Bray, in Berkshire, has sev-

continued on page 131...

parped on the synth. In conjunction with Josh's 'Oo-ar's and mangled dialogue, it's quite astonishingly out of keeping with the rest of the score's overdone urgency. (Just wait until the tendril pulls Josh into Axos, when the theme goes into a menacing minor key and the 'Oo-ar's get more desperate.) The rest of the music has the uncomfortable air of someone with a an electric organ improvising as the pictures are going out live, most notably in the scene where the nuclear power-station is about to blow up and everyone slowly ambles away.

4. In the last episode, Captain Yates and Sergeant Benton are seen sitting inside their Land Rover, which is rocking unconvincingly in front of a dark blue background. It's almost as if somebody was supposed to put a CSO backdrop in there...[33]

The Continuity

The Doctor He still can't remember much of his past, and for the first time it's explicitly stated that the Time Lords have put a block on his memory of 'dematerialisation theory' to stop him leaving Earth. [See **Why Doesn't the TARDIS Work?** under 9.5, "The Time Monster"] He can mentally calculate the trajectory and estimate the landing-site of the incoming spaceship faster than the Brigadier's computer. The Doctor also claims that he's been published 'elsewhere', meaning somewhere not in Britain [or at least, not *yet*].

The Ministry of Defence's file on the Doctor is empty [see **The Supporting Cast**], with the Brigadier assuming personal responsibility for him. The Doctor isn't a British subject.

When taking his leave of Earth, the Doctor uses the Master's laser pistol with enough accuracy to zap the revolver from Filer's hand without hurting him.

• *Ethics.* Having spent the last year or so telling human authorities that aliens aren't necessarily hostile and that Earth should make peace with them whenever possible, here he meets a bunch of apparently peaceful aliens and tries to convince the authorities to blow them up. [Possibly because he deems Axos an anathema to human life, whereas the Silurians and such can potentially be reasoned with?] He has no qualms about putting Axos into a time-loop to save Earth, and is remarkably unconcerned that the Master seems to have met the same fate.

The Supporting Cast

• *UNIT.* The Ministry of Defence feels obliged to screen UNIT personnel. The Emergency Powers Act gives the Ministry the right to issue orders to UNIT under extreme circumstances, and to allow the regular military to take over from the UN forces. However, unilateral deals with extraterrestrials are illegal.

Whereas UNIT previously had its own space tracking station [7.1, "Spearhead from Space"], there's now a tracking room inside UNIT HQ itself. UNIT's chief headquarters is, as expected, in Geneva. The British contingent seems based in a building that appears to be a Victorian mansion with whitewashed interior walls, and solid oak doors marked 'UNIT'. [This suggests, in conjunction with the comment in "Terror of the Autons" that a bomb going off outside would cause complaints, that they share premises with other agencies. See the accompanying essay. A girl in a very non-military mini is seen walking past - she's credited as a secretary, but might be the tea-lady.]

The corridor outside the office has a big yellow plastic sign with a number "6" on it, with red, yellow and green lights [presumably to indicate the level of alert].

• *The Brigadier.* Deems Chinn's "Britain first" approach with regards Axonite as illegal, up to the point of drawing a gun on the man.

The Brig keeps a photo on his desk of a woman and two girls. [Does Doris know? One of the many amusing things about Gary Russell's book *The Scales of Injustice* is the *True Lies*-style subplot of the Brig's wife thinking he works in a bank - see 8.5, "The Daemons" - and he's late home because he's shagging Corporal Bell. In this account, Bell's name is "Carol", but for fairly obvious reasons that will become clearer when the Whomobile turns up, she has to be called "Rosemary"[34]. Anyway, if the Brig *were* carrying on with someone, it wouldn't be Corporal Bell, but let's draw a veil over this well-worn joke.]

The Supporting Cast (Evil)

• *The Master.* Evidently prepared to believe that the Doctor might run off in the TARDIS and abandon Earth to its fate, so he doesn't know his old comrade that well [and he *still* hasn't got the picture by the next story]. He also seems inclined to behave while the Doctor holds him at gunpoint, as if he's convinced that his old friend might actually shoot him.

Where's UNIT HQ?

...continued from page 129

eral good claims. There's a big bit of Thames, a few other military / scientific establishments in the area (Aldermaston, Greenham Common, Harwell and now that ultimate haven of mad scientists, the Fat Duck restaurant run by boffin-ish chef Heston Blumenthal) and (a sentimental touch for us, but possibly practical in terms of plausible deniability of alien sightings) the Hammer Films studios nearby. That said, the nearest thing to any warehouses on the river there is right opposite Windsor Castle, so the complaints Benton anticipated for the Doctor hurling a bomb out into the river in "Autons" would have to be taken *very* seriously. (It would, however, explain the Doctor getting curious enough to pop in on the construction of the castle - 25.3, "Silver Nemesis". We also like the idea of UNIT being based right under Gerry Anderson's nose...)

So where is this new HQ, which lasts all the way up until "Pyramids of Mars" (13.3) and possibly "The Five Doctors" (20.7)? The most obvious suggestion would be Gloucestershire, the area where England starts to turn into Wales. Wales is said to be 'nearby' in "Day of the Daleks" (9.1), and there's a possibly-intentional West Country feel to much of the location work in this era. In "Planet of the Spiders", the HQ is conclusively shown to be around eighty miles from Mortimer in Berkshire, which just about works. It's also (roughly) seventy to a hundred miles from Cambridge, according to "The Time Monster". On top of that, "Day of the Daleks" suggests that UNIT HQ is north of Auderly, and Auderly is fifty miles north of London. We say "suggests" because we're assuming that "down" means southwards and south means due south.

This sorts out a lot of odd details such as UNIT HQ being on top of the ruins of a Priory ("Pyramids of Mars"), being spatially adjacent to 'Wessex' ("The Three Doctors"; 11.1, "The Time Warrior"), being a short helicopter ride from Devil's End ("The Daemons") and being close enough to Devesham for Benton to meet his sister after work (13.4, "The Android Invasion"). Even the "comedy" copper in the tedious chase in "Planet of the Spiders" seems to confirm this, as both he and Terry Walsh's 'Man With Boat' have the right approximate accent. So we're not too far from GCHQ, the British government's listening-post for radio transmissions from, you know... foreigners. But would Downing Street allow a UN agency to station itself so close to somewhere so sensitive?

Cheltenham is, at least, one town where someone like the Brigadier can slip by almost unnoticed.

Alas, not all the figures add up. It takes the Brigadier three hours to drive from the HQ to South Wales in "The Green Death", and it *really* shouldn't take that long from Gloucestershire, even if he's avoiding the toll-bridge over the Severn at Bristol. That said, it is a fairly small, rural area and anyone who's driven there will know that once off the motorways, the routes get a bit circuitous. The Doctor gets there in next to no time.

There's always the possibility, of course, that UNIT's UK contingent have two or more buildings at their disposal simultaneously, and that the lab in "The Green Death" is in another city from the "main" one. This has been seriously proposed, and we should ask ourselves: does the TARDIS know which is which? If this is the one by the canal, where is it? It's a bit of a step from wherever Wenley Moor is (supposedly the Derbyshire Peak District, but not named as such on screen), not as close to South Wales (but that still makes the Midlands plausible), and with ready access to space-tracking experts. Leicester, with the National Space Centre now based there, is a good bet. Note that the Brigadier only ever mentions the city once, in connection with tracking a spaceship (13.1, "Terror of the Zygons").

At this point, some would argue that there's only *one* UNIT HQ, and that the TARDIS would get confused if the Brigadier moved around too much. But as with the idea that the Doctor's arrival in a different lab makes Benton, Yates and the char-lady relocate all of a sudden, it doesn't really stand up to scrutiny. If the Time Lords are in control of the TARDIS, it's going to return where it needs *to be*. The problem's the same if UNIT occupy two buildings at once or move from one to another: if it's not London, where is it? The canal and Benton's mention of 'complaints' suggest a fairly built-up area, and the Midlands was the centre of canal-building in the late eighteenth century when the pottery industry and later coal-mining and steelmaking grew. In trying to resolve all of these, and make both HQs occupy the same district (perhaps unnecessarily), one obvious solution presents itself...

After much measuring and drawing on maps, the only area that seems to meet *all* the criteria is somewhere in rural Warwickshire, in the region of Birmingham, plumb between the north and

continued on page 133...

He's taken to carrying a 'laser gun', which does exactly what anybody would expect a laser gun to do, but can also open the TARDIS lock [q.v. 3.4, "The Daleks' Master Plan", and his less-successful attempt to pick the lock in 26.4, "Survival"]. He also possesses an electronic lockpick of sorts, which enables him to break into the Doctor's TARDIS. [He's never seen to use this handy little device again - perhaps the Doctor upgrades the lock.] Here he uses yet *another* face-mask disguise, albeit one that's breathtakingly unconvincing. [Nonetheless, it seems to fool Benton. Mind you, he seems to be having difficulty keeping a straight face. Maybe UNIT has standing orders to allow anyone they think is the Master access, so at least they know where he is.] Apparently he can make it look as if the greatcoat he's stolen fits, when it manifestly doesn't.

He can hypnotise people just by looking at them in the rear-view mirror, and can do daring leaps onto moving lorries. [British readers who remember the Milk Tray ads may find this scene irresistibly familiar.]

The TARDIS(es) The Doctor's TARDIS seems to contain a 'light accelerator', although confusingly an Earth-built light accelerator can compensate for the deficiencies in the Doctor's dematerialisation circuit and make the Ship operational again [cf 18.7 "Logopolis"]. This simple solution has previously been blocked from the Doctor's mind, although the Master spots it straight away. However, once the Ship is active, the Doctor discovers that the Time Lords have programmed it to return to Earth anyway [see 8.4, "Colony in Space"].

The Master believes that the Doctor's TARDIS doesn't have a proper stabiliser. The console contains an unnamed component that, when removed, prevents the Ship from dematerialising. The scanner, which used to be a TV screen in the corner of the console room, is now built into one of the roundels in the wall. [It returns to its normal state for the next story.] The Doctor's TARDIS can, with difficulty, store up and release the energy output of the Nuton complex. When linked to Axos, the TARDIS can put the organism into a permanent time loop which apparently removes it from the normal universe, although boosting the power breaks the TARDIS out of the loop and leaves Axos stranded.

The Master's TARDIS has become a chunky grey cuboid with a single door [evidently its "default" form, and not unlike the SIDRATs in "The War Games"].

The Non-Humans

• *Axos.* A single alien organism, which the Master says has no [surviving] planet of its own. [The Axons' claim that the "ship" was grown, rather than made, is perhaps unreliable as it's part of their cover story. Axos can be linked to technology such as the TARDIS, suggesting it was deliberately engineered rather than evolving. Then again, we have reason to believe that the TARDIS is itself an organism with technological aspects, so making this clear a distinction is misguided.] Axos moves from world to world as if it were a spaceship, and buries itself on arrival so that only its maw-like entrance is visible. Its interior is a mass of living tissue, its walls lined with tentacles and eye-like sensory organs.

Axos thrives by distributing chunks of itself - as Axonite, a substance which tries to defy analysis but which is apparently material from Axos itself, albeit in a dormant state - across the victim-planet before draining the world of every 'particle' of energy and every 'last cell' of living matter. It needs to begin its nutrition cycle within 72 hours of landing [it originated on a planet which also has a 24-hour day?]. Individuals drained by Axos are spewed out of its body dead, bleached and crumbling to dust. Its presence on Earth causes erratic weather conditions in the vicinity, and it has 'variable mass' when it's on its way to Earth, vanishing from the radar altogether when missiles are launched at it. It can read the thoughts of people in its grip, mentally entrance its victims [not actual hypnosis, but enough to "stun" the Doctor and Jo at the start of episode three] and project invisible force-fields within its own mass.

Axos is seemingly "crewed" by golden-skinned, golden-haired humanoids, but in fact these creatures are just drones of Axos itself [their bodies presumably chosen to put humans at ease]. Reverting to their natural form, the Axons become masses of red tendril-tissue, still roughly humanoid in shape. When subjected to the Nuton complex's particle accelerator, a lump of Axonite turns first into washing-up-liquid foam and then a brown duvet, chasing our heroes around the lab [perhaps it needs a "critical mass" to become anthropomorphic].

The "lumpy" Axons aren't harmed by bullets,

Where's UNIT HQ?

...continued from page 131

south of England. The present location of the National Exhibition Centre is as good a bet as any. It's very quiet but close to three motorways (a notorious interchange, "Spaghetti Junction" opened there in 1972), an international airport and a canal. It explains how UNIT can have a frantic chase from Inverness to London; pausing at a quarry in Brentford, Middlesex; and still have a chance to change their clothes ("Terror of the Zygons"). It makes just as much sense, in fact, as basing Torchwood in Canary Wharf or anything at all in Cardiff. (Certainly, it's a lot drier than a base under the Tower of London would be, right next to the Thames under foundations almost 1000 years old - see X2.0, "The Christmas Invasion".)

Anyway, Birmingham in the early 1970s has several advantages, not the least being that the city was undergoing a bit of a boom, albeit briefly, and a lot of major employers were setting up secondary bases there. The BBC itself had Pebble Mill as a base of regional drama (see 15.1, "Horror of Fang Rock"; 22.2, "Vengeance on Varos" and one of the essays with "The Green Death") and there were significant transport, tax and recruitment gains

from locating around the city. Sure, it had an image problem, but this was the era when most of Britain's rock stars came from the city or its nearby rivals. (Birmingham, Solihull, Wolverhampton and Walsall all sprawled into one industrialised mess, each with a sillier accent than the last.) With several good science-based Universities around (the fictional 'Wessex' University from "The Three Doctors" could be Warwick, based at Coventry, or it might be Aston Poly or University of Birmingham itself). There are various suitable buildings around the city's periphery, such as the Jacobean manor near Aston Villa FC's ground or the various mock-Tudor buildings around Bourneville, home of Cadbury's chocolate. A lot of houses of the right size and look to be the HQ that visits an anti-matter universe ("The Three Doctors") were bought up in the seventies by those rock stars, shortly before they relocated to LA.[39] They don't even have to be old, as the Priory only burned down in 1911.

The only downside to this as a theory is that - even compared to *Torchwood* - there are very few people with local accents around. But then, we never actually see or hear this mythical bun-vendor.

and can fire jets of gas from their arms which kill instantly, or extend long whip-like tendrils which make the target explode on contact. In fact, Axos seems able to shape bits of itself into just about *anything*, and can even make identical-but-bulletproof duplicates of human beings after taking the subject to the ship's replication section. [Some other alien shape-shifters use a similar process. See 13.1, "Terror of the Zygons" and 13.4, "The Android Invasion" and compare to *Torchwood* 2.09, "Something Borrowed", in which BEMs with a 'proteus gland' do the job just by sight. We should also mention how the Vespiform in X4.7, "The Unicorn and the Wasp", uses something looking like chip-fat for the same purpose, but that entails some kind of instant reversible DNA resequencing, something even Time Lords find hard to do (see X3.8, "Human Nature").] The Axon duplicate of Filer looks good enough but acts unnaturally stiff.

The Axons claim that Axonite can use the energy it absorbs to copy, re-create and re-structure matter, and although this is part of their "sales pitch" to the humans there must be *some* truth in it. It can certainly be used to make small animals

larger, or to reverse this process. The whole of Axos suffers "pain" when part of its mass is analysed. Individual Axons can "transmit" energy back to Axos [induction again? - see "Doctor Who and the Silurians"], as seems to happen when one of the Axos-lumps enters the Nuton reactor. [Baker and Martin just love this sort of "walking into a reactor" scenario; see also "The Hand of Fear".]

The organism's interest in Earth comes from the Master, though it's not revealed where it encountered him. It seems to know about Time Lords even without the Master's help, and claims it can break the blocks the Time Lords imposed on the Doctor's mind.

History

• *Dating*. [Late 1972. Comets were scheduled to pass in 1969, 1970 and 1975, so we *might* have a scripted last-possible date for the tracking-station boys to think they've detected an unknown comet. Nothing on screen this year contradicts this, although the tracking-station workers might be offhandedly presuming they've found a second comet in a year that they're due for one anyway.]

'Freak weather conditions' aside, England's drab enough to suggest autumn or winter. [Assuming the Master's only been travelling in space rather than history, enough time has elapsed since "The Mind of Evil" for him to have been captured by Axos and returned to Earth.]

Britain apparently has emergency missiles ready to take out incoming spacecraft, while Washington has taken an interest in the Master. [The CIA probably wants to recruit him.] Filer, the American agent, is evidently so well-versed in the Master's case-file that he doesn't find the TARDIS surprising. [We have to wonder whether the US branch of UNIT knows about the Doctor being a time-travelling alien and whether he's ever loaned out. Then again, we ought to wonder if the US, Italian or Indian branches of UNIT ever get anything to do, what with all aliens picking on just the Home Counties and occasionally Cardiff, as far as we can tell.]

The Nuton power complex is a nuclear facility supplying power for the 'whole of Britain'. [We presume that, at the story's end, there are nation-wide power-cuts. This might explain why London's population, as given in "Invasion of the Dinosaurs" (11.2) has suddenly spiked.] At the complex there's a research programme which is attempting to accelerate particles beyond the speed of light and therefore develop a form of time-travel. [The Doctor oddly has no objection to this.] Sadly, the Axon duvet-monster kills the scientist planning all of this.

Chinn has the power to relieve UNIT of duties allocated to the organization by the United Nations via Geneva. [See **Things That Don't Make Sense**. Chinn, despite his boss's low opinion of him, might be better-connected than we thought he was at the time. After all if UNIT *is* working to an internationally-agreed First Contact protocol, not even the US President or British Prime Minister can over-rule it. See X3.12, "The Sound of Drums"; "The Ambassadors of Death"; 13.4, "The Android Invasion" and our comments with "Spearhead from Space".) See also **All Right Then... Where Were Torchwood?** under 9.3, "The Sea Devils".]

The Analysis

Where Does This Come From? The most obvious thing to say about "The Claws of Axos" is that two wannabe film writers wrote it as a seven-part Troughton adventure in 1968, just after *2001: A Space Odyssey* came out. Slightly less obvious (if still fairly evident) is that one of the writers had just quit advertising when he turned thirty, and the other was an animator-*manque*.

What comes across time and again in the Baker-Martin scripts is a delight in the possibilities of fantasy to provide arresting visuals, and then the zeal with which they work on justifying these with pseudo-science couched in real science. Almost all of their scripts began life as odd images and were worked on and worked on *and worked on* until - presto! - a logical reason emerged for them. Or not. Either way, of course, the original idea was long gone. From London Zoo filled with aliens and the Brigadier flying a spaceship into a much bigger ship (the first draft of 14.2, "The Hand of Fear") to a negative world where anti-Time Lords ruled over the dead (their first go at 10.1, "The Three Doctors") and right back to the giant head in Hyde Park giving people what they wanted (this story's original *donée*), Baker and Martin consistently came up with things that the BBC could never have got away with. The irony is that by the time of Bob Baker's last go, "Nightmare of Eden" (17.4), they *could* do it but everyone else was doing something else.

In keeping with the new direction the series has taken during this gestation period, this story's full of thrills and off-the-shelf items from any number of other adventure series, but with no reason for most of them to be there, save that they usually are. So we've got yet another doppelganger sub-plot that goes nowhere, a token American (because shows made for export *always* have one) and Season Seven-style topical palavah about nuclear power and experimental stations. Even the Master is now doing daring stunts.

As with the director's bravura use of colour and crazy electronic effects, the sense we get is that the writers have decided that because something is possible, it *must* done. (Apologies for harping on about that bloody frog, but it's symptomatic of this go-for-broke approach.) The four episodes that compose this story are bursting with things that seemed like good ideas to someone, with Dicks and Letts weeding out the impossible or over-expensive ones. As we've said a couple of stories ago, the nearest thing to *Doctor Who* on screen is *Top of the Pops* (with belated showings of *Star Trek* and *Sesame Street* being a distant second and third) and an arms race is going on between these

Why Did We Countdown to TV Action?

All right, a quick quiz: who was the Doctor's first black companion? Assuming none of you fell into the trap and answered "Martha", it's likely that several of you said "Mickey". Roz Forrester might have sprung to mind for *New Adventures* enthusiasts, albeit with a lingering sense that it's not the correct answer. Some of you probably thought back to the early days of Marvel's *Doctor Who Weekly* and said "Sharon", for which we'll give half-marks.

No, we have to go back to 1972 and a different comic-strip entirely. Jon Pertwee's Doctor is facing a London where everyone's on autopilot reliving the previous day, save for himself and an American tourist - a teenager called Nick Willard - who slept in a Tube station and escaped the fiendish Zeron rays. The Doctor wakes up in his country cottage bed and runs shouting down Horseguards' Parade before he and Nick finally send a jamming signal from the Post Office Tower and get Nick's cousin, a Radio One DJ, to send out a warning.

Welcome to the bizarre world of *TV Action + Countdown*. The *Doctor Who* comic strip of the Glam era had gorgeous painted colour covers, meticulous artwork, behind-the-scenes features on the TV show and plots as bonkers as anything Bob Baker and Dave Martin could have devised. If ever a strip captured how the TV series *felt* to the kids watching at the time, it has only one serious rival: the 1960s Dalek serial in the same publication. That was widescreen baroque, freed from the stifling limits of Lime Grove studios; this was the tartrazine aesthetic unleashed without all that inconvenient acting and stopping to explain things.

You want a high-speed chase with Daleks moving as fast as they ought to and with dinosaurs assaulting them? You got it! Antarctica in a nuclear submarine? Not a problem. A story called "Planet of the Daleks" that's actually quite good? Amazingly, even this flowed from the pen of Gerry Haylock. But what you *won't* get is Jo or the Brigadier. Instead, the Doctor's rapid turnover of one-story companions led to a strange mix of oddballs and try-outs unlike *anything* seen in the broadcast episodes pre-1981.

Let's be careful, though - if we're discussing comics in a British context, there's two crucial things to bear in mind. One is that the majority of superhero titles were American imports, available sporadically and often out-of sequence. The other is that we had an indigenous tradition (about as old as Superman, as it happens) of comics that were, well, comic. Ours were expressly for children, and the front-runners all came from Dundee to

begin with. Even when the *Eagle* began in 1950 (see **What Kind of Future Did We Expect?** under 2.3, "The Rescue"), it contained strips like "Harris Tweed" that were more akin to the japes in *The Beano* and *The Dandy* than the all-action westerns and space-adventures around it. Generally speaking, our "funny papers" were as puzzling to foreigners as our pantomimes and came from the same basic source: the inversion of social norms on festive occasions. *The Beano* (even the name connects to this tradition), is all about children being in charge or adults and generic stereotypes acting like big kids.

That theme cropped up when the comics combined with the other big entertainment fad of the pre-war era, to produce *Radio Fun*. In this, caricatures of the biggest stars got into silly adventures connected with their on-air personae. (In those days, this was often the only clue kids got about what their favourites looked like until they broke into film - if they did - but the overall effect was odd. Characters played by Pertwee were drawn to look like they sounded, for example.)

The logical post-war extension of this was *TV Comic*, launched in 1951 just as the *Eagle* (and in particular its lead strip, Frank Hampson's "Dan Dare - Pilot of the Future") raised the standard for British comics. As we've seen, *Eagle*'s impact on the comics field was not just profound but paradigmatic. For the next twenty-five years, British adventure comics looked like the *Eagle*. The good ones, that is: the cruddy ones looked like *TV Comic*.

From the start, *TV Comic* was at the cheap and nasty end of the market, serving up crudely-drawn and crudely-conceived variations on TV staples such as *Muffin the Mule* (X2.7, "The Idiot's Lantern") and *Mister Pastry* (11.5, "Planet of the Spiders"). By the time *Doctor Who* arrived on the scene, it was being published by TV Publications, which was owned by ITV London franchise-holder Associated-Rediffusion (itself a spinoff from Rediffusion, the French equivalent of the Muzak corporation). It existed mainly to publish regional ITV listings magazines. When Rediffusion lost its franchise and the right to publish *TV Times* in 1968, the subsidiary was restructured as an independent concern renamed Polystyle Publications. Up until 1971, the *Doctor Who* strip had appeared in *TV Comic*.

This is something we've been trying to address throughout these books. For the British Public,

continued on page 137...

ABOUT TIME 1970-1974

two flagship BBC Pop-Art shows.

For these four weeks, *Doctor Who* is more Glam Rock than the real thing. It's as though a memo from the Sixth Floor of Television Centre read, "Everyone's got colour sets for Christmas, give 'em something worth seeing in colour". This organic spaceship is an exercise in making something as unlike a studio-set of a spaceship ever seen on TV before - free of flat planes, rigid walls and obvious controls - and is using all the techniques developed on *ToTP* to make it colourful and exotic-looking. *Doctor Who* can do things like this now, so once in a while they do *all* the things they can and showcase the variety in a single episode. ("We gotta bluescreen, and we're gonna use it!") All those ITC shows had stunts and comedy moments, all those BBC dramas had experienced actors and extraordinary sets and costumes, all the pop shows had psychedelia and girls in short skirts, but there was only one place - this one - where you'd get all of that and a score done on a state-of-the-art synthesizer.

Throughout this story's lengthy development, the question that's being asked and answered in different ways is what *Doctor Who* is for - not with regards to who's watching, but why the BBC should persevere in making it. Letts had wrenched it in a more moralistic and adventure-serial direction, but his starting point was far-removed from the state the series had been in when this story was first pitched. Derrick Sherwin and Peter Bryant had been chastened by the whole sorry tale of "The Dominators" (6.1) and writers trying to make Message Stories. To a certain extent they were responsible for a period where the series reserved comment more than ever before - there is, for instance, no editorialising on the ethics of the Cerebraton Mentor (6.3, "The Invasion"), nor indeed on converting people into Cybermen. "The Claws of Axos" seems out-of-place between "The Mind of Evil" (a barbed parable) and "Colony in Space" (a blatant sermon). Baker and Martin wound up writing a story that hid two basic concerns so well, what exists now on DVD and video is the residue of the sugar-coating with no trace of pill.

The clue is in the description of the Axon family: a golden couple and their offspring, with slight American accents, straight out of a Coca-Cola ad. Axos arrived offering people whatever they most desired, and in return took what we most need. Shall we say it again? Dave Martin had just quit a

lucrative job in advertising. His knack for slogans remained ('Eldrad Must Live!' in "The Hand of Fear", 'The Quest is the Quest" in 15.5, "Underworld" and 'Contact Has Been Made' in 15.2, "The Invisible Enemy") but here we've got a guilty conscience at work. Chinn, meanwhile, seems like a fugitive from a different series: specifically, the ministry types in *Doomwatch* who were the real enemy of the public. As we've seen, Pedler and Davis' pet project had touched a nerve with the public and the *Doctor Who* team, looking over their shoulder at the "grown-up" counterpart, attempted to make Whitehall types a shorthand for the "ordinary" world and cynical motives. Over the various drafts of this script, Chinn's role was built up and smoothed down again.

There are other factors, of course. We know from Baker and Martin's work on crime shows (and indeed, Baker's "Nightmare of Eden") that the whole concept of drug dealers nagged at them. We'll become very familiar with their interest in Greek Mythology reworked to include (and demystify) the Time Lords, so here the Trojan Horse gets a makeover as a lump of orange plastic. The main one, though, is that interest in striking images. The "Bristol Boys" lived just down the road from a nuclear power station and said to themselves "that'd make a nice setting for a *Doctor Who* script, that would". They'd get their wish in 1976...

Things That Don't Make Sense Anything Pigbin Josh says.

So, who the hell is Bill Filer? He doesn't present any ID and Chinn, the Government busybody, doesn't demand to know who this person with the variable accent is. Is he CIA? Well, no, because Chinn would've had great difficulty in keeping him out and certainly couldn't have arrested him along with the UNIT contingent. But if Filer really *is* from the US franchise of UNIT, he seems very unconcerned that Britain has a known time-travelling alien scientist on their team and Uncle Sam hasn't. Also, Filer is said to be well-versed in the Master's case-file, yet he entirely fails to recognise the villain on sight. [Maybe he thought the aliens had abducted the Spanish Ambassador.] He *does*, however, accept without being told that the blue box is a time machine, whereas Jo finds this out but forgets by next week [see 8.4, "Colony In Space"]. Ostensibly Filer's job is to track down the Master, but when Chinn tells him to leave, his first

Why Did We Countdown to TV Action?

...continued from page 135

Doctor Who was something embedded in a context of children's media lore alongside *Animal Magic* and *Sooty*, both of which got shoehorned into the *Beano*-style format (see 17.2, "City of Death" and 8.5, "The Daemons" for more on these series). *Doctor Who* had existed as a comic strip since 1964, but modern fans tend to see the medium through the version begun in 1979, when Marvel launched *Doctor Who Weekly*. *Doctor Who Magazine* (as it later became, henceforth abbreviated to *DWM*) defined the way a generation of fans interacted with *Doctor Who* (see **Did *Doctor Who* Magazine** Change Everything? under 18.2, "Meglos"). In reflecting upon the days before the series was considered analogous to *Star Trek* in any capacity, the pre-1979 strips were regarded - when they were remembered at all - as pretty much uniformly embarrassing. *DWM* sought to correct this, in features on the "heritage" of pre-Marvel *Who* strips, but the memory of *TV Comic* hung around.

They did, however, salvage one treasured memory from the 1960s. For this, we have to thank the programme's bitterest rival throughout the 60s: Gerry Anderson. His production company, AP Films (later Century 21), was a pioneer of synergy: the co-ordinated selling of a concept or series over different media. Anderson-based strips had been one of *TV Comic*'s staples in the early 1960s, but in 1965 AP had got organised. The likes of "Fireball XL5" and "Supercar" were pulled from *TV Comic* at the end of the previous year (the *Doctor Who* strip was drafted in as a replacement), only to re-emerge in a colourful new Anderson-heavy comic called *TV Century 21*. Though published by City Magazines, the editorial and creative side was handled directly by AP Films, so forthcoming series such as *Thunderbirds* and *Captain Scarlet and the Mysterons* could be trailed months in advance of their television debuts.

For its first two years, *TV Century 21* ran a strip dedicated to the Daleks, which is the main reason why Hartnell's *TV Comic* incarnation never met his arch-enemies and made do with cut-price imitators such as the Trods. The back cover of *DWM* reprinted these in all their lurid glory and made robot Anti-Dalek agent 2K a hero all over again. It looked recognisably like an action-strip, so made everything else in the Annuals and *TV Comic* (and, let's face it, on television) look a bit starchy. For copyright reasons, the Dalek strips had no overt connection with *Doctor Who*. The Doctor's comic-strip adventures took another seven years to catch up, and in between, only *TV Comic* sustained us while the series wasn't on.

The Hartnell Doctor strips are now largely remembered, if at all, for three things. First, they introduced the first off-screen companions: John and Gillian, who were supposedly the grandchildren of 'Doctor Who'. For better or worse, they've since become an odd part of *Who* folklore. In 1968, Jamie belatedly replaced them, though later the Polystyle Doctor would travel solo more often than not. The rights to use the TV characters cost money, and besides, companions were liable to have disappeared from our screens by the time they got into print. (In particular, World Distributors, publishers of the *Doctor Who Annuals* of the 60s, 70s and 80s, encountered this problem. They also ran comic strips, but these tended to be so awful that fandom has done its utmost to blank them out of its collective consciousness.)

Second, there'd been a pleasingly cartoony six-month run by artist Bill Mevin that looked like no *Who* strips before or since. On the plus side, Mevin's Hartnell seemed agreeably like the real thing, but some of the aliens were more ludicrous than any of the Delegates who went to Kemble (3.2, "Mission to the Unknown") or even the Monoids (3.6, "The Ark"). Mevin's brief stint on the strip lifted it closer to "Dan Dare" quality. (Despite this, we must point you in the direction of the Go-Rays, because nothing we could say would make these seem even *half* as daft as the strip looks.)

Third, in an early example of what we now call "cross-promotion", the strip ran a sequel to "The Web Planet" (2.5) within a week of its conclusion on BBC1. If this doesn't sound like cause for celebration of any sort, remember that in a medium when the Doctor usually faced off against mischievous goblins or the Pied Piper of Hamlin, the Zarbi were about as good as it got. Then in the run-up to Christmas 1965, Mevin gave us a story where the Doctor, John and Gillian helped Santa (not "Father Christmas", as they had an eye on the overseas market even then) make and deliver toys on a massive scale, then defeat a demon magician who makes snowmen come to life. Back on screen at this point, Katarina was hurling herself out of an airlock and Sara Kingdom was shooting her brother ("The Daleks' Master Plan").

continued on page 139...

move is to go and look at this alien ship for himself instead. Luckily for him (and conveniently for the plot), the spaceship proves to have his quarry inside it (a reversal of the usual *Doctor Who* procedure). So if Filer's from UNIT Washington he's been *really* badly briefed, and if *not*, then UNIT UK have to rethink their security procedures. Maybe he's just an FBI special agent who investigates UFOs as a hobby. [No, that's a silly idea.]

This brings us to the strange question of Chinn himself: what's his actual role, exactly? He barks 'Chinn, here, MoD' down the phone and is in charge of a 'committee of inquiry', yet gets the authority, somehow, to launch stock-footage missiles. If he's from the Ministry of Defence, he's been astonishingly ill-briefed (to the point that he's never *heard* of the Master); but if he's not - and is instead from the Treasury checking on how much taxpayer's money goes on paperclips or lateral molecular scanners - then he should have no authority to launch missile attacks on unknown vessels of unknown power.

The more one considers this, the more baffling it becomes. Neither Chinn nor the minister is in the chain of command, and the people we see in Chinn's first scene taking notes don't accompany him to Nuton. He's later able to place UN personnel under arrest, plus barge into First Contact situations and negotiate on behalf of Her Majesty's Government, despite not having even the remotest sign of any official mandate or military rank. He reports to a minister, who has absolutely no confidence in him at all. The minister himself, an honest-to-goodness government minister with a constant phone link to 10 Downing Street, might *perhaps* be able to do all of this legally, but even that is unclear: he's investigating some aspect of UNIT, but with no idea as to what they do. So that's *two* people the Brigadier has allowed in to his HQ who have no idea why they're present, and nobody tells them that they're in the way. [Suddenly the Master's comedy mask and oversized greatcoat seem a lot more plausible as a means of gaining access.] Anyway, shouldn't a complex as powerful and important as Nuton have its *own* government oversight committee, whose first task would be to shut Chinn in a room somewhere and get the Brig some regular army backup?

The missiles Chinn fires (illegally, it seems) are a piece of film of a Bloodhound and... a photo of the same missile perched in front of a camera

feeding a monitor. Whoops. When the missile strike is aborted, the photo reverses itself. Chinn arranges the missile launch by phone, and so far as we can tell, there's no security procedures to verify his identity. Nor is there any provision made against incoming aliens cutting off the phones. [Not as frivolous as it seems: what with Axos' arrival causing 'freak weather conditions', a 70s phone line could be blown down or interrupted by static.]

The Doctor reasons that the Axons must be lying, as they're apparently able to harness any form of energy but claim to need resources from Earth. Yet when the horrible truth about the Axons is revealed, it transpires that they want Earth's energy anyway, as if that motive makes perfect sense now that they've been identified as evil. If they can indiscriminately draw energy from a whole planet, then can't they just suck the power they need from a sun somewhere? Why waste precious energy skipping through time to avoid a tasty banquet of nuclear warheads their hosts have thoughtfully provided? Oh, and Axos has 'variable mass', which the Doctor describes as 'interesting'. Try "physically impossible", and you're closer to the mark.

Everyone keeps banging on about the well-nigh inconceivable amount of energy it would take Axos to travel through time, with the Doctor claiming that 'pure mathematics cannot lie'. Yet it quickly turns out that Axos just needs the energy of a single (albeit advanced) nuclear reactor on Earth. Surely, the whole of Earth's energy (which Axos was planning on draining anyway) would outweigh anything the Nuton complex can produce? Then again, Axos is an entity so stupid that after it drains the life from Pigbin Josh, it dumps his body outside so the next humans to come along can find it and get suspicious. Even so, Benton and Yates curiously take it on trust that the corpse - which has a beard and is dressed in rags, complete with a shoe in one pocket - must be Filer's.

Earlier, Axos determines that Pigbin Josh has 'atypical' intelligence - but as he's the first human they've ever encountered, how does it know? Did the Master provide some baseline quotient of human intelligence? [Perhaps he supplies every prospective invasion-partnership with a glossy brochure outlining Earth's suitability for conquest. It's also been suggested that Axos gets something of a clue regarding human advancement from the

Why Did We Countdown to TV Action?

...continued from page 137

Once Troughton's Doctor arrived - unannounced and unexplained at the end of 1966 - the strip incorporated more TV monsters including the Cybermen (but only the Mondas model from 4.2, "The Tenth Planet"), the Quarks (see 6.1, "The Dominators", for why this might have been more trouble than it was worth) and the Witches. (Or the "Carrionites", as X3.2, "The Shakespeare Code" rechristens them. Once you realise that Gareth Roberts is a huge fan of these silly strips, a lot of things start to make sense.)

Whereas the Hartnell stories had been aimless and whimsical, with an almost fairytale-like atmosphere, the Second Doctor's comic strip adventures were boisterous and - by contrast with the telly - bloodthirsty. For every madcap plot with the Quarks trying to conquer the universe with giant wasps (did we mention how much Gareth Roberts adores these strips? - see X4.7, "The Unicorn and the Wasp"), there was a story where the Doctor wins by blasting the villains with a ray gun and a cry of, "Die, hideous creature! Die!" (See Volume II for some of the more outrageous plots but understand that, when we made fun of the Scarecrow army, we had no idea that X3.8, "Human Nature" was on the horizon.)

You'd think nobody in the *Doctor Who* production office was paying any attention. But in fact, the job of vetting *TV Comic* storylines seems to have fallen to the assistant script editor of the day, including Terrance Dicks at one stage. The feedback was such that the later Troughton strips tied in closely with the on-screen events of the Doctor's exile (see 6.7, "The War Games", for more on this). By 1970, however, the general standard of the strip was giving Barry Letts cause for concern. The Third Doctor's first comics outing appeared a fortnight after the start of "Spearhead from Space" (7.1), and something was clearly amiss. The creative team were thoroughly settled in (artist John Canning - whose tendency to draw people raising their right index fingers and beaming triumphantly gets a lot of stick - had been turning out two pages or more every week for the past five years) and saw no reason to change anything now. Lip service was paid to the new TV format (the Doctor is shown to be in exile and working for a character called the Brigadier, who bears a passing resemblance to Nicholas Courtney), but the tone wasn't too different from the later Troughton strips.

Pertwee's first comic strip adversary is a trouble-making schoolboy who looks like Harry Potter. In a later strip he defeats a spy thanks to his newfound ability to levitate. In another, he goes on a cruise aboard the Brigadier's luxury yacht. You can see why Letts was concerned. Canning's energetic but clumsy art also failed to conjure up the series' visual texture of the new, colour episodes. (In fairness to Canning, this had suited the Troughton strips and he later developed a more polished style for his Tom Baker stories in the mid-1970s. Unfortunately, none of these have ever been reprinted.) In issue 999 of *TV Comic*, the Doctor had an adventure with a time-travelling bulldozer and then... stopped.

Letts and Dicks weren't happy and had tried to persuade Polystyle to revamp the strip into something closer to the new-look TV series. Liz Shaw was introduced (briefly, and when she disappeared the Brigadier went with her), as was the Doctor's car, here called 'Betsy'. Out went Troughton-era writer Roger Cook, who we presume isn't the doorstopping investigative journalist of the same name. In came Alan Fennell, a regular scriptwriter on Gerry Anderson's supermarionation series and former editor of *TV Century 21*. Fennell's scripts took what our lawyers advise us to describe as "a generous amount of inspiration" from the then-recent Season Seven. None of these alterations seemed to have pleased Letts, but Polystyle ruled out further changes as being too expensive.

Much later, when the TV series was off the air, Marvel's efforts to reclaim the whole of the programme's past led to a reappraisal of *TV Comic*. They published *Doctor Who Classic Comics* in the early 1990s, reprinting creaky thirty-year-old strips, albeit with new colour effects by artists who laboured under the delusions that Cybermen are pink and Jon Pertwee was bright yellow.

Two things are worthy of note here. First, *Classic Comics* divorced these stories from their original context. Rather than being just one item in an anthology of child-friendly strips based (more often than not) on popular TV series, they were repackaged as pure, concentrated *Doctor Who*. Back in the day, readers of *TV Comic*, *Countdown + TV Action* and *Look-in* got their favourite show in amongst all sorts of other hit series such as *Basil Brush*, *Follyfoot* or *Hawaii Five-O*.

Second (and despite an implausibly valedictory editorial in the final issue), no-one pretended that

continued on page 141...

missiles and radar sent in its direction - but termites can make vast hills, and an individual termite's none too smart. It still doesn't resolve the matter of them defining the one specimen they've surveyed as 'atypical'.]

Instances of people going deaf, blind (or both) when the plot requires: a UNIT guard fails to hear the "whoosh" / electric hum of Axos' main orifice opening right behind him, allowing the Master to sneak up and kill him. The Master also tells a hypnotized UNIT driver to get help from a guard who - as we discover in the very next shot - is standing right there, not at all curious about the sinister-looking man who's issuing orders to his comrade. [So *nobody* in UNIT, save the Doctor's little gang it seems, knows what the planet's most-wanted looks like.] Observe how the Master sneaks up behind a communications officer who's calling for Greyhound very, very softly, as if he's gently waking them up from a deep sleep rather than [as one imagines from the dialogue] calling them over a bad connection. Later still, the Master tinkers with the particle accelerator and thereby fails to notice the *five* troopers practically creeping on tip-toe to surround him. (Never mind that the soldiers encircle their foe in one of those "don't move, or we'll shoot ourselves" moments.) How come everyone within Axos can hear Jo scream, but not Filer's gun going off, repeatedly?

When Sir George asks about the police box that's cluttering up his research facility, the Brigadier at first responds, 'I've no idea', then turns around and spies the Ship, then turns back and says, with confidence, that it's part of the Doctor's equipment. Did he need to distinguish it from all the *other* police boxes that one might bring into a reactor room? Later on Axos, the Doctor becomes horrified as Jo nearly ages to death - but Jo herself seems awfully passive about the whole affair, not complaining or flinching in the slightest at being turned into a pensioner and back.

Not for the last time [see in particular 14.2, "The Hand of Fear"], Bob Baker and Dave Martin have trouble comprehending the scale and consequences of nuclear energy. In "The Claws of Axos", they give us the Nuton nuclear power complex - a facility so large that it powers most of Britain, yet which has pitifully few staff members, researchers and security guards, and which blows up as neatly as an empty warehouse. Indeed, the Master's amusing line about putting 'sticky tape on

the windows' would be funnier still if Baker and Martin weren't intent on treating an atomic explosion as if it were a World War II bomb going off, only a bit bigger. Speaking of which...

Strange things to do in a meltdown: 1) amble slowly down the road half a mile, then stop; 2) watch a nuclear reactor explode; 3) through binoculars; 4) then go back. [And don't give us that stuff about this detonation only being the light-speed accelerator going "pop" after the trigger-mechanism is removed... accelerating things past lightspeed requires a lot more energy than an atomic bomb anyway, and having something *that* powerful detonate *that* close to a nuclear pile is at least as dangerous as anything that happened at Chernobyl.[35] Besides, if the lab's concrete walls are blown off, the reactor's shielding must become compromised.]

The TARDIS is visible during the humans-versus-Axons battle in the final episode, even though it's already left the scene by then. [Let's call it a freak side effect of the Doctor's time loop - it makes as much sense as anything else.]

Once Axos activates its nutrition cycle, it need only let matters play out to win. Instead, it sends a cadre of spaghetti-monsters against the heroes, and in particular makes a bid to kill Benton and Yates before they can escape in their Land Rover. Honestly, why bother? What possible difference can it make, if you're about to consume the energy of the entire world? (Anyway, why physically lumber onto the jeep onto to get shaken off / blown up, when they could've just hit it with exploding tendrils?) During said fracas, why can't Yates cock his gun properly?

And one final note about Chinn: what are the *other* officials left at UNIT HQ going to make of his story when he gets back and what purpose did his inquiry serve?

Critique So it *was* too good to last. At long last, and after several improbable successes, the production-team's luck runs out and they hit upon a method of doing UNIT *Doctor Who* that doesn't really come off.

What's irritating is that it's not a case of any one thing being grotesquely off-key, so much as it's a *lot* of things just aren't in tune with each other or the previous stories. Each aspect of "The Claws of Axos" has been nudged just slightly too far: the characters are slightly more schematic than before, the design a tiny bit more cartoonish, the

Why Did We Countdown to TV Action?

...continued from page 139

they were any good. They were reprinted not for their own virtues, but as fan heritage. The earliest strips have a certain naïve charm, but seemed crude even in the mid-1960s, and fail to capture all but the most basic resemblance to the TV series they were supposedly based on. But this wasn't true of everything *Classic Comics* reprinted and it's in the middle of the Pertwee years that the *Doctor Who* comic strip became, briefly, something more than disposable spinoffery. Letts wanted a more exciting *Doctor Who* strip than *TV Comic* could carry. A way out of the impasse appeared in the form of a new Polystyle title - one better suited to run the *Doctor Who* strip than the relentlessly juvenile *TV Comic* - and this was called *Countdown*.

Countdown was edited by Dennis Hooper. He'd been art editor on *TV Century 21*, and cast his new comic from the same high-quality, colourful, puppet-filled mould. The big selling point was a strip based on the latest Century 21 series, *UFO*, but it was a tactical blunder. When *Countdown* appeared in February 1971, *UFO* was sinking fast. Aside from Anderson, the emphasis was on science fiction, with the title strip being loosely inspired by *2001: A Space Odyssey*. But Hooper liked *Doctor Who* enormously, and persuaded *TV Comic* to surrender the *Who* strip to his new venture.

Doctor Who's jump from *TV Comic* to *Countdown* was a stylistic leap as big as any seen in the TV series. Initially drawn by Harry Lindfield, the *Doctor Who* strip was now in colour - a big deal, when most of the country still couldn't see how gaudy "The Claws of Axos" (8.3) really looked. Lindfield's work wouldn't have looked out of place in the *Eagle*. The stories themselves were tighter and more sober than anything *TV Comic* had managed. With hindsight they're still full of padding, logical flaws and clichés, but the difference from the Cook / Canning strips was palpable.

Yet in many ways, the format hadn't changed *that* much. The Doctor is still seen as a solitary figure living in a moorland cottage with no constant companion other than 'Betsy'. UNIT is mentioned occasionally, in passing. The exile format was adhered to briefly, but was clearly chafing - the second serial, "Timebenders", has the Doctor going for a stroll and stumbling on a gang of WWII Nazis with an experimental time machine (as one does). In the very next story he "rediscovers the element of the TARDIS" and travels freely in time and space again, without resorting to such contrivances.

Hooper's interest in *Who* was such that he wound up writing most of the scripts himself, and these are notably sparkier than those by deputy editor Dick O'Neill. He soon struck up a good working relationship with Letts, the result being a rather more creative form of synergy than yet-another attempt to foist the Zarbi or the Quarks onto an audience that really couldn't care less. Soon, Hooper was editing *Doctor Who Holiday Specials* for Polystyle, revealing the name of the Doctor's home planet to readers months before it was mentioned on TV (see 11.1, "The Time Warrior") and visiting the set for exclusive photoshoots. The first of these was on location for "The Daemons", with pictures from this shoot were used as reference for the 1971 comic serial "The Celluloid Midas". (Hooper was photographed on location, and ends up in the strip as a soap star who's been turned into plastic by the eponymous villain.) It sounds weird, but this story is regarded as something of a high point for the *Doctor Who* comic strip. The stories were just as odd as anything being broadcast at the time. They had, however, one devastating advantage over televised stories: the draftsmanship. The magazine had a house-style that owed a lot to the star illustrator of *TV 21* in the 60s, Frank Bellamy. He drew the *Thunderbirds* strip and although he never worked on the *Who* adventures, his influence was *everywhere* in the new comic. Bellamy had as big an impact on the look of British comics as Frank Hampson. His work was colourful, detailed and dynamic. It used striking images and composition, and was "realistic" without slaving itself to realism. He sought to make his strips cinematic, and seemed incapable of drawing a dull frame. (Or certainly a rectangular one - his frames are asymmetric and urgent, to the point that every image seems to burst in from somewhere else.) He took over "Dan Dare" after the publishers forced out Hampson in acrimonious circumstances.

Just as *Countdown* was launching, Bellamy was becoming associated with *Doctor Who*. His illustrations for the series, published in *Radio Times* between 1971 and 1976, defined the off-screen "look" of the series at the time, and particularly well-remembered work includes his pieces for "Day of the Daleks" (9.1) and "Terror of the Zygons" (13.1). Nowhere is its influence more apparent than *Countdown*. If you were doing an action-strip in the UK (except for the curious ones that had

continued on page 143...

music a bit less richly textured, the acting a shade more (putting it politely) emphatic. Any of these things alone would have been forgivable (if not demanded) had the rest been reigned in. But the rot sets in early, with Peter Bathurst (as Chinn) opening a file with 'TOP SECRET' on it in huge bulbous letters. He's usually a fairly reliable performer, but here seems to have morphed into Peter Glaze (see 1.7, "The Sensorites" and various mentions of the kid's show you're all supposed to shout about). Then enter the Token Yank (except he isn't). It's still possible at this point to resign yourself to a story that involves these characters for four episodes - but then in comes Pigbin Josh with That Bloody Music. From then on, there's a whole string of things seemingly designed to suck out any possible enthusiasm on the viewer's part.

The funny thing is that we could indulgently enjoy this story if it were *all* bad, but unfortunately, enough goes *right* to make the wrongness all the more painful. Bizarrely, all the caveats we listed when reviewing "Terror of the Autons" (8.1) are plusses here. There's some good, honest greasy kid's stuff to enjoy with your sausage and mash on Saturday teatime; for a start, giving the Master any motivation beyond getting his TARDIS back would rob this story's villainy of its joyous absurdity (laser-guns, crap disguises and all). What with stunts and bangs being the new basic requirement for *Doctor Who*, anyone in the audience thinking, "it's been ten minutes and nothing's exploded", should be well served. And after six weeks of relatively orthodox drama with a malignant cookie-jar making people hallucinate (8.2, "The Mind of Evil"), the kids needed a good old-fashioned monster (preferably *not* a dragon).

And on that score, they got one of the greats. The Axon Monsters look like a seven-year-old boy drew them, and they blow people up with hugely Freudian tentacles. And they're not green! This is such a breakthrough, we hope a large percentage of the viewing public got to see it in colour. Even if you didn't, what we could call the "Tartrazine Aesthetic" informs everything else going on here. The detached Axos head floating about and revolving oddly is just one of the weird and purely televisual moments here. If nothing else, the programme-makers have figured out that colour *Doctor Who* shouldn't aspire to be second-rate feature films; it should be unique and trailblazing television. Compared to "Terror of the Autons", what's striking is how cautious the exposition

scenes seem. This story has a much stronger plot than the season-opener - not necessarily any more *sensible,* you understand, but the links from one set piece to another are less arbitrary - and it could've accommodated more wild camera work, abstract music and shorter scenes. If someone had realised that Baker and Martin had essentially written a comic strip for television, the director could have given full rein to his gleeful experimental tendencies.

So yeah, you can see occasionally some potential in all of this, *but...* (and here it comes) what we actually get falls between two stools. They had pretty much got "gritty realism" down pat with "The Mind of Evil", but here they keep pushing it in a new adventure where it just isn't going to work. The music is crass, over-loud and relentless. (Leaving aside Brian Hodgson's "atmospheres" in Season Six, this story has the least amount of unscored air time per week since the jumble of stock cues in 5.1, "Tomb of the Cybermen".) The acting is pitched somewhere between absolute conviction and *commedia del'arte* or the traditional British panto, sometimes by the same actor in the same scene. This is unmistakably the point at which *Doctor Who* moves from being a TV show to being a style of acting. Bathurst is just the most egregious member of a cast so stiff, even Richard Franklin is a welcome breath of naturalism.

There's no use denying it: a major goof in terms of script, performance and plot-logic is Bill Filer. Jo reacts to his apparent death and later hearing his voice as though they share a history, but no reason is given for this. Nor do Katy Manning and Paul Grist (who *can* be good in other things - we've seen him do it, honest) share any on-screen chemistry. We can *try* to be charitable, but Filer is just an embarrassment. Between his wonky accent and hopelessly stilted B-movie lines, you wonder if anyone making this had actually met any Americans, ever.

By any orthodox standards, then, this is a remarkably inept piece of television drama. Worse, as regards the later UNIT stories, it's the first harbinger of humiliations to come. It's so unprecedentedly clumsy, it actually comes as a shock if you watch the Pertwee stories in order. The strengths of "Terror of the Autons" (the abrupt editing, the blatant artificiality of the music and sets) have become catastrophic weaknesses, yet it's hard to keep your eyes off this story. This is often through sheer bewilderment (especially at

Why Did We Countdown to TV Action?

...continued from page 141

started appearing in *The Beano* in the late 60s[40]), you were in his wake, regardless of the genre. (Bellamy, in fact, preferred Westerns.) He was also Target Books' first choice to illustrate their novelisations, a gig eventually given to art student Chris Achilleos, who was asked to produce work in Bellamy's style[41]. (It seems that Bellamy was just too busy to do more work for Polystyle, and the *Radio Times* gig was more cost-effective than three colour pages a week all year round.) Apart from one curio for *Radio Times* (see 8.4, "Colony in Space"), Bellamy never actually illustrated a *Doctor Who* comic strip. It just *felt* as though he had.

As the Marvel reprints demonstrate, these stories aren't about plot but mood. The logic of the strips, even the ones that *don't* have Daleks in, is wonky, but the visual panache is entirely in keeping with the fast-paced, gaudy style of the Letts era. Fifteen years before "The Curse of Fenric" (26.3), the Doctor was whisked away to Nazi Germany - a topic *TV Comic* and even Season Seven would have struggled to avoid seeming tasteless. Things considered too risky to render on TV for the fear of looking underwhelming (fake alien invasions run from a lighthouse, soap-bubble spaceships, etc.) could be controlled and made to look plausible.

Although the start of 1971 wasn't exactly a bad time to launch a new TV-based comic, *Countdown* failed to catch on. It was expensive to produce - especially compared to the perennially tacky *TV Comic* - and the contents didn't prove as attractive as Hooper had hoped. In spring 1972, it was relaunched as *TV Action + Countdown* with a new emphasis on action series such as *The Persuaders!* and *Mission: Impossible*, while surreptitiously switching to a cheaper printing process at the same time. With Pertwee 'hai!'-ing his way round Peladon and Solos, *Doctor Who* fitted the "TV Action" description quite snugly and proved it by nabbing the cover.

By now Lindfield had been replaced by Gerry Haylock, another artist in the *Eagle* / Bellamy tradition, and his covers always included one large, fully-painted panel. The result was arguably the best artwork ever to grace a *Doctor Who* comic strip. Tying in with the relaunch, Polystyle ran the most high-profile "design a *Doctor Who* monster" competition outside of *Blue Peter*, with Letts, Dicks and Pertwee roped in as judges. The winner was one Ian Fairington, who won a colour television for

his family and got to see his creation - the Ugrakks - immortalised in newsprint. Pertwee himself came in to judge this, and his arrival was written up in exactly the same tones as teen mags such as *Jackie* would handle a visit by David Cassidy. That said, the Ugrakks were fairly generic villains in an overlong romp. The art remained striking, but the standard of the scripts was deteriorating and the comic was no nearer to finding an audience.

So at the start of 1973, it was revamped *again*, losing half the title to become *TV Action*. There was still a place for *Doctor Who*, but further format changes knocked it off the cover. Like the stars of the other major action strips, the Doctor now appeared on a rotating basis. His serialised adventures were interspersed with longer self-contained stories and short periods when his strip was "rested". Rather than inspiring audience loyalty, however, this turned out to be the kiss of death. The art, the scripts, the *everything* felt sloppier than ever before. Though it was still superior to *TV Comic*'s output, *TV Action* finally expired in the summer of 1973.

Its failure must have been galling for Polystyle. They had the format right, but they'd been beaten to the punch by arch-rivals Independent Television Publications, who had taken over *TV Times* in 1968. A month before *Countdown* first appeared, ITP launched their own brand new comic, a "junior *TV Times*" that interspersed features and photospreads with strips based on popular ITV series, including such obvious *Who* wannabes as *Timeslip*, *Freewheelers* and *Catweazle*. It was called *Look-in*, it was glossy and colourful and it sold by the bucketload, becoming one of the big British comics successes of the decade.

With *TV Action*'s demise, *Doctor Who* returned to the also-ran option, *TV Comic*. Haylock remained as artist, though his work - now exclusively in black and white - was no longer up to the standard he'd set himself on *TV Action + Countdown*. He left in early 1975 when it became clear that his rendition of Tom Baker wasn't terribly successful. By mid-1975, John Canning was back in the harness and would remain through various format changes (the comic growing tackier with each new revamp) until 1979. By the end, they'd stopped giving him new strips to illustrate but were content to reprint Haylock's work, with Canning doctoring five-year-old stories to replace Pertwee's likeness with that of Tom Baker.

continued on page 145...

where they've chosen to point the camera), but large chunks of it are tremendously pretty and, frankly, groovy. And that's the astonishing contradiction at the core of "The Claws of Axos": while the plot, dialogue, acting and music conspire to make the viewer mute the sound, the extraordinary visuals keep you from switching off.

Let's try to be upbeat, then. This story is hard to like, but easy to *love* and at least has the decency to look unlike anything else, then or now. If you remember our recommended method of watching "The Tomb of the Cybermen" (make a compilation of appropriate chart hits of the period, and play the story mute as accompaniment), you might do the same here. Maybe select a prog rock album from 1971 (not that you'd admit to having any, but you could borrow some - something by Gong or Tangerine Dream, perhaps) or even, appropriately, *Who's Next* by The Who. Then replace the chips 'n' dips with sweets from the time ("Spanish Tobacco" and Anglo Bubbly, washed down with Nesquik), or that seventies classic: a fondue.

The Facts

Written by Bob Baker and Dave Martin. Directed by Michael Ferguson. Viewing figures: 7.3 million, 8.0 million, 6.4 million, 7.8 million.

Supporting Cast Peter Bathurst (Chinn), Paul Grist (Filer), Donald Hewlett (Hardiman), David Savile (Winser), Derek Ware (Pigbin Josh), Bernard Holley (Axon Man), Fernanda Marlowe (Corporal Bell), Tim Piggott-Smith (Captain Harker), Patricia Gordino (Axon Woman), John Hicks (Axon Boy), Debbie Lee London (Axon Girl).

Working Titles "The Gift", "The Friendly Invasion", "The Vampire From Space" (see **The Lore**).

Cliffhangers Jo, exploring the organic interior of the Axon "spaceship", sees a lumpy red Axon loom out of the wall in front of her; the Doctor activates the dormant Axonite in the power centre, and he and his colleagues suddenly find themselves surrounded by irked Axons after a duvet-monster chases them around a giant Ker-Plunk!; the Master uses the power of the nuclear reactor to try to destroy Axos, but the Doctor and Jo are

trapped inside as the creature goes into spasm around them.

What Was in the Charts? "Pushbike Song", The Mixtures; "Power to the People", John Lennon & the Plastic Ono Band; "Hot Love", T Rex36; "Strange Kind of Woman", Deep Purple. (Careful, that fondue set's hot.)

The Lore

• If you've been keeping count, you'll have spotted that until now, Dicks has commissioned scripts from his former colleagues (Don Houghton and Malcolm Hulke), his predecessor (David Whitaker), his pet project (Robert Holmes) and several other seasoned writers who didn't make the grade. He's had submissions from *Who* veterans Bill Strutton, William Emms, Peter Ling and Douglas Camfield, but with the exception of "Inferno", everything that's reached the screen has been the work of writers he's used before on the series. Between "The Seeds of Death" (6.5) and "Inferno", Holmes wrote ten episodes and (allowing that Whitaker's work re-drafted into shape for "The Ambassadors of Death"), Hulke wholly or largely wrote twenty-four. Hulke aside, Dicks was finding that his gamble on hiring Holmes to rework "The Space Trap" had paid off (see 6.4, "The Krotons"), and he had a reliably inventive writer up his sleeve for contingencies. Maybe lightning could strike twice...

• We should back up a little. When a sitcom script was sent to Derrick Sherwin in 1968 (through the Byzantine processes of the BBC's Script Pool), he and Dicks made an appointment to speak to the writers. Animator Bob Baker and penitent former adman Dave Martin lived in Bristol and worked for a local film company. They had based *A Man's Life* (the sitcom pilot, the name coming from recruitment ads of the time) on a friend of theirs[37] and had no idea that the people who'd invited them up to London were the makers of *Doctor Who*. Dicks and Sherwin mentioned the new format and asked if the writers had any story ideas. As it turned out, they had lorryloads. A six-part Troughton script, "The Gift", began with a space-battle between jellyfish-like spacecraft and had a giant skull landing in Hyde Park and offering people whatever they wanted for a price, and making their human-sized nerve-cells become what anyone desired. Then on page two...

Why Did We Countdown to TV Action?

...continued from page 143

At this time BBC Enterprises were planning an in-house comic to rival *Look-in* and it was widely assumed that they would claw back the *Doctor Who* rights when Polystyle's licence expired. Brian Bolland - best known for his clean and bold artwork for *2000AD* - was sounded out as an artist for the new BBC strip. The *Eagle*-style was no longer as fashionable as it had been at the start of the decade, with a new trend in British comics - spearheaded by IPC titles such as *Battle Picture Weekly*, *Action*, *Starlord* and *Misty* - drawing inspiration from American and, especially, European artists rather than Hampson or Bellamy. After a wobbly start, IPC's *2000AD* was now becoming as influential as the *Eagle* had once been. (For its impact on *Doctor Who*, see 24.2, "Paradise Towers", and in fact most of Volume VI.) Though the "BBC *Look-in*" didn't happen, it wasn't entirely unexpected that Marvel employed IPC's *wunderkinds* Pat Mills and John Wagner to revitalise the *Doctor Who* comic strip in *Doctor Who Weekly*. They were already pitching material to the TV series proper (see 20.3, "Mawdryn Undead" and What *Else* Didn't Get Made? under 17.6, "Shada") and their work (along with Dave Gibbons' striking black-and-white art) marked out the Marvel approach as something a cut above what had gone before. At least, until they were given the push for being too expensive. What happened next is a much more complicated story and is still unfolding.

Dicks asked for a reworked version. Four months later, he got something that was almost as profligate, with memorable images but no logical connection between them. Barry Letts was now producer, and was particularly worried about the giant skull. So on the day the revised version arrived, Dicks asked for *another* revision (to be delivered more promptly if possible), and by the way could Baker and Martin include the Master in it. They went on like this for another six months and three drafts, whittling seven episodes' worth of material into a four-parter called "The Friendly Invasion" and later "The Vampire from Space". The Axons had difficulty with English at first, but later had mid-Atlantic accents. They were described as looking like "the adman's dream Coca-Cola family".

• No sooner has Dicks house-broken a script with too many ideas, than Letts gives it to the similarly inventive Michael Ferguson to direct. He's been very much in demand and had something of a "buzz" about him since "The Ambassadors of Death". Ferguson's first move was to book an experimental studio session and play with some fresh ideas - this is the first concerted attempt to get CSO to work with yellow instead of blue (they'd tried both with "Silurians"), and more ways to abuse a video-disc player to make it do exciting things. Also mentioned are a number of experiments concerning back-projection and the light-show effects used on *Top of the Pops* (an outfit called "Crab Nebula" usually did these).

Here's where the "growing frog"-effect seems to have originated. Earlier versions use a rat (possibly, it was considered too close to the phobiadeath in "The Mind of Evil" episode one). One script has Professor Winser running scared from the frog (this sounds to us like a leftover from the rat sequence). This session, which also included the first attempts at Axon transformations and the rice-dribble effect (see below) was just before Christmas.

• The various alien-looking Axons were mainly designed and made by freelancer Jules Baker, then better known for making large inflatable or polystyrene body-suits for carnivals and TV's *It's A Knockout*. They were made of chamois-leather covered in various other flameproof substances (because of all the explosions happening around them) and were thus mercifully warm on location, if almost unbearable in the studio. One of the ten-drilled Axons was resprayed and used as the Krynoid in "The Seeds of Doom" (13.6); the others were pressed into service for exhibitions. Letts, it seems, had misgivings about the monsters. Baker was actually touted for the job, even though the BBC's in-house costume teams jealously guarded this most high-profile challenge (thus, BBC regulations meant that he wasn't credited).

• On the 4th of January, filming started in and around the Dungeness nuclear power station, on the Kent coast. It's pretty bleak at the best of times, but that week the weather ceased to make any sense. Pigbin Josh's first appearance was supposed to entail heavy-duty cables hanging from the pylons leading to the station as a backdrop - but in the thick snow and fog, visibility was drastically curtailed.

As with "The Ambassadors of Death", Ferguson requested and got the services of film cameraman AA Englander (or "Tubby'" Englander, as he was called). He'd worked with Rudolph Cartier on the *Quatermass* serials, and had thus been instrumental in getting the quality of filmed inserts in television up to a far higher standard than had been budgeted for, let alone achieved. Even so, in January the available light resulted in a four or five-hour work day under normal circumstances (snow extends this a little, but the fog on the first day undid this slight bonus).

• Derek Ware took the part of Pigbin Josh eagerly, as he welcomed the chance of some straight acting. (No, we're not saying anything.) His dialogue was scripted, and written phonetically. A typical example: 'Ur bin oughta gone put thickery blarmdasted zoines about, gordangum, diddenum?' He took the role four days before filming began, on New Year's Day 1971. A lot of the first filming day was spent improvising the scrap-heap scenes, while they waited for the fog to lift so they could do the planned scenes. Havoc's deal with the BBC meant that they got a flat fee (which was welcome, in a precarious business), but resulted in multiple retakes being covered in the per diem rate. Ware had to plunge into the icy water of the drainage ditch on a child's bicycle that had been found, operating dodgy brakes with mittened and frozen hands. He claims it was warmer in the water. Englander apparently wanted another take, but the front wheel had buckled, allowing Ware to get away with the haphazard first attempt and then thaw out.

Ware did all the shots around the boats and the big stunt scene of Josh being pulled into Axos. (If you couldn't tell, he was shuffling himself along, as the two guys pulling the rope were too slow *and* the pebbles had frozen together.)

• Day Two saw the arrival of a BBC Outside Broadcast (OB) van. This hefty vehicle (used to ferry OB equipment to sporting events and royal weddings, and usually with a tiny studio inside) was fiendishly disguised with the UNIT logo to double for their Mobile HQ. (The interior set had been seen in "The Mind of Evil".)

• The regulars finally arrived after their festive break. With them were three guest artists and ten soldiers. Donald Hewlett (Sir George) had served with Pertwee in the Navy, and would later become famous in *It Ain't Half Hot Mum*. David Saville (here as Professor Winser, but previously Lt Carstairs from "The War Games") was just about to become more famous for *Warship*. We'll see him again in "The Five Doctors" (20.7). Peter Bathurst (formerly the betrayed governor in 4.3, "The Power of the Daleks") played Chinn - the part had been revised from petty annoyance to major antagonist to back. Bathurst had been in *The Quatermass Experiment,* but if you haven't seen the two extant episodes, you'll find it hard to credit what part he played[38].

• Some of Katy Manning's dialogue was dropped or moved to studio scenes, as she found it difficult to talk. In some shots her bare legs were blue. Make-up was used to cover the effects of the cold on her face, and her thin-soled boots led to her coming close to getting frostbite. Courtney's fake moustache kept falling off when the glue froze. (Conversely, between the latex "old man" make-up and tramp's clothing he had on, Ware was sweating. Everyone else, though, was swaddled in thick overcoats or standing over open car engines for warmth between takes.) In the scene where Yates and Benton find Josh's body, a wax face was made to crumble as they touched it. This scene was amended to a white-out on transmission.

• The following day, which was foggy (of course), Delgado arrived and did the scene where he shoots Stuart Fell. A small explosive charge provided the smoke; Fell was a trained acrobat (and fire-eater - see 14.1, "The Masque of Mandragora"), so he could do falls and somersaults with precision (see also Morbius' charming death-scene in 13.5, "The Brain of Morbius"). He also zapped other Havoc members from inside one of the Axon suits. Later, he became Manning's usual stunt-double. He'd been in the series before, as an extra in 3.10, "The War Machines" (directed by Ferguson).

• Thursday brought a change of location, to the Army's nearby training ground just outside Folkestone. Here the Master jumped onto a truck (Havoc's Jack Cooper did the actual jump, but Delgado really stood atop a moving vehicle as it went under a bridge) and Yates and Benton beat up a rather persistent group of Axon hitchhikers. As the footage shows, the fog had gone but it was raining, and driving over wet grass was awkward. Just to *really* mess up continuity, Friday brought bright sunshine. The team moved to Dungeness A, the nuclear power-station seen in the distance during Josh's early mutterings. Dungeness B was being built at the time (and for many years later) and sirens kept going off during filming.

• The studio recordings were in late January and early February. The frog used for the Axonite demonstration grew restless and had to be chilled-out: literally, the handler used ice to make it more sluggish. Bernard Holley, here playing the Axon Man (previously, he was blasted to death in 5.1, "The Tomb of the Cybermen" episode one), had been a *Z-Cars* regular and wore his uniform cap with the costume as a gag. Corporal Bell was given an extra line, saying that the arrival of the space-ship had caused freak weather conditions.

• The director got Bernard Fox to handle the technical stuff, and several experimental techniques were tried for this story. As noted, the spaceship was "flown" in the studio, using CSO and a moving camera (a technique that needed computer-driven cameras to get right, as John Dykstra managed for *Star Wars*). The Axos model was three feet long, made from fibreglass with gaps for a latex diaphragm to make it "breathe". Condoms were added later. Letts wasn't too keen on the "spaceflight" effect, and most similar shots would be done on film until the advent of Quantel in the late seventies (see 17.4, "Nightmare of Eden").

• The second recording block saw a logistical snag: Letts, Dicks and possibly Ferguson found the title "The Vampire from Space" a bit silly (not to mention misleading), so the titles for the first two parts needed to be re-done. By this time Frank Bellamy had already done the promotional strip for *Radio Times* to launch the next story (see **Additional Sources** under "Colony in Space"), hence the reference back to the earlier title.

• With the exception of the remounted cliffhanger with the man-eating duvet, episode three was a straight run-through in scene order, although there was a delay to find the keys to Delgado's handcuffs. They also attempted to mix between Manning and Mildred Brown (playing old Jo) using blue-dyed rice: the rice was drizzled in front of the face of one, and the locked-in image of the other was CSO'd onto the falling grains. Holley was placed on a swivel-chair and shot from two cameras at nearly right angles to one another, and the two images were mixed for the "floating head" scenes. The second cliffhanger, requiring a spark-generator and a fond farewell to the trusty Foam Machine (see Volume II), was done last.

• The Master's TARDIS had been described as being a white hemisphere, but a prop like the SIDRAT machines (from "The War Games") was used. It appears that an outside contractor, one Clifford Culley, constructed the new console prop. We'll hear more of his expertise later.

• All four episodes overran, although the first two needed the most severe pruning. Among the cut scenes, the Master claims that Axos ensnared him off Antares IV; Filer blags a meeting with the Brigadier, claiming that the CIA sent him to interrogate the man; Jo meets Filer in a Hollywood-style "cute" collision (the sound wasn't working, hence its omission); the Doctor mentions "Greeks bearing gifts", and later claims that his first loyalty is to science (if only as an excuse to pretend to side with the Master). Some of the other excess is available on the DVD, as well as some material from the first two studio sessions. (This includes the 'Vampire' titles, Josh's uncensored disintegration, Jo introducing 'Bill Washing... oh', much more stuff with the UNIT tracking station and the set-up for the Master hypnotising the UNIT driver. We might as well tell you... fans have amusingly redubbed this last to suggest that Nick Hobbs is being fellated.)

• By time of transmission, the press were full of reports that the series was "too frightening" for children. Indeed, during the story's broadcast, even William Hartnell was being quoted as thinking the new direction was unsuitable. The worries over this had begun even while the crew were in Dungeness, although it was comparatively late in the editing that Letts took the decision to over-expose Josh and Winser's disintegrations.

8.4: "Colony in Space"

(Serial HHH. Six Episodes, 10th April - 15th May 1971.)

Which One is This? Arguably the definitive alien-planet-in-a-quarry tale, with eco-friendly colonists trying to eke out an existence on a desolate world while being harassed by an evil mining company whose robot comes trick-or-treating as a lizard. There are future soap-stars a-plenty, and the record number of 'Hai's from the Pertwee era.

Firsts and Lasts The first "space" story of the colour / Pertwee era also introduces the early-70s version of the Time Lords, who aren't yet the glittery-robed university dons we see in later stories but *do* seem more down-to-earth than those seen at the end of the 60s. Whereas in "The War

Games" they're solemn, po-faced demigods in minimalist clothing, now they're a lot more political and like hatching secret plans amongst themselves. And when the Doctor describes the TARDIS as being outside the space-time continuum when it travels, it's the first real confirmation of what has become the standard idea of how the Ship traverses space and time.

The Master's TARDIS is shown to have its own, slightly more "sinister" console room for the first time. And the keen-eyed amongst you will just about spot the debut of the triangle-patterned walls that will blight BBC space-shows for a decade (see 9.4, "The Mutants" for their first proper use). Here, it's in Leeson's dome.

First story directed by Michael Briant. He'd been helping in some capacity make the Doctor's adventures since the Hartnell days, which makes the abnormality concerning the TARDIS' materialisation effect (see **Things to Notice**) doubly strange. After years as the voice of every monster worth hearing, Roy Skelton gets an on screen appearance as Norton. (He'll be back under odd circumstances; see 10.5, "The Green Death".) Havoc's Terry Walsh also gets dialogue here, for the first time, mere seconds before a fight breaks out.

Accompanying this story, we have the first *Radio Times* comic strip, illustrating the Doctor and Jo travelling to a new world. *Eagle* and *TV21* veteran Frank Belllamy drew this, also providing monochrome pictures beside the listings for each episode. It's the start of a tradition that lasts until Season Eleven.

Second and last appearance of the Master's laser pistol. (Shame.) And for the first time, the opening theme music goes the way everyone thinks it always did.

Six Things to Notice About "Colony in Space"...

1. This is the first colour-era story in which the Doctor gets to go to another planet but, since last week's 'galactic yoyo' shenanigans, the production team seems to have forgotten how to do the TARDIS' dematerialisation effect properly. As a result, the Ship doesn't do its usual slow-fade-from-view, but instead vanishes completely after a few seconds' worth of wheezing, groaning noises. Hardcore fanboys might want to develop an explanation for this, but it's *not* a side effect of the TARDIS being steered by the Time Lords - as the director himself suggested - since the Master's

TARDIS does exactly the same thing. The script obviously intends the Master's ship to slowly vanish as the Doctor shouts 'Look!' and points, whereupon we get a few seconds of nothing much happening and then the rocket's suddenly gone. (In later years this sort of prescience is restricted to companions, starting with Jo and reaching ludicrous proportions with Tegan.)

2. The IMC robot used to attack the colonists, in itself a lovely piece of clunky mechanical design (operated by John Scott Martin, in case you hadn't guessed), is accompanied by a device that projects a hologram of a giant reptile. In BBC effects terms, this means that two colonists look out from their home to find an enormously-enlarged image of an iguana moving in slow motion - just like in the 30s *Flash Gordon* serials - waiting for them outside. Since the lizard is *supposed* to be a fake, it's debatable whether this technically qualifies as a bad special effect or not. In the interests of verisimilitude, the robot is equipped with big claws that look like they come from a fancy-dress Foghorn Leghorn costume.

3. The name of the colony's technician and all-round repairman is 'Jim', thus giving one of the characters the chance to say 'Jim'll fix it'. Non-British readers should note that *Jim'll Fix It* was a popular children's programme of the 1970s, presented by the deeply unsettling Sir Jimmy Savile (see 3.10, "The War Machines"; 22.4, "The Two Doctors"). Since *Jim'll Fix It* was (like *Doctor Who*) a staple of Saturday-evening BBC entertainment, this sounds an awful lot like an in-joke.

Except... *Jim'll Fix It* didn't start until 1975. Admittedly, the phrase "Jim'll fix it" was a pre-War equivalent of "Let George do it" or "not my problem, mate", but it's pretty unlikely that Jo would have heard it, and very *very* unlikely that Mary-from-the-Future would have. Nonetheless, they giggle about the phrase, in a knowing sort of way. We're at something of a loss to explain this, although perhaps the joke seems funny to colonists with no discernable sense of humour, just as the IMC people curiously watch footage of the Vietnam War on their 'Entertainment Console'. To make it worse, that clip is accompanied in the transmitted version by a burst of Emerson, Lake and Palmer, reinforcing the connection between Prog Rock and evil (see 8.2, "The Mind of Evil").

4. The Master's TARDIS has several significant differences when compared to the (mercifully

tidied up) one the Doctor uses. It has inbuilt torture equipment, booby-traps on the doors and a whole bunch of Home Office-issue filing cabinets. Bear this in mind, both here and in subsequent stories, when the Master gloats about his access to 'the files of the Time Lords'. Then have a look in **Things That Don't Make Sense**, where you will also see a comment about the similarly daft IMC spaceship.

5. The torrential downpour that delayed location shooting makes the climactic fight between Terry Walsh and Nicholas Pennell (as the ship is about to leave) about six times better than it should have been. In a story where Pertwee is *Hai!*ing hither and yon, and a series that increasingly finds excuses for fights where none exist, we get a real fight with genuinely high stakes.

6. The Doctor and the Master engage in a moral debate refereed by a silly-looking godlike alien whose power the Master wants. It's identical to the ethical argument in the following story, except that here it actually makes sense. Older viewers may, however, find it hard not to think of *Basil Brush* when confronted with the glove-puppet deity.

The Continuity

The Doctor He *is* briefly tempted when the Master offers him the power to end war and suffering across the universe, though he ultimately concludes that 'absolute power is evil' [he doesn't hesitate to refuse when the same kind of power is offered to him again in 8.5, "The Daemons"]. Strangely, he seems to recognise the planet Uxarius just by looking at the scanner picture of it, even though he doesn't know anything about the place.

[Perhaps he had a crafty look at the controls while Jo wasn't looking, but they frequently don't tell him anything useful such as - oh, say - the name of the planet he's landing on or even which galaxy he's in. 19.2, "Four to Doomsday", at least, indicates that the readouts *can* say this much when they're actually working. But as we don't see him do this, we might conclude that the name 'Uxarius' just pops into his head the way things do these days.]

He claims to be an expert in agriculture. He also knows the staple "magic" trick of making a coin disappear and "finding" it behind someone's ear. [He acts as though he's never seen this talent, however, in 19.3, "Kinda".] He calls the alien god-

thing 'sir' at all times, and stops in the middle of fleeing for his life to thank him.

• *Ethics:* He favours colonisation to people living 'like battery hens', and displays no moral qualms about the thought of the colonists killing the 'giant lizards' who threaten them, saying, 'Whatever it was you saw can be destroyed'. Neither does he express any remorse after pointing out a threatening primitive to the Master, knowing as he must that the Master will (and does) shoot him dead. The destruction of the city-machine will undoubtedly cause massive casualties, but he still believes that its proprietor has acted with 'compassion'.

• *Inventory.* The Doctor still has the key to the Master's TARDIS [from 8.1, "Terror of the Autons" - the Master also has one, so making spares can't be difficult]. His sonic screwdriver seems to start beeping out a warning when he's in the vicinity of an alarm beam.

The Supporting Cast

• *Jo Grant.* Despite everything she's seen so far, Jo still has trouble believing that the TARDIS can take her to other planets. Granted, she's never been inside the Ship before, even though she must have been working with the Doctor for months. It's suggested that she's never really believed in the Doctor's ability to time travel either, and that she's always thought his stories were just jokes. [Given events in the previous adventure, it seems she's been having a go on the Brigadier's memory-wiping machine.]

• *UNIT.* Still on the lookout for the Master, with UNIT agents sending reports of possible sightings back to the Brigadier. Despite the Doctor's bluster, they persist in looking for the Master on Earth, and one especially reliable agent claims to have found him. [Possibly in a church in the West Country - see the next story. We never find out who these other agents are, but as Jo started out as one, we imagine their entrance exam wasn't too rigorous.] They've already arrested the Spanish ambassador by mistake. [UNIT's over-riding concern with this one man seems to prove that Bill Filer - see last story - really is from their Washington branch and not just some itinerant bounty hunter. As late as 9.5, "The Time Monster", finding the Master is still UNIT's top priority.]

UNIT still seems to be based in the same building [unless they took those green, arch-topped doors with them and built walls around them], but they've moved the TARDIS to a smaller room that looks less like a school lab, apparently downstairs.

The Supporting Cast (Evil)

• *The Master.* [A quick note on story placement: if we try to resolve the issue of why the Master is only *now* looking for an ultimate doomsday weapon of doom, rather than doing this first and *then* embarking on the Nestene / Axon / Alien Mind Parasite tag-teams, it's worth noting that he here knows the Doctor and Jo. In his own timeline, then, "Terror of the Autons" must occur first. It's been proposed that this story and "The Mind of Evil" are told in the order that the Master experienced them, but are reversed for Jo and UNIT - we'll look at this carefully in the essay with the next story. Either way, we're left with the problem of figuring out why he waited so long before tracking down the star-killer.]

Here he's said to have stolen files from the Time Lords, including a file pertaining to the doomsday weapon. [He must have done this before he first arrived on Earth in "Terror of the Autons" - see **The Time Lords** for our reasoning on this - which is presumably how he knew about the Doctor's exile.] Recently, he's been visiting a lot of planets in search of something. [The file on the weapon didn't give its exact location? If the Time Lords *did* know, then we have further grounds to suppose they have physical, written files and no back-up copies.] Here he carries pellets of knock-out gas and a respirator [also used in "The Mind of Evil"]. When surrounded by hostile IMC men, he doesn't attempt to use his powers of hypnosis [so it's possible that he can only hypnotise one subject at a time].

The Master seriously believes that there's a chance of the Doctor joining him in his attempt to take over the galaxy, *if* he plays up to the Doctor's altruism and claims that the doomsday device can be used to bring peace. It's notable, though, that he makes this offer when he doesn't technically need the Doctor's help... suggesting that he has some real regard for his arch-rival, or at least considers the Doctor to be generally useful. He sees it as a basic law of life that one must either rule or serve. [His inferiority complex again; he's a megalomaniac because he doesn't want to be bettered.] He seems unable to communicate to the priest-like aliens, suggesting that he isn't particularly adept at telepathy. [Is this the price he pays for a strong will and hypnotic ability? See **How Telepathic Is He?** under 1.7, "The Sensorites".]

The TARDIS(es)   The Time Lords state they 'immobilised' the Doctor's TARDIS. Here the Doctor builds himself a completely new dematerialisation circuit, whereupon the Ship is steered to Uxarieus by remote before he's even set it in motion.

Upon returning to Earth, the TARDIS rematerialises in a different location in the Doctor's lab. [As the Brigadier is seen unwisely crossing into the corner that the vanishing TARDIS has just occupied and "demanding" that it return at once, we might imagine that the Ship has a failsafe that sounds out landing-places and prevents it squishing people (or materialising inside them... yuk!) on arrival. This makes the Ship's next materialisation more worrying (9.2, "The Curse of Peladon"), but explains why so few people ever see the TARDIS arrive, and why it so often manifests itself in back alleys or store-rooms.]

The Doctor describes the TARDIS as being outside the space-time continuum when it travels - a Saul Bass-style pattern of coloured bars revolve on the scanner while the Ship is in flight, eventually giving way to a view from space of the planet where it's about to land. [See **Can the TARDIS Fly?** under 5.6, "Fury From the Deep".] The scanner itself is now a conventional TV screen again. On the outside, it takes four primitives to physically shift the Ship.

The door is operated by a knob on the corner of the console furthest from it [as when Susan used to have the job of opening them] and they make the same whirring noise as Dalek citadel doors [1.2, "The Daleks"]. The outside surfaces of the doors look like the interior, with inset roundels, but open directly onto the planet with no intervening mirrors [as in the last story] or black "atrium" [as per most Tom Baker stories]. From the outside, the exterior doors look like those of the police box, with no apparent gap. The doors apparently close themselves after a while, as Jo leaves them gaping wide open but the primitives find the Ship locked up tight.

The Master's TARDIS has a console room with the same decor and kind of console as the Doctor's Ship, although it's fitted with two transparent plastic tubes for holding prisoners [with a wall-panel made of embossed steel - *screamingly* early 70s!] and a lot of old-fashioned filing cabinets.

What's the Timeline of the Earth Empire?

What follows is an at-a-glance guide to the rise and fall of Earth's Empire, from 2100 to 3000. (For a timeline of the twenty-first century, see the essay accompanying 5.4, "The Enemy of the World".)

There are other accounts of this, such as Lance Parkin's *AHistory* (available, we have to admit, from the publisher of this guidebook). *AHistory* attempts to reconcile the on-screen references; the spin-off TV series; and the tie-in books, audios, videos and comic strips into a single chronology. However, for the sake of both sanity and clarity in this timeline, references made on screen have been given high priority, with connections to Virgin, Big Finish and BBC Books kept to a minimum.

In an attempt to reconsider matters and get everything correct (at least, as correct as a chronology based on *Doctor Who*'s haphazard history will allow), the version of this essay that appeared in the First Edition of this book has been altered a bit.

c. 2100. The end of the era in which humankind's adventures are restricted to the solar system, and in which Earth keeps getting attacked from its own doorstep (4.6, "The Moonbase"; 5.7, "The Wheel in Space", 6.5, "The Seeds of Death", etc). We don't hear much about the Cybermen for the next four centuries. According to "Nightmare of Eden", a "Galactic Salvage and Insurance" company was in operation but went bust. Most evidence from the TV series suggests that humanity starts to expand into deep space around the start of the twenty-second century.

We know we stated intentions to keep tie-in references to a minimum, but this one fits too perfectly: the Missing Adventure *Killing Ground* establishes that a massive drive towards colonisation begins in 2100 exactly, timed to mark the new century.

2116: "Nightmare of Eden" (17.4). Space travel is becoming more commonplace, as is exploration of the outer planets. Interstellar liners are becoming fashionable, even routine, but on the whole travel beyond the solar system is still a novelty. New laws are brought in to cover the whole of human-occupied space. There's a Space Corps by now, but individual planets have their own customs regulations.

2157 - 2167: "The Dalek Invasion of Earth" (2.2). Earth becomes less important in the grand scheme of things as the Daleks hit the planet with a virus, then take over wholesale. The population crashes. Until now things haven't changed much since the twentieth century, since London still has most of its landmarks. The colonies become less centralised as Earth falls, and a lot of them are probably cut off from the homeworld altogether, which might explain the kind of societies we see in stories such as 16.4, "The Androids of Tara".

(Mind, it doesn't *have* to. It's only recently that some members of fandom have declared that anyone who looks human must be descended from people from Earth. But whatever Russell T Davies' view on this, it's just as plausible that worlds such as Tara have no connection to Earth, and thus no reason to fit into the chronology at all. After all, Skaro had the humanoid Kaleds and Thals, but nobody's daft enough to suggest *that* as an Earth Colony. So for the rest of this list, we'll try to restrain ourselves to planets with an explicit link to Sol III. Fair enough?)

c. 2190: "The Space Pirates" (6.6). The Space Corps becomes increasingly important as commercial space travel opens up more and more of the galaxy. Piracy's an issue. At this time the phrase "outer planets" is being used to refer to worlds *quite* near Earth (say, eight light-years away), but beyond the solar system they still conversationally calculate distances in "billions of miles", not light years. The homeworld's having trouble keeping things together.

The 2200s: "The Chase" (2.8), "Paradise Towers" (24.2). More colonisation schemes across the galaxy. The Mechanoids in "The Chase" seem to have been built around now. According to "Paradise Towers", there seems to have been a fairly major war, one big enough to require a lot of space fighter-pilots and all able-bodied men and women. Which war is this? Well, we have a ready-made candidate...

c. 2250: "Death to the Daleks" (11.3). Now, we have to admit to changing our minds here. In the original Volume III, we went with the herd and placed this story in with "The Sensorites" and "Revenge of the Cybermen" in the 2700-2900 zone. However, the Daleks seen here are of a considerably less advanced design than those on Spiridon (in 10.4, "Planet of the Daleks"). They use

continued on page 153...

The Ship can fly like a spacecraft when it takes the form of one, complete with rocket-trails. The Doctor concedes that it's a slightly more advanced model than his own. As a security precaution, the Master carries a pocket-sized device which floods his own TARDIS console room with sleeping gas, and a little TV screen inside the gadget shows him what's happening there. He opens his doors with a switch on the panel nearest the exterior, and from the inside these doors look as though they've been camouflaged as part of the spaceship disguise. Built into the outer skin of these inward-opening doors is a beam which, if broken, alerts the Master that the vessel has been penetrated.

The Time Lords The Time Lords' files describe the doomsday weapon on Uxarieus, and they consider the Master's theft of this information such a threat, they use the Doctor to deal with the problem. [Again, there's clearly rules governing the degree to which they can intervene, or *be seen to* intervene. They're unable to track the Master precisely, but the Doctor's an acceptable agent, and for various reasons a reliable one. Obviously, as someone in exile in twentieth-century Britain, the Doctor is almost the last person anyone who knows of the Time Lords' affairs would expect to see. His arrival at another point in space-time could be plausibly excused as one of his attempts to fix his TARDIS. And his relations with the High Council are so notoriously bad, even the Master bought the Doctor's claim to be aiding Axos in return for revenge on the Council in the previous story. See "The Two Doctors" for an awful lot more in this vein.]

A heavyweight tribunal sits to discuss the Master's access to these files, suggesting the offence is at least as bad as actively intervening in a planet's history, as happened when the Doctor was tried. [See the next story for our thoughts on how and when the Master got hold of this. It's odd that the theft of a file on an ultimate weapon is only spotted some months - in screen time and therefore probably in Gallifreyan Mean Time (see **Do Time Lords Always Meet In Sequence?** under 22.3, "The Mark of the Rani") - after Bowler-Hat Man gives the Doctor a heads-up.

[It's not impossible that the Master returned to to Gallifrey and committed the theft after 8.3, "The Claws of Axos", but if *that* were true, you'd have expected him to gloat that such a breach was possible even when there's an APB out for him.

One might also expect that in wake of a security breach, the Time Lords would send someone a lot more ruthless to nip the problem in the bud, rather than alert the Doctor - of all people! - that such a thing is possible.

[Alternatively, a thorough audit of what's been pinched takes years. This might make sense if the files were merely copied without permission, but the tribunal's actions suggest the physical file has been taken and they have no backups. Again, the meaning of the word 'file' has changed considerably since this was made, so we have to apply a bygone paradigm for data-retrieval to understand what's supposed to be happening.]

The three Time Lords who make this decision wear austere black robes and seem to be some form of secret committee. [Are they High Council members? The Doctor implies as much later on. We're later told (10.3, "Frontier in Space") that it was the High Council that staged Doctor's trial in 6.7, "The War Games" - one of the Time Lords seen there (played by Clyde Pollett) and one of the three seen in "Colony" (played by Graham Leaman) return in "The Three Doctors" (10.1). Another of the original Tribunal was played by Bernard Horsfall, and he *also* appears later (14.3, "The Deadly Assassin") as a High Council member. That story, in fact, shows over a dozen members of said council.] The tribunal meets in a chamber with glass-brick walls, of the sort you got in municipal swimming baths built around then, or the dining area of a factory.

The Non-Humans

• *The Primitives*. The natives of Uxarieus once had a highly advanced technological civilisation, creating a super-race through genetic engineering and developing their "doomsday weapon". Though never actually used in anger, the weapon is capable of destroying suns and was responsible for the creation of the Crab Nebula during testing. The Master believes it to be 'the most powerful weapon ever created', and even the Doctor finds it unbelievable [because only Time Lords are supposed to have that level of solar engineering; see 25.1, "Remembrance of the Daleks"]. The weapon stretches for miles within the subterranean city that used to be the centre of their culture. Its radiation has not only blighted the soil and caused the people to physically decay, it's also reduced the natives' society to a primitive level.

Most of the primitives are more or less

What's the Timeline of the Earth Empire?

...continued from page 151

ships more like the saucers that landed in Chelsea, and the entire tenor of the story - with plagues and a loose association of Earth colonies - is more in keeping with stories set earlier.

It is, after all, unlikely that the Daleks would have come all this distance to conquer Earth yet haven't colonised or enslaved any other planets in this galaxy. Inevitably, the newly-liberated humans would have pressed home their advantage and launched a crusade across this sector of the galaxy. Let's not forget, they have captured Dalek ships and weapons at their disposal. At a pinch, Dalek subjugation could explain why none of the other intelligent races on our doorstep are active in the galaxy any time earlier in the broadcast stories.

With such scant evidence, we have to confess that this is a judgement call. However, good reasons exist to place this story well ahead of any Empire (see the entries for "Earthshock", and "Frontier in Space"). Chiefly, it's so the 'Dalek War' referenced could denote some of the outlying colonies from circa 2157, most of which seem to have escaped relatively unscathed. Had Dalek Wars occurred wherein it became obvious that humans had a distinct talent for opposing Daleks, this could have laid the foundations for the Federation (or the Empire, depending on which you think came first).

c. 2300: "Vengeance on Varos" (22.2), "The Macra Terror" (4.7), "The Caves of Androzani" (21.6, background detail), "The Happiness Patrol" (25.2), "The Twin Dilemma" (21.7). By now there are independent Earth colonies all over the galaxy, and have been for the last two centuries. The colonies still don't consider Earth to be particularly important. According to "The Sensorites", by the twenty-fourth century the lower half of England has become a vast Central City, so Earth's busily re-building and repopulating itself. Whenever "The Caves of Androzani" is set, the Doctor visited Androzani Major centuries earlier, before the spectrox trade got going, so the colony was probably flourishing a while before that.

c 2400 - 2450: "The Curse of Peladon" (9.2), "The Monster of Peladon" (11.4). For obvious reasons, people have assumed that the "Galaxy Five" mentioned as off-screen terrorists in "The

Monster of Peladon" is the same something-or-other that Zephon represented in "The Daleks' Master Plan" (3.4). Even though the same Hartnell season produced "Galaxy Four" (3.1), in which the eponymous place was a *planet*, not an actual galaxy, it's logical enough to conclude that "Galaxy Five" equals "The Fifth Galaxy". From here, it's but a small leap to deduce that "The Monster of Peladon" is set shortly before the year 4000 (in which "The Daleks' Master Plan" indisputably takes place) and thus that "The Curse of Peladon" - which takes place fifty years earlier - must be circa 3940. The only snag is that nothing visible in the Peladon stories confirms this.

On internal evidence alone, nothing makes even "The Monster of Peladon" look as if it's taking place any later than - say - 4.7, "The Macra Terror" or 22.2, "Vengeance on Varos", the latter pretty conclusively dated as 2350 or so. The other planets with representatives on Peladon are remarkable for their proximity to Earth. Alpha Centauri is the second closest system to ours (assuming there are indeed planets there), with Arcturus and Vega close enough for the Sylvester McCoy stories to have been viewed there by now. Mars is right on our doorstep. Moreover, there's no regular transmat / teleport - they all use shuttles and even Alpha Centauri treats the moving of a statue around the mines as witchcraft. The aliens have fairly crude weapons, and nobody seems to know much about Earth's customs (so we're not big players yet). As even *The New Adventures* authors deemed Galaxy Five to be a terrorist cell rather than an actual galaxy at war with Mutter's Spiral (and as everyone in this story treats the sonic cannon as near-mystical technology - not just the Pels, but Vega Nexos too), it's as easy and logical to put them here as there.

All of that said, we should reiterate what we said in Volume I: '...virtually everyone assumes [the Peladon stories] are set somewhere in the 3000s.'

(NB: After a long day and a few drinks, we could even suggest that the accoutrements on Peladon - the purple frocks, combination of standard-issue wooden banqueting chairs, and all-purpose curved bank of lights they borrowed from Gerry Anderson - form a clever clue and not just a piece of cost-cutting. If the former, then "The Androids of Tara" is also set in this period. We're going to have to make the same judgement call about

continued on page 155...

humanoid, with muddy green skins and faces not unlike the Easter Island heads, but within the darkened, dilapidated city live mutations of the species who have pale skins, walnut-like craniums and almost no eyesight. They're also shorter, wear ornate robes and obviously wield power as priests of some kind, but like the others they're telepathic and incapable of speech.

At the top of the hierarchy is the guardian of the weapon, who resembles an even more shrivelled version of one of the priests, around two feet tall and apparently incapable of moving from his seat of power. This guardian seems to be the only native who can speak [in English?], who can reason with the Doctor, and who understands the technology of the weapon he guards. This creature's "wisdom" is such that after he meets the Master, he's prepared to destroy the weapon and most of his species along with it. [He may feel it's a merciful release for his people, or possibly feel some self-destructive guilt about the damage his kind did in the past.] At one point he causes a gun in the Master's hand to instantly vanish.

Planet Notes

• *Uxarieus.* [The spelling's debatable here, since generations of fan-guides have gone for "Exarius", "Uxarius" or even "Agzarius". But "Uxarieus" is the scripted, BBC-approved version.] A rocky and largely barren world, with birds and insects but no larger animal life other than the primitives. [It's doubtful that no animal life *ever* existed here, or the primitives never would have evolved. Radiation from the weapon probably wiped out most other species.] Earth Control classified Uxarieus as suitable for colonization, but it turns out to be the richest known source of the durilinium that Earth needs for living units [i.e. houses].

History

• *Dating.* The colonists left Earth in 2471, and according to a calendar it's now Tuesday, 3rd of March, 2472. [Jo, not quite believing in time-travel yet, thinks that Mary's reference to things on Earth 'back in '71' means 1971 rather than 2471. This suggests that a) in her own time it's got to be 1972 at the very least and b) she's as thick as two short planks.]

At this point Earth is polluted, over-crowded and devoid of grass, although starvation isn't a problem. Dissent is met with incarceration. [The dialogue is unclear as to whether it's the state or the corporations who perpetrate this oppression, and to whether those "incarcerated" wind up in prison or a mental hospital. See "Frontier in Space", also by Hulke.] People die from epidemics, toxic spills and horrifying traffic accidents, but there's no mention of state-imposed birth control.

'Floating islands', rising to three-hundred storeys, are the latest scheme to house everyone. [They're probably the forerunners of the sky-cities mentioned in "The Mutants", circa 3000 AD.] A hundred billion people currently live on Earth. Living units are mainly made of the wondrous metal durilinium. Space travel is common but apparently expensive, and the colonists who settle on Uxarieus aren't ever expecting to go back. Everyone is expected to carry official papers, with interplanetary travel permits and spaceship registrations being mentioned.

The Interplanetary Mining Corporation (IMC) is a ruthless organisation run along military lines, with uniforms and weapons [usually hand-guns and sub-machine guns, as per 21.6, "The Caves of Androzani"], and can buy influence at government level. They can exploit legal loopholes and take what they want from unpoliced planets, holding trials and using the law to punish people for 'piracy' and 'trespass', both of which carry the death penalty (which they carry out themselves). Once a planet is given into IMC's jurisdiction, the ship captain becomes Governor [see 4.3, "The Power of the Daleks" for a possible sidelight on this] and acting against them is considered treason. The Corporation routinely harasses occupants of planets they want with bogus monsters and planted agents who sow dissent, but their actions, if exposed, are subject to galactic law.

Disputes on frontier worlds are settled by an Adjudicator, one of a team of peripatetic circuit-judges [mention is made of an 'Adjudicators' Bureau', and the ID of the *real* Adjudicator cites a 'Bureau of Interplanetary Affairs'] with their own spaceships. Their decisions can take years to reach, but although their word is 'final', Dent is confident that any Adjudicator who stands in their way 'can be dealt with'. Adjudicators wear vast collars on their black robes, with silver detailing [c.f. "The Mutants"].

Technology seen here includes hand-held medical scanners and 3D image projectors. Dent instructs that a message be 'warped' to IMC headquarters on Earth. IMC also uses a MK III servo-

What's the Timeline of the Earth Empire?

...continued from page 153

Amazonia's dress and the way all the women in Earth's government dress in "Frontier in Space", but that puts the Peladon stories into a packed area of Earth history where at least one of the delegates would have mentioned the galactic situation. Perhaps.)

2472: "Colony in Space" (10.4). Earth is now not only repopulated, but horribly over-populated. A new wave of colonisations begins, this time spearheaded by non-conformists who just want to get away from a miserable, oppressive planet, but Earth is trying to keep closer checks on its colonies than ever before. The Empire has its roots in this period, with a centralised government clamping down on dissenters and planning to build floating cities for the billions. Mining potential on other planets seems to take precedence over mass colonisation or agriculture.

2493: "The Rescue" (2.3). More colonisation. It looks like they've relaxed the restrictions on who gets a spaceship, where they can go and what help they can expect if things go wrong. Earth's ridiculously high population figures ease off in under half a century. Is this due to a war? A mass exodus? Cannibalism? Whatever the Southern half of Britain's like, Liverpool is still a separate city.

2500-ish: "The Caves of Androzani" (actual story). Another educated guess: the Sirius Conglomerate has no apparent connection to any external body. Morgus speaks of Earth in the past tense. The fact that the life-extending spectrox is a commodity within the Nine Planets but *not* galaxy-wide (even the Doctor was unaware of its existence) suggests that even a comparatively nearby system is totally beyond Earth's jurisdiction. Yet Earth is only nine light-years away.

Therefore, this is either long before the Empire or long after it. If we're forced to choose, the carbines and machine-guns used - plus the crudity of the androids and space-drives - indicates the former. As we discover in "Frontier in Space", Sirius is granted Dominion status shortly before 2540, and must be economically self-sufficient by then. (We say that even though a large amount of spectrox presumably floods the market once Jek and Morgus die, which inevitably causes hyperinflation and a generation who remain inconveniently active far longer than is good for the property

market. See also **Is This Any Way To Run A Galactic Empire?** under "Frontier in Space".)

2520: "Frontier in Space" (10.3, background detail). Twenty years before the Master's efforts to stir things up, Earth and Draconia fight a war. After this, a frontier was set up between their two spheres of influence. Yet no military dictatorship followed. No effort was made to resolve the causes of the conflict, and neither side mentions any trouble with Cybermen.

We have to wonder, then, just how big a threat the Tin Terrors from Telos really were. If they had any logic at all, they would have taken advantage of the Earth-Draconia conflict to stage lightning incursions on frontier planets. Both Earth and Draconia tend to go in very overtly, overpowering their opponents rather than infiltrating them, so the Cybermen's sneaky tactics are more likely to reap benefits *now* than at any other time since Earth started colonising the Galaxy. Perhaps the Cyber-War only lasts six years, starting with this confused situation providing cover for their activities and ending with...

2526: "Earthshock" (19.6). There's a conference being held on Earth, at which it's agreed that humanity (and apparently everyone else) should unite against the Cybermen. This obviously does a very good job of pulling the colonial powers together, and seems to be what cements the Empire. What follows is the last Cyber War, in which Voga's resources ("Revenge of the Cybermen") are used to (seemingly) wipe out the Cybermen for good.

Well, er, maybe. A wild card is the rather alarming implication that the only reason the Daleks avoid this galaxy after losing Earth in 2167 is that the Cybermen were too big a threat. But if you're acquainted with how often the Cybermen's plans fail (see most of Volume II), this isn't really on. As we'll see, the Daleks would welcome the prospect of humans and some other species engaging in a cosmic barney, so why were they absent during *either* the Cyber-Wars or the Earth-Draconia War?

Maybe they weren't. The dating for "Death to the Daleks", after all, is very ambiguous, whatever heroic steps one takes to fix it down. It occurs a generation after an otherwise un-recorded 'Dalek War', but so long after the Dalek Invasion of Earth that people don't automatically associate a space-

continued on page 157...

robot, an all-purpose digging machine operated either by remote control or its own programming, and which can be used to fake giant lizard attacks. The colonists have pre-fabricated domes, hydroponic food and a nuclear generator, although the relay system is close to collapse. They communicate by radio.

[As the doomsday weapon was used to create the Crab Nebula, we can date the decline of ancient civilisation of Uxarieus to some time around 5250 BC. In real life, Chinese astronomers saw the supernova that created the Nebula in 1054, and it's 6,300 light years away.]

The Doctor estimates that Earth's sun will burn to its core in 10,000 million years. [See also 3.6, "The Ark"; 21.3, "Frontios" and X1.2, "The End of the World".]

Additional Sources   "Colony in Space" was accompanied by a "teaser" comic-strip in the *Radio Times*, as drawn from the TV script by the legendary *Eagle* and *TV21* artist Frank Bellamy. Thereafter, he provided monochrome pictures beside the listings for most episodes. His magnificently lurid redaction of this adventure's opening scenes, with Jo's first trip in the TARDIS transformed into something impossibly exciting, also alludes to the previous story being called "The Vampire from Space" (to the confusion of many readers).

This extra splash of publicity may at least partly explain the pick-up in the programme's viewing figures after "The Claws of Axos". (As you'll recall from the essay in Volume II, the magazine came out on Thursdays, so a sneak preview of an early scene was a rare treat in itself.) The *Radio Times* illustrations continued until Season Eleven, although Bellamy contributed occasional *Doctor Who* work after that, including a superb version of the Skarasen from "Terror of the Zygons" (13.1) which is how many of us like to imagine the Skarasen looking.

Hulke's novelisation of this story, entitled *Doctor Who and the Doomsday Weapon*, develops the minor characters and fills in a lot of details. It's widely regarded as the single-most influential Target book, and to have inspired many future authors of tie-in books and audios (to say nothing of transmitted episodes) to become writers. It was written before the "Terror of the Autons" book and *long* before the intervening ones. As such, it introduced Jo to the reading public with a piece where

her uncle (a senior civil servant this time) gets her the UNIT gig after her first attempt to become a spy landed her a filing job in Bangkok. Not only does this make sense of her incredulity at the TARDIS, it makes a lot of "Carnival of Monsters" (10.2) more plausible.

The prologue even introduces pieces of programme lore that made it to the screen, with the Doctor stealing his TARDIS while it's in for repair with a faulty chameleon circuit (18.7, "Logopolis"), plus an elderly Time Lord in charge of the records. ("The Deadly Assassin", although in the book, he's aware of the Doctor and nearing retirement.) An audio version of this truly seminal work is now available, read by Geoffrey Beevers ("The Ambassadors of Death"; 18.6, "The Keeper of Traken"). He does the Master as Melkur (which is fair enough), but seems to think that the Doctor is C-3PO.

The Analysis

Where Does This Come From?   Space, the final frontier... and yet, if we're to believe the American accounts, it's exactly like the previous one. The big myth of stories about going to other worlds was that it was going to be just like the Europeans taming the West. There would be honest, hardworking settlers, then ruggedly individualist pioneers, then entrepreneurs and mass immigration, then finally a federal system of government.

People who knew a bit about space could protest all they liked - this was How It Was Going To Be. Gene Roddenberry pitched *Star Trek* as *Wagon Train* across the stars, and ponder the use of the Afrikaans word "Trek" in the title. It was all about farmers and savage natives, but Europeans have nothing comparable. It's impossible to go anywhere that nobody else has been, to leave one place and start again fresh without encountering the past somehow.

Those people-who-knew-a-bit-about-space understood that on a moonbase (or in a station in L5 orbit), rugged individualists would get everyone killed. Wide-open spaces were out of the question. The ideal people to colonise a new planet were Maoist kibbutzim with no sense of smell. Everyone would live in each other's pockets and drink each other's reclaimed waste (a bit like X3.03, "Gridlock") for the first few centuries. Mapping the Pilgrim Fathers (at least, the Thanksgiving version) onto space travel was so

What's the Timeline of the Earth Empire?

...continued from page 155

plague with Dalek softening-up tactics. The Marine Space Corps in "Death to the Daleks" has as much in common with early Space Patrols (like those of Hermack in "The Space Pirates" and Steven Taylor - see "The Chase") as it does with the semi-military surveys of the Sense-Sphere ("The Sensorites").

2540: "Frontier in Space" (actual story). The Doctor describes the era as the start of the Empire proper. Humans come face-to-face with the Draconians, and nearly start a war. The Dalek threat probably only makes the Empire stronger, though what happens to the Draconians after this is anyone's guess.

However, no galactic invasion seems to follow the discovery of the Dalek subterfuge to set Earth and Draconia at each other's throats, and the assault force on Spiridon ("Planet of the Daleks") is abandoned. It's unlikely that any more is heard from the Daleks until the year 4000. (See "The Daleks' Master Plan" - Bret Vyon doesn't know much about the Daleks' 2157 invasion in that story, and in 3.2, "Mission to the Unknown", Marc Cory has to tell his colleague Lowery what Daleks are. They've become semi-legendary.)

2700 - 2900: "The Sensorites" (1.6), "Revenge of the Cybermen" (12.5). "The Sensorites" is said to take place in the twenty-eighth century, so this is clearly an age of people in starchy uniforms exploring mysterious planets. "Kinda" (19.3) might also be set in this epoch, as the imperials on Deva Loka talk about an over-populated homeworld. More uniforms-in-space business goes on in "Revenge of the Cybermen", which the Doctor suggests is set in the twenty-ninth century, centuries after the Cyber War.

If "Death to the Daleks" goes anywhere later than 2400, it's here.

2986: "Terror of the Vervoids" (23.3). The Empire seems to be flagging by this point, since the alien Mogarians are grumbling about the way the humans have strip-mined their world, and they're not being lined up against the wall and shot. The view from Earth is ambivalent about Empire: if the Vervoids are desirable as a work force, it should be becoming obvious that any galaxy-sized socioeconomic unit is more trouble than it's worth.

3000-ish: "The Mutants" (9.4). The Doctor only establishes that it's 'the thirtieth century', although most tie-in lore (*The New Adventures* in particular) takes as read that it's the *late* thirtieth century. Earth is covered in endless grey sky-cities by this point, and the planet's said to be biologically and politically 'finished'. The Empire falls.

If you want, you can place the start of the Federation here. We tend to think otherwise, as we discussed under the two Peladon stories.

One last thing: while we're on the topic of humanity's space Empires, the new series references subsequent Great and Bountiful Earth Empires in phases of galactic history that we don't really experience in the pre-1989 series. Examples thus far include the 4100s (X2.8-2.9, "The Impossible Planet" / "The Satan Pit"; X3.7, "42"; and X4.3, "Planet of the Ood") and a Fourth Great and Bountiful Human Empire that was scheduled for 200,000 (X1.7, "The Long Game"), but was (we think) derailed by events in X1.12-1.13 "Bad Wolf" / "The Parting of the Ways". According to X1.2, "The End of the World", there's also a new Roman Empire in 12,005, which will undoubtedly push up the price of lark's tongues.

---

easy and frequent, it was almost unquestioned.

Instead of constantly striking out for fresh woods and pastures new, people in Europe (and specifically Britain) tend to take over a small place and remake it as their own (see **Did Sergeant Pepper Know the Doctor?** under 5.1, "The Tomb of the Cybermen"). Gardening is one manifestation of this. People who have small gardens or none at all could apply to grow vegetables of a piece of land the size of a stretch limo (Donna's granddad has one in X4.1, "Partners in Crime"). Allotments have been a part of the national psyche

for a century or more, since the great Municipal movement of the mid-nineteenth century (the same movement that gave us public libraries, parks with bandstands and swimming baths).

Our formerly unspoken wish is to become self-sufficient and never need to buy food again, with any other purchases made by bartering our runner-beans. Of course this was unrealistic, but everyone privately thought it until people said it out loud in the 1970s. Running an allotment was more than a hobby but less than a lifestyle choice (like everything worthwhile in British life). At one stage, of course, it became vitally important. We were told in the 1940s to "Dig for Victory" (much as the Americans had their "Victory Gardens"), and rationing meant that homegrown vegetables were a crucial part of running a household. (Besides, if you had tomatoes, you could name your own price.)

A related piece of wartime self-mythologising was the make-do-and-mend mentality, which veered off into the amateur inventor in his garden shed. Post-war, this fed into the boom in "Do It Yourself", not just for home improvements but as an act of self-validation for dads in boring jobs. For granddads, the improved diet (thanks to that rationing) and exercise meant they were more active in retirement than was expected. The original Wallace and Gromit film *A Grand Day Out* takes this to its obvious conclusion: we might laugh at the idea of building a space rocket in the cellar out of odds and ends (down to wallpapering the Command Module), but it comes from a specifically British attitude to machinery and domesticity.

Incidentally, Wallace is named after the inventor of the Bouncing Bomb, the film account of which (*The Dambusters*) told a story about simple home-made devices for targeting, and the application of cricket to a hitherto insoluble strategic problem with the Ruhr Valley industrial plant's defences. (As we saw in **How Believable Is The British Space Programme?** under 7.3, "The Ambassadors of Death", this same approach - when applied to rocket-science - could easily have put Britain ahead in the Space Race at one stage.)

We'll be looking again later at how the next generation took this attitude and habits, and tried to go for the self-sufficiency ideal with both food and energy. These days, everyone is looking back on this as a missed opportunity to free ourselves from the need for imported fuel. (See 10.5, "The Green Death"; 11.2, "Invasion of the Dinosaurs" and other sidelights throughout this volume.) An innate virtue is perceived in refurbishing something to make it "as good as new" (the anti-entropy thing can take on religiose overtones, especially in Protestant countries) and avoiding waste. DIYers can become obsessive about this make-do-and-mend ingenuity. The entire self-sufficiency boom of the 70s had some of the same roots as the American pioneering spirit - there's less of a gap than you'd think between *How The West Was Won* and *The Wombles*.[42] The colonists

aren't going to take what they need then move on, they're going to use what *little* they've brought with them in increasingly thrifty ways.

What we're saying is that if "Colony in Space" is a Western - as is sometimes claimed - then it's a bloody weird one. What kind of rancher has a notice-board with graphs and pie-charts and a desk with drawers full of paperwork? Well, an English one, obviously. Listen for what's *not* said: nobody claims that the planet is theirs because God brought them there, nobody says that burying their dead there and spending a year tilling the soil earns them the right to stay, nobody says that after failing on one planet they have to move to another one. They're only offered a return to Earth as an option. This isn't a frontier, it's a giant allotment.

On the other hand, Earth conforms to all the worst predictions of various professional doom-mongers. The checklist includes over-population (the Club of Rome's pet anxiety; this is the era when we calculate how big an island is needed for *everyone* in the world to stand up on it - why they should want to is another matter), pollution, warfare (surely a viable solution to the first problem) and running out of resources. We can also check off the sea-cities we were all supposed to be living in by 2001 (with everyone speaking Esperanto too, but in *Doctor Who* this is redundant, as everyone speaks BBC English except comedy yokels).

Remember that this is 1971, and nobody's figured out that most of these evils would either cancel out or be either-or situations. Authoritarian governments prevent over-population and waste; really regimented societies would force people to leave the planet or prevent them from polluting. We're still in the phase of single-issue dystopias, and Malcolm Hulke is simply overlaying one on top of another with no notion of how they would affect one another. Most attempts at forecasting the future were like this (this is the era of *Soylent Green* et al). However, with Hulke writing the script, the dialogue will be heavily slanted against unstoppable capitalism. Dent claims that 'What's good for IMC is good for Earth' (paraphrasing a widely-misquoted comment by the head of General Motors) and Morgan apologises for murdering the Doctor by claiming 'purely business, you understand: nothing personal'. Indeed, whilst the colonists berate over-regulation, it's left implicit that the lack of strong government, which allows "famines" and "epidemics" to weed out the excess population, is what allows the megacorps to get away with murder.

Ministerial types discussing the fate of nations - and opting to send the programme's hero in as a patsy - is a routine start for episodes of many spy series in the early 70s. In *Jason King*, it was Dennis Price (the suave murderer in *Kind Hearts and Coronets*) discussing King's use with Ronald Lacey (the Gestapo man Toht in *Raiders of the Lost Ark*) about one episode in every three. Prior to this, it had been MI5 and the CIA deciding McGill's next mission (in *Man in a Suitcase*). Later on, this would happen to Spider Scott (*The XYY Man* - see 22.2, "Vengeance on Varos") or Eddie Shoestring. What's happening here is very clear and surprisingly early: the Time Lords are being rethought as Whitehall mandarins and the Doctor is more or less a private eye.

Oh, and as an aside: the Uxariean city, a vast underground machine covered in the hieroglyphs of an ancient alien civilisation, is vaguely like *Forbidden Planet*, but the idea that they caused something in our pre-history (the Crab Nebula nova) is the first hint of von-Danikenism (the notion that aliens landed on Earth and influenced ancient societies). More, much more on this in the next story...

Things That Don't Make Sense Well, the broadest problem here is that the entire story is predicated on the notion that mining and colonisation / agriculture are mutually exclusive. Basically, the plot only works if the coveted duralinium is *only* accessible from the same tiny bit of the planet as where the colonists live, and that *only* their squitty little patch is capable of cultivation. To attain their goals, IMC need only go and mine on a different continent for a bit, then wait until the colonists starve. Moreover, the colonists could've tried growing crops elsewhere - at some distance from the Doomsday Weapon, they might've even succeeded. Surely, crops can grow *somewhere* on the surface (although why the colonists didn't go there in the first place is a puzzler), or Earth would have deemed this planet as "unsuitable for colonisation". [Then again, maybe they *did*. We're assuming that IMC were lying because they're the baddies, but maybe the colonists really were the victims of a computer error.] Either way, however much IMC insists there's been a computer cock-up, it should take an Adjudicator precious little time to contact Earth Central and figure out that Uxarius is tagged for the colonists. So exactly how long do the IMC boys think they can keep this deception going?

Major Issue No. 2: if Earth is as neurotically over-regulated as we're lead to believe, surely *someone* would have insisted that all planets designated as suitable for colonisation first be surveyed for mineral riches. What kind of half-baked dictatorship is this?

Major Issue No. 3: quick and unobtrusive it might be, the entire set-up of this story with regards the Master is bonkers. We're told that he stole the Time Lords' file on the Doomsday Weapon, yet he still doesn't know precisely on which planet it's located, whereas the Time Lords somehow know to send the Doctor to Uxarius ahead of him. Never mind if it's certain the Master will eventually show up there, they could've just dispatched somebody to wait around and properly arrest him. Along those lines, the Time Lords find their Doomsday Weapon file is 'missing', which suggests a physical file that can be stolen but (it would seem) not copied. Together with the sight of the Master's bank of filing cabinets, this leads us to suppose that the whole data-store for the Time Lords - the most advanced and omniscient race in the cosmos - is printed on A4 sheets of paper, held together with the occasional bulldog clip, and can be removed by stuffing manila files up your jumper or inside your copy of *Radio Times* (or whatever Time Lords read).

And considering the circumstances, it's somewhat odd that the Time Lords don't brief the Doctor on his mission. Whilst the non-interference palavah might prevent them from directly intervening, and force them to maintain the legal fiction of the Doctor just stumbling into politically-sensitive situations on the likes of Peladon and Solos, the Master is one of their own and he's *already* meddling. So stopping him should be perfectly justifiable. Anyway, the Doctor himself is bound to find out the score regardless, so the Time Lords being circumspect only serves to impede their own agent from doing his job.

And *why*, if they know about the Doomsday Weapon, has Gallifrey left it just lying about Uxarius all these millennia, waiting for someone to come along, flip a switch and start obliterating entire solar systems? Even under a policy of "non-intervention", this seems needlessly risky. Presumably they don't object when the Doctor's intervention results in the Weapon's destruction, so why not just get rid of the damn thing in the first place?

Major Issue No. 4: in his guise as the Adjudicator, the Master rules in favour of IMC. Why, exactly? The Weapon isn't what you'd call portable, so does he want IMC to begin full-scale mining sooner rather than later? Far better to keep the whole thing bunged up in legalities for years. Perhaps he's trying to pressure the colonists into showing him the primitive city, but he could readily do that without showing IMC such pointless favouritism. Anyway, the Master has a time machine. Why land on Uxarieus during this conflict *at all*, when he could just go there in a previous era and shoot a few primitives? If he wants to create an Empire as he claims, his entire scheme depends upon his fortifying Uxarieus as a power-base, and that's something better done when all these silly humans aren't underfoot.

It's a little bizarre that Earth authorities must know about the primitives and the remains of their ancient city, yet no teams of archaeologists have been dispatched to find any leftover goodies. [Given that the near-contemporary expedition to Telos in 5.1, "The Tomb of the Cybermen" needed private finance, it's almost as if Earth authorities were actively blocking archaeologists from finding anything potentially useful.] One might also expect that IMC would have someone on staff to evaluate any alien cities they might discover, and that such an astonishingly well-funded organization might have more than *one* talented miner (in this case, the "irreplaceable" Caldwell) per survey team. Especially when there's eleventy zillion citizens to choose from, Caldwell's "irreplaceable" status is extraordinary.

Everyone keeps insisting that the primitives are harmless, yet they constantly carry spears, routinely kidnap people to trade for food (odd in itself, since Ashe gives it to them voluntarily) and go so far as to *kill* an IMC guard. We might imagine that they telepathically sense he's a baddie, but they murder him to grab Jo as part of their kidnap scheme, not because it's morally the right thing to do. And once rumours of giant lizards start circulating, the colonists never wonder if a) the primitives, who constantly carry spears, can show them how to deal with them, and b) if the primitives are eating the giant lizards, which could become (so far as they know) an alternative food source while the colony gets its crops going. (This also brings us to Mary Ashe's self-contradictory statement: 'There's no animal life, just a few birds and insects.')

Right, time for the agronomy lesson. As we've mentioned, Mary tells Jo that the colonists left 'back in 2471', as though this was ages ago. But the next shot is a calendar showing '2nd March 2472'. Combine this with Ashe's account of the settlement's dismal agriculture, and it seems that the entire colony has undergone three or four failed harvests in just over one Terrestrial year. [Maybe less, even. If it's 2nd of March, then 'back in 71' refers to a maximum of fourteen months ago, but you've got to subtract the time required for the colonists to reach Uxarieus in the first place.]

All right, so maybe Uxarieus has a very quick orbit - but no, if that were true, they should have invented their own calendar, not kept using Earth-standard. Moreover, it seems as though the colonists have gambled a *lot* on getting everything up-and-running in one season, even though nobody with any sense does that. Even people who try to grow all their own food in present-day Britain calculate on three years minimum. True, they've been sharing their supplies with the primitives, but surely not to such an extent as to put them in jeopardy. Besides, what *did* the primitives eat, on their barren planet, before the colonists showed up? We're never told, and (just as annoyingly) the colonists never think to ask. Also note that the crops listed on the wall-chart include 'fungus' and 'algae'. If even *that* isn't growing, then the atmosphere wouldn't be worth breathing. Still another "crop" is 'hydro' - this presumably denoting hydroponics, although had someone asked how anything in the soil could affect *this*, they might've identified the source of the problem a lot sooner.

When the Leesons get slaughtered, nobody on the other end of the radio hears Jane Leeson crying out, 'Who are you?' - something one would hardly ask if being eaten by towering lizards. Anyway, the IMC members perpetrating this fraud really are *morons* to not realise that it seems odd that a 20-foot lizard could fit through such a small door, even if only the Doctor picks up on this. Then at the start of episode two, the Doctor captures the control box for the claw-sporting IMC robot - but instead of taking the machine back with him as proof of IMC's wrongdoing, he leaves it behind, helpfully allowing IMC to retrieve it and cover up their crimes.

Uxarieus contains the biggest duralinium strike IMC has ever come across, enough for... (adopts

Dr Evil pose)...one million living units! Sounds good, until you realise what a drop in the well this is, compared to the 100,000,000,000 people living on Earth. How did all the previous umpteen billion get anywhere to live? Companies along the lines of IMC must have mined over 20,000 planets to get as much as was required (and as Uxarieus is a particularly rich source, it's probably more like 40,000). Even *if* it's the case that a 'living unit' is more akin to an apartment block than just an apartment, this hardly seems feasible, does it? Anyway, they've got 100,000,000,000 people to deal with, and they've only *just* started building cities in the sea? Are people living inside each other or something?

Why does Caldwell let the Doctor drive back to the IMC spaceship, when he knows the way and the Doctor doesn't? Later, when the two IMC goons accept Caldwell's claim that he's killed Winton, they don't bother to take the body off his hands. (The front door of the IMC ship warns of 'Anti-Intrusion Vaporisors', so disposing of the incriminating corpse back at HQ is surely a lot easier than in a mineralogist's tent.) Anyway, how does Caldwell get away with this ruse? *Surely* the goons reported back to Dent, who might've thought it out-of-character that the moralistic Caldwell would plug a fleeing prisoner in cold blood. Similarly, when Winton shows up in the colony alive, why doesn't Dent wonder if there's some funny business going on? Come to think of it, why does Caldwell have a handcuff-unlocking beam when he's not involved in the fraud?

The captured Dent tells Winton he's holding 'A piece of very delicate equipment. Leave it alone,' in a manner that can only make Winton *more* suspicious, not less. We should also stop to consider the daftness of the IMC spaceship having filing-cabinets, desks and other office furniture and clipboards loose and capable of flying about whenever the ship manoeuvres - especially as we see it parked at 45° to horizontal.

Virtually nothing pertaining to Norton, the IMC mole who masquerades as a colonist from a "sacked" settlement, rings true. When Jim the engineer and his assistant, a primitive, die under mysterious circumstances, nobody calls Norton's story - that the primitive went berserk and Norton had to kill him, the only witness to the crime, in self-defence - into question. Never mind that Norton was asking about Jim's value to the colony beforehand. Eventually Winton comes to view Norton with *a bit* of distrust, but does he lock the

man up as a liability? No, he lets Norton get a gun and participate in the IMC shoot-out at the end of episode four. Whereupon Norton shouts out a warning to the approaching IMC men and Winton shoots him dead. Standing where he is on a very high walkway, Norton *must* know that hollering to his comrades will get him slain, yet he does so anyway. Such a sacrifice would make sense if he were part of some greater calling or purpose, but he's just a stooge who's evidently willing to die for his employer's bottom line. It's like watching someone "bravely" giving up their life to lift Wal-Mart's stock price.

Anyway, this gunfight only happens because the IMC boys show up to their appointed meeting with the Adjudicator armed to the teeth. Isn't that contempt of court or something?

We've already touched upon Jo's strange disbelief that the TARDIS can travel, or indeed do much of anything at all and her crazed willingness to accept [see **History**] that the colonists left Earth in 1971, even after she *just* hears a conversation about how Earth is a hellishly polluted police state. But now we've reached episode four, and as usual, the Master's arrival makes Jo and everyone else act even stupider. For starters, Jo shows the Doctor some cave-paintings done on glass. All right, but the detail is on the *other* side of the glass - almost as if they were explaining for benefit of TV viewers getting a reverse camera-view. The Doctor distracts one of the primitives with conjuring tricks before knocking the creature out and making his escape. But since the primitives are telepathic, why is the guard a) fooled by sleight-of-hand, which relies on the magician hiding his intentions from the audience, and b) unaware that the Doctor's about to hit him? Norton and Caldwell can mug primitives too, so it's not just a Time Lord Zen thing. Neither do any of the primitives or the height-challenged "priests" telepathically realise that the Doctor has incapacitated one of their number. During his meeting with the little puppet guy who runs the city, the Doctor never thinks to ask if he knows the location of the missing TARDIS. And why do wavy lines appear when the puppet guy's wall covering comes down?

None of the dozen or so people present find it remotely strange when Jo, upon seeing 'the Adjudicator' for the first time, blurts out 'It's the Master!'. According to Winton, Adjudicators can take *years* to rule, yet the Master - despite his saying he's thought 'long' and hard about the matter - delivers a verdict in the exact space of time it takes him to have a back-room chat with the Doctor. Nobody finds that remotely strange either.

During said chat, the Master tells the Doctor that whereas his own (forged) documents are 'immaculate', the Doctor has none, so insisting that the colonists check the Master's credentials would only backfire. Ten minutes later, the Doctor suggests that the colonists... check the Master's credentials. And once again, the Doctor enters the Master's TARDIS and is amazed to find it's slightly more advanced than his own. Has everyone been taking turns on the Brig's memory-rubber?

Frustratingly, there's a whole heap of idiocy surrounding the Master's booby-trapped TARDIS. Let's start with how this trap works: there's an infrared beam that only works when the doors are gaping wide open. Yet instead of automatically closing the doors and gassing the intruders, this activates an alarm in the Master's handset (known to generations of fans as "The Cherry Bakewell of Doom"[43]). The so-alerted Master must then flip open the lid and see who's broken in to his ship, whereupon he has the option of flooding the place with nerve-gas or something less lethal (even though there's just the one red button, suggesting that only one kind of gas is available). This might make some kind of sense if he has a cleaning lady coming around on Thursdays, but is otherwise (as is traditional with the Master) horribly over-complicated. One also supposes that the Master can override his own burglar alarm - the alternative is that at the end of episode six, when fleeing for his life, the Master has to rummage around in his pockets and operate his powder-puff to avoid gassing himself on take-off.

But worse, when they break in, the Doctor makes it absolutely clear to Jo that the doorway contains an alarm beam. To prove the point, they enter the Ship by sliding under it. Yet once inside, after *a couple of minutes* in the room, Jo gets so determined to leave that she walks all the way back saying 'oh, Doctor, do come on', before standing in the beam's path for over a minute. The subsequent release of gas is, of course, accompanied by a melodramatic "whooshing" noise and flashing blue lights, but only once Jo's stepped *back into the TARDIS where she knows it's not safe* do the doors close, thus allowing the concentration of gas to overcome the Doctor.

Moreover, the Master claims he used a gas that incapacitates rather than kills because he wants the Doctor's services as a guide to the alien city.

Okay, but he triggers his trap *before* learning that he needs the Doctor's help. It's almost as if he's refusing to kill his old school chum and finding excuses, the old softy. And whatever this gas was, the Master can walk around without a gas mask only a few minutes later.

The Master's dialogue at the end of episode five isn't the *quite* same in the recap at the start of episode six. As with the previous one (and episode two), they remounted and shot it differently so you wouldn't twig the situation would be resolved by Pertwee yelling 'Hai!'

The little puppet guy says that once the Doomsday Weapon's power source became active, his race started to decay - odd that they didn't see this coming. If they *had*, why didn't they build an off-switch? And if the irradiated soil is what prevents crops from growing, and the city's been chucking out rads for a few thousand years, what makes everyone so sure that the crops will magically start growing just because there's been a rather unimpressive explosion in a cave?

In the finale, why is the massacre of IMC's troops presented as a happy ending? Ethics and storytelling aesthetics aside, it just means that the colonists can expect reprisals on multiple fronts. A *real* Adjudicator is coming to judge their case after they've staged an armed insurrection and, unless they can detain Captain Dent indefinitely and get away with it, he'll probably just go off and send for reinforcements from IMC. There are troubled days ahead for the colonists - but at least their cover crops will grow now. Possibly.

And how did the Doctor get his TARDIS key back from Morgan?

Critique It's hardly subtle, is it? Younger viewers in 1971 might've regarded this story's good intentions as a revelation, but you can't watch it now without feeling like you're being lectured. We're given a linear narrative that requires otherwise intelligent and hard-bitten people to become gullible and guileless. Jo was never too bright, but here she's just hopeless. Caldwell's head must be stuck somewhere dark and soundproof. There's the vague hint that IMC got away with this sort of thing in the past because nobody thought that buying or replacing an Adjudicator was even possible - a notion that a single line of dialogue could have averted. But for lack of it, you can only conclude that either the Master or the entire Galaxy is stupid.

As is the case in many Pertwee stories, the biggest problem here is the sense that everyone involved is really, really pleased with themselves for "inventing" the hoariest clichés going. It's inconceivable that nobody in the production office had ever thought of any of the ideas before, or maybe *heard* them or *read* them or *seen* them, but somehow this was all considered good enough for their target audience. Throughout this story, we're presented with the grindingly obvious as though it were a miracle of suspense, surprise and drama. We're left with the uncomfortable impression that they commissioned "Colony in Space" just so they can broadcast these bits, and then tell other lazy hacks who think anyone can write SF that "we've already done that". It's either that, or Malcolm Hulke had some (ahem) compromising photos of Dicks and thus couldn't be held to a higher standard.

Even setting aside her abrupt bout of amnesia, Jo is here out of an obligation to sell the story to kids. After all, her main contribution is to get captured by two different sets of antagonists in the space of one episode. Then when the Master turns up, she's a hostage. Manning provides decent enough performances in other stories, but she's merely adequate when made to play a stooge. (Proof that she's largely decorative is that they make her wear a top in the same colour-scheme as the IMC boys.) Fortunately, for a large chunk of the story Bernard Kay (as Caldwell) and Roger Delgado occupy her usual role and are much more interesting to watch as Pertwee explains things to them. It's usual at this point to single out Morris Perry as Dent, but even though he's good, he's playing a baddie he can automatically get his teeth into. John Ringham has a much more thankless task with Ashe. Some reviews carp about his lack of charisma, although to be fair, he's the administrator of a settlement in dire straits, not a cult leader.

It's as if the production team thinks that taking the TARDIS to another planet in another time means audiences will demand *less* attention to detail than in a UNIT story. In that regard, the mistake with the dematerialisation shots (and it manifestly *is* a mistake, whatever Briant says now) represents the whole story. They think they can get away with it, purely because they haven't done this sort of thing in a while. It's not so much that the first alien world the series presents in colour is a quarry, but that it's the most *boring*-looking quarry in the whole history of quarry-based

Doctor Who filming. Indeed, Uxarieus is a grey, boring planet full of grey, boring characters (the leader's name being "Ashe", appropriately[44]) in grey, boring sets. One wonders if some BBC administrative chap with a clipboard came around and said they'd nearly used up the year's supply of colour making "The Claws of Axos", and now must ration it to make "The Daemons".

Just to rub it in, many viewers would have seen the first ten minutes of this rendered in the most thrillingly lurid manner imaginable in the *Radio Times*. Had someone taken the Frank Bellamy version to Michael Briant six months earlier and told him to make *that*, this story would be the most fondly-remembered and appropriate adventure of Season Eight. 1970s Britain had been made to look exhilaratingly wondrous and chock-full of futuristicness (compared to our everyday experience), so seeing a far-off world in 2472 that looked like a damp quarry with some tents was horribly deflating. Even the Time Lords seemed to be having a conference in the works canteen.

What's saddest is that we know everyone involved can do better. Later on, Hulke will sketch planets in far more deft strokes, and make points by showing rather than telling. His minor characters will be more interesting and alive than the major ones seen here (and that's *after* the cast rewrote the dialogue; see **The Lore**). Briant will make alien worlds and odd places seem either more Bellamy-ish or interesting to look at in other ways. (He even makes a quarry look genuinely alien, and the natives properly sinister, in 11.3, "Death to the Daleks".) In fact, in his next two stories he's going to make the Glam-era BBC visuals work *for* him rather than being an accidental side effect.

Then, as if this couldn't get more exasperating, the Master shows up and all hope of imaginative storytelling leaves town. Before now, the surprising nature of this new antagonist and Delgado's sheer charm has covered the fact that the Master is a crass plot-device on legs. The writers of *The Man From UNCLE* admitted they would think up arresting visual images, and if they couldn't think of a proper motivation to go with it, they'd simply admit defeat and blame it all on THRUSH. This is what the Master all too often brings to *Doctor Who*, as becomes clear when they shamelessly wheel him on to keep everything going for another three episodes. Ironically, "Colony in Space" is the nearest we get to a sensible (or at least comprehensible) reason for the Master's villainy, as opposed to some bloke in a bowler hat telling us "he's bad" or the Doctor claiming "he's bonkers". That it results in a climax where a sock-puppet alien is praised for his compassion for triggering an explosion that will kill all the primitives - a scene wherein the aforementioned alien "god" flaps about while the camera zooms in and out to try and make him look marginally less embarrassing - speaks volumes.

The Facts

Written by Malcolm Hulke. Directed by Michael Briant. Viewing figures: 7.6 million, 8.5 million, 9.5 million, 8.1 million, 8.8 million, 8.7 million.

Supporting Cast Nicholas Pennell (Winton), John Ringham (Ashe), Roy Skelton (Norton), Helen Worth (Mary Ashe), John Scott Martin (Robot), Peter Forbes-Robertson, John Baker, Graham Leaman (Time Lords), Bernard Kay (Caldwell), Morris Perry (Dent), Tony Caunter (Morgan), Norman Atkyns (Guardian), Roy Heymann (Alien Priest), Terry Walsh (Security Guard Rogers).

Working Titles "Colony"

Cliffhangers Alone in the one of the colony buildings, the Doctor's examining the aftermath of a "giant lizard" attack when the IMC robot trundles through the door towards him; in the same building, the same robot bears down on the Doctor *again*, but this time under the control of Morgan (the IMC second-in-command) and with fake lizard-claws attached to its arms; the primitives take a captive Jo to the underground city, and everything goes dark as the tunnel entrance closes behind them; during the firefight at the colony, the Master points a gun at the Doctor and announces that he's about to become the victim of stray bullets ('it's always the innocent bystanders who suffer'); outside the primitives' city, the Master prepares to push the remote-control button which will kill Jo with poisoned gas inside his TARDIS.

What Was in the Charts? "If Not For You", Olivia Newton-John; "Jig-a-Jig", East of Eden; "Double Barrel", Dave and Ansel Collins; "Malt And Barley Blues", McGuinness Flint; "My Brother Jake", Free; "I Did What I Did For Maria", Tony Christie.

The Lore

• Malcolm Hulke had voiced so many misgivings about the series' new Earthbound format, it was almost inevitable that he'd be the first writer to take the Third Doctor to another planet. The official commission came just days after Katy Manning was cast as Jo and a fortnight after "Inferno" finished transmission.

Hulke found a way to sneak his own political and environmental concerns into a story with obvious referents to Westerns. The original story had Quaker-like settlers on a planet whose indigenous life-form had degenerated into a cargo-cult. Unscrupulous prospectors set these two groups at one another's throats.

The plan also allowed for a spell without UNIT or the Master, both of whom were in danger of outstaying their welcome. The Brigadier was written in to top-and-tail the story, but more crucially, the story was conceived as two halves: the first just about the colonists and the prospectors, the second re-introducing the Master into an already complex situation. (Incidentally, the myth that all six-parters are four-parters with two extra episodes tacked on is something Robert Holmes said to Robert Banks Stewart, a means of encouraging a slightly blocked author to pull his finger out and finish an under-running story, i.e. 13.6, "The Seeds of Doom". It doesn't bear close examination, save in stories by Holmes himself or with his input prominently in the mix.)

• The provisional date for the story was 3000AD or thereabouts; robots and personal communicators were held to be commonplace by then. The date was later refined to 2971 (in one of those annoying instances of massaging the date to a comfy round number of years in the viewers' future, screaming *This is an allegory, people!* - see, for instance, 21.1, "Warriors of the Deep"). Ideas kicked around in early drafts include a more humanoid robot who serves drinks, and a specific sound for when the primitives are using psychic powers. The Priests and the name 'Uxarieus' were later additions, and the date was brought forward five centuries in the final rewrites in January.

• New director Michael E Briant (he added the 'E' to avoid confusion with then-popular actor Michael Bryant) had been assistant floor manager on 1.2, "The Daleks" (note the very similar way in which Jo finds an alien flower just outside the TARDIS) and 2.6, "The Crusade" (and look who

Briant has cast as the sympathetic member of the Bad Guy posse - Saladin, also known as Bernard Kay). He was also production assistant on two Dalek stories and "Fury From the Deep" (5.6), where he inadvertently created the single most useful plot-device ever: the sonic screwdriver.

Briant decided that for logistical reasons, the robot would be less of an android and more a mini-dump-truck. New designer Tim Gleeson devised a plywood and corrugated-card buggy, with pneumatic tyres, which was built by outside contractors. A man inside (John Scott Martin, inevitably) or the Visual Effects team was to operate this. As it turned out, it was more the latter on location, as the slippery sloping surfaces made stopping difficult and the rain caused them to have to rebuild it on location, plus physically lift it in some shots.

• Bernard Wilkie supervised the effects, with Ian Scoones as his assistant. Scoones, a recruit from the Gerry Anderson Century 21 stable, brought the Master's spaceship with him. It had been a jet fighter in a *Joe 90* episode ("Splashdown") and was flown on wires. The Colonists' ship (called the *Mayflower* in the script, but mercifully not on screen) was about the size of a roll of wallpaper. Its takeoff was shot (like most of the model work) at Ealing, and combined Scoones lifting it from the base out-of-shot with shots of it suspended in front of back-projected clouds, with a Schmerly flare in the base to provide flames and smoke. (It's an old *Thunderbirds* trick; Schmerly, as you doubtless recall from 15.1, "Horror of Fang Rock", make naval rockets, explosive bolts, that sort of thing.) One version of the ship was blown up with another explosive in the Ealing shoot. (You may have seen the rushes for this in the *Doctor Who Confidential* episode that accompanied X3.7, "42.".) A second was taken to the location for a forced-perspective shot alongside the IMC vessel.

• In the interim since being Saladin, Bernard Kay had been the first actor to voice Aslan, in ATV's 1967 adaptation of *The Lion, the Witch and the Wardrobe*. This version was by the people who'd make *Ace of Wands* later on, and made a huge impression at the time. Less impressive was Kay's turn as a slightly camp alien villain in the peculiar Amicus invasion flick *They Came from Beyond Space*. (If you were wondering - as Isaac Asimov did when told the title of the film he was asked to advise - "beyond space" means "the moon", which is here run by Michael Gough.)

As Robert Ashe (named "John" in an earlier draft, and again in the novelisation), Briant cast John Ringham. Amazingly, this is the same man who played the bloodthirsty Tlotoxl in 1.6, "The Aztecs". (He'd also been the misguided Customs man Blake in 4.1, "The Smugglers".) We heard Sheila Grant doing Quark voices (6.1, "The Dominators"). Morris Perry, as the main villain Dent, specialised in Russian agents and was a regular in action shows. Many of the smaller parts went to actors with whom Briant had worked when he was PA, such as Graham Leaman (the communications officer Price in "Fury from the Deep"), Peter Forbes-Robertson (a guard in 4.3, "The Power of the Daleks") John Herrington (Rhymnal in 3.4, "The Daleks' Master Plan") and of course Roy Skelton.

• Like Bernard Kay, Tony Caunter had been in "The Crusade" (as Thatcher, the Chamberlain's assistant). He had originally been cast here in a smaller role, and here's where we address a common misconception. Morgan was written as male, but Briant wanted a strong female number two for the principal antagonist in the first half. The previous year had seen a great many blandly positive women depicted on TV (even UNIT had Corporal Bell these days) and Briant, who had seen female crewmembers on commercial vessels and been impressed by their can-do approach, thought this would give a fairly flat henchman role a lift. It wasn't intended at any stage to give the Master a female sidekick, nor (as was sometimes stated) to create a new regular female villain. (Look in Volume VI to see whether this was a good idea or not.)

Anyway, Briant gave the role of 'Miss Morgan' to Susan Jameson, who was playing similar roles since her break in *Take Three Girls*. (Anyone reading this who was watching British television at the time will now have the theme tune stuck in their heads[45].) Then the Head of Drama Serials, Ronnie Marsh, suggested this might be misconstrued as a bit, well... kinky. If you think this tells us more about Mr Marsh than anything else, bear in mind that the violence in the serial was now under scrutiny from both the BBC's own Audience Research department and the tabloid press. (The scene where the Doctor overpowers Morgan with Venusian Aikido to the chest was singled out for comment in the final Audience Research document, so think about what would have happened had he - Morgan, that is, not the Doctor - been female.) This was resolved just prior to filming; as

Jameson had turned down other work for this part, she was paid and Caunter took over the role.

• The quarry used, Old Baal claypit near Plymouth, was nearly flooded during the same bad weather that blighted filming of "The Claws of Axos", which caused a major rethink of the shooting schedule. The plan had been to use lightweight cars instead of laying dolly-tracks for the cameras. The "futuristic" buggies used by the IMC were imported Haflinger cross-country vehicles on loan. This story's assistant floor manager suggested using the buggies in lieu of the cars for tracking shots. (This chap was called Graeme Harper - you'll hear more of him in later volumes.) The BBC lost an £80 deposit, partly as a result of Jon Pertwee being rather taken with them and going for joyrides when he wasn't shooting, and partly because of the scene with the rock pushed downhill as an ambush. (The polystyrene rock was weighted to roll right, and one of the stage-weights came adrift and hit the buggy.) The Colonists' domes were based on geodesic domes, then-widely believed to be the shape of all futuristic utility buildings. (See 2.8, "The Chase" for the first Buckminster Fuller-inspired design in the series.) They were intentionally cheap-looking; aside from the assumption that the colonists had scrimped and saved just to get a second-hand rocket (a theory that informed their clothing and kitchenware), it was hoped to recoup some of the overspend on "The Mind of Evil".

• There was originally a garden planted outside the dome, but more rain removed it. Unfortunately the prop robot was left outside in this rain and - being cardboard and plywood - was damaged.

• During the second block, rehearsing episodes three and four, some of the guest-cast took it upon themselves to rewrite the dialogue, making their characters' motivations consistent from episode to episode. Meanwhile, Letts took aside Pertwee and asked if he was taking this part seriously. Rehearsals were getting to be a laugh-riot and the star was allowing (or leading) practical jokes. Pertwee pointed out that everyone made sure they were on time for rehearsals, and they were getting through their scheduled tasks quicker than anticipated because of the increased enthusiasm.

• Studio recording was more or less an episode a day, on Fridays and Saturdays. Oddly, the Brigadier's two scenes - set as they were in different episodes, albeit using the same set - were recorded separately. The line about the Spanish Ambassador is widely taken as a reference to Delgado's previous role in *Sir Francis Drake*. Two days before recording started, Pertwee was called in to re-shoot some film excerpts in the BBC carpark - a ruse to get him there for *This Is Your Life*.

• The iguana was pre-filmed specially for this story, with one loaned from London Zoo. By all accounts, it was an unwilling TV star. (Perhaps it had the same agent as the frog from the previous story.) Some of the junk in the holding cell within the primitive city had been seen before, including one piece prominent in Liz's lab in "Spearhead from Space" (7.1). This prop is one of many from the Century 21 toybox and features heavily in the series *Star Maidens* (a show where, to be honest, the props are a lot more watchable than the cast). Lurking in the background as colonists are Les Conrad (see 21.6, "The Caves of Androzani", 21.7, "The Twin Dilemma" - he's been a number of UNIT troops already) and Monique Briant (yep, the missus) in the last episode. One of the priests is Stanley Mason, who's the nimble gargoyle Bok in the next story.

• Aided by Brian Hodgson, Dudley Simpson produced the music to be post-synched. He began work five days before episode one aired and continued for the next fortnight, providing about half an hour's music (some of which will, we fear, stick with you for days after seeing this). There are a couple of extra pieces of music: a bit of *Tank* by Emerson, Lake and Palmer can be heard in the "Entertainment Complex" scene (but not too much, as they were losing viewers rapidly enough by that stage, and it's obviously not on the BBC video release), and the flashy montage when the Doomsday machine self-destructs has another blast of *Build Up To...* by David Vorhaus (see 7.4, "Inferno" for Vorhaus' connections with the Workshop via White Noise).

8.5: "The Daemons"

(Serial JJJ. Five Episodes, 22nd May - 19th June 1971.)

Which One is This?   The Devil went down to Ambridge. The Master's a trendy vicar, stone gargoyles and Morris dancers threaten the destruction of the world, and the pub landlord's hens have stopped laying.

Firsts and Lasts   Season Eight (the "Master Season") ends with a story co-written by Robert Sloman and producer Barry Letts, which is something of a turning-point. From this point on, all the Pertwee seasons end with a story ostensibly by Sloman, but more or less co-written by the producer. As such, it's our clearest clue to what Letts had in mind for the show. "The Daemons" makes apocalyptic revelations about Earth's history and finally sees the Master captured after twenty-five episodes of naughtiness, while 9.5, "The Time Monster"; 10.5, "The Green Death" and 11.5, "Planet of the Spiders", are all pitched as important moments for the Doctor's character.

This is the last five-part story although - unlike the brace that opened Season Six - it was planned as one from the start. After the reasonably transparent 'Colonel Masters' (8.1, "Terror of the Autons") and the cryptic "Emil Keller" (8.2, "The Mind of Evil"), here the Master develops his habit of using a pseudonym that means "Master" in another language.

It's also the first time that most of the key UNIT members are seen in civilian dress (or in the Brigadier's case, pyjamas).

Five Things to Notice About "The Daemons"...

1. One of the best-remembered stories of the Jon Pertwee era (at least, among people who only saw it on broadcast in the 70s), "The Daemons" combines all the things you expect in a story of this kind, jammed up against each other. One minute there's a helicopter exploding, and the next there's a character-actor with a yokel accent leading a posse of armed Morris-dancers. (Anybody who's attended a real English May Day celebration will sympathise.) State-of-the-art electronic effects are juxtaposed with an old man adopting a "crikey, that statue's come to life and is about to kill me" pose for what seems like ten minutes. Then we're having an anthropological slideshow in a pub, while the Master's dressing up as the head of a satanic coven to summon the Devil. (Casual students of the black arts will notice that the Master misquotes Aleister Crowley, 'to do my will shall be the whole of the law', thus proving that he's evil.) This mix / mess is now so characteristic of 1970s Doctor Who, it's almost impossible to recall how downright peculiar it originally seemed that any one of these ingredients was in a story, let alone all of them at once.

2. Sadly, "The Daemons" is also notorious for having one of the *least* convincing endings of any Doctor Who story, in which the vast and all-powerful Azal, the last of the Daemons, explodes when Jo confuses him a bit. One of the better April Fool's scams in fan history claimed to have found "episode six", the end of which was tagged onto the broadcast episode five in desperation. When you see the last part of this story, you'll understand why people bought the hoax.

3. Miss Hawthorne supplies some archly contrived exposition, when she mentions the priest who's been replaced by the Master: 'I mean Canon Smallwood, our old vicar. *The one who disappeared in such mysterious circumstances.*' However, this being a Pertwee / UNIT yarn, the bulk of the info-dumping is done by a smarmy bloke from the BBC talking to camera on a television programme the Doctor's watching. We can't help but wonder if David Simeon was cast because he looked a *bit* like Michael Palin, who was then systematically parodying every one of Alistair Fergus' real-life counterparts in *Monty Python*.

4. Azal's appearance raised a few eyebrows when this story was finally shown in America. Here, however, the main thing that attracted attention was the exploding church effect. In Britain, we can tolerate all sorts of religious iconography popping up in a kid's adventure show, but you threaten ecclesiastical architecture at your peril.

5. And finally... 'Chap with the wings there. Five rounds rapid.' The Brigadier's unflappability becomes the stuff of legend.

The Continuity

The Doctor   He utterly refuses to believe in magic, or even use the word, insisting that all phenomena can be explained scientifically [compare with 26.1, "Battlefield"]. He sticks by this opinion, even when the local white witch convincingly argues that magic is the same thing as the Daemons' "psionic" science anyway. He's very bad at being polite when he's flustered, doubly so when someone accuses him of wearing a wig.

The Doctor can survive a drop in temperature that would kill a human being, and knows how to ride a motorcycle. Curiously he believes that humanity will 'probably' blow up the world. [Is he referring to future World Wars, or has he just forgotten future history? Is it contingent on his own actions? See 9.1, "Day of the Daleks".] He has no interest in gaining the Daemons' power even for altruistic reasons, believing that humanity should be left to grow up by itself. He appears live on national television as the Barrow is opened, and Jo is seen saying his name on screen. [That should keep the conspiracy theorists in business for a time, especially when the Prime Minister begs for the Doctor's help during a national broadcast in X2.0, "The Christmas Invasion".]

When he's fixing Bessie, the hankie in the pocket of his overalls matches the cravat he later wears. [So he's really getting into this "dressing-up" business.]

• *Ethics*. He has no objection to turning Bessie suddenly - and thereby causing the death of a helicopter pilot (Girton, one of the Master's minions) - as said pilot is intent on trying to murder him and Jo. He does at least look appalled when the chopper explodes, and (to be fair) had little chance of reasoning with Girton or breaking the Master's control.

• *Background*. He not only knows that something terrible is buried under Devil's End, but he also knows the Daemons' history in detail, suggesting some first-hand experience. [Failed attempts were made to open the Devil's Hump before - see **History** - so was the Doctor involved? A cut line suggests that the Master is worried that the Doctor knows about Daemons from personal involvement rather than as a mere "memory trace", perhaps suggesting that Time Lords have huge amounts of stuff dropped directly into their cortices for possible future use, as we've speculated elsewhere.]

He seems to have heard both Hitler and Genghis Khan speak [which more or less confirms hints respectively left in 26.3, "The Curse of Fenric" and X1.1, "Rose"]. Here he quotes the first line of an old Venusian lullaby [the same one he uses in 9.2, "The Curse of Peladon"], which translates as 'close your eyes, my darling... well, three of them at least'.

• *Bessie*. Here the Doctor fits a radio control device, which can be used to steer Bessie from a little gadget in his pocket. [He's never seen to use this again.]

The Supporting Cast

• *Jo Grant*. She's utterly dedicated to the Doctor by now, prepared to sacrifice her life to save him even though he spends much of the preceding day being rude to her. She's easily impressed, but makes a distinction between a vague belief in 'the age of Aquarius' and believing what Yates tells her

about psionic force-fields in the crypt. [She's seen so many of the Doctor's conjuring tricks, perhaps it's more comforting to believe that Yates is doing one than to accept the alternative.] She's become far less independent than in earlier appearances, although she's still prepared to impulsively rush off and get captured by the Master while she's zonked out by concussion and drugs.

The Doctor is never seen to thank her for saving either him or the world. Indeed, when she criticises the Brigadier in exactly the same manner as the Doctor always does, the Doctor gives her a stern lecture for doing so. [There's no pleasing some people...]

Jo knows her National Anthem [using the term 'knavish tricks', cf 9.3, "The Sea Devils"] and can get middle-aged men to do as she asks about once per episode.

• *The Brigadier*. He's seen sleeping alone [but see **The Lore**]. Despite his ire at being woken up to hear that his entire staff have gone AWOL with a chopper, he responds to - shall we say - unusual circumstances very ably. His trust in the Doctor's gadgetry means that instead of getting trigger-happy as was his wont, he's reduced to grumbling that he sometimes wishes he worked in a bank.

• *Yates and Benton*. Act as if they have a day off school when an impenetrable barrier separates them from the Brig. They're quite prepared to go off on an unauthorised jaunt in the Brigadier's helicopter, improvise rescue plans and get into fights with (generally hypnotised) locals. Benton can fly a helicopter and is a capable shot. [Yates also takes over from Jo as principal expository question-feeder.] Interested in watching the dig at Devil's End, Captain Yates nonetheless gets sucked in to the rugby and loses a bet with Benton.

• *UNIT*. The mobile HQ is now 'Greyhound 2'. Yates is 'Trap 2'; Benton is 'Trap 3'.

The Supporting Cast (Evil)

• *The Master*. He's not great at staying in character when trying to charm people, his impatience causing him to snap and start demanding their obedience. Tapping Azal's power [or so it seems], he can summon a small whirlwind.

Here he seems interested in obtaining Azal's power as a means of ruling humanity, which has become an end in itself. [Later stories will see him keen to have control of Earth, even when a whole galaxy or the cosmos is his for the taking. Exactly

The Daemons - What the Hell are They Doing?

Everyone knows that the end of "The Daemons" is - if you'll pardon the phrase - a *deus ex machina*. Azal becomes confused and blows himself up after Jo hurls herself in the way of thunderbolts intended for the Doctor. However, virtually nobody seems interested in asking *why* the Daemons were so keen throughout the ages for humanity to advance in the first place. What's in it for them?

Within *Doctor Who*, other beings that influenced humanity's development usually did so for very obvious and selfish motives. The Fendahl wants a posse (15.3, "Image of the Fendahl"), Scaroth needs a labour-force so he can get his head together (17.2, "The City of Death") and so on. Yet the Daemons' motives, like those of the unseen aliens in *2001: A Space Odyssey*, are unclear to the point of looking like mere plot-contrivance. Understandably, fandom has applied its mass intellect to the problem, with mixed results. So here, we'll attempt to fathom the cryptic aliens' motives and account for the sheer absurdity of the story's climax. The various scenarios presented by Azal's words aren't always in synch with what's said in the BBC Books and the Virgin *New Adventures*, but let's push onward anyway.

Tellingly, Azal speaks as though he's working on strict orders: 'My instructions are very precise', he claims. He *must* hand on his power and knowledge at a designated time, or dire consequences will occur. In short, an immensely powerful being has a "Best Before" date, and is under orders from an even *more* powerful entity to select someone from the planet being tested as a worthy successor. And the dialogue suggests that the Daemons have done this several times before. Why should this occasion be so radically different from the others?

In case you haven't guessed where this is going, consider the fate of Sir Percival Flint, an archaeologist mentioned in this story. At the time of the Industrial Revolution (the Daemons' last known intervention), his workers left him for dead. Now consider that Azal, as potent and omniscient as he seems, doesn't appear to know about Time Lords when even the Bandrils (!) are in the loop about them (22.5, "Timelash"). Now ask yourself what would actually happen to someone whom the Daemons found worthy - the ability to change size and animate gargoyles must entail some biological alterations.

To spell it out, maybe the role of Daemon doesn't entail physically travelling from Damos and sleeping for millennia. Maybe each selected worthy specimen is turned into a horned beast by the previous post-holder, following instructions from the original Daemon (who might in fact be the doddy spaceship) and is tasked with passing on this poisoned chalice before the power becomes too great to bear. From the Daemons' point of view, running each planet like the British Raj - guiding the locals towards the point where they can run things along the lines laid down by their 'masters' - is a simpler way of shepherding the galaxy towards whatever their desired end might be. Heck, the Romans did it, as did the Ottomans (until their selected "clients", the Mamelouks, became too much of a handful). Also, if we assume that Daemonicity is more akin to a meme than a planetary origin, a status conferred on suitable candidates like Sir Percy, what were the original Daemons like and what happened to them?

That's what bothers a lot of people about this backstory - beings *that* powerful should have made more of a splash in the galaxy than we've ever seen. Worse, if they were wiped out, powerful agencies must have done the deed. (Alas, the timescale is wrong for either the Osirians from 13.3, "Pyramids of Mars" or the Old Ones from the Dark Times - see X3.0, "The Runaway Bride" and others - to have been responsible.) The hypothesis in the previous paragraph still works, though, if the Daemons knew that they were leaving and wanted to make a mark in their absence.

Perhaps, and this is where we get really tentative, the Daemons are sterile and this is their way of reproducing themselves on a grand scale. Once we (or one of the other client races we hear about) collectively come up to scratch, maybe everyone will undergo the same process. (Of course, if this is what's happening here, then Azal - if indeed he was formerly Sir Percival - is planning to pass on his abilities and physical form to the chosen one, who will then supervise the process of turning *every* worthy human into a Daemon.[55] The hurdle here is that it's hard to see why the Master would want that to happen to him. We'd like to think he had a long-term plan, but this really isn't his strongest suit.)

Whatever actually became of Sir Percy, the term 'left for dead' might be significant. No body was found. Sure, Bok can *evaporate* bodies, but if we're positing a physical transformation from minor nobility to sulphur-breathing Daemon, what

continued on page 171...

why is unclear.] It's left unsaid how he finds out about the Daemon at Devil's End.

[We can assume that the Master's access to the Time Lords' files wasn't just some quick break-in and copious use of an office photocopier, so his learning about Azal from the information seems the most likely. However, the effort the Master later puts into trying to tap the Matrix (see Season Twenty-Three) indicates that he lacks total access at that stage in his criminal career. We also know that he's got the technical wherewithal to tap the APC Net (14.3, "The Deadly Assassin") even while at death's door, but if this tap were closed off, possibly as part of Engin's security review as requested by Acting-President Borusa, then the Master has good reason to hire Glitz and Dibber to obtain Matrix bootlegs from Drathro (23.1, "The Mysterious Planet").]

[We have no idea, however, when he initially starts siphoning off the Time Lords' data. One imagines that it's a big risk to place a trap-door inside the Matrix *after* the Time Lords alerted the Doctor to his impending crime spree on Earth in the 1970s, so perhaps the heads-up from Bowler-Hat Man in "Terror of the Autons" was prompted by the discovery of a lot of files about 70s Britain being opened in a short space of time. This makes the sudden decision to whip the TARDIS off to Uxarieus in 8.4, "Colony in Space" a bit more plausible.]

The Non-Humans

• *The Daemons*. Roughly 100,000 years ago, the Daemons came to Earth from Damos, a planet 60,000 light years away on the other side of the galaxy. They originally came to help homo sapiens kick out Neanderthal man, and have been 'coming and going' ever since. [So maybe Azal's ship hasn't actually been there for 100,000 years. Of course, 'coming and going' could just refer to the periodic manifestations, or something else entirely - see the accompanying essay.] The Doctor claims that Greek civilisation, the Renaissance and the Industrial Revolution were all inspired by them.

The Daemons were amoral by human standards, and Earth was a scientific experiment to them. They were known to destroy their failed experiments, with Azal telling the Master to 'remember Atlantis' [see, as if you couldn't guess, **How Many Atlantises are There?** under 4.5, "The Underwater Menace"]. Human myths of magic are just remnants of the Daemons' advanced science, Azal apparently being the inspiration for Azazael, the fallen angel. The Doctor describes him as the worst menace ever to be faced by humanity, thus shifting the Keller Machine from the number one position after just a few months.

The Daemons were humanoid in shape, but with goat-like legs, cloven hoofs, satanic features and - of course - horns, which therefore became a symbol of power throughout human culture. Azal, the last of the Daemons [probably in the universe, although he *could* feasibly just mean on Earth], is at least twenty feet tall when he manifests, but can cause both himself and his technology to change size. His spaceship is only fifteen inches long when the Doctor finds it, even though it weighs around 750 tons and was 200 by 30 feet when it arrived. When Azal is miniaturised, he's so small that he's practically invisible [not to scale with the miniaturised spaceship, then, or he'd be more like an action figure]. To grow he needs to absorb energy / matter from the environment around him; shrinking causes him to shed the surplus energy as a heatwave. He can thereby generate a heat barrier, a dome of energy ten miles across and a mile high. Anything that touches explodes. Azal himself can generate lethal energy from his fingers.

The Daemon sees Earth as a failure, and he's been 'instructed' [by whom?] to destroy it or to pass on his knowledge and power to someone else who'll oversee things. In fact procedure is clearly important to him, as he insists on appearing before the Master exactly three times, making his decision on his last appearance. It's not clear whether Azal's been conscious all these years, or whether he only wakes up when the Devil's Hump barrow is opened.

He's able to sense the alien presence of the Doctor at long range, and considers even a Time Lord's knowledge to be inferior [but presumably, the Daemons never cracked time-travel]. He believes himself so rational that when Jo tries to sacrifice herself to save the Doctor, Azal self-destructs, his own power turning against him. [No wonder he's the last of his kind. This is deeply strange, especially since self-sacrifice *isn't* illogical but a survival technique that even many animal species have adopted. The novelisation expands on this slightly, giving the impression that Jo's act of "irrational" intervention sets up a psychokinet-

The Daemons - What the Hell are They Doing?

...continued from page 169

made Percy the obvious candidate? We might suppose he had crucial knowledge of the arcana, the rituals or whatever, but there's a snag - we know his workers ran away. Fear is a strong emotion, but the rest of the coven needs to be physically present for the convocation to work. Perhaps the psychic force was enough to arouse the previous Azal, but not enough (or too fleeting) to protect Flint as he'd hoped. This would explain why the Master is so keen to have back-up for the last ritual.

However, if Azal really came from Damos in person about 100,000 years ago, on a mission to raise the local bipeds (the hairy bipeds, that is; the Daemons don't seem very fussed about chickens), the question remains: why did he bother? Are the Daemons so bored? Is braining-up species some kind of hobby? Did they do it just for company and how many other races have they unwisely nudged towards nuclear capability?

That last point is intriguing: the previous interventions all seem to be making H. Sap more proficient killers, and the earliest mention is that they helped us to 'kick out' the Neanderthals. This could mean they simply evicted our cousins and put them somewhere else - like, say, Mondas (4.2, "The Tenth Planet"), or any of the other planets that seem to have spontaneously acquired humanoid life-forms against all the odds. However, if we go along with the less charitable interpretation, then the Daemons are simply more eldritch versions of the War Lords from "The War Games" (6.7), training us up to become galactic warriors. Maybe the hippies of Atlantis were wiped out for setting a bad example. (See **How Many Atlantises Are There?** under 4.5, "The Underwater Menace".) At this point, the newly-revealed fact that the Sontaran-Rutan war started 50,000 years ago (X4.5, "The Poison Sky") might be significant, but we've got another essay on that coming up about that (see 11.1, "The Time Warrior").

One possibility that's been floated, along the lines of David Brin's *Uplift* books, suggests that all races are judged on how many new intelligent species they have raised to an acceptable standard in a given time. In other words, the Daemons are bucking for a promotion based on commission. If we take this cosmic pyramid-selling scheme seriously, Azal's main worry in judging us would be whether we have, in our turn, created or fostered any other intelligences. Under that scenario, WOTAN from "The War Machines" (3.10) would be a better advocate for humanity than the Doctor. The Master could simply mention whaling and our treatment of chimpanzees as proof of our lack of concern for potential fellow-intellects. (If the Master knows about *The Clangers* and King Crimson, he *must* have seen the PG Tips tea commercials with chimps in wigs pushing pianos up staircases.)

A more plausible theory is that they're keen to expand our consciousness. We already know that the fundamental nature of the cosmos is somehow linked to conscious observation. (This was more or less accepted within physics, but it also ties up a lot of loose ends in *Doctor Who*. See **What Makes the TARDIS Work?** under 1.3, "Edge of Destruction" and **What Do the Guardians Do?** under 16.1, "The Ribos Operation". Oh, and look - X3.10, "Blink", says it outright.) Maybe a "critical mass" of consciousness (the ontological equivalent of Dark Matter) is needed to "close" the universe, and the Daemons have been given the job of wringing every ounce of it out of this galaxy. It may be more a question of the right kind of consciousness (see **Does Everyone in the Universe Speak English?** under 14.1, "The Masque of Mandragora" and **How Many Significant Galaxies Are There?** under 2.5, "The Web Planet"). Intriguingly, on screen we only venture later than the Fifty-Seventh Segment of Time (see 3.6, "The Ark"; 21.3, "Frontios") after the Time Lords are gone, and our one glimpse of a Heat Death future - rather than the version fitted as standard in *The New Adventures* (the "concertina" theory) - is a scenario where humanity has devolved (X3.11, "Utopia"). At this point, the obvious question is why humans were more promising candidates than dolphins, Orang-utans or those dormant Silurians. This of course, requires us to know the Daemons' criteria.

As you'll see in **Are These 'gods' Related?** (under 26.3, "The Curse of Fenric"), we'd be quite prepared to accept that the motives of god-like aliens shouldn't be too amenable to mortal scrutiny, *if* the stories in which they appeared were less predictably plotted. (See also **Could It Be Magic?** under 25.4, "The Greatest Show in the Galaxy".) If the series weren't so rigorously empiricist in its overall approach audiences over the years - never moreso than here - we'd be more prepared to "buy" cryptic behaviour and beings moving in

continued on page 173...

ic field which causes Azal's power to rebound on himself, though this may be an over-generous way of seeing things. (See "The Curse of Fenric", for a more elegant use of a similar idea.) Either way, Azal's decision that if the Doctor must be destroyed if he doesn't want power is equally illogical.] If nothing else, Azal is considerate enough to tell those assembled to flee, once it's clear that he's going to detonate.

The Master calls on Azal's psionic power through ritual or pure concentration, and his coven helps as violent emotions produce psychokinetic energy. The power can cause weak victims to die of fright; overcome the will of specific targets, and turn them into murderers; create force-fields around people; and cause various poltergeist-like phenomena. Miss Hawthorn's "magical" incantations seem to hold the energy back. [Perhaps *any* kind of ritual sets up a psychic counter-charge, since the Doctor's Venusian nursery-rhyme keeps Bok at bay and part of the Master's invocation to Azal is "Mary Had a Little Lamb" backwards. See "The Curse of Fenric" and also 14.1, "The Masque of Mandragora" for an extended riff on this idea.]

The Hump is opened at Beltane, a major occult festival, and the Doctor believes this is significant. [It's hard to see how, unless the Daemon's psychic force somehow convinced Professor Horner to open the barrow on that particular night. Or did the Master hypnotise him?]

The Master summons Azal unaided, but needs the full coven to help him 'control' the Daemon. Azal has very precise instructions that at the third manifestation, he must donate his power to a worthy successor. Azal says the Master was only able to summon him because 'the time was right' [so presumably a timetable constrains these "omnipotent" beings]. The Master exerts some control over Azal by ordering him to obey 'in the name of the Unspeakable One'. [These days, we might assume that he's referring to the Beast from X2.9, "The Satan Pit". The Tennant story even names Damos as a planet where the Beast is worshipped, but the dialogue is so garbled it could mean practically anything.]

• *Bok, the Gargoyle*. [Named in dialogue but once, in episode three, and also in the credits.] A stone carving in the church cavern at Devil's End, animated by Azal's power. It's apparently indestructible - instantly putting itself back together even when blown into fragments - and can disin-

tegrate people by pointing at them. The Master can control Bok telepathically, but Bok has a mind of his own. [It seems odd that Azal's power should choose to settle in such a definite form, since he's no reason to show off. Either Bok's animation is the Master's idea, or one of the earlier witch-cults at Devil's End specifically made the gargoyle as a receptacle for the Daemon's energy.]

Bok can be scared off by something made of iron, the Doctor claiming that iron is an old magical defence. *He* doesn't believe in it, but Bok does. Sometimes Bok shows very precise control, destroying Mike's gun but leaving him unscathed, and usually he zaps items headed his way - like the odd brick, rather than the person chucking it. He normally kills individuals when instructed, but only evaporates people unprompted when it seems like fun. [So Bert (who's on his side) gets it, but Mike (who flung the brick as a demonstration) doesn't and neither does Jenkins (the marksman ordered to give him 'five rounds rapid'). Nor does he zap the Brigadier, who gave the order. This indicates a degree of autonomy, as does his refusal to obey the Master when scared off by Venusian lullabies and trowels.]

• *Venusians*. Evidently they have more than three eyes, and offspring who need lullabies.

History

• *Dating*. The barrow is opened on the eve of 30th of April. [Probably 1973. This makes it the same day that *The Wicker Man* - the good one, not the Nicolas Cage thing - is supposedly taking place.]

[The 1st of May is obviously not a Sunday, neither does it seem that 30th of April was. No services take place, and the local GP promptly responds to the first death and is expected to be available when Benton needs treatment. 1st of May, 1973, *was* a Sunday, but *Doctor Who* has more than one instance of calendar days being out of synch. (See 3.10, "The War Machines", for a classic example and 25.3, "Silver Nemesis", for our best guess at to why this is the case.)]

At some point, Neanderthal Man was removed from this world. [The Doctor is reticent about how this was achieved: genocide seems to be one option, but they might have been relocated. To Mondas, perhaps? It makes as much sense of anything connected to that planet - indeed, the whole business with a planet wandering off and coming back smacks of a daft experiment by god-like

The Daemons - What the Hell are They Doing?

...continued from page 171

mysterious ways. (By which we mean their actions in general, not how they get from A to B - even if, as with the Wirrn from 12.2, "The Ark in Space" and the supposedly powerless Daleks in 11.3, "Death to the Daleks", this remains an issue.) With "The Daemons" being a story that's emphatically about science defeating superstition, it desperately needs a logical, knowable reason for things to happen - but then it ends with a mystery. On this score, it's a bigger cop-out than the shameless fudge of "The Satan Pit" (X2.09), even though that story seems conceived primarily as a rebuke to this one's empiricist stance.

Overall, though, the *main* logical inconsistency with the Daemons is that either every other intelligent race in the known universe has undergone the same trial and somehow passed (despite the obvious shortcomings of the Ice Warriors, Kaleds, Zygons, Foamasi, Raxacoricofallopatorians, Arcturans and even the titchy demi-gods of Uxareius in the previous story, 8.4, "Colony in Space") or Earth has been singled out despite all these more promising candidates nearby. Unless the Doctor (or someone of similar stature and moral probity) also contrived to confuse each planet's Daemon into going "bang!" in every single case, some kind of get-out clause must permit spacefaring races to survive a Daemon's wrath. Maybe the *only* difference between Earth and the others is that we were unable to leg it to another planet when our mentor went ballistic. Maybe this is why Mars is so inhospitable, even to Martians these days.

---

beings. Theories of what happened to Homo Neanderthalis change about once a month - at present it's thought that either intermarriage or warfare removed them from the picture].

According to the Doctor, the horned Egyptian god Khnun [q.v. 13.3, "The Pyramids of Mars"] was in some way inspired by the Daemons. In the seventeenth century, witches hid from the witchfinder Matthew Hopkins in the cavern under the church at Devil's End; in the eighteenth century, the third Lord Aldbourne performed black magic ceremonies there. It was also apparently a site of importance in pagan religion.

In 1793, Sir Percival Flint attempted to open the Devil's Hump, but his miners ran back to Cornwall, leaving him for dead. Another attempt was made in 1939, but this is described as the 'Cambridge University fiasco'. The "tomb" inside the Hump is ostensibly the same shape as the Daemons' spaceship, though smaller than it would be at full-size. [This might indicate that human beings built the tomb around it. Throughout *Doctor Who*, Britain plays a remarkably large part in world history, even compared to what was taught in our schools in the 1950s, and most aliens attack it first. Is Azal's presence the reason for this? The Doctor mentions the industrial revolution, which *is* potentially the country's greatest contribution to global history, at least to date.]

BBC3 shows the broadcast from Devil's End. [In the real world, BBC3 didn't come into existence until the twenty-first century. Since the barrow's opening isn't punctuated by yet more reruns of *Two Pints of Lager and a Packet of Crisps*, and the continuity announcer isn't misguidedly convinced that she's a stand-up comedian, we assume that it's not the same station.] Miss Hawthorne claims that the last witchcraft act was repealed in Britain in 1951 [technically accurate, since the 1951 Fraudulent Mediums Act replaced the 1736 Witchcraft Act]. UNIT helicopters are worth £20,000.

The Doctor mentions the 'national power complex' [so the Nuton power complex (8.3, "The Claws of Axos") seems to be operational again].

Additional Sources When Target stepped up production of their novelisations, Letts adapted this story himself. *Doctor Who and the Daemons* is fondly remembered for its bravura use of Free Indirect narrative - not least an extraordinary passage about an anteater's tongue and a jelly-baby, only the second mention of these sweets in the series' oeuvre (see 10.1, "The Three Doctors" for the first). There's also odd incidental details such as Miss Hawthorne's cat (Grimalkin), the *Mapp and Lucia* subplot of Lily Watts' reigning over the village, the fact that the Daemons are Chapter Thirteen of the Galactic History primer that the Doctor read at school, and the time the Master persuaded the President of the Time Lords that it was the Doctor who put glue on the presidential perigosto stick. (Not the sort of behaviour we might expect from the *Damien*-like child as seen in X3.12, "The Sound of Drums".) At 170 close-typed pages, this is twice the word-count of the average Target book.

The script was also published in book form in 1992, although this was a transcript of what was broadcast rather than the original screenplay. A video-taped documentary (*Return to Devil's End*) has several of the cast revisiting Aldbourne twenty years later. At the time, the pub landlord had kept the "Cloven Hoof" sign for visitors - these days the place has changed hands, and you make the pilgrimage at your own risk.

The Big Finish audio "The Spectre of Lanyon Moor" picks up the story of Sir Percival Flint. Nicholas Courtney plays the Brigadier opposite Colin Baker's Doctor, so completists will be thrilled.

The Analysis

Where Does This Come From? Because "The Daemons" was so massively influential, it takes a while to realise how unprecedented and out-of-synch it was with every story beforehand. It also takes a bit of an effort to comprehend how far this story was in keeping with the overall mood of Britain in 1971. This story's roots will take more than a few mentions of source-texts to get straight, so you might need a ploughman's lunch[46]. Everyone ready, set? Here we go...

As we said when looking at Silurians, the early 70s was the golden age of people thinking up "explanations" for odd historical or cultural phenomena. The most widely-known is, of course, Erich von Daniken. Beginning with *Chariots of the Gods*, his books popularised an idea that not only were our ancestors incapable of doing the least thing for themselves, but that anything that isn't immediately explicable must be the work of aliens. Yes, indeed: Pyramids, Morris Dancing, Stonehenge, Atlantis - aliens are responsible for *all* of 'em.

For most middlebrow readers, this was only slightly more implausible than pop-anthropology bestseller Desmond Morris "reducing" all social interaction to something analogous to animal behaviour in *The Naked Ape*. If you go back far enough, the granddaddy of all accounts for odd human activities through basic needs being rerouted is Sigmund Freud. Certainly, the wider readership for paperback editions of *his* work

made publishers think that people could handle all sorts of things. Millions of otherwise sensible people bought, read and half-believed Von Daniken's account of prehistory.

However, the best starting-point for the *Doctor Who*-style of planetary events becoming folklore is Immanuel Velikovsky's book *Worlds In Collision*. We'll consider this again under "Death to the Daleks" (11.3), but it happens that Nigel Kneale wrote *Quatermass and the Pit* very soon after this book came out. Velikovsky theorises that the planet Venus was - somehow - exuded from Jupiter (thus causing the Red Spot), hurtled past Mars and skimmed Earth. So we get Zeus producing Aphrodite from his brow in Greek mythology and Moses "summoning" plagues, freak tidal effects (as in the Red Sea) and carbohydrate distillate falling from the air.

The words "yeah" and "right" might spring to mind, but his approach - so radical in the 1950s - caught the public mood. Space was synonymous with Tomorrow, not the deep past. If half-remembered silly stories were in fact detailed accounts of astral phenomena, then surely only the generation that had finally seen their own planet from *outside* just a couple of years previous could handle this. A whole culture suddenly felt very smug and superior, whilst at the same time humbled by the Earth's fragility and the bravery of the people who told themselves stories to account for it all. As we'll see, archaeology was providing proof of a lot of things that had been just stories (see "The Time Monster").

You'll remember from Volume I that BBC2 was consciously designed as an alternative to mainstream and commercial television, and often made a virtue of the fringe nature of its material. (You'll also note that Benton and Yates are watching BBC3; everyone would have taken this as code for the dig being less popular than recorded highlights of Rugby Union.) To get BBC2, you needed a 625-line UHF set - a rarity, but as colour also required this, people upgraded and suddenly had three channels. Up until that point, only affluent viewers had seen BBC2. If you look at the way people on the margins - or those with strong but unconventional opinions - were lent film-crews to make short programmes in the early years, a lot of the odd things we'll discuss in a moment make a bit more sense.

The weekend that "The Daemons" episode five was shown, the 12,000 people who went to the

What's the UNIT Timeline?

Since we've established that the UNIT stories are perfectly at home in the early 70s (see **When are the UNIT Stories Set?** under 7.1, "Spearhead from Space"), the next step is to establish a chronology that actually makes some kind of sense. Obviously, no chronology is going to be *entirely* acceptable to fandom-in-general, but what follows (we dearly hope) is one in which has the minimum possible number of glitches.

Summer 1968: "The Web of Fear". There's nothing in "The Web of Fear" to indicate that it's supposed to take place in the future, and the plan to set the UNIT stories a few years ahead of time obviously hadn't been made by this point. The story was written in 1967, but was broadcast in early 1968. The novel *Downtime* (a sequel to this story) insists on 1968 - this is feasible, and it should be noted that the Yeti incursion lasts for some weeks before the Doctor gets involved. See the main "Web of Fear" entry for more on why the Tube map is such a giveaway.

Autumn 1970: "The Invasion". Always controversial. The Brigadier recalls the events of "The Web of Fear" taking place four years earlier, but he *is* speaking from memory and on the spur of the moment, so here we've given him a little leeway and suggested just over three years instead. The alternatives are to move "The Web of Fear" backwards to 1966, which is *just* about possible but a little clumsy, or to move "The Invasion" forward. Which we don't want to do, because...

Late 1970: "Spearhead from Space". According to "Planet of the Spiders" (11.5), the Third Doctor arrived on Earth 'months' after the events of "The Invasion". The reason for dating "Spearhead" to late 1970 or early 1971 is simple: the shops still use shillings, rather than the decimal currency that was introduced to Britain in February 1971. Now, the truth is that if we can believe in a world where a well-known division of the UN fights aliens, then we can believe in a world where the British currency system changed at a slightly later date. But as the change was such a fixed "before" and "after" event in the British consciousness, it's an irresistible historical marker. To anyone alive at the time, altering it would be like altering the dates of World War Two.

Early 1971: "Doctor Who and the Silurians", "The Ambassadors of Death". The Doctor's settled on Earth by the time of "The Silurians", and not much time passes between that and "The Ambassadors of Death" as he's still harping on about the Brigadier's alleged act of mass-murder. (That said, you'd expect him to bring it up every time the Brig's tactics annoy him. But after this one mention, it's forgotten.)

[By the way, it'd be lovely to wish the whole Mars-Probe-in-the-era-of-8-Track-Cartridges thing away. It's fun to imagine that when the Doctor returns from the "Inferno" reality, he gets it slightly wrong and returns to a reality *exactly* like the one he knows, but with no British astronauts. Alas, the set-up returns some years later, when 13.4, "The Android Invasion" claims that Mission Control Wood Norton sent Guy Crayford into space in a denim spacesuit and cravat. So it's desperately hard to ignore.

[And *yet*, these days the Plucky Young Girl Reporter who claims to have covered the Crayford story doesn't believe that have landed humans on Mars yet - see the end of "Warriors of Kudlak", the third *Sarah Jane Adventures* yarn. It's been twice confirmed (X3.6, "The Lazarus Experiment"; X3.10, "Blink") that Americans made the first moon landing in 1969, so how is it that the well-publicised Mars Probe programme in "The Ambassadors of Death" (up to and including John Wakefield covering it live on global telly) has been so comprehensively forgotten? So far, nothing on screen accounts for this, but as other, bigger events have also been erased from the public memory (*before* the Time War, so we needn't bring that into the picture), it's almost inevitable that one day we'll find out. Maybe the global link-up used Archangel technology (see X3.12, "The Sound of Drums").]

July 1971: "Inferno." A calendar in the parallel universe says it's the 23rd of July, so unless the dates are all wrong in the other world (and given the sheer volume of fluky similarities between the two realities, this is unlikely) then this looks fairly solid.

[Just one thing: it's been plausibly suggested that if we swap the last two stories of Season Seven around, Liz's exit from UNIT makes more sense. She as good as resigns to help Cornish at

continued on page 177...

second Glastonbury Festival got to join Edgar Broughton in chanting *Out, Demons Out*. (It was adapted from the Fugs' chant - don't ask *us* to explain the Fugs, look it up - itself connected to an attempt to exorcise the Pentagon in 1967.) The 60s one-hit wonder band The Crazy World of Arthur Brown did their 60s one hit - a hybrid of Aleister Crowley and Screaming Jay Hawkins - wherein Mr Brown would cavort in proto-Gene Simmons make-up and a blazing crown danger-ously close to his luxuriant hair, then bellow "I am the God of Hellfire and I bring you...Fire!" ("Fire" got to Number 2 the week 6.1, "The Dominators" started.) The stage was a giant pyramid, aligned to the stars.

Glastonbury is now mostly associated with the Festival, held most years around the Solstice, but the town has a great deal of folklore and history around it. Joseph of Aramethea landed there (sup-posedly) when it was still an island and planted his staff, which flowered into a rosebush that blooms on Christmas Day[47]. A pair of skeletons tentatively identified as Arthur and Guinevere were found, still with red hair, in the Abbey. Oh, and Dr John Dee has associations with the place. Having a somewhat homespun rock music event there - with the more (shall we say) patchouli-scented portion of the nation's youth listening to Hawkwind, Gong, Melanie and Fairport Convention for free, then climbing the mound of the Tor overlooking the town or chilling in a near-by stone-circle (see 16.3, "The Stones of Blood") - seemed right and proper. So doing a rural *Doctor Who* story about ancient magic and maypoles was as obvious as doing one about Sat Navs (X4.04, "The Sontaran Strategem") or *Big Brother* (X1.12, "Bad Wolf") today.

And that's odd, because the *previous* Festival, where Tyrannosaurus Rex topped the bill just before elfin singer Marc Bolan dropped the other member of the band (bongo-player Steve Peregrine Took - yes, really) and went all-out for chart success as "T. Rex", was far more, err, "Daemonsy". Yet it's hard to think of a story *less* in tune with the flowers and Ley-lines vibe than "Inferno" (7.4), broadcast that same week. Something remarkable was going on in British culture for these simultaneous changes to both seem right and natural. This will take a bit of explaining, particularly with regards to something non-UK viewers often find puzzling about this story. (Let's face it, most of us here do too...)

Overseas readers may not realise this, but the tradition of Morris Dancing - however much we may mock it - is still popular in rural Britain. It's a sort of hybrid of much older fertility customs (see 21.2, "The Awakening", for another) and half-remembered or corrupted accounts of Dervishes seen by people returning from the Crusades; "Morris" deriving, we're told, from "Moorish". Helston, in Cornwall, has an older one involving a man wearing a wooden horse costume and the famous "Furry Day" dance-tune (older British readers will shudder at Terry Wogan's rendition of this as *The Floral Dance*).

So Morris dancing and maypoles both have roots in fertility rituals, but even as late as 1970, their origins were being downplayed. After all, it was becoming apparent that big money was to be had from such things, but also that otherwise charmed tourists were uncomfortable with the real origins. Look carefully at "The Daemons" and what's most interesting about that whole sequence is how the well-rehearsed villagers show no real interest in doing the dances for themselves. It's become an obligation, with the fun sucked out of it. We refer you to comments on the winter sol-stice equivalent (Mummers) under "Planet of the Spiders", but here let's look at the bigger picture.

... or to be exact, a bloody big picture carved into a hill just outside Cerne Abbas in Berkshire. Chalk Hills in parts of Southern England were often scraped strategically to produce pictures, such as the Bronze Age horse (you may know it from the cover for the XTC album *English Settlement*) or the Long Man of Wilmington. But the Cerne Abbas Giant is more... er, um, overtly connected with fertility. All right, we'll say it: he's got a hard-on the size of a tennis-court. The Victorians didn't talk much about it, but neither did they get rid of it. (*Tess of the D'Urbervilles* changes the name to "Abbot's Cernal", but the use of the place in ensuring healthy babies and good harvests is clearly reported from life.)

Then suddenly, in the early 70s, people were acknowledging that apparently "quaint" rural rit-uals had connections to more earthy matters and cycles of birth and death. By "people" we mainly mean "people on telly", and by "suddenly" we mean in the previous five years. Books such as JW Fraser's *The Golden Bough* and Robert Graves' *The White Goddess* were being reprinted in popular editions. The reasons for this are complex, but a big one was that TS Eliot had died, and so was

What's the UNIT Timeline?

...continued from page 175

the end of "Ambassadors", but is magically there again in "Inferno". This is far from being the only time the running-order of the stories is the main worry - keep reading, and also take a look at **Who's Narrating This Series?** under 23.1, "The Mysterious Planet".]

October 1971: "Terror of the Autons." The Doctor's been working on the dematerialisation circuit for three months, and he hadn't even touched it by the end of "Inferno". Liz's departure also seems to have happened a while ago. October makes sense, since it doesn't look like summer in the story and the heating's on inside Mr. Farrell's house. Promotions such as the daffodils tended to be in the school half-term. (See **When Did Susan Go To School?** under 25.1, "Remembrance of the Daleks" for more.)

Somewhere in 1972: "The Mind of Evil". Ah. Now we've got problems. In "The Mind of Evil", the Governor of Stangmoor Prison says it's been 'nearly a year' since the Master installed the Keller Machine there. It's unlikely that the Master arrived on Earth months before "Terror of the Autons" and secretly worked on the project for so long before revealing himself - why, after all, would he interrupt this delicate plan by dealing with the Nestenes? Besides, had he been up to such hanky-panky on Earth for so long, the Time Lords would surely have warned the Doctor sooner. (This assumes, of course, that the Time Lords were fully aware of the Master's activities; see **How and Why is the Doctor Exiled to Earth?** under 9.5, The Time Monster" for more.) Furthermore, on the face of it, it's unlikely that the Master even considered the Keller Machine idea before the Nestenes were defeated, because he just isn't the type for back-up schemes.

Unless - as we're dealing with a time-traveller here - he nipped back in time *half-way* through plotting the Auton conquest, fetching the alien mind-parasite as a means to attack the Nestenes if they betrayed him. (Here we must presume, for the moment, that the mind-parasite's powers could affect a monstrous cephalopod.) Or perhaps it *was* a reserve plan for Total World Domination, as his current scheme was fun but looked like going wrong. This almost makes sense of his abrupt *volte face* when the Doctor points out that the Nestenes are right on top of them - if Plan B is sitting in his TARDIS, miles away and immobilised, then he would need a Plan C.

We could conclude, then, than nearly a year really *does* pass between "Terror of the Autons" and "The Mind of Evil". (Isn't it strange, though, how we can easily accept large gaps between seasons but not between individual stories? As if the scheduling of a BBC TV programme would really make a difference to UNIT. Well, except *The Passing Parade* being on opposite a rugby international of course.) It's also a safe bet that it's autumn or winter - just look at the location filming.

But we have the problem that when the Doctor discusses Keller's plan for Total World Domination and says, 'Who else? The Master', it's as if he's been the *only* thorn in UNIT's side for some time. Accepting a year between stories is one thing, but a year of the Doctor's life where nothing remotely interesting happens would be almost unheard of. (Anyway, Jo doesn't seem all that much older, even if she's a lot more self-assured in this story than during her debut. But then, her apparent age and maturity fluctuates between stories - between scenes, even - so this isn't much help.)

The choice is, therefore, between whether you take 'nearly a year' to mean eleven or more months or just anything over six months. Or perhaps the Governor has been hypnotised, and it's really only three months. (Given that 'Professor Keller' would need to be accredited by a real, checkable, University in Switzerland and have published papers in real, checkable scientific journals for years before to get this post, and that making one man "remember" a false past is easier than creating the evidence for one, this is a safer option than time-travel or UNIT sitting around for a year waiting for the Master to do something nasty.)

Mid-to-late 1972: "The Claws of Axos", "Colony in Space". Some months have probably passed since "The Mind of Evil" - at least for the Master, given that the he's had time to explore the universe, find Axos and come back to Earth. Assuming that the Master habitually returns to Earth in "real time" - meaning if he's aged six months, then he deliberately returns to Earth six months after his last visit (Time Lords seem to keep doing that sort of thing) - then more time presumably passes between "The Claws of Axos" and "Colony in Space", as the Master visits several planets prior to landing on Uxarieus.

continued on page 179...

obviously a better poet than anyone had thought when he was alive. His epic anthropological treatise-cum-rant, "The Waste Land", owed a great deal to Fraser's book and was now on the school curriculum. There's also a whole sub-genre of fiction about séances and country-folk showing sceptical townies what's really going on (see "Planet of the Spiders" for more).

Okay, so everyone's going around "understanding" things at the tops of their voices - from Corn Dollies being fertility symbols and connected to those strangled men found in peat bogs from thousands of years back, to kids dancing around maypoles and people chucking confetti at weddings. You've got hippies tapping into Theosophy - itself partly inspired by Bulwer Lytton's *Vril-ya* (see "The Silurians") - and a dog's breakfast of bits from every non-Western belief-system they can lay their hands on. (See the triptych of essays accompanying 4.9, "The Evil of the Daleks"; 5.1, "The Tomb of the Cybermen"; and 5.2, "The Abominable Snowmen"; plus the notes for 4.5, "The Underwater Menace".)

You've got everything at all being either down to aliens or ancient wisdom that's been garbled down the centuries. You've got Orthoteny: the theory that if you correlate UFO sightings with the supposed locations of Ley lines, you can find the most powerful sites of astral power. (Guess what? They include Glastonbury, Cadbury castle - see "Battlefield" - Reading and, um, Tottenham. Nobody ever suggested that Alexandra Palace was built by astronauts, though.) There's a lot of credulity mixed with anxiety.

To outsiders, one of the oddest things about the swing back to magic was that the majority of its advocates were fairly old. The hippies adopted the iconography, but it was middle-aged flying saucer nuts who were publishing pamphlets and holding meetings in church halls. We'd now like you to look at Miss Hawthorne's contribution to "The Daemons". Director Christopher Barry wanted an older, madder woman, but Letts over-ruled him and was right on the money. The people making the loudest anti-establishment cries about ancient powers and lost wisdom were middle-aged and educated but also rural. The majority of them were single, but this was somehow turned into the stereotypical Anglo-Saxon virtue: they knew their own minds, and weren't going to be persuaded by city folk.

Among those who don't chug Kool-Aid with paraquat chasers, this eventually leads to the old debate between "revealed truth" (which the doubters can never know, so ha-ha-ha) and empirical investigation (whose results need a bit of work to understand - not nearly as useful if you're trying to start up a religion and tell everyone else what to do). We soon get to the tiresome impasse that results when the True Believers decide that if you can "do" science, you are biologically incapable of understanding the Truth. As you can see, it's very like the wholesale smugness of hippies who value the insights they got whilst tripping their nads off over things other people can actually see.

It's also very like religious zealotry of another kind: witch-sniffers. Even without Arthur Miller's play *The Crucible*, this was a topic taken up by contemporary authors' investigation of mass hysteria and the roots of Fascism. Hammer films touched on this in the lurid but sly *Witch-Finder General*, and soon the whole British horror-film industry (and "legitimate" cinema) kept on about devils. There was *The Devil Rides Out* (1968), the first film version of one of Dennis Wheatley's massively popular shockers. In the months following "The Daemons" we had *Blood on Satan's Claw* and the curiously similar Ken Russell film *The Devils*, based on Aldous Huxley's historical novel *The Devils of Loudon* (and more like 9.4, "The Mutants" than many people are willing to admit). We'll discuss *The Wicker Man* in a moment. The point is, having the Master step into the role of "local holyman who whips people up into hysteria and uses them for his own ends" is just as obvious as having him as a Bond-villain in "The Mind of Evil".

Of course, being British, we found a compromise between faith and science. Even in this book so far, you'll have encountered theories becoming accepted by the early 1970s that were crazy-talk when first expressed (Plate Tectonics, the various accounts of the moon's origin, over-population, the number of potentially life-bearing planets in our galaxy, decimal money...). And there's going to be more (pollution being a bad thing, Crete being Knossos, anti-matter, black holes...). "Science" as a body of knowledge is different from "Science" as a process of investigation, checkable and subject to revision. Men with Beards on BBC2 were constantly looking at old stories and recent fads and asking, "How can we find out if this is true?" Some, like Henry Lincoln ("The Abominable Snowmen", etc.), stirred a lot of trouble. Others,

What's the UNIT Timeline?

...continued from page 177

[As previously suggested, some have argued that "Colony in Space" occurs *before* "The Claws of Axos". In most regards this doesn't actually matter, because by the time we reach "The Daemons", the Doctor and the Master have experienced the same amount of time since "Terror of the Autons".

[However, swapping these stories would make better sense of Jo's perplexity with the TARDIS at the start of "Colony in Space". She's admittedly never stepped foot in the Ship before, but her comment to the Doctor, 'All that talk of yours about travelling in time and space, it was true!' seems utterly bizarre, given that the ending of "Claws" - which she fully witnessed - depends upon it. Admittedly, this line occurs in a story where she thinks it feasible that colony ships left Earth in 1971, but still...

[Additionally, if we're swapping stories, around there might be some merit in switching "Colony" with "Mind of Evil" to account for the 'nearly a year' problem. A strike against that, though, is that when the Doctor and Jo meet the Master on an alien planet, they seem shocked but not, apparently, because they believe him to be stuck on Earth.

[Whatever the case, the BBC showed these stories in a particular order. If they've placed them in the order that the Master experienced them, for ease of viewer-comprehension, then the logic is clear even if Jo now seems to forget whole invasions. The TARDIS travels into the far future and they find that the Master had "earlier" visited the same piece of futurity.

[Switching the story order also makes the Doctor's opening remarks in each adventure a *little* smoother. In "Colony in Space", he says, '[The Master's] TARDIS is working again now. He could be anywhere in space and time', as if it's a recent development. But in "The Claws of Axos", he's insistent on saying, '... keep telling you, he's left Earth by now'. He doesn't say outright, "I've just seen him on a quarry-like alien planet exactly five centuries in the future", but it's easy enough to imagine.]

30th of April - 1st of May, 1973: "The Daemons". "The Daemons" unquestionably ends on the 1st of May, and again, the Master's spent some time preparing his role as Mr Magister. Those who aren't convinced that nearly a year passes between "Terror of the Autons" and "The Mind of Evil" might prefer to conclude that it's actually May

1972 rather than 73, which is feasible but leaves some awkward loose ends later on.

Rugby from Twickenham is on television, so it's probably a weekend, and strictly speaking the 30th of April was a Sunday in 1972. It's slightly odd that they're playing rugby union at all that late in the year, especially as it's a club match and not an international. But days of the week *never* seem to match up with dates in the *Doctor Who* universe (see 25.3, "Silver Nemesis" for our theory on why). A 'BBC3' is mentioned, but we didn't get one until 2002 (and Sergeant Benton watching *Torchwood* is wrong on a dozen or so levels).

September 1973: "Day of the Daleks", "The Sea Devils". In "Day of the Daleks", it's the 13th of September when Jo leaves the present day. "The Sea Devils" probably takes place shortly thereafter, since the weather looks suitably autumnal, but the problem is...

December 1973: "The Time Monster". According to an interpretation of dialogue that borders on the autistic, it's Michaelmas, i.e. the 29th of September. Since "Day of the Daleks" is set in mid-September, the 'Michaelmas' comment would suggest that the whole of Season Nine takes place over the span of a fortnight and that the Master sets up the TOMTIT project in about a week. And yet, one of the lab-staff involved in TOMTIT suggests that she's been working with the Master for several months (again, let's keep the Blinovitch Limitation Effect in mind).

Of course, the phrase 'and a merry Michaelmas to you' is only said by a jocular Jo, as a sort of sarcastic "gee, thanks", so it's highly debateable how literally we're supposed to take this. *The Discontinuity Guide* suggests that "Michaelmas" might just refer to the Oxbridge autumn term, which begins in the last week of September, but it's anybody's guess how she would know a thing like that. It would be on the notice-board in front of Benton, but he wasn't *that* stricken with ennui, surely. Anyway, if we're talking about when school terms end, it's no later than December.

Along with everyone's decision to dress for warmth and look disappointed by the weather ('it's a doomy old day'), this could occur at any time of the year, really.

(Well, *almost* any time. Window-cleaners tend to be more commonly spotted in spring and

continued on page 181...

such as Bob Symes, had a lot of fun but always seemed to wind up debunking.

Patrick Moore, clean-shaven but dishevelled, was TV's best-known Astronomer and sceptic. (In the original Greek meaning of "one who doesn't stop asking questions", that is.) During the brief spells between moonshots, he invited members of the Alutherian Society (a bunch of Theosophists who believed Venusians had psychically contacted them), as well as Flat-Earthers and various others, to appear on a documentary he was making. (A book version of this, *Can You Speak Venusian?*, is worth tracking down.)

He didn't jeer, he didn't score points, he simply gave them enough rope and asked very simple questions. As Moore pointed out, the attempt to prove or disprove loopy theories frequently led to genuine insights and discoveries. (We have to bear in mind that, as we discussed in 2.1, "Planet of Giants", the myth of the maverick scientist who Proved Them All Wrong is a powerful one.) It's key that other broadcasters adopted this approach. Whatever the truth, the attempt to investigate made good television and yielded surprising answers often enough for the True Believers to come out of their dimly-lit front parlours and into the public domain.

As we've hinted, the best place to find the older beliefs flourishing was out in remote rural communities. It became almost commonplace that folks out in the sticks still did odd things to secure good harvests. (Predictably, Nigel Kneale had a crack at that one too, in his seventies anthology show *Beasts*.) The earliest use of it in mainstream drama was an early *Play for Today* (John Bowen's *Robin Redbreast*, TX 10th of December, 1970, just as "The Daemons" was being written) and the most obvious is Robin Hardy's 1973 film *The Wicker Man*. Here, the implicit threat of the Queen of the May (see "The Awakening") as a sacrifice for good harvest is made to seem relatively normal and the strictly Christian cop is the freak. A generation on from the discovery of Tollund Man, a miraculously preserved man who had been ritually - and apparently voluntarily - strangled thousands of years before, this idea was being looked at again. The old song "John Barleycorn Must Die" was re-recorded several times, and not just by folk-music archivists. (If you've not seen *The Wicker Man*, track it down: you'll want to have everyone involved in the dreadful Nicolas Cage remake burned in a giant man-shaped basket.)

It was almost taken for granted that the occasional chicken was being ritually slaughtered in places not too far from major towns in Britain. London-based media had a lot of barely-disguised contempt for rural ways - most people in the capital had fled these types of communities or only heard about them from people who had. It helped that these bits of Britain couldn't yet get 625-line transmissions, and thus wouldn't see anyone slagging them off on BBC2. They may, of course, have seen an episode of *The Avengers* called "Murdersville" (1967). In this, a corrupt millionaire co-opts an entire village to collectively act as a hitman. Little Storping-in-the-Swuff (not too unlike some real West Country names) has yokels straight out of central casting, but who use handguns and can chase Mrs Peel around in a helicopter. The village pub is the centre of all this, and its landlord is the ringleader. We're not accusing anyone of lifting this for "The Daemons" - just saying, that's all.

While the majority channels went hog-wild for space, BBC2 discovered the visual appeal of archaeology. Their *Chronicle* strand spent the 60s making archaeology look space age, using the stark monochrome of the early years and early Radiophonic Workshop sounds to give the deep past a sense of perspective and grandeur. Of course, TV archaeology had been a mixed blessing. Three-day time-limits are a matter of course these days, but in the weekend of the first moon landing, BBC2 offered, as an alternative, live coverage of a dig into a Bronze Age barrow at Silbury Hill. This was covered over the course of a year, but the moon-landing weekend was definitely billed as the highlight. It was in colour, and there was the promise of a British equivalent of Tutankhamun's tomb, even something like the Sutton Hoo finds (see 5.3, "The Ice Warriors"), only bigger.

A lot of people got very excited during the first televised dig the previous year, during which suspiciously little showed up. It was presented by genial Icelander Magnus Magnusson. (We say "Icelander", but actually his soft Scots accent made him seem all the more unnerving when he was the question-master on Nazi-themed quiz *Mastermind*. We're not saying that *The Passing Parade*'s "Alistair Fergus" is in any way like him by the time they've cast a smarmy youngster, but you can see the thought-process that went into the names.) By the end of the last day of this,

What's the UNIT Timeline?

...continued from page 179

autumn. Of course, if Wootton is connected to the University, the absence of any students would suggest holidays, which again makes the window cleaner a bit more plausible. Michaelmas term in some colleges ends in late November, which would explain the absence of any Christmas decorations - although when this story was made, people hadn't got into the silly modern habit of putting these up on 1st of December, and instead waited for Christmas Eve.)

All told, two explanations present themselves. One: more than a *year* passes between "Day of the Daleks" and "The Time Monster", and they're different Septembers. Two: Jo is just being overly chipper, and it's not really Michaelmas. We'll assume the latter, since a lot of the stories in Season Nine are off-Earth missions for the Time Lords, and if more than a year passes then the Doctor would have to spend most of that time sitting in his lab failing to get his dematerialisation circuit to work.

Early 1974: "The Three Doctors". Another season gap before "The Three Doctors" means that it could have been weeks or months since the Master's last sighting. Jo's travels in the TARDIS after this only take a few days, so she gets back to Earth in time for...

April 1974: "The Green Death". There are *two* calendars on display here, one in a security guard's office and one at the pit-head, the first claiming that it's February and the second claiming that it's April. Since a pit-head is more likely to keep track of these things than a lone security guard... and since the guard's calendar is a month-by-month one, and he might just like the picture... and since it's a hopelessly out-of-date 1972 calendar anyway... April is more likely, if only for the birdsong.

Mid-to-late 1974: "The Time Warrior", "Invasion of the Dinosaurs". The Doctor's still hanging around with UNIT even though his TARDIS is fixed, so it can't have been *that* long since Jo left him (even if he's trying to fine-tune the Ship, you can't imagine him waiting until it's 100% before running off again). "Invasion of the Dinosaurs" takes place a few weeks later. After this, the Doctor spends some time dragging Sarah around outer space, and then she goes back to her old life for a bit, so a little while elapses before...

March - April 1975: "Planet of the Spiders", "Robot". Two stories back-to-back, although three weeks slip by during "Robot" episode one, and the pass Sarah's issued by the SRS is dated the 4th of April. (The SRS is staffed by fascistic nerdy obsessives, so this is presumably more reliable than a security guard's calendar.) Now, for Harry and Sarah the next few days are hectic, and they return to Earth several months later.

September / October 1975 and thereafter: "Terror of the Zygons", "The Android Invasion", "The Seeds of Doom". There's no way of knowing how long it takes the Brigadier to use his space-time telegraph and bring the Doctor back to Britain, because there doesn't seem to be any correlation between the time the Doctor spends on the TARDIS and the time the Brigadier spends on Earth while he's gone. Awkwardly-placed *Missing Adventures* aside, from the TARDIS crew's point-of-view, only days pass between "Robot and "Terror of the Zygons", and more time *must* pass for UNIT. It looks sort of autumnal, although it could be a wetter summer than the real-life drought in 1975. (Those who consider the novels to be at least

continued on page 183...

absolutely nothing at all, not a sausage, had been found.[48]

Archaeologists weren't really "characters" back then... well, except the former *Brains Trust* panellist Sir Mortimer Wheeler, a rather donnish chap. TV eccentrics were either scientists or people who were abrupt. In the latter category comes the now-forgotten figure of "the rudest man on TV", Gilbert Harding. He was originally a *What's My Line* regular, then the first person in Britain to be famous simply for being famous. In "The Daemons", Professor Gilbert Horner is Harding to

fifteen decimal places. Professor Richard Atkinson - a less rebarbative character than Horner - led the BBC's sponsored dig, but the press emphasised that however much they were in it for the science, pay-off would be achieved if the fabled gold statue of King Sel on his horse showed up. The first few shovelsful were dug in April 1968, and no less a figure than BBC2's controller (and seasoned documentary-maker) David Attenborough handled the PR. It was a long-running colour Outside Broadcast, right next to a motorway, so the public got intrigued and came to watch.

Another thing often seen on BBC2 were men with van-dyke beards and horn-rimmed glasses saying things like, "The soul as such is a very dated concept... viewing the matter existentially...". Many of them were much-ridiculed advocates of the "Good News" Bible. (This was a new edition in less forbidding prose, intended to be more inclusive and accessible, but which made Psalms sound like an ICI shareholder's meeting.) As with Miss Hawthorne - who is, shall we say, from a different denomination - the people most prone to complaining about the traditional CofE service being "eroded" were those least likely to be regular churchgoers. The clergy viewed the sudden advent of a lot of kids with eyes like hoops believing any old tosh as a splendid opportunity to do a recruitment-drive.

As Britain increasingly stopped bothering with church, the attempts to appeal to the young seemed more embarrassing with each passing year. This is the golden age of the Trendy Vicar, in sandals (with socks) and driving a moped. The main legacy of this familiar figure in the nation's schools is a profound mistrust of any Christian who tried too hard to sound cool (eg Cliff Richard, Tony Blair). Anyone up late enough to be watching regional television when transmission closed down saw an awful lot of these chaps giving homilies and desperately trying not to use the "G"-word, in case mentioning God sent people straight to bed.

What we're saying, then, is that if ever there was a time for *Doctor Who* to pilfer whole chunks of *Quatermass and the Pit*, this was it. Nigel Kneale's brand of gothic paranoia was radically out-of-step with the orthodoxy in 1959, but was now so mainstream as to be innocuous. Nobody in the British Rocket Group would have been so glib about the "Age of Aquarius". Similarly, the more radical novel *Childhood's End* by Arthur C Clarke was - on the back of *2001: A Space Odyssey* - getting a reprint. In this, it emerges that Humanity is due for an upgrade (a naturally occurring one) and our mentors - big hairy guys with horns and sulphurous B.O. who've been sent to stop us blowing ourselves up before we get to Level Two - cause a psychic shock that resonated back through time and into our mythology. (The idea of humans evolving into Homo Superior and wiping out the original model is there in that year's album *Hunky Dory* by Glastonbury's bill-topper David Bowie - see **What Was In The**

Charts? for a drastically implausible cover version of *Oh! You Pretty Things* by the former frontman of Herman's Hermits - and lurks behind things such as "The Mutants", "Planet of the Spiders", 1973's Thames *Who* knock-off *The Tomorrow People* and various John Wyndham books.) The surprise in "The Daemons" isn't that the barrow contains a spaceship, but that the occupants didn't really tinker *that* much with the human race and probably didn't do anything to our DNA. They just scored a place in our folklore and nudged us towards the steam reciprocating engine.

Incidentally, if you didn't do Latin at school, the name 'Quiquaequod' - the "wizard" name Miss Hawthorne attributes to the Doctor - is made of three declensions of the word "Who".

Things That Don't Make Sense Nobody ever bothers explaining why the first victim of the Daemons' power, who dies of fright in the opening scene, is killed. The skittering noise that accompanies the event is usually associated with Bok, but why would he be scaring locals at this phase of the story? Is the Master doing a "test run" on someone with a weak heart? It's obviously not Azal, so what the hell is going on? [The novelisation calls the man 'Josh', the same name as the yokel who's the Axos' first victim, so it's obviously a jinx in rural areas. Similarly, the televised story has two 'Charlies'.] And as broadcast, the scene makes very little sense to anyone who doesn't know the book - owing to stock footage of a frog, a cat, a mouse, etc., it looks as if it's taking place in a petting zoo. On a similarly rustic note, no two villagers have the same bucolic accent. [This is an inevitable aspect of doing stories with rustic settings - see 22.3, "The Muaark o' the Ruanneh"; 18.7-A, "K9 and Company"; and way, *way* too many others to list, but it's especially obvious here.]

Garvin the verger, when allowing Miss Hawthorne her info-dump about Canon Smallwood, tells her that the new vicar is indisposed. Then Mr Magister suddenly appears a few moments later, from just behind her. So how did Garvin not see him coming and say, "Ah, here he comes now..."? Later, when the constable recovers from the Daemonic-influence (or something like that) that made him stalk Miss Hawthorne with a large stone, she never thinks to ask, "Why are you holding that rock?" And who, precisely, does she mean when she greets confirmation that the End

What's the UNIT Timeline?

...continued from page 181

semi-canonical might note that Paul Cornell's *No Future* suggests a date of January 1976 for the Zygon affair, ignoring the unseasonably mild weather and greenery everywhere. The novel itself is set months later, in June 1976, so everything fits neatly. Well, as "neatly" as everything can, in a book about the Meddling Monk disguising himself as Virgin boss Richard Branson and altering history, alongside a back-story of a Buddhist Brig who's set up a Special Ops division over several years, despite all the on-screen evidence.)

The Brigadier spends the last days of his stint at UNIT seemingly perpetually in Geneva on official business. If the Brig's abrupt departure is the result of unwelcome changes in UNIT's structure and mission (as *The Sarah Jane Adventures* Series Two hints), then a lot of high-level meetings might culminate in his premature retirement. Incidentally, "Seeds" manifestly takes place in autumn / winter (or spring / summer, if you're in Antarctica). Amusingly, people's breath makes mist in London but not the South Pole.

Lethbridge-Stewart retires shortly thereafter, and...

June 1977: "Mawdryn Undead". ...is working in a public school a year later. Everything is settled, and all is right with the world. Well, for a while.

Err... The Future: "Battlefield". Doris, whom he took to Brighton in 1964, is now Mrs Lethbridge-Stewart. The story told about her in "Planet of the Spiders" suggests that she was very young, but even so the apparent age of her "now" and the other peculiar details suggest that this story is set in 1989's idea of the year 2000(ish). Compared to our own memories of this year(ish) the incidentals are curious - there's no mobile phones, texting, email or laptops, but men wear pedal-pushers and apparently there's a king on the throne. There's an airport in Docklands (that, at least, is right), but a united Czechoslovakia, which is wrong for reasons nobody could have foreseen.

On the other hand, we have the new logo and senior officers who've read the files about the Doctor. The reformed UNIT, funded by the UN but no longer under its jurisdiction (or so it seems) appears to begin here and continues from "Aliens of London" (X1.4). Such dating problems fall into the whole Great Powell Estate Date Debate, however, which is another essay for another volume.

---

of the World is nigh with, 'What a tale I'll have for them now'.

So the Doctor arrives, yelling 'Stop that dig!' (as if that'll help), and then tells Professor Horner 'Don't pull that stone!' - at which point, he appears to go over and aid the doomed professor in removing it, releasing confetti. (A side-note from Dr Science: Azal's awakening is associated with a rapid drop in temperature, but a terrific blast of wind *from* the barrow rather than *into* it. So presumably the sudden growth-spurt that caused the big freeze was in a chamber with really *really* high atmospheric pressure that rapidly cooled and contracted to become merely really high. But how did a stone wall and some mud keep that in for centuries?) And later, when Bok's eyes peer out from the darkness of the dig, we might wonder how he got in there without breaking the security tape.

Benton spots hoof-prints from the air, and Yates says that whatever caused them is 30 feet high and walked into the woods. He says 'woods' as if to mean they can't follow the tracks any more - but something 30 feet high crashing through trees

would create a much *more* obvious trail, surely? We might also question Benton's priorities - with something *that* big rampaging around and treading on policemen, he seems to honestly think Yates wants to go off and have breakfast. The hoofprints become smaller on the ground, and they're rather close together too, as if Azal urgently needed the toilet after thousands of years asleep. [Well, that would explain why he headed for the trees.]

It's not immediately obvious, but that phone-call where the Brigadier exclaims 'My helicopter?!' isn't Yates contacting him [as the previous scene indicates], but the Brig lying in bed calling the Doctor some time around five in the morning. Is this usual? The Brig also advises that if the Doctor isn't available, they should 'wake Miss Grant' - is she living at UNIT HQ now? Still later, the Doctor ends a radio conversation with the Brigadier, who becomes alarmed, as if they've suddenly been cut off. They haven't, but if the Brig is so concerned, why doesn't he just ring the Doctor's party up *again*, as he did in the first place, and does again a few scenes later?

The Doctor claims that the "tomb" inside the Devil's Hump is the same shape as the Daemon spaceship. Well, okay, except that both the tomb and the spaceship appear to be roughly circular, whereas the Doctor later describes the ship as being 200 feet long and 30 feet across. [He means 30 feet *deep*, but either way it doesn't give Azal much leg-room when he's at full size.] Another geometry problem: the energy barrier around Devil's End is ten miles across, yet its perimeter is next to the one-mile-to-Devil's-End sign. The local signposts are embedded in concrete, so the council must have thought about getting the details right before planting them, but somehow they revolve like pinwheels without causing any damage to the roads. They also recover from being incinerated in a bread-van conflagration. Other nearby villages are called 'Satanhall', 'Lob's Crick', 'Little Coven' and the like - didn't anyone detect a theme here? And even allowing for the spinning signposts, *how* lost can the Doctor and Jo get? One spinning sign puts them within three miles of Devil's End, yet it seems they're out wandering for hours.

We explained under "The Ambassadors of Death" (7.3) why so many people leave their keys inside their vehicles, but here it reaches silly proportions as the Master's lumberjack-shirt-wearing minion makes off with the UNIT helicopter, left good-to-go by Mike, a *captain*. Actually, the whole scenario with the helicopter is a bit pointless. The pilot seems intent on "forcing" the Doctor and Jo to drive into the heat barrier, but it's hard to see what he can do, other than buzz annoyingly over their heads, if they just pull over and park. Maybe they're worried that he'll divebomb them kamikaze style, but if *that's* his plan, why doesn't he do it? He's got ample opportunity.

And why isn't Bessie equipped with seat belts? We might speculate that Jo getting flung from the car motivates the Doctor to install the "inertia dampner" seen in "The Time Monster", but the injury was preventable if they'd just buckled up. [Letts obviously re-thought this, and added a line in the novelisation where the Doctor wonders why Jo and indeed all young people these days (like the readers) don't "clunk-click".] And why does Plaid-Shirt seem impervious to Mike's punches? If the Master is - dunno - channelling Azal's energy to make the man invulnerable, it's never said. If, on the other hand, he's hypnotised all of his gang (despite the obvious problem that

causes with regard to 'violent emotion' as a fuel-source), why are they all so bad at obeying him?

When Bert the landlord returns from failing to kill the Doctor (remember, he was sent *after* the helicopter stunt failed, so it can't have been the plan to use the chopper to drive the Doctor off the road and into Bert's sights), he sheepishly tells the Master, 'I'm sorry' and is amazed, for some reason, when the Master deduces from this that 'The Doctor got away.' Benton, trained soldier that he is, gets an awful lot of grief from a hostile verger and an enraged Morris Dancer - why does the latter storm the pub anyway? He can't know that Mike is out, so it looks like he wants to take on Benton and Yates single-handed.

To aid in his plans for world domination, the Master has assembled the lamest group of cultists to ever operate in Britain's shores. When Miss Hawthorne snoops they don't just refrain from killing her, they lock her up where passers-by can hear her cries. They similarly spare Yates' life for no good reason, and they only bind his hands, allowing him to stand up and shamble off to get help. Before that, Yates demonstrates the presence of a psionic force-field by throwing a book at the stone. Fine, but as one of the Coven-members walks in, pages are still fluttering to the floor and the man utterly fails to notice.

Then Yates and Jo ensconce themselves in the worst hiding-place ever - a sort of large wheel where you can plainly see between the spokes. And a short while later, Jo is thick enough to dash out in front of the coven members and shout, 'Stop him! He's evil!' They're a Satanist cult, so it can only be taken as an endorsement.

Why do mothers fear their children being left outside when the Morris men come mincing up the main street? Unless they somehow know about their plan to wrap the Doctor up and publicly murder him, it presumably means that this "side" [the correct term] are notorious child-molesters or something. [Or worse, perhaps they fear exposing their children to Morris Dancing. Not a bad idea but it's actually popular in those parts - or at least, it was when this story was made. This might have changed if the Talkies have reached Wiltshire.] It's similarly bizarre that everyone emerges from their homes, looking care-free and sunny, immediately after the local church gets blown to pieces and there's all manner of robed cultists wandering about the place.

Here we must refrain from closely examining

the gullibility / fierce mood swings of the locals, or we could be here all day. It's worth mentioning, however, that Bert advises them to kill the Doctor because 'Thou shalt not suffer a witch to live' (Genesis 22:18 in the King James Authorised translation), but evidently following a Mephistophilean priest who uses an animated gargoyles to obliterate the town squire is perfectly all right. Maybe Bert is playing to the crowd, but he's taking part in the Maypole dance dressed in newspapers as part of the Morris Dancing. Really, citing scripture to kill someone for following pagan practices is a *bit* hypocritical if you're in the middle of doing one yourself. (Anyway, the last person to be executed for witchcraft was killed just before the government decided it didn't exist and outlawed burnings in 1735.) Benton's hearing must be exceptional to hear the Doctor mutter 'the weathercock on the church roof?' for him to know to shoot it.

Brace yourselves... Dr Science wants to talk heat-barrier physics. Azal generates a lot of energy by reducing in size, and evidently causes a blast of extreme cold by growing abruptly. So far, so good. [That is, if we accept that you can convert mass into energy and vice versa without blowing up a city - that generally occurs when you do it this quickly, as with Hiroshima. Incidentally, the novelisation has Benton making a more pertinent analogy with Boyle's Law and fridges, and the Doctor - the sod - tells him off!] The problem, though, is that the heat just reaches a certain distance and... stops. Two feet either side of this, and the ambient temperature is normal for a day such as this. Puddles even stay damp right up to the edge. Ordinarily, the only way to keep heat all in one place is with some kind of efficient insulation, like a vacuum or some very thick foam. And we might posit a force-field of some kind, but if such a thing existed, why not simply use *that* to keep unwelcome visitors at bay?

Now, if the entire village were overheated and the roads outside weren't, we could [at a pinch, and with the same "well it makes for a better story" shrug of resignation we reserve for people spontaneously turning into trees and such] just about live with this. We could *even* swallow the idea that it's not a perfect sphere but a very flat dome. [However, as the village's electricity remains on and the toilets aren't exuding hot smelly water, we must assume that the barrier doesn't extend underground. Not much of a problem in itself, but it makes both the Doctor and the

Brigadier look like dolts because they don't consider the possibility of just tunnelling under it.] But from a plot-logic perspective, it's baffling as to how the heat barrier is sustained when Azal grows again. Okay, so he never *quite* regains his full height, but how does he siphon off energy directly from a barrier a mile or more away, rather than cooling down everything around him and allowing the energy to percolate towards the newly-chilled zone? We can run with the idea that the heat barrier is actually two force-fields sandwiching a foot-thick dome of very hot air [yet mysteriously not affecting the helicopter's aerodynamics or the sky-colour], but if so, it ought to weaken when Azal grows. [In addition to privacy, maybe he needs the hot area not just for privacy as a sort of "mass-bank"; see **How Hard Is It To Be The Wrong Size?** under 16.6, "The Armageddon Factor".] Thus, unless there's an even *more* improbable funnel of heat from the barrier to the crypt, Azal must be channelling the energy through, um, hyperspace or something. [And *this* is the definitive story where science triumphs over magic?]

One more twisted science issue, if you're still following all of this: the technobabble the Doctor gives Osgood suggests that the 'heat exchanger' device will take the hot air's energy and spread it around so that the average air temperature becomes tolerable. But they achieve this by... adding more energy.

[This might, just *might* come off as described. The Doctor mentions a process akin to the way a microwave oven works, although instead of adding energy to water molecules making them move about faster (which is what "heat" basically is), he's 'buffering' them with 'a sort of controlled resonance', making the movement *slow down*. The device is designed to pulse out of phase[49]. This could actually work, despite apparently being almost as impossible as building a torch that shines out beams of darkness, if the whole of the barrier cools down evenly throughout.

[But that's not what we actually see on screen. Instead, we get a big generator that makes a hole inside the heat barrier, thus compounding the felony by making a small localised reversal of entropy inside a bigger localised reversal of entropy. The Doctor has told Osgood how to become Maxwell's Demon - symbolically appropriate, but a very silly thing to do in a story about how science beats superstition. Mind, the Second Law of Thermodynamics has never been the

Doctor's favourite bit of science - see 24.1, "Time and the Rani"; X3.11, "Utopia"; 18.7, "Logopolis" and indeed most of Volumes IV and V.]

Besides, if the air's *that* hot, how can Osgood see the Doctor's circuit-diagram without heat-haze or a prism effect distorting everything?

Then in the build-up to the finale, when Bok emerges from the church, take a gander at the utterly bored villager behind the two "terrified" young women. The Doctor tells the reformed villagers to 'spread out' and converge on the church. Doesn't he realise they'll be sitting ducks for Bok, or even coven-members with guns and knives? [Actually, they seem to have left these in their other cassocks.]

Azal suddenly turns into a computer and yells 'No Compute! Self-Destruct!'. [Or words to that effect. We've got an essay that attempts to resolve this, but it's far from perfect.] Jo's refusal to let a friend get killed is enough to cause this, but Matthew Corbett freaking out when a chicken is going to be cut up doesn't. Even after seeing Azal, the hayseed satanists sound really bored with all this chanting. If this is his idea of generating the required 'violent emotion' amongst his followers, the Master should get out more.

Fleeing for her life, Jo nips into the back room and picks up her old clothes in case someone takes her to "strip the willow" (the maypole dance we see at the end). Mind you, many people would welcome a blouse as nasty as that being consumed by hellfire. Talking of clothes, are Yates and Benton officially on duty in this story or not? If they are, why the whole "Man at C&A" smart-casual look (remember, they wore uniforms to watch telly and eat corned-beef sarnies)? And if not, shouldn't they be court-martialled for taking a helicopter and loaded weapons? And gawp in amazement as the Master's cloak doesn't just blind Benton, it *knocks him over* as if it's weighted with lead. [Maybe it is: all the mini-hurricanes, to say nothing of the helicopters he was evidently anticipating, cause enough of a draft to risk removing his dignity by flapping his cerements over his head at a crucial moment.]

Jon Pertwee isn't sure how to pronounce "Daemons" either.

Critique There was a time when every fan *knew* this was quite obviously the best *Doctor Who* story ever. Then we saw it again, and the great rethink of the previously unassailable Letts era got under

way. Then received wisdom became that "The Daemons" was smug, trite, occasionally incomprehensible and thoroughly misconceived - all of this is true, but it's so much more.

We went to town on **Where Does This Come From?** because this story is the clearest example of *Doctor Who* picking up on something in the air and processing it for family viewing just before it became too obvious. This is cut from the same cloth as Marc Bolan's move from folkie mysticism to child-friendly boogaloo. Now that we all know this story, the sheer shock of this combination of elements happening on Saturday teatimes is irretrievably lost. And, like *Citizen Kane* or *Be Bop A-Lula*, all of this story's startling innovations have been done so often, it's hard to see why they made such a splash first time.

The biggest of these is the hardest to see: for most of the first three episodes the Doctor seems to be acting against everything he's ever stood for and siding with the forces of ignorance and superstition. Until the slide show, there seems no reason for him to be using iron as a defence, rushing to stop a dig as soon as he hears that it's going to climax at midnight on Beltane or proclaiming that this is the greatest threat ever. It was, on first transmission, as much of a jolt as the first two parts of "The Invasion of Time" (15.6) or (for anyone coming to the series completely fresh) the Doctor's pathological dread and urge to kill a stranded alien in "Dalek" (X1.6). With familiarity, this whole subtext is lost and the slide show is just another info dump.

For better or worse, the mix of god-like aliens (in the general sense) and rural England is one we'll see a lot more. Here, though, the alien is flagrantly based on a "current" religious figure (i.e. the Devil / Satan) as opposed to one from an obscure mythology that nobody practices anymore (as far as we know; apologies to any Osiris worshippers who happen to be reading.) Conversely, the rustic setting is the most extreme oo-arr-dang-oi caricature of English village life we'll ever see (and that includes some pretty pungent competition). Here the story hits its big hurdle. Any adventure that concerns a Satan-like alien in a relatively realistic village *or* a goblin of unimaginable power in Pigbinshire would be pushing its luck. Later stories (notably 15.3, "Image of the Fendahl" and 21.2, "The Awakening") opt for one or the other, with good reason. Both at once makes this rather safe and manageable for viewers - at the expense of making us watch a cartoon for most of the five episodes.

But as "The Daemons" lacks the nerve to *be* a cartoon, this looks like an inept attempt to be realistic. The beginning and end of episode one are garbled, to the point that some shots are almost impenetrable without several viewings. This isn't just a function of the piecemeal preservation and recolouring, it's down to editing and shot composition. (And as most of these scenes are on film, there's almost no excuse.) Similar confusion surrounds whether Bok really can fly - it takes a combination of titanic goodwill *and* someone explaining it to you to make sense of the radiophonic chuffing sound and people looking in odd directions.

It happens that this story dared to confront something deeply sacred to the majority of 70s BBC viewers: *The Archers*. "Devil's End" is drawn less from real life than from "Ambridge". (It's another Thomas Hardy job, a fictional county called "Borsetshire" with towns called "Borchester" and "Pennyhassett": see **Where Is UNIT HQ?** under 8.3, "The Claws of Axos".) When *The Archers*, "an everyday story of country folk" started (on 1st of January, 1950), most people listened to radio and so any daily drama on the Home Service (the main channel, later to become Radio 4) would get millions of listeners even if they didn't stick around for much beyond the first few bars of the opening music.[50] It was intended to give farmers advice on how to get better yields without seeming like an information service (in the immediate post-War era, everyone was getting a bit sick of those), but got a huge following amongst suburban and city folks - not least for playing up to yokel stereotypes, me old pal, me old beauty. Generations of people who claim to loathe soaps have soaked up a working knowledge of the series, to the extent that the theme tune is shorthand for everything bucolic. Making *this* a "normality" for aliens to disrupt was a brave move.

Contrasting "The Daemons" with the previous UNIT stories only makes its take on rural life look all the more awkward. Until now, the UNIT adventures have either occurred in cities or remote scientific installations, with country folk mainly present as hapless victims or comic relief. "The Daemons", however, moves the ground from under our feet and shows us a rural community on *their* terms, with the Doctor and UNIT as outsiders. Unfortunately, as a whole it treats people

from outside London as either idiots or risibly self-important. Now, you could argue that this is hardly a change, as *Doctor Who* has hitherto treated people from Whitehall and Westminster the same way. True, but the difference is that politicians and civil servants are, to a certain extent, fair game because they chose to be that way. Picking on people from the countryside, reducing them to a set of second-hand stereotypes, is qualitatively different from bracketing all bureaucrats (or indeed all prisoners with cockney accents) as practically interchangeable and dimwitted.

That the only person to side with the Doctor is the mad old witch (and even *she* sounds like she was educated elsewhere) just compounds the crime. If they'd tried this nonsense with any other ethnic group or class, you would expect trouble. (See, however, "The Green Death" and "Terror of the Zygons" for instances where they *did* get away with it, just about.) The Master even inveigles his way into the graces of an authority-figure, then kills him to demonstrate his power. The odd-looking villagers, who until that point have been vaguely interesting, at that exact moment go from being a collection of stereotypes to one big one. They even carry blazing torches, for heaven's sake.

The good news is that whereas the Doctor often takes control of situations in an altogether too effortless fashion, here it's slowed down a great deal. The *bad* news is that pretty much everything about this story is some kind of delaying tactic to stop the Doctor / the Master / Azal having their final confrontation too early. After a while, you either become frustrated by this frantic backpeddling or accept that the detours are the whole point, and the stuff about the Master and the Devil is just a flimsy pretext. Anyone taking the latter view might conclude that the story's pinnacle happens when Benton dukes it out in a pub with a Morris dancer, because from that point, there's hardly anything left to do that they haven't tried, save for the scene where the Doctor gets burned at the stake (well, maypole) by the most bored-looking angry mob ever televised.

If, on the other hand, you believe that the story's crux is an immensely powerful alien adjudicating on whether Mankind deserves to live... well, then you have the problem of the abruptly stupid ending. Without Azal turning up and the Brigadier finally getting to shoot at something, this story would be nothing more than a compendium of things that could happen in a small village run by the Master. A *big* ending is required to make

"The Daemons" actually end rather than just run out of air-time, but it's so perfunctorily done they could've just had the Brig drop a bomb on the church, or the hand of God reaching down and a big echoey voice (Charlton Heston or Graham Chapman, the choice is yours) casting aspersions on everyone. If this is your take on the story, you also must acknowledge that, once he's done this gambit, the Master will never be able to top it. As a character, he becomes redundant or ridiculous in ways he wasn't before. After conjuring up the Devil, any other scam is going to look a little bit pathetic.

Most worrying of all, "The Daemons" sets a precedent that allows all the regulars to run through their party-pieces. As with the later season-enders, everyone's desire to let their hair down and play it for laughs mitigates against showing a new threat of unprecedented scale. Courtney plays with his usual aplomb, but the story entails him being stuck behind a force-field of sorts while the troops behave like they're playing hooky. Sergeant Benton really becomes the figure we all remember in this story, and John Levene gives the lines a bit more charm than was on the page. He's wisely made half of a double-act with the veteran Damaris Hayman, which might explain why he seems so relaxed. On the other hand, Richard Franklin seems *less* at ease than ever. He can't even watch television convincingly in episode one, although he's on somewhat safer ground when he's asking questions or beating people up. More than anyone else, Captain Yates is out of place here. That could have been a useful focal point of the story, for the viewers if not the writers. It ultimately doesn't harm this production too much, as the story is *about* a traditional holiday, but it's really an issue when the programme-makers overplay this hand in later stories. By this time next year ("The Time Monster"), UNIT become almost as out-of-their-league and folksy as the Walmington-on-Sea Home Guard in *Dad's Army*[51].

So for all the supposed audacity of the story's basic conceit, this is closer to children's television than even "The Claws of Axos". At least it's slicker than anything children were getting at the time, but that's of small comfort to the modern viewer. This story's reputation is based partly on the effect it had on the viewership (and to be fair, like all the stories reshown as compilations, it stuck in the public's memory better than most), partly on the

fun the cast and crew remember having on the shoot, and only *partly* for its actual quality. Watching it for the first time now, many people feel like they're seeing photos of a party they didn't attend. Others enjoy the era it evokes, when such things seemed possible. But without such indulgence, the flaws in pacing, performance and plot-logic outweigh most of the things they got right.

The Facts

Written by Guy Leopold (pseudonym for Robert Sloman and Barry Letts). Viewing figures: 9.2 million, 8.0 million, 8.1 million, 8.1 million, 8.3 million, *but* the compilation repeat just after Christmas - the start of a tradition until "Genesis of the Daleks" (12.4) - got a whopping 10.5 million, the highest ratings since "Galaxy Four" (3.1).

Only episode four exists in its original colour form, the other episodes released on BBC video having been reconstituted from various sources. The abrupt change in resolution between episodes three and four is hugely noticeable. (See **The Lore** for details.)

Supporting Cast Damaris Hayman (Miss Hawthorne), Don McKillop (Bert the Landlord), Rollo Gamble (Winstanley), Robin Wentworth (Prof. Horner), David Simeon (Alastair Fergus), Eric Hillyard (Dr. Reeves), Jon Croft (Tom Girton), Stanley Mason (Bok), Alec Linstead (Sgt Osgood), John Owens (Thorpe), Stephen Thorne (Azal), The Headington Quarry Men (Morris Dancers).

Working Titles "The Demons" (apparently Christopher Barry changed the spelling...)

Cliffhangers Professor Horner breaks into the Devil's Hump, and Jo finds the Doctor's motionless body in the aftermath; inside the Hump, the Doctor's about to explain everything to Jo when Bok the gargoyle prances down the tunnel after them; the village begins to quake as the Master performs the ritual to summon Azal, but even the Master recoils from the (unseen) apparition in front of him (the first time that a cliffhanger depicts a threat to the Master's life); Azal manifests himself in the cavern for the third and final time, expanding to full size in front of Jo and the coven.

What Was in the Charts? "He's Gonna Step On You Again", John Kongos; "Oh You Pretty Thing", Peter Noone; "Chirpy Chirpy Cheep Cheep"52, Middle of the Road; "Knock Three Times", Dawn (feat. Tony Orlando); "Devil's Answer", Atomic Rooster - it only made the Top 20 a few weeks later, but was getting a lot of airplay at the time. If you're going to split hairs you can have "Co-Co" by The Sweet, and serve you right.

The Lore

• So who *is* this Guy Leopold? Apparently he's a friend of David Agnew - in other words, he's a pseudonym for the producer and friends (see Volume IV). Letts had been toying with the idea of writing a story since becoming producer unexpectedly, in late 1969, but had pitched ideas for stories to Gerry Davis even before directing his first *Who* story (5.4, "The Enemy of the World", in case you'd forgotten). It seems that Letts and Dicks had discussed the vague outline of this story as a possible safety-net, to be developed properly if the 1971 run needed a new ending in a hurry.

We know that several ideas for stories were in various stages of development from mid-1970. We discuss Jon Pertwee and Reed de Rouen's "Doctor Who and the Spare-Part People" in **What Else Wasn't Made?** under 17.6, "Shada", but we have grave doubts about whether it could be considered a serious contender. Glyn Jones (see 2.7, "The Space Museum" and 12.3, "The Sontaran Experiment") had an idea or two, as did Ian Stuart Black (3.9, "The Savages"; 3.10, "The War Machines"; 4.7, "The Macra Terror"). Douglas Camfield, recovering from his tachycardia (see "Inferno") suggested something about a lost Amazon city (see also 14.2, "The Hand of Fear"). All of these ideas seem to have taken on board the original Bryant / Sherwin suggestion of UNIT as a global army, and the model of ITC shows where foreign locations are suggested with stock-footage, back-projection and badly made-up extras driving Citroens around Borehamwood on the wrong side of the road. Letts' idea of the format, however, was more homespun.

Another script being seriously considered at the time was Bill Strutton's "The Mega". Exactly what appealed about this (apart from the fact that Sutton's one transmitted story got the record viewing figures for its first episode - which sounds great until you see how quickly they tailed off once people had *seen* 2.5, "The Web Planet") is never discussed. All accounts suggest that it's more about big insects, but this time in London. As an aside, we know that tentative approaches had been made to John Wyndham shortly before he died in 1969. These concerned a *Doctor Who* version of something like his posthumously-published book *Web*, so it's possible that this is what Strutton was being asked for, *or* that people remembering it almost forty years later are just getting their wires crossed.

Be that as it may, "The Mega" never got anywhere, and Letts commented on how sad it was that supernatural adventures like the audition piece he'd written for Jo and Mike couldn't be made to fit into the programme's format. Dicks, apparently, suggested a way it could be shoehorned in. As producer and occasional director, Letts was on a wage-scale geared towards younger people, and needed to get back into writing. So it came to pass that Letts rounded off two years of telling people what he wanted in a script by having a crack himself. But although he'd written for television before, he was less confident of his ability to meet *Doctor Who's* specific and peculiar requirements and sought help from a collaborator. After failing to get anywhere with his friend Owen Holder, he contacted a near-neighbour...

• Robert Sloman, distribution manager for the *Sunday Times* (for which he wrote occasional reviews and features), hadn't written for television but had done a few well-received experimental plays, one of which was adapted into a feature film[53]. He was already involved in a writing partnership, which is cited as one reason for the *nom de plume*, to avoid letting it seem he was going solo. Another is that as producer, Letts could not - strictly speaking - write for his own series without permission. (Even asking for such leeway was chancy.) Sloman's son was called Guy, and Leopold is Letts' middle name, hence the pseudonym. Sloman seems to have suggested that the Von Daniken theme of a space-traveller who was woven into our mythology be combined with a dig at a Bronze Age barrow. Letts brought the Dennis Wheatley aspects and the idea that the Master should be finally defeated and eased out of the series.

• The script has a female hand giving the Brigadier the phone when a call awakes him in the middle of the night. Terrance Dicks had created an entire life for the Brigadier, involving a wife called Fiona. Nicholas Courtney found this a bit odd. Meanwhile, Benton was supposed to have a ballroom-dancing partner called "Mavis" (possibly the kid sister he takes dancing in 13.4, "The Android Invasion"). Anyone trying to locate UNIT HQ should know that Benton and Yates watch the Knockout of the Southern Area Championships. (The regions on the series Come Dancing , which followed the National Ballroom Dancing Federation categories in most particulars, would have included Cheltenham - one of our posited sites in the essay - as "Midlands".)

- Not to put too fine a point on it, but Christopher Barry had run away from Doctor Who in a bid to avoid typecasting. He had directed a well-received Out of the Unknown (see "Inferno") from a script by Owen Holder, and worked on Paul Temple (the racetrack episode that aired on 25th of August that year). But he liked the idea of archaeology as a theme and agreed to direct this story. He changed the title's spelling almost immediately, whilst rewrites were ongoing. He thought Miss Hawthorne should be old and mad; guest star Damaris Hayman wasn't quite what he had in mind and, as someone whose friends included witches, Hayman wanted to downplay the dottiness. Letts eventually sided with her.

Don McKillop, later the cop whose head gets chewed off in An American Werewolf in London, played Bert the Landlord. (Blink at the end of the film and you'll miss John Owens, who's Thorpe in this story, as a plod with a Zapata moustache.) McKillop was all over British TV, popping up in things like Z-Cars and The Likely Lads, and eventually Take the High Road gave him a long-term gig. (The documentation always calls him "Bert the Landlord". It's been suggested that his surname was "Ford", but if so, they couldn't have used it on screen. Bert Foord (sic) was the BBC's senior weatherman. Unlike other broadcasters, they used legitimate meteorologists from the Met Office - formerly part of the Air Ministry - so he was a civil servant as well as a TV icon.)

- Barry decided early on that the story needed more than the usual amount of filming, including night-filming (very expensive, with everyone paid time and a half) and a long time on location. Thus, this story had a fortnight's filming allocated - compared to five days for the previous story, which was an episode longer. Indeed, a fortnight on location was about as much as had been needed for the eight-part all-action story "The Invasion" (6.3) and longer than for "The Ambassadors of Death".

- Production assistant Peter Grimwade (more

on him in Volume V) found Aldbourne, in Wiltshire, on a preliminary visit to the West of England. It was near a Bronze Age barrow, an airstrip and a reasonably large town (Marlborough), and had an almost stereotypical village green. As part of the deal with Aldbourne's Parish Council (whose pond-drainage fund was the main beneficiary), the BBC wasn't permitted to film inside the church. Worries about potential religious objections had already led to careful wording in the script to avoid mentioning God, while making clear that the sabbat is taking place in a cave, not the crypt. Similarly, though, the precise details of Miss Hawthorne's beliefs were researched to avoid lazily or maliciously associating pagan and wiccan practices with devil-worship or making her seem silly. (That said, the reference to Azal as 'the Horned God' was amended to 'Horned Beast' - the BBC is an equal opportunities debunker.)

As those of you with the novelisation to hand will have spotted, the Master's "incantation" is 'Mary had a little lamb' backwards (a trick also used by Miss Hawthorne in the book). After recording, the Head of Serials, Ronnie Marsh, insisted that the shot of the Master holding a knife over Jo for sacrifice should be removed. (Not without reason, as it turned out - a nearly contemporary production, Spyder's Web, came horribly unstuck doing this. In the episode "An Almost Modern Man" [TX April 1972, guest-starring Rollo Gamble], a voodoo sacrifice of a naked woman was recorded, but the lady in question was hospitalised when the prop knife failed. The resulting press coverage prompted a review of ATV's safety procedures but caused a lot of small boys to tune in, which may account for why the series was cancelled. If we just say that both Robert Holmes and Roy Clarke wrote their oddest scripts for this series, you can see why this is a shame. The star, a chap called Anthony Ainley, will also be prominent in Volume V.)

- The beginning of the filming was the UNIT garage scene, shot at Membury airfield. They later filmed the UNIT garage scenes for "Planet of the Spiders" here, which is appropriate - it was during the filming for "The Daemons" that Letts and Pertwee saw autogyros being flown nearby. The menacing shape in the opening scene is a black furry hat owned by assistant floor manager Sue Heddon. The owl that looks like a piece of stock-footage was filmed especially for this scene on location. Just like Jo in episode one, Katy Manning really *did* get the map upside-down while guiding Pertwee to location filming earlier that year. This time she missed where some light-coloured stones had been laid out as a path for her to follow, and ran into a barbed wire fence.

• Pertwee was slightly injured falling off the motorbike, but not on film. This may have happened when he went joyriding to vent his annoyance at the protracted reshoots of the "diagram" scene. Nicholas Courtney had previously attempted to placate him, a reversal of the situation in "Terror of the Autons" (8.1). The line '...and it comes out here' is (as many of you will know) from "The Music Goes Round And Round", a Danny Kaye hit. (It's from the film *The Five Pennies*, and passing on this gobbet of information almost makes having to sit through that film on a wet Bank Holiday worthwhile.) It happens that Pertwee doubled for Kaye during the filming of *Knock On Wood* - you don't think a big Hollywood star flew all the way to Britain for a total of fifteen seconds of location footage, do you? - and "covered" many of his novelty songs on record. (Pause to say that the rumour that Pertwee's version of "Three Little Fishes" is used to extract confessions in Third World nations isn't true, but it *is* an extraordinary rendition.) Filming this scene took a lot of takes, and led to annoying lapses in continuity. Indeed, while the filming is fondly recalled *now*, this portion of the shoot very often got fractious, with snow on St George's Day delaying the heat barrier filming. Overall, however, the cast and crew maintained the feel of a working holiday.

The next day, Saturday, was the one with all the villagers on the Green. That gag about Yates and the Brigadier going for a pint was ad-libbed, a reflection of the fairly good-natured atmosphere. The local kids got rides in Bessie and the Headington Quarry Men got all the Morris dancing scenes out of the way in one day. Plans to film on Sunday were shelved as Pertwee had been booked to do a late-night cabaret in Portsmouth (due to *The Navy Lark*, he was much in demand here; see 9.3, "The Sea Devils"). This annoyed Christopher Barry, who'd had to miss his sister's wedding on the Saturday afternoon. (To this day, it's unclear how troubled the relationship between Pertwee and Barry was. The story doing the rounds is that they faked a row during their next story together, "The Mutants", to get Barry out of having to work on *Doctor Who* again. And yet, Barry directs the very first story with a new

Doctor, "Robot".)

• For once, they got a stuntwoman (Pamela Devereaux) to double for Manning rather than get Stuart Fell to drag up. This story was also a rare chance to see the face of Gerald Taylor, the van-driver whose cap appears to have eaten his hair. He was a Dalek operator back in the Hartnell days, as well as a War Machine (well, *the* War Machine with different numbers on) and the voice of WOTAN, with all that that entails (see 3.10, "The War Machines" for what this voice said that was so controversial). Later on, we'll see him as Vega Nexos, Peladon's very own Mr Tumnus (11.4, "The Monster of Peladon"). Jack Silk doubled for the Doctor the next day, during the motorbike shooting scene.

• Notoriously, the first take of the Master's arrest was slightly marred by the assembled kids cheering him.

• During the first day's camera rehearsals the then-ubiquitous Ed Stewart came to visit and had his photo taken in the crypt set. "Stewpot" was then at the apex of his popularity, branching out from being a Radio 1 DJ to hosting *Crackerjack* (go on... you know you want to) and having the jokes page (and often the cover) of *Look-in*. (It would take a book this size to fully convey what this show meant to kids at the time, but have a look at the aforementioned *Countdown* essay.)

• The music for the TV rugby broadcast, watched by Yates and Benton at UNIT HQ, is Berlioz's *Symphony Fantastique*. This is held to be a clever in-joke, but the next movement of the piece - wherein the protagonist goes to Hell - is woefully inappropriate for BBC sports. The bit we hear is actually a cheerful piece about going to be guillotined. (*Symphonie Fantastique* was "in" that year, as a COI "Public Information" film about motorcycle proficiency used the Third Movement at the same time.) Bill McLaren's commentary seems to suggest that five different teams are on the pitch, since it's pasted together out of fragments from several different matches (we have no idea why) with a short clip of film when we actually see the screen.

• "Charlie" (one of the villagers at the town meeting) is played by John Scott Martin, showing his face on-camera after years of being stuck inside Daleks, giant insects and mining robots. We'll see him again in "The Green Death" and "Robot", and thereafter whenever casting companies are asked for slightly dazed-looking old men. (We've mentioned some of these in other volumes, but keep an eye out in *Little Shop of Horrors* and the video for Peter Gabriel's *Steam*.) Rollo Gamble played Squire Winstanley. There's not much left to say about his other acting roles, but his biggest claim to fame is as a director on Rediffusion Television's quite literally poptabulous *Ready, Steady, Go!* Indeed, he helmed the episode wherein guest-presenter Dusty Springfield introduced the stars of Tamla Motown to the British public (TX 28/4/65). Someone called Jim Davidson is credited as one of the UNIT troops, but we can't be sure it's *that* Jim Davidson[54]. (We're more certain that the "Nicholas Courtney" who provides the voice of the BBC3 announcer is the same one who plays the Brigadier, and whose relatively small part in episode one allowed him to wander off into the next studio and watch Morecambe and Wise rehearse.)

• Stephen Thorne was originally to have mimed to the voice of Anthony Jackson (AKA Fred Mumford from *Rentaghost*) while playing Azal, but this was abandoned. Thorne, an experienced radio performer, delivered the lines himself, although the false teeth presented difficulties. Curiously, he wasn't allowed to keep the dentures as souvenirs as they were BBC property, even though nobody else could wear them (or would want to, one supposes).

• When this story was deemed a success, Sloman lost his coyess about writing under his own name. However, his next idea for a story ("The Daleks In London") was eventually rejected when it was decided to include the Daleks in Louis Marks' proposed time-paradox script (see "Day of the Daleks" and "The Time Monster").

• All right, we'll say it... one viewer wrote the *Radio Times* to complain about the BBC's apparent policy of blowing up historic buildings to make television programmes. Letts patiently explained that it was a model, but the letter was alluded to in *The Making of Doctor Who*, the only guide to the

series in print for most of the 1970s (see "The Sea Devils"). For years this anecdote was treated as a tribute to the ability of the BBC's effects team, but watching the episode again, it's more a tribute to the fact that some viewers are a bit over-excitable. (Licence fee payers will be relieved to hear that the BBC didn't blow up a helicopter, either - they bought a few inches of stock film.)

• 625-line colour copies of this story became hard to find. Letts asked for all of "The Daemons" to be kept, but only episode four was retained in the archives. There *had* been a compilation repeat just after Christmas 1971, but the copy in the archives was a monochrome telerecording. However, a U-matic copy from an off-air 525-line NTSC Betamax copy of the colour compilation existed, due to a Los Angeles station showing the story in the late 70s. (See **The Lore** under "The Ambassadors of Death" for more. The US was the first country to buy this story, as part of a package that included the first three colour seasons minus "Spearhead from Space".)

When BBC2 started showing re-runs of selected stories in the 90s, it was proposed that a shot-gun wedding of all of these sources could make a broadcastable copy. The two basic images - one in detail but lacking colour, the other in colour but scuzzy - were of different screen-ratios, so a bit of Quantel magic was needed to resize them both to the same scale. A gap where the Betamax tape had to be changed was covered by an even worse VHS copy. The process was covered in detail by gosh-wow technology series *Tomorrow's World* (then-edited by former Bedfordshire DWAS local group head Saul Nassé - we really *do* get everywhere) just prior to transmission of the rebuilt story in November / December 1992. Despite the tendency for NTSC conversions to make everyone go orange, this is currently the best-quality copy available.

9.1: "Day of the Daleks"

(Serial KKK. Four Episodes, 1st - 22nd January 1972.)

Which One is This? The Daleks fight UNIT (very slowly) in an English country garden. The Doctor visits a nightmare future where ice maidens massage keyboards while big apemen prance about and *everyone* wears Nehru suits, all as part of one big Dalek-inspired time paradox.

Firsts and Lasts Other than the two 1960s Peter Cushing movies, it's the first time the Daleks appear in colour. (None of them are red, despite what both the films and the Dalek comic-strips in *TV21* had told us.) And they now have pupils in their eyes, stupidly.

The Ogrons make the first of three appearances (including their cameo in 11.2, "Carnival of Monsters") as the Daleks' lackeys. The Blinovitch Limitation Effect a shameless piece of technobabble designed to gloss over the complicated problems of time travel, is mentioned for the first time and it'll go on to become a much-abused catchphrase of the series (indeed, we devote a whole essay to it under 20.3, "Mawdryn Undead"). Less obviously, it's the first time that spacetime is referred to as 'the vortex', and it *isn't* the Doctor who says it.

Katy Manning delights boys everywhere by flashing her pants on a number of occasions, which soon becomes a regular feature. The TARDIS console is seen outside the Ship, and installed in the Doctor's lab, for the last time. And in the tunnels, it's the final occasion that we hear the 'alien wind' sound from 1.2, "The Daleks".

This is the last story to credit Peter Diamond for fight arranging.

Four Things to Notice About "Day of the Daleks"...

1. As the plot involves a *different* successful Dalek takeover of our planet two centuries from now (see 2.2, "The Dalek Invasion of Earth"), the BBC went to town on promotion and played up to nostalgia by pastiching old publicity material from 1964. This means the BBC1 trailers contained shots of Daleks trundling across London Bridge, only this time in colour and nothing at all to do with the new storyline. And, if you thought the

Season 9 Cast/Crew

- Jon Pertwee (the Doctor)
- Katy Manning (Jo Grant)
- Nicholas Courtney (Brigadier Lethbridge-Stewart)
- Richard Franklin (Captain Yates)
- John Levene (Sergeant Benton)

- Barry Letts (Producer)
- Terrance Dicks (Script Editor)

Radio Times cover for X3.4, "Daleks in Manhattan" was a crass spoiler, try a Frank Bellamy cartoon depicting the cliffhanger from an episode they didn't air for another *two weeks*.

Despite this, and even though the word 'Daleks' appears in the title, "Day of the Daleks" continues the great *Doctor Who* tradition of not giving old enemies a proper scene until the end of the first episode. However, a clumsy "reveal" occurs about ten minutes after we see a bit of a Dalek and hear it speak. The Daleks in this story sound terrible (so you could be forgiven for not recognising the voice), but the cliffhanger is still is a bit of an anticlimax, even compared to the non-surprise surprises of other Dalek stories.

2. It's a great story for monsters acting out of character. Witness the Daleks' shocked response, when told that someone called the Doctor is interfering with their plans: 'DOC-TOR? DID-YOU-SAY... DOC-TOR?' (Not only that, but episode four contains the peculiar sight of a Dalek gingerly pushing open a pair of French windows with its sucker-arm.) We can top that, though: when one of the gorilla-minded Ogrons is asked what happened to the human victim he was sent to kill, his reply is a slow, half-witted, 'we... found... and... destroyed... the... enemy'. When a second or two later he's then asked if there were any complications, he off-handedly mumbles 'no complications' as if he's just forgotten to keep acting stupid. A mere five seconds into their debut, and they've already messed up continuity.

3. When the Daleks attach the Doctor to their mind analysis device, the psychedelic "brain-pattern" we see on the screen is quite blatantly the *Doctor Who* end title sequence, in an obvious attempt to save money on special effects.

Although this (weirdly) suggests that the title sequence represents the inside of the Doctor's mind, the effect is rather spoiled when the words "Doctor Who Jon Pertwee" *ever-so-briefly* flash up on screen. The other two cliffhangers are reprised with the "sting" still included, as the director thought that was how things were usually done.

4. One of the most memorable scenes - though not perhaps for the right reasons - is an extended chase sequence in episode three, in which the Ogrons persue the Doctor and Jo as they flee on a Honda trike conveniently left outside the Dalek control centre. It happens that Pertwee had just bought one, and persuaded Letts that it looked space-age enough for this sort of thing (even though they had to add a futuristic 'bibble' noise).

With hindsight, however, you just have to ask yourself to whom the trike belonged, since the Ogrons would topple over if they tried to climb onto it (older readers might recall Magilla Gorilla) and the Daleks' Nazi-style policemen would lose an awful lot of authority if they were using something this infantile to keep order. The shot of the trike pulling away from the centre, chased by a group of extras in oddly-fitting helmets and black leather tunics, looks for all the world like the evil-alternative-future version of the Keystone Kops. Adding to the affront, the pursuing Ogrons seem to be half-running, half-hopping, yet still keep pace. Dudley Simpson cranks his Bontempi organ up to eleven and adds flanged cymbals for extra urgency, but really, they'd have been better off with a Benny Hill-style burst of *Yakkety Sax*.

The Continuity

The Doctor Here the Doctor claims that a principle called the Blinovitch Limitation Effect stops time travellers constantly going back into their own pasts and making sure that everything turns out all right for them. Sadly, somebody interrupts him before he can explain it properly. [But see **What is the Blinovitch Limitation Effect?** under "Mawdryn Undead".[56] Here it's an odd thing to say, however, coming as it does in a story where the Doctor and Jo do the very impossible phenomenon he's just described, and meet their temporal counterparts while he's fixing the TARDIS.]

He's confident that the Brigadier will correctly interpret the phrase 'tell it to the Marines' as "This is a pack of lies." [It's old wartime anecdote about a similar situation, only with Nazis instead of

time-travelling guerrillas. The Third Doctor seems to be more prone to using "period" slang and topical references - the more time he spends in this era, the better at it he gets. Letts' radio play "The Paradise of Death" has him using terms like 'chuffed', and describing people watching soap operas as getting their 'fix'. However, all the other references in that story bewilderingly suggest that it's set in 1990s Britain-plus-a-bit-more *and* in a non-existent gap between 11.1, "The Time Warrior" and 11.2, "Invasion of the Dinosaurs".]

The Doctor has no problem using the word 'ghost' to describe apparitions and manifestations, provided there's a scientific explanation involved. He initially isn't bothered by the fact that Earth stands on the brink of global war [perhaps knowing that humanity isn't "scheduled" for World War Three yet]. He describes the Daleks as his 'bitterest enemies' and 'the most evil, ruthless lifeform in the cosmos'.

He's able to resist the Dalek mind probes, to the point that even extracting a simple admission of identity 'practically kills him'. For the first time since "The Keys of Marinus" (1.5), he proves himself quite the bon viveur and describes the plonk as 'sardonic but not cynical, good-natured... very much after my own heart'. He's rather taken with Chateau Quisling 2172 as well, and goes the entire story without any tea. He loves gorgonzola.

• *Ethics.* He's quite content to freeload off the state when it comes to Sir Reg's wine-cellar, both before and after insulting his host to his face.

At one point, the Doctor uses a stolen gun to disintegrate an Ogron who's pursuing him. [This is the first and almost only time the Doctor is seen to use a gun against an opponent; killing a sentient creature by *any* means seems out of character for him. Yet he doesn't seem to feel remotely guilty afterwards. It's starting to look as if the Third Doctor *dislikes* violence but is actually more willing to use it than most of his other incarnations. Even his non-lethal Venusian karate is overly aggressive by the Second Doctor's standards. Maybe he feels that the Ogrons aren't intelligent enough to count as "real" people, but even so, it's an unsettling thing to watch.]

Later, he's quite convinced that killing someone to save the lives of millions is 'still murder'. He even spares the Controller's life, persuading the terrorist / freedom fighters that the Daleks 'would always have found someone'.

• *Background.* The Doctor claims to have given

How Does Time Work?

Since the last time we tackled this essay, we've been presented with a lot more evidence. Fortunately (cue big wiping of the sweat off our collective brow), most of the new data confirms our basic hypothesis. Whilst there's an existing pattern for history that "ordinary" time travel tends not to reconfigure, the presence of beings biologically capable of "ungluing" causality can shift time-lines. The beings most suited to this are Time Lords and their TARDISes, but the Daleks eventually crack this and start (or at least prosecute) a Time War (understand that words like "eventually" are a little unstable in this context, but bear with us).

What the new series makes clear is that the Daleks have become able to rewrite history on a vast scale, making new time-lines such as the one running from X1.7, "The Long Game" onwards come into being. Arguably, *these* Daleks themselves hail from a new timeline, and thus aren't of a type that we saw in the original series. However, as the new breed bases their operations in phases of history that the classic series didn't visit (somewhere between the year 4000 and the 57th Segment of Time; see 3.4, "The Daleks' Master Plan"; 3.6, "The Ark"; and X1.13, "The Parting of the Ways"), our consideration of the state of affairs in "Day of the Daleks" in the original Volume III needs fewer refinements than might have been thought.

Even so, the previous essay's view of the relationship between Time Travel and Free Will is further from the *Doctor Who* orthodoxy of today than it was when we considered the issue in Summer 2004. We're obliged, therefore, to go back and look at this whole matter again.

Recently, it's been confirmed that when the Doctor and his companion(s) visit a timeline that's later closed-off by his actions, they all continue to remember these events. This had been our working hypothesis since "Carnival of Monsters" (10.2), but "Father's Day" (X1.8) actually says it out loud. (This is, mind you, just about the only uncomplicated addition "Father's Day" makes to our time-paradox database, and is one of the few things about this story on which everyone can agree.) In "Last of the Time Lords" (X3.13), this ability to revise time is presented as the main reason Martha left the Doctor, so it's pretty much set in stone now. (See **What Actually Happens in a Regeneration?** under 11.5, "Planet of the Spiders" for a freaky interpretation of this.) And in *The Sarah Jane Adventures* story "Whatever Happened to Sarah Jane?", we get a clear statement that a changed timeline is a different thing entirely from a parallel universe, divergent continuum or counterfactual history.

So it seems that crossing one's own timeline has become The Most Perilous Thing it's possible to actually do. The Doctor suggests it as a means of wiping out the Daleks ("The Parting of the Ways"), but only as a ruse to get rid of Rose and embark on the far-less complicated procedure of wiping out himself and every being with a nervous system in a parsec's radius of Earth in the year 200,100. And yet, when Rose needs to reset Donna's timeline (X4.11, "Turn Left"), she does so by dispatching the Donna from the aberrant timeline to fix things for her former self. (Donna then deploys the now-standard method of running into traffic and dying with Rose nearby.) Therefore, unless Donna2's death was part of the "pattern" of time in Donna1's world-line, we have to assume that Rose's plan was... err, for Donna2 to harangue Donna1 (and give Sylvia a long-overdue slap) and thereby unleash Reapers, the critters from "Father's Day" who show up to eat time-spillage and excrete anachronistic chart-hits.

There's corollary of this that needs a bit of thought. Although the available evidence is patchy, it looks as if the consequences of closed-off alternate timelines can be "real". As far as we know, Donna2's body doesn't wink out of existence once Donna1 turns left. (Although the fact of Donna2's death in a traffic accident seems not to have reached Donna1- perhaps Wilfred and Sylvia's news-management works retroactively.) Similarly, as far as we know, the UNIT troops killed at Auderly House in "Day of the Daleks" are still dead once Styles and company leave the building. Adam is still with his mum, augmented brain-spike and all (in "The Long Game"), even though there's reason to believe that the events in X1.6, "Dalek", have been superseded.

All of these artefacts have consequences that *themselves* have consequences, so the problems caused by their sudden non-existence are actually greater than any by their persistence in the "official" time-line. The alternative is that - to take Donna's trip back as the limit-case - she dies, her other self turns left, and the timeline with stereotyped Italians being rounded up by the military wing of Equity never happens... which means that Donna doesn't go back, and she turns right. And if that were so, we'd have two mutually-exclusive chains of events flip back and forth so rapidly, time

continued on page 197...

Napoleon the idea for his famous 'an army marches on its stomach' line, and says he knew him well enough to call him "Boney". [In "The Sea Devils" (9.3) he also claims to have known Nelson, one of Napoleon's arch-nemeses, so he likes playing both sides against the middle. A friendship with Napoleon is a lot more feasible than a friendship with Mao Xedung - see 8.2, "The Mind of Evil" - since Napoleon may have become a dictator, but began as an extreme example of the Enlightenment values the Doctor upholds. Most of Napoleon's British opponents weren't especially democratic anyway. At least Napoleon thought of himself as a scientist and did, after all, go to investigate Egypt with the aid of 150 scholars and an army of "liberators" instead of just conquering it. "The Reign of Terror" (1.8) actually takes place during Napoleon's rise to power but he and the Doctor don't meet on that occasion; either there's a missing adventure, or the Doctor is just making this up.]

The Supporting Cast

• *UNIT.* Here the government isn't using UNIT as standard security for peace conferences, but calls in the Brigadier's team when there's a special problem at the site of the summit. Styles' aide (Miss Paget) makes the request, not Styles himself. Either there's a new lab for the Doctor at UNIT HQ, or a whole new HQ. [It's usually assumed that UNIT HQ is near London, but here characters go 'down' - i.e. south - from HQ to Auderly, which is said to be fifty miles north of London. Wales is 'nearby'. And it's apparently not far from the HQ to the conference, meaning that this new centre of operations is in the middle of nowhere. Or Swindon, which amounts to the same thing. See **Where's UNIT HQ?** under 8.1, "Terror of the Autons".]

The soldiers on guard stand to attention as the Doctor runs in, but now have long hair and Frank Zappa moustaches. Once again, the Brigadier is far from camera-shy.

The UNIT canteen has definite opening and closing times, and the impending end of the world does nothing to alter this. [One presumes, then, that they've fired the privileged charlady - q.v. "Terror of the Autons".] The Brigadier is now assuming the Doctor to be popping off unannounced, and goes in person to check if he's in the building. The lab now has a firing range and a golden yellow corridor outside, just in case any

CSO shenanigans are called for.

Yates' call sign here is 'Greyhound Two'. UNIT HQ is 'Trap One'.

• *Jo Grant.* She's initially taken in by the Controller's platitudes. [To be fair, she's presented with very little evidence to the contrary, beyond a story of brutality told to her by people who want to shoot the Doctor and tie her up in a cellar.] She survives the time-transference, against all the expectations of the guerrillas, but not to the Doctor's surprise. [We know now that anyone who's ridden in the TARDIS is saturated with Artron energy - see X2.13, "Doomsday", "Attack of the Bane" and, by implication, the way the companions survive a trip through Interstitial Time in 26.1, "Battlefield".]

Jo's escapology doesn't fail her on this occasion, as she's able - unlike the Doctor - to wriggle out of the ropes the guerrillas tie around her hands. Rather sweetly, Jo says 'take care' when saying goodbye to Anat, even though the outcome of her return to 197somethingorother will likely result in Anat's death or wipe her from existence altogether.

• *Mike Yates.* According to Jo, he marches on his stomach. He has no qualms about depriving Benton of his snack.

The TARDIS The Doctor is still working on the dematerialisation circuit, trying to cut out the 'override' which allows the Time Lords to remote-control the Ship. [Here the Doctor has worked out that the High Council steered it in "Colony in Space" (8.4), but he's probably guessing, since at the very least the three individuals responsible weren't the *whole* High Council.]

While fiddling about with the console, the Doctor causes duplicates of himself and Jo to appear, but there's an explosion from the console and the duplicates vanish. The Doctor claims that this is a freak effect, and that the duplicates have gone forward into their own time-stream. [The duplicate Doctor says 'of course, I remember now' as he appears, and knows things will soon sort themselves out, implying that at some point in the future he and Jo will temporarily be transported back to this point... but if so, we never hear about it. Later in that episode, he speaks of seeing himself as 'a few moments ago', so the 'other side' of that encounter might happen then. He also seems to imply that he's not really there, as if it's not true time-travel but a moment's confusion in causality.

How Does Time Work?

...continued from page 195

would effectively stop.

One thing that *has* been made a lot clearer, however, is the status of historical events. Some are, no matter what version of Earth's history we're in, fixed points. Dickens always died in 1870 (X1.3, "The Unquiet Dead"). Others, such as the career of Agatha Christie or the eruption of Vesuvius (X4.7, "The Unicorn and the Wasp"; X4.2, The Fires of Pompeii") were up for grabs when the Doctor was around, but were established facts in Donna's past.

This point needs to be said clearly and - it appears from some of the utterly nonsensical comments online - repeatedly. Some people seem to think that if the Tenth Doctor causes an event in the past, then it *wasn't* true for the previous Doctors, even if they encountered consequences of that event. To argue this is to say that the Great Fire of London (which the Fifth Doctor started in 19.4, "The Visitation) hadn't happened in the 1911 that the Fourth Doctor visited in 13.3, "Pyramids of Mars", even though the Great Fire is mentioned. If this were the case, then the Cybermen in "The Invasion" (6.3) would have posed for photos beside a wooden St Paul's Cathedral with a spire, rather than the one Sir Christopher Wren designed as part of his post-fire rebuild of the city. More alarmingly, this logic holds that without Adric slamming a spaceship into Cretaceous-Era Earth, no *Doctor Who* story featuring humans would have been possible before "Earthshock" (19.6).

The same holds true for the exceedingly trivial suggestion that Torchwood didn't "temporally exist" until the Doctor and Rose went back and pissed off Queen Victoria. Yes, Torchwood was brought into being by the Tenth Doctor's were-wolf-related antics, but that doesn't mean that it wasn't around in 1880, 1881, 1882 and so on in the classic series. Anyway, Torchwood is mentioned by name in X1.12, "Bad Wolf" and X2.0, "The Christmas Invasion", so it's a definite historical event even before the Doctor went back and "caused it".

We've recently been told that there's no longer access to alternate universes (X2.5, "Rise of the Cybermen"; X4.13, "Journey's End") - but also that universes might exist where this injunction does not apply. Nothing anyone does in the Doctor's universe can create them, but *other* forms of creation can intersect with the Doctor's continuum. Moreover, there's now a distinct difference between an altered time-line and a parallel universe (hitherto, it had been routinely assumed that the former generates the latter). This still seems to be the case, but whereas it was formerly possible to access these variations on the original timeline with (say) a functioning TARDIS or Morgaine's magic (26.1, "Battlefield"), it's no longer possible. The analogy seems to be railway lines: you can reverse up to the "points", change something and proceed forwards along a different line, but not jump from one line to another and back *unless* some kind of breach is made by (say) a Void Ship (X2.12, "Army of Ghosts") or the Reality Bomb ("Journey's End"). But this is risky for both world-lines.

Moreover, the non-linearity of time in the new series clearly permits a *very specific category* of temporal paradox, wherein the Doctor is apparently permitted to get information from "else-where", outside an apparently closed loop of cause-and-effect. Whereas we had to squirm to excuse Leela inheriting immunity to a virus from her ancestors - who got it from *her* (15.2, "The Invisible Enemy") - it's now apparently licit for the Doctor to learn things from his future self (X3.10, "Blink"; X3.13-A, "Time Crash"). Moreover, with the aid of a drastically reconfigured TARDIS, the Master can bring the Toclafane from Humanity's distant future to paradoxically wipe out Earth's population in the present (X3.12, "The Sound of Drums"). And if the Daleks now have the *same* capability, all bets are off.

The point is that in the pre-1989 format, such shenanigans were expressly forbidden. Even now, rules seem to exist concerning 'wibbly-wobbly timey-wimey' stuff ("Blink" and "Time Crash" again), it's just we're not told what they are. (Our best guess is that using a small paradox to prevent a bigger one permits the TARDIS to soak up whatever ripples or Artron energy happen as a conse-quence; see also **What Is The Blinovitch Limitation Effect?** under 20.3, "Mawdryn Undead".)

And *now*, gentle reader, let's look at the time-paradox in "Day of the Daleks" afresh. To recap, this story has a timeline branching off from estab-lished *Doctor Who* chronology at the point when Auderly House blows up (let's call this Day D), and ends with the rebels sending the Doctor back to stop this (on Day Z, in the future). On Days W-Y (still in the future, just not quite as far from Day D), the time-travelling insurgents seek to assassinate

continued on page 199...

The Target novelisation of "Day of the Daleks" contains an epilogue in which the Doctor and Jo return to UNIT HQ and find their past selves there, meaning that the console briefly jumps into the future, which is taken from the cut final scene.]

The Non-Humans

• *The Daleks*. In the late twenty-first century, the Daleks invaded an already-crippled Earth, and they're still in charge several generations later, at which point the time-paradox is resolved and the invasion never took place.

[The gold Dalek says that the 'pattern of history' has been changed, and another Dalek tells the Doctor that they've invaded Earth *again*, which is taken as hinting that they remember their original invasion of 2157 in "The Dalek Invasion of Earth" (2.2). This seems highly strange, however, as such historical alteration - including events in the 70s triggering a string of world wars - would surely have averted the 2157 invasion from occurring at all. Anyway, the 2157 event was specifically to get the planet's core, in what *seemed* to be an early attempt to branch out from Skaro; by contrast, this is simple plunder as part of an overall expansion of the Daleks' already-impressive empire. That empire seems to be coeval with the oppressed Earth - there's no hard evidence of them travelling to and from Skaro in the remote future, nor do they seem to be ferrying Earth's plundered minerals through time.

[The Daleks talk as if their recent breakthrough in time-corridor technology has allowed them to pre-emptively launch an assault on Earth circa 2070 from their base in the twenty-second century. Everyone in this timeline - Daleks, the Controller, rebels and all - think of their version of events as the baseline history of Earth, which tends to suggest that these Daleks don't originate from another era. Rather, they're consolidating the past from this point.

[Nevertheless, it seems that Earth is something of a catch for the Daleks in *any* timeline. Perhaps significantly, the Dalek in "The Dalek Invasion of Earth" who tells Ian and the Doctor about the fall of Earth almost wets himself with excitement, repeating, 'We are the masters of Earth', as if he still doesn't quite believe it. Then there's the whole issue of Mavic Chen in 3.4, "The Daleks' Master Plan", and how the Solar System is counted alongside whole galaxies as powerful allies. Overall, the suggestion seems to be that acquiring Earth allows the conquest of an entire section of our galaxy.

[With this in mind, it's worth noting that the time-travel devices we see are designed for users with fingers. Perhaps human ingenuity *did* give rise to the time-corridor, even though the Controller thinks (or at least claims) that the Daleks made it. To be fair, time-travel seems easier on Earth than on some other planets - see **Why Does Earth Keep Getting Invaded?** under 13.4, "The Android Invasion" for why. Compared to the supposedly more advanced DARDIS machines of the later Hartnell Dalek tales (2.8, "The Chase" and "The Daleks' Master Plan") these portable gadgets are remarkably precise and powerful, despite coming from almost 1,500 years earlier. Either way, the Daleks have adequate tracking equipment and a Magnetron. We never see how they themselves reach the 1970s.]

The Dalek's time-technology is straightforward enough for the guerrilla resistance to copy it. Their "hand"-held modules can transport someone two hundred years into the past, and return the user even if he / she is no longer anywhere near the machine. Once the module is used to transport someone back in time, the two time-zones seem to be causally "linked" somehow, as the traveller will return after the same amount of time that he / she spends in the past [all part of the Blinovitch Limitation Effect]. Something resembling a 'mini-dematerialisation circuit' is part of the design, and the space-time vortex is mentioned [presumably the same one through which the TARDIS travels]. The Daleks' "time vortex magnetron" - which looks a lot like three oranges sprayed silver - can draw anybody using one of the modules to the Daleks' control room, provided the Daleks know the module's frequency.

These Daleks don't recognise the Third Doctor on sight, and require use of a mind probe to establish his identity, even though they know his appearance can change. [Once the Doctor is forced to admit to being the same person who gave them so much trouble in a different incarnation, the Daleks acknowledge the Second Doctor - despite there being no apparent way that they (or any Daleks from this time-period or earlier) could know about him. After all, neither of the Second Doctor's broadcast encounters with Daleks left any survivors capable of reporting to Dalek high-command. (Complicating the issue, though, the Daleks recognised the newly regenerated Doctor

How Does Time Work?

...continued from page 197

Styles; they arrive on 11th to 13th September, 197£ (Days A and C). Got that?

Additionally, both sets of time-travellers - Dalek and human - have limited time-corridor technology seemingly of the kind that the Daleks can access in the Davros Era (21.4, "Resurrection of the Daleks"). This preserves overall causality, even if the Daleks who employ Lytton are aware of the potential risk and expressly prohibit the use of out-of-period weapons or the leaving behind of corpses.

Events on Day Y cause Day C. We're all agreed on that, at least. All that changes is that Auderly House explodes with the delegates in it in one version, and with only Daleks inside in the other. So our first question is: were the Daleks around in the Day D that caused Days E-Z? How would things have been different if they had *always* come back and made sure their version of history prevailed? We could devise any number of scenarios where the knowledge that aliens were trying to sabotage the World Peace Talks might have ensured a new resolve amongst the governments of the planet (as opposed to Auderly House's destruction triggering political unrest and a series of global wars, as the folks in Day Z tell us, repeatedly), assuming anyone actually knew about the Daleks' involvement. So the BBC crew and UNIT must have all been exterminated. UNIT were only called in, remember, because of a botched assassination attempt on Day A.

We have therefore a second question: what, if anything, did the Third Doctor actually change? If he hadn't gone to the altered future, the Daleks wouldn't have become *personally* involved in the assassination of Styles et al. It seems that the main impact the Doctor has on events on Day Z is rescuing Jo. The rebel Shura would still detonate his bomb regardless. If UNIT had ignored the Doctor's advice to withdraw and let the Daleks get blown up, the result would be a lot of dead solders, but the bomb would still have taken out the Daleks in the explosion (slow as they are, the UNIT bullets didn't impede them any).

So again... what changed? In the aberrant history, not a lot. In the main one, Sergeant Benton and Captain Yates live to get involved in 9.5, "The Time Monster" et seq. This brings us back to the first question: if the Daleks came to the past because they knew the Doctor was back at Day C, then they were the determining factor. UNIT might

have repelled an Ogron-only assault, and then decided, just maybe, perhaps, possibly, that right after a squad of Ape-soldiers has tried to wreck them, the peace talks should proceed as planned. This would have been possible if the Brigadier failed to persuade Styles that the talks were under threat from the outside before the bomb went off inside. Styles is a bit of a knob, but not *that* stupid.

What this is looking like, then, is that time-travel rules out Free Will in what we're calling the aberrant time-line. But in the main one where the Doctor resides, individual humans can live their lives and make their choices unimpeded. Bah! That *can't* be right, can it?

Moreover, it seems to go against the grain *of the entire series* if humans don't have Free Will, meaning that nothing is worth fighting for or changing. In "Day of the Daleks" episode two (just before the first mention of "Blinovitch Limitation Effect"), the Doctor tells Jo that 'every choice we make the history of the world'. This is confirmed throughout the series, from "The Aztecs" (1.6) through "Pyramids of Mars" in Season Thirteen and right up until "The Curse of Fenric" (26.3). Indeed, the *one* story where the Doctor is confronted with a time-paradox that seems pre-ordained is 18.5, "Warriors' Gate", and the then-script editor, arch-Positivist Christopher H Bidmead, had kittens when he saw the original "Third World" conception of a four-part tale about a situation pre-ordained by the *I Ching*. Even then the Doctor must choose to do 'the right sort of nothing', but the end of this tale is instructive. Although it emerges that Romana is a 'time sensitive' (albeit not a very good one) roughly the same as the Tharils, she's able to offer them help with the plans for a TARDIS and something innate that they lack.

Bidmead's instinctive recoil from a *Doctor Who* story about pre-destination tells us a lot. It's fair to say most people reading this would be bothered by the idea. The whole history of *Doctor Who* has been about our ability to make a stand, make a difference and get involved. To give the Doctor, and he alone, this right seems like a betrayal of everything we thought he stood for, and renders him just another superhero. In fact, older fans whose experience of the series comes from when it was part of the BBC's mainstream output and had the same values as *Blue Peter* ("you can do it too, if you put your mind to it") undergo a Bidmead-esque gag reaction when confronted with *anything* that

continued on page 201...

on sight in 4.3, "The Power of the Daleks".)

[One possibility is that the Daleks *don't* outright recognise the Troughton version from the Third Doctor's memories, but nonetheless infer that he's another Doctor and advise their agents to keep an eye out for him. That makes the fact that the Second Doctor is here depicted with a still from "The Faceless Ones" (4.8) - a story in which the Daleks lay a time-travelling trap for him - rather intriguing. It's not impossible that the Daleks the Second Doctor encounters on screen are from the aberrant timeline created by Styles' death, something we'll discuss in **How Do You Set a Trap for This Man?** under "The Faceless Ones".

[The other, and of course far simpler, explanation is that the Second Doctor and Jamie met the Daleks in an incident that was too boring for the BBC to bother transmitting.]

The leader of the Daleks here is coloured gold [this may signify its position as head of one of the conquered districts on Earth, the Dalek equivalent of "governor"]. Normal Daleks are, as expected, silver-grey. 'Dalekanium' is a highly-effective explosive, the formula for which was stolen from the Daleks by the guerrillas. [This isn't the same as the Dalekenium mentioned in "The Dalek Invasion of Earth", which was a non-explosive metal christened by the human scientist Dortmun. But since both are Dalek-based materials apparently named by humans in the twenty-second century, there's an obvious historical parallel between the two.]

• *Ogrons.* Large, thick-skinned and very stupid, the Ogrons are higher anthropoids who used to live in scattered communities on one of the 'outer planets'. Though the Ogrons don't seem to offer much in the way of initiative, the Daleks use them as "policemen" because they're loyal, or at least not intelligent enough to be dishonest. [See 10.3, "Frontier in Space", for more on the possible history between Daleks and Ogrons, and note how this story and "Carnival of Monsters" establish that the Ogrons serve the Daleks in the "orthodox" history as well.] The Ogrons are armed with ultra sonic guns which completely disintegrate their targets. It's implied that the Daleks themselves are disintegrator-proof. These guns are manufactured locally, using metals mined in Wales, but are from a design that is two centuries ahead of anything on Earth in the UNIT era. [This is a bit confusing: the 'two centuries' line looks like the Doctor's first clue that the time-bandits are from the twenty-

second century even though - logically - it cannot be in any way connected. Moreover, we see Ogrons from the twenty-sixth century in "orthodox" time using the same weapons.]

History

• *Dating.* [September, probably 1973.] Jo establishes that it's the 13th of September when she leaves the twentieth century. [Annoyingly, the Controller says that she's already told him the year during their *off-screen* conversation, thus stopping anybody conclusively dating the UNIT stories.]

At this point there's a summit conference in Britain, this time hosted by Sir Reginald Styles at Auderly (pronounced "Orderly"), a government-owned country house fifty miles north of London. Styles, the 'Chief Representative at the UN', is apparently the only diplomat capable of convincing the Chinese delegation to reconsider their withdrawal. The world is shown as being closer to the brink of war than ever. [This was feasibly the Time Lords' biggest single reason for exiling the Doctor to Earth in the 1970s. His presence here means the survival of a free human species, but more significantly, a less powerful Dalek empire.]

Observation satellites report troops massing along the Russian-Chinese frontier. In South America and southern Asia, fighting has already broken out in many areas; and UNIT is put on maximum alert [there are news cameras at Auderly when the Daleks arrive, so presumably the Brigadier has to slap another D-notice on the press]. The Brigadier seems to believe that China was just being stubborn in refusing to negotiate. [See also the twentieth-century history in "The Chase".]

In the alternative future, a series of wars in the late twentieth century led to a hundred years of destruction. Seven-eighths of humanity was wiped out before the Daleks took over. The same spot fifty miles from London has been developed, and high-rise blocks tower over scrubland. Dalek Earth seems to be one enormous slave colony, where humans are worked to death under the scrutiny of human and Ogron guards. There's a human government, with a human Controller running the district where Auderly House once stood. The Daleks' staff have shiny faces and a tendency to talk like zombies [though they don't have big clunky mind-control helmets like the Robomen in "The Dalek Invasion of Earth"]. Authentic food such as fruit seems to be at a pre-

How Does Time Work?

...continued from page 199

makes the Doctor less imitable in everyday life or extreme circumstances.

The series' rhetoric makes something else equally plain: the Daleks aren't good at making choices. They follow orders, remove variables and demand certainty. That being the case, what if it's the presence of the Daleks in the aberrant "Day of the Daleks" world that removes Free Will? There seems little reason in allowing the development of time-travel to jeopardise what seems like a tasty set-up for them - they claim their discovery is the means by which they've conquered Earth 'again'. This is probably intended to refer to their previous "success" in 2.2, "The Dalek Invasion of Earth" but as the "destroyed Auderly House" timeline would surely have averted the twenty-second century invasion from ever happening, the statement makes virtually no sense unless they're talking about something very different.

Let's say that at some stage in the aberrant timeline (in honour of the Nestlé chocolate bars, we'll call this Day Q), somewhere between their initial opportunistic raid circa 2072 and Day Z, a Dalek develops a time machine and goes to the day the Daleks first came to Earth. (Just to annoy them, and as a token reminder of Terry Nation-style daftness, we'll call this Day J.) Any intervention before Day J would jeopardise their future success, but *afterwards* it can only strengthen their grip. A century of wars evidently occur before the Dalek influx but there's little to actually link the failure of Styles' mission with all of these. We're *told* that his undertaking is make-or-break, and that if he fails, the world will end in one mighty conflagration. Therefore, some time between Day D and Day J, someone must take steps to prevent a nuclear war. The logical way to do this is to dispatch an army of Daleks to Day F or whenever from Day R (or sometime around then) - however, that's no soap, as it would eradicate the history that Anat and the Controller remember. It's possible, then, that humans or Ogrons were sent to handle this (this, at least, would explain the controls being made for finger-bearing life-forms). However, there's no reason why a large Dalek contingent couldn't have been sent from Day R to Day K, as reinforcements for both the Dalek taskforce and the timeline. (This removes another recent objection - Earth being invaded when Torchwood have all this lovely alien tech. Raids from a secure base in the future can handle anything.)

The Auderly House conference is, therefore, the earliest possible day at which the future Daleks can intervene safely in their own history. They can bolster up their hold on Earth's history after their first arrival, but any other "fixing" of time raises issues for them of choice and contingency. Making a known past more secure is entirely in keeping with their usual methodology. Anything that went wrong there would be likely to reset the time-line to a situation where the Daleks still hold sway over Earth, but with fewer of them around. A Dalek from any stage after Day Q could go to any stage after Day J, and could even visit Day F as an observer.

Similarly, a Dalek from Day Y could visit the 1960s or earlier - in theory - but would have self-destructed rather than do anything to alter history. (Unless that is, it self-destructs right next to a young Winston Churchill or Abraham Lincoln and wreck the timelines by mistake.) That self-destruction would probably have been an order. In theory a Dalek could disobey and cling to life, but it's highly unlikely. Even if it *did*, though, anything it did in the past would be part of that past (as when the Daleks zapped the crew of the *Mary Celeste* in 2.8, "The Chase"). A deliberate attempt to change establish history would *only* happen if the Dalek Supreme ordered it - and no Dalek Supreme would risk changing a past that has ended up with Daleks in control. One Dalek Emperor did, and look what happened to him. (See 4.9, "The Evil of the Daleks" and **Who Died And Made You Dalek Supreme?** under 11.3, "Death to the Daleks".) That incident is worth noting, because it's only after the Daleks think they've converted the Second Doctor to their cause that they have the nerve to do this, even if they mistakenly seem to think that he's just a human who's become special by travelling in time.

This settles the issue: the three adventures where Daleks have apparently mastered free travel in time are the ones where they show the *least* knowledge of the Time Lords and their activities. Had "The Chase" only had one mention of "The time-machine of the humans" and distinguished between the Doctor and his human companions even *once*, we could let it go, but they keep calling the TARDIS a *human* vessel and never show the slightest awareness of the Doctor's alien physiology (not even when making an android duplicate). It's therefore looking as if this story, "The Evil of the

continued on page 203...

mium, with nourishment conveyed through pills and tablets.

The Controller seems able to read computer readouts by touch. [A minor detail in itself, but in concert with the way his girls seem to operate the time-scanning equipment by waving their hands over the consoles, it could be taken as evidence of some kind of augmentation in their skin. We could even go all 90s retro and claim it's nanotechnology, but it's probably something more interesting than that. The human guards lack this, so it's possibly a visible and practical effect of opting to serve the Daleks, like the colour-coordinated Nehru suits and matching Chelsea boots.]

The Doctor suggests that the Daleks still operate from Skaro in this period, and the Controller seems to agree.

The Analysis

Where Does This Come From? The use of the hoariest time-travel cliché *not* involving butterflies or one's parents is sanctioned by Chris Marker's 1962 art-house flick *La Jetée*. In this, a survivor of an apocalyptic war travels back to the time of his childhood to try to fix things. It was remade, less ambitiously in some ways, as *Twelve Monkeys* (1995). And if we're in a mood to show off, we could mention Harlan Ellison's scripts for *The Outer Limits*, especially "Soldier".

The key to understanding "Day of the Daleks", however, isn't so much the paradox shenanigans, but rather the footage of the devastated future. In common with many films of the early 70s, the connection between excitingly big concrete buildings and weed-infested wastelands is pretty much a given, so it's presented to us but not really examined or questioned much. Inevitably we have to mention the film that kicked off the Hollywood dystopia genre of the 70s: *Planet of the Apes*, released in 1968. In this, it's revealed that humans started a war, allowing a nightmare future where gorillas are running a police-state and enslaved humans wear rags and chains. The apes themselves wear padded leather chest-pieces and in some cases quilted leather headgear - like the security guards in this story. They also ride horses around weed-infested wildernesses from which odd-looking concrete dwellings emerged. Anyway, the British, low-budget version is a 1960s high-rise in a patch of scrubland with buddleia thickets and cow-parsley. The railway tunnel has

been left derelict, and there's no agriculture.

Just think for a moment about what such a shot tells us. By retreating into ever-denser conurbations and not tending or using the land outside, we've lost some kind of balance. It's part of a whole set of binary oppositions we get in films, TV series and books of the time: urban / rural, future / past, synthetic / natural, and the *big* one underlying a lot of SF, mind / body.

Originally, the Daleks were the extremes of each of the first terms in these pairs. They could never leave their city, had mechanical appendages and unnatural foods, and were brains in tanks. The implication (which Terry Nation laboriously spelled out in the 1973 *Radio Times* special) was that the Daleks were the ultimate future of humanity. It's almost inevitable that they'll be found in a concrete tower-block supervising the use of humans and Ogrons as mindless brute labour. Nobody lives in small towns or villages any more, and nobody farms or gardens. Thus the lurking fear behind many Pertwee stories - of an over-populated Earth smothered in cities and people living 'like battery hens' ("Colony in Space") - haunts even a future where the planet is under-populated.

Look at the location work in the car-park. Nice clean steel, no graffiti, no vandalism, and yet it's presented to us as a world that's collapsed. Even in films directly sold to us as being about society in free-fall (*A Clockwork Orange* can stand in for dozens), we see everything working as it should, and everyone either meekly acquiescing to it or running riot in a very orderly manner. What we're encouraged to notice is exactly this lack of any rebellion, any damage or any disorder. The thing we're supposed to find scary is the constant surveillance, the way almost all resistance has been crushed from within.

How did things get this way? It wasn't a single war that did the deed, but a century of smaller ones that wiped out 7/8th of the population. Specifically, Styles is clearly suggested as sorting out a conflict between China and the Soviet Union. This flashpoint scared many in the West, simply because there was so little anyone here could do about it, what with neither side listening to NATO. This isn't the old-style Cold War paranoia about infiltration, pollution of our Vital Bodily Fluids or an atomic conflagration. (Indeed, the words "nuclear" and "atomic" are completely absent from this story - remarkable, as it's a Dalek

How Does Time Work?

...continued from page 201

Daleks" and "The Daleks' Master Plan" come from a different timeline to the one that includes Davros ("Genesis of the Daleks" onward), the Daleks' limited time-corridor techniques and their plan to assassinate the High Council ("Resurrection of the Daleks"). The isolation of the 'Human Factor' was a key item in their plans in "The Evil of the Daleks", so this matter of the inability to handle multiple possibilities must go deeper than we thought. (See also **What Is The Blinovitch Limitation Effect?** and **What Makes the TARDIS Work?** under 1.3, "The Edge of Destruction".)

Looked at in this light, then, the Doctor's presence at Auderly is only really critical as a messenger to tell Styles to flee, then tell Shura that Daleks were coming but that Styles had already left. As we know, Time Lords can convey information to people in causal loops without necessarily being trapped in those loops themselves ('wibbly wobbly', etcetera). *These* Daleks, on the other hand, seem to have caused the unravelling of their own continuum by over-reacting to the threat they perceive from the Doctor. It's Shura and the Controller who exercise choice, not the Time Lord at the heart of it all. We can all rest easy, then, because the version of time-travel and causality offered in **Can You Rewrite History, Even One Line?** (under "The Aztecs") seems to hold good, even in this story.

adventure.) Instead, we have a fear of a systemic breakdown, and fear that the network of alliances and pacts would make any small-scale war escalate, the way the apparently petty Serb Nationalist movement brought about World War I with a single bullet.

It was commonplace that almost all of the liberation movements of the early 1970s were bankrolled or armed by either the Soviets or the CIA, to the extent that the Arab-Israeli conflict was a proxy war in the same way that Mozambique and Bangladesh (and to a certain extent the politics of South Africa) were, only more overt and better-reported. Coups were arranged in Chile, Greece, Argentina and the Philippines. Nations whose support the West needed had their human rights abuses politely ignored. Some strategists thought that there would come a time when all these brushfire wars would overstretch the West. But on the plus side, whilst the US was keeping the Chinese busy in Vietnam, the Soviets were rather more inclined to not antagonise their great rival.

It seemed that Nixon and Brezhnev were the only world leaders on speaking terms. The SALT meetings (that's Strategic Arms Limitation Talks - they liked contrived acronyms in the 70s) led to a new word catching on: détente. A realisation that if nuclear war came, it wouldn't be a result of imperial designs on either side, but of World Leaders not being able to sort out their petty differences in time. Suddenly, there was Summit Conference-frenzy. The Chinese didn't go in for this as much as other countries, though.

Think back to "The Mind of Evil". China was the intransigent party there too. Nixon said as much in 1965, shortly before Chinese and US jets got entangled in a brawl over the South China Sea. While the Cultural Revolution was getting underway, removing anyone with any education from contact with anyone they might "contaminate", the US expanded cultural and technical contact with the People's Republic. President Johnson tried to make a deal with the Soviets, and Premier Kosygin popped over to New Jersey. The Xinhua news agency (the Maoist mouthpiece) denounced this as the other two ganging up on them - by now, China had hydrogen bombs too.

All candidates in the US Presidential election started saying nice things about China. The winner, Nixon, talked about negotiation whilst secretly authorising carpet-bombing of Cambodia, and Mao ordered that Nixon's inaugural address be translated and published in the *People's Daily*. Since the first version of this guidebook, it's emerged that Mao's top advisors were advocating "playing the American card" to make Moscow think twice. Students visiting the Russian capital from China had been fighting with soldiers, and Beijing pointedly did not rebuke them or disavow their activities. It got steadily worse. In 1969 alone, there were four hundred clashes between Chinese and Soviet troops. In mid-1971, the scenario of China and non-aligned countries starting small wars that ran on for a century was horribly plausible.

This is one of the clearest examples of *Doctor Who* being too topical for its own good. Between the writing of the script and transmission of the finished episodes, the whole situation had altered.

It might seem odd to some that it's a British diplomat trying to stop a war, but under the so-called "Nixon Doctrine", the US at times stepped back from being a "Global Policeman" and encouraged other nations to broker deals.

By 1970, the Pakistani leader Yahya Khan, Poland's US Ambassador Stoessel and Romania's leader Nicolae Ceaucescu (see 25.2, "The Happiness Patrol") had been asked to intercede between the US and China. And about a month after this story was shown, Nixon and Kissinger went to meet Zhou Enlai (or "Chou En Lai", as we spelled it then) and Mao Xedung.[57] Three months after visiting China, Nixon was in Moscow, getting Brezhnev to sign the first SALT charter. China and America sent their Ping-Pong teams to play in each other's capitals, a link-up between an Apollo capsule and a Soyuz took place and everyone was chums again until 1980.

So "Day of the Daleks" was written at the end of the phase of geopolitics where the three superpowers were at each other's throats, but we should mention that it was also at the start of a different phenomenon: urban guerrillas. This is the era of Black September and of hi-jackings of jumbo jets. News footage played up the initial oddness of people in combat fatigues running around a bombed-out city like it was a battlefield. (Note that here, the Ogrons catch a future-freedom-fighter who's by a railway bridge with a train going over it.) With hindsight, it's hard to look at Anna Barry (as Anat) without being reminded of Patty Hearst holding up a bank. The use of cheroots and moustaches is clearly a hint that someone in the production team is thinking of South America.

However, with the rebels having Biblical names and a female leader, the main reference seems to be the Israeli army, but we have to remember that the first prominent female guerrilla - the Palestinean Leila Khalid - was in the news a lot in the year before this was written. (Chris Boucher was obviously paying attention to this, as we'll see in 14.4, "The Face of Evil".) After the Six Day War in 1967, the world got used to the idea that Israel could be an aggressor. The PLO had a lot of public sympathy, so long as they didn't kill too many civilians: the cause seemed just, but not everyone in Britain was entirely sure about their methods. (The same had been true, until about six months earlier, of the IRA; when they started bombing the mainland, they lost practically all support. We're like that - blowing us to bits just makes us cross.)

Things That Don't Make Sense How do the Daleks operate the hand-held time-machines with those fiddly knobs?

Thanks to the TARDIS generating temporal duplicates of Our Heroes, Jo is dumbfounded to see counterparts of herself and the Doctor. More amazing still, we should think, is the way the future-Doctor opens big heavy doors without touching them. [Is this some secret application of the 'door handle' from 7.4, "Inferno"?] Understandably, the future-Doctor doesn't dispense helpful advice such as "avoid the temptation to jump onto any trikes you might see" or "save the charlady, save the world", but Jo is remarkably quiet in both manifestations. Perhaps she can't believe that she really looks like that.

A conference to save the entire world is being held at Auderly, and when it becomes clear that the house is a security risk, the Brigadier's men are desperate to keep things under control despite all the ghosts, ape-men and vanishing UNIT personnel. Nobody suggests just moving the conference to another building instead. Amidst all of this, Sir Reginald Styles becomes irked at the security-caused delays, as he has to be at the airport 'in an hour'. A long search of the grounds later, he's still around and, bafflingly, refuses the Brigadier's offer of an escort (surely the only way he could get there on time, by that point).

If we're questioning Styles' behaviour, though, it can't escape comment that he's a man who's in denial, he won't admit to seeing his "ghostly" attacker even when presented with hard evidence, and won't allow the conference to be moved out of the house even when he can hear gunfire outside. This is bordering on mental illness, yet the fate of the world has been entrusted to this guy. The Daleks are similarly confused in the finale, barging into the house without considering the idea that the people inside might have seen them coming and left. Granted, they don't know the Doctor has already gone there with a warning, but the fact that they're being shot at indicates they've lost any element of surprise.

The future-humans' assault on Auderly consists of Anat, Boaz (who can't shoot straight) and Shura, all of them thinking their combat clobber is useful camouflage when it stands out against concrete, brick, foliage and everything else they're next to. To compound this effect, Anat insists that they postpone their incursion until it's light. [Z-Cars fans will also be amused by the call-signs

'ZV1', 'ZV 3', ZV10' and so on.] And for all their training and weaponry, they can be overpowered by one man, literally single-handed.

On meeting the guerillas, the Doctor perplexingly describes their time-travel equipment as as 'a bit antiquated', even though it's from two hundred years in the future and has only just been developed. Nonetheless, the commandos persist in thinking that this velvet-clad technocrat is Sir Reginald. And despite all the time he's spent in the Cold War era, the Doctor finds the idea that Styles could come back from Peking with a radically changed personality as a bit far-fetched. [Taken with X3.2, "The Shakespeare Code", it's looking as if "The Mind of Evil" has been tippexed from his memory completely.]

Even allowing that the guerillas aren't temporal physicists, they *should* be able to realize - as they're taking building-wrecking explosives into the past - that they're in danger of creating the very disaster they're trying to prevent, long before the Doctor warns them about it. What, they honestly believe that Styles caused all of this trouble by blowing up Auderly, so they're going to solve the problem, if needs must, by blowing up Auderly? That's what Shura seems to think. And Shura's bomb is the same size as the one Boaz uses to mangle a Dalek in a car-park without causing any structural damage, but *this* time around, it blows up a whole stately home and dispatches two Daleks to boot. (And um... what happened to the third?)

Upon examining the time-travel device taken from the first guerrilla, the Doctor presses a button and seems surprised when it activates. Then, upon being told by the Brigadier that the captured rebel "vanished", the Doctor never stops to notice that there's a connection with him triggering the device at the exact same moment. Later, while searching Auderly for the missing Doctor, Yates and Benton don't bother looking in the cellar (where he's being held at gunpoint) even though they know he's been raiding it for bottles of wine since he moved in. And upon being told that the "last hope for humankind" conference is going to go ahead after all, Yates asks 'oh, when's it fixed for?', like it was a charity cricket match. He's also able, somehow, to hear the Brigadier being told 'tell it to the Marines' from the Brig's telephone handset.

Fast forward to the future, where the Daleks have established one of the most ineptly-run police-states ever. For a start, they interrogate the

Doctor in a room with a very showbiz door that takes ages to raise and lower, and makes a bibbling sound as it does so. Worse, it's a mesh through which one can easily hear things such as 'I'm trying to help you' and 'ZV10 to Eagle, do you connect?', yet the the interrogator insists on making such remarks and showing his true colours. And somehow, in the course of overpowering him, the Ogrons get through the door without making any of those inconvenient bibbles.

The Doctor explains his plan of escape to Jo in a prison cell that's fitted with surveillance cameras, which relay the image straight to the Dalek control room... where the Daleks have got it on in the background with the sound off and are talking amongst themselves, making them look like gossipy old housewives. [Even the one who looks over his shoulder in X3.5, "Evolution of the Daleks" was more sensible than this.] At this point they're actually discussing the question of whether the Doctor really is the Doctor, so you'd think they'd be interested in what he's got to say for himself.

Moreover, the Daleks have gone to all the trouble of enslaving humanity and keeping them on pills, yet they've also got a supply of fresh fruit, evidently on the off-chance that some time-travellers will need to be lulled into thinking "The future's bright: the future's got oranges". For their part, the rebels have a packet of cigars that's somehow stayed fresh for more than two centuries, and they're blithely seen smoking them as if they've got an endless supply.

At one point the apparently confused Brigadier says, 'Even the Doctor can't just vanish into thin air.' [That settles it: he's knocking back Torchwood's retcon pills as if they were M&Ms.] The Controller tells the Doctor that, 'Nobody who did not live through those terrible years can understand' - even though he himself didn't either, what with his being the grandson of someone who did. And is the stuff that makes the future-humans' faces all shiny a sort of moisturising cream that comes in sachets they stick on the cover of *Evil Future Vogue*?

In episode two, how dim are the UNIT patrols (sans their two disintegrated members, admittedly) to not see five Ogrons walking, plain as day, across the Auderly House lawn? In episode three, the rebels in the tunnel shout, 'Run, Doctor!', and his response is to dash *toward* the oncoming trouble rather than away from it. Why do the Ogrons announce their presence with all that whistling anyway? And by episode four, the Doctor expects he can return to the modern-day via the tunnel because it 'hasn't been compromised', even though a Dalek was plainly seen there there at the end of episode two.

The Ogrons' guns aren't Dalek-issue, as the Doctor recognises them as being Earth-made twenty-second century technology, i.e. part of known history. But if they hail a twenty-second century in which global war sent humanity into a new dark age, then why do they end up being produced on Dalek Earth? On the other hand, if they're merely two centuries more advanced than anything on Earth, this implies that the Daleks have a head start on us in a strictly linear series of discoveries, pre-ordained, as it were. This being the case, why did no-one in "orthodox" history develop time travel in 2172? Moreover, the Daleks invade after a hundred years of wars, but the Cybermen and all the other races who come sniffing around Earth looking for minerals (Urbankans, Slitheen, Sycorax, Ice Warriors...) somehow didn't have the interest?

Right, here's a point that's probably lost on most viewers these days: the BBC report on the Peace Conference is done on film. In the early 70s, most BBC news reports were made on the same 16mm stock as *Doctor Who*. (Although it wasn't as well-lit, hence the washed-out colours that've led a younger generation to misconstrue the whole decade as a sea of brown and yellow.) Such clips were introduced in bulletins as being filmed earlier in the day or, if overseas, a few days ago. As late as 1978, the majority of major stories were reported a day or more after the event, and were told via a live report by phone, with a caption-slide of a map and the reporter's face. Film, after all, had to be taken by dispatch-motorcycle to London and developed and edited. (This is why the IRA timed their bombs to go off around 3.00pm, to get it as breaking news on the 5.50 bulletin.) In short, to the trained eye, any attempt to build up tension here is redundant because we're watching what looks like the Nine O'clock News' treatment of a big diplomatic story as proof that the world didn't end. Had the Auderly footage been on VT, we might have accepted it as "live" coverage and the uncertainty they were going for would have worked. But on film, it's just not feasible.

If Styles and his chums arrive at RAF Manston at 1800 hours (as the Brigadier says) and the date is the 13th of September (as Jo keeps telling us),

why is it still light when they get to Auderly? And observe how a guard outside the Peace Conference is the same one the Doctor beats up in "The Sea Devils". Yet in that story, he acts as if the Doctor is just someone who's causing trouble.

And finally, when Benton reports two men missing, Yates takes seriously his suggestion that they've nipped into Auderly House for a cuppa and a thaw-out, instead of patrolling the site of the most important summit in history after terrorists with teleports have been reported. UNIT has long since stopped recruiting the best of the best, haven't they?

Critique We all know (and **The Lore** will confirm it if you didn't) that Jon Pertwee really hated acting in stories that featured the Daleks. But if his disdain explains why he's a much more compelling a performer in this story, then perhaps the programme-makers should have unleashed the pepperpots in a lot sooner. Well, we say *perhaps*... if the Daleks alone were capable for ratcheting Pertwee up to a higher level, we'd then have to account for why the star seems on autopilot in the next two Dalek stories.

A closer examination shows that it's the scenes in episode three - where the Doctor is on the receiving end of this police-state's form of justice - where Pertwee really crackles, just as he did under similar circumstances in "Inferno". This Doctor is so rarely on the back foot, seeing him talk his way out of an interrogation (especially one that doesn't use *Top of the Pops* electronic effects) and witnessing the routine Pertwee gurning as a means of suggesting pain is genuinely unsettling. From that point, Pertwee is then at the top of his game (save for the pre-filmed material) until the very end - castigating the *collaborateurs* and guerrillas equally, and making the Daleks' fear of the Doctor entirely plausible. That we're dealing with the same actor who handled the earlier frivolity with ghosts and gorgonzola shows just how completely Pertwee has remade the series in his own image.

The thing is, whatever the overall merits of this adventure, all that's most annoying about Pertwee adventures is to be found here, in between the moments when the series is getting its act together. Although their collective experience with *Doctor Who* dates back to Season Five, Barry Letts and Terrance Dicks have treated the advent of colour as Year Zero - as such, they're exuberantly trying out all the most basic science-fiction concepts as though for the first time. And here, they've given one of the classics to a writer who left academe for ITC and soaps, and he uses it as the springboard for a relatively mature drama about making choices. The result, arguably, is much more successful than it deserves to be.

Yes, there's some bread-and-butter UNIT stuff (including the Doctor insulting the limited military mind as though he's contractually obliged so to do), and yes, there's some lamentable padding about Yates and Benton snacking on duty. But once we're past all of that, the story really comes alive. Paradoxically, it's the lengthy discussions that are the most exciting, with the sporadic chases and gunfights dragging despite director Paul Bernard's obvious wish to push a few boundaries. Still, he gets full marks for the near-misses when moving two separate cameras in a complicated CSO set-up, for deliniating an entire world in two episodes and three sets and for - best of all - most of his casting decisions.

But in the grand scheme of things, we're at a curious point in "the UNIT era". Most of the material in UNIT HQ is shockingly under-rehearsed, the Doctor's Venusian Karate has now degenerated to Pertwee shouting "Hai!" and some slapstick falls (one has him opening a door and knocking someone over, then beating that guy up without putting down his glass of claret - "neat" to some viewers, abjectly silly to others). As for the need for UNIT to engage a classic monster... well, it's tricky. What with the Daleks being shoved into a story where they aren't really needed, it results in something of an anti-climax. That said, sketching in a tyrannical evil future is a lot quicker when the tyrants have a resume. They're a known threat, big enough to justify a time-paradox and the ability to exploit it. Like it or not, audiences buy major-league abilities such as time-travel more easily when high-concept villains are involved, perfunctory though their inclusion might be.

Undoubtedly, as a pitch to floating viewers while ITV companies are trying to re-launch *UFO*, the idea of "Daleks from the future try to change their history by coming here" was a hit. It also allowed the *Doctor Who's* previously entrenched time-travel themes to co-exist with the UNIT / Yeti-in-a-tutu formula. In absolute terms it works well enough, with the caveat that - as we'll see in the rest of this book (not to mention at points during John Nathan-Turner's producership and the Wales series) - making a story to justify an attention-seeking gimmick isn't *always* the way to go.

The Facts

Written by Louis Marks. Directed by Paul Bernard. Ratings: 9.8 million, 10,4 million, 9.1 million, 9.1 million. An hour-long version was shown instead of a cancelled *Nationwide* on 3rd of September, 1973, and got a healthy 7.4 million; this edit was a lot more exciting, whilst lacking hardly any of the plot-beats or atmosphere.

Supporting Cast Aubrey Woods (Controller), Anna Barry (Anat), Jimmy Winston (Shura), Scott Fredericks (Boaz), Wilfred Carter (Sir Reginald Styles), Jean McFarlane (Miss Paget), Alex MacIntosh (Television Reporter), Oliver Gilbert, Peter Messaline (Dalek Voices).

Working Titles "Years of Doom", "The Ghost Hunters".

Cliffhangers After getting a fix on the twentieth century, the Daleks in the control room insist that all their enemies will be exterminated (as if anyone present didn't already know that); the Doctor pursues the time-travelling guerrillas into the tunnels near Auderly House, and is startled to see a Dalek materialise in the shadows; the Doctor loses consciousness on the Dalek mind analysis machine, while the Daleks once again chant 'exterminate' at him.

What Was in the Charts? "Stay With Me", The Faces; "Theme From 'Shaft' ", Isaac Hayes; "Ernie (The Fastest Milkman in the West)", Benny Hill; "Coz I Luv You", Slade.

The Lore

• In the years since Louis Marks had penned "Planet of Giants" (2.1), he'd written for commercial television and the BBC's *Doomwatch* (specifically, an episode called "The Islanders"). He'd been story editor for *No Hiding Place* and had also created ATV London's soap *Market in Honey Lane*. (Later called just *Honey Lane*. ATV had *Crossroads* for their Midlands arm and needed a Cockney soap - especially if they wanted to bag London in the forthcoming ITV franchise auction - so Marks provided them with an East End market series, which the BBC invented all over again in 1985.)

Now, it happened that one of the key writers on this show was a promising youngster called Robert Holmes, and the producer was a former

BBC set designer, Paul Bernard. Once Holmes had scored himself a regular place in the *Doctor Who* writing team, Terrance Dicks trusted his recommendations and this could account for why both Marks and Bernard worked on this story. Or, to be honest, it could all be a huge coincidence.

• Marks first submitted a straightforward time-paradox story (if such a thing can exist) with no Dalek complications. Such an angle hadn't really been tried since "The Space Museum" (2.7), but here the narrative hook made it look like a ghost story.

Marks was interested in the idea of time-travelling terrorists - a topical idea (as we've seen) of the kind he'd pitched to both *Doomwatch* and the earlier version of *Doctor Who*. In the first draft they were just that: a kind of futuristic Black September movement (see **Where Does This Come From?**) and on the run from tyrannical humans who employed hybrid dog-men as a police-force.[58] The revised version had the Doctor using their time-travel equipment to go forward to their time. (The original story seems remarkably similar to *Conquest of the Planet of the Apes* - a time-paradox adventure about an anthropoid-run future created after a nuclear war, and caused by people trying to prevent it. However, we should stress that *Conquest* didn't see release until June 1972, meaning Marks got there first. In fact, the version *with* Daleks ends up a lot more like *The Terminator*, a fact not lost on Ben Aaronovitch - see 25.1, "Remembrance of the Daleks", although *Terminator* itself was hardly original.[59])

• However, between talking about this story in late 1970 and the formal commissioning, two complications arose. One was that Marks formally joined the BBC, and the other was that Letts and Dicks had been in talks with Terry Nation. It happened that Huw Wheldon had been pestering Letts for more Daleks. As we saw in Volume I, Wheldon (whose name wound up being consistently mis-spelled), demanded Daleks at every possible juncture, and everything else the series could deliver was just a means of filling in time. Wheldon was now Managing Director of Television (a post they devised after the whole Donald Baverstock crisis, and one that looked suspiciously like a sinecure to keep Wheldon in the Corporation). He wanted Daleks, so we got Daleks. True, some of the public had been asking for them as well, but they could be placated by saying that it was a matter of waiting until a good

enough story came along. In any case, the official target audience were possibly too young to remember them. Producers generally took these lines when trying to keep Wheldon off their backs, but with Letts harping on about the older age-profile of viewers these days, the excuses were wearing a little thin. Anyway, they thought they'd found a good enough story...

• Robert Sloman had liked working on "The Daemons" and devised an idea about time-slippages caused by malign forces... and the specific malign forces he had in mind were Daleks. After the bid to launch the pepperpots in the US, possibly with their own series and Sara Kingdom as the lead (see "The Daleks' Master-Plan"), Nation was back in the UK working on Lew Grade's ultimate example of devising a pitch without a show to go with it: *The Persuaders!*. Although that show's long-term future was in the balance, as either (depending on who you ask) Tony Curtis or Roger Moore was causing trouble on set, Nation was story-editing like nobody's business and didn't look like he'd be free to write scripts in the near future. He *did* like the idea of pitting the Daleks against the new Doctor in colour, though. So as long as he got script-approval (he vetoed Dalek-Cyberman battles), a cash sum and on-screen credit for creating the Daleks, he was up for it.

• The public were told that maybe, if enough people asked for it, the Doctor and UNIT might one day run into the Daleks. However, Letts then had a brainwave. As with the advent of the Master, what the new season needed was an attention-grabbing gimmick to grab headlines and audience-share. The first story in 1972 should have Daleks. However, they decided that just after giving Sloman the nod for his Dalek script to *end* the season, in spring 1971, so the choice was either to pump him full of black coffee and lock him in an attic until he produced six episodes in a weekend or remove the Daleks from Sloman's effort and ask him for a time-slippage story with some other supervillain (like, ooh, the Master, perhaps?). That freed the Daleks up for addition to that year's *other* time-anomaly script, which was on the blocks for filming in September. (We'll pick up that bit of the story under 9.5, "The Time Monster".)

Dicks kept an eye on the new Marks script throughout late summer, whilst Letts was on leave. Nation received £25 per episode and the credit "Daleks Originated by Terry Nation". The strange choice of verb - "originated" rather than "created" - may well have been intended to gloss over the dispute between the BBC and Dalek designer Ray Cusick (see **Who *Really* Created the Daleks?** under 1.2, "The Daleks" for more on this), or possibly just to suggest that Nation didn't physically build the costumes. Their late addition to the plot explains why the Daleks appear, on average, for only two-and-a-half minutes in each episode.

• Letts' first task, upon his return in August, was to get freelance director Paul Bernard to explain carefully what the ITV companies were doing with CSO / Chromakey. Bernard had begun as a set-designer with Granada, ABC and BBC, and was one of the new intake of trainee directors that the start of BBC2 had required (see Volume I). He was also a gifted painter, and at times saw TV directing as a means to fund his real work (which eventually he did full-time). He had thence gone to ATV and risen to producer, but had also directed occasional episodes of soaps. (It was in this capacity that Letts, who had written a few of these in his time, first encountered Bernard.) He went freelance in 1971 and his first job was this story (so his earlier frustration at BBC working methods weren't as great as all that).

• As you'll have doubtless noticed, Letts was a CSO enthusiast, but even he was frustrated by the fringing sometimes caused by the strong blue. Thames, the world's pioneers at getting it to work in 625-line PAL, were also having trouble. The problem, apparently, was that the cameras used three sets of filters (red, blue and green) and the use of a blue so close to the filter colour was making the other two primary colours over-compensate. (That's putting it *very* crudely and anthropomorphically, but for pity's sake, this isn't a textbook.)

Yellow, which requires blue and green to be roughly equally mixed, caused less instability. ATV had found a shade of yellow that worked well and was readily available as a commercial house-paint, and Bernard had occasion to use it when directing *This Is.... Tom Jones.* (If you *saw* some of the costumes worn in that show, especially the knitted stripy body-stocking worn by Sammy Davis Jr, you'll understand why not removing certain colours from the wardrobe department's palate was a vital priority.) It hadn't been lost on Letts that they'd probably need to CSO a large blue object at some stage.

• Bull's Bridge in Middlesex had been suggested as the best location for the tunnel. It was next to Osterley Park House, a picturesque Robert Adam-built red-brick manor house near Brentford (used for the cover of Wings' *Band on the Run,* not that you can tell). Ultimately, though, they went to Dropmore Park to film the Auderly locations anyway. That's in Buckinghamshire, the other side of Slough. The trike chase and the multi-storey car-park scenes were filmed at Brentford, so the change to Dropmore must have been very last-minute.

• To explain all the confusion about the name of the house where this story takes place: the original script named Styles' pad as "Austerley" House (pronounced slightly differently if you're English, but not too far off "Osterley"). Then it became "Alderley" (as the Brigadier calls it in one scene, although in another he thinks it's "Alderney", which is in the Channel Islands). The director called it "Austerly", then "Auderley" and finally - in the on-screen caption - we see 'Alex MacIntosh Auderly House'. The novelisation (with maps and everything) reverts to 'Austerly' and reinstates the final scene, written by Dicks, which Bernard cut.

• Bernard found three and a half serviceable Dalek shells (a base served as the debris from the 'Dalekanium' attack in episode three) and had one painted gold. In studio scenes, observe the lengths they go to - such as shining green light on the Dalek to alter the tint - to avoid it being in the same shot as any CSO panels with the same colour. The pupils were added to the eye-bobbles as part of an overall refit, including new mesh, castors and sidelights. The presence of one Gold Dalek actually made the process of turning three shells into a strike-force much harder. Making them trundle smoothly over wasteground was also difficult.

• John Friedlander made the Ogron masks, based on an idea he'd had for a half-mask. (Bernard, it seems, came up with the idea of their being ape-like.)

• Courtney, Franklin and Levene were now booked on a story-by-story basis, as the current plan entailed three off-world adventures ("Carnival of Monsters" was made as part of this year's output) and a non-UNIT story with the Master this year. Courtney had filled his summer with an uncredited role in an Agatha Christie adaptation, *Endless Night.*

• Former BBC reporter Alex MacIntosh appeared as the reporter at Auderly. It's often suggested that the BBC was wary of using present newsreaders in fiction (hence former newreaders

Corbett Woodall and Michael Aspel turning up in *The Goodies* and *Doomwatch* - alas, not the only thing these series have in common) but the *doyen* of the trade, Richard Baker, had turned up shockingly in *Monty Python*. Also, Kenneth Kendall was in both 3.10, "The War Machines" and *Adam Adamant Lives!* (He also plays a reporter in the kitsch classic *They Came From Beyond Space*, mentioned under "Colony in Space".)

The key difference is that "newsreaders" (as the BBC called them) or "newscasters" (as ITN, the commercial news service, termed them) or "anchormen" (a subtle difference exists between the American and BBC meaning of the term, but you get the gist) were actors-turned-journalists and therefore had Equity membership. On the other hand, news reporters had to leave the NUJ before *playing* reporters - it's obvious, hopefully, why having trusted reporters appearing in advertisements was strictly regulated. Just to be on the safe side, the caption with MacIntosh was written in the same typeface as the end-credits, which is noticeably different to that used in BBC news bulletins of the time. Regular monster-performer Pat Gorman appears with a face for a change, playing MacIntosh's boom-mike operator.

• A gadget called a Chromotrope was used for the time-travel scenes. Although the patterns are very like the images made with two striated glass discs (as manufactured for Victorian magic-lantern shows), this was a bespoke device built for discotheques.

• Talking, as we were, of Sammy Davis Jr, his hit song "The Candy Man" was from the 1971 film *Willy Wonka and the Chocolate Factory* - and was sung in the film by Aubrey Woods, who plays the Controller in this story. Woods later appeared with even *more* odd face-paint as Krantor in the *Blake's 7* episode "Gambit" (which itself has a Wonka connection... no, you work it out) by Robert Holmes. The rebel Boaz was played by Scott Fredericks, who we'll see again as the treacherous Stael in "Image of the Fendahl" (15.3). And credited as 'Gypsie Kemp' is the actress later known to fans of the best-ever Australian soap *Sons and Daughters* as Sarah Kemp: she played the grandiose lush Charlie.[60]

Jimmy Winston, here playing Shura, was the original keyboard player for the Small Faces - he was dropped, at least in part, because he was taller than the others. By this stage he was telling everyone that he'd always intended to be an actor (his

late 60s band Winston's Fumb never set the world alight, but they weren't at all bad), and he'd just secured a big part in the British cast of *Hair*. So seeing his former bandmates, now trading as The Faces, on *Top of the Pops* every week ("Maggie May" was at number one throughout the studio recording in October 1971) wouldn't have been *quite* so galling. (See **What Was In The Charts?**.)

• The episodes were recorded in the now-routine two-per-fortnight pattern, on Mondays and Tuesdays. The set-designer (David Myerscough-Jones) had miscalculated the size of the felt CSO cyclorama, causing the floor to need repainting. This and a VTR mishap made the first episode's recording over-run. (You can see how stressful it was in the Brigadier's first scene, where the Minister on the phone - Peter Messaline again - replies to stuff Courtney hasn't said yet, and Courtney is uncharacteristically unsure of his lines.) Time-wise, however, the first episode *under-ran*, so the "feeding Sergeant Benton" scene and the 'Mike Yates certainly does' business were added.

• The Doctor's encounter with Napoleon - first mentioned here - formed the basis of the test-reading for actors auditioning to be the Eighth Doctor in 1995. (Indeed, the scene - specifically written to show off all the important points of the Doctor's character - was filmed several times over. See 27.0 for a list of some of those who tried it.)

• Unlike any other Dalek story, this one had the voices done in the studio without the ring-modulator. Peter Messaline and Oliver Gilbert did the voices, although they were never asked back.

• Bernard had to order the Ogron actors to move slowly while running after the Honda trike, in order to give the Doctor and Jo a chance to escape for a bit. (Admittedly, he wanted to make it more like the moon-buggy chase in *Diamonds Are Forever* - see the illustrations in the Japanese edition for some idea of what it could have been like.) Speaking of leisurely exits, Pertwee and Manning were nonplussed by the comparatively slow "escape" from the doomed mansion. This, plus the resolutely unthreatening Daleks, seems to have affected their opinion of this story.

• By now even Letts had noticed that the saturation use of electronic music was a mixed blessing. The amount of music per episode in this story is under a fifth of that used in the previous year, although this was often re-used as it had been in the 1960s. Simpson also used conventional percussion, albeit processed and "flanged", often relying on Tristram Fry. We'll have two stories this year with other composers, but in Simpson's three stories this formula of processed beats and primitive synth is the standard.

• So with the Daleks coming back, the obvious thing to do is tell the world about it... but Letts didn't *quite* play it that way. Although the BBC had sanctioned their use (with Nation's veto), they were rarely seen save for archive clips (usually accompanying "Is *Doctor Who* Still Scary?" pieces). By now former companion Peter Purves was presenting *Blue Peter*, and a viewer's query about whether it really was Steven the astronaut showing us how to make cakes and train dogs[61] allowed a showing of that clip from "The Traitors" ("The Daleks' Master Plan" episode four - that's why it still exists) and a chat with three Daleks, plus a hint that if enough people asked they *might* return. This was 25th October 1971 (the same edition where they celebrated Picasso's 90th birthday by having one of his paintings in the studio - along with two scary-looking security-guards). One of the Dalek operators for this was Cy Town, who later got to operate Daleks in *Doctor Who*.

• Shortly after this, the production team briefed the *Radio Times* and opted to launch the new season with a Christmas special: an edited one-episode compilation of "The Daemons". Only *then* did they announce the Daleks' return, at an event run by *The Observer*, an upmarket Sunday newspaper (see "The Sea Devils" for more on this event). Both this compilation and episode two of "Day of the Daleks" topped ten million viewers (the last time this had happened since that self-same Hartnell story, back in 1965), so *something* was working.

• Considering the ratings boost from "The Daemons" omnibus edition, it seems strange to note that "Day of the Daleks" was being broadcast as the BBC showed something they'd commissioned a potential replacement for *Doctor Who*. This was *The Incredible Robert Baldick* from Terry Nation, his first BBC gig since "The Daleks' Master Plan". Despite starring Robert Hardy as the eponymous Victorian scientist / adventurer, this project bombed. (It looked, it must be said, as the work of someone who thought *The Wild Wild West* was an altogether serious production, and wrote a parody of it:) Nation, between the pilot's recording and transmission in October 1972, re-approached the *Doctor Who* production team (see 10.4, "Planet of the Daleks").

• In time, the shot of Auderly House exploding was seen by more British viewers than any other part of *Doctor Who*. It was used as the punch-line for a sight-gag in the pre-credit sequence of the 1977 *Morecambe and Wise* Christmas Show - one of the ten most watched programmes of the decade (and therefore of any British TV ever) and the only one anyone now remembers watching.

9.2: "The Curse of Peladon"

(Serial MMM, Four Episodes, 29th January - 19th February 1972.)

Which One is This? It's *The Hound of the Baskervilles,* Glam Rock style, with mythical beasts, torch-lit dungeons, mad priests in Ming the Merciless drag, a big green penis for a comedy monster, storm-lashed Bavarian castles and - omigod! The Ice Warriors are back!

Firsts and Lasts The Ice Warriors return to the series after a three year break (see 6.5, "The Seeds of Death") to make their colour debut (big shock - they're green). Some of the characters seen here - along with most of the props and sets - turn up again in the story's sequel, "The Monster of Peladon" (11.4). For the first time, this Doctor wears a waistcoat and Jo covers herself up a bit.

Pay particular attention to the throne, actually an Art Nouveau chair that will crop up on most subsequent pseudo-mediaeval planets in the 1970s. The eagle lectern in the TARDIS console room will also become a regular fixture, in "The Time Monster" (9.5), "Image of the Fendahl" (15.3), etc.

First of about sixty thousand uses of the word 'interstitial' this year, but it's the last time they try to get away with using a wall-sized blow-up photo of fruit-packaging as a flat for the TARDIS interior wall. (They'd been doing this since day one; see 1.1, "An Unearthly Child".) Pertwee finally gets out of those black capes and puts on something more like a dog-blanket or a Volkswagen seat-cover.

Matt Irvine gets a temporary attachment to the special-effects team that will last for decades - and starts this impressive tenure by making a tiny TARDIS with a flashing bulb.

Four Things to Notice
About "The Curse of Peladon"...

1. "The Curse of Peladon" comes equipped with five, yes *five* different kinds of monster, a supporting cast dressed in *Flash Gordon* fantasy-wear, an extended fight scene in an arena and a great big castle on a lightning-wracked mountainside. It is, therefore, the *perfect* story for eight-year-old boys...

... were it not, that is, for the delegate from Alpha Centauri. With his great big domed head and single enormous eye, "he" is one of the great "rude-looking" *Doctor Who* monsters. (Anyone wishing to consider other candidates should examine the Eye of Axos, 8.3, "The Claws of Axos"; Erato the Tythonian, 17.3, "The Creature From the Pit"; the alarmingly testicular thing the Ogrons worship, 10.3, "Frontier in Space"; and the Vervoids, 23.3, "Terror of the Vervoids".) Still, the moment when the Ice Warriors menace Alpha Centauri into voting their way, and he sheepishly raises all his right pseudopods in favour of the motion, is quite lovely.

2. Set against this "epic" backdrop there's even an attempt at a love-story between King Peladon and Jo Grant, leading to some of the most unlikely romantic dialogue in television history: 'My mother was an Earthwoman, so you see, there *is* a bond between us' is always a favourite, as are 'I was brought up by wise old men, I hardly ever see anyone young or beautiful' and 'One minute you're condemning the Doctor to death, the next minute you're proposing to me'. Anakin and Padme just aren't in this league.

3. This and "The Monster of Peladon" were the only Pertwee yarns with no location filming. However, two "exteriors" were mounted on film at Ealing: one for rock-climbing and the other for the gladiator scene that no-one can watch without humming the music from those scenes in *Star Trek*. (You know the tune we mean - it's the National Anthem of Zoidberg's home planet in *Futurama*.) This last may or may not be intended to be "outdoors", as it has a roof and the spectators are all shot on videotape. (The novelisation depicts the arena as an enormous outdoor stadium, but also has the Doctor promising to 'float like a butterfly, sting like a bee'.)

4. The Doctor seems to be absolutely riveted by the dials on the TARDIS console. He simply can't take his eyes off them. We'll tell you why in **The Lore**.

The Continuity

The Doctor

• *Ethics*. He's prejudiced when it comes to Ice Warriors, believing them to be 'savage and warlike' before he finds out the truth; it's one of the few occasions when he's seen to be utterly wrong. He seems to enjoy the process of accidentally getting mixed up in interplanetary politics. Even without Venusian martial arts, he's skilled enough in armed combat to hold his own against the King's Champion.

• *Inventory*. The Doctor carries a spinning mirror which creates a strobing light and a soothing noise capable of calming a large, angry animal [see **The Lore**]. The same device almost hypnotises Jo, and even causes some more impromptu gurning from the Doctor himself [so it's not *just* a spinning mirror]. The Doctor calls this 'a kind of technical hypnosis', but also refers to a 'telepathic understanding' [between him and animals?].

• *Background*. He attended the coronation of either Queen Elizabeth I or Queen Victoria, but isn't sure which. Either way, he doesn't see any reason that he shouldn't go back and attend it again. [See, **What Is the Blinovitch Limitation Effect?** under 20.3, "Mawdryn Undead" and also - as if you didn't know - X2.2, "Tooth and Claw" and X3.2, "The Shakespeare Code" respectively for more on Victoria and Elizabeth I.]

He knows all about the people of Alpha Centauri, or something about their biology at least. [12.1, "Robot", hints at a prior visit.]

The Supporting Cast

• *Jo Grant*. She was planning on a night out on the town with Mike Yates before the Doctor dragged her off in the TARDIS. [Does this hideous relationship ever get anywhere...?] By now she's self-confident enough to bluff a throne-room full of alien monsters into thinking she's a princess, without even flinching. There *is* an obvious attraction between her and King Peladon, and just for a moment it looks as if she's genuinely tempted to stay [c.f. 10.4, "Planet of the Daleks"]. She seems shaken by the death of Hepesh, the high priest, and beforehand takes his side in an argument with Alpha Centauri.

The TARDIS It's still apparently under the Time Lords' influence, although the Doctor once again believes he's in control and says that this is the first

Aren't Alien Names Inevitably a Bit Silly?

It happens that unfamiliar names must be judged according to how much they *sound* like actual names, and how far good reason exists why nobody has called their child this in our culture. Names have fashions like anything else. Before 1800, nobody would have called a boy "Oscar" - it was the name of Ossian's brother in a fake Celtic epic that became wildly fashionable when everyone believed it was authentic. Nobody after 1940 would have risked it either, but now it's coming back. "Elsie" has become a lot more frequent than was previously the case. Nobody outside Wales was ever called "Dylan" before 1965, and the once far-more common "Blodwyn" is still a joke even there.

So that's our first rule: when we dub a name "silly", bear in mind that it's culturally-specific. In America, the name "Sharon" (originally Hebrew for "desert" and the name of a fruit that's somewhere between a plum and a mango) is a vaguely exotic name. But in Britain it carries connotations of housewives in Essex... Jackie Tyler is an archetypal "Sharon". Male equivalents would be "Darren" and "Kevin". (Imagine, then, how much we would have *loved* Sharon Stone and Kevin Costner to co-star in a film.)

A second rule would be: nobody would call any child something that couldn't be yelled. A handy rule for anyone seeking to think of a name for a child is to try saying "Is ____ coming out to play?" or "____! Put that down at once!". This alerts us to the possibility that some cultures physically cannot make the sounds of vowel / consonant mixes. The Japanese "L" / "R" problem is a cliché, but people from the Indian sub-continent have trouble with "W"[65] and Western Europeans have immense trouble learning some of the Greek consonants.

Unfortunately, the one time *Doctor Who* tried to capitalise on fact was Roslyn de Winter's decision that the Menoptra have long curled-up tongues for sucking nectar from plants, and would therefore over-enunciate vowels (2.5, "The Web Planet"). This might have worked if the author, Bill Strutton, had been told and the script rewritten with this in mind. Nevertheless, most of the character-names in this story sound as though they were handed down across generations and could (conceivably, but good luck if you want to lumber your own offspring with them) be real names. There's more to this than meets the eye, as we'll see.

But when it comes to alien name invention, there are three basic approaches, which we'll designate according to the writers who had the best signal-to-noise ratio. They are:

• **The George Lucas method:** listening to speech (especially jargon and out-of-the-way phrases) and writing down the ones that sound like characters or planets.

• **The J.R.R. Tolkien method:** learning several extinct languages and studying philology for decades.

• **The Ursula le Guin method:** steeping yourself with a lot of other cultures' systems of naming, then just staring into the air listening for anything that pops out of your head.

Doctor Who writers have tried various hybrids of these. The le Guin method presented an unusual snag, though - unlike fantasies written by a single author, *Who* writers had to cope with their predecessors coming up with similar names in earlier stories of which they were unaware. Steve Gallagher had leonine time-sensitives called "Tharls", but Terry Nation had got there first (18.5, "Warriors' Gate"; 1.2, "The Daleks"). In that case, the solution was to alter the spelling and shift the emphasis. Nation himself had this problem when he wanted to call a character something that, had it appeared in a *New Adventures* book, would doubtless have been spelled "P'taal". It looked daft when written as "Petal" (not that this appears to have stopped Nation), but as the similar-looking / sounding "Patel" appeared in the previous story, the character became "Latep" (10.4, "Planet of the Daleks").

This brings us to a subsidiary system: writer Wilson Tucker used to include the names of friends as characters in his novels, and "Tuckerisms" added to the shifted spelling method result in many of the silliest *New Adventures* names. You can make your own list, but be aware that Isaac Asimov did it a lot earlier and got away with it.

The George Lucas method has one obvious advantage: you can imagine people actually saying these things because, somewhere, they do. Instead of haphazard conglomerations of vowels and consonants, there's a history even with something like "R2-D2" and "Padme Amidala". The downside, however, is that if you know any comparative

continued on page 215...

test-flight since he got it 'working again'. [It seems the TARDIS can now travel around as much as it wants, but only to places where the Time Lords think the Doctor's presence might be useful. So if the Doctor kept making trips instead of leaving the TARDIS in pieces at UNIT HQ, would he keep having Time-Lord-sponsored adventures? Note how they more overtly hand him an assignment in 9.4, "The Mutants".]

The Ship is dematerialising properly again [after that little problem in 8.4, "Colony in Space"]. The Doctor believes the TARDIS is 'indestructible', or at least, it can fall off a mountain without suffering damage. [Yet the Doctor seems to think Jo is safer outside than in, so a lot of objects inside the Ship must be smashed to pieces. See 2.4, "The Romans" for a comparable instance.] The scanner's on the blink thanks to a tiny fault in the interstitial beam synthesiser, an element that's found underneath the console.

The Time Lords Having set Peladon on the path to joining the Galactic Federation, the Doctor believes it can't have been a coincidence that he arrived here at such a critical time in the planet's history, and concludes that the TARDIS must have been sent by the Time Lords. [The Doctor's suspicions are never confirmed, but it's a reasonable assessment - even if arriving at critical points in planets' histories is what he *always* seems to do.

[It's not clear why the Time Lords should want Peladon to join the Federation. There's reason to think that Time Lord technology requires obscure minerals found on planets in this galaxy and a narrow period of history (see 22.2, Vengeance on Varos"). But since the rise of the Daleks is such a concern for them (see 12.4, "Genesis of the Daleks" and arguably 9.1, "Day of the Daleks"), since the Federation needs Peladon's resources to fight Galaxy Five (in "The Monster of Peladon") and since the Fifth Galaxy will one day ally itself with the Daleks (3.2, "Mission to the Unknown" and 3.4, "The Daleks' Master Plan"), it's possible they're making a pre-emptive move in the Time War. (This assumes that Galaxy Five and the Fifth Galaxy are the same organisation, and that this story is further into the future than it looks.) More cogently, of course, a risk to the Federation's credibility might need nipping in the bud, and it may turn out that Peladon's future contribution to cosmic politics will be vital.]

The Non-Humans

• *Ice Warriors*. Since the Doctor last met them in the twenty-first century, the Ice Warriors have rejected violence 'except in self-defence' and are loyal members of the Federation [see **History**]. Here they don't identify themselves *as* Ice Warriors, but do represent Mars.

The two-person Martian delegation is headed by Lord Izlyr, his aristocratic rank denoted by a smoother helmet, less armour and what look like marks of status on his chest-plate. [We have to reiterate that no-one ever calls him an "Ice Lord", a phrase oft-used in fandom.] Despite this being a time of peace, Izlyr still demonstrates a distinctly military sense of nobility, and say that his people retain the 'aristocratic process'. Sub-delegate Ssorg carries a large firearm that can apparently kill any living creature, and is no longer physically incorporated in the Martian armour. Trisilicate, a metal used by the Ice Warriors, can only be found on Mars [but see "The Monster of Peladon"].

Mars and Arcturus are said to be old enemies. [So at some point after the twenty-first century, all the Ice Warriors presumably come out of hiding and create their own "empire", possibly run from Mars. Or maybe not. We note that Izlyr is called "Izlyr", whereas all other delegates - except the Doctor - are identified by planet. He represents people *from* Mars but who might be in exile, like de Gaulle in WWII or the Dalai Lama. Arcturus is sufficiently close too our system for antagonism with the Ice Warriors to have sprung up without any empire-building on either side, and we've no idea how old these 'old enemies' might be. For all we know, the Mars / Arcturus conflict might have been when Varga (5.3, "The Ice Warriors") was buried alive in the last Ice Age.]

• *Alpha Centauri*. A 'hermaphrodite hexapod', referred to as a "he", but with a squeaky and feminine voice, the delegate from Alpha Centauri is a yellow-green thing with one huge eye in the middle of his bulbous head and no other facial features. He has six arms protruding from the front of his body, and as he wears a robe, it's not clear what he's got for feet. ["Hexapod" means six limbs, all of which we can see, so he probably shuffles like an upright slug.

[Some brave attempts have been made to compare the scaredy-squid like Alpha Centauri with the Pierson's Puppeteers from Larry Niven's *Known Space* stories - i.e. that the only ones brave enough to leave their homeworld are considered mad and

Aren't Alien Names Inevitably a Bit Silly?

...continued from page 213

religion, the names "Padme", "Amidala", "Endor" and "Skywalker" are *too* familiar, and least said about "Salacious Crumb", "General Grievous" and "Darth Tyrannus", the better. It's a constant risk. J.K. Rowling must be praying that nobody who's familiar with Thomas Hardy ever reads her books.

In a classic case of transatlantic incomprehension, when the American producer of *Space: 1999* Season Two hired American writers, one of them thought that a name he'd seen in passing would sound good as an alien planet. But when the episode "The Rules of Luton" was aired *here*, those few people still watching the show fell about laughing. Luton is a small, dingy town with a famously none-too-hot football team (of whom Eric Morecambe was a director) about twenty miles outside London. They used to make straw hats there. It's been a punchline here for generations, not least because of the similarity to the word "loo". (This would've been a problem even if the episode hadn't sucked so horribly.)

Anyone seeking to suggest "otherness" through names, therefore, is walking a tightrope between giving a name some sense of a past behind it (rather than just random letters chosen by a hack writer) and bringing about an entirely wrong sort of associations. But what *are* the wrong associations? Broadly, those would be smut, bathos and crassness. Smut is obvious but terribly culturally-specific. (Edgar Rice Burroughs springs to mind, creating a villain called "The Mighty Jed of Goolie". Most people in Britain will get the "goolie" thing - the rest of you just think of what the Ogrons worship - but anyone familiar with Glasgow will find "Jed" risible. Mind you, it has overtones of Ol' Timers chawing tobaccy for Americans too.) Bathos is when the illusion is punctured, as in the "Luton" thing. Crassness comes when something is so patently intended to convey a meaning that you feel insulted: He-Man's arch-nemesis "Skeletor", for example (or, let's not forget, his henchman "Stinkorr").

Here we step nimbly from embarrassing merchandise to Terry Nation's *Dalek Pocket-Book*. This much-derided Dictionary gives both good and bad examples. We may mock it (come on, when Nation has a continent called "Darren", it's hard not to), but actually his strike-rate is pretty good. Names such as "Arkellis flower", "Flidor Gold", "Lalla Palange" and "Brindigulum" surely outweigh "Zeg" and "Wibbial". On a good day, Nation was one of the best exponents of the le Guin method.

It's curious, though, how little it gets mentioned that Nation was Welsh, even now that his native city is home to *Doctor Who* in its modern guise. In fact, he was pre-War Welsh, when the education system and employment opportunities forced the language close to extinction (see **Why Didn't Plaid Cymru Lynch Barry Letts?** under 10.5, "The Green Death"). It's now almost unimaginable that this comparatively ancient tongue was an underground cult within living memory, but when Nation was a child it would have been something mildly shameful.

This is the point where we must trot out that old fib about Nation making up the name 'Dalek' by looking at telephone directories. In a language with so many words starting with "Da" and ending with "liog" or "lech", 'Dalek' is about the most obvious name an alien could have. (The *most* obvious, of course, is one coined by another Welshman with a multi-lingual background: "Oompa-Loompas".) Yet Nation never mentioned that it was in any way connected to his roots. Anyway, which letter does the Welsh language lack? "J" (all those "Joneses" are mid-eighteenth century anglicised "Ioans"). Nation was doing something most people do when forced to invent odd-sounding names: dredging up things from childhood.

He was far from infallible, though. Planets with idiotically obvious names were a regular feature of his stories: 'Marinus' ("The Keys of Marinus") has oceans, 'Aridius' ("The Chase") doesn't, 'Mechanus' (ditto) has a lot of robots milling around and 'Desperus' ("The Daleks' Master Plan") is populated by convicts. Incidentally, the tradition even continues to this day: Series Four begins with fat-bunnies called 'Adipose' (X4.1, "Partners in Crime"), then volcano-beasts named 'Pyrovillians' (X4.2, "The Fires of Pompeii") and a planet called 'Ood-Sphere' (X4.3, "Planet of the Ood"). Then in X4.12, "The Stolen Earth", it turns out that the bees come from 'Melissa Majoria'.

Nation came up with an intriguing notion that people circa AD 4000 might have gone retro and used names from the seventeenth century. This also applies to having a companion called "Zoe" in 1968, and using the names of Saxon kings for the Pipe-People in 25.2, "The Happiness Patrol". One advantage is that these names are at least sayable - and for all his faults Nation got names to *sound* like names and not typos. Many of them, in

continued on page 217...

too disruptive to be allowed to stay. That doesn't explain, however, how someone from an obviously aquatic background (which would account for the high voice) functions on a planet where there's no rainfall. Perhaps that explains why he's wearing a shower-curtain. No? Please yourselves.]

Centauri is flustered by the very thought of violence, and the implication is that the people of Alpha Centauri are peace-loving, although he has a tendency to see other cultures as primitive and doesn't try too hard to stop them killing each other. He sneezes when exposed to dust [odd, for a being with no visible nose or mouth].

• *Arcturus*. A spider-like being with a humanoid face on a body just a few inches long, the delegate from Arcturus occupies a clunky robotic "body" with a life-support system that includes a 'helium regenerator' [so Arcturans can't breathe Peladon's atmosphere]. Arcturus lacks mineral deposits, which is why the delegate wants to make a private deal with Peladon instead of seeing it join the Federation. [Is he acting for selfish reasons, or on behalf of the Arcturan government? Either way, see **Things That Don't Make Sense**.]

They're capable of entering a metabolic coma, and have built-in weapons in their tanks, which they can use to perform extremely slow quick-draws on furniture provided by their hosts. The removal of the sensory array not only causes this coma but affects the 'memory circuits' [suggesting this is a proper cyborg, not an organic occupant of a tank, even if Arcturus is lying about his memory-loss as part of his scheme - Izlyr knows enough about their physiognomy not to be fooled by a lie so we'll accept this as true].

• *Aggedor*. The Royal Beast of Peladon, Aggedor is a large, shaggy, bear-like creature with a snout like a boar's, a single horn in the middle of its forehead and lethal claws. It's believed to be the last of its species, and up until this point was thought to be extinct - not surprising as young men used to hunt it as a rite of passage. The Doctor treats Aggedor as a male specimen, though it's not clear how he knows. Aggedor is not only the "heraldic animal" of the Peladon royal line, but also has a kind of religious significance, having its own sacred temple in the King's citadel.

Planet Notes

• *Peladon*. A planet with an Earth-like atmosphere and Earth-like inhabitants, Peladon has a culture and a level of technology which appear

mediaeval, but its people know about the existence of aliens and it's on the verge of joining the Galactic Federation.

Indeed, aliens seem to have visited Peladon for some time, as the current ruler's mother was from Earth. [Such royal inter-breeding might qualify the planet for Federation membership, although it *could* be argued that Peladon is a former Earth colony which has lapsed into a pre-industrial state. The letter "H" looks the same on Peladon as it does on Earth, which might suggest human ancestry... unless the King's mother introduced a human language as the language of court. Alternatively, the mysterious force which translates everything into English for our benefit might just be converting the symbol as well. (See X1.2, "The End of the World".]

The planet is rich in minerals, and is many light-years from Earth, which Centauri describes as 'remote' [from Peladon, obviously, since Earth and Mars are less then five light-years from Alpha Centauri itself and cosmically speaking, Arcturus is only around the corner].

Peladon has a single ruler, currently the young King Peladon, whose court includes a Chancellor, a High Priest and a very macho [and thus extremely camp] Champion. Only men of rank and females of royal blood are allowed in the throne room. Superstition is common, sacrilege is punishable by death and trial by combat is still possible for nobles. The royal citadel is, charmingly, still lit with flaming torches. As in imperial Rome, purple appears to be the royal colour.

• *Venus*. The Venusian lullaby previously used by the Doctor [8.5, "The Daemons"] now has a tune, which sounds remarkably similar to "God Rest Ye Merry, Gentlemen".

History

• *Dating*. [Harder to establish than you might think, although it's not any time between 2500 and 3100, because Earth hasn't got an empire. See **What's The Timeline of the Earth Empire?** under "Colony in Space" for the case that it's pre-2500, although it's commonly believed that it's just before 4000.]

The Galactic Federation includes Earth, Mars, Alpha Centauri and Arcturus. Earth is important enough for its delegate, Amazonia, to chair the Committee of Assessment. Alpha Centauri describes himself as a member of the Preliminary Assessment Commission [just on Peladon, or is it

Aren't Alien Names Inevitably a Bit Silly?

...continued from page 215

fact, sound like "Terence" or "Tel". We've noted before that Nation produced crap when he sat down and actually took time to come up with something; when he free-associated to a tight deadline, he struck (Flidor) gold. Just to confirm this, the introduction to the *Dalek Pocket-Book* follows the old Gothic tradition that Nation is merely translating a document he found one day. (We presume it washed up through the Time Rift in his native Cardiff.) He maintains the pretence that these words and stories are something outside himself. That alerts us to a very interesting and ancient tradition, so excuse what might appear at first to be a weird digression...

There's a huge body of research into the phenomenon of glossolalia, "speaking in tongues", where the making of vocal noises that aren't words as such tends towards baby-talk. The recording of people doing it reveals that there's a marked prevalence of open-ended utterances, with voiced labials and fricatives (Vs, Ms, Bs and Ls) or - as it's technically known - "yabba-dabba-doo". If you're talking without thinking (or singing without listening), it's easier to go "shoobidoobidoo" rather than "ents" or "ilk", constructions of harder consonants in difficult amalgamations. It's harder, though, to make a convincing planet out of baby-talk, so writers tend to set up a system of similarities and slight differences, starting from an original nonsense-word or two. With our innate ability to spot anomalies, we can usually gauge if one of these names is not like the others... one of these names doesn't belong.

We're now running the danger of turning this into a thesis on structural linguistics, so we'll leave a lot unsaid. However, what sets English apart from a lot of other languages is that a great many potential words that don't have assigned meanings yet. Philologists note that every potential monosyllable in Japanese has already been used, but so far "frad", "neesh" and "polg" are available for filling with semanticity. (Note that the computer on which this is written thinks that "semanticity" isn't a word either: you all know what it *ought* to mean, though, and that's going to be important in a few paragraphs.) There are groups of sounds - phonemes - that tend to go with others, and an experienced language-user has a brain trained to "fast-track" these through the processing department in the cortex just above the left ear, Broca's area (see 7.1, "Spearhead from Space"), and its interpretative counterpart on the other side, Wernicke's area. A possible name like "Snigsby" has bits in common with other, known English names, and so looks and sounds like one.

Moreover, the shape your mouth goes when you say some things (or even what happens when you imagine it being said; to the human brain, it hardly makes any odds) has an effect too. The Dutch language is very well-stocked for words with "K"s, "F"s and "P"s, but nevertheless people in Holland prefer swearing in English because our Celtic-derived expletives are more satisfying to say loud. Even if you don't speak the language, our swear words just *sound* rude. Velar consonants, affricates and fricatives (k','ng','sh''t') are a lot more satisfying. The physical characteristics of any made-up word should be more important than potential meaning and names, which are almost totally divorced from their original meaning (at least in our culture), so ought to work better as pieces of pure euphony than invented verbs. After all, what exactly does "Beyonce" mean?

This next bit might sound surprising, but the idea that poetry should rhyme is historically very recent. Just having the last syllable of one line sounding a bit like the last syllable of another *isn't* intuitively obvious as a method of forcing words into a pattern. In the Middle Ages as much if not more used alliteration, with the same consonant as often as possible at the start of each word in a given line, and no rhymes worth noting. Go back further and the key thing is metre. Each line has the arrangement of stressed and unstressed syllables as a constant, and, as far as we can tell, that preceded writing.

So what, then, was poetry for? The simple answer is that it's a high-density information storage and retrieval medium. In pre-literate cultures, the history of the tribe and the account of why we're all here is something passed down orally in a heavily stylised mnemonic system. That's why the Bible is in "Verses", why Homer uses all those stock phrases ("rosy-fingered dawn", "the wine-dark sea", "circumspect Penelope") and why, when Alex Haley was researching *Roots*, he waited eight hours for a simple answer to a straightforward question about Kunta Kinte's departure from Ghana. The Griots, Bards or Cantors found a way to convert complex information into a memorable and easily-passed-on form, and this was added to all the others accumulated over the century.

continued on page 219...

a standing body?], and political conflict is said to violate Federation law.

Despite the Federation's supposed commitment to peace, if Peladon were to execute a Federation representative, it would constitute an act of war and Federation ships would level the planet. Under the Galactic Charter - Galactic Articles of Peace, paragraph 59, subsection two - the Federation can't over-ride Peladon's holy laws [does this apply to all local laws, or just religious ones?], nor can it involve itself in internal politics unless a unanimous decision of delegates calls on emergency powers. Federation law only accepts unanimous decisions. The organisation's evidently rife with internal divisions, as a war would ensue if the Ice Warriors were accused of killing the delegate from Arcturus.

The King says that 'the memory of this unhappy day' shall be 'wiped from our history.' [Hepesh's insurrection probably is swept under the rug, but the Doctor's visit to Peladon is widely known in "The Monster of Peladon".] The delegate from Earth looks astonished when she sees the TARDIS dematerialise, as if nobody in this bit of the future has ever seen something teleport before. [Unless she's got a background in history, and can't believe she's looking at a police box. As she's got a place-name for a title too, we might assume that "Amazonia" denotes a nation-state of sufficient power to represent Earth, rather than any surgery to improve her archery or a sponsorship deal with a book distributor.]

The Analysis

Where Does This Come From? In 1972, Britain joined the EEC, with the Common Market giving the country closer links to Europe than ever (and, indeed, than many people wanted). By its writer's own admission, "The Curse of Peladon" is *Doctor Who's* version of a "current events" story. Some critics have taken this to extremes, found more exact parallels than close examination can stand and built elaborate theses on King Peladon's hairstyle (no, seriously).

But it's worth bearing in mind that Britain's formal entry into the EEC (as it was then) was just one of many such negotiations happening in those days. We're in the era of détente, remember (see last story), but we're also just coming out of a phase when African and South American countries are signing up for things their governments'

opponents found a bit scary. Development packages were treated with the utmost suspicion. After all, a lot of the miracle crops being offered to farmers in what they called the "Third World" needed repeat prescriptions. (The seeds were high-yield, but the resulting plants were sterile, so you had to go back next year and buy more, along with fertiliser. The same governments would unblushingly condemn said farmers for growing hashish and opium poppies, despite acting like pushers themselves.)

A lot of mining corporations had influence at the diplomatic level, nudging the treaties into giving them partial ownership of countries. Factions backed by multinational copper smelters overthrew the Golden Boy of 1960s Africa, Nkrumah, and this plunged Ghana into turmoil (see 2.8, "The Chase"). If you look at the story in this context, as anyone following the news at the time *would* have done, Britain is less like Peladon and more like Alpha Centauri - offering aid with strings, but talking all the while of the moral advantages of leaving feudalism and superstition behind. Progress, defined as always as "becoming more like us", was unequivocally a good thing in and of itself, never mind how much money was there to be made. US television gave us a version of *Tarzan* in which Ron Ely wrestled alligators and talked about how UNESCO could help preserve tribal artefacts for future generations.

So a lot of countries saw development as part of a mutual-backscratch process, by which they got what they needed in return for apparently small concessions given to nations or organisations much bigger than them. Since (effectively) 1946, there had been the World Bank - a body set up at the suggestion of economist John Maynard Keynes to provide overseas aid, in return for sometimes-strict restructuring of an entire nation's economy in order to meet loan repayments. (This got embarrassing when Britain needed it - see **Why Didn't They Just Spend More Money?** under 12.2, "The Ark in Space", but first **Who's Running the Country?** under 10.5, "The Green Death" to see how we got there.)

As mentioned in "The Tenth Planet" (4.2), the Chilean government took this into a new direction, employing cybernetician Stafford Beer to reconfigure the entire economy and social services to conform with information theory and neurology. (They might have even succeeded if an American-backed fascist coup hadn't overthrown

Aren't Alien Names Inevitably a Bit Silly?

...continued from page 217

Now here's where it gets a bit complicated: how do you make a war or a famine "portable" and "sticky"? Indeed, what happens when you compose a poem even today? Fortunately, there's quite a lot of information about this, because not only do poets love talking about themselves (and have done so throughout history), but we have NMR scanners and a lot of neurological investigation. Memory is best served by having multiple sets of associations: factual, biographical, sensory and so on. (We touched on this in **How Does Hypnosis Work?** under 8.1, "Terror of the Autons".) Actors learn lines by repetition of the words themselves, out of context, but also by connecting what they need to say with where they're facing when they say them, what they have in their hands and the like.

Actors with huge tracts of stuff to recite need more help, clearly. Sometimes they take the formal properties of the line, such as the metre, and sing it. (This is how Jon Pertwee got a handle on technobabble.) For example, if you know a line is a set number of syllables long, and that the word you're reaching for is three syllables (stress on the first) and almost rhymes with "elephant", it's likely to be "telephone". Semantically, "elephant" and "telephone" have nothing much in common (certainly not now that they've stopped doing trunk-calls... Peter Glaze is no longer with us, but his feeble one-liners live on). But formally, they're very similar. The bit of the brain struggling to remember the word "telephone" (look, it's just an example for most people, but as we get older this could happen) might rummage around for words that mean "communications device" and find "radio", "semaphore", "Tannoy" or whatever. But given "sounds like "elephant" to cross-reference, it could get to "telegram" and "telephone", as well as "elegant", "element", "Sellotape" and other non-communication-themed words. The more connections, the better.

However, we tend to favour the frontal lobe, and especially the left hemisphere. That's pretty much where "me" lives, and it's strongly linked to the references to the meanings of words. So an association from elsewhere, like "shape" (number of syllables, stress-patterns), sound, what the mouth feels like when saying it, where you were when you first heard it and so forth can seem like a prompt from elsewhere. Poets often describe the creative process as bypassing their everyday selves and letting something "out" (as in the case of Ted Hughes' famous example *The Thought-Fox*) or "in" (the Greeks blamed all creativity on Memory's nine daughters, the Muses, and put anything they'd made under the influence in a Museum)[66]. A writer who shuts up and lets the right hemisphere do the driving can find the verse-form or rhyme-scheme making him or her say things that wouldn't normally be said. Strict rhyme is actually a form of liberation, or so Auden said.

The neurology confirms it. They've done scans of musicians composing, people doing crosswords and people doing comprehension tests - and the results are markedly different for the latter but similar for the first two. So it's a common reaction amongst people fashioning new conglomerations of sounds, such as Terry Nation thinking up words or Paul McCartney writing "Yesterday" in his sleep, to think "Did I do *that?*".

So if the making of patterns is what's behind poetry and memory, then the similarity of unknown words to existing ones deserves close attention. Remember "semanticity"? It's obviously a noun denoting the possession of a quality (like "authenticity" and "ethnicity") and that quality is to do with the meaning of words. A synonym might be "meaningfulness", but that's clumsy (although the computer spellcheck likes it, which is what you get for allowing Bill Gates to arbitrate on the English language). By a complicated process of comparison and analysis, most English-speakers can figure out what such neologisms should mean. What about when the comparison reveals discrepancies between the contextual inference and the verbal similarities?

That's where it gets silly. Names shouldn't sound like things that people would say as technical terms, insults or slang (unless they're clearly intended as such), and should appear to follow some kind of rules inherent in that culture. We can buy an alien princeling called 'Turlough' (which, as we've noted, is a good old Irish name connected to the Norse god Thor - see 20.3, "Mawdryn Undead"). What makes less sense is that someone with *that* surname would have the first name 'Vizlor' (see 21.5, "Planet of Fire"). Suddenly, he's a Czech / Irish alien, and for some reason we have trouble with that. Our Absent Paradigm (the world-view of the place where these words are inferred to mean something) is jolted.

continued on page 221...

a democratically-elected government that Nixon and Kissinger didn't like. No-one ever tried anything like the Allende scheme again, so we'll never know. See 25.2, "The Happiness Patrol" for the next part of that story.) Every week saw a news story about somewhere that had been a wretched mess sorting itself out with a bit of cheap technology and a lot of goodwill. However, the next story was often a tale of how Western intervention in a small conflict had turned it into a humanitarian disaster. (Most spectacularly, and shamefully for Britain, there was the Biafran war of the late 60s.)

Oh, all right, let's talk about the Common Market. As soon as Georges Pompidou took over as President of France, it looked possible that Britain could finally get a place in the European Economic Community. (His predecessor, Charles de Gaulle, had been petulantly vetoing this since 1957.) During the intervening period the British economy had undergone a few transitions, such as decimalisation and the decoupling of Sterling from the Gold Standard, making Britain less intimidating to Belgium or Italy. So Ted Heath's negotiations for a belated entry coincided with the first draft of this story being written.

Does that make "The Curse of Peladon" a satire, as younger critics claim? Well, the idea of depicting national stereotypes as different beings was nothing new. Serge Danot had made an animated caricature of Europe as a garden full of animals and odd-looking farmers called Le Manège Enchante. The redubbed, rewritten version of this (The Magic Roundabout) had been a hit in the UK (and prompted the tiresome assumption that it was all about drugs[62]).

The thing is, unlike the French series, "The Curse of Peladon" has no obvious correlation between the aliens and the various countries involved (even Alan Barnes, in DWM #381, comes unstuck trying to push that one). Even if we try to link Hepesh's attitudes with the pro-Europe camp's depiction of their opponents as pig-headed and stuck in the past, the fact that the same author wrote a sequel that undermines this reading curtails any effort we might make. Like General Carrington in "The Ambassadors of Death" (7.3), Hepesh isn't so much evil as he's just obsessed with his own piddling local concerns. So it's a fable rather than a work of satire, which doesn't make any particular political point yet comes across as a cautionary tale about the fear of accepting the alien. And since "accepting the alien" is

one of the cornerstones of Doctor Who, it's no surprise that the Doctor's on the side of the Federation.

It's been said that the appearance of the Federation is another sign of Doctor Who (or at least Terrance Dicks) being influenced by Star Trek, and it's hard to argue with that. But there's a much more European slant on things here, meaning that any planet in this Federation is bound to find itself surrounded by neighbours instead of a wild frontier. And this Federation even feels comfortable threatening primitive planets with warships, which is something the Star Trek one probably wouldn't do. Bear in mind that Alpha Centauri mentions how other primitive planets have taken the Federation negotiators hostage in local power-plays. This isn't anything one can say of the European Union's member states even now, but wasn't unknown when UN observers went to fledgling democracies. It was (and is, regrettably) common with international aid and human rights organisations.

Note that the Star Trek Federation, even in the original series, is much like America's view of the UN: the humans / Americans are the important ones, and the other species are just funny-looking people from a long way away, who occasionally show up in the background. The Federation assembly on Peladon looks for all the world like a committee meeting in Brussels, except with better outfits. They're a group of diverse races, all with different agendas but forced to live alongside each other, and constantly at each others' throats as a result. It's a much more "global" view of the universe, a much more political vision. Let's not forget that Centauri is explicitly stated to be a civil servant.

In some ways, we're closer to the then-popular "Ekumen" stories of Ursula le Guin. In these, the various hominid races of the galaxy are getting back in touch. (Humans are around, but they're not in charge. If anyone is, it's the oldest space-travelling race, but they're all going into this to see what they have in common and what their differences can add.) Each of these races seems to be an experiment of some kind, so - to cite the most famous example, from The Left Hand of Darkness[63] - Gethen seems not to have fixed sexes. Suddenly, having Alpha Centauri flapping about seems a lot less of a wild improvisation. One wonders if Hayles and Dicks got hold of a synopsis and half-read it while watching Ted Heath make excruciat-

Aren't Alien Names Inevitably a Bit Silly?

...continued from page 219

But if people use words *as if* they mean something where they come from, we get a glimpse of their world and how it works. Nobody actually has a 'sonic screwdriver' - not a real one, anyway - but everyone can figure out what one ought to do and how it might work. That is, in the original concept of a thing that undoes screws by sound, not the tricorder / Stattenheim Remote Control / magic wand configuration we've got now. A natural tendency is to infer a rude meaning to any unfamiliar word. (The radio series *Round the Horne* - see 10.2, "Carnival of Monsters" - milked this one joke relentlessly. Using perfectly legitimate but odd-sounding and unfamiliar words turns everything into innuendo. Folk Singer Rambling Sid Rumpo would deliver ditties using the words "cordwangle","splod","bogle","grunge","posset" and "woggle" at strategic points and it never got old. The dirty minds of the listeners that did the rest.)

Throughout these guidebooks, we've hinted that there's more mileage in leaving the viewers to infer the off-screen details of a planet from dialogue than in any number of expensive (or less-expensive, but not always less effective) special effects sequences. However much money was spent to render New Earth (X2.1,"New Earth"; X3.3, "Gridlock") we inherently know it less well than we know Raxacoricofallapatorius (X1.5, "World War Three"), to pick just two examples from the same author. One name from an alien race might just sound like someone's kicked over a Scrabble board. Two or three, though, give a hint of some kind of underlying pattern.

And a problem occurs when you *try* to do it to order. In establishing a pattern, it's possible to make either very repetitive sound-lumps (which can be useful in itself, as the 'Trau' and 'Krau' of 21.6, "The Caves of Androzani") or to forget common sense. *New Adventures* readers will recall the outburst of punctuation-marks peppering people's names.[67]

The TV writers, however, know that actors need to *say* these words, and thus fall back on fairly well-established (if seldom taught or discussed) rules of which letters can follow which other letters."V" followed by "L" is a common combination in Eastern Europe, but not here. We all know about Nation's fixation with the name "Tarrant", so let's take a less well-worn but appropriate example: Brian Hayles. In his stories, the Ice Warriors seem to have three basic principles. The troops have monosyllables with double-S and / or a hard guttural (K or G) in there somewhere ('Ssorg' in "The Curse of Peladon", 'Sskel' in "The Monster of Peladon") and the Chiefs (oh, all right, Ice Lords) get multiple syllables and / or long-drawn-out ends ('Varga' in "The Ice Warriors", 'Izlyr' in "The Curse of Peladon", 'Azaxyr' in "The Monster of Peladon" and, stretching a point, 'Slaar' in "The Seeds of Death"). So it's remarkably regular - well, barring the first Ice Warriors story, in which we also get names such as 'Rintan' and 'Isbur', and a human with the great, unused Martian name 'Storr' (because Brian Hayles had yet to hear Bernard Bresslaw sibilantly rasping out these names).

Now, it would be possible for people to apply the basic tendencies and randomly generate Ice Warrior names such as "Spunk", "Snog" or "Shag" and Lords called "Ibrox" or "Rizla". These would be intrinsically a bit daft even for non-British viewers, however, as short vowels with hard consonants sound too Anglo-Saxon to be properly foreign. Around these parts, those words have unfortunate associations.

It's also been noted that two of the Chancellery Guards in successive Gallifrey stories (14.3, "The Deadly Assassin"; 15.6, "The Invasion of Time") were given names ending with 'red', so people who consider this stuff sometimes trick themselves into thinking that the suffix '-red' is a clan name. You can see the hazard of setting up rules for a species and their names - it might generate examples that are too close to home. In the Gallifrey example, they'd run out of names and wind up with a character called 'Inbred'. In itself it's a problem for the viewer / reader / listener, but it's even more weird if the characters themselves don't realise it.

This itself could form part of an Absent Paradigm. (After all, if we were to pop back a century and warn everyone that two of the most famous men of the next hundred years would be called "Adolf Hitler" and "Elvis Presley", people would laugh. Then we'd get onto war-criminals called "Slobodan Milosovic" and "Pol Pot"...) But better off-beam associations than none at all, it seems. Many of the more resonant names come with ethnic stereotypes fitted as standard: you want to suggest exactitude and remorseless efficiency, go for Germanic names ('Stattenheim' in "The Mark of the Rani", 'Dortmun' in "The Dalek Invasion of Earth", 'Emil Keller' in "The Mind of Evil",

continued on page 223...

ing speeches in bad schoolboy French.

Let's get into specifics. Plot-wise, this is overtly *The Hound of the Baskervilles*, but aesthetically we're in *Throne of Eagles* territory. For all the knicker-twisting about contemporary relevance, the Europe of the nineteenth century is at this story's heart. The design is overtly establishing a look of Bavaria, especially in the reign of the Wagner-mad (and later just mad) Ludwig II. Quite aside from dressing like a Teutonic princeling, Peladon talks about blood-alliances and royal hunting beasts. We're closer to the Hapsburgs than the Bundesrepublik, and the Federation is spoken of (and acts) like the Hanseatic League or the Holy Roman Empire circa 1500. We're going to get more of this soon (see "Frontier in Space").

However, the king's thigh-boots have a more obvious 1972 look. This is a story steeped in the Glam era; Peladon might almost have walked (well, minced) out of the *Top of the Pops* studio. (Think, in particular, of Brian Eno-era Roxy Music.) Grun is so like Overend Watts, the bass-player for Mott the Hoople, we had to check that *Doctor Who* got there first. Hepesh's robes aren't a kerjillion light-years away from what Rick Wakeman would have worn on stage. (The music's got a hint of Wakeman about it too, or - again - maybe vice versa.)

Things That Don't Make Sense We're told that Arcturus was in secret collusion with Hepesh to further a deal for Peladon's minerals, as Arcturus' homeworld lacks such deposits. Sounds reasonable, but we're *also* told that the conflict on Peladon is in grave danger of splitting the entire Federation asunder, with the member planets choosing sides between Arcturus and Mars and bringing everything to ruin. In this scenario, Peladon would almost undoubtedly get obliterated in the crossfire. So how, precisely, does this match with Arcturus' goals? Fair enough if his people *want* to cause all-out warfare - if, say, they're looking to settle old scores with the Ice Warriors or whoever - and they're using Peladon as the flashpoint, even though nothing is said about this. But as a means of securing Peladon's mineral wealth, triggering a conflict that will likely level Peladon seems like a staggeringly bad way of going about it.

Anyway, when Arcturus tries to shoot the Doctor at the end of episode three, how on Earth

(or Peladon) does he expect to get away with it? The room is full of eye-witnesses! And unless Arcturan and Martian weapons leave identical forensic evidence, any attempt to blame the Ice Warriors would be exposed as a stupidly wrong. Never mind that Arcturus' gun was previously shown to take about three weeks to aim and fire, and make a lot of noise in the process. The cliffhanger sort of relies on him doing it more stealthily than that.

Related to all of this, Hepesh encourages the Doctor - whom he thinks is the Earth delegate - to escape before his duel with the king's champion, claiming Peladon would suffer massive retribution if he were killed. But it turns out this is a ruse to get Aggedor to murder the Doctor and, when that stunt fails, Hepesh hopes the Doctor will die in combat after all. (Hepesh even throws the king's champion a sword when he's backed into a corner - surely this is against the rules?) So, er, what happened to the "massive retribution if the Doctor dies" bit? Is Hepesh just suicidally reckless? Even as late as episode four, he says he doesn't want the delegates as 'guests or hostages' because of the payback Peladon would suffer, yet he apparently arranges to destroy their communications devices and cut them off from help, and in general his actions are those of someone who's almost deliberately trying to invoke such reprisals.

But then, not much about the court set-up and the politics therein makes sense. The king, after all, is such a tosser that he evidently needs Federation backing to *replace his own high priest*. Never mind that he should've stringently excluded Hepesh from the negotiations from the start - does he enjoy having one of his own advisors standing there, blatantly sowing distrust and contradicting almost everything he says? Granted, Torbis' death leaves something of a void in the king's inner circle, but surely the king is within his rights to tell Hepesh to keep to his Aggedor-sanctum for a few days. And if he *doesn't* have that authority, what good will asking for Federation backing do? And how will he then persuade his people that joining the Federation won't unduly impede upon Peladon's sovereignty?

If the Time Lords are responsible for piloting the TARDIS to Peladon, then why don't they make a better job of the landing? Maybe they hope to fool the Doctor into thinking he's just performed a "normal" arrival (i.e. one that's less-than-perfect), but it runs the risk of their own agent falling off a

Aren't Alien Names Inevitably a Bit Silly?

...continued from page 221

'Nyder' in "Genesis of the Daleks"); sinister and inscrutable, wheel on the Chinese / Mongol handles ('Mavic Chen' in "The Daleks' Master Plan", 'Regos Krang' in "The Tenth Planet"). Exotic and borderline adjectival names have the hint of Celtic or Armenian roots. (We've no idea what makes a 'Taltarian' airlock any different from any other kind, but the word stays in the memory long after the plot of "The Chase" episode two fades into blissful oblivion. More recently, a throwaway reference to the 'Pentalion drive' from a transmit - 12.5, "Revenge of the Cybermen" - gave us the name of a really badly-designed spaceship in X3.7, "42".)

As we've noted, the fact that the majority of characters hearing these alien names are presented to us as native English speakers presents fairly limited parameters for defining alien names as alien or names. There are, of course, problems with this. A dead giveaway that English-speakers have thought up these names is the lack of consideration to where the stress falls. English is almost random in allocating the emphasis in some words, forcing some actors to guess at the pronunciation of alien names. Is the First and Greatest of the Time Lords Oh-mega or O-ME-ga? Are the little guys with the Probic vents 'Son TAR ans or SONT arans (see 11.1, "The Time Warrior" for how this was decided and X4.5, "The Poison Sky" for a comment on this).

Morever, English speech tends to centralise the pronunciation of unstressed vowels, which doesn't help. And here's where we recall the scene from 18.4, "State of Decay" about lexical entropy - that names alter over generations from the less probable to the more, as the Brothers Grimm theorised. As no Serbo-Croat editions of X3.4, "Daleks in Manhattan" have reached us, we can't say whether they give the aliens a different language's word for 'unwelcome foreigners', but we *can* state that the French for 'Judoon' (X3.1, "Smith and Jones") is in fact 'Judoon', but with a softer 'J'. (Even if Judoon-speak such as 'Torr Dorr Rorr Corr...' is reworked to avoid sounding too much like real French.)

But then, we might surmise that the TARDIS translates everything into Welsh anyway[68], and that when we hear Azaxyr call his people 'Ice Warriors' (11.4, "The Monster of Peladon") or Scibus refers to the 'Sea Devil Warriors' (21.1, "Warriors of the Deep"), they're actually saying "Rhyfelwyr Hiâ" or "Derdri Aic". (If the latter *do* speak Welsh, it explains the name 'Silurian'... "Wales" originally meant "far and distant things".) Most cultures have a name for themselves that means "people" anyway, so whoever narrates *Doctor Who* (see **Who Narrates This Series?** under 23.1, "The Mysterious Planet") must doing a bit of on-screen footnoting.

Alien names are *supposed* to be a bit out-of-the-ordinary, but the deliberate attempts to be silly are the most revealing. Douglas Adams - who could, when necessary, deliver memorably mellifluous exotic handles ('Salyavin' in "Shada", 'Jagaroth' in "City of Death", 'Soulanis and Rahm' and 'Qualactin' in *The Hitchhiker's Guide to the Galaxy*) - often risked bathos with knowingly daft names to show that something was amiss. (They sometimes had "Oo" sounds, but the most famous deliberately-embarrassing name is, of course, "Slartibartfast".) His mentor Robert Holmes delivered many of our treasured alien names but played for laughs: 'Dibber' in "The Mysterious Planet", 'Narg' in "The Two Doctors", 'Wurg' and 'Keek' in "The Sun Makers", 'Runcible' in "The Deadly Assassin" and dozens more. And these days we're all so used to tongue-twister planets and aliens, they can make a joke about Raxacoricofallapatorius having a twin planet called 'Clom' (X2.10, "Love and Monsters" - this is, we note, very close to "Clum", a real place in Wales). With the new series being made in a city that has districts called "Splott", "Gabalfa" and "Dinas Powys", all bets are off.[69]

---

cliff before he can perform his mission. Prior to arrival, Jo seems confused about the console room layout - she asks the Doctor to open the TARDIS door, but actually gestures to a section wall. Within the citadel, Jo seems remarkably well-groomed after clambering around on a storm-lashed window-ledge (even if her shoes change when she's outside). The guestrooms aren't in bad shape either - being warm, dry and completely free of "weather" noise even though the windows are just holes in the walls.

The quarters for the Ice Warriors only has one bed, so either their proud martial tradition requires one of them to stand up all night or they've got an equally proud martial tradition of snuggling up together. (See **What Are the Gayest Things in *Doctor Who*?** under "The Happiness Patrol" for a lot more in this vein.) Of course, Sub-Delegate Ssorg *might*, as was pointed out to us, be female, but one presumes that would've come up in conversation when discussing Alpha Centauri's bits. (We watched this story again and, to our immense frustration, Ssorg is never referred to with a third-person pronoun in the whole four episodes. It's like the production team knew that someone would eventually write an unauthorised guidebook in which this would be a hot topic.)

At the start of episode two, based upon Jo's description, the Doctor concludes that Ssorg must have left the tell-tale footprints by the upended statue of Aggedor. This presumes, however, that Jo can't distinguish between human and Martian feet.

Even back in the 70s (when we were smaller but no less pedantic), many of us found it deeply irritating that the delegate from the Alpha Centauri system is called 'Centauri' and the delegate from the Arcturus system is called 'Arcturus', yet nobody tries calling the Doctor "Sol" or even "Earth". (Mind you, as the king of the planet takes the planet's name, perhaps that's just a local custom. English monarchs used to do it with visiting nobles - see, for instance, *The Merchant of Venice*. So now we just have to work out whether the Ice Warriors really come from Mars or a planet called "Izlyr" - maybe, like "Amazonia", it's a region.) Delegate Izlyr goes on about how his people have renounced violence but nobody upbraids the Chairman Delegate for calling them 'Ice Warriors'. Either the Martians really like the name, or they think everyone on Earth is still living in the twenty-first century and being deeply patronising.

In demonstrating his weapon, Arcturus thanks his hosts for their hospitality by zapping, rather protractedly, a nice vase or urn they'd placed in his room. What if it contained someone's ashes? Then there's the faked "attack" on Arcturus, which entails removing his sensory array to induce a 'metabolic coma'. We can imagine any number of situations where a metabolic disorder would affect the senses, but not vice versa. Allowing for the ambiguity of where the Arcturans' physiology stops and their cybernetic implants begin, it's either an incredibly stupid design or their biology flies in the face of natural selection. (We assume that their evolutionary ancestors never played Blind Man's Bluff, except as a method of execution.)

Removing the sensory equipment also alters the 'memory circuits'. Was this life-support system built by Amstrad or something? It's a *really* shoddy design. It's also way too fiddly for the likely suspects, Izlyr or Ssorg, to have removed that circuit, what with them either having pincer-hands or wearing boxing-gloves. Later, Jo finds Arcturus' missing circuit in the Ice Warriors' room and it never occurs to her that a) it could've been planted there, b) as proof of the Ice Warriors' crimes, it's pretty flimsy evidence, and c) they could accuse *her* of planting it there if she speaks up about it. Then after her little confrontation with Ssorg, Jo makes herself look more guilty by trying to escape out the window. And when Ssorg tries to alert Izlyr to Jo's snooping, nobody comments that Ssorg has just waddled into the conference room with the missing / incriminating circuit.

We'll leave aside footling points such as the Doctor magically working out Hepesh's entire deal with Arcturus (and how Aggedor suddenly turned up to aid this plan) and instead consider a more substantial flaw. As we see in the sequel to this story, Hepesh is high priest of a religion that uses the spirit of Aggedor as an off-stage threat. But a *real-life* Aggedor cropping up is at best an embarrassment. Anyway, it would suit Hepesh's purpose far more to have the one remaining Aggedor put down before it starts shedding all over the place and humping the furniture.

If hunting Aggedor is the manhood rite-of-passage for Peladonian nobility, and if Aggedor is (supposedly) extinct, how did young Peladon, with his 'tainted' blood and everything, become king? It's clear that he's yet to be anointed, but the story ends with Aggedor chewing up the man responsible for that duty. So what are they going to do? Get Aggedor to lick Peladon in public and thus prove his regal worth? (No, wait - most likely, they'd then end up with the Doctor, whom Aggedor seems to like better, being crowned.) Besides, Peladon is half-human. If he *had* married Jo, it's likely that another coup would have occurred within hours. (To be fair, something like this occurred to Dicks and Hayles - see "The Monster of Peladon".)

"Amazonia", the genuine Chairman-Delegate from Earth, arrives and argues with Izlyr and Centauri as the Doctor walks in on the contrived "Doctor Who?" joke. Izlyr is looking directly at the Doctor when she asks, but neglects to point him out. And it's odd that the Federation didn't tell Centauri or the others who was going to arrive and what that person looked like. It's additionally strange that for the three or more episodes when they all had functioning communicators, nobody got a signal from the Earth ship saying, "We're running late, start without us."

To look at the Big Picture for a moment, we're liking the lateral-thinking pacifist idea of singing a lullaby to a semi-mythical beast in a labyrinth. It's all vintage *Doctor Who* stuff. But why, three stories later, does the Doctor immediately go into Ernest Hemingway mode and try to defeat the Minotaur with cape-twirling and karate? (More on this in "The Time Monster".)

Finally, the last shot makes it look as if Amazonia's doing the Sting for the end-theme.

Critique It's weird... nobody really hates this story, but curiously it's easier to list its faults than to find any reason to recommend it. It's undoubtedly a very likeable adventure, but any attempt to isolate its virtues just highlights the things that went wrong. It was a relief on first transmission to find that we weren't on Earth, yet even the setting isn't all it should have been.

Just like three of the last four stories, we're dealing with something that's among the first things that would pop into anyone's head were they saddled with a sudden unexpected tax demand and a desperate need to write a *Doctor Who* story. The TARDIS is working, and they go to a planet that's got feudal traditions and lots of different aliens (one of whom is in league with the local witch-doctor) and the Doctor gets into a gladiator-fight. There's a comic-relief alien who looks a bit like an octopus and a bit rude. If anything like this had occurred at any time in the last four years, this would look like a parody of *Doctor Who* on a sketch-show. So why does this story have such huge affection among so many fans?

It's first worth looking at the diet-Freud thinking that seems to inform such character as King Peladon is actually given. He defines himself as lacking in comparison to his absent father, and sanctifies his mum. (Peladon's romance with a girl who looks a bit like her, and is from the same planet, becomes a lot more icky if you think of it that way. Lest you think we're going out on a limb here, the novelisation confirms it in rather noisome detail.) It's hardly uncommon for *Doctor Who* to show boy-kings facing crises and being left as adults when the Doctor departs (21.3, "Frontios" is a clear parallel, and 3.5, "The Massacre" is a warning of what happens when this fails). And in this particular story, we can't have a lad who's pushed onto the galactic stage after being / still being moulded by old men, so Jo has

to step in.

Amazingly, this is the first time we've had an on-screen romance with a TARDIS crewmember since 3.3, "The Myth Makers". Obviously it can't go too far (although we don't actually know how much time elapses between Hepesh's death and the coronation...), but at some stage in the writing, the clear intention was that Peladon and Jo would have a more conventional relationship than what the strained dialogue heard on screen illustrates. So the first thing to say in this story's favour is that it's written for Jo and not for the Doctor. She's placed at the heart of all this, and to our considerable relief, Katy Manning chooses this story to make her acting debut. Ordinarily her performance is split between relatively normal (i.e. bright and perky) when the star's not in the scene, and making big goo-goo eyes and putting on a baby voice when he is. But most of this story, it's the reverse: she's normal with the Doctor, and downright impassioned when he's not around. The first episode threatens to become run-of-the-mill Jo Grant material, with occasional flashes of perkiness and a brief moment of dizzy blonde, but she's neither (pardon the phrasing here) pert nor twee.

Strangely, for most of the story, Jo's usual function is taken by Alpha Centauri. Even more weirdly, it's done so well that it's hard to be upset about it. By use of this one character, we get a feel for an entire species and their place in the scheme of things. We also have a rare moment of culture shock, when Jo is confronted with Centauri's as a hermaphrodite (still not convinced that the writers were thinking about sexual politics?). The discrepancy between Centauri's voice, look, official function and manner are enough to sketch in a whole galaxy.

The Ice Warriors, on the other hand, were never that good an idea on paper. They succeeded for two stories because some clever directors and ingenious actors found ways to make beings who move at three miles a fortnight seem menacing. Fair enough, but in "The Curse of Peladon", we're merely asked to accept the Doctor's word that they're bad. Running counter to this, we're cut to a scene where Izlyr seems a lot more civilised than Hepesh or Arcturus. True, numbering the Ice Warriors amongst the goodies is probably intended to play on pre-conceived notions. But if you're coming to this without knowledge of their past appearances (and it's been three years since "The Seeds of Death", remember), it's hard to see why the Doctor's making such a fuss. Even viewers who *did* remember them, however, would likely split into two camps: those who had trouble accepting that they've genuinely changed their ways, and those who wondered why they were ever *that* serious a threat in the first place.

Whatever the case, they get the same team from last time, and somehow Alan Bennion makes Izlyr into a different character even though he's working with much the same dialogue as last time around. (It's occasionally *very* similar, and the shift of emphasis from military conquest to Federation membership is less abrupt than you might think. The lines are still staccato declarative statements for the most part, and the emphasis on duty and suspicion is constant.) As lumbering, hissing red herrings, the Ice Warriors have a job to do but otherwise they're purely decorative. In an odd way, this story could easily have functioned with Izlyr as the detective.

To finish up looking at the aliens... Arcturus is yet-another idea that anyone with a vague notion of *Doctor Who* tradition would use as a first attempt before deciding to do something a bit more original. It's almost as if they took Terry Nation's one-line description of the Daleks and gave it to a different designer, just to see how else it could come out (see **Who *Really* Created the Daleks?** under 1.2, err, "The Daleks"). Even the humanoid head with tentacles is the part of the Dalek they chose not to show until 1983 (compare Arcturus to the modern Kaled mutants, e.g. Dalek Caan in X4.13, "Journey's End", and this is really obvious). Just to make the comparison complete, the voice-effect that Brian Hodgson provides makes it work. Even the bubbling water on the life-support system is something they did better later (22.2, "Vengeance on Varos").

For all the aliens on display, then, they're largely window-dressing and the *real* story here is with the humanoids. Regrettably, that's where it all falls down. There's just no escaping it: at its core, this is a rather dull and obvious tale of an old man clinging to the old ways, with only the murder-weapon to make it novel. (It's just about possible that some of the very youngest viewers hadn't heard of *The Hound of the Baskervilles*, after all.) By this point, we're getting perilously close to arguing that so long as the punters got twenty-five minutes of pretty pictures and groovy burbles, nobody cared about anything else. There's more than a grain of truth to that (see **Does Plot**

Matter? under 6.4, "The Krotons"), but for anyone watching it *now*, the curious thing is how much a viable plot-strand is mixed right down. We've already touched upon the Doctor's bigotry when it comes to Ice Warriors, and should specify that the production-team uses this as much as they dare to avoid the kids spotting that Arcturus is near-as-dammit carrying a flashing sign saying I AM THE VILLAIN.

Regrettably, just having Jo accept that Izlyr is a goodie isn't enough - we need a sign of contrition from the Doctor, and we never get it. In one way that's good, as the Doctor's reflex is to save even his enemies' lives, but this just highlights the way that nobody actually *learns* anything in this story. Peladon is finally allowed to follow his natural inclinations, without old men with raspberry-ripple beards blocking him, but the only character who changes as a result of the experiences here is, er, Aggedor. It's four episodes of puppy-training.

So if it's not the plot, the funny aliens, the "scary" aliens, the dialogue or the acting that give this story its feel-good factor, where does it come from? The directing? Hrm, this is interesting to consider. Lennie Mayne got his design team onto the same page to make a cohesive world, even if the dialogue of occasion thwarts this effort. (We're told that Peladon was 'taught... to hunt and ride', and yet this planet seems all rocks, tunnels, steep mountains and lightning.) Most significantly, though, the flaming torches on the walls required the lighting to be low, and not all from the ceiling as per usual. The result is a *chiaroscuro* effect that makes the aliens seem less like plastic and glass-fibre, and the repetitive masonry and rock-face effect walls look that bit more like a place than a studio. On this level, Aggedor is a bit of a mixed bag. In the cave, with its low lighting and carefully selected angles, he seems menacing (although less so than the Prince in *The Singing Ringing Tree*, the 1950s East German film the BBC was serialising for kids at the same time). But the reveal of him in the throne room is one of all-too-many shots that make obvious that it's a man in a teddy-bear suit.

The story's overall colour scheme, at least, is restricted but well-judged. (The episodes are made to work without colour, as was needed in 1972.) By having purple for the locals and green / red mixes for the visitors (including the Doctor), the darkened sets make almost any frame of the story look thought out. (It also makes Amazonia more of an outsider than ever, and shows that Jo's choice of dress was more fortuitous than we'd suspected.)

To liven all this up a bit, they throw in some swordplay. Generally these are long, boring and flatly directed, and in particular the fracas in the throne room has too few camera-angles. It's well-choreographed, but looks for all the world like a set-piece to make episode four run to the correct length. There's a tradition of sword fights in *Doctor Who* past and future, but when it winds up looking less violent than Pan's People dancing on *Top of the Pops*, it's time to rethink the value of such scenes to the series.

The good news is that the gladiatorial fight is well-enough executed. But the *bad* news is that even this just shows up how far *Doctor Who* has become a matter of inserting set-piece A into tab B. All of episode three is build-up to this fight, just as most of episode four is build up to the next one. Just shoving in incident after incident isn't the same as storytelling. A clear link between cause and effect is required. Without it, when they run out of set pieces, the story grinds to a halt about five minutes into the last episode. Perversely this makes the ending work better (certainly for audiences used to the lachrymose endings of stories in the Welsh series[64]). Because it's less obviously a "tag" scene, the conclusion of the Jo-Peladon storyline has time to breathe and we're given a sign that she's growing up, even if most of her impressive moments here are when she drops the cutesy act she routinely does for the Doctor's benefit. The space-based stories in this era underline this, although once Jo returns to UNIT, she reverts to her irritating cute old self. For a series in the custody of two old soap hands (and this story was written by another), this dichotomy is baffling and lamentable.

To pull everything together, then: there's a distinct feeling that some of the production team thought that if "The Curse of Peladon" had a *Scooby Doo* plot where the suspects were funny-looking monsters and added a few fights, the kids would be happy. Fortunately we get a bit more than that in the finished episodes: they could have used a bouncy-castle, a traffic-cone and a Kroton from their monster storage depot, and it would have been substantially the same tale. This story's redeeming grace, then, is that some thought has gone into the design. The fundamentals are unchanged, but Mayne and his crew have taken what Hayles gave them and gone to town on it.

And *that's* why it's so beloved.

Besides, if nothing else, they've managed a whole planet without any quarry locations. Things are definitely looking up.

The Facts

Written by Brian Hayles. Directed by Lennie Mayne. Ratings: 10.3 million, 11.0 million, 7.8 million, 8.4 million. (The abrupt slump between episodes two and three was mostly due to power-cuts; see **The Lore**.)

Supporting Cast   David Troughton (Peladon), Geoffrey Toone (Hepesh), Alan Bennion (Izlyr), Sonny Caldinez (Ssorg), Stuart Fell (Alpha Centauri), Ysanne Churchman (Voice of Alpha Centauri), Murphy Grumbar (Arcturus), Terry Bale (Voice of Arcturus), Gordon St. Clair (Grun), Nick Hobbs (Aggedor), Wendy Danvers (Amazonia).

Working Titles   "The Curse".

Cliffhangers   At the entrance to the throne-room, the King's Champion tries to push the huge stone statue of Aggedor down onto the delegates' heads; after the Doctor commits sacrilege by entering the temple of Aggedor's inner sanctum, the King has no alternative but to sentence him to death; the Doctor beats the King's Champion in the arena-pit, but in the gallery a weapon slides out of Arcturus' casing and there's a sudden shot from Ssorg's big ray-gun.

What Was in the Charts?   "Son of My Father", Chicory Tip; "Theme From 'The Persuaders' ", John Barry Orchestra; "Family Affair", Sly and the Family Stone; "Horse With No Name", America.

The Lore

• Stop us if you've heard this one before... director Lennie Mayne, a rather outspoken Australian, was irritated with the restrained, British way in which the cast reacted to the mythical beast entering the royal chamber. He castigated them, insisting they should be thinking "holy f***ing cow!" After a break, during which Pertwee circulated amongst the cast, and as Barry Letts showed a party of (according to some sources) boy scouts and / or a vicar around the set, they filmed the scene and an entire cast of character actors as aliens shouted 'holy f***ing cow!' in unison at Aggedor.

Unsurprisingly, this story has been embroidered a lot over the years. The more plausible account, though, is that this took place during camera rehearsals before lunch *and then* Letts took the vicar to the studio, whereupon Mayne moderated his language for the rest of the day. DWAS founder Jan Vincent Rudski was also in the studio during one of the recording sessions, but he doesn't remember any such activity.

Right, have we got that out of our systems? Back to the start, then...

• Brian Hayles had just got into hot water for adapting a novel (*Deathday* by Angus Hall) into an episode of the new-look, spooky *Out of the Unknown*. By "adapting", of course, we mean "junking everything except the title and chucking in full-frontal nudity, because nobody watches BBC2". Alas, the author was one of about five people who *did* watch this, and he got rather irate. The producer of this last gasp of a once-great series was BBC hack Alan Bromly (of whom more later, some of it actually good - see 11.1, "The Time Warrior").

Hayles had sent in a couple of new ideas for *Doctor Who* stories in early 1971, and Dicks and Letts had met him to kick ideas around. One of the two spec scripts ("The Brain Dead") had the Ice Warriors and the other ("The Shape of Terror") had an enclosed base on an alien planet, a whodunit theme and no location filming. Dicks thought it was dull and samey, and was especially unimpressed with the rather anonymous monster. So they mashed the two together and added a pretext for a gladiatorial fight for the Doctor. Hayles developed the Baskerville-style "curse" plot, plus thought the Ice Warriors were such obvious villains, they should be made to help the Doctor instead. It was on Letts' mind to do two successive stories that weren't wholly UNIT-based, with returning "classic" monsters to remind viewers that the Master wasn't the only shot in the show's locker. This seems to explain why "The Curse of Peladon" was pulled ahead of 9.3, "The Sea Devils" in the running-order, although spacing out the two space stories ("Curse" and "The Mutants") was a sensible precaution. The rest of the explanation will come in that story's listings.

• In the original script, the "Venusian lullaby" used by the Doctor to soothe Aggedor was the Tibetan chant 'om mani padme hum', because

there really were an *awful* lot of weekend Buddhists working on *Doctor Who* in the 70s. Dicks proposed the re-cycled "Klokleda partha mennin klatch" from "The Daemons", and Pertwee added the tune. About half the cast and crew guessed where it came from, the rest went in for wild speculation based on Pertwee's knowledge of folk music. (As you've hopefully figured out, it's based on "God Rest Ye Merry Gentlemen".) Dicks added justifications for Jo to be wearing something other than hot-pants or a mini (her "date" with Mike Yates), why there's wind and lightning but no rain and - apparently - the end-scene where the Doctor figures out that the Time Lords have manipulated him. A large part of episodes three and four, in fact, were rewritten by Dicks and further amended by Mayne.

• "Lovely Lennie Mayne" (as he was almost credited for one episode, apparently) had been a director with the BBC since the mid-1960s, working on things like *Vendetta* (popular in its day, circa 1966, but slated by Huw Wheldon). Before that he'd been a dancer on breakthrough Associate Rediffusion show *Cool for Cats* (a sort of proto-*Ready, Steady, Go!*). He'd directed a few *Doomwatch* episodes, including one featuring Terry Bale, and another where Patrick Troughton proved that life existed after *Who* (see 10.1, "The Three Doctors").

Patrick's son David Troughton, returning to the series after his cameos in "Enemy of the World" (5.4) and "The War Games" (6.7), was sharing a flat with Colin Baker. Katy Manning developed a huge crush on him (David, that is, not Colin) but didn't act on it - and discovered, too late, that it may have been mutual. As you've all now no doubt seen, he returns again in "Midnight" (X4.10). Ysanne Churchman's other claim to fame is as Grace Archer, wife of Phil and the character unexpectedly killed off in the episode of *The Archers* broadcast on the day ITV began transmission in 1955. (The BBC running spoilers and publicity-stunts? Unthinkable!) In voicing Alpha Centauri, she was told to think of the character as "a prissy, homosexual civil servant". (It wasn't her first alien voice-over; she'd done an episode of the puppet show *Space Patrol* too.) Alan Bennion seems to have been the only choice for Izlyr (he previously played Slaar in 6.5, "The Seeds of Death"), but, amazingly, Sonny Caldinez only came on board as Ssorg after two days with David

Purcell in the role.

• The script didn't really detail how Alpha Centauri should look. Barbara Lane designed the costume around a basic wicker frame, and made the eye close with the calliper brakes used on motorbikes and bicycles. There was a one-way mirror for the operator to see through. Mayne's reaction to seeing Alpha Centauri was, so the legend goes, "it looks like a f____ing prick!" So they added the cape - and would up giving them to every alien (making the Doctor's instant acceptance by the delegates far more plausible) - at which Mayne is reported to have said, "Now it looks like a prick in a cape".

The Ice Warrior was a composite of the bits they had left over since the 60s but with a new gun. Bennion's old costume from "The Seeds of Death" was taken out of mothballs and given a new sparkly cape. Arcturus' magic tea-trolley was later re-used in the "Future" section of *Blackadder's Christmas Carol*, occupied by "Bernard" (linguistically appropriate if nothing else). It included working hydraulics from fish-tanks, and a red light for when "damaged". The tank's occupant, Murphy Grumbar, operated the gun by shoving it with his foot.

• As previously noted, this is the first and only story to credit 'Profile' - Terry Walsh's stunt troupe - with episode three crediting Walsh alone. Walsh had got onto a cushy number as Pertwee's stunt-double, so when he formed Profile he kept the *Doctor Who* gig and Havoc (Derek Ware's troupe) sought work elsewhere. (Notably they worked on *Some Mothers Do 'Ave 'Em*, a slapstick sitcom with a protagonist who kept bad impressionists in work for years.) Then Equity got onto Ware's case about his simultaneously being a stuntman and an agent, so Havoc bit the dust.

Oddly enough, former Havoc members who'd worked on *Doctor Who* found themselves being hired again (keep an eye out for Stuart Fell playing monsters, starting with this very story), whilst Ware wound up teaching fight-arranging at a Theatre school. Walsh was put in charge of directing the fight scenes, which were left deliberately perfunctory in the scripts to accommodate whatever the budget and running time required. Gordon St Clair was another member of Profile, so did his own stunts as the king's champion Grun, but Walsh doubled for Pertwee wherever necessary. He was still officially a Havoc member when the contracts went out, which *may* be why the credit is split.

• Another split credit was for Special Effects. Ian Scoones and Bernard Wilkie did the work after Jack Kine had to drop out through illness, but an oversight left Wilkie uncredited on the first two episodes. Scoones used a colleague from Century 21 to light his model of the citadel "properly", and the fall-out from this led to his going to other studios for filming to avoid further antagonising the BBC's staff by using freelancers. (See "Frontier in Space" for more.)

• The studio recordings were on Mondays and Tuesdays, this time one per day. Episode two was recorded after a photocall; after this, it was noticed that Manning still had one of her curlers in her hair, as you'll see in nearly all the stills for this story. Owing to reasons we'll discuss in "The Sea Devils", speed became of the essence... the final edit of episode two's score, in fact, was made hours before transmission. Similarly, episode three was recorded two days after episode one had aired.

• In this episode, a device to hypnotise Aggedor was furnished from components from a plastic model aircraft with a battery-powered bulb and a spinning dental mirror (not the sonic screwdriver, as is often suggested). The wall-mounted torches meant that the lighting was kept low, so the shadows would look right. That scene where the door opens too far and hits the Doctor was an unrehearsed accident, but they kept it.

• The power cuts which affected most of Britain that month led to the continuity announcers giving "The Story So Far" summaries before each episode. (The scheme was that different parts of the country had their power switched off at different times, and rotas were published in the press. You knew in advance when the lights were due to go out, unless you were Christopher Barry - see "The Mutants".) The miners originally called the strike, but railway workers had a connected grievance, so they co-ordinated their disputes to cause maximum inconvenience. The BBC knew in advance when they couldn't make programmes, but not always who would get to see them on transmission - paradoxically, the ratings show that more people saw this story than "The Sea Devils". It's not known whether Arcturus was deliberately made to look like miners' union leader Joe Gormley, but a lot of people thought it was.

The miners eventually accepted a pay settlement fractionally higher than the meteoric inflation-rate, although it didn't end there as the deal didn't include overtime. (The management took this as a signal that they could demand more work per week from each miner than the pay-rise covered... this will get nasty by the time we get to this story's sequel; see also "The Green Death".)

• On 5th of March, the day after "The Sea Devils" episode two went out, Alpha Centauri made another appearance in *The Black and White Minstrel Show*. (See **Did *Doctor Who*** End in 1969? under 6.7, "The War Games".) In a stroke of bad luck, the power cuts failed to prevent people seeing this.

• So why *is* the Doctor staring so fixedly at the console in the TARDIS scene? Apparently, the one of scene-shifters played a prank by putting a dirty photo on the prop to try to put Pertwee off. We've tried looking for it, purely out of the academic diligence that this guidebook requires.

9.3: "The Sea Devils"

(Serial LLL. Six Episodes, 26th February - 1st April 1972.)

Which One is This? Duh! It's the one with the Sea Devils in it - seven foot turtle-men in string vests come out of the sea and launch commando raids on naval institutions. There's plenty of Navy larks, stuff with speedboats and hovercraft; and music quite unlike anything you've *ever* heard...

Firsts and Lasts As the serial code indicates, "The Sea Devils" was filmed before "The Curse of Peladon" but shown afterwards, the first time that *Doctor Who* stories had been shot out of sequence. If you've read Volume. I, you'll realise how big a deal this is and how much things have changed since the 60s. *Doctor Who* was becoming a much more structured kind of programme, at least in theory.

On screen it's the first of two outings for the Sea Devils, the marine branch of the Silurian family. For the first (and only) time during the Pertwee era, there's a menace to modern-day Britain and UNIT doesn't get involved. (Presumably because UNIT doesn't have a naval division at this point.) And curiously, this is the last story to not mention the TARDIS. (13.6, "The Seeds of Doom" nearly took that honour, but then they went and added an epilogue scene with the Doctor and Sarah arriving in Antarctica.)

This is the first story to have music (as opposed to "atmospheres" that could be sound effects)

entirely composed and executed by the BBC Radiophonic Workshop. As it turns out, Malcolm Clarke will also be the *last* in-house composer to work on the series (23.3, "Terror of the Vervoids").

A nation's eight-year-olds sob as, for the final time, the caption 'Action By Havoc' appears. In a related incident, the ubiquitous Terry Walsh - here playing a guard named Barclay - finally gets a line of scripted dialogue in episode three.

Six Things to Notice About "The Sea Devils"...

1. The most memorable visual thing about "The Sea Devils" is the assault on the island in episode five, in which a whole legion of reptile-people marches out of the ocean and onto the beach. Anyone watching this as an adult will observe six men in baggy overalls and string vests, with goofy turtle-masks on their hats, wandering around looking a bit confused. Anyone who's familiar with the end-credits of *Dad's Army*, in fact, will have extreme difficulty taking it seriously. But anyone who was a child when the episode was first transmitted will tell you that this was - honestly - one of the best things *ever*.

2. The Master specifically asks for a colour television, and watches *The Clangers* on it. Yes, terribly sweet and his use of it to bamboozle Trenchard is wonderful. He'll do this same trick several lifetimes later with the Toclafane and *Teletubbies* - "The Sound of Drums" (X3.12), but stop and look at the set he's using. *Look* at it! It's a Venetian blind painted yellow. This is apparently supposed to suggest the "near future", but viewers would have discerned it as... well, as a yellow-painted Venetian blind, of the sort used for keying in CSO of fake news reports elsewhere.

Funnily enough, this same blinds-TV trick turns up in just about every episode of *The Goodies*, which is sort of like *Monty Python* meets Tex Avery, and uses many of same effects, cast[70] and back-room staff as Pertwee-era *Who*. Only, er, *The Goodies* does the blinds-TV effect slightly more proficiently and for deliberate comic effect. A newsreader would announce some variety of slapstick catastrophe on these *faux* tellies, so if the Master and Trenchard were acting true to *The Goodies* form, they should rush out of the studio and onto a filmed insert, whereupon speeded-up cartoon-like action would ensue. And nothing in the lone Sea Devil / landmines sequence dissuades us from thinking that Tim, Bill and Graeme (the eponymous Goodies) are about to arrive.[71]

3. It's impossible to talk about "The Sea Devils" without mentioning the music. As in "Doctor Who and The Silurians", it divides opinion between those who feel it's daringly inventive and those who feel it's just repellent noise. However odd it sounds now, imagine how much odder it seemed at Saturday teatime in 1972. There are moments when it's impossible to imagine any other kind of music working with this story but some things - like the *wheeeeeee-ker-dunk* used for when Trenchard and the Doctor are playing golf - that make you wonder why they bothered. See also **Just How Important is the Music?** Under 9.4, "The Mutants", for more on this year's experiments with sound.

4. Although it looks like a Navy recruitment film at times (and indeed nicks footage from a couple of these), the Senior Service doesn't come out of this too well. They're the latest British institution (after the Church of England and the Prison service) to be infiltrated by the Master, and watch the way he takes the salute when impersonating an Admiral - perhaps they mistook him for Haile Selassie. Their security is woefully lax in other ways; this being a Malcolm Hulke script, the sirens and security lockdown start just *after* the escapee gets through a cordon unchecked. And the climax of episode five has an eight-foot lizard in a smock sneaking up on a guard - not from behind but *straight in front of where he ought to be looking*.

The Navy does, however, have one unexpectedly advanced piece of equipment: along the lines of Reegan's Magic Breadvan (7.3, "The Ambassadors of Death"), they have an Air-Sea Rescue helicopter that changes from a blue Sea King to a red Wessex in mid-flight.

5. Jo gets the "exposition" duties this time, reminding the audience about the Silurians by asking, 'That was that race of super-reptiles that had been in hibernation for billions of years, wasn't it?' without even taking a breath. (And: billions...?) Then in episode four, the Doctor sternly commands her to 'Let me take over the explanations.'

6. The Doctor sabotages the Master's electronic lash-up - described, in a catch-phrase of the era, as 'analogous to the laser' - by 'reversing the polarity of the neutron flow'. This is destined to become another catchphrase of the series, even though this marks the *only* time it's used during the 1970s.[72]

The Continuity

The Doctor He's an accomplished swordsman, a trained diver and good at playing golf while blindfolded. He's moved on from shouting 'hai!' when performing martial arts moves to shouting 'akira!', and is prepared to make a point about his superiority in combat by handing a weapon back to the disarmed Master in mid-combat. The Doctor states that the Master used to be a 'very good friend' of his, and establishes for the first time that 'you might almost say we went to school together' [quite possibly the Prydon Academy; see 14.3, "The Deadly Assassin"]. The Doctor admits to feeling sorry for the captive Master, though it seems that the Master can't conceive of this and believes the Doctor's just suspicious.

The Doctor is still a bit of a git towards Jo. After a ten-mile walk, he forbids her to eat sandwiches and wolfs them down himself. He also claims that violent exercise - such as swordplay - makes him hungry.

• *Ethics.* Here the Doctor's prepared to destroy the Sea Devils, killing thousands of them by blowing up their base, but only when he believes that war is inevitable otherwise. [Compare this with 21.1, "Warriors of the Deep".]

• *Inventory.* The sonic screwdriver is capable of detecting and detonating landmines. The Doctor's UNIT pass is numbered '10'. [They appear to have been made on site, outdoors, with photos of the Doctor and Jo in the clothes they're wearing in that story, but standing outside in a strong wind.] He now carries tenners around, in case he needs to bribe anyone.

• *Background.* The Doctor claims that Nelson was a good friend of his [q.v. 9.1, "Day of the Daleks"]. He implies that he may have been involved in the Crimean War, and - though he never states he was there - casually mentions Gallipoli and El Alamein [from the First and Second World Wars, respectively] in the same breath.

The Supporting Cast

• *Jo Grant.* Impressively, she knows enough karate to knock out a highly-trained guard with one chop. She also tosses aside two guards in the course of making an escape. Her attachment to the Doctor is such that when he insists on putting himself in a dangerous situation, she looks down at her shoes and very nearly starts sniffling. [At the very least it's become a kind of father / daughter relationship by now.]

She can abseil, drive a hovercraft, jimmy hand-cuffs with a couple of jeweller's screwdrivers, politely avoid Trenchard's rather slimy advances and get a naval officer she barely knows to call her 'Jo'. She's evidently read a number of confidential files on UNIT cases before her time, and says that the Brigadier told her about the Silurians. She apparently [unlike Manning] has phenomenal eyesight, able to spot the Master from very high up and three hundred or so yards away.

The Supporting Cast (Evil)

• *The Master.* Like the Doctor, he knows how to handle a sword - even though he's put on weight in prison. He uses *another* mask of his own face to fake his death, the last time he's ever seen to do this. His motive for helping the Sea Devils appears to be pure malice, wanting to hurt the Doctor by eradicating the human species; yet he *does* seem rather touched that the Doctor, and more particularly Jo, came to visit. Arguably, his obvious enjoyment of *The Clangers* proves he isn't completely sociopathic.

It's once again implied that the Doctor is a much better scientist than the Master, who's apparently becoming less and less of a genius as time goes by and increasingly relies on the Doctor for technical assistance. The Master has pieced together events pertaining to the Doctor's last meeting with the Silurians, somehow.

The Time Lords The Master says he knows about the Sea Devils from the Time Lords' files, which suggests the species is of note to the Doctor's people. [But then, presumably every species is. Anyway, the Master can't possibly have stolen *all* the Time Lords' files. He may have taken a particular interest in files which relate to Earth, after discovering that the Doctor was there, which might explain his knowledge of Azal in "The Daemons" (8.5). If so then the Time Lords may have expected the Doctor to come across the Silurians, and cross-referenced the "Silurian" file with the "Doctor in exile" one.

[Alternatively, and perhaps more plausibly, the Master's original attempt to conquer Earth with the Autons (8.1, "Terror of the Autons") was one of a number of schemes he devised to humiliate the Doctor before starting his *real* plan of cosmic domination in 8.4, "Colony in Space" and the Sea Devils were potential allies he considered, reject-ed, then remembered once captured. With his knowledge of high security prisons in the UK - 8.2, "The Mind of Evil" - he may even have anticipated that he'd be sent to Fortress Island if caught and kept this plan as a contingency. Granted, it requires an unusual amount of foresight, but it's not impossible.]

The Non-Humans

• *Sea Devils.* A half-delirious witness to the attack on the sea-fort coins the term "Sea Devil", so it's not the name used by the reptiles themselves. [But again, see "Warriors of the Deep". They could, with equal justification, be called 'Green Gilberts' (which is how the captain of the submarine describes them) or 'Those Lizard-Things'.]

The Sea Devils are reptiles, marine relations of the creatures from the Wenley Moor caves, generally known as Silurians even though the Doctor now believes they should have been called "Eocenes" [see **What's the Origin of the Silurians?** under 7.2]. The Doctor believes they're a different species [with perhaps a common ancestor, but not capable of inter-breeding], adapted for life underwater.

[Even if the Sea Devils *are* 'cousins' of the Silurians, as the Doctor claims, they probably aren't close ones. "Doctor Who and the Silurians" proved that the Silurians were cold-blooded (Quinn keeps his cottage very hot, the cave-base is swelteringly warm, etc.), and it's hard to see how seven-foot reptiles might stay conscious in chilly seawater this far north. Nor is it clear why something cold-blooded with *that* much skin-area (including all those crinkles and the fins on their heads) wouldn't immediately head for the nearest radiator or light a fire. The obvious inference is that they're warm-blooded, which explains why they're so active on their commando raids without eating a whole sheep each, then sleeping in the sun for a year or so.

[This is just about possible, and raises another significant factor: the Sea Devils can float. Most creatures that live in the sea, or spend a lot of time there, have fat-reserves. Just as humans are better swimmers than most Great Apes because of our adipose tissues, so the Sea Devils seem to have adjusted quite significantly as far as their diet and metabolism are concerned. We use the word "seem", of course, because we never see either species eat. What's most plausible is that they're

All Right, Then... Where Were Torchwood?

So here we are in the mid-1970s (ish), and a suspicious number of vessels vanish without trace in the busiest shipping-lane in the world. Prehistoric reptile-men connected with earlier incidents in Derbyshire assault the Navy, and an alien terrorist is held on an island and keeps escaping. There's threats to Britain from non-human intelligences, and useful technology to be plundered - who ya gonna call?

Wouldn't it be great if there was some kind of secret army, like in *Men in Black*, but more rabidly xenophobic and entirely staffed by people who got bullied by the school chess club? Who protected us from all this and found ways to make the hoarded science and technology work for themselves? What would be *really* funny is if they were sworn to secretly protect and restore the British Empire, so we could finally tell the Yanks to sod off and learn to spell "colour" properly. And wouldn't it just be a hoot if they'd been going for all this time, and yet UNIT never managed to run into them?

If you've been sleeping *very* soundly since the First Edition of this volume, you might need to be told that BBC Wales' All-New *Doctor Who* introduces an organisation called the Torchwood Institute (later the star of its own spin-off series), whose main aim is to obtain and exploit any alien artefacts that might be useful to the British Empire whilst containing any perceived threats to same.

The first and most important "threat", as it happens, is the Doctor. Torchwood was set up in 1879 by Queen Victoria (X2.2, "Tooth and Claw"), although Captain Jack Harkness later reconfigured the Cardiff branch's remit and resources after New Year's 2000 (if we're going by *Torchwood* 2.12, "Fragments").

Some years later, Torchwood central - portrayed as a private army with Jatharr Sungliders and complete access to every CCTV camera in the UK - perishes with the destruction of its headquarters (the Canada Square tower in Canary Wharf) in X2.13, "Doomsday". When that occurs, Torchwood becomes limited to Jack and his dysfunctional Scooby gang, who operate in a hole in the ground in Cardiff that comes complete with pizza delivery and holding cells full of ravenous Weevils.

All well and good, but if we look at the number of potential threats and useful objects that we *know* happened in *Doctor Who* stories set between 1880 and 2007, there's a number of interesting non-events. Quite simply, where the hell were Torchwood when - just to pick an example - the Yeti turned up (5.5, "The Web of Fear")?

Close examination of the BBC Wales series in relation to the *Doctor Who* made from 1963 to 1989 (even though the two are obviously compatible) causes a fair amount of trouble. Are we to assume that the Time War changed everything? Is the Sarah-Jane Smith we meet in "School Reunion" (X2.3) the same person we saw in "The Hand of Fear" (14.2)? If so, why doesn't she seem to remember events in "The Five Doctors" (20.7)? And is the spin-off series *Torchwood* canonical as *Doctor Who*? If so, how many psychic nasties called 'Mara' are we dealing with?

The previous *About Time* volumes have tended to assume that the majority of readers want it all to be on the same ontological footing, even when time-travelling beings have rewritten the past *and* are said to have done so in the stories as broadcast (X1.7, "The Long Game"; X1.12, "Bad Wolf"; X2.0, The Christmas Invasion"; 9.1, "Day of the Daleks"; 12.4, "Genesis of the Daleks"). It would be nice to pretend that we could consign some stories to limbo, but for the purposes of this essay we'll maintain the same policies we stuck to in **What's the Dalek Timeline?** (2.8, "The Chase") and **What's the Timeline of the Far Future?** (3.6, "The Ark") and **How Does Time Work?** ("Day of the Daleks").

We shall therefore assume that the Torchwood Institute were around in the same continuity as "Terror of the Zygons" (13.1) - in fact, we *have* to, as that story is referenced in "School Reunion", which falls directly after the episode where the Institute gets set up. Furthermore, Sarah's continuity in her very own spin-off series (not to mention X4.13, "Journey's End") indicates that all three BBC Wales shows inhabit the same timeline as the UNIT stories of the 1970s. Deal with it.

If this is so, then Torchwood Mk I must have been as much use as a marzipan lifeboat. Think about it: all these amazing alien devices and techniques drop into the British Empire's lap, and *still* we went from being Top Nation circa 1920 to runt of the litter by 1975. Even in the *Doctor Who* universe, in which there's manned Mars launches and people building timescoops, the Brigadier constantly pines for better days. There's a Cold War, an Energy Crunch and an Arms Race. *Doctor Who*'s history has coincided enough like the one we've actually lived through for the British Empire to fade away, even though it's got a crack team of xenobiologists and well-paid boffins let loose on

continued on page 235...

descended from shoreline-dwelling reptilians, and have retained a lot of their more useful land-based facilities, such as broad feet and five-fingered hands.]

Lacking the third eyes of the Silurians, the Sea Devils' faces resemble sea-turtles, with fin-like growths instead of the Silurians' crests and skin which appears either orange or green. [This could be a racial difference. Then again, they tend to be green when they're on land and orange when they've just come out of the sea, so possibly it's something to do with damp pores.] They breathe air, but can evidently survive underwater for some time.

Like the Silurians, the Sea Devils are generally aggressive but aren't obsessed with war, their leader being prepared to consider peace with the humans until he's attacked. There are thousands of Sea Devils in their underwater base off the coast of Britain [no more than a few hundred miles from the Wenley Moor caves, so these two species were common in western Europe], and potentially millions more in installations around the world. The leader seems sure that the Doctor's telling the truth after mysteriously holding his hand over the back of the Doctor's head [this is either some form of rudimentary telepathy or just Sea Devil posturing]. It's not clear whether they were woken by operations on the sea fort or something the Master did, but their hibernation devices have deteriorated over time and the reactivation mechanism doesn't work. Unlike the Silurians, they apparently just need a certain signal to wake them up, and they don't have to drain power from other sources.

[It seems odd, though, that the hibernation devices in *all* the installations across the world have somehow broken down. If, as we are told, the trigger was supposed to fire after a catastrophe that never occurred, is it not possible that one re-awakened cell in Derbyshire would be enough to trip the rest?. Again, see the audio *Bloodtide* for a less-than-bulletproof explanation.]

Unlike their 'cousins', the Sea Devils use ultrasonic communicators to rouse themselves; the Master uses this to give commands. [The device Dr Quinn was given in "Doctor Who and The Silurians" acted as a homing beacon for a lost Silurian, but the gizmo the Master builds with government-issue components works almost like a joystick, sending a Sea Devil through a minefield like it was Sonic the Hedgehog.] Only their leader

is heard to speak - the rest utter eerie cries when injured.

Also unlike the Silurians, the Sea Devils wear garments not unlike large - but fetching - string vests. [Who knows? This may be a weird camouflage. As they've only just encountered human activities, maybe they think that fishing-nets are commonplace on land. (And for anyone who thinks we've here gone mad, we humbly suggest a close look at 4.5, "The Underwater Menace". If the Sea Devils' resurrection is in any way connected with the destruction of *that* Atlantis - a more plausible means of resetting their alarm-call than the fort getting retrofitted, surely - maybe their first contact with humans was, Heaven help them, via the Fish People[73].)]

Their technology resembles that of their land-going cousins, since the "diving bell" they use to take humans into their underwater lair is almost organic in appearance. The Sea Devils' standard side-arm is a weapon which projects a concentrated beam of heat, intense enough to burn through rock or metal. They have some way of immobilising a submarine at long range, and their base can be entered via a huge undersea cavern, the mouth of which can be closed off by a force-field.

Sea Devils "shake hands" by pressing one palm against the palm of the person they're facing.

History

• *Dating.* [1973, probably autumn. The Master speaks of colour television as if it's still something of a luxury, again suggesting the early 70s rather than the late 70s - see 11.2, "Invasion of the Dinosaurs". He's watching *The Clangers*, which aired November 1969 to October 1974; the BBC didn't next air the series until 1986.]

The Master is being held prisoner on Fortress Island, conveniently close to the Sea Devil base. Many people wanted to see him executed, although the armed forces don't seem to know about him. [The novelisation expands on this, claiming that the Doctor argued for mercy during the trial. It also claims that the public were aware of the case - but not that the Master was an alien - and that the Brigadier wrote a letter to the Prime Minister about the problem of keeping him confined.] He's being held in remarkably luxurious conditions, even taking into account the hold he has over the governor, and the guards call him 'sir'. [Conspiracy theorists might think the British government is buttering him up, maybe trying to

All Right, Then... Where Were Torchwood?

...continued from page 233

captured spaceships.

At a very simple level, it seems that Torchwood has missed trick after trick. Travers brings back advanced robots from Tibet some time in the 1930s (5.2, "The Abominable Snowmen"), then sells one to make ends meet. Not only does Julius Silverstein ("The Web of Fear") grab it for his crummy little museum (still lit by candles in 1968), but he's never, in so far as we can tell, approached / coerced by people with impressive-looking credentials and friends in high places into giving it up. It's not like Travers is even that obscure. In his dotage, he's still the first person the Government thinks of to investigate this web-fungus clogging up the Tube, even though to begin with not everyone thinks his Yeti is connected. He's famous for developments in electronics, a professor (in the UK that means he's permanently attached to a University in a very senior position; unlike in the US, where anyone with a teaching post can call themselves this) and listened to. He also knows the Doctor, and trusts him.

More importantly, Travers didn't know anything about the Doctor when they first met. Even if we're presuming that his trip to Tibet to find the Yeti didn't arouse Torchwood's interest, wasn't funded by them or assigned to anyone who joined the expedition at the last minute and sent cryptic messages back to London or Cardiff, why did his return with alien goodies not get noticed? Why was there *nobody* from this supposedly high-powered organisation in the Goodge Street bunker? The killer punch is that their original base is about half a mile away from Loch Ness, and they failed to spot Broton's ship or a giant lizard ("Terror of the Zygons") - and indeed, neglected to investigate the single-most famous Mysterious Happening in Britain.

Once you ask questions like that, all sorts of past *Doctor Who* stories become interesting. How did someone calling himself 'the Doctor' turning up to see WOTAN (3.10, "The War Machines") fail to get Her Majesty's Geek Infantry out in force with pepper-spray and straight-jackets? Why were Jago and Litefoot (14.6, "The Talons of Weng-Chiang") not taken in for questioning? (We can't swear that they weren't, but the Doctor doesn't hesitate to get them involved and neglects to warn them. And as we'll see in a minute, by *that* incarnation he should have been told about Torchwood.)

It might be countered that the spooks and nerds were dealing with a Charter that mentioned a skinny guy with plimsolls and an annoying fake cockney accent, so all these middle-aged men calling themselves 'Doctor' and dressing up as Edwardian gentlemen-adventurers might have slipped through the net. It's just about possible that they failed to spot that *every single time* someone tried to invade Earth using the Home Counties as a bridgehead, one of these oddly-dressed chaps is on hand to stop them. It's *remotely* conceivable that they somehow failed to get into UNIT's records. (These were filed, you will recall, by Jo Grant - a blonde so dizzy she hides by closing her eyes - in a top-secret organisation that every journalist in Britain has heard of. We also know from Season Eleven that a least one such journalist can walk into a UNIT operation on the flimsiest of cover stories, along with any passing spider-tormented ex-travelling salesman.) But this is really pushing it, you must admit.

The point is that if Torchwood entirely failed to think that a time-traveller with a police box and two hearts - and who goes by the name 'the Doctor' - *might* be the same person as a seemingly younger time-traveller with a police box and two hearts and the same name, they don't deserve to get their own spin-off Chad Valley *Give-a-Show* slide strip. To be fair, the recruitment system of this secret brotherhood seems a little haphazard. After all, thirty-odd years after the UNIT era, they're led by a woman who allows two invasions within twenty minutes (X2.12, "Army of Ghosts"). Cybermen come to our planet by personal invitation of Yvonne Hartman, and they proceed to take over the entire world and use her HQ as their base of operations before the Daleks sweep in to crash the party in their millions. Worse, Hartman's "replacement" (by default if not the actual chain-of-command) is a man who doesn't exist, is a known associate of the man Torchwood was set up to hunt and has severe staff discipline issues.[79] And under his watch, the Beast of Revelations wipes out a good amount of the population of Cardiff. That's all right, though, because Captain Jack is doing all of this in the Doctor's honour (X3.12, "The Sound of Drums")[80]. Moreover, it isn't even clear whether Torchwood has a monopoly on alien tech: the clear hint in the second episode of *The Sarah Jane Adventures* is that UNIT, not Torchwood, cleared up after Slitheen tried to soak

continued on page 237...

get his help with scientific research projects. There's one obvious possibility, though, that we'll examine in the accompanying essay.]

Walker, the Parliamentary Private Secretary, has the Minister's authority to blow up the Sea Devils. He's familiar with UNIT's file on the Silurians, and suggests there's an "official line" that these creatures are to be destroyed.

The Analysis

Where Does This Come From? It would be stupid to ignore that both the producer and star of this series had served in the Navy in World War II. Letts had also been in the film *San Demetrio, London*, made by Ealing Studios just after the real events on which it was based. Pertwee's wartime experiences might have made a story like this inevitable, but there was also the small matter of *The Navy Lark*.

This was a knockabout radio farce based on the worst suspicions of the serving ratings about the incompetence and self-interest of their superior officers. Leslie Phillips played a clueless Lieutenant whose grasp of navigation and naval terminology was so poor, his usual instructions for steering were "left hand down a bit". Reporting to him was a Chief Petty Officer from the East End whose uncle was a scrap-metal dealer, and they had a symbiotic relationship. (With disarming simplicity this character was called "CPO Pertwee" and always referred to himself in the third person, as in "Pertwee's got and idea" or "Abandon ship! Women and Pertwee first!")

The series started in the 50s but was still running into the 70s, recorded on Sundays at the BBC's Regent Street studio. (Bear this in mind when looking at the filming schedules.) By 1972, Pertwee was playing several other characters, alongside Michael Bates, Ronnie Barker, Tenniel Evans, Phillips and Stephen Murray. One semi-regular character from the early days was Sir Willoughby Todhunter-Brown, a pompous diplomat who repeatedly got put in charge of small colonies who all immediately made bids for independence. Sound familiar?

But if Pertwee had come to represent the Navy as former servicemen remembered it, the abandonment of National Service in 1960 had caused the Senior Service (we *all* called it that; they even had their own brand of cigarettes) to buck its ideas up with regard to recruitment. The Air Force

had all the glamour and the army had a catchy slogan ("It's A Man's Life in the Army" - see 8.3, "The Claws of Axos") but the Royal Navy had two big advantages. One was that our nuclear capability was all in Polaris subs (see the essay with "The Ambassadors of Death"), and the other was Prince Charles. Back then he was quite the dashing playboy (and easily the world's most eligible bachelor), so seeing him flying RN helicopters on the news almost once a fortnight was a crafty way to reinforce the idea of the Navy as up-to-date. *Doctor Who* coming along and asking for help *just* as the Prince of Wales returned to civilian life was exactly what they wanted. You can almost hear both the Navy and Letts saying, "Look! We've got Hovercraft!"

Helicopters over the waves featured in other news items of the time, notably the seemingly endless pieces about the impending energy bonanza in the North Sea (see also 5.6, "Fury from the Deep"). Michael Buerk, the BBC's Energy Correspondent, was never more than five feet from a life-jacket. In "The Sea Devils", the abandoned-fort sequences echo these reports.

Long before space, the children of Britain heard tales of weird life and bizarre adventures from sailors home on leave since Shakespeare's time. (*The Tempest* is a compendium of accumulated tall tales, but a century earlier Sir Thomas More passed off Utopia as a series of anecdotes from a returning mariner.) The sea was presently a blank canvas for imaginary tales, with the added bonus that what little was known for certain was as amazing as any tale. There has always been a place for stories of lost civilisations, undersea cities and ancient powers sleeping; indeed, this season ends with a trip to Atlantis, by writers oblivious to the shameful precedent in this series. (See **How Many Atlantises Were There?** under "The Underwater Menace".) In English folklore there's a specific one that's hard to ignore: Lyonesse, where Arthur was taken by Nine Maidens (see 26.1, "Battlefield" but also our comments on "The Daemons"). We all grew up knowing things were asleep under the sea, waiting to re-emerge. In the early 70s, we also knew the sea contained weirder things than anyone had thought. It *must* be true: it's on telly every week....

Here it's worth reiterating the TV schedules of the time. On Saturdays you got *Doctor Who*, followed by *The Generation Game* and so on. Mondays at twenty past seven was always an

All Right, Then... Where Were Torchwood?

...continued from page 235

up all Earth's energy.

Nonetheless, people with an interest in reconciling all of this have expended a lot of ingenuity trying to link the 70s stories with what we now surmise must be happening off-screen. The fact that Professor Fendleman (15.3, "Image of the Fendahl") calls in someone called 'Hartman' to dispose of a lot of dead bodies and step up security around his sonic time scanner has been leapt on. (It *can't* be Yvonne, however - she would have been about eight and possibly less effective than she was at Canary Wharf - but it may be a relative.) Then you have to ignore the number of Tylers clustered around this time-rift. Mind you, we're told in the first *Torchwood* episode that a fourth Torchwood branch used to exist, and even Jack doesn't know what happened to it.

Whilst the ULTIMA machine seems not to be connected directly with Torchwood (26.3, "The Curse of Fenric"), Commander Millington's actions plausibly stem from their orders. The scheme to let the Soviets have a booby-trapped decoder (plus Millington's knowledge of an alien toxin, and the willingness to use it on Moscow) is classic Torchwood. Unfortunately, it's also classic Whitehall, so we don't need this interpretation to make the story work any better.

More helpfully, Torchwood involvement gives us a seemingly plausible explanation for Chinn's bizarre behaviour in "The Claws of Axos" (8.3). If he's working for Torchwood, then it makes sense that he'd move Heaven and Earth to remove the Doctor from UNIT protection, grab the Axonite for Queen and Country and pull rank whenever he can. On closer examination, of course, this all falls down. For one thing, if the Doctor's listed as a threat, what about the Master? Doesn't anyone in Torchwood know about him? Chinn, at least, is completely in the dark about someone who recently caused a lot of deaths and attracted notice at ministerial level (8.1, "Terror of the Autons") and obtained Home Office approval for a scam that almost caused a Third World War (8.2, "The Mind of Evil"). It's been suggested that the Master was spared from execution after his arrest (8.5, "The Daemons") because someone with a lot of clout put in a bid for his services. But then we'd have to ask how Torchwood - if they pulled this string - could have allowed the Doctor to see his old foe (9.3, "The Sea Devils"), let alone failed to capitalise on their good fortune. This becomes

especially odd if we recall that it's the Doctor's intervention that seems to have tipped the balance.

As hinted a while ago, the Third Doctor's activities (and we presume those of all subsequent incarnations) had UNIT sanction. Apprehending UNIT's semi-official Scientific Advisor might have triggered international repercussions, even for a body that could conceivably replace him with an android duplicate that rubs its neck and says 'good gwief!' just like the real thing. Fair enough, but we still have to account for Torchwood's remarkable ability to stay undetected when earlier Doctors thwart alien incursions - the sort of thing they could likely detect well before UNIT or the regular army, allegedly. There's a hint that this crosses the Doctor's mind at the end of "The War Games" (6.7), when he's threatened with exile to Earth in the twentieth century, and he's concerned that he might be recognised.

This, of course, assumes that he knew he'd be spending his exile on Earth in Britain. (*We* know that was the only place the BBC could afford to base the new series, but he doesn't.) If the Second Doctor knew that Torchwood existed, it must have been in an unscreened adventure, because the instances of him saving twentieth-century Britain must count among the most gobsmackingly obvious things that Torchwood should have been onto before the Doctor arrived. Thousands of teenagers going missing from Gatwick airport (4.8, "The Faceless Ones") is precisely the sort of thing they were set up to prevent. This even occurs a good two years before UNIT were even set up (going by our own dating, and the helpful hint from President Elect Toadthrush in "The Sound of Drums" that a First Contact protocol was established by the UN in 1968). If a police inspector is onto the alien conspiracy, surely professional alien-catchers might have gotten a whiff of Chameleon Tours' nefarious activities. But it seems they didn't. If that's the case, can we get a rebate on all the tax revenue Torchwood have wasted on tube trains to Cardiff and pterodactyl-chow?

But we do have a smoking gun - or rather, a glowing orange Disintegrator. Think Tank (12.1, "Robot") have all the hallmarks of being a Torchwood outfit, or at least having Torchwood members amongst their number. Miss Winters knows all about the Doctor. The group has got technology way beyond what the rest of the

continued on page 239...

imported film series such as *Mission: Impossible, The Virginian* or *Star Trek*. (They'd tried putting *Trek* on in the *Doctor Who* slot, but it wasn't really getting the audience they wanted. So with the second and third seasons, the show was shifted into the Westerns / Spies bit of the schedule. It hardly mattered as everyone was probably watching *Coronation Street*.)

Friday was a film, usually a *Carry On* (amazing to think a time existed when they hadn't yet received a dozen showings). Thursdays was the pantswettingly thrilling combination of *Tomorrow's World* and *Top of the Pops*, but Tuesday? Ah, well, Tuesday was Jacques Cousteau night. Seriously, the youth of the nation would wolf down beans on toast or sausage and mash (or lamb cutlets, if they were posh) before watching undersea creatures gouging lumps out of one another and men in woolly hats using space-age machinery to film it. The 60s conception of the oceans dealt with what was there for us and how humanity could live there soon (see "The Underwater Menace"). However, the early 70s more entailed what had always been there, and what we had thoughtlessly done to it.

Cousteau was one popular advocate of this new respect for the seas, but the advent of colour television made it a rich vein of spectacular and relatively cheap documentary footage. Luckily for the smaller regional ITV companies, we had an alien world no more than eighty miles from any of us. It had the added bonus that, around Britain's shores, a lot of groovy archaeology was done, with boats from Elizabethan times to World War II transforming themselves into micro-ecologies. It was a human-interest story, a scientific goshwow moment and a wildly colourful extravaganza, just sitting there waiting for any TV crew with a waterproof camera and an empty slot to fill. Notorious cheapskate stations Anglia and Westward cleaned up in this field. In short, the arrival of colour TV triggered a resurgence of interest in the life aquatic, and no producer in their right mind would refuse a chance to do an underwater story.

One other strand of this story needs a bit of contemporary glossing: humans are seen from the "outside", as it were, a lot more in this story than usual. In many films of the time, the camera assumes the point-of-view of a non-human observer, either overtly (as in, for instance, all the films about computers observing us dispassionately, such as *The Forbin Project* or the insect-eye-

view from *Phase IV* - see 10.5, "The Green Death") or implicitly (*Planet of the Apes* can stand for one habitual stance; Brechtian or pseudo-objective distancing methods as in *A Clockwork Orange* or *Slaughterhouse Five* for another).

Of course, the granddaddy of all of these is Stanley Kubrick, who did both styles in *Doctor Strangelove* and *2001*. So look carefully at the grotesque close-up of Walker eating, then put that in context with the odd camera-angles and the astonishing music. We'll pick this up in **The Critique**, but we should note how close the avant-garde was to the mainstream circa 1972.

Things That Don't Make Sense Three ships have been sunk in a month. In the English Channel, no less. Not only has this not made the headlines (as it did when two were damaged in 2003 in the same month), but UNIT haven't heard a dicky-bird about it. Captain Hart seems equally misinformed, as he's acquainted with Trenchard enough for the two of them to chat about golf, yet he doesn't know about the Master, the *only* prisoner in Trenchard's care. There's not even a "Have You Seen This Man?" poster in sight, in case the Master might, perhaps, escape and head for the nearest supply of electronic components and weapons. Moreover, it's said that 70 ships (!) have disappeared in the area near the Sea Devil base in the last decade, yet it *also* appears that they've only recently woken up. Maybe the base has automatic defences, but the loss of so many ships to - say - futuristic heat rays that fire on *anything* that approaches would surely have warranted investigation before now, wouldn't it?

Once the Doctor and Jo have reason to suspect the Master participated in the electronics raid, they do the sensible thing and immediately use Captain Hart's phone to call UNIT to come and investigate. Oh, hang on a minute - they *don't* call UNIT, instead opting to dash off and check out the prison themselves. Then, before learning anything of help, the Doctor tells Jo to return to the naval base from which they've just come and... to phone UNIT. At this point the Doctor suspects that Trenchard is complicit in the Master's schemes, yet he *tells* him that Jo is headed back to base (allowing Trenchard to order her capture) - as opposed to extending her head start by claiming that she's just popped out to the loo. Clearly, Our Heroes have spent so long in the Master's proximity, they too have lost the power of forethought.

All Right, Then... Where Were Torchwood?

...continued from page 237

world, and indeed UNIT, can get their hands on. They're led by a power-dressing zealot and seem to be as sexually ambivalent as the Cardiff bunch. However, they aren't especially secret. Maybe they're just a front, to cover the embarrassment of nicking alien discoveries and passing them off as Made In Britain, or to allow commercial exploitation of pilfered gadgetry without having to deal with cosmic Intellectual Property law. But if that's the case, they they're a mess of it, because their plan relies upon the world's nuclear arsenal and not anything they've built or retrofitted. Admittedly, Think Tank aren't quite following the Torchwood rulebook (it's hard to see, after all, how a nuclear holocaust would help to protect the Empire) - but then, neither do the Cardiff sector even before Canary Wharf. And besides, technically it's the Scientific Reform Society who are doing bad things. If Torchwood were funding Think Tank - and allowing alien tech to slip into their hands but keeping a discreet distance - this scenario *might* still be possible, given Torchwood's characteristic negligence.

So, we have to account for a well-funded and talented organisation that's not terribly good at its job. One possibility is that - as we saw in X1.4, "Aliens of London" - the really savvy extraterrestrial invader stages hoaxes and distractions to keep Earth's authorities out of their way. This could explain why the UK has traditionally been where the largest concentration of crop-circles are to be found. Another possibility is that even before he officially joined then, Captain Jack might have been running interference. We know that he was recruited against his will in the late nineteenth century - thirty years after returning to Earth - and

a century later wound up in charge of the Welsh contingent ("in charge of" meaning that he was the only one left alive). However, it's hinted that his investigations into Mara activities (*Torchwood* 1.5, "Small Worlds") and weird circus folk (*Torchwood* 2.10, "From Out of the Rain") were for a different outfit. The *real* puzzle here is how he stayed so low-profile as to avoid Canary Wharf and not get reprimanded for his pro-Doctor leanings.

That said, Jack (or someone like him) must have persuaded the head of Torchwood not to use alien tech to prevent World War II, and thereby set up all manner of time paradoxes. Torchwood also seems to have avoided influencing the development of radar or the Manhattan Project. Jack did spend about 130 years here with nothing better to do and with a keen interest in Doctor-sightings, so it's workable. But even this is unsatisfactory, as Torchwood would have to be immensely stupid not to spot someone *who can't die* cropping up all over the place every time they're just about to apprehend the Doctor.

No matter how you slice this, if we posit the original version of Torchwood was active from the 1880s to (more or less) the present day within the orthodox *Doctor Who* continuity, their track record is abysmal. They have three functions: to stop the one they call the Doctor (they screwed that up royally); protect Britain from alien incursions (we'd've been better off hiring the Chuckle Brothers[81]); and use such alien devices as come their way to sustain and expand the British Empire (we started off running a quarter of the planet and wound up with McDonalds, Nickelodeon and Starbucks, making the UK feel like an occupied nation). In short, even compared to "Time Monster" era UNIT, Torchwood's a bit crap.

Furthermore, some swords are set on the wall just outside the quarters where the Master's being held, yet this doesn't tip anybody off that he may not be *quite* as imprisoned as he's meant to be. Even allowing that Trenchard helps the Master out of a misplaced sense of patriotism, he doesn't appear to have thought that perhaps a good reason exists for the Master to be locked up for life on an island miles from anywhere, surrounded by armed guards and landmines. (Keeping so many windows open isn't the best idea, either.)

For their part, the Sea Devils seem to believe that attacking any ships which come into their waters is a good way of wiping out the human

species, rather than - oh, say - just drawing attention to themselves. [Maybe the Master's *really* misinformed them about modern humanity.] It's never explained why the Sea Devils capture the submarine that's sent to investigate them, instead of just blowing it up the way they do with everything else. If their goal is to inspect state-of-the-art human technology, perhaps they should have considered doing so *before* starting a war against unknown aggressors.

The surviving lifeboat from one of the early Sea Devil attacks, which is supposedly being kept at a top-secret naval base as evidence in an official investigation, is lying around on the beach exposed to the weather. Even in the 70s, forensic science was a little more advanced than *that*. Had they run out of tarpaulins? And while we've already mentioned that the Magic Helicopter that seems to be some sort of Transformer, why - when the Doctor and Jo need rescuing - does Hart send this out instead of calling the HMS *Reclaim*, which we later find is right on the sea-fort's doorstep?

Hart keeps a detailed map of all the ship sinkings, yet he's apparently never wondered - until the Doctor points it out - if there's a correlation with the sea-fort that's smack dab in the middle of the incidents. Trenchard states that the Master is fattening up a bit because he 'can't get the exercise', but when the Doctor and Jo walk in, the Master is working out on exercise equipment. The lone Sea Devil that attacks the sea-fort has a strange sense of priorities, as he kills one of the crew, but leaves the other alive as gibbering wreck for no good reason. Maybe he spares the crewman to spread a sense of fear but why, then, would he sabotage the radio to stop the distraught man calling for help? And we might also wonder how two blokes performing maintenance on the abandoned sea-fort was enough to wake the Sea Devils up from their long slumber, yet the fort's initial construction, however many years ago it occurred, didn't do the trick.

On the fort, Jo finds the corpse of the skinny maintenance man and shouts, 'Look!', whereupon the Doctor stares straight ahead and says, 'What is it?' (It's a fully illuminated dead body, you fool!) Soon after, Jo refers to 'Those things that attacked us', when it was just the one, really. She's also repeatedly sceptical that the Doctor can turn a transistor radio into a transmitter, even though she's seen him hotwire all manner of advanced / alien technology by now (in the previous story, for instance, where he brought Arcturus out of his coma).

Security Guard Barclay (Terry Walsh, of course) has, apparently, been crouching in the middle of a field on the off-chance that escaping UNIT personnel would be heading for a precipice behind him. The prison guards' main mode of transport is a fleet of Citroen 2CVs with no doors - haven't they considered the possibility of it raining? And do *all* the guards on this island think they look good with moustaches? Is it an entrance qualification or something? Between those, the mini-capes, berets and blanco'd holsters, it's like the Pink Panther is about to saunter in.

There's rich picking in that beach scuffle at the end of episode three. From his vantage point, the Master can see that the Doctor and Jo are stuck between a minefield and a quintet of guards with shoot-to-kill orders. But instead of letting events play out, he uses his summoning device to bring forth a Sea Devil, thus instigating such chaos that Our Heroes can escape. Moreover, it seems as if that *one* Sea Devil overcomes the armed guards, even though he's outnumbered five-to-one and Sea Devils (as we repeatedly discover) aren't bulletproof. Okay, perhaps he kills the first two guards thanks to the element of surprise, but how can the remaining three men fail to shoot him dead, when he's just standing there in the open like that? And while we ordinarily wouldn't mention the boom-mic that's visible when the Doctor and Jo traipse through the minefield, it becomes a Thing That Doesn't Make Sense when it appears that the Special Effects boys have planted an explosive charge exactly where the guy holding the boom was standing.

Shortly into episode four, the Sea Devil that invades the submarine appears to push his way through a scalding hot, near-liquified metal door, yet suffers no injuries. The castle shoot-out that follows almost convinces you that the Sea Devils are bulletproof; the castle guards are *terrible* shots, missing their opponents at close range. Trenchard appears to shoot and wound one of the three Sea Devils outside the Master's cell, but there's no corresponding body on the floor afterward. (There's also an odd sequence where the Sea Devils look at one another, then one of them nods and looks to the first one into the room, and then the camera zooms on the Master - as if there was dialogue here originally. It looks as though they're deciding which one is going to ask Delgado for an autograph.) A minor quibble: there's no mark on Trenchard's body when the Doctor and Hart find it, even though he was presumably shot by the Sea Devils' flash guns.

In trying to wipe out the Sea Devils, Walker seriously thinks it a good idea to unleash a nuclear strike on a sea-fort that's less than five miles from a major naval base and which is significantly close to French territorial waters. Apart from rendering most of Southern Britain uninhabitable for generations (and so soon after Sir Reginald Styles narrowly averted a full-on holocaust[74]), can a Parliamentary Private Secretary actually do this? If he can, then this guy has a stiff upper lip and then some. Rather than make a will or drive away from Ground Zero very fast indeed, he just asks for more tea.

A problem we know of old, from "Doctor Who and the Silurians": the Doctor again winds up advocating a peace accord between humanity and another species that he must *know* historically didn't occur. [Maye he thought he could keep it out of the history books by giving the reptiles the Master's supply of rubber masks.] Meanwhile, the Master keeps insisting that mankind is weak, even though the missile assault on the Sea Devil base would seem to prove otherwise.

Something even old sailors don't immediately spot: when they go onto HMS *Reclaim*, the matelots pipe the Doctor aboard and not Hart. Does the Doctor outrank a Captain? [Maybe they were just reeling from the shock that it's really Katy Manning climbing a rope-ladder, and not Stuart Fell in drag.] Why do the naval personnel (from reversed stock footage, or so it seems) take off their headphones *before* their ships fire, only to whip 'em back on again? It's also odd that they reel in the diving bell so quickly - maybe everyone in the Navy knows that the Doctor is a Time Lord and doesn't get the bends. And from a moral standpoint, it's a little odd that the Doctor deliberately hands the submarine captain one of the Sea Devil guns, then is appalled when the man actually uses it. This happens shortly after the Doctor finds a Sea Devil who was apparently incapacitated by falling debris - even though there's not a bit of debris about the place.

When the Doctor sabotages the Master's device for waking up the reptile-people, causing all the Sea Devils in the area to roll around in agony to a painful high-pitch shriek, it goes on for well over a minute before the Master thinks to ask what's going on. Curiously, the Master expects the reptiles to understand the term 'teething troubles'. Even more curiously, the Doctor tells a random sailor assigned guard the Master: 'keep an eye on him', followed by 'watch him' - surely the *last* things you should say to someone guarding a hypnotist. All of this happens, of course, because the Master has suddenly decided in episode six he needs the Doctor's help to perfect the Sea Devils' reactivation device, even though he was quite happy to let the reptiles haul the Doctor away to his death in episode five.

As already noted, the boys at HMS *Seaspite* are guarded by someone who's mugged by a giant reptile who walks up in front of him and pinches

his nose. They're on a pebble beach, so the guard should have heard Green Gilbert if he weighed any more than a cat. Talk about Ninja Turtles! [Then again, such demeanour would explain, if not excuse, the Samurai drag in "Warriors of the Deep".]

Ultimately, the Master escapes in a hovercraft, into a narrow section of sea where half the Royal Navy is massing. Did they all go home, about ten minutes after readying to bombard the Sea Devils into oblivion?

Critique Better than any story we've seen in this volume so far, "The Sea Devils" illustrates the polarisation of *Doctor Who* under Letts into two basic schools of thought. On the one hand, we have instances where writers and directors seek to evoke a world like ours, and show what happens when something from outside is introduced. Most of the drama in this approach will be lit, shot, designed and acted like any other TV drama of the time, with irruptions of "otherness" into this treated as events in themselves, especially as they usually involve complicated set-ups and tight editing. ("The Mind of Evil" is a good example of this.)

On the other hand, some stories have tried to create a comic-strip world that includes elements from all over - putting domestic drama, avant garde cinema and non-narrative trickery of the kind used for Glam bands on *Top of the Pops* all on a roughly equal footing. Before now, the best attempt at at that approach was "Terror of the Autons". Where these two schools of thought differ is *whose* world is being represented: ours with the Doctor in it, or the world of the Doctor himself - one that's just enough like ours for all the other stuff to be equally real and thrill kids (and many adults). A lot of stories in the latter camp ground themselves in solid performances and mundane (in its original meaning of "wordly", as well as the common definition) dialogue but - and here's the rub - director Michael Briant's rendition of "The Sea Devils" goes further down this path than ever before.

This story is set in a world where the Sea Devils are "normality", and everything the humans do is alien. If you look at the story in this way, a lot of the odd incidental details fit into place. The extreme close-ups of Walker's mouth as he eats (and indeed the way humans seem obsessed with food and drink); the odd camera angles inside the fort; the Continental look of the Security team's uniforms and cars; and the fact that the escaping sub is shown on their monitors as being in negative.

In fact it's remarkable that - apart from the slightly dodgy ferry-man - all the humans present are service personnel.[75] The dialogue makes few concessions to the fact that children are watching and stuffs in jargon, naval slang ('I've brought you some kai') and rank designations as ordinary conversation. Apart from Trenchard's car (which has the story's villain hidden in the boot), all the vehicles here are odd. Even the motorbike Jo borrows is unusual, and the Land Rovers have naval flashes. From this perspective, the use of unfamiliar music makes perfect sense. We're watching a drama set in a world where incidental music sounds just like this.

Most of the time, this more or less works. True, a lot of scenes just come off as a kid's adventure show, with peculiar burbles and buzzings, and a lot of the time we're confronted with the now-familiar Pertwee routine of capture / plot-exposition / escape / chase. That said, there's something far more interesting in the overall debate between the Doctor and the Master as to whether mankind is trustworthy, and deserves to be spared the Sea Devils' wrath. Once again, Hulke's script is preachy and rather obvious, but it helps he likes the characters here a lot more. Even Walker is a big kid in the wrong job rather than a coldhearted villain such as Dent ("Colony in Space"), who literally chained Jo to a bomb.

What this story demonstrates above all is a script and a production not so much at loggerheads as almost incapable of comprehending one another. Where they overlap is in the stuff Letts and Dicks asked for up front: the "Join the Navy and see the World" material, the chases and the fights. (As Anton Chekov almost said, if you show a pair of swords on the wall in episode one, you have to use them by the end of episode three.) Hulke, describing the process of getting this story to the screen in his *The Making of Doctor Who*, claimed: 'It begins with the script'. It acutally doesn't and this very story, from his own script, proves it. Nothing in the edited stock-footage or the choreographed swordplay has any of Hulke's input, and the ostensible author chose very little of the content. His own conception of the story is almost drowned out by the rest of what's on offer.

What's particularly noticeable is how the Doctor has now resorted to the Brigadier's methods, yet there's not a single line of dialogue to underline this. In many scenes he's trying to find a peaceful solution... but then we're made to clap like idiots when the Navy and the army of Sea Devils start shooting at each other. Even the Master is only half a step away from being Von Gelb from *Freewheelers* for the first half of this story, and the plot makes the Sea Devils his pawns. We've all but lost the sense of the Silurians being creatures whose mere presence sends adults into primordial panic. The Sea Devils look out of place in a submarine or a naval base - but then, so do Pertwee and Manning (although getting into the right clothing for the mission, once again, lends the Doctor a lot more credibility as an expert).

There are a few other complaints. Unlike their cousins, the Sea Devils don't have that almost supernatural element to them, and they're just troops (as they're more blatantly portrayed in "Warriors of the Deep"). Save for their leader, they can't even speak - so when the Master sends one into a minefield with a twitch of his handset, we've no idea whether the creature is a willing accomplice or a victim who has no choice to obey. The poignancy of their plight as a species is squandered too. As with the Silurians, they've a viable case for their actions (far more than most *Doctor Who* monsters, in fact), but they're seen helping the Master in his bid to wipe out humanity just because... err... because he's bad and this is what bad guys do.

Yet again we return to the big problem with stories of this kind: we like seeing Delgado back and tricking the authorities, but the Master's presence lobotomises the storytelling. Wait, we should rephrase that - we *love* Delgado, and that's the real trouble with this adventure. All the regulars are doing exactly what viewers want to see, but the rest of the enterprise is just there as a pretext. If you're not watching this as an eight year old in 1972 on Saturdays, just like every Saturday, all the flaws and missed opportunities stand out a mile.

Indeed, watched out of context and by anyone not besotted with this era, it's difficult to see why anyone could have any affection for it. People on the outside see 1972-ness of it all - you need to take it on faith that in the 70s this was something entirely "other". Like the aquatic wildlife in those documentaries, it seemed real and had connections with the everyday world, yet it existed on its own terms. If you can somehow get into that headspace, there's *far* more here to enjoy than to groan at. Lots of newer fans and casual viewers of the DVDs and repeats manage it, but if somehow you can't, just accept that however much the bedrock of this is a dumb adventure story, the director was trying for something else.

The Facts

Written by Malcolm Hulke. Directed by Michael Briant. Viewing figures: 6.4 million, 9.7 million, 8.3 million, 7.8 million, 8.3 million, 8.5 million. (Those power cuts affected episode one, hence the "story so far" recap shown before the second part.) This story was repeated in compilation form, twice - a cricket match was rained off in the week between episodes four and five of "Planet of the Spiders", and it was serialised again in 1992 as part of BBC2's first batch of repeats.

Supporting Cast Roger Delgado (The Master), Edwin Richfield (Captain Hart), Clive Morton (Trenchard), June Murphy (3rd Officer Jane Blythe), Alec Wallis (Ldg. Telegraphist Bowman), Terry Walsh (Castle Guard Barclay), Donald Sumpter (Commander Ridgeway), David Griffin (Lt. Commander Mitchell), Christopher Wray (Ldg. Seaman Lovell), Colin Bell (CPO Summers).

Working Titles "The Sea Silurians". (D'oh!)

Cliffhangers Marooned on the sea-fort, the Doctor and Jo have just found the dead body of one of the crew when they hear something shuffling down the corridor towards them; having lost his swordfight with the Doctor, the Master unexpectedly produces a knife and hurls it at his opponent's back; as the Doctor and Jo are pursued across the beach by the guards, the Master activates his calling-device and a Sea Devil emerges from the water in front of them; the Doctor's diving-bell is pulled up out of the sea, and Jo realises that it's empty; the Doctor, Jo and Captain Hart are heading across the naval base when a Sea Devil - one of the first to attack the facility - appears in front of them and takes aim.

What Was in the Charts? "Hold Your Head Up", Argent; "Say You Don't Mind", Colin Bluntstone; "I'd Like to Teach the World to Sing", The New Seekers; "Morning Has Broken", Cat Stevens; "Brand New Key", Melanie; "Sleepy Shores", Johnny Pearson[76].

The Lore

• Barry Letts was curious to see if the coercion he'd used on the RAF to get "The Mind of Evil" made so effectively would work again - besides, as an old naval man himself, he wanted the Senior Service to get its moment of world-saving glory. In June 1971, Letts asked the MoD if he could borrow the requisite helicopters, sailors, shore facilities, boats and a diving bell. For once, the helicopters were the sticking-point: they were allowed a hovercraft instead, and decided to try to use stock footage of air-sea rescues.

The plan was to film "The Sea Devils" in reasonable weather in October and transmit it in spring, after the cheaper Peladon story was made after Christmas. (You would think that trusting the weather, at sea, in October, was asking for trouble, but this time they got away with it.) Luckily, the range of equipment and action sequences were enough like a training exercise to get the marines involved.

• The last story to significantly exploit the nation's coastlines had been "Fury from the Deep", shown four years earlier (a generation in Doctor Who terms). The production assistant on that story, Michael Briant, was now a director. Malcolm Hulke had demonstrated in "Colony in Space" that he could write well for the Master, and the villain's return for just one story this year seemed like a good idea (Roger Delgado was starting to worry about typecasting). Guess what - Hulke had been in the Navy too. The story was being written as the negotiations with the Admiralty were underway, and the use of locations and naval facilities in Hulke's scripts expanded accordingly.

Letts took the scripts with him on that six week holiday in July and amended them. This was mainly a matter of trimming over-running episodes, but also of fixing the whole issue of when exactly the so-called "Silurians" had gone into storage. There were valiant attempts to introduce us to the adjective 'Eocenic', removed before the episodes went out. Hulke took advantage of the opportunity to make the new reptile-men less prone to making speeches, but kept many of the same moral points up for debate among the human (and Time Lord) characters.

• Hulke kept a closer-than-usual eye on this story's progress from script to screen, as Pan Books' junior imprint, Piccolo, had asked Letts and Dicks to produce a behind-the-scenes book. Both were working flat out actually making the

TV show, so Hulke largely wrote *The Making of Doctor Who*, with input from Dicks on the series' past and some gosh-wow science pieces on the Fourth Dimension. The penultimate chapter is a detailed breakdown (at least, by 1971 kid's book standards) of the technical, logistic and artistic processes of making a six-part story; as a bonus, a picture of the Doctor being stalked by a Sea Devil appeared on the front, mere days after they last appeared on our screens. If this weren't exciting enough, the Schools TV series *Television Club* - which had previously shown how to produce a hit record and make it in the fashion industry - did a behind-the-scenes programme about the making of "The Sea Devils", which got its first showing a week before episode one.[77]

• John Friedlander was asked to make the new reptile masks. His basic turtle-face design was the same for all size heads but the gill-fins were subtly different for each one. The actors inside - as you can probably tell from the Sea Devils' height - could see through carefully concealed eye-holes in the throat. The costume designer (Maggie Fletcher) along with Friedlander and Briant looked at a lot of textbooks on turtles before drawing up the final designs. It was intended that the costumes would be big enough to permit oxygen cylinders, so that divers could play the Sea Devils. The eventual bodies were simply boiler-suits coated in brown and green latex, thus giving the Sea Devils the appearance of being stunt-men in turtle-hats, wearing boiler-suits on which they'd spilled latex.

• The script called for an oil-rig or something similar. Briant looked into using some of those offshore platforms he recce'd as PA on "Fury from the Deep", but the Shivering Sands complex was now potentially unsafe and the nearby Rough Sands fort was now claimed as "Sealand" by entrepreneur Roy Bates. (Or Prince Roy, as he's now called. Despite several reversals of fortune, the micronation has 160,000 official citizens - three of whom actually live there! It must be the only nation whose power requirements are entirely met by a wind-turbine.)

The fort they used (following re-writes to make it a fort being refurbished and not a rig being built) is about a mile off the Isle of Wight, just north of Bembridge. Nearby were a handy castle, several slightly different-looking bays and the HMS *Frazer*, a training facility with a lot of different forms of artillery. (Side note: the designation

"HMS" can apply to land-based installations as well as ships.)

The *Frazer* gunnery range was the first location used. (Those unaware of British geography should note that the Isle of Wight is only slightly smaller than Manhattan and is a popular tourist destination. But it's also in the inlet leading to Portsmouth, which has been the Royal Navy's main base of operations since Henry VIII's time. Thus a lot of yacht-clubs, hotels and famous beaches are right next to top-secret and well-armed military installations and defences built to keep out Napoleon.) The No Man's Land Fort is in fact on a peninsula, but shot to look as though it was out to sea.

• The filming began with the Doctor examining the scorched lifeboat, and all of the Seaspite sequences were filmed first. Pertwee, who had been stationed at "Pompey" (the reasons why Portsmouth is called that are lost in the mists of time) was in his element.

• On arrival at the location, Briant realised that the Sea Devils looked oddly like stunt-men in turtle-hats wearing boiler-suits covered in latex. Moreover, they needed belts to keep their guns in. Belts on otherwise naked reptiles would look silly (see 11.4, "The Monster of Peladon" for an example), so the Sea Devils needed to be dressed. Fortunately, Fletcher had some blue fish-net material left over from another series. (Well, probably. We're trying hard to think of *any other* BBC series from the early 1970s that would entail people dressing in blue string vests, and have drawn a complete blank. Indeed, the only other show where anyone dressed like this was Gerry Anderson's *UFO*, where the submarine crew flounced around in rather tighter mesh and looked even more idiotic.) Briant ultimately decided that a big string vest for each Sea Devil (and a cape for the leader) broke up the human silhouette effectively. Terrance Dicks has always maintained that this was a mistake, and that the monsters looked "bloody stupid" when dressed in string vests - this is proof, if nothing else, that Dicks' judgement on 70s *Doctor Who* isn't always on the button. (Those wishing to see a Sea Devil "streaking" should skip to the first episode of *Blake's 7* Series Four, but be warned that even *Blake's* fans find that story a bit of an ordeal.)

• Stop us if you've heard this one before: Katy Manning, like Delgado, had to be seen to drive an SRN5 military hovercraft. Manning, typically, pressed the wrong button and deflated the starboard side of the air-cushion, causing a dozen sailors to fall on top of her.

• Edwin Richfield (Captain Hart) was occasionally mistaken for a real officer. This came in handy when the BBC crew wanted to use the pom-pom gun seen in episode six. Although the gun was officially forbidden for non-service use, we're told that Richfield simply walked up and asked if he could have a shot, whereupon Briant filmed it. Richfield had been in just about every long-running series going, including assorted villainous foreigners in any ITC shows being made. (He was the only regular to appear in every episode of *The Buccaneers*, despite his atrocious Spanish accent.) He'd just played an Admiral in *UFO*.

• Many of the rest of the cast (twenty-three speaking roles in total) were actors with whom Briant had worked in some capacity. June Murphy (Hart's assistant, Jane Blythe) had been Maggie Harris in "Fury from the Deep", Royston Tickner (Robbins, the boatsman who shuttles the Doctor and Jo to the prison) had been in 3.4, "The Daleks' Master Plan" (as an on-screen director in that Christmas episode, alas). Norman Atkyns (here a Rear Admiral) had been the voice of god (sort of) in "Colony in Space". Peter Forbes-Robertson (the head Sea Devil), as should have been noted in Volume II, was the guard who towered over Ben in 4.3, "The Power of the Daleks". The person who gives this story's monsters their name (Clark, the delirious fort worker) is played by Declan Mulholland, later to be Till, Count Grendel's manservant, in 16.4, "The Androids of Tara" (where we list one of his other claims to fame).

For Trenchard, Briant cast Clive Morton, a veteran of the Ealing Comedies. He had been the Vice-Chancellor in *Lucky Jim* and had played a governor of a small colony just about to get independence in an episode of *Man in a Suitcase*. He's also the subject of a memorably bitchy anecdote concerning Sir John Gielgud mistaking him for someone else and saying, "at least I wasn't stuck with that bore Clive Morton".

• The majority of scenes with Sea Devils needed big guys in the suits. For stunt falls (especially that big one in episode five) they needed Stuart Fell, while specialist diver Mike Stevens handled the shots of the lone Sea Devil clawing his way up the boat in episode one. Fell also doubled for Katy Manning in some shots, as did a Marine for the first take of the abseiling sequence. (The result wasn't convincing so the stars tried it themselves.

Pertwee remembered to wear gloves, Manning didn't.) The cliff-top and minefield scenes were in fact shot at a caravan site.[78]

• Pertwee injured himself again, this time bruising his ribs on the sonic screwdriver while lying flat on the barbed wire. Although he wasn't drastically injured, this was his last significant stunt scene until "The Green Death". His back injury, a long-term complaint from - as he put it - "too many prat falls", would make the action increasingly difficult. Surgical supports would eventually be involved. In fact the sonic screwdriver seen here is a new prop made for this story.

• The Navy let the BBC play with one of their boats, HMS *Reclaim*, which was used to carry diving bells for training. It was only available for one day before sailing for Scotland. Briant, a keen yachtsman (and latterly author of several guidebooks to sailing around France), and Pertwee were unaffected by sea-sickness; others weren't.

• Dawn on Wednesday saw high tide and the Sea Devils rising from the deep in multiples of six. When the Havoc team were called on to play Sea Devils striding ashore from underwater, they found the heads were buoyant and the people wearing them couldn't duck down below the surface. (Sensibly, they had selected a piece of shoreline with a gentle slope.) Someone (probably not Derek Ware) decided to half-fill the headpieces with sea-water. This caused trouble as the kneeling stunt performers rose from the waves and choked on brine. They tried filming the scene backwards, but *this* resulted in dry Sea Devils emerging from the water. Ware had secured twenty-five guineas a day for his crew but (for reasons discussed under the previous story) this was the last time he or Havoc worked on the series.

• As the bulk of the Sea Devil action would be on film, Briant wanted to avoid "zap" effects using video trickery. In collaboration with principle special effects designer Peter Day, he devised a simple gun containing wire-wool and small gunpowder flashes (like pre-War photographers used). Unfortunately, this meant that any one gun could only fire once in a take. (Note especially the naval base assault, in which the Sea Devils take turns coming around a corner and firing but once.) Although the guns sometimes misfired, this technique proved fairly easy to remount.

• Another costume oversight gives rise to this story's first urban myth: they only had one Master costume with them, and Delgado was worried about getting this wet during the Buccaneer sea-

245

scooter chase. Admittedly he wasn't crazy about water and couldn't swim all that well, but calling it a phobia is probably pitching it a little strong. He *did* need to steel himself for the bits of the chase he filmed himself, leading Pertwee to dub him "the bravest coward I ever knew". (If you've read the listing for "Day of the Daleks", you won't be surprised to learn that this scene was a late addition, after Pertwee had seen the Buccaneers in action.)

Sea-sickness was a big reason why Delgado was so anxious in the hovercraft rescue - he wouldn't have driven the hovercraft in the next scene, had he been totally incapacitated. Derek Ware, although too short to play a Sea Devil, was the right size to double for the Master if required. He did so at short notice - Delgado had received bruises to his chest in a small car accident just before recording the swordfight, so Ware donned the toupee (Delgado was wearing a "piece" by this stage) and took part as well as choreographing. (Some sources claim that it was Terry Walsh on the other Buccaneer, or Ware, or Delgado. Walsh was more Pertwee's size and build, so if he were to double for anyone, it would be the star.) By now, Briant was asking the stunt team about the feasibility of additional "gags" - they were on good money but a flat fee per day, so it made sense to get the most out of them.

• A fortnight after filming ended, they were into the studios on Mondays and Tuesdays. There had been a small amount of model filming at Ealing, where Peter Day and his assistant Len Hutton worked on the submarine scenes. They had been to Admiralty House (another coup for the *Doctor Who* team) and been allowed to examine plans of nuclear subs - despite a technical hitch when their passes were queried and they were detained - and had modified a basic Airfix kit bought from Woolworths. Briant thought that the propeller in the model was a strange size and shape, so they devised a replacement that looked more aesthetically right. After transmission - stop us if you've heard this one - the MoD had words, asking how the BBC had been allowed to see secret designs for Polaris subs.

• In the swordfight, the complicated shot of the Doctor dodging the Master's blows whilst supine on a table were recorded on a video-disc machine and played back slightly faster. Ware doubled in parts for the Master, as we said, and that was the end of his association with *Doctor Who* - which

had begun with the caveman fight in the very first story.

• The record playing on the fab groovy DJ's show was the non-copyright backing track from *Johnny Reggae* by the Pipkins, a Jonathan King project. The version with words would have been a) too rude and b) too expensive. Jo's "favourite DJ" was Briant himself.

• In the later episodes, the "king" Sea Devil had a radio-controlled mouth to synch with the dialogue. Forbes-Robertson's spoken lines were processed in real-time, as the Daleks' voices had traditionally been. Recording ended a week or so before Christmas, and the pre-filmed fights and climbing for "The Curse of Peladon" took up the last working days of 1971.

• Owing to the vast cast (long enough to warrant the full version of the end-theme to be used in all six episodes), Briant decided early on to cut costs with the music. Dudley Simpson was reliable but rushed off his feet, often submitting the finished electronic components of his scores mere days before transmission. As BBC employees, the Radiophonic Workshop was paid less than outside contractors like Simpson, and Briant was keen to see how "far out" (look, it was the early 70s) the music could go.

The technology was developing very fast, yet *Doctor Who's* music had rarely been as innovative in the 70s as in the early Hartnell days during the era of Tristram Cary and Les Structures Sonores. Briant wanted to use John Baker, whose jazz-inflected twangs and syncopated chimes were used by many local radio stations and occasional TV plays. He had provided the ambient music (as we'd call it now) for Tobias Vaughn's office in 6.3, "The Invasion".

Baker was one of the "old-school" concretists, happier with tape and scissors than banks of potentiometers. However, he was taken ill and Desmond Briscoe, the Workshop's head, suggested a slightly controversial figure: Malcolm Clarke. He was one of the new intake, more at home with voltage-controlled oscillators and peg-boards, and had rather daringly suggested that the Workshop (whose utilitarian approach to soundmongering is reflected in the name) might consider the construction of sounds from the raw material of vibrations up as an art-form in and of itself (whilst not excluding the practical problem-solving for which they were originally set up).

The majority of this story's music was composed to the video-tape (a time-coded Shibaden copy) over Christmas and realised on the then state-of-the-art VCS3. (It's the one that has a joystick - if you found that clip of Roxy Music doing *Ladytron* we mentioned in the notes for "The Curse of Peladon", you'll see Brian Eno having way too much fun with one.) EMS, the makers of the VCS3, had been refining the device and made a customised amendation: the Synthi 100, which went on sale in 1974. The prototype, though, was donated to the Workshop (it became known as the "Delaware", after the road on which the converted ice-rink the Workshop used as studios was). Clarke developed something of a rapport with it. The VCS3 was, of course, a monophonic device, playing one note at a time, so even simple chords or harmonies had to be worked out in advance and laboriously recorded onto multi-track tapes.

• As transmission approached, the BBC pushed the boat out (sorry) and teamed up with the Young Observer (the kids' page of the *Observer* colour supplement) to plug... sorry, *discuss* the series at the Planetarium. Peter Purves (ex-companion and now *Blue Peter* presenter) interviewed Letts and Pertwee just before Christmas and unveiled the new monster. The forthcoming *Making Of...* book was announced and the screening of "Day of the Daleks" (which had been given the works as well) was accompanied by a *Radio Times* competition to win a radio-controlled Dalek. They timed announcement of the winner for episode one of "The Sea Devils". Not everyone saw that, however...

• Power cuts made a hole in the ratings, after the steady improvement over the last year. Episode two had a three-minute recap made of clips from episode one (this is reconstituted on the DVD). On the whole, though, the series' profile was growing. The monsters from Peladon appeared at the Ceylon Tea Centre (right next to the Paris Studio where radio sitcoms such as *The Navy Lark* were recorded), Kelloggs Sugar Smacks (see A4, "Dalek Invasion Earth 2150 AD" in Volume VI) gave away free badges and depicted Pertwee on the packet advocating "timeless energy". The badges included Bessie and Mike, but the free UNIT badge was actually slightly more realistic than the real thing (see the essay with "The Monster of Peladon"). All that was left was a novelty record, and someone had an offer for Pertwee. (Be afraid. Be *very* afraid. *I Am the Doctor* might have seemed like a good idea when Benny Hill

was at Number One with *Ernie*, but it really wasn't.)

• The day after episode two went out, in addition to seeing the shameful "return" of Alpha Centauri on *The Black and White Minstrel Show*, was also the day Pertwee appeared on *Ask Aspel*. Here the former newsreader and host of *Crackerjack* (you know the drill) introduced requested clips from recent BBC shows. Take our word for it: at the time, this was a rare treat. And the *Radio Times*' guest reviewer for the week ending 31st of March was Katy Manning. And then there was that *Television Club* item about the making of episode one and the *Making Of* book launch. Compared to the relentless puff surrounding the Tennant episodes this may not seem like anything special, but for 1972 this was a blitz of publicity.

• Fans with a malicious sense of humour and time on their hands contacted the National Audit Office and cross-referenced statistics on suicides in the UK with transmission dates of Pertwee episodes. Apart from the fact that "The Ambassadors of Death" and "The Daemons" seemed to rob more people of the will to live than any other stories, the main finding was a sharp rise in the numbers of self-drownings during the six weeks that this story was broadcast.

9.4: "The Mutants"

(Serial NNN, Six Episodes, 8th April - 13th May 1972.)

Which One is This? The Doctor and Jo travel a thousand years into the future, only to find the Earth Empire falling and the fat colonials oppressing some tribal planetary natives in order to stop them turning into big black insect-creatures. Geoffrey Palmer's back, but he once again plays a high-ranking official who dies horribly. And if that's not enough for you, it's the story that opens with a shot of what appears to be Michael Palin's "It's..." man from *Monty Python's Flying Circus*.

Firsts and Lasts First serious use (after its discrete preview in 8.4, "Colony in Space") of the hexagon-based plastic "wallpaper" which became the bog-standard BBC background for every space-based series from *Blake's 7* to *Come Back Mrs. Noah* (don't ask). More pedantically, it's the first story to state the year along with the 'BBC' copyright notice at the end of the credits. This story has

Tristram Cary's last music score, but James Acheson's first credit for costumes.

Six Things to Notice About "The Mutants"...

1. Theoretically a story about a violent clash of cultures on the edge of a collapsing empire, "The Mutants" is perhaps most notable for its excitable (and not in a nice, Robert Holmes way) dialogue. Sample quotes include: 'Die, Overlord, die!'; 'We want our freedom and we want it now!'; 'Am I left with nothing but mutants?'; 'You are a fool, Varan, a *fool*'; and 'You will die for a cause, the cause of Varan's revenge!' Along those lines, the old man in the warrior Varan's village defies all expectations and both under-acts and over-acts at the same time, somehow. Meanwhile, the off-screen voices (radio transmissions, computer announcements, etc.) are a mixed bag of accents, in an attempt to make Earth seem like a melting pot. There's Australian, American and Caribbean, as well as visible characters suggested to be German, Afrikaners, Yorkshire and old Etonian. Yet they all speak interchangeable dialogue.

2. "The Mutants" is also notable for the characters of Cotton and Stubbs, two "ordinary blokes" working for Earth's Empire, whose job seems to be to constantly chip in with "ordinary bloke" comments as the planet goes to hell around them. This is, depending on how you look at it, either an ingenious script device or deeply annoying. Cotton's most famous exclamation, at the final cliffhanger: 'We'll all be done for!' (And it might have worked, if he'd had the accent the writers were thinking of.)

3. Frustratingly, for every effect that doesn't quite work, there's one that surpasses expectations. People float about badly in inept CSO line-ups (Varan apparently loses a hand), but the guns have real incandescent flashes built in. Ky becomes a radiant, iridescent being, but flies down corridors looking for all the world like he's standing in front of a blue screen waving his arms about. The Earth investigators arrive in an electric toothbrush, but Skybase itself is a genuinely impressive model. The video effects and filmed models merge properly... about half the time. There are some scenes where it's so hard to work out what the intention *was* (such as the stuff in the crystal cave), we can't decide if the effect is botched or brilliant. We'll give them the benefit of the doubt, but for most viewers, it's probably a matter of whether they saw it in colour.[82]

4. Intentionally or not, Jo pulls whenever she's offworld, to such an extent that her autobiography could be called "Another Guy, Another Planet". This time around, she's won the heart of a long-haired lad from a different species entirely. (That would be Ky, whose name causes giggles amongst those familiar with water-based lubricants.) Alas, he pupates into Rick Wakeman[83] before he can ask her out. Note, though, that the scene where Jo run short of breath, and Ky has an attack of conscience and goes back for her, reaches the screen looking more like a randy gypsy responding to a come-on from the farmer's daughter.

5. There's a very odd scene in episode four, set in Professor Sondergaard's cave / laboratory, which involves violent rockfalls shaking the room. To emphasise this, one of the set cameras has been pointed at a sheet of Mirrorlon (see 5.3, "The Ice Warriors") to distort the picture, stretching the scene to make it look as if everything's been rocked out of shape. But the director seems to have forgotten about this halfway through, and filmed some shots through the rigged camera even when the rocks *aren't* falling, making the characters squash sideways in mid-conversation for absolutely no good reason.

6. Dudley Simpson's still on holiday, so this story has a return for 60s odd-sound maestro Tristram Cary. His previous form includes the much-recycled score for "The Daleks" (1.2), plus "The Gunfighters" (3.8) and its singalong plot summaries. Can any story's sound be odder than these? Well, someone's let Cary play with an early synthesizer (as a reward for helping build the prototype), so he gives it a shot. The Doctor himself describes one piece - the fanfare for "Overlord Broadcast" - as 'bombastic', yet it sounds almost exactly like the squeaky music used on the original BBC Video releases in the mid-80s. Other than that, it's unlike anything you'll hear in the series - including the previous story's different but equally, um, "challenging" soundtrack.

The Continuity

The Doctor He's incredibly resistant to radiation - or at the very least, he's better equipped to withstand radioactive thaesium than a man in a protective suit. [Alas, he forgets how to 'prepare myself' by 11.5, "Planet of the Spiders". Of course there's radiation and there's *radiation* - to judge by X3.1, "Smith and Jones", he can absorb a lot of routine Roentgens and channel it all into his foot. This is obviously *not* a normal Time Lord ability, though, or else the plot of 1.2, "The Daleks" would have been markedly different.]

Here he no longer seems to object to the Time Lords sending him on errands, believing that if they want something from him, it must be important. [If he's familiar with this sort of covert operation, it lends weight to the suggestion in 22.4, "The Two Doctors" that his pre-exile life was peppered with similar off-the-record tasks. See 12.4, "Genesis of the Daleks" and 13.5, "The Brain of Morbius" for comparable missions. However, if we compare all of these onerous and politically-sensitive tasks with the stuff he's made to do in Season Nine, two possible conclusions come to light: either the Time Lords were training him up for bigger stuff later - see **Is There A Season 6B?** under "The Two Doctors" for a sidelight on this - or the little local difficulties on Peladon and Solos were more significant than they seemed. We note that Peladon is the first planet he voluntarily returns to after a "business" trip there.]

• *Ethics*. He's quite prepared to sabotage the lab equipment lethally, in order to stop Professor Jaeger on Skybase. Yet earlier, he stops people shooting at Mutants because they're intelligent beings. He's also quite happy to let Jaeger know about technological feats ahead of his time, as he thinks the high stakes are worth the risk. [That, or he's already decided Jaeger's fate - a fairly alarming judgment call, as it's only episode two.]

Once it becomes clear that the Marshal and Jaeger are planning not just any old genocide, but that of a species unique in the cosmos [this seems to make a difference to him], the Doctor is entirely unforgiving. [For that matter, it's left unclear - owing to Ky's last-minute intervention - if the Doctor would have yielded to the Marshal's threats against Jo and transformed Solos' atmosphere or killed the deranged leader himself.]

• *Background*. The Doctor already has familiarity with the scientific process of 'particle reversal', and says it's a very useful technique. He claims to be qualified in 'practically everything' [again, see "Spearhead from Space"], and is familiar with Edward Gibbons' *The History of the Decline and Fall of the Roman Empire*.

• *Bessie*. The Doctor's making a minimum inertia superdrive for her. This defies several popular and important laws of physics [see 9.5, "The Time Monster" and **What Are the Silliest Examples of Bad Science?** under 10.4, "Planet of the Daleks"].

The Supporting Cast

• *Jo Grant*. She's fairly savvy in this one. She bluffs the Marshal into thinking that she and the Doctor are connected with the official investigation into his conduct and delivers a succinct, off the cuff, summary of the crisis to the Investigator. She can escape from thirtieth-century handcuffs too [although maybe the Doctor helped a bit].

The TARDIS Its instruments can identify the century in which the Doctor has landed, but on this occasion not the planet. The Ship here decides to land in a cupboard, with the door almost up against the wall. [For something similar, see 26.2, "Ghost Light".]

The Time Lords They supply the Doctor with a message pod, containing ancient Solonian tablets, for delivery to Ky on Solos. It materialises in the Doctor's lab without any of the usual TARDIS sound effects. [Again, it's not clear what stops the Time Lords teleporting it straight into Ky's possession. Nor is it explained where the Time Lords get the tablets from, or why they want to help the Solonians anyway. It doesn't seem to have anything to do with getting in the way of the Daleks or the Third Zone ("The Two Doctors").] The container is seemingly indestructible [TARDIS material?], but starts to open in Ky's presence. The Doctor states that these things are only sent in a 'real emergency', so much so that he's reluctant to let Jo go with him to Solos.

Planet Notes

• *Solos*. A remote part of the Earth Empire, Solos has a two-thousand year elliptical orbit around its sun, and lacks recognisable seasons because it doesn't tilt on its axis.

In truth its seasons are five hundred years long, so as the planet passes from "spring" to "summer" the temperature rises and the humanoid Solonians undergo a severe metabolic change. They become 'Mutts', their bodies taking on insect-like plating and their hands turning into clumsy pincers, until eventually they even have a separate thorax and abdomen. In fact this phase is only a brief one - though the atmospheric changes made by Earth's Empire triggers it too soon - and before long they take on an altogether different form.

The fully-developed Solonians are humanoid but sheathed in a multi-coloured glow, capable of killing with beams of energy or causing humans to collapse with a touch. They communicate through thought transference and can float through solid walls. [This looks remarkably like Light from "Ghost Light", but we'll leave you to speculate on the possible connections.] The Doctor considers this adaptive change to be unique in the history of the universe, but the untransformed Solonians are completely unaware of the process. [Because Earth has destroyed their culture, or because of the process itself? It perhaps doesn't help that they're made, as part of this, to revert to barbarism every half-century or so.]

Approaching the change, Solonians find themselves drawn towards a radioactive cave system [one of many on the planet] where one particular crystal acts as a bio-catalytic agent, drawing in thaesium radiation to drive the metamorphosis. The crystal appears to be man-made, but its origin isn't explained. [And what the crystal has to do with the planet's orbit is anyone's guess.]

The soil on Solos contains a nitrogen isotope unknown on Earth, so during the hours of daylight the ultra-violet rays create a poisonous mist that's lethal to humans within an hour. The Solonians, however, can breathe a human-friendly atmosphere with no ill effects.

During its pre-metamorphosis phase, Solonian society is tribal and has a roughly iron-age level of technology. The Empire has a Skybase in orbit, and it's a segregated society. Solos used to be rich in thaesium, used by the humans as fuel for Skybase and for its spaceships, but now it's been virtually mined out. The Marshal's globe of the planet suggests Earth-like oceans. [There's more on Mutts in "The Brain of Morbius".]

The tablets supplied by the Time Lords are carved in a lost Solonian language, cited as being 'the language of the Old Ones'.

History

• *Dating*. The thirtieth century, towards the end of Earth's Empire. [See **What's the Timeline of the Earth Empire?** under "Colony in Space".]

At this point Earth is 'politically, economically and biologically finished'. The Doctor describes it as grey, land and sea, with grey highways linking grey cities across grey deserts. Nobody lives on the ground, as the air's too poisonous, but in sky-cities [q.v. "Colony in Space"]. Earth can no longer afford an Empire, and Solos is one of the last planets to remain under its control. The Doctor states that humanity only moved on to the outer planets

after sacking the solar system.

[This would appear to contradict 15.2, "The Invisible Enemy" - by the same authors - in which we're told this started two thousand years later circa 5000 AD. Neither of these accounts, for that matter, chimes with the story we're told in 5.3, "The Ice Warriors" (a story that also seems to take place in 5000) concerning a new Ice Age caused by attempts to feed millions. Granted, there's reason to think that "The Ice Warriors" takes place in 3000 AD, but frankly that dating works even *less* well in conjunction with this story.

[It's perhaps relevant that the society seen here is unlike the "regimented" Earth life of 2986 in 23.3, "Terror of the Vervoids". Were it not for the Doctor actually dating this story on screen, we could happily assign it a date after the year 4000 (3.4, "The Daleks' Master Plan"), but before the fifty-first century culture in which Captain Jack 'dances' his way across the galaxy (X1.10, "The Doctor Dances"). But as we're stuck with the Doctor's dating, we have to assume that humanity cleans up its act, then returns to Earth's system and starts *again* for some reason, then makes all the same mistakes *again* by the time Magnus Greel starts monkeying around with Zygma particles (14.6, "The Talons of Weng Chiang").

[The Solonians' two-thousand year life-cycle indicates that whenever the Mutt turns up on Karn at the start of "The Brain of Morbius", it's some multiple of that length of time after the thirtieth century. At a pinch, this could place the Cult of Morbius in the much-talked-about fifty-first century. But as the Mutt - identified as 'Krizz' in Terrance Dicks' "Brain of Morbius" novelisation - is smart enough to fly a spaceship, it's possible that some changes have occurred in the manner of the metamorphosis, suggesting a much longer period of the Solonian life-cycle. (The alternative explanation is that Solonians have their own spaceships and Krizz started pupating whilst in flight. This is unlikely without any thaesium nearby, but perhaps his pupation was a symptom of his ship springing a leak when the Sisterhood of Karn wrested control and crashed it. So Condo's killing Krizz prevented a being of god-like psychic powers taking on the Sisters and making that story even more complicated and Prog Rock-ish.)]

Humans first arrived on Solos five hundred years previous to this story. Prior to this, it seems, the Solonians were farmers and hunters. A Marshal now oversees the planet, while his men -

What's Going On With This Music?

It can't have escaped anyone's notice that the incidental music for this phase of *Doctor Who* is markedly different from what has gone before, what will come and - for that matter - anything else on television before or after. All but five of the scores are by old hand Dudley Simpson, but he's doing things hitherto unheard (and unheard *of*) with the first generation of synthesizers. The remaining five scores include two oddly transitional works by Carey Blyton (with eccentric orchestration but very conventional Children's TV scoring), one taken from stock-music (we'll treat this separately later) and two consecutive purely electronic soundscapes. These have obvious connections to what other people were doing with the early machinery, especially in Europe, but those connections are part of a wider trend that's often overlooked; in fact, they're part of *three* other trends, which we'll only be able to sketch in here.

As a general point, though, the advent of the synthesizer is to the sound of *Doctor Who* what CSO was to its look, and was deployed by directors and the producer for the same reasons: it was cheap (if laborious); it was something nobody else could get away with using to this extent; it helped give stories set on other planets (or with weirdness afoot in present-day London) a feeling of "otherness".

If we step back and look at what cinema-goers were hearing in the huge wave of Science-Fiction films made between 1970 and 1975, two big trends come to light. First, we have reclaimed classical music, or music made to sound like it. (The former category includes *A Clockwork Orange*, with old recordings mixed with Wendy Carlos' reworkings of Beethoven and Rossini and deliberately naff pop. It sits alongside more obvious examples like *Soylent Green* and *Zardoz*.) The second is freaky burbles. They had a more established place in SF flicks than borrowed Beethoven, predating *2001: A Space Odyssey* (the film that legitimated showing off your highbrow vinyl collection[87]) by a dozen years. Bebe and Ford Barron's sounds for *Forbidden Planet* (1956) weren't officially music because the Musician's Union objected to a film with a whole score done without their members, hence the credit for their "Electronic Tonalities". Nonetheless, it woke people up to what tape and oscillators could achieve.

As the BBC Radiophonic Workshop would later explore, the Barrons found that despite the minute attention to detail in the preparation of each cue, the technology made the end result unpredictable. The oscillators and amplifiers used valves (or "tubes" as Americans call the pre-transistor switching arrays) that performed differently the hotter they got. The *Forbidden Planet* score acts as a handy signpost for three other things that will become hallmarks of Science-Fiction's use of electronica - and specifically *Doctor Who*'s resorting to it over the years - and alerts us to one specific feature that's practically unique to the series in this time.

The first is an assumption that audiences were after "weirdness". For better or worse, the SF audience is exposed to music that's close to (or derives from) the highbrow and experimental music of the mid-twentieth century at precisely the time that the gulf between the avant-garde and the mainstream is widening almost hourly. The second is that compared to most forms of screen drama, SF music is less prone to draw a sharp line between diegetic and non-diegetic music, and indeed diegetic and intra-diegetic. (Don't panic, we'll explain this in detail in about three paragraphs.) *Doctor Who* often makes no distinction at all and, later on, plays with the audience's expectations.

The third is that for budgetary reasons as well as any desire to create a specific aesthetic effect, the sound of specific films is usually either *all* electronic or totally *non*-electronic. Dudley Simpson deserves a lot more credit than he gets for finding ways to bridge, ignore or exploit this gap.

In the early 70s, a purely electronic soundtrack was staking a lot on a developing technology. We're in the earliest days of voltage-control, with Robert Moog and Peter Zinovieff launching companies to build and sell synthesizers in the late 1960s - each one almost built to order. To summarise crudely, these made the sounds from the wave-forms up, so one circuit would generate a buzz, hoot or hum, and another would manipulate it. (The Moogs initially had the monopoly on keyboards, and Zinovieff's EMS instruments used joysticks like radio-controlled cars and pegboards like telephone exchanges.) The sounds they made could be wildly unfamiliar or approximations of known instruments (trumpets and flutes being easiest, and even these related to the real thing as strawberry-flavoured *Pink Panther* chocolate bars related real strawberries). They were almost insultingly crude as ersatz instruments, and even on

continued on page 253...

'Overlords' to the Solonians - have black-and-silver uniforms and carry energy weapons. Solonians and Overlords appear to speak the same language. The Marshal answers to an Administrator in a similar uniform, sent from Earth to oversee Solos' move towards independence. The Investigator from the Earth Council, dressed in a white robe and skullcap, arrives in a Hyperion space shuttle. [This probably isn't the same as *the* Hyperion, from "Terror of the Vervoids", although the dates tally.] His staff dress in a similar way, while his guards wear white helmets and uniforms (rather less functional, with what seems to be gold lamé trimmings) quite different to those of the local imperials.

Earth still has a Bureau of Records, and seems to be run by a Council. "Earth Control" is mentioned. The Skybase staff get 'videos' from home. Technology on the station includes a lab researching atmospheric control, but a good old-fashioned hydroponic garden supports the station's environment. Ionisation rockets are used in an attempt to change the environment. The whole of Skybase is due to return to Earth after the crisis [so it seems to be a "ship" rather than a fixed station].

There's a teleport system to the surface. [This appears to work on a "wormhole" principle rather than disintegration / reintegration or quantum entanglement (see **How Do You Transmit Matter?** under 17.4, "Nightmare of Eden"). We can say this with reasonable certainty, because the Doctor is cheekily waving to the guards as he leaves in episode three, but is seen in a normal stance when he arrives.] The teleport booths are racially segregated and have helpful signs reminding people to take Oxy-Masks when walking on the surface.

The Analysis

Where Does This Come From? The big clue is something so obvious, we almost miss its full significance. The teleports are segregated. In Britain, this was unthinkable even when it was a fact of life in America.

The British reporting of the American Civil Rights movement was relatively straightforward - the system was self-evidently wrong, and while it persisted Americans had no right to tell anyone else how to live. Gandhi had used the same methods to make Britain step back from India as soon as Hitler was out of the way, which made the

NAACP more obviously right than they would otherwise have been. (Whatever the colonial administration made of him, Gandhi was popular in Britain itself. His visits in the 1930s to cotton factories and the East End clothing districts of Stepney and Bethnal Green - wearing a loincloth in our weather - rather endeared him to Joe Public. He was, after all, a university-educated lawyer who had taken to wearing loincloths by choice, so he stepped outside the usual racial categories. Not that Churchill agreed. We could stretch a point and offer Sondergaard as a rough analogue, but only half-heartedly.)

There's a Wartime film made for GIs posted in Britain, where the narrator and co-writer Burgess Meredith (of *Rocky* and *Batman* fame) has to patiently explain to US audiences that a British girl dating a Black GI wouldn't raise as many eyebrows in the UK as in the Deep South. It's the one moment where the cocksure, wise-cracking narrator becomes tongue-tied, and it's hilariously awkward. (Of course, in Wartime we were actually rather keen to show ourselves as diverse, as against the monolithic and reductivist Nazis.)

In making the Overlords seem foreign and the Solonians live in tribes, the most obvious parallel is Apartheid. Again, in Britain this played badly, not least because (apart from any moral revulsion) it was so impractical as to be grimly comic. An episode of *The Goodies* from the time shows different races only permitted to use different parts of a pedestrian crossing. Later, they had Philip Madoc as an Afrikaans governor trying to impose a system segregating against short men (apartheight); he was overthrown by an army of jockeys. Granted, there was horrific and casual racism in Britain, but it wasn't enshrined in law[84] - nor, officially, had it been anywhere in the Empire. (That is, apart from forbidding serving officers from marrying women from other races, for a complicated historical reason we won't get into here.)

In some ways, this analogy makes for a curious anomaly. Not once does the Doctor oppose Ky's militancy. The *one* thing on which Ky and Varan agree is that the Time Lords should have sent weapons instead of stone tablets. And even when Ky has supposedly advanced to a higher plane of being, he zaps the Marshal into nothingness - yet the Doctor doesn't intervene. (Admittedly, it's hard for him to do so without getting shot, but not even a word to Ky about using his new powers for good? It's very odd.)

What's Going On With This Music?

...continued from page 251

their own terms, they tended to grate.

This jarring quality isn't just a matter of opinion, you understand, it's maths. Close examination of the wave-form of most naturally-occurring sounds shows that the sound is "crinkly" and that those crinkles are made up of smaller crinkles and so on. (You can keep looking - and listening - in closer and closer detail and it won't smooth out.) However much you add waveforms generated from scratch together to make crinkles (waveforms inside waveforms), those crinkles will eventually resolve into chunks if you examine it closer. It's the difference between looking at a tree in finer and finer detail, always seeing more; and looking at a television image of a tree, which eventually becomes dots in primary colours. (This is also why your dad is right and albums on vinyl *do* sound better than MP3s or CDs. Fractal geometry strikes again.)

You could also notice that, in sounds that originate in nature and most orthodox musical instruments, the relationship between crinkles and crinkles-upon-crinkles seems to be constant. This holds good for birdsong, violins, trombones and even the majority of electric guitar settings. Voltage-controlled oscillators don't have this property. (But then, neither does the human voice. Some researchers suggest this is why Electro, Hip-Hop and House have an affinity with Rap, whereas earlier attempts to combine speech and music sound slightly odd unless saxophones - the nearest conventional instrument to voice in this regard - are also involved. It's no coincidence that bebop and beatniks got jazz and poetry to mix best before this.)

Even though EMS's VCS3 had three separate oscillators putting in their two-penn'orth to the overall wave (hence the name "VCS3"; clever, eh?), the resultant composite generally lacked the subtlety of even a slowed-down and harmonically-filtered recording of a lampshade being clouted. (You can hear this in 7.4, "Inferno" and on the Pink Swirly Album as *Blue Veils and Golden Sands*.) That's subtlety *and* innate familiarity: however novel and bizarre these tones on the surface, at the deepest level the processed found-sound had a mathematical "realism" that synthesizers wouldn't match for a decade.

That unearthliness wasn't always a liability, of course. In many ways, the lack of crinkliness offered a purity of tone similar to what a lot of music over the centuries had aspired to become. When the Theramin was used in Bernard Herrmann's score for *The Day the Earth Stood Still* (1951), it suggested that the Venusian visitors were from a higher plane; the triangle-waves used for Klaatu were like an impossibly good choirboy. Verity Lambert, quite obviously, was after something similar when she sought to get *Les Structures Sonores* (Parisian instrument-builders and recording artists) and then Ron Grainer and the Workshop to make something similar for the *Doctor Who* theme. (See, if you haven't already, **Why Did the "Sting" Matter?** under 7.3, "The Ambassadors of Death".)

The French outfit are an interesting counter-example here: they made real, physical instruments, but the ambition was to make sounds unlike anything hitherto heard. They specialised in variations on the Glass Harmonica (a device often attributed to Benjamin Franklin) and used new materials for their assorted tuned-percussion instruments. (There's a whole field of this, especially in California, oddly enough. Recent developments in ceramics have re-opened this can of worms and maybe future historians will see synthesizers as a blind alley.) The ones used in "The Web Planet" (2.5) were from commercially available recordings[88].

So even though it was made with more basic tone-generators, the *Who* theme was in a tradition of electronica dating back half a century. The Theremin, as most of you know, is played by using the operator's body to affect electromagnetic fields - usually one hand for pitch, the other for tone (although not everyone uses hands). There's a keyboard equivalent, the Ondes Martinot, for which French composer Oliver Messien scored his symphony *Turangalila* - and if that name rings a bell, it's probably because Matt Groening is a huge Messien fan. Perhaps appropriately, this instrument requires the player to wear a particular kind of ring.

Like Herrmann's score, Messien's symphony exploited the tension between a ninteenth-century Romantic orchestra (of the kind developed by Wagner) and the "alien". *Unlike* Herrmann, however, it found a synthesis by stepping outside the Western tradition and veering towards an Indian classical style. This wasn't entirely unfamiliar as a technique even in the early 1950s. The composer Arnold Schoenberg had started a move away

continued on page 255...

An American series would have made a bigger deal of this, but Britain is more pragmatic about watching former terrorists become statesmen. David Ben Gurion and Eamonn de Valera went from British jails to become world leaders, with airports named after them; Pandit Nehru did the same, but only got a collarless jacket worn by *Doctor Who* villains named after him. Mandela went from Robbin Island to find thousands of student union bars with his name on, but Oliver Tambo got the airport gig posthumously. George Washington got a city *and* a state.

The early 70s was - so to speak - a boom time for terrorist movements seeking to extract political concessions (see 9.1, "Day of the Daleks"). A generation had read Franz Fanon's *The Wretched of the Earth* and agreed that as colonialism is in and of itself an act of violence, it should be opposed by violence. America was hardly in a position to object (as it had been founded by precisely those means and with that justification), but Britain had told itself a story that defying anyone who bombed the cities was a defining characteristic of our national character. It might seem odd that in the year of the worst mainland bombing in the IRA's campaign, *Doctor Who* is giving tacit approval to armed insurrection. However, as we've just said, the Overlords are more obviously the Americans, who were generally agreed to Have It Coming, and the South Africans, who were morally wrong and (far worse) annoying. Nevertheless, with Barry Letts in charge, the fact that evolving into something with psychic powers doesn't automatically equate to outgrowing violence is interesting. (You can bet that we're going to return to this: see "Planet of the Spiders".)

Britain used to have an Empire once, odd as it seems now, and the temptation is to make "The Mutants" into some kind of analogy for that whole historical process. But as we'll see in **Is This Any Way to Run a Galactic Empire?** under 10.3, "Frontier in Space", this metaphorical process is flawed and limiting. Yet it *is* fair to say that a lot of the accounts about the post-War relinquishing of sovereignty in far-flung countries came to us from ex-Colonial personnel who never saw it coming. The abrupt change from sedate and relatively luxurious life in a hot country to 1947 Britain - with rationing, bomb-craters everywhere and the worst winter in living memory - made for good stories. It's just that it's not the story we're told here.

Instead, the man clinging to power after the

Government has decided that an Empire is more trouble than it's worth is one we normally heard in novels about commerce. The Marshall is straight out of a Graham Greene novel, except that instead of any national administration putting him in place it would have been a multinational company. Or maybe half a century earlier, this would have been someone in South America whose wealth and ego enabled him to order people around without any interference from the official authority.

Think of it in this light and suddenly we're in the territory of Werner Herzog's films, such as *The Dream of the Green Ants* with our own Ray Barrett (2.3, "The Rescue") or *Cobra Verde* and more especially *Fitzcarraldo*. These were all made shortly after "The Mutants", but illustrate the point that stories such as this are a whole genre unto themselves. The entire thrust of this story is that the Marshal has nobody in authority to stop him. Under British rule, the opposite would have been the problem... someone in a crisis would have been too bound up in bureaucracy to act quickly and decisively.

This isn't to say that the story is entirely unconnected with the Imperial past. There's a vague resemblance between the Solonian objections to the Overlords, as well as the "Quit India" campaign and its brutal counter-assaults, but it's so nebulous as to be laughable. The sarcastic offer of a light role in admin for the Marshal is a fair approximation of what a lot of formerly influential people did when coming back to Blighty. The BBC had more than a few. The main resemblance is the characterisation of Stubbs and Cotton as figures straight out of a Kipling poem, something like *Tommy Atkins* or *Gunga Din*. To be honest, the shift in emphasis to the salt-of-the-earth infantry carrying out the daft orders was one British audiences found more familiar and congenial. A lot of people knew someone who'd served in India and South East Asia in the War. Even if their stories made less heroic films, they had tales to tell, usually about the absurdities of military life.

Don't forget, Baker and Martin had originally got into the loop by pitching an Army sitcom; we're now only a couple of years away from *It Ain't Half Hot, Mum*. That 1980s boomette in dramas about the officer-class and posh young ladies caught up in the struggle for independence is one mainly made for the US market (see 10.2, "Carnival of Monsters"). Most British viewers

What's Going On With This Music?

...continued from page 253

from the orthodox scale decades earlier, and his tuning system was derived from numerology but came close to approximating the traditional scales of Indian instruments. Schoenberg's lead was followed post-war by Karlheinz Stockhausen, and through him we connect to *Musique Concrête* and Pierre Schaeffer. More on him in a minute.

What's notable is that the route to this occurs by way of a quest for a spiritual dimension that's apparently lacking in Western classical music after Wagner. Some composers were coming to similar end-products through a desire to remove any human or mystical "mush" from their music and refine it to a form of mathematics. Some, however, are just bored with violins and want to find something else. So you got mutually antagonistic groups of purists competing, with the end result being a large and passionate following for music that nobody voluntarily listens to these days.

When Pierre Boulez conducted some of these pieces at the Roundhouse in Camden, he got bigger crowds than when The Who played there. Another Roundhouse gig was the "Million Volt Light and Sound Rave", a 1966 Happening involving Peter Zinovieff, Delia Derbyshire and Paul McCartney. A huge tranche of the British Public were prepared to put in a bit of work and listen to anything new without judging it by the criteria appropriate for Petula Clarke or Tchaikovsky. For these people, a lot of material was becoming available on disc or via the Third Programme / Radio Three. The freaky burbles and occasional angular score you'd get in *Doctor Who* stories such as "The Savages" (3.9) were just the tip of an iceberg. A lot of avant-garde techniques were being plundered by (or from) popular culture. In its broadest sense, feedback is the quintessential art-form of the decade, either making loops or self-replicating processes (think of the Warhol screen-prints) or setting up systems actually intended go out-of-control "to order" and generate new forms independently of the artist. Jimi Hendrix's solos, Cornelius Cardew's "Process" music, the Beatles' *Tomorrow Never Knows* and Bernard Lodge's *Doctor Who* titles are all from the same trend. With the theme music, the BBC were smuggling something very like experimental art into the front rooms of millions.

One of the key tools in the Radiophonic Workshop's armoury was the tape-loop. It's one of the most important changes in the approach to

sound after 1945; the Nazis had found a new way to make a physical and malleable object with sound on it. Discs were a step in the right direction, with a couple of generations discovering the fun to be had with playing things on the wrong speed or backwards, or getting annoyed when a small piece of the recording reiterated because of a scratch. Just as the end of the American Civil War led to a lot of abandoned military instruments lying around in the Deep South (now thought to be a reason why Jazz happened), so the end of the War led to a lot of left over tape-machines, valve amps and microphones. Schaeffer's use of cut-up recordings of found sounds may have offended the post-Schoenberg generation of purists and mystics, but it led to sounds with that fractal similarity to orthodox instruments.

Anyone could do this; not everyone could do it *well*. Above all else, what the success of the Radiophonic Workshop in the 1960s shows is that access to technology or resources is a different thing from the imagination to use it; from the deep-grained understanding of sound. There's an awful lot of *Music Concrête* out there that nobody listens to these days (and a couple, like the Beatles' *Revolution 9*, explain why nobody bothered to make it after a while). Quite frankly, by 1969 everyone was sick of backwards guitar solos and mellotrons.[89]

However, these reified sounds (that is, sounds made into objects) afforded a lot of new noises at a time when the commercial quest for novelty in music was matched by the questing spirit of musicians, who'd got it into their heads that making girls scream wasn't enough any more. Just before Beatlemania, George Martin collaborated with the Radiophonic Workshop's Maddelina Fagadini on a single called "Time-Beat", and the crossover between the Workshop's string and sticky-tape approach and the massive success of Joe Meek's similarly ingenious use of ludicrously scant resources is similarly intriguing. (See **Did Sergeant Pepper Know the Doctor?** under 5.1, "The Tomb of the Cybermen".)

Before Psychedelia this was dismissed as novelty music, but by 1970 it had become the musical *lingua franca* as much as the Fender Stratocaster or the Hammond organ. Moog and Zinovieff changed that practically overnight, and now the sounds of futuristic cities, minds being blown and experimental collages of sonic texture from even

continued on page 257...

(especially those with family in India) wanted these boring toffs to get out of the way so we could see more of the scenery - and they *certainly* didn't want to hear Sir Alec Guinness doing his Peter Sellers impression.

Typically, *Doctor Who* looks at these big projects from the ground floor. Later on, we go to an anti-matter planet at the end of the Universe, and it's the crewmen Ponti and De Haan who get our sympathy (13.2, "Planet of Evil"). Still later, we go outside the universe altogether in a paradoxical realm filled with Cocteau-escapees, and we look at it from the point of view of two scousers who have to shift the heavy equipment (18.5, "Warriors' Gate"). BBC television was telling its heavy drama about the British in India (*The Regiment*, with episodes by Robert Holmes and Brian Hayles), but the definitive statement on this was *Carry On Up The Khyber,* where Sid James plays the Viceroy of India and the story revolves around what underpants the squaddies are wearing. So the real surprise in "The Mutants" isn't that Cotton winds up taking care of the transitional government, but that they kill Stubbs an episode before.

Even the 'Mutt-hunt' has an unsavoury precedent. In 1953, the Kenyan armed insurrection (the Mau Mau) was treated as an affront to decency. The insurrectionists were brutal, but nothing like as vicious as the reprisals. It became a Safari, with landowners offering bounties of five shillings for each one killed. This stopped once news of it got out in Britain, but Hollywood lapped it up. A whole rash of African movies had butch men treating the Africans as game. American audiences wouldn't have taken to virile Englishmen, so it was Victor Mature and Rock Hudson protecting the white women, while effete Englishmen objected and were invariably proved fatally misguided.[85]

We should also mention that the big cultural event in Britain, 1972, was the loan of the Tutankhamun exhibition to the British Museum. Huge numbers of people came and saw the Rosetta Stone, and *Blue Peter* told the story of the translation of Hieroglyphics all over again. As we're going to see (**Why Didn't Plaid Cymru Lynch Barry Letts?** under 10.5, "The Green Death"), access to an indigenous language and culture was becoming part of liberation politics closer to home...

Look, there's no polite way of saying this: Ky and Varan and the others look like stereotyped Welshmen (or as Hinks would call them, "Taffs"), all beetling brows and shaggy dark hair. As Ky, Garrick Hagon even sounds like he's attempting the accent (there's lovely). The Overlords have virtually wiped out the Solonian language, and there's no sign of their culture other than hippy beads. In South Africa at the time, the exact opposite was taking place (as we see in the "Frontier in Space" essay), so this is less a specific Apartheid parable than it's a generalised swipe at cultural homogeneity. Some in Wales claimed to be victims of this as much as the Maoris / Aborigines / Native Americans were. The point is that in the story, recovering this language allows comprehension of the problem and a solution that overthrows the Overlords. Back in the real world, people were prepared to go on hunger-strike to get more Welsh-language broadcasting. Baker and Martin, living in Bristol, *could* have seen enough television in Welsh to have converted to the cause, but in this period it was hardly out of their local news anyway.

We could also mention, if only in passing, the glacial Russian film of Stanislav Lem's *Solaris*, which has a space station (well, more a floating platform in the upper atmosphere, a literal "Sky-Base") over a mysterious and cloud-obscured planet, a plan to bombard the planet with high-energy X-ray beams and some abstract electronic music. (Direct comparison is only advisable if you're a big fan of Andrei Tarkovski's other films. Saying this influenced "The Mutants" in anything but an abstract manner - such as Baker and Martin reading a three-line review in the papers, perhaps - is like claiming that the horrible events in the shower and the unannounced cameo by the guy in charge makes "Spearhead from Space" resemble *Psycho*.)

Another thing that might have been in the authors' minds is Franz Kafka's "Metamorphosis" - which (apologies here if we're explaining what's widely known) tells of someone who wakes up to find he's turned overnight into a six-foot roach. It's a metaphor for alienation, clearly.

Things That Don't Make Sense As with "Colony in Space" and "The Curse of Peladon", the Time Lords use the Doctor as their agent but seem intent on hampering his effectiveness. Surely, sticking a post-it note saying "For attention of: Ky, the rebel leader" on the message pod would have been sensible. For that matter, why do the Time

What's Going On With This Music?

...continued from page 255

a year before seem to come from the same era as magic lantern shows and sepia photographs. Pink Floyd may have used tape-effects on their album *Dark Side of the Moon* but for commentary - the odd sounds they used for music were all VCS3s[90].

The *big* change in *Doctor Who*'s music, however, wasn't the instrumentation or sound-generation mechanisms so much as the use to which the music was put. From 1970 onwards, crucially, the music was written and performed after the recording of the episode rather than before. So whereas a 60s composer would be asked for four or five "moods", and perhaps a specific piece for a set-piece (such as the jingles and festival music in 4.7, "The Macra Terror", or the silent-movie music in 3.4, "The Daleks' Master Plan" when they do the Christmas episode), all of the music is written around the on-screen action. Hitherto, the sound of the world in any adventure was a combination of music and sound effects, but the music was itself a glorified sound effect. In the case of stories such as "The Wheel in Space" (5.7) or "The Krotons" (6.4), this distinction was almost academic, with Brian Hodgson providing both.

So the switch to music underlining the drama ("Mickey Mousing") rather than creating or sustaining the mood (diegetic music rather than non-diegetic) happens at almost the same time that synthesizers become the characteristic sound of the series. (There is, it has to be said, a lot of re-use of stings and short excerpts later in the story, or - in the case of Simpson's cut-and-paste of the "Master Theme" - every time Delgado does his stuff.) Something similar happened with Series Two of the new version, as the BBC Wales Orchestra was only available for a few sessions. Although various themes go through permutations in the course of each series, Series Two entails a few mood-pieces being recorded and slotted in at various points throughout (something which becomes very obvious if you watch the whole year in one sitting).

The scores of most *Doctor Who* stories, then, were simultaneously more like conventional film scores in one way and less like them in another. As we've said, this is the era when mainstream SF films are going down the route *Doctor Who* has just abandoned, fudging the distinction between a music score and the ambient sounds of the fictional world. In Season Eight it gets more complicated - there's at least two instances where music

from outside sources sounds a bit like what Simpson and Hodgson have devised for the adventure, but transpires to be what various characters are listening to within the story. (8.2, "The Mind of Evil" has the Master switching off Robert Fripp; 8.4, "Colony in Space" has the Doctor subjected to Emerson, Lake and Palmer. Music the character can hear as well as the viewer is intradiagetic music. Use this knowledge wisely, but don't try to impress people when watching *American Graffiti*.) However, we're going down the more conventional route of using music to instruct audiences in what they should be feeling at any point.

Of course, the simple assumption that anything a bit weird will do for Science-Fiction was finally torpedoed by George Lucas using the most unchallenging and backward-looking form of soundtrack possible for *Star Wars*. As he'd helped to pioneer the sound of film in his previous two movies (with help from sound editor Walter Murch, co-author of *THX 1138*), this wasn't an accident. Lucas hired John Williams to provide a safe, familiar and unthreatening score, pastiching earlier works (mainly by Prokofiev, who was himself parodying and affectionately subverting nineteenth-century Russian composers).

To be brutally honest, it's a score that assumes that audiences are too dumb to know what's going on. However, it highlights the way film music had been taking one of Wagner's better ideas, the *leitmotif*, and deploying it with less subtlety. Instead of just a theme for a specific character used the same way again and again, Wagner devised a complex coding system using themes for combinations of character and storyline and instrumentation to give this shade and texture. These motifs interact across the whole of the story (which, in the case of the *Ring* Cycle, is four three hour operas) and alter one another. To a lesser extent most diligent, film music did the same.

During the late 70s, Dudley Simpson also had a go at this. There's a recognisable Fourth Doctor theme that gets a cunning disguise in each story, but there's also similar ideas for the various monsters and a clever change of emphasis to differentiate the two Romanas. Nothing quite like this happens in the Pertwee era - unless you count Bessie getting the same music in two stories running (9.5, "The Time Monster"; 10.1, "The Three Doctors") and UNIT having a theme for "The

continued on page 259...

Lords send not-terribly-useful tablets rather than, say, the crystal that catalyzes the Solonians' transformation? And why send the tablets to Ky, who can't even read them, as opposed to Professor Sondergaard, who can?

Why is the teleporter on Solos - apparently the only one in operation - not near any of the mines or factories we hear about, but in the middle of nowhere? It seems that the Overlords have been controlling a whole planet from a zone about twenty feet in diameter from the teleport bay. No guards or support staff are stationed at the bay. They don't even have *password protection* on the teleport, which means that everyone - including all the rebellious elements - can pretty much come and go as they please. Note especially the mutant who teleports to Skybase and walks unchallenged into the Marshall's office, when the plot requires that the Earth Investigators see the creature and get spooked. Overlord security is *so* awful, in fact, that Ky's palm-print can open doors (even the sort where the palm-print key drastically slides back and forth, as if it's not fastened down properly - watch as Varan bursts into the room in episode one). Nor has access been restricted to Skybase's life-support systems. The hydroponics section doesn't have its own air-lock, even though - if the mutants are plague-carriers as the Marshall keeps insisting - the vivarium and the hospital ought to have been the first places isolated.

That's a point. In addition to it being poor security, why does the Marshall allow everyone to come and go, willy-nilly, to and from Solos when there's an outbreak of "plague"? Even segregated teleport bays (a sensible precaution under such a scenario, rather than an affront to humanoid rights) wouldn't fix this - especially as they both go to and from the same reception terminals. This whole system is wasteful and silly. A separate building would have made the rather-laboured moral lesson more effectively, plus avoid a number of plot flaws. [Anyway, if they seriously wanted to make a point about this, perhaps the Solonians should have been bussed to Skybase in overcrowded space shuttles. It's a more humiliating and thematically neat. They could even stage a re-run of the partition of India and Pakistan, just to keep Sir Salman happy.]

Moreover, there's no transport from the reception area on Solos to anywhere else on the planet. So even if the Mutt-hunts are conducted on foot, are we to presume that the Overlords have sub-

dued an entire planet's population with no vehicular transport of any kind? And they've maintained this control for five hundred years? If that's the case, Varan and his ancestors are the most useless insurrectionists in galactic history. Perhaps the Overlords only do the hunts for fitness-training (in which case, it's not working for the Marshal). If they had even so much as a bicycle, they could have caught the Doctor in episode five.

Come episode two, it transpires that the Marshal didn't lock the door to his own office before he dispatches Varan's son, enabling Varan to walk straight in and find the Marshal with a smoking gun (so to speak). Varan then insists on performing a "last rite" of sorts for his son, evidently not worried that he's handed the trigger-happy Marshall the perfect opportunity to plug him as well. As for the Marshal / Varan scuffle to follow... exactly what the *hell* is going on? Terrance Dicks' novelisation has Varan scoop up a chair and fling it at the Marshal, hitting him in the shoulder. Not a bad idea, save that on screen, it looks as if Varan just slaps a piece of furniture as if it's a naughty, *naughty* piece of furniture before he dashes out, even as the Marshal declines to leisurely shoot him in the back. And why does Varan insist on referring to himself in the third person when no other Solonian (save for the post-transformation Ky) does?

In the caves with Ky, Jo speaks of Earth as if it's completely the same in this time period as in her era [something of a habit whenever she travels to the future - see "Colony in Space"]. She's heard the Doctor describe it as a giant cat-litter but then she's also heard Stubbs and Cotton wanting to leave Solos and get back to Blighty - no wonder the poor mite's confused. [But then, Cotton seems barely able, halfway through episode two, to speak words such as 'oxygen treatment', so she might not have been following what he was saying.]

Stubbs, the supposedly "sympathetic" Overlord, seems awfully happy and chipper at the prospect of shooting Varan dead. Then Stubbs opts to turn against the Marshall and lie that he "eliminated" Varan - but when the Marshal discovers that Varan is still alive, he somehow puts this down to Stubbs' incompetence rather than treachery. (Mind you, this seems entirely right based on later evidence: he's a *terrible* shot.)

At the cliffhanger to episode two, Varan seems awfully intent on strangling the Doctor, even

What's Going On With This Music?

...continued from page 257

Ambassadors of Death" and "The Mind of Evil".

Yet Simpson's scores for Season Eight, however silly they may seem now, have this within individual stories, and take it to the extent of more-or-less inventing a new instrument for each species. Before and after the Season Eight experiment in all-electric scoring, he uses frequency modulation ("flanging") on conventional percussion and pianos to suggest that the story is set elsewhere, just as a "local" style occurs in stories set in historical periods or other countries.

Later he switches from saxophones to bass clarinets to suggest menace in places other than present day Earth, but the synthesized keyboard sounds remain the main method of suggesting "Wrongness". (For instance, when Simpson wants us to feel at home on an alien planet, he'll use something with known connotations - say, the church organ effect in 14.3, "The Deadly Assassin" and 16.1, "The Ribos Operation".) Once he returns to conventional instruments, the relationship between the scoring and the characterisation becomes more appreciably codified. His knowledge of how his music sounded on small speakers makes him select instruments (such as marimbas and bass clarinets) that most film or stage composers wouldn't think to use. By the time Simpson has to do a story about a space-war after Williams institutionalised the idea of a big capital-R Romantic score, this is only acceptable in Doctor Who as a joke. (Note the 'Young men are dying for it' scene at the start of 16.6, "The Armageddon Factor".) In this, we're given a blast of what might equally be the piano music from 1950s US soaps or the Rachmaninov piece from Brief Encounter.

Making the analogy between film music and television music has its limits, however. The makers of music for 1960s and 1970s television had to deal with the fact that people would talking in the room where the show's being watched, but also for the mono speakers with no tone-controls and restricted frequency range built into sets before 1985. However distinctive it is, what with the dialogue, the sound effects and the people eating their teas on their laps, the music is in a struggle for survival. (Simpson knew this and made arrangements with Hodgson, and later Dick Mills, to leave gaps in his score for big sound events.)

This is - if we can get a bit more academic for a moment - the main problem with recent attempts to try and co-opt film-maker and musician Michel Chion's theories of rendu. (It could best be translated as "rendering", and relates to the use of sound to mediate between the on-screen word and the audience.) Chion would have us believe that the filmgoer doesn't so much follow a story as "swim" inside a cinema soundscape and puzzlement occurs when an unmotivated or source-less sound is introduced into the narrative. Regrettably, this isn't the place to explore all of that. (The interested reader is directed to some of the essays in the recently-published Time and Relative Dissertations in Space book, especially Louis Niebur's exhaustive analysis - be warned, it might make you actually want to watch 6.1, "The Dominators" - and the introductory piece. Chapter Five is brilliant, by the way.)

One of the many interesting social factors in the watching of old-school Doctor Who was the use of home tape-recorders to capture the soundtrack of episodes, for which we should be particularly thankful, in cases where the BBC lost or destroyed the visuals. It's safe to say that no other programme - certainly no other drama - elicited this response, so obviously the programme's sound mattered greatly to some viewers. Yet most people would have thought this a bit weird. Hushing your relatives for half an hour or so isn't a practice that even the most attentive BBC2 viewer would have done, so for a BBC1 popular drama the main response was partially collaborative, involving a discussion of what was going to happen next. Ask anyone watching even the new series with children. These days, however, they aren't asking how the theme tune is made.

Pulling back to the transitional period of Seasons Seven to Ten, there's one obvious question to ask, one that the various composers and Douglas Camfield (assuming he was the only one who compiled the stock-music for "Inferno") all had to try to answer in different ways; does the music in television actually have any effect on audience perceptions at all?

In the past, the odd noises were part of what made Doctor Who known to most people. We've already investigated the extent to which this was as much a series of environments for younger children to explore as a set of narratives (see **Does Plot Really Matter?** under "The Krotons"), but we have to reiterate that each story's mix of conventional and electronic sounds was different. The degree of involvement at a sensory level was dif-

continued on page 261...

though the Doctor both spared his life and seemed eager to conspire against Varan's enemy, the Marshal. All right, maybe Varan is just an ungrateful savage, but explain how they can be wrestling outside the teleport at the end of episode two, and grappling *inside* the teleport (with the door closed and all) at the start of episode three. [Magic! Or horrible directing.]

Varan keeps insisting that the mutants are evil and diseased, yet he entirely fails to notice, somehow, the dirty, great mutant-ish lumps on the back of the old geezer who gets up to bang the gong. Stubbs has been told repeatedly that the Marshal wants him in constant contact when hunting for Ky in the caves, yet he entirely forgets this and rabbits on to the Doctor and Ky about bringing down the Marshal - thus exposing his true colours to the fat guy with the detonator and gas grenades.

Fast forward to the end of episode three, where the Doctor is informed about the impending gas attack yet insists on sitting around studying the tablets, enabling everyone to get caught flat-footed when, sure enough, the assault occurs. The group includes Stubbs and Cotton, who actually *have* oxygen masks, but insist on not wearing them. Shortly thereafter, the Doctor doesn't seem to recognize a man in a radiation suit (Sondergaard) when he sees one, telling Stubbs, 'Whatever it is, we'd better follow it'. And shortly after *that*, the Doctor insists on risking death by cave-in so he and Sondergaard can make use of the professor's records about life on Solos - records that they're never seen to actually use. Is he feeling quite well? One has to wonder: when Sondergaard passes out, the "moralistic" Doctor barely spares him a passing glance. Also, it's strange that Sondergaard knows that Solos has a 2,000-year orbit around its sun, yet he's labouring under the misassumption - until the Doctor corrects him - that Solos has no seasons.

Come episode five, the Marshal orders his guards to wait outside while he has a confidential chat with Jaeger. Fine, but he allows Jo and his other prisoners to remain, thus enabling them to hear a detailed account of his various crimes. And even though the Marshal orders his troopers to take the Doctor alive, they wilfully shoot at him as he uses the teleport terminal - the *only* teleport terminal on Solos, let's not forget. Anyway, why bother as he's 'porting up to Skybase, from which (if the Overlords get their act together) he theoretically can't escape? Still later, the lone idiot

guard left to watch the prisoners sits down, turns away from his captives and puts down his gun. The Overlords really don't have their hearts into this whole "maintain an Empire through force" thing, do they?

After the prisoners get loose, and the Overlord troops decide - without having benefit of actually knowing that a jailbreak is in progress - that they should charge into the Marshal's office with their guns drawn. Amid the subsequent chaos, Professor Jaeger seems awfully oblivious to the repeated sound of gunfire outside his lab. And why does the Marshal insist on detaining the Earth Investigators, when he's duped them into ruling in his favour? He *must* be a raving nutter, if he thinks this won't hamper his goals.

As ever with Bob Baker and Dave Martin (who try *so* hard, bless 'em), much of the space-science here is rubbish. In a space station, a door malfunction is basically a death-sentence unless fixed right away, yet Stubbs and Cotton ignore two of these to play chess. Then they arrange, on the Doctor's behalf, an even more lethal power cut. By day, humans can't breathe Solos' atmosphere, but this is conveniently ignored when Sondergaard accompanies the Doctor onto the surface and all of Jaeger's missiles are falling on this one small part of the planet - it's the missiles which make the Professor unwell.

Not to worry, Professor Jaeger has a Cunning Plan for converting Solos' atmosphere... well, maybe. Assuming for a moment that particle reversal works as we're told in episode two, of what possible use is it in fixing Jaeger's botched experiment? If so applied, Solos' soil and magma would appear outside the atmosphere. Whilst a suddenly hollow planet occupied by people with their organs hanging out is a promising idea for a future story (in print please, if possible... eww), it's a far more likely outcome than using particle reversal as a planet-sized reset button.

No, we can't avoid mentioning any longer... after a great big hole's blown in the wall of the Skybase at the end of episode four, the air rushes out of the station for just a few moments before the pressure "balances" and everybody shuffles out of the room as if nothing's wrong. But the door is still open, and the wall-gash is still there. The rush of air can *only* stop when there isn't any more air to rush, yet everyone exits without bursting open or even running a bit short of breath.

The scientific blunders continue... thaesium

What's Going On With This Music?

...continued from page 259

ferent each time. When the sound was made with distressed tape, there was an essential warmth to the sound-worlds - this was common to *Bleep and Booster* and the slightly melancholy mid-60s theme tunes the Workshop churned out[91], but the voltage-controlled oscillators placed a distance between viewers and story-world. In other ways, though, it allows us to engage with the story-world on its terms, rather than shoehorning it into a conventional format like a love-story, a war-story or a comedy. To some extent all music for film or television is slightly alienating. When we get productions such as "The Claws of Axos" (8.3) with saturation music (most of it as loud as the dialogue), there's little leeway for the audience to be beguiled, so they either take it or leave it. Fundamentally, though, Simpson is in the camp that believes that the music is intended to enhance the mood of each scene.

Season Nine's two "other" soundtracks, however, make no such concessions and have a different aim. Neither Malcolm Clarke (9.3, "The Sea Devils") nor Tristram Cary (9.4, "The Mutants") is trying to make us "feel" anything except lost and bewildered. The choice of settings for the synths in either case is significant, but not in itself the point of the music. If someone wanted to transcribe

either score for conventional instruments, they would still sound discordant. If anything, the odd intervals between notes would be more arresting. (We could get very technical and point out that they're both prone to use scales more associated with blues and jazz, but that's a subject for a whole book.) In some ways, we're blinded to the inventiveness of these pieces by the fact that they're being played on custom-made machinery. Although this was one of the hallmarks of the early years of the series, it's almost the last time we get anything this innovative presented to the viewing public, and the music of the series will play increasingly safe until it reaches the depths in the mid-1980s (list your own examples), and thereafter in the safe and mundane scores of John Debney and Murray Gold. Rather than a place for us to explore with the characters on screen *Doctor Who*, it's now a story that is going to make you *feel*, dagnabbit, even if it has to pull every cheap emotional blackmail trick in the book. A commonplace of the few criticisms actually allowed of Gold's scores is that they are, essentially, the soundtrack to war-movies. Just as the episodes have moved from being about exploration and discovery to safeguarding what we know, so the music became less adventurous and more reassuringly bland - a process that begins under Barry Letts and is still underway.

radiation knows, somehow, to go towards Ky. If it's conventional radiation (like heat), this is rather like having a light-bulb that illuminates everything in the room until you open a book, at which point the rays *know* that it's time to start going in one direction only. Maybe the pupating Solonians become some kind of radiation-magnets, but if so, why don't the large number of them near the caves suck the harmful rays away, allowing Sondergaard walk around without his romper-suit on? And if it's the crystal acting as a lodestone, why is Sondergaard still alive? Even with a lead-lined room as a base, he's been walking around in his version of plain-clothes carrying the crystal (because apparently, there's only *one* magic crystal to help transform the entire Solonian population) and should therefore have been fairly well poached by now. Then again, maybe this explains how he got such a good tan after twenty years (or whatever) spent in a cave.

In episode six, Sondergaard and a mutant beam up to Skybase, despite the macrophisor (which is

vital to the teleport's function) having been removed for Jaeger's experiments. Sadly, unless they're able to remove and replace this in about fifteen seconds, the end of the story doesn't work [unless the teleport is still u/s]. The complete Solonian transformation, from human to mutant to superhuman, is so severe that even Ky's clothes change. [Perhaps the radiation destroys his original clothing, and his robes as a super-being are some kind of telepathic illusion. Or maybe the augmented Solonians' native state is lycra body-stockings, shoulder-pads and tinfoil capes.]

Most importantly out of everything we've mentioned, what possessed them to cast Rick James?

Critique Well, you can't fault them for ambition. However much fandom knocks this story - and however one judges its implementation - it has a scale we haven't seen since "The Ark" (3.6). The monsters are scary and sad-looking at the same time (no mean feat) and there's still a lot of mileage in ex-colonial governors making dodgy deals to cling to power. (4.3, "The Power of the Daleks" was a potentially series-length variation of this, but it still works.) And allowing for a few predictable flaws with CSO, parts of this story look much better than they deserve. So if you're coming to this after seeing the officially-designated "classic" Pertwee stories, you're in for a few pleasant surprises.

More than anything, though, we're dealing with a story that looks *odd*. It's not just the music, or the tilted camera (we had those last time as well), and it's not the jumble of accents or the picture-quality (it looks strange on *any* screen, even in black and white, and even the clips on the DVD of "The Sea Devils" look, well, Australian). Somehow, "The Mutants" doesn't seem to belong in Season Nine - or indeed, as part of any show made by the BBC. Unlike their trips to Peladon and Uxarieus, the Doctor and Jo seem to have actually travelled to a strange place - even though we have it on good authority that it was made in Studios 3, 4, 4a and 8 at Television Centre, directed by Christopher Barry and shown on Saturdays in Britain in 1972. And we even know that one relatively important person saw it, because Salman Rushdie (even if he spectacularly missed the point of the one episode he saw) sort-of references the Mutts in *The Satanic Verses* as evidence that everyone in Britain sees foreigners as aliens.

Pinning down precisely where this weirdness / "otherness" stems from is a bit of a challenge, though. The basic plot seems obvious *now*, but when "The Mutants" was made, the idea of a planet with a long year hadn't appeared in the series (nor, we've got to say, had it cropped up in *Star Trek*). The notion of mutation as a cyclic pupation was also fresh. True, John Wyndham had milked the metaphor of butterflies and psychic powers in (ahem) *The Chrysalids*, but this wasn't a recurring process. Meanwhile, Baker and Martin have taken the opportunity to make a few timely swipes at South Africa. Or America...

Hang on a minute, that's *three* extended metaphors at work in one story. Any rhetorical effectiveness gained from the 'stinking, rotten hole' material is weakened by trying to make Solos stand in for several other "issues" as well. This story is a polemic about - er, well - something or other, *not* an attempt to tell a story about a world that exists for anything other than polemical purposes. Baker and Martin have grand goals, but now they're over-reaching, and it's creating knock-

on troubles for the production team.

Christopher Barry doesn't have time to clear up what this story is actually about, so he just gets it made on time and on budget. He's got a vague intuition that if this is the "future" and Earth stands for England, then one of the "chorus" should look different from everyone else. Not a terrible idea, but then he goes off the deep end and casts Rick James as Cotton, instead of someone who can actually say the lines. Was Rudolph Walker (formerly Harper, one of the soldiers in 6.7, "The War Games") on holiday? Well, no, he was off making the astonishing race-themed sitcom *Love Thy Neighbour*, but what we're getting as is that if you're casting people *just* on skin-colour (and we can't fathom why else James got hired), then you've missed a major point of this story. Or maybe you've just asked too many people what the point was, and got too many answers. Whatever the reason, Barry is clearly tiring of this story very early on.

Where he doesn't falter is with regards the music - fan-opinion will always be divided about it, but in truth the score is the only element anyone seems to be giving extra thought. Barry had a knack of getting composers to view *Doctor Who* as an invitation to stretch themselves, not just as a means to pay the mortgage and impress the kids. Like the then-contemporary electronic music coming from Germany - or muddy fields where thousands of enthusiastic stoners were listening to Gong or Hawkwind - the music seems to open up a new world, albeit not necessarily one you'd like to stay in for more than a few minutes.

Even in this regard, Barry has a problem. He didn't get to actually hear the music before recording started, so he doesn't try to live up to it. Compare this to "The Daleks", where he had the soundtrack well in advance, and you'll see the difference. As a result he makes visuals that are generally as uninspired as the music is innovative. This story has occasional moments of very bright colour but it's set in one of the blandest space-stations ever, with the bad guys in black and the "cavalry" in white. That set, with the vacuum-moulded triangle-patterns in beige, seems remarkably flimsy. Maybe spaceships *would* look like that, but it seems almost as though they'd made the scenery out of rice-paper so that Paul Whitsun-Jones (as the Marshall) can chew on it. At least he's putting some effort in, though...

Yes, that seems to be the problem - it looks as

though we're watching rehearsals. It's as if they've accidentally recorded the run-throughs of each episode, then dubbed music and sound effects on. Episode one contains a scene where Katy Manning has her glasses on, and right at the start, Pertwee famously flubs the 'I couldn't open it even if I wanted to' line. Everyone apart from Whitsun-Jones (as the Marshal) is behaving as if they're doing it for the benefit of the camera technicians trying to line up shots, not for viewers.

In Manning's case this is a pleasant change (as we've mentioned before, she seems to "perk down" for space stories). Also, veteran actors such as Pertwee, Geoffrey Palmer (as the Solos Administrator) and Peter Howell (as the Investigator) know what they're about, and deliver their lines right regardless of whether they think it's a take. We could maybe offer a defence of the actors playing Solonians, on the grounds that it's impossible to underplay lines as horrendously over-written as they're given, but it would be a half-hearted defence. And someone, it seems, has looked at a calendar and realised how long it's been since George Pravda (as Professor Jaeger) was last in the series, so they've given him a role, any role, regardless of his suitability.

There's a good four-parter in here, somewhere. (Maybe the extra two weeks could have been given over to making a good four-part story about a time-experiment and a different four-parter about Atlantis, sparing us from two freakishly incoherent six-parters in a row.) There's so much potential here that seeing it frittered away - with the cast bumbling about trying to figure out what they're doing and the director making so many big visual statements, then losing our interest in the very next scene - is outright painful. Some might even see it as a deliberate, clever ploy to "prove" that *Doctor Who* belongs on Earth in the present day and shouldn't waste its time in expensive space-yarns. Some moments here are as good as anything in the series, even to date, but most fans come away with a few jokes about the music, and a lot of bad memories of Sidney Johnson as the Old Man and a few other odd performances. Indeed, right at the end, it looks as if the Investigator (Peter Howell, not the Radiophonics one) can barely believe he's being asked to say, without gagging, that Cotton (Rick James, not the *Superfreak* one) should become the acting governor, which speaks volumes.

At a very basic, infantile level, it's possible to quaff some fizzy drink with too many chemicals, then watch "The Mutants" while saying, "Ooh! Pretty!" This is true of Baker and Martin's other contributions to the Letts / Pertwee canon, and - to be fair - it was an integral part of the programme's appeal back then. (Indeed, to a certain extent, BBC Wales is no different.) And if you miss the strangeness and charm of the scores for Hartnell and Troughton stories - or are a fan of early electronica - the music gives it all a fresh feel. Watch "The Mutants" with someone who doesn't know the plot, and see how long it takes for the basic idea to sink in. Watch it with friends who've all seen it before and join in with dialogue and sardonic comments. (This is up there, after all, with "The Five Doctors" and "Dimensions in Time" as far as audience-participation goes.) Just don't judge all Pertwee stories by this one.

The Facts

Written by Bob Baker and Dave Martin. Directed by Christopher Barry. Viewing figures: 9.1 million, 7.8 million, 7.9 million, 7.5 million, 7.9 million, 6.5 million.

Supporting Cast Paul Whitsun-Jones (Marshal), James Mellor (Varan), Garrick Hagon (Ky), Geoffrey Palmer (Administrator), Christopher Coll (Stubbs), Rick James (Cotton), George Pravda (Jaeger), John Hollis (Sondergaard), Peter Howell (Investigator).

Working Titles "Independence", "The Emergents".

Cliffhangers Escaping from the Skybase, Ky kidnaps Jo and drags her into the teleporter, just as the guards open fire on them; the Doctor and Varan both attempt to escape the Skybase at the same time, ending in Varan grabbing the Doctor around the throat and shouting 'die, Overlord, die'; the Marshal seals the Doctor and his new pals in and floods the Mutt caves with gas; the Marshal (rather stupidly) blasts through the hull of the Skybase, resulting in Varan being sucked out into space while Jo and her chums hang on for dear life; trapped in Skybase's refuelling lock with Jo and Ky, Cotton suddenly realises that the refuelling process is about to begin and that the area is going to be flooded with radiation: '*We'll all be done for!*'.

What Was in the Charts? "Back Off Boogaloo", Ringo Starr; "Alone Again, Naturally", Gilbert

O'Sullivan; "Heart of Gold", Neil Young; "Amazing Grace", Band of the Scots Dragoon Guards[86]; "Stir It Up", Johnny Nash; "The Young New Mexican Puppeteer", Tom Jones.

The Lore

• As we noted earlier, Barry Letts developed the idea of the Solonian life-cycle in 1966, and then-script editor Gerry Davis rejected it as being too complex. (This tells you all you need to know about how Davis regarded *Doctor Who*.) Letts also suggested adding it to Baker and Martin's basic story about an Earth colony on the brink of independence.

After a promising first episode, Terrance Dicks wrote to the authors about his concerns. Once again, the Bristol Boys were shovelling on out-there concepts thick and fast (mainly thick) and the storyline was becoming lost in a welter of other ideas. Entire sub-plots about cloning and asylum-seekers from Earth (see "The Invisible Enemy" and the comments on Dave Martin's *Make Your Own Adventure* books in the essay with 22.5, "Timelash"), a Vietnam parable and Ky becoming spherical (!) had to be removed and an ending included. The original script of "The Mutants" also referred to the mutations as "munts" instead of "mutts"; "munt" being Afrikaans slang for a black African. Go on - guess why it was changed. (And see 12.3, "The Sontaran Experiment" for the authors' continued interest in South Africa - then again, "Munt" was a not-uncommon surname in the East End of London.)

• This is the first of eight stories to have costume design by James Acheson. Among other things, he's responsible for Tom Baker's overall look, two separate rethinks of the Time Lords and - as with this story - collaborating with latex miracle-worker John Friedlander on a groundbreaking design for 13.1, "Terror of the Zygons". After 1980 he went into films, first with low-budget comedy / fantasies such as *Sir Henry at Rawlinson End* and *Time Bandits*, then bigger ones such as *Brazil, Highlander* and *Dark Crystal*. He also did a lot of work with Bernardo Bertolucci (literally a cast of thousands for *The Last Emperor*, and more detailed work for *The Sheltering Sky* and *Little Buddha*). He's done a few costumes for super-heroes (all three of the recent *Spider-Man* flicks, but alas he's tainted by association with *Daredevil*) and got a brace of Oscars (*The Man in the Iron Mask* and *Mary Shelley's Frankenstein*, but don't bother watching these just for that).

For the mutants themselves, Acheson also enlisted his friend and neighbour Alistair Bowtell, a sculptor and painter who had made bizarre props for *Monty Python*, the Bonzo Dog Doo-Dah Band and *The Goodies* (and Rod Hull's Emu). We could list his other achievements all day, but suffice it to say he had a long, stripy hand-knitted scarf that caught people's attention (see 12.1, "Robot", and also 12.5, "Revenge of the Cybermen" for his rethink of the monster design).

The mutant masks were constructed with the working mandibles operated by the wearers; they were attached to the actors' cheeks with clothes-pegs. These heads were Friedlander's design. One of Acheson's main concerns was that the clothes of the various parties should be distinct from one another but not include any of the CSO colours. He was advised that not everyone had colour televisions, which also informed his use of stark uniforms with piping for the two sets of Earth soldiers and neutral coloured smocks with beads for the Solonians and Sondergaard. Varan's tribe were scripted as Samurai-like, and this is mainly retained. People recall seeing Acheson working well into the small hours the night before filming to get things right.

• Garrick Hagon (Ky) hid his Canadian accent on screen but did many of the PA voice-overs (John Hollis did the rest). He's since done a great deal of radio and provided voices for films such as *The Dark Crystal*. He also popped up in *Moonbase 3*, but nobody talks about that. His other claim to fame, of course, is as Biggs - the guy with the Village People moustache who used to shoot Womp Rats with Luke Skywalker, and is in the bits of stuff George Lucas filmed but didn't include in *Star Wars Episode IV: The Good One*.

Hollis (Sondergaard) took the Lucas shilling too, as "Lobot" (if that really was his name) in *Star Wars Episode Five: The One Everyone Pretends to Like Better*. He'd been the sinister industrialist in the two *Andromeda* serials of the early 60s (see 3.10, "The War Machines"; the second serial is out on DVD and BBC4 did a remake recently with the dodgy company tactfully renamed). He's all over *The Avengers* and ITC like a rash, and was the uncredited Blofeld in *Thunderball*. Paul Whitsun-Jones (the Marshall) was the original James Fullalove in the original *The Quatermass Experiment*, and was Porthos opposite Roger

Delgado and Laurence Paine in the 1950s BBC production of *The Three Musketeers*. In *Who*, he'd been the Squire in 4.1, "The Smugglers". Peter Howell (the Investigator) is the Professor in *The Prisoner* episode with the lamest ending ("The General"). Rick James (Cotton) can also be seen in the barking mad 1920s-Expressionist-style penultimate episode of *Blake's 7*, struggling to retain his dignity in a loincloth and Marge Simpson's hair.

• Just for a change they filmed the exteriors in a quarry. This particular one, a chalk quarry near Dartmouth, had been used in the production of Portland cement. (If you're one of those people who goes looking for locations, prepare yourself for a shock - the bit they used is now the Bluewater shopping complex.) The location filming included reference photos for the CSO work of the thaesium cave in episode four. Baker and Martin had specified much more than was actually shot there, but Letts opted for more controllable (and cheaper) studio model-work.

• On the first Monday of 1972, Chris D'Oyly-John and new production assistant Fiona Cumming (she'll be back a lot in Volume V) decorated the wilderness with spray-painted buddleias. (Not hard to come by in London, as they usually sprout up as weeds and create thickets in under a year.) Manning had another of her mishaps, spraining her ankle slightly when she couldn't see where she was putting her feet. The local press came just as Pertwee was adopted by a field mouse and also took off-duty shots of him and Manning getting friendly with a donkey and a llama.

• Finally they went to the Chiselhurst Caves. As if the cold and tedium were not enough, the same power cuts that affected viewers hoping to see how "The Curse of Peladon" ended caused problems. Everyone in the country was issued with rosters (often printed in the newspapers for good measure), so they could work around the pre-arranged electricity switch-off in their area. Alas, the film crew seem to have forgotten theirs. Not only did people forget to bring wind-up alarm-clocks, they had an unexpected cut-off of lighting when deep inside a cave. The hexagonal symbols were carved (with permission) into the cave walls.

• Although the finished version doesn't look like it, the idea was that the Skybase model was to use a forced perspective, suggesting it was a vast construction with two equal-sized spheres and a long connecting tunnel. The end result, though, looks like two spheres of very different sizes.

(Frank Bellamy's *Radio Times* illustration only confirmed this.) The planet Skybase orbited was painted on glass and lit differently for different times of day, and some of the more complex insert shots were filmed upside down to avoid the perennial problems of BBC models: visible wires above the prop and debris from explosions falling downwards. Unfortunately, they were so proud of this innovation that Ian Scoones told everyone in the *Radio Times* Tenth Anniversary Special (see 11.1, "The Time Warrior") and audiences got wise. John Horton, this story's effects supervisor, also had to provide a "magic" cave (a fibreglass model that was backlit in pretty colours, mainly red to make a contrast with the blue lightning from a spark generator and not cause trouble with the yellow CSO keying. Some of the scenes in episode four used the now-standard video-disc technique to slow them down (see 7.3, "The Ambassadors of Death").

• The machinery for mass-producing vacuum-moulded set panels was proudly displayed on *Tomorrow's World* at around this time. Apart from the triangle panels we'll be seeing on practically every planet from now until Peter Davison, they made the rhomboid "bricks" for the BBC News studio. Jeremy Bear, in his first and only solo *Doctor Who* set, had difficulty getting the sets constructed as he requested and later specialised in children's series (although he was slated to design 13.6, "The Seeds of Doom" and gets a co-credit on the first two episodes).

• During rehearsals, Pertwee got a bit of karate coaching from Walsh and recorded his interview for *Ask Aspel* (see "The Sea Devils"). They more or less recorded an episode per session. A gallery-only day of experimental CSO work was needed for the effects in episode six, as well as make-up tests for the super-ageing of Ian Collier in the next story.

• Episode six was recorded ten days before the first episode was broadcast. Barry had a very early home video system (the Shibaden set-up used by the BBC that provided black and white time-coded copies - see the DVD of 17.2, "City of Death"), so did trial runs of his edits before the proper sessions.

• Since providing the score for "The Gunfighters" (3.8), Tristram Cary had taken his interest in electronic music to the obvious next step and designed the business end of the VCS3. He'd contributed a *musique concrète* piece to achingly trendy Swinging London spy-hokum

Sebastian in 1967 (his first film score, as you will recall, was *The Ladykillers*) and a lot of the music for the Montreal Expo 68. Although perfectly capable of writing melodically (as the "Ballad of the Last Chance Saloon" in "The Gunfighters" proves), he was more interested in the tone-colours available with voltage-control than in simply building a fake orchestra with which to play conventional music (see **What's Going On With This Music?**).

Whereas Cary had previously attended recordings to figure out what spot-effects were required, he now worked from the script and the video-recording. (This was less fun, he said. Certainly, the one effect that he would have been asked to make, the klaxon, is in fact recycled from 7.4, "Inferno".) "The Mutants", along with the sound-track for Richard Williams' memorable animated *A Christmas Carol*, was almost his last work in Britain before he relocated to Melbourne (the University had a job for him) and then to Adelaide, where he was a revered lecturer and composer. He was still working until his death, aged 81, whilst this guidebook was being revised.

9.5: "The Time Monster"

(Serial OOO, Six Episodes, 20th May - 24th June 1972.)

Which One is This? 'Hail! Atlantis'. The Master's back, and chatting up girls with odd accents (both his and theirs). We get a whole episode of him and the Doctor just bitching at each other, and the Doctor gives the Minotaur a pat on the back. Jo's feelin' groovy, Ingrid Pitt hears 'strange music', UNIT's outgunned by Roundheads and Benton his enters second childhood.

Firsts and Lasts "The Time Monster" isn't a story that gets an easy ride from *Doctor Who* fans, but what's surprising is just how much of the series' later mythology starts here. This is the first story which dwells on the idea of the TARDIS as a living, feeling thing, and the first time the Ship's 'telepathic circuits' get mentioned, as well as the first time the Doctor acknowledges the existence of the 'vortex' through which it travels. For the first time on television (the comic strips also did this), we see the Ship revolving on its axis as it travels - an idea not intuitively obvious but, once the precedent is set, it'll become inescapable for the rest of

the series, eventually getting enshrined in Sylvester McCoy's title sequence.

It's the first story in which the Doctor explicitly talks about his youth, and the first time he mentions the old hermit who used to live on his homeworld. This is also the first time we see the Doctor dreaming, although it's technically possible that the whole of "The Mind Robber" (6.2) counts. He also briefly abandons 'Hai!' for 'On Y Va!' (That's yer actual French, and more widely-used than "Allons-Y".) "The Time Monster" sees the only appearance of the re-redesigned TARDIS console room, which was changed *again* for Season Ten as almost nobody liked it.

Perhaps most strikingly, and with benefit of hindsight, it's the last time the Master and the "classic" UNIT line-up lock horns. (Even though the Brigadier never explicitly says that the search for the Master has been called off, the villain slips right down their "to do" list henceforth.)

Six Things to Notice About "The Time Monster"...

1. Not since the halcyon days of "The War Games" (6.7), when characters were brainwashed into forgetting something they'd seen in a time-killing set-piece, just so they could do it all over again, have we witnessed such blatant padding as episode three contains. If you've not seen it, the Doctor laboriously searches for various kitchen items and constructs a 'time-flow analogue', a sort of teeter-totter that - with the addition of a mug of tea on top (thus allowing a trial run that doesn't work, killing one minute and fifteen seconds right there) - lights up and makes 'deedledeedle' noises. Apparently this prevents the Master from conquering the universe, for about another fifty seconds. The eponymous monster is a 'Chronovore', which literally translates as "time-consuming".

Other delaying tactics include an entire episode of the Doctor and the Master teleconferencing, hoax phone-calls, Bessie finally turning into the Batmobile, the Doctor's subconscious apparently muttering 'it's so hard' and Sergeant Benton playing hide-and-seek with the Master. Twice. Strangely, this story has a reputation for being a bit silly.

2. The two "ordinary" supporting characters here - Professor Thascales' lab-assistants, Ruth and Stuart - are notable for delivering dialogue that makes the Atlanteans' prose-poetry sound believable by comparison. Ruth spends most of the story complaining about the way she keeps get-

ting patronised by men, while Stuart, whom she patronises in turn, gets to slouch about the place in a very 70s-sit-com fashion (and in a very 70s-sit-com moustache). His worst line: 'May God save the good ship Women's Lib, and all who sail in her.' Her worst line: 'Simmer down, Stu.'

But then, Ruth and Stu are only two components of the wildly diverse acting styles and occasionally arch dialogue on display here. Aiden Murphy (as Hippias, pronounced 'Hippy Ass') thinks he's being recorded on wax cylinders and yells everything in a high-pitched whine, whilst not actually moving his face or body. Well, except once, in a supposedly rabble-rousing speech when he raises his arm at *exactly* the wrong time. Older actors make huge gestures (as the Master's stooge Percival, John Wyse gets bonus daftness-points for the way he turns to the camera when Krasis appears), and we get a funny accent competition reminiscent of the glory days of "The Space Pirates" (6.6).

3. In amongst all this, we have a bizarre generation gap. The younger characters are written in a very self-consciously "trendy" way (back when that was a term of approval), with Disco Stu eating marmalade sandwiches and treating the appearance of a Biba-chick he doesn't recognise at the side of his bed with a weary nonchalance. (In those days a cravat, a big moustache and a poster of Elton John didn't *necessarily* warn girls not to bother - although Stu's telling Ruth, 'Listen, Luvvie, I'm not "men"...' doesn't aid his case). For her part, Jo often talks like a middle-aged writer's idea of a 70s girl. Contrary to popular belief, Katy Manning *was* capable of embarrassment, and cites the dialogue here as one instance - although, to be fair, you'd not guess from her game performance.

4. Dudley Simpson isn't especially helping matters. With his charcoal-burning VCS3 and a friend on kettle-drums, he's valiantly trying to catch the story's mood. On the plus side, he finally gives Bessie a sprightly (yellow) piece of music and furnishes Atlantis with some Arabian Nights flourishes. Unfortunately, he does parpy Bullfight music for the Minotaur fight, and tops off a genuinely toecurling scene where Jo taunts the Master by saying, 'Curses, foiled again', with a squelchy Vaudeville 'bwaa-bwaa-bwaa-bwaaaaa'. But even *this* fails to match the way he flags up the arrival of a non-speaking character who looks like Terry Walsh with some "Oh-ho, here comes a stunt" drum-rolls. (Oh, did we not mention the comedy window-cleaner in the "time-wasting" section?)

5. Episode three sees the UNIT troops assaulted by various military forces from history, including a V-1 buzz-bomb. Since the BBC could hardly be expected to build a brand-new V-1 for this brief sequence, stock footage of a V-1 is used. Unfortunately, the stock footage - unlike the rest of the episode - is in black and white. Best of all, when the Doctor tells the Brig to listen to the sound of the doodlebug, you can hear the crackle on the vinyl record of World War II sound effects. Typical - the one time we really need Dudley's Magic Piano and he keeps schtumm.

6. Those searching for traces of the psychedelic influence on *Doctor Who* need look no further than episode six, which starts in the New Age version of Atlantis (which looks an *awful* lot like a school production of *Joseph and his Amazing Technicolor Dreamcoat*) and culminates in the Doctor and the Master facing each other in a rainbow-coloured void, where they both end up facing an enormous floating female god-head in mystical face-paint. Lady Jo-Jo's verdict: 'Groovy.'

The Continuity

The Doctor He dreams about the Master and the Crystal of Kronos shortly before the *real* Master begins tapping the Crystal's power, suggesting some kind of telepathy or precognition. [Alternatively, this might be a further extension of the Doctor and the Master being Time Lords and "in many ways having the same mind"; see 18.7, "Logopolis".] The nightmare-version of the Master is gloating, triumphant and larger-than-life [much like the Master's vision of the Doctor in 8.2, "The Mind of Evil"], which suggests genuine fear or insecurity on the Doctor's part. [Alternatively, the dream has important clues such as the Crystal of Kronos and the four-headed axes (the "labrys" that gave the Labyrinth its name), so it might be a telepathic taunt on the Master's part, as with 14.3, "The Deadly Assassin".] He's obsessed with - even paranoid about - finding the Master at this stage.

The Doctor claims his reactions are 'ten times faster' than Jo's, and he knows how to bullfight. When Kronos slows down time, the Doctor and the Master aren't affected as much everyone else, and the Doctor's capable of running in slow-motion when everyone else is frozen. [See 11.2, "Invasion of the Dinosaurs" and **How Does Time Work?** under 9.1, "Day of the Daleks".] According to the Doctor, everybody has race memories. His own are causing trouble as he forgets things Jo told him the previous night, and can only half-remember stuff about Atlantis, Interstitial Time and so on. The Master believes, understandably, that the Doctor can't stand not having the last word. Remarkably, the Doctor seems to honestly think he can get the Master to relent from his fiendish plots just by *talking* to him, even when it's blindingly obvious that his opponent is a) totally refusing to listen, and b) hoping to lure the Doctor outside the TARDIS' protection so he can do something exceedingly nasty to him.

Once again [as per 7.3, "The Ambassadors of Death"], the Doctor's companion offers him a cup of tea, and he hands it back without appearing to drink any. [We've had to watch this scene again and again at half-speed, all in the interest of substantiating the theory that the Doctor can imbibe tea through his eyes. True, here he claims to have enjoyed the tea after looking directly into the cup, and Jo doesn't complain. He could just be distracted after awakening from his unsettling dream about the Master and simply handed the cup back - but if he didn't consume any of the tea, it would seem that Jo only gave him a quarter of a cupful. Another stroke against the "eye-drinking" theory is that he doesn't use this freakish superpower when quaffing char to complete the Time Vector Analogue; perhaps this is because Stu forgot to use a strainer and the mug has tea-leaves in it.]

• *Ethics.* The Doctor doesn't want anybody to suffer eternal torment, not even the Master, and even goes as far as asking Kronos for the villain's freedom. He admits to having subconscious thoughts of which he's not proud. [They sound like a Donna Summer record.]

• *Inventory.* Here the Doctor rigs up a handheld 'time sensor' which detects disturbances in the time-field, revealing the distance and bearing of the nearest active time machine. The distance is given in Venusian feet.

The Doctor also builds a 'time flow analogue' from a wine bottle, some cutlery, two corks and a mug with tea-leaves in it, stating that 'the relationship between the different molecular bonds and the actual shapes forms a crystalline structure of ratios'. He claims that he and the Master made these at school to spoil each others' time experiments, and here the lash-up temporarily jams the Master's TOMTIT equipment, spinning around even though it doesn't have a power-source.

[The word analogue" suggests that the very shape of the creation is supposed to mirror the

movement of time, perhaps even resonating with the vortex. This might mean that the energy which makes it spin comes from the vortex itself - the Crystal of Kronos does much the same thing, and funnily enough it's a similar shape - and it certainly suggests that tapping into time is much easier than you'd expect. This *could* explain why Waterfield is able to summon Daleks from the future using a carefully assembled collection of mirrors (4.9, "Evil of the Daleks"). Maybe. A bit.

[By the way, the January 2004 edition of *Scientific American* has details of a theory of 'loop quantum gravity', which is essentially interstitial time / space. The implications of this allow us to dispense with the eleven dimensions needed in Superstring theory, and muddle through with three spaces and time. Not only does this unify Quantum theory and Relativity, it helps poor hacks such as ourselves, who are writing guidebooks to science-fiction series of the 1970s. It would be nice if theoretical physics could go all 70s-retro.]

• *Background.* When he was a little boy, the Doctor lived in a house 'halfway up the top of a mountain' [sic]. Behind the house was a brittle old hermit who sat under an ancient, twisted tree [see 11.5, "Planet of the Spiders"], a 'monk' who'd ostensibly been there for half his lifetime and who'd learned the secret of life. On 'the blackest day' of the Doctor's existence [he doesn't explain what caused this unhappiness, although he tells Jo that he'll explain one day - anyone who wants can see X3.12, "The Sound of Drums" here], he asked this hermit for help.

Up on the mountain it was cold and grey, with weeds and a few sludgy patches of snow, but the hermit said nothing and simply pointed to a flower 'just like a daisy'. Looking at it through the hermit's eyes, the Doctor saw it glowing with life, and on the way down the mountain everything shone in the sunlight. [This is closer to Buddhist parable than anything we've heard from the Doctor before, and it's remarkably similar to the story of how the spirit of the Dharma was passed on to Mahakasyapa by Buddha. It's possible that it isn't supposed to be taken *entirely* literally. Note that the Doctor says 'I laughed too, when I first heard it' as if reciting a story someone told him.]

Explaining this part of his past to Jo, the Doctor seems more open and more "human" than ever before, and there's no sense of him feeling the need to surround himself with an air of mystery.

How Chauvinistic was the Pertwee Era?

This seems a good enough time to talk about the subject of sexism in the series, since in "The Time Monster" Ruth won't shut up about it. And it's this story, with Ruth constantly complaining about male prejudice and Stuart constantly being sarcastic to her afterwards, that's often cited as a test-case for the way 70s *Doctor Who* treated the feminist issues of its era. The cynical view is that Ruth represents the series trying to come to terms with the "new" feminism of the era - the subtext being, "because *Doctor Who* is a series where all the women are just ditzy assistants who scream a lot" - and forcing contrived and rather embarrassing pro-emancipation messages into a supporting character's mouth. Except ... it's far more accurate to say that Ruth represents *Doctor Who* trying to come to terms with " Women's Lib" as a popular subject.

The truth is, by this stage the series didn't *need* to prove it was in touch with the times. Like *The Avengers*, and like a lot of the other adventure programmes of the late 60s, it had introduced "emancipated" female characters long before equal rights became the hot topic of conversation. Even Barbara Wright, despite some occasional sarcasm from Ian Chesterton, was no shrinking violet and *that* was in 1963. ('I do wish he wouldn't treat us like Dresden china', she says to Susan before blundering into a lethal booby-trap in "The Keys of Marinus".) In fact, the 60s female companions were consistently shown as intelligent, resourceful and at least as capable as the boys, with only one real "screamer" (Victoria) among them. What chauvinism there was came from occasional, off-handed comments by the male characters, not from any stupidity or weakness in the women themselves.

It *is* hard not to wince, of course, when the soldiers in "The Invasion" agree that Zoe is 'much prettier than a computer', even if it's exactly the kind of thing you'd expect a bunch of annoying squaddies to say. Yet the infamous scene in "The Moonbase" (4.6) when the Doctor asks Polly to make the coffee while he gets on with the *real* work seems perfectly reasonable, insofar as that the Doctor says that kind of thing to humans all the time, male or female. (Bear in mind, during the UNIT era it's the dead butch Sergeant Benton who gets the tea-making duties, and in "The Time Monster" itself it's Stuart who's asked to put the kettle on rather than his female counterpart.) Anyway, the coffee provides the vital missing clue in "The Moonbase". Either way, the fact remains that it's only in the early 70s that the ditzy assistant

(Jo Grant, although even *she's* ostensibly a highly-trained agent) comes into fashion. Right before her were Liz Shaw and Zoe Herriot, both of whom were blatantly cleverer than any of the male supporting cast and *almost* as clever as the wise old man at the heart of the series.

Looking at this more carefully, though, Jo is part of a bigger shift in the programme's nature. As ex-soap personnel are now making *Doctor Who*, the stories are no longer discrete entities that offer viewers almost a different series every four weeks, but instead form part of a longer-term narrative. In principle, Jo is on a learning-curve. In *practice*, however, she's on a learning-roller-coaster, with different writers and directors assuming differing levels of experience and natural smarts. She was intended to be the novice who learns at the Doctor's side over a number of years - Jamie did something similar *within* stories, but rarely showed any sign of learning anything from one year to the next. And what with Third Doctor taking on the male companion's duties with regard to fisticuffs and daring leaps, it was perhaps inevitable that the companion / "novice" role would fall to a girl.

However, we have to admit that Terrance Dicks - the script editor in this phase - didn't see entirely eye-to-eye with producer Barry Letts on this topic. Dicks' conception of the girl companion, to be blunt, was that she was there to get rescued. He'd even introduced a moustache-twirling villain in Season Eight to cause her and the Doctor trouble, but whereas the Master *did* eventually offer Jo up for human sacrifice (in "The Daemons"), he only got to hypnotise her once that season (in 8.1, "Terror of the Autons"). The second time he tried, in their final encounter (10.3, "Frontier in Space"), he failed because she'd matured over the intervening three years.

This might seem like a good point to praise Jo's acquired resourcefulness and shout, "You go, girl!", but to look at her overall (forgive the phrase) "story arc", this process of individuation - of her becoming entirely her own woman, of her no longer needing the Doctor, of her no longer fearing the Master, of her standing up to the Brigadier - seems to be preparing Jo for her true role in life... as Mrs Clifford Jones. And that's the same Clifford Jones whom she outright admits to thinking of (in some respects if not more) as a 'younger' version of the Doctor.

continued on page 271...

[An actual love for humanity comes across in this period, something which seems unique to the Third Doctor. He's always had an affection for Earth, but it's hard to picture most of his other incarnations opening up in this way. Certainly, it's impossible to imagine - say - the Fourth Doctor displaying either the frailty or the sentimentality that the Doctor demonstrates here. The only comparable instance - again, featuring his old mentor - is in 18.4, "State of Decay" and that's with someone from his own world.]

The Doctor knows the location of Atlantis, and knows about both Kronos and the Crystal. He's been outside time before. [The vortex the TARDIS travels through, or perhaps he's referencing 6.2, "The Mind Robber"?]. He also speaks of the 'place that is no place' - Chronos' domain - as if from first-hand experience. [Either his memory-blocks are eroding, or this is where he went in 7.4, "Inferno". As he has knowledge of Chronovores, the former is more likely (although Craig Hinton's novel *The Quantum Archangel* - the sequel to this story - suggests that these beings are responsible for the paucity of alternate universes in *Doctor Who*; more on this in a bit).]

King Dallias calls the Doctor 'a true philosopher'. [It's true that the Doctor's calm acceptance of things that seem unlikely shows a lot more curiosity about such deep matters than we've seen lately. He's also rather sanguine about being chained up in a cell as the Master threatens to unravel the whole of creation.]

• *Bessie.* She now has a "super drive", which can accelerate her to ridiculous speeds. The brakes work by the absorption of inertia, so the Doctor can stop at high speed without the passengers flying through the windscreen [the thing the Doctor was fitting in 9.4, "The Mutants"]. The Doctor indicates that Bessie might be in some way 'alive', in the same way the TARDIS is.

The Supporting Cast

• *Jo Grant.* She's now starting to think scientifically, at last. She may know a smattering of Greek, enough to know that the word 'Thascales' means 'Master'. [That, or she's finally figured out the Master's *modus operandi*. Or perhaps she's benefiting from the TARDIS' translation system.] Jo figures out what a 'Time Ram' is faster than you might expect. [In Season Eight, she would probably have thought it was livestock from the Doctor's home planet.] Talking of which, she finds the

Brigadier's comment about 'the entrails of a sheep' about six times funnier than anyone else does.

Upon seeing Kronos "devour" the Doctor, Jo faints, then (somewhat crazily) expects that the Master - who sicced Kronos on his opponent in the first place - will "help" him. Her own fate doesn't seem to concern her once the Doctor is "lost".

• *UNIT.* There seem to be UNIT HQs all over the world, and every section of UNIT has the search for the Master written into standing orders, priority A1. [This might be confirmation that Bill Filer (8.3, "The Claws of Axos") really was a UNIT agent and not just some stray cop.] Under subsection 3A of the preamble to the Seventh Enabling Act, paragraph 24G, the Brigadier can have UNIT take over from a government investigation during a crisis like the TOMTIT affair.

Mike Yates is here referred to as 'Greyhound Three'; the Brigadier is 'Greyhound'. He takes a lot of persuading to take his head wound seriously.

• *The Brigadier.* He's less prepared to believe the Doctor's claims than ever before. [A result of the Doctor moving away from "aliens", which he understands, and towards "unlikely ancient gods". He becomes even more cynical by the time of 10.1, "The Three Doctors", so he's not coping very well under the strain of the job.] He calls Yates 'Mike', both in the cliffhanger to episode three (not repeated in the reprise) and to his face later. He has a map of Europe behind his chair, with the Mediterranean prominently displayed.

• *Benton.* If there's a prize for the most uses of the phrase 'the oldest trick in the book', he gets it. However, he's astute enough to outwit the Master, decisive enough to get the scientists to do something and - considering it's his day off - rather keen to investigate the possibilities of TOMTIT (even explaining it to the Brigadier). He doesn't even seem to mind suddenly finding himself stark naked in front of two young women and his superior officer.

The Supporting Cast (Evil)

• *The Master.* Here he's more blasé, arrogant and power-mad than ever before, once again posing as an academic in England even though this puts him perilously close to the Doctor. [More on this in **Things That Don't Make Sense.**] He demonstrates the ability to exactly replicate the Brigadier's voice (but not a Greek accent), and he's skilled at seduction. [Indeed, his relationship with

How Chauvinistic was the Pertwee Era?

...continued from page 269

Once you start thinking about it in those terms, the Pertwee era is rather worrying. Starting with Liz Shaw, Season Seven has a lot of bright women in big government projects, but they're almost inevitably called 'Miss'. It's not just that they're implicitly filling in time before marriage and motherhood, they're being made into appendages of the various middle-aged men who run things. Liz Shaw has a few doctorates, but she's almost never called 'Doctor Shaw'[96]. Miss Dawson in "Doctor Who and the Silurians" is implied to be hanging on for Dr Quinn to notice her (the novelisation makes a lot of this frustrated spinster status). Miss Rutherford in "The Ambassadors of Death" is apparently so much a part of Professor Cornish's harem that she's replaced, without comment, by an anonymous 'First Assistant' wearing the same costume (mini-skirt and high white boots, of course).

Finally we get one with a first name, Petra Williams in "Inferno", but her soon-to-be-boyfriend Greg Sutton at first assumes her to be a secretary, and she clings pathetically to Professor Stahlman as a role model. Evil Parallel Petra is even more of the stereotypical ice-maiden until she cracks and starts literally clinging on to hunky Greg2. The very next story, of course, debuts Jo Grant. Except... the Jo we got, midway between Tara King and Goldie Hawn, is almost entirely Katy Manning's invention. They'd intended her to be a trainee secret agent. Both versions were obviously meant to be decorative - but so had *all* the companions been to some extent, including the male ones. The main thing that changed was what surrounded the principal girl.

There's no getting away from it: a series with lots of soldiers in it will have a strong appeal to boys. Even if the soldiers include a few female ancillary staff to answer phones and act as straight-man to a sweaty corporal who thinks he's detected aliens (7.1, "Spearhead from Space"), this is part of the near-future thing, like the original UNIT uniform. Come Season Eight, some of these soldiers become regular characters in an ongoing story. The series' focus shifts to a lot of competent men (insofar as the Brigadier and company actually act competent, that is), so the outsider who needs to be told stuff becomes the key audience feed-person. It just so happened, by sheer coincidence of course, that this feed-person was small and blonde and had big brown eyes and was shot from slightly above more often than not and made mistakes and giggled and idolised the Doctor.

But even formula this is too simple. "The Mind of Evil" (8.2) requires so many UNIT regulars in so many subplots, Jo is left to overpower big hard criminals and stop a prison riot because there's no *time* for her to be girly and goofy. And there's never any question of her not being trained for "men's work", so eventually we see her driving a hovercraft in "The Sea Devils" (9.3), with no comment from Captain Hart or the sailors she ferries to the base. (Along those lines, we again refer you to "The Moonbase", in which Ben and Jamie's macho posturing is deflated by Polly's insistence that the Cyberman-killing plan was *her* idea, so she's going with them to carry it out.)

Nevertheless, the series' entire emphasis is now on spectacle, and Jo's skimpy outfits often became part of the same package as 'Action by Havoc', big explosions, scary monsters, lurid electronic effects and impressive military hardware. (However, the records reveal that *John Levene* was the real eye-candy of the series, with the female staff of at least one factory sending in fan-mail by the sackful.[97])

So the picture is already more complicated than it seems at first sight. Within the UNIT set-up, Jo is almost a mascot. That she's infantilised owes as much to her youth as the fact that she's female, and matters only become interesting once she leaves HQ. Her first story, after all, entails her charming off-screen authority-figure Mr Campbell and the bereaved Mrs Farrell, demonstrating people-skills the Brigadier (and crucially the Doctor) lack. (In itself that's a mildly sexist assumption, and one that the BBC Wales series is perpetuating ad nauseam.) Yet the HQ package deal has the "UNIT family", now in increasingly in rigidly codified roles. Mike Yates asks as many questions as Jo, but his inquiries typically stem from the writers getting something important across, not resolving plot logic or prompting info-dumps. He also explained as much as he asked - usually to Jo. It's Benton, meanwhile, who often gets to say 'I still don't get it' and prompt more explanation.

Thrust into other spheres, Jo's function becomes closer to the old-fashioned companion. She's our eyes and ears, either in alien worlds or other institutions. The most revealing example is "The Sea Devils", where the Navy treats her and the Doctor as equals (except for the diving bell

continued on page 273...

Queen Galleia is curious. He could get what he wants through - say - hypnosis or blackmail, but chooses to try his luck simply charming her into doing his will. She seems to find this domination appealing, at least to start with. What with all the hoo-hah about Lucy Saxon's abuse - see X3.13, "Last of the Time Lords" - this takes on a very disturbing complexion.]

The Master wears a TV-wristwatch which can apparently monitor outside events without the need for cameras, and which can tap in to UNIT's radio signals. He also owns a handy map of Atlantis, and he's still smoking fat cigars.

The Doctor describes the Master as 'paranoid' for wanting to take over the universe, and the Master replies 'who isn't... the only difference is, I'm a little more honest than the rest'. [It's a curiously awkward line, the first time that the series tries to bring cod-psychology to the Time Lord psyche. Compared to what's offered in "The Sound of Drums" - "duh-duh-duh *DUM* duh-duh-duh *DUM* ... I must dress up as Ali Bongo and steal Concorde" - it seems subtle and almost sensible.]

He doesn't seem to mind risking the destruction of the entire cosmos in the course of achieving his goals. After exploiting the strengths of those around him, and their strongly held beliefs, the Master now returns to dominating the weak-minded: 'it's quite like old times'. He appears to have chosen Wootton as his base for the sheer number of military exploits there down the years - perhaps as a means to humiliate Captain Yates. He certainly seems to have it in for Mike, from the running commentary he gives to his timescoopery.

At one point the Master tells Percival, 'Nobody, nothing can stop me now!' [See the previous Atlantis story, 4.5, "The Underwater Menace", for why this is worrying.]

The TARDIS(es) The Doctor's TARDIS has telepathic circuits, and TARDISes communicate telepathically, so when the Doctor is lost in the vortex he's able to use the Ship to communicate with Jo in the console room. This connection seems to be the TARDIS' idea, not the Doctor's own [the Master doesn't have such a good rapport with his own Ship, which is perhaps why he's not expecting the Doctor to do this]. There's a control on the console marked 'extreme emergency' which, when pulled, can retrieve the Doctor from the vortex again and make him materialise inside the

Ship. The Master can use the telepathic circuits to predict the Doctor's words before he says them, and force them to come out of his mouth backwards. [Though a pedant would point out that if you play the Doctor's backwards speech backwards, it still sounds like rubbish.]

There's now a swan-neck microphone in the console, and a handy hole for the hand-held detector. The volume control on one TARDIS can be over-ridden by an adjustment on the other's telepathic circuitry. Both vessels are said to be on the same 'frequency', whatever that means.

Both the Doctor and the Master have renovated their TARDIS console rooms, so now they look suspiciously similar [more telepathy?] and once again the scanner is set into a roundel. The Doctor claims to have done 'a spot of redecorating', so the remodelling was his decision. [By 15.2, "The Invisible Enemy", we'll see signs that the Ship does the actual work rather than hiring decorators or gnomes with ladders and trowels.]

For the first time, the TARDIS is said to be outside time when it travels. According to the Doctor, the duration of a journey depends on the TARDIS' 'mood' [so it's less to do with the distance or period]. Here he's able to land the TARDIS in the same location as the Master's, thanks to the time sensor.

When the Doctor's TARDIS and the Master's TARDIS occupy roughly the same space, the Doctor's TARDIS materialises in the Master's console room but at the same time the Master's TARDIS materialises in the Doctor's console room [see also "Logopolis"]. The Doctor's vaguely surprised by this, so it seems that he's never tried it before. Weirdly, however, the exterior of the Master's TARDIS is also seen in his laboratory on Earth at the same time.

[This suggests that the TARDIS' exterior is just a handy interface to the extra-dimensional interior, and *not* a real "outer shell" to the craft. This was the usual assumption in late 70s stories and some scenes in "Logopolis". The Master's TARDIS might therefore generate *two* interfaces, one on Earth for the convenience of its pilot, the other leading into the interior of the other TARDIS trying to co-exist alongside it. This is possibly a result of the dimensional instability and it's not a normal function of the Ship(s); otherwise, the Doctor could have escaped his exile by popping up inside someone else's TARDIS. The nearest parallel to this is whatever happens at the start of 20.4, "Terminus", in which the TARDIS "bonds" with a

How Chauvinistic was the Pertwee Era?

...continued from page 271

sequence), and where both she and the female Lt Blythe are viewed - first by Trenchard, then by Walker - as ornaments and children. But unlike Blythe, Jo is permitted to actually speak her mind to Walker, and is more effectively critical by simply ignoring him and doing her job (such as crawling through vent shafts and driving hovercraft). Blythe is stoically professional when dealing with pompous older men, much as Liz had been with General Scobie in "Spearhead from Space". The point is that the writers preferred displaying sexist idiots and then showing them up to having the female leads making speeches.

Like many series of the same time, *Doctor Who* is in a cleft stick. If they show competent women getting on with jobs, those women can become part of the problem for the male characters and nothing else. But when making the traditional speech about not letting your job take over your life, a male protagonist often puts his foot in it and mentions the female character's attractiveness. Or if nothing else, we get two male characters discussing the female ones in locker rooms or elsewhere. Considering that it was the early 70s, *Doctor Who* admirably has few such scenes (perhaps because they got them all in ahead of the pack, as in 5.7, "The Wheel in Space"). Watch a few episodes of Gerry Anderson's *UFO* for searingly inept examples of what we mean: SHADO has a 50% female staff, but the dress-code (designed by Sylvia Anderson) has tinfoil minis, body-stockings and string vests (not to mention purple wigs, which are apparently part of the uniform). Within the Pertwee stories it's only in a Terry Nation script, "Planet of the Daleks" (10.4), in which the male leader finds the presence of a woman a snag. (But that's a different case... Rebec's his lover, so his total commitment to the mission has thus been compromised. If they'd dared to show gay couples, a male version of her could have been just as big a problem.)

The UNIT format - with its conventions of military protocol - removes any prospect of relationships moving beyond professional, but the inherent patriarchal nature of the show's set-up comes right to the fore. Much of the rhetoric is enacted by contrasting the "bad" male authority figures (various big-science project bosses, the Master's various aliases and the Brigadier) against the "good" one, the Doctor. And once Jo arrives, the whole of UNIT revolves *around* the Doctor - they

work for him now, not vice versa. The Doctor always had the potential to be an autocrat, by virtue of his knowledge (or his ability to know where to look when he was in the dark), but had previously reserved this power for when the need arose to escape from nasty situations.

However, the Pertwee era sees the Doctor's formerly pseudo-parental relationships with his companions evolve into power-relationship between him and his 'assistants'. Even the supposedly enlightened Malcolm Hulke and the formerly pro-female David Whitaker combined to give "The Ambassadors of Death" (the first time we have the usual 70s description of the leads as 'the Doctor and the girl') a taint of this. The Doctor's alien-ness is brought to the front just as it looks like women might think of him as male, rather than just old and wise.

The situation becomes even murkier when Letts, possibly after reading *Cosmopolitan* in the toilet (as most men did), decided in 1973 to assertively demonstrate a liberated modern woman. Ruth Ingram gets on everyone's nerves now (and may have deliberately been intended to), but the main thing to notice is how far her stooge assistant is emasculated and made a loveable doofus. Once Sarah Jane Smith arrives in 1974, we're in altogether messier times. Like Ruth, Sarah spends her first year making speeches. What's interesting, again, is how everything around her aligns itself to allow this. Linx (in "The Time Warrior") makes that famous / notorious comment about the female human thorax and announces that Sontarans have dispensed with such procedures. But notice how they still call Linx 'he', even though 'he' is androgynous, a clone and severely contrasted to the big hairy men whose clumsy weapons are less effective than his exotic (meaning "feminine") techniques of hypnosis and stealth.

A year or so later, we see the future-male Noah becoming, in effect, female (12.2, "The Ark in Space"). Just before that we'd had an extreme caricature feminist, Miss Winters, who's clearly meant to be both a Nazi and a lesbian (12.1, "Robot"). Aboard the fake spaceship (11.2, "Invasion of the Dinosaurs"), it's Ruth (a different one) who advocates Sarah's execution, not the rather feeble men. Cumulatively, it looks as if the repertoire of "bad" authority figures is widening, just as the Brigadier starts becoming an uncle-figure. Nevertheless, the

continued on page 275...

passing spaceship by creating a door. Alternatively, and other scenes in "Logopolis" seems to confirm this, they may be topologically inside one another like a Klein bottle. This would chime with the conversation the Doctor has with King Dalios about Ideal Forms, conducted - if we follow the archaeological dates for Thera's destruction as confirmed by the Doctor - a thousand years before Plato had the same idea. See **How Indestructible is the TARDIS?** under 21.3, "Frontios".]

While the TARDISes are linked, the Master [and possibly the Doctor as well] can place a 'time-lock' around both Ships so they can't escape one another. The Master's vehicle can fling the Doctor's off into the vortex, but the Doctor can't do the same. It's also established that if the atoms of two TARDISes attempt to occupy *exactly* the same point in space and time, the result is a 'time ram' that will utterly annihilate both Ships.

According to the Master, $E=MC^3$ in the extra-temporal physics of the time vortex.

The Non-Humans

• *Kronos, the Chronovore*. Chronovores are creatures 'beyond human imagining' which live outside time [in the vortex], and Kronos is the fiercest of the lot. When Kronos first manifests himself, he appears as a roughly humanoid figure with wings and what looks like a Grecian-style helmet for a face, although he's glowing so brightly that the light blots out his features.

In this form, held captive by the Master and held back by the seal of the high priest from Atlantis, he doesn't seem capable of speech but screeches like an animal. When he attacks the Doctor, the Doctor ends up lost in the vortex, supposedly 'alive forever' in the nothingness. The Doctor believes that creation is finely-balanced, and that when the Master opens the floodgates of Kronos' power all order and structure will be swept away.

Only once free of the Master does Kronos reveal himself in a different form, claiming that shapes are meaningless and only wishing to go back outside time. Though the people of Atlantis know Kronos as a male deity, here "he" appears as a huge female face, existing on the boundary between 'your reality and mine'. Kronos is beyond human morality, as she's capable of destroying a city without remorse but also thanks the Doctor for her release. She wishes to cause the Master eternal

pain for what he did, but allows him to escape after the Doctor's request for mercy.

Stu knows the name of Kronos after he encounters the Chronovore, something the Doctor puts down to 'race memory'. Kronos herself recognises the Doctor 'of old', though he doesn't seem to know her personally.

[These days, the activities of the Chronovores chime with what little we know about the Reapers in X1.8, "Father's Day", although the details of that story are so self-contradictory we're going to have to lie down in a darkened room and come back to this some other time. Other beings feed on the energy released by time going wrong, notably in X3.10, "Blink"; X4.11, "Turn Left"; and the *Sarah Jane* story "Whatever Happened to Sarah Jane?"]

• *Venusians*. Venusian feet are about a yard in length, so they're always tripping over themselves, and one Venusian mile is roughly the same as four and a half Earth miles. An old Venusian proverb goes 'if the thraskin puts his fingers in his ears, it is polite to shout', although 'thraskin' is a word seldom used since the twenty-fifth dynasty and the modern equivalent is 'plinge'. [We *thought* Spike Milligan coined this term, but it's actor slang. "Walter Plinge" is the theatrical equivalent of "Alan Smithee", or is used in cast-lists printed before all the parts are cast. The Doctor could be making this up as he goes along.]

Planet Notes

• *Atlantis, Earth*. Believed to be part of the Minoan civilisation, circa 1550 to 1500 BC, Atlantis bears obvious cultural similarities to classical Greece. The Doctor refers to the Atlanteans' 'cousins in Athens', and its royalty seems to intermarry with other monarchies, the King's wife herself being the daughter of kings. Many of the non-speaking characters appear Asian or African, and the Queen has a Persian cat. Perhaps thanks to Kronos, distinctly supernatural powers are at work in the city: the doomed King Dalios was there when the Temple of Poseidon was built, 537 years ago, although this great age is unique even in Atlantean terms. [The Atlanteans don't seem to *know* he's that old, so he can't have been King for long, and something must have gone wrong with the line of succession. Or is clouding their minds another of his powers?]

Once Atlantis worshipped Kronos and the city prospered, but the result was imbalance; a decadent society and natural disasters seem to have

How Chauvinistic was the Pertwee Era?

...continued from page 273

original conception of Sarah was a retrograde step.

In this light it's worth considering how far Sarah gained in popularity when she became a more aspirational character. Once the Doctor had transformed into a scruffy art student, we started to *see* Sarah having it all rather than just hearing her demand it. From "Robot" on, she's dressing more playfully, sorting out her work-life balance and at some stages making the Doctor jump through hoops to get her to come with him again. Dads and lads might have had a "thing" for Lis Sladen, but girls wanted to be Sarah - not for the time-travel, but for the fun she was having whilst working.

Prior to 1973 this was a lot harder. To accurately depict women in any known historical situation or show at least vaguely three-dimensional characters in fantasy worlds meant talking about sexism in a way that risks itself being sexist. Television drama, especially fast-paced stuff like this, can only use broad strokes in a six-part serial. Whilst the regular characters are amenable to slow incremental change and development (however much Letts and Dicks may be accused of botching this with Jo), guest-cast characters haven't got time for depth. In female characters, professionalism is hard to dissociate with clinical detachment. The much-praised grown-up women of David Whitaker's Troughton scripts were either fanatics, widows or some odd combination of the two (respectively Janley in 4.3, "The Power of the Daleks"; Ruth Maxtible in 4.9, "The Evil of the Daleks" Gemma Corwin in "The Wheel in Space"; and Astrid Ferrier in "The Enemy of the World"). To get any further under their skins would take a slower, longer kind of drama.

And however many assertive women he wrote into his stories, Whitaker was not above exploiting the plight of women caught by male desire and chicanery. Fariah in "The Enemy of the World" is clearly implied to be blackmailed into being Salamander's mistress, and El Akir in "The Crusades" has an actual, no-messing harem full of international women with no body hair. However, it's hard to comment on sexism without risking complicity. The casting of such roles requires women to audition and be measured up, literally and figuratively and then appear on national primetime television to be scrutinised on their plausibility as sex-objects. Thinking about Jo in

this context is revealing. The plot of "Terror of the Autons" sees her *given* to the Brigadier, who then *gives* her to the Doctor. It isn't until "The Mutants" (9.4) that Jo asserts her right to choose whether she helps the Doctor, and does so against his will.

We mentioned earlier that Jo was part of an overall "spectacle". This isn't just a matter of dads gawping at Katy Manning's thighs (although there was a fair amount of that), but something more fundamental, connected with the whole nature of television drama and fantasy. It's usually assumed that audiences "identify" with the female companion more than with the Doctor or the villains. This might be simply a matter of her better anticipating what *you* would do under those circumstances, but at a deeper level it's more troublesome. Conventional film theory claims that male audiences see themselves in male characters (especially assertive ones who get the girl) and observe the female ones as part of the display put on for them. Yet in most cases, monster movies have female characters as the spectators looking at something else that's defined by its bodily appearance. They then, traditionally, scream.

Moreover, the whole *point* of the Doctor is that we can't entirely identify with him, as many of his motives are unknowable. In theory, that is. Relatively undiscerning viewers who take the BBC Wales series to be a very conventional romance have rather missed the point, hence their perplexity at later events. Less traditionally - but just as interesting as a counter to the theories of the 'male gaze' - is that we've seen right from "An Unearthly Child" (1.1), that the point-of-view of *something* looking at Our Heroes is always a threat. Looking at things or people without actually engaging with them is what bad guys do, that's why the Doctor decided not to be a Time Lord any more. So even at the level of shot-composition and camera angles, *Doctor Who* is at odds with the inherent (as the theorists claim) tendency of television and film to be patriarchal and reinforce society's male bias. Not that Letts and Dicks saw it that way themselves; they were quite happy to put in as many car-chases, punch-ups, explosions and violent deaths as they could get away with in any given story, safe in the assumption that mainly boys would be excited by this.

In effect, then, the "popular" feminism of the early 1970s (meaning, the media fuss about bra-burning rather than what was practised by *actual*

continued on page 277...

followed. Though the Crystal of Kronos is kept in the Temple of Poseidon by a high priest, the secrets of controlling the Chronovore have been lost for five hundred years, so only the Crystal and the seal of the high priest (currently Krasis) remain. [Krasis' medallion was intended to show the concentric ring islands of Atlantis - see the essay with "The Underwater Menace" - but closer examination reveals the intersecting circles and arc-segments we now associate with the TARDIS scanner in the BBC Wales series. If you want to think of this as incredible forward planning, do so but please keep quiet about it.] The city has been in decline ever since, and is now close to starving, apparently in need of rainfall. There's mention of a council under the King.

The Crystal of Kronos, seemingly just a trident-shaped piece of quartz, can draw power from outside time to fuel the Master's TOMTIT machine. The priests of Atlantis used the Crystal, and some complex geometric calculations, to draw Kronos into time. It's not clear where the Master gets hold of the Crystal he uses, but the Doctor states that it's made the jump through interstitial time; that in the 1970s it's linked to the original Crystal, thousands of years in the past; that it is the original; but that its essence is outside time, with its appearance here. Dalios claims it's just a fraction of the whole Crystal, split from the genuine article during an attempt to destroy it.

[This can get *very* confusing, as - alas - our account in the First Edition of this book demonstrates. A lot of readers wrote in to suggest how the crystal might work, but none of them could agree, so we're back at Square One. Here, with a nod towards the story's sources as our guide, is our best guess...

[The original crystal is a big quartz trident. The fragment is a small quartz trident. Either, then, the original started off with a smaller trident-shaped extrusion - which opens up all sorts of fractal possibilities - or the process of "splitting" removed some of the essence and created a smaller version of the original without changing the original's apparent shape. We know that the crystal's "essence" is outside time, and all manifestations in our sensory realm are illusory anyway (this is all covered in **Where Does This Come From?**). So far, so good.

[But then we have *another* problem with how many fragments are in Atlantis at the end. The "real" crystal is in the Labyrinth and one fragment

is worshipped in public, but the fragment vanishes, somewhere, long before the Master draws Krasis to Cambridge using TOMTIT and... er, the fragment. The two are linked via Interstitial Time, apparently, and the story in every other regard suggests that events in Atlantis happen at the same pace as events in Cambridge, so that as much time passes for Krasis between arriving in the lab and stepping out of the Master's TARDIS in Atlantis as passed for Hippias, Dalios et al.

[Therefore, something must have happened in Cambridge in episode two to make the fragment leave its sconce. It's still there when Krasis vanishes, but Hippias later claims that it went at the same time as the High Priest. In bringing Krasis to Cambridge, therefore, the Master melded the fragment he had with its earlier self. Uh? Exactly how he found the fragment in the first place, God only knows. (Did he buy it on eBay? Or did the volcano hurl it up from the subterranean depths, as we speculated in "Inferno" and that story's essay?) But if the fragment ceased to have been in Atlantis in episode two, where (and when) did the one the Master have come from? That the Master has found the fragment and built a machine around it seems clear enough. Apparently, the process of doing this causes earthquakes and gives the Doctor nightmares - a cut scene shows Dalios having similar dreams when the Master sets off for Atlantis, so the connection was intended. But then the Master arrives with the fragment in Atlantis, where the big crystal *and* the same fragment had been.

[Now, we can assume that the crystal's ability to soak up time energy covers any Blinovitch hassle - although bringing them together might cause something not unlike a Time Ram. The point is that Master leaves his device behind in Atlantis, with the fragment still in it, and makes off with the *big* crystal. So we might conclude that when Atlantis sinks, there's two fragments in one place and time - the one in the Master's machine, which is itself the one he later (or earlier, from his perspective) found and built into TOMTIT. In which case, the Master's search risked setting up a huge temporal paradox that could have freed Kronos just as effectively as smashing two TARDISes together. *Or*, if we accede to the story's internal logic and toss common sense under a bus, the fragments are temporally-distinct aspects of the big crystal. In other words, they're *both* really "avatars" of the true crystal - like shadows on the

How Chauvinistic was the Pertwee Era?

...continued from page 275

feminists) did more harm to *Doctor Who* than good. It convinced the programme-makers that "feminism" meant "constantly *talking* about feminism", something which eventually made the women involved seem a lot more two-dimensional than they had been half a decade earlier. If you want proof, look no further than Jo's predecessor. Liz Shaw was already at *least* as "liberated" as Sarah, so much so that she wasn't just smarter and more self-possessed but also capable of treating the boys at UNIT with the same sarcastic derision as the Doctor himself. But again, Liz never felt the need to prove these feminist credentials. Unlike Sarah, she didn't overtly mention Women's Lib in her very first story. She didn't insist on dressing like a tomboy. She didn't object to the Doctor calling her 'my dear', and there was no reason why she *should* have done, since at the same time he was a lot more patronising to the butch, moustache-wielding Brigadier. It's a definite instance of "show, don't tell", whereas by the time we reach "The Time Monster", you have the curious bi-polar effect of Ruth speechifying while Jo, not Liz, is in the companion role.

One last point: the first actual mention of 'Women's Lib' in the series is Jo commenting on the Draconians in "Frontier in Space". In the same story, she makes jokes about Ogrons having girlfriends. However, a year earlier she'd had a salutary lesson in making assumptions when confronted with Alpha Centauri (9.2, "The Curse of Peladon"). The fact that they're even making jokes about other forms of reproduction (including one cut from 10.2, "Carnival of Monsters", for timing purposes) indicates they're trying to make kids think about these things and look at human society as if from outside. For a family show in the early 70s, this was remarkable - the people whinging about the supposed "gay agenda" of the BBC Wales series are as *nothing* to the inertia within the culture about sexism back then. Mainstream "serious" dramas, even supposedly worthy ones like *Doomwatch*, were nonchalantly treating women as dim stooges and clever women as threats. Even the sober coverage of the 1970 General Election had a title sequence that resembled the credits for a Bond movie. Judged against this background, *Doctor Who* in the early 70s seems as radical as *Spare Rib*.

wall of a cave cast by the same object - so one simply ceases to exist, like Cho-Je being absorbed into K'anpo ("Planet of the Spiders"). The big crystal is, of course, confiscated by Kronos herself.]

Nobody can move the fragment while there's energy in it, for some reason, even though they can touch it. When the Master taps the power of the fragment, it's capable of drawing whole armies through time to the present day; slowing down local time to a stop; pushing a window-cleaner off a ladder, for some reason; turning Benton into a baby; and causing Stuart's personal time to accelerate, so that he becomes an old man in seconds. [This isn't just a case of speeding up time, since if his whole *timeline* were pushed forward, he'd end up in a different location and have fifty years' worth of extra memories. The same problem occurs in 18.1, "The Leisure Hive".] His clothes remain 1972-vintage, tragically.

The *big* Crystal of Kronos, of course, is hidden in the depths of Atlantis, protected by a guardian who was once human and a friend of King Dalios. While human, the guardian was a human athlete who wished for the strength of the bull and a long life in which to use it; Kronos gave the man his desire by making him half-man, half-beast. The

Doctor recognises him as the Minotaur, though the word isn't known in Atlantis. [This suggests that the Doctor hasn't met the "real" minotaur or the "real" Theseus at this point; see 17.5, "The Horns of Nimon" and 17.3, "The Creature From the Pit". The thing he encountered in "The Mind Robber" was just a story, so it doesn't count.]

In the 1970s, there's volcanic activity around the Thera group of islands off Greece, AKA the Santorini islands, shortly before the Master begins using his fragment of the Crystal. The significance of this is never explained. Atlantis obviously isn't in the Atlantic, although strangely its inhabitants refer to it by that name anyway. [It's being translated into the term we know for convenience, we expect, but it's possible that the people seen here are founders of a spin-off city. See **How Many Atlantises Are There?** under "The Underwater Menace".]

History

• *Dating.* [Late 1973.] Ruth has been working on the TOMTIT device for 'months', presumably with Professor Thascales, so it must be that long since the Master's escape from prison in 9.3, "The Sea Devils". [Jo says, while chatting on the phone with Benton, 'And a Merry Michaelmas to you too'. If you're the sort of person who accepts everything Jo says as literal and true, then it's the 29th of September, but this jars with the date in "Day of the Daleks". See **What's the UNIT Timeline?** under 8.5, "The Daemons", for a full account.]

Atlantis is at first said to have existed 4,000 years ago, though the Doctor later specifies 3,500 years ago. [The latter is more likely, since by the time he gives the later date he's seen the readings on the TARDIS console. The secrets of Kronos were lost to Atlantis five hundred years ago, so the first date marks Atlantis at its height and the second marks its destruction. 1500 BC is, indeed, the traditional date for the fall of Atlantis and the actual date of the eruption of Santorini.]

The TOMTIT project - Transmission Of Matter Through Interstitial Time - takes place at the Newton Institute in Wootton, Cambridge, seventy to a hundred miles from UNIT HQ. It's explained that time isn't smooth but made up of bits, and that with TOMTIT it's possible to transport objects through space by breaking them down into light-waves and pushing them through the interstices between 'now' and 'now'. Even though conventional science (or at least, Dr Cook, one of the observers) believes this to be nonsense, the Doctor doesn't seem surprised that humans are attempting something so advanced. [We've seen that some research into time has already been taking place ("The Claws of Axos") and will soon see the full extent of British involvement in time-travel research ("Invasion of the Dinosaurs").] The Doctor knows what the acronym 'TOMTIT' stands for and was originally planning to go with the Brigadier to investigate - even if apparently, he doesn't expect it to work until he finds out that the Master's involved. [See **How Do You Transmit Matter?** under 17.4, "Nightmare of Eden".]

The Doctor refers to World War Two as 'the Hitler War' [is this how it's seen by the Time Lords?]. The Brigadier has heard a V1 before.

The Analysis

Where Does This Come From? Jo talks about 'all that Cretan jazz' as if it's positively trendy. Which of course it was: you couldn't move for Erik Satie "gymnopedies" and pseudo-classical interior décor, thick eyeliner and elaborate hairdos straight out of the Oresteia. Greek-Key patterned

dado-rails and Sanderson wallpaper was replacing the late-60s William Morris styles. Terracotta was that year's colour. As the frock worn by Jo in "The Curse of Peladon" (9.2) and the more garish one in "The Green Death" (10.5) indicate, the classic grecian lines of the 1890s had made a comeback.

And Greece had come to us. With the coup in 1967 (a military junta took power, and retained it until 1974), a number of fugitives settled in North London, alongside the Greek Cypriot community already in the Tottenham / Wood Green area and elsewhere. Other cities had similar experiences. As always, the mainstream British population first learned about this with the advent of Greek restaurants, usually called "Zorba's" or "Parthenon". Later on, this resulted in the usual late-night post-pub snack, the Doner kebab, but at the time it meant that bazoukis and ouzo became almost as familiar as sitars and tikka masala. People still went on holidays to Cyprus, at least until 1974, and Crete and the Palace of Knossos were on the tourist map like never before. Memorabilia from the Mediterranean was suddenly a lot more common.

In short, if ever a year existed to do a vaguely Greek-themed *Doctor Who*, it was 1972. This was the year, after all, that Nana Mouskouri broke through into the charts. At the time, every school-child knew that Atlantis was Crete and the Labyrinth was a real place. Documentaries, including many for children (usually presented by pre-*Newsround* John Craven), were made about the truth behind old myths. The idea had been floated in 1909, and again more forcefully thirty years later by a Greek archaeologist with the *astoundingly* Terry Nation-ish name of Spiridon Marinatos. By 1964, it was sufficiently ingrained as an idea to seemingly need a vigorous rebuttal from French scholar Pierre Vidal-Naquet. Aside from the ancient astronaut / Velikovski stuff about myths being half-remembered cosmic events, this was the era when Linear B (a syllabary used for writing Mycenaean) had been decoded and was confirming a lot of the ancient stories.

We're seeing in the *Doctor Who* adventures of this period a lot of folkloric things being investigated (including ley-lines, gypsy curses, cave-dwelling "ancient ones" and what have you), and what's more obvious than to go for the *motherlode*: ancient Greek legends? As we saw with "The Myth Makers" (3.3), Schliemann's excavation of Troy triggered a lot of stories about what *else* might be

How and Why is the Doctor Exiled to Earth?

The activities of the Time Lords are always curious, but occasionally they seem self-contradictory. In "The War Games" (6.7), we're led to understand that the Doctor is to be punished for interfering in the normal flow of events, and yet this entails him being sent to the planet in whose affairs he's been diddling with most regularly, right after his peak diddling activity. They allow him to keep his TARDIS, even though he can't operate it, except in those stories where they need him to do exactly that. Judged by the standards they expected of the Doctor when sentencing him, their decision to exile the Doctor to 70s London, or 'twentieth century Earth' as it's called here, is just daft. They *must* have an ulterior motive, mustn't they?

One thing is clear: even before the Master turns up - when the Doctor's very *presence* will jeopardise all life on Earth - the brief period of his exile involves the planet being doomed several times over. This is worth bearing in mind, because these days it's become commonplace to assume that the Time Lords crucially want any agent of theirs on Earth to deal with the Daleks' aberrant time-line (9.1, "Day of the Daleks"). Yet surely, the safest way to stop Earth being invaded in the aftermath of a 1973 catastrophe is for Stahlman's Inferno project (7.4, "Inferno"), or any of the other threatened disasters in Seasons Seven and Eight, to destroy the planet circa 1971. Logically, therefore, the Time Lords have deemed the *status quo ante* as the right course for Earth's history in the early 70s and beyond.

The more you think about it, the more peculiar this seems. The Doctor's exile and activities on Earth aren't just restoring the orthodox time-line so much as actively *creating* large chunks of it. Without his presence, the Nestenes - an immeasurably superior race to *Homo Sapiens* - would have overwhelmed humanity. His involvement similarly tips the Silurian conflict in UNIT's favour, despite the reptile-men's superior abilities and better claim to this planet. It's as if the Time Lords are working to a script that has humans becoming significant players on the cosmic scene. Moreover, the Doctor intervenes at several points to help create (or at least, "un-prevent") events he's already experienced the consequences of in earlier adventures.

This becomes more all the more paradoxical when you consider that the two parallel worlds the Doctor visits on screen are resolutely similar to "home". Even if it's not blatantly stated, the production team were explicit in their insistence that the Doctor had no equivalent in the alternative world seen in "Inferno" (7.4), and yet it seems as though this Earth has survived a remarkable number of Doctor-sized threats in its past (Sutekh in 1911, for example; see 13.3, "Pyramids of Mars"). Meanwhile, Pete's World (X2.4, "The Rise of the Cybermen"; X2.13, "Doomsday" and others) seems to have been created in 1879 and never had *any* Time Lord supervision, yet it resembles ours in all but a few trivial matters. (See **Is Pete's World the Empire of the Wolf?** in Volume VII.) So much so, in fact, that the Doctor can safely leave his monocardial doppelganger there with Rose (X4.13, "Journey's End").

Oddly enough, though, this *might* explain the curious and apparently inconsistent means by which the TARDIS is immobilised. From what we can piece together on screen, the Doctor's memory of the TARDIS' dematerialisation codes is blocked off, along with a lot of Galactic History that he learned in his schooldays (8.5, "The Daemons" and apparently 7.3, "The Ambassadors of Death"). The Time Lords also, discombobulate the Dematerialisation Circuit (first mentioned in 8.1, "Terror of the Autons") and *might* - judging by "The Ambassadors of Death" - have done something unpleasant to the Time Vector Generator. (This is tricky, as little we know about this unit comes from 5.7, "The Wheel in Space", where removing it messes with the Ship's internal dimensions. So it's possible that this just explains how the Doctor got the console out of the TARDIS in Season Seven, and that it's not a real fault at all.) Once he has been to Nazi-World and met jackbooted versions of all his chums he learns (or, apparently, relearns) about the role of choice and Free Will in time travel (at least for people like him). From that point on it becomes almost a matter of replacing worn or locked-off components. Memory-blocks persist, despite Axos claiming to be able to release them (8.3 "The Claws of Axos"), but the conceptual and theoretical aspects of Time Travel are available to him.

Two key factors should be noted here. One is that the Ship is *pretty much* operational by "The Claws of Axos", to the extent that the Master can get her flying when need be. This is probably true from a point shortly before "Terror of the Autons", as the Doctor thinks that a small repair job on his Dematerialisation Circuit (or a crafty swap with the Master's Ship) will get him spacebourne again.

continued on page 281...

true. Let's not forget, Victorian efforts to find Atlantis (paid for by Prime Minister William Gladstone, who also wrote the intro for the English translation of Schliemann's account of finding Troy) were being re-evaluated by serious scholars as well as Theosophists. People who wanted a more romantic account of how Aztecs and Egyptians both came up with the idea of pyramid temples than the ones on offer. (More romantic than Thor Heyerdahl sailing across the ocean in a raft? There's no pleasing some people.)

In Volume II, we featured many essays about various concepts of the world as a physical manifestation of abstract ideas. So a lot of what needs to be said about "The Time Monster" should be very familiar. (If not, look up **What Planet Was David Whitaker On?** under 5.7, "The Wheel in Space"; **Why Was That Portrait in Maxtible's Study?** under 4.9, "The Evil of the Daleks"; **Did Sergeant Pepper Know the Doctor?** under 5.1, "Tomb of the Cybermen"; and **How Buddhist Is This Series?** under 5.2, "The Abominable Snowmen".) The Doctor finally makes the equation between the TARDIS and Plato's idea of pure form in this story, which ties in with the idea of "temporal grace" in "The Hand of Fear" (14.2) and should have made the console-room asphyxiation in "Planet of the Daleks" (10.4) impossible.

Variations on this concept didn't stop with Romanticism. The German philosopher Arthur Schopenhauer wrote *The World as Will and Representation* to develop a more pessimistic variation wherein conscious souls are trapped in a physical world running to a pre-ordained script, like passengers in a roller-coaster (see 20.3, "Mawdryn Undead"). Against this was a newer strand of Existentialist philosophers following Soren Kierkegaard - the Doctor paraphrases him when he points out that 'being without becoming' is 'an ontological absurdity'. Stuart's rapid ageing is an example of what we mean. His body has been pushed sixty or so years into its own future, but he has no memories of things that will happen along the way. Conversely, Dalios is five hundred years old, but his physical body stopped aging at (let's say) eighty. Their souls. like the true forms of the Crystal of Kronos and the TARDIS, are outside space and time and are unaffected.

The thing to note isn't so much how Sloman derived this idea, but that he's quite happy for the Doctor to idly mention it. We've already seen in stories this year that Existentialism has become

the basic assumption of *Doctor Who*. (The essay with "Day of the Daleks" should reinforce this even if "The Mutants" fails to make it entirely clear. If changing into a big insect, and then an angelic bloke in spandex, isn't a process of continual "becoming", then what is?)

As many of you will know, these philosophers are routinely thrown in for comic effect in *Monty Python's Flying Circus*. We're not claiming that absolutely every single ten-year-old in Britain was *au fait* with Kierkegaard[92] in the early 70s, just that it was more mainstream than now. Back then, people were less embarrassed by knowing things that weren't sport- or work-related. As we established in the first two volumes, the availability of paperback editions of the key works - plus the self-improving zeal that came after World War II - meant that people who'd missed out at school (or indeed, missed school in the Blitz) were filling in the gaps in their education and trying to look beyond the nine-to-five. Penguin books were doing for the mind what Charles Atlas was offering to do for the body: stop you feeling ashamed.

The ideas we've just mentioned were in wide circulation, even if the names weren't always known (or dropped for effect). In some ways, this is characteristic of BBC drama in this era; these days, people think it's pretty clever that characters in *Lost* are called "Rousseau" and "John Locke". Rather than slowly and patiently explain it all, Sloman's script runs through all the (supposedly) amusing ramifications of the idea for the kids and lets the adults figure out the connections. We've left Sydney Newman's original didactic model of *Doctor Who* far behind but the clear intention of this script is in keeping with the original idea of making drama of the same quality as that for adults, based on a fantasy premise and for a family audience. (About the *execution* of it, however, we'll remain silent a bit longer.)

So at a very fundamental level, this story's based around conflicting philosophies - or, to be more accurate, it's taking the story-ideas from one view but making the story say something antithetical to where that view comes from. The Crystal of Kronos and a great deal of the thinking behind the TARDISes and their abilities is from the same source as the original stories about Atlantis, Plato, but the idea of Interstitial Time has a hint of Leibniz. (See **Can You Rewrite History, Even One Line?** under 1.6, "The Aztecs", for some idea of where we're going with this.) Given that this

How and Why is the Doctor Exiled to Earth?

...continued from page 279

All his subsequent tinkering seems to be geared towards either bypassing the fault in this circuit *or* rebooting with new codes. (Notice how he's capable of steering the ship into a time-loop in "The Claws of Axos" and seems not to need help getting into spacetime, even if his arrival on Peladon in Season Nine was unexpected.)

However, as much as anything else, the memory-blocks have to do with limiting the Doctor's access to knowledge that could enable him to get revenge on the Time Lords. He's lost all but the vaguest grounding in alternate universes ("Inferno"), and has no idea - until a crisis-point arrives - that Daemons are asleep in darkest Pigbinshire. So the Time Lords seem to have staked a lot on the Doctor sorting out the correct time-line from a number of choices, without him actually knowing much about any of it.

As we've recently discovered (X4.2, "The Fires of Pompeii"), this is an innate ability Time Lord ability, so it's possible the Doctor can intuit which events need a bit of a nudge and which are set in stone. Removing his recall of what he and the Master were taught at school is a little redundant, *unless* the goal is to force the Doctor to intervene and learn how these events are shaped. Maybe, perhaps, it's not just that the Time Lords need someone on hand to mould the history of early 1970s Earth, but that they require a *specific* Time Lord to do the job.

Several interesting possibilities arise from this. One is that this is all for the Doctor's benefit as well as that of Earth, meaning that the Time Lords are training him for something. Another is that he has skills and a perspective that they lack. A third is that he's a known opponent of the High Council, and thus his arrival on Solos, Peladon or Uxarieus ("The Mutants"; "The Curse of Peladon" and "Colony in Space" respectfully) has plausible deniability.

Taking the first notion seriously affects how we perceive not just the UNIT stories, but - in fact - every story made in colour. After his next regeneration, the Doctor is not only sent on increasingly delicate missions by his fellow-countrymen (see 12.4, "Genesis of the Daleks" especially), he's responsible for saving Gallifrey from disintegration (14.3, "The Deadly Assassin") and two separate invasions on the same day (15.6, "The Invasion of Time") but alters the outlook of those in authority. He's appointed President once and offered the job twice more. And shortly before we lose sight of his activities, he's entrusted with *awesomely* powerful Time Lord artefacts which he uses on solo missions - apparently with High Council sanction but never with any collusion (25.1, "Remembrance of the Daleks"; 25.3, "Silver Nemesis").

The most interesting thing to infer from this is that the Time Lords chose a new body for the recaptured Second Doctor that was capable of martial arts and operating vehicles more precisely than hitherto, as he'd need those skills for the missions they had in store for him. A *more* tenuous supposition, as we'll see (**Is There A Season 6B?** under 22.4, "The Two Doctors") is that it's not the Time Lords of the Doctor's own time who are looking out for his future development, but those from later.

That second option - about his outlook on life, and especially on a Time Lord's duty to intervene on behalf of justice - seems to be supported by the comments during his initial trial. The main speaker (can we just cut through the speculation and agree that it's the future Chancellor Goth?) claims that the Doctor has a part to play in this fight. And we later discover (in the first two stories of Season Fourteen) that Time Lords swear an oath to do exactly this. How this squares with their non-intervention policy is never made clear. Perhaps having a rogue who's more loyal to the original precepts of the Time Lords than the present administration is their get-out clause. If any major cosmic power accused them of using the Doctor as their catspaw, they could point to the paperwork showing that his memory of how things historically played out had been blocked, so he was a free agent and making it up as he went along.

That makes another detail of the TARDIS' clamping interesting: the Doctor's memory becomes a lot less foggy once the Master shows up in Season Eight. This might be some kind of telepathic backwash from having an old school chum around, but it makes more sense if the Time Lords alter the terms of the Doctor's exile without telling him. Whatever these Dematerialisation codes are, they don't seem to matter when taking the TARDIS into the Master's vessel, escaping from Atlantis or returning to Wootton in "The Time Monster" (9.5). In the first two instances, he supposedly piggy-backed on the Master's Ship but that's not the case in the third. Maybe Kronos helped him.

continued on page 283...

adventure grew out of the ashes of a story concerning time-paradoxes and was being discussed at the same time as the attempted definitive statement on this ("Day of the Daleks"), it's perhaps inevitable that the story should end with an idea that everything the Doctor had seen was preordained. All the stuff about daisies serves to prepare Jo to accept the inevitable: that Atlantis is doomed no matter what they do.

Things That Don't Make Sense The fundamental flaw with the story's first half is that the Master has decided that basing his evil scheme somewhere close to where the action is, maybe Athens or Crete, is too much hassle [what, he had a problem with Greece being run by Fascists in the early 70s?], and that Cambridge, right next to where the Doctor is based, is a far more sensible option. He's also decided that rather than be a reclusive millionaire he's going to insinuate himself into a university science department, with all the peer-review complications and red tape that entails. The only possible benefit from this is use of hard-to-obtain facilities - but what, we might ask, is there that a Time Lord can't get? Well, there's people, but that would mean that he's at Wootton because TOMTIT actually benefits from Ruth and Stu's input. No, that doesn't seem terribly likely, does it? So maybe he's got a strange need for military observers and university funding oversight groups. Then he takes matters a bit further, and for no conceivable reason attempts to summon Kronos in the presence of the Brigadier and the funding committee.

During said demonstration, when everything appears to be going wrong with TOMTIT, the Master yells, 'Come Kronos, come!', yet no-one seems to notice. With hindsight, we also have to ask how the Brigadier (who's heard the Master speak on a number of occasions) and Benton (who can identify his voice on the phone after hearing it once before) didn't spot 'Professor Thascales' as a ringer the moment he entered the room. This becomes even more silly, once we later discover the Master's facility for vocal mimicry. [If Martha can recognise Harry Saxon's altogether less recognisable voice - "The Sound of Drums" - we might deem this some kind of auditory hypnosis, but there's no evidence of the Delgado Master even having time to do this and he's wearing a radiation suit that would get in the way.] Later, the Brigadier bizarrely claims that there's, 'no reason

[the Master] should know we're onto him'. Other than the Brig and Benton being *in the room* during the Master's botched attempt to summon Kronos, no... there's no reason whatsoever.

Why has the Doctor, who's been stuck on Earth for a number of years now, measure everything in Venusian SI units? How do Venusians (said here to have huge plates and to keep tripping over) play hopscotch? [See 11.3, "Death to the Daleks". All right, you don't *have* to watch it just for that.] And if the time sensor allows the Doctor's TARDIS to materialise in (roughly) the same place as the Master's, then why doesn't the Doctor plug it straight into the console and go directly to the Master from his lab at UNIT HQ, instead of roaring around the country in Bessie telling Jo that they have to hurry? [Incidentally, Bessie's new gadget - the inertia-damper - would make faster-than-light travel a realisable dream. Instead it's used to break various British traffic laws.]

Dr Percival is the sort of person who becomes enraged upon thinking the Master a fraud, and looks for all the world like the sort of stubborn individual with the willpower to overcome the Master's hypnosis [for comparison, see 8.1, "Terror of the Autons" and "The Daemons"]. Instead, he succumbs to such a degree that the Master says it's been a 'long time' since his hypnosis has worked so well. Stuart has exceptional eyesight to spot that the Land Rover accompanying the committee members has UNIT markings - except that he hasn't, because he thinks it's a Jeep. Later in Stuart's space-age bachelor pad, the Doctor asks for a wine bottle; it turns out there's an empty one right at this foot of the table, where he's assembling the parts for his 'time-flow analogue,' that he entirely failed to spot. And the fact that Benton falls for the Master's "look behind you!" trick is the sort of thing that makes one despair as to UNIT's effectiveness. It's also goofy that Benton asks *Stuart* - a lanky, goofy civilian - to frisk the Master for weapons. No wonder the fiend escapes.

The medallion the Master gets from Krasis can not only summon a Chronovore, it can scare it into submission. This is odd, as it only has a few geometry puzzles on one side. Taken alongside Azal's defeat when Jo sets up a logic-problem and BOSS being bamboozled by a paradox ("The Daemons", "The Green Death") it's amazing the same author's final story ("Planet of the Spiders") didn't end with the Doctor defeating The Great

How and Why is the Doctor Exiled to Earth?

...continued from page 281

More pertinently, many of the threats to Earth during the Doctor's exile are *caused* by the Master, who's attracted to Earth primarily - it must be said - because the Doctor is there. Perhaps the Time Lords want the Doctor and the Master to sharpen each other up (this sounds altogether more plausible, now that we've heard all sorts of tales about their exploits in the Time War). Or maybe the Master's less circumspect intervention in Earth's development is part of the Time Lords' plan for humanity - allowing that he can't be permitted to destroy Earth, but *is* allowed to get as close as anyone has. Perhaps the Doctor is simply there as a safety-device to train the Master, or perhaps he's there to draw the Master to Earth. But if the Doctor is, ahem, "Master-bait", he needs his wits about him to prevent catastrophe - hence his sudden ability to recall Lamadine welding techniques, and how to defuse what we're going to call a Sontaran Fragmentation Grenade in deference to the "Terror of the Autons" novelisation.

All of this does, however, fit a pattern we see throughout the exile period, wherein the safe steering of the TARDIS is somehow more important than just getting it from A to B. This is partially confirmed in "Planet of Giants" (2.1), which suggests that materialisation is the most delicate part of any flight through eternity. For that matter, it's possible that the billowing smoke and funny noises aren't actual faults, but the Ship's peculiar brand of Error Message. (See also 1.3, "Edge of Destruction" and again "The Wheel in Space". And at long last, we have a sensible reason for the comedy sound-effects in 17.5, "The Horns of Nimon".)

Maybe, then, it's not that the TARDIS is actually unable to dematerialise without the correct codes, but that it *refuses* to on the grounds that the passengers won't survive such a trip. After all, the Doctor's first attempt to bypass the code results in him being flung into the vortex and winding up, flukily, in a parallel universe where all his friends are in charge. He has an 'extreme emergency' switch (seen in "The Time Monster") fitted to fish him out of spacetime should this happen again. Note also that whilst he's willing to go on missions for the Time Lords alone if possible ("The Mutants"), his own test-flights see him cautioning Jo about the danger, and then doing what he can to get her to come along. We have a partial hint from "The Two Doctors" of what might happen to a non-Time Lord passenger if things aren't right.

After the Doctor has shepherded the humans through a period when they seem to be hell-bent on either self-destruction or enticing passing aliens to destroy them - and after he's rebuilt the TARDIS practically from scratch and *almost* put down roots - the Doctor is given a new Dematerialisation circuit and gets his memory unblocked in "The Three Doctors" (10.1). Allegedly this is a reward for his saving the Time Lords and defeating a being from their mythology, but it took *three* versions of himself do it, and only after the President pulled rank on the High Council to achieve that team-up.

So is he being rewarded, has the term of his sentence been served but then a crisis intervened, or has something more significant changed? It's interesting that we've never seen the President get involved in the Doctor's affairs (he doesn't appear, for example, with the Time Lord Tribunal in "Colony in Space"), yet he knows all about the Doctor's exile and his work with UNIT. It's also interesting that the Master loses all interest in 1970s Earth after the Kronos business ("The Time Monster"), yet - somewhat bizarrely - wishes it as a reward for services rendered to the Daleks in 2540 (10.3, "Frontier in Space").

Clearly, there's something tremendously important about Earth, but it's something that - for the Master at least - has a small window of opportunity that coincides with the Doctor's involuntary stay and again nearly six centuries later. And perhaps this "something" is a temptation the Time Lords couldn't risk the Doctor knowing too much about, hence his memory blocks. Maybe they feared him turning up on their home world thirty feet high, breathing sulphur and zapping them if he'd out about Azal ("The Daemons"), or perhaps they didn't trust him with the Crystal of Kronos ("The Time Monster").

One last thought: the new series yields a thundering amount of evidence that the *most* delicate time for Earth, vis-à-vis alien intervention, is circa 2005 to 2010. However, it's also well-documented that Britain alone has at least three agencies who wouldn't have been up to the task without significant earlier interventions from the Doctor (especially during his exile and the immediate aftermath). One in particular is empowered by a Prime Minister whose own career is significantly affected by the Doctor's activities, and who's motivated simply by knowing that he's no longer reliably around to deal with whatever threat arises.

One by waving a book of Sudoku at her. This medallion, though, is powerful enough to make the stack-heeled budgie-man that is Kronos' main form stay put in a room with flimsy walls and open windows.

The doodlebug falls on Wootton in the same place that a doodlebug fell in 1944, the idea presumably being that the Crystal of Kronos draws it through time but not space. So why does one of the locals remember the 1944 bomb going off, when transporting it to the 70s means that it never hit the ground thirty years earlier? We might also question why, exactly, the time-displaced knight and Roundheads feel the urge to attack the armoured UNIT convoy, as opposed to either soiling themselves in awe or - at the very least - pausing to wonder just what these strange sights are all about. But luckily for Our Heroes, the Master has summoned the one group of Roundheads who can't hit a stationary target from ten yards away. Weirdly, the Doctor claims the Master brought these people 'back in time' - he means "forward in time", surely? When Benton leaves the lab to set his fiendish trap for the Master and Percival, he walks past an ambulance - does it really take twenty minutes to get Stu out of bed, or was the ambulance summoned for the comedy window-cleaner, and is now hanging around in case anyone else gets hurt?

Dr Science has a couple of points about TOMTIT's temporal effects... Terry Walsh, playing the comedy window-cleaner, falls off his ladder in slow motion. He's injured as if time had flowed at the same rate for him as for the floor he hit, which isn't the case (otherwise the camera's point-of-view would have run at the same time). The Doctor is able to run into a field of distressed time and rescue the Brig and Ruth by taking their arms and making them jog in the opposite direction. But if they're jogging they're moving forward in time (however slowly), so why do they not remember anything, even though when Stu gets blighted he gets access to race-memories *and* everything that happened? In similar vein, if the Brigadier's stuck in a permanent hole in time, why is any light - let alone the sound of birdsong - emerging to get as far as the window? [Come to think of it, shouldn't the slowed-down time in other scenes cause the wavelength of the light to shift? Dr Science says that it might turn to heat, but we'd have to build TOMTIT to find out.] We can only explain all of this, alas, by reverting to

our original conclusion: that TOMTIT's effects amount to whatever Barry Letts thinks would be fun to include in a story one day.

And incidentally, TOMTIT is so wondrous a machine that it fixes all of the various time-buggery problems (the frozen UNIT troops, Baby Benton) even when the supposedly vital Crystal of Kronos has been removed. Moreover, the idea of time flowing at different rates in different places - amusing as the results might be to some - is diametrically opposed to the idea of granular time. If time is made of particles and there's 'a gap between *now* and *now*', then opening up that gap ought to allow more particles through, not make them flow slower. It also makes nonsense of the Doctor's later claim ["Invasion of the Dinosaurs"] that localised time-eddies are impossible. [That comment also means that the Cardiff Time Rift can't work, so we might suggest that the Doctor is just wrong on that occasion.]

It's readily becoming obvious that every time the Doctor rearranges his TARDIS layout, the Master does too. Every time. This tradition continues in the 80s, but it's readily apparent here. So either the Ship-to-Ship telepathy extends to interior décor horrors, or the High Council of the Time Lords are enforcing the equivalent of a dress-code. [We had an elaborate riff about desktop themes, but someone beat us to it.] It's also curious that the Doctor has the perfect opportunity to sabotage the Master's TARDIS but doesn't even consider the point, instead opting to go back inside his and hitch a ride to Atlantis [unless he's leery of setting off a trap in the short time allotted - see 8.4, "Colony in Space"]. People with nothing better to do with their time (and clever computers with samplers) might like to try to work out the Doctor's supposedly backwards dialogue in episode four.

Some supervillain silliness follows the Master making his "big arrival" in Atlantis in what looks like a computer bank, when his TARDIS has a working chameleon circuit. Then when the Doctor and Jo arrive, they evidently fail to check the scanner before leaving the Ship - meaning they just blunder outside to face Krasis (who they know is hostile to them) and a bunch of trident-bearing guards. In episode three, King Dalios tells Hippias about the Minotaur, and explains the importance of protecting the Crystal of Kronos. By episode five, however, it takes no time at all for the Queen (and / or Krasis) to convince Hippias to try to kill the Minotaur and bag the crystal. Hippias has no love for the Queen at that point, so why does he ignore the King's wishes and agree to do this? And it seems *incredibly* stupid that Hippias plans to kill the Minotaur using only his bare hands and maybe a torch.

Then, once the Doctor and the King learn that Hippias has gone to the chamber beneath the temple (pursued by Jo) why does the Doctor decide to fight the Minotaur with his bare hands? Why not get the King to shamble down there and nicely ask his old friend to back off? Or would that just take too long?

Someone off-camera coughs during the Master's "seduction" scene with the Queen, as if to punctuate his statement that Atlantis will become 'Rich, powerful, magnificent among the nations of the world.' Seconds later, it sort of sounds as if there's footsteps (possibly the cougher exiting) when the Master says, 'Purely because of Dalios' great age...'

Being charitable, we can accept that Aiden Murphy (Hippias) thinks he's on stage. Or even, at a pinch, that they cast him to make us think more fondly of Rick James in the previous story. However, the Minotaur itself make us *less* than charitable about everything else in this story. It's obviously Dave Prowse going 'Ooo-arrrr! inside a rubber head, and they didn't bother to dub on a real bull. And talking of silly men going 'Oo-arr', what's with the tractor-driver counting 'One two six heave!'? Even by Pigbin standards, this is unacceptably patronising. At the end of the story, the Master handcuffs Jo but she's not bound after the 'Time Ram' impact. [Kronos magically and benevolently released her? Or maybe Jo *can* do escapology in her sleep.]

We're in a story about Atlantis and a Chronovore capable of obliterating entire worlds, but aside from some loose metaphorical talk, absolutely nobody (except Dalios, as he dies) comments or seems to suspect that they're caught up in the very historical events that led to the city's destruction. The Master, in particular, desperately wants Kronos' power yet never pauses to think that bringing Kronos through in Atlantis itself might end very, very badly for him. He really doesn't think these things through, does he?

Critique As you'll have seen, every script has to go through a script editor and the producer, then the Head of Serials and usually the Head of Drama at BBC1. Then something like thirty other people involved in making and designing things get a copy. Then all of the film-crew, the studio technicians and a dozen or so actors have the chance to reject things or opt out. Then, once the story is recorded and being edited, the Head of Serials watches the rough cut and decided on things. And yet, not a single member of the one hundred or so people involved in making this story seems to have said, "Wait a second..."

It's worth considering this slowly. All sorts of people could have prevented this story from reaching our screens, and so they must all have thought it was appropriate. Moreover, there are none of the usual rumours about Pertwee storming off the set, and no comments from the cast or crew about how they all foresaw from the get-go that this was going to be a disaster. Everyone made this story voluntarily and deliberately... They can't *all* have been on drugs, surely?

What's *really* shocking is when you compare this to the earnestness of the previous story by the same director, just six months earlier ("Day of the Daleks") and note how things have changed since the last UNIT story. The more obvious (and deceptive) comparison is with "The Daemons", but "The Time Monster" isn't just an attempt to make lightning strike twice, it's a concerted effort to make an iconic and groundbreaking story. That it fails doesn't owe to any lack of effort. True, it has some daft ideas, some ludicrous plotting, some obvious and exasperating padding, some of the *worst* acting ever committed to tape and an ending that's off-the-scale embarrassing. At heart, however, is a story that only *Doctor Who* could have done (although *The Tomorrow People* had a good go about once a year). It's also one that uses all of the facilities available in this uneasy hiatus between *Doctor Who* being purely UNIT and Yeti-in-the-loo and predominantly being Adventures in Space and Time again. It's the UNIT / Master / Time Paradox mix that a lot of people *think* was always happening, but in fact this is the only time where all these ideas coincide. (In the very next story, they end the Doctor's exile, and thereby remove one of the cornerstones of the format they've had since colour started.) Still, they've gone for broke and decided to make a thoroughgoing, self-conscious epic...

Unfortunately, to accomplish this, they have to sell the audience on each new concept laboriously and illustrate with examples. Really stupid examples. It's all done in such a fashion that nothing seen in any episode is too drastic a shift from how that episode started and yet, after six weeks, we've arrived at a fanciful yarn with a Minotaur, Benton in a nappy and a man in a pigeon suit destroying Atlantis before turning into a gold-faced lady in a really cheesy CSO inlay. The point isn't where the story ends up, it's how we got there.

Every other Season Nine story has taken a basic type of *Doctor Who* idea and done it a bit more emphatically than before, as if to get the definitive take on each sub-genre. "The Time Monster" looks like someone sat in the bath devising a list of ideas to try in a story about time-experiments and Atlantis, then cobbled together a story to use them all in six episodes. In this, it's one of the most inevitable stories ever. Not only is this *exactly* what you'd anticipate a *Doctor Who* story from 1972 being like, but it's the kind of story that would only have been attempted that year. In many ways this is what a certain strand of early 70s *Doctor Who* was always trying to become.

As if to confirm its status as period kitsch, enter Ingrid Pitt, Hammer icon and rhyming slang, who finds whole new ways to make Sloman's dialogue grate. An adventure that's already had attempts at early 70s youth dialogue (UNIT dating is severely messed up by Jo using 'groovy' in all seriousness any time between 1970 and 1992), its caricatured "ordinary bloke" lines for Benton and its stilted "epic" language for the Atlanteans *might* be thought to be running out of options for wrongness. And then, just to cap everything off, Ingrid speaks.

As with our previous low point in the series - 2.5, "The Web Planet" - there's some clever and insightful attempts to suggest a wholly different world-view, but they're smothered in the dialogue and mangled by some truly eccentric performances. Worse, they all but admit this by devoting a whole episode to Pertwee and Delgado bitching, because these two are reliable and can make any silly idea sing, right? Wrong. The point of the Doctor and the Master, especially played by these two, is that they work best when they're disrupting someone else's cosy world. An episode of them teleconferencing from their TARDISes is marking time, and raises the technobabble-levels to new heights. This is all punctuated, you understand, by the sequence of Stu and Ruth making a baby. Had they done it by conventional means, the result couldn't have been less broadcastable.

(Side note to say that even though the story's ending - with John Levene looking embarrassed -

gives reviewers an open goal, the *real* shame about is that Benton in Atlantis could have livened up the last three episodes to no end, yet nobody thought of it. Everyone's going by the tick-box approach that keeps UNIT for domestic duties, and official capital-c Companions for TARDIS travel. But that just yields a sense of including things that "ought" to be there. Conversely, this thinking explains why so many people who *haven't* seen "The Time Monster" think this must be a great story.)

Again, as with "The Web Planet", if they hadn't tried something beyond what they'd previously achieved, we'd be griping about their lack of ambition. For all its faults - no, dammit, *because* of its faults - "The Time Monster" is infinitely more fun to watch than much of Season Eleven. This is damning with faint praise, but Seasons Nine and Ten are concerned with seeing how far they can push a particular type of story in a particular direction. That they manage only two or three real duds (one of those self-consciously retro, and written by Terry Nation) out of ten stories is remarkable.

So we're excusing "The Time Monster" by placing it in context because - however much fun can be had pointing at Aiden Murphy and calling him "Naboo" whilst jeering - this is the only thing that can cogently be said about it. They tried something, it didn't quite work, they moved on. It isn't remembered well by the public (the last two episodes were shown while everyone was on holiday) and fans shudder at the thought of it, even though so many of the series' core concepts start here. It's axiomatic that in a quarter-century of production, pretty much *any* science-fiction serial will produce period pieces. This is a really vibrantly early-70s pop-culture artefact, like hot-pants or an eight-track cartridge of Maureen McGovern. For that reason alone, it is to be cherished - albeit through gritted teeth.

The Facts

Written by Robert Sloman. Directed by Paul Bernard. Viewing figures: 7.6 million, 7.4 million, 8.1 million, 7.6 million, 6.0 million, 7.6 million. (Perhaps mercifully, no AI figures were recorded.)

Supporting Cast Roger Delgado (The Master), Wanda Moore (Dr. Ruth Ingram), Ian Collier (Stuart Hyde), John Wyse (Dr. Percival), Terry

Walsh (Window Cleaner), Donald Eccles (Krasis), Aidan Murphy (Hippias), Marc Boyle (Kronos), George Cormack (Dalios), Ingrid Pitt (Galleia), Derek Murcott (Crito), Susan Penhaligon (Lakis), Michael Walker (Miseus), Dave Prowse (Minotaur), Ingrid Bower (Face of Kronos).

Working Titles Err... "The Daleks In London". (See **The Lore**.)

Cliffhangers At the first demonstration of the TOMTIT project, the power builds up beyond the machine's limits and the Master calls out to Kronos to manifest himself; the Master re-activates the TOMTIT device, and the priest from Atlantis materialises in the control room; the Master causes a V-1 doodlebug to appear over the UNIT convoy, and the Brigadier loses radio contact with Yates as its bomb explodes; having condemned the Doctor to the vortex, the Master uses the control on his own TARDIS which sets the Doctor's Ship adrift, with Jo still inside it; Jo finds herself locked inside the catacombs beneath Atlantis, and a bellowing noise rings out along the passage.

What Was in the Charts? "The First Time Ever I Saw Your Face", Roberta Flack; "Me and Julio Down at the Schoolyard", Paul Simon; "Rocket Man", Elton John; "Rockin' Robin", Michael Jackson; "Metal Guru", T Rex; "Oh Babe, What Would You Say?", Hurricane Smith.

The Lore

• We'll assume you've read a bit of the prehistory of this story in the entry for "Day of the Daleks". Robert Sloman's original script involved the Daleks experimenting with time and summoning "historical" opponents for UNIT, hence all the messing-about with Roundheads. Although it was relegated to mid-episode padding here, the "timescoop" idea turned up again in stories such as "Invasion of the Dinosaurs" and "The Five Doctors" (20.7).

As late as May 1971, "The Daleks In London" was going to be the six-part season climax, and Sloman - after lengthy negotiations with Terry Nation - got the official go-ahead on 25th of May. Less than ten days later, Barry Letts and Terrance Dicks presented Louis Marks with the task of rewriting his script to include Daleks. Sloman had now blocked out a six-part storyline, which he

promptly junked and began again. Letts had a few ideas he wanted to try out, and Sloman, in the course of devising a new story that echoed the mythology-is-forgotten-science theme of "The Daemons", was guided in how to incorporate them in a UNIT-based story that also had a historical thread (apparently by popular demand) and a radical rethink of the Doctor's motivation...

• Although religion has traditionally been what bad guys do in *Doctor Who*, and Dicks frequently cautioned against weakening the stories with polemic ("selling out the audience for a pot of message", as he often put it), Letts was becoming increasingly concerned that the Doctor being right all the time was dramatically limiting, and that showing even someone as wise and ancient as him to be on a steep learning-curve (spiritually, at least) made for a more interesting long-term narrative. Letts added the 'daisiest daisy' scene, as part of his project to make the Doctor's heroism and wisdom seem more of a work-in-progress. Bizarrely, heroic playwright Dennis Potter said something which echoed it almost verbatim in his final interview. (In his last few months, he made unkind references to then-BBC Director General John Birt as a "croak-voiced Dalek". Unkind to Daleks, that is.)

• With the Daleks removed, it seemed opportune to give the Master an unscheduled re-appearance along with UNIT, with the bonus of exploring what made the evil Time Lord tick. Sloman had a few ideas on that score, which he proposed in passing as a possible "grand finale" for the Third Doctor and his nemesis (see "Planet of the Spiders"). Letts supervised the planning for the new six-part story very closely, whilst Dicks oversaw the re-writes of "Day of the Daleks" to add various items. (Not just Daleks, although Nation had a few notes on their dialogue. The time-paradox element needed a bit of cleaning-up - or at least showing that they'd thought about the same problems the audience, but weren't going to attempt a proper answer.)

Dicks went on holiday for a fortnight while the Letts-Sloman huddle was going on, returning just before the submission-date of 3rd of August (by which time Letts was off for six weeks - rank hath its privileges). Sloman himself took the opportunity a little later to go to Crete for a holiday - purely research, you understand - but in no way is this connected with the scripts for episodes three to six being delayed. Honest.

• A last-minute script alteration prevented

years of dull fanzine articles: Jo mentions that she doesn't speak ancient Greek, so the Doctor flips a switch under the console to solve the problem. How Benton could understand Krasis, though, would have been a puzzle even with this *deus ex machina* in place. The Master's 'My dear Benton' slip was added to cover an even more crass mistake, this time by the writer(s) - unless Benton's first name, as they seemed to think, is also 'Mike'. Oh, and an under-running episode three *was* bulked out with the scene about making a time-flow analogue out of odds and ends.

• As this story was being written, Paul Bernard's debut story as director ("Day of the Daleks) was being broadcast. Set designer Tim Gleeson, who had overseen "Colony in Space", was assigned. The Atlantis set is taken almost unchanged from the reconstruction of the Central Court or the Palace of Minos - excavated by Sir Arthur Evans in 1901 and painted, from the plans, by Piet de Jong for the books Evans and his wife published between 1921 and 1936. The costumes for the women derive from frescos and statuary, especially the famous snake-goddess votary (although no nipples were exposed at prime-time). His rethought TARDIS interior only made the one appearance, officially because it was damaged in storage. His rendering of the Master's console retained the Time Rotor from the last Gleeson-designed story.

• At the end of recording "The Mutants", Bernard and the earlier story's director, Christopher Barry, shared a studio day experimenting with effects techniques. Gleeson and the EM-Tech company (see "Day of the Daleks") tried out some new lighting effects and an experimental ageing make-up for Ian Collier (as Stuart Hyde) was examined.

Two days later they began pre-filming at Ealing. The scenes of baby Benton were shot on film but, for some reason, remounted with a different child in studio recording (perhaps the original sprog acted the rest of the cast off the screen). This and the scenes of Dalios, Hippias and the neophyte seeing the Crystal "afire" were done while work on "The Mutants" drew to an end. Pertwee went straight from recording that story to filming the dream sequence in late March. That day they tried various forms of fowl to make a suitable Kronos, but after experiments with chickens, owls, seagull and cockatoos, they plumped for an out-of-focus dove.

• David Prowse plays the Minotaur in episode six. Well, *officially* it's him, but Terry Walsh is inside the cow-head for a lot of that fight. Prowse had just made *A Clockwork Orange*, a part that mainly required him to carry Patrick Magee around. He was a body-builder from Bristol (and his accent had helped him when playing a giant kid to advertise Tonka Toys: *real tough toys for real tough boys*) but many casting directors only wanted him (so to speak) for his body. Even when he played his most famous role, the Green Cross Code Man (because "Splink" - discussed a lot later in this book - had gone horribly wrong, so they needed a superhero to stop kids getting hit by cars), he was originally redubbed by Peter Hawkins. By 1980, he was doing the voice himself. By 1983, there was an animated one, voiced by someone (Hawkins again?) approximating Prowse's accent.

What had changed? Prowse had a busy few years, both serving as a physical trainer to Christopher Reeve for *Superman* (a part Prowse himself auditioned for, although he was mysteriously rejected in favour of an American), but also being squeezed into leather and a tin gimp-mask to play the Film Doctor's sidekick in *Star Wars* and the sequels. As a result, Prowse went on Saturday Morning TV as himself (imagine James Earl Jones on *Tiswas*) and became a household name.[93] Everyone recognised him from the Green Cross TV spots, but they now had a name to go with it and knew what he really sounded like. There was widespread dismay (not least in the Bristol area) when *Return of the Jedi* revealed someone else's head inside Vader's helmet. His day in *Doctor Who* was 30th of March but, not being a registered stuntman, he wasn't in the costume when the Minotaur ran into the foil mirrors or the fake wall.

• In the first week of April, the location work began with the Wootton scenes (it's a swizz, readers - this was done in Berkshire and not Cambridge at all). A lot of the film was done at different speeds, to create the time-slowing effects and Bessie going at super-speed. Ian Collier's make-up was removed in three phases to provide the "reverse-ageing" effect.

Later in the week they relocated to Hampshire and did the skirmishes with Roundheads and the knight. A collision between the horse and the Land Rover affected filming of the latter, and a tangled negligence suit was avoided only by diligent paperwork. The actor / stunt-man hired as main driver, Marc Boyle, also played Kronos. He was in on that experimental session at the end of March, wearing the "glowing" Kronos costume. On the basis of this session, it was decided to keep the Chronovore's physical manifestations to a minimum *and* to use Vaseline on the lenses, with everyone crossing their fingers that nobody would look too closely.

This was Boyle's first on-screen credit - at least on television. If you've seen the extraordinary British zombie-biker-gang flick *Psychomania* (1973), in which John Levene and Alan Bennion play policemen killed by the most well-spoken Hell's Angels in history - never mind confirmation that Beryl Reid (see 19.6, "Earthshock") has *no* shame - you'll see Boyle and his colleagues doing some pretty accomplished bike stunts. And Roy Scammell falling off tall buildings. And George Sanders worshipping a frog. (It may even be the same frog from "The Claws of Axos", but regrettably IMDB doesn't list livestock.) Much of the rest of the cast should look pretty familiar too.

• In order to avoid the perennial "let-me-put-on-the-handbrake-and-tell-you-the-plot" syndrome that afflicts many of the Pertwee stories, it was decided (possibly by Letts, who seems to refined this technique for "Planet of the Spiders") to attach a small camera to Bessie's wing-mirror, rig up a tape-recorder and send Pertwee and Manning off to drive around country lanes doing their scenes. Orson Welles had pioneered this in *A Touch of Evil*, sending Charlton Heston through a dusty, crowded Mexican street. (And if you doubt that Chuck Heston and Jon Pertwee have anything in common, watch *The Omega Man*. It's impossible to view this film with a straight face once you've seen a few Third Doctor stories.)

There is, of course, a typical snag connected with Katy Manning and navigation (see "The Daemons", again), and eventually Bernard sent out search parties. A scene where they were stuck in a herd of cattle was planned, and cows were even hired for the occasion, but it never happened. (Maybe they needed Equity cards or something.)

• Ingrid Pitt had already worked with Pertwee (who proposed her as Galleia) in the film *The House That Dripped Blood*, a movie notable for being one of the very few films where you can hear Pertwee doing something like his "normal" voice instead of a funny accent. He plays a rather prima donna-ish horror actor who wears cravats and frilly shirts, but he's possessed by a vampire's

cloak as sold to him by Geoffrey Bayldon (see "The Creature From the Pit"). This means that Pertwee sounds - and dresses - exactly like the Doctor but, um, he's a vampire.

Pitt, whose autobiography *Life's A Scream* has some curious entries about unlikely celebrities, went straight from this story to her landmark movie, *Countess Dracula*. She'd reunite with Donald Eccles (Krasis) in *The Wicker Man* the following year.[94] Susan Penhaligon, later a big name in 70s TV, got her break here because the person originally cast as Lakis (Anne Michell, who, spookily, is in *Psychomania* and looks a lot more Greek than her replacement) was fired for being consistently late.

Ian Collier (Stuart Hyde) eventually wound up wearing "old man" make-up based on tissue-paper and honey, which we can't honestly say looks much different from the more laborious latex techniques used at the time. He'll return as Omega in "Arc of Infinity" (20.1). Letts suggested George Cormack for the role of Dalios, and in "Planet of the Spiders", he'll return as the self-same Wise Old Mentor the Doctor mentions in the gaol sequence.

• Pertwee improvised the Spanish dialogue himself (he spent his summers in Ibiza, before it was fashionable).

• By now Roger Delgado was losing work simply because casting directors assumed he was constantly on *Doctor Who*. He was asked to return once in the next series, in an off-Earth story ("Frontier in Space") but requested that the Master go out in an emphatic blaze of... well, glory was optional, but a definite end to the character (at least in this body) was a must. After this story (but filmed slightly earlier), he appeared as an Italian police captain in *Jason King*, as a member of the Spanish Inquisition in the BBC's *Don Quixote* (recorded now and shown the following year) and as the soothsayer[95] in a multinational production of *Antony and Cleopatra*. As it turned out, the recording of episode three was the end of the "UNIT family" (more on this in "The Green Death"), although they saw each other socially from time to time. The UNIT material for the last two episodes was recorded earlier to release Courtney and Levene.

• The Time Ram element obviously appealed to Letts, who referenced it in "The Paradise of Death" radio drama in 1993. As scripted, Jo initiated the Ram with her foot, as she was manacled to the walls of the Master's TARDIS. Episodes five and six were recorded after episode one went out on air, and the filming for "Carnival of Monsters" (10.2) began two days after episode two aired. The week after the last episode saw the TV premiere of *Doctor Who and the Daleks* (starring Peter Cushing - see the Appendix in Volume VI). This was rather better-received, it must be said, than the story itself. This film and the sequel, shown just under a month later, got 10 million viewers.

10.1: "The Three Doctors"

(Serial RRR, Four Episodes, 30th December 1972 - 20th January 1973.)

Which One is This? It's a birthday party for the series, so the First and Second Doctors get invited back on board the TARDIS and someone's even sent anti-matter-flavoured jelly. The villain is revealed as the very first Time Lord of all (he'd like to come and meet us, but...), though not before he steals UNIT HQ and drags it through a black hole. The Brigadier goes a bit special too.

Firsts and Lasts Nominally the story marking *Doctor Who's* tenth birthday (it was actually broadcast shortly after its ninth), "The Three Doctors" sees multiple Doctors meeting for the first time (almost passé now, but *ludicrously* exciting in 1972), as well as revealing more than ever about Time Lord history and Time Lord politics.

Here we meet Omega, who's not only the first historical Time Lord but also the first Time Lord to be given a name (of sorts) rather than a title such as "Doctor" or "Master" or "that Monk", and learn that the Time Lord planet has both a President and a Chancellor. Since the story's end sees the Doctor rewarded with a new dematerialisation circuit, it's not only the end of his exile on Earth - even if it isn't, in itself, the end of the UNIT era - but also the start of a whole new era in which he actually has *some* control over where the Ship's supposed to go. What's more, the TARDIS gets yet another 70s re-fit, this one lasting until "Pyramids of Mars" (13.3) and arguably to five minutes before the start of "The Masque of Mandragora" (14.1). Debatably, it's also the first time he saves the entire universe. This story also sees the beginning of the programme's fascination with black holes and, right from the start, the assumption is that Time Lords are responsible for them.

First time the Brigadier goes inside the TARDIS, although his inability to believe what he's experiencing jars if you watch "Spearhead from Space" (7.1) again soon afterwards. (Notice how Benton, who blunders in some time earlier, takes it all for granted.) From now on, the Doctor will wear a succession of very big, very 70s bow ties, completing his sartorial transition from Edwardian masher to night-club bouncer.

Season 10 Cast/Crew

- Jon Pertwee (the Doctor)
- Katy Manning (Jo Grant)
- Nicholas Courtney
  (Brigadier Lethbridge-Stewart)
- Richard Franklin (Captain Yates)
- John Levene (Sergeant Benton)

- Barry Letts (Producer)
- Terrance Dicks (Script Editor)

First story to credit Dick Mills with 'Special Sound' (a responsibility he'll oversee for the next seventeen years), but alas it's the final appearance of William Hartnell. The Doctor - in this case the Second Doctor - carries jelly-babies for the first time. (Sadly, the jelly theme pervades the story.)

**Four Things to Notice
About "The Three Doctors"...**

1. "The Three Doctors" sees William Hartnell's swan song as the First Doctor, though he was too ill to even attend the studio recording sessions (he died in 1975, at the age of 67) and shot all his scenes on film. As a result, the First Doctor only addresses his successors from a monitor screen in the TARDIS, and spends most of that time chiding them for missing the obvious. Conventional wisdom holds that this is a sad way for Hartnell's time on the programme to end but, really, it just makes you remember where the series came from. The First Doctor *wasn't* an action hero, and his role as oracle and peacemaker to the Other Two is pitched perfectly, even if he looks distressingly unwell at times. He'd be so much less interesting if he had to run up and down corridors like everyone else. (See 20.7, "The Five Doctors" for something closer to what was originally planned.)

2. "The Three Doctors" also sees the first real appearance of the Stupid Brigadier. Though he's increasingly found it hard to accept anything the Doctor has told him over the last three years (compare "Spearhead from Space" with 9.5, "The Time Monster"), here he goes into a state of denial the like of which we won't see again until Donna in "The Runaway Bride" (X3.0). He refuses to believe that the TARDIS interior is anything but an illusion, convinces himself that an alien world is

actually a beach in Cromer and concocts his own paranoid theory about the Second Doctor's presence, even when everybody else tells him it's wrong. The Doctor finally seems to have broken his mind (a plot idea developed more fully in 20.3, "Mawdryn Undead").

His staff's reactions, mind, are just as unlikely. One UNIT soldier's now-notorious response to the gel-guards, as they wobble towards UNIT HQ: 'Holy Moses! What's *that*?' On the plus side, Benton's reaction to the TARDIS interior is as down-to-Earth as we might expect.

3. As for the force against whom our hero(es) is/are fighting... well, it's Omega, the man who wasn't there. In theory, the conception of a man so angry with the universe that even the destruction of his body isn't enough to stop him is wonderful. In practice, the result is Stephen Thorne shouting a lot in a glam-rock Muu-muu. This is almost enough, but when we're told that the singularity is attuned to his will - meaning he can create anything he needs - then the story desperately requires an impressive display of the force of his mind. But what we *get* are Gel-guards (who sound like the Soup Dragon from *The Clangers*, and look like someone's dipped a Yeti in marmalade) and one scene where Omega tries to impress the Doctor by creating a chair.

4. Scientifically-minded viewers who've ever wanted to observe a singularity - the one-dimensional point forming the nucleus of a black hole, where all physical laws break down - will be interested to learn that it looks like a hole in the floor with a BBC dry-ice machine in it. See also **What's With All These Black Holes?**.

The Continuity

The Doctor(s) There's immediate tension between the Second and Third Doctors when they meet, so their personalities aren't compatible even if they seem to have the same sense of ethics. The Second Doctor doesn't even like the new-look TARDIS console room, and frequently tricks his "younger" self into doing all the dangerous work [well, if *he* got killed, there'd be an enormous paradox].

When they're together, the Doctors can telepathically "conference" by shutting their eyes and concentrating. [We might conclude that only iterations of the same Time Lord can do this, as none of the other people on the Doctor's homeworld are seen to try it. But if so, it's not clear how the Doctor *knows* he can do it, if Time Lords are never supposed to meet themselves.]

The Doctors' force of will is stronger when they team up. Both the Second and Third Doctors defer to the First, as if the First Doctor's older *personality* grants him wisdom beyond theirs, despite the fact that they've got more experience. The President of the Time Lords describes the First Doctor as the 'earliest' Doctor, establishing for the first time that there are no prior versions [see 13.5, "The Brain of Morbius"].

Neither the First nor Second Doctors are surprised to find themselves in the Third's company, meaning that they must receive some kind of "briefing" from the Time Lords before they're dispatched, but it's unclear whether they retain any of their memories when they go back into their own timestreams [see also "The Five Doctors" and **Is There A Season 6b?** under 22.4, "The Two Doctors"]. The Second Doctor remembers meeting Benton during the Cyberman invasion [6.3, "The Invasion", which Benton claims happened 'all those years ago'], but hasn't seen him since and has no knowledge of the Third Doctor's adventures. The First Doctor can mysteriously identify Omega's energy-creature as a 'time-bridge' when his successors can't.

Neither the Second nor Third Doctor will admit to knowing the lyrics of "I Am the Walrus" by The Beatles. [We can't vouch for the First Doctor on this point; see 2.8, "The Chase"]. The Second Doctor thinks best to music, which the Third Doctor doesn't appreciate. The Third Doctor now takes a lot of sugar in his tea, which he stirs with a silica rod [of the type typically used for corrosive substances].

• *Inventory.* The Second Doctor arrives on Earth with his recorder, although it's destroyed along with Omega's realm. [Is there a point after "The Invasion" when it vanishes from the Second Doctor's adventures...? Granted, we never see it after this. Well, nearly. Against all odds, the animated version of that story shows that what we thought was a telescope is actually the recorder with lenses in.] He's also equipped with jellybabies.

The Third Doctor carries a pencil and a bunch of fake flowers, which he can produce from his jacket as a conjuring-trick, but these too get left in Omega's world. The Second Doctor tosses a coin to decide which version of himself is to do something dangerous; the Third Doctor acts as if this is

What's With All These Black Holes?

Perhaps the most surprising thing about "The Three Doctors" is that the science is almost exactly right. That is, as far as was known in 1972, the material about black holes was at least permitted by the scientific theories. Contrary to what Barry Letts seems to think in interviews *now*, there's a solid scientific idea behind the fantasy trappings - even if, at the time, no-one had any way of knowing if such bodies even existed.

Although the original speculation about collapsing stars dates back to the Enlightenment mathematician Laplace, it was only in 1967 that physicist John Wheeler coined the term "black hole". In itself this was a case of rebranding what had previously been called "Frozen Stars", but it got people interested. Between 1799 and 1964 Einstein happened, fortunately so did quantum theory - the two don't quite mesh, which is where the fun starts. Einstein says, crudely, that mass and energy are the same thing from different points of view. He also says that space and time have a similar relationship. And mass distorts space (or energy distorts time, or another combination). The amount by which mass dents space is called... gravity. (And, yes, it can sometimes be treated as something that travels in waves. Like we said, Quantum theory is apparently equally true but doesn't quite fit.)

If you get enough mass / energy in one place (like a star), it noticeably affects spacetime. Even before Einstein, it was known that Mercury's orbit doesn't follow the path that Newton and Kepler say it should. Being so close to a huge mass like the Sun means that spacetime was "misbehaving" for the tiny planet, yet making it act according to the Relativistic model. (That's why people wasted a century and their eyesight looking for an inner planet, the notional 'Vulcan' mentioned in 4.3, "The Power of the Daleks", to account for the discrepancy.)

Now, a seriously large mass in a small space will become a denser mass in a smaller space. Once gravity overcomes the far stronger forces within an atom, the matter becomes superdense and behaves very oddly (see **Why Are Elements So Weird In Space** under 22.2, "Vengeance on Varos"). Once you get *so* much mass in so small a space, it keeps getting smaller and denser until the escape velocity is beyond the speed of light. In other words, to get away from it you need to move faster than anything in the universe can move. So even light can't escape this "black hole", and, er, that's *nearly* all we know about it.

We've become so used to these terms we forget exactly what's being said. The Event Horizon - which can be pretty big - is the stage beyond which we cannot know anything about it. If an entire Galaxy became a black hole (and some think the whole Universe in inside one), then it'd be about a third of a light-year across. (In fact it has to be fairly large for anything to remain as matter at all. With smaller black holes, atoms are wrenched apart as tidal forces pull the object - or person - into a long thin line of particles and, eventually, energy.) The surface gravity wouldn't be intolerable, but it's inescapable and no-one would even know you were there. From the outside, your life would be seen to slow down to a halt and you'd softly and suddenly vanish away. So far, Omega's place seems plausible, but what he does while he's there doesn't make sense. Yet.

Further in it gets more sticky. A lot of mass in a small area tends to become infinite mass in a one-dimensional point - the Singularity. This will destroy everything it encounters, possibly *everything* given time, and remove it from the Universe entirely. However, depending on what the original mass was doing before becoming a black hole, the singularity could be a revolving torus (doughnut-shaped) with a central aperture big enough to fly through.

According to the physics, taking a flying leap at a rolling doughnut is a nifty way to get around inconvenient spacetime snags like "causality". (Quantum theory says otherwise, claiming there's no way a one-dimensional point can exist because all matter is waveforms and there's no room for a waveform to vibrate. Sort of.) Even though black holes can "boil off" particles and x-rays through quantum effects (what's now called "Hawking Radiation", and we'll talk about *him* later), the Singularity is eternal, if big enough. So one created at the Big Bang (which was, after all, a large mass in a small area) should still be around.

You should (although in the early 70s this was thought impossible) also get "naked" singularities, with no remaining black hole around them. If 1% of stars implode this way, there should be a billion in this galaxy, and if only the top 1% of *those* are eternal, that's 10 000... except that they "eat" each other on contact. The "whirlpool" shape of galaxies is now thought to be super-massive black holes draining everything else out of the cosmos. (Here's where the rewrite of this article from the First

continued on page 295...

a con. [The novelisation suggests that this is a two-headed Martian crown, so "tails" never comes up (see also 16.2, "The Pirate Planet").] The Second Doctor uses a small Philips screwdriver to fix the Brigadier's radio. The Third Doctor's sonic screwdriver acts as an anti-matter detector (making the same Geiger Counter noise as the anti-matter in this story), but it's useless in Omega's world, for some reason.

The Supporting Cast

• *UNIT.* The Brigadier describes UNIT HQ as a 'top secret security establishment', even though there's a great big sign outside which says "MINISTRY OF DEFENCE, UNIT HEADQUARTERS", and it's even got his name on it. [It's already been established that UNIT's existence is common knowledge. The Brigadier presumably just means that top-secret operations are being run from the base.] In the Brigadier's office there's a video link to the security council in Geneva. Dr Tyler contacts them as a matter of course for Mr Ollis' disappearance, but was already planning a visit after seeing anomalous results from his 'cosmic ray' research. [This only occurs, however, after he shows his results to the Yanks and whoever (the Belgians?).] UNIT here uses the same garage as appears in "Planet of the Spiders" (11.5).

Captain Yates is nowhere to be seen. [Perhaps this story occurs right on the heels of "The Time Monster", meaning he's still on sick leave after a doodlebug landed on his head. This means that Mike misses out on his chance to travel in the TARDIS and, as far as we see on screen, never does (but see 22.5, "Timelash" if you dare). See also **Who Decides What Makes a Companion** under 21.5, "Planet of Fire", and note how Mike and Liz Shaw - who didn't travel in the TARDIS either - are sent as phantoms to manipulate the Third Doctor in "The Five Doctors".]

Oddly, the President of the Time Lords is fully up to speed with the Doctor's attachment to UNIT. [It seems strange to hear so powerful a being talking casually about a bunch of comedy soldiers restricted to one planet, so it's possible they become much more significant in the future. *The New Adventures* suggest they evolve into the 'Knights of Geneve' in the Benny books, and perhaps even the Grand Order of Oberon - see 22.6, "Revelation of the Daleks".]

• *The Brigadier.* Here he sees the TARDIS interior, and visits an alien world, for the first time. The shock of this may partly explain why he's less willing to accept anything the Doctor says than ever before. [Nevertheless, he adapts to somewhat bizarre circumstances better than is generally recognised. The thing which he finds hardest to accept is that the Second Doctor has somehow come back. But to his credit, he overrides Benton's incredulity when the Doctor advises that they guard the drains, and later he improvises a cover story for the Security Council (the Second Doctor is the third's 'assistant' - presumably they don't have a photo of Jo on file) and at every weird turn of events he's immediately thinking of damage-limitation. When UNIT HQ is transported somewhere, he's worried about the diplomatic repercussions if it's on foreign soil - 'this could be construed as an invasion' - which few other officers would be smart enough to see so quickly. As his last major case involved a teleport system (see "The Time Monster") this is a sensible reaction. In short, his brief reaction to what he thinks might be Cromer is an anomaly, and his assumption that a Time Lord messing with a time machine has resulted in something going wrong with time isn't unwarranted. Nevertheless, it's worth noting that his next trip in the TARDIS triggers a nervous breakdown (see "Mawdryn Undead").]

• *Benton.* He, at least, copes with this well and comments, 'Nothing to do with you surprises me any more, Doctor.' He's rather pleased to see the old Doctor back and suggests that two Time Lords should be able to create a door in a world created by one Time Lord. Unfortunately he causes trouble with the anti-matter beast by chucking a sweet-wrapper at it.

The TARDIS Re-decorated, again, and the Third Doctor has "fiddled" with the controls so much that the Second Doctor has trouble using the scanner [he was having difficulty with it in 6.5, "The Seeds of Death", so it might have needed fixing anyway]. The Time Lords ultimately reward the Doctor with a new dematerialisation circuit, and return his knowledge of time-travel law and 'dematerialisation codes'. It's possible to boost a walkie-talkie through the TARDIS' communication circuit. [We're led to believe that when the force-field isn't working, radios and other communications systems within the Ship can function - see the pilot version of the first episode (1.1), the Master's trimphone (8.2, "The Mind of Evil") and practically all of the BBC Wales series.]

What's With All These Black Holes?

...continued from page 293

Edition comes in handy: active galactic masses are now observable, and there's a great picture of M87 shooting out 5,000 light-years of plasma and x-rays, courtesy of the Hubble array.)

Draining to where, though? It seems counter-intuitive even by these standards that all that energy / matter goes nowhere. Some of the earliest theories connected this '"funnelling" effect to the then newly-discovered Quasars, the oldest and most powerful objects known. The idea was that "white holes" spew out matter and energy elsewhere in the cosmos. This was invoked to explain another anomaly: the theories say that anti-matter should be as plentiful as matter, but can't coexist with it. So where is it? Either an anti-cosmos (as whimsically postulated in "The Mutants") or the other side of space and time, whatever that means. As the process of entering a black hole strips particles down to their charges as part of stretching them into infinitely-long lines with no elapsed time - a chronosynclastic infundibularisation, or as scientists call it, "spaghettifying" - the difference between matter and anti-matter becomes academic. (See **What Does Anti-Matter Do?** under 13.2, "Planet of Evil".)

The problem is that term: "black hole" is a catchy name, but suggests perforation. It's possibly more helpful to think of them as places where space-time is tied in a knot that gets tighter and harder the more energy is exerted. When someone theorised places that repel matter ferociously, these things got called "White Holes" and the whole idea of wormholes and anti-matter universes got tied up with our nice simple gravitic tar-babies. The big difference though is that whilst we *now* have lots of observed objects that are either black holes or something much odder, nobody's found anything that exactly fits the predicted qualities of a White Hole.

The most interesting developments in this phase occurred when Roger Penrose, a British mathematician, figured out a few odd side effects of this. His paper in the May 1972 edition of *Scientific American* (Vol. 226, No. 5) formed the basis for the *Sunday Times* article by Brian Silcock; Baker and Martin read it just before starting work on "The Three Doctors". (Luckily they don't appear to have read the *rest* of that issue of *Scientific American*, because it also had a study calling into question the efficacy of Transcendental Meditation - something that wouldn't be wise to

bring this up in front of the boss.) Silcock pointed out that actually, some particles can evade this force simply by *being* particles and doing quirky quantum stuff. (See **How Do You Transmit Matter?** under 17.4, "Nightmare of Eden", but note that Entanglement doesn't necessarily produce metallic Rice Krispies as a side effect, as suggested in *The Sarah Jane Adventures*.)

Similarly, if we're dealing with anti-matter, one half of the particle-antiparticle pair could be swallowed and the other left free to roam. (Which could explain the discrepancy between the amounts of each - note that the maths suggests that anti-matter black holes behave exactly like any other. Gravity doesn't discriminate.) It was already predicted that the matter being squeezed would, on the way to the Event Horizon, produce powerful X-Ray emissions (which is how they found Cygnus X1, the first ex-star to be identified as a probable black hole). Now it seemed that these freakish objects were subject to the laws of Thermodynamics like everything else, but not in a nice orderly way. If the randomness of any emissions is such a threat to the orderly laws of physics, why doesn't the existence of black holes make *everything else* not work as it should? The answer was that the Event Horizon cut us off from the effects of this and made everything run on what passes for clockwork post-Einstein. He called it "The Law of Cosmic Censorship".

So, at the point when "The Three Doctors" was written, the idea was that you could "fall" down a black hole and - if your angle was right - cross space and time and either emerge as a stream of particles at the beginning of time *or* into an anti-matter cosmos equal and opposite to this one. (Gerry Anderson made a very lavish pilot for a series called *Into Infinity* based on this premise, and most of it was spent explaining the science to the viewers - which probably explains why it didn't become a series.) Good old-fashioned Relativity ensured that with anything approaching infinite mass, the speed of light or one dimension, time and space exhibit pretzel logic.

If you throw in quantum theory, black holes become a one-way anti-entropic hoover, restoring energy and mass to the universe in unpredictable ways and thus defying the Second Law of Thermodynamics (which states that everything will eventually become the most probable state, tepid and inert - see 18.7, "Logopolis"). This seems

continued on page 297...

Under the TARDIS console is the Ship's force-field generator, a portable device [used again in 17.5, "The Horns of Nimon"] which not only creates a force-field around the Ship, but also seems to have a force-field operational within itself. The Second Doctor's recorder, trapped inside this field, isn't converted into anti-matter along with the rest of the Ship when Omega draws it into his realm. The suggestion seems to be that nobody can leave the Ship until the force-field's disconnected. [So it's not a normal defensive feature of the TARDIS, although indications are that it was built shortly before 3.1, "Galaxy 4" - where the Doctor is inordinately proud of it - and obviously after 1.5, "The Keys of Marinus", where he's confused when Arbitan places a force-field around the Ship. These days, of course, the force-field is fine-tuned enough to protect people standing outside the ship (X1.13, "Parting of the Ways") and to serve as an environmental barrier ("The Runaway Bride").] The generator makes a noise similar to the one the TARDIS made when Ian and Barbara first burst in ["An Unearthly Child"], and the Third Doctor ends this story planning to build a new generator to replace the one that was lost.

The console room also has a ceiling and the odd cylindrical "booths" to one side, like in the original design. The monitor is colour, at last, but once again is a TV set suspended from the ceiling. It can show the TARDIS itself from outside, as if from a camera placed ten feet away. It also does sound and appears to transmit pictures and sound to other places [making teleconferencing with Omega possible, much as what occurred in "The Time Monster"].

The Time Lords The three high-ranking Time Lords seen here all speak of the Doctor as a near-equal. [In later stories he's half-forgotten, or anonymous. It's possible that there are just fewer Time Lords at this stage - not for the last time, it's strongly hinted that Time Lords equate to angels, with the "fallen" all part of some cosmic plan - see **Where Does This Come From?**.]

Two of the Time Lords here present have been before: the Chancellor was at the Second Doctor's trial [6.7, "The War Games"] and the other was on the tribunal [8.4, "Colony in Space"] that sent him to Uxarieus. [Fans who believe that the Second Doctor had a series of "secret" Time-Lord-sponsored missions after "The War Games" - see **Is There a Season 6B?** under "The Two Doctors" -

have latched onto as the Chancellor's qualms about investigating the Doctor's time-stream as proof of these side-adventures. The theory suggests that the Chancellor knows about the Second Doctor's covert missions, and is trying to stop the President investigating the Doctor's timeline just so he doesn't get found out. Which is fine... as long as you can believe that he's prepared to jeopardise the future of a) the Time Lords and b) everyone else in the cosmos in order to keep things hushed up.

[Similarly, some take the hint from Omega's original name - 'Ohm', even though it was never used on screen - that the Doctor is somehow his mirror-image, and was always intended to land up being the last Time Lord. The Romantic notion of the Doctor not just as an exile, but the sole survivor of his race (like Superman), first appeared in the subtitle of the Coast to Coast Movie version first announced in 1986. You know, the one that was supposed to star Rutger Hauer / Donald Sutherland / Howard the Duck. Anyway, Johnny Byrne (18.6, "The Keeper of Traken") claimed responsibility for this notion. We've recently seen a version of this idea worked into the series, but there's no indication that this was ever planned.]

Time Lord operations appear to be run from a "control room", where robed figures observe instruments and monitor screens. Mention is made of a 'time travel facility' [are TARDISes berthed there?]. The Time Lords have a Chancellor and a President [credited as 'President of the Council'], the President being deferential to the Chancellor and calling him 'excellency' [c.f. 15.6, "The Invasion of Time"], although ultimately the President seems to have the final word. [After 14.3, "The Deadly Assassin", the Chancellor is subservient to the President. Perhaps the power-structure remains unchanged, but custom is altered.]

When Omega drains 'cosmic energy' into his black hole, threatening the whole of space-time with collapse, the Time Lord planet seems particularly hard-hit and is so depleted of energy that it's effectively paralysed. The Doctor's TARDIS doesn't work during this period [suggesting that it might, as speculated after the TV Movie's botched continuity-references, take its power directly from Time Lord central: see **What Makes TARDISes Work?** under 1.3, "The Edge of Destruction" and 27.0, "Grace: 1999"]. However the Second Doctor's arrival removes this problem, so it's prob-

What's With All These Black Holes?

...continued from page 295

wrong - and indeed it is (eventually Hawking sussed out why, but this essay is focused on what people thought in the 70s[101]). Still, the possibilities this opened up were worth a look, whilst the effort of bolstering the accepted law of Conservation of Energy and the Second Law of Thermodynamics led to other discoveries.

The new theory suggested that particles and energy can skip around the Event Horizon, because they're not solid "lumps" but waves of probability, and the "gap" each one makes in the surrounding energy-state forms an anti-particle elsewhere. This may seem nigh-incomprehensible to the layperson, but the upshot is that if one half is created one side of the Horizon, the other half could pop into being "outside". (If you think this is weird, think about exactly how your watch or mobile phone work - this is mainstream physics, and has been since about 1920.) If treated right, then, a black hole is an inexhaustible supply of energy, just from bunging waste matter in its direction.

Hang on, though, doesn't Quantum theory *also* suggest that the very act of observing an event affects the outcome? So instead of just a "halo" of Hawking radiation, if a conscious mind were to go near a singularity, it could bias the random output and create whatever it feels like?

Strange as it sounds, a couple of years after "The Three Doctors" was broadcast, Steven Hawking gave a lecture saying pretty much that. Obviously, there's no way of involving a conscious observer in the process, but yes - the random nature of the emissions of "fuzzy" black holes as they fizz away into nothing, leaving these naked singularities, is such that a grand piano, a Bandril Ambassador or a book exactly like this but with "Pertwee" changed to "Twerpee" every time is equally as likely as heat or light. Without predictability, science might have returned to being a branch of philosophy. And if Cosmic Censorship is circumvented, we might as well give upon trying to understand anything. This isn't the place to explain exactly what happened next, but there was an apparent get-out clause in the small-print of General Relativity.

About a year later, the fat hit the fire again. The journal *Physical Review D* published a paper entitled "Rotating Singularities and the Possibility of Global Causality Violation" by Frank Tipler. In this,

he suggested that by a geometrical trick, you could 'swap' space and time, and travel back and forth to any point *up to the creation of the singularity*. (*New Scientist* got hold of it in the summer of 1980, and did a feature illustrated with a publicity photo from "The Masque of Mandragora", so obviously we read it avidly.) Tipler later concluded from this that anyone able to do this would have done, so obviously we are the most advanced species in the cosmos and it's all for our benefit. He called this the "Anthropic" principle and it was briefly fashionable. Also a fad of its day was Adrian Berry's pop-science book *The Iron Sun*, about building black holes as tunnels through space-time and traveling around thereby. This provided the basis for both 15.4, "The Sun Makers" (in a very early draft) and 17.5, "Horns of Nimon". [NB: as with "The Deadly Assassin"; "The Horns of Nimon"; X2.8, "The Impossible Planet" and by implication "Terror of the Vervoids", Omega's star is artificial in origin. In *Doctor Who* terms, a "natural" black hole has yet to appear. X2.9, "The Satan Pit" even has the Doctor claim that 'my people practically invented black holes... well... in fact they *did*'.]

Of course, by that stage, black-hole theory had moved on from the state of play in the early 70s. Despite the jets from Active Galactic Centres being visible and everyone these days sort-of knowing that there's an accretion disc, the attempts to depict them in *Doctor Who* have traditionally been more about their effects (slowing down time and causing traffic accidents) than their appearance. Deplorably, the good people at BBC Wales chose to do a less accurate one simply because it looked "cooler" - indeed, with the freakish and stupid properties of this particular stellar anomaly, it's worth wondering why they bothered calling it a black hole at all. Nonetheless, the name is instantly recognisable, and made a rather daft fantasy look approximately scientific.

Still, the prize for the *worst* representation of all goes inevitably to Season Twenty-Three's effort in "Terror of the Vervoids", but we can't just blame director Chris Clough as the script (by those noted advocates of accurate science in the series, Pip and Jane Baker) ignores what going *that* close to a black hole would do to a spaceship once the story moves beyond the cliffhanger. This is, however, interesting as the lack of anything going *in* or being jetted *out* sort of indicates that it's a long

continued on page 299...

ably the Third Doctor's memory that's at fault.

During the crisis the Time Lords feel they can't spare anyone to help the Doctor, as everyone is needed to combat the energy drain. [Meaning that they can't spare anybody capable of helping the Doctor? Admittedly, most Time Lords would be useless in the outside universe.] However, they do have the ability to make the Doctor's own time-stream cross itself, even though it uses up a great deal of 'temporal energy'.

Crossing one's own time-stream and meeting one's 'other selves' expressly contravenes the First (and most important, according to the Chancellor) Law of Time. [This has changed by 23.3, "Terror of the Vervoids", and the reference may be the first insinuation that a complete change of form is normal for Time Lords rather than being a quirk of the Doctor's.] When the First Doctor is caught in a 'time eddy' he's only visible by scanner, where he's seen sitting in a triangular 'transportation unit'. [The Second Doctor doesn't have one of these when he arrives on Earth, so it probably only exists in the vortex.]

The worst thing about this crisis is not that the Time Lords are facing destruction, but that they will have failed 'those we are pledged to protect'. [This is the last time that the Time Lords are seen to be so selfless, but it doesn't seem to be out of keeping with anything said about them so far, including what they have the Doctor doing in their name. In later stories, they'll apparently sanction assassination and all manner of extreme actions (see Season Twenty-Three in particular). Alternatively, 'those we are pledged to protect' might just mean other Time Lords.]

At the conclusion of this crisis, the destruction of Omega's realm creates a supernova out of the black hole, and the Time Lords see this as being a whole new source of energy. [This is bizarre. The black hole, referred to the President as 'the black hole', is apparently the power-source originally created by Omega and therefore the lynchpin of all Time Lord society. At the end of the story, it's replaced by an entirely new source of energy - but the lights come back on and all their gadgetry starts to work again, suggesting that no rewiring is needed. You'd think at the very least, the technology of the entire planet would need to be re-engineered to run off a supernova, like converting from gas to electric. Is this what causes such a huge social shift in Time Lord society before "The Deadly Assassin"?

[That said, "energy" is always a vague concept in Doctor Who, and it could be anything from heat to this mysterious Artron energy we keep hearing about. Beings such as the Exxilons (11.3, "Death to the Daleks") seem able to tap all form of energy with equal facility, er, save for instances where the plot requires that they can't. Either way, it's safe to assume that the ancient Time Lord technology can adjust without its present-day operators noticing.

[All we can say for certain is that they refer to 'vital cosmic energy'. We could be picky and latch onto the word 'vital', speculating that refers to its original meaning of "life-giving" or "made by life", but this could complicate matters. Similarly, the fact we're told in the same breath that this compromises the Time Lords' 'time travel facility' might lead us to believe that Omega is sapping a very specific form of energy that's used by the Time Lords but is essential to all life. Take a look at our speculations under **What Makes the TARDIS Work?** (under "The Edge of Destruction") and **What Is The Blinovitch Limitation Effect?** (under Mawdryn Undead") for our line of reasoning here.

[It's also worth mentioning that the Time Lords don't have much idea about black holes at the start of this story, and later on - "The Deadly Assassin" to be exact - they don't even realise what Rassilon did to found their society. And just to reiterate, the nucleus of a black hole, assuming it can be put inside the sort of pointy cupboard we see in "The Deadly Assassin", must be the singularity. The whole star could not possibly be - as is said in that story - 'set in an eternally dynamic equation against the mass of the planet' unless that planet weighs as much as a few thousand stars. So Omega's star and Rassilon's are two different stellar remnants.]

The Time Lords don't know how anything can exist in a black hole, and have difficulty believing that any force in the universe is their equal. The President seems [maybe, see **Things That Don't Make Sense**] to have been aware all along of Omega's survival. [In a pinch, this might indicates that the version Omega tells is no paranoid fantasy but an accurate summary of a genuine betrayal - the first hint that Time Lord history might largely be seen as propaganda. The novelisation of 25.1, "Remembrance of the Daleks", like the later New Adventures, hints that Rassilon deliberately sent Omega to his doom.]

What's With All These Black Holes?

...continued from page 297

way from any useful matter. The problem being: a black hole has no reason to *that* far from anything else. The obvious conclusion is that this too is a construct, a nice long way from any star-systems or passing spaceships (ordinarily) and therefore very likely some kind of research station. For that matter, the Master's most recent attempt at grand-scale naughtiness involved 'black hole converters' inside missiles, somehow.

It's looking very much, then, as if every single black hole in the *Doctor Who* universe is home-made (except, maybe, perhaps, the Eye of Harmony - if that's *not* the same one as Omega's star, which most sensible people now think). You can speculate on why that is for days - we've suggested at least one idea in these books, namely that at some point it became necessary to slow down the universe's expansion. (As we've said, the observed Red Shift gives a figure that cannot be right according to all the other available data. So either Hubble's Constant isn't as constant as it should be or absolutely everything else is wrong.) In theory, one might could cross the beams of two powerful lasers to create micro-singularities, but these wouldn't last long enough to be noticeable (see 4.9, "The Evil of the Daleks" for some frantic attempts to use this to cover an embarrassing line of dialogue). This in itself allows BBC Wales to write K9 out of *The Sarah Jane Adventures*, so let's not discount it completely. Much of the most exciting work in this field was later discredited, and we have only inferential evidence that Cygnus X1 is indeed a black hole, although a lot of work went into figuring out what else it might be.

Nevertheless, the simple fact that *Doctor Who* writers had not only the opportunity but the means to use something from *real* science before any other series, accurately and dramatically (as opposed to picking between the two as usual) makes this period special. By the time we get to "The Deadly Assassin", of course, black holes have become all-purpose means to make space / time shenanigans seem legitimate and scary, with Rassilon's journey being told like Moses climbing Mt Sinai. However, as a symbol of Gallifrey's sovereignty over time, the idea that the Eye of Harmony is *the* black hole, from the Big Bang, is very potent. Unlike the Time Lords by this stage.

• *Omega.* Considered legendary by the Time Lords, and even the Doctor admits to honouring him as a hero. As a solar engineer [see "Remembrance of the Daleks" for more on how this was done; the Doctor here refers to Omega as '*the* solar engineer', perhaps denoting a formalised office], Omega made time-travel possible for the Time Lords by turning a star into a black hole, something which he claims happened 'thousands of years' ago. [23.4, "The Ultimate Foe", suggests millions. Either Omega has lost track of time or it just doesn't pass in the same way for him, which is entirely possible. In fact, it would unavoidable *that* close to an event horizon.] It was his duty to 'find and create' the power-source to give the Time Lords the energy they needed, but it was always going to be a dangerous mission and he was lost in the supernova he created [which then turned into the black hole, apparently]. According to the Doctor, he's been revered ever since. The Doctor also suggests that Omega could 'resume' a place on the High Council, meaning that the High Council pre-dates the Time Lords.

In fact Omega survived the mission, and now exists inside a realm of anti-matter inside a black hole. He constructed this world through his own will, turning the power of the black hole's singularity to his own ends, with the result being that can create solid objects out of nothing. [It's not explained how Omega's brain and body survived the black hole for long enough to allow his will to build his new world, nor does anybody explain what anti-matter has got to do with black holes. See also **What Does Anti-Matter Do?** under 13.2, "Planet of Evil".] Omega is incapable of leaving his realm without another mind to keep it stable, and he seems to need a Time Lord to do the job. Here Omega suggests that his brothers only became Time Lords *after* his sacrifice. [But even before then, his people must have possessed greater-than-normal mental powers, or he wouldn't need another Time Lord to take over from him.] He cannot even create a being with such a consciousness to preserve his realm as he departs.

Omega primarily wants revenge on the Time Lords for abandoning him, believing that they should have made him a "god". Constant exposure to the singularity has a corrosive effect due to the acceleration of the particles in the 'light-stream', hence the mask he wears, but in fact there's no physical substance under his armour and his will is all that's left. The 'dark side' of his mind can telepathically wrestle the Doctor, appearing in this psychic sparring-match as something bald and hideous. [What does the Second Doctor see when the Third Doctor is fighting Omega's 'dark side'? Do both antagonists disappear into a dreamscape? If so, is Omega connected to the Matrix? He might be, if 20.1, "Arc of Infinity" is to make any gesture towards sense.]

Omega somehow recognises the two Doctors in his world as being the same individual, and knows about the High Council's Laws of Time even though he presumably left the universe before they were devised. He also appears to know about terrestrial mythology, describing himself as the 'Atlas' of his world. [Prometheus is another parallel; see **Where Does This Come From?** and also Rassilon's fate in "The Five Doctors".]

It amuses Omega to use the Doctor as the instrument of his revenge, as if he's aware of either the Doctor's strained relations with his people or his future. [Again, Rassilon in "The Five Doctors" seems also to have foreknowledge of both the Doctor and the Master. Unlike "Arc of Infinity", this isn't wickedness against the Doctor per se.]

The Non-Humans

• *Gel-Guards.* [Never named as such on screen, and the spelling varies according to which source you use.] Omega can dispatch lumps of anti-matter from his own realm into the "normal" universe, sending them along a stream of faster-than-light 'compressed light', although he states that these organisms can exist in either the world of matter or the world of anti-matter without the usual colossal explosion. The anti-matter splodge on Earth apparently has some limited intelligence, and has been scanning Earth [and presumably many other planets] for a Time Lord. Anything targeted by the anti-matter can be transported into Omega's world, something the First Doctor calls a 'time-bridge', though everything snaps back to its original location when the realm is destroyed.

Objects entering Omega's realm are converted into anti-matter [and so is the TARDIS interior, which is presumably in another dimension]. The entity seems to home in on the Doctor's mental energy, as it takes people and places that have a vague trace. However, it also processes the first conscious being it encounters (Mr Ollis). It's eventually re-enforced by almost-humanoid lumps of jelly, each one with a single eye in the middle of its forehead and pincers that function as energy weapons. Omega also uses these creatures to guard his palace [simple humanoid shapes seem easier for his will to maintain than proper "people" - and are certainly easier to mass-produce than the Ergon from "Arc of Infinity"]. These hubba-bubba nightmares burble as they move.

History

• *Dating.* [Probably early 1974. See **What's the UNIT Timeline?** under 8.5, "The Daemons".]

Dr. Tyler suggests that Britain's space research isn't as well-funded as NASA's [but have NASA got a man on Mars?], his cosmic ray monitoring device being the most sophisticated this side of Cape Kennedy. The box is marked 'Wessex University' [so it may be that body's space research which isn't NASA standard[98]]. Houston has recently put up a 'space monitor', and the Cold War still seems to be [back] on, with Tyler referring to 'Yanks' and 'the Other Lot'.

Dr. Tyler's research balloon lands at a wildlife sanctuary at Minsbridge, England. [Where the locals - or at least Mr and Mrs Ollis - have a generic "rustic" accent that comes and goes depending on which universe they're in. Assuming this is a thinly-disguised Slimbridge, it suggests that UNIT HQ is in Gloucestershire or thereabouts. On the other hand, there's a 'Mins*mere* fairly close to Cromer, on the other side of the country. Logically a portmanteau of the two would be in the middle, roughly where our first guess of UNIT's base was, around Bray. However, 'Wessex' suggests the former far more clearly (see also 11.1, "The Time Warrior").]

Additional Sources The antagonist's name being a Greek letter follows the lead of *The Making of Doctor Who* (1972 edition), which was, in its day, the only guide to *Doctor Who* available in the shops and therefore a comfort to a generation. The catalogue of the Doctor's adventures in *The Making...* is presented as a transcript from the Doctor's trial, in which his Time Lord name is given as a pseudo-mathematical series of Greek symbols. Specifically, the Doctor's name is (brace yourself as we now answer a question that vexed schoolchildren for generations): $\Theta^3 \Sigma X^2$. This trend, begun in the book and put on screen in "The Three Doctors", eventually taken as read in Baker & Martin's last joint *Who* script "The Armageddon Factor" (16.6). Drax in that story calls him 'Feet', and the Doctor himself later claims that 'Theta Sigma' was his 'nickname' at school. (See 25.2, "The Happiness Patrol", and also "The Five Doctors" for more on Old High Gallifreyan.)

As with "The War Games" and the novelisation of "Terror of the Autons" (8.1) before it, this book claims that the Doctor's fate - had he been found guilty - was both execution and removal from the Time Lords' records. This is far more in keeping with their later, quasi-Soviet way of handling things than the usual fate in the novels of the time, to have your "life-stream" reversed.

The Analysis

Where Does This Come From? People cite supposed influences for this story as diverse as *The Wizard of Oz*, Harry Harrison's *Deathworld* books (see 14.4, "Face of Evil" for what happened when someone who'd actually *read* the books had a go) and Ingmar Bergman's film *The Seventh Seal*. But right or wrong, these alleged sources are a side-issue.

What Bob Baker and Dave Martin intuitively grasped is that the Time Lords needed an equal and opposite force to make the Doctor's actions important enough to tip (or preserve) the balance. This conception of paired opposites extends into the sequence most often criticised in this story, where the Third Doctor gets to wrestle with 'the dark side' of Omega's will. Think about it: if the equal-and-opposite force has within *himself* equal-and-opposite forces, it makes the symbolism of an anti-Time Lord agency redundant. It *is*, however, in keeping with both of the Baker-Martin stories so far (and into the future, notably "The Armageddon Factor") and the overall trend within fantasy fiction of the time.

What eventually emerges on screen, however, is the residue of various attempts to take *Doctor Who* out of the rut of attempting *Star Trek* with BBC facilities, and moving it back into an older British tradition of symbolic fantasy for kids. The first draft (as discussed in **The Lore**) explicitly invokes not just Narnia but Lewis Carroll, as well as L Frank Baum. It also had a malignant echo of *Peter Pan*, with the death-world occupied by figures from various mythologies - just as in the original stage-play's version of Neverland.

Now, as we examined in Volumes II and VI, the main thread in many such stories is a tendency to think of two opposing forces as representing

Good and Evil, and to assume that the one you're following is good. When many of these stories end, it's by the protagonist realising that both sides need the other to exist, *or* that the battle was more like a dance and the two sides are part of a greater whole. Remember that when Baker and Martin previously wrote for the Master, he was motivated by Axos holding his TARDIS, not any overt malice (8.3, "The Claws of Axos"). In England's literary tradition, there's an obvious touchstone for this...

John Milton's day-job was reading everything being printed in England to see what people were saying about the new, King-less government (not so much to stop it as just to keep tabs). When he got home from a hard day at the chapbooks, he wrote *Paradise Lost*, and made the Biblical story work as a faux-classical blank-verse epic. This, he hoped, would get the general reader to see how human intellect was actually part of God's plan, rather than going against it as the regime's opponents (especially the Catholic ones overseas, who were thought to be harbouring the nation's enemies) claimed to believe. He made plain that Lucifer's fall was part of a celestial masterplan to make humans use their free will properly. If the Devil had a point, this was - somehow - better because people were actively thinking about it and then *choosing* God, rather than just opting for the creator because he's the only game in town. After all, if God wanted yes-men, he would have made sheep the dominant life-form.

The trouble is that later generations of readers thought Milton did too good a job. God doesn't get a speaking part (for obvious theological reasons, this wouldn't have crossed Milton's mind), and his emissary Raphael refuses to give straight answers to basic questions such as, "Does the Sun go around us or what?" So Lucifer, the fallen angel, God's original right-hand-man, is the *only* person who says anything memorable. Added to this disconnect, the account in the first Book of the creation of the capital city of Hell, Pandaemonium, is one of the most impressive accounts of how something literally unimaginable can be evoked.

A century later, William Blake used the fact that the establishment (all of whom lumped rebels like him in the same bucket as the "misguided" government of Milton's time) referred to him as a "devil" to invert the whole vocabulary of the state, and thereby pointed out what is *now* the majority view. Milton, Blake said, "was of the Devil's party but did not know it". In other words, the version of religion being practiced by the Church of England relied on the kind of blind obedience that actually went *against* God's will. A repressive church, in Blake's view, is worse than none at all. And here we can't help but note that Omega's mask is flagrantly Blake-like (although *which* engraving it most resembles is a matter of personal choice; the consensus is that it's closest to the face of the fallen tyrant Nebuchadnezzar[99]). Even though the script asked for the mask to look Etruscan.

Of course, not every Romantic rebel was brave enough to identify openly with even a fictional devil. Shelley used the nearest available Classical substitute: Prometheus, the Titan who stole fire from the gods of Olympus and gave it to mankind. As punishment, Zeus chained him to a rock in Tartarus and got eagles to chew his innards, daily (the internal organs regenerated at night). Then they gave Pandora a box to keep the humans occupied.

What we're getting as is that these figures are in the vocabulary for self-dramatising outcasts, the sort of people who would later be called "Byronic" and would provide us with ambiguous figures such as Dracula, Oscar Wilde, the Phantom of the Opera, Heathcliffe, assorted Bond villains and the Doctor.

Milton intended "Better to reign in Hell than serve in Heaven" as a statement of Lucifer's hubris, but it struck a chord. However much Stephen Thorne's performance makes us think of Omega as a moustache-twirling villain, the script makes character sympathetic, something that *wouldn't* be true of such a figure in a *Star Trek* story (think of "The Squire of Gothos", for instance). In fact, it's possible to imagine this story reconfigured slightly to make Omega a kind of King Arthur, sleeping in a timeless tomb until the Time Lords' greatest need (see, again, "The Five Doctors"). You never know, we still might - ideally he'd be played by Paul McGann.

And as we mentioned in the first volume, there's a strong tinge of Hans Anderson about Omega, especially the story "The Scholar and his Shadow" (beloved of Jungian analysts) and - this will freak out anyone who's only familiar with the abhorrent Disney version - "The Little Mermaid". As we've seen, Baker and Martin's outline for "The Three Doctors" gave the name of the antagonist as "Ohm", which is an almost-obvious joke. This point would be easier to argue if the *name* "Who"

were actually used in the series itself. (See **Is His Name Really 'Who'?** under 3.10, "The War Machines". We should also point out that some have suggested that there's a pun involving Transcendental Meditation - "Ohm" and "Aum" being alternative, mainly American, attempts to spell what we write as "Om", the various meanings of which were occasionally stretched to suggest yet *another* Buddhist subtext[100].) In the final script, of course, it's changed to "Omega". (See **Additional Sources**. More physics-fun can be had if you remember that Ludwig Boltzmann first floated the idea of the Heat Death of the Universe. He wrote a grim equation we'll examine a lot in Volumes IV and V. His version had the letter W as the number of unobservable states, but everyone else used Ω.)

We'd also better mention that everything in this story about black holes and anti-matter was sort-of accepted fact. As we'll see (**How Does Anti-Matter Work?** under 13.2, "Planet of Evil"), there were lots of bonkers ideas about this sort of thing then. black holes had an instant appeal, the way lasers almost immediately caught the public imagination in the early 60s. Baker and Martin read an article in the *Times* about it, and this was *also* read by the writers of the serial "Vidar and the Ice Monsters" in the Saturday-morning kid's show *Outa Space!* (See also 11.2, "Invasion of the Dinosaurs" and the essay with the next story.) In their story, done in the old *Bleep and Booster* tradition of drawings with rostrum cameras moving around and actors speaking the dialogue, a new Ice Age in the future (see, naturally, 5.3, "The Ice Warriors") was threatening the end of the world, but a rebel hero found a cave full of alien intelligences who looked like dinosaurs and had been here before. They thought of a way to pull the ice back with black holes over the poles. This gives you some idea of the appeal these things had for British ten-year-olds. Books about these then-largely hypothetical objects replaced *Did Ancient Atlantean Astronauts Create The Archers?* on the bookshelves. We could even stretch a point and say that the thunder whenever Omega loses his temper is an allusion to the way King Lear's madness is somehow connected to the exterior storm in Shakespeare's play, but there's a whole tradition of such obvious symbolism in literature; the Victorians called it "the Pathetic Fallacy".

One last thing... as Dicks claimed that starting Season Ten with a team-up was a sad and fannish idea forced on him (see **The Lore**), so he leaned toward downplaying it and originally asked for a story about the Doctor and Jo in a realm of the dead, where the first two Doctors sacrifice themselves to let Our Hero escape. Had a story like this been screened, would Letts be proclaiming it as an existential / Buddhist parable?

Things That Don't Make Sense Let's get this straight. Omega wants revenge against the Time Lords for abandoning him, and he's found a way of draining off their energy and bringing them to their knees. But while this scheme is in progress, he abruptly decides to surrender his power in the interest of leaving his anti-matter realm. How, then, does he plan on exacting his vengeance once he's regressed to being just him? If he's out to *destroy* the Time Lords, he'd best finish the job before returning to our universe; if he wants to conquer them, well, yielding his ability to hold their energy to ransom perhaps isn't the best way of going about it.

But then, Omega's captivity doesn't make a great deal of sense either, since he's capable of sending gel-guards all the way to Earth with specific instructions to find the Doctor, yet has never tried sending a request for help to anybody in the whole of space and time. At the very least, couldn't he have abducted someone from the Time Lord planet millennia ago? Furthermore, this story requires Omega (who's stuck in a tiny home-brewed cosmos since the Dawn of Time) to know a great deal about the Doctor, yet not have the faintest idea what his previous incarnations looked like.

Later, it's agreed upon that *both* Doctors will take Omega's place. All right, wouldn't that cause several temporal shenanigans, if the Troughton Doctor can't complete his lifetime to create the Pertwee one? Even more curiously, it appears that Omega hasn't taken his hat off in several hundred years and is unaware that his body's not there any more. It's also strange that Omega acts as if he needs the Doctors' help to do so, even though he whips it off easily enough a few moments later.

And why *can't* Omega create a conscious-but-obedient life-form to hold the door open for him when he leaves? Surely a moderately bright psychedelic bloodhound can't be any less effort than thirty or so gel-guards? Unless Omega is mentally controlling all of these, but then you have to wonder about the whole "Oops! I ate Mr Ollis" thing that got the story started in the first place.

Speaking of which...

When a man disappears in 1500 acres of countryside, Dr Tyler gets immediately onto UNIT, not the police or the man's wife (who later says there's 'nothing unusual' about her husband going off for the day). What if he'd just gone for a pee in the bushes? And yet, the Brigadier feels the need to personally take charge of this investigation. Maybe Chinn ("The Claws of Axos") had a point about UNIT wasting taxpayers' money. (Incidentally, a sign claims that Ollis manages a 'Wild Life Sanctuary', not a "Wildlife Sanctuary", raising the prospect of an altogether more exciting kind of *Doctor Who* adventure.)

It's debatable whether Bob Baker and Dave Martin actually *meant* this story to have the feel of a Christmas pantomime, but either way, it's a story full of characters so stupid that they seem to be asking the audience to shout "behind you!" or "don't pull the rope!" at them. Sergeant Benton is left alone to guard a highly volatile cosmic space-pizza that the Doctor desperately wants to keep calm, but then he petulantly throws a gum-wrapper at it as soon as nobody's looking. And as we've suggested, the Brig seems not to have realised that he's been in a series about a time-traveller for the last five years. [Arguably, this is proof that the UNIT stories are set in the near future, as he's apparently auditioning for *Rentaghost* a year before the pilot episode.]

Then there's Dr Tyler, a man with no motives in life other than to do whatever's convenient for the plot. He shows no sign of activity for an episode and a half, and then - when the script under-runs by a couple of minutes - changes his entire personality by making a sudden attempt to escape from Omega's palace, just so the gel-guards can chase after him for a while. Where, in fact, does he think he's going to go? (No wonder Tyler himself comments about this little side-adventure: 'That was a bit of a waste of time, wasn't it?') Despite his being a high-ranking scientist with an obvious interest in extreme physics, plus a habit of finding everything he sees absolutely fascinating, Tyler just walks out of the TARDIS saying, 'Well, I think I've seen enough for one day, thanks', as soon as the story no longer needs him.

If the hunter-seeker pizza can travel faster than light, then why does it hide in the drains and crawl around so slowly? Why not zoom off to Minsbridge and cut out the middleman? And why does the Third Doctor hope to use the TARDIS to 'lure' the hunter-seeker away from Earth?

Remember, the TARDIS isn't working until story's end. [It's possible he intends to do his 'galactic yo-yo' stunt - see "The Claws of Axos" - as a means of confusing it. The short hop that the "disabled" TARDIS performs in Omega's realm, at least, might be a result of the goofy laws of physics there.] We also have to ask what exactly the Gel-Guards contribute to the scheme. If Mr Ollis is fair game for a confused disco-lighting hunter-seeker, then UNIT's brave lads should also be applicable for the one-way trip over the rainbow. So why does the energy-splodge instead summon these *It's A Knockout* rejects to come and get shot at by the squaddies from central casting?

The Time Lords, possibly *the* most technologically advanced race in existence, require a quick briefing on what a black hole actually is. This would seem odd no matter what, but it makes even less sense the more we discover more of their past. (See "The Deadly Assassin" and accompanying essay.) Moreover, Baker and Martin bust a gut getting their terminology right, and then give us stuff about 'a flash of kinetic energy'.

Whilst getting energy from chucking things into a black hole is possible (desirable, even) and has kept physicists happy for years with dreams of unlimited power in one form or another, making a black hole turn into a supernova by throwing an "anti-recorder" at it is just daft. You'd get a burst of energy equivalent to the mass of two recorders times the square of the speed of light - enough to blow up New York, but not a whole dimension. And considering how long Time Lords live, it's a puzzler as to why everyone's so pleased that a source of energy that will last forever has been replaced by one that will last about a few hundred thousand years. [Dr Science, who's been vaguely impressed by this story so far, offers the observation that for a star to be big enough to become a black hole, the mass must be too big for a supernova *and* for light to get away. If only half the mass were inside this universe, and it was only the smallest possible black hole, then the finale just about works - even if the sudden accessibility of a lot more energy in the Universe would speed up entropy just a bit. Either way, the High Council should put the champagne on ice, and perhaps not celebrate that they've just lost an energy source that could've serviced their needs until the end of time.]

In episode three, the TARDIS has the amazing ability to display itself on its own scanner. The same episode provides some of the best opportunities in the entire series for glimpsing that the back "interior" of the police box is just a wooden wall. The door to the Doctor's lab is open when it's transported away from Earth, but mysteriously locks itself once it's transferred to an alien world [more proof that natural laws really *don't* apply there]. Later the anti-matter draws UNIT HQ into Omega's universe, but leaves behind a flat stretch of ground with no foundations, disconnected plumbing or gaps in the grass. And can anybody explain exactly *how* the Second Doctor's recorder slips into the TARDIS force-field generator like that? Or why it materializes with a TARDIS groaning noise, in episode one, before the Doctor himself? (Here we're glossing over the fact that the recorder is in plain sight, just lying there on the console, the entire time that it's "arriving".) As things start to look bad, the Brigadier suggests that the Second Doctor 'consult his superiors', i.e. the Time Lords. Thanks for the info-dump, but why does he say it now? He doesn't know about the various communications / help from Gallifrey, and he's never advised contacting the Time Lords for aid during all the crises with the powerful entities such as the Axons, Azal and such.

Suddenly, in episode two, Tyler knows that the source of the 'space lightning' is a black hole. [On the advice of our Scientific Advisor, we recommend that anyone with a smattering of physics puts his or her fingers in his or her ears and sings the yodelly bit from *Hocus Pocus* by Focus while Tyler is drawing equations in the sand and going from $E=MC2$ to 'I must have been travelling faster than light' by way of concluding that acceleration is the same as gravity.] Suddenly, in episode three, the President knows Omega is behind all this. Suddenly, in episode four, the First Doctor can come and go across the Event Horizon whenever he feels like being condescending to someone.

In the anti-matter universe, the Brigadier and company drive Bessie from Omega's lair to UNIT HQ - the two Doctors resort to running, yet only arrive a couple of moments later. And while it might be churlish to say it, you can hear everyone's footsteps in the finale, even after they've "disappeared" up Omega's magic steam column on their way back to Earth. *Really* nitpicking now, but how come the credit says "BBC 1973" when the whole thing was made in 1972, and the first episode went out 30th of December that year?

Critique No other story, not even "The Daleks" (1.2), has such a clear divide between those who saw the first and (in those days) unrepeatable broadcast / experience, and those who got to know it through the subsequent repeats, video and DVD releases. For anyone who's blasé about multi-Doctor reunion stories, this a silly run-around with naff monsters, a panto villain and actors doing their party-pieces; in which everyone's either a one-note caricature or woefully out of character. The sets are shoddy - even if you generously interpret Omega's plight as causing a world that's as insubstantial as a dream, a couple of the effects look like they're trying to *homage* the Hartnell era's more risible moments. The dialogue revisits the excruciating attempts at "ordinary bloke" speech from "The Mutants" (9.4) and Dudley Simpson's music is taking it less seriously than the previous story ("The Time Monster").

But for anyone who saw it on BBC1 in 1972-3, there was a giddy thrill of the sheer unprecedented nerve of the thing. The bickering between Doctors was implicit in the title (although a lot of people were curious as to how this would be achieved), but it was the scale of the story - with even the Time Lords up against it because of a figure that even the Doctor found intimidating and legendary - that made the initial impact. The way that the Time Lords need to explain to one another what a black hole is gives the game away, even if that detail has become an amusing period piece. But for most of us, this was honestly the first we'd heard of them (indeed, science programmes for another five years used "The Three Doctors" as the point-of-entry for any features on singularities). In much the same way, let's not forget, Goldfinger had to introduce Bond and the audience to lasers in 1964.

That *frisson* of real science underlying all the fantasy trappings is what almost every *Doctor Who* story had been trying to get right since 1963, and would never quite manage again. Alas, the story loses a lot without it. Perhaps appropriately, the image from *The Wizard of Oz* of peering behind the curtain and spying a shabby huckster pretending to be a magician is what happens here. If you go in knowing how the series progressed after this, and what the story winds up doing, then the on-screen result is flat. We're all so used to this story, we can join in with the atrocious dialogue ('Liberty Hall, Dr Tyler', 'Ho-ly Mo-ses, whass that?', 'I'm fairly certain that's Cromer' and so on).

That being the case, it escapes our notice that the aliens have come *straight to UNIT HQ*, penetrating the one place that's been inviolate in every previous invasion. Simultaneously, the Time Lords are exposed and vulnerable in ways we'll never see again. Remember: the humiliation in "The Invasion of Time" (15.6) was that of the gnarled and crumbly society we'd seen about a year earlier (in 14.3, "The Deadly Assassin"). But the Time Lords prior to "The Three Doctors" were abstract and seemingly omnipotent. Nothing like this crisis had ever happened before, and the only hope of saving themselves and the beings they guard was to break their own laws.

This sets us up for what is, by the story's own logic, a one-off transgression of the Laws of Time - something that sets the Doctors up for a lot of set-piece rows. Unfortunately, even these are a con: this isn't the Troughton we got for 124 episodes in the 60s, but a half-remembered mulch of gimmicks and Victoriana ('I may call you Jo, mayn't I?'). He's a "potty professor" instead of the avuncular wolf-in-sheep's-clothing he'd played before. Even this fails to remove anything from Troughton's performance (by definition, meeting his future self was the *one* thing that could never happen during this Doctor's "spell", so it's yet another facet to an ever-changing persona), but in this and subsequent reunions, he plays 'The Second Doctor'. He's a Time Lord dressed as a tramp, and not "The New Doctor Who" as he'd played in the past.

Similarly, the one thing that the original Doctor would *never* have done is sit by and watch. The only real precedents for this are "The Chase", in which he spends much of episode one testing his time-telly; and "The Tenth Planet" (4.2), when he knows perfectly well how history must unfold, and is very active in making sure nobody jeopardises it (when he's conscious, that is). So the idea of the Doctor watching his own adventures on some kind of monitor is a pretext for this most impatient of Doctors to be out of the action. By which we mean to say: this is emphatically a Pertwee story with cameos.

Ranged against the Doctors is a being of unimaginable power, whose abilities we're, er, left to imagine. The programme-makers don't overburden Omega with the trappings of god-like majesty. This is, alas, the main weak-point of the story. The sense of fatigue with imagining a whole universe should have been reinforced in the dialogue, not left for the novelisation. We're given a vague inkling that the gel-guards are extruded from the walls, but we never actually see it. We have a notion that the wilderness is almost notional rather than physical, but what we see is a quarry filmed with a tilted camera.

What we *don't* get is a sense that Omega is the Doctor's true antithesis. He's pure thought, whereas the Doctor we know now is almost pure action. With Hartnell's forcible removal to a similarly constrained state of intangible willpower, the apparent idea to have Omega as a counterforce to a) the Time Lords and then b) the Doctor is weakened. In theory, and to many of those watching at the time, it's a beautiful allegorical idea. But watching it again now, even Stephen Thorne's barnstorming and scenery-chewing is inadequate to the task of making the idea work on that budget.

But what do you want out of a *Doctor Who* story anyway? If you're watching this to see how multi-Doctor interactions work (with regard to Blinovitch and temporal paradoxes), or for details of Time Lord society, you aren't going to get a lot out of this. If you're a fan of the UNIT era and want action-packed adventure, then the gel-guards' assault won't going to float your boat the way "The Ambassadors of Death" (7.3) might. But on the plus-side, there is nostalgia here for lapsed Hartnell and Troughton viewers who thought they'd outgrown the show. The Brigadier's memory is wiped and Jo becomes thicker than ever - but only dedicated viewers would know, and besides, talking in detail about earlier Pertwee stories would be pointless in this situation. The characters are pared down so that new viewers can start here (or rejoin). At the time, we liked our emotional scenes downplayed - the Brigadier's half-embarrassed salute to the Doctors tells us more than hugs or tears could, the same way we would all rather have watched *Brief Encounter* than *Love Story* (unless we needed a laugh).

So for people who want to watch something that 12 million people loved in 1973 (and half that amount nine years later, on a minority channel) and that broke new ground for the series, "The Three Doctors" is there to be taken on its own terms. Criticise it all you want for falling short of Baker and Martin's ambitions, or for that ambition flying in the face of all reason and experience. Just *don't* blame it for not being what nobody wanted back then. Sometimes you need a three-course meal, sometimes beans on toast is exactly the right thing. This is what Saturday teatimes were for in 1973, and it can be a slightly guilty pleasure now.

The Facts

Written by Bob Baker and Dave Martin. Directed by Lennie Mayne. Viewing figures: 9.6 million, 10.8 million 8.8 million, 11.9 million. You have to go back to the Hartnell era for ratings like that. (Episode five of 2.5, "The Web Planet", in fact.)

Supporting Cast Patrick Troughton, William Hartnell (Dr. Who), Rex Robinson (Dr. Tyler), Roy Purcell (President of the Council), Laurie Webb (Mr. Ollis), Clyde Pollitt (Chancellor), Graham Leaman (Time Lord), Denys Palmer (Corporal Palmer), Stephen Thorne (Omega).

Working Titles "The Black Hole".

Cliffhangers The Third Doctor leaves the safety of the TARDIS to face the anti-matter organism in the UNIT lab, but Jo insists on running after him and the creature causes them both to vanish in a flash of 'kinetic energy'; the whole of UNIT HQ disappears from the landscape, and hurtles into the black hole; locked in telepathic combat in a featureless black limbo, the Doctor finds himself losing to the dark side of Omega's mind and slowly being strangled to death.

What Was in the Charts? "Crazy Horses", The Osmonds; "Mouldy Old Dough", Lieutenant Pigeon; "Crocodile Rock", Elton John; "Jean Genie", David Bowie.

The Lore

[Before going any further, let's get onto the same page with the recording order. "Carnival of Monsters" was made immediately after "The Time Monster", then they had a holiday. The next batch began filming in September, with "Frontier in Space", then "The Three Doctors" in the run-up to Christmas. After the hols, they went ahead with "Planet of the Daleks", "The Green Death" and "The Time Warrior". That was May, then Letts and Dicks concentrated on *Moonbase 3* for a while.]

• With hindsight, it seems like the world and his mum had asked whether we'd ever see a team-up story with the three actors who'd played the

Doctor. Terrance Dicks wasn't too struck on the idea, but suddenly he asked Bob Baker and Dave Martin to furnish him with just that. In the version he told the writers, it was a visit by an elderly gentleman he later realised was William Hartnell (and had to chase after, once he twigged that he'd accidentally snubbed the man to whom he owed his job) that led to the idea being floated.

As we'll see, Hartnell barely knew what day it was and was virtually immobile, so this is very implausible. Why Dicks had to excuse his *volte face* is unclear: the idea is rather less gimmicky than pairing a new arch-villain with the Autons, or bringing back the Daleks to fight UNIT ("Terror of the Autons"; 9.1, "Day of the Daleks"). As a season-opening ratings-grabber, it was entirely excusable. It also allowed them to eliminate the inherited format of the Doctor being exiled to Earth in the present-day.

Anyway, Dicks asked the writing team to think of ideas along the lines of "The Mutants", and left it to Letts to find out if Hartnell and Troughton were available and willing. (This is in February.) Troughton was willing but busy; Hartnell was available and, despite his public misgivings about the direction the series had taken under Letts, enthusiastic. The only stumbling block was Pertwee, who was so possessive of the series that getting him to appear with the Daleks took a lot of coercion. However, so long as it was obvious who was Top Doc, he didn't object in principle.

This was March, during recording of "The Mutants", and Dicks sent a pre-release copy of *The Making of Doctor Who* to give the Bristol Boys a few pointers. So it was agreed then; Bob and Dave would write the first story of the new season, which would be recorded third, and the three Doctors would team up to fight something or other too powerful for any of them and Pertwee's Doctor would win.

Anyone who can't see at least three flaws with this plan should probably re-read this book from the start.

• Problem No. 1: Baker and Martin had too many ideas. The original story was for the Doctors to meet in the realm of the dead, but Dicks deemed this too scary. Note, however, episode two - in which the Chancellor says the Doctor is dead and Jo wakes up believing this. (She does this a lot.) They would be whisked to an alternate dimension through a gateway in a graveyard, and meet an army of mythological beings who worked for Death.

The BBC bigwigs weren't into the whole cemetery thing (how times change), so instead the Doctor and Jo were sent to limbo by an accident in the lab (trying to fix the TARDIS, most likely). The Doctor's two previous selves were trapped there and would team up to fight Death (who was playing games with the President of the Time Lords in full Ingmar Bergman style), and the earlier two would sacrifice themselves to distract Death so the Doctor and Jo could get away. The fate of the Universe rests on this conflict, as Death is in charge of an alliance of evil beings who are vying with the Time Lords for control (see 16.1, "The Ribos Operation" for a similar idea).

Other amendments were that the anti-Time Lord agency had fungal servants. As late as mid-September, the story included Jamie as the Second Doctor's foil. (He would've had a mild flirtation with Jo, as they teamed up to keep their Doctors in line.)

Dicks stated in his next letter to Bob 'n' Dave (late July) that the Brigadier should get a more meaty part in this story, exploring his character and giving him more to do than explain the plot and order people to shoot at things. (That's not *exactly* what we got. Never mind...) It appears that the villain split himself into three facets (one per Doctor) at one stage - or possibly into one good, one evil and one neutral. By this time, the writers had seen the item in the *Sunday Times* (16th of July) about black holes and "Cosmic Censorship" (see this story's essay for more on that).

About a month later, the scripts were submitted with Omega as a Time Lord version of the Wizard of Oz, projecting an image more powerful than he really was. Most of Jamie's dialogue was now given to Benton, although the team hoped to have a final, "Where have you been?" scene as the Second Doctor rejoins his own timestream. The details about the black hole's ability to amplify his will - and the notion that this enabled him to resolve matter and anti-matter - gave the script a fantasy feel but a hard-science justification. So this time, Baker and Martin's fertile minds were working *with* the programme's limitations, end of Problem No. 1.

• Problem No. 2: William Hartnell. Although he had responded favourably to Letts' call, the fact remained that he was sporadically lucid and had days when he didn't recall ever being in the series, days when he blamed dark forces in the BBC for kicking him out and days when he just sat in a wheelchair glaring at people. His wife, Heather

Hartnell, suggested that even if he was on form, the stress of going into a studio to record would be too much. Baker and Martin had enjoyed writing the bickering dialogue for the three-personned Time Lord (confusingly, they refer to Pertwee as 'Doctor One' and Hartnell as 'Doctor Three') and given them all something to do - perhaps wary of having them together too much in case of personality clashes in rehearsals. As they were now too busy to rewrite the whole thing, they permitted Dicks to do whatever needed to be done. A first pass cut down the old Doctor's activity, but had him on hand to help.

By this stage it was becoming apparent that Jamie would not be around for even the re-drafted cameo at the end. (*Emmerdale Farm* was just beginning and in those early days Frazer Hines' character, Joe Sugden, was at the heart of the story, so the timetables clashed.) For a while it was thought they could get Wendy Padbury back as Zoe, but the general mood - and certainly Pertwee's feeling - was that the emphasis should be on the series as it was in 1973. Dicks was told to do a second rewrite to place the Hartnell Doctor on film, in a celestial sedan chair. (In fact three of these were made, from Perspex and wood, suggesting that the effects requirements were specified before the last rewrite.)

A few other things were amended along the way: Daunton Tyler's whimsical Yorkshire phrases (and silly first name) were trimmed, along with the Doctor's rude outbursts, a scene where Omega feeds the captive humans and the Second Doctor's envious examination of his later self's clothes. Later in the story the more obvious padding crept in, such as Tyler's futile escape-bid and the Doctor's conjuring trick. (Manning still has the flowers.)

• Although the team-up idea had been floated a while back, Pertwee was seemingly unaware that the story, still called "The Black Hole", would be made until the script arrived through his letterbox. This would have been in late September, just after the BBC announced the story still claiming that Jamie would be in it, and when contracts were being issued for Hartnell and Troughton.

• This brings us to Problem No. 3: the timetable. This story was to be made after "Frontier in Space", and scheduled to finish on 1st of November. Filming was supposed to start for "The Three Doctors" on 6th of November and recording would end on 12th of December...

eighteen days before transmission of the first episode. As you'll recall, they began the year under similar tight deadlines through the efforts of director Lennie Mayne. He was called in for this story too: he'd recently directed Troughton in *Doomwatch* and had a small cadre of actors he could rely on. (We'll see Rex Robinson a couple more times after Tyler, both in Mayne-directed stories.) The late filming of this story, necessitated by Patrick Troughton's many other work commitments, made this production more like a 1960s *Doctor Who* than had been planned.

• When the *Radio Times* cover of the start of Season Eight had featured Roger Delgado more prominently than the ostensible star, Pertwee had been put out. So when, for this year's debut, the three Doctors were photographed (some time in October), Letts saw to it that Pertwee's natural height advantage made him the focal point of all the publicity stills. However, when the rehearsals began, the other regulars were on tenterhooks to see how Troughton would get on with Pertwee, apparently unaware of the previous encounter at the photocall.

• Jim Acheson returned on costume design, and it seems was briefed to keep a hint of the original Time Lord "look" from "The War Games". (At this stage, though, they're fairly generic priest / senators.) He also had the job of making a lightweight metal-looking helmet for Omega; the design was Acheson's but the execution was Alistair Bowtell (see "The Mutants"). The look was inspired mainly by Grecian theatre masks.

• 6th of November was the tussle with what the script calls 'Omega's Champion' (namely Alan Chuntz in a rubber suit and mask), interspersed with Hartnell's scenes. The Doctor's dialogue was written on idiot-boards and delivered to camera. By all accounts, Hartnell was disorientated, but he was delighted to be working again on a series he'd loved. (Heather reported that he seemed to have been partially rejuvenated by the experience.) Nevertheless, he could only do brief moments of filming.

• The next day was the material at Mr Ollis' house (Summerfield Cottage) and the Minsbridge (Springwell Reservoir) and the beginning of the quarry shoot at Harefield - at a lime-works that is now, apparently, a lake. This was cold, wet and miserable, and Manning needed make-up applied to her legs to make them the right colour. (Baker and Martin scripts always seem to do this to her.)

It was at around this point that she decided to leave at the end of the transmission year, more for the work opportunities than just to stay warm. (On the whole she was having the time of her life, but worried that if she didn't leave soon, this would be her last job.)

• After a couple of days of this they returned to Summerfield to film the same house from behind (this was Hartnell's only location work). Troughton's insert for the Time Lords' monitor was also filmed at the lime-works (it's not a clip from 4.7, "The Macra Terror", as earlier guidebooks solemnly told us). The second day of the quarry shoot had seen the first use of the Gel-Guards (to much giggling from the assembled onlookers as they were taken from the van). Inside these were the usual Dalek operators, Murphy Grumbar, John Scott Martin et al. The blisters on the surface broke easily and often, with the operators unable to see where they were going and tripping over regularly.

• The last day of filming was at the YMCA in Denham (again nearby) which was UNIT HQ this time. With the still photos taken here, the model team were able to send UNIT beyond the blue event horizon during a two-day model shoot prior to recording (which also furnished the black hole, light beam and the anti-matter flash graphic, most of which had to appear on monitors at various times in the story).

• Rehearsals started on the following Wednesday. To keep a low profile, Troughton read a book on Transcendental Meditation between scenes, and the rest of the cast walked on eggshells for the first few minutes. His imprecise manner with the scripts threw Pertwee off; unused to improvising, Pertwee found his predecessor's advice ("it doesn't matter what we do, they're all watching the monsters") infuriating. He preferred to work from the scripted cues throughout, whilst Troughton said something *approximately* right in rehearsals until he'd got his marks down, and would then get word-perfect in studio. Apparently, an unscripted addition during the scene where they find the recorder in the force-field (something along the lines of "it's dark in here") caused friction. As Pertwee was the star, Troughton agreed to play it by the book. Nevertheless, as a consequence, their scenes together in "The Five Doctors" were kept to a minimum.

It was still hoped that Hartnell could do one scene on VT, probably the final debriefing to the President. (The lines the Prez says about Omega 'providing' once again seem to have been the First Doctor's originally.) Nicholas Courtney ad-libbed the 'Cromer' line, as well as his salute when leaving the Doctors behind.

• In order to preserve some sense of continuity, both designer Roger Liminton and soundmaker Dick Mills went back to the source for this story. The TARDIS set was rethought from photos of the Peter Brachaki design from 1963. (Hence the return of what are sometimes called "transporter pads": the drum-like ceiling fixtures, even though they pre-dated *Star Trek* by three years.) Liminton also re-used components from his previous story (10.2, "Carnival of Monsters", made five months earlier) for Omega's palace and the Time Lord hall.

• Both Graham Leaman and Clyde Pollitt, seen in the control room, had been senior Time Lords before (in "The War Games" and "Colony in Space", respectively). As the idea of regeneration hadn't really taken hold yet, except with regard to the Doctor, the re-casting could have been meant to indicate that these were the same people. We do know that Lennie Mayne had looked at "The War Games" in the run-up to this story's production, so it's probably not just an accident. The President was played by Roy Purcell, who'd been the chief warder at Stangmoor prison in "The Mind of Evil". It was decided very early on that Mike Yates would not be aboard the TARDIS; Richard Franklin was directing for the stage at the time.

• The anti-matter "scout" was a fun-fur rod-puppet (or, according to some sources, a feather-boa), subjected to grey-scale differentiation (i.e. shot in black and white with high contrast, so that the shades of grey become more distinct, on three levels instead of around twenty). Each shade was then given a false colour. This was one of the basic tricks used on *Top of the Pops* at the time, usually to distort the faces of pretty-boy Glam rockers. As you might guess, the humans' re-appearance in the UNIT lab was done by getting everyone to jump and cutting from the high-point.

• This story was recorded more or less an episode a day, on Mondays and Tuesdays. The small exceptions were that the corridor material for episode two was done with episode three, giving Pertwee and Manning a day off, and the Time Lord scenes for episodes three and four were done with episodes one and two, to avoid building the set twice. Dudley Simpson was able to get the orthodox music for the first two episodes recorded and dubbed a week before Christmas (i.e. a fortnight before transmission began) and did the other two the day after Boxing Day. Dubbing the sound effects (and synthesized portions of the score) was done over the two days after each music-dubbing session. The trailer included a different rendition of the theme tune, which we'll discuss in the next story's notes.

• In November 1973, David Bowie, under the influence of an incredible amount of recreational pharmacology, told *Rolling Stone* the plot of his "Ziggy Stardust" stage-show. Some have seen the maunderings of this stoned buffoon as reminiscent of the plot of this story, but anyone reading the popular-science journals (or just the *Sunday Times*) would have picked up stuff about antimatter, black holes and the like. Ziggy meeting multiple versions of himself, however, seems like our story. Almost. A bit. Bowie was in Britain when "The Three Doctors" was broadcast, recording *Aladdin Sane* (or at least, his body was physically present). The phone box on the back of the album isn't really much of a clue, though, no matter what people say. Now, if Hartnell had actually *said*, "Let all the children boogie"...

10.2: "Carnival of Monsters"

(Serial PPP, Four Episodes, 27th January - 17th February 1973.)

Which One is This? The blurb on the Target novelisation puts it best: 'The Doctor and Jo land on a cargo ship crossing the Indian Ocean in the year 1926... or so they think.' Everyone is running from rubber dinosaurs, but forgets about it twenty-five minutes later. Meanwhile, Jo is appalled that people *enjoy* watching her and the Doctor being chased around oversized electronics by giant rampaging caterpillars.

Firsts and Lasts The Doctor mentions the planet Metebelis 3 for the first time, and spends much of the next two years either trying to get there or regretting having been there. Given that for the first six years of his TV existence the Doctor had no control over the TARDIS at all (it took a stolen Dalek time machine just to get his first companions back to Earth, remember), this marks a new phase in the Doctor's existence: having a TARDIS that's *supposed* to work but doesn't quite.

Ian Marter - who goes on to play Harry Sullivan

in Seasons Twelve and Thirteen, and to write some of Target's best *Doctor Who* novelisations - makes his first appearance here as Handsome Young Officer Andrews on the *S. S. Bernice* (see 8.1, "Terror of the Autons" for his near-miss). Conversely, Brian Hodgson, maker of "special sounds" since the start, leaves to found his own company. He goes out with a bang, or rather a banshee - the Drashig scream still sends grown men scurrying for cover.

First appearance (out of several, what with various hallucinations and flashbacks) of the Drashigs, voracious caterpillar-like aliens which caught the imagination of anyone watching at the time. People born too late thinks they're a bit silly, but the public response was so favourable that "Invasion of the Dinosaurs" was given priority the following year. (Not Barry Letts' best move although, in his defence, the Drashigs rock.)

First use of marsh-gas as a handy distraction, a Robert Holmes speciality. (It's not, however, his first joke about this sort of thing.) This is also the last story to be made as part of Season Nine, but it doesn't look especially cheap.

Four Things to Notice
About "Carnival of Monsters"

1. Robert Holmes is now often remembered as the greatest of all *Doctor Who* scriptwriters, renowned for the way he applied eccentric, even bizarre, characterisation to the kind of science-fiction being peddled by the BBC. He regularly created scenarios which were part space-opera and part music-hall. And "Carnival of Monsters" is the story in which the real Robert Holmes comes across for the first time.

A year away writing about the British Raj (see **The Lore**) seems to have made him more willing to get *Doctor Who* away from Earth, so as to talk about it more clearly. He therefore returns with a clever story of petty bureaucracy and tawdry showbiz that pre-empts Douglas Adams' best work by more than half a decade. An alien keeps miniaturised human beings inside his viewing-machine as part of an intergalactic sideshow, yet when the Doctor meets him face-to-face, the "bad guy" isn't a twisted, megalomaniacal villain but a second-rate showman in a spangled jacket who doesn't even know how to work the machinery. It's recognisably from the same place as the circus scenes from "Terror of the Autons", but stepped up a notch or three.

Was 1973 the *Annus Mirabilis*?

As many of you will know, one of the hit shows on British television lately has been *Life on Mars* - in which a by-the-book cop from present-day Manchester is somehow brought face-to-face with the old-skool policing of *The Sweeney* when a car hits him and he wakes up in 1973. Or rather, it's a distorted version of 1973 that shows it to be drab, grim and generally unpleasant.

This is a lie. Manchester was like that then, but it was like that in 1983, 1993 and 2003 too. In 1973, everywhere *else* in the UK had bits that were exciting and gaudy, until about Halloween. (We'll take as read a bit of prior knowledge of the Yom Kippur War, and why many people count the end of "The Sixties" as 6th of October, 1973; **Who's Running the Country?** under 10.5, "The Green Death" will tell you all you need to know). The resolution of *Life on Mars* (such as it was) made clear that no real reason existed for the story being set in 1973, other than that it was a year the writers liked.

But for *our* purposes, we have to start by asking ourselves if there's anything about 1973 that made it a more-than-usually appropriate year to plunder for archive repeats. Is the *Doctor Who* of 1973 qualitatively different, or was the year itself special, so that any fondly-remembered TV from that time will automatically be chosen? We're going to confidently answer "yes" to both of these, then we're going to look pityingly at anyone who thinks otherwise.

(We're well aware that today's kids will probably, in future, find themselves trying to argue something similar about 2008 and defend David Tennant against whoever's got the part in 2043 - Winston Fox, maybe? - while occasionally screaming "How can they call themselves *Doctor Who* fans if they only watch the 3D episodes?" But we can only argue from the facts we have available now.)

To start, consider that 1973 is statistically more popular with BBC schedulers. Of the eight Pertwee stories that the terrestrial BBC channels have re-run in their original form since he left the series, *four* have been from Season Ten, with only "Frontier in Space" denied its place in the sun. "The Three Doctors" and "Carnival of Monsters" were shown in *The Five Faces of Doctor Who* season that launched the idea of "Out of Doctor" repeats in 1981. "The Green Death" got a repeat on Sunday mornings in early 1994, weeks after "Planet of the Daleks" was shown at prime time on BBC1 on Fridays as part of a retro-themed evening schedule using other hits from that era. (The remaining

four were all on BBC2 in the "cult TV" slot: "Spearhead from Space" and "Doctor Who and the Silurians" were shown in late 1999 / early 2000 after an abortive relaunch, and "The Sea Devils" and "The Daemons" aired in 1992. They also showed re-edited 50-minute episodes of "The Curse of Peladon" in 1982.)

Many commentators have pointed out that 1973 is the year that most of the people *now* working in television were ten years old. But even though that's sort-of true in 2008[102], it obviously wasn't in 1993 or 1981. Once *Doctor Who* had receded into the soft rich loam of the public memory, Britain may have settled into a collective impression that Tom Baker was the One True Time Lord, but the specific stories repeated were almost all Pertwee. If you saw a Fourth Doctor adventure post-Davison but before 2005, it was three separate showings of "Genesis of the Daleks" or one unannounced re-run of "Pyramids of Mars". Black and white repeats were even more scarce (a mere four in twenty-five years). To all intents and purposes, vintage *Who* meant Jon Pertwee, and the Pertwee era stopped with "The Green Death". By comparison, there's only been one repeat of a 1974 story - an omnibus showing of "Planet of the Spiders", done to lead in to "Robot".

This can't be a coincidence. We'll talk about what was different about 1974 in a while, but we need to think more widely about what the viewers had been living through the year before. Stand by for 1973: a crash course for the ravers.

For most of that year people were looking to the future, but from November on (after Princess Anne's wedding) everyone was peering into the past, and the rest of the decade was on long series of revivals and nostalgia-crazes. The next big fad was a garbled version of the 1950s, with Teddy-Boy suits (see 24.3, "Delta and the Bannermen") and the first inkling that Grease was the word. After that it was a rolling programme of revivals of Mods (see 2.8, "The Space Museum"), Skinheads and Doir chic. Then of course we got Punk (which we invented, so CBGBs can sod off), the cult that expressly claimed that there was "No future in England's dreaming".

Of course, the 1950s of 1970s pop wasn't quite right, and had a strange ambivalence. (If you can get past the shock of Deborah Watling with her kit off, the film *That'll Be The Day* is a classic of re-imagined 50s Britain for a 70s British audience.) In

continued on page 313...

311

2. "Carnival of Monsters" can be (and often has been) read as a commentary on *Doctor Who* itself, with Vorg prodding his exhibits into jumping through viewer-friendly hoops and referring to the most vicious of the monsters in his collection as 'great favourites with the kiddies'. (Although it's probably a coincidence that when his Miniscope / TV screen shows us a Cyberman - the only time we see a one of them during the entire Pertwee run - Vorg's assistant refers to it as looking like 'a blob in a snowstorm', exactly how the Cybermen *were* introduced to us in 1966.) Kids in those days used to feed the little men they thought lived inside the television set (they still do, if you don't stop them) and this story picks up the motif in the Troughton stories that the Doctor could see out of TV screens and runs with it.

3. Although the 1920s setting aboard the *S.S. Bernice* is effectively realised, the main thing that people generally take from this story is the sheer vibrancy of the design. The down-at-heels entertainers are the most colourful thing on a planet that's populated by civil servants, who are literally grey-faced bureaucrats and talk about themselves in the third person. The best example of this: 'One has no wish to be devoured by alien monstrosities, even in the cause of political progress.' The Scope's interior makes electronics look like an adventure playground, even if bits of it are suspiciously familiar (see **The Lore**). Inter Minor itself is somehow both a bold step at delineating an alien world *and* a pop-art set worthy of exhibiting in a gallery or permitting Slade or T Rex to perform on.

The other thing that people take away, however, is the Drashigs - the series' first attempt at using puppets on scaled-down sets to suggest huge, tyrannosaurus-scale alien monstrosities. Though some of the Drashig close-ups work quite well, especially when they're tearing their way into the hull of the ship, the sight of them popping up through the deck like Sooty and Sweep is one of the series' most unintentionally funny moments. And yet, since this is a story about the need to watch monsters on television, you'll be forgiven for loving them anyway.

4. Now that a fight-scene between the Doctor and some authority figure is part of the package, the excuses to include this are becoming increasingly tenuous. This story has Vorg, the showman, twiddle a knob on the Scope to demonstrate that the 'Tellurians' can be 'made to behave in an amusingly violent way'. As a result, everyone on the ship gets bellicose, and Lt Andrews decides to have a punch-up with the Doctor for what the script acknowledges is no good reason. Note that even when engaging in fisticuffs, the Doctor can't resist the urge to shout *HAI!!*

The Continuity

The Doctor Orders a large scotch on the *S. S. Bernice*, and doesn't seem to be doing it just to blend in. He's happy to be referred to as a vagabond. [See 9.1, "Day of the Daleks" and 21.7, "The Twin Dilemma" for more on the Doctor and alcohol.]

Whatever mechanism translates alien languages for the Doctor's benefit, it doesn't translate carnival lingo. Or he doesn't want to admit that it does. [Similarly, he gets the period slang wrong, saying '99 skidoo'. Either he's forgotten that the correct term is "23 skidoo", or he's saying '99' because that's the thing doctors want people to say during check-ups.]

For once, he's reckless enough to leave the Ship without checking the outside gravity, atmosphere, etc.

• *Inventory.* The Doctor carries a string file around his neck [in the next story, it's hidden in his shoe]. The sonic screwdriver can, with a simple flip of the cap, ignite pockets of marsh-gas and cause impressive explosions as a result. Nonetheless, the Doctor says the sonic screwdriver only works on 'electronic locks', not the metal door lock that keeps him and Jo in Major Daly's cabin. [The new series similarly claims that the screwdriver doesn't work on 'deadbolt sealed' locks. See the next story, however, for when the Doctor adapts the screwdriver into a magnet of sorts.] In the TARDIS there's a magnetic core extractor, a device not unlike the sonic screwdriver which can open the hatches inside the Miniscope.

• *Background.* He's been to Metebelis 3 before, and obviously enjoyed the experience as he's keen on taking Jo there. [This conflicts with the hostile terrain and fauna he encounters in 10.5, "The Green Death".] He knows the history of the *S. S. Bernice*, even though he seems to change it here: see **History**. He recognises a plesiosaurus on sight [q.v. 7.2, "Doctor Who and the Silurians"], and claims he took boxing lessons from John L. Sullivan. [He was the legendary American boxer who, in 1889, became the last heavyweight cham-

Was 1973 the *Annus Mirabilis*?

...continued from page 311

British popular culture, then, Glam and associated fads were the last time that "futuristic" equated to "fashionable". (Yes, we had the early 80s "Futurists", the New Romantics whose self-publicity ran parallel with Seasons Eighteen and Nineteen, but their idea of the Future was warmed over Bowie and Eno from 1972.) But even the future was starting to be tinged with wistfulness. The fact that we'd seen the last Apollo moon landing just before Christmas 1972 seemed very appropriate in a year where *Dan Dare* strips and *Astounding* covers were being plundered for retro chic.

This had always been part of the basic notion of Glam anyway. The style and content (like there could be a difference) was rooted in an idea of pop musicians being mutants from the future who were trying to blend in with us by assembling "authentic" versions of period clothing and getting it wrong. They had 50s shoulder-pads and Elvis-like lamé suits, but eyeliner and lipstick. They had Victorian urchin clothes in primary colours. The music referenced Phil Spector, Chuck Berry and Muddy Waters, whilst the lyrics touched on clichés of 30s gangster movies and Humphrey Bogart - alongside spaceships, motorbikes, aliens and jukeboxes.

If you've been following the hints in the **What Was In the Charts?** entries, you'll have encountered a cross-section of these already. It may have started in art-schools and been terribly conceptual to begin with, but once rough-looking blokes took it over, all sorts of odd stuff hit the mainstream. Despite what various compilation CDs from the 90s tried to suggest (largely as an attempt to cover the subject without including Gary Glitter, the great unmentionable of Glam), the whole thing ended in a blaze of glory with Christmas 1973. The Biba boutique, which had started the vogue for mixing decades, went bust when everyone did it themselves. Former Glam stars spent 1974 writing elegiac songs about how the party was over[103]. Even the ringmaster of it all, David Bowie, moved to America, put on a business suit and became a soul singer, for a bit.

But for three solid years, the thrust of British Popular Culture (note the caps) was a mix of deeply ironic nostalgia and over-coloured spangly futurism (sound familiar?) that had got teenage girls screaming again and made parents grin when these bands appeared on *Top of the Pops*. In case the essays in Volume IV didn't fully convince you, we'll say it again: *Blue Peter* and *Top of the Pops* are the sister-programmes to vintage *Doctor Who* in ways that *Blake's 7* could never have been. The Who / ToTP crossover was never more overt than in the Glam era (or the Jo Grant phase, as the dates coincide almost exactly).

To remind you of a few more obvious examples: the effects used on Azal's face as he melts down ("The Daemons") or Stevens' as his mind becomes a battleground between BOSS and the Metebelis Crystal ("The Green Death") are the quintessential Glam-era effect for T Rex or The Sweet. The Eradicator effect in "Carnival of Monsters" is one tried out here, then used for Alice Cooper performing "School's Out". The costumes worn by bands like Mott the Hoople or Chicory Tip look, as everyone's dad said, "like something off *Doctor eff-ing Who*". The ToTP set-design tended towards black backdrops with a lot of coloured geometrical shapes hung from the ceiling and raised diasses for the performers.

Now look at the space-bases we've had over the Pertwee era. (They're not always black, but usually a neutral colour to offset loud clothing and attention-grabbing lumps of set. Look at Jaeger's lab in "The Mutants", for example.) There's a lot of crossover before and after, and the comparison of the two series over the twenty-five years they were both on would prove illuminating to anyone unfamiliar with one or the other. However, this three years is a particularly rich seam, and when fashion and the music became less *Who*-friendly in 1974, the world got a little less ebullient. Suddenly "Now" wasn't the optimum time to be in, and Britain wasn't the most exciting place.

This is quite an important moment, as the public (rather than the usual stream of experts) were confronted with a multiplicity of possible futures and the power to choose between them. This was the year when people started thinking about loft insulation, Salter Ducks and wind-powered televisions. Even without the miners going on strike or the Arabs hiking up the price of crude, it was dawning on people that energy wasn't something to squander. Pollution, energy-crunch, population explosion and all were familiar news items, but 1973 is the year the ordinary members of the public were encouraged to do something about them. Programmes such as *A House For the Future* were shown with helpful DIY tips about lagging and tin-foil behind radiators, as well as the more outré

continued on page 315...

pion to win his title in a bare-knuckle fight... although it's ironic that the Doctor insists on Queensbury Rules here, since Sullivan went into a decline after they were introduced. Presumably, this was around the same time that the Doctor wrestled with the Mountain Mauler of Montana (see 2.4, "The Romans").]

At some point, presumably before leaving his own world, the Doctor campaigned for the banning of the Miniscopes. [This is the only known indication of the Doctor having a crusading streak before he left his own people.]

The Supporting Cast

• *Jo Grant.* Still carries her bunch of skeleton keys, somewhere [as she did in Holmes' previous story, "Terror of the Autons"]. She can pass for a memsahib [the Major, at least, assumes she can play Bridge or Mah-Jongg, so she must be from a good family] and can improvise a story for the Major about coming aboard at Port Said. [Either she has A-Level geography, then, or she's been abroad a lot as a child. The novelisation of 8.4, "Colony in Space" suggests the latter, claiming she spent two years at spy school learning languages before becoming a file-clerk in Bangkok.] On the other hand she hasn't read Edward de Bono or even heard of 'Lateral Thinking' - very odd for the early 70s, when it was second only to *The Joy of Sex* as the book everyone was lending everyone else.

The TARDIS The new dematerialisation circuit allows the Doctor to 'program' the Ship, not 'steer' it. At least it works that way in theory, although it obviously isn't very reliable as he ends up on completely the wrong planet here.

The Time Lords Though the Time Lords don't interfere in the affairs of other cultures 'as a rule', at some point in the past the Doctor 'had a great deal to do with' the Time Lords banning of the Miniscopes; he convinced the High Council that the machines were an offence against the dignity of sentient life, and made such a fuss that the Time Lords outlawed them. [Some fans have claimed that the Miniscopes were actually banned because they threatened the Time Lords' monopoly over time-travel, but that *isn't* the suggestion here. As in all stories before the 1980s, the suggestion is that Time Lords are non-interventionist through a combination of lethargy and a strict moral code -

not out of a respect for causality - and are prepared to intervene when someone like the Doctor makes life hard for them. See **How Involved are the Time Lords?** under 15.5, "Underworld".]

All the Miniscopes were officially all 'called in' and destroyed. The Doctor indicates that when the Time Lords banned them, the one owned by Vorg somehow slipped through the net. [He doesn't consider the possibility that he might have ended up inside this one at a point *before* the Time Lords dealt with the problem, so it's probably fair to assume that the Time Lords erased them from history altogether rather than just collecting them. Which might mean this is the only one in the "current" version of the timeline, so perhaps he *was* steered there by the Time Lords anyway....]

Here the Doctor suggests that there's an intergalactic *law* against Miniscopes, suggesting - for the first time - that the Time Lords have direct political contact with worlds outside their own. [This is also the case in 22.4, "The Two Doctors", also by Holmes, and which uses much of the same terminology as this story. If the Lurmans and the people of the Third Zone are indeed related, then the culture which connects them may be one of the few which has overt dealings with the High Council. The obvious question is whether the law was passed by the Time Lords (who then expected everyone else to abide by it), or whether it was agreed by a wider confederacy of powerful beings who have to accept a majority decision. In the new series, the range of races who know something about - or were directly impacted by - the Time War makes this more plausible.]

The Miniscope A 'miracle of intragalactic [sic] technology' containing miniaturised life-forms from across the history of the universe, all of which can be observed live on its screen, the Miniscope itself is apparently capable of scooping its "exhibits" from any point in space and time. The Doctor returns everything in the collection to its proper place, but only by hooking it up to the TARDIS and reversing the 'original settings'. [This means that the Miniscope must have played *some* part in collecting its specimens from history, and isn't just a receptacle for beings collected by other means, but it may not be capable of "scooping" things from elsewhere in time without some greater power source (c.f. 17.4, "Nightmare of Eden"). It's obvious that whatever process the Scope uses takes the actual life-forms and a ver-

Was 1973 the *Annus Mirabilis*?

...continued from page 313

ideas with methane extractors and pigs. News reports about Alternative Energy (and the scare-quotes around "Alternative" vanished pretty quickly) went from "well, isn't *that* clever? to "better get yours now". It's significant that even in the summer, when the power-cuts seemed like a brief fad from last year, a story like "The Green Death" was nowhere near as controversial as it had seemed when commissioned.

The world was catching up with the series and soon overtook it. *Doctor Who* had been a place where such present-day concerns were discussed in the abstract, with hypothetical futures and planets or social problems that were safely in the past. Viewers took stories more obviously allegorical of the daily events to be sermons; Letts and Dicks could get the Population Explosion (as it was called then) into the background of space-stories, but having a story about a miners' strike or power-cuts somehow cheapened the rhetorical strength of the series. Even if "Death to the Daleks" (11.3) and "The Monster of Peladon" (11.4) *had* been exciting and well-made, they would have lost the casual viewers' support just by preaching. The real-life concerns of Seasons Seven through Ten were about the near future, not the present.

For the previous thirty years (and indeed, right back into the Victorian era), the idea held sway that progress was linear and your only choice was to accept it or resist it. 1973 was the year when it dawned on the public that not everyone was going to get to wear reflective spandex whilst riding a jet-pack to a job that required you to take Esperanto lessons (in pill form). Whenever a novel or a film projected a version of the future, it was based on one single trend extrapolated. *Doctor Who* had, at least, attempted to take two or three of these grim or groovy forecasts and mix them up a bit. In "Frontier in Space", we get a cacotopia comprising over-population, a police-state that locks dissidents on the moon for life without trial and a space-war brought about by xenophobia. Expansion into the galaxy hasn't liberated humans the way *Star Trek* said it would.

Here we should stop and point out that *Star Trek*, as well as many other similar American models of the future, thought along these lines: *Item* - the future will see the continuation of the trend towards an enlightened, democratic state. *Item* - the future will see humans going into space. *Item* - the trend has been for women's skirts to get short-

er. *Therefore* - by the twenty-third century, the galaxy will be filled with happy, prosperous and broad-minded people who barely notice that all the women are wearing what amount to stretched T-shirts. For the record, we single out *Trek* not just for its cultural hegemony (just then beginning to get oppressive), but because of the big omission in its word-view. In classic *Star Trek*, we repeatedly see lots of alien planets with One Big Thing wrong with them. They're single-issue planets, but Earth is never shown unless it's a comedic time-travel episode (or "The City on the Edge of Forever"). Earth is some kind of Utopia they daren't show, just in case it weakens the arguments for its superiority over whatever backlot or orange-and-purple desert set they're on this time. But in Pertwee-era *Doctor Who*, however bad things are on any planet they visit, it's worse on Earth.

There's something very obvious to say about early 70s SF films that younger readers will need to take on trust. Nobody who went to see them seriously thought, "That's the future I'm going to grow up in." They went to see a certain degree of spectacle and a moral tale made simpler by using figures in a landscape. The whole trend between *2001: A Space Odyssey* (1968) and *Star Wars* (1977) was to make something that looked arresting on screen and have people who weren't happy living there. This was part of a general appetite for anything not seen before or (in the case of the soundtracks) not heard (see **What's Going On With The Music?** under 9.4, "The Mutants"). This is entirely at odds with the trend before 1968 and to a great extent after 1975 (when, as we discuss elsewhere in these books, the entire emphasis of the big-budget Hollywood movies went from social concerns to treating people as meat). Whilst this resulted in many inadvertently amusing futures (such as *ZPG*, where Zero Population Growth somehow turns into Zero Population and children are banned - that can't end well), it brought mainstream movies closer to what, for budgetary as well as culturally-specific ones, *Doctor Who* had always done. For three years or more, the filmmakers were playing catch-up with the BBC.

(Just to reiterate something that that's particularly crucial here: although *Doctor Who* partook of a lot of the issues and values of the SF films and occasionally had some cross-over in subject-matter with *Star Trek*, the public's mental bracketing of

continued on page 317...

sion of their environment, suitably amended for maintenance, rather than any 'sampling'. Vorg got his Miniscope from a Wallarian, though who *designed* it isn't clear. Since cultures like that of the Lurmans don't seem to have time-travel at this point - see "The Two Doctors" - we might also conclude that Vorg has no idea how valuable his doomed Miniscope really is.] Contained within the Scope, and eventually returned to their home eras, are... the S. S. *Bernice*, a plesiosaurus, an Ogron, a Cyberman and a colony of around twenty Drashigs.

The Miniscope's exterior plates are molectic-bonded disillon, and anything which leaves the machine's compression field returns to its normal size within a few seconds. [The internal dimensions may be unstable, as the tiny Doctor walks for 'miles' through the internal circuits but is Action Man / G. I. Joe sized when he leaves - perhaps the further within one goes the smaller one becomes.] The Eradicator beam disrupts a great deal of the Miniscope's circuitry. [Pletrac, whose colleague Orum identified the metal used in the Miniscope's construction and can thus be considered an authority on the subject, believes that the beam will destroy the entire machine and not just kill the organic life-forms within. Orum himself knows about the Eradicator's power and is not expecting an explosion.]

Those inside the Miniscope find themselves repeating the same actions over and over again, without knowing anything's wrong. [They're in a time-loop rather than just being hypnotised, even though they can almost-remember past loops; otherwise they'd starve to death. Matter seems to "teleport" inside the machine's circuits, the hands of the clock on the S. S. *Bernice* resetting themselves without help, and the decanter refilling despite all the drinking we see, so it's not just in the minds of the passengers. Even so, as outside participants the Doctor and Jo are immune. The obvious comparison is with the 'chronic hysteresis' in 18.2, "Meglos", but that was imposed on a time-machine in vortex and broken by two Time Lords.]

A simple 'aggrometer' control on the front of the Miniscope can change the subjects' levels of aggression, but the Drashigs have no intelligence centres and can't be controlled. On the other hand the plesiosaurus *does* seem to be controllable, which says a lot about the stupidity of Drashigs. The Miniscope's power generators [though

apparently not the Miniscope itself] were built by the Eternity Perpetual Company to last forever; that's why they went bankrupt. The Scope came with a handbook. [So it was probably a mass-produced object. A custom-made handbook *is* conceivable, but not in the hands of someone like Vorg. If one exists, then perhaps the Time Lords *did* simply impound them all, rather than prevent them from ever having been created. If, however, it "escaped" into a version of history otherwise lacking in scope, so to speak, this may explain how the fate of the S.S. *Bernice* became a mystery even it's here returned to Earth, preventing the enigma from ever happening.]

The Non-Humans

• *Lurmans.* A space-going species from a place nowhere near Earth, Lurmans appear indistinguishable from humans even if they're technologically superior. The Lurmans know of humans, but refer to them as 'Tellurians' [q.v. "The Two Doctors"]. The similarity between Lurmans and Tellurians has caused some scientists to refute Voldek's theory that life in the universe is infinitely variable. Improbably, Vorg speaks the carnival lingo of Earth, and claims he's worked 'many a Tellurian fairground', even though it's said that Tellurians hail from 'a distant galaxy' and nobody knows how they reproduce.

Lurmans are apparently part of a super-culture of many worlds and species, since Vorg and Shirna frequently refer to their past experiences of other planets. Shirna worked with the All-Star Dance Company, while Vorg did National Service with the Fourteenth Heavy Lasers, his battery sergeant being a crustaceoid mercenary [mentioned again in the audio play "The Paradise of Death", written by this story's director].

The Lurman version of the gambling game Find-the-Lady involves three magum pods and a yorrow seed. They use credit-bars as currency, have translator diodes which allow them to communicate with the people of Inter Minor, and refer to spacecraft as "thrusters".

• *Drashigs.* Huge, vicious, omnivorous-but-flesh-loving animals, like hundred-foot-long caterpillars with dragon-shaped heads and mouths big enough to swallow most dinosaurs, Drashigs are native to the swamps on one of the satellites of Grundle. They're blind, but hunt by scent and have various knobbles over their heads which appear to be sensory organs of some kind.

Was 1973 the *Annus Mirabilis*?

...continued from page 315

the series with other shows was not like it became in the late 80s. There was no such thing as "Cult" - except as a catch-all researcher's category for shows such as *The Magic Roundabout* and *The Pink Panther* that had unexpected demographics. *Doctor Who* remained firmly mainstream, alongside *The Onedin Line* and *Bagpuss*, until 1980 or thereabouts.)

For most people, the thing about 1973 was that it was lurid and reckless (until suddenly it got bleak and scary). It was, after all, an age when new things were coming on the market and newness was good in and of itself. It was a period when conspicuous consumption - the display of new things as a show of status - was finally catching on here after a generation of make-do and mend (which came back with a vengeance at the end of 1973). There was disposable paper furniture. There was a bewildering array of instant food. There were, until that autumn, mini-skirts and hot pants. The last point is something people not alive at the time can't grasp - it was as if someone had arranged a meeting for all women in the country and secretly agreed that on the stroke of midnight, they would all don mid-length skirts, blouses with wide collars over brown jackets and bobbed hair. When Elisabeth Sladen saw what she was to wear in "The Time Warrior", she thought it made her look schoolmarmish. That was May. By the time the story was screened (December), it was what girls wore on dates. It was like somebody had flipped a switch.

Looking at magazines from November 1973 (the week of Princess Anne's wedding), the thing that strikes one is how many hints and tips for using leftovers and making new clothes from old ones fill even the aspirational ones. The thing about this wedding was that many people remembered Her Royal Highness being born, around the time things stopped getting worse after the War, and had seen her embodying all the trends of the early 70s. (She landed up presenting *Blue Peter* in tight shorts and a big hat, like the one from 7.3, "The Ambassadors of Death".) This wedding triggered a day off from school, and most families used it as a benchmark. After this, it was a few weeks to Christmas, and this year's looked like being a bit forlorn. The last major Royal Wedding had been in 1962, when Princess Margaret got hitched to a glamorous photographer, and it now seemed as though it happened on another plan-

et. *This* one looked like being the last bit of cheer for a while, so thereafter people began facing up to the new austerity. Meteorological data confirms our overall impression that the summer of 1974 was wetter than the previous one, but not that every day after Princess Anne's wedding until the following Christmas was a torrential downpour. The golden summer of 1973 and the miserable one to follow are both the products of hindsight.

You're getting the general idea. In Britain there were trends and social forces that had been developing since the late 1950s and came to a peak, then a new climate came along. What historians call "The Long 1960s" lasts from the Suez crisis of 1956 (when Elvis and Pop Art happened) to late 1973 (The Yom Kippur War and the Three Day Week). So 1973 is the year when these things got as far as they were going to go. Even without the drastic hike in oil prices, the fear of terrorist reprisals and Heath's reaction to the miners being to shut off all the power, these trends had almost run out of steam. In some ways older citizens grabbed the crises of Winter 1973 as an excuse not to try to be "with-it" any more.[104] The hunger for anything new, anything at all, was replaced by a yearning for comfort and familiarity. In Britain this was noticeably at the same time as austerity measures were re-introduced and connected with memories of both the War and the immediate worsening of conditions post-war (see **How Believable is the British Space Programme?** under "The Ambassadors of Death".)

However, something similar was going in stateside too. America's version of nostalgia was something they'd also been dealing with since 1973 and is an ironicised one, found in Robert Altman's *The Long Goodbye*, most of Peter Bogdanovich's films, *Chinatown* and Randy Newman's "Good Old Boys". An Americanised version of this sense - that dreams of the past were inadequate but all we had - was in things like *Goodbye Yellow Brick Road* (the album, not just the single), which really launched Elton John in the States. It was a time when film-writers were re-examining all the old movies without the Hays office breathing down their necks, making sure no kisses were longer than four seconds. It was also a time when they could look back on their own youth with sufficient hindsight to be analytical. Everything that had occurred since Kennedy had been shot could be hinted at by making stories set before this. George

continued on page 319...

Legend has it that when a [Lurman] battle-thruster landed on the Drashig's home-satellite, with a crew of fifty and all the latest armaments, a scout-orbiter later found the thruster eaten except for a few scraps of the reactor ventricle. Even so, Major Daly kills one with a tommy-gun, and Andrews' stick of dynamite slays another. In their native habitat they're only seen to come to the surface of the swamp in order to feed.

• *Wallarians.* They're notorious gamblers, and Vorg won his Miniscope during the Great Wallarian Exhibition, at which he also met a Wallarian wrestler called the Great Zarb.

• *Dinosaurs.* The plesiosaurus identified by the Doctor technically has more teeth than you'd expect from the species. [As fish-eaters, it would lack molars.] According to the Doctor, it's been extinct for 130 million years [more like 140 million according to fossil evidence, but then, the Doctor's actually been there].

Planet Notes

• *Inter Minor.* Obviously a highly technological planet, but also deeply insular and paranoid, Inter Minor broke all links with other worlds after the Great Space Plague thousands of years previously. It's evidently in a part of the universe which contains a number of civilised worlds, and it's nowhere near Earth, although it may be close to Metebelis 3 since that's where the Doctor's heading when the TARDIS lands there. [A cut scene has Vorg refer to the planet as being in the Acteon System, which puts it in the same region as Metebelis 3.] President Zarb, his Council and the Central Bureau have recently decided that aliens are to be re-admitted, with Lurmans being designated as the first visitors, though visas are required. The planet's Interstellar Ecology Commission forbids the transference of zoological specimens between planets, and there's a three-member Admissions Tribunal to oversee the Lurmans' arrival.

The inhabitants of Inter Minor are divided into at least two classes. The rulers of the planet are officious, bureaucratic, grey-skinned humanoids referred to as 'the official species' who have very little sense of humour and a limited understanding of the word 'entertainment'. The workers - 'functionaries' - have the same grey skins but near-bestial features [two species descended from the same roots, so they're no longer biologically compatible]. While the rulers speak primly, referring

to themselves in the third person throughout, the functionaries just grunt [except when Shirna is getting out of her space-suit, when they make Kenneth Connor-esque 'phwoarr' noises]. Functionaries seem to be treated like animals, or slaves at best, and rebellious functionaries are killed without compunction. There's currently some unrest among this underclass, which Zarb - whom we never actually see - has put down to a lack of diversion. Amusement is prohibited, but Zarb is considering lifting this restriction. Treason still carries the death penalty for the official species.

Zarb has already disbanded the army, and Inter Minor has defence pacts with all its neighbouring planets. Its only internal defence now is the 'eradicator', a mounted energy weapon which destroys any organic molecules in its path, although a new type is apparently being developed. The bureaucrats carry smaller hand-held weapons which can either kill or stun. Their technology is apparently compatible with that of the Lurmans. There's an Inner Constellation Corrective Authority, which seems to cover this whole group of worlds, not just Inter Minor.

• *Demos.* Mentioned by Vorg, who's come to Inter Minor from there. [If it's the same as 'Damos', the former homeworld of the Daemons - see 8.5, although the spelling is admittedly different - then other species have over-run it since the Daemons' extinction. This might give us some idea of Inter Minor's location, and that of the world/s inhabited by the Lurmans; "The Daemons" states that the planet is on the other side of Earth's galaxy. This contradicts other lines in the story where Vorg claims that Tellurians come from another galaxy. The Lurmans know about Earth but generally speak of human beings as something far-away and rarely-seen. Vorg claims more familiarity with humans. This might just be part of his showman-spiel, but he seems to know a lot about his livestock, getting the details of the Drashigs right and telling Kalik things we know to be true about Ogrons. However, as Earth is termed "Tellus" and humans 'Tellurians', we have to assume that Greek-sounding planet names simply appealed to Holmes: 'Demos' meaning "planet of the people"?]

• *Metebelis* 3. The famous 'blue planet of the Acteon group', according to the Doctor, who also states that the air there is 'like wine'. [By episode four, Metebelis 3 has become the blue planet of the Acteon *galaxy*. 'Group' seems more likely,

Was 1973 the *Annus Mirabilis*?

...continued from page 317

Lucas conflated style and substance with *American Graffiti*, and the US went into its Bicentenary partying like it was 1962. Next thing you know, they're remaking *Superman* absolutely straight and electing a 40s film star as President. This is a Big Subject, but we're just trying to say that it's not just BBC dramas and pop stars that withdrew from the idea of a better future.

Time to get controversial: we're pretty much sure that 1973 was the year that *Doctor Who* was most popular. Here we don't mean "most-watched", but it was more loved than ever before or since. The stories were capable of being re-watched with more pleasure than any isolated tales from any other period. They were, if you will, more likely to "stick". However many millions tuned in for a Davison story, you rarely heard anyone talk about the day after (except for when Adric died, of course. Even then, it was a brief case of "Did you see..?", "Yeh", "Serves him right" - neither a national trauma nor a cause for street-parties.) For that matter, no matter how many people saw - for instance - 16.5, "The Power of Kroll", it's been erased from the public memory (even the naff effects and men looking like Old Greg from *The Mighty Boosh* doing aerobics) whilst Drashigs and Gel-Guards and inevitably Giant Maggots remain unbudgeable.

Throughout these guidebooks, we've been trying to establish the extent to which the context in which these stories were made - and the conditions under which they were originally intended to be seen - determine the content, style and decisions about future stories. In terms of episodes and stories, Season Ten is approximately the midway point to the series in its original configuration. But more significantly, it's the period at which *Doctor Who* is closest to the national mood and is most firmly established in Britain's collective imagination. In its own way, *Doctor Who* helped us decide who we were and who we wanted to be.

This is a contentious view - according to some loud voices among the generations of fans not actually alive at the time (or just in their infancy), the series was only genuinely popular when Billie Piper was in it. Others point to the ratings and conclude that (even if you take the ITV strike of September 1979 out of the equation) Tom Baker is the only iconic Doctor, and his term of office was *so* popular and successful that nobody thereafter could compete. A third camp, mainly of older fans

but with significant support from those who were kids in the 80s and investigated via video, is that the black and white era was the peak of the programme's potency because there was absolutely nothing like it anywhere else, yet it was entirely in keeping with the mood of the times.

Before examining the reasons *why* 1973 was the climax of the programme's rise to institutional status, we'd best counter these rival claims. One thing that is emphatically *not* a clue to anything is ratings. Even if the BBC had really taken that much notice of these in the 70s, the big question is which system of counting was being used. The advertisers who kept ITV in business used the JIC-TAR system, which wasn't the same as the BBC was using (they didn't get onto the same page until 1981). If you believe the figures *both* sets of research give, then 108% of viewers were watching the two main channels (presumably the anomaly was resolved by -8% watching BBC2). Furthermore, the Pertwee era is the one where the Audience Appreciation figures were only sporadically recorded. In any case, the ratings recorded *households* watching, not individuals (assuming a figure of 2.2 viewers per household, which was questionable for a child-centred series like *Doctor Who*, even if the correct number of set-top boxes was being tallied). True, in crude numerical terms, more people supposedly watched 9.2, "The Curse of Peladon" than the oddly-similar X1.2, "The End of the World", but we aren't really in a position to use ratings as a guide to overall impact.

(Similarly, anyone who thinks that X2.13, "Doomsday" being the tenth most-watched thing in the hottest summer on record, in an era when nobody really watches television with the intensity they did in the past, means that the first showing of that story had a bigger impact than the *only* broadcast of "Frontier in Space" is using the same logic that says that Westlife[105] are better than the Beatles because they had more UK Number Ones. We're not saying "Doomsday" *didn't* have such an impact, just that the evidence has to be different and this might take years to assess. What effect the constant repeats of the BBC Wales episodes on cable channels will have on how well they're remembered - if at all - ten, twenty or thirty years hence also remains to be seen. The highest ratings of *any* form of *Doctor Who* post-Season Seventeen were for the *Children in Need* special "Dimensions in Time", which mercifully means that 13.8 million

continued on page 321...

since galaxies are very big places and most must surely have more than one blue planet. It's probably safe to say that the Doctor gets absent-minded later on, especially since he talks about the 'group' in detail. It's Jo who mentions the 'Acteon galaxy' after (mis-)hearing what the Doctor says, so possibly her mistake probably influences him later on. Anyway, there's no indication that this is the Acteon region, and surely even the TARDIS couldn't miss by an entire galaxy...? Well, there was that one time on Zeta Minor (13.2, "Planet of Evil"), but even then the Doctor had some inkling that something had gone wrong.]

History

• *Dating.* The S.S. *Bernice* vanished from Earth en route to Bombay [Mumbai] from England on the 4th of June, 1926, according to the calendar in one of the cabins. [The calendar has the layout of a calendar for 1925, proving that days of the week really don't match the dates in the *Doctor Who* universe.] According to the Doctor, the S.S. *Bernice* disappeared even though the Indian Ocean was perfectly calm, a freak tidal wave being the popular explanation. He also says that it was as famous a sea mystery as the *Mary Celeste* [see 2.8, "The Chase"]. This version of history is apparently changed at the end of the story: see **Can You Change History, Even One Line?** under 1.6, "The Aztecs" and **How Does Time Work?** under 9.1, "Day of the Daleks". On board the ship, Claire mentions Fred Astaire. [In 1926, Astaire was the star of a hit show in London and Liverpool, which is where Claire must have seen him in *Lady Be Good*, since he didn't start making movies until 1933. Then again, the histories of showbiz personalities are clearly different in the *Doctor Who* universe... q.v. 3.4, "The Daleks' Master Plan".] *Chu Chin Chow* was another West End smash of the late 1920s [unlikely to be revived these days].

Jo refers to 1926 as being 'about forty years' before her own time. [Suggesting that the UNIT stories aren't set in the late 70s, or she would have rounded up to "fifty". But since forty years after 1926 is 1966, at *least* half a decade out, this is damning proof that off-hand statements made by companions shouldn't be taken at face value. The clobber she's wearing is absolutely bang-on fashionable for summer 1972 (the promo clip for *All the Young Dudes* by Mott the Hoople shows a whole street full of teenage girls dressed in pretty much the same rolled-up jeans and boots).]

The "real" date, from Inter Minor's point of view, isn't established. [Many fan-histories have suggested that the 'Great Space Plague' which did such damage to Inter Minor is the same disease we hear about in 11.3, "Death to the Daleks". Since the plague was a thousand years ago, this would date the story to somewhere in the mid-3000s. But this is dubious, as the plague in "Death to the Daleks" seems confined to Earth's sphere of influence, whereas Inter Minor is in a completely different galaxy.] The Doctor suggests that Jo was born about a thousand years too early to know the principle of anti-magnetic cohesion that holds the plates of the Miniscope in place. [This *needn't* mean the Miniscope was built a thousand years after her time, though, just that human beings discovered the principle then.]

The Analysis

Where Does This Come From? At the time, the BBC hierarchy were undergoing one of their seven-year itches concerning the Corporation being patronising, patrician, metropolitan and so on. Lord Reith's original conception of the BBC was something that elements within its own management found objectionable, or - as is more often the case - thought the public should *believe* they found this heritage objectionable.

During the last round of this in 1964, the then-Controller of Television, Stuart Hood, culled any sections he thought were harbouring such unwelcome tendencies. He and his assistant, Donald Baverstock, made a lot of enemies. Hood, a former Marxist and university don, was quoted as calling the BBC "too bloody middle-class" (the irony of this seems to have eluded him) and quit abruptly at the end of 1963. Baverstock, smarting from what he considered a demotion, quit rather than head the launch of BBC2. (See Volume I for the fall-out from this, but it's a complicated story.)

Many things prompted their departure but the people brought in to repair the damage Hood caused (such as completely shutting down the Children's department) were themselves coming to the ends of their contracts by 1971, and younger staff were rising though the ranks. So a period of reflection accompanied the BBC's 50th birthday, and a lot of drama about working-class history and struggles against patrician, metropolitan, educated authorities was commissioned. The

Was 1973 the *Annus Mirabilis*?

...continued from page 319

people have blanked it out.)

The unreliability of official figures was known at the time. In Malcolm Hulke's *Writing for Television*, Robert Holmes observes that no matter how many people the BBC say saw *Z Cars* or *Doctor Who*, the latter got his elderly relatives, neighbours and colleagues talking even if the former was more high-scoring. This reminds us of another salient point: most of the massive ratings hits of the 70s were things nobody can recall in any detail. Admittedly the most-watched thing of the decade was the splashdown of Apollo 13[106], but the rest were spectacularly unmemorable for the most part. (Go on, who won the 1973 Eurovision Song Contest? Or Miss World 1970? Or that year's FA Cup Final? Who was on the 27th of April, 1977 edition of *This is Your Life*? You don't know? These were all in the top ten[107].) Apollo 13 and Princess Anne's wedding were pretty much the only events talked about after getting these astonishingly high viewing figures; the rest melted into oblivion within hours. Ask anyone who was in Britain at the time and they'll tell you about giant maggots, the Master and where they were when they saw all the Doctors meeting for the first time. Oh, and something about newsreaders dancing with Eric and Ernie.

The claim that Hartnell era had the biggest impact because of its sheer uniqueness, however, needs a look. We've some sympathy with this, but would like to remind the reader how much of Volume I was given over to suggesting that the elements of each story were off-the-shelf and just combined in new ways. True, Hartnell didn't have a story-editor looking enviously at *Star Trek*, but *Doctor Who* was far from being the only game in town even then. The freshness it offered was that the entire family could participate, and that each story was unlike the one before, not *necessarily* unlike anything else ever broadcast. The Pertwee era did the same, as enough time had elapsed since the one and only broadcast of each Hartnell adventure to re-invent the wheel for a new generation of kids. We've noted how much of Season Nine is stories that have really obvious premises being re-introduced to the viewers as though it's the first time anyone's done such things.

By Season Ten, they're confident enough to revisit old types of story and give them a daring twist. Even "Planet of the Daleks" has a joy of doing this in colour, and the thrill of being able to talk about old stories as historical events. Season Ten is stuffed with comments on the usual way these sorts of stories go, and this generally ages better than doing something for the first of many times. By contrast, Season Eleven does everything *again*, because they know they can do it. It's emphatically risk-free because the production team are pre-occupied with *Moonbase 3* and the whole team are looking to move on. Also notice how the middle three stories of the season are, effectively, remakes of stories the kids watching might have actually seen. (Another small but significant change: the Radiophonic Workshop's facilities were hitherto at Dudley Simpson's disposal. After 1973, this is curtailed and Simpson buys his own synthesizer and uses fewer settings and more "conventional" musicians. The sound of the series from 1974-80 is pretty much constant, whereas before this it changes considerably from story to story, even with the same composer and equipment.)

Doctor Who in the context of a Saturday Night is the other thing that changes. More than before or since, *everything* else on BBC1 in early 1973 seemed to cross-over into *Doctor Who* territory, with Jimmy Savile's bizarre and seemingly random show *Clunk Click* having Daleks on (to tie in with, um, "The Green Death") and Mike Yarwood doing spoof news bulletins from 2003 to the curious ragbag of items linked by a time-travelling computer supposedly hosting *Outa Space!* (This had even worse dinosaur puppets by Colin Mapson, so getting Cliff Culley in to do "Invasion of the Dinosaurs" might have seemed like a good idea.)

Or to put it another way, *Doctor Who* was only the furthest-out extreme of a whole tranche of popular television, from Bruce Forsythe's *Generation Game* to costume dramas such as *The Onedin Line* and popular science shows such as *Tomorrow's World* and *The Burke Special*. (These last two are intriguing as they were both shown on Thursdays, separated by *Top of the Pops* and *Some Mothers Do Have 'Em*. If you watched any one of these series, you watched *Doctor Who* and all the others.) *Clunk Click* became a lot more sober in its second and final run, just after "Invasion of the Dinosaurs". Then in 1974, the whole of light entertainment went into wholesale nostalgia mode. It's odd how much of the 1970s was spent dwelling on the 1930s. (Hmm.... if only someone had done a show about a 70s cop like Derren Nesbit in *Special*

continued on page 323...

1929 General Strike was now A Good Thing and the BBC's complicity in Churchill's attempts to break it was now officially shameful. We'll pick up on all the stuff about Welsh coal-miners and Lancashire millworkers later in this season.

We should note in passing, though, that Verity Lambert did a series about the Suffragettes that might not have been commissioned before this. Not only was the British Empire the subject of a documentary in exactly the same tone and style as the epic about World War I (*it's a human tragedy, why was this allowed to happen*, etc.), but a high-profile series about the Raj took as its starting point the unquestioned assumption that it was A Bad Thing and The Wrong Answer. (We're not saying it wasn't, just commenting on how basic this assumption was even by 1971.) *The Regiment* will be lurking under a lot of this year's stories the way *United!* did in Season Four.

So after he'd written two episodes of a series set in India at the start of the twentieth century, it's inevitable that Robert Holmes had a lot of reading under his belt, and almost inconceivable that he hadn't read *A Passage to India*. The similarity of Claire Daly's interest in the "real" far east, one presumes, is at least influenced by Adele Quested's curiosity about "the real India". More cogently, Paul Scott's Raj Quartet of books was three-quarters done in 1971 and the press (and television) were becoming interested. (You may have seen an adaptation of the four books as *The Jewel in the Crown*.)

Freed from the need to be scrupulously accurate, Holmes indulges in his trait of over-egging period dialogue with everything that might be expected from that time, rather than just what would normally be said under those circumstances. But then, he also overdoes the Tribunal's admin-speak. Most notoriously, one scene has Vorg trying to talk to the Doctor in palare. Although show-folk indeed used this as a secret lingo, this mix of Romany and backslang was mainly associated with the gay underworld and was introduced to the wider British public through *Round the Horne*. In this (as we saw with Ramblin' Sid Rumpo in **Are Alien Names Inevitably A Bit Silly?** under 9.2, "The Curse of Peladon"), the use of an unfamiliar word was deployed to suggest something far ruder. But as these were here spoken by Julian and his friend Sandy, where it provided a smokescreen for far more naughty lines in plain speech.

For mainstream BBC radio (when homosexuality was still technically illegal) this was daring stuff. Vorg's lines are less racy, and translate as follows: 'Varder the bonapalone' equals "Look at the pretty girl"; 'Nanti dinari ye jilks' is "No money here, understand?" The Doctor's inability to understand this less-than-alien language might be a sign that, unlike Vorg and Shirna, he hasn't got the means to translate automatically - or simply that he won't admit to being familiar with this slang.

It is, however, in keeping with a debunking of the clichés of previous generations of space opera that Holmes has picked up from his reading. The script refers to the Scope as 'looking like a cross between a jukebox and a samovar', and this lack of awe is entirely in keeping with 50s magazine SF. (Notably Robert Sheckley and Frederik Pohl, whose "Tunnel Under The World" resembles this more than slightly. It was adapted for BBC2's *Out Of The Unknown*, the series to which Holmes submitted "The Space Trap", which became 6.4, "The Krotons".)

Little signs of Holmes knowing his SF and having paid his dues come in the use of the term 'Tellurian', a Greek-derived word associated with the *Lensman* books (more on them in the next two essays) and in the throwaway asides. The fact that someone called Kalik ridicules the Lurmans for having 'ridiculous' names such as 'Vorg' and 'Shirna' is pure Sheckley. Indeed, the entire set-up is very like one of his stories about Joe the Galactic Junk-Yard-Man, with miraculous alien tech winding up at his place without instructions and with slight faults. The lived-in terms such as 'credit-bar' and 'cargo-thruster' sound like *Galaxy*-style space-talk too. (*Galaxy*, founded by Horace Gold in 1950, went for the more urbane, satirical and character-led stories and was given to using the innovations of earlier magazines as backdrops rather than as the main point of the story. In 1960s Britain, if you knew of any SF at all it was probably stuff from *Galaxy* repackaged in anthologies, often selected by Kingsley Amis or Brian Aldiss, or adapted for television. This is where Douglas Adams derived his approach.)

The Doctor has always been a spanner in the works - drop him into a "serious" SF scenario, and he'll mess things up within minutes - but here we see him interacting with environments even more erratic than *he* is. When things go wrong with the Miniscope, Vorg talks about 'bric-a-brac' caught

Was 1973 the *Annus Mirabilis*?

...continued from page 321

Branch, where he was hit by a car and woke up in the era of Bulldog Drummond and the British Union of Fascists.) Pertwee-era futuristic *Doctor Who* seemed out-of-key with the new line-up.

We also see the start of a more worrying long-term trend. At certain phases the public (if not the professional critics who get paid to say anything at all, regardless of whether they contradict themselves) took *Doctor Who* as a whole, with no interest in who wrote or directed a specific story. The series itself was an author, and cumulatively *Doctor Who* had what's called "institutional charisma". Like NASA or MI5, it embodied a set of values and got public support just for existing, until a drip-feed of small mistakes and wider concerns overtoppled this. For better or worse, we're living through another phase like this now. The BBC Wales version could put out forty-five minutes a week of a guy peeling bananas to music and the public would lap it up, *if* it had the usual title-sequence and was on BBC1 at 7.00 pm or thereabouts on Saturday. Conversely if the public have decided (or been told to think) that the show isn't for them, then even the inventive and competently made highs of the last two years of Sylvester McCoy's run wouldn't get a look. In 1974, the Writers' Guild gave the production team a special award simply for being *Doctor Who*. From this point on, the series undergoes a backlash - starting with Mary Whitehouse and Jean Rook (see Volume IV) but eventually from the public.

These guidebooks have been written in the hope that we're being at least *objectively* opinionated. Any impressions one or both writers might've had in childhood have been scrutinized for verification (not always successfully, but one does the best one can). A lot of people have the feeling that 1974 was the hangover after the party of the previous few years, but it's hard to get a numerical index to demonstrate it arithmetically. It *is*, however, one to which anyone who was in Britain then - especially those in school, but not exclusively those active within *Doctor Who* fandom - will attest. The single most important factor about 1973's *Doctor Who* output was that almost nothing new added to the programme's repertoire after "The Time Warrior" hit on the right mix of history and monsters. Every story from then on was, to a large extent, a variation on something developed in the early 70s and using techniques tentatively tried then.

As we saw in the essay on Polystyle comics (under 8.2, "The Mind of Evil"), the Pertwee era's format was infinitely malleable, and there's an almost unlimited number of ways that this character and the kinds of things he encounters could go. The elements are more "portable", can be taken out of the television context and played with by writers, artists and kids playing in the streets more than ever before. Nobody really pretended to be the Hartnell Doctor in the school playground; they all wanted to be Daleks or Cybermen. The public's mental template of *Doctor Who*, even now, is one formed at this point. 1973 was the high-water mark of this whole style of making the series, and the point at which everything stopped changing. With hindsight, it looks like they had reached the place the series had always wanted to reach. It's wrong to think this, and consigning the first decade of the series to the category of "trial runs" is extraordinarily stupid, but a lot of people feel it to be true. It isn't a coincidence that when the 1988 chart-topper "Doctorin' the Tardis" mashed up the theme, some sampled Dalek dialogue and two Glam classics, one of the latter ("Block Buster" by The Sweet) was No. 1 throughout "Carnival of Monsters". (The other charted just after "The Time Monster".) Comedians who avoided the obvious "Daleks can't climb stairs" jokes all referred back to non-existent stories from 1973. (See 26.1, "Battlefield" and the various *New Adventures* references to "the Wondarks of the Wataii Galaxy", supposedly defeated by Pertwee, from *A Bit of Fry and Laurie*.)

As the second most popular figure on British TV that year would say - pausing in the doorway on his way out - just one last thing. As we've seen throughout this volume and in an essay in Volume II, the *Radio Times* was an event in itself. Being on the front cover was an achievement; getting two in a year was a milestone, and getting a special souvenir magazine for a tenth anniversary was unprecedented. 1973 also saw the magazine running a competition for schools to win a real Dalek (or at least, a genuine prop shell) and a follow-up article talking to the bemused winners. After the "Time Warrior" item, with famous and non-famous fans talking about why they watched (reproduced as a pdf on the DVD), the next cover was for "The Five Doctors" (20.7) in 1983, then "Dimensions in Time" ten years after that.

up in the circuits instead of relying on pseudo-science. The Minorians want to get rid of the Doctor because he's a bureaucratic nightmare, not because they want to conquer the galaxy - in fact, they don't want *anything* to do with other worlds. In itself, this is a *very* different sort of adventure story to anything else in the popular media of the 1970s. (With the possible exception of *The Avengers*, which is full of devious scientific masterplans by English eccentrics, although not even *The Avengers* has anything as casual as a space-time-scooping-device whose user has lost the instructions.)

Indeed, it isn't too far away from the serious dramas about Whitehall that the earlier scenes of Time Lords mimicked ("Colony in Space"), but even before this, Holmes had a Time Lord appearing in a bowler and pinstripes as though this were the usual dress-code for people like himself. *Doctor Who*'s war with petty officials began in "The Reign of Terror" (1.8), but has its origins in World War I. People at the sharp end of *any* job, especially trench warfare, can't see the logic of what they're being asked to do. By the early twentieth century, it was axiomatic that neatly-thought out schemes - whilst useful for running railways - weren't always flexible enough to adjust to and assimilate unexpected eventualities. Indeed, the love of order was symptomatic, in the public mind, of a psychological flaw.

With hindsight, Holmes' work had often hinted at the sadism of petty officialdom, starting with the ham-fisted satire of "The Krotons" (in which a machine consumes the best brains and covers it up with euphemisms), through to the minor bureaucrat Maurice Caven (6.6), who gave it all up to become a more ruthless space pirate than the "professional" Dervish. And in "Carnival of Monsters", we have Kalik, who gets off on wielding power. As actor Michael Wisher observed, "He had his whips in the cupboard." We'll see this taken to extremes in "The Sun Makers" (15.4) and "The Caves of Androzani" (21.6).

This is only a slight exaggeration of how most people had always thought Whitehall functioned. The caricature pen-pusher is a figure of fun in Dickens (see 23.4, "The Ultimate Foe") and a symbol of a harsh, incomprehensible universe in Kafka. The fight against this is generally akin to King Canute ordering the tide to turn back.

Then in World War II, we got a champion who cut through the red tape and made progress on his own terms. You think we're talking about Churchill, but he was Admiralty through and through and only opposed bureaucracy that he hadn't personally set up. The *real* hero, someone on whom Pertwee (as the Doctor) imitates as much as anyone, is General Montgomery. (Pertwee had played a Monty-like character in *The Avengers*. The first colour episode, "From Venus With Love" has him play a Brigadier (!) with the beret, moustache and glasses of the hero of Alamein, plus a lot of his verbal mannerisms.)

Monty, however, was arguably following in the footsteps of the great military iconoclast and hero of Mafeking (see 3.4, "the Daleks' Master Plan"), Lord Baden Powell. His inventive and cheeky tactics in the Boer War seem to underlie the Doctor's similar ruses in "The Time Warrior" (11.1), so perhaps this anti-authoritarian strand of the Doctor's persona derives from the same source as the most hidebound paramilitary organisation of all: the Boy Scouts.

For a lot of the story, the Doctor is trapped in another kind of system entirely. Again, the metaphor of machinery and people stuck inside it is one with a long pedigree... Charlie Chaplin's *Modern Times* makes it explicit, though Marx said it earlier. Children of the early 70s would have seen a strange serial, "Oliver in the Overworld" as part of *Little Big Time*, a sort of ITV *Crackerjack* spoiler. The kids in the audience had an entirely different thing to shout: *Hiya Freddie*. In this, Mr Garritty (formerly of Freddie and the Dreamers) told bad jokes and ran around, accompanied by dodgy CSO, inside the workings of a giant grandfather clock with talking components. It even spawned a hit song, "Gimme Dat Ding", which you've heard on the underscore of *The Benny Hill Show*.

However, the machinery in "Carnival" has more in common with the obstacle courses of *It's A Knockout* (see 8.3, "The Claws of Axos"), although the viewers would have found that this technology, like that of T-Mat (6.5, "The Seeds of Death"), was closer to home. Is it *really* coincidental that the Miniscope works the way a child thinks a TV set works? It was a commonplace of the time that everything complicated had tiny little men inside, operating levers and running around on treadmills to provide power. Many sketch-shows played up on the person inside the telly reacting to what went on in the viewers' front rooms. Occasionally, the designers of *Top of the Pops* played up to this and built stages that looked like circuitry, as though the studio were the interior of the viewers' set. This also applies to the existence of contiguous "zones" which only the Doctor can enter at will. Symbolically, he's channel-zapping.

It also suits a generation raised on war-surplus bits and bobs, with an awareness that if it goes wrong, you thump it. Welcome to the world of 1970s tech. The look of the Scope interior is familiar to anyone who'd taken the back off a television or transistor radio - which in 1973 meant anyone who had a dad. We saw in "Colony in Space" how far gadgetry and repair had become ends in themselves, and with the construction of consumer electronics still conceptually graspable by anyone with the will and time (note the Doctor's improvised radio transmitter in 9.3, "The Sea Devils"), a lot of people took it on themselves to construct machines from designs in popular magazines. A lot more took to using electronics without wanting to admit that they didn't know how it worked. Just calling the manufacturer or buying a new one weren't really options then.

More to the point, the national mythology had people lashing up devices triumphing against the "professionals". It was a handy wartime story (see, for instance, *The Dambusters*) and provided endless amusement when underdogs entered sporting events (Eddie "The Eagle" Edwards is only the most recent example). The virtues of thrift, pride in ingenuity (Watt looking at kettles, Fleming discovering penicillin...) and the little-guy-against-the-system all made these stories attractive, but we were self-aware to the point of knowing that there were limits, hence the popularity of William Heath-Robinson's drawings. However, this is less relevant here than another well-worn notion - the short-sightedness of people who, on encountering something truly mysterious, try to milk it for a fast buck.

A penultimate point: our spell-checker reminds us that 'Miniscope' is very like "Kinescope", the old "What the Butler Saw" machines. (You wouldn't believe the fun we've had spell-checking these books.) A final point: the way in which the humans have been 'conditioned' not to see things is so reminiscent of "The War Games" (6.7), the precise amount of Terrance Dicks' rewriting can only be guessed at. Similarly, the characters stuck saying the "lines" they're given echoes "The Mind Robber" (6.2), although Jo never looks directly at the camera when expressing horror at people watching her misfortunes for 'kicks.'

Things That Don't Make Sense Why doesn't the plesiosaurus turn up outside the ship at any point during episodes three or four [is it scared of the Drashigs]? Why does the Doctor materialise inside the Miniscope in his characteristic lying-down position, since he was standing up when he vanished from the outside world, and the device presumably isn't programmed to bend people's limbs around for no good reason? Why does Orum doubt the Drashigs will succeed in breaking through the Miniscope's 'molectic-bonded disillion', when he's seen the Doctor do just that?

How did the Doctor know he was going to need rubber boots that day? Why do they have dynamite in the forward hold? Why do sticks which would only be - comparatively speaking - the size of dandruff cause so much damage to the scope's workings?

And why - complicated issue here - does whatever magical process resets the clocks, rebuilds the hull after a Drashig attack and foregoes the need for anyone on the *Bernice* to regularly eat or visit the loo not re-seal the way out into the works? [The logical answer is that a Time Lord caused this, and thus it's somehow "immune" to the re-set process, in the same way that the Doctor and Jo remember all the previous times they've had *that* conversation with Major Daly. Then again, the Doctor also causes said conversations, so why do Daly, Claire and Andrews not remember any of it? Perhaps they're brainwashed, to the point of not seeing alien technology around, as a form of belt-and-braces procedure. But then we return to the problem of the ship-people eating regular meals, in which case it's probably more a temporal effect than simple hypnosis. Anyway, the whisky doesn't run out because the Doctor has some.]

Why do he and Jo gawk when a giant metal pick (wielded by Vorg) is repeatedly stabbed at them, instead of doing the sensible thing and dashing for cover? And when the *Bernice* temporally "resets" for the final time, why does Jo shout at Andrews, Daly and Claire - as if she's *surprised* that they've forgotten recent events - and get herself captured yet again? Has she not been paying attention?

Why do the innards of the 'scope, which were never (presumably) designed to house organics, have so many convenient walkways? [Well, all right. Maybe it *was* made for miniaturised maintenance crews, hence the fact that there are portals - doors with handles, in fact - out of the works into the various zones. This doesn't explain why there's an iron bar across the doorway, though.] Considering he's broke and the Scope is outlawed, why does Vorg claim he's got insurance on the device but not its livestock? Why does "Five Foot Two, Eyes of Blue" start playing every twenty minutes when the only people who would have a gramophone are talking in a different room?

Why did anyone think the theme tune needed re-doing, especially when the result sounded like Rolf Harris humming along to a Stylophone and a Bontempi organ in a pinball arcade? [American readers will be amongst the minority of people on the planet who know *Doctor Who* but not Rolf Harris. Lucky bleeders! Just type "Stylophone" into an online search and he'll show up, possibly painting, possibly swimming, probably wearing a hideous shirt and wobbling a piece of stiff cardboard.]

Why does the story end with Vorg being honoured for killing the escaped Drashigs and saving Inter Minor - instead of being locked up for bringing them to the planet in the first place? This is doubly odd, when you consider that nobody save Orum (who has reason to keep his mouth shut) *knows* Kalik released them.

Critique Frankly, we worry about the head-health of anyone who doesn't realise that this is what *Doctor Who* is for. Admittedly, it's a simple adventure based around a clever idea that allows spacemonsters, period costumes and dialogue and a distorted-mirror view of something we recognise, but *above all* it permits all the colour and pace of Light Entertainment, early-70s style, to happen for plot reasons. If *Doctor Who* is, as stated occasionally, *Top of the Pops* with plots, this is the Pan's People / Glam Rock story *par excellence*. Even the electronic effects leave a grin on your face.

Strangely, people tend to miss how the two plot-threads within this adventure mirror one another: the unrest amongst the Functionaries isn't what this story is "about" any more than the Doctor is going to upbraid Major Daly for casual racism. Affairs on Inter Minor are a backdrop for Vorg and Shirna (a Doctor / companion surrogate), just as the *S.S. Bernice* is there for Major Daly and Claire. (Another director might have, in fact, had the same actor play Vorg and the Major, just to ram home the point.) As above, so below, and the Sahib and the Wallahs become Zarb and Wallarians. With accurate and in-character costumes in the historical section taken from stock,

the space-age showbiz couple can look gaudy and fanciful with a clear conscience.

The key aesthetic concept here, once again, is "spectacle" - both as part of what this story *does* and what it's *about*. However, the story also allows us to savour the look and sound of three alien worlds and a period setting, plus the exciting 3D set of the circuitry itself. Brian Hodgson wraps up his tenure on 'Special Sounds' in style, making the Drashig noises and the Scope interior sound alien and exciting. Even Dudley Simpson seems to have pulled out the stops for this one. Listening to his scores in sequence, this story is where it goes from squeaky synths and percussion to a chamber-orchestra with varied tone-colours and an overlay of electronics; it was like this in 1969-70, but with the line-up of instruments (based around a clarinet and brass) that will dominate the rest of the decade. He uses electronics within the planet scenes more, but still has the conventional instruments handy for use when appropriate (such as when Shirna explains "entertainment" to Pletrac). Without wishing to overstate the point, Peter Halliday's deadpan punch-line to that gag is arguably the point when the *Doctor Who* that we all understand and cherish really comes into being.

It's very easy to oversell this idea, but a lot of commentators have pointed out that practically no stories of this type existed before "Carnival of Monsters", but there's dozens afterwards. Robert Holmes' background in political journalism and love of the 1950s "social comment" form of science-fiction was the reason he initially hated *Doctor Who*. His revenge was to remake the series to his own specifications, but this story is where he rolls his sleeves up and gets down to it in earnest. Barry Letts observed this linguistic turn as being the root of the programme's (and Holmes') uniqueness. The line about fossil fuel being stored in hygiene-chambers is a direct parody of a pre-war cliché about the working-class and (or so Letts claimed) is meaningless to anyone under thirty - but that alone justified it for him.

Meanwhile, as director, Letts gives the story a sense of place and time. As the sun moves across the desert on Inter Minor as the day progresses, subtly underlining how time is running out for the Doctor and Jo, it's not moving at all for the Bernice's passengers. Holmes gives the Major lines that are, for the majority of viewers, the verbal equivalent of sound effects, giving a period feel to it. However, to anyone who knows what a Madrassi or a Laskhar are, the inference is obvious: imperialist, racist attitudes and snobbery belong in a museum. That's not the main thrust of the story, but it's a consequence of the more radical and interesting idea: that watching other people in lordly detachment is itself a form of imperialism. (He even comes back to this when the Time Lords get rethought and given a 'Panopticon'.) Thirty years before *Big Brother*, we have a *Doctor Who* story ridiculing the idea and showing the viewers themselves to be, at best, parasites. There's a lot more said about this in future; watch as this theme develops over the 1970s.

And from a technical point of view, this is a textbook example of using the medium in ways that film, radio or theatre could never hope to match. Moreover, it's a near-perfect specimen of how to organise four twenty-five minute episodes. Each cliffhanger moves the story into a new phase without contriving any menace. The Doctor is in trouble, but for reasons laid out in advance. You can start watching at *almost* any point and have as much of an idea of the set-up in five minutes as anyone who's been with it from the start - but not through the crass use of repetitive exposition.

Indeed, if any one episode of this were your first-ever exposure to *Doctor Who*, you'd have some idea of the full potential of the series right there. No previous Pertwee story allows such a range of the series' arsenal to be used, and no other episode does so whilst being so completely entertaining. There are two pieces that look like padding - when the Doctor and Jo are chased around the ship in episode one, and when he and Andrews have a punch-up in episode two - but these are both giving us information we need later and showing us things we've not seen before. More to the point, although we get glimpses of the shipboard location in each episode, it serves a different function each time. For a story about people and beings confined inside little bubbles, it has an amazing sense of scale - far greater than many stories that have entire worlds being traversed. There's practically no waste: even scenes cut for time contain dialogue that would've been the saving grace of many other adventures.

This is a story whose "moral" - such as it is - is against hierarchies of any kind, including audiences over performers and Kalik's xenophobia. Some gripe about the primary-coloured look, whinging about the lack of this precious "gritty realism" that made "Colony in Space" such a win-

ner. (Next year, these people will get "Death to the Daleks" and "Invasion of the Dinosaurs", and good luck to them.) As much as anything else, this story's look kept small children entranced, whilst a story too clever for them was being told. The reach of the viewers should always exceed their grasp.

Anyway, what the hell does "realism" mean in that silly phrase? Does it mean characters reacting as they *would* if this situation were to occur? If we're being honest with one another, we get that more here than in "Inferno" (9.4). Does it mean looking as though the story were actually happening? It happens that the 1926 sequences are far more "realistic" than the version of rural life in "The Daemons", or the British Mars missions launched when the Beatles were still together. Who among us has ever walked around inside a Miniscope *so often* as to carp that they don't look like the one seen here? Anyone who'd seen a 70s TV with the back off knew what was really happening here.

The reason it's not as well-remembered outside fandom is, perhaps, that it's entirely self-contained. For almost the only time while Letts and Dicks are running the show, it doesn't really connect to any other story (barring mention of Metebelis 3, and a couple of cameos by Drashigs later on). It's not part of any longer-running storylines such as UNIT or the Master, there's no sign of the Time Lords being involved, and the threat is only to a few beings in a box and a few more watching them.

That is, however, its strength. Anyone with only the vaguest inkling that *Doctor Who* existed before Billie Piper can watch this with no crib-notes. The fact that "Carnival of Monsters" was cleared for DVD release ahead of more apparently obvious choices *and* got included in the 1981 repeat season 'The Five Faces of Doctor Who' (alongside "big" stories such as 18.7, "Logopolis" and 1.1, "An Unearthly Child") speaks volumes.

Astoundingly, we've not even mentioned how good the cast is yet, nor how comfortable they seem in this world. Note that Leslie Dwyer (as Vorg) seems to be ad-libbing in character with the term 'credit-bars', as if he's been doing this for ages. There's a few slightly iffy CSO shots, a slightly repetitive running-around-a-boat scene and one or two wonky bald-wigs... but other than that, this is about as close to perfect as you can get.

The Facts

Written by Robert Holmes. Directed by Barry Letts. Viewing figures: 9.5 million, 9.0 million, 9.0 million, 9.2 million.

Supporting Cast Tenniel Evans (Major Daly), Ian Marter (John Andrews), Jenny McCracken (Claire Daly), Leslie Dwyer (Vorg), Cheryl Hall (Shirna), Peter Halliday (Pletrac), Michael Wisher (Kalik), Terence Lodge (Orum), Stuart Fell (uncredited, but he's the Functionary Who Gets Shot Down and Does a Somersault).

Working Titles "Labyrinth", "Peepshow".

Cliffhangers A huge hand reaches down into the hull of the *S. S. Bernice*, and plucks the TARDIS out of the Miniscope in front of an astonished Doctor; in the "swamp" circuit, Jo is horrified to see the Drashigs rearing up out of the sludge; on Inter Minor, Shirna screams as a tiny, miniaturised Doctor stumbles out of the hatch at the side of the Miniscope.

What Was In The Charts "Blockbuster", The Sweet; "Superstition", Stevie Wonder; "Hocus Pocus", Focus; "Papa Was A Rolling Stone", Temptations.

The Lore

• This is a story created out of managerial expediency. Barry Letts had noticed a couple of potential side-effects of the shift to making two episodes a fortnight and pre-filming a week ahead. One was that if you were making a story in January, the locations were cold and miserable. But if you made it in June, you were more likely to pull it off without getting the flu. The other was that if you made one lot of actors do one bit of the story all in one fortnight, you could pay them off and not have to bring them back a fortnight later.

So Robert Holmes was asked to devise a story where two sets of characters who never meet are influencing one another for four episodes (allowing the largest possible number of sets per episode). His solution, "The Labyrinth", was first proposed in May 1971.

A third corollary occurred to Letts: namely that if they made a story in summer and held it over until later, they could all go off on their holidays and start the next block of recordings with the scripts all ready. Pertwee was by this time very much in demand and so allowing him two months off seemed like a good way to keep the star enthusiastic. (We refer you to the trouble Pertwee's cabaret appearances caused on location during "The Daemons", at around the time this story first emerged.)

• Once again, Letts volunteered to direct Holmes' four-part script (as per "Terror of the Autons"). Whilst Holmes had been writing for a number of other series, he delivered workable proposals around Christmas (just after "The Sea Devils" finished production) and the first proper scripts (now called "Out of the Labyrinth") by the following February. Knowing that he'd drawn the short straw with the budgets, he surmised that the monsters would made with dish-rags (hence the anagram 'Drashigs').

The cliffhanger to the first episode was initially the revelation that aliens are observing Our Heroes; the material on Inter Minor began in episode two. The terminology was slightly different, with a 'Strobe' rather than a Miniscope and a 'Glo-Sphere' showing the occupants. The Inter Minorian capital was called the 'Vol-Dome'. For at least one more draft, the planet Inter Minor was called 'Odron' and the various Odronites had number-letter combinations to denote rank. Kalik was 'X10', and the subplot of an attempted coup against his brother was introduced here.

By the time rehearsals began, the story was called "Peepshow" and a few smaller changes had been made. The Palare scene was added, as was the string-file to make the sonic screwdriver less of a "get out of jail free" item. The Doctor and Jo were no longer forced to hide in the chicken-pen from Vorg's hand and the "lateral thinking" sequence was inserted.

• The story began filming at the end of May with the Marsh sequences. The two leads had to stand on boards to spread their weight when filming close-ups. Manning made a mis-step and began slowly sinking in the boggy soil. That was in Burnham-on-Crouch, in Essex. The SS *Bernice* scenes were filmed a few miles south in Kent, on the river Medway, where a mothballed Fleet Auxiliary Vessel was moored permanently. (Letts shot it carefully to make it seem as though the ship were at sea and not tethered to anything. The establishing shot of her in the middle of a body of water is a rare example of CSO working better than many of today's CG effects.)

Here they were joined by several Indian extras, Andrew Staines (you've seen him as Goodge in "Terror of the Autons" and will see him again at the end of this book) as the captain and Ian Marter as Andrews. Marter had been in a few films, usually as policemen (you may have seen him in *The Abominable Dr Phibes*: if not, why not?) but had been taken very ill and hadn't worked much in the previous year before playing Andrews.

During the filming of these scenes, an incident involving a nautical compass took place, the details of which altered every time Pertwee told the story at conventions. We've tried to get the definitive version, but life really is too short.

• Into the studio on 19th of June and Tenniel Evans, who had first persuaded Pertwee to consider playing the Doctor, joins the cast as Major Daly. As Pertwee's co-star on *The Navy Lark* since 1959, Evans had a head start in bonding with the regulars. However, a lot of the rehearsal time was spent on gossiping and joking. Jenny McCracken (Daly's daughter Claire) had done *Counterstrike* and *Crossroads*, but her most recent telly had been as another 1920s flapper in the PJ Hammond *Ace of Wands* yarn "Peacock Pie". (Later she was in football-themed kid's sitcom *Jossy's Giants,* written by surrealist Darts commentator Sid Waddell, and was credited as Milla Jovovich's acting coach in *The Fifth Element*.)

• During the filming, someone had pointed out that the Indian Ocean at that time of night should be pitch-dark, so Letts had a line added to the dialogue. Far from being dishcloths, the Drashigs were fashioned from hose-ducting and the mandibles of terriers in latex hand-puppets. (This sets a grisly precedent for the use of fox-skulls in the giant maggots later this year - see "The Green Death".) Although the majority of the scenes with Drashigs had been pre-filmed, they and the Plesiosaur - also a puppet, if you'd not guessed - were used "live" in the studio with operators dressed in yellow manipulating them for CSO inlay.

• In both recording blocks they did some of the Scope interior scenes. Designer Roger Liminton, on his first *Doctor Who* out of two (we've just looked at the second, "The Three Doctors") based his idea on printed circuit boards rather than the cogs and mole-drives hinted at in the script. Letts used the lighting gantry of the studio in some shots, to give a sense of scale (see also 19.6, "Earthshock") and a few models for forced-per-spective scenes. Liminton's contribution earned him an interview in the *Radio Times* Tenth Anniversary special, where he said that he'd taken his cue from the TV cameras and *Top of the Pops* sets. As you'll have seen, "The Three Doctors" - made six months later - re-used elements, making the Scope interior less impressive than it could have been for regular viewers.

• The original ending for episode three was recorded in this session. In this, the Doctor is trapped by a charging Drashig and a vertiginous drop. He finds his ankle trapped in wiring. The Drashig approaches and goes off the edge (this is the one the Doctor finds dead in episode four as shown). Astute readers will, of course, notice the similarity to the second cliffhanger in "The Caves of Androzani", also by Holmes. Terry Walsh doubled for the Doctor in the stunt where he's hanging on the ledge by the wires, as you'd expect by now.

• A fortnight later the Inter Minor bits began, with the first day given to the scenes without the Doctor or Jo. Michael Wisher came back as Kalik, after his stint as Rex in Letts' last story as director - this means, counting his Dalek voices, that he's in the cast for three consecutive stories this year. Peter Halliday (Pletrac) had been the head stooge Packer in 6.3, "The Invasion" and had done voiceovers in Season Seven. Terence Lodge (Orum) had been was the dissident Medok in 4.7, "the Macra Terror". All three of them will return later in the series.

Cheryl Hall (Shirna) had just been in *A Clockwork Orange*, but would really find fame in *Citizen Smith*. (It's a sitcom about a none-too-bright group attempting a Marxist insurrection in Tooting - this says more about the 70s in Britain than any number of textbooks.) She later wound up on the Arts committee of Kent County Council (so DVDs of this story might be easier to find in their libraries). Leslie Dwyer (Vorg) has his claim to fame in a later sitcom, *Hi-De-Hi!* (see 24.3, "Delta and the Bannermen"), wherein he played a grumpy Punch and Judy man who hates children. Dicks picked up Vorg's line about a 'carnival of monsters' and made it the new title, to Holmes' slight chagrin.

• One shot recorded here, but not used in the final edit, is a Drashig chewing Kalik. It may have been too gory for kids or (more likely) have looked exactly like a glove-puppet eating an Action Man doll in Interminorian clothing. Jim Acheson made the Lurman costumes distinctive even for people watching in black and white by giving them texture and contrast. Shirna's hair had spring-mounted polystyrene balls (something Acheson found in a seaside gift-shop, ten years before Deeley-Boppers were bafflingly popular) and Vorg had a Perspex bowler hat (which steamed up periodically). The Inter Minorians had grey make-up (after a brief flirtation with masks modelled on casts of the actors' faces) and bald skull-caps that wrinkled and came unglued. One scene at the end has this happen to Halliday so obviously, Letts trimmed it for the repeat.

• The Functionaries had a one-size-fits-all mask, covering the faces of stalwarts Murphy Grumbar and Stuart Fell. His ascent to the Upper Level was one of the scenes the BBC included in their behind-the-scenes documentary *Looking In*, which celebrated fifty years of the Corporation, and this scene was a script excerpt in Malcolm Hulke's *Writing for Television*, with notes by Holmes and Letts. The Eradicator effect in this instance was a variation on howlround, using feedback from the camera looking at a monitor but with deliberate interference introduced. As we've noted elsewhere, this effect was later adopted for *Top of the Pops* and accompanied Alice Cooper's rendition of "School's Out" in August that year. This effect was too fiddly to use when another CSO input was added to the equation, so some shots with the big Eradicator simply used a red glow. Some of the material shown on the Scope was pre-recorded *Bernice* shots which had used a fish-eye lens. Others, using the lens again (Rick Lester as an Ogron, Terence Denville as a Cyberman), were fed from another part of the studio against CSO backdrops or a filmed model-shot of Drashigs.

• As we've already hinted, much of the running-order of material recorded was changed in editing. A lot of "colour" was taken from episode one and the gaps filled with expository scenes from episode two. A few of the trimmed scenes are on the DVD, including one where the Lurmans are spoken to the way the English are "supposed" to talk to foreigners, and Shirna replies in Pidgin.

In fact, DVD-buyers will have seen a longer episode two than we did then, because the Australian company ABC bought this serial and were sent an earlier edit. The differences are small and marked up in the notes: on this is the attempted re-make of the theme tune, the notorious "Delaware" version. Letts had got it into his head that a purely electronically-realised version would be more up-to-date. Paddy Kingsland gave it his best shot with the Workshop's new EMS rig (see the essay with "The Mutants") but Ronnie Marsh heard it and ordered them to replace it with the previous take. This slipped the scissors when the Australian copy was shipped out. (The only time *we* heard it was on a trailer.)

Simpson's score for this story was dubbed on in late October, almost four months later. He had a band of five musicians and extra electronic sounds (we assume that Dick Mills did these, although Brian Hodgson and Simpson were collaborating on the theme for *The Tomorrow People* shortly before this).

10.3: "Frontier in Space"

(Serial QQQ, Six Episodes, 24th February - 31st March 1973.)

Which One is This? *Doctor Who* finally does space opera properly, as the Doctor gets locked up in prisons all over the galaxy in order to prevent some terrible force of evil stirring up a war between humans and Draconians. Who's behind it all? You get two guesses, and they're both right.

Firsts and Lasts First story of Season Ten to be filmed. This is a big change (see 9.3, "The Sea Devils") and, as the production codes indicate, everything else is complicated by it.

It's also, of course, the last appearance of the original Master; Roger Delgado's death in June 1973 meant that the character didn't return until well into Tom Baker's reign, and was then radically rethought. Overall it's not a bad goodbye to the series - full of quality gloating and some elegant wit - but on the other hand, our very last sight of him leaves much to be desired (see **Things to Notice**). This also marks the first time a Time Lord affects a fake cockney accent and it's a real cockney - Delgado was born in East London - who does it. Sadly, this will be repeated by the Doctor (11.2, "Invasion of the Dinosaurs"), Drax (16.6, "The Armageddon Factor") and the Tenth Doctor's perpetual Kenneth Williams impression.

Though previous stories have suggested that the TARDIS somehow materialises in space on its way from planet to planet (5.5, "The Web of Fear" and 8.4, "Colony in Space" both spring to mind), this is the first story in which we actually see the

TARDIS spinning through a black void, as if it's started flying around the place like a spaceship. The first of these, though, is stated as being in hyperspace (which has an odd light-blue patch when seen on monitors, strangely) and the last has no stars. That's a point... first use in the series of the term 'hyperspace'.

First use of the space-gun props, one of which will crop up again and again, notably as the Doctor's dinosaur-stunner in - oh, you guessed - "Invasion of the Dinosaurs". Oh look, it's Terry Walsh firing one of them.

A small but significant point: this is the first time that Dudley Simpson has used a bass clarinet to signify aliens - one of the hallmarks of the so-called "gothic" phase coming in Volume IV, even though he used it for a creepy jungle as early as 2.8, "The Chase" - and the first story on which Dick Mills actually did 'Special Sound'. For the rest of the 70s, the Mills-Simpson collaboration will give the series' sound an equally distinctive feel.

Last time the TARDIS makes the "flanged" rematerialisation noise, used since "The Seeds of Death" (6.5) four years earlier. Things go back to normal now.

Six Things to Notice About "Frontier in Space"...

1. Designed as an epic, galaxy-spanning piece of SF adventure (and with some politics thrown in for good measure), "Frontier in Space" has a sense of scope not seen in *Doctor Who* since "The Daleks' Master Plan" in 1965-6. In fact it's just the first half of a twelve-part saga which ultimately sees the Doctor go to a Dalek-infested planet and dispose of their army ("The Daleks' Master Plan" was also split, more or less, down the middle by two writers). There's another unconscious flashback to the 1965 story: the Doctor's space-helmet is recycled from one of the delegates in "Mission to the Unknown", the one we've tentatively identified as 'Beaus'. (See **Which Sodding Delegate Is Which?** under "The Daleks' Master Plan", but be advised that information has come to light that makes some of those findings questionable. No, we're not going to re-do Volume I just for that.) It also gets used as the dead pilot's helmet in the next story.

However, in "Frontier in Space" the Daleks only reveal themselves in episode six - the only occasion on which their return was kept secret from the viewers instead of being massively advertised by the BBC. The following week, though, saw a *massive* campaign.

2. "Frontier in Space" uses model spaceships and latex-faced monsters like they were going out of style (which, in one way, they were). Notably, it contrasts with the previous Pertwee future romps, where it's all been colonials griping about over-population whilst stomping around in quarries.

These days, the models might look a bit ropey but it's worth repeating that BBC audiences had only the Apollo coverage and *Star Trek* for comparison, and the latter was already notorious for re-use of a few stock model shots. But it's what those space journeys connect that's important. What's really striking is that although the Doctor sees such a huge swathe of the galaxy - an Earth vessel under attack, Earth itself in the twenty-sixth century, a penal colony on the moon, a prison ship owned by the Master, the heart of the Draconian Empire and finally the planet of the Ogrons - he does most of it from inside a variety of prison cells. Meanwhile, Jo is locked up mid-way through episode one and, apart from a brief visit to Draconia and her permitted "escape" in episode five, she's only free right at the end.

3. The future-Earth settings have a slightly familiar look. The Draconian compound is a genuine building, very 70s-looking. The Draconian Embassy also has the last word in advanced technology 1972-style: a spherical TV set that can only get a black and white picture. (Waddaya want? Hovercars?) Similarly homely (though we never thought we'd say it at the time) is the concrete penal block that is obviously the South Bank complex. We're led to believe that the Doctor and Jo are incarcerated in the Hayward Gallery, and that Ogrons-pretending-to-be-Draconians launch an assault from the Festival Hall.

4. We're actually rather pleased to point this out: Louis Mahoney as the info-dump dispenser is an incidental detail that passes most viewers by these days. But in 1973, a black man reading the news was more futuristic than hyperdrives, mind probes or a Lunar gulag. And most heartening is that he retains a Jamaican accent, rather than attempting Received Pronunciation. (He'll be back twice, in 13.2, "Planet of Evil" and X3.10, "Blink".) How people speak on the 2540 version of BBC Radio 4 is another matter - Patel (one of the Peace Party convicts on the moon) and the President are clearly aiming at some kind of standardised English that isn't American.

5. The final cliffhanger and its resolution is one of those moments where Dicks' background in

soap operas pays off. The regular viewer has been following Jo's progress from irritatingly ditzy hanger-on who gets captured to self-controlled and independent agent (i.e. more or less the character Letts originally created in 1970 before redrafting it to suit Katy Manning). Anyone watching the stories in order will recognise her defiance of the Master's hypnosis - and the *second* parade of old monsters in two stories - as a sign that she's not long for this show.

Yet what's remarkable is that this is one of a number of Jo-moments where they acknowledge the show's usual practice and play with expectations. Here, Jo's plucky and imaginative escape from a cell, allowing her to contact the Doctor with the Ogron planet's co-ordinates, is *exactly* what the Master hoped she'd do. Also bear in mind the start of episode two, where she lays out a couple of well-worn escape plans, and the Doctor calmly asks what they'd do when they escape. She suggests hijacking the ship and going to Earth - whereupon the Doctor says, 'but we're *going* to Earth'. This sort of self-awareness will become a useful time-saver in later stories, especially once we change Doctors.

6. At the conclusion of the final episode, the Doctor activates one of the Master's fear-generating devices and causes all the Ogrons to scatter. Two things are noticeable here. One: as they panic, the Ogrons make a noise much like a crowd of Gumbies from *Monty Python's Flying Circus*. (Though elsewhere in the story the Master's relationship with the Ogrons is almost exactly like Basil Fawlty and Manuel, while his response to the Daleks' orders is like Basil Fawlty and Sybil.) Two: the Master also vanishes at this point, Roger Delgado's final appearance in the series being utterly bewildering as he's simply in the middle of things one minute and gone the next. Presumably he runs off with the panicking Ogrons (bizarre in itself, since the Doctor's unconscious by this point and he can't be terribly worried when *Jo* snatches up his gun), but surely we should at least be able to see which way he goes...? (See **The Lore** for the probable reasons behind this muddle.)

The Continuity

The Doctor He feels something like a 'premonition' when Daleks are near [the same feeling he gets in 3.10, "The War Machines"]. Conversely, he can't hear the high-pitched squeak of the Master's 'fear-box'. [It would be sensible if the Master designed it not to work on Time Lords.]

• *Ethics.* He overtly states that he's acting on behalf of peace, although for only the second time in his career he's seen to use a gun - and once again he's shooting at Ogrons [q.v. 9.1, "Day of the Daleks"]. Curiously, when the Ogrons assault the cargo ship, the Doctor flings one of the crewmen into the attackers - even though such a move is likely to result in the crewman's death. [It happens that the Ogrons want the crew alive, but the Doctor doesn't know that.]

• *Inventory.* Reversing the polarity of the sonic screwdriver's power-source allows the Doctor to use it as an electromagnet, powerful enough to pull back huge metal bolts. The Doctor carries the string file from "Carnival of Monsters" (10.2), but it's now in his boot, not around his neck. It's capable of sawing through prison bars. He has a hand-held radio direction-finder and there's a small watchmaker's screwdriver in one of the frills of his shirt. [Honest! It's in episode six.]

Prison authorities confiscate his sonic screwdriver in episode three and don't return it. [So we can assume that he has a ready supply of them, as seen in X3.1, "Smith and Jones". This does, however, make its non-use after 19.4, "The Visitation" perplexing.]

• *Background.* The Doctor claims he was once captured by the Medusoids, hairy jellyfish with claws, teeth and a leg. They put him under a mind probe to ascertain where he was going, and he told them he was going to meet a giant rabbit, a pink elephant and a purple horse with yellow spots; technically true, as all three were delegates at the Third Intergalactic Peace Conference. At least two mind probes had nervous breakdowns as a result, and the Medusoids eventually had to let the Doctor go. [All of this sounds, however, like one of those spurious Terrible Zodin anecdotes (see 20.7, "The Five Doctors"; 22.1, "Attack of the Cybermen"). But as we now know that spacesuited rhinos are acting as galactic police (again, "Smith and Jones"), we can't be entirely sure that he's making this cobblers up...]

The Doctor has been to Draconia before - see **Planet Notes** - and knows its customs well. He claims that he only 'borrowed' his TARDIS, and that it was hardly the latest model at the time. He shows no surprise at the offences with which he's charged by the Master - including beating up

Is This Any Way to Run a Galactic Empire?

We've been talking a lot in this volume about the various ways that *Doctor Who* took off-the-shelf items from American Science-Fiction (and in particular the 1940s *Astounding*, beloved of Terrance Dicks and *Star Trek* writers) and gave them a sardonic, low-budget British spin. Yet the most peculiar manifestation of this is something the majority of viewers, on both sides of the Atlantic, never seem to question.

Since before World War II, but especially since what was (at the time) a radical reconfiguration in the late 1940s and early 1950s, American writers of varying degrees of talent and integrity have attempted different kinds of Space Operatic tales about Galactic Empires. Black and white-era *Doctor Who* had occasionally shown various militaristic imbeciles stomping around planets where they didn't oughta, be claiming such-and-such a quarry / set in Lime Grove in the name of the So-and-So Empire. Yet it's only in the Pertwee era that the idea that Earth has a Manifest Destiny on a pretty grand scale really kicked in.

For the majority of BBC viewers, it seemed relatively obvious as the stories that did this were trading on notions of a future pretty much along the lines that American shows had established, just with actors who could talk properly (well, by-and-large; see 9.4, "The Mutants"). But the matter was more peculiar for those who knew the source-material, and the basic question that was never asked out loud was this: why are American hacks so obsessed with Empires? The more complicated query, however, troubled us earlier in this volume, so we'll state it here: why did British TV hacks, most of whom actually knew what running an Empire entailed and why it had eventually done nobody any favours, go along with the American hacks' model so uncritically?

We'll have to step back and define terms first. The Galactic Empire is a hoary idea from the earliest days of the pulps, pre-Gernsbach. (That's Hugo Gernsbach, after whom the award Steven Moffat keeps winning is named. He - Gernsbach, that is, not Moffat - coined the term "Science Fiction" in 1926 and has thus caused a lot of misunderstandings. See **Could It Be Magic?** under 25.4, "The Greatest Show in the Galaxy", **Is This An SF Show?** under 14.4, "The Face of Evil" and a lot elsewhere.) We're talking about an era when the terms "Galaxy" and "Universe" were interchangeable (something David Whitaker never got the hang of even in the 1960s). It's a quick and dirty shorthand for a big off-stage power that makes demands on protagonists and antagonists, and thus justified any number of outlandish plots.

The idea was refined over the years, mainly under the auspices of the most powerful and diligent editor of the era, John W Campbell. He took over *Astounding Science Fiction* in the late 1930s, and sternly weeded out a lot of the lazy thinking that misplaced Western-writers and Pirate Adventure peddlers had got away with when turning their hand to space-yarns. When we're looking at Galactic Empires, we're basically dealing with a combination of three authors, two of whom were on his roster. First up is the gonzo baroque of AE Van Vogt. His works have the same kind of plot logic as a Terry Gilliam animation from *Monty Python,* albeit motivated by paranoia (his books had a resurgence of popularity among 70s stoners). A hero who discovers dormant psychic or cognitive powers is chased across the Solar System by repressive regimes who betray him at every turn, but always fail to catch him because he suddenly learns to teleport / hypnotise / stop time.

Van Vogt's galactic empires come in two flavours: the benign observers who cannot interfere, but shepherd humanity on to a higher plane of being by telling Our Hero what's going on in a dream or something[111] *or* the more interesting but less potent humans who squabble and feud over vast but finite power-sources. In the latter category comes *Empire of the Atom,* a shameless reworking of Robert Graves' *I, Claudius.* In many ways the original configuration of the Time Lords (6.7, "The War Games") and the more venal and factional version (14.3, "The Deadly Assassin") both have echoes of this, as does - strangely enough - the second radio series of *The Hitch-Hiker's Guide to the Galaxy.*

However, Van Vogt was following a trail blazed by an earlier and even more lurid author, E.E. "Doc" Smith. If read in the order of publication, his *Lensman* books each step back from the previous story to show that the affairs of one scale are shadowy reflections of a bigger battle between older forces. What begins as a simple tale of fairly anal-retentive space-cops with a bit of telepathy for routine stop-and-search purposes becomes the Grand Battle between forces of Order and Chaos, with a bit of police procedural stuff involving stopping crime by smashing one planet between two other larger ones. Imagine, if you will, Lt Hugo

continued on page 335...

policemen and stealing spaceships - which suggests he may well have done these things at some time, past or future. He also claims that he's never been 'employed' by anybody [possibly true, allowing for his unique standing at UNIT].

The Supporting Cast

• *Jo Grant*. She seems to think she's being used as a general dogsbody at UNIT, who mainly makes tea and does filing. She finds filing really complicated. We finally get on-screen confirmation [after 8.1, "Terror of the Autons"] that her uncle got her the job there.

While extemporising to keep the Master from realising that the Doctor's gone for a space-walk (wherein she uses 'I mean' a lot), she claims that it's unfair of the Doctor to keep refusing the Master's offer of a share of whatever power's on offer. She keeps up the pretence even after the course-correction apparently sends the Doctor off into deep space forever. She later insists that she's never going in the TARDIS again after she gets home.

When the Master's fear-machine shows Jo what she's most afraid of, she sees a Drashig, then a Mutt, then a Sea Devil. [It's working its way backwards through her monster-memories, although the Master himself is apparently no longer giving her nightmares.] By now she's learned techniques to prevent her falling for the Master's hypnosis by filling her mind with nonsense, or at least more nonsense than usual. Jo mentions a film where someone overpowers two 'big fellers', which suggests that she watches a lot of gangster movies.

[By the way, when they get back in the TARDIS, Jo is wielding a gun. Did the original ending have her shoot the Master? See **The Lore** to find out.]

The Supporting Cast (Evil)

• *The Master.* Once again, the Master would apparently rather save the Doctor's life and gloat than see his rival die quickly, genuinely feeling that a long-range killing lacks 'the personal touch'. [See **Things That Don't Make Sense** for more on this.] He knows some Earth poetry, specifically Tennyson. Here he's moved on from watching *The Clangers* and is seen reading Wells' *The War of the Worlds*. [Obviously there's some sense of irony here, but nobody is watching him read, so he's not just showing off. If nothing else, this suggests that he's capable of enjoying a good book, and that he's not wholly sociopathic.] He denounces the

Doctor's 'usual sickening lovability'.

His stated part of the deal with the Daleks is to become ruler of Earth, although he's planning to make a move on the entire galaxy, somehow. [One bizarre detail: if his reward for helping the Daleks is to become ruler of a post-war Earth, what is there about our planet that he craves so much? He can't be doing it to get back at the Doctor, whom he doesn't know is operating in this time zone. Or is it just a stepping-stone to his betraying the Daleks and grabbing a bigger prize?

[Another small but significant point: at no time does the Master show any sign of having a TARDIS at his disposal. All right, keeping it hidden is a sensible precaution - especially given how often it was broken into in Season Eight - but is it possible that he's stranded in this time? After all, we don't actually know what Kronos did to his Ship (in 9.5, "The Time Monster"), but at some point between this story and the next time we see him - on Gallifrey, where TARDISes are easier to come by - he's fated to get stranded on Tersurus, on almost literally his last legs (14.3, "The Deadly Assassin").]

Oddly - and unlike his guise as the Adjudicator ["Colony in Space"], he appears to have really put in some time as a high-ranking official in the government of Sirius IV, since he's using a real spaceship [not a disguised TARDIS] and his documents are good enough to fool the President. Indeed, he may well have been present at the High Court of Bassat, when indictments were brought against the Doctor and Jo for tax-dodging and defrauding the Sirius Union Bank.

The Master uses a few colloquial British turns of phrase when talking with Jo, suggesting that she will 'rot in here for the rest of yer natural', and later telling her, 'Thank you Miss Grant, we'll let you know'. When impersonating a police vessel captain, he adopts the traditional voice of a London bobby such as George Dixon [see 2.1, "Planet of Giants" and 14.6, "The Talons of Weng-Chiang" - presumably radio, or whatever FTL comms they use, distorts his voice so that the Doctor doesn't twig his identity]. The Master equips his Ogron underlings with portable hallucinatory hypno-sound devices, which work on the fear centres deep within the mind and make the Ogrons' victims see whatever they're most afraid of [an offshoot of the Keller process from 8.2, "The Mind of Evil"?]. Even so, Jo sees the Ogron ship briefly change shape just like the

Is This Any Way to Run a Galactic Empire?

...continued from page 333

Lang (21.7, "The Twin Dilemma") developed Jedi powers and became the agent of the White Guardian (16.1, "The Ribos Operation") who was in turn a pawn of something even bigger. Other writers followed Smith's lead, none of them quite managing to be as outrageous or as banal (it *is* possible to be both, as he also proved with his even more preposterous *Skylark* stories[112]), but the general trend is that a story with a galactic empire in it has some kind of mystical agenda.

The other Campbell writer to really make this sort of story his own was a kid from Brooklyn who changed the rules. Sort of. His contribution takes us back to the problem with *Doctor Who* doing this but by a strange route...

So this teenager, Isaac Asimov, has meetings of fellow fans in a room over his parents' candy-store. The New York / Brooklyn SF fraternity includes a lot of future big name writers in the field and many of them, being scared of Fascism for various reasons (it's not coincidence that Campbell asked them to write under more Anglo-Saxon sounding names), hang out with teenage Marxists. After all, Marx's theory of Dialectical Materialism and of History following rules as basic as those for gasses under pressure looks scientific - a set of Laws underlying History and making Sociology into a predictive science.

Fast forward to after the War. Asimov is less enamoured of the idea, but still intrigued. He does a string of short stories about a mathematical genius who can predict what society's going to do (because when you're dealing with a whole galaxy, the actuarial probabilities become like the statistical behaviour of the molecules of gas in a vessel being heated). Asimov cheats a bit, however, by having the "predictions" turn out to be like the conclusions drawn by Edward Gibbons in *The Decline and Fall of the Roman Empire*. Campbell comes along and says "why not make these a series?" (this, if you haven't guessed, gestates into Asimov's *Foundation* trilogy - as it was until 1985, when a fourth book came along and things got out of hand), even as those self-proclaimed Marxist chums of his are all hauled before the McCarthy Witch-hunts. So the start of Asimov's story is the mathematician Hari Seldon and his followers being hounded and exiled for saying that the empire is going to topple in a few centuries' time.

We could sit and tick off the pilfering in *Doctor Who / Blake's 7 / Star Trek / Star Wars* all day (everyone in this field owes Asimov big time, even if they don't know it), but let's be brief. Seldon has cannily manoeuvred the Galactic Emperor into doing exactly what the Seldon Plan needs: the followers are sent to a worthless planet on the edge of the galaxy, where they are ostensibly preserving all the knowledge of the Empire in the *Encyclopaedia Galactica*. In fact they're using this accumulated science to parlay their limited resources into first holding the balance of power when nearby planets secede from the Empire, then passing off their science as miracles and starting a cargo-cult religion, *then* becoming economically vital. The thing is, although Asimov models his Foundation on the way the Arabs took advantage of having the best versions of what ancient knowledge remained after the Library of Alexandra burned down and Rome fell to the Vandals and Goths, the planet is also a version of New York. So is Trantor, the Capital of the decaying Empire. (It's a planet entirely covered in skyscrapers, which are later demolished and the rubble sold for scrap. Later on, we get a spaceport based on Grand Central Station.)

Just pause here and consider...out of all the fictional Galactic Empires we've just outlined, do *any* of them in any way resemble the British Empire? Hardly, and less so the closer you look.

In 1972, as you may recall from Volume II, the BBC Radiophonic Workshop did a version of the *Foundation* Trilogy that is, in many ways, the closest thing to *Doctor Who* without the Doctor that one can get. It was conceived by David Cain, one of the old school soundmongers who had, unlike his contemporaries, adapted to the new age of voltage control (see **What's Going On With This Music?** under "The Mutants") and provided a score / atmospheres more oblique and challenging than anything in Season Nine. What's worth noting is that it was transmitted on the "quality" station, Radio 4, and had lots of instantly recognisable character actors. (You'll know many of whom from *Who* - an argument between Lord Stettin and his consort, played by Peter Pratt and Prunella Scales, is irresistibly like a version of "The Deadly Assassin" with Sybil Fawlty.) Lines written to be said in Brooklyn accents were delivered as though this were a dramatisation of a nineteenth-century novel. Characters that Asimov had written as hustlers straight out of Damon Runyan stories were transformed into self-made entrepreneurial engi-

continued on page 337...

Earth people do. [So some of the humans' responses to the device might be programmed into its signal to guarantee that all afflicted Earthmen - including the crewman who seems level-headed about the current political tensions - see the Ogrons as Draconians, when at least some of them might fear (say) snakes, spiders or otters more.]

The Master is, once again [after 8.3, "The Claws of Axos" and "Colony in Space"], packing an energy weapon of some kind, as well as a bulky signalling device that's somehow concealed in his rather tight tunic.

The TARDIS It appears in the path of the Earth vessel during its 'hyperspace transition', and the Doctor pulls off a last-minute course correction to land inside the ship 'in normal space'. [See **Can the TARDIS Fly?** under 5.6, "Fury from the Deep".] Ultimately the Doctor uses the Ship's telepathic circuits to send a message to the Time Lords [see the next story]. Given an accurate data, he can work out the correct course coordinates.

The Non-Humans

• *Draconians.* Human-like but with reptilian scales on their faces, crests on their heads and a tendency to hiss, here the Draconians are portrayed as Earth's rival power in the galaxy, the only time any other species inside human-space is shown to *have* a serious Empire. They're also more than a little Japanese, with a male-dominated society that forbids females to speak in the Emperor's presence and a culture of aristocratic warrior-nobility. [Although rather more has been made of this in fan-fiction than the author intended.]

They claim they never lie; the President of Earth doesn't dispute this and claims that the 'honour' of the Draconian race is well known. Their homeworld is, logically, Draconia. Like Earth, Draconia is expanding and colonising planets. The Doctor speaks of only *two* great empires in the Milky Way at this point. More significantly there isn't a higher authority to whom Earth and Draconia can go to for arbitration.

Humans refer to Draconian ships as being 'galaxy class' and fitted with neutronic missiles, and insultingly refer to the Draconians themselves as "dragons". [Is Draconia actually in the constellation of Draco, the dragon? If so, it's a remarkable coincidence that they're reptilian. Perhaps Earth's sun is in the Draconian constellation of "the Great Ape". Draco, a long, windey constellation, contains 130 stars visible to the naked eye, as well as several juicy galaxies. There are three plausible G-class stars (like ours) within 100 parsecs: 63_ (Tyl), 14_ (Aldhibah) and 23_ (Alwaid).]

Draconians see humans as 'inscrutable'. The title of Emperor is hereditary, the Emperor being addressed as 'majesty', but Emperors rely upon support from the 'Great Families' and have been deposed before now. (As we will see, this makes the Draconians more akin to the Hapsburgs). The Emperor's son is referred to as a prince, addressed as 'highness'. 'My life at your command' is a typical Draconian statement of respect between people of noble rank, Draconian or otherwise.

The fifteenth Emperor ruled five hundred years ago [their years, but how long these are is anyone's guess], and made the Doctor an honorary noble of Draconia. There's still a legend among Draconians of a man who helped their people when they were almost overwhelmed by a 'great plague' from outer space, and the Emperor still knows the names 'Doctor' and 'TARDIS'.

[This event has plausibly been argued to have taken place some time before 1970, and that Draconia is the fabled "Planet 14" where the Cybermen observed the Second Doctor and Jamie. See 6.3, "The Invasion" for an alternate theory. The connection between Cybermen and plague shouldn't need elaborating; see 12.5, "Revenge of the Cybermen" and 4.6, "The Moonbase". Then again, it's the season for such things - Inter Minor once had a 'Great Space Plague', and look what the Daleks brew up in the next one.]

No reason is ever given for forbidding females to speak. [It's presented to us as simple sexism, but they tolerate Jo as part of odd 'alien' customs. As we never see a Draconian female, nor hear one speak, this is debatable. Perhaps they have sultry voices which drive their menfolk wild with desire, or perhaps they really are stupid, being "breed-mares".] Draconians are said to have mind probes at their disposal.

• *Ogrons.* The Doctor establishes that Ogrons are mercenaries, and that a lot of life-forms employ them, not just Daleks [q.v. "Day of the Daleks", "Carnival of Monsters"]. Ogrons are apparently resistant to mind probes because they're too stupid (although they can at least fly spaceships). The weapons carried by the Ogrons here can stun as well as kill, the Doctor believing

Is This Any Way to Run a Galactic Empire?

...continued from page 335

neers midway between I.K. Brunel and a Trollope novel. Cocky Pentagon types became petulant public schoolboys. And this is our biggest clue as to what exactly is going on in *Doctor Who's* attempt at the same thing.

In Earth's history there is, with one significant exception, a single thread running through all successful empires that were actually honest enough to proclaim themselves empires: they started by accident. They tend to begin when other, larger empires threaten trading routes, and military means are used to reinforce the safe ones. With the Romans, it was Carthage that was perceived as the enemy; politicians on the make could always get an ovation by demanding action. (*Cartago delenda est* - "Carthage must be destroyed" - is still perhaps the most successful slogan in the history of electioneering.)

Now let's flash forward and consider how an Industrial Revolution will produce more stuff than a tiny island full of farmers can possibly use. The British were happily selling mass-produced goods and getting raw materials in return, but then Napoleon decided this had to stop, in the interest of his dreams of making the kids who bullied him at school shut up coming true. Thus his campaign in Egypt made the British presence in India more vulnerable and put them on a war-footing.

Up until then, the story of Britain and India was a lot more complex and bilateral than is widely supposed. (See **Did Sergeant Pepper Know the Doctor?** under 5.1, "The Tomb of the Cybermen" for one aspect of this.) Similarly there's General Wolfe in Canada and the whole anti-slavery campaign (which was to the Napoleonic wars what Palestine was to the Cold War) and thence the Louisiana Purchase and the US-UK War of 1812. What had been a lucrative set of arrangements, lending military and economic support to any local Maharajah who agreed to let us swap cotton for Huntley and Palmer biscuits or Lea Enfield rifles, perforce became a series of garrisons.

By the time this crisis was over, the other big advantage of empire became obvious... you always have somewhere to dump your losers. India had begun as a last-ditch attempt by failures such as Robert Clive[113] to scam their way out of bankruptcy and now every misfit and also-ran had a place to go - a blank canvas, a chance for re-invention. The simple fact was that without wars or any worthwhile plagues, this was the solution

to the perennial problem of established families: what to do with too many sons reaching adulthood. Rome had almost exactly the same problem, but it was a more violent age, so mothers could tell their sons, "Come back with your shield or on it." So small nations punch above their weight, struggle for survival against bigger opponents and prevail, then get defensive and go through a phase of denial, acting like the little kid that gets picked on when it's often the bully itself. Does this sound in any way familiar?

In a lot of ways, this is not only the creation-view America has of itself, only with the other countries replaced by the vast empty continent to the west of New York (which wasn't actually empty at all, allowing for the nations of the Sioux, the Navajo, the Comanche...). The reason galactic empires seemed natural to American writers is that either case - being opponents of a pre-existing Empire or forging one for themselves - fits what they tended to tell themselves. The difference is that the United States actually set out to do it, getting into huge tussles with anyone who differed with them (remember the Alamo) and providing a fresh start for all those leftovers who got beaten by Napoleon. (This is, incidentally, why Americans drive on the wrong side of the road[114].)

Only one official Empire in recent times has ever said, "Let's make an Empire!" - and that was the Belgians. Don't laugh: whatever atrocities the British perpetrated pale when compared to the brutality of this brief abomination. Whereas the British Empire was formed, as iconoclastic historian AJP Taylor put it, in a fit of "collective absent-mindedness", Leopold II of Belgium staked everything on carving out a trench in the as-yet unexploited bits of Central Africa. (The Belgian Congo, as it was called until 1960, formed the hub of it.) The rapaciousness of this appalled even the most jingoistic British imperialists, and was analysed by Joseph Conrad in *Heart of Darkness* (see 19.3, "Kinda"). As Britain had got rid of slavery about a century earlier (although slave *owning* in other countries wasn't scrapped until 1833), the Belgian slave trade was seen as appalling. Britain wriggled out of accusations of hypocrisy by pointing out how much investment of time and resources went into getting India educated, fed and safe. Most people in Britain believed this. Many in India did too.

And that's the major problem with trying to

continued on page 339...

they're 'neuronic stun-guns', but the Ogrons themselves don't get any brighter.

After the Doctor adjusts the Master's 'fear-box', it works on an Ogron. Curiously, the Ogron sees a Dalek, and not the giant orange scrotum that his people worship.

• *Daleks.* For the second and last time, the commander of the Daleks is shown to be gold. [The superiority of this Dalek could be connected to better armaments or shielding. As we've recently seen, gold Daleks can do things that the old grey models found impossible (had the one in X1.6, "Dalek" been around in 2.8, "The Chase", the series would have finished ten minutes after the Beatles appeared). We *might*, were we in the mood, link this up with the properties of Flidor gold, as mentioned in the *Dalek Pocket-Book* and elsewhere. So perhaps in the Time War, the Daleks tried to get as many of their (for want of a better word) foot-soldiers armoured up to the eye-stalks for combat against their first serious opponents, the Time Lords. See also **Who Died And Made You Dalek Supreme?** under 11.3, "Death to the Daleks".]

The Daleks' plan is to take over the galaxy once the human and Draconian empires have destroyed each other, although it's not clear how the Master got in touch with them. They know the Doctor at this point in their history, although it seems to be the Master who identifies him.

Planet Notes

• *The Ogron Planet.* [Otherwise unnamed.] A 'barren and uninteresting planet' on the remote and otherwise uninhabited fringes of the galaxy, the world of the Ogrons looks like a quarry and the Ogrons themselves seem to inhabit caves, with primitive paintings on some of the walls. One of these paintings describes a large, puffy, orange "Ogron eater", a 'reptile' worshipped by the Ogrons out of pure fear. When we eventually see this creature at a distance, it appears to be something like [and this is us being charitable] a dinosaur-sized carnivorous air-bag.

Galactic co-ordinates of the Ogron planet: 2349 to 6784. Earth seems to have done a survey of the world, but doesn't know much about it. [With the massive overpopulation mentioned back in "Colony in Space", in 2472, this seems very odd. Two things of note: one is that neither the humans nor the Draconians of 2540 know about Ogrons, despite their careers as mercenaries clearly begin-

ning two centuries earlier. (They even use the same weapons they had in "Day of the Daleks".) Similarly, the route to the Ogron homeworld from Earth infringes on Draconian space, so if Earth *did* survey that bit of the galactic rim, it was probably with Draconian compliance or before Draconia had a space-fleet of any size.]

• *Sirius IV.* There is a High Court somewhere called Bassat, either on III or IV. The months are long and oddly-named, with the Doctor's malfeasances committed on 51st and 52nd of Smalk. General Williams explicitly describes Sirius IV as part of the empire, albeit in a discussion of how it's no longer as compliant to Earth's will, and despite its Dominion status.

The Sirius tax regime is fairly strict, with the death penalty for non-payment of 'Planetary Income Tax' as well as vehicle landing taxes. Dominion status allows Sirius IV leverage with the Galactic powers apart from Earth, gives it the right to try and punish its own citizens, and makes mistreatment of Sirian officials a political hot potato. The currency is measured in 'Sc' [presumably Sirian Credits]. The Commissioner of Interplanetary Police from Sirius has the power to take wanted criminals from Earth's jurisdiction, with the President stating that relationships with colony planets are always difficult and that if there's a war then Earth will need all the help it can get. [So the colonies are closer to Earth than they used to be, but remain independent for now. This story's essay will investigate why this doesn't fit the usual pattern for empires.]

Sirius IV has a logo on their ships and the Master's tunic: a circle that's black in the lower half, with three white horizontal stripes and white on top with a black circle inset. [See 21.6, "The Caves of Androzani", for more on Sirius.]

History

• *Dating.* 2540, according to the log of the pilot, and the Doctor confirms that it's the twenty-sixth century. [The SOS also makes mention of the date, and includes the number '72'; is it the 72nd day, i.e. 12th of March, it being a leap-year?] The Doctor describes this period as being the beginning of the Earth's Empire [see the chronology under 9.4, "The Mutants"] and it's definitely the same Empire that he and Jo saw falling in the thirtieth century.

Earth has a world government and a single President, who has a Cabinet, although civil

Is This Any Way to Run a Galactic Empire?

...continued from page 337

map the American-model Galactic Empire onto Britain: nobody who set out to create an empire would do it the way Britain did. You don't take a vast area with forty different languages and teach them yours, in case they use it to a) gang up against you and b) tell the world what you're up to. The Apartheid regime in South Africa went to great lengths to prevent the various tribes getting access to English for precisely that reason. And if you're going to build churches and church schools, you should perhaps issue Bibles that omit Moses, Ruth, David, Judith and the various bits of the New Testament concerning Rome. Never, ever, mix up peoples of different religions without first making sure they don't all resent you enough to overcome their differences (and if you do get simmering antipathy going, don't suddenly announce that you're leaving and let them knock lumps out of each other for the next sixty years). On no account should you educate the people over whom you rule up to degree level and let them become lawyers, permitting them to travel around the Empire and see what else is happening. You *definitely* don't let people from one bit who've got a grudge emigrate and settle all over the place, revelling in their "victim" status and collecting money for terrorist groups every St Patrick's Day. The catastrophe of the Empire was a mix of cynicism, brutality and incompetence.

So what's happening in the *Doctor Who* version of Empire is deeply strange to anyone who recalls - or knows people who recall - the British Empire in its later years. The overwhelming majority of the people who worked overseas in Imperial times were not pioneers, preachers or peddlers; they were admin or soldiers. The soldiers were never treated as any better than the locals, except when opposition had been overcome (as was the case in Fashoda or Khartoum) or overwhelming opposition had inflicted a spectacular defeat (as in Spion Kop). Even then, as George Orwell points out, Kipling writing poems about these guys was an uncomfortable reminder of the price middle-class Britain was paying for the convenience of Empire. Yet in *Doctor Who*, the nearest we get to acknowledgement of this is - oh, dear - Stubbs and Cotton in "The Mutants".

If Earth is meant to be Britain, then, it's running things in reverse. According to "Frontier in Space", Sirius IV is granted Dominion status some time before 2540, but this is supposed to be the *rise* of the Empire. "Dominion" is, historically, what happens just before full independence. (Even if, as in the cases of Canada and Australia, it drags on for so long that the practical difference between the two is confined to things like the ability to get jobs in London without visas, whether you can get a knighthood and how easily you can get NHS treatment when visiting an aunt in Sheffield.) Dominion is what you do when you inherit an empire you don't particularly want, but can't risk abandoning it outright in case there are massacres. It's your exit-strategy from empire, not a means towards it.

If they *were* systematically trying to model the fictional Galactic empire on the British Empire, Solos would have been a Dominion for decades before the story started and there would have been a vast infrastructure of pen-pushers and their families in pressurised, air-conditioned domes on the planet's surface. Rhetorically, this would have been a better parallel to the British in India (building summer retreats up mountains that look like small commuter towns in Surrey, but halfway up the Himalayas) and the Elizabethan campaigns in Ireland (whence the term "beyond the pale") *and* South Africa *and* the Deep South - as they tried to do with the segregated teleports. This isn't just hindsight or backseat driving. The conclusion *has* to be, with so many professional and well-read people involved, that systematically making the direct analogy with the British Empire simply wasn't in the Letts-Dicks gameplan.

Of course, they aren't the only ones playing; two of the key stories of this period are by left-leaning writer Malcolm Hulke. His criticism of both economic expansionism and the administration of justice in an empire that's on a war footing is as trenchant as anything we've seen. However, he never gets to say - or make the Doctor say - that Earth shouldn't *have* an empire, just that they've messed up the lives of the citizens thereof. Oddly, the very lack of a firm galaxy-wide government is the root of the IMC's apparent *carte blanche* and Earth's economic woes in "Colony in Space" and, whilst Hulke has the President refuse to declare martial law or take military action against Draconia in "Frontier in Space", he gives General Williams a good case for stronger control on the Dominions through the implication that Sirius IV is so corrupt that it's given the Master a high office.

Unfettered capitalism and militarism are, in

continued on page 341...

unrest is widespread across the overcrowded planet and she's having difficulty keeping control. The apparent attacks by the Draconians on Earth's ships have led to demands for war from many people, with rioting reported in Tokyo, Belgrade and Peking, while the Draconian consulate in Helsinki is burned to the ground. The President is burned in effigy in Los Angeles, and certain senior officers feel a military dictatorship is required. General Williams suggests that if the President isn't seen to act decisively, she can and will be replaced [by Williams himself, perhaps].

Space travel is now commonplace, hyperspace being involved in the process. There are references to 'battlecruisers' and luxury liners on the Mars-Venus cruise. Despite the prior claim that Earth hasn't a single blade of grass by the twenty-fifth century ["Colony in Space"], here the President's building is surrounded by lush fields, seemingly for miles around. Space-port ten is apparently nearby. Spaceships are still transporting commodities as simple as flour, and the doors of the cargo vessel are 99% durilium [in both "Death to the Daleks" and 11.4, "The Monster of Peladon", the generic outer-space-building-substance is called 'duralinium', which is probably related]. Even small freighters are issued with hand-guns, although these are locked away. It only takes hours for Earth ships to get from the homeworld to the frontier.

The Arctic areas have recently been reclaimed, the Bureau of Population Control announcing that they're ready for habitation. [But do they mean Arctic or Antarctic? The newsreader says 'Arctic', then tells us about the first 'totally enclosed' cities so plausibly, they could be floating on whatever's left of the polar ice-caps or in the sea.] As a special inducement to get people to live in the enclosed cities of New Glasgow and New Montreal, the 'family allowance' has been increased to two children per couple. [Taken in conjunction with the population figures given in "Colony in Space", by the same author, it seems that Earth's population has been halved in sixty-eight years. Maybe the Draconians got closer to wiping out humanity than we generally think.] There's evidently a Congress, with Congressman Brook being the leader of the opposition. [He might be an American, if we assume that accents have changed a bit in five centuries.] Mention of rioting in Los Angeles suggests that at least some of the United States is habitable [see **Whatever**

Happened to the USA? under 4.6, "The Moonbase"]. Earth uses mind probes to ascertain the truth from suspects, and the probes evidently aren't harmful as long as the subject tells the truth.

Relationships with the Draconians have always been strained. During the first encounter with the Draconian Empire twenty years ago, a Draconian ship 'arranged' to meet an Earth ship in peace, but the Earth ship was damaged by a neutron storm which also destroyed the Draconian ship's communications equipment. Both ships were supposed to be unarmed, the Draconians sending a battle-cruiser with empty missile banks, yet on board the Earth ship General Williams made the decision to attack and destroy the Draconian vessel.

The result was a war, and humanity is still anxious that another might occur. Since then, a treaty between the species has established a frontier between Empires which the Draconians have never violated, leading to trade treaties and cultural exchanges. The treaty also forbids espionage and subversion between species. Williams is, despite this, still an adviser to the President [see **Things That Don't Make Sense**].

In military matters the President's authority is limited, and the General takes charge. [His position must be fairly secure and independent of the President's office, in fact, given how much the two of them argue.] The President can only overrule him with the backing of the full Earth Senate. [There's a Senate and a Congress and a Cabinet? Obviously, it's not the kind of Cabinet we have in Britain.] The President is rather hands-on, and personally supervises interrogations, negotiations with visiting police commissioners and reparations for damage caused by riots. All women in the Presidential service have similar high-collared ballgowns and long gloves. [Amazonia (9.2, "The Curse of Peladon") is somewhat in keeping with this, which yields - if you're in the mood - a bit more evidence that the Peladon stories occur in this period.]

Many forms of dissent aren't permitted on Earth [it's much the same society mentioned in "Colony in Space", only slightly worse], with the Peace Party being outlawed. Thousands of political prisoners have been permanently sent to a high-security penal colony on the moon, where the influence of the peace movement's spokespeople won't spread. The Special Security Act allows prisoners to be sent there without trial, although

Is This Any Way to Run a Galactic Empire?

...continued from page 339

Hulke's stories, symptoms of badly-run empires and bad things in themselves, not a sign that empires are a cause of these miseries. (The pre-War left in Britain, after all, were enamoured of power as a means to do good - hence their willed blindness to Stalin's atrocities, since they believed that orderly, scientific societies would create model citizens who looked after one another and would one day not need a state to control them. Hulke's generation saw this idea come under cogent criticism but were more concerned about the internal contradictions of control-freak states of any political hue.)

What's funny is that "Colony in Space" doesn't actually hint that there *is* an empire - we infer it from the same writer doing a story set seventy years later and which necessitates that one have been around for a while. It's interesting that, whilst Hulke has the Peace Party rounded up and shipped to the moon, he also shows a sympathetic President whose solution to the warmongers is to try to control the news media. War is judged as the worst-case scenario (to the point of over-riding basic civil rights) in "Frontier", yet Hulke's next script starts out as a dig against the appeasers of the late 1930s. Letts and Dicks are coming to it from different perspectives and individual writers can add to the mix, but they don't control it. Moreover, the main concern here all around is to make exciting and stimulating television for a mass audience of all ages. Attempting to apply a direct and absolute political tone to any *Doctor Who* script of this period is going to be tricky, given that there are so many intervening stages.

The obvious point to make about the Pertwee space stories is that there are two that involve a multi-species Federation as well. Admittedly, having more than one kind of alien around in stories such as "The Mutants" and "Frontier in Space" causes more problems than a simple six-part allegory can handle, but they aren't even mentioned. The tie-in novels / CDs, chronologies such as the ones in these guidebooks, and even fan-fiction can make all sorts of connections, but as the Draconians are *such* a big part of the galactic situation in "Frontier", it's amazing they're never mentioned on screen again. Similarly, no hermaphrodite hexapods appear in the judicial inquiry into activities on Solos. As we mentioned before, the proximity of all the named planets in the two Peledon stories makes an earlier dating of those adventures more plausible, but they're so near to Earth and so powerful, it's inconsistent that they don't intervene in the Earth-Draconia dispute. Yet because each story is about a different kind of interaction between human / British and "Other", the attempt to make a consistent "future history" - of the sort that Campbell had all his *Astounding* authors try at some time with their own works (most obviously with Heinlein) - is a recipe for disaster.

And if we're back with *Astounding*, there's a wider issue that needs a mention. A lot of early twentieth century theorists took Marx's idea of history as a predictive science (which Hegel sort of started) and ran with it. The German historian / philosopher Oswald Spengler tried a more right-wing take (notably in *The Decline of the West*, published in 1918), and posited a model of all great cultures running through a cycle of struggle, expansion, stagnation and decay. The English economic historian Arnold Toynbee took the view that any sphere of influence big enough *not* to get engulfed by another would get so big, its own internal contradictions would shrink it down again. The idea that Empires have a lifespan is ingrained. Notice how Asimov's *Foundation* had a definite purpose - to preserve the collapsing Empire's good points and prevent thousands of years of wars and ignorance. However, Asimov got one thing across very clearly that the Letts-Dicks stories skip - a galaxy is a *big* place, and an Empire spanning even a relatively small section of it would take centuries to create, and have an inertia that will keep it going for millennia even after it's peaked. The Pertwee stories take it as read that an Earth Empire will somehow just happen, then with equal suddenness be over because Empires always do that.

Looked at with this in mind, the anomalies mount up: two hundred years before this collapse, the Earth ships were still exploring (1.7, "The Sensorites"); peripatetic Adjudicators take up cases based on whether they're in the area at the time the appeal gets made, rather than there being regular circuit-judges or a galactic court of appeal ("Colony in Space", "The Mutants"). Earth is still over-populated and polluted, whilst whole planets are left unexplored.[115]

As either a copy of the American model, a parallel for recent history or a logically self-consistent story of Earth's future, none of this makes much

continued on page 343...

ABOUT TIME 1970-1974

hardcore prisoners are shipped in specially to act as trustees.

There are heavily-armoured security guards on Earth itself, carrying energy weapons. The Peace Party ostensibly has friends in the media and the government, and its sign is a very twentieth century two-fingered "Peace" salute. The Lunar Penal Colony has its own logo, another circle with three vertical black stripes (like prison bars).

Earth in this period has a Historical Monuments Preservation Society. The Doctor knows something of this period in history, but doesn't foresee the Daleks' involvement in this crisis. [Does the Master's involvement change known history, or do the Doctor's actions in the next story make their activities unknown to historians? The fact that the Time Lords agree to steer the TARDIS to the Daleks' base suggests that these events could alter galactic history.] He doesn't seem to believe there should be a war between humans and Draconians.

The Analysis

Where Does This Come From? Well, it's another Malcolm Hulke "... in Space" story to follow "Colony" and once again the Big Social Issues dress themselves up in futuristic shoulderpads for the family audience. Many viewers see this story as a Cold War parallel, but for the most part this doesn't hold up - there's no crude racial metaphor here, no suggestion that the Draconians should remind us of the Russians, the Chinese or any other Communist state, nor even the Nazis. If anything they occasionally turn Japanese, but that seems to owe to the costume designer making the imaginative leap from "reptiles with a fear of females" to "Samurai" unprompted. Theodore Sturgeon once observed that the overwhelming majority of "alien" civilisations are really Meiji Japan. Here it's more of a whim than actual commentary.

If the script takes anything as a "source", it's manifestly Anglo-Spanish relations. The obvious model, if not the most exact, is Elizabeth I and Sir Francis Drake. Bear in mind that Hollywood did this sort of thing to death. (As "Geoffrey Thorpe" in *The Sea Hawk*, Errol Flynn gets to do the fighting whilst Flora Robson makes a speech about taking a stand. It was clearly aimed at the US audiences of 1940 who were dithering over Hitler whilst England faced a fresh Armada.) This version is closer to the probable truth than ITC's *Sir Francis Drake*, but still has Roger Delgado as a tricky ambassador.

However, the more accurate historical parallel here is the War of Jenkins' Ear, an object lesson in how politicians who want to start a war for their own advantage should think carefully about how to stop it again. The crux of it is that a vague anti-Spanish sentiment, plus resentment over the terms of the Treaty of Utrecht, were manipulated into a clamour for war over a single incident ten years earlier.

This may not have happened as claimed - Captain Robert Jenkins claimed his ear was severed by Spanish coast-guards out of malice, but for all anyone knows he may have committed a murder or even hacked it off himself. (It happens that bullfighters claim the ears of their victims, which is why Vincent Van Gogh sent his to a love-rival.) Ten years on, and with no documentation, Jenkins displayed his ear at meetings to whip up war-fever. To make the parallel clearer, the subsequent nine-year conflict in the Caribbean caused Britain to involve its nearby dominion colonies, making this the first war in which America was involved.

However, Hulke's expressed aim was to make an analogy of late-nineteenth century Europe, with the Draconians as surrogate Hapsburgs and the obvious analogy with the causes of World War I. The final version obscures this, but that's hardly surprising. Apart from anything else, they'd just done a planet like that ("The Curse of Peladon"). Moreover, the anxiety over the present-day Superpower conflict was inevitably going to exert a distorting power. Its vision of Empire-versus-Empire is so obviously seen through the filter of James Bond. (As in "The Mind of Evil", the Master is once again playing Blofeld. The 'third party' scenario was the original plotline of "The Daleks" as well.)

If this has *any* direct message to send to the Cold War cultures, it's that the fear of the "enemy" is a bigger problem than the "enemy" itself, with the Doctor making it quite clear - especially during his interrogation - that the whole espionage game is a pointless waste of time. There's an obvious parallel here with the *Star Trek* episode "Balance of Terror", but even *Doctor Who* at its most *Trek*-like is still notably more humanistic. (Fans of American media SF, however, will no doubt enjoy the similarities between the start of

Is This Any Way to Run a Galactic Empire?

...**continued from page 341**

sense, does it? Actually, the thing that makes least sense is the idea that empires *have* to end the way the British one did, because very little about that process (certainly not the messy partition of India and the two Pakistans) could have been foreseen even twenty years earlier. Without the two World Wars, the British Empire might well have developed into a looser confederacy - a Federation even - but only because the education of everyone running it (Indian, African, Canadian, Caribbean, Australian *and* British) included Classics, so they'd all sucked in Greek ideas of Democracy along with Biblical teaching and Latin oratory.

The idea of the Nation State is a Western one we exported. Of course, for an essentially action-orientated series - and indeed, for a genre developed from adventure-magazines - sedate contentment is not what you need. Decaying empires tottering is much more exciting, and can be shown as the work of a few plucky individuals taking a stand, as opposed to socio-economic forces at work over centuries. However, *Doctor Who* never went as far down that route as *Star Wars*, and the British take on this is the more pessimistic view that a bureaucracy *that* big and that efficient would keep going no matter what. We'd *like* a Federation like in *Star Trek* - but we know it would turn into the one from *Blake's 7*.

the Earth / Draconia war and the start of the Earth / Minbar war in *Babylon 5*. The Draconians, like the Minbari, approach the humans with their gunports open. This is, in turn, appropriated from the much-misunderstood satire *Starship Troopers* by Robert Heinlein, possibly by way of Joe Haldeman's *The Forever War*, serialised shortly before this story's broadcast and causing a stir. And we should note that a similar misunderstanding led the Mysterons to declare war on Earth in *Captain Scarlet*.)

Hulke, of course, was not blind to the atrocities committed by both sides of the Cold War and was doubtless very familiar with Alexander Solzhenitzin's *The Gulag Archipelago*. He's almost forgotten these days, but this Soviet dissident made stringent criticisms of his former nation whilst not entirely preferring the West. But as we've been saying, the Cold War - whilst it used popular media to reinforce stereotypes (or rather, allowed the stereotypes to become associated with political views that suited the governments on both sides) - is only the most obvious and (therefore) ineffective manifestation of this kind of thinking. The nineteenth century had just the same clichés about the Russians, and the British had almost exactly the same arms-length respect for them. The shadow-boxing across Eurasia was still thought of as The Great Game" - Kipling's *Kim* is a better model for British espionage than the "Gangbuster"-derived American model. More cogently, the period after the Armistice in 1918 had British and French agencies covertly trying to influence the outcome of the Bolshevik uprising and do "Scarlet Pimpernel"-style raids to free sym-

pathetic nobility who had assets we could use. The First Lord of the Admiralty, one Winston Churchill, oversaw this and the subsequent clampdown on left-wing sympathisers in the UK (such as, er, Hulke's friends and family).

The detail of the Peace Party organising in exile is also vaguely similar to Trotsky's travels. (Hence, perhaps, the mildly amusing sight of Professor Dale putting on a spacesuit whilst wearing a *pince nez*.) The lunar compound is flagrantly Botany Bay (the increasing Australian presence in the UK meant that we were reminded about this every bloody day). The President of Earth is female - not absolutely unique in SF at the time, but notable nonetheless. Possibly she's an allusion to Golda Meir, Israel's president (the Arab-Israeli conflict was heating up again that year, and her appointment of the alleged "warmonger" Moshe Dyan as defence minister was hugely controversial). The President is Eastern European, Brook is almost certainly Barry Goldwater (a prominent US Republican Senator and presidential candidate, although the accent's wrong), and the newsreader is a black Jamaican (three years before Trevor McDonald - now *Sir* Trevor - was trusted to give bulletins).

Things That Don't Make Sense We'll mention it here, as it's the last time it happens: what kind of evil genius can't figure out, after seven previous adventures, that you can't snap your fingers while wearing leather gloves?

The Doctor views the monitor screen of the Earth cargo vessel when a "Draconian" appears on it to demand the humans' surrender, but he doesn't seem to see either a Draconian or an Ogron. So what *does* he see...? It's repeatedly established that the device doesn't work on him, yet the Doctor never says, "Look, Jo, it's an Ogron who's learned to read off an autocue." This exchange, curiously, isn't recorded for training purposes - what with all the political tensions at work, you might think that the Earth authorities would wire at-risk ships to get proof of the Draconians' wrongdoing.

Overlooking the oft-cited "idiocy" of starting a war over a consignment of flour (it's *deliberately* petty, like Jenkins' Ear) we have to ask ourselves how the Ogrons got all that flour off the cargo ship in so little time. The obvious way is to open the bags and get a giant Hoover, but they're not bright enough for that. Maybe they just left the air-lock door open. [Although one might expect the Master to get upset at a vast cloud of flour leading right to their hideout, especially if he were also planning to steal large numbers of eggs and a stick of butter the size of Gloucestershire, then threaten the Universe with a giant éclair. Now that we've seen his turn as Professor Yana (X3.11, "Utopia"), it's harder to rule this out.]

So the Hardy boys (the crewmen of the flour-laden spaceship) see a blue box in hyperspace and tell everyone about it. Later, when General Williams interrogates the Doctor, a blue box turns up in his mental images. Everyone still fails to believe his story about how he arrived on the cargo ship. And twenty-sixth century spaceship with 1940s readouts and a control desk looking like a Bang and Olufsen music centre is one thing, but they have pin-ups from *Woman's Realm* on their walls. [Actually, it's not: they come from a Science-Fiction magazine - the top one looks suspiciously Roger Dean-ish - and seemed retro even back then, but now look like someone's plastered a painting on the wall of a really dull planet and a 1940's-style pin-up. The script suggested Jane Fonda as Barbarella, thinking that these guys were basically truckers. Maybe the designer had never met any.]

The Earth authorities make the obvious mistake of locking the Doctor up in a cell *and* allowing him into the President's office without searching him for potential weapons; he's still got the sonic screwdriver when he tries to escape. Nor do the Draconians search the captive Master thoroughly enough to find the gadget he uses to signal the Ogrons. Why is the Doctor allowed his old clothes (and pocket-contents) back when he's sent to be brain-scanned, whilst Jo is forcibly changed into Kung-fu PJs? Why are no forensic tests done on the dead guards shot by obviously non-Draconian guns? And why don't the President and Williams realise that confronting the Draconians with the Doctor and Jo - who are sure to refute the claim that they're Draconian spies - will just make their complaint sound petty?

Crucially, why does the Earth prison contain no CCTV? Had anyone had eavesdropped on the Doctor and Jo in their various cells, the whole story would have been different. In this supposedly paranoid future, no "objective" shots of the Ogron raid on the Hayward Gallery Detention Centre exist. And consider the extreme recklessness of the Draconians in episode two, when they trick the Earth President into moving the Doctor *and then* stage a foray in which they're plainly seen to gun down Earthmen ، an overt act that's guaranteed to ruin diplomatic relations, if not trigger outright war. Yet what to they hope to gain from this? The chance to privately interrogate the Doctor, like he's going to reveal anything. Jo's arrest-warrant claims she did 'Committ' crimes.

There's no segregation of gender in the lunar prison, so presumably contraceptives are in the milk-shakes. [It's a pretty rum sort of prison, after all, that creates whole generations of dissenters, even if the life-support systems could cope.] Besides, why don't they use "chill-out" drugs to keep the dissenters from escaping or flicking V-signs at the guards?

The Doctor's spacesuit being zipped is audible on the cabin monitor, yet the Master just continues with his reading - is he deaf? Shortly after this, a door opens and closes very audibly.

Bill Wilde, as the Draconian pilot, persuades everyone in episode four that the aliens are called 'Triggonians' or 'Trick Onions'. The Draconians prefer to guard prisoners with their backs turned. (But then, so do the Ogrons. The one guarding the prisoners in episode six, in fact, is *exceptionally* dim because he can presumably overhear them plotting to escape, yet does nothing about it.) The Doctor unwisely says aloud, in front of the Master, that getting on the Draconians' good side all depends on how you approach them. Fortunately, the Master just ignores this advice and tramples all over protocol, irritating his Draconian hosts.

On the way back to Earth, the Doctor secures the Ogron they've taken for Show-and-Tell in the very cell he's already sawn his way out of, even though there hasn't been time to fix it. Hardly a surprise, then, when the captive breaks down the door with his bare hands. It *is* odd, though, that we join the action after the captive Ogron has broken down his cell door and very neatly set it aside - all without his Draconian guard noticing - before going up the walkway and overpowering him.

As with "The Mutants", we have a pressurization issue - it's questionable as to whether even the Doctor could close, using just one arm, the airlock door whilst the air is still escaping. Anyone who quibbles about the Master's 'sonic' device being able to work in the vacuum of space probably (and understandably) went postal on seeing and hearing the "sonic grenades" in *Attack of the Clones*. Another schoolboy science-error: by converting his sonic screwdriver into a magnet, the Doctor forgets to switch off the "physics-defying" circuit, so the magnet *repels* the metal bolts.

The backstory regarding General Williams and the Earth-Draconian war is simply nuts. We're supposed to swallow Williams staging a pre-emptive strike on a Draconian ship on a peace-mission - one that was travelling with its gun-ports open as a gesture of their honest intentions. Did nobody think to inform Williams about this tradition, and how is it that the Earth ship was carrying weapons, in violation of the arrangement? [Unless he destroyed the Draconians flagship by some other means, despite his own ship being ravaged by the ion-storm.] So Williams is a bloodthirsty warmongering xenophobe with no sense of military protocol, who gunned down an unarmed opponent, yet he was allowed to keep his job and rise through the ranks after this catastrophic blunder.

Worse, nobody - not in the aftermath of the war, and not in the twenty years of truce, 'cultural exchanges' and frantic diplomatic manoeuvres performed to avert another conflict - has brought Williams' mistake to his attention. In fact, the Draconian prince looks as if he's been posted to Earth for some time but he only tells Williams the truth when the plot requires that Williams become one of the goodies. And Williams, oblivious to his error and having spent the last couple of decades seething with contempt for the Draconians, accepts the prince's unproven claims within seconds. [See **The Lore** for more on this, as well as an explanation as to why 'Sheila', a non-speaking role, is oddly credited in episode three.]

Dr Science is in da house: while chasing the Ogron ship in orbit around the planet, Williams instructs the pilot to 'increase speed' and overtake them. As any ten year old could have told them (especially given all the moonshot coverage and James Burke studio simulations on telly at the time), this takes you into a higher orbit, so you'd take *longer* to go around the planet. [When we commented upon this in the old Volume III, someone wrote in and suggested that the space-ship was in the atmosphere and thus behaved like an aeroplane - but this isn't the case. The model shot shows space, and the view from the window is blackness, not sky or flames. Williams talks about 'completing an orbit', and the Master later describes the Doctor 'orbiting this planet'.]

When spacewalking on the outside of a ship in hyper-drive, the Doctor is sent flying by a course-correction. He should've had the same velocity (speed and direction) as when he was on the ship, so how does squirting a bit of air out of a bottle make him magically catch up with a ship now going away from him at several times the speed of sound? Or possibly several times the speed of *light*, which makes his catching up even more impressive? Later, as with the similar scene in X3.7, "42", we see an orange-spacesuited Doctor clinging on to the outside of a ship, busting a gut to do repairs, but most of the damaged area is more accessible from inside the spaceship and could be fixed with tongs and a glue-gun with a long nozzle. Unlike Chris Chibnall's effort, here at least we get a *vaguely* good reason for a spaceship's controls being on the outside; to whit, allowing access to vernier control mechanisms of some kind. Then the panel bursts into flames: if they're in space that must mean that the ship's oxygen supply is passing through the electrical system and right past the surfaces that get incredibly hot on re-entry.

For one last time, the Master as played by Roger Delgado goes to incredible lengths to avoid killing the Doctor. First he saves his foe from asphyxiation, on the grounds that his 'employers' want him alive, then he dispatches his Ogrons to overrun the captured prison ship as opposed to just blowing the Doctor out of the sky with a missile volley. Fine so far, but when the Daleks show up, they don't want the Doctor alive at all, and recommend exterminating him. The Master then does a complete about-face and asks that they kill the Doctor later, so he can 'suffer' the horror of witnessing the Dalek subjugation of the galaxy. All right, maybe this behaviour isn't *so* strange for the Master, but what's utterly baffling is that the Daleks tend to categorise all non-Dalek beings as either a) potential slave labour or b) killable, yet agree to this anyway. When have they *ever* bothered with causing suffering as an end in itself?

Between episodes five and six, the TARDIS somehow rotates 90 degrees and turns its door away from the wall, so the Doctor and Jo can get in. And did the makers of the "Ogron Eater" have any idea what a 'large, savage reptile' - as Williams describes it - might look like?

Critique We've repeatedly suggested that getting into the mindset required to see *Doctor Who* as it was meant to be seen will help you appreciate some of its odd features.

For better or worse, this is especially true of this clump of six episodes. Although "Frontier in Space" is occasionally repeated as a feature, and is available as a video (annoyingly, with a cover that gives away the surprise ending), this shouldn't be seen or examined as a discrete story so much as watched in between "Carnival of Monsters" and 10.4, "Planet of the Daleks".

Because however much one can fault "Planet" for not having any connection to this story once the TARDIS lands on Spiridon, "Frontier in Space" is presented as a six-week chunk from a longer serial, like it used to be. It was very consciously made to be watched over six weeks (or to be more accurate, over the entire twenty-six weeks of Season Ten). Anyone who considers it as a two and a half-hour story is going to lose something. From that point of view, it looks like a lot of locking-up and escaping.

What *does* come across, though, even if you swallow this story whole in one sitting, is that the scale increases week-by-week. What begins with a deliberately petty *causus belli* is left to resonate until by episode six, we're on the brink of an intergalactic war between Earth and Draconia, with the Dalek fleet poised to take over. It turns out that the real enemy, as FDR said, is fear itself. At the same time, though, this story needs the viewer to get the full impact of the longer-term character-development. Crucially, Jo Grant winds up being the person who overcomes fear.

If you've been watching for a while, week after week, the sight of Jo willing herself to see what's *really* in front of her - as the Master tries to hypnotize her, thus defying him - is immensely satisfying. It also sets up her otherwise rather abrupt

departure two stories later. By "The Green Death", she's acting independently of the Doctor and UNIT and only really needs help in a situation the Doctor would have found daunting. Notice how "Carnival of Monsters" has Jo taking the initiative with Major Daly and the escape plans, and how "Planet of the Daleks" has the Doctor relying on *her* twice. Granted, in "Frontier in Space" she hasn't *quite* outgrown the Doctor, and some of their exchanges entail her slipping back into the pupil-teacher thing a bit too readily for modern audiences. But she's stoic, she keeps going and she actively contemplates spending forty years in a twenty-sixth century prison rather than trust the Master. Although these adventures are watchable in isolation, the cumulative effect is far more impressive.

Blunders and goofs occur here and there, and some of the info-dumps are downright clunky. As is so often the case in Pertwee stories, they have a newsreader to fill the viewers in on what's been happening. (Note, though, the ticker-tape scroll under the pictures - another detail lost on anyone who's never known a time before CNN or News 24.) The details of this future society don't entirely add up - empires don't usually have Presidents, for example. But this isn't *necessarily* a bad thing, as a too-cohesive fictitious world can look suspiciously like a parable. Looked at it that way, the rough edges and apparent inconsistencies here are tantalising rather than annoying, just as they would be in any foreign culture.

Nevertheless, we're finally seeing Earth after hearing so much about it from expats and colonised aliens, and it looks... well, like viewers in 1973 sort of expected it to. The Lunar Penal colony is one of those anomalous details but it, too, has a sense of rightness to it. Cheekily, they recycle real NASA footage of a low-orbital flight across the moon to partly offset the obviously string-mounted model spaceships (see also "The Seeds of Death"). This was made for Joe Public in Britain in 1973, and so inferring the world beyond the story from throwaway comments was still hard work, even though viewers now had the assorted clichés of *Star Trek* and then-current films with various nasty futures to draw upon. Having spent Season Nine re-inventing the wheel, the production team can start taking the audience's basic competence for granted and tell more interesting stories.

Week after week, this story has to find something new to offer the casual viewer, and in so doing allows a lot of the set-pieces of space-opera to get the *Who* treatment. We see spacewalks, the old standby of an oxygen tank and Newton's Third Law (taken from every kid's book about building space stations[108]), even when it wouldn't work because they're in hyperspace at the time. (Two episodes later, this scene is reworked with the same terribly early-70s orange spacesuit.) We get lizard-like imperialist aliens who aren't a bit Japanese, really. In episode two they're shown to have different personalities, different agendas (and security clearance) and a degree of sophistication way ahead of most not-really-Japanese scaly aliens. Understandably, fandom hasn't let the Draconians go (even though they never returned on screen), to the point that the tie-in novels and semi-pro videos wheeled them out every so often. We want to know more about this odd culture, even though it's flagrantly one (or more) of ours repackaged and sold back to us. Visually, as with a lot of this story, the Draconians are one of the programme's truly great designs. The Ogron Bollock God, erm... isn't, but at least its screen time is kept to a minimum.

A lot of stories from this period seem dated when seen again or contain details that wouldn't have struck anyone at the time as odd. "Frontier in Space" has no irritating anachronisms beyond the obvious "vintage" CSO and Synthesizer (and even here, we're doing better than in Season Nine). There's no casual sexism, not a lot of heavily dated hardware and there's a bit of lateral thinking with the National Theatre being a listed building (unimaginable then, entirely plausible now), so we know that Earth's capital is London. Of course. The future dates faster than anything else, but this story has weathered better than just about anything made in the US in 1973. If we're all still here in 2043, we can dust off DVDs of the BBC Wales series and see if that's aged as well - assuming we can find something to play old-style DVDs on.

The Facts

Written by Malcolm Hulke. Directed by Paul Bernard. Viewing figures: 9.1 million, 7.8 million, 7.5 million, 7.1 million, 7.7 million, 8.9 million.

Supporting Cast Vera Fusek (President of Earth), Michael Hawkins (General Williams), Peter Birrell (Draconian Prince), Harold Goldblatt (Professor Dale), Madhav Sharma (Patel), Bill Wilde (Draconian Captain), John Woodnutt (Draconian Emperor), Stephen Thorne (First Ogron), Ramsay Williams (Congressman Brook), Michael Wisher (Dalek Voice).

Cliffhangers The Earth rescue team arrives on the cargo ship, and the crew insists that the Doctor and Jo are traitors working for the enemy; the Ogrons burst into the Doctor and Jo's cell on Earth; the Doctor and Professor Dale, attempting an escape from the lunar prison, find themselves trapped in the airlock while someone pumps out the air; held captive on the Draconian ship along with the Doctor and Jo, the Master surreptitiously activates a signalling device, and elsewhere an Ogron picks up the message on the bridge of his *own* ship; in his quarters on the Ogron planet, the Master turns his hand-held hypno-sound device on Jo.

What Was in the Charts? "Cum On, Feel the Noize", Slade; "Why Can't We Live Together?", Timmy Thomas; "Part of the Union", The Strawbs; "Roll Over Beethoven", ELO; "Nice One Cyril", Cockerel Chorus[109]; "Get Down", Gilbert O'Sullivan.

The Lore

• After the success of "The Sea Devils", Letts and Dicks pondered doing a drama series about the Royal Navy. As you'll recall, they were told that someone else had got there first, but this is the point where they start looking for a way off *Doctor Who*. As it turned out, they were there another two years - the BBC heads believed that the series was on a roll, and changing the staff was too risky. Nonetheless, a large part of the thinking behind "Frontier in Space" was to put together a Plan B. Much of this story's technical legerdemain was a rehearsal for *Moonbase 3*.

Another key factor was the series' big anniversary. This story was commissioned before "The Three Doctors", and the plan was self-consciously retro. They could now get the Doctor off Earth and so planned, essentially, "The Daleks' Master Plan II", only in glorious CSO and with as much of the show's past in as possible. A quick chat with Douglas Camfield, director of that adventure, suggested that twelve weeks was too long for an audience to follow a story. The protracted negotiations with Terry Nation left the production team in an interesting position: they had agreed to give Nation first refusal on any subsequent Dalek story commissions but could only use them as solo stars, even though their last outing had introduced the Ogrons (as neat a way out of the perennial "stairs" problem as any).

Thus the idea of making a twelve-part story in two halves, with Nation providing six weeks of Dalek thrills, became increasingly attractive. With this tacitly agreed, the first six weeks needed to be sorted out. The obvious contrast with Nation's simplistic action yarns was Malcolm Hulke, the obvious counterweight for the Daleks was the Master, and the obvious monsters to bring back were the Ogrons - a hit with kids and (best of all) still in storage. Ergo, a director who's done Daleks, Ogrons and the Master (Paul Bernard) was the obvious choice. And they had just got hold of a lot of ex-Anderson models, so Ian Scoones was asked to pull out the stops and brace himself for a big space-epic.

Introducing the Daleks as unseen puppet-masters made more sense with a smaller-scale war, so the end of episode six led into a threatened invasion of the entire galaxy. As we've just mentioned, Nation was reluctant to have other monsters going head-to-head with the Daleks. He *had* been asked repeatedly about Dalek-Cybermen battles during the late 1960s. However, we note that a terribly subtle reminder about the Ogrons in "Carnival of Monsters" (recorded just before this story) was followed by a cameo from a re-modelled Cyberman. Designs for glam-era cyber-costumes were made, and Letts had been considering a return visit of the Telosian villains for a while. (He even announced it in the letters page of *Radio Times* - see 12.5, "Revenge of the Cybermen" for how it turned out, and see also "The Monster of Peladon".)

• The Draconians were a late addition. Early scripts are said to feature 'Andromedans', so presumably this would have been an intergalactic war. Instead of a 'fear-box', the Ogrons would have worn, um, rubber masks to fool everyone into thinking it was humans or Draconians raiding spaceships. (All we know of Andromedans is that they are 'aquiline' - birds rather than reptiles? It had the virtue of not having been done so far in the series, but look at 21.7, "The Twin Dilemma" before deciding if it might have worked. With Hulke thinking along the lines of nineteenth-century Europe, the Hapsburg eagle is an obvious

visual cue for viewers.)

• Letts and Dicks were planning their escape with an adult-oriented near-future series, *Moonbase 3*. This story's model-work and set-design was a trial run, although *Moonbase 3* has aged far less well. Paradoxically, the "futuristic" design for the far-off year 2003 (in which time Europe would run the third Moonbase) looks so much like the set for *Look! Mike Yarwood* (another stalwart of Saturday nights in the Pertwee era) as to make one nostalgic.[110] The official go-ahead from the BBC's drama department was given just before Christmas 1972, but the plans were well-advanced when filming for "Frontier in Space" began in September of that year. The consequences of this decision will be outlined over the rest of this book.

• Paul Bernard was contracted shortly after completing work on "The Time Monster". As an artist and former set-designer, he took a keen interest in the visual aspects of the story, drawing the Draconian faces and scouting interesting-looking locations. John Friedlander, who sculpted the masks, was later quoted in *The Sun* as saying that the Draconian heads were modelled on Dave Allen's plaster-cast head. This is apparently a Chinese Whispers version of a comment about how long it took to dry the latex.

The main masks for speaking-part "Dragons" were moulded from the actors playing the roles (and contrary to what you might have read elsewhere, Peter Birrell is not the same Pete Birrell who was bass-player for Freddie and the Dreamers, who would in any case have been too busy doing *Little Big Time* on ITV). Incoming costume designer Barbara Kidd seems to have suggested the Japanese influences, taking her cue from the face-design. This design had practical reasoning behind it: the whiskers concealed the join between the half-mask and the chin make-up and the lumpy skin made the masks more comfortable for actors to wear for long periods. All parties were keen to ensure eye contact between the Draconian actors and the other cast-members after the awkwardness of working with Ice Warriors.

• Stop us if you've heard this one before... Pertwee liked the Draconian masks. During filming he got chatting to one of the actors, an amateur astronomer, about Cepheid variables and globular clusters and - so he claimed - forgot it was just a man in a mask. Stop us again if you've heard that the various homeless folks who congregated near the National Theatre wandered around during the shoot. One story claims that a drunk woke up, saw a Draconian and started praying.

• The next two days were spent at a gravel quarry in Reigate. (Proverbially where every single alien planet in 70s BBC space-shows were filmed, but probably not true as gravel makes too much noise. Certainly, this story's exterior dialogue needed redubbing.) This was the first and, as it turned out, only use of the orange "Oberon Eater" (as the brochure of the company that made it calls it). Written as a fearsome lizard that could chow down on Ogrons, it was a giant orange blob like a partially deflated bouncy castle, and so was limited in its screen time. We'll see more trouble with this ludicrous prop in studio.

• Finally, they went to Highgate. Although Naomi Capon never directed Doctor Who, her place in the programme's lore is assured for making the Out of the Unknown story that needed lots of grey robots that could be re-painted white (see 6.2, "The Mind Robber" and "Carnival of Monsters"). The veteran director / producer's husband designed the house where they lived, and Barry Letts had been there. He proposed this as another "heritage" twentieth-century location. The script suggested 'an astonished Draconian gardener' should see the Doctor escape.

The final day's filming was the space-walks and so forth, for which only Pertwee was needed. You'll be astounded to hear that they used the same spaceship prop for both vessels, redressed for the two episodes where it appeared. Equally amazing is the revelation that they used Kirby wires for the Doctor. What you might *not* have spotted is the technician hanging around holding the hatch closed at the end of episode four's EVA. Then they filmed the first batch of models and let the actors get on with rehearsals.

• Ian Scoones' use of outside lighting technicians had caused trouble in the past (see "The Curse of Peladon"), so he filmed the models at Bray studios. Officially Bernard Wilkie and Rhys Jones were in charge of effects but the majority of the work was Jones and Scoones, with Wilkie co-ordinating and doing the paperwork. Scoones took a number of the models from his old job at Gerry Anderson's Century 21 studios. The shuttle's spherical nose was a lightbulb, left unpainted in one rectangular patch to make a window. Mat Irvine made an even smaller model for one shot.

The "docking" problem was solved by attaching the smaller model to the front of the camera and moving both towards the larger model rather than faff about with wires. Fans of UFO will recognise at least two of the spaceships.

• The episodes were recorded two a fortnight, but done more or less one a day. The first batch were recorded at the beginning of October and went almost without a hitch. (Although the end-credits for episode two had a slide from episode one, meaning that Louis Mahoney and Roy Pattison got credited all over again, whilst Timothy Craven and Laurence Davidson didn't get any. The caption scanner broke down, which may account for it.) The cargo ship set (which we'll see again redressed as the Master's ship) had a feed from another camera on the left monitor and the right from a telecine machine showing model-work already filmed. These were reversed for the Master's craft in episodes three and four.

• The director had already changed the timing of the episodes in the early stages, moving material from the last episode to the previous one, shunting that episode's cliffhanger to earlier in the episode and so on. It was later discovered that the middle three episodes needed reworking in editing. The main casualty was episode three, which lost a whole character's dialogue. Sheila, the Presidential masseuse, had lines covering the troubled history of human-Draconian relations, including the detail that Williams had used his exhaust-jets to attack the Draconian battleship and start the first war - see **Things That Don't Make Sense**.

• The lady operating the Mind Probe (if you've not seen 20.7, "The Five Doctors" you'll not understand why we have trouble with that phrase) had previous form, playing Danielle (the sister who helps tend to Barbara and Susan) in 1.8, "The Reign of Terror". Cross, the surly Trustee at the Lunar Colony, was Governor Lobos in 2.7, "The Space Museum". Madhav Sharma, as the incarcerated Peace Party member Patel (or 'Doughty' in the scripts), played Rao in three episodes of Moonbase 3 and an endless string of doctors in the 80s and 90s. He's now a National Theatre player, so is often at the location for the Earth prison.

• The Saturday before the recordings had been Katy Manning's birthday, and her agent brought along another of her clients, Stewart Bevan, to the party. We'll hear more about him in 10.5, "The Green Death".

• The final two episodes were made out of order, largely because the Draconian make-up for the throne-room scene was expected to be time-consuming. Episode six was delayed and was thus recorded on the Tuesday (Halloween). In attendance were photographers from *TV Action +Countdown* (see the essay with "The Mind of Evil"), who snapped John Scott Martin getting into a Dalek shell, Delgado reading the papers in a quiet moment, puppeteers preparing to operate the Drashig and Pat Gorman being helped into his Sea Devil costume. A couple of their portrait shots appeared as a taster for the new season but most were withheld to avoid spoilers. The Dalek props were the ones used in "Day of the Daleks" a year earlier, but as the voices hadn't really worked, Letts proposed Michael Wisher (who's been seen twice already and was doing voiceovers before this). Cy Town had also been in the series before (lurking around as one of Evil Parallel Stahlman's technicians in 7.4, "Inferno", an observer for the Keller Machine demonstration in "The Mind of Evil" and we *think* a waxwork in 7.1, "Spearhead from Space") but only started operating Daleks when he appeared as one in *Blue Peter* (see "The Sea Devils").

• Episode five's cliffhanger was shot with episode six. For the final episode, the director was asked to help devise a better lead-in to the next story. His ending had the Ogrons seeing the Doctor as the 'lizard' and causing a commotion, thus avoiding his being shot dead by the Master. The Ogrons had succeeded in capturing the Draconian Prince and Williams, who pursue the Master as the Doctor and Jo chase the Daleks to their lair. For reasons that should be obvious, this was reworked once Bernard had seen the "Bollock Monster". Instead, Jo operates the fear-box and the Master is caught up in a melée of panicking Ogrons. Even this was deemed not to work when Letts saw it in editing. Bernard claims that the new TARDIS scene was dropped into his lap at no notice.

• Editing of these episodes began a couple of days later, just before filming for "The Three Doctors" began. Letts was still not happy with the ending. Dicks had been working with Terry Nation on the revisions for "Planet of the Daleks" and drafted a better dovetail with that story's start (with a wounded Doctor and Jo unaware of where the TARDIS is heading). This was recorded in January as part of the next story and only needed

Pertwee, Manning and a small section of the set. Delgado went from this story to make an episode of ITC's new drama *The Zoo Gang*, and then secured a part in a comedy called *Bell of Tibet*, to be filmed in Turkey.

• Although the Daleks' appearance in episode six was (for once) kept secret, the following week saw a massive Dalek-based publicity campaign, centred on the *Radio Times*' "Win A Dalek" competition. (Ultimately this was won by a class of primary school children, who looked less than thrilled at being photographed with it.) The competition required entrants to think up a new story for the Skaroine terrors, something which (if we're being honest) Nation himself hadn't done in nearly a decade. The main author of this volume still insists that his entry was better than the winner's.

• This was Bernard's last *Doctor Who* contribution, but his connection with the series personnel didn't end there. When he went to Thames to make the first story in a new *Who*-clone called *The Tomorrow People*, he brought Dudley Simpson along to do the theme-tune (easily the best thing about the series) and Brian Hodgson (now a freelancer working with Simpson on a new project called Electrophon) to do the special sound. Hodgson also provided some of the incidental music (from stock album tracks by him and Delia Derbyshire). Electrophon did the synth renditions of light-classical pieces heard in 14.5, "The Robots of Death". (As well as provided a - shall we say - novel form of "special sound" for a short film about French variety artiste le Petomane. Look him up if you can't guess the noises we mean.) Simpson found that working with Hodgson's replacement, Dick Mills, developed into a sort of telepathy and the rest of the 1970s will see them work together very well. Bernard's later freelance work was sporadic, mainly to allow him to return to painting whilst paying the bills. A vile rumour connects him with the creation of TVAM's second biggest star, Roland Rat (see 23.3, "Terror of the Vervoids"). An equally odd rumour had General Williams being played by the same "Michael Hawkins" who is Christian Slater's dad. Seven years and several thousand miles separate them.

10.4: "Planet of the Daleks"

(Serial SSS, Six Episodes, 7th April - 12th May 1973.)

Which One is This? "Terry's All Gold": a selection-box of Nation's greatest hits, but this time in colour. *Way* too much colour. Lurid green jungles, aliens in bright purple furs, Thals in pastel space-suits and a Dalek Supreme sprayed black and gold, all on a planet with the biggest Dalek army ever assembled (apparently), made up of the smallest Daleks ever assembled. Oh, and one of the Daleks is invisible but immobile.

Firsts and Lasts Err... it's the first Pertwee story not to have any significant first or last things happening, which says it all, really. He wears a purple suit that makes him look even more "Superfly" than ever, and the Thals have a legend about him that's a variation on a story we've seen (as opposed to one from an adventure too preposterous to broadcast, as per the last story).

Digging around, we find that this is the first time since 1964 that new Dalek casings have been constructed. Except it isn't, because the Peter Cushing films had some, one of which turns up here - that's a first *and* a last. This is the only story with costumes by Hazel Pethig, best known for her work on *Monty Python*. Really reaching now, it's the last time the Dalek control car-alarm sound is used.

Oh... *got* it! For a generation of schoolkids playing at being Daleks (non-British, non-old-enough readers will have to take this on trust), it's the first-ever use of, 'My vision is impaired, I cannot see!' and it's Michael Wisher who says it. Truly, a watershed.

Six Things to Notice
About "Planet of the Daleks"...

1. Terry Nation returns to the series for the first time since 3.4, "The Daleks' Master Plan" in 1965 - a seven-and-a-half-year gap, during which four other writers and various production teams have re-defined and re-created his most notable creations. Nation's response to this? Ignore everything that had happened while he'd been away, and go back to first Dalek principles by writing a *King Solomon's Mines*-style adventure story on a jungle planet.

Nation "standards" on offer here: vegetation that (all together now) 'seems more like animal than plant', invisible monsters, people escaping by hiding inside Dalek casings, a bacterial weapon and a countdown to the apocalypse. And the dialogue is pure *Biggles*, with the word 'space' attached to make it futuristic. Sample lines: 'I'm qualified in space medicine, I'll do what I can'; 'Spiridon... one of the nastiest pieces of space-garbage in the Ninth System'; 'you've been infected by the fungoids'; and 'it's an area of huge boulders'. And the Thal leader is called 'Taron' - not quite "Tarrant" but close enough.

2. The conclusion of the story sees tidal-waves of "molten ice" destroying an army of 10,000 Daleks deep inside their cave-system base. It was always going to be a challenge for the visual effects boys, and the designers' solution - to fill a model set with an army of toy Daleks (the Louis Marx models with "Tricky Action", as used in 4.9, "The Evil of the Daleks"), then chuck water at them - is a prime example of *Doctor Who* using its own merchandising as a special effect. Clifford Culley, a freelance effects designer, will return to the series to deploy some terrible dinosaurs (see 11.2, "Invasion of the Dinosaurs") and a truly astonishing sequence with a toy tank and a giant robot (12.1, "Robot"). That said, his model Dalek floating up the flue is at least as good as Ray Cusick's efforts of 1963, and he gives us one of the better Dalek ship arrivals.

3. The jungle's "animal noises" - the same ones used in every space jungle from "Mission to the Unknown" (3.2) to "Meglos" (18.2) - are just as inconvenient, especially during the scene when Taron pours his heart out to Rebec in the middle of the wilderness. He says 'I love you', and the response is the remarkably ill-timed sound of a rutting wildebeest. It happens again while the Doctor's giving his final, serious-minded speech about the futility of war. Almost as good is the scene in the darkening jungle clearing, in which the Doctor and company see the glowing eyes of predatory animals surrounding them in the undergrowth - this basically involves several pairs of tiny electric lights being switched on all over a darkened set, much in the vein of *Scooby Doo*.

4. We'll tackle the ramifications of this in **The Continuity**, but... this is the story in which we learn that if an air-tight seal is put over the door of the TARDIS (i.e. an unimaginably complex space-time vessel with a near-infinite interior, which spends most of its time either in space or the vortex), then everyone inside will suffocate. The cause of this calamity? Ejaculating toadstools.

5. There's a very entertaining moment in episode three when the Doctor and Codal, in a lift inside the Dalek city, open the doors on one of the lower levels; find a Dalek waiting for them outside; close the doors; descend for a while longer; open the doors again; and find an identical corridor outside, but this one empty. You can almost see the stage-hand giving Jon Pertwee the signal: "It's all right, we've moved the Dalek. You can press the button again now." (And try to watch the Doctor's rope-climb out of the ventilator shaft in episode four without imagining the Thals shouting, "Lynch him!".)

6. Until the "Dalek War" DVD - announced just as this book was going to press - episode three of "Planet" was only available in black and white. Curiously, it's the one episode that really relies on the Daleks casting eerie shadows on the walls and scooting around their base like they did back in the day. A suspicious mind might conclude that they arranged the loss of the colour print on purpose. Some omnibus versions made available to public television in America skip the missing episode entirely, which means the icecano, Latep's relationship with Jo and the Doctor and Codal being reunited with the rest of the party have to be inferred from internal evidence.[116]

On the other hand, the grand finale to this twelve-part attempted epic is an episode that absolutely relies on the impact of colour, with the gaudy exterminations, the lurid jungle chase and the arrival of the Dalek Supreme - with personalised livery - in a steel spaceship with pink jets. And the colour-schemes for the costumes are only slightly more odd than they looked in monochrome, with purple fun-furs, Jo's worst outfit *ever* and Pertwee in a maroon ensemble that makes him look like he's fallen in a vat of Ribena. Hazel Pethig, credited for 'Costumes' for this adventure, never worked on *Doctor Who* again.

The Continuity

The Doctor Ice begins to form on the Doctor's face, and he falls into a coma-like state, after he was winged by the Master's gun [in the last story]. Jo points out that the Doctor was in this state once before. [8.5, "The Daemons", although that occasion was accompanied by an external temperature drop and there isn't one here. Can Time Lords "freeze" themselves when they're injured?]. He only has a minimal pulse (Jo says that both hearts

beat about once every 10 seconds) and breathing-rate during this period, but he recovers after an hour or so. He talks about Susan as though she were just another companion, not his 'granddaughter'. His blood is red [cf 18.4, "State of Decay"; 22.4, "The Two Doctors"], but the wound clears up completely in a matter of hours.

• *Ethics.* He states, once and for all, that he 'abhors violence' - just after he murders a Dalek with obvious relish. He gives a "feel the fear and do it anyway" speech, which even he terms "a tutorial on courage" to Codal, the rather vague scientist who seems to have a crush on him.

• *Inventory.* His sonic screwdriver is magically back in the jacket of the magenta velvet ensemble he's opted to wear in a moment of oxygen-starved sartorial insanity, even though it was left in a cupboard on the moon halfway through the last story. [See 11.5, "Planet of the Spiders" for more on this strange development.

[This is a good time to stop and ask where the Doctor got the screwdriver in the first place. In 5.6, "Fury from the Deep" and 12.1, "Robot", he talks about it as a gadget he's made. That's plausible, as we know from 17.5, "The Horns of Nimon and possibly 17.2, "The City of Death" that Romana can build one for herself. So maybe he's got a whole toolbox full of them, as X3.1, "Smith and Jones" seems to suggest. Notably, when other people identify its use (12.5, "Revenge of the Cybermen"; X4.1, "Partners in Crime"), they're from societies at least a thousand years ahead of us. Given that Miss Foster ("Partners in Crime") and Sarah Jane Smith have their own versions, there must be a cosmic branch of Do It All that supplies them, or at least the key components.]

The Supporting Cast

• *Jo Grant.* Given the chance to visit anywhere in the universe, Jo simply wants to return home to Earth. The implication is that although she likes her work with the Doctor, she doesn't like the travel [the next story suggests that she's a lot more concerned about her own planet than we thought]. Yet another wet alien boy falls for her here, and the way she mopes after she leaves him - despite the fact that they barely knew each other - suggests that she's already getting lonely. She veers wildly between competent guerrilla and kooky chick, especially in one scene where she goes from planning an assault on the Daleks to saying '...and then I was rescued by this bowl...'

What are the Silliest Examples of Science in *Doctor Who*?

As everyone (or at least, every fan) knows, the silliest ever bit of science-gobbledygook in *Doctor Who* ever is the line in "The Faceless Ones" (4.8) in which we discover that the Chameleons' plight was caused when they (all together now) lost their identities in a colossal explosion. Unfortunately, the cumulative effect of *Doctor Who* being written over more than a quarter-century, then a sixteen-year gap (some of it by people with a good grasp - or at least, an *interest* - in actual science, some not) leaves a lot of other scientific cock-ups to be accounted for. There's even cash-in books on the science of *Doctor Who* now, although some of these aren't *so* much about the science actually used in the show, because that would have entailed those involved actually watching it.[118]

Given that Sydney Newman admonished writers for making abstract science more enticing that practical, hands-on engineering, it's astonishing how often a basic knowledge of the latter highlights flaws in scripts where characters rhapsodise on the former. Therefore, what follows in this essay is a selection of - shall we say - "curious" scientific claims that mainly fall into the domain of Physics, although biological goofs exist a-plenty. (We've mostly covered these in other essays, but reserve the right to rant a little bit about 18.3, "Full Circle".) More to the point we should specify that, with most of the writers of the BBC Wales version deriving their fanciful conceits from the thinly-veiled magic of *Star Trek*, nearly all of the following examples of bad science from the old series are outstanding mainly because the writers *tried* to get it right. They did their homework - as far as getting the terminology sounding plausible, if nothing else - but they fall down when applying simple logic to the fruits of their researches.

For the purposes of this piece, we'll also set aside the tottering pile of half-baked assumptions and fairy-tale logic that we've elsewhere designated as "Whitaker-Science". (The curious are advised to look at Volume II, and the essays **What Do Daleks Eat?** and **What Planet was David Whitaker On?** under 4.3, "The Power of the Daleks" and 5.7, "The Wheel In Space" respectively. Then ask yourself whether Helen Raynor's risible *deus ex machina* end to X3.5, "Evolution of the Daleks" was a deliberate nod to the first incumbent of her job as script editor, or was simply very bad indeed.) Along those lines, we tried, really *tried* our best to resolve the matter of time travel through the use of 144 mirrors when in 4.9, "The Evil of the Daleks" (funny how Parallel-UNIT gets

by with a mere dozen in X4.11, "Turn Left") and by now we've more or less given up on Whitaker, Robert Holmes and Terry Nation when it comes to using words like 'galaxy', 'constellation' and 'universe'. Furthermore, we won't our time repeating any other elaborate discussions of daft examples that we've devoted whole essays to, or which have detailed extensions in the **Things That Don't Make Sense** entries. (We refer you to "The Underwater Menace" and "The Invisible Enemy" for especially piquant examples.)

In the interest of fairness, *Doctor Who* 1963-1989 often tried to keep up with science that was itself superseded. Sometimes a subsequent revision of scientific theory would - through no fault of theirs - catch various authors with their pants down. After all, anyone trying to explain (say) penicillin or atomic bombs a century ago would be in serious trouble. So we're going to at least try to redeem these ideas and salvage some vestiges of plausibility - not least because earlier volumes have lain us open to criticisms of picking on Terry Nation now that he's not around to defend himself. Heck, even in 1928, Sir Arthur Eddington (the guv'ner of astrophysics) was using the term "Island Universe" to mean "Galaxy".

Before we start, we should also refer the interested reader to the essays **How Hard Is It To Be The Wrong Size?** under 16.6, "The Armageddon Factor"; **How Can The Universe Have A Centre?** under 20.4, "Terminus"; **What Were Josiah's 'Blasphemous' Theories?** under 26.2, "Ghost Light"; and **What Does Anti-Matter Do?** under 13.2, "Planet of Evil", for much, much more in this vein.

Icecanoes: Gawd luv 'im, Terry Nation gave it his best shot. He read the word "allotrope" somewhere (see **Where Does This Come From?** under 10.4, "Planet of the Daleks") and tried to apply a bit of real-life science to Spiridon, his fantasy-world of invisible monsters and wanking lilies.

In case Taron's explanation went over your head (most likely because you'd dozed off), allotropes are molecular anagrams (meaning different forms of the same element, such as graphite and diamond being allotropes of carbon). There are, in fact, many exciting and baffling allotropes of ice - alas, water is just about the *least* understood liquid anywhere. Nothing about this stuff makes sense. Most liquids are at their densest when they

continued on page 355...

The TARDIS When the plants on Spiridon put an air-tight seal on the TARDIS, the 'automatic oxygen supply' turns on even though the air outside is breathable, and the Doctor begins to suffocate as the supply runs out... suggesting that the Ship takes in air from the outside. The warning 'Automatic Oxygen Supply Exhausted' appears on the screen when the air is getting thin, in 70s art-nouveau computer-lettering. [This is so overwhelmingly stupid that it's almost impossible to get a grip on. The TARDIS' passengers *can't* seriously depend on external oxygen, since the TARDIS travels through the vortex and frequently lands in places with no atmosphere. And if the door isn't normally air-tight, then what stops air leaking out into the vortex while the Ship's in flight? What about all the planets with toxic atmospheres?

[You could argue that the Ship stores air when it's in an air-rich environment, and that the supply is simply depleted here, but this seems hard to swallow. If the Ship is as vast on the inside as we've always been led to believe, then it shouldn't take the Doctor just a couple of hours to exhaust the supply once the doors get sealed. Besides, why should the crack in the doors be the means of drawing in air, when the TARDIS is supposed to be able to change shape?

[Some cross-referencing on this: in 2.8, "The Chase", we had a hint that the TARDIS can't stop in outer space in case of air-loss, although the very next story (2.9, "The Time Meddler") has the Doctor learning of the Monk's refinement to allow this very facility, and he even has a poke around the Monk's console. By 4.6, "The Moonbase", it's assumed that there's an air-lock and no leakage. At the end of 5.4, "Enemy of the World", the doors are left open and a tremendous wind issues into the vortex - so the bits of the Ship that we can't see must contain a lot of air. And if this *is* the same Ship from the Hartnell days, then it should have the living quarters and food machine bay we saw in 1.2, "The Daleks" - so Nation should have known better. The Doctor should have hours left, even on that basis.

[For this to make any sense at all, it *has* to be assumed that the TARDIS is currently experiencing some kind of technical fault in its life-support systems, and that the seal on the doors is almost incidental, despite the Doctor's claim that all the circuits are in order.] Luckily, the Doctor keeps an emergency supply of oxygen canisters in the console room, inside a cabinet on casters that we've never seen before. [See also 11.3, "Death to the Daleks", from the same author, for a similarly idiotic notion of the TARDIS doors working with a crank-handle.]

Decorative panels on one wall of the console room display a peculiar pattern never seen before [this looks not unlike a frame from the title sequence]. There are cupboards in the room, which also look new. [It's all horribly 70s formica, the stuff you'd see advertised by the two main cheap-and-nasty bedroom furnishers of the era, MFI or G-Plan. Maybe the constant TARDIS refits are being done by their Venusian branch, MF-Hai!!?]

The bottom drawer of this unit sends out a bed on a little motorised divan. [Jo knows how to use this device. Does she sleep on it? Surely they don't, you know... both use it at once.] The refit that added the cupboards and drawers has built the scanner into the wall, rather than hanging it from gimbals as we saw last time [in 10.1, "The Three Doctors"]. The picture on the scanner currently seems to be in black-and-white [more proof of a systems fault], but can relay sound. A handheld 'log', basically a tape recorder, is found in a locker just above it. [Jo discards this recording in the jungle, and the Doctor later finds it - the same scenario as (what a surprise) a previous Nation story, "Mission to the Unknown".]

A switch on the TARDIS console can put an image of Earth up on the scanner. Various other worlds, Skaro included, also appear on the screen. [The Doctor has apparently programmed Earth into the controls as a standard destination, but this suggests that the scanner has a "memory" for places the TARDIS has already been; something similar is seen in 1.3, "The Edge of Destruction".] As the Doctor is dragged from the Ship, it's obvious that the police box exterior is matched with a police box interior on at least two sides, so apparently the doors of the console room open onto an intermediate space between the two dimensions. The doors' outer face as seen from inside is, this time, blue.

The Time Lords When the Doctor sends them a telepathic message for help, the Time Lords guide the Ship to the planet where the Dalek army's been assembled, apparently by remote control. [Two things are striking here. One: the Doctor is prepared to ask them for help, the only time he

What are the Silliest Examples of Science in *Doctor Who*?

...continued from page 353

become solids, but water does it 4°C above that point. Most liquids increase in viscosity as the pressure goes up, but water decreases when under 20°C. (NB: we've tried to verify this - as with a lot of the factual matter in *About Time* - by cross-referencing several textbooks. One source we were told about claims it's 33°C. If you're one of those people who take all their information from Wikipedia, then complain online about how our facts are all wrong, please observe our candour on this point and belt up.)

The specific heat capacity of water is *twice* that of ice or steam, so it takes half as much energy to heat a cubic centimetre from -10 to -5°C as from 5 to 10°C. If there's a liquid you'd expect to behave stupidly and conveniently capriciously for a Terry Nation story, it's water. However, water doesn't even behave oddly to order. You get allotropes of ice that lack a regular molecular structure but are solid (in other words, a glass made of hydrogen and oxygen). You get alternative crystalline arrangements of the atoms under extreme pressure (Ice V and Ice XIII are the most common - the core of Saturn might have lots of these), but so far no liquids at sub-zero temperatures.

It gets worse. Allotropes is that they need exceptional purity and very rapid freezing, which the inside of a planet isn't likely to provide. If it did, the first thing any miraculously pure spring water would do on contact with the balmy heat of a jungle (at least by day) is either boil or sublime (like dry ice, which skips that whole liquid phase and goes straight to gassy carbon dioxide).

Alternatively, and from the look that the turquoise gloop in "Planet of the Daleks" shows us, we might suppose that the water has been doped with some kind of cryoprotectant like diethylene glycol (the anti-freeze most famous for its use in German wines) to stop the water forming ice-crystals. That's really not an allotrope, although we still can't discount that Nation *might* be hitting on something interesting. So what kinds of substance could be in the water to allow it to run that cold? Sugars are a possibility, glycerols another, alcohols a third. So is the cyan-coloured witches' brew we see the Doctor dip his finger in just a very sticky Piña colada? Well, the substance it most resembles is one that *does* stay liquid for a while at low temperatures (by domestic standards) until exposed to air, and which resembles naturally occurring compounds: wallpaper paste.

Invisibility (General): When the Doctor bamboozled an invisible monster with an egg-timer in "The Face of Evil" (14.4), you could almost hear Chris Boucher - that story's author - grinding his teeth at the corny way this idea had been used hitherto. The point is that anything not absorbing light in the visible spectrum couldn't interact with light on those frequencies *at all*, and so logically wouldn't be able to see.

That's not the end of it, though. The entities we're dealing with aren't just capable of letting light *through*, they don't affect light at all, so there's no prismatic effects. A glass alien would still be visible, unless we're dealing with beings whose bodies miraculously have exactly the same refractive index as air. If you've tried finding broken glass in water, you'll know the problem: light slows down when it hits glass, water or any other transparent medium (it's only *in a vacuum* that light is the fastest thing possible). But if the medium and something *else* transparent slow it down by the same amount, that thing becomes invisible. If the medium's properties change - as when warmer air mixes with cooler, making heat-haze - the difference is noticeable.

As neither the Daleks nor the Doctor can tell where they are, the Visians (3.4, "The Daleks' Master Plan") and the Spiridons ("Planet of the Daleks") must have exactly the same temperature as the air. Even if the Daleks lacked infra-red vision, the lack of dew forming on the locals - despite their living in a steamy rain-forest or swamp such as Mira or Spiridon - or the fact that objects behind them don't shimmer suggests this is the case. (Just as well, given that they're wandering around naked.) The Refusians (3.6, "The Ark") seem to perceive that the Doctor and Dodo are different from the Monoids, but are *also* able to chuck statues around. So we might assume, more or less, that they're bodiless psionic forces (this isn't exactly scientific, but it's not trying to be), although Wester in "Planet of the Daleks" assuredly isn't. He picks up objects to look at them, knows Jo on sight (or maybe smell) and becomes visible when he dies.

This last bit's the real problem, actually. If the Spiridons' invisibility is willed, they might be performing some form of "funnelling" effect on light, bending it to go around their bodies. If you hold your breath and screw your eyes up really tight, you might just be able to believe that - but it would take an awful lot of concentration and

continued on page 357...

does this other than the Omega crisis in "The Three Doctors", "Attack of the Cybermen" (22.1) and of course his fateful decision in "The War Games" (6.7). It seems odd that he does this now, but never tries it again, not even when - for example - the entire universe is threatened in 18.7, "Logopolis". Since this can't *wholly* be a matter of pride, he may feel that he can still ask for favours after saving them from Omega, or alternatively he may just feel that the Master's intervention in Dalek history will startle them into action. And that's the second notable point, the fact that the Time Lords are so willing to help. Once again, Dalek influence, and / or the development of this galaxy, could be of major concern to them.]

The Non-Humans

• *Daleks.* The Dalek army assembled on Spiridon, ready for the conquest of 'all solar planets' and thereafter the galaxy, is 10,000 strong. The Doctor calls this 'the mightiest Dalek army there's ever been'. They're interested in this particular planet because of the invisibility of its natives, but its army is in suspended animation, so presumably the planet's subterranean low temperatures are also useful [indicating that these Daleks have been here for some time, waiting for the invasion]. Some Daleks have indeed been made invisible, but the process requires large amounts of power and they can only remain unseen for around 'two work-cycles', in addition to which the process seems to make them break down at least occasionally.

Here Dalek operations are run from a "central control" area in their base, and there's at least one section leader, although it's revealed that they have a Supreme Command somewhere off-planet. The Dalek Supreme - part of the Supreme Council - arrives in a smooth, featureless, dumbell-like vessel, and is revealed to have a subtly different body-shape to the rest of the Dalek line, with chocolate-and-gold livery and oversized "light-bulbs" on the dome. [The *real* reason for this is that it's actually a Dalek salvaged from the 1965 / 1966 Dalek cinema films and given a new paint-job, but it looks significantly different to the normal Dalek form. As the Doctor asked the Time Lords to take the TARDIS to the departing Dalek ship's destination, it's possible that the Supreme's vessel is the same one which left the Ogron planet, although there was no Dalek Supreme on show in the previous story. The Supreme recognises the section leader

on sight, even though the leader's casing is the same colour as all the other Daleks. The Supreme exterminates subordinates who fail in their duty. His eye-stalk, which looks suspiciously like a torch from Woolworth's, also lights up when he speaks [see **Things That Don't Make Sense**].

The vertical panels around a Dalek's middle are 'sensor-plates', according to the Doctor. He also states that most Daleks have an automatic defence call, a transmitter which may keep functioning even after the Dalek's deactivated and which is apparently triggered when the dome is lifted. [Again, there's no indication of how he knows this. There doesn't seem to be any such transmitter at work in "The Daleks".] He also knows that Daleks are susceptible to low temperatures, the creatures inside instantly dying of shock when their casings are exposed to sub-zero levels of cold.

Their internal guidance systems function by high-frequency radio impulses, so positive feedback can jam them and give them temporary seizures. [This might explain why the light-waves cause them to sicken and die. Electromagnetic waves wouldn't ordinarily penetrate their shells, but if they are making themselves translucent, the possibility of other wavelengths - such as microwaves - getting in and causing interference is greatly increased. This may be the 'light-wave sickness' of which Codal speaks.]

Dalek guns are still capable of disabling instead of killing - the last time they're ever seen to do this - and two Dalek guns in unison are powerful enough to make an entire Thal spaceship go up in smoke. Dalek sucker-arms can lift non-Dalek-designed objects, while one Dalek is seen with no sucker on its arm and a heat-based cutting-tool in its place. [So their weapons are enough to blow up spaceships, but not to blast open metal doors?] Dalek guns can make other Daleks explode, which is good to know. One Dalek uses an 'anti-gravitational disc', a *very* slow floating platform just big enough for a single unit.

Inside their city, the Daleks are experimenting with blood-destroying bacteria which can destroy all life on the planet within a day, Daleks included [so Daleks have blood]. However, they and their servants can be given immunity. Victims die within an hour of exposure to infected air.

Faced with death, the Daleks display fear.

• *Thals.* The other inhabitants of the Daleks' home planet have only recently developed [deep]

What are the Silliest Examples of Science in *Doctor Who*?

...continued from page 355

energy to do this, the way it's presented on screen. After all, if this is something mental (so to speak), why do they need fur coats in the chilly bits of the complex? Why not just stop being invisible and conserve energy to stay warm? If it's an involuntary mental process, then how do they find mates? Again, maybe by smell, although Jo doesn't comment on it. But surely predators would find a really pungent Spiridon as easy to hunt as a visible one, so what's the point?

Invisibility (Daleks): Back in their pomp, the Daleks were wont to boast about their many powers and abilities. In Volumes I and II, you'll have encountered some of the strange claims made on the Daleks' behalf in the *Dalek Pocket-Book and Authentic Space-Traveller's Guide*. However, mention of the Voltoscope, the Hypno ray and other such developments seem petty compared to the 1965 *Dalek World* book, in which we discover that Dalekenium is worth £100,000 an ounce (in 1965 money!) and is so light that a Dalek only weights 2 1/2 lb. (Evidently, they never converted to metric on Skaro.)

However, one extraordinary weakness was proclaimed loudly in amongst the braggadocio: the Daleks can't see red. (Figuratively they did little else, but not *literally*.) Apparently their electronic eyes are unable to register this frequency, so their perception-range lacks the ability to register anything red. They even have a cartoon of a Dalek colliding with a post-office pillar-box to prove it.

What makes this more remarkable is that the *Dalek Pocketbook* has a photo on the cover from the Peter Cushing film version, *Doctor Who and the Daleks*, where the massed hordes of Daleks are given orders to fire-extinguish the Thals into submission by... a Red Dalek. It has the usual brass fittings, but is mainly a big rosy lump. Do the Daleks perceive this as a floating cummerbund? (According to X1.9, "The Empty Child", red is 'a bit camp', so it's possible that the Daleks don't want anyone laughing at them.)

When we finally got a Red Dalek in the broadcast episodes (X4.12, "The Stolen Earth"), it had strap-on accessories and stood in a big spotlight giving orders. "A-ha!", we all thought, they *must* be able to see him. Yet, looking back on the previous seventeen Dalek adventures, and especially the dozen in colour, there's nothing to indicate that the Daleks use any red instrumentation (save for Spiridon - but that control-complex, with handles on the doors and all the rest, seems not to have been built for them). Maybe the latest breed of Daleks responds better to red than any before. Obviously, having vision that lacks a colour in the visible spectrum is something of a tactical error, especially after they developed infra-red targeting (25.1, "Remembrance of the Daleks"). Presumably their spectrum ends at orange then starts again; any Thal agent worth his salt could just wear red clothing and a ski-mask. If only the Zerovians in the *TV 21* strip had thought to respray their robot agent 2K (oh, wait... the comic-strip Daleks *also* had a red boss)...

Either way, Terry Nation took it upon himself to rectify this curious anomaly by making the Daleks not only able to see everything - including events on far-off planets with *incredible* telescopes - but to become invisible. Not with any Spiridon help, though. This gem of Dalek lore is actually found on the wrappers of the Dalek Death-Ray ice-lolly from 1975. Since you ask, it was chocolate fudge with a mint-ice coating and very nice, but the wrappers, alas, revived the tradition of stupid Dalek gloating. Dalek scientists, we were solemnly told, had found a way to become invisible using the miraculous power of infra-green light. Even if you don't know Latin, the obvious parallel is infra-red, which is the bit of the spectrum going towards heat. So logically, "infra-green" must mean "yellow".

Supernovae: Perhaps part of the reason Kit Pedler got his reputation as TV's Mr Science is that compared to his colleague Gerry Davis, he looks like Archimedes of Syracuse. When Pedler was rushed to hospital, Davis wrote "The Tenth Planet" episode three, in which the scientist Barclay gravely suggests that the use of the Z-Bomb could potentially turn Mondas, an Earth-sized (and Earth-everything-elsed) planet, into a supernova.

As most of you probably know, a nova is the colossal release of energy when a large amount of hydrogen starts fusing into helium under the pressure of its own gravity, thus creating a star. Most stars are born in "stellar nurseries", and therefore have a lot of other nascent stars nearby. A supernova, however, is the opposite - a big star on its last gasp. Or maybe it's two stars: one dying and the smaller neighbour having its mass sucked in.

continued on page 359...

space flight, and state that they come straight from Skaro. Nobody has ever travelled this far before. There are apparently Daleks still on or around Skaro, since the Thals know something of the Daleks' plans. [Even though this story is set after the era of "The Daleks", when the Skaro-based Daleks are wiped out... the space-travelling Daleks must have moved back to the old homeworld.]

As ever, the Thals are all pretty-faced humanoids with blond hair, but they have a lot more determination than before; the Doctor clearly has concerns about them becoming overly military, even though they're still a bit pathetic as warriors go. They carry stubby little energy-weapons, and have a sizeable military, with Codal speaking of a 'division' of over six-hundred people in which he's a scientist. Some of those on Spiridon have seen action before.

The Thals know of Earth, but it's just a name in their old legends. Likewise, they've heard of the Doctor and consider him mythical after his help in defeating the Daleks 'generations ago'. This era in Skaro's history [i.e. the events of "The Daleks"] is known as the Dalek War [both the Doctor and the Thals know the term, so the Doctor must have done some checking-up on Thal history since], and the Doctor claims they're famous as one of the most peace-loving peoples in the galaxy. They still don't shake hands on Skaro.

• *Spiridons*. The natives of Spiridon are humanoid, but invisible thanks to an 'anti-reflecting light wave', though they can be seen by the huge, purple, furry pelts they wear [so there must be huge, purple, furry animals somewhere on Spiridon]. They become visible on death, revealing themselves to be humanoids with lumpy faces. Though wholly sentient, only one of the Spiridons we meet here is remotely civilised, their artefacts appearing rather stone-aged despite having a fully-developed language and "natural" cures for the local killer fungus. There are ruined statues and ancient-looking buildings in the jungle. [We might conclude that, like the Exxilons in the *next* Dalek story, they're survivors of a fallen civilisation. If so then their invisibility may have been artificially generated at some point in the past, since evolutionarily speaking it seems improbable. Wester the benevolent Spiridon seems to imply that it was the Daleks who destroyed his culture.]

Planet Notes

• *Spiridon*. A planet seemingly covered in jungle and teeming with life, Spiridon is nonetheless unique as it has a core of molten ice; a cold, gooey allotrope of ice rather than just water. The ice occasionally erupts through ice volcanoes. The planet is tropical in the day, sub-freezing at night, and after dark there are boulders which give off heat absorbed during the day. These tend to be popular with the local animals, which include large, unseen predators with glowing eyes [the big, furry, purple things that the Spiridons skin?] and huge - but equally unseen - flying animals.

The plant-life on Spiridon includes large flower-like 'fungoids' which spit sickly yellow slime at their victims. This spores in this slime spread across the flesh of anyone it "infects" until it engulfs the victim. There are also eye-plants, which amusingly turn to stare at anyone who passes, visible or otherwise; and a creeping tentacle that creeps through the undergrowth and grapples something.

Skaro is 'many systems' away, and the Thals refer to Spiridon as being in the 'Ninth System'. The Dalek city on Spiridon is either a Dalek pre-fab base that's been constructed inside the shell of the native Spiridon architecture, or a Spiridon city that's just been re-fitted. [The latter is considerably more likely, as almost all the equipment seems to be designed for beings with hands.]

History

• *Dating*. Presumably 2540 [following directly on from "Frontier in Space"], and obviously generations after "The Daleks".

Once the army's buried in the molten ice of Spiridon, the Doctor believes it'll take centuries to melt the Daleks out. [Presumably the Earth Empire later deals with them, unless these Daleks end up being used during the next invasion attempt on Earth in "The Daleks' Master Plan". The tie-in writers and fandom have often pondered what happened next: Paul Cornell did a strip in *DWM* in which Davros converts the Spiridon Daleks all into his white and gold lot (in 25.1, "Remembrance of the Daleks") but *faux* time-travelling fanzine "Chronic Hysteresis" did a spoof review of 2013's big Anniversary story "Tomb of the Daleks", in which the Brotherhood of Logicians yadda yadda (5.1, "The Tomb of the Cybermen" if you hadn't figured it out). Nick Briggs did his own take on what became of the

What are the Silliest Examples of Science in *Doctor Who*?

...continued from page 357

Either way, it involves things that have a lot of mass and are already chucking out energy. Mondas has the opposite problem - it's rather the point of the story.

Judging by what we're shown on screen, a Z-Bomb is a warhead the size of a Winnebago trailer. Stars are a lot bigger than planets, and planets are a lot bigger than Winnebago trailers. Even if it turned *all* its mass into energy on detonation, a Z-Bomb would *maybe* make an Australia-sized hole in Mondas (which, funnily enough, also has an Australia). And if aimed at a fissure, it might, conceivably, rend the planet asunder.

To turn a planet into a *supernova*, you'd need to borrow energy from elsewhere, not to mention an awful lot of hydrogen. If humanity had a weapon that could obtain these from other sources - maybe by use of a wormhole, with one end conveniently close to a large gas-cloud - then it's astonishing that *any* alien race managed to invade Earth, let alone the comparatively pathetic Mondasian Cybermen. Seriously, why is Earth space-control faffing about with Zeus Four when they can whip across the galaxies?

Of course, in a very technical sense, Barclay might have been almost right. A bit. The standard mechanism of a supernova, as was understood in 1986 when "The Tenth Planet" is set (and, more to the point, in 1966 when it was written) involved the release of as much energy in a day as the star had put out in its lifetime, as gravitational collapse makes the star's atoms give up any attempt to remain as matter, becoming energy again. If (and it's a big *if*) the Z-Bomb does something with gravity, then maybe the effect on Mondas would be a rapid implosion and a colossal release of energy by the same process as a supernova but not on the same scale. However, a Z-Bomb of that design would need a much bigger rocket to launch it - one the size of Canada maybe - and would do far more damage to our planet than the invading Cybermen, a near miss with another world or that world going bang in close proximity to Earth. This all makes you wonder if Pedler was hospitalised after Davis announced that this was going out with both their names on it.

Elsewhere, we have the more orthodox use of stellar events in both "The Three Doctors" (10.1) and "The Edge of Destruction" (1.3). As we've already mentioned, the comparative brevity of the thing in the former story makes its use as a power-source for the Time Lords rather silly - unless they're already planning on *not* being around forever - but how exactly the Second Doctor's small Dolmesch treble recorder could detonate an entire anti-matter universe and make a black hole turn into a supernova is a mystery. If anything, it should have made the Event Horizon slightly wider. (The same confusion about how a "hole" can actually contain any mass, let alone theoretically an infinite one, persists even to the 2007 *Children in Need* skit "Time Crash", in which where the coincidence of a black hole and a supernova makes the total mass added to the universe balance out. Not the stupidest idea in that *feutillon*, but still very wrong.)

In the other case, why does having a solar-system-sized mass all in one place make it *more* attractive than when it was a solar system? The only way this works is if the TARDIS was inside the proto-planetary mass, in which case it would all balance out (as with the centre of the planet in 15.5, "Underworld").

Space Travel That's Just Like Sailing: When discussing General Williams' instruction to his pilot in "Frontier in Space" (10.3), we noted that the idea that speeding up will let you orbit a planet faster is plain daft. This also, as we noted when discussing the much-mentioned Mars - Venus rocket run (**When Did the Doctor Get His Driving Licence?** under 7.1, "Spearhead from Space"), applies just as much to a solar orbit. We've even commented on how often the analogy of space travel to sailing crops up in Hartnell stories, even though they don't make as much of this as *Star Trek*'s earliest episodes (which look so much like *South Pacific*, you almost expect Nurse Chapel to wash that Vulcan right outa her hair).

However, as you might expect, the worst and most embarrassing instance of this sort of thing occurs when Kit Pedler and David Whitaker team up - as happens in "The Wheel in Space" (5.7). It's a bigger issue than it seems, especially when you remember that director Tristan de Vere Cole was hauling Pedler in for script-conferences during rehearsals, and TV's Mr Science got it wrong again. What's most distressing is that the biggest blunder of all occurs in the scene that introduces Zoe to the Doctor as little miss know-it-all.

To recap, Zoe is puzzled as to how a ship (the *Silver Carrier*) can travel 87 million miles when it's

continued on page 361...

Spiridon Daleks in the "Return of the Daleks" audio, and linked it into Big Finish's "Dalek Empire" mini-series.]

The Analysis

Where Does This Come From? Above all else, this adventure is about recycling the writer's back-catalogue with nothing he didn't invent to get in the way. We can criticise Nation for this approach (and will, later) but this is, in fact, what he was asked to do. The entire scheme of doing what amounted to a twelve-episode serial was consciously nostalgic and commissioned *before* anyone had thought of "The Three Doctors", so it shouldn't surprise us that the script is knowingly retro. These days it's easy to forget but a "long-running" adventure serial, in that era, was one that lasted for three or four years. By this point, *Doctor Who* had been breaking new ground constantly for a decade, even though most of the original target audience were expected to have moved on, and the *present* viewers were babies or unborn when the whole thing began.

In this period, repeats were almost unheard of and "classic" repeats, from a different phase with a different cast, were actually against Union rules. So this is one of the very first stories to exploit the public's "folk memory" of *Doctor Who* - something less detailed than the archives. As this story was commissioned right after the first TV showing of the Cushing movies, this notion was just beginning to dawn on Letts and Dicks. Before this, anything vaguely recognisable from the show's long past was admissible (see, for instance, the parade of B-list monsters that supposedly made up the sum of the Doctor's fears in 8.2, "The Mind of Evil"). *Afterwards*, the invocation of the show's heritage had to be handled more carefully - alluding to the past meant being either accurate or imaginative, making up unseen adventures or looking up the details. (Unless you were Terry Nation - see 12.4, "Genesis of the Daleks" and the Doctor's "memory" of the film version.)

Nation has also gone back to the sources of his original (if we can call it that) script. There's a lot of Rider-Haggard-style "lost civilisation" material, although nowhere near as much as his next go ("Death to the Daleks"), filtered through Edgar Rice Burroughs (more *Tarzan* than Barsoom) and Alex Raymond's *Flash Gordon* comics (assuming a kid in Cardiff ever got to see them). To be honest,

these had been copied and parodied so often, it's hard to tell what's a reference and what's a pastiche of a form, like trying to find a specific film where Mickey Rooney actually says "Let's do the show right here!"

Additionally, Nation hasn't let the grass grow under his feet while he's been away. There's evidence that he's been thinking about the implications of the stories he wrote back in his pioneering days. He's considered how to immobilise a Dalek, and how this can be prevented from making them less scary (see his next story for a development of this). He's thought about what kind of space-army the pacifist Thals would assemble and their level of technology. Above all, he's been rethinking jungle warfare. Inevitably, any writer who'd spent the late 60s in America would have a few thoughts on the subject. Earlier Dalek jungle adventures had used real flamethrowers, like Hollywood's version of the WWII South Pacific campaigns, but Nation seems to have thought about the logistics of doing it in TVC and seen footage of Vietnam. So here we see the Daleks experimenting with (to all intents and purposes) Agent Orange.

Nation has also done a bit of homework on allotropes. Now, obviously, anyone on the fringes of Science Fiction in the early 70s would have come across the word via Kurt Vonnegut's novel *Cat's Cradle*, in which an allotrope (Ice-9) causes all orthodox water to turn to crystalline ice on contact, so the world is abruptly ending as people drink, rain falls and so on. It could have been a good *Doomwatch* premise, but Vonnegut uses it for a sly dig at how people cope with inevitable doom. Nation's version of this theme entails doing what you can in the hope that something turns up. In this, he's part of a very long tradition of Anglo-Saxon storytelling. And whilst the Daleks are their old selves - half a plunger-length away from being called "Fritz" - the Thal leader Taron displays the first signs that fighting them too ruthlessly removes your moral right to defeat them. Nation will touch upon this again in later Dalek stories, as well as the bits of *Blake's 7* he actually wrote.

In the past, Nation was writing war-stories based on the time-honoured idea of the Englishman who'd rather be at home smoking a pipe and tending his herbaceous borders, but is forced to fight and make a stand for decency against the Beastly Hun / Johnny Frenchman /

What are the Silliest Examples of Science in *Doctor Who*?

...continued from page 359

only got enough fuel for 20 million. As most of you will know, in space it takes as much effort for a ship to stop or change direction as it does to get started, and carrying on in a straight line is inevitable as long as no planets or other gravitational fields get in the way. You'd only need fuel for course-corrections, *and* Zoe knows the ship was out of control. She says it was reported overdue seven million miles from Station Five, which is 87 million miles away. And what, precisely, *is* there between 80 million and 94 million miles from Earth orbit? Nothing. It's literally the middle of nowhere. Even Mars halfway around its orbit from us would be the wrong distance. (If the ship had fuel for 20 million miles, then it was either over-stocked or - if they anticipated missing a big planet and drifting off - severely underpowered.)

And even if this *was* en route for Mars (and if that's the case, why not say so instead of 'Station Five'?), at a point when Mars is 80 million miles away and it's headed in from the asteroids (and went AWOL seven million miles from touchdown), there remains the problem that to go that far inward - towards Earth's orbit in nine weeks - requires you to slam on the brakes so hard that you'd plummet into the Sun. But that slamming wouldn't require any more fuel than they had.

If it's an issue that a ship that vanished somewhere near Venus came to be in close Earth orbit, then thrust is a problem. If, as we're discussing here, a lost ship has crossed space in a *shorter* time than expected, then Zoe needn't worry about its fuel supply. A burst of thrust will send a spaceship into a bigger, faster orbit around the sun, i.e. further out towards Jupiter or wherever. Whether any human could withstand that amount of acceleration is another matter, but we're pretty certain Zoe isn't asking that. She would've interrogated Jamie an episode earlier instead of talking about spanking. To "descend" the gravity-well takes some delta-V too, but to avoid just falling into the Sun it needs to be done gradually, so the time factor is again more important than fuel.

However, listen closely to what Zoe says and it's actually odder than that. It's claimed that the *Silver Carrier* was lost nine weeks ago near Station Five. Given that the Wheel is W3, we might assume that 'Station Five' another Wheel-like station in Earth orbit. If all the stations *are* in Earth's neck of the woods, the five Lagrange points are good candidates. (These are points where the Sun's gravitational pull and the Earth's are in equilibrium, so one is right over the other side of the moon, and two are in the same orbit but 60 degrees around in either direction. And one is a long way out, on the opposite side of Earth from the moon. This is L1, and the best bet for a stable orbit. Even if you're steering well clear of Earth's gravity-well, it's a short hop. Off-the-shelf in the books that have wheel-like space stations and delta-wing shuttles like *Silver Carrier* is the description of L5 as the most likely first base.)

So, if anything, nine weeks is unreasonably slow for such a journey, even if stations Three and Five are the furthest apart. (Note how it took three days to reach lunar orbit in 1969.) Similarly, Venus - if we go with the idea that it's at its closest to Earth, just to stop us quibbling about the distances - is too near for this to make sense. Zoe was so precise on this point, it's inconceivable that even Whitaker got it wrong.

It might be countered that we're restricted to thinking in terms of orbits tangential to the plane of the ecliptic, like all the regular planets' orbits around the sun. But there's the rub: without planets and their handy propensity to orbit in a flat plane, the possible trajectories get a lot longer. To go "over" or "under" the Sun would take a lot longer than nine weeks, unless the Doctor and Jamie were zooming around encased in some kind of jelly and zonked out to withstand acceleration of a dozen Gs. Avoiding the Sun and hopping out of the ecliptic wouldn't be as bad, but it's still so much more time- (and fuel-) consuming. Using the orbital velocity of your starting-point is pretty much a given, unless you've got magical *Star Trek* engines.

And what's more puzzling than any of this is that Zoe says, 'that ship must have been refuelled in space, provided with at least another twelve more fuel rods.' We know from *later that same episode* that there's three boxes of Bernalium on the ship's manifest. So what's the bloody problem?

Just So Stories: As we all know, *Star Trek* hired physicists to make heartbreakingly pointless claims that the science within the show was all checked out before any attempt was made to turn it into realistic dialogue. But as is also clear, they haven't the first clue about molecular biology or the rudiments of evolution, and have silly stories where spare bits of DNA are activated and make

continued on page 363...

Killer Robots / Morris Dancers. The Thals had been an extreme version of this, based loosely on the Swedes, but in the original Dalek story, it was the even-tempered Ian Chesterton who found his inner Bulldog. Now, however, there's no such male lead and the Doctor - who Nation had used more as a comic figure and exposition-dispenser - is at centre-stage. Hence we get the rather awkward scenes where Taron and Codal ask the Doctor's advice on how to be a male lead in a 1960s *Doctor Who* story, since the Doctor is himself in a curious limbo between Ian and the Hartnell version. Logically, *Jo* would be the one to undergo such an initiation, but this is the 1970s and it wouldn't have occurred to anyone involved, except perhaps Letts (who'd not get taken seriously). The "tutorial on courage" and the lecture to Taron about not becoming like the Daleks are examples of Nation clumsily but gamely retooling his approach to the series on screen. He has another go in his next story, but by "Genesis of the Daleks" he seems to have been guided in the right direction.

Things That Don't Make Sense Even if he didn't know the story's title, the Doctor requested that the Time Lords send the TARDIS after the escaping Dalek ship. He winds up on a planet where he meets some Thals from Skaro, the Daleks' homeworld. The Thals are on a military expedition to stop '...*them*'. When he sees 'what we're up against', he gasps in shock: 'A Dalek!' He expected, maybe, Yartek, Leader of the Alien Voord?

Why is the invisible Dalek just running around loose anyway? The Daleks are performing invisibility experiments, fair enough, but what makes them let their test subjects just wander out of the city until they die and need retrieval? You might reply "They got past because they're invisible" - but we're talking about the Daleks, who are used to obeying orders and will stick around if told. Or if they're too ill to know where they're going, you'd think the Dalek scientists would have just locked the doors and kept a lookout. They're invisible, after all, not intangible. (Hrm, maybe the Daleks cast out their own sick and lame to die in the wilderness. They're ruthless enough, but on the downside for them, anyone with a handful of flour could find a dead Dalek, nick its gun and start massacring the pepperpots.)

Even allowing that he's rather delirious, why does the Doctor - in his moment of consciousness remaining - tell Jo to record what happens in the

log, as opposed to something more helpful such as, "Whatever happens, don't leave the TARDIS"? The Ship is supposedly invulnerable, and she could've just explained things once he woke up. As matters stand, it's a bit rich when, in episode four, the Doctor wants to know why Jo didn't stay put.

Odd things to do in between recovering from a near death coma and collapsing from hypoxia: 1) decide to rethink your outfit; 2) after changing into a natty purple ensemble, *now* you decide to repair the ship's systems. Telepathically, the Doctor seems to have divined that purple is this year's colour on Spiridon, and that he'll need boots for the swamp adventure in four episodes' time.

Mind you, he does all this after his body temperature drops below zero, which makes less sense the more one thinks about it. If he's got as much water in his body as humans [and all his tea-consumption makes this likely, to say nothing of all the times he's almost died from dehydration], then ice-crystals in his blood would have shredded his internal organs. If he's as icy to the touch as he appears, then either his body would normally be below zero [unless his circulation is overcompensating], or something is happening inside his body that requires all of his blood-heat *and* any available heat around his person.

Even apart from the malarkey about the TARDIS' air supply, a small amount of goo from the local plant-life is apparently strong enough to seal the TARDIS doors shut, even though they're powered by great big motors and open inwards. And when the time comes for the Thals - who are on the run, and eluding the Daleks, remember - to extract the Doctor from the Ship, they magically produce plastic body wrap, large knives and even protective helmets from nowhere to do so.

Once again, Terry Nation doesn't seem to grasp quite how large the galaxy is. 10,000 Daleks is supposed to be a shockingly huge number and enough to conquer the galaxy - even though 10,000 is just a tiny fraction of (say) the 350,000 troops who were evacuated at Dunkirk. The Daleks "search" Marat's body and find the map of the Thal bombs' location remarkably efficiently, considering that they can't even bend down to roll him over. Anyway, how do the Daleks know straightaway what's to be found there? Did Vaber mark, "Here there be bombs", on it?

When the Doctor opens the hatch that over-

What are the Silliest Examples of Science in *Doctor Who*?

...continued from page 361

people turn into spiders, or travel at transwarp speeds and thus become what humans will "inevitably" evolve into some day.

In case the stupidity of this eludes you, bear in mind that evolution works on the simplest principle of all: if it ain't broke, don't fix it. Species have random mutations and odd genetic quirks every generation, but if that small change doesn't enable the individual who's got it to eat something extra, out-run predators better, have healthier offspring or merely function about as well as the rest of the species, it won't survive to another generation. If things don't change, it doesn't make any odds. If things *do* change and the rest of the species finds it harder to cope, then it's an advantage to be different that way. So anything suggesting that humans (or human-like aliens) are "more evolved" has missed the point, and anyone saying that the next developments are pre-ordained is either Terry Nation or an idiot.

It might be countered, however, that as the process of figuring out how Species A became Species B is conjecture and cannot be tested without a time-machine and a number of identical Earths (so that you can change one thing and see what's different), evolutionary biology isn't quite science. It does, however, make doable science happen. And in *Doctor Who* terms, it allows the attentive viewer to ponder that many of the odd features of aliens are things that, looked at in this light, should have wiped out the species long ago.

Indeed, from this point of view, some species should never have come into being at all. In 6.4, "The Krotons", the titular aliens have a number of curious features that rather militate against them ever getting space-flight, any form of technology or indeed doing anything other than slopping about in puddles. This might be why their scheme to harvest the Gonds' brain-power looks like a selective-breeding program to stop their slaves ever having brain-power again. They pick the cleverest male and female students, then kill them before they have clever babies. No wonder the Krotons have been stranded for centuries.

You may have seen earlier in this book similar conjecture about the odd arrangements Arcturans have made (9.2, "The Curse of Peladon"). We could mention that the Sensorites' reaction to darkness (in 1.7, "The Sensorites", naturally) is the exact opposite of the most useful thing to do (pupils contract when the lights go off), or that

their cousins the Ood (X4.3, "Planet of the Ood") are as spectacularly unsuited to life on an ice planet as it is possible to imagine. But the latter can wait for another volume, after we've gone into the sheer silliness of the Abzorbaloff's biology.

By the mid-70s, you start getting signs that the writers are thinking these things through - part of how the Williams era script-team devises stories at such short notice was that they "built" aliens, then thought of stories to go round them. We were left only wondering how anyone found out that you could snort powdered deep-fried Mandrell (17.4, "Nightmare of Eden").

Then in 1980, the computer-nerds rose to power and messed thing up all up again. We've looked at the daft idea that the Time Lords somehow "dented" reality and made all advanced species look like humans (**How Does "Evolution" Work?** under "Full Circle"), and the notion that external form somehow reflects mental processes (**What Was Josiah's 'Blasphemous' Theory?** under "Ghost Light"). But any geneticists who want to get good 'n' angry should watch "Full Circle" for a Lamarckian fantasy, with the unpleasant taint of Rupert Sheldrake's barking mad nostrums of "Morphic Resonance", tarted up with the language of genetics. In this story, after all, we find that Marshmen evolved into humanoids because - um - everything eventually does so, as long as it really, *really* wants to. There was some guff about spider-bites too. It all looks as though someone had an A-Level biology book handy, but only grabbed some scientific-sounding words from the index and didn't actually understand any of it.

Still, we all thought that nothing as excruciating as Reg Barclay's ludicrous T-cell anomaly "reverting" him into a man-spider (the *Star Trek: The Next Generation* episode "Genesis") could blight *Doctor Who*. Then we saw X3.6, "The Lazarus Experiment"...

Driving Planets: More Terry Nation insanity, but this time vouchsafed by Kit Pedler (TV's Mr Science) and Christopher H Bidmead (TV's Mr Algorithms). Both the Daleks (in 2.2, "The Dalek Invasion of Earth", by Nation) and the Tractators (20.3, "Frontios", by Bidmead) attempted to move planets around as mobile bases of operation in their plans to conquer the Universe. Meanwhile, the Cybermen were already on a planet that's moving either eccentrically or crazily. In "The Tenth Planet", Mondas is in a strange orbit, but it may

continued on page 365...

looks the Dalek army, it's fitted with two little round handles. Is all Dalek furniture built this way? Apparently so, as all the electronic equipment is designed to be used by beings with hands. Maybe they stole the city from the Spiridons [whose technology seems to have been quite good within living memory, but nobody there knows how to use it - a shortage of science teachers perhaps?] or the Daleks were expecting the Ogrons to come along and defrost them when the time was right. [This shows a *lot* of faith in the Ogrons, however.]

One minute we're told that if a Dalek will die instantly if its bumper-skirt gets a bit chilly, the next the Dalek Supreme is planning to drench a whole Dalek army up to their indicator-lights in the same stuff. The Doctor says the Daleks are 'vulnerable' to extreme cold, yet this story revolves around 10,000 of them being frozen - see the problem? [At risk of launching a hundred thousand fan-fics, the most sensible explanation for much of this and "Frontier in Space" is that the Master has hypnotised the Dalek Supreme as a pre-emptive move in the Time War. What other reason can exist for the Top Dalek's repeated idiocy?]

So this being a Terry Nation story, the Daleks have an interest in plague, albeit as a means of overkill. "The Daleks' Master Plan" saw them dealing sternly with a handful of spies by burning down an entire forest, but there it was disproportionate in an *exciting* way. Here, they opt to wipe out a similarly scant handful they don't actually know to be dangerous with a virus that will eliminate every living thing on Spiridon - and which requires that every single Dalek present queue up and get a shot [and a lollypop?]. Dalek security is so crap that Wester can bluff his way into the section where they're brewing the planetary plague, *and* they've left the lid unsealed on the bacteria culture. What, they don't see the need to keep it sealed until they're ready to release it? (Because Daleks *never* bump into things by accident.) But then, the Daleks also - in full knowledge that there are rebels, invisible natives and dangerous wildlife about - leave the door to their spaceship open.

Nice idea though it is, the escape using body-heat and a tarpaulin to rise up the shaft isn't quite that simple. In theory the cold air at the bottom would be denser, but the air from the jungle ought to be laden with moisture. (That's why we call them "rain forests".) At the very least, the shaft ought to be filled with impenetrable fog, and ideally (from a Saturday-teatime cliffhanger perspective) rimed with ice. (If nothing else, this could have made a more hazardous ascent, with icicles threatening to fall from a great height or rip the Doctor's improvised balloon.) You would expect the precipitation from damp air meeting cold air to cause a slight drizzle, possibly enough to cause a heavy puddle on top of the balloon and sink Our Heroes. Why have the Daleks left a handy tarp there anyway?

Assuming the Spiridons are natives of Spiridon [and the name is a bit of a clue], why did no other beasts have their handy invisibility talent? And how do they find mates? What does a Spiridon male look for in a female, if they have such things? In evolutionary terms this is a non-starter. And if it's technological, what happened to their advanced science, and why couldn't the Daleks have developed something similar unaided? And if they can *see* in another part of the spectrum, then they can be seen that way too? Worse, as it takes the Daleks a heck of a lot of energy to achieve the same effect, how come the Spiridons don't eat all the time? [See this story's essay for more in this vein.] Even if they've got a means allowing light to hit and somehow indirectly affect their retinas [else, *we'd* see a pair of retinae floating about], the remarkably abrupt transition from day to night and back should affect their visibility. Besides, if it gets that cold that quickly, you'd think a carnivore could learn to hunt by seeing into the infra-red, spotting all the warm prey against a suddenly cooler background.

The Thal spaceship, which seems like a flatpack DIY kit, has doors like a Barratt home and loose objects like fire-extinguishers and trimphones - very helpful, if the gravity systems fail or they go into a tight spin. It's as if they expected invisible heavy-breathing aliens to reveal their presence by picking things up menacingly. Presumably, their base of operations really needs the cobwebbed corpse of the pilot [the much-missed Myro?] stuck in a chair, on the off-chance that some visitors need scaring. And the decision to put the door in between the two rocket exhausts is just silly. Furthermore, the Thals' space-suits don't seem terribly airtight; gloves might have been a good idea. Especially if, about once per episode, you're going to stick your fingers in liquid suggested to be -100°c.

If the both the Daleks and the Thals are still

What are the Silliest Examples of Science in *Doctor Who*?

...continued from page 363

have been natural. (Although it appears to stop and start again, so we're forced to bring it into the discussion about Earth and Frontios. Eric Saward added the detail about Mondas having a huge motor in 22.1, "Attack of the Cybermen", so we'll count him among the guilty parties.)

In the case of Earth and Frontios (which is Earth-like enough to support the colonists there, without benefit of terraforming), the planets involved are fairly hefty ones. The obvious problem is they're both orbiting stars, and shifting Earth from its orbit would take a fair bit of welly. We're going around the Sun at 30 Km a second (or about sixty thousand miles an hour, if you must) on a planet that's 6X 1024 kilogrammes. That velocity makes for equilibrium with the Sun's gravitational pull. "Velocity" is the key word here, plus the fact that the orbit means the planet is moving in an ellipse - thus changing its direction constantly.

If the Sun's pull abruptly stopped for whatever reason, the planets would all whiz off in a straight line following whatever bearing they were last on. So Earth would hurtle off into space at a hundredth of the speed of light. (Similarly, if the Earth were to one day vanish but leave the moon behind, our satellite would go on an endless jaunt unless Earth disappeared at *precisely* the moment that the moon's trajectory around Earth was parallel to Earth's around the Sun. What are the chances of that happening?) If Earth happened to be facing the right way when the Sun's gravity cut out, it would arrive at Proxima Centauri in a mere 420 years. However, the Sun *is* pulling, so Earth has to reach the escape velocity of the Solar System, about 1000 Km/s. So that's (deep breath here) 600,000,000,000,000,000,000 tonnes accelerated to 1/3 the speed of light. We're back to Delta-V and now we're looking at an *absurd* amount of it.

Of course, the wily Daleks have thought of this. They've decided that Earth is to be denuded of its magnetic core. Generously assuming this to equal about half the mass of the planet, this is still a tall order and Earth - with no magnetosphere and a much lower gravity - will lose all its atmosphere and quickly become very radioactive, moving as it would be through the cosmic radiation at that kind of lick. And at a third of lightspeed it would stay fresh for longer, with relativistic effects meaning that everyone they hope to invade will prepare for impending Dalek onslaughts faster than the Daleks can unleash them (not *much* faster, but

enough to be noticeable).

Never mind that, if Earth lost half its mass, the gravity would be commensurately less, and at *that* speed this could be a problem. The Daleks had better have good brakes. They could, perhaps, use some kind of inertial damping system. This is actually accepted within *Doctor Who* lore (such as for Bessie's brakes; see 9.5, "The Time Monster"). In fact, all of those stories where they generate artificial gravity must use this type of technology. If you can switch off inertia, then the world's your shuttlecock. ("Doc" Smith, of the *Lensman* and *Skylark* books we mentioned in the last essay, and who himself contributes to allotropic amusement with a fuel-source richer even than copper, allotropic iron[119], had this as his ultimate deterrent: a weapon called a "Nutcracker" that was two planets bashing into each other with your ship in between. At a crucial moment, they switch the inertia back on.) But here's the kicker: if you *can* do this, then hurling planets around is almost the least interesting use of the technology. (The absolute epitome of a banal use, however, would be making brakes for your sprightly yellow roadster.)

Let's be fair, though. The Daleks never *say* they plan to send Earth out into interstellar space by brute force, simply that they're placing an engine within to move it and then conquer other worlds. If, as we've speculated before, there's a handy wormhole just past Jupiter (**Why Does Earth Keep Getting Invaded?** under 13.4, "The Android Invasion"), they only need to heft the planet a mere half-billion kilometres. This also covers the odd arrival out of nowhere of Voga (12.5, "Revenge of the Cybermen") and possibly Mondas' trip 'to the edge of space'. However, even pushing Earth to past Jupiter would require moving quickly enough for tidal forces to do nasty things to the planet (especially if it's now lacking a core, and has considerably lower gravity holding it together). They *could* be planning to hurl a large number of meteorites at an opponent, but then we return to the basic problem underlying this whole premise: why Earth? If they want to push planets around, surely better, less inhabited and less troublesome ones are available nearby.

The Tractators are a different matter. Let's assume that Frontios' gravitational pull is constant without their help, and that it has Earth mass. Let's also assume that the species doesn't need to do anything for long periods of time and can lie dor-

continued on page 367...

based on Skaro, how is it the Daleks have the means of conquering [or at least menacing] entire star-systems, yet they've left a society of people on their homeworld free to develop weapons, space-travel and an anti-Dalek force? And as the Thals return home in a stolen Dalek ship... well, let's hope the Thal anti-aircraft guns are as efficient as their crap pistols.

Latep comes to the conclusion that the Daleks found the Thal explosives and blew themselves up - but why would he think that, in the absence of all Dalek shrapnel and wreckage? And why does Jo even have to *think* about whether she'll go back to Skaro [a war-torn world that's presumably crawling with Daleks] with Latep, who she barely knows? [Maybe she's stalling to think up a polite lie, like "I've got a boyfriend back at UNIT HQ".] Meanwhile, it's curious that Jo knows which console knob will punch up a photo of Earth in episode six, but she couldn't open the door in episode one.

Some final notes: an allotrope of ice at significantly low temperature bubbles to the surface on a tropical, steamy, sultry planet, yet somehow, none of the local wildlife has adapted. Why will it require, as the Doctor estimates, a thousand years to dig the Dalek popsicles out? A few days with a stirrup-pump should be all that's needed. Oh yes, and the invisible Spiridons only leave footprints in the ground when there's an ominous close-up involved - and only one foot. Apparently, they hop everywhere.

Critique For anyone unfamiliar with 60s Dalek stories or Terry Nation's usual obsessions, this is an entertaining enough romp if quite slow and clunky. It has flaws to be sure, and in a lot of ways the subsequent stories with David Maloney as director see him trying to solve problems encountered here: chases through alien jungles (13.2, "Planet of Evil"; 14.3, "The Deadly Assassin"); making three Daleks look like an unstoppable onslaught ("Genesis of the Daleks"); making Prentis Hancock actually seem interesting as a hot-head in conflict with a more experienced officer; and making invisible monsters not look like something from *Rentaghost* or Michael Bentine's *Potty Time* ("Planet of Evil" again). Given that Maloney is facing *all* of these problems at once, his solutions this time around are quite effective. Except that...

We can't deny it: there's something not quite

right about all of this. If you want a one-word review of "Planet of the Daleks", that word is probably "perfunctory". This story hasn't got nearly as much pep in its step as "The Chase" (2.8), which means that - paradoxically - there's less that can go wrong. As we discussed in Volume I, what makes "The Chase" so funny is that they had huge plans for it, then gave it to a director who couldn't handle it. *This* time they have a director with a proven track record of salvaging stupid-looking monsters and absurdly ambitious stories and they've given him just about the safest and most unadventurous production of the Pertwee era. The Maloney of the Troughton and Baker years is such a distinctive director, seeing him do such bread-and-butter work is frustrating. The only sign that we're dealing with the same person lies in his casting.

It's unclear whether Terry Nation had actually bothered to watched any *Doctor Who* since he legged it to Hollywood, but the evidence suggests not, since "Planet" ignores virtually every change made to the programme in the interim. Ostensibly the theme of the story is "the meaning of bravery" - various Thals overcome fear, let concern about others jeopardise their mission and indulge in acts of impatient and / or suicidal stupidity, even as the Doctor gives lectures on both the nature of courage and the importance of not glamorising warfare. But these feel like trivial, lightweight ideas, to be covered in just a single scene of any other story. Besides, the rules we "learn" about bravery here only seem to apply to characters in gung-ho adventure stories (usually starring Dana Andrews and set in the Philippines).

Still, as we've pointed out in **Where Does This Come From?** Nation is figuring this all out on the hoof. He's still remarkably unsure of what the Doctor's role in a story should be these days, yet Taron and Codal aren't the right material from which protagonists of this kind of story are made. The Doctor gives moral lessons because otherwise, what is he *for*? Nation can't get away from the idea of the Doctor as lawgiver and advisor, even though he's dealing with a Doctor who's much more physical.

But this assumes that the Dicks-Letts model, derived partly from *Star Trek*, is the best way to make *Doctor Who*. It's not, in fact, compulsory to make topical references or big moral points in every single bloody episode. (Thinking along those lines leads to things such as 11.2, "Invasion

What are the Silliest Examples of Science in *Doctor Who*?

...continued from page 365

mant for centuries, millennia or maybe aeons. It doesn't require a Gravis to organise them once the wave-guide is built. They could plausibly exert their control over gravity and move this planet to anywhere in the galaxy, so long as they're confident that the star at which they're aiming will still be there when they arrive.

(Here's where we make a slight detour, and refer you to the sort of thing that popped up in children's books about the Wonders of the Universe circa 1970: Roche's Limit. Basically, if a small solid body gets too close to a bigger solid body, the tidal forces pull the smaller one into a lot of very small bodies - as with Saturn's rings. This is only true if the smaller body had been orbiting the larger, as it's the tension between the orbital vector (angular momentum) and the gravitational force of both bodies that does the shredding. We mention this because the Silurians in 7.2, "Doctor Who and the Silurians" seem very clever in these matters, yet they're scared of the moon (or whatever) hitting them in one lump. So whatever it was they saw coming, it was coming straight at them, not leaving a hitherto stable orbit. The other reason we mention Roche's Limit is to cover ourselves, as it's very unlikely that we'll do a guidebook to *The Sarah Jane Adventures*.)

Once we get out of Terry Nation's borderline-plausible double-talk, and step into the realm of complete mumbo-jumbo (X4.12, "The Stolen Earth"), things actually get a bit clearer because they aren't trying any more. Instead, we have 'electrical fields' holding subatomic particles together (like, um, electrons?) and Earth being towed through normal space across half a galaxy in an afternoon. Once you get into that sort of thing, all you can hope for is that the double-talk "explanations" are consistent with the other ones used in the series, or at least by the same author. This isn't the worst offender here by a long chalk, but it's still a long way behind the ingenuity of "The Pirate Planet" (16.2) when it comes to thinking out the consequences of these things. Putting Earth *back* at the end of X4.13, "Journey's End" makes the weather go wrong, but removing the moon and tides and spending three days with no sunlight caused absolutely no ill effects.

In any case, as with the previous attempts to move planets around by conventional means, the net effect of dragging Earth and its magnetic field through conventional space should have *at least*

been some amazing aurora borealis / australis effects, even without Torchwood sending up a magical magnetic version of Topo Gigio's magic spaghetti. Logically, nobody on Mondas should have been able to use radio or any kind of dynamo. Indeed, without any kind of shielding beyond what the planet itself provides, the Mondasians should have dreaded their world's accelerated return to proximity with the Sun for the sudden spike in cancers it would cause. (And of course, moving the whole Solar System for a giggle would spark off massive solar flares; 23.1, The Mysterious Planet".)

Whereas Mestor's plan in "The Twin Dilemma" (21.7) technically falls into the "planet moving" category, it's so ludicrous that we can't bring ourselves to discuss it.

Black Light: As anyone with hippy parents will know, 1970s bedrooms and poster-designers used to call ultraviolet "black light". From the rough use of this to describe the torch that the Doctor uses to display Linx standing at the top of the stairs (11.1, "The Time Warrior"), this seems to be what Robert Holmes understood by the term in 1973. (Although, to be fair, the term was only actually applied to the gadget in the script and then the novelisation, which Holmes was involved with but didn't finish. It was used again, however, again in "The Two Doctors" book, which is pure Holmes.)

By 1986, this means something else entirely - we're just not sure what. In "The Mysterious Planet", 'black light' denotes an immensely powerful source of energy, both allowing the robot Drathro to run for centuries and power a whole underground city of five hundred people and their food-growing operations (whatever those actually were). And Drathro could *only* run off this stuff, so it wasn't just your commonplace solar energy in a specific frequency (like, say, ultraviolet). There would be a lot of this about, after a solar flare, as the Earth's magnetosphere would have taken a right old pummelling. Whatever this stuff was, it could spark off a chain reaction that could destroy the universe.

Uh?

The funny thing is, if we think back to the beginning of the twentieth century, there *was* a predicted ultraviolet catastrophe. That was a calculation that if energy was radiating off at all frequencies and all possible amplitudes, then a mug of coffee

continued on page 369...

of the Dinosaurs".) There's a lot in "Planet" that will make modern viewers gag (episode four sees the two male leads - the Doctor and Taron - chide their female companions for being vaguely independent within minutes of each other), but the production-team had to *try* to see if this stuff could still entertain viewers and work in colour. Don't forget, this is the first Dalek story made since the TV debut of the very first colour Dalek adventure (with Peter Cushing as the Doctor). A vast chunk of the target audience had only seen TV Daleks wandering towards Auderly House and shouting about how they run an Evil Future Earth - they'd never observed them in their natural habitat of a space-jungle (making space-jungle noises, BBC-style), and never witnessed such groovy psychedelic extermination effects.

Comparison with Maloney's next Dalek story is intriguing. "Genesis of the Daleks" mutes the colours down, drops the lighting to bare minimum and almost completely separates the action sequences from the lengthy speeches. In "Planet", he's trying to keep everything moving during debates, and to keep people talking during chases. Effective though "Genesis" is, the Daleks need to be garish intruders, not the dullest things on any planet they invade or occupy. ("Remembrance of the Daleks" got this about right, and made the link with the TV21 comic strip explicit.) In "Planet of the Daleks", the Daleks themselves are drab and functional - although the Dalek Supreme's arrival is a suitably comic-strip moment and easily the high-point of the story. Meanwhile, the cast - although usually good in anything else they've been in - are clearly struggling with this material, and *especially* when forced to fly up a chimney. Bernard Horsfall, in particular, seems to be visibly composing a letter to his agent as the fourth episode begins.

In the 60s, a Dalek story resulted in the designers and cast putting in just that *little* bit extra effort. But in the 70s (with the exception of "Genesis"), everyone slackened off a bit when the Daleks showed up, thinking that people would watch anyway, so why bother? Most of the cast and the costume designer are going through the motions for this story. The set designer has put in more effort, but it's only partly successful. The city looks great from the outside, and the interior has a lot of exciting dials and Dalek-ey things, but it's also full of hand-held gadgets and handles. Was there a cut line about the Daleks stealing the city

from its original builders? Apparently not; it was just a case of the designer not thinking it through.

Daleks worked in jungles before, so why not now? The thing is, a 60s studio jungle looked like a jungle in a studio (with visible cameras, lights and floor-managers, if Richard Martin was allowed to direct). In colour and 625 lines, it, er, looks like a studio made to look like a jungle. The only times colour stories get away with jungles is on film ("Planet of Evil"; 14.4, "The Face of Evil"; 17.3, "The Creature from the Pit" and some of 17.4, "Nightmare of Eden"). Nation starts off thinking that what worked in black and white at Riverside or Lime Grove would work better in TVC and with the facilities for colour. He's had CSO explained to him and thinks, not for the first time, that if the BBC made the original Dalek story look better than he could have possibly imagined, he can imagine a bit *bigger* and they'll cope. Alas, the jungle set has one of the stupidest attempts to cut costs (by suggesting wildlife through lights), and one of the most abrupt and inadvertently amusing daybreaks ever. That's not entirely Nation's fault, but it shows how the people assumed the presence of Daleks is enough to make a story like this work.

As we said when reviewing "The Three Doctors", you can't blame a story for not being something it never set out to be. This time around, however, you *can* blame it for not setting out to be anything special. In its own way, "Planet of the Daleks" recaptures a bit of the flavour of the old stories, and the Daleks themselves cast ominous shadows and move with a speed and agility we won't see again until they're flying around (X1.13, "The Parting of the Ways"). It does the job it was designed to do well, like a deftly-made sandwich or a paperclip that doesn't snap. But that's it.

The Facts

Written by Terry Nation. Directed by David Maloney. Viewing figures: 11.0 million, 10.7 million, 10.1 million, 8.3 million, 9.7 million, 8.5 million (what was it PT Barnum said...?). Episode three only exists in the BBC archive in black-and-white, a fact mentioned in *Queer as Folk*.

Supporting Cast Bernard Horsfall (Taron), Prentis Hancock (Vaber), Tim Preece (Codal), Jane Howe (Rebec), Roy Skelton (Wester, Dalek Voice),

What are the Silliest Examples of Science in *Doctor Who*?

...continued from page 367

would produce infinite energy. To get around this, Max Planck suggested treating it as a subatomic cash-dispenser that only gave out notes, which as simple a description of Quantum theory as you're going to get.

Is *that* what the Doctor's on about here? Well, no. He's suggesting that this energy-source links all powerful bodies in the cosmos, so that igniting one will set off a trail of them. It's like a truck leaving a trail of petrol from its leaky tank to the last place it refuelled, with another trail from the tanker to the depot and *that* leading to the refinery. (If that stretched analogy sounds familiar, it's reworked from that standard text on science, *Plan 9 from Outer Space*.)

It gets worse. If this stuff is a wavelength, then Glitz's ruse to Drathro - that they have a lot of black light in their ship - is amazingly stupid. Do they keep in cans or sacks? The lame gag Dibber makes about having so much they can't see is only slightly less sensible than the original premise. Yet Drathro, the alien super-computer, falls for this trick.

To reiterate: "Uh?"

Venderman's Law: This is, as you'll recall, the idea that governs the Space-Time Visualiser "The Chase" (2.8). It operates on the principle that light absorbs mass and that therefore everything which has ever happened is recorded on "light-neutrons" (wher?) somewhere - complete with sound and camera-angles, it seems.

Let's start with the idea of light absorbing mass. Light doesn't *have* mass, which is how it can travel at the speed of light without becoming a singularity of infinite mass (which is what happens if anything with any mass at all tries this). Now let's ponder exactly how many types of mass a photon might hit in the course of its duties - it seems likely that more than anything else, you'd see a star. Other items might include people's retinas and the inside of a filament in a lightbulb. So how do you single out Shakespeare's codpiece from all the things any given photon might have been in contact with on its itinerary? And why would the ones that weren't in the visible spectrum be excluded? (By the way, apologies for the gremlin that got into p174 of Volume VI and did what silicon does, changing 'photons' into 'electrons' when discussing particles with no mass.)

You want to know the *really* stupid thing about this? The idea wasn't even Terry Nation's. It was from a short story called "The Dead Past" by Isaac Asimov. Fortunately, Asimov had the good grace to use neutrinos (about which little was known at the time) rather than light (which even small children knew was disseminated in photons, not neutrons). "The Dead Past" was adapted, without the mumbo-jumbo, for *Out of the Unknown* shortly after "The Chase" was shown. Even the non-science-minded John Gorrie (director of "The Keys of Marinus") and adaptor Jeremy Paul (writer of episodes of *Lovejoy* and author of *The Flipside of Dominic Hyde*) baulked at this attempted pseudo-science. Trusting a biochemist on particle physics isn't always advised.

Tachyonics: The arch-nerd and script editor for the phase of the series, Christopher H Bidmead, later devoted the best part of an episode (in 19.1, "Castrovalva") to people swapping lectures about recursion when facing death, and claiming that 'if' is the most powerful word in the language. For Bidmead, "somehow" is a much more useful one.

All right, tachyons are kosher physics. It's *theoretical* physics, admittedly, but still legitimate. They're fast (hence the name - like "tachycardia": it's yer actual Greek), but are basically like faster-than-light counterparts of your basic "bradyons" such as electrons, W-Vector bosons and Higgsinoes. (Exactly when these stopped being called "tardyons" is another matter - quantum theory even has the *names* of particles changing if you stop looking at them.)

The trouble comes when you try doing anything with tachyons, assuming they really exist. Not only are they likely to disintegrate very quickly (which from our perspective means very shortly before they come into existence), they can't actually interact with anything we can perceive. The problems we had with the Space-Time Visualiser are magnified here - since the particle can *only* travel faster-than-light, it might just as well not be there.

Anyway... in 18.1, "The Leisure Hive", the titular facility somehow uses particles that are *never* going to be detected to send information back in time and defy several important laws of physics. How does this help the Argolins to reduce the seven signs of ageing, though? If they irradiate the subject with tachyons (somehow) and thereby make the cells of the subject's body go back in

continued on page 371...

Michael Wisher (Dalek Voice), Hilary Minster (Marat), Alan Tucker (Latep).

Working Titles "Destination: Daleks!" (no, honestly).

Nation, showing the in-depth research that made him the legend he is today, still thought individual episodes needed titles and gave luridly melodramatic ones here: "Destinus"; "Mission Survival"; "Pursued"; "Escape or Die"; "The Day Before Eternity" and "Victory". If you're wondering, the planet was called "Destinus" before Dicks put his foot down.

Cliffhangers The Doctor and the Thals trap an invisible opponent on Spiridon, and when it's coated with liquid colour-spray it's revealed to be a Dalek (oddly, the Doctor seems surprised by this); after another Thal ship crashes in the jungle, one of the survivors tells the Thals that there are 10,000 Daleks on the planet with them; in the lower levels of the Dalek city, the Doctor's escape-plan seems to be failing as the Daleks burn their way into the room where he and the Thals are trapped; Vaber heads through the jungle on a solo mission to sabotage the Dalek city, and gets ambushed by Spiridons on the way; the Doctor and company sneak into the Dalek headquarters dressed in Spiridon furs, but one of the Daleks sounds the alarm after noticing their shoes.

What Was in the Charts? "Hello Hello I'm Back Again", Gary Glitter; "Drive In Saturday", David Bowie; "Also Sprach Zarathustra", Deodato; "See My Baby Jive", Wizzard; "Twentieth Century Boy", T Rex; "One and One is One", Medicine Head.

The Lore

• When they decided to use the Daleks as Season Nine's attention-grabbing opening gambit, Barry Letts and Terrance Dicks re-opened negotiations between the *Doctor Who* office and Terry Nation for the first time since 1967. Now, with Nation's series *The Persuaders!* on ice, and a delay while he waited to see if *The Incredible Robert Baldick* would become a series (it didn't, even though every other play in the *Drama Playhouse* series it was in got picked up), he was in a position to exercise the right they negotiated last time: namely, that he got first refusal on any Dalek stories the Corporation wanted to commission.

So in the spring of 1972, just after the Louis Marks story had been shown (9.1, "Day of the Daleks"), Nation sent in a proposal for "Destination: Daleks" with a lot of tried and true elements that had, at least, not been done in colour or when the majority of the country's ten-year-olds were old enough to have seen it. Dicks had a few concerns with the characterisation of the Thals - namely, that there wasn't any - and suggested that at least some of them should live past episode four. Moreover, Nation had suffered a slight injury (his leg was in plaster), so he planned to write the whole story in one go once he was back at his desk. Dicks had concerns that this strategy would complicate the re-write process, were he unable to see each episode as it came in and gave notes. He suggested a few basic character-traits for each Thal, and wanted to see these and at least one "moment of charm" for Jon Pertwee to play. Dicks' comments also explained how CSO might make the Spiridons blurry when seen, and that the Head of Serials had voiced many of his concerns with regards to earlier stories.

• Although David Maloney had distanced himself from *Doctor Who* since directing the last black and white story (6.7, "The War Games"), he was intrigued by the prospect of doing a Dalek story in colour. He'd made episodes of *Owen MD* and *Paul Temple* and directed the whole of the classic serial version of *The Last of the Mohicans*[117]. By the time he joined in late November, the script's wrinkles were resolved almost completely... Petal had been renamed Latep and made more overtly fond of Jo; Rebec (named after Nation's daughter, for whom he later wrote his only children's novel, *Rebecca's World*) was made Taron's ex and 'Destinus' was renamed 'Spiridon'. Meanwhile, the start had been reworked to give Jo a reason to leave the TARDIS and get separated from the Doctor.

Maloney assembled a cast he could trust: Bernard Horsfall (the Thal leader Taron) eventually appeared in four *Doctor Who* stories, all directed by Maloney. Tim Preece (the scientist Codal) had played King John in the Maloney-directed *Ivanhoe* from 1970. Roy Skelton (the invisible Wester) had done voice work on "The Krotons" (6.4) and many other stories. Jane How (token woman Rebec) had appeared in another classic serial, *A Little Princess*, directed by *Who* veteran Derek Martinus a few weeks earlier. As we'll see, Maloney later collaborated with Nation in

What are the Silliest Examples of Science in *Doctor Who*?

...**continued from page 369**

time without making him, her or it forget everything that he, she or it has ever experienced, *and* they make the cellular changes stick (somehow), all that will happen is that Mena (or whoever) will have wrinkles and cellulite from the future sent back to her younger self, creating a temporal paradox by losing her custom before you start. If we're lucky, this is the limit of the silliness, because we have somehow to account for the end of the story and relate this to tachyons.

You remember that Pangol got made by the Argolins donating cells and shoving them in the magic time-telephone (somehow). And he consequently was able to make hundred of hims (somehow), but that these (somehow) got the Doctor inside Pangol's clothing (with his scarf hidden in the pointy hat) without the original Pangol knowing anything about it. So now tachyons are making something very like the much-derided end of "Planet of Evil" (13.2) happen, mainly because they use vaguely-scientific-smelling words such as 'anti-baryon shield', 'tachyon' and 'Schrödinger Oscillator' and everyone happily swallows this garbage.

"Genesis of the Daleks" and later became *Blake's 7* producer. With that in mind, it's worth noting how Nation's script here called for blasters with telephone-style coiled cables connecting them to belt-mounted power-packs, an idea that was carried over to *Blake's*.

• One piece of location filming occurred, on 2nd of January, 1973, at a Fuller's Earth quarry in Surrey. For this, the effects team provided dry-ice for mist and bubbles in the lake. Apart from the impression of cold and gloom, this covered up the fact that the Daleks were running on wooden boards. There were currently three fully working Dalek props, and it seems all three were taken on location (although only two were used in the filmed sequences). John Scott Martin operated both of them. (So why did the Thals capture just the two? At this stage, the script still had Codal inside a shell at the start of episode five.)

While this was being filmed, the first new "proper" Dalek shells since 1964 were being built, including four working props suitable for the "crowd" scenes and some vacuum-moulded "dummy" shells. The rest of the week's pre-filming was achieved in the Ealing complex and the model stage. Many of the sequences of defrosting Daleks were realised using Louis Marx models painted in the colour-scheme Maloney had devised for the story, then placed on cards to be moved in threes or fours. A number of the shots of the allotropic ice used a mixture of gelatine and wallpaper paste.

• Between the location shoot and the recording, Katy Manning got her hair done. This caused a slight continuity glitch in episode five, but also when the finale of "Frontier in Space" was remounted.

• One of the problems was that the production-team were trying out a method of linking cameras, so that if one zoomed in on a person or object, a slave would zoom at the same rate onto whatever was being keyed in by CSO (a prototype of the "scene synch" process trialled in 18.2, "Meglos") This was used for scenes like Wester investigating the Thal ship (where he finds a phone prop lifted from *The Prisoner*). The script indicated that the ship was a glorified glider and couldn't get back into orbit once a mothership dropped it onto the planet. The excitable flowers had their seed squirted with the aid of a stirrup-pump (it was the same gelatine and polycell mix as the icecano shots on film).

• Alistair Bowtell furnished the Spiridons with purple furs and the first of the newly-built Dalek shells was sprayed glossy black for the start of episode two (there are surprisingly few cliffhanger reprises). If you didn't guess, the Dalek cutting through the door at episode three's cliffhanger was equipped with a heated blade and an expanded-polystyrene door-panel. Stage-hands hoisted the floating Dalek in episode four. (The upward-parachuting scene was made by an outside contractor but *not* Westbury Design and Optical Ltd, who did the main effects work - specifically Clifford Culley, of whom more elsewhere in this book.)

Although the script had included two Thals disguised as Daleks, this was reworked when the number of working shells was revised down to three. However, one scene needed a fourth, so Tony Starr was added to the roster of Dalek operators. John Scott Martin had been joined by Cy Town and Murphy Grumbar for the studio work. (A convention anecdote claims that Jean McMillan, the new make-up supervisor, insisted that they have make-up: as a protest they turned up to one rehearsal with lipstick, eyeliner and fake tits, with Skelton and Michael Wisher doing camped-up Dalek voices.) As stated, the Dalek Supreme was a redressed prop from the Peter Cushing films - Nation hadn't been keen on David Whitaker's idea of an "Emperor Dalek" as devised in the original spin-off book, the comic strips and "The Evil of the Daleks" (4.9).

• The first episode was shown twenty minutes later than usual because of various sporting fixtures on *Grandstand* that afternoon (the Oxford-Cambridge Boat Race chief amongst them). Concerns were noted that the Thals' protective gear in that episode looked like polythene bags and children might try to copy them.

This is the only 70s story to have been repeated in prime-time on BBC1 in the 1990s. It was shown on Friday nights, as part of the programme's 30th anniversary not-really-celebrations, immediately before a revived *Bruce Forsythe's Generation Game*. They delayed episode four to allow for that year's *Children in Need* (see Appendix A2, "Dimensions in Time" for the full horror of this weekend) and in that week showed the first (and botched) *Thirty Years in the TARDIS* documentary.

Each episode was preceded by a five-minute film, especially made for the occasion, about some aspect of the series such as the history of police boxes or what it's like inside a monster costume. The feature on "missing episodes" before episode three looked like nothing so much as an apology for the fact that one-sixth of the story was in black-and-white. For some baffling reason, *only* episode three was wiped in 1976; the rest is all in the archives on videotape.

10.5: "The Green Death"

(Serial TTT, Six Episodes, 19th May - 23rd June 1973.)

Which One is This? Giant maggots, look you.

Firsts and Lasts It's Jo Grant's last appearance in the series, and for once the companion gets a send-off that's both set up in advance and relatively dignified. (This is Jo and her future husband's story more than it is the Doctor's.) There's even an epilogue showing a lonely, reflective Doctor slipping out of the engagement celebrations early and

driving off into the night, complete with a slow fade into the end credits. "The Green Death" also sees the last appearance of the Pertwee "flame" title sequence (including a first upside-down use), and the last appearance of the early 70s logo until its surprise comeback for the 1996 TV Movie. This is the last story (bar one, which we'll tell you about next time) in which the episodes are called 'episodes' rather than 'parts'.

This is the first time that Wales has appeared as itself, rather than as a fake Tibet (5.2, "The Abominable Snowmen"). Therefore, it's the first time that an entire country of people who've been paying for this show to get made have any acknowledgement that their loos might also harbour Yeti. On the downside, though, the treatment of the Welsh characters is a thing best watched from behind the sofa. (These days, of course, the TARDIS seems to go to Wales all the time.) This is the first outing for the new-improved Bessie, and the differences are obvious once you know to look for them. (Among other things, the bonnet's noticeably longer.)

For the first time ever on screen ("The Abominable Snowmen" being a possible exception), the TARDIS is told to head for a specific place and actually gets there unaided. And for the first time since "The Highlanders" (2.4), the Doctor gets into drag, when Jon Pertwee exercises his repertoire of comedy voices by disguising himself as a cleaning-woman. It's not a pretty sight. He also poses as a randy old Welsh milkman, and gets to indulge his love of fast-moving vehicles by driving a milk-float through a barricade at high speed.

The Doctor finally calls Captain Yates 'Mike' in episode five. And to celebrate ten years of *Doctor Who* (or near enough), we finally get a little green man (John Scott Martin) and a bug-eyed monster. Sydney Newman's comments aren't recorded, but the father of the series couldn't really complain.

Six Things to Notice About "The Green Death"...

1. Despite only appearing in a single story (and then only briefly), the giant maggots are anecdotally the best-remembered monsters of the 70s, so much so that the first question non-fans tend to ask about classic *Doctor Who* is "oh, which was the one with the giant maggots?". To be sure, this story features far scarier insect movement than anything in "The Web Planet" (2.5). These aren't any old common-or-garden giant maggots; they're serious two-foot grubs that crawl, jump, hiss and

have, um, teeth. And they have a green slime that's toxic in itself.

This effect is achieved in a variety of ways, all of them pretty obvious when you see the story, but the basic *ick* factor of maggots doesn't make this any more agreeable. Sometimes they're real maggots in goo, and actors CSOd on to the scene. Sometimes the maggot is a rod-puppet CSOd onto the action. Sometimes it's a close-up of a glove-puppet and sometimes they just make a model slag-heap, drag a model Bessie along it and put maggots on a revolving backdrop like a model train-set owned by really sick kids. And wait until you find how they made "extras" for the long-shots...

2. For years, fan-lore held that "The Green Death" was one of the very few *Doctor Who* stories that had a deliberate "topical" point to make. Though analysis of most of the rest of the Pertwee run proves this to be wrong, what's different about "The Green Death" is that Barry Letts went out of his way to commission a story based on environmental issues rather than letting Nature take its course. Given the touchy nature of the subject, the debate is given to us from both sides... sort of. One side is led by a groovy young scientist whom Jo fancies and who is *always* proved right, the other by a slimy capitalist who is the slave of a mad computer trying to take over the world. Which side do *you* think is responsible for creating the giant toxic maggots?

3. Like the B-movies of yore, this is one of those giant insect stories in which (1) a perfectly ordinary substance turns out to be lethal to the monsters and (2) this discovery is made by accident when somebody spills something onto a laboratory slide. In this case the maggot-killer is a type of edible fungus being produced by the eco-people, something which leads to some odd-looking scenes as the Doctor drives through a maggot-infested landscape while Sergeant Benton stands up in the back seat chucking Quorn at them.

4. Aside from the maggots, the star of the show here is John Dearth as the voice of BOSS, the unhinged computer who runs Global Chemicals. A world away from the usual "does-not-compute" sort of mad machine, BOSS mumbles when it's embarrassed, quotes Oscar Wilde and hums Beethoven while it prepares to take over the world. Even HAL wasn't this good. Regular viewers were just slightly puzzled, though, when BOSS didn't turn out to be a front: you can just about imagine Pertwee turning to Manning and saying, '

"BOSS?" The infernal gall of the man. "Boss" is a slang word for "Master"!' Fortunately that's not the case, but Dearth's turn here is worthy of comparison to Delgado.

5. It's a good time for bizarre and unwieldy dialogue. Cliff Jones' opening gambit with Jo is 'you'll contaminate my spores!', while later on Jo has to say 'I'm up on a slag heap with the Professor' and make it sound urgent. Extra marks, too, for the Brigadier's summary of the first corpse found at the polluted mine: 'This fellow's bright green, apparently. And dead!' And everyone, BOSS included, loves mixed metaphors.

Conversely, the dialogue for the Welsh characters is stuffed with every conceivable cliché, with grown men forced to say 'here we are nattering like the women in the chapel' and 'I take my hat off to you, boyo!' We've somehow arrived in Theme-Park Wales (Croeso y Parc Cymru), and the Londoners get away with treating the locals as sub-human because everyone knows this version of pit-village life is as realistic as *Fraggle Rock*. Listen out particularly for the moment when Jo refers to Bert - the miner who's just been putrefied to death while trying to save her life - as a 'funny little Welshman'. The BBC Welshmen (Mostyn Evans, Roy Evans and, of course, Talfryn Thomas) are all present and correct. Much fun can be gleaned from watching them delivering these lines whilst trying not to let their eyes betray how much they want Robert Sloman to be spatchcocked and roasted over an open fire (ideally at some London millionaire's second home in Gwent, torched by militant Welsh Nationalists - see this story's first essay).

6. Episodes one to four feature Tony Adams as Elgin, Stevens' right-hand man (or PR man, according to the novel) at Global Chemicals. In episode five he suddenly disappears, to be replaced by *another* right-hand man who fills exactly the same space in the plot, played by Dalek / Zippy voice-artist, Roy Skelton. It's almost as if somebody got sick and dropped out of filming halfway through... (See, if you couldn't guess, **The Lore**.)

However, what's really interesting is not how everyone acts as though Mr James, the abruptly-introduced newcomer, has been around for the entire story but how his first meeting with Yates (the last cliffhanger) plays out as a result. The reprise at the start of episode six is thus almost incomprehensible to anyone who'd missed a week. Yates meets James and breaks his conditioning with a *Top of the Pops* psychedelic effect (somehow - the effect of the crystal is introduced in the previous episode). Then, as though James trusted Yates, he gasps 'Four O'Clock' and dies.

The Continuity

The Doctor Here he graduates from using Venusian karate to using Venusian aikido. [If it's anything like Earth Aikido, it should work by avoiding being hit by one's opponent unless they would hurt themselves more in the process, but instead it's mainly shouting 'Hai!' and making them turn somersaults.] He actively enjoys this, and comes as close as he ever does to saying "come and have a go if you think you're hard enough" to Hinks, the doomed guard.

Proving once again that he has a closer relationship with Jo than with most of his sidekicks, the Doctor's obviously devastated when she leaves him, but earlier he's hurt even when she declines to take a ride with him in the TARDIS. His reaction to Professor Jones is much like that of an over-protective father. He's sharp enough to see what's happening between Jo and Jones before anyone else, and briefly tries to stop them getting any closer before he accepts the inevitable. [His description of Jo as a 'fledgling' suggests that he sees himself as her mentor, something that's not particularly true of his relationships with any of his previous companions. The suggestion here is that Jo's being growing up under his supervision.]

Now the TARDIS is in working order, the Doctor initially refuses to investigate the colliery at the Brigadier's behest, even though he really should be interested in what's happening there. He is, of course, immune to BOSS' brainwashing. He seems to be using UNIT HQ as a fixed starting-point for all test-flights [possibly just because Jo has been travelling with him]. He also regards the peculiar dragonfly-like creature that hatches from a giant maggot chrysalis as 'beautiful'.

BOSS claims to have read the Doctor's computer file at UNIT [he didn't appear to have one in stories such as 8.3, "The Claws of Axos"].

• *Ethics.* The Doctor seems to prioritize his joyride to Metebelis 3 over investigating the mysterious death that the Brigadier tells him about that morning.

• *Inventory.* As well as displaying its usual ability to open all electronic locks, here the sonic screwdriver can emit a high-pitched shriek that alarms maggots. He acquires, then parts with [and will later wish he'd never set eyes on] a blue sapphire from Metebelis 3.

• *Background.* The Doctor has read Professor Jones' paper on DNA synthesis, and considers it 'quite remarkable' for the era.

[That's perhaps a bigger point than one might think. The implication in a number of stories is that there's a linear progression in the development of science on all planets - to the point that nobody discovers, say, antibiotics before the development of the microscope. This is absurd on first sight, yet stories such as "Day of the Daleks" (9.1) and "Carnival of Monsters" (10.2) do indeed indicate a strict timetable of discoveries. Perhaps the Doctor's otherwise unnecessary comment is a hint that Cliff's Nobel Prize is for something that changed the course of human development from what the Time Lords have pre-ordained. *How*, exactly, the Nobel Committee could have known that is another matter.

[Yet it's also notable that the idea of DNA synthesis isn't especially novel, and a lot of the details were already known at the time. So whatever Jones' paper was about *has* to be something extraordinary - perhaps he's found a way to synthesize it in a lab from scratch. Without reading this non-existent paper, we can't determine whether it's about how DNA is synthesized naturally, or how to do it with domestic appliances. It could well be ahead of its time... the Human Genome Project, after all, took supercomputers and clever ultra-violet dyes and scanners, and only really started delivering results in 1999. But if Cliff could do *that*, why go mollicking up the Amazon looking for a toadstool he could probably make with everyday household items?

[Coupled with the fact that a paper on 'the teleological response of the virus' was apparently published in the 1950s - 11.1, "The Time Warrior" - it seems that molecular biology in this version of the 70s is as peculiar as the British take on rocket science (see 7.3, "The Ambassadors of Death" and accompanying essay). We might also want to examine X3.6, "The Lazarus Experiment" in this light, but Richard Lazarus had help with his homework.]

The Supporting Cast

• *Jo Grant.* She's interested - to the point of ranting - in Professor Jones' work even before she goes to Llanfairfach on UNIT business, so much so that

Why Didn't Plaid Cymru Lynch Barry Letts?

(Incidentally, if you don't know, "Plaid Cymru" is pronounced to rhyme with "Fried Humvee".)

Had any other minority been treated the way the Welsh get treated in "The Green Death", the producer would have faced immediate dismissal and pressure groups would be onto the BBC demanding the axing of the series. Sure, the Scotland of "Terror of the Zygons" (13.1) is affectionately parodied by Scots in front of and behind the cameras, but South Wales is here populated by every known cliché and caricature. It exists merely as a backdrop for people from London, and it's scripted with a mean spirit.

1973 was very possibly the worst year in which to do this, as the Welsh were rampantly self-assertive and culturally confident. Moreso even than 1997 (of which more later), this is a suicidal time to send up Wales or treat it as an appendage to England. That said, modern-day Wales - even when it's deemed to be "cool" - is always the butt of jokes. (This explains why non-UK viewers will never comprehend the basic absurdity of *Torchwood* until they find out why this is the case. Imagine if they made *CSI: Saskatoon*, and you're a tenth of the way there.) With Cardiff now the yardstick for normality in *Doctor Who*, and conditions in Wales markedly different to how it was under Edward Heath, this repays a detailed examination. It will help if you have access to a map of Great Britain.

If we're beginning at the beginning, and just in case you didn't know, Wales isn't a region of England - it's a country unto itself. In essence, the bits of the British mainland that didn't take to the Saxons coming in the seventh century became Scotland and Wales (and there's a good case that Cornwall should count too). The Romans had encountered enough difficulty with these bits, and garrisoned large chunks of Wales because of guerrilla attacks by the Siluri and Ordovici. (They were Celtic tribes from the heart of Wales, both immortalised in names of rocks and thus geological eras, as you must know by now.)

The borders were porous and trade took place, but the post-Roman consolidation of England under Alfred the Great and the Norman conquest a century later (2.9, "The Time Meddler") just made the Scots and the Welsh more certain of their own separateness. The Normans built castles, but the newly-appointed Lords of the Marches (the bits on the edges of England) were autonomous and ignored the English kings. Edward I forestalled a war by appointing his baby son Prince of Wales (still the official title for the Heir Apparent).

We could go on all night about the Mediaeval attempts to kick out the Norman lords (and many in Wales do). Eventually we wound up with a Welsh noble, Henry Tudor, as King of England. He looked like the foretold Son of Prophecy, the figure destined to free the Welsh from foreign oppression, but his son, Henry VIII, caused a lot of trouble by overseeing the first serious attempt to make Wales part of a united British power. The 1536 Act of Union made English the official language of Wales. Subsequent Acts confirmed this, especially after Scotland's king, James VI, took over from Elizabeth I and started telling all his new subjects to call his giant kingdom "Britain".

Here's the thing: since before Alfred the Great, the Welsh language had been the core of cultural identity. Something identifiably like modern Welsh was being written just after the Romans left. Welsh literature took from the Bardic tradition (see our notes on Griots in the essay with 9.2, "The Curse of Peladon") and even their legal system was a work of art. Epics like the *Mabinogion* were being composed under the semi-autonomous Lords of the Marches, and even in the early fifteenth century, the self-mythologising Owan Glyndwr was able to command huge support by claiming to be the man charged with defending the language and culture. (Oh, and overthrowing the English by the sword.)

We explained briefly, in the notes for "Delta and the Bannermen" (24.3), the conventions for written Welsh. What we can't avoid saying now is that spoken Welsh sounds to the uninitiated like a recording played backwards. Quite simply, this is a harder language to learn than French or Russian, which makes it an easier language to keep secrets in and plot with, when you're dealing with non-Welsh speakers. By the start of the twentieth century that language was almost extinct, and the reasons for this are the same as the reasons why Wales was such a joke.

First off, we have the Industrial Revolution. This needed coal, iron ore and manual labour. It turned out that South Wales had more coal than Newcastle or Yorkshire combined, although it was in deeper mines. Economically and demographically the centre of gravity shifted to towns built in the steep valleys, especially those with access to the ports, Cardiff and Swansea. Row upon row of pokey cottages stacked up on hillsides amid spoil-

continued on page 377...

she refuses the Doctor's offer of a trip to Metebelis 3. She's prepared to defy the Brigadier in order to join the protest against Global Chemicals. [It's odd that someone with such a tenuous grip on science is so concerned about ecology, so either the Doctor's really getting through to her or she's just being trendy. Here she displays the same zeal for the environment that she had for the Age of Aquarius in 8.5, "The Daemons".]

Jo overtly states that the Professor reminds her, sort of, of a younger version of the Doctor. [Then again, she says this before actually meeting him, and doesn't even know what he *looks* like.] Inevitably, as soon as she introduces herself, she becomes her klutzy old self from 8.1, "Terror of the Autons" [the camera even shoots her through laboratory equipment, exactly like her first meeting with the Doctor] and she becomes eager to please all over again.

[We have to say that after such a rom-com "cute meet", it seems almost preordained that Jo and the Professor will argue until they are in a life-threatening situation, after which it's a matter of counting the minutes until they become engaged. But with Jones so much like the Doctor - albeit looking like previous alien boyfriends she's had - it seems a bit like a rebound romance. Nor does she seem to object to Professor Jones constantly patronising her.]

Jo claims to be trained in First Aid [although this is part of an overall ploy to get down the mine and nab some goo for the Professor to analyse, and so might not be true]. She also tells the miner Dave that she's with UNIT; technically not true either, at this stage. She mentions to Cliff that she never quite got around to just passing the Doctor his test-tubes [see "Terror of the Autons" again], which rather contradicts what she told the not-really-there Doctor in 10.3, "Frontier in Space".

Jo and Cliff plan to marry, then do the usual romantic thing of going to the upper reaches of the Amazon to search for a legendary super-nutritious giant toadstool. The Doctor gives her the sapphire from Metebelis 3 as a wedding present, and she takes it with her [it's sent back in 11.5, "Planet of the Spiders"]. She also gets her uncle at the UN to have the Nut Hutch declared a 'United Nations priority one research complex', stating that it's only the second time she's asked him for anything. The Doctor's hope that she 'might turn into some kind of a scientist' seems vindicated, as she can fix a radio with a screwdriver she carries

around in her afghan jacket. It's her turn to be 'Trap One'.

• *UNIT.* The Brigadier speaks to the minister who helped draft the Third Enabling Act [see 9.5, "The Time Monster"], now the Minister of Ecology. [See also 13.6, "The Seeds of Doom", in which there's a World Ecology Bureau.] They seem to have spoken before. The Brig also claims to be able to 'bring influence to bear at Cabinet level' [the same minister, or does everyone in this story have a pet Secretary of State?]. The Brigadier tries to quote article 17 of the Act, but the minister overrules him with article 18, paragraph 3. This states that in matters of domestic concern, UNIT will place itself at the disposal of the host nation in all respects. Consequently, the Minister orders the Brig to obey Stevens' wishes.

HQ is about three hours' drive (or twenty minutes in Bessie) from South Wales. The Doctor has a computer record at UNIT, which claims he talks a lot.

• *The Brigadier.* Visibly flustered when the Prime Minister gives him orders. He was once stationed in Aldgate [but then, given how often UNIT used to change its HQ, he must have been stationed virtually everywhere]. In civvies, he dresses like Terry-Thomas or the Eric Idle "nudge-nudge" man [see 20.3, "Mawdryn Undead"] and drives a two-seater Mercedes. He seems enthusiastic about giving Global military protection from patchouli-scented hippy scientists - until, that is, Stevens tries to tell him how to do his job. Despite apparent jealousy when Cliff acts like Jo's keeper, this is the most relaxed we ever see Lethbridge Stewart until his retirement [26.1, "Battlefield"]. At dinner, the Brig is seen enjoying a cigar.

• *Captain Yates.* He's the first UNIT officer since the lorry driver in "The Invasion" (6.3) to go undercover [unless Benton disguising himself as a flasher in "The Mind of Evil" (8.2) counts], but he's not strong enough to fight BOSS' mental conditioning. Mike is left emotionally damaged by events here [see 11.2, "Invasion of the Dinosaurs"] and he seems oddly relieved when Jo and Cliff get engaged. [Well, maybe - it's hard to decide if Richard Franklin is going for "disappointed that Jo's getting hitched" in this scene, or if he's just distracted by what the hippy scientists are wearing.]

The TARDIS The Doctor no longer has any problems with the dematerialisation circuit, and believes he has total control over the Ship, but the

Why Didn't Plaid Cymru Lynch Barry Letts?

...continued from page 375

tips, and slag-heaps greeted anyone on a train into these cities. Even today, to get to the Riviera-like splendour of Swansea (err, comparatively speaking) you have to pass through the dystopian vistas (and smells) of Port Talbot. A lot of people got rich on the back of all this industry, but they made a point of not sticking around in the Rhondda Valley. Anyone with any money taught their kids to speak with an English accent - so they could leave. (Hence the disproportionate number of actors from Wales in those days, and Dylan Thomas' job at the BBC poetry department in London.)

A second reason is more specific to Wales. As the Normans and Vikings and Angles and Saxons never really got to do much rape (or pillage, for that matter) and made a point of not going near the local girls, the Welsh were genetically shorter and darker than most people in England and Scotland. There was an influx from elsewhere when the mines opened, and areas near docks tend to have much more genetic diversity (hence Dame Shirley Bassey, from Tiger Bay, Cardiff) but whilst they made wholly Welsh-speaking households a lot rarer, they had less of an immediate effect on the look of the nation's citizens than the advent of better food, the NHS (largely an invention of Welsh politicians) and the M4 motorway. Even today, ask most people in England what someone from Wales looks like and they'll describe Talfryn Thomas ("Spearhead from Space", "The Green Death") rather than Catherine Zeta Jones.

The third reason is that the fragments of the indigenous culture we have now are held together by a half-remembered, half-invented version of Druidic lore concocted in the Enlightenment (see the Doctor's comments on John Evelyn in 16.3, "The Stones of Blood") and, well, they look bloody stupid. Men in sheets blowing trumpets to the four corners of the earth, and girls dressed in a "national costume" that looks like Heidi going trick-or-treating in a witch's hat with a buckle on it. Outside that written work, nobody knows much about the real Welsh heritage prior to the church taking on the function of social cohesion (and the evangelism that went on in the nineteenth century is a matter for book-length works). The church ran the schools, and - even if they didn't put it in these terms - wanted to remove the contaminated Welsh language and its associated barbarism.

By 1847, the use of Welsh in schools was condemned as leading to sedition although (despite what's been said elsewhere) not actually outlawed. The use of the stigma of the "Welsh Note" (a wooden emblem hung on people caught speaking Welsh in school) was nowhere near as widespread as 1970s textbooks made it seem, but the *perception* of its use by the evil imperialist English was a potent rallying-point later on. The idea of insurrection to liberate a culture of bed-linen, goats and silly hats was absurd to everyone elsewhere.

The fourth and final reason is the most profound of all: the very name "Wales" comes from the same linguistic root as "Walnut", i.e., "from over there". These are people defined as the outsiders, the people off the edge of the world. They speak English full of easily-parodied idioms (see X4.2, "The Fires of Pompeii"; there's lovely) and with a sing-song lilt very like the usual thing people do when pretending to be Swedish for comic effect. They come from a place that's wet and miserable *even by British standards*. And they were especially vulnerable to economic downturns, so the only time anyone from Wales was on the news was when they were on the breadline. As a result, even the Doctor thinks he's slumming when, in "The Unquiet Dead" (X1.3), he winds up in Cardiff.

Of course, there are a lot of people who disagree, especially in Wales. The issue of self-determination is, for most of the twentieth century, one the Welsh associate with the right to speak and write in their own language. Plaid Cymru, the main Independence movement, was founded shortly after World War I along the model of Ireland's Sinn Fein - and, following the Irish model, they started planting bombs in 1925. For the most part the Welsh Nationalist movement restricted its civil disobedience to non-violent means, but there was the contentious issue of English people buying holiday cottages, pushing up property prices beyond the locals' means and only staying in summer. Fire-bombing of empty cottages got headlines, but it was the indirect protests that caused mass arrests. By 1967, an Act of Parliament advocated bilingual road-signs and stipulated that broadcasters in Wales had to observe a minimum number of hours of Welsh-language broadcasting.

Ah, here's where things get spicy! When ITV started in 1955, the Tory government of the day wanted to encourage competition and thus set up

continued on page 379...

space-time co-ordinate programmer is nearly worn out and he states that the TARDIS is 'getting on a bit'. He gets to Metebelis 3 by wiring the co-ordinates into the programmer rather than just feeding them into the console.

The Non-Humans

• *Giant Maggots.* The lethal, luminous, stinking green slime being pumped into the mine at Llanfairfach apparently causes an 'atavistic muta-tion' in the insect life there, causing eggs to grow to abnormal sizes and hatch out into vicious, bul-let-proof maggots around two feet long. [The goo apparently converts the DNA of human cells into maggot cells, so the maggot DNA might somehow have got into the slime itself. The thing the mag-gots turn into isn't exactly a giant fly, which means the effects on insect genes aren't just size-related. 'Atavistic' suggests they're reverting to an earlier evolutionary stage, perhaps like the giant dragon-flies of the Cretaceous age.]

Eventually, a maggot will enter its chrysalis state and emerge as a glistening dragonfly-like creature, capable of spitting slime. However, the fungus-based meat substitute eaten by the eco-researchers at the Nut Hutch conveniently kills the maggots when they try to consume it.

• *BOSS.* The Bimorphic Organisational Systems Supervisor, a sentient computer that runs Global Chemicals from the top floor of the building. [Note: sources differ on whether it's "Bimorphic" or "Biomorphic". Dearth seems to say the former, and the novelisation agrees. "Bimorphic" suggests two shapes, as in analogue and digital, or organic and electronic; "biomorphic" suggests "life-shaped" which it isn't really.]

Named BOSS by its designers, it's 'the only computer ever to be linked to a human brain': Stevens, the nominal head of the company, from whom it learned that the secret of human creativ-ity is inefficiency. It's now self-controlling. It's in constant contact with its "agents", meaning the human beings it brainwashes with sonic signals delivered via headphones. Its aims: efficiency, pro-ductivity, profits for Global Chemicals and world domination. BOSS isn't permanently trapped by a hoary logical paradox set by the Doctor. [It's the Epemenides Paradox.] It is briefly confused by the logic-paradox, however. [This might suggest that its brain is analogue rather than wholly digital, and programmed with some sort of Bayes filter (an algorithm for calculating shades of grey

instead of "either-or", a cousin of the briefly-fash-ionable "Fuzzy Logic"). If so, then instead of sweating the details, BOSS steps back and looks at overall patterns the way a human mind does, rather than going through programs step-by-step.

[Since there was at least one sentient computer in Britain as early as 1966 (3.10, "The War Machines"), it's not surprising that others exist, and BOSS seems to be a more complex machine than WOTAN. It's possible that some of BOSS' technology was taken from the Dalek battle com-puter in Radcliffe's shed (25.1, "Remembrance of the Daleks") or Tobias Vaughn ("The Invasion"). It's not clear how BOSS got to be in charge of Global Chemicals, but it probably wasn't *meant* to be. The link with the director's brain seems to have been Stevens' own idea, so this is doubtless where the rot set in. (It's odd that a chemist - the inventor of the 'Stevens process' - should be such a groundbreaking computer engineer as well. One possible answer is that Stevens is a programmer who linked up with a computer, and that togeth-er they developed the petroleum-cracking tech-nique that bears his name, covering up the extent to which a mad computer did all the work.)]

Intriguingly, BOSS knows about the Doctor from the UNIT computer, and is aware that the Doctor isn't human.

Planet Notes

• *Metebelis 3.* Though the Doctor has fond memories of the place ["Carnival of Monsters"], on returning he discovers that it's a nightmare-world full of howling blizzards, nasty-looking snakes, aggressive giant birds and shrieking things which throw rocks and spears at him. Metebelis 3 is blue all over, with a blue sun. [Or so the Doctor says - on his arrival, it looks yellow / pinkish in sunset. "Planet of the Spiders" has the Doctor claiming that Metebelis 3 is called the 'blue plan-et' because it looks blue in moonlight, which does, almost, reconcile what we see of the planet in the two stories. We still have the blue sun to explain, however.]

The Doctor takes one of the planet's famous blue sapphires from a bird's nest, a crystal that 'clears the neural pathways' when someone stares into it. [There's no mention of its psychic powers yet, just its ability to break hypnotic condition-ing.] It seems to glow while doing this, and even mesmerises the Brigadier. Metebelis 3 has life-forms capable of making and hurling spears, and

Why Didn't Plaid Cymru Lynch Barry Letts?

...continued from page 377

the franchises to cover regions - four at first and with a split between weekdays and weekends, making eight possible companies. (In fact it was slightly fewer, because people like Lew Grade got a weekday slot in one region and weekends in a different area.) To a certain extent the BBC followed this pattern, because as the access to television spread across the country, they were the people building the transmitters, with the local ITV franchise brought in on each new one. By 1969, the BBC's set up - six non-London studios and transmitters - was looking a bit cumbersome. There was a massive expansion, with previously poky studio facilities stuffed into nooks of Victorian office buildings replaced by purpose-built complexes like Pebble Mill in Birmingham (see 15.1, "Horror of Fang Rock").

By 1970, there were a dozen regional BBC television centres, each doing local news and contributing to that compendium of all that's most weird about 70s Britain: *Nationwide*. Each region developed a particular speciality, such as current affairs (Manchester, possibly as a response to the local ITV service, Granada, establishing a strong track record in this) or single dramas (Birmingham, under the leadership of David Rose; see 22.2, "Vengeance on Varos" for more).

However, commercial television in Wales was a political and cultural minefield for two obvious reasons: one, the law stipulated how much of its output should be in Welsh, even though advertisers were terrified of paying for this; two, the ITV companies were almost all owned by rich men in London. The BBC, paid for by license-fees, was ostensibly more responsive to local conditions but was perceived as being primarily English.

It's often forgotten that HTV (the ITV station for Wales and bits of Western England after 1968) began as a joke that got out of hand. The Franchise-holder, TWW, was run from London by Lord Derby, a chum of the regulator (Lord Hill of Luton, who in wartime had been "The Radio Doctor"), and a lot of Welsh writers and broadcasters in exile in London thought that they could do better. The whole thing began as a conversation in the offices of *Private Eye*, a satirical magazine. There had been a Welsh-language service in the early 1960s, but it had shut down (it's the only ITV franchise-holder ever to go bust) and while TWW took over its facilities and "footprint", it but didn't really do a lot in Welsh. The main effect of this was

to get the BBC's Wales service to buck its ideas up, and once HTV started (rather earlier than expected, as TWW stopped everything eighteen months early in a fit of pique, despite spending a fortune in getting ready for colour), its Welsh half (we say *half* because it had Bristol and Liverpool in its area, and so couldn't do an all-Welsh service) began to try to undercut BBC Cymru.

So, obviously, the BBC's Cardiff-based service fought back and made Welsh-language programmes of general interest, which - for various technical reasons - got relayed around various transmitters and took up long chunks of non-primetime broadcasting in London, Manchester and Birmingham. You would be watching a schools broadcast or *Boomph with Becker* (we could describe it as "like Fanny Craddock with a leotard, scaring pensioners into keeping fit", but then we'd have to explain Fanny Craddock) and then the announcer would say, "The next programme is in Welsh and on certain transmitters only." Three minutes of Radiophonica later (*Tros Y Gareg* a piece of music that still causes goosebumps, arranged by John Baker and finally out on CD as we write this), we'd get live coverage of the Eisteddfod or their long-running soap *Pobol Y Cwm*[126], which originally looked so much like *Emmerdale Farm* that many people swore off drink after coming across it accidentally, thinking they'd forgotten how to speak.

In the early 70s this meant that Wales didn't just look exotic, it was that most prized of all things then: "authentic". It meant that we were in a position to look at this vigorous place with its own language and compare it to what we'd been told Wales was like. And because the use of Welsh in schools had only really come back in the 1950s, most of the people speaking it on telly were young and fashionable. Wales was sexy!

Naturally, it helped that they were going through a bit of a boom. Not economically (as the coal strikes were cutting into the whole economy of the nation) but socially. Anything England did, Wales did as well and with no compromise. The national sport - rugby union - was played in every town in Wales but nationally against England, Scotland, Northern Ireland and France; Wales just couldn't be beaten. Laurence Olivier could be trumped with Richard Burton; WH Auden with Dylan Thomas; Mick Jagger with Tom Jones; Yorkshire brass bands with Welsh male voice

continued on page 381...

is (when we see it here) roughly the same colour as the TARDIS, making it extra tricky as the Doctor tries to find his way off the planet.

• *Venus*. In addition to the aikido, the Doctor tells a story ending with the moral 'never trust a Venusian shanghorn with a perigosto stick'. Everyone apparently finds this funny.

History

• *Dating* [Early 1974, probably April. See **What's the UNIT Timeline?** under "The Daemons", for the evidence.]

Global Chemicals has its headquarters near Llanfairfach colliery, South Wales, the National Coal Board having closed the pit a year earlier. Newport is the nearest large town [so it's in Gwent, probably, around the Rhondda valley]. Britain is still obsessed with energy, and 'the Ministry' grants Global Chemicals the authority to restrain people under the Emergency Powers Act, with UNIT once again called on to protect the project. Professor Jones, meanwhile, indicates that he won a Nobel Prize. There are computers all over the world by now, with BOSS planning to extend its power by connecting to 'seven other complexes', including Moscow and Zurich.

The Prime Minister at this point is called Jeremy. [Someone else is in charge by the time of 13.1, "Terror of the Zygons", unless he had drastic surgery or the Brigadier's taking the piss - see **Who's Running The Country?**.] The current Minister for Ecology drafted the Seventh Enabling Act, and thus knows precisely how far he can coerce UNIT into serving the country's interests.

Additional Sources The Target novelisation of "The Green Death" (by Malcolm Hulke) changes the name of the company from Global Chemicals to Panorama Chemicals, since a real company called Global Chemicals objected to the original TV broadcast, on the grounds that it had never knowingly made giant insects.

Still, if you thought the TV version's habit of playing up the link between the company and Nazism was too subtle, this is the book for you. The TV story begins with the company's representative addressing the Welsh villagers with a parody of Chamberlain's "Peace in our time" speech, and has BOSS mention both Nietzsche and Wagner; the book goes one step further by pointing out a direct parallel between BOSS' 'one world, one people, one BOSS' philosophy and

Hitler's "ein Reich, ein Volk, ein Fuhrer". Indeed when Arnold Bell (AKA the doomed Ralph Fell on screen) is brainwashed he babbles, 'God is love... today Europe, tomorrow the world... when I hear the word "culture" I reach for my gun... the meek shall inherit the Earth' (to which Stevens replies 'Panorama Chemicals shall inherit the Earth').

Just in case the criticism seems to be coming just from the Left, the Brigadier objects to multinational corporations eroding national sovereignty and buying political influence (but the phone call from the Cabinet is faked by BOSS anyway). Cliff's courtship of Jo begins at least ten minutes before the end of the story, with a crafty snog just before she knocks over the fungus-powder. (She also tests that Cliff isn't listening by offering to serve the coffee *topless*, a detail that often comes up when older fans discuss this book.)

The novelisation also gives a citation for the origin of the word 'serendipity' which suggests (tenuously) that the Doctor knew Horace Walpole (as Walpole was instrumental to the development of Gothic Horror, this is very intriguing), gives the miners far more dignity and individuality than the televised version and shows Malcolm Hulke (who later criticised it implicitly in "Invasion of the Dinosaurs") tackling difficulties which the original script papered over. Furthermore, it gives the Brigadier an opportunity to say what had often been implied on screen: that he believed the one ordering people to do dangerous things should be the first in. (Dave the miner, though, uses this to over-rule him - claiming that in a mining accident he, not a soldier, is the man in charge.) Llanfairfach is shown as a community scarred by half a century of resentment after the 1926 General Strike, and where the hippy scientists are more alien than the maggots or mad computers - mainly because they make people question their own way of life, rather than just dumping on it like the English always do. There's even a scene described (oh yes) from a maggot's point of view. Barely a page goes by without Hulke showing that he's thought about this rather more than Sloman did. Shame about the pictures, though...[120]

Many fans have taken the hint from off-screen life that Jo and Cliff eventually parted company, with the novel *Genocide* (1997) being the most prominent BBC-authorized confirmation of it. The Big Finish audio *The Doll of Death* (2008), however, shows them as together about ten years on from the book.

Why Didn't Plaid Cymru Lynch Barry Letts?

...**continued from page 379**

choirs (if you've not heard either, investigate). Abruptly the prime-time schedules had people such as Max Boyce (folk-singer, stand-up and player on the ethnic stereotypes in much the same way Billy Connolly did a few years later for Glasgow) and the less famous but fondly-remembered Ryan and Ronnie. These two, with Boyce to a lesser extent, capitalised on the London-based media version of Wales, especially the one from BBC costume dramas.

Oddly, though, the easiest way to illustrate this is to detour into 1930s Scotland. One of BBC Television's biggest hits was *Doctor Finlay's Casebook*. These began as adaptations of stories by AJ Cronin, but rapidly exhausted the available copy and started inventing new situations for the energetic young medic, his crusty older colleague and their starchy housekeeper / nurse. These were set in a rural idyll, Scotland in the 1930s, with nice cars and lots of colourful characters. (This formula later worked for *All Creatures Great and Small* and *Heartbeat*; see Volume V.) The books, however, were altogether more spiky, being about why medical practices in remote areas could benefit from a more organised and co-ordinated system with adequate cover for hard-up farmers... a National Health Service, if such a thing didn't seem too utopian.

Cronin, you see, had axes to grind. Indeed, he was far more polemical in his novels about idealistic young doctors going to practice in rural Wales and pit-villages in the Rhondda Valley. Cronin was born in Scotland, trained as a doctor, and was a Navy surgeon in World War I (there was a book in that too). He established a practice in Tredegar (a mining town in Wales... you see where we're going with this?) before becoming Medical Inspector of Mines for Great Britain. His bestseller *The Citadel* exposed corruption in medicine for miners and was one of the reasons the idea of an NHS caught on; it was adapted into a film, as was *The Stars Look Down* (that film is now regarded as a classic). But before we go thinking that Cronin was some kind of radical, let's note that when he began writing, he had a lucrative consultancy in Harley Street. The success of his books led him to move to America before World War II, then go into tax-exile in Switzerland. *Doctor Finlay's Casebook* allowed the BBC to cash in on his reputation without ruffling any feathers.

Why we've mentioned all this is sadly obvious:

any story set in Wales in the 1930s was inevitably about bronchial complaints and mining accidents. Robert Sloman's conception of Welsh coal mining communities comes almost wholesale from the film versions of Cronin books. There was no end of other material in the same vein on television, with period dramas having actors doing BBC Welsh (see **What Are the Dodgiest Accents in the Series?** under 4.1, "The Smugglers" for the all-purpose Welsh / Geordie / Gujarati voice) and declaring, "It's Dai Pugh! The Pit's collapsed on him it has!", in the same sets and costumes where the same actor had last week run in and said "Trouble at 'tmill!" in bad Yorkshire. (These were a sufficiently distinct sub-genre for *The Goodies* to do a parody, with a conspiracy led by an Archdruid played by, um, Jon Pertwee.) But these were all in Cronin's shadow.

Many in Wales itself were amused by this as much as annoyed. Dylan Thomas, himself fighting that self-loathing we mentioned earlier, tried to write a more lyrical version of life in ordinary Wales once he was certain he'd never have to go back there permanently. *Under Milk Wood* has to be seen within a tradition of writers re-working and parodying their roots from afar (such as James Joyce in Zurich or Lennon and McCartney in the Stockbroker Belt), but a lot of people in the rest of Britain and worldwide took it at face value. Those same late-eighteenth-century dandies who'd recreated the Druidic Order in Primrose Hill, NW8, had launched a whole movement for the exaltation of all things Celtic (see 23.1, "The Mysterious Planet") and made a big deal about the (fake) Irish epic of Ossian and Oscar. Welsh mysticism was much more in vogue than anything London had to offer (which is the start of the cult of John Dee, whose artefacts all wound up in Horace Walpole's possession - Dee was Welsh and claimed to be descended from Merlyn).

When this flared up again, first with the Celtic Twilight fad of *fin de siecle* Theosophists and then the (ahem) Age of Aquarius, it became self-evident that anyone Welsh was automatically, genetically, closer to the source. You had an excuse to have a chip on your shoulder (because the English were to blame for everything bad, ever), you could play the Bard card and make out that you had access to some ancient Celtic wisdom and you could drink a lot and shag everything that moved as a form of honouring Dylan Thomas. Like the

continued on page 383...

The Analysis

Where Does This Come From? We should discuss the whole idea of doing a story about pollution, but **The Lore** is the place for that. Suffice to say, the precise nature of this story - the *kind* of anti-pollution polemic we get - is more interesting.

For a start, the half-baked attempts at a political conspiracy-theory thriller seem odd when seen in the context of real-life news items concerning kickbacks (see **Who's Running the Country?** for a gloss of John Poulson) and the unfolding farce of Nixon's botched cover-up over Watergate. Even when compared to thriller films of the time (we'll elaborate on these in "Invasion of the Dinosaurs"), it seems naïve. CCTV linked to a computer is presented as such a bizarre transgression that the Doctor never once thinks about it.

But that's not this story's basic genre... this is a bug-eyed-monsters-caused by-pollution yarn with Wales standing in for Arizona. We might try to dignify it with some spurious claim to its place in a tradition from John Wyndham to *Doomwatch*. (The latter did its own "poisonous bug" story in a story by former *Doctor Who* script editor Gerry Davis - it was called, imaginatively, "The Web of Fear".) But we should be thinking more of 50s drive-in fodder like *Tarantula!* or *Them!*. These would have plucky youngsters and bearded scientists pitted against the engorged arthropods, but here both roles get combined into Professor Jones - who talks about changing the entire planet to suit him, yet somehow isn't presented as being as big a menace as BOSS.

There's a long tradition of having big versions of unpopular creatures - insects especially - running amok in remote communities. It's often set in America, usually in the 1950s and frequently the result of atomic tests. In the 70s, we got our thrills from supposedly more mature dramas where pollution of "the balance of nature being upset by man" was the culprit, but it wasn't always any less hokey when looked at now. We could, for instance, consider Saul Bass' directorial debut, *Phase IV* (1974, set in Arizona but made in the UK[121]), wherein ants get themselves organised in ways that look like - what a surprise - complex graphics sequences from the start of a thriller movie, like the ones Saul Bass used to do.

More pertinent - and a lot funnier - is *Night of the Lepus* (1972), in which giant killer rabbits run around in slow motion. (We could list this film's hilarious inadequacies all night, so look it up for yourselves. There's a clip of it in *The Matrix*, if you can be bothered.) Both were released ahead of a whole slew of vengeful-insect flicks set in remote areas populated by people called "Cletus" and "Jeb". Logically, then, the British version should be in South Wales.

The Greeks theorised that maggots and flies were a product of decay, not its cause. What happens is that *animus*, the spirit that animates animals, is a finite quantity but can be divided. One creature with a *lot* of it can donate it to thousands that don't have much. A cow dies and its soul transmigrates into loads of maggots[122]. Letts and Sloman have already dealt with the Devil (AKA Beelzebub, Lord of the Flies) and Atlantis, so obviously they would have to take the New Age into the everyday world - and there's nothing so effective as a Sephiroth in a loo in Tooting Bec.

In this scheme of things, "soul" is the result of a perfect balance between the four elements - which is why a dry lake (earth and fire) when doused by rain (air and water) produces frogs. Maggots result from a slight imbalance which is the cause of all decay. (The Catholic Church found ways to unite Aristotle, which is where this stuff can be found, with Christianity; all change is decay, with decay and sin being the same thing.) The next Sloman script will deal with a bigger imbalance caused by ambition, ego and greed: in this story, pollution is less to do with *chemical* waste than with a company's immoral quest for profits above all else.

The business about Global Chemicals' refinement being based upon 'Bateson's Polymerisation' is used as a pseudo-scientific smokescreen but the *real* cause of this physical symbol of corruption was moral decay, specifically greed and selfishness. The polluted country was a macrocosm of an unbalanced self. Jones gives lots of speeches about why Global Chemicals was part of the rich West's monopolising of resources, and that the entire industrial process is unsustainable. Look at the way Cliff and Jo's revised first meeting stresses how Wholeweal is 'logically, aesthetically and mortally right'. And Hilda (who ties herself in knots at parties) is writing a book on 'Self-Actualisation', which should tip you off to what's really occurring here.

'Self Actualisation' was one of the more benign psychological theories wherein humans could find meaning without religion or therapy, although it never really took off in Britain, where

Why Didn't Plaid Cymru Lynch Barry Letts?

...continued from page 381

Irish, the Welsh had a reputation for being imaginative outsiders, iconoclasts and closer to nature. It's that old Romantic thing of the "noble savage" again, but given a college education.

The "faults" of the Welsh, therefore, were now in keeping with the times. Just have a look at how many dramas of the era focus on David Lloyd-George (Prime Minister in World War I and instigator of a lot of what the 1970s was about, such as welfare programmes and votes for women, but also notorious womaniser and drinker; see X1.4, "Aliens of London"). Meanwhile, the past - with coal looking like it was on the way out - was there to be sentimentalised. The makers of *Bagpuss* and *The Clangers* had earlier produced *Ivor the Engine*, about a steam-train who sang in the chapel choir and had a dragon hibernating in his boiler. It looked like it was set in the 1920s - until they started talking about decimal money.

Somehow, Wales was unspoiled by cynicism or change for its own sake, a fact not lost on advertisers. Exiled Welshmen made strenuous efforts to get away from all that (re-inventing themselves as aristocrats; how many people were even aware that Kingsley Amis was Welsh is open to question), but the rest of Britain romanticised Wales and indulged their whimsy. If we couldn't understand what they were saying, it meant we weren't sufficiently attuned (a fact which makes many American scholars' interpretations of Dylan Thomas' poetry very funny).

These days, we all cringe along to Jo's speech about the 'funny little Welshman' Bert but what's less notorious is Cliff's way of comforting her by giving her the Big Picture, and getting all mystical about one dead miner's place in the Scheme of Things. Put simply, Cliff Jones is as inevitable a character for 1973 as Ben Jackson had been in 1966, or Donna Noble was in 2006. They even cast someone who looked like either a member of Welsh-language prog band Man or (if you squinted) JPR Williams, doctor and rugby international.

But look at the town he inhabits. Many of the throwaway comments in "The Green Death" could come straight from *Under Milk Wood* (especially the Doctor as the randy old milkman, and Jones the Milk talking about "Tom the Sea Captain"), the rest from *Ivor the Engine*. Not only is the milkman called 'Jones the Milk' (the traditional way of telling all the Joneses in one village apart was adding their job after, hence the old joke about "Jones the Spy"), but he says everything with a question-style ending ('there's lovely, isn't it' and things like that) and calls the Brig 'Boyo'. "The Web of Fear" (5.5) had this kind of ethnic humour with Evans the Driver, but now we get a whole village of them playing rugby (the dead miner Ted Hughes was 'best prop-forward we ever had', despite being played by the scrawny John Scott Martin) and suffering from various ailments. This is like having a small town in the American Midwest full of people called "Cletus" and "Jeb" who lack teeth and have fewer great-grandparents than is traditional. It allows a quick and easily-assimilated depiction of a community from available materials, the same way "The Daemons" (8.5) managed to caricature every bit of England that isn't a city. *Doctor Who* Wales is an entire nation of Pigbins. So now we have to ask: *how did they get away with it?*

The answer is that however politicised the struggle for autonomy and the fight for the language had been, by 1973 the then-vast and contradictory repertoire of stereotypes about Taffy and Blodwyn, leeks and daffodils, sheep-shagging and stupid place-names were *known* to be wrong but provided at least a distinctive identity. It made for a Wales-of-the-past, as cosy and safely vanished as the England of bowler hats and pea-soupers, against which we could measure the hip, raw Wales of the go-ahead 70s. If someone in 1973 had set a *Doctor Who* story in a London inhabited by Pearly Kings with barrel-organs and the kind of accents Americans do when they think they are talking like us, riots would have broken out. But "The Green Death" and also "Delta and the Bannermen" seem to have been made under a special dispensation the people of Wales have for clueless Londoners who are unaware that the joke's on them. ("Bannermen" is odd, as the Americans Hawk and Weismuller seem present chiefly to make comments that nobody in England would dare to any more, even as the script and the rest of the cast lay on the clichés thick and fast. Mainly thick. Some scenes have about six layers of irony.)

Quite simply, the fact that *Doctor Who* even *acknowledged* the existence of Wales was a breakthrough in the 70s, and seeing monstrous maggots in familiar settings was a lot more scary and welcome for Welsh viewers than aliens in a London they only knew from telly.

In 1997, within months of Tony Blair being elect-

continued on page 385...

the majority of people thought it a bit, you know, Californian. (This explains why EST never really caught on here either.) Abraham Maslow and Carl Rogers were big names then, trying to get beyond Freud or Behaviourism, and their theories were discussed by the kinds of people founding their own Wholeweals. Sadly, the emblem of this school, the "Pyramid of Needs" resembled the totalisers they used to show how many stamps or shoes had been contributed to the *Blue Peter* Christmas appeal. As we saw in 9.4, "The Mutants", this was also close to what Barry Letts was thinking at the time (Maslow, not the *Blue Peter* shoes thing).

A real-life version of Wholeweal - Biotechnic Research and Development, in Wales - got a bit of publicity (including the *New Scientist* piece that Letts read), but the emphasis was on the practical engineering being done, not on the ideals. As we'll see, the self-sufficiency notion that had been a remote dream in 1971 was increasingly looking like the only viable long-term option. Terry Nation milked it for maximum melodrama in *Survivors* (see 11.3, "Death to the Daleks" for more). Individuals dropping out were quixotic and doomed, or would simply be parasites and hypocrites. Smaller collectives, on the other hand, stood a chance of literally ploughing their own furrows without having to interact with the overall economic system. In the process the whole malaise of anomie - not feeling like you belong within society and that nothing you do has any worth or brings you any satisfaction - is circumvented.

Wholeweal, for all its hyper-qualified membership, is a sort of Kibbutz based on personal freedom but tempered with personal responsibility. You don't eat if you don't work. This is a remarkably resilient strand in British life, running through various semi-revolutionary movements such as the Levellers and Diggers of the 1650s. (Gerrard Winstanley, founder of the Diggers, got a cheaply-made biopic by the people who made *It Happened Here* - 7.4, "Inferno" - in which the only professional actor was the guy who played the villain: Jerome Willis, who here plays Stevens.)

Suddenly everyone was doing it, including several of Sloman's friends. The sitcom *The Good Life* (the first episode of which, by a wonderful quirk, was shown the same month as the debut of *Survivors*) touched a nerve simply because instead of chasing after status and goods, Tom and

Barbara were living how they wanted without compromises. This is why The System (note caps) that makes people go against their supposedly innate sense of justice and proportion is represented by a Mad Computer. *Real* environmentalists, the ones who knew their stuff, were rather keen on cybernetics, but the idea of a self-sustaining system out of anyone's control had to be represented as something not just non-human, but anti-human too.

There's something very unpleasant running through the whole of the Pertwee years that becomes unavoidable here. Many of the writers view the proletarian characters as being stuck in drab lives by choice; it's not just that they don't know any better, it's that they can't imagine any other life. However, the key difference between Sloman's script and Hulke's novelisation of "The Green Death" is that Sloman seems to have decided that anyone working in a mine deserves nothing else. Hulke, at least, believes compelling reasons exist why the miners' solidarity in the face of hard and dangerous work over generations makes it difficult for anyone to have left. He depicts the smug Professor Jones from their point of view: an outsider who's come to patronise them.

As much as anything, this is a generational shift. The access to opportunity within education had greatly expanded since the 1926 General Strike (the Strike didn't cause this change, but it's such a big benchmark that everyone used it). We had seen a similarly big change in the 1950s. The last two Prime Ministers had each been the first in their family to go to University. (Harold Wilson brought his ability to transcend his roots into the conversation at every opportunity - paradoxically reinforcing the stereotype of Yorkshiremen who go on and on about how hard their childhoods were when exhorting people to break out of stereotypes.)

There was, of course, a deep ambivalence about this within the BBC, albeit not from the usual sources. In general, writers who touched on this were motivated by self-loathing. We have to be careful with terminology here: Americans use the term "middle class" to mean something like what we call "working class", but in Britain it refers to a whole range of non-aristocratic, non-proletarian income bands. It's axiomatic that people from middle-class backgrounds use "middle-class" as an insult (generally prefixed by words such as "nauseatingly") and think the desire to make more

Why Didn't Plaid Cymru Lynch Barry Letts?

...continued from page 383

ed Prime Minister, Wales voted for its own assembly. There had been attempts to get this and a Scottish parliament going in 1978, during the last days of the previous Labour government. At around this time, the charts were full of Welsh bands (one album, "Mwng" by Super Furry Animals, was entirely in Welsh and was commended in the House of Commons for reaching the top twenty in the UK and selling in America.) There has been a Welsh-language channel, S4C, since 1982.

S4C (Siriol Pedwar Cymru, which translates as "Channel Four Wales") is co-run by BBC and Channel 4, making it the only BBC station to run advertising (now almost all in Welsh). The expansion of the main BBC Wales, to cope with the Assembly and a big push for new drama, began in this new ebullient phase but really made an impact on the rest of Britain in 2005. That's a story you may think you know, and is another essay for another time. But the point is that even five years earlier, this would have been unimaginable.

of one's life is exclusively a middle-class trait. This is patronising, but nonetheless a regular phenomenon.

It's commonly observed that writers from impoverished (either financially or with regard to their prospects and ambitions) backgrounds hold anyone who *didn't* get to London and become famous in complete contempt. However, the BBC's remit is to provide quality stuff for everyone, and it couldn't help but offer broader horizons to those viewers who tuned in for soaps or pop music. For every person terrified that giving equal opportunity to all would make him or her somehow less "special", a dozen donnish were chaps keen to make sure the best the world offered was made available to everyone (see **Did the BBC Actually Like *Doctor Who*?** under 3.9, "The Savages") and a whole slew of professional Northerners and part-time Cockneys writing for and about people like themselves. Yer actual working class, of course, used the BBC - especially those allegedly "insufferably middle class" manifestations like Radio 4 and Blue Peter, - as a way out of the limited horizons they were presented at school or work, and only people who'd already got to this exalted state begrudged them the chance. (See "Carnival of Monsters" and our comments on Hood and Baverstock.)

Nevertheless, there's an uncomfortable sense that the Llanfairfach natives are victims because that's all they're good for and both the problem and its solution must come from London. We'll see the same problem in Sloman's other stories, but please note that he's swimming with the tide. In some ways it's perfectly true that Welshmen *themselves* traded on the stereotypes, but 1973 was not the year to go around saying it - see the essays with this story.

For the benefit of anyone who doesn't spot the quotes: Neville Chamberlain came back from Munich, having conned Hitler into signing an agreement not to do anything bad like invade a country, and stood at Heston Aerodrome proclaiming, "I have in my hand a piece of paper... peace in our time". Stevens later declares that 'What's good for Global Chemicals is good for the world', an adaptation of Charles Erwin Wilson's similar remark about General Motors.

BOSS' fanfare, 'Tarantara!', is from *Iolanthe* (he seems not to know the tune, though). 'Jocelyn Stevens' was the editor of the *Sunday Times*, not to mention Sloman's boss. 'Nancy with the Laughing Face' is a Frank Sinatra record (we're certain that Professor Jones was a huge fan). BOSS refers to 'Der Tag', and calls Stevens 'My little *ubermensch*', amid a few hints that he or Stevens have read Nietzsche but not actually understood it. You might find yourself hankering for the comparative subtlety of the Daleks talking about a 'final solution' (2.2, "The Dalek Invasion of Earth"). Even Jo's serendipity is a straight steal from Fleming discovering Penicillin (see 2.1, "Planet of Giants" for how this story was adapted for wartime use).

All right. Here we have an existentialist protest against corporatism, but couched within the terms of a Renaissance world-view with a set of received ideas about the Welsh. Sometimes, though, a maggot is just a maggot. Sloman wasn't crazy about critters, and found maggots almost as unnerving as spiders. He'll be back in a year to deal with *that* phobia too.

Things That Don't Make Sense The roster of words that Jon Pertwee can't pronounce now includes "chitinous". Jo knows all about Professor Jones from the newspapers, but has apparently never seen a photograph of him in print, as she doesn't recognise him on sight. Nor does she realise that the person labouring over a dish of mushrooms might be the notorious 'mushroom professor'. And leaving aside the rapidity of their courtship, isn't it traditional for couples to get their first snog *before* they become engaged? [See **What Are The Oddest Romances in** *Doctor Who*? under 24.3, 'Delta and the Bannermen", for more on this strange Welsh version of speed-dating. There's also an entry on BOSS and Stevens.]

Prior to the crisis with Jo being trapped down the mine, why did the Nut Hutch people seek to borrow cutting equipment from Global Chemicals (the very company against which they're protesting) and did they honestly expect them to lend a helping hand, rather than condescendingly-but-politely telling them to piss off? Even though the maggots can leap yards through the air, none of the thousands of maggots in the mine try to hop on the Doctor's cart as it slowly rolls past them. The same shot entails a glaring misuse of CSO, as the cart's wheels seem to disappear entirely. There's a surveillance camera in the waste-pipe at Global Chemicals - handy as it lets Elgin know that the Doctor and Jo are there, but it's probably going to be less useful on the 364 days of the year when the pipe's just full of sludge.

All the miners are stupid enough to want to touch the glowing green slime even after they've seen people die of it. And when one of the doomed Welshmen makes a telephone call from the mine in the first episode, a mysterious hand appears in the tunnel to give him his cue. [This ghostly limb will make an even more spectacular appearance in "Pyramids of Mars".] Bert says, once he and Jo have nearly plummeted to their deaths in a lift, 'It felt like brake-failure; can't happen in theory'. If it can't happen, how does he know what it would feel like? Oxyacetylene cutting equipment has to be fetched from Cardiff, but a cherry-picker lorry from the South Wales Electricity Board is no problem. At the start of episode four, Stevens' stooge Hinks goes to great lengths to sneak into the Nut Hutch while utterly failing to see Jo just sitting there on the floor in front of him.

Why does the military perform bombing runs with a helicopter labelled as belonging to 'Twyford Moors Helicopters, The Heliport, Southampton'? Why does Jo react with what can only be called absolute alarm at the prospect of the Doctor and

Cliff experimenting with human body cells? Is she unfamiliar with the concept of scraping a bit of skin or drawing a bit of blood? When he sees Jo go running pell-mell through the maggot field, Cliff doesn't shout for Benton and his men to come help him get her out.

The maggot that hatches in the Nut Hutch does so fully grown. Okay, but think about the comparative size of the maggots to their eggs - how large must the mamma maggots be, not that we ever see them, to lay such whoppers? [Alternatively, if you think it makes more sense that the eggs were tiny when laid and grew on contact with the goop, how much nutrition was in the goop and how did the eggs ingest it? Is it something else Jones the Mushroom can get us to eat? Come to think of it, we have no idea where Sunny Delight comes from...] Once it's established that the Nut Hutch maggot died from eating the miracle fungus, the Doctor doesn't consider that an extract of the stuff can cure the deathly ill professor, and instead wastes precious time figuring out the 'serendipity' clue. 'I should have guessed', the Doctor says upon realizing the truth. Yes, he really should. He also cuts it *really* close by only according the Brigadier three minutes to get in and destroy BOSS if necessary - is this even enough time to properly get in the building, or is the idea that the Brig will just bomb it into ruination?

Jo's uncle arranges funding for the Wholeweal commune, which Cliff interprets as 'work for the Valleys'. Is Jones the Milk going to become Jones the Mycoprotein? And it's not as if he's going to be on hand to train all these ex-miners to become research biologists, because he's gollywhacking up the Amazon at the first available opportunity. So Hilda, the woman who stands on her head during dinner-parties, will be running the training schemes, we presume. And why is everyone over thirty in this village ill?

We also have to ask what, precisely, the Brigadier says in the end scene. According to sources who have too much time on their hands, Nicholas Courtney can be heard saying, when one of the dolly-bird extras asks him to dance, '...it's one thing I would never do in public... ah, well, there you are... what I'd like is to make love to you all...'. [No wonder Pertwee leaves in such a hurry.] Of course, he could be talking to Yates and Benton. [Unsurprisingly, there's a whole section on UNIT's apparent abandonment of the chain of

Who's Running the Country?

On the face of it, the effort at "realism" in the Pertwee stories means we can assume a governmental system almost identical to that of the real Britain at the time. As with many of the items in this guidebook, we can measure what's said and shown on screen against the real-life news, treating *Doctor Who* as a dramatic reconstruction (see **Who Narrates This Series?** under 23.1, "The Mysterious Planet" for more on this'). In that case, if we accept the dramatic license and "names changed to protect the innocent" clause, you can see how the political fall-out from various invasions, plagues and freak daffodil fatalities would accumulate.

For the benefit of children and foreigners, a crash-course in real early 70s politics follows. Around the time "Inferno" was broadcast (June 1970), Labour PM Harold Wilson narrowly lost the election caused by the economic instability following his Chancellor's decision to uncouple the pound from the Gold standard in 1967. (The Chancellor of the Exchequer makes all the economic decisions - this one, Jim Callaghan, will be Prime Minister later.) This election was too close to call until polling day, with the decision to give 18-year-olds the vote seeming to confer the incumbent Labour Party with an advantage almost outweighed by the sense that it was time for a change.

Two days before the election, England were knocked out of the World Cup after an ill-judged penalty. Football was intimately connected with national prestige (see 3.10, "The War Machines") and it was assumed that the national side were going to walk it. As the bad news from Mexico sank in, the public felt let down, depressed and in the mood to punish someone. And so the Conservatives, led by confirmed bachelor Edward Heath, formed a government with a slender majority. Jeremy Thorpe, leader of the Liberal Party, didn't trust either of them but was more inclined to support Wilson's policies.

(NB, British politics, even today, is less vituperative than the American version and "Liberal" still doesn't have the pejorative connotations that right-wing Americans have given it in the States. The current Liberal Democrat party is an amalgamation of this party, itself formed from the wreckage of the Whigs caused by Gladstone's position on Home Rule for Ireland in the 1850s, and the SDP, a party made from bits of the Labour Party after it went through a schism in the early 1980s. More on that in a while.) Nevertheless, as the Tories (a traditional name for the Conservatives, an Irish word for "bandit") were officially the Conservative and Unionist Party of Great Britain and Northern Ireland, and as the violence in Northern Ireland escalated, Heath looked safe.

However, Heath was finished by February 1974. To list all the things which went wrong would take a book as big as this, so here are the headlines: Chancellor of the Exchequer Anthony Barber had managed to defy the laws of classical economics and get inflation *and* unemployment rising exponentially. (One week saw us passing two milestones: beef at £1.00 per lb and one million unemployed.) Trade and Industry Secretary Peter Walker narrowly avoided being jailed along with his business partner Jim Slater.

Meanwhile, Home Secretary Reginald Maudling was implicated in a series of corruption cases that arose from the bankruptcy hearing of his friend John Poulson, an architect. Poulson had designed a number of prominent buildings, including the rebuilds of Cannon Street tube station and Waterloo railway station, but had been caught up in corrupt town-planner T Dan Smith's schemes to regenerate Newcastle[127]. The hapless Maudling's love of money meant that once a link to questionable dealings was uncovered, the press looked for more - and found them. Another property company with whom he had an association was investigated for fraud and the boss committed suicide. Revisions to Government payments to the Maltese government had his dabs all over them. He'd also made several controversial moves, including introducing internment without trial when in charge of Northern Ireland. Oh, and he introduced revised immigration laws that weren't racist at all, goodness no - they just wanted to keep out people from Commonwealth Countries other than Australia, Canada and anywhere else that was predominantly white. So the discovery that Maudling was on the take fell as a gift to people who wanted him out of office for other reasons.

At the same time, relations with the Unions were deliberately confrontational. In order to be seen to be strong, both sides became intransigent, causing power-cuts and rail-strikes. Heath was simultaneously pro-Europe in an era when Europe didn't want Britain, and pro-America when anyone could see that Nixon was a crook. Nixon's intervention in the Arab-Israeli conflict resulted in the

continued on page 389...

command in **What Are The Gayest Things In Doctor Who Ever?** under, of course, 25.2, "The Happiness Patrol".]

Finally, it can't escape mention that in Jo's last story, she's dim enough to somehow think she and the Doctor can manoeuvre an ore car through a collapsed tunnel.

Critique Looking at it now, the single most interesting thing about "The Green Death" is how colourful it is. When Season Eleven arrives, you'll look back at Season Ten and marvel that so little time elapsed between 1973's gaudy excess and the drab and drained look of 1974's stories. The whole thing lands up looking as though that year's most popular colours are fighting for supremacy.

Forget the *Life on Mars* propaganda; the three main colours for curtains, shirts and dresses in 1973 were bright green, deep blue and burnt umber. Between that and what we were eating at the time[123], it's amazing anyone held down a meal. Watch this story's climax, when the trickery usually reserved for *Top of the Pops* or title-sequences is put to narrative use, and it's clear that something extraordinary is happening to kids' television. Orange, associated throughout the story with BOSS, is combating blue (the crystal, here a force for good, but later deployed to represent the Spiders of Metebelis 3 and countered with orange sparks from the Doctor's gizmo).

Earlier in this volume we've used the term "Tartrazine Aesthetic" to try to describe this process. It's a belief that the larger-than-life quality of some of these stories needs a suitably bold visual equivalent, in which viewers can see bits of their own world, only how they would like to *think* it was. It's like the version of Manhattan that Woody Allen created, or how London appears in American films (or BBC Wales' *Doctor Who*). However, "The Green Death" is largely absolved from the horrible patronising way the Welsh are portrayed by the way this story fictionalises Wales. The English characters (including the mad computer) are equally unbelievable and it's all in a world more akin to how a film crew from the future would evoke 70s Wales. Plot logic and nuanced characterisation are an optional extra.

Viewers latch on to these things and subconsciously think, "This is set in a world where things like _____ can happen". Most of *Doctor Who's* assaults on the senses during the Glam era were set in versions of present-day Earth that owed as much to comedy shows as to drama. (Here we can't help but note that the Victorian 'Dispensing Chemist' sign in Cliff's pad is the same one used when Stanley "Bok" Mason was hidden in Terry Gilliam's raincoat - that *Python* sketch about Halibut after-shave.) Helicopters dropping cherry-bombs by hand onto a Welsh slagheap covered in giant maggots is straight out of *The Goodies*. This is, regrettably, the last time this level of bright colour and visual panache is applied to present-day settings until the 1980s. It's almost, in fact, the last time we get it anywhere, with the slightly garish Mediaeval castle of the next story being a late flourish, but nothing similar occurs until 13.2, "Planet of Evil" and 14.1, "The Masque of Mandragora". As we've seen, 1973 is the year they pushed *Doctor Who* as far as it would ever go in this direction.

So even without Jo's departure, there's a sense of an era ending. Pertwee will stick around for another year but this is effectively the end of the style of *Doctor Who* he's been associated with, and the next clearly-defined phase of the series only gets under way with "The Ark in Space" (12.2). Watched without this hindsight, the story is nonetheless remarkable for two things. First, the Doctor is more than usually redundant. Once he's found the crystal and the cure for the maggot-infection, he's really there to ask Cliff questions and be rude to everyone. This adventure could just about work without the Doctor in at all; if a means to overpower BOSS were somehow found, this could be *any* series where a young couple get into trouble with a sinister megacorp that's polluting and brainwashing with impunity. Annoying and rapid though Jo and Cliff's courtship may be, at least it's relatively plausible and dignified. The Doctor's reaction to this is now widely seen as being some kind of romantic entanglement, but in fact is more poignant without this. He's *not* like the assembled humans; he will outlive everyone he knows. It's not that Jo has been dumped him for a younger model, it's just that he isn't needed any more. It's like *Puff the Magic Dragon* or the end of *Peter Pan* where the oblivious adult Wendy shuts the window on him.

The second thing is the maggots. Even ven though they only popped up just this one time, this is the story that anyone who discovers you know your old-fashioned 25-minute *Doctor Who* will ask about. Some of the maggot props - the ones with fox-skulls inside especially - are mag-

Who's Running the Country?

...continued from page 387

Yom Kippur war and subsequent oil price-rise. Heath was prompted to introduce petrol rationing and a Three-Day working week. (Not because fuel was all that scarce; it had to do with making the public lose sympathy for miners. Within hours of calling an election, he conceded that they were to be exempted from his statutory pay-restraints.) Before this forced an election, we also had a series of hilarious sex-scandals, notably Lord Lambton (a senior defence minister) and Norma Levy (who ran "cream-cake" parties).

You can see any number of points at which it could have gone differently. Curiously, "Grocer" Heath himself was never involved in any breath of scandal. Most of the worst threats to his administration were apparently small to outside observers, and the more-damaging material from the Cabinet papers (released thirty years later, and so just beginning to filter though in recent years) was unknown by the public.

Unlike today's media feeding-frenzy for ministerial scalps, gentlemen's agreements to not mention particular things hushed up pre-Watergate British politics. Most of what happened in *Doctor Who* stories would have been just as circumspectly reported. Stately homes blowing up on the Nine O'Clock News would have been tomorrow's chippapers, and official cover-ups for ships being sunk in the Channel were par for the course. (You think we're kidding? Four thousand people died in one night in 1952 due to smog - the "London Particular" that *Murder, She Wrote* viewers think are still common, like steam-trains - and coroners' offices were instructed to make the cause of death seem natural. The Housing Minister responsible was future PM Harold Macmillan. Soldiers were asked to walk through deserts in the Australian outback where atomic bombs had gone off, just to see what would happen, and vast numbers of London orphans - and some non-orphans whose parents couldn't be traced after the War - were shipped to Australia to start new lives, whether they wanted to go or not.)

Everyone in *Doctor Who* behaves as though politicians are still in fear of being voted out, so the threatened insurrection appears not to have happened in the fictitious 1970s. But if power-cuts could cause an election, how might the repeated interruptions caused by Wenley Moor, Nuton and project Inferno going offstream have affected ministerial careers? Unlike our history, oil and coal seem to have been totally abandoned by generating companies (all government-run, or privatised as happened in the 1980s?) some time before UNIT formed. There's a well-established Ministry of Ecology (in "The Green Death"), run by someone with prior cabinet experience (either in defence or the Foreign Office) who drafted UNIT's charter. If an Ecology Minister is among the Cabinet posts, not amalgamated with - say - the Department of the Environment (which also handles housebuilding, county boundaries, local council regulation and so on), it must have been a priority distinct from other ministerial duties.

Certainly the World Ecology Bureau from "The Seeds of Doom" (13.6) seems to be run from London, not Brasilia or Athens. This government, in "The Green Death", has been in power for a while. If other data on UNIT dates are valid, then the election has either taken place during the "gap" year between "Terror of the Autons" and "The Mind of Evil" or not at all. This means that the demise of three Permanent Under Secretaries and a Minister must be explained to the public as by deaths by "natural causes". In the case of Sir James Quinlan ("The Ambassadors of Death"), this is only possible if the "live" global telecast never went further than the studio. (The issues with Sir Charles Grover - see 11.2, "Invasion of the Dinosaurs" - *might* be swept under the carpet by the fact that outside the bunker itself, none of this story "happened". This does not, of course, excuse Barry Letts' radio play "Paradise of Death", unless Sarah can remember two personal histories at once.) The alternative is a by-election every week and a rapid turn-over of Cabinet ministers even by Tony Blair's standards.

Let's assume, therefore, that the most sensible version is Jeremy Thorpe in Number Ten from spring 1972; Thorpe, of course, is obviously supposed to be the Prime Minister named "Jeremy" in "The Green Death". With hindsight this seems terribly unlikely, but no-one in that period knew all of his secrets. Thorpe was leader of the Liberals from 1967, following a period when they'd gone from being the second party in British politics to a lame-duck fringe party in the early 1960s. They were unlikely to win a general election in their own right, but occasionally found themselves in a position to tip the balance between Labour and the Conservatives. Between 1977 and 1979 they kept the minority Callaghan government in power.

continued on page 391...

nificently menacing, but the majority are just real-life maggots and genuinely creepy, simply because you know they *aren't* being operated by a BBC effects guy.

More than any of this, though, John Dearth owns this story. No previous off-screen voice has ever carried so much of the story so well. You almost want BOSS to win, as he's wittier, more charming and more full of insight than anyone else here. Certainly the Brigadier's occasional lapses into "Three Doctors"-style idiocy are aggravating, complete with a sitcom-style musical "zinger" in episode four, and the Doctor is rather less eloquent than usual. Cliff gets all the grindingly "cute" types of lines that Disco Stu got in "The Time Monster", but in a Welsh accent. In a story full of stereotypes and clichés, it happens that only the Mad Computer gets any realistic or worthwhile dialogue and characterisation.

The Facts

Written by Robert Sloman. Directed by Michael Briant. Viewing figures: 9.2 million, 7.2 million, 7.8 million, 6.8 million, 8.3 million, 7.0 million. (The lowest ratings of the year - unsurprisingly, given the weather. However, as with all the most fondly recalled Pertwees, it got a Christmas compilation repeat, and *that* scored 10.4 million.)

Supporting Cast Jerome Willis (Stevens), Stewart Bevan (Clifford Jones), Tony Adams (Elgin), Ben Howard (Hinks), Mostyn Evans (Dai Evans), Talfryn Thomas (Dave), Roy Evans (Bert), Mitzi McKenzie (Nancy), John Scott Martin (Hughes), John Rolfe (Fell), John Dearth (BOSS' Voice), Terry Walsh (Guard), Roy Skelton (James).

Cliffhangers Jo and Bert-the-funny-little-Welshman go down into the mine, but the lift mechanism's been sabotaged and makes them plummet towards the bottom of the pit; a mine tunnel collapses in front of the Doctor and Jo, and they get their first good look at the maggots when several of the creatures crawl out of the rubble to hiss at them, like maggots always do; Jo, on her own in the Nut Hutch living-room, fails to notice that there's a maggot shuffling across the parquet towards her; the Doctor discovers the true nature of BOSS on the top floor of the company building; Mr James - whoever he is - is killed by a sonic pulse in the offices of Global Chemicals, and

Captain Yates turns round to find Stevens and the security guards standing in the doorway.

What Was in the Charts? "Rubber Bullets", 10CC; "Frankenstein", Edgar Winter Group; "Live and Let Die", Paul McCartney and Wings; "Can the Can", Suzi Quatro; "A Walk on the Wild Side", Lou Reed[124]; "Stuck in the Middle With You", Stealer's Wheel. (If you've seen *Reservoir Dogs*, you'll be imagining what Hinks did with Elgin in that room with chains hanging from the ceiling.)

The Lore

• To begin at the beginning... Barry Letts was increasingly concerned that he was unable to reconcile his job making exciting stories set in the future with his belief that there probably wasn't going to be one. As with "The Daemons", Terrance Dicks asked the obvious question: "Why not do a *Doctor Who* story about it?" The book Letts names as the source for his thoughts on ecology, *A Blueprint For Survival* by Edward Goldsmith, seems a pretty good match for the fictional *Last Chance For Man*, the book Sir Charles Grover wrote before the events of "Invasion of the Dinosaurs".

This shouldn't be too surprising: one of the many odd features of that story is that it was written as "The Green Death" was being broadcast, and seems almost to have been a rejoinder to its perceived naivety. (We will pick this up in two stories' time, but should state for the record that Edward Goldsmith at was at no point involved in building fake spaceships in disued tube stations and attempting a pre-emptive genocide with the aid of oddly bendy reptiles.) Indeed, as Hulke's first script for "Bridgehead From Space" (what it was called before any dinosaurs were included) includes a corrupt Prime Minister quoting Neville Chamberlain's "piece of paper" moment, it's possible that the overt identification of unchecked capitalism with the Nazis was a means of keeping Hulke in line when asking for a drastically new story (i.e. telling him "it's been done" stopped him doing it).

• It seems to have been decided very early on that Robert Sloman should be given the brief. From now on, Letts and Dicks were looking to branch out from *Doctor Who* so where possible they looked to hire safe pairs of hands who could manage crises without badgering the production

Who's Running the Country?

...continued from page 389

Thorpe, a thin, quiet-looking man who himself could easily have been one of *Doctor Who*'s ministerial supporting characters, had been a well-known figure in Soho's then-illegal gay bars. He'd often socialised with Brian Epstein (who managed *The Beatles*) and Kit Lambert (who managed *The Who*). There's even a photo of Thorpe on stage with the Jimi Hendrix Experience. The problem for Thorpe being: back then, an "out" gay politician would have been as unelectable as an IRA bomber.

Following the two elections of 1974, Wilson could only just sustain a minority government, largely owing to sugar shortages and a bread crisis caused by the invasion of Cyprus, just as the new potatoes were due. Thorpe looked like a king-maker, travelling to the hustings by hovercraft and helicopter. But while his flair for PR was making him a plausible Leader of the Opposition, one of his ex-lovers - Norman Scott, a rather soppy male model - contacted Marion Thorpe, the trophy wife (or Lady Macbeth, depending on who you believe). In fact, Scott was blabbing to anyone who'd listen, and Thorpe's circle quickly thought it'd be nice if he'd shut up - for good.

What follows was a case that, at the very least, highlights the Ealing Comedies nature of British scandal. In America, political assassinations are supposed to involve CIA mind-control experiments, ex-marine sharpshooters hired by the Mafia, that sort of thing. But the details of this murder attempt, as they emerged in a hysterically funny trial, kept us in stitches during the crisis of late 1978. The conspirators even included a carpet salesman who, amusingly, had the same name as one of the cast of *Dad's Army*. But the gist is that the attempt on Scott's life entailed the world's most incompetent hitman - former airline pilot Andrew "Gino" Newton (who muddled up Dunstable with Barnstable, towns on opposite ends of the country) - shooting Scott's dog, Rinka, then completely failing to hit his target. This took place on Bodmin Moor, so *Hound of the Baskervilles* parodies were rife.

Take a moment to consider this: the leader of the third biggest political party, at a time when the balance of power between the other two was at its most precarious, was suspected of attempted murder even as the press got hold of a letter from Thorpe to Scott with the cryptic message, "Bunnies can and will go to France." (This has never been satisfactorily deciphered.) What makes it even *more* peculiar is that a junior Labour minister (Jack Straw, later Home Secretary...) looked for Scott's financial details when trying to prove PM Harold Wilson's suspicions that the South African secret police were trying to overthrow him. Straw says the file was empty, but he's been implicated with the way the contents were leaked to the press to try to help Thorpe. Anyway, just after the 1979 election, Thorpe and three others were found not guilty of conspiracy to commit murder, after a trial widely regarded as a complete farce. Thorpe was diagnosed with Parkinson's Disease shortly thereafter, so he withdrew from public life. Scott lives in a palatial house, and nobody's sure how he paid for it.

Had an election been called in 1972, the Liberals would have had the advantage of no-one in their front bench being associated with any of the catastrophic decisions the other two parties had made (assuming that the Tories had been in at any time since 1964, in this version). As a coalition with Labour, they could have called on the broadly sympathetic but more experienced second-string figures of the Wilson government. (They would include Tom Driberg, Richard Crossman, Shirley Williams - indeed, many of those who formed the SDP in the early 1980s to avoid the more doctrinaire socialism of Labour then, and later amalgamated with most of the Liberals into the Lib Dems of today: future Foreign Secretary David Owen, but probably not SDP founder Roy Jenkins. As Wilson's Home Secretary, he might have been too "contaminated" in the public mind.)[128]

Britain has a female PM by the time of "Terror of the Zygons", c. 1976; assuming, of course, that when the Brigadier calls the person on the other end of the hotline 'Madam', he's actually talking to a woman and not just being bitchy to Mr Thorpe. That said, mapping known public figures onto the various ministers who crop up is a tricky manoeuvre. Most of them aren't apparently, minister for anything in particular.

However, just as an Ecology ministry is more plausible in a Thorpe government than any other, so the "Big Science" energy-generating projects of Season Seven and "The Claws of Axos" make more sense if technophiliac socialist Anthony Wedgewood-Benn had centralised all power production, and gone for a big, shiny prestige project.

continued on page 393...

office. Their not-quite-spin-off project *Moonbase 3* was heading for production almost as soon as this story was out of the way. ("The Time Warrior" was made immediately after this adventure, but that was made almost concurrently with the botched first recording of the pilot.)

• Another consideration was that Katy Manning had decided to leave. To go at the same time as the main star would minimise any publicity she'd get (and it was clear that Pertwee would be unlikely to stay beyond five years), and she was getting offers that were unsuited to the star of a series popular with children. (Fans of tacky smut will recall that Manning and *Play School* demi-god Derek Griffiths attempted to bring down a government through sleaze in *Don't Just Lie There -Say Something,* whilst she remained resolutely fully-clothed in *Eskimo Nell,* a farce *about* porn films rather than being one per se, honest, guv[125]. It had the second most bewildering cast imaginable... keep reading for the winner.)

It's also known that there was an idea for a full-time replacement / part-time source of fresh stories. The latter was probably a reporter called "Smith" who would stumble across odd things for the Doctor to investigate, reducing the reliance on UNIT and big obvious problems. (The clearest comparison would be Mickey's role in X2.3, "School Reunion".)

• The first episode was submitted at the end of December 1972, after discussions in October about the kind of story this should be. The final scripts were all in by the beginning of February, with a little leeway in them for whether Yates or Benton would be the "inside man" at what was now called 'Global Chemicals'. The Company was originally to be called "Universal Chemicals", but there really *was* one of those. It later turned out that there was a "Global Chemicals", too, but not in the UK. One of the chief scientists at ICI was called Bell, so the character "Bell" became "Fell". This is one of those stories in which two characters accidentally have the same name, since both the villain and one of Sergeant Benton's men end up being called "Stevens" (see 19.4, "The Visitation" for another). Benton also has a recalcitrant 'Private Dicks' to contend with.

• Stewart Bevan was Katy Manning's real-life fiancé by this time (see "Frontier in Space" for how they met), and director Michael Briant resisted everyone's suggestions that he was perfect for the part of Cliff. Bevan had done a bit of telly (later

he'd be a fixture in *Crown Court*) but not much yet. With very little time left, Briant auditioned Bevan and then decided to risk it, despite misgivings about big parts being given to "family".

• Briant recalls that it got a bit fraught. He took two film units and had been granted a larger special effects team than usual, led by Ron Oates. The main unit was busy at the mine-shaft (granted permission by the National Coal Board for the lifts, but not anything in the disused mine, as the dampened coal released the gases that canaries used to detect). Mostyn Evans (here the miner Dai Evans, and who'd been in 7.2, "Doctor Who and the Silurians", briefly) and Talfryn Thomas (the helpful miner Dave, and last seen in 7.1, "Spearhead from Space") were in these scenes, as were Pertwee and Nicholas Courtney (still in civvies after the earlier scenes with Manning).

When Briant saw the second unit's contribution for the Doctor's departure (shot through a star-filter), he was nonplussed but decided to use what they'd got instead of sending them all out again to film what he'd asked for. Day two saw Manning and Bevan talk to the press and announce plans to marry in Wales. Pertwee found the filming irksome enough without children watching and ridiculing his attempt to look scared when the incline he was supposedly hanging from was a shallow one with a tilted camera.

• Stop us if you've heard this before: the bombs dropped from the helicopter were lavatory ballcocks; the maggots in some of the long-shots were inflated condoms. More of the same sort of thing happened on the Thursday, with the flying insect scenes kept to a minimum because of strong winds. The Friday had everyone go to the old RCA magnetic tape factory at Bryn Mawr (the one in Wales, not the college in Pennsylvania), although they had trouble finding it at first as it had been renamed. This was abandoned over a year earlier.

Joining for that day were Jerome Willis (Stevens) and Tony Adams (Elgin), for the opening sequence of the story, and Roy Evans as Bert the Funny-Little-Welshman. Evans had been in 3.4, "The Daleks' Master Plan (see **Which Sodding Delegate is Which?**), and he'll return in "The Monster of Peladon". Adams is, as those of us who were in Britain in the 70s all pretend not to know, the actor who became *Crossroads* smoothy Adam Chance. (In the misguided 2001 relaunch, he became a curious hybrid of Hannibal

Who's Running the Country?

...continued from page 391

(Such as, for instance, Concorde or the Post Office Tower. See 3.10, "The War Machines" and 19.7, "Time-Flight": Benn officially opened both projects, and Concorde was largely built in his Bristol constituency, oddly enough). Think Tank (12.1, "Robot") also has many of the hallmarks of his pet projects, making its infiltration by fascist nerds more ironic. However, as Professor Kettlewell sees himself as a voice in the wilderness regarding renewable energy, it's possible that the Ministry of Ecology was disbanded after the Llanfairfach incident in "The Green Death". It's certainly not doing its job, if "Invasion of the Dinosaurs" is to be believed, as Operation Golden Age has no shortage of support. With a dynamic Science and Energy ministry (they seem to save been amalgamated) outgunning him at every turn, no wonder the Ecology minister is so vulnerable to overtures from Global Chemicals.

This may be the time to note that Northern Ireland is about the only contemporary "issue" never touched in *Doctor Who*. There was a terror campaign happening on the mainland, prompted by religious warfare (there's no other word for it) and a virtual police state *in a part of Britain*. Ireland had been split between the World Wars into the Irish Republic (Eire) and Northern Ireland. In the latter, the Catholics were a minority and subjected to routine abuse by the Protestants, abuse escalating into open and sustained violence. The British Army was sent in as a peacekeeping force (ostensibly to protect the Catholics) and landed up staying for decades, a situation resented by all sides. The Unionists, mainly Protestant, believe that Northern Ireland should remain part of the UK - as it has been since the rest became a Free State in 1922. (NB if you're confused about the difference between "The United Kingdom" and "Great Britain", the former includes Northern Ireland - and used to include *all* Ireland - whereas "Great Britain" - "Great" as in "Extended" is England, Scotland and Wales, and existed earlier. Olympic athletes from Northern Ireland (AKA Ulster) got very annoyed at the UK team being called "Team GB.")

On Halloween 1971, the IRA planted a bomb in the Post Office Tower (3.10, "The War Machines"), but it was two years later that the mainland bombing campaign began for real. Every time Irish home rule was on the agenda, a murder or scandal would push it beyond the pale (and that phrase is carefully chosen, as you'll recall from earlier in this book). The twentieth century was the time of armed uprisings and concerted moves towards a Republic. The Republicans, however,

continued on page 395...

Lecter and Swiss Toni from *The Fast Show*.)

• This story's Terry Walsh moment sees him playing a jobsworth security guard at Global Chemicals. In terms of lines and screen-time he does better than Jones the Milk, but his main contribution is the episode two fight, for which he gets a credit and is more obviously playing the Doctor than ever before (again, see "The Monster of Peladon").

• A week of rehearsals later, they were in the studio for episode one. The episodes were recorded, pretty much in order (except for the scenes of Dai in the mine-lift). This is John Burroughs' only story as designer, but his main claim to fame is as producer of *Full Swing*, a golf-themed celebrity quiz show that may be mentioned in Nostradamus (but, hey, it ended Jimmy Tarbuck's game-show career, so it wasn't a total loss).

Much of the BOSS set uses the Century 21 Computer Prop repertoire, notably the one with the curved bank of dials and the pea-bulbs linked to a sequencer that's rapidly becoming the Xeron Freezing Machine of the 70s. (Just wait until Volume IV: Tom Baker gets to wave his sonic screwdriver at it in practically every story. It comes as a shock to see the Moonbase control in *UFO* and find that these curvilinear gismos in their original habitat - that is, if you can pull your eyes away from Gabrielle Drake's purple wig.)

• The scene in which Jo and Cliff meet for the first time was a last-minute rewrite. A character called 'Face' had been removed from the story, and his lines given to Nancy (Mitzi McKenzie, who appeared as Mitzi Webster, an entirely incidental character in "Colony In Space"). However, she was otherwise engaged come the day of the shoot, so no-one else was around at Wholeweal and the scene we all know was created. (The novelisation retains the cut dialogue, if you can bear it.)

• A lot of scenes had their beginnings and ends trimmed. Hughes' auntie has to be told of his death, but Elgin tries to keep the company's name out of it and two GC goons try to intimidate Dai. There's a lot of Cliff-Jo stuff about how the world's gone wrong as well. Episode three saw the first major use of the rod-puppet maggots, which unnerved even the hardiest of cast-members and floor-crew. Manning, however, took off her glasses and couldn't see what she was supposed to be looking at (which caused a remount for one shot at the cliffhanger when they recorded episode six).

• The Minister for Ecology was played by Richard Beale, previously Bat Masterson (3.8, "The Gunfighters") and voice-overs for the Refusian (3.6, "The Ark") and the work-shift controller (4.7, "The Macra Terror"). Letts hedged his bets about a possible election or accusations of bias by hinting that the Liberal Party had come into power (see **Who's Running the Country?**). In episode four, Franklin ad-libbed the 'handbag' line and Pertwee improvised the business with the sticky moustache.

• Before recording the final two episodes, Adams was rushed to hospital with peritonitis and Roy Skelton was hurriedly drafted in as Mr James. (As Elgin is last seen getting brainwashed by BOSS, it's easy enough to imagine that he was killed and his corpse dumped in a ditch somewhere. The "Global Conspiracy" feature on the DVD, however, provides an alternative explanation.) At the same time, Elisabeth Sladen was auditioned and introduced to Pertwee (who gave an enthusiastic thumbs-up behind her back).

• Over the course of the story, several methods were used for the green death itself. Sometimes they stuck latex on the skin of the actor and scattered on Scotchlite paste (see "The Monster of Peladon" for the principal of Front Axial Projection) and sometimes they mixed this powder into a paste. It would be nice to think that the party scene was the last one recorded, but in fact the dragonfly scenes were remounted with CSO. In the intervening weeks, there had been a filmed model sequence using a bicycle-pump filled with pea-soup inside the proboscis of the insect prop. It seems that all the title captions were recorded in this last session, which might explain why the film of the "flame" effect graphics was upside-down in some episodes. Rather than rewinding the film and starting again, they may have just swapped the reels and shown it all backwards.

• The philistines who do the notes for the DVD seem to think that Wagner wrote Beethoven's Violin Concerto. For all the dialogue's references to Nietzsche, there ain't no Wagner to be heard, and they miss Beethoven's Fifth Symphony (surely the single most famous piece of music ever, although the version John Dearth performs goes

off-track pretty quickly). The way BOSS tells Stevens to "connect" is sung vaguely ('co-o-nect co-o-nect') to the tune of the third Brandenberg Concerto (Bach, if you needed to be told), which is sadly best known hereabouts for early episodes of *Antiques Roadshow* and Wendy Carlos' *Switched On Bach*. The music played at the party is from stock, by Electric Banana, who were mod nearly-men The Pretty Things under an assumed name.

The official music has a lot more electric guitar than usual, as Briant wanted a folksy, contemporary sound (suggesting John Denver as a starting point). Simpson made something vaguely Welsh-sounding that fit the bill. By this time, he'd been hired to do three other theme tunes in rapid succession. We've already mentioned *Moonbase 3* and *The Tomorrow People*, and - going rather up-market - Simpson provided a majestic theme for Dr Jacob Bronowski's astonishing visual essay *The Ascent of Man*. With all this income and so much of his work using electronics, it seemed wise for Simpson to invest in a synthesizer of his own. This coincides with a decision from somewhere in the BBC hierarchy that he should have less free access to the Radiophonic Workshop facilities. You'll note that the sound of the music changes from the next story on.

• The production team braced themselves for a storm of protest over the use of *Doctor Who* for a polemic about such a sensitive issue. But all they got was a pronunciation guide, in a letter saying 'the reason I'm writin'/is how to say "chitin" '. Hilarity ensued. Although the Daleks had been vanquished a week earlier, the first episode of this story got a tie-in appearance of a Dalek in Jimmy Saville's Saturday-night gallimaufry *Clunk-Click*. A couple more were dispatched to Wales to appear in a Welsh-language programme and didn't make it back. The publicity this generated carried on into the autumn (see "Death to the Daleks").

• The Monday after the transmission of episode five was the day Roger Delgado died. It was national news, and the elegiac feel of episode six was heightened, although obviously none of the cast or crew could have known this when filming. We'll pick up on this in the next story.

• In real life, Katy Manning's immediate future involved presenting a hippy-ish crafts programme called *Serendipity* (how to macramé and batik, that sort of thing) and those films mentioned earlier. There's also the small matter of the cheesecake photos she did with a Dalek. She did occasional

Who's Running the Country?

...continued from page 393

had little overt support in Westminster because their most visible activities at the time were mainly terrorist campaigns and the occasional tarring and feathering of suspected informers. Any form of republicanism was tainted by association.

All of this was happening, yet the nearest to a "controversial" present-day story *Doctor Who* got was "The Green Death". Quite aside from the raw nerve it would touch (especially for the relatives of anyone killed in a bombing on the mainland or shot in Belfast - the BBC covers the province too, and license-fee payers have the right not to be portrayed as green scaly monsters in half-baked allegories or, more appropriately, scaly *orange* ones), the issues were too complex to be turned into a six-week romp with Pertwee solving it all by platitudes and martial arts. To get some idea of

how well a Barry Letts treatment of the Troubles would have gone down, American readers should think back to 2002 and imagine a *Dawson's Creek* episode[129] where an Al-Qaeda member is portrayed as a noble and heroic freedom fighter who persuades everyone to stone Joey to death for harlotry, and has Dawson make video-taped messages threatening to destroy the US.

Still, alien incursions aside, is this the big "political" difference between the UNIT world and our own? Are we to conclude that the key divergence between our world and that of the series is the absence of religious demagogues and politicised gangsters exploiting a divisive issue? Is it the apparent diminution of American influence (see **Whatever Happened to the USA?** under 4.6, "The Moonbase")? Or is it simply Geoff Astell's free-kick in Mexico 1970?

---

television drama, including playing a junkie in a well-received episode of *Target* (written by Bob Baker and Dave Martin, who were actually very good at that sort of thing) and moved to Australia. There she co-starred with Barry Crocker (Aussie hero and star of *Barry McKenzie Holds His Own*, which has *the* most bewildering cast of any film ever, including all the ones they haven't made yet) in *Educating Rita*. Manning and Crocker have been an item for getting on for twenty years. She's become involved in *Doctor Who*-related works again, but usually not as Jo but instead as Iris

Wildthyme (the Doctor's supposed ex), while her most recent memorable TV appearance was alongside an "exuberant" Liza Minnelli in an edition of *Ruby Wax Meets*. (Manning and Minnelli are old schoolfriends. Their joint TV appearance involved both of them turning up late for an interview in a hotel room, in a state that was politely described in the media as "the worse for wear", and pretending to be dogs in front of an unusually speechless Ruby Wax. It really was quite wonderful to behold.)

season 11

11.1: "The Time Warrior"

(Serial UUU, Four Episodes, 15th December 1973 - 5th January 1974.)

Which One is This? A Humpty-Dumpty man from beyond the stars crash-lands in the Middle Ages and starts abducting scientists from the 1970s. Loud men in period beards have cunning plans (that's *exactly* the term they use, ten years before *Blackadder*). Meanwhile, a displaced *Cosmo*-reader tries to give the serving-wenches a lesson in female emancipation, and the menfolk a display of commando-raiding (although it's a short-sighted scientist and an archer who find the alien's g-spot).

Firsts and Lasts Though "The Time Warrior" isn't the first pseudo-historical story (i.e. a historical story with alien interference other than that of the Doctor; the first was 2.9, "The Time Meddler"), its balance of aliens and period costumes sets the tone for virtually all the "past" stories of the late 70s and 80s, because the source is less known history than known costume-dramas. Dennis Spooner tried it back in 1965, David Whitaker refined it (in 1967 with 4.9, "The Evil of the Daleks"), but here Robert Holmes and Terrance Dicks invent a whole new way of getting time-travel back into the programme's arsenal.

Other things, people and ideas making their debut here are: Sarah Jane Smith, the Doctor's new companion and only link to humanity for much of the next three-and-a-half years; the Sontarans, destined to become one of the series' Top Five Monsters, immediately making an impression here; the new "time tunnel" opening sequence (still not quite right, with the cut-out Doctor looking especially naff and the opening shot very reminiscent of the "Pearl and Dean" cinema ads), complete with the diamond-shaped *Doctor Who* logo which will come to represent the series more than any other piece of design. And as part of this change, we switch from "episode" to "part" in the titles for each, um, instalment (although for reasons of style, we'll sometimes refer to them as them "episodes" for the remainder of this guide-book). The protagonist's credit settles down as "Dr Who" from now until 18.7, "Logopolis".

Season 11 Cast/Crew

- Jon Pertwee (the Doctor)
- Elisabeth Sladen (Sarah Jane Smith)
- Nicholas Courtney
  (Brigadier Lethbridge-Stewart)
- Richard Franklin (Captain Yates)
- John Levene (Sergeant Benton)

- Barry Letts (Producer)
- Terrance Dicks (Script Editor)
- Robert Holmes (uncredited,
  Script Editor with Terrance on 11.2, 11.3)

This also is the first appearance of that cheesy "spade" TARDIS key, with the irregular blocks on one side and the star-system the Doctor's from (with three suns, contrary to what we later discover) on the other. For the first time *ever*, the Doctor names his home planet. It's called 'Gallifrey', apparently.

It's also the last story to be made as part of Season Ten, but the first story to debut on days other than Saturdays (if you were watching in Wales, that is). Later on this year, they'll shove the series all around the week, setting an unfortunate precedent for eight years later...[130]

Four Things to Notice About "The Time Warrior"...

1. As written, Linx the Sontaran is a warmongering idiot who gets too caught up in stopping the Doctor to complete his mission. What happened between script and screen is that the designers took a simple and comical idea - an alien whose head fits *exactly* into his helmet - and ran with it. The mask is quite simply the best in the programme's history, with lessons learned from the Draconians (10.3, "Frontier in Space") and the Ogrons (9.1, "Day of the Daleks") applied to a single alien rather than a batch.

Yet what lifts it into the classic status is what Kevin Lindsay does with the part. His physical performance, always writhing and strutting, allows Linx to convey moods even while wearing a tin hat and not saying anything. As with Bernard Bresslaw (5.3, "The Ice Warriors"), an entire species has been sketched in by one actor. Fortunately Lindsay returned (in a less-good mask, though) the following year and cemented

What Caused the Sontaran-Rutan War?

All comments on this - even our own in these guidebooks - have treated a lot of assumptions as facts. We know that the Sontarans and the Rutans have been at war for a long time. We also know that the Sontarans are not impressed by the idea of reproduction through genetic variation (sex, in other words) and that by the time of the Solar Flares that led to Earth being abandoned (12.3, "The Sontaran Experiment"), they're clones. We know that they've been adapted to feed and do various other things through their probic vents. We know that one phase of the war was being prosecuted 10,000 years after Earth was abandoned because of Solar Flares. We know that they needed a breeding planet in the early twenty-first century (X4.5, "The Poison Sky"), at which point the war was fifty thousand years old. But in *absolute* terms, we have very little reliable information to go on - and frankly, even those dates wobble if looked at too closely.

However, we *also* know that at least one side has time travel facilities. The Sontarans have the ability to pull things from the future even in Linx's era (11.1, "The Time Warrior", and notice how *he* knows about Gallifrey). Later Sontaran ruses involve bootlegging the Time Lord DNA sections involved in full control of time (22.4, "The Two Doctors") and launching an assault on Gallifrey (15.6, "The Invasion of Time"). Recently, we've heard that they considered themselves in the running for a role in the Time Wars. That might sound like the standard Sontaran bluster, but if they'd even *heard* about this conflict, there must have a grain of truth in it. For this to be even conceivable, they must be at least at the level of the Time Lords in the era of Rassilon. Thus, linear chronology might be a red herring. And even if we rule out time-shenanigans on their side, the Rutans are also riffing on Time Lord skills in 1901 (15.1, "Horror of Fang Rock").

It's when we look at the Sontarans as they have appeared over the course of the broadcast stories that the next flaw in the story appears. If they're clones, why do they all look so different? Well, the Doctor identifies Linx as a Sontaran Warrior, as though they had other types. As the only Sontarans we've ever seen have all been soldiers, it's hard to make any generalisations. The point, though, is that we haven't got any on-screen confirmation that Linx and the two we encounter 1985 - Stike and Varl - are clones *at all*, let alone all cloned from the same stock. Assuming them all to be identical forever and across all categories leads to logical absurdities when speculating on their military nature - how there can be a chain of command, how you get a promotion and so on.

So even if Stike and Varl were scientists rather than warriors (and hold military ranks simply to get the troops to obey their orders), the four "standard" height troop-types vary considerably, even if troops from any given era look the same as one another. You might expect a lot more variation had they experienced a using atomic weapons - this might in itself be a good reason to start cloning, to minimise the risk of harmful or unpredictable mutations. But the entire plot of the 2008 two-parter is that they need a whole new planet on which to breed - and yet, unlike practically every other story that season, it's not because their homeworld has mysteriously vanished. Although the Sontarans are keen to establish Earth as a clone-world, despite there being so many better candidates with suitable gravity and pink sunlight, this seems to be an extraordinary measure for them.

That being the case, it's possible that we've been misled by something we were constantly told: that Holmes crafted a detailed history of the Sontarans for Bob Baker and Dave Martin before a word of "The Sontaran Experiment" was written. It's widely assumed that this document was devised before or during the writing of "The Time Warrior", but this is doubtful. The plans for that story (along with the details in Holmes' contribution to the novelisation) make clear that Linx came from a race of *cyborgs* - and we know from the background paperwork to this story that it was a last-minute piece. It's entirely possible, then, that Holmes' future-history was written up only *after* he'd seen Kevin Lindsey in that mask, and that his conception of the Sontarans was influenced by the alterations and improvisations that happened during the making of the story. (Holmes *did* apparently go to the filming, but only remembered incidental details about British Rail breakfasts when asked later.) All we can say with absolute certainty is that it was routine for Sontarans to be cloned by the twenty-first century (X4.4, "The Sontaran Strategem" and "The Poison Sky"), but that a quarter-century earlier - during the Madellon Cluster campaign ("The Two Doctors") - there were at least two officers significantly taller than is usual.

Of course, the whole cloning issue only came up in "The Sontaran Experiment". It was one of

continued on page 399...

ABOUT TIME 1970-1974

the Sontarans as one of the greats.

2. So the producer has decreed that the Doctor's new companion is into Women's Lib, and what do the writers do? Give her something to complain about by giving *all* the characters sexist dialogue. "The Time Warrior" seems distinctly ruder than any other *Doctor Who* story of the period. All the women are 'wenches', and all the guards are 'lusty'; and Irongron refers to Sarah's 'taille', while Linx inspects her differently-shaped thorax. When it comes to the Doctor's relationship with his companion, Professor Rubeish becomes the first character to speak for the audience's mind with his, 'I should've thought he was a bit old for that sort of thing.' Rubeish also offers several other comments that were cut, concerning female brains not being good enough for science. Even Lady Eleanor is commented on, and she's Dot Cotton in a wimple.

3. Great cost-cutting dialogue of our time... observe how Irongron and his lads stall investigation of the falling star until daylight (to avoid a night shoot); marvel at the way all of Edward's men are at the Crusades; witness Rubeish cutting off an objection from one of the scientists, so they don't have to pay one of the extras 25 guineas for spoken dialogue; gaze in wonder at the lack of any food on Irongron's table. Then look at where the money went: a *lot* more extras than usual, but nowhere near enough to storm a castle (certainly not with that squitty little ladder).

4. One scene in Part Three, in which the Doctor and Sarah dress up as monks in order to get into Irongron's castle, is notable not only for the atrocious period acting of the two guards (relatives, perhaps, of the two from 14.1, "The Masque of Mandragora", who fear going down into the catacombs). But Comedy Accent of the Week comes from Jon Pertwee dressed as a monk - it was his comedy "Postman" voice from radio sitcom *Waterlogged Spa*, the same as he'll use for *Worzel Gummidge*, half a decade later.

The Continuity

The Doctor Still seems to see Earth as a base of operations, even though his TARDIS is in full working order and with Jo gone there's presumably nothing keeping him here. [The Third Doctor might still feel an affectionate attachment to UNIT, though this changes after he regenerates at the end of the season. It certainly seems convenient

for him. As he tells Linx, 'I'm just a tourist, I like it here.' Since we last saw him he may have spent some time working on the "Whomobile", which turns up in the next story, and he seems to be looking for things to occupy his time on Earth; see also the IRIS experiments in 11.5, "Planet of the Spiders".] He says he's not much of an artist, and would like to study under one of the great masters, preferably Rembrandt.

The Doctor seems to like Sarah Jane Smith on their first meeting, but principally because he enjoys annoying her. Here he's deliberately sexist in her presence [just to see the look on her face]. He's also of the opinion that the Brigadier 'means well.'

• *Ethics*. The Doctor believes that if Linx gives the secret of firearms to the people of the Middle Ages, then humanity will have nuclear weapons by the seventeenth century, before they're 'civilised' enough to handle the technology. [This is exactly the same point he made when the Monk tried to re-fit human history in "The Time Meddler", this story's direct ancestor. But the Doctor's vendetta with the Monk came across as a matter of personal pride rather than an attempt to save history, whereas here he finally seems to be acting like a Time Lord by defending the timeline. His implication that twentieth-century humans *are* civilised enough for nuclear weapons is questionable, especially in light of his comments in 8.5, "The Daemons".] When dining with the nobility, he demonstrates a willingness to fit in with their customs. [Even though Charles Laughton, playing Henry VIII, invented the "custom" of throwing a chicken bone over one's shoulder.]

• *Inventory*. He uses a pen-torch to break Linx's hypnosis. [This isn't powerful as his original one (going all the way back to 1.1, "An Unearthly Child"), which was bright enough to make paint fade. As you'll recall from Volume I, this was almost the original Doctor's only gadget, and in Volume II, we note that it was converted into the original sonic screwdriver.]

He also uses a kind of parasol - a discoid Venetian blind - to shield himself from Linx's gun. [This looks like a bigger version of the portable reflectors used by photographers, but we can't find any evidence that any were available in that size in 1973. We even asked for a look at catalogues from the time.]

What Caused the Sontaran-Rutan War?

...continued from page 397

those attempts to use a new and catchy scientific buzzword. (The same authors did this with 'black holes', as we saw in 10.1, "The Three Doctors". They also tried cloning again, less successfully, with 15.2, "The Invisible Enemy".) Fandom sometimes fools itself into thinking that the cloning angle goes back as far as "The Time Warrior", but in truth there's no explicit mention of this. For all we can tell from Linx's comments about this ('a million cadets are hatched at each muster parade'), baby Sontarans might have budded off from adults. Certainly, there's no mention of their being identical. Recently, "The Last Sontaran" (the start of *The Sarah Jane Adventures* Series Two) established that they don't even have children, so the Sontaran hatchlings must be born fully-grown.

Indeed, in later comments Holmes rather backtracked from the original idea of the Sontarans being totally devoted to war. True, they were entirely committed to winning this conflict against a thoroughly-determined opponent, and had subjugated all else to the need to victory for the duration - not anticipating that "the duration" would be measured in millennia. Holmes claimed that they switched to cloning as a desperate expedient. That's borne out by some of what we see on screen, especially in "The Time Warrior" (in which Linx sagely advises that a primary-secondary reproductive cycle, i.e. male-female, is inefficient and that we should 'change' it).

What we can say with certainty is that a cloned species *can't* just evolve. But if they're adapted, and seem to be a warrior caste of another species, then from whom? Moreover, *by* whom? Well, Styre ("The Sontaran Experiment") speaks of 'liberation'. Is it possible that Rutans created the Sontarans as slaves? This has been proposed a number of times, and it's appealing. Not only do the adaptations which make them warriors *sans puer et sans reproche* work equally well for slaves, but they're adapted for a high gravity environment. When we do finally see a Rutan, the jelly blob has difficulty with Earth's pull, and has a crystalline spaceship. However, as they're seemingly aquatic, the Rutans could conceivably come from the same world as the Sontarans - provided they could build spaceships underwater. Both species have the ability to absorb energy directly. The Rutans aren't the most practical of species and might have *made* themselves manual labourers, even though anyone who'd designed a race to do this would have per-

haps put more thought into the hands. Or, and this is possibly more plausible, they enslaved another race on their world (or a nearby one) and selectively bred them. Neither of these scenarios explains how the Sontarans got spaceships, but we don't really need to. So long as no theory rules out anything we've seen, we can speculate along these lines for ages. After all, it's only the marketing department of BBC Worldwide that claims that the Sontarans were "Bred for War".

But does it *have* to have been the Rutans? Many other races claim to have conquered half the cosmos. The Dominators (6.1, you can guess the title) test indigenous species to find out if they form a threat or a potential workforce, as do the Sontarans (in the eponymous "Sontaran Experiment"). The Doctor describes their servants, the Quarks, as 'machine-creatures' and they recharge themselves - just like Sontarans. Even the hunched, dome-like profile of a Sontaran seems hauntingly familiar if you look at a Dominator side-on.

More intriguingly, though, the war *can't* have lasted for fifty thousand years without the Sontarans and Rutans alike possessing space-travel and similar scale abilities for most of that time. Had either side been confined to any one planet, the other could have wiped them out fairly early on. (For that matter, it's hard to credit that a war in which only one side has time-technology could go on for so long without the other side suffering an absolute defeat. It's easy enough to imagine that Rutan shape-changers *have* infiltrated the Sontaran army and had a look at their technology, as some of the novels claim.)

According to the Doctor, the 50,000 date is the time they've been fighting a space-war - so the two species could just as easily be from opposite ends of the same galaxy, or two different galaxies. It's unlikely that a maladroit species such as the Sontarans developed their technology unaided. (Why *else* would Linx kidnap human scientists to work in his? Why else would Styre test humans for their resilience?) Certainly, unlike most beings in the Third Zone, the Sontarans have no qualms about 'diluting' racial purity in order to secure victory (even though they are originally said to be 'rabidly xenophobic'). Neither, if the Doctor's comments are to be believed, did the Rutans who made themselves 'shape-shifters'.

Intriguingly, that date also puts the start of the

continued on page 401...

• *Background.* The Doctor recognises Linx as a Sontaran, and knows the Sontarans' history. [It could be argued that he remembers them from the events of 22.4, "The Two Doctors", but this seems unlikely as the garbled implication of that story is that his personal history's being changed. Well, perhaps. More to the point, in "The Two Doctors", even the Second Doctor seems to know of the Sontarans - suggesting an encounter early on in the Doctor's travels.]

He's familiar with the work of Sarah's aunt Lavinia, having read her work on the teleological response of the virus, published at least a decade and a half ago [once again, he's taking an interest in "modern" human science]. He hints also that he's a member of the Royal Society.

Perhaps most intriguing is that he recognises Professor Henderson - an as-yet unnamed abductee - who's wandering around the castle in his pyjamas. [There *might* have been an unscreened meeting at the Hostel, but as transmitted, the implication is that the Doctor is well-enough connected to have been to colloquia with prominent scientists of the day and may be trying to get any missing doctorates for his collection. However, this makes his ignorance of Professor Whitaker's work in the next story more singular.]

The Supporting Cast

• *Sarah Jane Smith.* A young, smart, resourceful but determined journalist, Sarah quickly becomes the Doctor's new sidekick, even though - unusually - she initially regards him with distrust. [Sarah's character, it must be said, is vastly different in this story to her later appearances. After Season Twelve, she becomes a lot more playful, almost child-like in her relationship with the Fourth Doctor, but here she's constantly determined to show how tough she is. She'll always be pro-active, but here it's at her own behest.] She adopts the persona of serving-girl-pretending-to-be-noble very convincingly, improvising in character better even than 'Princess Josephine' in "The Curse of Peladon" (9.2). She loudly objects to being patronised and struggles like a trooper when man-handled. By story's end, a bond is obviously beginning to form between her and the Doctor.

Sarah has an aunt, Lavinia Smith, who's a renowned virologist and currently on a lecture tour in America. [The date in the script is 1974, which means that Lavinia's "The Teleological

Response of the Virus" was written in the mid-1950s, just after DNA's structure was deduced. If that's the case, Lavinia must have been more assertive than Rosalind Franklin, who got side-lined by Crick and Watson when the quest for the double-helix was written up. We now know that Lavinia raised her niece from infancy.]

• *UNIT.* Unsurprisingly, Sarah's heard of it. Surprisingly, she doesn't know it's involved in investigating missing Government scientists [uh?] and doesn't seem to recognise Lethbridge-Stewart from all his TV appearances [She never actually talks to him in this story, but he somehow knows her in the next story.] The Doctor working for UNIT comes as more of a revelation to Sarah than the time-travel or extraterrestrials.

[All right, let's stop and deal with the inconsistency of what Sarah does and doesn't know about UNIT's workings. There's an interesting possibility concerning her involvement with them in the Pertwee stories that explains a lot about her later career...

[Consider that nobody at Guy Crayford's reception committee (13.4, "The Android Invasion") seems even slightly surprised to see the Fourth Doctor and Sarah at the Space Defence Station, even though they hadn't known that anything was afoot there. It happens that the nation's space-security is falls UNIT jurisdiction, with the Brigadier having a permanent office at the station and Harry Sullivan being in charge of the medical wing. Sarah *must* have had a security pass to cover the story about Crayford being lost in space, which might suggest that she met Harry *before* she met the Doctor. Certainly, she seems to know Harry better in "The Ark in Space" (12.2) than their brief meetings at the comatose Doctor's bed-side in "Robot" (12.1) would seem to allow.

[So did the World Ecology Bureau call the Doctor direct for help (13.6, "The Seeds of Doom"), or did Sarah's sources *know* that something was up? And without benefit of such a source, how would Sarah have even known of the Think Tank's existence in "Robot"? For that matter, in her own series Sarah has a UNIT training manual in her attic - she may even have written it (her name's on the cover). As you can see, it's starting to look as if Sarah is better connected to UNIT than her "haphazard" meeting and association with the Third Doctor might suggest.

[Two obvious possibilities present themselves, then. It's possible that UNIT goes beyond the nor-

What Caused the Sontaran-Rutan War?

...continued from page 399

war firmly into the period when - in this galaxy at least - the Daemons were up to their horns in genetic and cultural mischief. We've hazarded some guesses about *their* motives (see **The Daemons - What the Hell Are They Doing?** under 8.5), but whilst the Rutans might plausibly have been a client race of theirs, the cloning thing - had it begun right at the start - seems out of keeping with the Daemonic notion of giving a species a nudge and then seeing what happens. Perhaps this is itself a clue: if you want two species to evolve faster, set them at each other's throats (provided they *have* throats). Indeed, as the Sontarans don't seem to learn from their endless defeats, it might be that they were bred simply to give the Rutans target practice, to put *them* onto an evolutionary fast-track scheme. Genetically and technologically, with a few odd R&D schemes here and there, the Sontarans remain static, their culture "on hold" forever.

But whichever race created them, if the Sontarans were made to fight and found an opponent that didn't give in, that fight would go on indefinitely, regardless of whether their makers survived. For all their intelligence, they see themselves as walking weapons, not people.

Conversely, whilst the Rutans were getting good at strategy, they weren't exactly made for combat. The detail that makes this intriguing is that their morphing technique ("Horror of Fang Rock") - which is obviously very handy for surveillance and investigation, and is used by a being able to analyse alien anatomy and cognition (and accents) very fast - is said, in the novelisation by the TV story's author, to be 'experimental'. Certainly, the Doctor isn't automatically making any connections to Rutan activity in 1901 when he deduces that he's dealing with an ice-cold, electrophilic shape-shifter.

The big worry, therefore, is that there's no reason for a war between a race like this and the Sontarans to have lasted so long *unless* the Rutans have superior WMDs. Even then, considering they're up against a mighty and rapidly-replenished infantry, things might get difficult for the Rutans. The Sontaran military strategy calls for vast numbers of foot-soldiers in hand-to-hand (or appendage-to-appendage) combat. Conversely, the Rutans - possible points for their ability to wield electricity (although the Sontarans would surely insulate themselves), but minus for their comparatively fragile frames - are going to be rub-

continued on page 403...

---

mal secret-agent stuff, and employs a few civilian operatives - such as the odd science / human-interest journalist - to keep an eye out for things that might warrant investigation. Indeed, UNIT might well have a number of "stringers" who get a little extra if they take something they've found to the Brig before the editor gets to see it, the same way reporters for *The Times* or *The Daily Telegraph* were on a retainer for MI6. Did UNIT pay Sarah's way through university or the National Union of Journalists' college in return for first-call on her skills and contacts? It seems a bit odd, given the "random" means by which she stumbles into the Doctor's life in "The Time Warrior" - and the fact that she's able to pose as her aunt, and infiltrate a UNIT-guarded facility without anyone recognising her - but nothing especially discounts it. Note that, the way Sarah reacts to the Doctor being from UNIT in "The Time Warrior" is more "Why wasn't I told?" than "UNIT are involved in this?"

[The other possibility is just that she's been enough of a nuisance that the Brig has authorised her to work with him, as opposed to their tripping over one another, and she therefore got training in weapons and exobiology.

[These days, of course, we almost have the opposite problem: *The Sarah Jane Adventures* confirms that Sarah had UNIT training, but the very same episode ("Warriors of Kudlak" Part Two) hints that the manned landing on Mars has yet to happen. See "The Android Invasion" and 7.3, "The Ambassadors of Death" for why this matters. That adventure also sees Sarah build a teleport-detector (with a nod to the video for *Cloudbusting* by Kate Bush - see Volume V) using skills obviously not gained at the NUJ college in Harlow.]

[A last bit of UNIT business: assuming Linx's time travel is a corridor with no spatial displacement, the security building where the scientists are housed is in the West Country somewhere. It's *not* UNIT HQ, as the Brigadier and the Doctor have to travel there, the Brig isn't running the operation and they need to show passes. That doesn't rule out its being near to wherever UNIT is based this week, as it's clearly staffed by UNIT troops (seen nattering in the corridor when Sarah first arrives - not very military). Then again, as the scientists have been vanishing from all over the country, it's likely that Linx *is* using a spatial as well as temporal corridor.]

The TARDIS There's coffee-making equipment inside the Ship, as well as a reflective fan that can block a Sontaran hypno-weapon. The Doctor summons up the equipment to build a "rondium sensor" which detects the delta-particles involved in Sontaran time-projection.

There's also a 'black light' box [see 23.1, "The Mysterious Planet"] that reveals the ghost-image of Linx at the research centre, apparently high-lighting the point where the Sontaran materialised in the twentieth century, and the Doctor uses it to track down the source of the matter transmission. The Doctor uses this device to track the source of the matter transmission. A time-journey seems to be enough to remove equations that Rubeish chalked on the TARDIS exterior [see also 18.1, "The Leisure Hive", but cf. 25.2, "The Happiness Patrol" and X1.5, "World War Three"].

The *main* thing to say here, though, is that the Doctor pilots the Ship to Linx's base of operations straight off, with no detours. [As far as we know, but any longer in flight and he would probably have found Sarah hiding. For the second time in two stories, he's got where he wanted to go. From now on, unexpected landings will be less frequent and often prompted by SOS calls or outside influences.]

The Time Lords The Doctor's homeworld is Gallifrey, and the Doctor states that the Time Lords are keen on stamping out unlicensed time-travel, telling Sarah to think of them as 'galactic ticket inspectors'. [The first time this is ever established, but it's key to the way they're portrayed in later stories. "Unlicensed" suggests that they license certain people to travel in time; unlikely, but see 24.3, "Delta and the Bannermen"; "The Two Doctors" and 22.5, "Timelash".]

The Doctor indicates that Time Lords are no longer young once they're over two hundred.

The Non-Humans

• *Sontarans.* Squat, powerful beings with dome-shaped heads and no visible necks, the Sontarans have leering gargoyle-like faces. The species has no females, its culture being so utterly obsessed by war that sexual reproduction is too slow and hap-

hazard. The suggestion here is that while creatures like the Daleks and Cybermen are ruthlessly determined to conquer the universe, the Sontarans just want a good fight.

At the Sontaran academy, a million cadets are hatched at each muster parade. The gravity on the Sontaran planet is many times that of Earth, and Linx is said to weigh 'several tons' there, so Sontarans are physically strong but designed for load-bearing rather than leverage. Conveniently, this makes them easy to tie up. Rather than eating, a Sontaran "recharges" through a probic vent at the back of the neck, but the vent is vulnerable and a blow to it easily fells Linx. [The armour leaves it uncovered, so it must be important to keep the vent, um, ventilated.] Sontarans like to see this weakness as a virtue, since it means they always have to meet the enemy face-to-face.

The Sontarans have been at war with the Rutans for millennia [see 15.1, "The Horror of Fang Rock"], and Linx claims that there isn't a galaxy in the universe which his species hasn't subjugated. [This sounds like the stuff of propaganda - presumably, they didn't hold every galaxy at the same time.] Linx crashed to Earth while on a reconnaissance mission, though he states that Earth is of no strategic importance [this changes thousands of years in the future for 12.3, "The Sontaran Experiment"]. Like many military imperialists, he sees the war as a struggle for 'freedom' and anything without a military function is an irrelevance to him. He's Commander of the Fifth Army Space Fleet in the Sontaran Army Space Corps, and has his own 'squadron'.

The flag of the Sontaran Empire is white with a little 'S'. [Perhaps it's being translated into an Earth-based alphabet for our benefit... q.v. the 'H' that the King's Champion scribbles in "The Curse of Peladon". But it might be a spiral galaxy, as on closer inspection it looks more like two crescents with a bulbous join. The sound made as the flag pops open is stated as being the Sontaran National Anthem in the book (see **The Lore**).] Linx knows of Gallifrey and the Time Lords, but Sontaran intelligence believes them to lack the morale to face a determined assault.

Linx's spacecraft is an egg-like metal pod, only big enough for one soldier but, like its owner, it's 'tremendously powerful' for its size and the technology on board is evidently impressive. Linx adjusts his ship's 'frequency modulator' to project himself several hundred years in the future and

What Caused the Sontaran-Rutan War?

...continued from page 401

bish at that. So it's probably best to conclude that the Rutans use a lot of intermediaries. We know that the Sontarans are interested in the potential of humans as cannon fodder, even though they're vastly superior to us as warriors. Perhaps the Sontaran Experiments were about determining what use, if any, incoming Rutans could have put the humans to rather than Sontarans using them. The fact that we keep hearing how such-and-such a planet (usually Earth) is strategically important or unimportant makes less sense if you think of it as a conventional space-war (if such a thing can exist) and more a matter of supply-lines and materiel.

But if humans are being evaluated for use in a war between Rutan-backed forces and Sontarans, are the Sontarans themselves - in the stories and time-periods where we encounter them - being used as proxies by another race? This might have been plausible when the earlier stories were written, but "The Invasion of Time" calls the point into question. In this story, the Sontarans are themselves using the Vardans as patsies in a campaign to conquer Gallifrey. They needed a great deal of subterfuge to get this close, but even in the thirteenth century, Linx thought that the Time Lords lacked the wherewithal to keep the Sontarans out of their homeworld indefinitely. Exactly how the Sontarans know this is another matter. As we said, they knew about the Time Wars, but were forbidden to participate. They also knew a great deal about the Third Zone and sponsored the Kartz-Reimer experiments into time travel.

However humble their origins possibly were, then, the Sontarans have become - cosmically speaking - players. After a point, nobody who could use *them* as they used the Vardans would need to. So we can pretty much rule out the Daleks and the Time Lords as either their creators or the instigators of the war. Whoever is doing the actual fighting, the Sontarans were one of the original combatants. It might - and this sort of twist is in keeping with the species and their real-world creator, who was much more proprietorial with them than, say, the Drashings or Autons - turn out that a pre-emptive strike by time-commandos actually started the war. We cannot know, although it might be significant that the Dalek-Time Lord conflict is called the '*last*' of the great Time Wars' on a number of occasions.

Symbolically, however, the point about the Sontarans being clones and the point about the war lasting forever are the same. The Sontarans and Rutans are knocking lumps out of each other, unchangingly, for all of time. The fact that the war seems not to have a reason beyond itself is part of what they represent. The Sontarans, with their bullet-heads, moustaches and wasp-waists, are Teutonic officers, lacking only monocles *unt tcherrrmen exhents*. They live for war, and that's all we need to know until we see them in action again.

take scientists back to his own time. The ship's 'osmic projector' is an important part of this process. [It seems incredible that the Sontarans have this sort of technology, let alone that such a small vessel is equipped with it. Compare this with 15.6, "The Invasion of Time", in which the Sontarans want the time-travel secrets of the Time Lords. Indeed, see "The Two Doctors", in which they have considerably less advanced technology than we see here, despite that story being set in 1985.

[Two possibilities arise: either the Sontaran-Rutan war went really badly and the Sontarans were set back millennia (as "Horror of Fang Rock" tenuously indicates), or Linx is using the time-corridor technology to escape the Rutan scout by travelling back to the thirteenth century. Evidence for the former comes from comparing the Scout probe sent by Styre ("The Sontaran Experiment") with the vastly superior ones used by Kaagh (*The Sarah Jane Adventures*: "The Last Sontaran") a minimum of 11,000 years earlier. The technology obviously improves and suffers in cycles.

[If we go with the latter theory - which makes more sense in many ways - then perhaps Linx is wrecking Earth's history to cause a big enough disruption in the timelines that his own people will spot him, a kind of "beacon". It's an intriguing theory, but a flawed one: you would first have to account for the fact that he's kidnapping twentieth-century scientists as opposed to (ooh, let's see) 1813, where there's genii aplenty, and interfering with *their* history and contributions to science would be far more damaging (see 22.3, "The Mark of the Rani"). Or Linx could just have pick 'n' mixed from Quattrocento Florence or carted off the entire Manhattan Project. In any case, if he were *seriously* attempting this, he shouldn't have sounded quite so surprised when a Time Lord sticks his nose in.]

Linx also has the resources to build a robot "knight", unkillable even when beheaded but with only rudimentary intelligence. Sontaran 'space-armour' consists of a silver-black body-suit and an imposing domed helmet, while Linx carries a wand-like firearm that can kill, stun, burn metal, make weapons fly out of people's hands or hypnotise human captives with its light. There's a translator-box on his belt.

On this occasion, Sontarans have two fingers and a thumb on each hand. Linx's skin is brown rather than grey [c.f. "The Sontaran Experiment"]. The Doctor seems to indicate that not all Sontarans are in the military, since he instantly recognises Linx's species but needs confirmation that he's a Sontaran *warrior*.

• *Rutans.* Though not seen here, they have squadrons of fighters.

History

• *Dating.* [On UNIT's timeline, mid-to-late 1974 seems likely; see **What's the UNIT Timeline?** under 8.5, "The Daemons".]

Linx crash-lands on Earth during the early Middle Ages, in the region of Wessex at a time when all the troops are fighting 'interminable wars' abroad. ['Interminable wars' is usually taken to suggest the Crusades. It's possible that Robert Holmes had this in mind, since every British schoolchild is supposed to know about Richard the Lionheart, and the Crusader era is one of those historical backgrounds that TV scriptwriters used to take for granted. When a generic "man from history" is accidentally brought to the twentieth century in "Invasion of the Dinosaurs" (11.2), he too insists on talking about Good King Richard.

[In "The Sontaran Experiment", Sarah states that Linx died in the thirteenth century rather than the twelfth. Then again, she's panicking at the time. It could be time of King Steven (1135-54), and the conflict caused over the right of Queen Matilda / Maud to rule despite having her genitals on the inside (why this isn't counted as our first Civil War is a mystery), which would make the "votes for women" comments in episode four especially apposite (see also 11.4, "The Monster of Peladon"). This period was much studied in the mid-70s - unsurprising, as it involved an attempted coup because of runaway inflation and Womens' Rights (see **Who's**

Running the Country under 10.5, "The Green Death"). Technically, Wessex ceased to exist a decade or so after the Norman conquest of 1066, but the only character who uses the name here is the Norman-hating Irongron, who's perhaps pining for the good old Anglo-Saxon days (even though these have been over for four generations at least). In itself, the use of the word 'Norman' might suggest the 1100s and not the 1200s. There is now a real-life Edward, Earl of Wessex (the Queen's youngest son got the title re-created as a wedding-present in 1999).] Lord Salisbury is also mentioned.

Meanwhile, in the present... the British have a high-security top-secret research facility full of scientists, working on space hardware and 'new alloys'. Professor Ruebish states that the loop theory of time has been 'arrogantly dismissed by Crabshaw and his cronies'. [Compare this with time-travel research in "Invasion of the Dinosaurs".] Somehow, the military restrictions on hair-length for men have been relaxed for UNIT personnel.

The Analysis

Where Does This Come From? Producers and BBC accountants like historical romps; writers and some viewers don't. The compromise, aliens jeopardising the "correct" run of Earth history, is now possible simply because the public are in on the gag. In "The Time Meddler", half of episode four is spent explaining why it's a bad thing to rewrite the past. Here, half of episode two is spent with Sarah the butt of the audience's ridicule for *not* twigging that she's been whisked nine centuries back in a dimensionally transcendental police box and that the Doctor is a friendly alien. As with "The Time Meddler" back in 1965, the big joke is that our technology is as good as it will ever get. This ultimately dates back to the first use of time-travel for humour, Mark Twain's A Connecticut Yankee in King Arthur's Court (1889). Of course, it shouldn't be forgotten that the middle ages were a common subject for historical dramas; the BBC adaptations in the early 1970s ran out of Tudors fairly fast. The availability of sets and costumes from stock must have made it irresistible.

At the basic level, the Sontarans are a parody of the martial traditions of ninteenth-century Europe, especially Germany. Holmes took the concept of a culture mentally prepared to sacrifice anything for victory to extremes. We might also note that the two named Saxon warlords are given warrior names: Irongron was a Danish chieftain and Erik Bloodaxe was the father of Leif Erikson (see, once again, "The Time Meddler"). Erikson had been used in at least one fairly recent book Holmes seems to have read, Harry Harrison's *The Technicolor Time Machine* (1967), in which a Hollywood company films epics on location in the past. We know that Dicks also read Harrison, and that Holmes had a very similar style and view of the world to the iconoclastic American author. But why might this book have been on his mind?

Linx is stranded on a backward planet and becomes unpaid scientific advisor to a local military leader. Sound familiar? This "fish out of water" set-up is something Holmes would revisit to better effect in "The Talons of Weng-Chiang" (14.6). Holmes' original plot breakdown played on the idea of the Japanese soldier refusing to believe that the war was over and Japan didn't win. In combining this with Thomas Hobbes' *Leviathan* (the source quoted when the Doctor labels Linx as 'nasty, brutish and short'), in which a monarchy is the only bulwark against "a war of all against all" (written soon after Charles I was beheaded), Holmes had a laboratory ready-made for his thought-experiment. It's a cliché to have advanced aliens seeing humans as "primitive", but what if one landed when we really *were*? Moreover, what if the alien, for all his technology, was in favour of all the things we like to think technology will cure us of liking? Can we really say we're so much better than Saxon warlords if we've invented the Winchester 67 and the atom bomb? Just because it's an alien in the Middle Ages who's collected all these scientists to build weapons, is that any better than Her Majesty's Government and UNIT doing the same? Coerced into doing a story in history, Holmes obeys instructions and rebels at the same time.

Once again, Holmes is using SF as a satirical distorting mirror. And once again, *Galaxy* magazine in the 1950s routinely did this sort of story. We should also mention Poul Anderson's novel *The High Crusade* (1960), in which members of an English village hijack a crashed spaceship and then attempt to sack - er, sorry, *liberate* - France and the Holy Land, but wind up capturing a galactic empire instead. In various forms, hubris can be found in every Season Eleven story, with human achievements belittled and human dignity compromised. As is that of the Time Lords: the saints of the story that began the previous season are now reduced to the status of 'galactic ticket inspectors'. Some might snivel at the choice of the name 'Gallifrey'[131] for the Doctor's home planet, but it sounds like a place rather than a kicked-over scrabble-board and is a lot better than the name proposed in *TV Comic*, "Jewel".

In the end, though, "The Time Warrior" marks another turning point for the series. Since the advent of the colour / Pertwee era, *Doctor Who* has been a mixture of pseudo-topical Earth-bound stories and tales set on dystopian quarry-planets, but this looks like a series that wants to try something a lot more lush (its period setting suggests much higher production values than something like "Frontier in Space", but then again, the BBC has *always* been better at historicals than space-operas) and much more escapist. There are also notable similarities to Robert Holmes' next pseudo-historical, "The Pyramids of Mars" (13.3), including a trapped alien, a big bang at the end and an unlikely attempt by the Doctor to disguise himself as a servitor robot.

Yet Holmes wrote this under protest to suit Dicks' plans to get the series back doing what it did when he arrived before all of the Earthbound UNIT stories. And Dicks was himself adjusting awkwardly to the demands of an audience fed up with bimbos who get captured and scream. After all, this is the first time a new female lead has been introduced since the UK edition of *Cosmopolitan* began in a blaze of publicity. However much Sarah becomes Lois Lane by "Robot", she's emphatically rooted in the magazine culture of *Cosmo* and its native precursor *Nova*. And however much we might find fault with the sexual politics of this story, it's worth noting that *the Doctor* doesn't find anything strange in a woman writing a groundbreaking paper on virology twenty years earlier. What will become interesting is how far Sarah tries to live up to an image that's already current in the media of strong women who can do everything - Shirley Conran's book *Superwoman* is only just around the corner - and occasionally falls short ("The Ark in Space" is a prime example, in the way the Doctor teases her into succeeding). Sarah becomes a character at precisely the point where she *fails* to be a stereotype. Proof of this is that the only way anyone can follow her once she leaves the series is by being completely wilful and semi-feral, or completely cerebral and sardonic. Or a computer that looks like a dog.

Things That Don't Make Sense Starting with the most notorious point: everyone *seems* to know the gaffe about Sarah peeling potatoes, evidently three hundred years before Sir Walter Raleigh brought them here. Except that, er, this glitch was in the novelisation, and (insofar as we can tell, after giving the DVD some intense root-vegetable scrutiny) doesn't appear on screen. Sarah doesn't actually peel anything, and the one thing that *might* be a potato - the first vegetable she picks up off the table - is probably an onion. However, British viewers who spend a lot of time at the greengrocer's would have spotted that the apple that Irongron uses for target practice is a Cox's Orange Pippin, a variety not grown until 1825 (and widely held to be the most apple-ish apples on the planet).

Irongron is eating and drinking when 'it wants but an hour 'til dawn'. So how late, exactly, did they stay up? Or did they all say Matins? A bigger problem with the same scene is why neither the supposedly-devious Linx nor the supposedly-dim-but-experienced-and-not-killed-yet Irongron don't think to let the messenger continue on his errand, his memory of the interrogation discreetly wiped. They could thus get the drop on Edward, now that they know precisely how few troops he has, but before his reinforcements arrive.

And isn't it a little odd that in making weapons for Irongron, Linx starts by making guns that look *exactly* like human firearms from later centuries, as opposed to making low-tech weapons based on Sontaran technology? 477

It's been argued that Linx pilfers his arsenal from a twentieth century arms supply - but if so, why does he have rifles and bullets, rather than something more formidable such as machine guns? Or why doesn't he lift the Dematerialisation Gun from Think Tank ["Robot"] or - if that's too powerful a weapon to give to primitives, for some reason - just a tank? Would that spoil the sport of it all? Anyway, it's clear he's got his kidnapped eggheads actively *building* the guns, which makes even less sense if they're mostly, if not all, theoretical physicists or eminent virologists.

In fact, why are *these* goofy boffins the optimum R & D team that Linx requires? The two tasks he requires help with, let's not forget, are fixing his spaceship and arming Irongron. So how does Linx, some time in the Norman occupation of England, know who's going to be available in the 1970s *just in England*, for some reason, with the

practical skills to help him? Obviously, he's not after raw brain power [if that were the case, then it's bizarre that he captures clever people and then stuns them into drone-like compliance]. He *must* be after technical prowess, but if so, he'd probably have been far better off abducting Victorian engineers. They're not just closer to his time (making it all the easier to transport them in larger numbers), they're better at making guns with a small forge.

Back in the modern-day, exactly how crap is security at the research facility, if UNIT doesn't realise that Sarah isn't her aunt Lavinia, who's a *lot* older? Even Professor Rubeish deduces that Sarah is a ringer, yet UNIT - tasked with protecting the world from alien invaders - somehow doesn't. And for what reason does Sarah suggest to Rubeish that the Doctor is a spy? By that point, other than being condescending to her, what has he done to warrant such a charge? [Unless it's a double-bluff to maintain her cover?] And why does the Doctor ask Sarah 'Have you ever heard of UNIT?' in Part One when, setting everything we've seen about the group's high profile over the past four seasons, the fact that UNIT was guarding the scientists (Sarah included) should have been a bit of a clue? And if we're being honest, Sarah doesn't really seem to notice or acknowledge that the console room's abnormal size beyond a very cursory comment of, 'still only a police box' once she exits the Ship. This is especially puzzling, considering that she must have deliberately hid in the interior rooms so the Doctor wouldn't discover her.

Which brings us to a bigger point, one we've pussy-footed around in various instalments of **The Continuity**... why the hell is the Doctor, who's spent five years or more trying to leave 1970s Britain and explore the universe again, lurking around UNIT HQ and wasting taxpayers' money on a stupid new car, some ESP experiments that could alter history if he's not careful, and the occasional jaunt in Bessie for the sake of it [20.7, "The Five Doctors"]. If we take the novelisation's hint - that the Brigadier involved the Doctor in this case specifically to help him get over Jo's dumping him - this is an *especially* odd thing to do. Why hang around a building and people with so much emotional baggage, when you can just go golliwhacking around space and time? [Later, we'll see in 12.5, "Revenge of the Cybermen" that the Doctor has set up a paging system - a 'space-time telegraph' - for UNIT to summon him in a crisis. But here, it's hard to see how a little local difficulty with a few missing boffins is big enough to warrant calling the Doctor back from the assorted pleasure-planets we always hear about but never see. Just imagine: he's confronted with an army of Raston Warrior Robots, armed only with his Venusian Aikido and a halibut, and the phone rings...]

Anyway, when did the disappearance of government scientists automatically become a matter for UNIT? And if it *is* of importance, then why wasn't of Professor Whitaker's abrupt absence a top priority matter for the Brigadier? This wouldn't be so irritating if it didn't come up in *the very next story*, in which the Brigadier recalls Whitaker being turned down for a government grant, but is unaware that the man has vanished. Worse, nobody speculates that Whitaker's disappearance might be related to Linx's kidnappings. Okay, *we* know they aren't, but the last thing the Brigadier hears is the Doctor's suggestion that the scientists have been taken back in time, and then suddenly dinosaurs start turning up in London. A single line of dialogue might have solved all of this, but for once, Terrance missed a trick.

The Doctor tells Sarah that he's concocted a smoking mixture of 'saltpetre, sulphur and fat, with a few little extras thrown in' - but once it's put to use, Sarah *still* feels the need to ask, 'What was that stuff, Doctor? Some kind of gas?' We might also wonder how the Doctor obtained saltpetre at short notice in a besieged castle in Wessex - the main way was to sieve dung through ash and leave it for a year. Even *then*, it was a waste-product of soap-making; using it for anything - fertiliser, then glass - came a century later. (And let's not worry about how *Linx* got hold of enough to make gunpowder.) During the scuffle at the end of Part Two, Pertwee's stunt-double grabs a spear just as he falls - yet it mysteriously vanishes in close-up.

Something that *looks* like a goof, but probably isn't: one of Rubeish's colleagues (the one wearing a grey sweater and brown jacket) twitches his head and mouth in time to the line, 'Can I ask...', whereupon Rubeish replies, 'Oh, Morrison, don't start asking a lot of awkward questions.' But when it's time for the scientists to go home, we discover that Morrison is the bald gentleman in the grey stripy shirt. Rubeish is *probably* talking to this man after all, but he's standing off camera, making the other bloke's head twitch seem very odd. If it's a joke at the expense of Rubeish's eyesight, it seems

odd that his hearing and voice-recognition haven't compensated.

The story concludes with Linx's spaceship exploding and Irongron's castle going up in smoke along with it. In line with the usual morality of TV programmes, the Doctor makes sure that everyone gets out of the cataclysm except for the two main villains. The trouble is that nobody stops to think about the wenches in the kitchen, all of whom presumably get blasted into pieces.

Critique The first and most obvious thing to say is that Pertwee seems perfectly happy doing a historical story. Remember, apart from the whole Atlantis debacle (9.5, "The Time Monster"), this is his only real trip into the past. In other stories (notably his last), he encounters pseudo-mediaeval planets, but the only real precedent for what happens here is - unsurprisingly - the 1920s sequences from Holmes' previous script (10.2, Carnival of Monsters").

Yet there's a simple reason why this formula was repeated afterwards: everyone involved knows what they're doing. The set designers can get a historically accurate set partly from stock and mainly from looking up or visiting the real thing, and the actors have familiarity with what's expected of them. Moreover, in *those* days, audiences had seen something similar and knew that different attitudes and customs existed back then. (These days, worryingly, any suggestion that the past wasn't like a fancy-dress version of either *The Sopranos* or whichever *Beverley Hills 90210*-surrogate you care to pick apparently cannot be comprehended by the viewers who've been brainwashed by The History Channel. Hence disasters such as *The Tudors* and - to a lesser extent - much of X3.2, "The Shakespeare Code". Indeed, the modern-sounding family in X4.2, "The Fires of Pompeii" have to be treated as a *Flintstones*-style joke that backfired.)

Meanwhile, everyone knows what a *Doctor Who* monster should be like and assumes that you can throw one at *any* historical setting and make a classic. That's the kind of sloppy thinking that led to "The Visitation" (19.4), and making it work requires more effort than even "The Time Warrior" seems to have taken... *seems* being the operative word. Because we know how smooth the production was, with regard to the filming and studio recording, we assume that this story was made almost negligently. Not so. A few of the effects are a little underweight, but the director consciously went in that direction. Alan Bromly's approach was to get everything done in the simplest way possible, then to rework the scenes into longer, more stagey takes. This would've seemed weird in any other story, but as he's apeing costume dramas anyway, the retro style doesn't seem too out of place.

This all seems more like a play than a four-part adventure serial. It shifts the emphasis onto the things that *aren't* right for the period, such as the alien and the visitors from the 1970s. Linx is a dominating presence even amongst louder, hairier and taller characters, and the reveal of his face at the end of the first episode is a textbook example of how to do such a thing. Kevin Lindsay's performance, *even from inside a tin hat*, is the focal point of the story. In many ways Linx is a re-run of the Master, not just for his gleeful messing with humans for his own ends, but for the poise of Lindsay's movements and the way he's Pertwee's physical opposite.

But before we get carried away with praise for this story, let's admit that a few features of it seem a little tiresome. The robot subplot is one of the weaker elements of the script, and the execution on screen doesn't redeem it any. The whole monk-disguise scene seems like an excuse for a Pertwee funny voice, Sarah's clunkily-scripted outbursts about being patronised are there for the Doctor to make jokes about, and his Venusian Aikido has firmly become a first-resort solution for all problems. It also gets a bit wearing that everyone is amazed - *amazed!* - by how great the Doctor is and talks about it. (Although to be fair, this is far less annoying than it could have been when taken with the scenes that occasionally poke fun at him, such as Irongron calling him 'a long-shanked rascal with a mighty nose' or the Doctor talking, from within the robot costume, like Bertie Wooster.)

Another sign that things are getting a bit comfortable and self-parody is that the music is starting to "Mickey Mouse" the action and play up the frivolity. Simpson has had his Radiophonic Workshop privileges withdrawn, and the music now uses whatever instruments he has handy. There's a keyboard element, but the settings are more conventional - the sort of thing found in mainstream pop - and the music for Season Eleven will be more like what comes later than what came before (except of course the one he didn't score, 11.3, "Death to the Daleks", which is just wrong).

But we can forgive so much of this, because of the confidence with which this adventure is conveyed. Just take a look at how - and this is a distinctly Season Eleven-ish feature - the Doctor gets in with the locals by eating with them. In one form or another, food is much more obviously significant in historical stories - but in particular the whole idea of doing a tale set in a castle lends itself to kitchens, trestle tables and tankards of ale. In fact, as with so much of "The Time Warrior", it looks at times like it was intended to be shown over Christmas all along.

The Facts

Written by Robert Holmes. Directed by Alan Bromly. Viewing figures: 8.7 million, 7.0 million, 6.6 million, 10.6 million. (See? The public thinks the series starts in the New Year.) The first and last episodes got AIs of 60%, but the rest weren't recorded.

Supporting Cast Kevin Lindsay (Linx), Donald Pelmear (Professor Rubeish), David Daker (Irongron), John J. Carney (Bloodaxe), June Brown (Eleanor), Alan Rowe (Edward of Wessex), Jeremy Bulloch (Hal), Sheila Fay (Meg).

Working Titles "The Time Fugitive", "The Time Survivor".

Cliffhangers Watching from the cover of some barrels in Irongron's courtyard, the Doctor sees Linx take off his helmet, and we're exposed to the face of a Sontaran for the first time; Irongron raises his axe to behead the Doctor; Linx replies to the Doctor's offer of help by raising his gun and firing.

What Was in the Charts? "Gaudete", Steeleye Span; "I Wish It Could Be Christmas Every Day", Wizzard; "Keep On Truckin' ", Eddie Kendricks; "Merry Xmas Everybody", Slade

The Lore

• As 1973 started, it was becoming obvious that Katy Manning would leave at the end of the run of episodes just starting on BBC1. As was the case twice before, Terrance Dicks gave Robert Holmes the task of writing in the new female lead. Holmes had submitted a storyline called "The Automata" that wasn't thought special enough to start a new season, so Dicks took him to lunch and suggested the Season Eleven Opening Night Gimmick - a return to time-travel into Earth's past. Viewers had occasionally requested this, but nobody was very enthusiastic about the idea. It didn't help that Barry Letts had got it into his head that the Hartnell-era historical stories were ratings disasters (although we suggest a look at Volume I to check this out for yourselves).

Holmes had decided to never do a "straight" story involving historical figures: while it was annoying to get lectures from bright eleven year-olds over scientific blunders committed in a modern-day or futuristic story, it was intolerable to be harangued by history teachers *and* bright eleven year-olds for stupid historical howlers. Dicks proposed an innovative, original, never-been-tried idea (sort of): namely, that instead of properly-researched history, they should chuck the Doctor into genre-history and have another time-traveller wreck it. This eliminated what Letts saw as the logical absurdity of historical stories - that Earth's history was sacrosanct to the Doctor, but every other planet and any period after the present-day was fair game. Dicks suggested an *Ivanhoe*-style setting with perhaps a hint of *Robin Hood*. (If you've still got Volume I handy, look at our references to the early days of Lew Grade's ITC and William Russell's previous star role.) The twist would be that someone was arming the Saxons with twentieth-century weapons (the ground-breaking new idea last seen in "The Time Meddler").

• Holmes *still* wasn't entirely happy, and his frustration at the whole process of proposals and outlines led him to send the document as a faked medal citation for the late Commander Jingo Linx of the 5th Sontaran Army Space Fleet, marked "For the Attention of Terran Cedicks". The fan publication *Cosmic Masque* reprinted this mock-military communiqué, and it has intriguing differences with what's seen on screen. Using fairly infantile language with lots of Vietnam slang (humans are termed 'gooks' and the guns are intended to help Irongron 'pow-zap' the forces of 'kingjohn'), Linx's records tell how he disguised himself as a local by wearing a suit of armour, and went in person to abduct technical support from 1,000 years in the future. The Doctor identifies him when the armour's helmet comes off and aids in dating the source of the time-corridor. The Probic Vent was still important to the story's climax. This led to a more orthodox script which is

pretty much what occurs on screen, and which was finished by the beginning of April. Letts had decided to proceed with this story immediately after "The Green Death", as had happened with Holmes' previous four-parter, "Carnival of Monsters". Indeed Letts fully intended to direct this too, as the end-of series treat to himself. However...

• The Head of Drama, Shaun Sutton, had given the green light to *Moonbase 3* - the project that Dicks and Letts saw as their means of escaping from *Doctor Who*. This was given the budget for six hour-long episodes by virtue of a partnership with Time-Life Films, but had to be made during *Doctor Who*'s summer break. The pre-filming was to be done in late April and early May and the studio recording from late June to mid-August for a September launch. That being the case, Letts reluctantly handed over the directorial duties on "The Time Warrior" to Alan Bromly, a veteran of the early days of live TV and a director who'd moved into production (the later, colour series of *Out of the Unknown* and the early episodes of *Paul Temple* - see 7.1, "Spearhead from Space").

Letts apparently had some input into the casting of this story, with Jeremy Bulloch (here the archer Hal, but see 2.7, "The Space Museum") having been in *The Newcomers*. (At one point Hal was briefly considered as a Jamie-like male companion[132], once it looked like a new Doctor would be needed - possibly less athletic than Pertwee - and Pertwee himself was increasingly immobilised by back problems and the hamstring strain that Manning and Delgado had been helping him cope with before.) Letts tried to get Bob Hoskins as Irongron but Hoskins, still a relative unknown before *Pennies from Heaven* (the 1978 TV drama, not the 1981 film), was booked and suggested David Daker. Classically-trained performer June Brown (as Eleanor) was also the producer's idea (she's now Dot Branning, formerly Cotton, of *EastEnders*).

• Bromley took several goes at amending the script to his own style (longer scenes and simpler shots as per live TV from the 1950s), but seems to have asked the author along to the shoot just in case. Letts and Dicks also travelled up to the location shoot - odd by any standards, but even odder when you realise that this is the most northerly shoot in the programme's history (even counting Vancouver; see 27.0, "The TV Movie"). It's even *more* odd when you remember that the two of them had other things to worry about, such as launching a whole new series and keeping Manning's departure quiet for the moment. That said, the castle used (Peckforton) was a Victorian mock-up, albeit potentially just as unsafe as a real mediaeval one. It's in Cheshire, so - who knows? - the idea of going on local television in Manchester may have appealed to the producer.

• Now, this is where it gets messy. It *appears* that someone else was cast as Sarah Jane Smith before Elisabeth Sladen. While this might sound too much like the known facts about Elizabeth Shepherd's gash episode as Emma Peel in *The Avengers*, Barry Letts says that someone was as-good-as hired as the new companion and then Lis came along. However, Letts gallantly refuses to name the lady, and at time of writing says he'll take the secret to his grave. But it's more complicated than that.

It seems the original plan was for a semi-regular reporter called 'Smith' to replace / augment UNIT as a source of present-day stories (sort of like Mickey's role in X2.3, "School Reunion" or Martha in X4.4, "The Sontaran Stratagem"), while another girl would travel with the Doctor. (So it's entirely possible that Sladen was always going to be Smith, but someone else was pencilled in for the full-time TARDIS-traveller before the producers realised the ideal sidekick was right under their noses.) While we don't know the identity of the companion-that-wasn't, two names keep cropping up...

One is Fiona Gaunt, who - just after this - was cast by Letts in *Moonbase 3* as *Helen* Smith (this may have caused the confusion), the station Psychologist whose patients all topped themselves. Her contract was issued for this role on the same day that Sladen met Pertwee. The other is Michelle Dotrice, who'd been in the last major black and white costume drama (*Middlemarch*, 1969) and was Frank Spencer's long-suffering wife Betty in *Some Mothers Do Have 'Em* (Action by Havoc). Thing is, it's fairly well-reported that Sladen herself was shortlisted for the same role. (A generation of us can't hear that without doing the Frank Spencer impression that kept school bullies away and provided work for bad mimics for a decade - the same impression now works for David Beckham.) Instead, she got a small but significant part as Judy the Greengrocer in one episode (the one with the hospital visit). So is *this* the only reason Dotrice's name has been raised in this connexion? Apparently not, but nobody can

find proof.

• Either way, whilst Pertwee signed a contract in January 1973 for everything up to Story ZZZ (as yet undecided, but they later put "Planet of the Spiders" into that slot), Manning didn't. Sladen had been doing rep in the north of England (including a lot of work in Scarborough, Alan Ayckbourn's base of operations and a prestigious gig) and had come south with her husband when his acting roles needed him to be London-based. (He's Brian Miller, and you'll come across him in Volume V.) Sladen herself did a few television appearances - including two in very different roles in *Z-Cars* (revived in 1968 and shown twice-weekly) and playing a student (also called Sarah) in a nuclear-terrorism episode of *Doomwatch* - and then made a few commercials. One of these, for Cointreau, had over-run into the small hours. On returning home from the shoot, she found a note asking her to audition for a part in *Doctor Who*.

• Sladen had three auditions in all, and after a day of talks and trials with Letts, she did a scene with Stephen Thorne about a man Sarah was interviewing who turned out to have a snake's tongue. This was in the rehearsal building where "The Green Death" was also being worked on, and Pertwee introduced himself to Sladen shortly afterwards. It was at about this time that Sladen realised that she was being tried out for a substantial role. It's reported that it was still unclear whether Sarah was to be the permanent assistant or a semi-regular like Mike Yates, but she was contracted for a year.

• A week's interim occurred between the end of recording "The Green Death" and the start of filming on "The Time Warrior", during which time Sladen was contracted to play Sarah Jane Smith (she signed on the 4th of May, a Friday) and Pertwee went to Stockholm (at least partly to film links for the BBC's Bank Holiday product-placement-fest *Disney Time*). The Monday saw the start of shooting in Cheshire. Sladen's first scene was the one where some guards manhandle Sarah. In one take, she got worked up and slipped into Scouse; Sladen was mortified, but no-one minded. Pertwee offered his support by setting his shooting-stick down to watch over her (right in her eyeline - a shooting stick, if you didn't know, is a combination stool / cane used for grouse shooting and watching field-sports).

• The woodland scenes were done on the first day. (However, they forgot to change Sarah into the pageboy outfit for one small scene; this needed a rethink of the costumes when in studio later - possibly because the female changing room was the chapel and in use a lot by the vicar.) Bulloch had been given archery drill. Several others, such as Daker and John J. Carney (Bloodaxe), were given a bit of riding coaching. Bromly suggested that the alien race should be pronounced 'SONT aran', but Kevin Lindsay quilted up as Linx, pulled rank as a resident of the planet and gave it the pronunciation we're all familiar with now (see X4.5, "The Poison Sky" for a reference to this). We should also mention that one of the extras is Ray Dunbobbin, later to become famous as Mr Boswell in *The Liver Birds*.

• The second day was all the courtyard material. Those of you used to spotting Terry Walsh will be frustrated to learn that he wasn't on hand in the first two days, so Marc Boyle did a lot of the supervision of stunts. Walsh seems to have been double-booked, but is definitely back for the studio work (although Letts seems to think Walsh doubled at least one scene for Pertwee on film). The bangs and flashes and a brief use of fire were all done on the last day, as one would.

• The studio recording was done almost entirely in sequence. Bromly had been uncommunicative in the filming, to the point that the cast worried that something was wrong. Sladen was flummoxed by getting so little feedback, and Pertwee found that the efficiency of the recording (some sessions actually ended half an hour *ahead* of schedule) was unnerving. As it turns out, the only real problem was a slight over-run in episode one, so a scene with Hal flirting with Mary the serving wench was lost. (This left Jacqueline Stanbury with no dialogue, so her credit was removed.) Similar exposition scenes in episodes two and three were trimmed, so Sarah never asks for male clothing and never explains that she's from another time. As you probably knew, one of the kitchen-hands is Bella Emberg (see 7.2, "Doctor Who and the Silurians", X2.10, "Love and Monsters").

• Jim Ward built the headpiece that Linx makes the Doctor wear. The bank of switches and lights the Doctor faces when trying to avoid getting his brain fried, however, should be very familiar. In episode four, Bromly refused the use of a model for the exploding castle and opted to cut to stock-footage of an explosion in a quarry.

• So the material was all in the can by 12th of June, and Letts knuckled down to work on Moonbase 3, with half an eye on how to announce Manning's departure and Sladen's arrival. Then on 18th of June, under a week later and two days after episode five of "The Green Death" was shown, it was announced that Roger Delgado had died. The film *Bell of Tibet* (a Franco-Turkish co-production, never finished as far as we can tell) was being made in Turkey, and Delgado had always tried to be prompt. If necessary, he would take a much earlier train or taxi. But this time, he and two technicians took an unregistered cab that went off a cliff near Nevishir. For once his wife wasn't travelling with him.

Manning, who had dined with Delgado just days earlier, was very upset but threw herself into her promotion work for *Serendipity*, with the news of Jo's departure breaking the following Friday. Pertwee appeared with Sladen to introduce the new girl the following week, then left for a holiday and some theatre work. However, by the time filming resumed for *Doctor Who* in September, he was obviously lacking his former enthusiasm, and found Manning's absence a bit disorientating. 18th of June was also the day recording began on the first episode of *Moonbase 3*, which was scripted by Letts and Dicks.

• For the new season, Letts had commissioned a new title sequence, this time not using howl-round from TV monitors but a variation on the Slit-Scan process used in *2001: A Space Odyssey*. For this, Bernard Lodge required a rostrum camera and a lot of patience. Essentially, this is a process of zooming in on a point or slit of light in a blacked-out setting without moving the frame of film. You then resume the original position, move whatever it is you've zoomed in on a bit and do it again. In this case, it was a mask cut out around the photo of Pertwee, then a diamond-logo-shaped mask and later a circular one for the end credits. Beneath the mask was a frame of film showing a polarised-light photo of a stretched portion of a polythene shopping-bag. This was moved right-to-left from frame to frame to provide the "loop" effect within the differently-shaped "tunnels".

• This story has a couple of odd side-issues apart from the whole "Who was the first Sarah?" red-herring. (We would love to think it was Jane Asher, just to add a whole nother layer to *Sarah Jane Adventures* story "Whatever Happened to Sarah Jane?"). Namely, why did they decide to label it UUU rather than VVV (as it had been in the contracts and notes well into the summer), and what possessed the BBC1 bosses to bring transmission forward two weeks to ten days before Christmas? A lot of viewers were caught out by this, despite Dicks going on *Nationwide* and the whole anniversary hoo-hah. The *Radio Times* Tenth Anniversary Special came out just ahead of episode one and had both an interview with Sladen and a rare treat - listings for stories as yet unscreened, including a couple that had yet to be made.

11.2: "Invasion of the Dinosaurs"

(Serial WWW, Six Episodes, 12th January - 16th February 1974.)

Which One is This? 'Ullo Jon, gotta new motor? With the logic of a *Scooby Doo* villain, someone's making unconvincing dinosaurs appear in central London to scare off the population. Meanwhile, Sarah gets stuck on a shoddily-built spaceship taking BBC2 viewers to the Promised Land (narrated by Martin Jarvis, of course). UNIT relocate to a classroom, so the Doctor and the Brigadier take turns to give lectures but spend most of the story in various land-rovers.

Firsts and Lasts First of two appearance by the "Whomobile", a road-worthy car / hovercraft / spaceship actually built by a custom car designer to Jon Pertwee's own specifications. (Pertwee just called it "the Alien". Now he's got a special "mobile" that bears his name, it's almost as if the Doctor's finally qualified as a true action hero. Fortunately, he never gets a utility belt to go with it.)

Part Six gives Sarah gets her first chance to escape through a ventilation shaft, but another series regular does something really unprecedented: Mike Yates goes over to the Dark Side without the aid of an Evil Parallel Universe.

The show's first female director gets her first colour story: Paddy Russell, who'd helmed 3.5, "The Massacre" and was a BBC staff floor manager since the *Quatermass* era of Rudolph Cartier in the mid 1950s, is finally trusted with a sixteen mil self-blimping Arriflex colour camera and CSO.

Six Things to Notice
About "Invasion of the Dinosaurs"...

1. Some *Doctor Who* stories are classified as "legendary", burned on the memories of those who watched them as children. Others are "notorious", also etching themselves on the viewers' minds for all eternity, and "Invasion of the Dinosaurs" is one of the latter. Pleased by the way the Drashigs had turned out in 10.2, "Carnival of Monsters" (don't mock, these were simpler times), Barry Letts saw the possibilities of using puppets to fill the screen with large-scale monsters. Unfortunately, these dinosaurs suck - literally. The models have bendy teeth so that in the tyrannosaurus / brontosaurus fight at the start of Part Six looks like fourteen-year-olds in the back row at the movies. Though the (three times actual size) triceratops and the stegosaurus aren't bad - perhaps because they barely have to move, the dino-on-dino action is perhaps the most embarrassing special effect in the history of the programme, a mess of latex and CSO so badly-executed that at times it's hard to believe the story was ever broadcast.

Or rather... in *long shot* the tyrannosaurus may be the worst special effect in the programme's history. The close-up shots of it, filmed using a larger and more detailed dinosaur prop, are actually quite acceptable. (The Kong-like scenes in the hangar, when a doped tyrannosaurus suddenly wakes up and breaks free of its chains, work rather well until the monster has to stand up.)

Other odd motions include the Tyrannosaurus Hop, where the leg with the cables operating the mouth is attached to the floor, but the other one is hovering in the air. There's also an *amazing* scene, reminiscent of FW Murnau's *Nosferatu*, when the dormant T-Rex rises to its feet by levitating itself through ninety degrees. With hindsight, it appears the glove-puppet pterodactyls were a way to break to us gently that the monsters are this story's weakest feature.

2. The first episode's got the wrong title, being merely "Invasion" instead of "Invasion of the Dinosaurs". This caused a lot of ruckus at the time, and is widely seen as a mistake. Not because hiding the dinosaurs' presence was necessarily a bad idea, but because if they were planning to do this, the advent of a pterodactyl halfway through the episode rather spoils the surprise. Not to mention the big picture of the same scene (looking rather more impressive in Peter Brooks' drawings)

in that week's *Radio Times*, and the fact that the *Radio Times* anniversary special had already given the full title three months earlier.

3. It's 1974, so everyone's doing paranoid conspiracy theories. We've had one already in UNIT-style *Doctor Who* (7.3, "The Ambassadors of Death"), but this one takes the biscuit. Not only is practically *everyone* who's not a regular cast member in on the loopy scheme, one of the UNIT "family" is too. And although Sarah's ambiguous status within the UNIT set-up will put us through our paces in the notes to follow, she's obviously being treated as a fully-paid-up staff-member by whoever operates the Brigadier's brain-rubber. First she idiotically trusts Mike. Then when he betrays her, she teams up with Sir Charles - the Minister with Special Powers, wearing a pinstripe suit, who might as well have I AM A TRAITOR tattooed on his forehead. Then, once she escapes from the spaceship she's locked up in to keep her quiet (don't worry, it's rather easier to get back from this than it appears), she sides with General Finch - who refuses to believe in time-travel despite the large numbers of dinosaurs appearing and vanishing before people's eyes, so is even more obviously covering something up.

4. They've found a new wrinkle on the perennial Pertwee plot of capture-exposition-escape by here having the army - and especially UNIT - as his captors. Twice. This allows for a whole episode of the Doctor running around a deserted London tricking the pursuivant squaddies, even though they have a helicopter at their disposal. (Residents or visitors to the Putney area watching the chopper scenes might like to confirm how rapidly a forest has grown up since the populace was evacuated.) Ingenious ruses used by the wily Doctor include: terrible cockney accents and badly-faked fights; leaving a false trail and doubling back (a favourite of his - see 14.3, "The Deadly Assassin" and ponder that Robert Holmes began shadowing Terrance Dicks on this very episode, Part Five); overpowering Sergeant Benton with the Vulcan Neck-Pinch... sorry, Venusian Aikido and, um, hiding in bushes.

5. Once again, UNIT tea comes into the spotlight. The final episode entails the Brigadier asking one of his men, Bryson, to make some and the Private grins as if he's been ordered to go undercover at the filming of a porn movie. Take a moment to consider the context: the city's being assaulted by more prehistoric monsters than ever, the regular army is led by one of the people

behind the fiendish plot, the government liaison is yet another conspiracy-member, in under an hour this evil gang will reverse time to prevent any of the assembled company ever having been born and Bryson wants to know if the order to get the hell out of there has been rescinded. He's then told that they're staying put, and is asked to brew up a cuppa whilst everyone waits to be chewed by dinosaurs. Yet he couldn't be happier. What is it with UNIT and hot beverages? (Go directly to 11.5, "Planet of the Spiders", if you think this is only confined to tea.)

6. Anyone who thinks that wobbly sets only began with the Graham Williams era five years later has obviously not seen this story. Sarah pulls a vent-shaft cover off and almost brings the wall down on her (actually an easier method of escape, all things considered). The Doctor has a similar problem when overpowering Martin Jarvis with his underarm deodorant. (All right, we *know* that's not really what happens, but the alternative is yet another instance of this Doctor using violence as a first resort. If we take it seriously, it's very unpleasant.)

But on the plus side, the script detail that UNIT have based themselves in a school allows for lots of pictures and diagrams on the walls, so you can while away the long exposition scenes and repetitive sequences of Sarah trusting the wrong person by looking at kids' drawings of planes and rainbows. You even get to learn about the structure of the human eye from the blackboard in the lab.

The Continuity

The Doctor When Professor Whitaker stops time, the Doctor can still think and act, albeit slowly. Sarah suggests that this is because he's a Time Lord, and the Doctor agrees. [Again, Time Lords seem to exist outside the normal flow of history. See **How Does Time Work?** under 9.1, "Day of the Daleks".] He takes multiple sugars in his tea [he's reached four before the camera turns to the Brigadier]. but at least he drinks it properly this time. [Rather than staring it into his stomach - see "The Ambassadors of Death" and 9.5, "The Time Monster". Incidentally, anyone who persists in denying that there's a connection between tea and Time Lord abilities is directed to 15.6, "The Invasion of Time" episode three.]

The Doctor's 'Venusian ooja' - as Benton calls it - can knock someone unconscious with a pinch to the neck or a finger to the ribcage [the first real

Mr. Spock influence in the Doctor's character, sadly]. Somehow he identifies a pretty anonymous park as being in London [there is a bus-stop around the corner, so if he squints really hard, it's possible he can make out the London Transport logo] and seems confident that he's landed the Ship close to UNIT HQ. He becomes very fed up when people ask him what he's doing.

Here the Doctor seems to imply that the Blinovitch Limitation Effect must be overcome before *any* time travel can be attempted. [Not exactly true, as we'll learn in 20.3, "Mawdryn Undead"; see also "Day of the Daleks".]

• *Ethics.* The Doctor recognises Sir Charles Grover as one of the founders of the Save Planet Earth society, and author of the book *Last Chance for Man*, so once again he's up to date with contemporary human concerns. The Brigadier believes him to be 'keen' on the whole anti-pollution movement. [See 12.1, "Robot" for Terrance Dicks' take on this.]

• *Inventory.* He has a watch on a chain [utterly useless for a space-time traveller, unless you're planning on hypnotising something, but the Doctor still plays with it impatiently while waiting for a bus]. He has lacy hankies for detecting air-conditioning, and in episode four appears to put a set of skeleton keys [did they belong to Jo?] to good use.

Here the Doctor cobbles together a stun-gun that uses a 'simple molecular reaction' to temporarily neutralise a dinosaur's brain cells, resulting in unconsciousness. This uses a technique that's not yet developed on Earth.

• *Background.* The Doctor states that the Vandals were 'quite decent chaps', and says it as if he knew them personally. When he describes a 'time eddy' caused by Operation Golden Age, in which time briefly runs backwards, he likewise speaks as if he's seen one before. Strangely, though, he's never heard of Professor Whitaker and doesn't know about local research into time-travel.

• *The Whomobile.* [Never named on screen. The programme-makers coined the term "Whomobile", and it's doubtful that the Doctor would ever use it, though the other members of UNIT might.] The Doctor's new car - and 'car' is the only word he uses to describe it - has been brought to London from UNIT HQ. A machine with no visible wheels and a sleek UFO-like shell, it's his vehicle of choice when he wants to get somewhere in a hurry [odd, since it doesn't move as fast as the turbo-charged Bessie]. The number-plate reads WVO 2M. [This means that the car was registered between August 1973 and July 1974, and the Doctor describes it as "new", again suggesting an early-to-mid-70s date for the UNIT stories.] It's basically in the shape of the 1960s "Lifting Bodies", such as the "Mustard" vehicle. [See **How Believable is the British Space Programme?** under "The Ambassadors of Death".]

The Supporting Cast

• *Sarah Jane Smith.* Here says that she's twenty-three years old. [With a vast amount of hindsight, this is glaring evidence that the UNIT stories occur at time of broadcast. The *Sarah Jane Adventures* story "Whatever Happened to Sarah Jane?" establishes beyond any doubt that Sarah was born in 1951, so she would have been twenty-three in... 1974, the year that "Invasion of the Dinosaurs" went out. Incidentally, Elisabeth Sladen was born in 1948, making her a little older than the character she played.]

The Doctor formally acknowledges Sarah as his 'assistant', but even before that, the Brigadier doesn't seem bothered by the fact that there's a journalist around the place. Sarah likes cities rather than quiet places, and once interviewed Lady Cullingford - now a member of the People - about a Private Members Bill about the pollution of rivers. Her qualifications for taking over from Jo Grant are established when she's knocked unconscious by a falling piece of masonry. She recognises most of the people on the alleged spaceship, including an Olympic athlete, a writer and the former Lady Cullingford. Her contacts include the editor of *Nature* and the science writer for *The Times*. [So her ability to sneak into top-secret scientific establishments obviously comes after a long campaign of getting science scoops.] The Doctor obviously trusts her enough to allow her to use the TARDIS haircutting facilities, and to borrow a leather jacket.

• *The Brigadier.* By now he's starting to regard the Doctor's eccentricities with some affection. His inability to listen to the Doctor is worse than ever, though, since he finds the existence of a secret government bunker under London 'difficult to believe' even though he's spent the last few weeks chasing dinosaurs. Despite this, he still has trouble discerning the difference between a tyran-

How Good Do the Special Effects Have to Be?

At the time of writing, this question seems to have been settled: you can do so much with computers and a green screen, audiences no longer even *think* about it. These days, they tell us, the quality of effects technology means that it's all down to the storytelling and acting, and we're more worried about whether we "buy" what we're shown as plausibly motivated than what the scene looks like. This is perfectly true, but it was also true in 1974.

What everyone is forgetting is that every generation of effects-mongery looks sufficiently different from what audiences think of as "a special effect" that there's a hiatus between the first use of it and everyone ceasing to be impressed or convinced. This is often misinterpreted as a matter of generations of viewers or moviegoers "processing" the images differently to how a previous generation did. This is codswallop. Unless there's some kind of genetic difference in TV viewers born ten years apart - one that makes their brains physically different from birth - the observed difference between how people saw an exploding church in "The Daemons" (8.5) when broadcast in 1971 and how people *now* perceive a fair-to-middling model-shot must be equally true of people who saw it then seeing it again now. This is, indeed the case. Ask anyone who saw it then and got taken in to watch it now, as we have. Anyone who still holds to this theory should mull over how much more impressive the early episodes of *Buffy the Vampire Slayer* looked then compared to now, or how naff *The Matrix* seems when seen again these days.

Now look back a few decades and think about how people related to special effects that weren't "up to" today's standards. Looking at what people wrote about these things at the time (something that's only slightly more accurate than what we remember, but provides an agreed baseline), the hallmark of a convincing effect is whether the viewer could figure out how it was done. For instance, nobody has ever seen a space beacon going into a low orbit around one of the moons of Jupiter, so we can't say whether the climax of 12.5, "Revenge of the Cybermen" is in any way "realistic". But we *can* make a confident guess at how the scene was made. This goes for models on wires, puppets, and - once this had been explained on factual shows like *Magpie* and *Multi-Coloured Swap Shop* - Chroma-key. Or at least, sometimes it does...

In a lot of circumstances, knowing how an effect was done is half of the fun. Think of Ray Harryhausen's stop-motion stuff. This is a process that's about as old as cinema, but chiefly people remember that it's laborious and requires real skill to do well. Half the joy of *Jason and the Argonauts* (1963) is the expectation built up in the moments before a set-piece begins. To take a more obvious comparison, the significant difference between *King Kong* and "Robot" (12.1) is that when we suspect an effect is afoot, we consciously (or otherwise) think "go on, impress me". We're expecting a spectacle, and in *King Kong*, we get spectacle a-plenty. In "Robot", we get an Action Man tank.

Here's where we come to the big difference between 1970s *Doctor Who* and the present-day revamp: audiences today expect the spectacle to be purely mimetic. We'll pick up on this in Volume V (**Is "Realism" Enough?** under 19.3, "Kinda"), but consider, for example, the climax of "The Green Death" (10.5). The focus of our attention is Jerome Willis' face being electronically coloured blue, orange or its usual hue, and occasionally going slightly out of focus. It's a style of television that, on first broadcast, everyone watching would have recognised as what routinely happened to Noddy Holder, Marc Bolan or Brian Connelly on *Top of the Pops*. Nobody thought it was *actually* happening, or that the singer was suffering. (The studio was full of dopey teenagers and the occasional mum bopping absently whilst looking for their own faces on the monitors, so rest assured that they would've rushed to the aid of any pop star who'd turned Day-Glo in real life.)

Top of the Pops and 60s / 70s *Doctor Who* use the sort of trickery normally reserved for the title-sequences of programmes within the "text", and both have their own titles and set-design that create a fantastical space where anything could conceivably happen. By 1960s standards, *Doctor Who* was fast-paced, exhilarating and above all *weird*. No other programme had visual "events" like exterminations or inlay split-screen shots of people looking at alien cities. In effect, the plot was about as important as those of Fred Astaire musicals - you were hoping it had one, but you didn't tune in for that or remember it.

For anyone under, say, seven, the pretty pictures and crazy burbles and whooshes were a sensual pleasure (think about how every record released in that time had its own "sound"). *Doctor Who* wasn't a programme, it was a place you visited for twenty-five minutes, and after that gobsmacking

continued on page 417...

nosaurus and a brontosaurus. He's quite prepared to face a mutiny charge to stop a superior officer from apprehending the Doctor.

• *Sergeant Benton*. Despite the constant friction between the Doctor and UNIT, it's a sign of the men's trust in their scientific advisor that when General Finch orders Benton to arrest the Doctor as a traitor, Benton offers to let the Doctor knock him unconscious as soon as they're left alone. [The process leaves no marks, however, so he could've just played possum. Perhaps he was having trouble sleeping.] Benton seems to enjoy beating up a General. He recognises Sarah, somehow, from a photo. He's willing, if the Brig so orders it, to level a gun at his fellow soldiers.

• *Captain Yates*. He's just got back from leave after the events at Llanfairfach [10.5, "The Green Death"], which he discusses with Sarah as though she knows about it. When he unexpectedly turns out to be a traitor working for Operation Golden Age, Yates is obviously confused, not wanting to harm any of his friends at UNIT even though the scheme will erase them from history altogether. He also believes that the Doctor might side with them, proving that he doesn't understand the Doctor as well as the more "lowly" ranks of UNIT. [It's long been held that Mike Yates' defection to Operation Golden Age is a result of temporary madness, triggered by his brainwashing in "The Green Death", though this is never explicitly stated. It makes sense, though, that he'd turn to a rabidly pro-environmental "cult" after what BOSS and Global Chemicals did to him. If the brainwashing isn't directly responsible for him changing sides, then at the very least stress must be getting to the Captain, as he shows definite lapses of judgement here. Evidently, he's only an efficient soldier when he's fighting for the good guys.]

Ultimately the Brigadier arranges for him to have a few weeks' sick leave and the chance to resign quietly [See "Planet of the Spiders" for his next move.]

The TARDIS Obviously its navigation isn't perfect yet, as the Doctor gets back to London some distance from UNIT HQ and some weeks after he left. He states the space-time co-ordinates are 'a bit out'. He doesn't seem to have the spares he needs for his tracking device anywhere in the Ship's stores.

The Non-Humans

• *Dinosaurs*. Brontosaurs, tyrannosaurs, triceratopses, stegosauruses and pterodactyls are all in evidence here. This time the Doctor positively identifies a tyrannosaurus rex [cf. 7.2, "Doctor Who and the Silurians"], even though its hands are the wrong shape and it's powerful enough to knock down whole buildings. The Doctor describes it as 'the largest and fiercest predator of all time'. [Assuming that he means *land-based* predator, and *on Earth* rather than anywhere in the universe... he's apparently never heard of the Giganotosaurus, discovered in 1995, so his dinosaur-knowledge isn't complete and may be informed by the received wisdom of Earth c. 1974. Here the tyrannosaurus is an active predator, not just a scavenger as some palaeontologists now claim.] He states that it's been extinct for sixty-five million years. The triceratops faced by the Brigadier, meanwhile, is a truly huge specimen of its type.

The Doctor pedantically corrects the identification of a brontosaurus. [Note that the beasts UNIT encounter really *are* cold-blooded and slow, in the face of all subsequent investigation and computer modelling.]

Planet Notes

• *Florana*. Probably one of the most beautiful planets in the universe, according to the Doctor [see 11.3, "Death to the Daleks"]. It's always carpeted with perfumed flowers, the seas are like warm milk, the sands are as soft as swan's down, the streams flow with water clearer than the clearest crystal... and so on. [Oddly enough, the Doctor doesn't seem to have gone there with Jo, nor does he seem to venture there to ease his sorrows after she leaves him for fungus-boy.]

History

• *Dating*. At least a few weeks after the Doctor and Sarah left Earth. [See **What's the UNIT Timeline?** under 8.5, "The Daemons". The map of the London Underground seen here is a mid-70s one. It has to be pre-1979 because the London *Evening News* is still going.] Rental shops are promoting colour television sets as a new, exciting thing. [Not that they were a novelty, although being able to buy or rent one at that price *was*. The fact that they specify this in the ads rather than just assuming all sets are colour, however, puts the story as pre-1977.]

How Good Do the Special Effects Have to Be?

...continued from page 415

title sequence and theme you knew the rules were changed. (See **Does Plot Matter?** under 6.4, "The Krotons".) As we've commented throughout this book, the Pertwee stories walk a tightrope between this tendency (what we're calling "the Tartrazine aesthetic" until anyone comes up with a better name) and the insistence on strict mimesis within the BBC's guidelines on violence and swearing (what the first wave of fandom called "gritty realism", like it was a budgie cage). CSO made what writers wanted more-or-less possible, so the effects took on a more functional aspect. The idea was that now you weren't supposed to notice that they *were* effects. In many cases the plot had key moments - often at twenty-five minute intervals - where we went from montage (cutting between something normal and something odd) to *mise-en-scene* (the normal and the odd in the same shot - see **Is This Really About the Blitz?** under 2.2, "The Dalek Invasion of Earth").

This had happened before, and memorably (Daleks on Westminster Bridge, Cybermen outside St Paul's - even if the story doesn't need it, this sort of thing makes great publicity shots). In a story like "'Planet of Giants" (2.1), it was strenuously avoided, and not just for technical reasons. When it was done, it was done in mid-episode, not as a cliffhanger (as would have been the norm even a year later). The story relies on there being two overlapped worlds that can't meet. A similar situation makes "Carnival of Monsters" (10.2) a fruitful comparison. The three cliffhangers, and indeed the plot, turn on things being seen in the same shot that belong in different realms.

Moreover, as would happen a great deal from now on, an electronic effect would be tried on *Doctor Who*, then if they got it right it would appear in *Top of the Pops*. In many cases, it would even become standard (CSO became the backdrop for News bulletins). "Destiny of the Daleks" (17.1) and "Meglos" (18.2) were test-beds, with the producers loaned Steadicam and Scene-Synch (respectively) at reduced rates. But "Carnival of Monsters" marks a turning point, as it's almost the last time we're encouraged to "look at the pretty pictures". From now on, we're supposed to *believe* what we are seeing. In "Carnival", the Pleisiosaurus effect is partly effective because it *looks* like an effect; it doesn't belong, so it stands out. A similar shot at the end of "Terror of the Zygons" (13.1) - far from being a bold, gaudy pop-art moment - is

considered an embarrassment because the rest of the story is so "realistic".

So by 1974, there are two schools of thought on this. One is that the effects are merely storytelling devices, to provide some idea of why the actors are doing what they're doing. The other is that by disrupting the normal rules of television narrative, you're taking the viewer "elsewhere" and should make that other place as exotic as possible. In the first point of view - taking our present case as an example - so long as everyone behaves *as though* a dinosaur had appeared outside Moorgate Station, everything's fine, and Shari Lewis can do the effects with sock-puppets. (Her Lamb Chop was briefly tried out on British kids just before the Season Ten episodes. We demanded Basil Brush back.) In the second case, so long as there's a groovy electronic effect or two (both sound and visual) as part of the narrative instead of a bolt-on as would be the case in *Top of the Pops* around that time, there's a point to watching this programme. However, CSO and the synthesizer made what *had* been *Doctor Who*'s Unique Selling Point available to any Tom, Dick or Harry. (Or TIM, Carol and Tyso - *The Tomorrow People* managed almost as well for a less critical audience.)

People who couldn't handle the fact that *Doctor Who* is a series of made-up-stories - which seemed to be most of fandom in the 1980s - were persuaded by *Star Wars* and the various American SF series that a "good" effect was one which didn't say "hey, I'm an effect". In some ways, this is understandable. *Star Wars* works because the whole project is an exercise in world-building, not just the real world with extra bits added (not something you can say about *Star Trek* in any of its recent forms), but that isn't the way *Doctor Who* works. Some of the worst excesses of modern Hollywood have been movies which are effectively just showcases for effects-work, so it's easy to see why viewers would be distrustful of anything that goes out of its way to impress. Even if teen-audiences are happy to go "ooh" at a computer-generated Transformer, it's just because it's so *big*. For them to remember anything about it after the credits roll there needs to be more.

Of course, there's nothing *wrong* with verisimilitude - but it should come from people's reactions to the shots. Instead of telling us "the rules have changed", the standard shots in too many programmes are the equivalent of establishing shots

continued on page 419...

Eight million people have been evacuated from London in the wake of the dinosaur appearances, with the government relocating to Harrogate. The city's under martial law under the Emergency Powers Act. [In reality the population of London was only seven million in the mid-70s, and hadn't even reached eight million by the end of the century, unless the meaning here is "Greater London". The evacuated zone seems confined to north of the Thames but extends to Chiswick and - from the map - Cockfosters and Enfield, outside the North Circular Road. But see 8.3, "The Claws of Axos", for at least one good reason why a baby-boom in Britain might have occurred over the last two years.]

In the vicinity of Whitehall, there's an underground shelter that was built 'back in the Cold War days', twenty years before. [It seems massively unlikely that the entire Cold War has ended by this point, since the stories made / set in the 1980s seem to suggest a world where there's still a schism between the US and USSR. See especially 19.7, "Time-Flight". Given that the mid-70s was a period of détente between East and West, Grover probably means that the shelter was built in the *worst* days of the Cold War. Certainly, in the era of détente when this was made, a thaw seemed the most likely option. Or possibly he means the early 60s, post-Cuba, as he states that the situation 'eased' after the plans were drawn up and that he was a back-bencher at the time. Incidentally, this suggests that nuclear technology in the *Doctor Who* universe is in advance of our own, if they were able to build a reactor that small in the mid-1950s. The nearest real-life equivalent, PINDAR, was completed in 1995.] Grover has only been a governmental minister for six months but had been in on the construction of the complex. Cryogenics technology seems to be functioning, allowing the putative "colonists" to keep their colleagues in suspended animation [Torchwood had this trick at the turn of that century, so let's not rule it out even though so much else of this is a hoax].

The athlete John Crichton successfully performed a [high] jump of 2.362 metres at the last Olympics [clearly supposed to suggest a world record, which it would have been; Gerd Wessig set a record by jumping 2.36 metres only (if the word "only" applies here), and that wasn't until 1980]. Eco-concern is so great that all manner of generals, politicians and scientists are prepared to work together on Operation Golden Age in an attempt to erase humanity from the planet. The "colonists" selected to re-populate the prehistoric world believe they're being taken to another planet on a spaceship. [Unlike most "cult" members they're not entirely stupid and fairly well-informed, so for this to be remotely feasible, there must at least be some talk of space-colonisation in this period.]

Human research into time-travel is unexpectedly advanced here, with Professor Whitaker not only developing the technology to snatch dinosaurs and Medieval peasants from their own time but also planning to wind back the whole of the Earth to the prehistoric era. [To the age of the dinosaurs, or just to the pre-human epoch? Maybe the yeoman in Part Two, is a clue that they want to go all William Morris and stop the Renaissance happening.] He applied for a government grant and was refused, since nobody believed his theory of time-travel would work. Whitaker was an outsider, always getting into arguments with other scientists. [Compare with 11.1, "The Time Warrior". Was Whitaker a victim of Crabshaw and his cronies? Some of the science used here may come from alien sources such as the Master, whose TOMTIT project in "The Time Monster" must have made *some* impression on the academic community. At least one scientist was aiming at time-travel in "The Claws of Axos", and the same kind of technology we see here is put into effect again in 17.2, "City of Death". Whitaker's theories were dismissed as nonsense by government advisors, and TOMTIT also appeared to be nonsense to most researchers on Earth.]

The end of the story sees Grover and Whitaker sent hurtling back to the "Golden Age" on their own, and their fate remains unknown [but if anyone can settle the argument about the age of the Silurians, it's them]. The duped colonists aboard the fake spaceship used in Operation Golden Age believe that many of their colleagues are in suspended animation. [As we see some new "arrivals" in Part Six, this might be true.

[Incidentally, some have proposed the theory that when Whitaker's machine is activated at the end of the story, time is rolled back by several weeks before the Doctor can switch it off, so that the dinosaur crisis never happened and nobody outside the room remembers it. But that's not the implication of the script, which seems to suggest

How Good Do the Special Effects Have to Be?

...continued from page 417

in cop-shows showing the precinct building with traffic outside. It establishes "normality" and they frequently use the same shot every episode. In no way are they supposed to imply that this event is special - they're "ordinary effects".

This ties in with the logic of these programmes as, in effect, soaps set somewhere else. We revisit the same world every time, and so we don't need to figure out how this world is different from ours. No conscious effort is required on the part of the viewer to correlate what's happening on screen to what's known of the world we inhabit. In short, it's a no-brainer. Classic *Star Trek*, for instance, had been firmly in the tradition of shows such as *The Outer Limits* and *Lost In Space* in presenting Scary-Looking Critter Of The Week in the pre-credits sequence. (At least, that was true in the first season, before we knew enough about the amusing ethnic stereotypes for one of them to act out of character as the "hook".)

Conversely, *Doctor Who*, even at its slickest and most routine, has the viewer is solving puzzles throughout. One of these is reconciling what we *can* see to what we're *expected* to see. "How different would the world have to be for this shot to make sense?" is a question subconsciously being asked by viewers, even whilst consciously thinking "that's a man in a rubber suit" or "Blimey! That dinosaur's crap!" If the tentative solutions to these puzzles chime with how the actors are behaving, you have a different world for very low capital outlay. (The astute reader will be recalling a similar line of argument about the real nature of Science Fiction in **Is This an SF Series?** under 14.4, "The Face of Evil". If it's still not clear, we're arguing that contrary to what dullards, claim *Doctor Who* is closer to literary - "proper" - SF than *Star Trek* or the Hollywood blockbusters post-1976. Anyone who disagrees hasn't read enough. The analogy goes deeper: nobody reading SF really believes in flying saucers or Atlantis (contrary to what Mundanes think) and most know enough about science and human nature to be judging the storyteller's skill in crafting a good scam. Similarly, the experienced media SF fan will be judging the effects not on whether they look "real", but on what's done with them within the story.) If the effects tell one story and the actors another, no amount of money and resources can save you - nor matter how many buxom Vulcans you show in their undies (or former teen pop-stars, if it's *Primeval*).[135]

So why is the twenty-first century incarnation of *Doctor Who* spending the equivalent of the Hartnell era's entire budget per episode getting The Mill to fake up spaceships and black holes? Especially when we're constantly being told how much more emotionally intense the new series is compared to the more phlegmatic and stoic old series - it seems almost like a vote of no confidence in Billie, Freema and the gang. The simple answer is that whilst a lot of the primary audience (overseas fans and the British Public in their millions) have a lot invested in the characters week-by-week, the show is also being made with an eye toward export overseas. They can't rely on the redubbed episodes having the same impact and they *certainly* can't expect everyone to know who Andrew Marr is (X1.4, "Aliens of London").

If anything the effects are *too good* now. In general the base level of digital effects - in the stuff in-between programmes, as well as the content itself - has been raised to a level where anything out-of-the-ordinary is almost ordinary. When BBC1 linked programmes with a little model globe spinning in front of a camera, anything *more* exciting or dramatically-justified than this would pass muster. The "interstitial" (as the BBC calls them, amusingly to all Pertwee fans) introducing X3.13, "Last of the Time Lords" was more technically accomplished than the CG sequence of the Guinevere probe colliding with the Sycorax ship (X2.0, "The Christmas Invasion"), but we've curiously stopped noticing.

We are asking you, therefore, to be kind to the Pertwee era's shortcomings when compared to the BBC Wales stuff or any other shows. These days, the bog-standard effects are sufficiently detailed to give any formerly-impressive feat of technical legerdemain a veneer of what the public would call "realism" and critics would term "verisimilitude". All this *really* means is that we must rely on the actors and storytelling to make us believe in anything. We're almost back to square one, with television owing as much to theatre as to film. (Note how big-budget effects-driven films and shows always hire theatrically-trained British actors[136].) Those rubber dinosaurs are there to stand in for what "really" would have been seen, just you'd hardly expect a real bear to show up in a stage production of *The Winter's Tale* (see 25.3, "Silver Nemesis", if this allusion eludes you). However, be aware that even small children in 1974 weren't fooled into thinking these or the spaceship were real, but were nonetheless worried about what was happening to Sarah.

that the machine's just warming up when the Doctor gets to it. This "forget the dinosaurs in London!" theory also creates a number of horrible paradoxes that aren't worth mentioning, even in a volume as pedantic as this one.]

At some point a Chinese scientist called Chung Sen will experiment with time-travel, but according to the Doctor he hasn't been born yet.

Additional Sources Hulke's novelisation is, as always, full of little gems. In place of the looter in episode one, we have the sad story of Scottish football-fan and drunk Shughie McPherson (a name suspiciously like the chef in *Crossroads*, played by Angus Lennie) who comes to after the Cup Final in a deserted London and is killed while praying over the dead milkman. We also have a definite date when the story takes place - alas, it's 1977. And there's an epilogue wherein the Doctor speeds around Charing Cross Road in a jeep, pausing to loot a Bible from Foyles to show Sarah the bit in Ezekiel where something like an alien encounter is described.

A lot of Sarah's thoughts are remembering things older journalists have told her - much of this is Hulke editorialising, but at least she has the "colonist" Mark down as running the Three Minute Mile, as opposed to some obscure jumping record that she improbably remembers. The novelisation also gives us the hint that Blinovitch was a Russian of the near future, explains Butler's motivation and gives him a scar to make him identifiable to readers (even when a character seeing Butler doesn't recognise him; apparently Butler was a fireman who fell through a window and has since been judged on his appearance).

Best of all, the book had a cover that takes the publicity photos from the story and - thanks to Chris Achilleos' alchemical touch - makes the story seem a whole lot more exciting. (Even if Target bosses objected to the big Roy Lichtenstein-style "K-KLAK!" as the pterodactyl menaces the Doctor.) The work is now available with this same cover (hurrah!), as a talking book read by - who else? - Martin Jarvis. We should also mention that, curiously, the US imprint changed a few small details to make the book a Fourth Doctor adventure.

The Analysis

Where Does This Come From? It's not much of a stretch to see this as Mac Hulke watching "The Green Death" and thinking "Right, let's show 'em how it *should* be done", but realistically this story has longer roots. Hulke was a writer for the early Cathy Gale-era series of *The Avengers* and his scripts for that show a willingness to do as much research as possible and then cherry-pick the bits that worked best as drama, however much making this sound like natural dialogue annoyed Honor Blackman. We've already devoted far too much space to his decision that 'Silurian' is a catchier name for a *Doctor Who* monster than "Ogilocene" or "Kimmeridgian", and now we have him writing a story that is in many ways a case for Steed and Mrs Peel.

One of the odd things about the 60s fantasy / spy series was that the villains were almost always cults made up of exaggerated versions of half-expressed small-c conservative notions of How Things Should Be. This is especially notable when you watch defrosted Edwardian hero Adam Adamant, whose entire schtick is that he's not used to Swinging London, defending the progressive and enlightened against people who want to send Britain back to the time he remembers. Hulke's last *Avengers* contribution was a collaboration with Dicks to salvage unfinished Tara King stories; they re-configured the extant footage into a story about salvaging Britain's art treasures underground in the eve of an emergency (and with guest-start Gerald Harper, AKA Adam Adamant, curiously). The idea of corrupt soldiers being in charge of an evacuation is one you get in another story of that year, "The Morning After", wherein Brian Blessed is using martial law to stop anyone opposing his crime-spree. That cheekily used footage from the film *Seven Days To Noon* which we mentioned under "The Invasion" (6.3), but which is very relevant here because the nuclear blackmail was perpetrated by a former government scientist who wanted to scare the world into abandoning nuclear weapons.

So taken alongside "The Invasion" and the near-contemporary *Freewheelers* episode mentioned earlier, you're doubtless getting the idea that there's a whole sub-genre of Abandoned London stories. That's correct, and it started long before even *The War of the Worlds* (1898), which is the motherlode of catastrophe tales where the beauty and horror of the metropolis derelict and deserted is evoked. It wasn't the first, though: *After London* (1885) by Richard Jeffries (whose *Bevis* is still readable) depicted an eco-catastrophe wherein pollution had led to a flood over the south of England and an invasion by Welsh, Scots and Irish. A generation or so before this, the Romantics had an ambiguous relationship with the capital. Shelley said that, "Hell is a city much like London / a smoky and populous city", but he was poncing about in the Alps off his face. In general the consensus was that London was somehow against Nature, and would undergo some kind of retribution one of these days. There was also the fun to be had contrasting this emblem of modernity with great antiquity, not least the idea of dinosaurs wandering around. It's obvious to mention that the Professor Challenger book *The Lost World* ends with a pterodactyl running - or flying - amok, and that the 1911 film ends with a brontosaurus at Tower Bridge. Half a century earlier, the opening paragraph of *Bleak House* involves the same image.

So, nothing really new here. What's interesting and very indicative of the shift in the public mood is that the reactionaries and thwarted boffins are in most particulars a cult. Here they don't try to brainwash Sarah, despite having *Ipcress*-ery available to send her to sleep so they can get her into one of those horrid Mao suits, but try to convert her through peer-pressure. This is, after all, the golden age of the Baghwan, of EST and of the Moonies. At time of broadcast, Pattie Hearst was photographed holding up a bank after being abducted by, and sympathising with, the Symbionese Liberation Army. And notice how the cultists heading for a new Eden in "Invasion of the Dinosaurs" call themselves *the People*, suggesting the language of the Jesus-Freaks (whose manifestation in Britain, the Festival of Light, included Cliff Richard, Mary Whitehouse and Malcolm Muggeridge), and they see 'permissiveness' as one of the problems facing humanity.

We got that a lot in the late 60s, and even more in the early 80s, but a whole tranche of eccentrics such as Sir Gerald Nabarro (a Conservative back bench politician) thought that the world was going to hell because clever people kept making things legal. Nabarro presented himself as "colourful" rather than "deranged" by driving steam-trains, but he was curiously keen on flogging and had a style of handlebar moustaches that made his pathological fear of homosexuals seem

like he was trying to hide something. The naming in "Dinosaurs" of 'usury' as one of the main things wrong with the world seems odd, until you remember that this is kind of a code-word for "Jews" - at which point the whole healthy-living and country walks aspect of this strand of environmentalism becomes horribly familiar. Note that we have no indication that this new world is going to have any non-white residents. Possibly because of our near-miss with Oswald Mosley (see 7.4, "Inferno") the normal reaction to things like this, even when Enoch Powell was popular, was sarcasm. We resent anyone telling us about their beliefs too loud (or, indeed, at all unless asked). Such cults as tried to open branches here weren't nearly as organised as the Manson Family or Jonestown: we tend not to take such things seriously enough.

Whilst we note in passing that this plot is almost fingerprint-identical to the ersatz-Bond machinations of Salamander in 5.4, "The Enemy of the World" (and has a villain with the same name as that story's author; not that Hulke had any issues with David Whitaker or anything - see Volume I and "The Ambassadors of Death"). This is also quite unmistakably the first post-Watergate story. Everyone is part of a conspiracy. The plucky journalist who "follows the money" finds that she can't trust anyone. What's not often stated about *All The President's Men* (the book Woodward and Bernstein wrote about their scoop) is that it's set out as a thriller, with plot-twists at strategic points even though most of them happened as described. It fits in with a whole category of paranoid conspiracy stories from the time. Since *The Manchurian Candidate* (Richard Condon's 1959 novel, then the 1962 film), it had become a cottage industry. Stoner films such as *The President's Analyst* play on the sense of a connected-up world of which the protagonist isn't really a part and there was a slew of big-budget Hollywood films during the Pertwee era that make this their theme. At the time of filming this story, there was *Three Days of the Condor*, then around time of broadcast you got *The Parallax View* and *Chinatown*, plus *The Conversation* and - stretching a point - we'd had the Eliott Gould version of *The Long Goodbye*. One of the key ideas common to stories of this kind is that the protagonist has to find concrete proof one way or the other, and is in a state of limbo for most of the story, unable to know if s/he is going mad or onto something huge. This would soon morph into the whole *Exorcist / Omen* cycle of supernatural horror, but right now a generation of young(ish) directors want to combine Hitchcock and student politics. (We'll get onto this more in the essay.)

Of course, the dinosaurs themselves are almost a side issue, and rightly so (Part Four contains about twenty seconds of pterodactyl action, and that's about it). It should be noted that in the mid-1970s, popular culture was going through one of its "dinosaur phases", as it does from time to time. While the children of the 90s had *Jurassic Park*, the children of the 70s had *The Land that Time Forgot* and - later - the seminal B-movie *At the Earth's Core*. Of course, the makers of these had time and money, but the results lack even the charm of this story. Kids are always going to be interested in anything with dinosaurs in, even dead ones: one of Pertwee's next projects after quitting was a 1920s Fu Manchu spoof for Disney, *One of Our Dinosaurs is Missing* - with model effects by Cliff Culley! Although the Japanese *Godzilla* flicks weren't big box-office here they found their way onto television and, at certain times of the year, got promoted as major prime-time premieres. The lamentable *King Kong Vs Godzilla* (1962) got onto our screens, over ten years after release, on a Saturday night in summer around the time Hulke was being asked to revise his original pitch. (All else is, these days, speculation but we can't help noticing the *Kong*-style capers with a misguided robot who changes size, just like Jet Jaguar, shortly afterwards: see "Robot". And note that the furry-suit Kong shows up in *King Kong Escapes* (1967), where he's led astray by a white-haired, cape wearing villain called "Doctor Who" who's built a robot Kong.)

Another thing to look at in passing is so obvious, we hardly dare point it out: the time-travel technology is that of television. Even the term 'roll-back' used by Whitaker about every fifteen seconds is the same as the "rollback and mix" that makes the TARDIS appear and disappear. The scoop has a scanner (somehow) and peeps in on the dinosaurs (like the then-recent Saturday morning kid's show *Outa Space*!). CCTV, the big "threat" in "Day of the Daleks" and "The Green Death" is routine in this story. The whole surveillance and processing aspect of this story is crucial: in Part One, the Doctor and Sarah are treated as numbers by a bored officer who's heard all the excuses before. Later there's a long chase with helicopters. London is both a giant prison and as

unregulated space for adventures to happen in while everyone's away. We saw this in "The Invasion", and now it's turned on its head and the Doctor is part of the problem for a lot of the story, instead of working for the apparatus of control.

Which brings us to the biggest point: despite being made just *before* the Yom Kippur War (see **Was 1973 the Annus Mirabilis?** under "Carnival of Monsters" and **Who's Running the Country?** under "The Green Death"), this is the first story of the mid-70s. Everyone in the early 70s knew that there was a problem or two with continued economic expansion and population growth. What could be done about it was the main concern; the small sustainable semi-drop-out communes mentioned in the notes for "The Green Death" became increasingly appealing as people in cities underwent power-cuts and lay-offs as the year ended. Most people were compromising and making do - as always happens when there's a strange crisis in Britain - but immediately afterwards the majority went back to how they'd always lived. You got that a lot in the mid-seventies. Nixon cancelled the Apollo programme to pay for Vietnam, a war he kept going to get re-elected. While America was losing faith in its leaders, in Britain a crippling economic crisis or two confirmed that the wheels had come off. The Club of Rome, a German-based global think tank, warned everyone about a population timebomb, and the idea of oil running out was no longer a thing that might happen "one day" but "next month". On the surface, the message of "Invasion of the Dinosaurs" is that there's no going back and we have to make what we can of the future.

Everyone waited for someone else to start first. Everyone knew they'd have to adjust to a long-term change but not right now, thank you, so the obvious solution was getting everyone to do it at once, ideally by consent but - if needs be - by force. Thus we come up to that old chestnut of the ends justifying the means. This is traditionally seen as a bad thing in television drama, as it makes the antagonists at best hypocrites and at worst monsters. In real life writers from the left, like Hulke and - more like him than many realise - Pip and Jane Baker would be intrigued by what can make someone switch off his or her conscience. This is, for anyone who'd been active in politics in the 1950s and 60s, a live issue. Do you support absolutely everything done in the Soviet Union just because your politics and their start from the same place? Do you sell out to get into a position of power to actually do something? It would seem that somewhere under all the silly rubber monsters and pompous homilies about greed is a better story just about Sir Charles Grover.

Once this moral dilemma is identified, Dicks can take it and make a superficially less serious story about the same idea - see "Robot", in which the eco-protester and mad scientist are combined into a more flawed and sympathetic figure, although once again this is very low down in the mix. If this looks like a stretch, look what the series says about the scientific rebel who puts his money where his mouth is and protests in a self-consistent way. It's possible to conceive of Cliff Jones in "The Green Death" as turning out like Kettlewell, but the story-logic is that he's a goodie not just because he's Welsh, young and Jo fancies him, but because there's no inconsistency between what he believes and how he acts. There's no suggestion here that the series has actually changed its stance, since the Doctor insists that he sympathises with Operation Golden Age before adding a serious 'but'. It'd be going too far to say that this injects a sense of realism into the eco-argument after "The Green Death", since realism seems less at home here among the rubber dinosaurs than it did among the giant maggots, yet there is a sense of *Doctor Who* reining in its optimism.

Things That Don't Make Sense This point seems so central to the story it's astonishing that it wasn't mentioned... the obvious paradox of Operation Golden Age is that the conspirators believe they can wind back time and live on prehistoric Earth, even though this will ensure that their ancestors never existed.

But even assuming everything *did* go ahead as planned - would it actually make a blind bit of difference? Could a few dozen, or even a few hundred, middle-aged Hampstead residents wipe out *anything* in prehistoric Earth (presuming for the moment that they're going there)? Isn't it a lot more likely that they'll just die off? Insofar as we can tell, they don't even have any equipment beyond their bare hands - taking tractors along would be hypocritical, even if they knew how to get petrol. Ditto with guns, which it seems aren't effective against dinosaurs anyway.

And if they're going to become part of *recorded* history, things get clearer but more pointless. Precisely which bit of the past they're planning to

relocate to with this doohickey is unclear (fandom assumes, understandably but illogically, that they're all going to the Cretaceous)... logically any time before 1750 is fair game, but realistically, it makes just as much sense for them to go to America circa 1200 AD. Then they could happily make a mess of their lives without affecting history much, because the Comanches would slaughter them and leave no trace. Or if they went to the late Cretaceous age, either Adric would come and kill them all [19.6, "Earthshock"] or the Xeriphas [19.7, "Time-Flight"] would melt them down for recycling as lycra-clad spirits. Or they could be dino-chow, Smilodon-snacks or mashed by mammoths. [Maybe the thirteenth century plot-dispensing man in the garage is more of a clue than we thought. Maybe they're going to the time of King John, and will make an idyllic William Morris-style mediaeval utopia with smocks and nice wallpaper, then die of smallpox in under a month. Of course, if they *really* wanted to wreck history, they could just sabotage the signing of Magna Carta... no, hang on, that's a silly idea.]

If Whitaker's time-field would rewind history on Earth but not anywhere else in the universe, then what would happen to the Doctor? Presumably he'd vanish from Earth at the beginning of "Spearhead from Space" as his exile ran backwards, but where would he go after that...? Or, as the time reversals don't seem to affect him, would he just be permanently stuck in a "frozen time" zone in a "1970s" that's mutually exclusive with the Golden Agers' revised history?

A few of the colonists seem to "wake up" in episode six... so do the baddies genuinely have hundreds of people alive in suspended animation or not? [This would, in fact, be a big breakthrough even for *Doctor Who* space-travel.] If it's just part of the deception, then they must have moved with *amazing* speed in the final phase - loading almost everyone involved [save for the overseers, such as Adam] into the "spaceship" and "awakening" them at near enough the last minute.

We should also mention that the colonists have been hand-picked to become the progenitors of the "new" human race, yet they're not the brightest bulbs on the tree. Notice how Adam tells Ruth, 'All our friends are waking up', which concerns him to the point that he fails to spot Sarah re-entering the faux airlock right in front of his eyes. Soon after, Ruth *twice* becomes alarmed that everyone present will die if Sarah "leaves the spaceship", totally forgetting that she can just shut the "airlock" behind her. And aren't they wearing a lot more suede than most vegetarians? [All right, if they're going to make it on a new world, they'll probably have to raise and slaughter livestock for at least the first generation. but this lot look incapable of existing without Waitrose doing home deliveries.] They're oddly credulous when it suits them, believing that middle-aged ministers are fit enough to do space-walks with no training. Then there's Mark, who swallows the idea that the whole thing is a front for evil time-travel experiments, yet can't conceive of a politician lying. And the fake spaceship is made with shaky windows composed of kitchen cling-film, with no sound-proofing at all. Mr Robinson, upon discovering that the 'colony' is a fraud perpetrated as a pretext for genocide, says 'We looked into it all very carefully - I sold my house' as though this settles the matter. And how do even these po-faced zealots keep straight faces when the documentary in the Reminder Room talks about how, 'the very seas, where life began, are now becoming lifeless and stinky...'?

"Deserted" London is amusingly busy, with traffic sounds clearly audible under the Doctor's statement that no vehicles are moving. And why, we might ask, isn't the public telephone that they try to use working? Sarah's suggestion - that it's down to vandalism - sounds dubious, unless you think that looters would feel the sudden urge to tear down phone lines. [Did the military deliberately cut the phones as part of a news blackout? Or did the dinosaurs just happen to sever the phone connections in that area? It's very odd.] Oh, and when the Doctor and Sarah walk past a branch of Allders, we can see - reflected in the shop window - not only the boom-mic operator but several passing cars. And just look over Benton's shoulder in the stand-off with Finch at the start of episode six.

Mike claims the air in London is 'clean' after three weeks without cars. Even if that were possible, one might suspect that the stench of rotting food would overcome this. Anyone who lives in the parts of London where they recently tried fortnightly refuse collections will know that the Doctor's nose should alert him to something being very wrong in this city, but it doesn't. No smell...not even any rats. There's a single dog chewing something in a Renault, but no packs of dogs, as one might expect. As foxes take advantage of even a Bank Holiday lull in traffic, you'd expect to see a lot more of them, too.

Dinosaurs in the Doctor Who universe genuinely are the most powerful creatures to ever inhabit the planet. In particular, a tyrannosaurs rex is strong enough to smash brick buildings and metal beams, and is bulletproof. At least, we think it's bulletproof... it's actually a little hard to tell, what with the tyrannosaurus rex offering such a big target, but the UNIT troops aiming for a spot some fifteen feet to its left. Then, once the monster on film has left them standing there on VT, the soldiers return to film and amble slowly to the Land Rover without even checking on their prisoners.

So Benton figures out a link between radio interference and the arrival of '... them' [it's all a bit Terry Nation - trying to make a mystery out of this, despite showing us two separate dinosaurs in the first fifteen minutes], but not even the Brigadier wonders if it's possible to triangulate the source of the transmissions. Had UNIT done so, we could've been spared three episodes of mollicking about in search of Whitaker's base. Oh, and it's a remarkably well-informed peasant who assaults Our Heroes in a garage, after spending three minutes loafing not quite out-of-shot waiting for his cue.

In a briefing, the Brigadier mentions that the military base is 'on the periphery', and points to Perivale. Well, what bloody use is that? Even with no traffic, it would take half an hour to reach any dinosaur sightings in, say, Piccadilly. And the Doctor refuses to believe that the time-eddies can be confined to London, or any similar-sized zone. [If this were true, then Torchwood wouldn't have happened.] Helicopters are conveniently available, but instead of being used to spot large reptiles arriving out of nowhere, they're used solely for hunting the Doctor [in a vast forest that appears to have sprouted up in Wimbledon overnight, somehow.]

In Part Two, Mike sabotages the Doctor's stun-gun. What's odd about this is that the gun uses a technique as yet undeveloped, but Whitaker - without even seeing it, and in the space of about five minutes - devises a small gizmo that will deactivate it. [And yet the Brigadier hired Liz Shaw...] Never mind that the Doctor checks his gadget three times (we counted), yet fails to see this rather visible add-on. Also, just prior to this undertaking toward the end of episode two, the UNIT troops give an extremely curious salute - as if they're pointing their guns at their superiors.

We discussed in the last story how it's possible that Sarah did some work for UNIT prior to her meeting the Doctor, but that's largely conjecture. On screen - and while the Brig and company obviously know Sarah's true identity when this story opens, possibly because they investigated her disappearance in "The Time Warrior" - it's odd that UNIT seems awfully eager to allow a plucky young female journalist about the place, her being a friend of the Doctor or no, as if that wouldn't pose a security risk. Just as odd, Mike talks to Sarah about 'that business in Wales with the giant maggots', as if she knows what he's talking about.

And while we've already mentioned Sarah's repeated habit of trusting people she really shouldn't, we should highlight the way she doesn't pause to wonder why Finch [who's setting her up for death by T-Rex] would give her a pass to photograph the sleeping dinosaur, as he's *supposed* to be keeping the existence of the monsters a secret, and would ever allow such a scoop to see the light of day. (Anyway, did Finch order the guards *in* the hanger to go outside while he hacked though the T-Rex's chains? Shouldn't the Brig and company have found this - and the fact that nobody was directly watching the dinosaur when Sarah showed up - a bit suspicious?) And after the attempt on her life fails, Sarah doesn't seem to consider that that Finch set her up, allowing him to re-capture her in episode five. As part of this, she only considers that maybe, possibly, taking some back-up along is a good idea once she's back in Grover's office... and it's much too late.

Sarah is *such* a geek that she can remember the world high jump record to three decimal places, despite never showing any enthusiasm for sport even in her capacity as a journalist. She can't, however, figure out that using a flash camera to take photos through a closed window will result in lots of shots of very bright windows, nor that it might jolt the sleeping tyrannosaurus awake. And we might fault her for leaving her camera behind as she escaped from the T-Rex, purely on the grounds that Lois Lane wouldn't do that. She also fails, in her note to the Brigadier about the "spaceship" she's just escaped from, to leave the location of the villains' base. Our Heroes have already figured that out, but it might've been a helpful thing to mention.

In his quest to track down the localised time-distortions, the Doctor has forgotten that he already built a handy portable gadget to locate TOMTIT ["The Time Monster"], and instead has to build a portable detector from scratch. [It's possible, though, that the previous locator only worked because the Master's TARDIS was part of the TOMTIT system.] Also, he stresses the need for speed, but winds up whizzing about in his space-age pimp-car, as opposed to charging about the place in Bessie. Mind you, he only uses his "Whomobile" after zooming about in a jeep for an episode. And he rather foolishly mimics Sarah's pattern of not taking along any back-up while he goes looking for the villains' base, thereby necessitating that he drag the Brigadier back there and try to prove his findings all over again.

Part Four ends with Finch and his men walking into the hanger just as a stegosaurus appears, and taking this as proof that the Doctor is behind the dino-manifestations. In what way, though, does this incriminate him? There's no equipment present, and dinosaurs have been materialising at random for the entire story, yet it's treated as if the Doctor were hunched over a bank of controls singing, "Nyarr harr harr ! I am the villain behind it all!" (Furthermore, if the Doctor *were* the Head Villain, why would he conjure forth a dinosaur at the hanger? Surely it's not much use there?) It's also odd that the traitorous Mike Yates leaves the Doctor with Benton, never expecting that Benton will just let the Doctor do a runner. There's what appears to be a chair-squeaking noise from off-camera, a fair amount before the Doctor gingerly renders Benton unconscious and also afterward.

The baddies' secret base has two entrances - a lift in Whitehall and another under Moorgate Station - so we're to believe that they built a vast complex the size of a village under the busiest city on Earth in the 1950s without anyone noticing. We might be charitable and presume their predecessors did, then were whisked off to remote Hebridean islands under the Official Secrets Act. All the same, it's odd that this place was off limits when the Yeti showed up [5.5, "The Web of Fear"]. More strangely, it *can't* have been connected to the Goodge Street base, or else the Brigadier - who first met the Doctor there - would remember it even if the UNIT mind-rubber was set to maximum. But if that's so, why didn't they use it during all the other End-of-Civilisation-as-we-know-it events of recent years, such as "Day of the Daleks"?

A demonstration of Whitaker's time-machinery - done for Grover's benefit - has Butler smashing a tea cup and then being put into temporal reverse.

But Butler's reaction afterward is to look smugly at Grover - not to immediately smash the mug again. [Think about it... what with the cup-shattering being temporally undone, Butler shouldn't have been aware that Grover indeed witnessed the event. Against the odds, Butler somehow knows which part of the "cycle" he's on.]

But then, it looks as though the whole of London is stuck in a time-eddy long before the climax. Hours pass, but a semi-permanent rosy-fingered dawn makes everything look pink and cast long shadows - including, in Part Six, the film crew when the Doctor walks towards Finch's Land Rover [but not when he's filmed from behind]. So unless the entire six episodes take place in under ten minutes - or at 23 1/2 hour intervals - we have to attribute this as a side effect of the time-scoop. Fortunately, that might also explain why big puddles and wet pavements seem to dry up between shots, and how autumn seems to come with a terrible suddenness and then go away again.

Happily for children everywhere, Operation Golden Age snatches five types of dinosaurs from the past, and they just *happen* to be the five most famous dinosaur species. Of course, many of them weren't even native to prehistoric Britain [and, as everyone points out, the tyrannosaurus rex with three fingers is a sub-species as yet unknown to science], so Whitaker's technology must be able to reach a long way through space as well as time [as logically it would *have* to]. The problem then being: if Whitaker can grab objects from any time and any place, he could kidnap the Doctor whenever he liked, purely by setting the machine to "UNIT HQ, a few seconds ago". But then, the conspirators think that the best way of dealing with a nosy reporter like Sarah is to put her on the fake spaceship with their stooges and let her unravel the least reliable part of their scheme, so devious planning isn't their strongest suit. They also decide to take Sarah back in time with them after re-capturing her, presumably so she can cause *more* trouble for them in the distant past. And then they lock her in the only room with an accessible ventilation-shaft. Do they *want* to be stopped?

There's a curious piece of editing during the interminable chase in Part Five. We cut between shots of the soldiers as seen from sixty feet away and ten feet higher up, and a view of the Doctor standing in open ground about ten feet away and three feet higher than the camera. We're encour-aged to interpret this editing as if we're seeing the soldiers from the Doctor's point of view. But if that's true, he must be standing right in front of them, in plain sight. And on at least two occasions, they're looking straight at him. Then he hides in bushes close by, but without the obvious sounds of rustling being heard by the soldiers under whose noses he's now ineptly secreted. Alas, these troops have earlier shown that they can't see Land Rover tracks right in front of them, but the Doctor can see one through trees (or he somehow heard the engine over the noise his own vehicle is making). The vehicle-maintenance staff have equipped all the Land Rovers with cut-out switches - helpful, whenever the plot requires them to malfunction. At least UNIT are better equipped, possessing very selective explosives that can blow up a wall and kill a triceratops without damaging a flimsy litter-bin.

Why did the production team, who prior to this have witnessed Pertwee's style of delivery for *four years*, tortuously given him the line: 'It's a stegosaurus; a splendid specimen'? [They were manifethtly taking the pith; see 11.4, "The Monster of Peladon", for further apparent mockery.]

And why was a story about dinosaurs given to the writer who'd caused the production team so much hassle over naming his prehistoric reptilemen 'Silurians'?

Critique Once again, a fondly-remembered novelisation has led a generation of fans to think well of this story, and contend that the execution was muffed. "Invasion of the Dinosaurs" is fundamentally sound, they argue, but with a few crap dinosaur effects. In fact, its flaws are a lot more basic.

This story has all the hallmarks of a last throw of the dice. The production team has finally resorted to catchpenny gimmicks such as dinosaurs, UNIT hunting the Doctor and a gigantic conspiracy. The plot is illogical and relies on stupid coincidences. For anyone watching it in one gulp *now*, this adventure has the common Pertwee-era blemish of a slowly simmering story punctuated by abrupt and repetitive cliffhangers (see, for instance, 10.3, "Frontier in Space" and obviously 8.2, "The Mind of Evil") and a chase that consumes a large slice of Part Five but is forgotten almost immediately afterwards. And it's got the sodding Whomobile.

Still, as ITV's recent rather desperate *Who* clone *Primeval* shows, kids and unfussy adults will happily watch dinosaurs in present-day London and a conspiracy plot where things explode periodically - *even if* the dialogue is tedious and the characterisation is virtually non-existent. Evidently, all the punters really need are halfway-convincing dinosaurs, a cute blonde flashing her undies and ministerial shenanigans that stop the heroes from doing what needs to be done[133]. Alas, "Invasion of the Dinosaurs" only has one of these elements.

It *is*, however, as well-directed as a story of this kind could be, with clever use of locations and a cast more than adequate for the demands of the script. The good news here is that although there's little scope for creeping around in dark alleys or gloomy corridors, Paddy Russell finds ways to make the serviceable sets serve the mood. Even this is a mixed bag, and the flipside of what's being attempted is inescapable when you watch Season Eleven in rapid succession. As soon as we leave Irongron's castle, the sets and costumes all opt for muted and drab colours, culminating in an entire planet where colour-sports socks go to die after they're washed with jeans ("Planet of the Spiders"). We don't get anything like the gaudy primary colours of Season Ten until "Terror of the Zygons", and this just draws attention to the fact that the sets in "Invasion of the Dinosaurs" are functional, but nothing more. While this is a bit of an asset (part of that whole "Yeti-in-a-loo" thing they keep trying to make work), it just adds to the overall sense of Season Eleven being a year in which the predominant question is, "Will this do?"

Ironically, if there's *one* person visibly putting in an effort, it's the one operating the video effects. For all that fandom (understandably) likes to give the dinosaur puppets a drubbing, anyone who actually *watches* the story will observe a couple of very good model shots of the sleeping tyrannosaurus being roused. When staying still, the dinos don't look altogether bad. It's only when they're forced to move, or - notably - to participate in the utterly lamentable "tyrannosaurus snogging a brontosaurus" scene that the effects look as heinous as their reputation suggests. And before you can say it, no - CGI effects could only redeem the sleeping / still shots, as the *truly* ropey ones have CSO actors inlaid. Like it or not, we should accept that better effects won't redeem this story for a great long while.[134]

It's been argued that a lot of the Pertwee stories

seem more acceptable if watched over a period of some weeks or days (i.e. as was originally intended), as opposed to swallowing the whole story in one go. Some stories have changes in what key characters know coming at twenty-five minute intervals but others, like this and "The Mind of Evil", need longer to develop story threads and so have to contrive cliffhangers that come out of nowhere and go away again. If you think of "Invasion of the Dinosaurs" as a two-hour play punctuated by a rubber monster going 'raaah' every so often, it's *less* misleading than seeing, for instance, "Carnival of Monsters" edited into a feature that removes a lot of the original impact. Even so, this isn't paced like a conventional thriller and shouldn't be judged as one because, as with *all* pre-1981 stories, the fact that we got one episode a week affected how we saw the story on transmission. (Or even *if* we saw all of it: see **What Difference Does A Day Make?** under 19.1, "Castrovalva".) Nonetheless, those of you who saw or participated in the fevered and sometimes demented online speculation about the end of "The Stolen Earth" (X4.12) should be aware that back in the 70s, a more civilised debate happened in school playgrounds every Monday morning following *every single episode*. So the implications of Mike Yates joining the bad-guys were as much a topic of debate on 21st of January, 1974, as trying to make "HANG ET ROSE" make sense as an anagram of 'Osterhagen' in the week leading up to 5th of July, 2008. Sarah waking up in "Dinosaurs" on a space-ship three months out from Earth was even *more* sensational.

Watch this adventure an episode a week (and okay, it doesn't *have* to be Saturdays at ten past six), and you see a different story from the one you get by just slapping on the video and letting it run. In fact, watching the Pertwee stories an episode a day will take just over two months; one a week will be eighteen months and you'll appreciate the ritual aspects of watching it (with Len Martin reading the Pools results just before each episode, or whatever equivalent you invent or discover). The soap-opera character-dynamics have a more potent cumulative effect, so that Jo leaving, Mike betraying UNIT and the build-up to the regeneration work on a deeper level than if you know abut them from guidebooks or cursory viewings of the stories as discrete stories.

However... even allowing for *all* of that, the sad fact remains that even on the first transmission, the kids of Britain thought the monsters in

"Dinosaurs" were rubbish and that the latter half of the story was just killing time. You can come at this week by week or all in one go, yet it *still* looks flimsy from a story perspective. Indeed, anyone who sells you a notion that there's a cracking story here is just overselling the point.

Who knows? Maybe this story *could* have worked with better dinosaurs, and if so much hadn't been staked on the puppets being good enough. Or perhaps without any dinosaurs at all, the story might have functioned with just a faked alien invasion or something. (Although it doesn't augur well that this story's basic plot is identical to the element of "The Enemy of the World" that's deemed to have fallen flat.) Regardless, what we *have* is the story they made, where the floundering attempts to find new ways to do the same old UNIT set-pieces grind on beneath a generally competent production of what was once a clever idea. It's all done with conviction, but no enthusiasm.

The Facts

Written by Malcolm Hulke. Directed by Paddy Russell. Cast: . Viewing figures: 11.0 million, 10.1 million, 11.0 million, 9.0 million, 9.0 million, 7.5 million. AIs (where recorded) hovered around 62%.

Supporting Cast John Bennett (General Finch), Terry Walsh (Warehouse Looter), Noel Johnson (Charles Grover M.P.), Peter Miles (Professor Whitaker), Martin Jarvis (Butler), Terence Wilton (Mark), Carmen Silvera (Ruth), Brian Badcoe (Adam).

Working Titles "Timescoop" (a word which eventually finds its way into the programme nearly a decade later, for 20.7, "The Five Doctors"), "The Bridgehead from Space".

Cliffhangers A tyrannosaurus ('raaah!') stops the military vehicle that's transporting the Doctor and Sarah to a detention camp; the Doctor's stun-guns fails to work on an apatosaurus after Yates' sabotage, which isn't a problem until *another* tyrannosaurus appears (and after the Doctor has already said 'mind you, I wouldn't want to try it on a tyrannosaurus', too); having been rendered unconscious by the Operation Golden Age conspirators, Sarah wakes up on what appears to be a

spaceship and is told by 'Mark' that she left Earth three months ago; the Doctor arrives at the hangar just as a stegosaurus materialises, giving General Finch a chance to arrest him on suspicion of being the monster-maker; the Doctor hurries across London but once *again* finds a tyrannosaurus appearing in his way. The last episode ends with the Doctor offering to take Sarah to Florana, the planet they're aiming for at the start of the next story.

What Was in the Charts? "The Show Must Go On", Leo Sayer; "Tiger Feet", Mud; "Forever", Roy Wood; "Top of the World", The Carpenters; "Radar Love", Golden Earring; "Dance With the Devil", Cozy Powell.

The Lore

• "Invasion of the Dinosaurs" is a hybrid of two ideas kicking around in early 1973. One was a parable about Vichy France, with aliens invading London and the government-in-exile in Harrogate giving over more and more powers to the occupying forces, until the Brigadier leads a resistance movement. The other was a trip back to prehistoric times to milk some more from the effects developed for "Carnival of Monsters". In the proposal, the Prime Minister was to fly to the alien ship to show it was all right, and be seen returning in a shuttle waving a computer printout - even as the aliens took up residence in the Tower of London and left eggs around the city to hatch into monsters that kept it free from humans.

The "monsters in deserted London" angle was the one thing Dicks liked about it, with the added incentive that it made it easier to talk Letts out of trying to do too much with model dinosaurs and CSO. So the first draft of what was then called "Timescoop" was discussed in January, just as it became clear that Katy Manning was leaving. As with all the scripts for the 1974 series, a big concern was allowing reliable writers to produce the material, allowing Letts and Dicks to oversee *Moonbase 3*. This story was slated to begin production in September - just as they would be finishing work on the lunar drama. Indeed, Dicks had Robert Holmes along for the last two episodes as uncredited deputy script editor (how "deputy" he was is a matter for debate), freeing Dicks up for another job he had coming (see "The Monster of Peladon").

• Officially the location filming began on 2nd of September, with the shots of deserted London. However, it can't all have been done then. Some of what we might term "Second Unit" material (actually filmed by the same people who did the main filming) was achieved "guerrilla" style without official sanction from the Police or the BBC - this probably happened very early one Sunday (so it could have been 26th of August or 9th of September, but possibly as early as June) before the final scripts were even commissioned. At least one batch was done just after a rainfall, but other shots show the city bone-dry. Director Paddy Russell took with her cameraman Tony Leggo, who had been much in demand for documentaries and had also worked on "The Massacre". These opening scenes included a lot of the same locations used in 2.2, "The Dalek Invasion of Earth" and one from "The Web of Fear" - as no sound was required, only the director, the cameraman and a camera assistant went.

• For benefit of intrepid souls planning to look for the filming locations, we here present them in order of appearance. There's the Embankment (strictly speaking, the Albert Embankment) just along from which is Westminster Bridge ("Earth hath not anything to show more fair"), the Cenotaph, Trafalgar Square (you knew *that* one, right?), Margaret Street (the other side of Oxford Street, about a hundred yards from Oxford Circus tube station and near Broadcasting House), Haymarket (where all the theatres are), Billingsgate (the fish market: at that time near Monument and the new-ish London Bridge, although the market moved to near Canary Wharf in 1982 and Lord Rogers supervised converting the listed building into offices), Long Lane (it's near Barbican tube and handy for the Museum of London - look, you might as well get the big picture if you're going on some kind of tour, but be careful of the complicated pedestrian walkways over roads. the system that partly inspired "Castrovalva"), what at the time was ceasing to be the flower market at Covent Garden (it's now the London Transport Museum) and Regent's Park, the Outer Circle. If you start at Margaret Street, go anti-clockwise - cross Westminster Bridge, walk along Albert Embankment to Waterloo Bridge, and then via Covent Garden to Billingsgate, and thence to Long Lane, you'll go through all of these and a few more locations used later in the story in about ninety minutes. However, this isn't the order in which they were filmed. Covent Garden

and Billingsgate were done later than the rest of the shoot, on the listed start-date of 2nd of September.

• All right, we'll talk about the dinosaur puppets... from 8th of September to 6th of November, various model shots were executed. Clifford Culley at Westbury Design and Optical Ltd, Pinewood, had been granted a larger than usual budget for effects, but soon realised he'd need help. In the time allotted stop-motion animation was impossible, so the majority of dinosaur effects were wire-operated models in real-time - either on film or in the studio on yellow backgrounds. He subcontracted to model-maker Rodney Fuller, but found that Fuller's models didn't always move as desired. A major problem was that the cables often fed through from under the base via one leg - meaning that walking, or in fact any other large-scale motion, was just impossible. Amazingly, Culley and co did some rather better model effects in the film *One of Our Dinosaurs is Missing*, released by Disney shortly afterwards, in which Pertwee and many other actors you'll know from 70s *Doctor Who* appear.

The filmed model work proceeded after recording of the episodes had ended, but some of the "interactive" shots on VT would be done "live" with actors inserted via CSO. From 23rd of September onwards, the proper location work with actors and sound-recordists began in the vicinity of Smithfield meat-market, near Long Lane and Moorgate tube station. The rest of the week's shoot was all to the West of Central London, in the Ealing, Kingston and Finchley districts.

• At the Smithfield location, the scripted scene of the Doctor on a motorbike taking readings when looking for the Timescoop was amended when - to Russell's astonishment - Letts agreed that Jon Pertwee should show off his new car. Back in January, and while opening a Ford dealership in the West Midlands, Pertwee had seen custom-designer Pete Ferries' display model (the Black Widow), and asked about getting himself a futuristic ride. He'd suggested the idea of contrasting Bessie with something space-age, but Letts pointed out that the budgets were getting squeezed enough with Pertwee's annual pay rises and the rising cost of everything else. (See **Why Didn't They Just Spend more Money?** under 12.2, "The Ark in Space".) So Pertwee and Ferries designed a car to look like it could fly but be street-legal. It had the engine of a Hillman Imp

(British motorists will be giggling here, but it could get up to 100 mph), the chassis of a Bond Bug (the most 70s car imaginable - a three-wheel sports car in various shades of orange and purple), aluminium wings and body, a rubber skirt (like a hovercraft; indeed, they tried to joke that it *was* one on *Blue Peter*) and a dashboard with a trim-phone and flashing lights simulating a computer. The windscreen would eventually be adapted from a motor-boat, but at this stage Visual Effects fashioned a temporary one just to make the car roadworthy. The obvious conclusion people have drawn is that - at least at the start of 1973 - Pertwee was looking to stick around for a while and cash in on being TV's Mr Space-Age when making personal appearances. But by the time Part Four was screened, things were very different.

• As with "The Web of Fear", the BBC had difficulty getting permission to use London Transport property, but were granted the use of the exterior of Moorgate tube (the gates were opened for no extra charge). The following day was spent in Ealing at various light industrial sites such as the Central Electricity Generating Board substation (the temporary UNIT HQ - a real school was used for the detention centre, oddly) and a storage depot owned by Pickfords' removals, wherein we're supposed to think ptero-dactyls are lurking. (Unlike the other prehistoric beasts, the pterodactyls were done either as hand-puppets or flown on wires - as you doubtless guessed - thus allowing the actors, usually Pertwee, to make physical contact with them.) A lot of the following day's planned locations were changed at short notice to use the Southall Gas Works, which you may recall was used in "The Ambassadors of Death".

• A scene cut from the first episode had a loot-er picking up the scattered money and then being attacked by a pterodactyl. It was probably elimi-nated for reasons of over-running, but might've been lost to avoid spoiling the surprise of the dinosaurs (more on this in a bit). As such, it's presently the only colour footage from the episode.

• Clayponds Avenue, Brentford, served as the street with the dog eating something from an abandoned Renault 4 - the house in ruins was apparently demolished soon after. Much of Thursday's material was filmed around Ham and Kingston, conveniently close to the director's

home. The TARDIS actually materialises near Wimbledon Common, which became the site of pilgrimage for the nation's children when *The Wombles* began transmission. The TARDIS needed a lick of paint and the doors fixing, as well as new 'Police Box' signs on each side.

• Whether by luck or design, most of the cast had previous form in *Doctor Who*. Carmen Silvera, later to star in *Allo Allo*, had been various female characters in "The Celestial Toymaker" (3.7); Martin Jarvis, more famous by this stage for *The Forsyte Saga* (but later much more recognisable and called upon to narrate everything) had been Captain Hilio, the insect Hamlet, in "The Web Planet" (2.5) and would be the Governor in "Vengeance on Varos" (22.2). Peter Miles had been Dr Lawrence in "Doctor Who and the Silurians", and had therefore gone from not believing in pre-historic beings to summoning them. He'll be back in 12.4, "Genesis of the Daleks", but you probably knew that, and he'd just done an episode of *Moonbase 3*. Charles Grover was played by Noel Johnson, hitherto the King of Atlantis (4.5, "The Underwater Menace").

The main exceptions to this list were Ben Aris (Lieutenant Shears), who played military types left right and centre in the 70s, and John Bennett, star of *Market at Honey Lane* (see "Day of the Daleks"). He later did another *Who*, however (14.6, "The Talons of Weng-Chiang", although you probably knew that too). One last minute addition was Colin Bell, late of the Royal Navy (well, 9.3, "The Sea Devils", at least) as the private in charge of radio for the last episode. George Bryson had played Private Ogden, but he was unavailable for the last day's recording, so 'Private Bryson' took over. Brian Badcoe (Adam) was the sort of experi-enced actor who might have been expected to pop up in *Doctor Who* at *some* point, and he was mar-ried to Hilda Braid. (She played little old ladies for so long, she actually became one.)

• We should also mention that collectively, many of the cast and crew recall Pertwee as being really apathetic about everything (except his cos-tume, according to Russell). And here's a small distraction for you: in episode two, it's alleged that Pertwee had his lines secreted around the set when the Doctor argues with Finch. John Levene joked that Pertwee was always looking at *him* when he said that the brontosaurus was 'large, placid and stupid', so the production team made sure Tom Baker did likewise in "Robot".

- The episodes were recorded almost one per studio-day, on Mondays and Tuesdays. The Timescoop (never actually named as such on screen) includes a curved back of lights flashing in sequences - doubtless, you'll be starting to recognise this set-feature. Much of the rest of the lab came from stock, and the stun-gun was also a seasoned veteran.

- Although nobody has any idea what dinosaurs looked like, or how they sounded, a few decisions were made early on. The stegosaurus was made green to make a contrast with the browns of all the others. The tyrannosaurus voice was a recording of a cow played backwards. Russell suggested that the brontosaurus would have a smaller voice-box and would thus be more feline-sounding. As so much post-synched sound was required, there was no point going to the expense of firing blanks from the rifles on location, so all the artillery noises were added later.

- Between recording the middle two episodes and the last batch, Pertwee took part in various anniversary celebrations for the show's tenth birthday in November, showing off the Whomobile on *Blue Peter* during their extended feature on ten years of the series. (This is supposedly the point when Episode Four of 4.2, "The Tenth Planet" went on its walkabout.) This also had the script about the "Monsters' shopping list" at the end of 6.7, "The War Games", which was used verbatim twice more. That was 5th of November, the same week that the Whomobile was shown off at a circus. Meanwhile, the rights for the comic-strip adaptation had gone back to *TV Comic* (see **Why Did We Countdown to TV Action?** under "The Claws of Axos") and they sent a crew to photograph the making of this story.

- The ambitious use of CSO continued. For this story the main problem was getting the image of the actors small enough to fit in with the already-filmed model shots. (Some of the technical team tried to persuade Sladen that CSO worked like ultraviolet light, making nylon transparent, and that she required special underwear to preserve her modesty.) A lot of jiggery-pokery with video-disc machines was involved in some of the time-slips and a caption with red lines radiating out on a CSO-shade yellow background was used for temporal displacement. In the climax, Pertwee's image was fed over a freeze-frame that was itself fed back, with a blue shading, rather as the original title-sequence had been made. There was, in fact, so much complex image-processing and monkeying about with pictures, they booked a gallery-only day to complete it without the actors. Letts attended this and took careful notes. The next time this was required (15.5, "Underworld"), it took a lot of negotiation to clear it with BBC bosses.

- Almost all of the episodes overran and needed trimming. One obvious anomaly created by the cuts is Grover suddenly knowing Sarah, as their meeting is removed from episode three. Episode five lost a nice scene where, due to staff shortages, the Brigadier orders Benton to keep himself under guard. Episode six is missing the explanation of why Sarah's been put with the Golden Age mob and not killed - Grover tells Yates that her resourcefulness is something most of his recruits lack and will need. However, the biggest edit came long after these...

- According to Letts, it was Russell's idea to retitle the first episode "Invasion" to create suspense and surprise about the dinosaurs appearing. Two days after broadcast, Hulke wrote a stiff letter to Dicks about this. Apart from the potential loss of viewers, there wasn't much logic to it, as the presence of dinosaurs had been widely advertised in advance. The decision must have been made before 5th of January, as the continuity announcer called it "Invasion" at the end of the previous episode. Switching title after one episode made the production team seem indecisive, Hulke added. He was already planning to move on and concentrate on the novelisations and his own projects, but this ended his connection with the broadcast series.

However, the change of title to one already used (6.3, "The Invasion") is *not* the reason the first episode went AWOL. In the First Edition of this book we discussed the widely-held belief that the wiping of the colour tape was an error. In fact, the opposite is true: in August 1974, the decision was made to erase this story but the last five episodes were inadvertently spared. August 1974 is something of an odd time to be wiping a story, because whilst officially the BBC were within their contractual rights to do so (the Doctor had been recast, so the Equity arrangement said the Pertwee stories were now unbroadcastable in Britain), the new Doctor had yet to appear. Moreover, the stories were usually held whilst overseas markets were sounded out - and 1974 is the start of the big push to sell the Pertwee stories to Australia and Hong Kong. It's not impossible that Letts arranged for its erasure, but he wasn't producer any more.

Whatever the reason, a 16mm black and white "engineering copy" of episode one was obtained by a fan almost by accident, and returned to the BBC in 1983. (The same batch gave us 5.2, "The Abominable Snowmen" episode two and 4.6, "The Moonbase" episode four.) And indeed, episode six was selected as a prime specimen of Pertwee-era *Who* in 1983 as part of the BFI's celebrations of the show's twentieth anniversary - so obviously not everyone thinks it's a dud. It remains, however, a sore point with Letts.

• Grover's spacesuit is one from *Moonbase 3* - so obviously, they were determined to salvage *something* from the series. By the time recording on "Invasion of the Dinosaurs" finished, it was obvious that *Moonbase 3* was a ratings disaster and a critical war-zone.

11.3: "Death to the Daleks"

(Serial XXX, Four Episodes, 23rd February - 16th March 1974.)

Which One is This? Ever wondered what would happen if the Daleks lost the use of their guns and had to outsmart everyone instead? No, neither did anyone else - but this is what *did* happen. Humans and Daleks have to live together in less-than-perfect harmony, on a planet whose living city / ancient monument eats a lot of energy. Any leftover Rider-Haggardry not used in "Planet of the Daleks" is present and correct, with the music leading you to expect that Sarah might turn to the camera and say, "Hello. I'm being a sacrificial victim. Why don't you all join in?"

Firsts and Lasts Though this isn't the first time that an ominous alien force drags the TARDIS off-course and forces it crash-materialise on a strange planet, it's the first time that it's happened since the Doctor got the Ship's dematerialisation circuit working. In other words, we're now entering the era of the programme in which "ominous alien force" is a plot device to get the Doctor to go to interesting places. Or, in this case, a quarry.

It's the first occasion that Sarah gets 'What is it, Doctor?', and also the first time she gets to wear a swimsuit. (Although if anything, this just proves that she's not the dolly-bird type.) Conversely, it's the last appearance of the "proper" Daleks (meaning pre-Davros), and the last time Murphy Grumbar is inside one of the shells.

First story script-edited by Robert Holmes, as Terrance Dicks was busy rushing "The Monster of Peladon" through. Holmes obsessions on display here include booby-trapped ancient city / temples, living cities with roots, names sounding a bit like 'Epsilon' (as in 'Rassilon'), sacrificial religions and so forth. (Holmes gets full control of the script commissioning and overall tone of the series in Season Twelve, whereupon the programme becomes a much more horror-driven affair. Note that "Death to the Daleks" is a much more brutal-looking story than those around it, and the attempted ritual sacrifice of Sarah seems so much more sordid than Jo Grant's "altar-piece" in 8.5, "The Daemons".) A lot of ideas thrown in here get re-used whenever a story is under-running or needs a rewrite in a hurry. Nation, meanwhile, tries out the idea of living machines with roots that behave like snakes, similar to what we'll see on *Blake's 7* with the *Liberator*'s defence system and - surprisingly late - calls a character 'Tarrant'.

More important than Holmes' contribution, though (if that's possible) is the final breakthrough in production. This is the first story to be made completely out of sequence; it was filmed set-by-set, rather than episode-by-episode.

Four Things to Notice About "Death to the Daleks"...

1. Carey Blyton's back, folks: and he's brought the London Saxophone Quartet with him. As with his last, equally distinctive score (7.2, "Doctor Who and the Silurians"), it's split between eerily evocative and infantile. Most people plump for the latter, and the "Three Blind Mice"-style Dalek theme that occurs when they're plodding around being picked on by troglodytes, hologram 'antibodies' and a few roots (!), coupled with a soundtrack wherein a clarinet is fed through a ring-modulator to make it sound like a Dalek is playing it (!!)[137], is, sadly, the main memory of this story for many people. And yes, Daleks *can* plod, as this adventure amply demonstrates.

2. Yet the one really memorable effect (for the *right* reason) is the living city's glowing, touch-sensitive wall designs, accompanied by groovy mock-Inca decals and a maze such as the ones Vladimir Koziakin used to do in those books you got in dentist's waiting-rooms. (The script specifically named him, that's how ubiquitous these were.) The Doctor claims to recognise the city's design from Peru; although viewers paying atten-

tion might recognise most of it from Atlantis (9.5, "The Time Monster"). A floor design in the city, however, provides us with a scene that those watching the omnibus version of this adventure wouldn't have recognised as the single most underwhelming cliffhanger in living memory. Due to the editing jiggery-pokery that resulted when one episode *over*ran and the one before it *under*-ran, Part Three doesn't so much end and it just... stops. (See **Cliffhangers** for more.)

3. When we first met the Daleks back in the 60s, Barbara mentioned that they smelled like a fairground ride. This has occasionally popped up in other ways, such as their DARDIS machines resembling penny arcades, and the procession of Daleks coming out of one resembling the cars at the start of a roller-coaster. Not to mention their decision to fight the Doctor in a haunted house at the Festival of Ghana. (Here we're chiefly thinking about 2.8, "The Chase", but there are others... *many* others.) But we here learn that the Daleks have their own shooting gallery. On even a small scout ship such as this, they have the means to replace their exterminator-sticks with what sound like BB guns and take pot-shots at little model police boxes. Now, either they do this whenever they're bored - and so were able to arm themselves when unexpectedly robbed of their power - or they've got the means to do this with no energy-reserves at all. Either way, the obvious inference is that they have toy TARDISes just lying around on their ships. The Doctor has really made an impact on their culture.

4. As ever in a Terry Nation script, the human supporting cast really is astonishingly wet. Observe how the Marine Space Corps are made up of polite people in blue jumpsuits called 'Jill' and 'Richard' (more the sorts of people you'd see at a fondue party in a 70s sitcom than hardened Space Marines, of the kind James Cameron *et al* offered us in the 80s). Breaking the mould is Galloway, the big gruff Scotsman, but *he* turns out to be violent and treacherous. Guess who's going to be carrying out the suicidal act of redemption? There's a spooky alien who turns out to be friendly and ever so helpful, Sarah finds the Doctor's lamp with blood, misleadingly (although not as bad a cop-out as 1.5, "The Keys of Marinus", which also had hooded figures creeping around booby-trapped temples).

Worse, as with "Planet of the Daleks", Nation's script glosses over the idea of the TARDIS as an unimaginably complex interdimensional organ-ism, and instead portrays the Ship as a box with some engines in it. Whereas in "Planet" the Ship doesn't even have its own working air supply, in "Death to the Daleks" the Doctor has to open its doors with a crank-handle when some of the power gets drained. Fortunately, Nation's been asked to ring the changes just a bit, so instead of yet another studio-bound jungle we get filmed location work with moody lighting and a sense of space. That's right, we're actually saying, "Thank goodness they made this in a quarry."

The Continuity

The Doctor His comment regarding a Root that attacks a Dalek suggests that he knows his *Hamlet* ('A palpable hit'), and that he's been to at least one cricket match. [See 3.4, "The Daleks' Master Plan" for when he didn't know owt about the game, and 12.2, "The Ark in Space", for his apparently abrupt acquisition of knowledge and enthusiasm for the sport. Then see also 16.1, "The Ribos Operation"; 17.5, "The Horns of Nimon"; and all of Season Nineteen.] When the Exxilons threaten to sacrifice Sarah, the Doctor abandons all pretence of having a plan and physically charges a crowd in the hopes of rescuing her. He's noticeably tactile with Sarah, Jill Tarrant and Bellal. [Indeed, at times in Part Four, it looks as if Bellal will join the TARDIS crew.] He can't whistle too well.

• *Ethics.* His usual belief in the sanctity of intelligent life obviously doesn't apply to Daleks, as he takes a great deal of pleasure in seeing the Exxilon City blow them up. [He doesn't consider beings with no individual identity to be intelligent. Note that he has no qualms about killing the City, either.] He tells Sarah to go with the Earth ship if he doesn't escape the City, so presumably he thinks she can cope in this future. In classic Nation style, he states his pragmatism thus: 'Why not, when the only alternative to living is dying...'

• *Inventory.* In the City he loses a five-piastre coin, which he says he probably won't need [so he's been to either post-war Egypt or Lebanon]. The sonic screwdriver can be used as a "mine-detector" to find explosive charges in the floor of the City, and to de-hypnotise his Exxilon ally Bellal [see also 14.4, "The Face of Evil"]. Curiously, the sonic screwdriver is unaffected inside the City, even though Dalek guns are still inoperative.

• *Background.* The Doctor implies that he's been to Florana more than once, and each time he comes back feeling a hundred years younger. [This seems odd, since he's only just managed to get his TARDIS under control. Does the TARDIS keep going back there of its own accord, or did the Doctor spend much longer travelling before "An Unearthly Child" (1.1) than is sometimes believed?] He's seen a temple in Peru that was allegedly too impressive to have been built by primitive man.

The Supporting Cast

• *Sarah Jane Smith.* Whisked out of her own time and off into space, she's already starting to lose some of her self-will and become reliant on the Doctor, often sounding like a little girl looking for reassurance. [This peculiar new environment is stripping away her independence. She gets some of her nerve back later, but after this she's never *quite* as brash as she was in her first appearances - or, at least, not without some redeeming perkiness.] The Doctor makes an attempt at "bonding" with her which is reminiscent of his relationship with Jo, though he doesn't take the same fatherly / mentor-like approach to her.

Sarah claims, in defiance of the Doctor's description of the fizzy seas of Florana, that she can sink anywhere. [With hindsight, this is making light of what must be a touchy subject - see *The Sarah Jane Adventures* story "Whatever Happened to Sarah Jane?", in which we find that Sarah's fear of heights might also be connected to a childhood incident.] This is the last time she *really* screams.

The TARDIS When the Ship gets too close to the energy-draining influence of the Exxilon City, it's incapable of taking off and the interior lights go out. [Since 'the power of a sun' supposedly fuels the TARDIS - see **What Makes the TARDIS Work?** under 1.3, "The Edge of Destruction" - it's unthinkable that the City might have completely drained its energy reserves. If the console draws power from some nigh-inexhaustible source, then it seems likely that the City drains the energy only as it reaches the TARDIS systems.]

The TARDIS is supposedly on its way to Florana when it lands on the Exxilon planet, and the City appears to make it "crash". [That should be unthinkable, unless the City is capable of reaching into the vortex? As on the many occa-

sions when we see the TARDIS hovering in space, the implication may be that the Ship briefly materialises in "real" space to get its bearings during the journey, and pops into existence too close to the Exxilon planet this time.] The TARDIS doors won't open when Ship is powered down, but alternatively, a manual hand-crank for the doors is kept in the console room alongside a paraffin lamp. In a nearby cabinet there's an electric torch. A red light flashes on the console when there's a 'mains' power failure, but the TARDIS has emergency power units *and* emergency storage cells. Oddly, there's still a hint of light in the console room even when the power goes out. The Doctor describes the TARDIS as a living thing, and believes that its energy sources should never stop. The lights inside the central column are still green [next time we see them, one will be red].

An Exxilon gets into the console room here, and menaces Sarah. [She leaves the Ship as soon as she's knocked it out, so it's entirely possible that the Exxilon wanders further into the TARDIS corridors and is still there even now. There's certainly no sign of it leaving.] There are sea-side clothes and items on board [Sarah may have brought them specially for the trip to Florana but they aren't really her style even during Season Eleven's horrific fashion-parade.]

The Non-Humans

• *Daleks.* [Side note to say that these Daleks have almost the same livery as the ones from "The Chase" and "The Daleks' Master Plan", and *exactly* the same as 4.3, "The Power of the Daleks". Their spaceship resembles the one from that story as well (but even so, the Doctor here fails to recognise its design). It's not unlike the one from 10.4, "Planet of the Daleks" either, but these Daleks seem to be less well-equipped (from what we see when they have their power restored).]

The Doctor regards them as the 'most technically advanced and ruthless lifeforms in the galaxy'. [He means at this point in time - they *can't* be as sophisticated as extinct species such as the Daemons, or indeed the Exxilons and certainly not the Time Lords.

[Still, this begs the question: which galaxy are we in? In "Planet of the Daleks", the Daleks were poised outside, with a forward base on Spiridon waiting for the Earth-Draconia war to play out. Nation's other scripts, notably 12.4, "Genesis of the Daleks" and "The Daleks' Master Plan", main-

Who Died and Made You Dalek Supreme?

One advantage of doing this volume again, only even more gooder, is that we can respond to comments from readers of the earlier edition. This essay (originally planned to be a mildly amusing run-down of preposterous boasts made in various Dalek Annuals and *Dalek Death-Ray* ice-lolly wrappers) is prompted by a question asked by a ten year old at a meeting of veteran fans to watch the premiere of "Smith and Jones" (X3.1): "If Daleks are all grown in bottles, how does one of them get to be Dalek Supreme?"

At first sight it's an easier problem than the similar trouble we had with the Sontarans (22.4, "The Two Doctors"), because whilst Daleks were originally created in a lab, they were each "brewed" separately and so could plausibly breed. There *could* be bloodlines - whilst anything that isn't a Dalek is inferior to anything who is, this doesn't mean that all Daleks are created equal. Indeed, with such ingrained conditioning towards obedience and leadership, it would be odd if Davros hadn't factored that in right at the start. And with such a neurotic attitude towards genetic purity, it would be weird if they didn't have a leaning towards aristocracy. (Unlike with humans, at least, there's a rational basis for this - the *aristoi* are genuinely a cut above and were genuinely born to rule.) The half-dozen or so made by Davros (12.4, "Genesis of the Daleks") began again without his help after the Doctor had blown up the incubator and so could be "founding families". So far, so good, but does this match what's actually on screen?

Well, err... sometimes. Sure, we get definite evidence of mixed-ability Dalek taskforces (most obviously in 2.8, "The Chase" where Dalek is noticeably stupider than the rest; when you look at the rest of the Daleks in this story, that's something of an achievement). But in pre-Davros stories, the only real sign of it lies the bafflingly pointless practice of self-destruction rather than face one's superiors. This practice is self-defeating (in 11.3, "Death to the Daleks", a small force is diminished when a Dalek lets one prisoner escape... whereupon he blows himself up and lets the rest go), but is entirely in keeping with the practices of military / aristocratic such as like the Romans or... *seppuku*. (Yes, Terry Nation has managed to get a completely different ethnic stereotype in and combine two of the three Axis powers. In having Daleks chase brave Earthmen through jungles where - all together now - the plants seem more like animals, he's tapped into the American version of World War II. So it makes sense that the Daleks should get enslaved humans, i.e. GIs, and natives to work to death building railways. The main surprise is that the beacon on top of the Exxilon City isn't used to hang the body of the Dalek Leader from, and thus get Mussolini in there too.)

Interestingly, Nation's got it into his head that - at least once the Daleks leave Skaro - there's a chain of command that demands absolute obedience. Only three of his scripts posit a Dalek *Fuhrer* who isn't Davros actually getting his plunger dirty and joining the troops (one of these is 17.1, "Destiny of the Daleks", so we can leave this to one side for now). In 10.4, "Planet of the Daleks", this one has a noticeably different shell and survives to give the customary Muhammed Ali-style taunt to the camera. However, in "The Dalek Invasion of Earth" (2.2) it appears that the Dalek *Capo* has died. How, then, did they select a replacement?

Obviously they don't put it to the vote, which leaves two equally flawed possibilities. Either the title is inherited by the next-in-line or, um, it isn't. In the former case, we have to wonder what the heir-apparent actually *does*. Is this prize specimen out on active duty, making the succession that bit dicier and raising the possibility of hostage-taking (much as was mooted when Prince Harry went off to serve in Afghanistan)? Is he (look, we'll assume for now that all Daleks are male - if Dalek Sec were female, X3.4, "Daleks In Manhattan", would end on a *very* different note...) kept away from combat and living the Dalek equivalent of a Hugh Hefner lifestyle? If the Supreme-in-waiting is not a descendant but a twin, why does one get the gig and not the other? (What with the *Richard III* quotes in the novelisation of 25.1, "Remembrance of the Daleks", you might be imagining a Dalek shell filled with Malmsey wine.) It's possible that the most militarily and socially plausible solution is to put *all* the other candidates into suspended animation until the incumbent dies. Then the only problem is taking the new Dalek Regent (or whatever title they use) to the place where his predecessor died and inserting him into the shell.

Or maybe they make a *new* shell for each one, customised. The on-screen evidence suggests that the resources put into a Dalek casing - with the hi-tech sensor arrays, impenetrable armour and colour-coded shells - gives them the status of family heirlooms; the shell *is* the job. (The Creepy Schoolgirl in "Remembrance" curses 'may their shells be blighted', which might be evidence of

continued on page 437...

tain that the Daleks come from a far-distant galaxy. Despite all the signs that this story is set well before humans branch out to other galaxies, and the risibly small populations mentioned, this probably isn't just Nation getting 'galaxy' and 'universe' muddled up (he has the Doctor talk of 'The Seven Hundred Wonders of the Universe', after all). So either the Daleks have settled, or he's trying not to worry the Earth expedition unduly by letting slip that the Daleks conquer whole galaxies.] He attributes their success to their 'inventive genius'. Mention is made of Dalek colony worlds that are home to millions of Daleks. [It's possible that this just part of a cover story that the Daleks feed the Earth crew regarding their intentions for the parrinium. If true, however, this is a formidable expansion of Dalek territory.]

These Daleks recognise the Doctor on sight, and move by psychokinetic power, i.e. their brains fuel their casings. However, their guns must have a different power-source, as the City of the Exxilons can drain their weapons but not stop them moving [see **What Do Daleks Eat?** under "The Power of the Daleks"]. When the guns aren't functioning, it doesn't take the Daleks long to fit themselves with projectile weapons instead. One Dalek self-destructs out of shame when its prisoner escapes. [This sort of thing only happens once more, in 25.1, "Remembrance of the Daleks", unless you take X1.6, "Dalek" at face value (see that story's essay for the debate about this). It's difficult to find any logic in this suicide, unless the Dalek is unstable and considers itself to be a *serious* liability to the Dalek species. Perhaps Daleks become extra-paranoid when their guns don't work properly. They visibly panic when they realise they're can't back up any of their threats.]

The Daleks have a 'plague missile', perhaps suggesting that they started the plague which is currently ravaging the human colony worlds, though this is by no means clear. [Plague is a standard Dalek weapon; see 2.2, "The Dalek Invasion of Earth" and "Planet of the Daleks".]

Their plan is to blackmail the 'space powers' into acceding to their demands, which is unusually subtle for them. Dalek ships are, as ever, featureless silver vessels with simple geometric forms. The Doctor states that the Daleks have a 'scorched planet policy' [meaning, they destroy any resources they can't use to stop anybody *else* finding a use for them]. After a 7,000-volt electric shock, one Dalek has its non-conductive shielding

burnt out but survives.

In this era, the Daleks recognise the Doctor on sight and use TARDIS-shaped targets when testing weapons. [They might know him from 10.3, "Frontier in Space", again suggesting that this story might take place later than the twenty-sixth century. But then we have to explain how they knew him on that occasion.] However, rather than take advantage of the Exxilons' capture of their greatest enemy - or use his brains to assist them in their quest for power - they allow the locals to sacrifice him.

• *Exxilons.* Inhabitants of Exxilon, a world that's full of rocks and not much else, Exxilons are humanoid but with hairless skins and blank, oversized eyes [so they *look* like they all live in the dark]. Once a highly sophisticated civilisation, they explored space but came unstuck when they made their City a living, thinking thing, as the City had no need of them and drove out those it didn't destroy. They're now primitive savages who see the City as a shrine and insist on sacrificing visitors to their gods. Though the "heretics" in Exxilon's breakaway group retain their civilised ways and want a return to the days of science, members of the main faction just grunt and chant their way through life. Weirdly, the skins of the exiled Exxilons look like glittery rock even though they seem to be dissenters rather than a subspecies. [A mineral-rich diet? Maybe they eat parrinium.] They seem to have a solid surface, but the Doctor *Hail*s two of them in the cobblers without bruising his knuckles. The Exxilon skeletal remains seen in the City look very humanoid.

• *The City.* Possibly one of the Seven-Hundred Wonders of the Universe, but it gets blown up here. [The Doctor says it 'must be' one of the Seven-Hundred Wonders, so it may just be a figure of speech. Anyway, even if it had been properly catalogued as such, there no evidence of it attracting more interest, or having crashed alien spaceships intent on taking a look.]

Though the City of the Exxilons looks like any run-of-the-mill high-tech futuristic city with shiny white corridors, it's actually alive. Its underground "roots" have a habit of slinking through the subterranean tunnels and blowing things up on contact, while the pulsing beacon at its highest point can steal any type of energy in the area, so long as it looks a bit like electricity. [It curiously doesn't affect anyone's synapses (which are electrical impulses), but that might be considered a sensible

Who Died and Made You Dalek Supreme?

...continued from page 435

this but probably isn't.)

This raises the other possibility. Maybe there's no genetic difference between the ranks and it's simply which shell you were put in at birth that determines your role and responsibilities. The Daleks' ingrained obedience and sense of duty would allow this to work. It might explain why the squad sent to hunt the Doctor, Ian, Barbara and Vicki ("The Chase") had such a moron on their team, although as these are the first Daleks with free access to time travel, they're faced with choice and free-will for the first time. So some un-Dalek-like hesitancy is only to be expected. (See **What's Wrong With Dalek History?** under 3.4, "The Daleks' Master Plan" for more on this.)

Alternatively, perhaps one inherits the position through experience. All Daleks start off as grey-cased "squaddies" and get promoted through surviving battles. Once the Supreme is killed, the next most seasoned officer is placed in what's left of his shell and repairs are made.

This all works until someone other than Nation gets to do the scripts; in particular, David Whitaker went and invented a Dalek Emperor (4.9, "The Evil of the Daleks") who's manifestly different from the other Daleks. Now, with the story's overt use of the analogy of bee-hives or ant-hills, the logical first suggestion is that they've taken a normal Dalek "drone" and pumped it full of hormones to make it grow and change. It's been suggested at times that he's Davros, although there's no particular evidence to support this. (Anyone inclined to favour this theory, however, will need to explain why the Davros-Emperor seems to think of the Doctor is a human who's been changed by time-travel. Many people think that "Genesis" began a totally different time-line from the one that culminated in "Evil"; the recent revelations concerning the Time War seem to back this up.) Davros *does* get to be Emperor too, of course, albeit one who's leading an Imperial Dalek race that he's made from dead people (22.6, "Revelation of the Daleks"; then "Remembrance"). Presumably their hierarchy depends on who they were before they died.

But the "Evil" empire is run by a dedicated Dalek wired into Skaro city. As the Daleks on Skaro all died the last time we saw the place (1.2, "The Daleks"), this one must have been off-world at the time. Logically, that Dalek couldn't have been in this state back then, so it *must* be an alteration that comes with the job, rather than the job going to a Dalek who can shout with intonation. But as the story ends with the Dalek Emperor and his entire world being destroyed in a civil war, it's safe to say that this set-up failed.

As discussed under 9.1, "Day of the Daleks", it's possible that this timeline is closed and that all other Dalek stories branch off from it, just as both Dalek stories with free time travel ("The Chase" and "The Daleks' Master Plan", with the Daleks travelling in DARDISes) seem to diverge from the rest of the non-Davros time-line. The message seems to be that having an Emperor is a liability, as on the two instances in the pre-2005 series this led to Skaro being destroyed, or near enough ("The Evil of the Daleks", "Remembrance of the Daleks"). In "Daleks in Manhattan", Dalek Sec even recalls *another* instance of Skaro blowing up in the Time War. (Maybe it was the same one, though. It seems reasonable to assume that the Time War starts with the Time Lords sending the Doctor on a pre-emptive sortie in "Genesis", and *seriously* gets under way when the Daleks start trying to grab Gallifreyan tech in "Remembrance". This does, however, makes the pre-credit sequence of 27.0 "The One We Don't Like to Talk About" all the more silly.) Sec earlier responded to Rose claiming to have destroyed the Emperor (X2.13, "Doomsday"), so there must have been one when he and his gang hid in a giant shaker-maker.

In Volume II, we suggested that this Emperor was Theodore Maxtible, the Victorian alchemist from "The Evil of the Daleks". He's converted into a Dalek (psychologically if not physically), isn't shown to die during the Dalek-versus-Dalek violence on Skaro, and is last seen screaming that the Daleks will be prevail. Some eye-witnesses (who saw the broadcast story twice, don't forget) claim he died in the crossfire, but there's no evidence of this in the soundtrack or the surviving telesnaps, and in fact the script has him walking into the smoke declaring Dalek victory. So *maybe* he grows up to be the new Emperor Dalek seen in X1.13, "The Parting of the Ways". A Victorian mentality might, after all, explain all that "god" business. Then again, if he'd been the Emperor killed in "Evil", there's all sorts of Blinovitch-related reasons why this would have been a disaster. It's not impossible, but we can perhaps dismiss this theory as the result of going to bed after eating cheese.

Let's posit, then, that this time-line ends - as the Doctor says - with the Dalek civil war. If so, there's

continued on page 439...

design precaution so as to not wipe out Exxilon's indigenous species. Likewise, the city's interior systems must be insulated from the effect, but not to such an extent that the Daleks inside the city can zap people.]

Anyone entering the City is exposed to a number of potentially lethal logic puzzles before they can reach the City's brain; the Doctor believes it has a reason for doing this, but he never explains what it is. [It clearly wants minds that are useful, possibly as servants. There's an ancient corpse sitting in the chair in its "control room" - which curiously vanishes when the Doctor and Bellal enter - though the City seems to function perfectly well with no staff at all.] The City's control centre can generate zombie-like "antibodies", basically human / Exxilon types with a mean streak and half-formed features.

Planet Notes

• *Florana*. Following his sales pitch to Sarah [see the previous story], the Doctor now adds that the water is effervescent, so you can't sink in it. [So it's like bathing in fizzy warm milk. Delightful.]

• *Venus*. The Doctor adds to the already-lengthy list of "Venusian" things in his repertoire by mentioning Venusian hopscotch. [As their feet are so big, it must be murder - see "The Time Monster"].

History

• *Dating*. It's an era in which Earth has a well-established space-going military, and humanity knows about the threat of the Daleks. [It can't be before 2200, and the old-style names would indicate a time before 3000. Human concerns involve a plague that's sweeping all of space, not just domestic problems on the homeworld, suggesting a time either long before or some time after the wars and riots of "Frontier in Space". A date between 2600 and 2900 would be plausible.

[However, the same evidence can be used to suggest it's very much earlier than this, as we saw in **What's the Timeline of the Earth Empire?** under 8.4, "Colony in Space". They use colour photographs on paper - clearly not something a ship would have as standard if they relied on video-screens, and hardly the first thing you grab from a crashing spaceship unless you have the facilities for this as standard kit. The overall look of the technology, even when making allowances for the lack of energy - indeed the fact that they

have this stuff handy - suggests they don't rely so heavily on it as one would expect, which sort of suggests an earlier time (in keeping with the stories about "pioneers"). Mind you, that would also include 1.7, "The Sensorites", clearly stated as being in the twenty-eighth century.]

The father of one of the humans was killed in the 'last Dalek war'. [So there have been several Dalek wars, starting with the events of "Frontier in Space"? Or is this one of those that broke out around the Earth Colonies at the same time that the home planet was under the Dalek yoke in 2157-67 ("The Dalek Invasion of Earth")?]

The Marine Space Corps (MSC) has been sent to Exxilon because the chemical parrinium is as common as salt there, whereas it's priceless on Earth. And parrinium is the only known way to cure / immunise against the 'space plague'. Ten million people on the outer planets and colonies will die without it. The MSC people use sulphagen tablets as pain-killers, and Galloway mentions a new 'Z-47' spacecraft they've been planning. Hearteningly, English people in the future still say 'leftenant' rather than "lootenant". Their badge is the same as that of the Federation in *Blake's 7*.

Carvings in the City of the Exxilons closely resemble the carvings of the Peruvian Incas, and the Doctor believes that the Exxilons travelled to Earth to teach the Incas how to build their temples [c. 1000 BC]. Bellal claims that Exxilon had grown old before life began on other planets. [That's the way his people remember it - probably not accurate, but we don't have any evidence either way.]

The Analysis

Where Does This Come From? So there's a network of tunnels hewn from the rock protected by big serpentine things, a sacrificial religion, people turning to stone and a lost civilisation in the back of beyond. Even if you somehow missed the huge early 80s trend for Sword 'n' Sorcery flicks based on 30s pulps, you must have an inkling that this was well-worn boys' adventure territory. Edgar Rice Burroughs produced these by the lorryload. Even in just the *Tarzan* and *Barsoom* books, you'd have this sort of thing fairly often (although not as often as is sometimes said) and comics-strips of the inter-war period made the borderline Freudian element of a snake in a tunnel into one of the most ridiculed clichés. Lost civilisations

Who Died and Made You Dalek Supreme?

...continued from page 437

little or no hope of anyone genetically altering Maxtible and following him into a war against Time Lords. He's also unlikely to be the Emperor Sec knew, and we've no guarantee that the one Rose dissolved into all-purpose-deus-ex-machina-orange-sparkly-dust-effect oblivion ("The Parting of the Ways") was Sec's Emperor either, even though that seems to be the implication.

An alternate answer is that this Dalek Ayatollah is the one Rose "contaminated" (X1.6, "Dalek"), who transmatted instead of self-destructing (fiendishly not shouting "E-mer-gen-cy Tem-por-al Shift!", as this would be a bit of a giveaway). This would help to explain why the game shows of AD 200,100 are all ones that a Dalek downloading the whole Internet in 2012 would know about, although you'll have to decide for yourselves if it cheapens the ending of "Dalek" if the title character survives and was being typically crafty instead of poignantly misunderstood and in need of a cuddle. He gets to be Emperor by dint of being the only Dalek left. It *would* explain why Rose is zapped straight to the Mothership instead of being made into a Dalek in a lab out past Pluto. Running with this for the moment, let's presume that Rose's Dalek is a third Emperor, Davros became the one Sec knew (err ...probably, we think), and the "original" was destroyed in at least one time-line. However, it's starting to become obvious that no matter how you slice this one, Emperors are just a bad idea.

Yet in what we *hope* was their final appearance for a while (X4.13, "Journey's End"), there was a big red Dalek Supreme leading an army bred from Davros' chest - but who were giving Davros a hard time anyway. As Davros was salvaged from inside the bubble of time containing the 'locked off' Time War, maybe Big Red was too. The alternatives are: that Davros once again created an army who don't think much of him; that always something happens when making a Dalek Supreme that makes that particular Dalek turn against Davros; that the whole subplot of the Daleks keeping Davros in a shed was something inserted for a reason that everyone forgot in the rewrites.

The second of these possibilities is the one most useful to us: either a Dalek Supreme is made with different abilities, possibly a special brew of nutrients (again, the bee analogy is enticing) or the process of becoming Dalek Supreme favours those with a particularly arrogant streak even towards other Daleks. Ah! This idea holds some potential, especially as it's rather unlikely that Davros created them all equal from his spare ribs, and they *then* fought among themselves for supremacy whilst hiding in the Medusa Cascade. Even presuming they had enough time to hold fights for status - like bull elephant seals (presumably with their guns switched off and possibly with a written test instead of butting their shells like dodgems) - the sheer number of Daleks required to hold regional heats makes this unlikely. Admittedly, they *could* have bred a few hundred, held the rant-offs amongst this first wave and set the genetic Xerox going once a clear leader emerged, but, again, this would take time. The signs are that the now-demented Dalek Caan, so vital to their plan, has a "best-before" date.

It looks, therefore, as if this particular Dalek Supreme was simply made that way. From this, you can infer what you like about the social stratification of Daleks in stories from 1965, 1975, 1985 or 2005. Then again, it seems that the Cult of Skaro ("Doomsday") were genetically engineered for cleverness and lateral thinking and *that* was almost certainly Davros' work. Although Caan's trip into the Vortex has rendered him as mad as a porridge-knife and able to prophesy some extraordinary plot-devices, this is probably not a genetic ability. Time Lords have some kind of genetic thing going on with time and Artron Energy, but Daleks neither regenerate nor come into direct physical contact with anything. So the Dalek Supreme *could* have been a Caan clone, making his disgust at the 'abomination' rather interesting.

Thus, the model we're suggesting for Dalek hierarchy (at least in stories made before 1975) has a minimum of genetic tinkering happen after the original creation (by whatever means) of the Daleks. Even if we suppose that the ones in the DARDISes require some kind of "Rassilon Imprimatur" (if this really existed - see "The Two Doctors"), most Daleks accept their place in the scheme of things. Davros began the whole business of racial purity, then thought better of it when he started again. The Time War made the Daleks more prepared to compromise on this. (We know from Jack's comments in "The Parting of the Ways" that the Daleks withdrew en masse from orthodox warfare some time long after 4000 AD, so we might have further grounds to assume that the Time Destructor in "The Daleks' Master Plan" closed off the "Chase" / "Master Plan" timeline, but not the experiments into time travel as whole.)

such as Opar and Pellucidar were themselves part of the whole late-Victorian adventure repertoire, with Sir Henry Rider-Haggard slyly parodying the Queen Empress as "She Who Must Be Obeyed".

Even the fact that this version of the sacrifice cult lacks a jungle setting is not an insurmountable objection: apart from the whole Burroughs-derived, Bulwer-Lytton schtick of a land at the centre of the Earth (see "Doctor Who and the Silurians"), there was at least one film adaptation of *She* that moved the story to the North Pole and had the lost city look distinctly Germanic. (It's the RKO version, designed by Van nest Polglase - he made those weird multi-dimensional stage-sets on which Fred and Ginger cavorted on the same sound set that would later be the USS *Enterprise*.) These lost civilisations were always slightly older than Europe's and fallen from a great height. *King Solomon's Mines* suggests the age by having the bodies of the first kings placed under dripping water that contained a saturate solution of calcium carbonate, so that the bodies became giant statues (as happens in some caves in the North of England - "Old Mother Shipton" will fossilise your teddy-bear in under a year).

As with the remarkably similar scene in the novelisation of 2.5, "The Web Planet", the idea is that the entire landscape has been made from the centuries of dead kings. There were real-life lost cities in Africa, some of remarkable complexity in the middle of relatively basic subsistence farming or hunting. There were two characteristic responses amongst European archaeologists to cities such as Zimbabwe (after which the country of Rhodesia was named after independence). One was to assume that, as Africans were innately inferior (as every pith-helmeted Victorian knew), someone from further north must have built these and then either fled or been eaten. The other was that the descendents of the people who built this were reduced to poverty and ignorance to the extent that they didn't have a clue where these ruins came from, so there must be a tendency for mighty empires to fall. (See **Is This Any Way To Run A Galactic Empire?** under "Frontier in Space".)

The Von Daniken fad we discussed under "The Daemons" suggested a third idea, clearly daft but more comfortable than either of the others. That fad was comparatively brief (certainly compared to others like the Loch Ness Monster or the Bermuda Triangle), but had a long-term impact on

Doctor Who - it permitted the use of ancient mythologies with only the flimsiest of pretext, by ascribing the mysteries of the gods to alien visitors. Phenomena-writer Charles Fort (whose name is now a byword for gaps in our knowledge that attract wild theories, i.e. "Fortean") had proposed something similar in the 1920s, but he was ridiculing dogmatism in science. Erich von Daniken, Swiss hotelier and convicted fraudster, was saying it for real. At the very least he was proposing where people should look for clues, even if they all turned out to be wrong. *Doctor Who* writers in the 70s could just use spaceships as a hand-wave and then get on with retelling much older stories.

With the fuss about Von Daniken's *Chariots of the Gods* (1968) dying down, the whole "ancient astronauts" idea was now just another part of the *Doctor Who* toybox. Perhaps the most significant thing to mention here is that the Doctor's revelation that the Exxilons went to Peru is not a major plot-twist but a throwaway aside. Nation's done this sort of thing before, after all. The 1965 *Dalek World* annual announced that a crashed Dalek ship in 2000 BC led to the building of the Great Pyramid at Giza and that Dalek mutants - lost in the Himalayas and adapted to the cold - are the "real" Yeti.

We can trace this idea back from Nation and Von Daniken to Velikovsky (see "The Daemons", and "Doctor Who and the Silurians") and through Fort back to the Theosophists and the whole Celtic Twilight movement that manifests itself in WB Yeats and Richard Wagner and (with the Theosophists' notions of Aryan superiority amplified a little) to the Nazis. There's a whole strand of European thought that loves the grandeur of a falling empire, especially one so great and so fallen as to leave virtually no trace. Whatever majesty one can find in Mediaeval church architecture and Roman aqueducts, it's as nothing to the ruins - especially the impossibly vast and epic ruins in Piranesi's engravings (one of the real starting-points for the Gothic movement on the late eighteenth century).

Egypt captured the imagination of Napoleon, and thereby everyone in Europe at that time, because it was incomprehensible. Shelley's poem "Ozymandias' picks up on this thread. Whilst science and the Enlightenment exhorted everyone to move forward, the Romantics spoke up on behalf of cycles. The first two-thirds of the twentieth century was all about progress... except, of course, Nazi Germany, where Hörbiger's *Welteislehre* "proved" Teutonic mythology by demonstrating that the moon changes shape every month because it, like the stars, is made of ice. Every so often it hits Earth, wiping out dinosaurs and the Gods. Two Gods escaped into the centre of the Earth (it's hollow, you realise) and will re-awaken next collision and lead the pure into a bright future. This was published in 1911, and by 1935 Goebbels had to issue a proclamation that you could be a good National Socialist without needing to believe it, that's how common the idea was (see "The Ribos Operation"). With this in mind, go back and read the plot of Wagner's *Ring* cycle (or the dumbed-down and relatively incest-free versions peddled later by Tolkien and Lucas). It's about decay and loss. *Twilight of the Gods* sounds a bit sad: in German it's *Götterdammerung*, far more triumphantly catastrophic-sounding.

Nation, as we've already said, was blessed with instincts that were a lot smarter than his thought-processes. His original Dalek script and his next one will revisit the idea of a ruined civilisation trying to shore itself up with fragments, as will *Survivors* - the civilisation in that case being ours. Tempting though it is to credit Holmes with the idea, Nation has hit on something potent with this story. With the Daleks becoming mythologised Nazis and then something more primal, Nation has been tapping into the emotional connections Hitler made for his followers even while he (Nation that is, not Hitler) was plundering the iconography to occasionally turn the Daleks into comic-strip Bosche. Although the majority of Holmes / Hinchcliffe stories will in some way entail a threat from the distant past making a comeback, it's in 17.1, "Destiny of the Daleks" (a splendidly Fascist title) that Nation finally makes the link between the Daleks and this idea of loss, rebirth and cycles by having Davros disinterred and then encased in ice.

But we're missing the obvious: once again they've sent Michael Briant to a quarry and told him to make a western. The scene when the dying captain tells Galloway that he's too vainglorious for command is so familiar, it's amazing they didn't go the whole hog and call him "Custer". And we're missing something really *really* obvious. The opening sequence where the TARDIS loses power sees the Doctor fall back upon a naff paraffin lamp, of the kind everyone went out and bought in 1971-2 when the miners went on strike, and

dusted off shortly before this story aired. See the next story for more in this vein.

Things That Don't Make Sense Yet *again*, Terry Nation has difficulty understanding the scale of space. "Planet of the Daleks" is based on the assumption that 10,000 Daleks is a huge army in galactic terms, whereas here it's said that ten million people on the outer planets will die without parrinium. Is that *all*? So, the death-toll for a plague that must have spread across huge swathes of the galaxy is a figure not much more than the population of a decent-sized city? [Maybe humans can cure most plague cases without exotic alien chemicals, but the parrinium is needed to cure those few plague victims who don't respond to the drugs. In other words, perhaps it's the only *guaranteed* cure rather than the only possible treatment.] Anyway, good luck to the Daleks in their quest to hold the *whole galaxy* to ransom with the lives of such a relatively small number of people on the outer planets.

And if this wonder-drug is *only* plentiful on Exxilon (or near enough), then why did the human authorities send the tiny force seen here? If time is so short, surely it would make sense to mobilize every warm body that can be spared? Then again, we might have to presume a single ounce of parinnium can cure something like 300,000 people - otherwise, buggered if we know how Sarah and Jill were able to single-handedly load enough material to cure ten *million* victims into the Earth spaceship in the short time available to them, without any sign of loading equipment about the place. But if we walk that route, then this talk about Earth only having "minute quantities" a bit silly, if so little can cure so many.

Besides, a mineral *that* valuable must have sparked a Klondike-style rush. And we still have the problem of how a planet whose technological marvel is a device that absorbs all energy - to the point of overcoming a TARDIS - didn't suck the juice from the prospecting satellite [which had to pass close enough to take an accurate reading].

Nobody involved in this story, not even the Doctor [who knew all about Tom Mix in his first life; see 3.8, "The Gunfighters"], appears to have seen a Western. If they *had* done, they might've come up with a better plan for evading an ambush by arrow-shooting natives than hiding in a hole and wasting what few arrows they have returning fire. If nothing else, the Daleks - brilliant master-tacticians that they are - should have realised that they were arrow-proof and... you've guessed it... formed a circle. It's also strange that the Daleks stand less than five feet away from the humans while bellowing out their plan to betray them, yet not even The One They Call The Doctor hears them conspiring.

As part of his mission to reawaken memories of the Hartnell Dalek stories, the director has done what he can to draw attention to the fact that they have three working Daleks, so a little fun can be had observing how the fourth, non-operational one just stands there immobile while his fellows twitch nervously. Moreover, we're told that the Daleks are now using 'psychokinetic' force to levitate / move around, yet they force two of the Earth crewmen to climb up and plant bombs on the top of the city, as opposed to just floating to the top of the tower themselves. This living city has elaborate internal defences, yet - as we see - nothing to challenge anyone intent on tinkering with its all-important power-tower. The city's power-drain is a bit inconsistent too: radiant heat isn't a problem (so oil-lamps and burning Daleks are permitted), but rocket engines are neutralised - even though, as far as we can tell, the Dalek ship uses chemical rockets to land.

The Doctor seems more than a little brash in this story. Not only does he wander off soon after arrival - thus leaving Sarah in the lurch - but toward the end of Part Two, he decides to leave Sarah behind while he reconnoitres (or so he says) *half a mile* ahead. Does he *honestly* think he's going to hear her screaming a warning, or get back in time to help? Later, the City triggers a loud sonic blast that makes Bellal temporarily psychotic, yet the Doctor - who has his back turned - doesn't notice anything happening until he turns round and sees the Exxilon pointing a gun at him. [Maybe the sonic blast only affects Exxilon senses? Either way, the Doctor's hearing declines further by the next story.] How did the Doctor salvage the gun from the slaughtered Dalek without the fiendish Root killing him?

Ultimately, the core of Part Four - the tests to reach the City's heart - are thoroughly pointless. As with "The Tomb of the Cybermen" (5.1), the nature of the tests is a red-herring, as it only needs *one* member of the party to be smart enough to open the gates and let in a whole army of thuggish morons. We also have to wonder about the intelligence of the Exxilons who starved to death in the first round of tests - they were smart enough to

deduce the symbol-test outside the city but didn't consider that the altogether simple-looking maze pattern was more than a pretty wall-design.

The lurid scarlet Bath-Mat of Doom at the end of Part Three is just about as silly, standing out as it does in these magnolia-painted corridors (as if to say "This Is A Trap"), and anyway there's enough of a run-up for Pertwee to hop across it, no bother. Bellal could probably have done the same. Keep watch as the Doctor waves the sonic screwdriver over the Bath-Mat - first it bleeps over the red sections, as if to warn, "This is unsafe", but on the second row, it bleeps over the *white* tiles, which are safe. Despite this discrepancy, the Doctor seems to know that red is always off limits. But then, the Bath-Mat is an exceedingly bad way of testing the intelligence of wheeled invaders [meaning that, for once, the old joke about Daleks and stairs can be trotted out with a clear conscience].

And viewed from a narrative point of view, the tests to reach the City's heart are, if anything, *more* meaningless. The Doctor triggers a nervous breakdown in the city's brain, but that becomes irrelevant as the Earth Marines blow up the beacon and allow everyone to escape. [Some have countered that the tower could have rebuilt itself save for the internal breakdown, but this is implausible given the tower's importance (surely, it would warrant an independent repair system), not to mention that the Doctor couldn't have *known* that such a double-whammy would be required.] The breakdown may save the future of the Exxilon species, but even that isn't connected to the rest of the plot, and Bellal doesn't even get the time-honoured epilogue speech about being able to build a better future for his people.

So the Daleks advance their plans, and believe that their plague missile will make it impossible for future human missions to land on - or collect parrinium from - Exxilon. First off, have they never heard of robots? Second, as parrinium is 'as common as salt' on Exxilon, is their single missile capable of polluting *the entire planet*? Never mind about the ten million plague-victims on the outer planets, this is a truly alarming WMD. And third, isn't it a bit silly to send a plague missile to a planet where the cure for the plague is so commonplace? [All right, fine... the Daleks' strain of plague *might* be more severe and instantaneous than the one troubling the outer planets, but you must admit that it's a bit ironic.]

We'll leave aside the question of whether the Daleks brought shovels and sieves or whether the Exxilons had them handy and ask what motivates Galloway to decide that the Exxilons must be treated honourably in Part Three, considering he seemed happy enough to agree to execution squads in Part Two. Why does a Dalek in episode four say, 'explosive *device* in position', rather than using the plural? (The plot rather needs them to not know that Galloway kept one of the tower-wrecking bombs.)

Special mention also needs to go to the suicidal Dalek who guards all the slaves. The gist is that after Jill escapes, the Dalek has such a crushing sense of failure that it refrains from sending for reinforcements, organising a search and shooting a few work-units *pour encourager les autres*. Instead, it self-destructs... and thereby enables *all* of the prisoners to escape. [We'll attempt to rationalise this in **Who Died and Made You Dalek Supreme?**.]

Around the end of Part Two, the Doctor rotates into Vila Restal from *Blake's 7*. He makes lame jokes ('The root won. Dalek Nil', among way too many others), lets Sarah pull him to safety, exhibits comic cowardice and calls everyone 'my friend'. Finally, while we can *just* about accept the presence of blazing torches in a network of tunnels, despite nobody (allegedly) ever going down there, the presence of Woolworth's candles on a planet with no technology is harder to swallow.

Critique A little game for you, to relieve the monotony of watching this story... see if you can spot the precise moment when Jon Pertwee decides to quit the series. Is it when a very good actor, John Abineri (as the expedition captain), expires after about fifteen lines of dialogue? Is it the cold, wet location shoot - especially the scene where they're in a ditch and the Doctor has to say that stupid line about 'the only alternative to living is dying'? Is it when he has to feign enthusiasm for watching a vacuum-cleaner hose assault a Dalek? Is it the bathmat? Or was it when this script plopped onto his doormat? Because however much effort went in to disguising it, the script is the real problem here - quite simply, there's very little to make the prospect of lying face-down in gravel in November seem like a good idea even if you don't (as Pertwee *did*) have a slipped disc and a lot of other tempting offers you're having to reject.

We have to concede, however, that although this story was stitched together from the usual Nation material, these four episodes are sufficiently unlike the ones before and after to be worth a look. The first episode has a wonderfully doom-laden atmosphere, and although the Doctor and Sarah are separated in the traditional Hartnell-era manner, they're in a world far worse than anything we've seen to date. Nation and company will get this right next time ("Genesis of the Daleks"). It's true that the TARDIS malfunction takes us back to the less-welcome aspects of Season Two (like it or not, "Death to the Daleks" is more like "The Web Planet" than is normally acknowledged), but at least we've not seen this since the show went into colour. Michael Briant was quite right to try to find new ways to do the old staples of the series and, if that meant getting someone in to do music with saxophones, so be it. Many of the programme's great moments, after all, occurred after people said, "that'll never work". The rest of 1974's output commits the cardinal sin of *Doctor Who* - playing it safe - so this was worth a try. It's possible that we'd think even *less* of this production if the attempt to make this look and sound a bit different had been dropped in favour of business as usual.

Unfortunately, the experiments that failed remain the only memorable parts of this story. Nation has to shoulder a lot of the blame for deciding to make a *Flash Gordon* script mixed with World War II clichés, while simultaneously missing the point not just of the series as it had developed after he left in a huff, but even of his own adventure. Potentially interesting plot-strands are squandered. The humans bargain trade the Doctor's life to the Daleks in order to save millions, but this is frittered away in a tiresome sacrifice sequence straight out of *Tarzan*, a mere three minutes after the first mention of the deal. Similarly, the ethics of "killing" a living city are never questioned.

Then again, it's not just Nation who's at fault. *Some* of the blame here can go to Robert Holmes, for not standing up to the veteran and demanding something worthy of Nation's reputation. (His reputation with the public, that is... this kind of story is exactly what Terry Nation is known for amongst fans.) There are so many similarly intriguing ideas mentioned in passing - more than worth a story in their own right, actually - that seeing the flaccid set-pieces which deliver them makes you want to switch your allegiance to *The Tomorrow People* right there and then. The

Exxilons have visited Peru! A city is alive and creates antibodies! The descendents of the city's builders have a cargo-cult based on its power! This city can absorb energy and creates "roots" that hunt! The implications of *any* of these would keep a hungry and astute writer inspired for ages. We've haven't always been kind to him, but Nation knew how to make high-concept adventures. The problem here, though, is that he had so many concepts to choose from, yet wound up dithering and picked the least interesting one.

A final point: the trouble with watching "Death to the Daleks" now is that some of what it entails will become clichés in future - meaning that it looks thoroughly derivative when in fact it's only about 70% recycled. Over the next three years, Holmes will re-use a lot of this adventure for reworking stories that aren't going anywhere (we refer you to the last episodes of 14.2, "The Hand of Fear" and 13.3, "Pyramids of Mars", just for a start). The spooky stalker who turns out to be a staunch ally is something essayed in "Planet of the Daleks" with Wester, and will crop up again with Tyssan in "Destiny of the Daleks" and, of course, Sevrin in "Genesis of the Daleks". To his credit, Bellal is by far the *most* interesting of the bunch, because he's startling-looking and because Arnold Yarrow plays him as a big bush-baby, endlessly curious. So yes - we can give the production team some credit for their ideas and ambitions with this undertaking. Alas, very little of what's actually on screen warrants praise or interest of any kind.

The Facts

Written by Terry Nation. Directed by Michael Briant. Viewing figures: 8.1 million, 9.5 million, 10.5 million, 9.5 million. AIs were in the low 60s.

Supporting Cast Duncan Lamont (Dan Galloway), John Abineri (Richard Railton), Neil Seiler (Commander Stewart), Julian Fox (Peter Hamilton), Joy Harrison (Jill Tarrant), Mostyn Evans (High Priest), Michael Wisher (Dalek Voices), Arnold Yarrow (Bellal).

Working Titles "The Exilons".

Cliffhangers The Daleks roll out of their spaceship to face the humans, and open fire (although the tight close-up of a Dalek gun goes on for so long, it's fairly clear the weapons aren't working);

in the subterranean tunnels, one of the City's snake-like "roots" rears up over the Doctor; and rather infamously, the Doctor stops Bellal treading on a funny-coloured stretch of floor inside the Exxilon City.

What Was in the Charts? "Living for the City", Stevie Wonder; "Teenage Dream", Marc Bolan; "The Man Who Sold The World", Lulu; "The Air That I Breathe", The Hollies.

The Lore

• This year's attempt to make the Daleks interesting came from Terrance Dicks' desire for a quiet life. He asked Terry Nation - a writer he knew could churn out Dalek scripts without any real bother - to deliver a four-part story with the theme of a lost and decayed civilisation that had the solution to a plague affecting humans. Nation was given a few hints about Sarah, then left to get on with it. By now Dicks was planning his escape to *Moonbase 3*, so he didn't chase the story breakdown. When it arrived, it had Daleks chasing a small party of humans running around in a jungle, with both parties trying to make deals with the locals. This might strike you as a little familiar ("The Chase", "Planet of the Daleks"); it certainly struck Dicks that way.

• One novel item that attracted the script editor's eye was the living city. It was enslaving the natives, but destroying it might raise an interesting ethical dilemma. One option was to have the Exilons (a rough anagram of "elixir", sort of, a bit; alternatively it's a take-off on "exile") keep Sarah as a hostage, although as more detailed character-notes for the new assistant developed, this looked less interesting. Another was the Daleks running off with the precious substance and "starving" the city, so that it died and the humans could help the natives move on.

Even before a director was assigned, the decision had been made to switch from a studio-bound jungle to a quarry. The humans were now living in a base-camp, rather than in their space-ship. One idea was to make the token woman the leader to avoid a dull character like Rebec had been in the first draft (even compared to the finished product) of "Planet of the Daleks".

• A few myths have grown up around this script's next stage. According to legend Dicks handed over to Robert Holmes with the words, "good luck - the Aspirins are in the bottom drawer" and after years of Holmes saying, "how hard can it be?", he quickly found out and wished he'd kept his mouth shut. Some sources claim that Holmes devised the title "Death to the Daleks" as a heartfelt wish that they would never, ever return after this. Whilst it's well known that Holmes suggested making the sought-for plague remedy a mineral rather than an elixir, we can't say for certain whether the new name 'parrinium' was a pun on "perineum", suggesting he thought the Daleks were a pain in the arse. What we *do* know is that Dicks concentrated on *Moonbase 3* and the drastic revisions to 11.4, "The Monster of Peladon", leaving Holmes in charge of this one while retaining on-screen credit (the scripts give them both the honours). Completed scripts were delivered promptly and made more of a distinction between the Exxilon factions (Holmes added the second 'X', apparently). They were now seemingly made of stone, a feature that caused the costume and make-up teams a few headaches. Director Michael Briant baulked when he saw the script, as it looked too big to do as television.

• By the time production began, the series was into its big anniversary bash but the road ahead looked very different. Despite *Moonbase 3*'s disastrous ratings, it was increasingly obvious that Barry Letts was considering his future outside *Doctor Who*. He'd tried to leave what he'd taken on as a temporary job twice before. By the time the location filming for the story, began it was known that a script editor from ATV, Philip Hinchcliffe, would replace him as producer.

• An unexpected publicity boost came when two Dalek props went walkabout. The shells had been sent to Wales to appear in *Mewn Pum Munud* and had not come back. *Nationwide* and *Blue Peter* covered the story and the press loved it. They were found in peculiar places and nobody was ever caught (or confessed).

• Although Jill's speeches about women being more than decoration were cut (more because they were irrelevant to the plot than any moral objection to them) the male cast were all, with the obvious exception of Pertwee and Mostyn Evans (as the High Priest - he was the doomed Dai Evans in 10.5, "The Green Death"), shorter than Joy Harrison. Most of the rest of the cast were old hands at this sort of thing, but this didn't help with the *déjà vu* Pertwee experienced when filming yet another Dalek romp in yet another quarry.

• By the time the filming started, Briant had got

the Dalek shells repainted in the old Hartnell / Troughton livery (the first time this was seen in colour) and devised a cunning plan to put the Daleks on the same rails used for the camera dollies. Filming, in a totally new quarry to them (in Dorset), began on 13th of November. This was a fairly bright, sunny day - just what you need for filming snake-like things on wires that will show up a treat on 16mm film.

It was, however, chilly. They set Terry Walsh on fire early on in the day (it wasn't a desperate measure to keep warm - he was inside the Exxilon robes when the Probe-thing hit and ignited the hapless slave in Part Three). The regular cast missed this, as they were still in the studio trying to figure out how to drive under a brontosaurus. (You'll note that the last two episodes of the previous story have the UNIT scenes taking place in the radio-room, freeing the TARDIS prop for transport to Lulworth over the weekend.) Walsh's costume for this scene was a variant from the "religious" Exxilon design. Newcomer L Rowland-Warne had made a costume that looked like rock for the basic "skin" for all of them, including the "nice" ones Bellal and Gotal, and more swaddling for the cultist Exxilons. All of this was extraordinarily risky near fire (terylene, glue various plastics and latex). Meanwhile, the full slapstick potential for Daleks on rails that inclined slightly was becoming apparent. Amazingly none of the operators was injured, but some slight repairs were needed for the shells.

• It was decided that the effects would be handled entirely in-house - an administrative decision, honest - and announced after Clifford Culley had been assigned. He was replaced by Jim Ward, who found a suitable "practical" pellet-gun for the Daleks (although nobody realised how badly the sound would resonate inside the shells) and operated the probe with help from Colin Mapson. The team had also built two model cities and two Dalek ships, one for pre-filmed destruction and one for use in the studio in each case. John Friedlander once again helped with the costume masks and was given an on-screen credit for the Exxilons. The rock-like shrouds resulted in a couple of the extras vanishing against the sand when they took a nap.

• The location shoot was partially hampered by it being November, so the working day effectively ended around four in the afternoon. On the other hand, the weather held and the quarry didn't turn into a quagmire, as had happened last time Briant had used one ("Colony in Space"). A couple of the action scenes required a point-of-view shot of the Dalek in the thick of the action, and this was done by putting a cameraman inside the bottom half of a shell with a reflective tube on the front of the lens. The half-Dalek would be pushed along the dolly-rails by stage-hands and assaulted by Exxilons. The blazing Dalek shell had already been filmed around the same time as Walsh's incendiary scene.

• Later in the week, the scenes requiring the filter on the lens for the gloom of night were shot. Terry Walsh died on screen yet again in the opening scene of the story, using a shot of an arrow pulled out of the padding on his chest, filmed in reverse. Lis Sladen earned her spurs as a *Who* girl by spraining her ankle in the slippery sand but, like a true pro, waited until the last shot Sarah was in before doing so. That was mid November, and the recordings were in early December, so in between rehearsals the cast joined in with more anniversary-related stuff. In the interim, the previous season won the series a BAFTA award for the writing, earning Dicks an interview on *Nationwide* in which he puffed the forthcoming season and explained the concept of what we now call "pseudo-historical" stories. They showed a few familiar clips, such as the speedboat chase from "The Sea Devils".

• As we've mentioned, the recording timetable was unlike anything they'd tried before. If you've read the essay with 1.8, "The Reign of Terror", you'll know how the series was traditionally made an episode at a time and recorded at the end of a week's rehearsal in a forty-five minute session. Over the course of this book, we've seen the development of a new pattern: two episodes per fortnight and the pre-filming at least a week before recording to allow time between stories. (The later Troughton adventures were supposed to be free of this problem, but the timetabling of time off to do a location shoot in the middle of recording the previous story was getting ridiculous, and kept threatening to recur as late as 6.4, "The Krotons".) So now we have the logical next step: making a story set-by-set.

To ease the cast into this procedure, Briant took advantage of the two days per fortnight pattern and did the camera-rehearsals on Monday and the recording on Tuesday. Unfortunately, the first day was hugely delayed (it appears that the TARDIS prop and the Dalek shells were sent to the wrong

studio after a last-minute change of venue).

In one regard, the recording was *very like* the 1960s stories - they began with the TARDIS interior to get it out of the way. You'll also note that the set is slightly refitted since "Planet of the Daleks", with return engagements for the lectern and the chest (if this is the same one, then it's the only post-Troughton appearance - unless anyone can prove that the same item shows up in 22.5, "Timelash") and a few of the hexagonal lights we saw in the fake spaceship in the previous story. A large chunk of the first recording block (4th of December) exists on video-tape (you may have seen some in *More Than Thirty Years in the TARDIS*), including the lining-up of the CSO panel and the model Dalek ship. In this scene, the fourth Dalek shell is empty and pushed along by a stage-hand. This footage also includes Sarah's first sight of the city, with the model lines up and shot with a star-filter to make the light on the beacon more imposing.

• The more "liberated" Exxilons - Bellal and his chum Gotal - were played by small actors. Gotal was Roy Heyman, who was a Priest in "Colony in Space" and Bellal was Arnold Yarrow, an experienced script-writer (lately one of the stalwarts of *EastEnders*, and then just finishing as script editor on *Softly, Softly Task Force*, a spin-off from a spin-off from *Z-Cars*). In order to suggest that they somehow fed on (or absorbed) radiation from the caves, their costumes were coated with veins in a reflective material used for Front Axial Projection. In this, the light that hits the paint is bounced back precisely along the same line. So if a lamp is attached to a camera, it means the actor can glow brightly on screen without having to do anything dangerous like have 100 watt bulbs in his clothing or eat Strontium 90. The rest of the studio lighting swamped the effect in the first session, but they later cracked it. They then did the same with the symbols on the temple exterior and the maze on the wall. As mentioned, the Daleks' new weapons were "practical" guns, firing real projectiles or blanks, and thus required special precautions such as plexiglass for the cameramen's safety when the Daleks tested their guns (oddly enough the script doesn't specify a miniature TARDIS) and a bulletproof vest for Terry Walsh as one of the 'Antibodies'. Recording ended a week before Christmas.

• Since his last score for the series, Carey Blyton had gone up in the world and was now Visiting

Professor of Composition for Film, TV and Radio at the prestigious Guildhall School of Music and Drama. It appears to have been Briant's decision to contact the London Saxophone Quartet and commission a score with no synthesizers. The Quartet were gaining a reputation for a can-do approach to any kind of music (and eventually had their own series on BBC Radio, reworking pieces composed for other brass by Purcell and Haydn, amongst others). Whatever the case, Blyton's score was written fairly rapidly but is still occasionally performed as a concert piece.

11.4: "The Monster of Peladon"

(Serial YYY, Six Episodes, 23rd March - 27th April 1974.)

Which One is This? The clue is in the title (see 9.2, "The Curse of Peladon"): we're back on the planet of purple, only this time for a whole six weeks. (They had enough trouble filling *four* episodes last time...) Aggedor, Alpha Centauri and the streaky-haired nobles are back, with the Ice Warriors returning in a move that surprised maybe two people.

Firsts and Lasts It's the first time that TARDIS returns, on screen at least, to a planet other than Earth (here we're not counting references to past adventures, such as the Doctor's visits to Dido in 2.3, "The Rescue". And no, 4.9, "The Evil of the Daleks" doesn't count either, because that trip to Skaro was done under Dalek power.)

First story with a Production Unit Manager, which is more important than you might think (see **The Lore**). This story sees the Martians refer to themselves as "Ice Warriors" for the first and only time. Oh, and to date, it's the last appearance of the Ice Warriors on TV (see, however, **What Would the Other Season 23 Have Been Like?** under 22.6, "Revelation of the Daleks" and **What About Season 27?** under 26.4, "Survival" for some attempts at bringing them back).

Other than that there's not much to comment upon here, which says it all, really....

Six Things to Notice
About "The Monster of Peladon"...

1. This is an unabashed sequel (i.e. remake) of the earlier Peladon yarn, with the same sets, cos-

tumes, props and cliffhangers, only this time it's a naïve young *Queen* embroiled in offworld political machinations and - in a lame attempt at topicality - unrest among miners caused by rabble-rousers and stirred up by alien agents. But *this* Peladon story features Vega Nexos - a faun-like alien from (apparently) the planet Luvvie, whose renown in fandom far outweighs his actual screen-time. It happens that he's killed something like ten seconds after his memorable entrance, but he's immortalised to a generation through the collectable cardboard stand-up figures given away with Weetabix breakfast cereal (See **Why Was There So Much Merchandising?**). Watching it now, it's amazing he wasn't in the story more, so fondly is he remembered. And surely, he's *far* more deserving of an unannounced guest-appearance than the Macra (X3.3, "Gridlock")?

2. The *most* immediately striking thing about "The Monster of Peladon", however, is the fashion sense. Particularly the hair. Director Lennie Mayne, not content with the usual signifiers of social class used in Pertwee stories (say, the overuse of 'aye' to mean "yes" and the adoption of a West Country accent to indicate being gullible, contrasted with the Received Pronunciation - with optional lisp for women - and almost always being right for the toffs), wants to suggest that the classes are in fact genetically different. The miners are shorter, uglier, and have Bride of Frankenstein streaks in their frizzy hair - making their heads look like giant mint humbugs. The aristocrats are tall and slender, wear the precise shade of metallic purple associated with Cadbury's chocolate. They also have red hair with a single white streak. (Except for Ortron, who has a white mane and beard striped with crimson, as if he's been eating very rare steaks rather clumsily; the queen, meanwhile, hides her flash under her dinky all-purpose crown.) Once upon a time, we called this the "Dickie Davies" look, after the silver-streaked sportscaster; more recently it was "the Rachel". You can only assume that since the miners are supposed to be "burrowing folk", the costume department thought it'd be fitting for them to look like badgers.

3. Even without benefit of the *huge* clues in the *Radio Times*, the majority of viewers had a fairly good idea concerning the identity of the surprise villains. Even without basic knowledge of Brian Hayles' resume (because people back then didn't think of *Doctor Who* as having individual authors - apart from maybe Terry Nation - but as an

author in and of itself), the way that the production team has bust a gut to establish this as the same planet where we *last* saw the Ice Warriors makes their absence really noticeable. The fleeting glimpse of green scaly giants lumbering behind frosted glass is the most inept attempt to make a mystery out of what we already know since... ooh, "Planet of the Daleks" and the first revelation of '..*them*' (10.4).

4. Everyone knows (or at least likes to entertain themselves suspecting) that George Lucas ripped off the look of the Ice Lords (they're never actually called that, but you know what we mean), right down to the heavy breathing and the cloak. But a scene in episode four has also led younger viewers to wonder if the folks at *2000AD* were paying *ve-e-ery* close attention. Azaxyr, standing tall, with a bullet-shaped helmet with inset eye-shields and a jutting jawline covered in fuzz, tells the Doctor 'I am the law' and 'that *was* your trial', much like Judge Dredd. Then again, with his disco cape, pointy hat and big utility belt, Azaxyr could almost be a green Batman.

5. Back on form after her screaming-and-asking-stupid-questions phase in "Death to the Daleks", here Sarah Jane Smith makes the most overt feminist statement (that's "overt", which isn't the same as "good") by giving the Queen of Peladon a lecture about Women's Lib, apparently changing the course of the planet's history with the words 'there's nothing "only" about being a girl'. An inspiration for girl-adventurers everywhere? Or a clumsy attempt at tackling hip social issues by someone (not necessarily the accredited writer) who didn't bother to include any speaking parts for female characters *except* for the companion and the lisping Queen? (Presuming for the moment that Alpha Centauri doesn't count.)

6. Fans of Terry Walsh - the series' stalwart stunt expert and Doctor-double - will enjoy the protracted fight sequence in Part Four, which not allows him to show off his moves, but also lets us get a good look at his face when he's supposed to be doubling for Jon Pertwee. He also plays the Guard Captain who's killed at least three times, and various other guards. Maybe the Pels have cracked cloning. Other things you shouldn't be able to see include the leg of the man inside the Aggedor costume, when the furry trousers come away from the furry boots during his death-scene.

The Continuity

The Doctor Deliberately goes back to Peladon to see how the planet's getting on, the first time he's seen to follow up "old cases". He's capable of going into complete sensory withdrawal when necessary [not here described as an innate Time Lord ability, but see 23.4, "The Ultimate Foe"], and obviously has experience of trisilicate. He claims there's nothing he likes more than a quiet life, but it's impossible to believe him.

• *Ethics*. When cornered, the Doctor has no compunction about using Eckersley's heat-ray to kill one of the Ice Warriors. He goes on to kill several others who are threatening the miners. [Initially he uses the device because it's the only chance of survival he and his friends have, although subsequent uses suggest that he's ready to fight military-style campaigns when he feels it's needed.]

• *Inventory*. The Doctor uses the monocle he's reverted to carrying in his waistcoat pocket [see Volume I] to induce 'light hypnosis' in Aggedor. He performs another distracting conjuring-trick with a coin from his pocket, so he's obviously never short of spare change.

The Supporting Cast

• *Sarah Jane Smith*. Much more independent here than during her last "adventure", and much less prone to rely on the Doctor, though she's no longer arguing with him every step of the way. [Now she's used to space travel, she's starting to settle down.] She's certainly taking the "exploring alien planets" idea in her stride, so much so that she's ready to criticise the Doctor for landing in 'another rotten, gloomy old tunnel'. She also claims that the Doctor has always told her 'where there's life, there's hope'. [Since we've never heard him say anything of the sort to her, the suggestion might be that more time has passed between them than we know about. Anyway, did they ever get to Florana? The 'where there's life...' line foreshadows the Third Doctor's dying words in the next story.]

The Doctor decides to take her back to Earth at the end of the story, without her asking, perhaps demonstrating that he doesn't see her as a full-time companion. Yet. [Oddly, he grabs her by the ear and tugs her inside: hardcore feminist Sarah lets this go, but try to imagine Leela, Ace or even Mel putting up with this.]

Sarah seems to figure out how to use a zap-gun pretty quickly, and seems quite prepared to use one on Eckersley. [We see her being very familiar with terrestrial weaponry in stories such as 12.1, "Robot" and 13.3, "Pyramids of Mars". In the latter, she's very confident of her marksmanship - more signs of UNIT training? - and the former sees her willing to shoot Miss Winters.] She mourns the Doctor for a good ten minutes before going to see his "body".

The TARDIS The scanner's on the blink. [It might be a result of the power-drain in the last story. The Doctor says the scanner is 'still' malfunctioning at one stage - suggesting an ongoing fault, which wasn't the case when they landed on Exxilon. This seems to be a recurrent problem when he goes to Peladon.] The Doctor says the Ship's 'spatial coordinates' have slipped a bit too, explaining why it lands half a mile from the Citadel.

The Non-Humans

• *The Pels.* They still have a ferociously-maintained class divide, and a disregard for non-royal females. They're sometimes called 'Peladonians', sometimes 'Pels'; even the Doctor can't decide.

• *Ice Warriors.* Commander Azaxyr [again, not referred to as an "Ice Lord"] is in charge of the Federation troops sent to keep order on Peladon, so the Ice Warriors would seem to be the "UN peacekeepers" of the Federation. However, Azaxyr is actually loyal to a faction which wants a return to the Martians' military past. Alpha Centauri suggests that only the Doctor refers to the Martians as 'Ice Warriors', yet Azaxyr later refers to his troops as 'Ice Warriors', the only time this happens on screen. They don't recognise the Doctor here. The standard Ice Warrior weapon is now a small handheld rod which kills instantly [the special effect seems to suggest that it makes people implode] and can burn through metal. Warmth makes them dizzy and sluggish. They no longer refer to Mars as their home; nor does anyone else.

As in their first appearance, one of the Ice Warriors in Azaxyr's retinue has a differently-shaped helmet to the others [see 5.3, "The Ice Warriors"].

• *Alpha Centauri.* The same hexapod who was on Peladon fifty years previously, and there's no sign of ageing other than 'a little grey around the tentacles', so the species must be quite long-lived. He's now the Federation's ambassador on Peladon, and he's willing to vouch for the Doctor - even

though he must know that the Doctor faked his credentials in their last meeting.

• *Vega Nexos.* The representative of the planet Vega is satyr-like, with furry legs and cloven hooves but a human top half, and no modesty as he prances around naked even in the company of the Queen. His slitty eyes just emphasise his animal-like appearance, and the claim that the people of Vega are experts in mining techniques underlines the fact that he's obviously supposed to be some kind of burrowing mole-person. "Nexos" would seem to be his name or title. His people have been miners for centuries and are biologically adapted for the task. [As we saw in 22.2, "Vengeance on Varos", this is consistent with the side effects of Zeiton 7, which might have an impact on attempts to date this story. See **History**.]

• *Aggedor.* The Royal Beast of Peladon is the same specimen the Doctor met last time, so it's another long-lived species. He makes a good tracking-animal. Aggedor dies here, and the implication is that he's the last of his kind.

Planet Notes

• *Peladon.* Fifty years after the Doctor's last visit, Peladon is established as a member of the Federation but still regarded as primitive by the other planets. A single individual acting as both Chancellor and High Priest now advises Queen Thalira. [Odd that she doesn't call herself 'Peladon', like her father.] The old King died when the Queen was young, and everyone on Peladon now knows the story of the Doctor, while Chancellor Ortron took over the day Hepesh died. [Allowing that fifty years have passed, he must have been *very* young for a chancellor, unless the Pels age well. This detail contradicts Gary Russell's book *Legacy*, which claims that the Pels have shorter lifespans than humans, living about sixty-five years at most.] The monarch still has a big butch Champion who can't talk. Women of non-noble rank are now allowed in the throne-room though the miners aren't usually allowed in the citadel, which is overlooked by Mount Megeshra. Peladon has ostensibly never dishonoured a treaty.

The miners, being commoners, are generally superstitious idiots who don't trust alien technology unless they can shoot someone with it. Still, the story ends with better relations being forged between the workers and the nobles. It turns out that Peladon is rich in trisilicate. [A mineral which, in "The Curse of Peladon", was said to be found only on Mars. In "The Curse of Peladon", the Doctor blamed the Ice Warriors for an attack on the other delegates simply because he found traces of trisilicate in the area, so with hindsight the fact that the stuff is found all over Peladon makes him look rather silly]. Federation membership has benefited the ruling classes, but not the miners.

[Incidentally, Thalira looks plausibly like a child of Peladon, but also unnervingly like Katy Manning. Fan writers have picked up on this for stories about what Jo did later.]

History

• *Dating.* 'About' fifty years after the Doctor's last visit to Peladon. [We have to assume that they do, in fact, mean fifty *Earth* years, as various parties have the opportunity to say 'eighteen of your Earth years' or whatever but don't. See **What's the Timeline of the Earth Empire?** under 8.4, "Colony in Space" for more.]

The Federation is currently involved in a war against Galaxy Five, and desperately needs trisilicate for use in circuitry, heat-shields, inert microcell fibres and radionic crystals. Eckersley states that the Federation's whole technology is based on trisilicate, and that whoever has it will win the war. [The Federation must have known about Peladon's trisilicate before the planet joined the Federation, which may be why Peladon was given membership despite its rather backward society. If trisilicate is so vital, then Mars must have been a major power in galactic politics until now, and the discovery of *another* source of the mineral might have been the reason behind Azaxyr's revolt.]

Alpha Centauri claims that the Federation was the victim of a vicious and unprovoked attack, and that Galaxy Five refuses to talk, but it becomes anxious to negotiate a peace treaty after its plot on Peladon fails; Centauri baldly states that the war is over. Trisilicate is a transparent yellowish ore in its natural form, and the Federation uses sonic lances [see also the Doctor's use of a handheld 'sonic lance' in 22.1, "Attack of the Cybermen"] to mine it. Duralinium is this week's futuristic-sounding building substance, while the agents of Galaxy Five use a matter-projector and a directional heat-ray to fake the appearances of Aggedor's spirit.

Federation law usually forbids summary executions, and doesn't allow natives of 'primitive' plan-

ets to get hold of sophisticated weapons [from other Federation worlds, although it's notable that Peladon is *described* as primitive despite its status as a member-planet]. Alpha Centauri sends for security troops, but the troops can't be recalled once they've been summoned, leaving their commander in charge of Peladon and able to declare martial law. Azaxyr's strong-arm tactics wouldn't be tolerated in time of peace [so Centauri must believe that a State of Emergency is in effect Galaxy-wide].

The Analysis

Where Does This Come From? This time, most of what you need to know is in **The Lore** section, because this story is conceived almost from the start as a topical response to current events. So first off, we have to ask: why did the production team think that *Doctor Who* was the place to debate these issues?

Well, in a sense it always had been. Right from "An Unearthly Child" (1.1), the stories have taken current concerns and developed analogous situations (notice how the arms race and the relationship between technology and democracy is discussed with reference to the first technology - fire - and patrilineal leadership). If anything, it was the brief joint tenure of producers Peter Bryant and Derrick Sherwin, rigorously refraining from discussing anything outside the self-contained world of the story, that's the anomaly. Even then, the cast slipped in a few sly allusions, such as the Krotons having South African accents (see, guess what, 6.4, "The Krotons").

Nothing goes as far as "The Monster of Peladon" in winking at the audience and hoping they get the reference, but the problem is that even British children in 1974 needed more than the broad strokes used here. It wasn't, after all, a theoretical or abstract concern like Apartheid or censorship that they was being talking about - it was the coal-strike, the power cuts and the Three-Day Week. Everyone over the age of four knew what was happening. Or rather, what *had* happened, as this story was broadcast after the whole situation had ended, a new government was in power and the Eurovision Song Contest had sparked a coup in Portugal - a news item of *far* more interest to the nation's kids. To make a story so minutely topical as to be out of date in the month between recording and broadcast looks

Why Was There So Much Merchandising?

No-one growing up after *Star Wars* or in another country would bother to ask such a question. Indeed, looking back at it now, the idea that a chocolate bar, a cereal packet freebie or two, some comic strips, a "Fluid Neutraliser", the Chad Valley "Give-A-Show Projector" (just don't ask), toy Daleks and the occasional 7" record is some kind of marketing bonanza is absurd. *These* days every supermarket has sonic screwdrivers, Face of Boe tanks, 'Destroyed Cassandra' figures (your price: £7.99 for a rectangle of white plastic strips) and rows and rows of unsold Dalek Sec voice-changers, which are advertised on Nickelodeon. The notion that what was around in the 1970s was overkill is hard to explain to anyone who wasn't there, because it misses a crucial point: by law, there shouldn't have been any. The BBC didn't need the revenue to finance the programme, and was, in fact, officially required to *avoid* overt cashing-in on any programmes it made.

The BBC started television broadcasts in 1936. Only Hitler's Germany had anything similar, and the Nazis used it for sport (the Olympics), DIY, home-making hints and trite documentaries about the lives of ordinary people (what an unthinkable waste of the medium). It wasn't until 1955 that the government allowed commercial television - which is to say, with advertising breaks but no sponsorship of programmes. As a quid pro quo, the commercial network was allowed to keep all the revenue from advertising and the BBC kept all the revenue from the Television Licence, with which everything from Benjamin Britten being commissioned to write *Peter Grimes* down to the cost of *Blue Peter* badges was financed. *Doctor Who* came out of the Drama Department's budget, along with all the Jane Austen adaptations, soaps, one-off plays (at least four a week back then) and serials. Any revenue from selling any of these overseas or making "I Heart *Dixon of Dock Green*" tea-towels went into the overall budget, not to the individual programme. Any merchandising was to be available at near-enough cost-price. BBC Enterprises, who supervised this, maintained strict quality control.

Christmas 1964 was something of a surprise to British parents. Instead of nice, ordinary toys like jigsaws and teddies, kids wanted anything with either the Beatles or a Dalek on. There had been TV spin-off fads before, including Davy Crockett hats and Robin Hood stuff (not to the extent popularly imagined, any more than everyone lived exclusively on Spangles in 1972). Still, the scale of that year's commerciality was unprecedented. The next ten years would see a steady stream of *Doctor Who* merchandising - other guidebooks can tell you all about these, and what they're now worth on the open market, but that's not the point. To the kids, they were priceless.

This is what most people failed to realise then (except, of course, Gerry Anderson). Any programme which invites you into a world generates an excitement about "relics" from that world. Sure, these days they're collectable and you're supposed to "need" the set, but to a child in those days, it was an emotional attachment, the prospect that it might all be real (you knew it wasn't, but only when anyone asks you). By being all BBC-ish about it, the *Doctor Who* office maintained a level of craftsmanship and "good faith", so that the attitude of the programme carried on throughout. With founding script editor David Whittaker ghosting much of the material in the early annuals and supervising the Dalek comic-strip, it was logically and aesthetically self-consistent, which is what children love most about fantasy.

One important factor needs to be recalled: these were mainly toys bought for the kids by indulgent adults. Odd as it seems, the items available for pocket-money prices (yo-yos, marbles, Matchbox model cars, Ladybird books and... well that was about it) were worthy but unconnected with mass popular culture. By the time you were getting enough money for this sort of thing, you'd be shelling out seven shillings and sixpence (32 1/2 p) on a 45 rpm single and were deemed to be too grown-up for toys. The big-ticket items like PVC Dalek suits were for kids with rich uncles, and the waiting for the birthday or Christmas invested the items with special value beyond even the cost. (This, incidentally, is why old merchandise is so collectable... these items were literally loved to bits so only the unsold ones are in good nick now. Nobody thought to buy bubble-bath as an investment.) The big change came when Twentieth Century Fox found that they could make back the outlay for an expensive science-fiction film in collectable units, like action-figures and stickers, at kid-friendly prices. The film that launched this child-exploitation bonanza was, of course...

Beneath the Planet of the Apes. What, you think George Lucas ever had an original idea in his life? No, it was the move from one-off hit to franchise,

continued on page 453...

like making unnecessary hostages to fortune. So is that *really* what's going on here?

Perhaps it's worth looking at what the 1973 miners' dispute was actually about. The 1971-2 one was simply about pay. Getting enough to live on seemed like a reasonable request and eventually the government came around to the same view as the miners' union and the majority of the British public (who gamely managed throughout the power cuts partly due to a lot of residual goodwill - with an admixture of guilt - about coal-mining, and partly because there's nothing the British like more than being seen to muddle through in adversity and tell everyone about it).

The 1973 dispute was about respect. Although the miners had enough coming in, the amount they got - for all the risk and illness they endured - was only as much as someone else got for working in a factory or an office. Why did they bother? Because of tradition, but also because the areas with the coal had so few other jobs. This was something that was true of other industries that were supposedly or genuinely in decline. Until the fall-out from the Yom Kippur War made the assumption look shaky, most economic forecasts were based on the idea that oil would replace coal (except in power-generation - which would be nuclear, of course). As both 10.5, "The Green Death" and 22.3, "The Mark of the Rani" explore, people far removed from this life either respected it in a mildly patronising way, or disdained it and thought any notion of community built around industry was sentimental and damaging.

Here's where we get to the nub of it: the relationship between people in authority a long way away and people at the business-end who feel they're not being listened to is the main focus of this story as broadcast. The original scenario Brian Hayles submitted was exactly the opposite, with the people who were dishing out aid being benign and gullible, but the people for whom it was intended not getting any benefit.

In the broadcast version it's the intermediaries (such as the Doctor and, eventually, the miners' leader Gebek) who bring harmony and respect back. The antagonistic factions simply haven't talked to one another for too long. However much this might be offered as a diagnosis of the dispute between the Heath government and the National Union of Mineworkers, it's a total inversion of the first draft's claim that the intermediaries are getting fat on siphoned-off aid. So whilst we could

identify Gebek with Union leader Joe Gormley and the rebellious Ettis with his firebrand deputy Arthur Scargill (who saw the strike as a means to a more widespread disruption, thus bringing about deeper political change), you have to accept that doing this leads you to seeing the miners as superstitious dimwits prey to any passing rabble-rouser. There are specific topical concerns, such as the excruciating scene where Sarah discusses "Women's Lib" with the Queen, but the story's overall emphasis is more general. Also, despite being set largely in mines (which allow the same sets to be reused again and again, especially the ones that were straightforward tunnels last time we were on this planet), it's actually less directly about an identifiable single issue than the proposed story.

In another reversal, Aggedor had previously been a real animal turned into a vengeful spirit. In this story, the miners take Aggedor as their spectral mascot. This is a familiar theme in British (especially English) popular culture. Since the middle ages, there have been stories of lost leaders who will come back at a dark hour, such as King Arthur or Sir Francis Drake (whose drum is supposed to sound at times of national crisis). During the crisis that accompanied this story's making, there were many on all sides who evoked the Dunkirk Spirit - the modern-day version of Drake's Drum.

Things That Don't Make Sense Understandably, it's forbidden for less-advanced cultures get their hands on the Federation's sophisticated weaponry. Yet the Federation has installed a sizeable armoury on Peladon that contains laser guns. As the official number of off-worlders numbers exactly three (Alpha Centauri, Vega Nexos and Eckersley) when the story opens, this is, surely, a stupid thing to have about the place? After all, any Federation security troops summoned to Peladon would surely bring their *own* guns, so installing the armoury just creates the scenario that any insurrection will be able to shoot at any Federation soldiers with advanced firepower.

Once again, Brian Hayles (in the bits of this story that he actually wrote) gives us a future where the whole of technology and society changes in the blink of an eye. We can *just* about buy that, in "The Seeds of Death" (6.5), the advent of T-Mat causes rockets, cars and clothes shops to vanish into the history books in the space of about

Why Was There So Much Merchandising?

...continued from page 451

with the appalling TV series and all, that made the *Apes* films into toy commercials. *Star Wars* only really differed by having a really nerdy director who supervised each and every R2-D2 pillowcase. In this, he was inadvertently following in Verity Lambert's footsteps, while *she* had been half-consciously following Brian Epstein's diligent Beatle brand-management. Back then, the BBC's disdain for commercial concerns meant that not only were the spin-offs assiduously monitored for quality-control purposes (because a kid scalded with a shoddy hot-water bottle was a bad mark against the Corporation as a whole, not the manufacturer), but that the department heads gave that *little* bit more money for Dalek stories, so long as they kept a-coming.

By the time of "The Chase" (2.8), the requirement to churn out Dalek adventures outstripped the production team's desire to make them. By "The Power of the Daleks" (4.3), the toys were written into the story as a cheap and not-too-embarrassing way of suggesting an army of them growing in secret. So much of a buzz surrounded the Daleks back then that there were two films made (see the Appendix in Volume VI) and the BBC found itself thinking of cross-promotion and marketing. However, there isn't any record of the TV adventures having blatant plugs for Sugar Smacks, as was seen in the second Peter Cushing *Dr Who* movie.

That said, Kellogg's' made the first real "collectables": badges of the Doctor, Jo, the Brigadier, Mike and the ultimate prized item, a UNIT badge that was rather better than the ones worn by Messrs Courtney and Franklin. Sugar Smacks were linked with *Doctor Who* the same way that Ricicles were with *The Magic Roundabout*. Weetabix, the homegrown (literally, to start with) rival cereal, topped this a couple of years later with the pasteboard figures that made Vega Nexos, Hieronymus and the White Robots briefly rival the Yeti and the Cybermen for schoolyard kudos.

By this time Target books had launched what would be the single most important form of merchandising: novelisations of broadcast stories (See **How Important Were The Books?** under 2.6, "The Crusade". Calling these "merchandising" seems somehow wrong, as - for those of us in the UK in the era before video - they were the *only* available record of what happened in the stories.) What's important here is how these were also at pocket-money prices but - crucially - neither numbered nor published in any obvious sequence, so that "collect the set" mania wasn't fanned until the mid-80s commercialisation of fandom. Just as on screen, the stories being told were the main point of interest.

While the BBC maintained rights over the programme, the TARDIS, Bessie and so on, there were two big anomalies: the face of the lead actor and Terry Nation's (contentious) claim over the Daleks. Nation and Pertwee cashed in big time. Any long-term fan will have his or her favourite crass example (we've already listed the Dalek ones; Pertwee did Col Public Information films advising kids to SPLINK[140]), but what's interesting is how far they stuck within the BBC's overall guidelines. Pertwee (or a badly-drawn avatar) promoted a breakfast serial for giving "timeless energy", but it was phrased as general dietary advice for kids. He released a novelty single (a snatch of which is running under the end credits of *More Than Thirty Years in the TARDIS*), but plugged it on BBC radio only. Reading the *Dalek Pocket-Book and Space Traveller's Guide*, you can see that Nation was as big a fanboy as any of us, in love with the world he was making up, even though that led to absurdities such as the ones we've mentioned in earlier essays (and many more you can find for yourself). The commodity-fetishism of poseable action-figure sets and eBay are a long way from this almost infantile delight. It *mattered* to writer and child-viewer alike.

The show's Tenth Anniversary saw a small change in this. For better or worse, Barry Letts managed the publicity for the series personally and maintained close links with the staff at *Countdown + TV Action* (see the essay on this). The *Radio Times* anniversary special, which opened a can of Drashig-sized worms (see **What Are These Stories Really Called?** under 3.2, "Mission To The Unknown"), allowed tantalising glimpses behind the scenes, something never really done before. (Troughton had been dead against it, except for children who won competitions; Lambert and Wiles never thought to do it.) This became the hallmark of all subsequent merchandising, culminating in Marvel UK launching *Doctor Who Weekly* in 1979. Even then, it took a while for the magazine to get into the groove of regular behind-the-scenes material, with the early issues pretending that the Doctor himself was the editor and acting

continued on page 455...

five years. But here, he asks us to swallow that in the fifty years since the last Peladon story, the entire galaxy has switched to - and become totally reliant upon - a substance so rare that only Peladon and Mars (according to "The Curse of Peladon") seem to have it.

One of those planets, of course, is Peladon - where mining operations are only *now* being modernized. So prior to this, how did the entire galaxy get so dependent on a mineral still being mined at most two sources, at least one of those *by hand*? And as far as know, trisilicate on Peladon is only found in the tunnels in about a mile's radius from the Citadel. Besides, given its alleged reserves of this all-important mineral, how has Peladon warranted such little interest and resources? There are no permanent armed orbital stations, and no smugglers?[138] Anyway, the use of trisilicate would presumably make any planet that's got it ridiculously wealthy, so why aren't the Ice Warriors buying everything in sight? Or if they insist on supporting Galaxy Five, why don't they just blockade Mars and cut off the Federation's supply of trisilicate, which is as good as getting the material to Galaxy Five, if not better?

[Ah, you might counter, Azaxyr's group aren't officially connected with the Martian government, and are a part of a breakaway faction. Even if this were so, Galaxy Five *must* have a trisilicate source of its own, and the wherewithal to stop Peladon's comparatively feeble production. This would make Mars' ability to supply all of what the Federation needs to fight a war the deciding factor. If that much dissent exists on Mars already, the Federation would have to declare martial law on the very planet where at least some of their police force originates. Therefore, the rebel Ice Warriors have a ready-made source for dissent, almost guaranteed to bolster their support. Either way, the fact that Galaxy Five immediately surrenders after Eckersley and Azaxyr's plan goes south just shows how badly messed-up their strategy was. Somehow, they've lost in a win-win situation.]

In defiance of all the civil unrest that's afflicting Peladon, the goodies stubbornly refuse to post guards on the communications room - even though it contains a vital radio link with the Federation, has a switch that can open the Federation armoury *and* is the vantage point from which someone can monitor the entire citadel on CCTV. Locking the door would be a start.

Over at the refinery, Eckersley's choice of installing a security system that literally causes brain damage is curious. We later discover that the device can be set to temporarily disorientate any interlopers (as occurs when Eckersley turns the device against the Doctor) rather than cause permanent damage. Somehow, though, it has "Fry" as the default setting... and Eckersley wonders why the miners resent his presence. As his fiendish plan relies on making the miners get superstitious and providing genuine visions of Aggedor that genuinely zap Vega Nexos, leaving his burglar alarm set on "trippy visions" might be a better idea all around. Moreover, Gebek says in Part Three that 'several' of his people had 'their minds destroyed' by the device. That's a Health and Safety issue worth mentioning to Ortron, surely? Are we seriously supposed to think that the Pel royals wouldn't take issue with some of their subjects getting brains obliterated?

Ortron claims that he took over as Chancellor immediately after Hepesh died. Even allowing that King Peladon said that day would be wiped from the planet's history, it's hard to fathom that Ortron didn't know how Hepesh died and, besides 'everyone' on Peladon knows the story of the Doctor. So why does the Doctor's surviving being thrown to Aggedor confuse him? Why does he know so little of the Doctor's activities, including what he looks like? Then again, why does the Doctor show no concern about wandering into the temple in Part One, considering it resulted in an automatic death sentence the last time he was there? Why does he forget to sing to Aggedor until after a few life-threatening lunges? What kind of High Priest is Ortron, to ignore such an obvious sign of Aggedor's favour and spend the rest of the story opposing the Doctor? If there's a heretic on this planet, it's the man in the purple frock. He's also dim enough to open this story with the incredulous complaint, 'Where are these saboteurs?', as if it's impossible to think that they might be hiding.

But even with 'everyone' on Peladon knowing about the Doctor, it's strange that when a citadel guard spots the TARDIS arriving, he doesn't approach or challenge the travellers. Nor does he inform the royals about this, instead preferring - for some reason - to tell Gebek. Then at the start of Part Two, Ettis, Gebek and their colleagues display *amazing* battle skill - they're caught empty-handed and flat-footed, yet they're able to parry

Why Was There So Much Merchandising?

...continued from page 453

as if it were all "real". By this time, *Star Wars* and all those annoying US series with cute robots and kids for "audience identification" had happened, and they needed merchandising to pay for it to be made... hence the cute robots and kids.

So, from the BBC point of view, exploitation of money-spinning rights to things was a means to an end, of preserving the bond with the audience. Don't forget, prior to 1970 *Doctor Who* was a brand image for oddness, not a series of individual adventures. It was a "zone" where the laws of TV narrative were bent; somewhere you visited, not something you watched and followed. Most of the public couldn't remember the plots, but knew the sort of thing that might happen. The illustrations in the *Radio Times* and the programme's aesthetic of "difference" all helped viewers participate with this. In the pre-video, pre-channel-zapping age, once you selected a channel you were there for the night, and Saturday nights belonged to BBC1. *Doctor Who* belonged to Saturday night, and if you wanted to continue inhabiting the "place" it created you needed your Target novelisations, records of Jon Pertwee and Deep Purple performing "I Am The Doctor" ('I cross the void beyond the mind...'), Rolykin Daleks and "Masterplan Q" chocolate bars

(and, if you're strange, your underpants with Tom Baker on).

After the 1983 Anniversary, the position changed again. It's been argued that this was the point when *Doctor Who* became something you bought, not something provided as a "public service" which you opted to participate in or not. Certainly the number of reunions, returns of old characters, settings and monsters and gimmicky collectables increased exponentially. (This was the era of *The Doctor Who Cookbook* and many other items which have now attained a certain kitsch status. We have dealt with some of these oddities in a later essay, **Why Did They Think We'd Buy This Crap?** under 22.5, "Timelash".)

When people wax nostalgic about spin-offery, we forget that it was Colin Baker who (until recently) had the largest number of such items, not Pertwee or Hartnell. However, most of these were forgettable or unavailable in the high streets. By this stage, the actual programme was an embarrassment in many quarters As with his mentor Letts, producer John Nathan-Turner managed the merchandising at least as well as the programme, which was increasingly looking like "product" itself. To an extent, of course, this was simply a

continued on page 457...

---

the Queen's sword-wielding guards with some sticks. (And as they're in the mines, where did the sticks come from?) Later, a guard spies the miner Reba and shouts, 'There he is!' - as if they were looking for him specifically when, um, they aren't.

Come Part Three, the Doctor gets caught sneaking out of the Citadel, but doesn't mention to Ortron that the Queen ordered him to go and see Gebek. Does he *want* to get locked up? Suddenly, Sarah relays to Gebek the Doctor's concern that the rebels will try to capture the sonic lance - even though we don't see him air such worries to her. [This might have occurred off-panel, but it's a strange oversight.] And suddenly, Sarah miraculously knows all about Ortron's bid to secure the benefits of Federation membership for 'him and his aristocratic friends'. Even presuming this were true [and frankly, there's no clue that it is], it's a subplot from the earlier version of the script, in which the Ice Warriors were still the good guys and Sarah was duped into joining Eckersley's faction [see **The Lore**]. Then in Part Five, Sarah's idea of militant feminist action is...

getting the Queen to pretend to faint. [Either Terrance Dicks hasn't been listening to Barry Letts' readings from *Spare Rib*, or he's taking the piss.]

The Queen, Ortron, Gebek and the Doctor are united in their plan to make everything look normal when the Federation troops arrive. Yet when Azaxyr gives his "the story so far" info-dump in episode four, it's obvious that they've all done a massive about-face and told him *everything*. What happened to the "Nope, nothing to see here..." plan? Anyway, how did Azaxyr walk into the communications room mere seconds after the Doctor and Gebek opened the refinery door to discover the Ice Warriors within? The Martians are supposed to be in hiding, but to make such an entrance, Azaxyr would practically have to be skulking outside, ready for his dramatic entrance.

Peladon obviously treats its miners much more fairly than we're led to believe, since the mines are fitted with a heating system that can be adjusted for comfort like a great big radiator. Mines with air-conditioning would seem *remarkably* luxurious to anyone watching the news in 1974, so why are the Pel miners whinging? And why are they on about how great it was before the Feds arrived, seeing as that none of them look old enough to remember what the mines were like fifty years back? Later, Azaxyr tries to force the miners to co-operate by removing the fresh air from the mines and sending in his Ice Warriors. As the Martians have difficulty breathing Earth-type air anyway, how would heated air be better? Fine, the CO_2 content would be higher, but so would everything else, especially with torches burning everywhere.

Eckersley expects a Martian to know what 'argy-bargy' means. Yet Azaxyr does indeed know the phrase. Ditto 'jiggered'. The fall of the Ice Warriors on Peladon fails to account for their orbiting spaceship/s - you know, the one/s that are causing all the jamming. Assuming they exist, these same ships singularly fail to detect Alpha Centauri's activation of the Spatial Distress Beacon - or at least, they don't tell Azaxyr about it, for some reason. Elsewhere, the sonic lance is capable of destroying the entire citadel, yet it's left unat-tended and out in the open for about two episodes. And in springing the Doctor from his cell, Gebek is able to knock a *helmeted* guard unconscious with a single punch.

But then, if we're being honest, the Doctor isn't at his best this adventure. His hearing is once again questionable, as several guards in clanking armour file into the temple of Aggedor behind him without him noticing. We should also ques-tion his judgment in telling Ettis' band of rebels how they can open the Federation armoury [from the communications room], as if it's unthinkable that they'll capitalise on this information. His mar-tial arts skills must be failing him as well - Ettis beats him in one-on-one combat, even though we've frequently seen him trounce combat-hard-ened opponents twice the stupidly-afro'd miner's size. Curiously, before the sonic lance detonates, the Doctor is lying fallen on his back; *after* the explosion, he's apparently in the same spot of floor, but on his stomach.

In Part Four, Jon Pertwee is credited as playing the Doctor, yet it's plainly Terry Walsh for some-thing like three-quarters of the episode. Equally puzzling is how the Doctor figured out that Aggedor could follow a scent - the species was for-merly the royal hunting beast, so it presumably *makes* one that other animals can follow (we hear about this in the second cliffhanger), but that's all. If stepping into the temple is blasphemy, what

about using their god as a sniffer-dog?

Why does *anyone* listen to Ettis after a certain point? True, he uses the sonic lance (and kills the Queen's Champion), but later on he leads his sup-porters into a disastrous raid on the Citadel, get-ting them all mown down by Ice Warriors, even as he legs it before numbering among the casualties. Yet he still enjoys popular support, we're told. [Maybe they just want to embarrass the Queen by making her say his name a lot.]

The baddies try and fail to close the refinery door properly, helpfully enabling the Doctor and Gebek to spy on them. Max Faulkner, here cred-ited as 'miner' is shot dead in Part Six... then exactly seven scenes later, Eckersley shoots him dead again. And after several years of writing for Pertwee (whose inability with sibilants made words such as 'Interstitial', 'Venusians', 'Silurians' and 'Sarah Jane Smith' has provided so much fun), those sadists on the production-team have up and given Nina Thomas lines such as 'the use of the sonic lance is essential' and 'Thank you, Ambassador: the audience is at an end.' And that's just in her first scene! The later ones, where she converses with Pertwee, are like a *Two Ronnies* sketch. Ms Thomas doesn't talk like that in real life, so this is clearly the director's idea. [Bathtard!] Why would he do such a thing, if he wanted peo-ple to take this story seriously?

Critique As you'll read in **The Lore**, this story was made under trying conditions. Anyone who's read the whole of *About Time* will realise that this is usually a guarantee of something outstanding - crises in production accompany stories such as "Spearhead from Space" (7.1), "The Greatest Show in the Galaxy" (25.4), "The Mind Robber" (6.2), "The Androids of Tara" (16.4) and of course "The Daleks" (1.2). It is, however, certainly not a *guarantee* of inspiration, quality or any on screen interest - and "The Monster of Peladon" is, in fact, the classic counter-example. If this adventure has any distinguishing feature, it's the woeful lack of any zest, ambition or merit. More even than the story before it, it's the most dismal example of the series and its star functioning on autopilot.

This was obvious even to children watching at the time. The ostensible target-audience - the pre-text for all these actors making idiots of them-selves on national television - were only mildly intrigued by Alpha Centauri, and not even the less-than-entirely-surprising revelation that the

Why Was There So Much Merchandising?

...continued from page 455

result of the length of time the programme had been on the air. Some of the people making the series belonged to a generation that had known it all their lives, so it's not surprising that fetishising the past became part of the programme. Once video releases of the old stories were permitted, the content of the newer ones began to dovetail with what was on sale - see 22.1, "Attack of the Cybermen". *Doctor Who* was a shop-window. Once it was no longer on air the spin-offery, videos, books and audios of various kinds kept the money rolling in, just as much as it had when new episodes were being made. Sporadic repeats seemed almost like pretexts for the continuity-announcer's hucksterish reminders of what was available in shops right now. By that time the whole idea of "cult" had taken hold and the assumption was that *Doctor Who* was something for collectors to purchase: one of the most successful family entertainment series ever made was now of interest to a coterie.

A final word about the second most involving form of merchandising: games. The Annuals had no end of variations on Snakes and Ladders (1976's had a "Foam Rubber Avalanche" as a hazard), but specific shop-bought board-games are comparatively rare (making the poor sales of the Eccleston one really odd). There was a pretty generic space game from Strawberry Fair with Tom Baker's face on the front in 1978, but fewer people played that than made the "Theatre" from cut-outs in the *Radio Times* and hints on *Blue Peter*. There was a puzzling Games Workshop one from the 80s boom-ette (copyright law meant that they had Ice Warriors who were men made of ice, and someone called "Mary Jane") but the real period-piece is Jotastar's *Top Trumps* cards. They had the rights to all sorts of monsters (including Davros - against all expectations if you knew the Nation team's litigiousness). Unfortunately, they muddled up the Ogrons and the Sea Devils, and the Doctor's peculiar trans-temporal army - the Legendary Legion - were a random selection of non-copyright historical and mythical figures. Shaka Zulu and Annie Oakley against Cybermen and Silurians (there's a Big Finish audio we'd all like to hear). Quite how Sherlock Holmes had a "Mental Powers" rating higher than Omega or the Giant Spiders of Metebelis III is another question for another time. The picture of the Doctor on the reverse of each card looks like the Dalek Sec Hybrid from "Daleks In Manhattan" (X3.4), only wearing a fedora and feather boa. Somehow the recent Playstation *Doctor Who* Top Trumps game is a lot less fun. Those who played any games other than this may also recall the 1988 game, which was like a more obsessively inclusive version of "The Five Doctors" (20.7) with absolutely every concept, character or monster possible crammed in. Shockeye has an Inner Force of 80 and a Dodecahedron skill of 50, if you were wondering.

Ice Warriors were behind it all lifted this out of the humdrum. At this point, *Doctor Who* is in a comfort-zone, providing a set menu of monsters, stunts, homilies and caves. What Terrance Dicks (the main culprit, it seems) never quite grasped was that the main influence of *Star Trek* on *Doctor Who* should have been as a warning, not a role-model. *Trek* was cancelled after three years partly because it fell in love with itself, but mainly because the increasingly desperate attempts to break away from the formula reminded everyone that there *was* a formula.

But to be fair, each *Trek* episode pressed the re-set button because the series needed to be shown in any order once the original NBC broadcast concluded. However self-contained any *Doctor Who* story - or indeed episode - was or wasn't, the one thing it *not* meant to be was something the BBC could repeat. So while there's nothing wrong with making a sequel to a story set on a planet we've seen (after all, all the UNIT stories are set on Earth), each adventure had to be intriguing in its own right and not just ride the coat-tails of an earlier one. The Sea Devils entertained sufficiently and scared kids who'd not seen "Doctor Who and the Silurians" (the ones who'd really liked the earlier story were the later one's only real critics), and "The Sea Devils" itself works perfectly well as someone's first introduction to the series. (Quite what they make of the next two stories is another matter.)

It's not like anyone is really putting in less effort on screen than before. Pertwee's incapacitated and can't do the stunts, but he's finding new ways to deliver plot information now that his assistant isn't asking dumb questions and isn't Katy Manning. Alan Bennion is playing his third "Ice Lord" and makes it a subtly different mix of the basic qualities. As the Queen, Nina Thomas is given a *terrible* part and copes as well as might be expected. The old hands behind the cameras do well with overly-familiar material too. Director Lennie Mayne's six-episode budget has been augmented by re-use of old sets and costumes, so he could have gone to town exploring this world had the script had permitted it. If the story had been allowed to *be* a story about exploring an odd planet we've partly seen before, this would've been exactly what *Doctor Who* was intended for.

Alas, Dicks has decided that this story needs to be "about" something, and has given it the most crass subtext imaginable. Without knowing what he was getting at, and without a handy guide to British politics circa December 1973 (which we've thoughtfully provided elsewhere in this book), this is just a dull romp in a cave. With it, it's an *embarrassing* romp in a cave. Granted, a lot of stories that were rejected for the unmade Season Twenty-Three were about as unpromising as this, but "The Monster of Peladon" at least has the virtue of being made first. At the risk of overstating the point, all subsequent political allegories in cave-mines with pseudo-feudal societies are to some extent kicking against this adventure as much as against they are against *Star Trek*. Because they did a sequel to "The Curse of Peladon" that was about Arthur Scargill, a generation of later writers thought of this as standard *Doctor Who* procedure - and thus stories such as 22.2, "Vengeance on Varos" and 17.3, "The Creature from the Pit" got made. (Some might include that in the counts against this story.)

You'll have noticed that we're locating this story in the context of what it was apeing, and what happened as a result. But the thing is: we can't evaluate "The Monster of Peladon" on its merits, because it hasn't really got any. Nothing goes particularly wrong, because they're playing it safe and don't try anything they haven't done before. We *could* make fun of stuff such as Rex Robinson's performance... but this requires more effort than the story really deserves.

The Facts

Written by Brian Hayles. Directed by Lennie Mayne. Viewing figures 9.2 million, 6.8 million, 7.4 million, 7.2 million, 7.5 million, 8.1 million. The only recorded Audience Appreciation figure was for episode three, at 64%.

Supporting Cast Donald Gee (Eckersley), Nina Thomas (Thalira), Frank Gatliff (Ortron), Rex Robinson (Gebek), Ralph Watson (Ettis), Ysanne Churchman (Voice of Alpha Centauri), Stuart Fell (Body of Alpha Centauri), Gerald Taylor (Vega Nexos), Graeme Eton (Preba), Terry Walsh (Guard Captain), Roy Evans (Rima), Nick Hobbs (Aggedor), Alan Bennion (Azaxyr), Sonny Caldinez (Sskel).

Cliffhangers Aggedor's "spirit" appears before the Doctor and the Queen's Champion after they're sealed into one of the caverns of the mine; beneath the temple, the *real* Aggedor looms out of the darkness towards the Doctor and Sarah; the Doctor opens the door of the (supposedly deserted) refinery, and an Ice Warrior shambles out; in the cave overlooking the citadel, Ettis beats the Doctor in one-on-one combat, but the sonic lance self-destructs when Ettis uses it; the Ice Warriors burn their way through the door of the refinery where the Doctor and company are hiding.

What Was in the Charts? "Seven Seas of Rhye", Queen; "Jarrow Song", Alan Price; "Remember You're a Womble", The Wombles; "Judy Teen", Cockney Rebel; "A Walking Miracle", Limmie and the Family Cooking; "Shang-a-lang", The Bay City Rollers.

The Lore

• As we saw with "The Curse of Peladon", the thinking behind Peladon's relationship with the Federation was more UNESCO than EEC, despite how those involved rationalised it later on. This is doubly true of the first draft of "The Monster of Peladon", which was commissioned in January 1973 (i.e. long before the Yom Kippur War, the Oil Crisis and the Three Day Week).

However topical it turned out to be, the original premise was of a faction within Pel society keeping all the benefits of the sudden high price of Trisilicate for themselves, and not letting it trickle down into schools, hospitals and what-have-you. Indeed, King Peladon was in the story and Thalira - originally intended as his wife - was suborned to the opposition after the whole 'Princess Josephine of Tardis' business. So it was a genuine sequel, not just a bigger remake. Once the peacekeeping force of Ice Warriors turned up to restore order, the as-yet undefined new companion was to be misled by slight xenophobia into supporting Eckersley. Ortron was an opportunist, taking advantage of the rebellion and 'invasion' to set himself up as Viceroy.

• Lennie Mayne's availability as director was checked, and as many costumes and personnel as possible from the 1972 story were to be used. (As it turned out, only designer Gloria Clayton and, of course, Dudley Simpson returned.) This was always planned as a six-parter, and would, if possible, be done entirely without location shooting as per last time. However, while Barry Letts and (particularly) Terrance Dicks found Hayles' palace politicking and dynastic shenanigans interesting, they imagined it would be hard to "sell" to small children. In this light, the interview in *Doctor Who: The Unfolding Text* seems to suggest that what they call a *Sanders of the River* story - meaning of the Federation bringing prosperity and enlightenment to the "primitive" Pels - wasn't so much ideologically objectionable as implausible to the 1970s generation (not to mention dramatically inert), at least according to Letts and Dicks. They don't name names, and frame it very much as a hypothetical alternative to what was broadcast, but it looks as though Hayles was the target of their criticism. At the very least, he was asked to simplify the story.

• Although Robert Holmes was de facto script editor by this stage, Dicks was keeping an eye on the last two stories of the year to ensure that Holmes had a good starting-point for his official debut. Hayles was a writer with whom Dicks had worked repeatedly in various capacities, and Dicks' first substantial crisis had been reworking "The Seeds of Death" (6.5) to cope with Frazer Hines quitting and then un-quitting (consequently, the whole of Episode Four of that story was pretty much by Dicks). The *hope* was that this time there wouldn't be any need to rebuild a story from the ground up...

• Thankfully, Hayles' second pass clarified matters. The minor character Megeshra became a mountain and a coup on Mars meant that the Ice Warriors were back to their lootin' and a-shootin' ways. Alpha Centauri defended the Doctor in court, but Our Hero was then to be framed for killing Vega Nexos. We get scenes filmed in a quarry, a literal cliffhanger and the situation is resolved by the Doctor getting word to Federation HQ - whereupon the Feds, er, threaten to blow up Mars if they Ice Warriors don't withdraw. Sarah's part was greatly increased, although she was still

in "plucky girl" configuration and not the speech-making *Cosmo*-reading Libber that Letts wanted. The Doctor was still a fairly passive arbitrator, either on trial or under house arrest.

The scripts still needed work for a number of other reasons but - crucially - they couldn't abandon it as by this time (it was now 23rd of November, 1973 - the Doctor's tenth birthday), as the *Radio Times* special published a fortnight earlier had informed the nation's kids that "The Monster of Peladon" was going to be shown between "Planet of the Spiders" and "Death to the Daleks". By this point Hayles had been paid for *two* different versions (thereby hangs a tale, but not a very interesting one), so there was no option but to delay the start of production and pump Terrance full of coffee. (Well, he was arguably pumped full of *something*, as the stage direction get increasingly whimsical. By the end of episode five, a scene where an Ice Warrior is clouted on the head with a rock notes '...good for kiddie winkies - pleasant dreams', and the sabotaging Eckersley's burglar alarm recommends, 'Take the money! No, Open the box!' Readers unfamiliar with 1960s game shows will have to take it on trust that this is a catch-phrase from the era of Associated Rediffusion. However, as we've seen, Lennie Mayne tended to add his own comments to camera scripts, so this is hardly out-of-keeping even if Mayne didn't write them himself.)

• In case you were unaware, the last couple of months of 1973 were a bit fraught, so it was almost unavoidable that a story with striking miners would take on a few more topical notes. The main problems with making this story during the fifth State of Emergency that Edward Heath had imposed in just under four years as Prime Minister were, however, logistical. Heath had imposed restrictions on the use of fuel and electricity in order to make the public resentful of the miners' refusal to work overtime without more pay (see "The Green Death" and **Where Does This Come From?**) and so most workers were on short-time and the television companies were ordered to close down transmissions at 10.30pm. Power restrictions were reintroduced, and there was talk of petrol rationing. (In fact there was more than enough fuel. Heath eventually conceded that the miners were a special case, but it was too late; he'd called a snap election so backing down wasn't an option.) Between January 1st and March 8th, 1974 (so after Heath had been humiliated in the polls), all companies had to make their employees only work three days in any working week. This, coupled with Dicks' desire to tackle more immediate "issues" in the series, had an obvious influence on the broadcast story.

Yet there was another, more practical, concern: by kicking the production into the New Year at the precise moment that the BBC had opted to launch the new season in mid-December, the episodes would have to be recorded much closer to transmission than was comfortable. One way the BBC management had decided to handle the complexities of making television in a period of power-cuts and 20% inflation was to give the financial and logistical co-ordination of certain intricate shows to what was termed a Production Unit Manager (PUM). The idea was that if Series A had a set that Series B could re-use, and A and B had the same PUM they could do a deal. Or if Series B and Series C were in studio in the same time, they could swap props or... you get the idea. These people would each have a handful of series on the go at any given time. The first PUM for *Doctor Who* was George Gallaccio (later to get a peculiar cameo - see **Who Are All These Strange Men in Wigs?** under 13.5, "The Brain of Morbius"). It was a formal version of the kind of ad hoc arrangements that had seen *Doctor Who* and *Doomwatch* go halves on a space-capsule (7.3, "The Ambassadors of Death").

• Just before Christmas, Barry Letts made it known that he thought it was time to produce something else. Pertwee was now unlikely to want to carry on unless the BBC *really* pushed the boat out and gave him a pay-rise significantly above inflation. The search for a successor began with a few tentative calls to people such as comedian and writer Michael Bentine (who wanted to supervise the scripts as well); character-actor Fulton Mackay (see 7.2, "Doctor Who and the Silurians"), who was waiting to see if the pilot for a new sitcom he'd made with Pertwee's chum Ronnie Barker was going to series (it did); and several others (to be continued in the next story's notes). Another potential Doctor was children's favourite Bernard Cribbins, then riding high as the voice of *The Wombles* and with previous form as Tom in *Dalek Invasion Earth: 2150 AD* (see Volume VI). As you probably knew, he finally returned to the fold as Donna's granddad in the BBC Wales *Who*.

Pertwee was asked to keep his intentions quiet for the time being; the early start for Season Eleven had already cost about a million viewers.

By the time filming began (in the second week of 1974), the search was getting frantic but it was several weeks later - the day "Invasion of the Dinosaurs" episode five aired - that Pertwee's bombshell was made public. (By this stage, recording of the last three episodes of "Monster of Peladon" was about to start and a new Doctor had been cast in an unlikely process.)

• Mayne assembled a cast who knew what was expected of them: Rex Robinson had been Dr Tyler in 10.1, "The Three Doctors" ('Liberty Hall, Dr Tyler, Liberty Hall'); Donald Gee had worn tin-foil in the line of duty in 6.6, "The Space Pirates"; Ralph Watson had been a UNIT captain caught by the Yeti in 5.5, "The Web of Fear"; Gerald Taylor had been Daleks and War Machines before getting his bread-van blown up (8.5, "The Daemons"); and the various stunt-men included Max Faulkner and Terry Walsh (inevitably), plus Nick Hobbs and Stuart Fell inside costumes as Aggedor and Alpha Centauri respectively.

Just to make it seem even cosier, Alan Bennion (Azaxyr) and Sonny Caldinez (Sskel) led the Martian contingent as before. Roy Evans, former-ly Bert the Funny-Little-Welshman from "The Green Death", here plays a miner identified in the credits as 'Miner'; in the earlier script, the *Radio Times*, most guidebooks and on screen, he's called 'Rima'. Nina Thomas (Thalira) had just made her *other* notable screen appearance, as Jimmy Lea's wife in the grime-encrusted British rock musical *Slade in Flame*. (In her big scene, she just about holds her own against Noddy Holder and some horrific wallpaper.) Frank Gatliff (Ortron) had been playing pompous men for ages, but is prob-ably most familiar as the unconvincingly-named Soviet agent Grantby in *The Ipcress File*.

• Other items returning were those Art Nouveau wooden chairs, the secret passage behind the tapestry in the throne-room, the right-arm-across-chest salute and the Second Doctor's anti-anti-matter gadget ("The Three Doctors" again), here redressed as a sonic lance. The Alpha Centauri costume was rebuilt slightly, with a bet-ter cape (we can only speculate on what the Black and White Minstrels had been doing with it), and Ysanne Churchman was asked to provide 'his' voice. One actor not hitherto seen in the series was Frances Pigeon, here The Woman In The Purple Dress[139], who joins Petra and the Uxarian dinner-lady as characters where the director cast his wife (7.4, "Inferno"; "Colony in Space" - there are many others where the director's missus got a job). Needless to say, the Refinery equipment contained a lot of those old Century 21 props we've already seen as part of BOSS.

• The people of Peladon - as anyone who's seen this story will remember - have very distinctive hairdos. Ortron was given a white wig with red streaks, as were the brothers Hepesh and Torbis last time we saw the planet (this indicates that Ortron was a blood-relative of theirs, unless it comes with the job). Thalira was given a white streak in Thomas' own red hair. The Miners had stripy afros. This was Elizabeth Moss' only story as make-up designer on *Doctor Who*, strangely.

• Pertwee's back condition flared up considerably during the week of filming, and he was advised to keep his action scenes to a bare minimum. He did, however, record a few voice-overs for the fight at the end of Part Four, in an attempt to cover for Walsh's face being so much more visible than was planned. Oh, and contrary to the (admittedly appealing) claim made in various other guidebooks and fanzines, the words mouthed by the Doctor when Aggedor appears at the end of episode one are 'what the *blazes* is it?', *not* "what the bloody hell is it?" or anything ruder.

• After the red glow used for the Ice Warriors' weapons in "Curse", Mayne reverted to the use of the Mirrorlon trick from their first two outings. This is partly because the red glow was now reserved for the Spirit of Aggedor evaporating unbelievers, and partly because they were also using Mirrorlon shots for sonic lancing, rockfalls and the like. Heck, it may also have been an early manifestation of fans telling the production team what went down well. Whilst this story was being made, a letter to the *Radio Times* asked why so few "classic" monsters were appearing, apart from the Daleks. Letts replied that forthcoming story "The Monster of Peladon" would include the Ice Warriors (an openness which rather wrong-footed the magazine's carefully-vague listings during broadcast; these were accompanied by illustrations by Peter Brookes in Frank Bellamy's style), and furthermore promised '... a Cyberman adventure in 1975'.

• During transmission, the first of the new Target adaptations of Pertwee's earlier adventures were published. The star signed several of these, just prior to his successor being named as some guy they'd found on a building-site. Demand for these books had persuaded Dicks to turn freelance and given Hulke a source of income after his

row with Letts over the retitling of "Invasion of the Dinosaurs" Part One. Hayles jumped in with a version of "The Curse of Peladon" soon afterwards, but his main work from now on was fantasy film scripts and script editing *The Archers* (so anti-EEC sentiments expressed by characters with curious versions of English were a recurring theme). He wrote the films *Warlords of Atlantis* and *Arabian Adventure* (the latter was being filmed when he died in 1978) and the six-part paranormal series *The Moon Stallion*. (In which promising youngster Sarah Sutton played a blind girl to great acclaim. See 18.6, "The Keeper of Traken" for why she isn't more famous now.)

11.5: "Planet of the Spiders"

(Serial ZZZ, Six Episodes, 4th May - 8th June 1974.)

Which One is This? "I can't believe it's not Buddha." It's the end of an era in so many ways, as we've reached the story where the Doctor has to confront his own worst fears (represented as huge, blue cackling spiders) and thus liberate himself from his past and begin life anew (represented by his lying on the floor with one knee in the air and turning into Tom Baker). Along the way there's car-chases, spooky goings on in cellars, a whole *planet* full of Pigbins (absurdly hairy ones too, not so much Mummerset as Marmoset) and some atrocious CSO.

Firsts and Lasts The last story of the Third Doctor's run (although Jon Pertwee will be back for 20.7, "The Five Doctors"), and the final application of the Pertwee Death Pose as he changes into Tom Baker. Though the next season opens with a half-hearted attempt to get the Fourth Doctor to work with the same old team, this is the last time the Doctor, the Brigadier, Sergeant Benton and Mike Yates all come together as a "family". In fact, the real Yates will never be seen again after this (he turns up in cameo as a phantom, again in "The Five Doctors"). Naturally, Pertwee gets his last few opportunities to shout 'hai!' before his departure. Total number of 'hai!'s in the Third Doctor's run: 73. Total number of other martial arts exclamations ('akira!', 'on y va!', etc): 7.

The word 'regeneration' is used to describe the Doctor's transformation for the first time, wherein it's explained that *all* Time Lords can do it. The

Brigadier mentions UNIT's medical officer, Dr. Sullivan, who doesn't show himself here but becomes a regular fixture in Season Twelve.

For the first time, the Doctor calls the Brigadier 'Alistair', and the Brig's relationship with Doris is mentioned (see 26.1, "Battlefield"). Last appearance of the sodding Whomobile. Oh, and we get a close-up on Stuart Fell's face at last. He's the tramp hovered over in the chase scene in episode two, which makes him the end of the long, dishonourable run of comedy yokels (unless you count the entire population of Metebelis 3).

It may seem trivial, but it says so much: it's the last use of Oscilloscope traces to represent "science-ness". From now on, it'll be fake computer graphics.

Six Things to Notice
About "Planet of the Spiders"...

1. In later years it was an accepted rule of the programme that when one actor left the series, the Doctor simply had to receive a major wound before he could turn into his replacement, but in the 1970s the series still felt there should be some deeper reason behind it. In this case, the transfiguration of the Doctor is given a religious element (the word 'regeneration' usually had the prefix "spiritual" for most of the previous century) and specifically an overlay of Theravada Buddhism. The Tibetan Master Cho-Je sets the rules in the first episode. ('A man must go inside, and face his fears and hopes, his hates and his loves, and watch them wither away... the old man must die, and the new man will discover to his inexpressible joy that he has never existed.') The references to the world we know being 'the world of change' sound as if they're directed straight at the audience. The Third Doctor spends his last episode facing his greatest fear, even though he knows it'll destroy him. (Compare this with 24.1, "Time and the Rani", in which the Doctor regenerates after unexpectedly getting a bump on the head, and see **When Was Regeneration Invented?**) This being the early 1970s, the destruction of the personality isn't presented as *necessarily* a bad thing and the monster is a giant-sized ego. As the whole of this book has tried to show, ideas of this sort were very current. In some ways, then, this is the most 1974-ish story possible.

In others, however, it could almost be a relic from the 1950s. For every up-to-date reference to fork-bending (we're only four months on from Uri Geller's TV debut) and people getting into Transcendental Meditation 'these days', there's a glimpse of a bygone age where people calling themselves 'Professor' do mind-reading acts in variety theatres and girls called 'Doris' go off to Brighton with dashing subalterns who get given watches.

UNIT lack both vending machines and instant coffee, so Benton has to make it properly. Lupton's incredulity that they let girls work as reporters these days fits in with this curiously retro story. So this apparently timeless parable on an apparently massively topical theme is set in a context that children watching would know only from old movies. (As the Buddha taught, this world is a veil of illusions.) Sadly the scene that most exemplifies this story is one where a rural copper watching the car-chase and making his report; he's got no reason to be on patrol in that stretch of quiet road, and you'll note that he's as bemused by the idea of cars going at 90mph as he is at what those cars look like. On the other hand, he's in a Panda car and using a radio rather than a police box.

2. That car-chase involving the UNIT crew and Lupton (the story's human villain) takes up twelve minutes - that's *half an episode* - and ends with the shocking revelation that it needn't have happened at all. The pursuit involves Bessie, the Whomobile, a gyroplane, a speedboat and a one-man hovercraft, not to mention the police car that gets dragged into things for comic relief. And only *after* all of this do Lupton's spider employers decide to teleport him to safety, making the whole exercise a bit pointless.

But then, as much as anything else, this story is intended to trot out all the Pertwee-era's set-piece specialities in a row. We get the cars, the Venusian Aikido (the end of episode three, in another scene that seems to slow down time), the cod-mysticism (along with some real mysticism) and a few unscripted returns of trademark items from this phase of the series. Once again, John Levene ad-libs a classic Benton line (the stuff about hairdryers) and once again Barry Letts tries to get CSO to do things just *slightly* beyond its grasp. As director, Letts pilfers the cast from other stories, and as co-author he's amassed a lot of ideas from earlier stories he wrote. (Watch Mike showing Sarah the cellar and explaining not to step on the Mandala, and you'll have serious "Daemons" *déja-vu*.) On the plus side this means that a lot of running storylines all meet here - with the Metebelis Crystal, the

Doctor's old mentor, Mike's breakdown and Jo's honeymoon all dovetailing. And we get John Dearth, Cyril Shaps, Ysanne Churchman, Kevin Lindsay and George Cormack back. The downside is that this story, more than any other before it (even 5.6, "Fury from the Deep"), looks like a stew made from leftovers.

3. However, along the way we get glimpses of a more mature show, one that uses the editing to make more innovative use of flashback than we've had so far. Notice the particular style of "stuttering" repetitive fast-edit when Tommy recalls important details, and short inserts for the Doctor recalling his worst fear. Both of these were becoming accepted in Hollywood dramas in that period, whilst films for family audiences still used wavy dissolves from the 1940s. Similarly, the sound isn't made to echo the way old films and 70s television characteristically conveyed "this is a flashback". Within the dialogue itself, Lupton's explanation of how middle-management disputes led him to want to get revenge on the world sounds sensible and appropriately petty, but it's written in terms that remove this scene from the slightly *Trumpton*-ish world of Sergeant Benton's ballroom dancing. In every sense except for explicit sex and swearing, this emerges as the most "adult" form of *Doctor Who* seen to this point.

4. Then again, there's *one* portion of the story that belongs in Children's Hour: the population of Metebelis 3. Whilst the menfolk wear sheepskin and buskins and have Zapata moustaches, the women have shawls and shoes from British Home Stores. The result is part Spaghetti Western, part Isle of Wight Festival, so you're not sure if the next arrival in the township is going to be Jimi Hendrix or the Bolivian Army on the trail of Butch Cassidy and the Sundance Kid. Although the Doctor keeps telling us this is all in the future, it's the most 1974-ish planet imaginable. L. Rowland-Warne has designed a police uniform for the Spiders' guards which combines tight waistcoats (with no shirt) and huge, *huge* flared trousers. Then when the villagers start talking in yokel, it's supposed to mark out Sarah and Lupton as not-from-around-these-parts - except that Neska doesn't talk like any of her kids. And just as the shock of Jennie Laird's shoes wears off, the full impact of her underpowered performance takes over. 8.8 million people saw her absent-mindedly deliver this aria: 'No I shan't you shan't take him. Sabor my husband my love why did you do it why, why? I shan't let you take him I shan't I shan't.' 8.2 mil-

lion people tuned in the next week.

5. After the embarrassment of putting the word 'Dinosaurs' in the title of a story that would have been better drawing attention *away* from the rubber monsters, it would be a brave writer / producer / director who emphasised the spiders without first checking that it was doable. Here Letts was walking a tightrope: the BBC guidelines and arachnophobes would be gunning for him if the spiders were too scary, and everyone else would despair if they aren't scary enough. So when you're watching, be advised that a genuinely unpleasant model spider was made, but he rejected it. You might also bear in mind that a spider *that* big would be squashed on the floor unless its mobility was somehow assisted by psychic force or balloons, so *obviously* the Metebelis spiders won't move like real ones on Earth.

6. For some people, the single scariest thing in the whole of *Doctor Who* is in Part Five, when the Great One plays with the Doctor and makes him march around in a circle against his will. Seeing the Doctor frightened and close to tears is *way* more disturbing than watching him die. All those previous psychic assaults he's overcome with gurning and sheer mental force, yet here all he can do is plead with her to stop. The next few years will see a lot of stories themed around possessions of various kinds, but starting the cycle with the Doctor himself almost devalues the subsequent ones. It also adds another of those oddly mature moments in the middle of a story that has so much that is purely for kids. Philip Hinchcliffe's stint as producer starts in two stories' time, but with Robert Holmes already established as script editor in all but name, the future starts here.

The Continuity

The Doctor At UNIT HQ the Doctor has built the IRIS machine (the Image Reproducing Integrating System) as part of his experiments into human extra-sensory perception; psychometry, telepathy and clairvoyance are all covered by his 'particular field'. He nonchalantly states that psychic powers lie dormant in most humans, but that psychokinesis is a rarely-developed faculty. [So he's performing non-TARDIS-related experiments on Earth, unexpected since he's now got a fully working Ship. Nor does he give a second thought to IRIS after this story. Is he starting to think of Earth as home, and just looking for excuses to stay? If so, then this doesn't survive his regeneration. It's not known how he finds out about the psychic Professor Clegg.] The IRIS machine displays the thoughts of anyone attached to it on a video screen. Contact with the blue crystal from Metebelis 3 kills Clegg, and the Doctor acknowledges that he's responsible. [It may help him accept what K'anpo says, to whit...]

K'anpo believes that the Doctor's greed for knowledge is his own personal demon. [The Master surmised as much, and the Doctor acknowledges that he's got a curiosity problem *again* just before he dies in 21.6, "The Caves of Androzani".] His self-sacrifice almost comes across as a form of atonement for causing all this trouble. He feels fear when the Great One takes over his mind, and she states that he's not used to it [nor is he used to his enemies being mentally stronger than he is, which is probably what scares him]. When he goes to face the Great One in her cave, he does it even though he knows it'll kill him; afterwards he says that facing his fear was more important than just going on living.

The Doctor states that when a Time Lord's body wears out it "regenerates", which is why they live such a long time, the first time this is made explicit. The 'crystal rays' in the cave of the Great One devastate every cell in the Doctor's body, and he returns to UNIT HQ in the TARDIS after more than three weeks away. [At least from UNIT's point of view. The novel *Timewyrm: Revelation* charmingly suggests that it actually takes the Third Doctor's body ten years to reach the point of regeneration, and that the Doctor lies helpless on the TARDIS floor for the entire time. Whether you believe this or not, there *is* the suggestion here that the Doctor has been suffering for some time before he gets back to Earth.] He states that he got lost in the time vortex, and that the TARDIS brought him 'home'. The Doctor seems to be dead at first, and it's apparently only K'anpo's presence which gives the cells a 'push' and forces change. K'anpo warns that he'll be a little erratic once he becomes a new man. The Third Doctor's last words: 'While there's life, there's...'

The Doctor doesn't recognise K'anpo on sight, though the man seems familiar to him [see **Do Time Lords Always Meet In Sequence?** under 22.3, "The Mark of the Rani"]. Indeed, although he claims to have seen his mentor's face in the Metebelis crystal while looking into it, the Doctor is completely unaware that the old man to whom he meets at the end of Part Five is a Time Lord, let

alone one he's met. [This flatly contradicts X3.12, "The Sound of Drums", where we're told that Time Lords always know one another regardless of appearance, although 21.7, "The Twin Dilemma" seems to substantiate it.]

• *Ethics.* Even knowing that he's dying from radiation poisoning, the Doctor valiantly tells the Great One to refrain from completing the crystal circuit (and thereby perishing) instead of just letting her get on with it.

• *Inventory.* Seen in close-up here, the sonic screwdriver has blatantly changed shape in the last year or so. [Professor Clegg identifies the screwdriver as the very one the Doctor used against the Drashigs (10.2, "Carnival of Monsters"), which pre-dates its being confiscated - and seemingly never returned - in 10.3, "Frontier in Space". Clegg even hallucinates scenes from that story, via IRIS. So it must be the same device, at least in part, even if the Doctor's modified it.]

In a leather bag in the TARDIS, evidently in a locker in the console room (but not one that we've seen), is a device that looks like a carpenter's plane. With this, the Doctor can discharge the adverse effect of the spiders' energy bolts. [As with 10.5, "The Green Death", the colour-coding is interesting. The machine generates, or perhaps *pulls* from the Doctor, an orange spark with the opposite effect of the blue one. It's very tempting to connect this with all the spangly orange energy-clouds associated with Time Lord abilities in the BBC Wales series, but if we do so, the jade-coloured haze surrounding the apparition of the K'anpo in the Doctor's death-scene becomes tremendously significant. We'd then have to explain, after all, why the UNIT lab seems to suddenly become an obvious hotbed of Artron energy, yet it's the one place the TARDIS can never find (as opposed to the obvious refuelling-site that Cardiff has become these days).] The device also acts as a mineral analyser and a shield to the spider-energy, and gets left on Metebelis 3.

• *Background.* The Doctor claims he 'borrowed' a TARDIS as a means of leaving his homeworld, and that he 'had to get away'. [Possibly this just reflects his desire to travel the universe, although 18.7, "Logopolis" mentions that there were 'pressing reasons' for his hasty departure.]

He knows the traditions of Tibet [see 5.2, "The Abominable Snowmen"] as well as a little of the Tibetan language. He claims to have been a friend

When Was Regeneration Invented?

When William Hartnell left *Doctor Who* in 1966, one of the most bizarre (but nonetheless great) decisions in television history was made: to get a younger and significantly different actor to fill his role, and use the Doctor's alien biology as an excuse to make this sort of thing seem perfectly acceptable. According to received wisdom, this is how the concept of "regeneration" was born, the idea that Time Lords can change their bodies whenever they're badly damaged and thus ensure the series' longevity.

Received wisdom, however, is dubious at best.

We tend to forget, now, how the Hartnell / Troughton change was pitched to its original audience. In episode four of 4.2, "The Tenth Planet" and episode one of 4.3, "Power of the Daleks", there's no suggestion that it's normal for the Doctor to change his whole persona whenever he's injured. The word used in the script is renewal, and even that comes from an incredulous comment made by Ben, to which the apparent newcomer responds with another question. The Doctor isn't giving anything away at this stage, and his claim that the change is 'part of the TARDIS' hints that this isn't just some kind of biological super-power.

The implication, weird as it seems now, is clear: Patrick Troughton's Doctor is supposed to be an extension of William Hartnell's. Perhaps not simply a younger version, but at the very least they're aspects of the same identity, the Second Doctor drawing a parallel with a caterpillar turning into a butterfly.

And there *is* a kind of logic there. At heart the First Doctor is just as mischievous as the Second, but too old, tired and impatient to extol the virtues of anarchy in the way the Troughton version does (the original idea, according to then-script editor Gerry Davis, was a "Jekyll and Hyde" transition). They're the same individual to a far greater extent than the Third and Fourth Doctors are, or the Fourth and Fifth, or the Fifth and Sixth, or the Sixth and Seventh. It should be remembered that *Doctor Who Monthly* - the only half-reliable source of *Doctor Who* information, until the mid-80s boom in programme guides - believed as late as 1982 that the First and Second Doctors were supposed to be the same man. A "Matrix Data-Bank" column from that year informs its readers that they shouldn't confuse "regenerations" (e.g. Pertwee into Baker) with the "rejuvenation" of Hartnell into Troughton.

So if the writers and producers didn't invent the idea of "regeneration" in 1966, then when did they come up with it? In "The War Games" (6.7), when the Second Doctor turns into the Third? Again, no. In "The War Games" the Doctor is utterly horrified by the idea of the Time Lords changing his face ('you can't just change what I look like!'). Though later fan-lore insists that the Time Lords "force" a regeneration on him, this isn't what the story says and it's obviously not what Terrance Dicks and Malcolm Hulke had in mind when they wrote it. As it's described in episode ten, the Doctor is undergoing some peculiar Time Lord surgery to alter his form as part of his punishment. It's certainly not a natural part of Time Lord life, and in "Spearhead from Space" (7.1), the Third Doctor's personality seems to have several hold-overs from the Troughton days, as if he's been changed on the outside but hasn't been completely re-formatted on the inside. And throughout the Pertwee era, when the phrase "Time Lord" becomes common currency and the Doctor frequently discusses his people's politics with the Master, there's no mention of regeneration as a standard fitting of the species.

By the time the Third Doctor turns into the Fourth, the audience is used to the idea of a different actor taking over the Doctor's role... but still doesn't take it as read that the power to change is one of the Doctor's built-in abilities, and still requires the story to explain it. Even given that enough time has passed since "The War Games" for a new audience to come along, there's no assumption that parents will tell younger viewers "oh, yes, this is what he does".

In "Planet of the Spiders" (11.5), it's stated for the very first time that regeneration (a new word!) is what happens when a Time Lord's body gets worn out, and it sounds suspiciously like an attempt to justify the events of "The Tenth Planet" and "The War Games" to viewers who are about to meet yet another version of the Doctor. It's a word that's hitherto been more commonly used in a religious context, to suggest spiritual re-awakening, which is what K'Anpo seems to have been through in order to astrally-project to UNIT HQ. It's noticeable that even here, the Doctor can't regenerate without turning the whole process into a life-changing ritual, and he seems to need K'Anpo's help - a 'push' - to make the final change.

Regeneration isn't really taken for granted until "The Deadly Assassin" (14.3), and even here there

continued on page 467...

of Harry Houdini, who taught him a thing or two about escapology. He states that Sergeant Benton makes the best cup of coffee in the word 'next to Mrs. Samuel Pepys'. [Odd, as she didn't actually like the stuff, although the Pepys' diaries note her delight in this new thing called "tea" that's being imported. Deb, Pepys' mistress, apparently loved coffee... maybe the Doctor was being discreet.]

Here the Doctor reiterates that when he was young a hermit lived behind 'our house', and that he spent some of the finest hours of his life with the old man [q.v. 9.5, "The Time Monster"]. It was from the hermit that he first learned how to look into his own mind.

• *The Whomobile.* It flies. It's also a nippy mover on land, capable of at least 90 MPH.

The Supporting Cast

• *Sarah Jane Smith.* Writes articles for *Metropolitan* magazine, selling them to someone called Percy [as before, she still has a life on Earth and hasn't become the Doctor's full-time travelling companion]. The Doctor calls her his 'assistant' even outside the context of UNIT.

Intriguingly, Sarah *agrees* to letting the Queen use her as a Trojan horse on condition that the Two-Legs are set free. Whilst under regal domination, she's as perky as ever [and as skittish as we later see her with the new Doctor]. Perhaps significantly, the Queen never fires psychic lightning at the Doctor or K'anpo. The Doctor confirms that Sarah held the Queen in check better than most would have. Still, the most interesting thing about this whole subplot is that the Queen seems to play fair and sticks to the deal when controlling Sarah - so the "host" must be able to run interference to a certain degree.]

• *Jo Grant.* She's still in the Amazon, at her twenty-ninth native village, and she and Professor Jones haven't found their toadstool yet. She sends the blue crystal from Metebelis 3 back to England because the Indian porters say it's 'bad magic'. Her letter suggests that she knows her Evelyn Waugh, in that she jokes about 'cleft sticks' [as in Waugh's *Scoop*], but nonetheless she can't seem to construct a sentence properly.

• *UNIT.* UNIT's Medical Officer is called Sullivan [12.1, "Robot", etc]. Despite UNIT HQ being a top-security establishment, Sarah is allowed to hang around there three weeks after the Doctor vanishes and she loses her "I'm his assistant" excuse. Even the Brigadier doesn't know

she's there.

A minor member of UNIT staff has obviously been given the job of servicing the Whomobile. Benton is in charge of brewing the Doctor's morning coffee, some time around 9.00 AM. The HQ is around eighty miles from the Buddhist retreat near Mortimer. [That's near Reading, Berkshire, so the location is plausibly Gloucestershire or Hereford and Worcester. See "The Green Death" and 9.1, "Day of the Daleks". The garage seems to be the same one from "The Daemons" and "The Three Doctors".] The lab has a stuffed crocodile suspended from the ceiling [see **Where Does This Come From?**].

• *The Brigadier.* Owns a watch that was given to him in Brighton hotel eleven years ago, by a young lady named Doris ["Battlefield"]. The watch was a thank you for something the Brigadier doesn't want to talk about. Here the Brigadier's at his most bluff and impatient, his response to the Doctor's regeneration being 'here we go again'. He's let his hair grow.

• *Captain Yates.* After his fall from UNIT, he's getting his act together at a Buddhist retreat . He seems almost completely "cured" here [again suggesting that he *was* temporarily unbalanced during 11.2, "Invasion of the Dinosaurs"], and Sarah trusts him even though she was on the receiving end of his treachery. His 'compassion' protects him from the spiders' attacks, proving that he's ready to sacrifice himself out of principle, not just because it's his duty as a soldier. He drives a nice red sporty number. His last words: a rather feeble 'Ooh! I feel fine' after magic brings him back from the dead.

• *Benton.* Volunteers to look into the Metebelis crystal, even after it's resulted in Professor Clegg's death, on the grounds that he's more expendable than the Doctor.

The TARDIS The co-ordinates for Metebelis 3 are still wired into the programmer ["The Green Death"]. When the Doctor goes there to find Sarah, the Ship lands in exactly the right location [and the right time-zone] even though the Doctor has no idea where she might be, the Doctor noting that the Ship is 'no fool'. [The TARDIS might be able to home in on its "crew". On the other hand, this could well be the only inhabited area on the planet; the TARDIS certainly seems to have a habit of landing in populated places.] The TARDIS key is currently a medallion on a chain.

When Was Regeneration Invented?

...continued from page 465

are anomalies, as if Robert Holmes is being cagey about formalising things. It's said that Time Lords can regenerate twelve times, the closest thing we've had to a "rule" so far, yet Runcible asks if the Doctor's had a 'face-lift' as if that's more likely than a full bodily change. (In retrospect we might assume that Runcible-the-Fatuous is just being casual about regeneration, but that doesn't seem to be the way the scene's written.) The Doctor's reply was written as 'three so far' but changed to 'several, so far' in order to preserve the impression, fostered in "The Brain of Morbius" (13.5) that even before Hartnell the Doctor had worn many faces.

For obvious reasons, "The Invasion of Time" (15.6) has to assume the existence of regeneration as a given in order for Borusa to return without actor Angus Mackay. Leela is familiar with the idea because the Doctor's been so off-hand about it, dismissing the Rutans' lack of ability in this field. The idea has become a standard fixture even among casual viewers by the time we reach "Destiny of the Daleks" (17.1). By this point the change of actors is so familiar to the audience that producer Graham Williams and script editor Douglas Adams can be casual, even jokey, about the phenomenon. Romana apparently changes her form in much the same way that she might change her wardrobe.

Far from being a clever device invented in 1966, regeneration actually emerges as a way of tying together the various approaches taken by the programme's various production teams, and the idea only becomes "solid" once people have stopped questioning it. When Tom Baker's Doctor was scheduled to leave the series in 1981, young fans who'd never seen a regeneration accepted it without hesitation, because they'd read all about it in DWM and The Making of Doctor Who. But even here, the script is wary of taking too much for granted. When the Fourth Doctor becomes the Fifth in "Logopolis", writer Christopher H. Bidmead still feels he needs a "reason" to have the Doctor change. He creates the character of the Watcher, a deliberate echo of K'Anpo's intervention in the previous change-over story, to help the transformation go smoothly (but see 18.7 for more).

By the time of "The Caves of Androzani" and the Fifth Doctor's shift into the Sixth, the Doctor's constantly using the word 'regeneration' to describe his ability to re-create himself, but as a writer Robert Holmes still doesn't want it to seem completely normal. The dying Fifth Doctor states that 'it feels different this time', and well it might. This is the first time it's happened unaided, the first time that one person - one person, remember, since the First and Second Doctors were basically the same man - has turned into another without outside assistance. The first time, in short, that the process runs the risk of being arbitrary (see also **Who Are All These Strange Men in Wigs?** under "The Brain of Morbius").

The fact remains that in the classic series, the only "normal" regeneration for the Doctor - the only one pitched as a routine rebirth-of-an-injured-body, is the last and least convincing change of the entire BBC run - the moment at the start of "Time and the Rani" when the Sixth Doctor bangs his head on the TARDIS floor and becomes the Seventh, a metamorphosis so bland that it's accepted as a purely functional part of the programme. But it took twenty-three years to get that far.

The Time Lords

• *K'anpo*. The hermit who played such an important part in the Doctor's formative years [see "The Time Monster"] now turns out to be the Abbot at the Buddhist retreat which Mike Yates is attending on Earth. [Pure coincidence, or is something mystical going on here? It would seem that K'anpo left Gallifrey first, so has he been keeping track of the Doctor's career? "Rinpoche" is a traditional title given to the Abbot of a monastery, but it's also used to describe a reincarnated lama, which seems apt.] He goes by the Tibetan name of K'anpo, and seems to know more about what's going on than anyone could possibly have told

him. He can "see" the spider that's possessing Sarah, as can the Doctor after being told to 'see through my eyes'. [Telepathy, or more zen? Compare this to the Doctor's anecdote about the daisy in "The Time Monster".] The Doctor refers to him as a 'guru', and he says that the Doctor was 'always a little slow on the uptake'.

K'anpo is a Time Lord, but states that 'the discipline they serve was not for me'. He knows of the Doctor borrowing a TARDIS, and regenerated before going to Tibet. The Doctor's comment - 'I had to get away, I hadn't your power' - indicates that K'anpo left via mental, rather than mechanical, means. [The hint is left that K'anpo's regeneration and TARDIS-less travel are the same process. Along similar lines, see 17.6, "Shada" - in which the Doctor uses mental power to "swim" to the Ship - plus 7.4, "Inferno", and of course "The Time Monster". Throughout these books we've speculated on the links between mental power, regeneration and time travel (see **What Makes the TARDIS Work?** under 1.3, "Edge of Destruction"; **What Is the Blinovitch Limitation Effect?** under 20.3, "Mawdryn Undead"; and **How Do You Transmit Matter?** under 17.4, "Nightmare of Eden"). We also can't avoid saying again that the same effect - the "traditional" Tom Baker title sequence - is used for the Doctor's mind in 13.5, "The Brain of Morbius" and 14.3, "The Deadly Assassin", and for the spacetime vortex in "Shada".

[In "Shada", it's scripted that the Doctor was taught by 'a space-time mystic in the Qualactin Zone' (because Douglas Adams is involved, and he uses names like that a lot). But in the actual recording, and in the Big Finish audio version starring Paul McGann, this becomes 'A space-time mystic in the Quantocks'. That's a range of hills near Taunton in Devon. Quite a few railway stops away from Mortimer, but intriguingly close.]

Cho-Je, a spiritual guide at the centre, is also a Time Lord 'in a sense, but in another sense he doesn't exist'. He's a projection of K'anpo own self, something which even the Doctor doesn't immediately grasp; K'anpo apparently knows everything Cho-Je witnesses. [Symbolically, he represents the "new man" in the Buddhist parable about the old man dying and being replaced.] K'anpo seems to sense the death of the Doctor and his *own* death approaching, and when he dies, his body vanishes for a moment before that of Cho-Je replaces it. This produces an individual who looks like Cho-Je but speaks of himself as K'anpo. [The similarity with the Watcher from "Logopolis" is striking. Is Cho-Je projected backwards through time from the regeneration, as the Watcher seems to have been? If so, this is presumably how the old K'anpo knows that his time is almost near.

As with the similar transition / transmission of Panna and Karuna [19.3, "Kinda"] the new, young priest is a composite of both personalities, finishing Cho-Je's last sentence and then talking to Sarah as though both sets of memories were in this body. The new K'anpo can levitate and materialise out of thin air, surrounded by a glowing aura [hinting that he isn't really "there"]. He also

seems to be the catalyst which triggers the Doctor's regeneration. [These things are all part of the 'power' the Doctor speaks of, they're not inevitable results of the regeneration. K'anpo's move to Tibet is a relatively recent event in his life, yet his new body looks and sounds Tibetan, perhaps a sign that powerful Time Lords can influence their biological change to match their mental state. See also "Logopolis"; 27.0, "The Abomination"; X1.13 "The Parting of the Ways" and 17.1, "Destiny of the Daleks".]

Cho-Je / K'anpo is never heard of again, and the Doctor never expresses an interest in meeting up with his old mentor. [Does K'anpo stay on Earth? Does the retreat stay open, after meditation goes out of fashion? All we can say for certain is that by the 2005 series, the Doctor is convinced that there are no other Time Lords around. Mind you, maybe the old mystic has a way of hiding.]

The Non-Humans

• *Spiders.* Normal-sized spiders came to Metebelis 3 with the human colonists, but grew in size and intelligence after being exposed to the blue crystals. The humans didn't find out until it was too late. The 'eight-legs' we see are cruel, arrogant and predatory without exception, and all are female, certainly those who make up the council under the queen spider Huath. [Is this a species that eats the males after mating?] The prospect of a 'coronation' thrills the Spiders. [They even make 'mmMMMmmm' noises when it's proposed - as one might suspect, the novelisation suggests that a deposed queen is eaten.]

When a spider jumps onto a human being's back, it vanishes but can still be "heard" by its carrier / victim, who gains the spider's power to kill, hurt or stun with bolts of blue [mental] energy. A level of clairvoyance is also part of the bargain, plus the ability to teleport objects over short distances. [People can quite comfortably sit in chairs while they've got spiders on their backs, so the spiders in some way join with their hosts' bodies instead of just turning invisible.] The spiders themselves have acute telepathic senses, and can 'twist the minds' of their bodyguards and servants. They can also figure out how to fly an autogyro, apparently. The body of the dead spider on Earth vanishes [it returns to Metebelis?].

Buddhist-style rituals can be used to summon spiders to Earth from Metebelis 3. The rites performed by Lupton and his friends can also make

What Actually Happens in a Regeneration?

Whilst nothing we wrote in **How Does Regeneration Work?** (18.7, "Logopolis") is actually invalid, we now have - thanks to the BBC Wales series - a lot more available data and some knotty recent problems that have generated quite a bit of spittle-flecked debate online. As we just covered in **When Was Regeneration Invented?**, the idea of regeneration was never in any series "bible". Eventually, the various ideas of who the Doctor was and how he changed settled down into what *might* be called the "standard" model, although other theories have been proposed. So here we're going to combine both series' approaches, and see if we can't account for all the weird side effects of a television series being improvised by a succession of writers, coinciding with special-effects technology developing in fits and starts.

Here in 2008, we've been repeatedly presented with a fairly standard "regeneration pattern" involving the orange swirly effect so beloved of BBC Wales, only cranked up a notch so that flame erupts from the sleeves and collars of whoever's changing into a new body. If nothing else, it streamlined the storytelling so that casual viewers and small kids could understand that what the Master (in X3.11, "Utopia") was doing was what the Doctor had previously done (in X1.13, "The Parting of the Ways"). The explanation in *that* story was fairly minimal too: Eccleston's Doctor said that all the cells in his body were changing and he didn't know what he'd soon look like - then suddenly David Tennant was standing there licking his new teeth and carrying on the conversation.

Tennant's Doctor (X2.0, "The Christmas Invasion") later spoke of the Eccleston version in the third person ('I miss him') but had all the same memories - or so it seems. (This is an issue of contention, as we're going to discuss.) Still later, the regeneration-that-wasn't (X4.12, "The Stolen Earth" / X4.13, "Journey's End") added a complication, showing the orange swirly stuff to be *physically* present and divertable, rather than a visual conceit in same the way that we see the swirling Time Vortex when anyone remembers something from a previous episode. Oh, and since the First Edition of this guidebook, we've also learned that within the first fifteen hours of a new body, severed limbs can conveniently grow back ("The Christmas Invasion").

The thing is... *none* of what you've just read could be inferred from any episode broadcast before 1990. If you look back over the whole of *Doctor Who*, this neat picture is actually very messy, and the safe conclusions we can draw from the BBC Wales episodes are a lot more conjectural. The Doctor is the only Time Lord we actually *see* regenerating on screen (other than the K'anpo in 11.5, "Planet of the Spiders"; and no, what with Romana darting in and out of the console room, she doesn't count), and no two of his transformations in the classic series are the same. Moreover, *all* of his body-changes (save for Sylvester McCoy turning into Paul McGann) take place either in the TARDIS or with the help of an outside influence, usually a superior Time Lord (as with, again, the K'anpo). By the way, here (as we just elaborated upon in **When Was Regeneration Invented?**) we're taking it on trust that the first two occasions where the Doctor's appearance changed actually *were* regenerations. (And please, let's not get started on how many times he might have changed bodies before we joined his adventures - **Who Are All These Men In Wigs?** under 13.5, "The Brain of Morbius" takes up *that* story.)

The supposedly simple Pertwee-Baker transmogrification at the end of "Planet of the Spiders" - the first to be outright *called* a 'regeneration' - is more complicated than it looks. K'anpo says, 'I will give the process a little push and the cells will regenerate. He will become a new man.' The K'anpo who says this isn't the one we first met, though - he mentally projected a second and younger self, Cho-Je, and relocated into his body (er, sort of) after dying.

More to the point, before this, the previous K'anpo commented upon his departure from Gallifrey - claiming that 'I regenerated and came [to Earth]...', as though the two were cause and effect. It's further established that he didn't steal a TARDIS (the Doctor did, he says, because 'I hadn't [the K'anpo's] power'). All told, we're invited to conclude that the K'anpo astrally projected using the psychic energy produced in the regenerative process - and if *that's* the case, then regeneration and space-time travel are linked.

This reinforces an odd detail from the Doctor's first shape-shift. The older Doctor we'd known since the start became a debased, younger, shabbier model... and his clothes changed to match. The Hartnell Doctor collapsed on the floor, wearing his usual garb, then he changed and the Troughton Doctor woke up wearing his own togs and the previous Doctor's ring (which fell off). At the time, everyone accepted this as part of the

continued on page 471...

illusionary tractors appear on Britain's roads, which may or may not have something to do with the spiders' influence. The spiders are apparently drawn several centuries through time, as well as across vast tracts of space. A naturally-occurring mineral on Metebelis can block the spiders' power, and the energy bolts are less effective on compassionate or innocent minds [which may be why the Doctor isn't killed when he's hit by one].

At the heart of spider society lies the Great One, a spider vastly bigger and more powerful than the queen, at least sixty feet across and surrounded by a "web" of the planet's blue crystals which should - she believes - give her infinite mental power when completed. Even without it, her power is such that she can control the Doctor's actions. The Great One's aim is to conquer the universe, though her followers just see Earth as being rightfully theirs. She insists she's searched all of time and space for the 'perfect' crystal taken by the Doctor. [Meaning that her mental powers are almost on par with Time Lord technology - although as she isolates the crystal's 'vibrations', this isn't necessarily as rigorous a search as the Time Lords might undertake. (The difference seems to be like the difference between reading a telephone directory and rummaging in your pocket for the phone as it rings.)

[It's possible that Lupton's faux-Buddhist rituals are meaningless in themselves, and just act as a psychic focus for the spiders; a convenient bridge-head at almost the right space-time coordinates. You'll notice that this is the same excuse we used to cover the embarrassing silliness of Waterfield rupturing the space-time continuum with 144 statically-charged mirrors in 4.9, "The Evil of the Daleks" - but then, the two stories aren't dissimilar. In any case, the creatures *can* move between worlds and centuries on their own, but it uses up a lot of their mental power. The Great One must be aware of or subject to the Blinovitch Limitation Effect, or she would have taken the crystal from Metebelis 3 before the Doctor ran off with it.]

Ultimately, the completed web destroys the Great One rather than making her infinitely powerful. The other spiders seem to be destroyed along with her.

['In another sense', as Cho-Je might have said, 'they don't exist'. It's strongly hinted that the spiders are the 'demons' produced by a clouded mind meditating for power as opposed to for the sake of meditation. This is clearly what Cho-Je

believes has happened, and under the circumstances he has as much claim to trust as the Doctor in these matters. The story of them evolving as a result of the crystals and being on the spaceship by accident doesn't bear close examination (look at **How Hard Is It To Be The Wrong Size?** under 16.6, "The Armageddon Factor" for some reasons why, and ask yourself what reasons space-travellers might have for taking genetically-modified spiders with them).

[For once, though, we're offered an alternative: that they're manifestations of Lupton and his friends projecting their evil out of conventional space and time. 20.2, "Snakedance" offers a pseudo-science figleaf for the same idea, again using blue crystals. This doesn't make much literal sense, but then, very little of this story does. We can accept either interpretation depending on age, taste and what time of day it is.]

Planet Notes

• *Metebelis 3.* Here it's a very different world to the one the Doctor visited before ["The Green Death"], and this is a later point in its history. It's no longer blue all over, the Doctor now claiming that it's called the blue planet because the *moonlight's* blue. [In "The Green Death" the Doctor claimed it had a blue sun - which it clearly doesn't - but it *was* indeed a blue-lit night during his last brief visit.]

The planet is inhabited by humans, descendants of human colonists who've been kept in a Mediaeval state by the giant spiders. The 'eightlegs' have been known to wipe out whole villages of wayward humans, including Skorda, and there's a strict curfew. Both humans and spiders eat sheep, which were brought to the planet on the ship, although spiders prefer human meat; their victims are stored in webbing. The spiders now live in great artificial citadels, while the humans live in pseudo-Mexican villages.

In addition to its power to cure brainwashing and spider-possession, the blue crystal from Metebelis 3 alters the brain of the "backward" Tommy, turning him into a potential genius - or at least, a fully functional human being - within hours. It causes a localised "wind" and earth tremors when Lupton's people are performing a spider-summoning ceremony, and kills the psychic Professor Clegg who's holding it at the time. The Doctor states that he went to Metebelis 3 deliberately to get the crystal, but he had no idea

What Actually Happens in a Regeneration?

...continued from page 469

very peculiar recasting of the lead role. After all, how many other series changed their lead actor on screen in those days?

Not long after, it was implied that the act of travelling in time had made the Doctor immortal and immune to human frailties - or so the Dalek Emperor believed (4.9, "The Evil of the Daleks") and the Master of the Land of Fiction hoped (6.2, "The Mind Robber"). Even in the last moments of black-and-white *Who*, the Time Lords suggest that the Doctor's ability to change his appearance was a freakish effect and not routine for them (6.7, "The War Games"). Again, modern fans might think they know better, but the ambiguous evidence from the new series makes this more likely than the purely biological explanation as offered in - say - 1987 in "Time and the Rani" (24.1). At that phase of the programme's development, the idea that a new Doctor would awaken with new clothes was laughable. The flak that Peter Grimwade (who directed "Logopolis") copped for Peter Davison waking up in shoes, whereas Tom Baker had died with his boots on, made anything *this* mystical beyond the pale for the fanboys. These days, for better or worse, things are different.

The much-quoted dialogue from "The Power of the Daleks" (4.3) that whatever the Doctor has just done is '... part of me... part of the TARDIS...' is less help than it might be. It *looks* like he means that the one causes the other, but everything else about it is conjecture. Yes, the TARDIS travels through the vortex and occasionally stops of in Cardiff to soak up a free meal, and yes, it seems as though the Doctor somehow chucks out a load of Artron energy when regenerating (enough to attract passing spaceships; "The Christmas Invasion") but this isn't as conclusive as all that. Fire and life both need oxygen, but you can't resurrect the dead with a welding torch. Because time travel and regeneration both involve this weird stuff, it doesn't necessarily mean that regeneration is an aspect of time-travel.

What we can't help noticing about the new series episodes is the Doctor's amazing ability to walk around in a newly-altered timeline, and remember things that - from his point of view - have only just become historical facts. The Daleks and the Jagrafess seem to outright change history (X1.7, "The Long Game"; X1.12, "Bad Wolf") and the Doctor, after half an hour in the *Big Brother* house, remembers old gameshows such as *Bear With Me*.

In "World War Three" (X1.5), Harriet Jones is naggingly familiar to him until the changes in history caused by the Slitheen assassinating half the Cabinet settle down, and a future with Jones becoming Prime Minister and netting three consecutive landslides comes into being.

But what if it works the other way around, too? When seeking to account for the weird effects of the Sixth Doctor somewhat turning into an Androgum, owing to his second self getting a genetic makeover (22.4, "The Two Doctors"), we speculated on the possibility that the Doctor's *own* past was being rewritten without affecting the outside universe. (See also **Can You Rewrite History, Even One Line?** under 1.6, "The Aztecs"). It might seem like over-egging the pudding to suggest such historical revision in a series that innately tries to avoid such things, but this looks like as plausible a mechanism for regeneration as any.

And if this *were* the real process of regeneration, would the effects be any different to what we've seen? Not since 2005, certainly, but a few of the earlier regenerations might be more complicated. Has there been anything that can only be accounted for by this proposal?

Well, there's that raincoat. The Doctor, fresh from saving the world in his pyjamas and growing a new hand (in "The Christmas Invasion"), selects a coat we've never seen before, and which couldn't have fit any of his previous selves nor any of the known male companions. Yet from "The Christmas Invasion" on, we could accept that he just had it lying around. Moreover, in "Gridlock" (X3.3), it emerges that Janis Joplin gave him the coat. Leaving aside the odd notion of Hartnell's Doctor going to the Fillmore, the problem here is obvious: why would anyone give a coat to someone obviously either too short or too broad in the shoulder to wear it?[144] Now, you're going to raise the objection that the TARDIS wardrobe probably has such an array of different sizes, it can cater to nearly anyone's physique, so the raincoat isn't as odd as all that. Well, true... but that still doesn't explain the complication with Janis. She can't have foreseen that one day the Doctor would fit a coat she'd decided to give him, even if she'd been around when he had regenerated.

The theory doing the rounds a few years back was that a regeneration makes it so that once - say - Jon Pertwee turns into Tom Baker, the Doctor had

continued on page 473...

of its importance. The Great One describes it as the 'one last perfect crystal of power', necessary to complete the crystalline web which reproduces the pattern of her brain. [It's bizarre that she *knows* there was once a perfect crystal on Metebelis 3, even though there are presumably none in her own time. It's also bizarre that the Doctor just stumbled across it on his last, hurried, visit. Did it *want* to be found ...?]

History

• *Dating.* [On Earth, it's probably early 1975 by now; see **What's the UNIT Timeline?** under "The Daemons."]

Here the Brigadier establishes that there was a period of 'months' between the Second Doctor's last appearance on Earth [6.3, "The Invasion"] and the Third Doctor's arrival [7.1, "Spearhead from Space"]. The Buddhist retreat is near Mortimer [in Berkshire] according to the sign at the train station but Sarah refers to 'darkest Mummerset'. [Look at **What Are The Dodgiest Accents In The Series?**, under 4.1, "The Smugglers" if you still think that this is a real place. Mummers were strolling players, usually amateur, who put on Christmas plays in neighbouring villages - anonymously, in disguise, pre-Cromwell. Somerset is a county where they don't really talk like that, but Londoners think they do. Ergo, 'Mummerset' is the generic oo-arr accent adopted by actors.]

The parts of the story set on Metebelis 3 are harder to date. [The planet's people are human and have been there for centuries, so must be well after 2100, but the Doctor only describes this as 'the future'. There also remains some dispute about whether Metebelis is in the Acteon *group* or the Acteon *galaxy*. "Group" seems more likely - see "Carnival of Monsters", for the reasons - but if it's "galaxy" then the Earth ship must have landed there a long way into the future, since humanity doesn't appear to have intergalactic travel even in 3000 AD.]

It's been 433 years since the human ship crashed in the mountains where the blue crystals are found, and it happened just after the ship came out of 'time-jump' with insufficient fuel. [Implying time-travel, so these humans might be *very* advanced; no human beings anywhere else in the series are said to have reliable time-ships, not even tens of thousands of years from now. Then again, all faster-than-light travel needs a time-dis-

tortion of some kind, so we might equally date the launch at the same period as the 'space-time ships' mentioned in 22.2, "Vengeance on Varos", i.e. the twenty-third century.]

The Analysis

Where Does This Come From? We saw in **How Buddhist Is This Series?** under "The Abominable Snowmen", this story's reputation as the definitive statement on the subject comes mainly from Barry Letts having to go around telling everyone *this is a Buddhist allegory!* His very public statement regarding the story's intent was prompted by letters to the *Radio Times* (see **The Lore**), and makes everyone miss something rather more obvious.

What Lupton and his pals are up to in the cellar is nothing more nor less than a séance - and the spiders are *exactly* what Cho-Je says they are: demons. All the iconography (except the prayer-wheels and other window-dressing) is straight out of an MR James adaptation. It's a country-house, with a meek little host and a simple servant, the townies who visit are sceptical until eldritch sendings chase them, and a rather grandiloquent "sensitive" bewails his cursed state and dies. This was the sort of thing the BBC did practically every Christmas (and officially designated as an M.R. James-led thing from 1971, pausing only for 1976's Dickens tale *The Signalman*). Additionally, Jacques Tournier (of *Cat People* fame) had done a big-screen adaptation of one, released as *Night of the Demon* (and shown regularly afterward[141]).

You'll spot a lot of the Sloman / Letts material in these stories. If the whole thing with a tractor appearing out of nowhere to menace Mike and Sarah isn't conclusive, the death of 'Professor' Clegg confirms it. He's psychically assaulted by demonic forces chasing after something he's just been handed. And Clegg's death alerts us to something even more flagrantly pilfered: we've said that "The Daemons" had more than a hint of *Quatermass and the Pit*, but the Doctor's IRIS machine is stolen wholesale from it (especially the clip of spiders "dancing" on the screen when Our Heroes play back Clegg's last moments).

More fundamentally, though, this story represents the way that the various attempts to establish the existence of ESP were assumed to have succeeded. It was no longer a matter of "whether", so much as "what are they?" and "how do we har-

What Actually Happens in a Regeneration?

...continued from page 471

Junior".)

magically *always* looked like Tom Baker unless you happened to meet an earlier incarnation. (In which case, your memories would be copy-protected the same way Rose remembers the past where her dad didn't die but everyone else did; X1.8, "Father's Day". Ditto, apparently, photos taken by those people.) An exception or two (notably 22.5, "Timelash") exists to this theory, but it might explain why, if "Rose" (X1.1) took place soon after the Doctor regenerated, there were copious photos and drawings of the Eccleston version visiting the *Titanic* and the Kennedy Assassination. And this is *perhaps* why the Doctor who stepped out of the Tachyon Recreation Chamber (18.1, "The Leisure Hive") was still Tom Baker, even though we know from benefit of hindsight that he'd become Peter Davison long before reaching the five hundred years that he ages in that story.

So, according to this theory, the very *second* that the new Doctor says his first, "Hallo", a garment that had hitherto been a good fit for (say) Sylvester McCoy or whoever altered so that it had *always* fit (say) David Tennant. You scoff, but that's as good a means as any of explaining the Hartnell-Troughton clothes issue, and we've much less reason to discount this proposed mechanism now than we had in 2004. (Of course, it doesn't explain why McCoy looked as if he were swallowed inside Baker's Technicolor dreamcoat, or why Hartnell's ring fell off Troughton's finger.)

This doesn't, however, explain the projection of alternative selves that sometimes accompanies the regenerative process. The K'anpo maintained Cho-Jo until they fused into one body, the Doctor himself produced the Watcher ("Logopolis") and both seem to have been pre-ordained. The secondary selves reverberated back in time from the regeneration and seem to have arranged events to make this event happen "properly". Romana, who is (predictably) better at this sort of thing (albeit possibly just because she's a newer model of Time Lord) tried out several potential looks before picking one. (We might extrapolate from "Castrovalva" that she's actually in the TARDIS' Zero Room, and is sending avatars to chat with the Fourth Doctor.) Most recently, the Doctor managed to channel the orange swirly stuff into his spare hand and thereby grow a whole new self. (For reasons obvious to anyone familiar with *Carry On* films, the single-hearted Doctor seen in "Journey's End" has become known as "Oddbod

These "alternates" are all real / solid bodies, it seems (although the Watcher's precise nature is hard to fathom from the scant information we get). Certainly, the signs are that Cho-Je has been around for a while and eaten with his brethren at the monastery. Even if we conclude that the orange swirliness of regeneration is the fabled Artron energy, it's a bit of a leap to make this stuff - which seems to power both the TARDIS and regenerations - solid enough to eat mung beans. And even if the original Time Lord somehow sustains these "projections", they seem to possess independent properties and characteristics. The Fourth Doctor in "Logopolis" was largely unaware of what he was going to actually *do* on the Pharos dish, even though his future self had (evidently) sent back a plot-device. So unless the Doctor was simultaneously dying, having flashbacks and operating the Watcher by remote control, we have to assume that the Watcher was a conscious individual apart from the Doctor's awareness. More recently, we see Oddbod Junior in possession of a complete "self" (albeit one inflected with Donna's traits). It's looking, then, as if regeneration includes the production of an entirely new consciousness.

Whenever the topic of regeneration is introduced, it's typically stated that this is how Time Lords "cheat death". This becomes interesting when we remember what death actually does in the *Doctor Who* universe. When metabolic processes end, the memory and consciousness are often moved elsewhere, such as into another body (19.3, "Kinda"; 24.2, "Paradise Towers" and many more). More alarmingly, the specific moment of death can be interfered with, leading to odd half-life processes. In 17.6, "Shada", Professor Chronotis is outside time and effectively immortal, but still drinks tea and eats crumpets. Under similar circumstances in *Torchwood* Series Two, Owen Harper is unable to eat, recover from injury or (when the director remembers) breathe, but he's also able to lay down new memories and talk to people.

To cite a bigger example, since Rose-as-Bad-Wolf zapped Jack back into life ("The Parting of the Ways"), he's been unable to stay dead or, apparently, sleep. This could be another instance like Chronotis, where Jack's life-stream (whatever that is) has been removed from time at a significant juncture, or that more simply (if you feel com-

continued on page 475...

ness these?" Like the existence of "Greys" in the 1990s, psychic powers were popularly assumed to exist. Anyone who questioned this was obviously part of a sinister cover-up. This had been a thread running through twentieth century culture since the Theosophical Society had its big surge of popularity in World War I (see **How Many Atlantises Are There?** under 4.5, "The Underwater Menace" and **Why Is That Portrait in Maxtible's Parlour?** under 4.9, "The Evil of the Daleks"), but had undergone a fashionable shift in the 1950s.

The editor of *Astounding Science Fiction*, the arch-rationalist John W Campbell (see **Is This Any Way to Run a Galactic Empire?** under 10.3, "Frontier in Space") had been swayed first by Dianetics / Scientology (this happened despite, or perhaps because of, its marked similarity to the stories of his regular writer AE Van Vogt - who also converted) and then by the almost laughably slight evidence concerning something called the Hieronymus Device. Campbell heard T. Galen Hieronymus describe how this thing was supposed to work by processes "outside known scientific laws" and built one to debunk it. To his surprise, it worked for him, revealing "eloptic" radiation from all living things and unique emanations from every element. (This is doubly odd, as the people who go for this stuff claim that "negative psi", or scepticism, means it only works for believers... odd how these things always work that way.)

Campbell was more surprised when he replaced the circuitry with a *drawing* of the circuit and it *still* worked. The theory behind it is worryingly close to the idea in "The Time Monster" that tea-leaves and bottles of Moroccan Burgundy can jam crystals from Atlantis through the ratio of their molecular shapes (and the places where Hieronymus devices are advertised also offer Atlantean crystals, although not trident-shaped). Over the course of the 1960s people investigated psychic phenomena in labs, using Zener cards and skin galvanometers (and thus launching the whole biofeedback fad), but the most promising results seemed to be coming from the Soviet Union. Well, we should emphasise the word *seemed*, as the research wasn't replicable, but it was enough to get the US to shove a lot of money at the problem - just as they'd done when scared about brainwashing (see 8.2, "The Mind of Evil"). Princetown University had rather a large depart-

ment, but this was closed down after several years of inconclusive results (funny, we had a feeling that was going to happen).

To the extent that anything connected with the mind invariably became mysterious and therefore "Eastern" in popular culture then, the crossover between meditation and psi-powers was natural and obvious. We note that the Doctor dredges up the word 'guru', with a pedantically correct pronunciation, as though Sarah wouldn't have heard of it. There's a one-size-fits-all approach that equates Zen with ESP, and this with teleportation. It was obvious, therefore, to anyone at the time that the Doctor's mentor would possess both wisdom and formidable psychic powers.

Yup, there's no getting around it... the Doctor's spent four years beating up security guards and paralysing UNIT personnel who get in his way with Venusian Aikido, so the fact that he had a childhood mentor whose face he sees in times of crisis shouldn't come as a surprise. The presence of this person in the Gompa is hardly unexpected (where else would he be, a chip-shop? - or wait, a motorcycle repair shop, obviously), but they missed a trick not having George Cormack bald-headed and with contact-lenses, suggesting blindness and thus insight. Calling the Doctor "Glasshopper" would have sealed the deal.

Anyone unsure about what we're getting at should note that the Universal TV show *Kung Fu* was on ITV opposite *Doctor Who* in some regions; in this, David Carradine played Caine, a former Shaolin monk on the run in the Old West, who kept having flashbacks to Keye Luke as his old mentor giving him wise advice, usually involving bending like a reed in the wind, finding your own level like water in a cup, going round like a circle in a spiral, et cetera. The entire story we're told here is about the Doctor facing his fear and being reborn, which smacks rather of an initiation rite.

Except, it's not *particularly* Buddhist even then. Many cults do this sort of thing, including the Freemasons and the Yakusa. And no way is Tom Baker's Doctor a Ninja. Ahhh, but the Great One is supposed to represent the Ego, and the Doctor has to surrender this to become reborn. At least, that's what they tell us, even if this means that *The Prisoner* (under all the overt Catholicism) was also a Buddhist parable. (Sorry to spoil the ending of a forty-year-old TV show here, but ultimately the hero confronts the mysterious Number One who is... himself! Somehow, a surprising number of

What Actually Happens in a Regeneration?

...continued from page 473

fortable labelling such a concept as *simple*) that he's been given an involuntary ability to reverse time for himself only to the moment before death. The latter is unlikely from his various comments on how terrible coming back feels, and that he's very slowly ageing. We also have the odd detail that the TARDIS got the jitters and tried to shake him off because he 'shouldn't be' ("Utopia").

Something related seems to be happening in "Mawdryn Undead" (20.3), where the mutants need to be reunited with mortality via either the Doctor's remaining regenerations or the huge blast of Artron energy when the two Brigadiers touch. Not for the first time, we're dealing with a kind of Cartesean Dualism - a separation of mind and body - which puts the body into a very subsidiary role. The mutants' bodies are stuck in time, but their minds might not be. And not for the *last* time, we get the odd notion that minds somehow create bodies. (See **What Were Josiah's "Blasphemous" Theories?** under 26.2, "Ghost Light" and **How Does "Evolution" Work?** under 18.3, "Full Circle".) Whilst this seems to help explain Omega's status in "The Three Doctors" (10.1), it makes "The Brain of Morbius" more pointless than ever. If regeneration works like *this*, then the Doctor's consciousness is the same one throughout.

Unfortunately for our quest for a neat answer (but fortunately in other regards), the indications are that the opposite is the case. The new Doctor gets a new consciousness but the old memories, albeit in jumbled form. Each dying Doctor is losing the "I" that has been speaking for the last several years, as "The Parting of the Ways" makes plain. This might well be how he can shake hands with previous selves (as in 20.7, "The Five Doctors") without "Mawdryn Undead"-style flashes of Artron energy (see **What Is The Blinovitch Limitation Effect?** with that story), but we could go around in circles asking if the new body creates the new self or whether the old self created the new body.

Minds creating bodies also opens up a lot of other potential oddness - such as, say, the Doctor summoning the Master into being after eating cheese before bedtime - but until recently this wasn't an issue. And we're no better off considering the role of Artron energy in the creation of Oddbod Junior. The original Tenth Doctor has no qualms leaving his doppelganger behind in a TARDIS-free universe[145] for Rose to keep as a pet - so obviously, the spare Doctor can sustain himself by the usual breathing and eating. Sure, the new boy has the original's memories (and some of Donna's), but the "main" Doctor views his augmented hand as being someone else.

But if we're plundering evidence from the new series, it's hard to ascertain how the Chameleon Arch (X3.7, "Human Nature", etc.) fits into this. True, the Doctor acquired a new body and a new consciousness at the same time (or rather, John Smith did) and yes, the half-hunter he carried had definite swirls of orange fairy-dust whenever Tim opened it, but this is hardly conclusive. There's seepage of the Doctor's memory into Smith[146] and the TARDIS is clearly prompting new-old memories of John's parents, dance-steps and a whole fictitious past.

Once again, a throwaway line that the TARDIS is doing all of this looks like a solution. It seems reasonable that the dying Doctor pops his memory into a back-up aboard his Ship and the new body - with its brand-new "me" - gets a download (possibly via the telepathic circuits, especially in instances where he doesn't actually "change" within the Ship). The potential snag here is that in "Utopia", the Master regenerated aboard the Doctor's TARDIS. His own - assuming it even survived the Time War and is still in working order (likely true, as he must've used equipment aboard his Ship to hide his memories inside a watch) - is presumably somewhere around the Silver Devastation. His plan, such as it was, clearly didn't rely on the Doctor happening by on his way somewhere. So conceivably, there *could* be a telepathic link across ten trillion years and several galaxies, but this would suggest that *all* Time Lords need a TARDIS or similar to regenerate... and we know that K'anpo didn't. (Anyway, Romana only had the Doctor's Ship, which would raise questions about why she didn't turn into *him*. That said, it's interesting that the Doctor's next life was young, blond and pert, even as Romana became a lot less aloof and considerably more skittish.)

If death results in the consciousness being removed from time (a dodgy proposal, but one *Who* writers occasionally employ in the face of theological and philosophical complexities) and yet such a consciousness is able to take on board new memories, then we might have a get-out clause. This opens up far more problems than it

continued on page 477...

people *didn't* see that one coming and rang in to complain.) In fact, what's supposedly the most Buddhist story of all has a lot more in common with Mediaeval Catholicism, which also considered curiosity to be the cause of all sins, and ego as something to be beaten out of you. Indeed, many forms of Buddhist doctrine suggest that deliberate ignorance is the cause of suffering. Is the Doctor really intended to become self-less (literally) or just Self-Actualised? (See "The Green Death" for more on this.)

So what is the message we're supposed to take from this? As we all have spiders on our backs, temptations or fears that control us, we're supposed to kill ourselves and try again next lifetime? Not likely, even when the BBC was more courageous than it became in the 80s. No, this is another parable about existential liberation, getting out of bad habits of thought and not accepting anyone else's domination. We've been seeing this emerge as a theme across the latter half of Pertwee's Doctorate, often couched in terms of metamorphosis (9.4, "The Mutants"), not trusting dodgy authority-figures who claim to have "the answer" ("The Daemons", "Invasion of the Dinosaurs"), accepting responsibility for the consequences of your actions ("Day of the Daleks"; "The Green Death") and so on.

Just to confuse the issue, the clearest expression of this hitherto comes from the Master in "The Time Monster". Now, though, the whole story makes it abundantly clear that self-governance is the only way to avoid domination by others, but it comes at the price of total responsibility. Domination, as with the show's previous dalliance with Buddhism, comes with other people talking through your mouth ("The Abominable Snowmen"). From now on, possession will become a standard tool in the show's arsenal at least until K9 shows up, and occasionally thereafter ("The Armageddon Factor"; 19.7, "Time-Flight"). There's a simple and obvious reason for this (*The Exorcist*, released in 1973 but based on a bestseller from three years before - go on, you thought the objects flying around when Clegg dies had a familiar ring to it, didn't you?), but more complex underlying reasons exist why *Doctor Who* should be more prone than any other series.

To summarise very crudely, *Doctor Who* was a television series made by people who read novels. There's more of a tendency to celebrate (or even accept the existence of) an introspective and indi-

vidual self in literature than with cinema or television, which rely on individuals temporarily becoming part of a unitary collective consciousness called "the audience". Literacy is part of the way an internal monologue is inculcated. (There's neurology involved but - to your inexpressible joy - we won't investigate it here.) Loss of this "selfhood" is more scary for people who read and have more invested in that self. We mentioned *The Exorcist* a while back - this and others of its kind (*Rosemary's Baby* for example, or *The Stepford Wives*) were adapted from novels by people who were *hoping* that the subjectivity of the novel-reader's identification and acceptance of the book's world-view would transfer to the screen. The simple point is that Peter William Blatty adapted his own novel into the screenplay for *The Exorcist*, whereas Steven Spielberg (who claimed that he barely reads novels) adapted *Jaws* and made it a collective cinematic experience by making the shark treat people as objects.

Television, especially action / fantasy shows, had another tendency: namely making "human nature" a fixed and innate object. Thus, no matter what psychic menace afflicts Jim or Bones, it'll be completely forgotten next week, and their personalities will remain unchanged from any previous or future episode. Granted, this is partly so they can show "segments" in any order, but mainly it's because advertisers discovered that people who don't believe that advertising or any other form of conditioning has any real or lasting effect are the best subjects for their voodoo. (This is the upshot of their own internal memos, and is a matter of record.) Brainwashing and hypnosis were staples of successful American shows (plus the ones made here for the US market as much as our own consumption), but were curable.

As we've seen, early 70s *Doctor Who* straddles these two tendencies through it's innate soapiness. Terrance Dicks read English Lit at Downing College (so he may have been taught by FR Leavis... those who know what this implies can mull it over the coffee to their heart's content), but adored *Star Trek* and sought to emulate it in his own show. However, unlike *Trek*, his version of *Doctor Who* had unfolding character-led "arcs" (not that they were called that then), so characters such as Mike and Jo developed as a result of brainwashing and hypnosis. And characters *did* change over time and make sacrifices that had consequences - after all, "Planet of the Spiders" is

What Actually Happens in a Regeneration?

...continued from page 475

solves, though - if all that makes a new Doctor 'the Doctor' is the same DNA and access to the old memories, then is it really the same person? Donna-as-Supertemp had the Doctor's mind, and he seemed to treat her as one of his other selves. (A glance at **How Do You Transmit Matter?** under 17.4, "Nightmare of Eden" will give you a taste of the existential can of worms waiting to be opened when you start on this topic.)

What appears to be happening, then, is that a crisis induces a surge of Artron energy which somehow stimulates a Time Lord's DNA to provide structure to that energy - with said structure being a new body that's sort of an anagram of the previous one. This looks like the silly business of the Doctor's DNA somehow causing cosmic rays to behave like lightning in such a fashion as to form new Dalek-Human-Time Lord hybrids (X3.5, "Evolution of the Daleks"), but we have to remember two things. One is that in the real world, DNA is essentially a template for making proteins out of any passing material. The other is that, unless we're very wrong indeed, Artron energy is somehow connected with probability (see **How Does the TARDIS Work?** under 1.3, "Edge of Destruction").

A new consciousness comes into this new body, in which the freshly-minted neurons restructure themselves whilst retaining old memory-traces and motor skills. (Or maybe not: "Kinda" suggests that the Fifth Doctor must relearn conjuring, even though some of his previous selves had the talent; ditto Nine in "Rose". Then again, it's possible they remember *how* and are just acclimating to their relatively new fingers.) The DNA seems at times to have a "repertoire" of potential faces (as in "The War Games"; see also **Why Are There So Many Doubles in the Universe?** under 20.1, "Arc of Infinity"), and is sometimes susceptible to outside influences. "Castrovalva" both suggests that 'ambient complexity' causes odd effects, and that the Doctor never quite knows what he's going to be like. (Let's quickly acknowledge the McGann movie's contribution to this debate, then run away.) Furthermore, this wondrous orange sparkly energy stuff can seeps into the DNA of anyone *else* who travels in time, to the point that that Mickey can activate the Genesis Ark (X2.13, "Doomsday") and Miss Wormwood can trace Sarah (the *Sarah Jane Adventures* story "Invasion of the Bane"). This *might* even be connected to Ian and Barbara getting knocked unconscious on their first journey. (If they were the first non-Gallifreyans to travel in the Doctor's TARDIS, the Ship might have needed to adjust to their presence and fix their language skills.)

Hang on, though... if there's *that* much power

continued on page 479...

---

a story where the hero dies and is reincarnated as a different character.

In case the origin of the entire plot of the wizard killed by a witch-queen who traps him in a cave of crystal *still* eludes you, the designer has helpfully put a stuffed crocodile in the UNIT lab, suspended from the ceiling. We're in Arthurian territory, a region of British folklore we'll revisit periodically from now on (16.3, "The Stones of Blood", wherein a thinly-disguised Morgan le Fay / Nimue has ravens as familiars and traps the Doctor in hyperspace; see also "Battlefield", which spells it out for dullards). This and this alone excuses the fact that the demonic forces in this story all have female voices (there must, logically, be male spiders *somewhere* on the planet). It's only a European trait to assume that all spiders are female and (therefore?) manipulative. Nevertheless it's a commonplace of folklore, even down to the level of the Basil Rathbone *Sherlock Holmes* B-movies. But then, as we've suggested,

everything from this story seems rooted in the immediate post-War era and given a veneer of topicality. Even the Variety acts that the Doctor and the Brigadier witness as the story opens come from a bygone age, despite the topical gag about streakers.[147]

Things That Don't Make Sense So there's this UNIT engineer, in the garage, fixing a car. Some bloke comes up and asks 'where is the Doctor?', and the engineer automatically assumes the stranger means the medical officer. Even if this engineer is very new to UNIT, surely he'd know that there's an elderly civilian sporting the fashionable "mutton-dressed-as-lamb" look who calls himself 'the Doctor', and that, er, everyone in UNIT probably lost a mate because of something he did and / or owes him his life. And even if this was his first day on the job, he'd surely know that the owner of the stupid-looking space-car he's fixing *as this conversation takes place* isn't standard

UNIT equipment, and is owned by the same person who's got a sprightly yellow roadster called Bessie - and who isn't Harry Sullivan. Besides, if this guy is trusted enough to conduct repairs on the Whomobile, he's probably someone the Doctor or the Brigadier has hand-picked for the job, and may have been there long enough to remember when Jo Grant was wiggling around in mini-skirts.

There's also something screwy with the time-scale. Lupton is clearly and repeatedly stated to have jaunted from the speedboat to the Gompa at '10.30', but as it's still light and clearly not summer, it must be 10.30 in the morning... which means Sarah has been wearing the same clothes for two days. (But when the Doctor opts to investigate Lupton's disappearance, it would seem that he makes a detour to South Croydon so Sarah can change into that hideous stripey ensemble.) Even if we allow for artistic license and ignore the way the shots of the Doctor and the Brigadier at the theatre are intercut with Yates walking around in broad daylight, we still have the whole question of why the Doctor and the Brigadier are treating the stuff at the lab as a new day while Lupton and Cho-Je are still on the previous one.

In one of those shocking coincidences that the story requires to function, Jo just happens to send the Metebelis crystal back to the Doctor at the exact time that the Metebelis spiders make a bid to reclaim it. And it's not so much a mistake as a loose end, but... the blue crystal causes a miniature earthquake and lethal poltergeist-like phenomena when Lupton's renegade choral society perform a summoning ritual some miles away, which is reasonable. But this is the *second* time they've performed the ritual, even if it's the first time that the spider fully materialises. Since the blue crystal was still in the post and on its way to UNIT HQ at the time, are there several dead postmen at the local GPO? [Or does the crystal only turn lethal when a psychic such as Professor Clegg holds it?] Why does the Doctor revert to calling Clegg 'Professor' after the poor feller's *Quatermass*-lite death?

Come to think of it, how did the Doctor know to *find* Clegg? If he had some kind of meter to detect psi ability, then why wait for the stage-act? Why not just visit him in his digs or at rehearsals? As the Brigadier seems to know nothing of what the Doctor is up to with UNIT funds, why did he go with him to this tacky night-spot? What made the Doctor think that taking the Brig along was a good idea? And why is the woman laughing heartily at the terrible comedian also to be seen in the Gompa meditating the next morning when Sarah arrives? Is she paying a penance?

In trying to scare Sarah off her investigation, Lupton resorts to *Scooby Doo* logic - that the appearance of a ghostly tractor will frighten her and Mike to the point of helplessness, as opposed to just stoking their interest. The Brigadier, usually a crack shot even in a crisis [see "The Mind of Evil"] can't bring Lupton down with his revolver even though Lupton's moving at hobbling-speed and they're facing each other across an empty car park. Bessie, which formerly had the power to move at impossible speeds across Britain's countryside, now struggles to match the Whomobile's 90 MPH. [Admittedly the Brigadier - who lacks the Doctor's lightning reflexes - is driving it, but on an empty road with magic inertia-damping brakes ("The Time Monster"), this shouldn't make any odds.]

It's said that pure, well-balanced minds are supposedly less prone to the spiders' attacks than others, yet K'anpo is killed by a single blast from one of Lupton's crowd. Even if he's old and weak, surely his great wisdom and all-round niceness should give him more of a shield? And whereas the spiders possessing Lupton's friends can sense the vibrations of the crystal when they're in the same building, the one "riding" Sarah can't sense it when she's in the same room. Besides, if Lupton's spider can track the crystal to the UNIT lab, *eighty miles away*, why can't she find it in the same building, in a shoebox in the cupboard under the stairs?

Right, time for the accent discussion. First off, a lot of odd assumptions about intelligence crop up in Tommy's steep learning-curve. There's the way that his rapid intellectual growth removes his comedy yokel accent; the fact that he can deduce the pronunciations of counter-intuitive spellings (within minutes, he's figured out 'we weigh and measure'); his supernatural ability to figure out how to use a dictionary and an encyclopaedia; and his ability to construct complicated sentences with correct syntax with no previous coaching, even though everyone who might've provided an example has been talking to him as if he's a baby for his whole life. In fact, if he's copying the positive role models for examples of how to behave now that he's intelligent, shouldn't he have a com-

What Actually Happens in a Regeneration?

...continued from page 477

inside a regenerating Time Lord then surely when one dies, he / she must blast a hole in the ground. Unless every single dying Time Lord we've ever seen was on his last life (and 15.6, "The Invasion of Time" makes this improbable), this can't be right. So maybe they borrow it from somewhere. The obvious answers were to be found in the Master's attempt to reboot himself using the power of the Eye of Harmony (in 14.3, "The Deadly Assassin"). Just as the screen into which the Second Doctor disappeared before turning up as Pertwee was obviously (albeit with hindsight) the Matrix ("The War Games"), so the fact that the Master was after this power and that President Borusa offered him a new regeneration cycle ("The Five Doctors") indicate that either proof that the Master is amazingly deluded, or that this is indeed possible.

Ergo, it seems, the Doctor's regenerations - and those of Time Lords who seem to be able to change bodies with considerable ease - were governed by Gallifrey. This was fine, when there *was* a Gallifrey. The Doctor and the Master have both demonstrated the ability to regenerate without it, although we're no longer sure that the "Thirteen Strikes and You're *Really* Dead This Time" rule (established in "The Deadly Assassin", and reiterated in places such as "Mawdryn Undead") even still

applies now. Of course, it may just be that the available Artron energy apparently seeping *out* of the Doctor while he's crashed out in Jackie's bed was - when seen in reverse by those of us bound to normal, sequential time - seeping *in* over a period after the regeneration (say, about fifteen hours) and he was fiddling with time to get a sort of energy overdraft. This makes as much sense as a lot of the other suggested explanations but, um, still seems wrong.

Either way, rather than the sedate lying on the floor and blurring that we witnessed in old regenerations, every regeneration in the new series has entailed this OTT orange-swirly-from-the-clothes thing, and every one has taken place aboard the TARDIS. No two regenerations were alike until 2007, so something significant has apparently changed. Just because Gallifrey's destruction is the most significant change that we know occurred in the interim, it doesn't mean it's the *only* one, nor even the one that's most important here. As a ponderous textbook had it, *Doctor Who* is an unfolding text - so simply by tracking changes in how the makers of each series perceived the show, we can get a handle on some of the ideas and obstacles that shaped the key concepts of the series. But the main thing you learn is that while it's still being made, there's no way you can get the whole story.

---

edy Tibetan accent like Cho-Je, rather than talking like the bad guys? [Not for the first time, the assumption is that "intelligent" equates to "educated", that the hallmark of this being Received Pronunciation (RP). As this assumption was so widespread, Tommy *could* have deduced that someone who wants to be thought of as smart wouldn't gabble in a Mummerset accent - save that there's no indication of there being a radio or television anywhere in the building.]

By the same token, why should 433 years on a remote planet cause the descendants of the original colonists to talk like the cast of *The Archers*, especially when they have the frightfully well-spoken Eight-Legs around setting them a good example? [Less frivolously put... the West Country accent these actors are affecting is one that's the residue of an older indigenous set of vowel-sounds that were supplanted in more affluent areas around the time of the Battle of Blenheim. (Queen Anne's reign, although some philologists put it earlier.) It's not something that anyone who

speaks RP would slide into if they'd not heard it before - we know from several islands around the world what happens to the language when it's left alone. If they were going to represent this as a realistic response to being left to their own devices for centuries, then Arak and Tuar would talk like Bob Marley or converse in Tagalog. As we're made to see it, this could only occur if the Eight-Legs are amusing themselves by *making* their two-leg slaves talk like a bunch of Pigbins. (Or just hiring anyone who can't do the Walter Gabriel voice to work as their bearers and bodyguards, as Max Faulkner and Walter Randall are excused from Mummersetting. So, see? That fourth cliffhanger *could* have been worse after all, me old pal, me old beauty.)]

How does Lupton fail to spot Sarah, who's just standing in the open, plain as day, once they both arrive on Metebelis? How come Arak can openly wander around the village yelling 'Aye!' when he's wanted by the law? And really - *for telepaths*, these Eight-Legs are rubbish at running a police-state.

They can't spot Sarah five feet away, can't get straight answers from the villagers and don't even bother getting the truth with mind-probing. Are they scared that they'll pick up the colonials' accent and lose credibility? [Besides, Arak is plainly visible through the door when Sarah is apprehended, so the guards must be stupid *despite* their using BBC English.]

Incidentally, how do the Metebelis residents *know* that 433 Earth years have passed since their spaceship arrived? Did they have a ready-reckoner handy just in case someone from Earth popped up and wanted the story? Or if Metebelis and Earth have the same year, against all the odds, why bother saying 'Earth years'? [We might have to write this off as a translation problem.]

The big one ('mmMMMmmm'... all praise to The Big One!): the Doctor realises that his old mentor is advising a suicidal return to the mountain and asks, 'Is there no other way?' In allegorical terms, confronting his biggest fear is well and good, but here he isn't confronting it, he's *surrendering* to it. The Doctor's strategy is to give the Great One [and we hope American readers can avoid thinking of Jackie Gleason when they hear that name] exactly what she wants and allow her to win and conquer the Universe. K'anpo doesn't know that this will cause a positive feedback loop and a model explosion.[142] Therefore, at the time the advice was given, the proposed course of action was for the Doctor to permit the end of everything in the service of his personal growth. It's all "me, me, me" with these Buddhists, isn't it?

Critique So it's come to this... half an episode of Pertwee driving various vehicles because he can; half an episode of the Doctor lying unconscious and the plot stopping until he revives; five minutes of *Hai!* and Terry Walsh in *that* wig; almost a whole episode of Jenny Laird wondering if it's a take; and some impossibly ambitious attempts to make a whole planet with CSO. It would seem that *Doctor Who* now aspires to be like *The Tomorrow People*, with psychic powers replacing plot or motivation.

Let's turn that paragraph around and get a little perspective. In essence, we're criticising this story for having a car-chase with hovercraft and autogyros; too many set-piece stunts; a lengthy sequence of the Doctor performing martial arts on numerous opponents; a scene revealing yet another little detail about his childhood and a climax where he saves the universe from a psychic force in an elaborate Buddhist parable. Oh, and because the TARDIS is used as a shuttle service between his normal Earthly base and a planet occupied by giant spiders. Because they've *finally* got giant spiders into the series (unless you count 2.5, "The Web Planet").

Now think back to the start of this book. Try to imagine explaining what the problem actually is to someone who's just seen "Spearhead from Space" or even 6.7, "The War Games". Little by little, the Barry Letts-Terrance Dicks team have completely overhauled this series and taken vast numbers of viewers with them. They've done something else that is hardly ever mentioned - namely, using the complexity of soap-opera scripting. Whilst people who don't watch them might sneer, the thing about soaps is that they require a lot of long-term character-relationships and plot developments to be held in the viewers' minds, a skill supposedly only needed for hefty novels. The number of plates being spun by the viewers of *Lost*, *Mad Men* or *Damages* are equivalent to those for someone reading *Middlemarch* or *Mary Barton*.

Take a moment to consider what someone watching "Planet of the Spiders" has to bear in mind: the crystals, how the Doctor found the all-important one, what they did to BOSS and why Jo had it; Mike Yates, his reasons for not contacting UNIT, his reasons for taking up meditation, his relationship - if any - with Sarah; the Doctor, his interest in human psychic ability, his travels to other worlds (including the Miniscope), his friendship with the Brigadier after a shaky start, his childhood mentor, his previous irresponsible actions and his cars; Jo, her marriage, her trip up the Amazon, the fact that she doesn't know Yates has left under a cloud...

You get the idea. In 1974, the only other drama series with *this* many threads running in a single episode were soap operas or adaptations of novels. Letts and Robert Sloman even keep the viewers up to speed without lengthy "Previously..." catch-ups or obvious info-dumps and the only flashbacks (well, apart from one clip of the sonic screwdriver and Drashigs, edited to avoid having to pay Katy Manning) are from earlier in the story. We've been trying to think of an original drama from Britain or America circa 1974 with that much faith in its audience, *especially* one with set-piece stunts, car-chases or special effects and a primary audience under fifteen years old. They have made "The Children's own programme that adults adore" (as the *Daily Sketch* referred to it in a review of "Spearhead") into something as sophisticated as anything being made on British television, and as mature as possible without leaving children bewildered.

The drawback is that by the end of the previous recording block they'd done everything possible with this Doctor and this format. As you'll doubtless recall, everything from "Invasion of the Dinosaurs" on was reheating old ideas. Even so, Letts pulls out the stops and has a good go at making his script-contributions and directing style create an all-embracing atmosphere. He takes the gimmicky tricks Michael Ferguson did with the videodisc (7.3, "The Ambassadors of Death"; 8.3, "The Claws of Axos") and puts them to narrative use. It's a grand attempt, however...

It's sad that such an event, something consciously made to *be* an event, has so many longeurs and misfires. This was to be *the big one*, the story that tied up all the long-running storylines into one final epic ending and do everything that *Doctor Who* was now known for doing - all in one glorious six-week package. The last episode contains a major revelation that should have been the story's focal point - the introduction of someone who's effectively the Doctor's role-model - but it's made simply a piece of plot exposition in among the chases and monsters. In many ways, the whole of Season Eleven is like this story: made in the realisation that it's the last time they can do anything like this.

You'll notice that this is pretty much what we said about "Invasion of the Dinosaurs", and it's the same fundamental criticism that holds for *all* the stories in this block - that everyone is playing safe just to get to the end. "Invasion of the Dinosaurs" at least had a director who'd not done a story in colour before, whereas the rest involved a slew of old hands (both in front of the camera and behind it) treading water. Even this much-vaunted Buddhist parable amounts to an ego becoming ambitious and leading everything out of balance through greed and curiosity, the same as BOSS's back-story.

But let's focus on the positives. Most of the cast *do* know exactly what they're doing, and do it better than was required. We've latched on to Jenny Laird's underpowered performance simply because it stands out, but the regulars are all on form. Nicholas Courtney finds new ways to do the same old stuff (shoot at things, say 'good grief' and

be British in unlikely circumstances) and Elisabeth Sladen hasn't tired of being the viewers' benchmark for normality.

Appropriately, we have to make special mention of Jon Pertwee, who has to take the character he's been playing for five years into a completely new area and be frail, scared and out of his depth. He grades his performance to give the six episodes a definite progression towards an inevitable death. Flashy as the later regenerations got, all subsequent Doctor-Doctor hand-overs are attempts to top this one. The difference is that this time it really *looks* like a death, as opposed to a bored actor having electronic jiggery-pokery committed upon his face. True, we can snipe about the Licence-fee-payers funding Pertwee's mid-life crisis, we can gripe about the padding and a few iffy effects, and we might even ponder how realistic the "present-day" setting is... but ultimately, we have to admit that "Planet of the Spiders" was state-of-the-art for 1974 and still has a lot going for it. It could have done more, but nobody would have been ready for it.

The Facts

Written by Robert Sloman. Directed by Barry Letts. Viewing figures: 10.1 million, 8.9 million, 8.8 million, 8.2 million, 9.2 million, 8.9 million. (Reaction figures give a lamentable 56% for the last episode. The highest figure is 60% for episode two, the one with the seemingly unending chase. That's right, the dull one got the best response.)

Cliffhangers   The sinister meditators perform their ritual in the cellar of the retreat, and one of the spiders appears in the middle of their mandala; after a protracted chase sequence, the Doctor finally catches up with Lupton on a speedboat, only to find that the man has vanished from the driver's seat; attempting to rescue Sarah on Metebelis 3, the Doctor is brought down by an energy-bolt from the hand of one of the spiders' guards, collapsing before he can crawl back into the TARDIS; in the spiders' larder, a web-bound Sarah is overjoyed to see the Doctor arrive, until she realises that he's being led in by the guards; Lupton's "gang" at the Buddhist retreat, all of them possessed by spiders, team up against Tommy and hit him with energy-bolts. (It's strange that the last cliffhanger of the Third Doctor's era doesn't involve the Doctor at all; note also that the scenes are in a different order during the re-cap.)

Supporting Cast John Dearth (Lupton), Cyril Shaps (Professor Clegg), Christopher Burgess (Barnes), Terence Lodge (Moss), Carl Forgione (Land), Andrew Staines (Keaver), Kevin Lindsay (Cho-je), John Kane (Tommy), Terry Walsh (Man with Boat), Kismet Delgado (Spider Voice), Gareth Hunt (Arak), Geoffrey Morris (Sabor), Jenny Laird (Neska), Joanna Munro (Rega), George Cormack (K'anpo).

What Was in the Charts? "Seasons in the Sun", Terry Jacks; "Remember Me This Way", Gary Glitter; "Spiders and Snakes", Jim Stafford; "Year of Decision", The Three Degrees; "Emma", Hot Chocolate; "This Town Ain't Big Enough For Both of Us", Sparks.

The Lore

• After the fight scene in "The Green Death", Pertwee's occasional back problems had been growing worse and he was thinking of moving on. He had been considering this for a while, but by this stage he was looking for reasons *not* to go. Although already paid far more than most BBC stars, he put in a bid for a 20% pay rise just to see how much the BBC valued him. The Head of Serials, Shaun Sutton (who had known Pertwee since RADA, although unlike Pertwee had not been thrown out) calmly stated that the next year's budget had already been allocated. When later asked about his departure, Pertwee cited this reason - however, Letts and Dicks have queried it. It's entirely possible that Pertwee told the story so often, he started to believe it. (At time of writing, the same story is being told in some of the more louche online discussions about David Tennant's announcement of his departure; it obviously fits some people's idea of how stars behave.)

• The quest for a new Doctor, conducted under the radar until midway through recording "The Monster of Peladon", continued. As usual they started with variations on the previous incumbent. The production team approached Richard Hearne, star of children's show *Mr Pastry,* to play the Doctor as a much older incarnation but still able to do stunts. (Hearne made himself up as a doddery grandfather, and did slapstick routines that required considerable athleticism.) Letts had in mind a sardonic older man, possibly Scots - his first choice was Graham Crowden, then Fulton Mackay. (We could be wrong, but it looks as if

they were basing the new Doctor on a specific idea and finding men to fit.) But Letts was also considering younger actors - former pop heart-thob and *Carry On* leading man Jim Dale was approached, possibly on Pertwee's suggestion. (For American readers, Dale is the narrator of the *Harry Potter* audiobooks and *Pushing Daisies,* even though everyone here knows that Stephen Fry is the only possible voice for Rowling.) Dale had co-starred with Pertwee on the first Rock 'n' Roll show, *The Six-Five Special,* before - as with Pertwee - he worked on various *Carry On* films (see 2.4, "The Romans"). Britain's first rock-n-roller, Tommy Steele, was also in the frame. He'd gone all Disney on us and was in West End musicals like *Hans Christian Anderson* (based on the film starring Pertwee's doppelganger, Danny Kaye). Meanwhile, on a building-site not half a mile from Television Centre, an ex-monk was wondering why he'd ever thought he'd make it as an actor...

• Robert Sloman had submitted the storyline for "The Final Game", intended to be the last story with the Master, three months before Roger Delgado's fatal car crash. Conceived as the final, climactic showdown between the Doctor and the Master, the initial idea was that the two Time Lords would be revealed as parts of the same persona. The Master was Id, and the Doctor was Ego. (Sloman admits that he pinched this from *Forbidden Planet.* However, given the nature of "Planet of the Spiders", it's possible that this Doctor / Master relationship was going to be implied through metaphor rather than being explained scientifically.) At the end of the story, the Doctor and the Master would be caught up in some form of Reichenbach-Falls-style mutually-destructive act, during which the Master would finally see the error of his ways and sacrifice his life to save the Doctor and the universe. The sadder and wiser Doctor would move a significant step closer to spiritual awakening, although with a long way to go. Some of what Letts intended can be found in the flying reptile cavalry charge from the 1993 radio story "The Paradise of Death", especially the conversation about 'untying the knots in my mind'.

• Back in the real world, where "Planet of the Spiders" was made instead... once again, Letts more or less co-wrote this story (at least in the plot stage) allowing Sloman sole credit. One specification that Sloman found especially hard to meet was the chase in Part Two. Letts provided a booklet of notes on Buddhist thought, especially the Vajrayana way. Sloman wrote much of the dialogue phonetically, such as the Doctor's breaking into Tibetan and Tommy's garbled speech. (Sloman later admitted to regretting the patronising way Tommy had been treated in his script, and found the scene where he's "cured" of both learning difficulties and a West Country accent deeply uncomfortable.)

The script had a mention of a UNIT M.O. called 'Dr Sweetman' (retained in the novelisation), but this was changed to 'Sullivan' when the new male companion was decided upon. This character was a precaution, just in case they found an older man to play the Doctor and needed a Jamie / Ian / Steven sort of backup for action sequences. Nobody is sure if the character of Harry Sullivan was created before or after Letts checked Ian Marter's availability (see "Carnival of Monsters", "Robot").

• The script stated that the Gompa - where Cho-Je and the boys did their non-stuff - was located in North Wales, not in Mortimer where the train station is. (The Hovercraft chase mentioned that the river involved was an upper reach of the Thames, consistent with the Buckinghamshire / Oxfordshire locations speculated on earlier in this book. Be that as it may, the finished story leaves out all such details and yet has the "comedy" characters speak with generic yokel accents.) The backstory had the Min-Dol-Lin retreat set up by exiled Tibetans fleeing the Chinese invasion in the late 50s. Lupton was the first European to join. (This seems improbable with all of the interest in things Eastern in the late 1960s, unless Lupton had come several years earlier and nobody spotted anything amiss.)

• Letts assembled a cast largely drawn from actors he'd worked with before, but also people who'd worked on Jon Pertwee Doctor Who stories; partly this was to avoid lengthy explanations, but also it was to make the star feel more comfortable during a troubling time. It's well-recorded that Pertwee was more withdrawn than usual during rehearsals, answering his fan-mail rather than socialising.

• The filming began with Elisabeth Sladen and Richard Franklin travelling from Mortimer BR station to the Gompa (Tidmarsh Manor provided the exteriors) and on the second day (12th of March), the epic chase filming began at the Membury airfield used in "The Daemons". The autogyro owner doubled for both Pertwee and John Dearth (who returned, in vision this time, after his scene-stealing voice-over as BOSS in "The Green Death"). Pertwee's back problems began to affect his work around the time of "The Green Death", though he persevered with painkillers and trusses - at least, as far as stunt-doubles would allow. Terry Walsh was also a trained masseur, and so took it upon himself to help (something Katy Manning and Roger Delgado had hitherto volunteered to do).

Often Pertwee would be in his dressing-room wearing hair-curlers and a "corset", leading to raised eyebrows. While filming at Marchant Barracks with the Wessex Regiment, a Sergeant walked in on him and yelled: "Bloody Hell! Doctor Who's a pooftah!"

The last two days saw the use of the hovercraft (for which Pertwee received a brief but thorough instruction before being allowed to operate one without crash-helmet or lifejacket). He stopped, on his way back get out of the wet costume and shower, to talk to children who had found his hotel. Letts recalls that any vehicle Pertwee hadn't already bought, he obtained shortly after this story ended.

• The new faces in the cast included two fairly new actors. John Kane (Tommy) had been Bottom in Peter Brook's almost-legendary 1970 production of A Midsummer Night's Dream (the one with the trapeze). This was, however, his first main television role, so John Levene took him under his wing (note that the "cured" Tommy speaks with an accent like Benton's). Later on, he provided scripts for the notoriously bland sitcom Terry and June and Thames' Aztec-themed children's drama The Feathered Serpent. (It wasn't just Aztec themed but "The Aztecs"-themed. The plot is that a benign Emperor thinks human sacrifice is wrong, but his evil High Priest - played by Patrick Troughton - has other ideas. And oh look!... George Cormack's in it.) To complete the circle, the actor who played Tonila in 1.6, "The Aztecs" is Walter Randall - whose last Doctor Who appearance is as the guard who zaps the Doctor and sends him to be webbed-up for dinner.

• The life insurance for Roger Delgado was a shambles, since he died in an unlicensed taxi. His widow, Kismet Delgado, was left in dire financial straits. Pertwee and his wife Ingeborg took care of some of the problem, whereas Letts arranged an Equity card so she could play Huath the spider-queen and get some money coming in while the legal hold-ups ran on. She went on to marry William Marlowe ("The Mind of Evil"; 12.5,

"Revenge of the Cybermen"). Gareth Hunt (Arak) was later a household name after *Upstairs, Downstairs* and *The New Avengers*, but he's best remembered for a series of instant coffee ads. (The same brand kept Peter Davison in work immediately after leaving *Doctor Who*, and later made Anthony Stewart Head famous here long before he was Giles on *Buffy*.)

• As most *Who* fans seem to know, Tom Baker was plucked from obscurity and bricklaying to be the Fourth Doctor. The details can be found in Volume IV, but it's worth mentioning that Bill Slater had just taken over from Shaun Sutton when the APB went out from the *Doctor Who* office for a watchable nutter. The decision had been made to make the first story of the new season not *just* in the same recording block as the previous one, but to run both productions more or less concurrently. (It's also worth pointing out that photos of Baker circa 1960 show him looking very like his shorter fellow ex-Merchant Seaman Tommy Steele...) Thus, Baker's first day of recording was whilst "Planet of the Spiders" was still being made. He had been presented to the world in a photocall with Pat Gorman as a Cyberman, but was still able to walk down the street unrecognised.

• "Boris" (the "walking" spider) became an emblematic effect. Mat Irvine appeared on many childrens' television programmes giving hints to young modelmakers, and frequently displayed Boris - partly to reassure people that it *was* a model. Lis Sladen wasn't too keen on spiders herself; Pertwee took steps to make her get on with the job by showing her the workings and making her touch each and every model spider. Irvine himself, of course, was later seen as one of the judges on *Robot Wars*. The Spiders were made inhouse (Ian Scoones again) but operated by the Barry Smith Theatre of Puppets. Letts hired them again for his productions of *The Invisible Man* and *Pinocchio* (the latter outraged parents by sticking to the book and not being cutesy Disney garbage).

• The episodes were recorded out of sequence, but more-or-less two per fortnight (on Tuesdays and Wednesdays). The Earth scenes were all done in the second block, the Metebelis scenes in the third and the lab scenes for the whole story in the first. Meanwhile, "Robot" began preparatory shooting (we can't say "filming" here as it was all done on VT - locations, effects and all) on the Saturday after the Earth scenes of episodes five

and six of "Spiders" (which were recorded along with Part One). Tom Baker, who'd already filmed his "arrival" on 2nd of April (along with all the other scenes in the UNIT lab), began in earnest on the 28th at the Wood Norton location where Pertwee had made his own debut in the role ("Spearhead from Space"). Courtney and Levine were able to shoot their location scenes for the later story (their contribution to the regeneration sequence being in the can), while Pertwee was squaring up to the Great One, reminiscing about Houdini and beating up Max Faulkner and Walter Randall.

Some doubt persisted as to Sladen's availability for both shoots, but the production team thought they could manage as a lot of the driving sequences needed a double (Sladen hadn't passed her test yet). There were also various hairstyle anomalies had to be ironed out - literally in Baker's case. The main snag, though, was Sladen's change of style when they remounted, nearly six months later, the scenes of the Robot picking up Sarah.

• A less successful effect involved the assault on the spider citadel. Even Letts admitted that the CSO wasn't up to snuff and the scenes were cut. This made Part Six under-run by about five minutes, hence the drastic re-configuration of the cliffhanger at the start of the episode. This wasn't the only one: the 'hai!' scene which ends Part Three, and is protractedly reprised in the next instalment, was filmed for Part Four. Part Three under-ran badly, and should have ended with Sarah's line 'sorry, Doctor'.

• It's alleged that "Planet of the Spiders" led to a nationwide outbeak of arachnophobia, but the main source for this is yet another religious-based anti-television pressure group. Information from the National Bureau of Statistics casts doubt that such a widespread fear occurred, not that Letts was at all upset at the free publicity the complaint generated.

All in all, this seems to be the result of a few publicity-seeking vicars who'd run out of Carpenters records to play backwards in the hope of finding things that sound a bit rude. There were a few letters of complaint from parents, who were mainly - it seems - the sort of people who thought the title "Planet of the Spiders" gave insufficient warning. The arachnophobes weren't the only ones with grievances, however. Angry Buddhists - if such a thing can be imagined - wrote letters of complaint to the *Radio Times* about all of this.

Letts patiently explained it all, rather condescendingly, which is why this story is sometimes regarded as "Buddhism 101".

• After this story, Richard Franklin returned to theatre. He became a familiar figure on the convention circuit in the 1980s and even had a panto-style play on the Edinburgh Fringe (which is where hopeful theatre companies and comedians go every August to be spotted - or so they hope) called *Recall UNIT, or the Great Tea-Bag Mystery*. He later got into local politics and ran for Parliament (see "Invasion of the Dinosaurs").

• Pertwee returned to the stage in a West End farce, and took over as host of a murder-mystery game-show, *Whodunnit!* (yes, everyone made the same joke) and continued with *The Navy Lark* and advertising voice-overs. He also took one of the crystals home as a souvenir for his young son Sean. A few years later, this was traded for a skateboard. By the time of his father's death, Sean Pertwee was already making a name for himself as a beefcake actor (1994's *Blue Juice* gave him higher billing than Ewan McGregor or Catherine Zeta Jones) and he's now one of the most in-demand voice-over artistes in advertising.

• Bizarrely, the week between Parts Two and Three saw an unexpected repeat of the omnibus of "The Sea Devils" (9.3). Then "Planet of the Spiders" was itself repeated three days after Christmas 1974, in a one-episode format, as a lead-in to 'Robot' - which began the next day. Golly, it was exciting!

• Jon Pertwee is the only Doctor to have had entries in either the *Guinness Book of Records* or the *Guinness Book of British Hit Singles*. The former was for the longest continuous mono-ski run, the latter was with a novelty record based on the theme for *Worzel Gummidge*. Although "Worzel's Song" only scraped the bottom of the Top 40, it earns him a place in the book, just above the Pet Shop Boys[143].

Worzel Gummidge was a children's book by Barbara Euphan Todd. It was first published in 1936 about a scarecrow who came to life; writers Keith Waterhouse and Willis Hall, creators of *Billy Liar*, adapted the original book in the early 70s and offered the part to Pertwee whilst he was saving the world from shop-dummies and spaghetti-men. Pertwee's enthusiasm got the project off the ground, and it first reached the screen in 1979.

Then when Southern (the ITV company who made the first run) lost their franchise, he found ways to get it relaunched in co-production as *Worzel Gummidge Down Under*. (It had already been established that he had an Australian cousin played by *Hancock* veteran Bill Kerr, for whom see 5.4, "The Enemy of the World".) This was easily his favourite role - he even arranged for a Worzel doll to be attached to his coffin when he was cremated. This series finally removed any typecasting Pertwee had to face, although his back pains interfered with work. He never thereafter took on a long-term part, but did things as diverse as play James Abbott McNeil Whistler in the prestigious arts series *Omnibus* (and when you see portraits of Whistler, you'll admit this is perfect casting), Death in an video-game version of one of Terry Pratchett's *Discworld* books, and a World War One air-ace in *Young Indiana Jones and the Attack of the Hawkmen*. Moreover, he was a regular on the convention circuit, telling tall tales and teasing about his alleged rivalry with Patrick Troughton. He appeared in many of the BBV video projects that provided apprenticeships for many of the people who later made the BBC Wales series. Although the painkillers occasionally made his life difficult, he continued working until mere weeks before his death, making an ad for mobile phones with Kyle McLachlan and a documentary about gourmets who eat insects. He also gave interviews for *DWM* that offer no hint that he thought he was ill. It was only two years before this that he gave up riding his motorbike.

Even in death, he managed to upstage his successors: Pertwee "crossed the void beyond the mind" just under a week before the first UK transmission of the Paul McGann TV Movie in 1996, thus ensuring that everyone was measuring that film against childhood memories.

the end notes

1 We don't know precisely why Pertwee spent so many Bank Holidays driving the wrong *faux* vintage car around fêtes, yet it's something everyone here remembers when you mention him. Photos of this exist - proving that it's not a misremembered Bessie - and posters advertising this team-up appeared in local newspapers. Many people are surprised to find that Pertwee wasn't in the film as they'd thought. Obviously, the car was a celebrity in its own right and needed a driver of similar stature - ideally someone who was associated with old cars that had surprises - but there were many other candidates.

2 Dennis Spooner, former *Who* story-editor, created the show as a possible answer to "who would investigate the Mary Celeste if it happened today?" He was obviously obsessed with this mystery, as 2.8, "The Chase" shows. So it had a New York cop, a mini-skirted boffinette and a flamboyant dandy novelist - yes, in velvet and frills with a vintage car - whose job was to think "outside the box" and get the girls. Unlike UNIT they had a regular UN contact, their "M" figure Sir Curtis Seretse (having a black authority figure reportedly made some US stations reluctant to show it). Jason King, the novelist, was played by Peter Wyngarde, who we'll see in 21.5, "Planet of Fire", and got his own show when Germans liked it enough to pay for him to drive around Paris being suave.

Spooner took the money and made the show as a wholesale joke at the expense of his gullible paymasters. Jason King was based on Churchill's special team of intelligence advisors, thriller writers like Dennis Wheatley and Ian Fleming. Note that Wheatley got Aleister Crowley into the War Office (see "The Daemons"), and that Fleming took note that the Elizabethan intelligence division hired John Dee, who gave himself the caballistically-derived code-name "007".

3 As is so often the case with Pertwee, there's a long and - frankly - implausible story attached. Essentially, Pertwee was attached to Military Intelligence (!) towards the end of the war and was sent to keep tabs on comic actor Eric Barker's allegedly seditious routines about the Admiralty. However, he made his presence known (Pertwee claims to have shouted "Hello, I'm a spy" from the audience) and wound up becoming part of that night's act, then traded a favourable report for a gig with Barker after the war - hence *Waterlogged Spa* and his reputation as the "funny voice" man.

4 It'll save time to say this now: most jobbing actors in those days were attached to local theatres. Thus, any one performer could be up to twenty characters in a year. (The usual practice was to perform for one week and rehearse the next part during the "off" week - this may be the origin of the theatrical superstitions about *Macbeth*, as hearing a guaranteed moneyspinner being unexpectedly rehearsed might mean that your less successful play was being yanked early, putting you out of a job for three weeks.) Many *Doctor Who* performers either began there, went back to it or took roles involving latex and built-up shoes to *avoid* going back to it. For some, it provided valuable training in adapting to unusual circumstances or keeping a straight face - Nicholas Courtney's unflappability in the face of eyepatch-related malarkey in "Inferno" is a testament to this. Most people saw it as a means to learn the craft quickly, then hand on what you'd learned to the next generation of hopefuls.

5 There was a hint that Michael Ferguson wrote the *Radio Times* piece when he was visiting in the run-up to 6.5, "The Seeds of Death", which makes the anomalous details of 7.3, "The Ambassadors of Death" interesting.

6 A regular route between Mars and Venus is almost a contradiction in terms. The two planets are orbiting the Sun at different distances, both in elliptical trajectories. At times it might be quicker and more fuel-efficient to go closer to the sun and out the other side to reach the target planet - as opposed to waiting for a convenient conjunction when they're at their nearest to one another, which would only happen about once every sixty years. But at other times, a slingshot past Earth might cut a few months off your travel time.

It's the same problem we encountered in "The Invisible Enemy" (15.2), when people were going from asteroid A to asteroid B willy-nilly, forgetting the huge cost in what they call "Delta V": the ability to change velocity and get out of gravity-wells (remember, "velocity" means speed and direction). Unless (as is usually posited in these sort of stories) the spaceships have magically efficient rockets that can go straight from planet to planet in no time, and don't need to worry about conserving fuel to get home again. Even then, you're probably dealing with space-warps within close proximity to populated planets and perilously near a star. Cut corners with stuff like that, and you find yourself 65 million years in the past making an appointment with destiny at the very end of the Cretaceous Age (19.6, "Earthshock"). We'll discuss a lot more of this sort of thing in the essay with 10.4, "Planet of the Daleks".

7   In the copy of *Doctor Who and the Day of the Daleks* being used as research material for this guidebook, the title 'in preparation' for a forthcoming novelisation is *Doctor Who and the Sea-Monsters*, making the parallel with the "Cave-Monsters" book more exact. We can date the later book more precisely with the internal illustrations, which are by the notorious Alan Willow and not the earlier Target illustrator, Chris Achilleos. These are marvellously evocative but also easy to recaption for comic effect, as fanzine editors have shown over the years.

8   So what *do* the early 70s taste like? Original-flavour Hula Hoops and Anglo-Bubbly, of course, washed down with Cresta - "It's frothy, man". We hope you can track these down and eat some before watching each story. We've tried it on experimental subjects to whom we've shown these stories, and found that even people who weren't born at the time get Proustian rushes and access buried memories of previous lives in the Nixon era. Don't have all three in our mouth at the same time, though, because that would be yucky.

9   If you've not seen either series, the parallels are interesting. *Secret Service* has professional gibberishmonger Stanley Unwin as a priest who speaks gobbledegook (rather as Pertwee had done in *Waterlogged Spa*), and who is secretly an agent for an organisation called B.I.S.H.O.P. Unwin, represented by a puppet version of himself for most scenes, dashes about in an old car that has been souped-up to go at 120mph. *UFO* is about the near-future - 1980 - and has a secret military organisation dedicated to defending Earth from

evil flying saucer creatures. The Moonbase set, or parts of it, will turn up throughout 70s *Doctor Who*. In that phase Gerry Anderson made a feature film (*Doppelganger*, AKA *Journey To the Far Side of the Sun*), with the devastatingly original premise about a parallel planet that's in the same orbit as Earth but hidden by the sun, and where everything is back-to-front. Perhaps we can be forgiving about this, as it's been *weeks* since anyone proposed this as a *Doctor Who* storyline. This film also had the Nehru-collar and de Laurean car aesthetic of *UFO*, and the whole near-future British space programme looked like what 7.3, "The Ambassadors of Death" was probably intended to be. It's even got Nicholas Courtney in it, at Mission Control. More by luck than judgement, the last three months of Season Seven wound up resembling a cheaper remake of this film, but without Barry Gray's usual bullfight music.

10   To tackle a myth that's manifested at times: the alleged pastiche of Procul Harem's 1967 hit *A Whiter Shade of Pale* (see also 22.6, "Revelation of the Daleks") wasn't an in-joke. Whilst showing a clip of docking with the real record - the sort of thing seen in retrospectives of the year 1967 - that piece wasn't actually used for the Apollo XI coverage. As might be expected, the BBC went with Richard Strauss, although Apollo VIII's Christmas extravaganza (see "The Invasion") had Pink Floyd's *Lucifer Sam* as its theme-tune. You'd think that going from a riff-heavy piece about a ship's cat with supernatural powers to Cliff Michelmore (the nation's collective uncle) talking about yaw manoeuvres and inertial guidance was the most absurd mis-match imaginable. However, Michelmore also presented *Holiday 72*, which used a version of the theme from *Shaft*. American readers might like to imagine Mr Rogers on Ritalin, then imagine him being the black private dick who's a sex-machine with all the chicks. The Floyd also jammed over the live feed of the approach to the Lunar surface, which might have backfired had the spaceship crashed or failed to leave orbit. Before you ask, the BBC wiped that tape too.

11   We mention this because in the opening scenes with Liz, as with later in "The Time Monster," they do a set-up where the Doctor is handed a cup of tea and returns it a few moments later without ever raising it to his mouth. It's pos-

sibly the case that he just forgets to drink because he's distracted with weighty matters, but the fact that it happens twice *and* Liz's baffled reaction (very funny, if you're looking for it), we might speculate that he's absorbing the tea as vapour, getting it to teleport into his body in keeping with the 'transmigration of object' scene.

You think this is far-fetched? In the second instance, he actually returns the cup to Jo and tells her, 'Thanks, I enjoyed that.' And when we *do* see him drinking tea, it's from from an enamelled tin mug ("The Time Monster" again and 11.2, "Invasion of the Dinosaurs"). Perhaps metal impedes his ability to stare tea into his body. UNIT tea, in particular, seems to be a lot more significant than we supposed - see 8.1, "Terror of the Autons" and many others. If we're further pursuing this line of thought, it's interesting that the Doctor's ninth regeneration is aided by the TARDIS drinking tea for him (X2.0, "The Christmas Invasion").

We'd refrain from mentioning all of this, but this otherwise random super-power can resolve several odd examples of the Doctor acquiring objects without us seeing it. For example, at the end of 14.3, "The Deadly Assassin", he says goodbye to Engin and Spandrell and departs, apparently leaving his coat and scarf in the museum cabinet. He can't pop back and ask for them without the Time Lords raising the Transduction barriers all over again, so how does he retrieve them, the sonic screwdriver and whatever else was in his pockets before meeting Leela? See also 10.4, "Planet of the Daleks".]

12 EA Sports have managed to programme their Playstation game *Fifa09* with simulacra of real-life commentators Clive Tyldesley and Andy Grey reacting to events more coherently and articulately than the originals. David Coleman, however, was the undisputed master of sports-commentary goofs, to the extent that the magazine *Private Eye* named its long-running column of mixed-metaphors, inanities and misused 'literally's "Colemanballs". However, it was his use of the phrase 'quite remarkable' to cover for when he had nothing to say that was most widely parodied.)

13 British readers have been expecting this comment since this story started... When dealing with John Abineri in a context when the word

'ambassadors' keeps cropping up, we have to acknowledge ads for Ferrero Rocher, long recognised as the cheesiest campaign of the 1990s. In these, he plays a butler who carries a tray of these nasty chocolates around a reception, to the delight of various mittel-European stereotypes. Nicholas Courtney was up for the same role.

14 We bite the bullet and here discuss a subject shameful to all who were in the country between 1964 and 1988...

Crossroads, created by Peter Ling and Hazel Adair (see 6.2, "The Mind Robber" and 20.4, "Terminus"), was the astoundingly inept and glacially slow soap made by ATV, possibly as a money-laundering or tax-evasion scam. Nobody will admit to watching it, but it ran and ran, providing work for struggling writers and actors with no shame. It was about a motel just outside Birmingham - see, if this could run for decades, you can just about image how *Triangle* (see 23.3, "Terror of the Vervoids") might have seemed like a good idea to someone. Even by 1966, it was notoriously the worst thing on telly.

Yet for better or worse, it *has* provided us with folklore. The woollen hats sported by Mike Nesmith in his Monkee days are known here as "Benny hats", after the dim but supposedly-loveable mechanic with the Mummerset accent who always wore one, and gave the soldiers a handy nickname for the Falkland Islanders they were supposed to be rescuing. Victoria Wood's *Acorn Antiques* is flagrantly based on it, with Amy Turtle becoming "Mrs Overall". Paul McCartney recorded a version of the theme - it's on the Wings album *Venus and Mars*, pop-pickers - and former producer Reg Grundy went to Australia with a burning desire to make something like it but cheaper. We all know where that led...

Anyway, Terrance Dicks began there and, in the process met Malcolm Hulke, Ling and Don Houghton, which might explain why the UNIT stories are so much more interdependent and have character "arcs" (see **Is Continuity A Complete Waste of Time?** under 22.1, "Attack of the Cybermen"). The motel burned down several times when they got desperate for a ratings-grabber (in one instance they dragged it out over five episodes - apparently nobody called the fire brigade). In one notorious incident, they appeared to kill off a major character played by someone whose private life was dominating the press coverage, then relented due to public pressure and produced a *deus ex machina* that makes Bobby Ewing in the shower seem worryingly plausible. As with *Dallas*, however, this stunt spelled the beginning of the end. They tried to go upmarket (with hilarious results), and only a few hardened fans mourned the ending.

Then in 2000, they tried to revive it for day-times, and the results were mesmerically wrong-headed. They took it off, retooled as something deliberately camp (this failed, and alienated those few of us who were still watching out of sheer dis-belief) before revealing in the last episode that the whole revival was a bizarre fantasy of Jane Asher's character Angel, who worked on the till in a supermarket. It would be nice to think that, if nothing else, this launched a few careers, but so far Freema Agyeman is the only casualty to have crawled from the wreckage - and even *she* was cited as a "newcomer" when she was introduced to the world as Martha. The top lesson that TV executives learned from this was that 60s and 70s revivals were more trouble than they were worth, and it was safer to stick to lame-brained quizzes and reality shows. Luckily for us and everyone reading this, BBC Wales weren't listening.

15 It's also written about as being called *Snowy White*, just to confuse the issue.

16 David Jacobs did the famous announce-ment "Jah-nay... intooooo Spaa-a-a-ace". In the last episode of the first series, he said, "...the part of the Venusian Time Traveller was played by Deryck Guyler". Maybe you have to be British for this to be funny, but it is.

17 Specifically, it was the Space Shuttle as orig-inally conceived before Nixon's cost-cutting demands bit into the plans. The shuttle we all know is a compromise and lacks the re-usable launch plane that took the smaller Orbiter to the right height. They wanted to get it off the ground before 1976, so they developed it quickly and did all sorts of stunts with jumbo-jets and the cast of *Star Trek*. Mustard was a three-stage delta-wing, with the two that weren't going into space being flown either by pilots or radio-control and possi-bly carrying enough surplus fuel to load up the Orbiter for a lunar orbital insertion. One design has all three stages identical, so they can be mass-produced and used in many combinations.

18 Somehow the idea that the first Englishman on the moon would eschew NASA's multi-million dollar bacon-flavoured toothpaste for Kendal Mint Cake seems irresistibly right.

19 Britain's use of the metric system seems to cause some confusion in America. Yes, we've adopted it for formal use and when talking about science, and yes, we weigh food in kilos these days - er, except when we don't - and yes, every-one has been taught it in schools since about 1970. But that doesn't mean we use it for every-thing. Distances are still given in miles and speeds in miles per hour, although the translation is often available. People are weighed in stones (the American thing of giving someone's weight in pounds is so unfamiliar here, we have to translate it into kilos and then into imperial measure-ments). Temperature is always in Celsius because - frankly - it makes a more handy mental image. (When the weather forecast gives a figure under ten, wear a coat; over twenty, shirtsleeves; over thirty, take drinks with you.) Milk bottles are in pints, but cartons or polythene jerry-cans are in litres.

And unlike decimal money, there was never a switchover-day announced, so generations differ slightly on their emphasis. Occasional scare-sto-ries in the tabloid press make it seem like we're going to be forced to use it, but that says more about tabloid paranoia about Europe (despite those papers being themselves foreign-owned) than about the EU or schools.

20 Although surely the most characteristic example - and yet another reason why it stands among the best stories in the whole of *Doctor Who* ever - is Simpson's decision to give the last scene of 17.2, "The City of Death" a *downward* chord progression into the theme to match the slow pull-out from the Doctor and Romana running away from the Place de la Concorde, as they go off into Paris for the holiday they intended to have when the story started.

21 So you'd go into Woolworths with 50p and look for an album you could afford, and there was something called "Top Space Themes or "TV Theme Bonanza". Geoff Love and his Orchestra would have a crack at *Battlestar Galactica* (the original one) or *Lost In Space* along with the easier ones such as *Star Wars*. Invariably there would be

a dreadful attempt at the *Doctor Who* theme using a soprano saxophone or Fender Stratocaster to do the main melody. Until Keff McCulloch, this was as bad a rendering of the tune as was imaginable. Other band leaders had a pop, as you'll recall from our comments in Volume II concerning Don Harper. Murray Gold's attempt to cudgel Ron Grainer's theme into a John Williams-ish shape is part of a long, sorry tradition.

22 Non-UK readers might want to notice the seemingly constant references to chips and beans on toast in the new series. As you probably know, chips are deep-fried sections of King Edward potatoes - not any old spud will do, and not in the flimsy toothpick-sized pieces that Americans call "French fries". But "beans on toast" seems to have caused a great deal of confusion. It's simple enough: heat the contents of a tin of baked beans (small haricot beans, like "Navy beans", usually in tomato sauce and sometimes with tiny sausages, but better not) and place them onto buttered toast. Marmite or HP sauce are optional, as is grated cheese (which can be melted into the beans if you want). Lots of iron, vitamins, protein and carbs in three minutes, and best eaten with the plate on your lap watching something like "Carnival of Monsters" or "Pyramids of Mars". Only posh kids had lamb cutlets.

23 People had such fun with that name. The best was the *Daily Express*' headline for his second journey, *Dr Fuchs Off to Antarctica Again*.

24 "Contra-terrene" was a phrase adopted by pioneer SF writer Jack Williamson in the 1930s for what is now called "anti-matter". However, he's also credited with popularising the term "Android", although Albertus Magnus (thirteenth-century scholar and alleged owner of the talking brazen head) is the supposed coiner of the word, so we have to ask why "CT" hasn't caught on the same way. It does, after all, suggest a moral dimension to this stuff other than just particles spinning the other way around, which is pretty much how *Doctor Who* has used the stuff.

25 This might sound strange to non-UK readers, but is entirely normal. To anyone from 1970s Britain, the idea is that a little old lady goes around with a trolley, oblivious to what's happening around her, like in any ministry or major company. The very last Virgin *Doctor Who* book, *The Well-Mannered War,* has one wandering around a battlefield. It's proverbially the lowest job in any firm - see, if you can stomach it, Hugh Grant as the Prime Minister in *Love, Actually*, being smitten by Martine McCutcheon. Forget Steven Seagal in *Under Siege* and think of how American offices use the mail-cart and the water-cooler. Combine these functions on a trolley with biscuits, toast and an urn full of char, pushed around by a lady (generally of mature years) with flat heels and a hairnet, or a lad straight out of school.

Studies repeatedly show that offices with this arrangement work better and reduce sick-leave, as the tea-lady's arrival breaks up the working day and provides gossip, whip-rounds and - for people working in basements or secret government installations miles underground - a clue as to what the weather's like. See 11.2, "Invasion of the Dinosaurs" for more on that. They often did the cleaning as well - see 10.5, "The Green Death" for Pertwee dressing as one. *Torchwood* has Ianto Jones, an all-purpose Mr Fixit who makes coffee and does things with stopwatches, but compare their success-rate and *esprit de corps* with 70s UNIT - and note that it's around the time that Sergeant Benton takes over the refreshment duties that Mike Yates goes mad and starts trying to kill his colleagues. Mind you, he prefers cocoa anyway.

26 (Err... actually, Pop Art began as the British response to US culture, then was co-opted by people in New York. Led by Richard Hamilton and Eduardo Paolozzi, the first wave exhibited in 1956 at the Whitechapel Art Gallery's *This Is Tomorrow*. Peter Blake, Derek Bolshier, Pauline Boty and Peter Phillips had the prestigious *Monitor* BBC series given over entirely to them in a film introduced by Sir Huw Wheldon, but directed by Ken Russell, in 1962. By that time, along had come Warhol and that lot. The original Pop Artists all became lecturers and their pupils included David Bowie, Ian Dury, Pete Townsend and Bryan Ferry, so there's a definite connection.

27 *Top of the Form* was the most anachronistic children's programme of the era. It had begun in the 1950s on radio, back when schools were divided into "forms" instead of "years", and had well-scrubbed youngsters answering questions on classic books, trigonometry and geography whilst

wearing school uniforms with caps and clinging to stuffed toys called "Gonks": a Dutch fad imported around the time of Beatlemania. Humpty from *Play School* was the nation's most famous Gonk and they had their own novelty record - a remix of which is under the end credits of *Shaun of the Dead*. We would suggest a look at freakish British Pop Musical *Gonks Go Beat*, but don't. Seriously, don't.

28 He's in a Third Programme production of *King Lear*. It was broadcast on 5th of September, 1967. What makes this interesting is that Paul McCartney has just read about John Cage's Zen experiments in composition and aleatory influences - i.e. trusting to luck and including something random - and has decided that one of the pieces of a sound-collage they're doing to end one of John Lennon's similarly opaque new songs should be a feed from whatever's on the radio when they're mixing. Listen carefully to the last few moments of *I Am the Walrus*...

29 It wasn't a sister's birthday but an unexpected abduction by Boy Scouts: *Three Times a Lady* by The Commodores - a merciful relief in the summer of *Grease*; O-Level Computer Studies (which meant learning to read punched paper-tape and program in CECIL and BASIC - the latter of which was months later); not telling; thinking of the phrase "author's parachute".

30 If you've read Volume VI you'll be dying to know... that's the same Lord Boothby who's alleged to have been shagging the Prime Minister's wife at the same time. See X1.4, "Aliens of London" for a sly acknowledgement of this sort of thing. Incidentally, Ronnie wasn't politically biased; Boothby was a Tory but Ronnie also supposedly slept with Labour minister Tom Driberg. There's no evidence that he ever hallucinated a giant hedgehog called Spiny Norman, but his friendships with Judy Garland and Frank Sinatra shouldn't come as too big a surprise.

31 The first, the two-parter *Now You See It, Now You Don't* has a sinister scientist played by Christopher Benjamin - Sir Keith from 7.4, "Inferno", Jago in 14.6, "The Talons of Weng-Chiang" and Colonel Hugh in X4.07, "The Unicorn and the Wasp" - and location filming in a nuclear power station. The second, *The Nightmare*

Gas, has people killed by their own phobias, but in a more prolonged method including vivid hallucinations that taxed even Thames' proficiency with ChromaKey. In both cases, the baddies lived in bohemian pads - Falk (Benjamin's character) had a TARDIS-like houseboat; Thalia, the nasty lady with the gas, had a converted windmill rigged with tripwire-activated cameras to detect Tarot's motorbike. Whether either had a garage with an electronic key is unknown. And whether the wiping of *Ace of Wands* Series Two is a bigger loss than *Doctor Who* Season Three is a debate that has run throughout *Who* fandom for decades, and will only end if both are found.

32 Apparently, another prison visit was needed; an anecdote doing the rounds has it that the person contracted to do the prison uniforms was himself locked up, and Bobi Bartlett needed to go and ask him where he'd put the material. This seems a little too good to be true, so we've asked around. It appears that it's another case of two stories being conflated, which is a shame.

33 Little did we know, when we wrote this in the original edition of this volume, that people would give us such a hard time for this one throwaway comment. The wise ones who pore over the minutiae of the filming schedule solemnly informed us that no studio filming was documented and this was down to location footage shot at dusk with the hazy crepuscular sky looking like a blue screen.

Except that the two different scenes where this is apparent - Filer's arrival in episode one, and Yates and Benton battling Axon monsters in episode four - were filmed on different days with different weather conditions: thick fog for the Filer scene on 4th of January and persistent rain for the Axon / Land Rover stuff. The background in the close-ups is the same and doesn't look like either. With a camera crew *that* experienced, it's improbable they would have attempted to light shots like that on locations, even in the first week of January when the sun sets at 4.00pm. They had enough difficulty with the shot of the Axon walking around Dungeness A's aerial corridor (the one they show at half-speed but obviously didn't film that way). It makes even less sense when you see how light it is when they blow up the vehicle.

We've seen these clips in extreme slow-motion on DVD and there are artefacts in the corners of some shots that could be clouds or wrinkles in a backdrop, but nothing unambiguously a result of location filming. Moreover, we know that Michael Ferguson was keen to try new ways of doing things with CSO, and indeed a special experimental session was booked for 22nd of December to try out a number of exciting / innovative / harebrained ideas, as **The Lore** explores. Combining blue-screens with film and back-projection was on the agenda.

Had such a technique come off, the rest of this book might have included some very different memorable scenes, but film and CSO never mixed happily, despite the best efforts of the *Monty Python* directors. However, the one day set aside for studio work was (apparently) reallocated for location-work to make up time for the weather-afflicted location schedule.

34 Obvious to *us*, anyway: if you've somehow avoided seeing *Hong Kong Phooey*, it might be too hard to explain. If you have but never made the connection before, you'll now take Venusian Aikido, the flying car scene from 11.5, "Planet of the Spiders", and Corporal Bell a lot less seriously, although Benton beginning each sentence with "Ooh! Ooh!" might have been an improvement. What if the Doctor wasn't really UNIT's scientific advisor, but just Pertwee the Mild Mannered Janitor?

35 A persistent account claims the Chernobyl disaster occurred because they used a candle to inspect wiring when the power was switched off, then forgot it. With all the hullabaloo about building more nuclear reactors as a means of bringing down greenhouse emissions, one hopes that engineers have made the new models candle-proof.

36 Incidentally, the word Marc Bolan says 2:14 into the song isn't, as far as we know, "Torchwood" but probably "Touchwood", the name of Catweazel's familiar, a toad.

37 Namely Keith Floyd. British readers will be thinking now of Floyd - a flamboyant, boozy TV chef - in a sitcom like unto *Get Some In*, a Tony Selby vehicle from the late 70s about National Service in the late 50s. Floyd in such a setting is quite amazingly wrong - imagine Tom Baker playing Bilko and you're halfway there. Overseas readers will have to accept that Jamie Oliver and

Gordon Ramsay are only the *least* freakish of our TV chefs, which is why we're less concerned with other people seeing them.

38 The answer is: he was an astronaut on the first manned flight into space (British, of course). The idea of "The Right Stuff" took a while to permeate here.

39 This conjures up the wonderful image of Ozzy Osbourne forgetting that he's moved out and blundering into the lab just as Cho-Je starts the Doctor's regeneration. "Liberty Hall, Mr Osbourne...". If he, or whichever rocker owned the place, had only leased it and still popped in occasionally, it would explain the Brig's memory-lapses. Inhaling close to a seventies musician would invariably have adverse effects.

40 These days, when you describe *Billy the Cat and Katy* to anyone, they look at you oddly. Nobody in 1970s Britain thought that rubber-clad, whip-wielding nine-year-olds with strange masks and high boots was in any way kinky. Or, at any rate, as odd as anyone old enough to make the connection still reading *The Beano*.

41 Achilleos' covers soon developed their own identity, still very much influenced by comic imagery - see 11.2, "Invasion of the Dinosaurs" for the obvious example - but every time he threatened to leave, Target's response was always to get on the phone to see if Bellamy was available to replace him. Achilleos was hugely popular with Target readers but couldn't cope with the demanding schedule; significantly, he was only able to make the break just after Bellamy's death in 1976.

42 We'd better get this out of the way, as they'll be mentioned a lot later. In the books by Elizabeth Beresford, these are small furry beings who collect the litter on Wimbledon Common and use it for their burrows. The five-minute animated puppet show, beginning in 1973, simplified the stories but confirmed voice-artist Bernard Cribbins as a national treasure (see B4, "Dalek Invasion Earth 2150 AD"; X4.0, "Voyage of the Damned" et seq. and 11.5, "Planet of the Spiders").

The series was a hit, and Mike Batt's annoyingly catchy theme was released as a single. Then it got a bit silly, as people in Womble costumes promoted the single - think of the Yeti (5.2, "The Abominable Snowmen") with hats and scarves and glasses, then add Gibson flying-V guitars. Inside the costumes were many famous and "credible" musicians who loved the idea of going on *Top of the Pops* without anyone knowing it was them and accusing them of selling out.

Then there was a follow-up single, the even-catchier *Remember You're A Womble*, then another, then another... then a film was made, not with stop motion but with the suits (dry-cleaned) and Bonnie Langford. There was a new series in 2003 with different actors (rather than just one doing *all* the voices), but that vanished. Most recently, Cribbins has done the voices for a protest about the curtailment of Children's television in the UK, and the reliance on imports and co-productions that Americanise everything for export, entitled *The Bad-Ass Wombles of Central Park*.

43 British fans have made this joke for decades, but then in X3.11, "Utopia", it turned out that the Master had gone undercover as Mr Kipling - the fictitious maker of 'Exceedingly good cakes' from the long-running ads - and built a spaceship from toffee. Suddenly, sending the Ogrons to steal flour from the Earth freighter in 10.3, "Frontier in Space" fits into a pattern.

44 This might, just, perhaps, maybe, possibly be very clever indeed. Assuming that Mac Hulke was as much of a jackdaw in his reading as his scripts and novelisations indicate, it's conceivable that he knew that the Arabic version of Adam was called "Ash". In which case, his having a daughter called "Mary" is skipping a whole Testament.

45 It was a rewrite of *Night Flight* by Bert Janch's folk-rock outfit Pentangle. Seriously, if you've heard it once, you'll be humming "bay-bap-pa-doo-dah/bay-bap-pa-doo-dah dah" all bloody week. Download it if you don't believe us. They did a sequel, *Take Three Women*, in 1982 just to cement it in our heads. Nobody can remember anything about the plots, just the song.

46 Victorian fast-food, invented by 1960s ad-men: it's a hunk of fresh-baked bread, with as thick a crust as you think you can manage (you'll have to wrench this apart by hand); butter, ideal-ly salted, to melt onto the bread and ameliorate the forthcoming strong flavours; a lump of proper

cheese that tastes of something, ideally cheddar or stilton, the size of your fist; a pickle or two, if possible home-made and a bit tart, either piccalilli or apple-chutney - commercially-bought stuff like Branston if you're slumming - and if you feel up to it, a pickled onion or two; optional salad or coleslaw. Some places have some kind of rural sausage, a Cumberland or a Lincolnshire or the dreaded Black Pudding, but this misses the point. Originally that was "buy more cheese", then "get back in touch with your roots (of at least an approximation of them)", and now it's "I haven't got time to wait for my microwaved vegetarian lasagne". Wash all of this down with some kind of ale, even if it's only ginger.

47 We can confirm part of this. After the first Fan Olympiad, the *Who* fan version of Glasto, a party of us went to the Tor on 6th of January. The Glastonbury Thorn was just in flower, which means that miracles respect the change of calendar in 1753, even if *Doctor Who* dating doesn't.

48 As it turned out, this was even more exciting from the purely scientific view, and the "nothing" was found to include grass and ants that simply shouldn't have been there. In the 1968 dig, the only real find was a few snail-shells (dating the construction of the hill to long before the Bronze age, ergo before any gold). This was itself interesting, just not very spectacular.

The thing is, it was a lot older than anyone thought - Mesolithic rather than Bronze Age - and wasn't built as a barrow at all. Essentially, Silbury Hill was a man-made geographical feature, intended to be seen from miles away (especially when covered with chalk) to act as a staging post of some kind, probably on pilgrimages to various other nearby stone circles. As with most such objects, remember that whatever the reason for doing it, it mattered enough for people to get their act together and coordinate a complicated logistical exercise over generations. In many ways, that's harder for people today to get their heads around than the idea of aliens coming for no good reason and tagging their handles across the West Country.

49 The novelisation claims that Doctor's gadget is, like so many Pertwee-era contraptions, 'analogous to the Laser', so presumably the idea is to arrange the heat energy into a nice coherent stream of infra-red photons. All those photons, in a nice tight beam, have to be sent to somewhere else. It would make a very effective weapon, so maybe the Doctor doesn't want the Brigadier to listen too closely when he explains it all. In fact, if Osgood blabs to anyone - like, say, Miss Winters (12.1, "Robot") - Britain will have a phenomenally-advanced ray-gun by 1975, and there'd be no need for North Sea Oil, Axonite or Bateson's Polymerisation (13.1, "Terror of the Zygons"; 8.3, "The Claws of Axos"; "The Green Death", and many other Pertwee era stories about the need for new energy sources).

Of course, since that was written the idea of using lasers to cool things has developed in a totally different direction, resulting in the 1997 Nobel Prize for Physics. This isn't the place for a detailed explanation of how that works but remember all the stuff about quantum jumps between atomic shells in **Why Are Elements So Weird In Space?** (see 22.2, "Vengeance on Varos") and ponder where the energy to make an electron jump might come from. They can get rubidium down to a fraction of a degree above Absolute Zero by getting the atoms to absorb exactly the right coloured light.

50 We are reliably informed that Americans generally don't know it. Weird. It's a jaunty little piece called *Barwick Green* by Arthur Wood and after being broadcast twice a day, six days a week for fifty-eight years, it must be etched into the collective consciousness of the planet by now. Molluscs probably know it, so you have no excuse. It's almost impossible to hear without breaking into a dopey grin, even if you happen to be foreign. The irritating music for irritating yokel Pigbin Josh has plausibly been suggested to be an inept parody of this - it was possibly changed for legal reasons, or maybe because you simply don't mock an institution like *that* without a much better reason. Josh's bizarre monologue might be a backhanded tribute to Ambridge legend Walter "ooh-arr me old pal me old beauty" Gabriel (see 6.6, "The Space Pirates"). Billy Connolly, speculating that the reason we never win anything in the Olympics is our National Anthem being such a dirge that we're all disincentivised, proposed that we should adopt the *Archers* theme instead. It has, he said, the big advantage that everyone knows the words: "tum-ti-tum-ti-tum-ti-tum, tum-ti-tum-ti-taaa-daaa". There was a recent fuss when Brian Eno was asked to remix it. You tamper with such things at your peril.

51 Another piece of fundamental BBC culture: *Dad's Army* was a sitcom about a real piece of social history, wherein the threat of Nazi invasion in 1939 led to men rejected for active service through age or infirmity being turned into a last-ditch civil defence force, the Home Guard. A small town in the most vulnerable part of Kent is a microcosm of 40s Britain, and the obvious slapstick potential is offset by having people putting their lives on the line for values that are also the source of all the character-humour. A self-important bank-manager puts himself in charge, with his aristocratic but louche assistant as a wonderfully vague 2-I-C but the real tension is with regional command trying to make them more "professional", i.e. more like the stereotypes of the Germans they are fighting. The series produced a lot of quotable lines, one of which is (apparently) in the forthcoming *Star Trek* prequel, and lots more are in Paul Cornell's *New Adventures* book *No Future*. Incidentally, although Arthur Lowe's performance as Captain Mainwaring is part of the national consciousness, he only got the part because Pertwee turned it down after making a successful pilot. Or so Pertwee claimed. There's no evidence that any such pilot episode was even made.

52 'Five rounds rapid'.

53 Since you ask... *The Wild and the Willing*, VT *Young and Willing*, stars Ian McShane as an "Angry Young Man" - terribly fashionable in 1962 - who gets drunk a lot and seduces his professor's wife. It's the sort of film you expect Rita Tushingham to be in, but she isn't. Lots of promising youngsters play the other students (John Hurt, Jeremy Brett, Samatha Eggar, Denise Coffey) and the script, from Sloman and Laurence Doble's play *The Tinker*, was adapted by Mordecai Richler and directed by Ralph Thomas. It has a brilliantly period poster - lurid and prim at once - and still gets churned out as an afternoon filler, especially on Australian TV.

54 Non-British readers will be unaware of this person (a comedian whose chaotic private life is far funnier than his material) who effectively killed off the most successful game-show in British TV history when he hosted *The Generation*

Game. He also, bizarrely, appears opposite Ken Campbell and Geoffrey Palmer in Peter Greenaway's *A Zed and Two Noughts*.

55 And there we were, very proud of ourselves for thinking of this, when the second story of *The Sarah Jane Adventures* did something oddly similar. There ain't no justice!

56 In the spirit of Sherlock Holmes and Thomas Hardy, we propose that if the BBC are making this series as dramatised reconstructions of real events with the names changed - so that Slimbridge becomes "Minsbridge" and Warminster is "Tarminster" and so on - then the more-recent (all right, mid-1980s) publication of a paper suggesting a limit on temporal paradoxes is the true Onlie Begetter, and that really we're talking about the Novikov Self-Consistency Principle. It's real, look it up!

57 Three or so months earlier, however, the former chief of the military, Marshal Lin Piao, was killed in a plane crash en route to Moscow. Whilst Mao seemed to think that his enemy's enemy might be a friend, not all in Beijing agreed. We now know that Kissinger was in China at around the same time. It has since emerged that he gave the Chinese a briefing on Soviet deployments on the Chinese border that was so secret, not even senior US spooks knew about it.

58 At almost exactly the same time as this story aired (3rd of Jan to 9th of Feb), there was a six-part serial, *Man Dog*, with a remarkably similar premise except that the eponymous "man-dog" was one of the fugitive time travellers with his mind hidden inside the body of the kids' Border Collie. The series has been shown in the US, but never released commercially here. Clearly, something was in the air at BBC television.

59 James Cameron let slip that he took inspiration for *Terminator* from two *Outer Limits* episodes ("Soldier" and "Demon with the Glass Hand") by Harlan Ellison. A settlement entailing cash and credit to Ellison occurred after he threatened to sue.

60 Apparently, her birth certificate has "Gypsy" and she changed to "Sarah". If you spent the mid-80s in Britain or Australia, you will now be imagining all sorts of bizarre "accidents" that might have befallen Corporal Bell so that Charlie could get her job, and UNIT's new radio operator pouring martinis and addressing the PM and various Geneva bigwigs as "*dahlin*'".

61 And do things with Sticky Backed Plastic. To correct an erroneous footnote in Volume IV, the term "sticky backed plastic" referred to a product called Fablon, which was an adhesive vinyl with various textures - wood effect, *faux* brick and so on - used in DIY to cover chipboard. In the early 70s, everyone's dad had tried to make a cabinet or shelf with this stuff. There was also a transparent model used for cheap laminating of photographs or covering your school textbooks with wallpaper or posters of pop stars / footballers / Katy Manning (as everyone was obliged to at the start of the school year, for reasons nobody ever quite explained). Sellotape was always referred to as "sticky tape" or even "Sellotape". It was Thames' cheap and tawdry *Blue Peter* clone, *Magpie*, that got into trouble for product promotion. By *not* naming it, *Blue Peter* was allowed to exhibit endless faith in Fablon's ability to turn corrugated cardboard boxes into Barbie-Doll kitchens, of the sort you might pay several pounds for in the shops.

62 In the original, Pollox the dog was the British, hence his prodigious consumption of sugar-lumps. Flappy the rabbit was the Spanish, with guitar and *mañana* attitude; the Germans were a clumsy cow; the French peasant farmers a snail with a cheroot; the Dutch had beards and trikes and grew lettuce; the Belgians had pointy heads and clogs and ran the barrel-organ and the eponymous roundabout; and so on. Eric Thompson, *Play School* presenter and one of the cast of "The Massacre" (3.5), re-dubbed it without any idea what the original stories were, so just made up characters for the various figures based on what he could see. Hence Dougal, the dog, was a self-important busybody based on Tony Hancock. His antagonist was, logically, a snail who talked a bit like Sid James, less so as time passed. The rabbit was renamed "Dylan", and like, talked in a drawl, man. Ermintrude the cow was very cheerful and called everyone "dear heart" - think of Miss Hawthorne from "The Daemons".

All of these, and Florence (the girl who seems to have been the "everyman" figure in the original) simply accepted the odd situations - except for Dougal, who got irate and tried to take control. And the situations *were* odd. So everyone these days thinks of it as being all a big druggy allegory, and they made a godawful CGI film version with many drastically wrong voice-artistes - Tom Baker, hang your head! - and many more in the even wronger American version, retitled *Doogal*. This ought to be an insult, but having a title that distances this abomination from the Thompson classic is actually a relief.

The original for Ermintrude - Thompson's widow, Phyllida Law - was considered for the part of Barbara Wright. She never got around to doing *Who*, but was the elderly home resident who knows something about aliens in *The Sarah Jane Adventures* story "Eye of the Gorgon". The originals for Florence are their two daughters, one of whom got an Oscar for *Sense and Sensibility*.

63 Fans of non-skeddo spin-off audios will know that there's a BBV CD of the same title, featuring Sophie Aldred as not-Ace-at-all, honest, dealing with issues concerning her mum. Antagonising the author of a Very Famous Book is a silly thing to do, although thus far, it seems, they've been below Doubleday Books' radar.

64 People berate us for calling the post- 2005 episodes "Welsh", as if that were an insult. Anyone who's been in Wales when a new episode is transmitted will have heard the pride in the BBC Wales announcer's voice as he or she says "... and now, made in Wales, *Doctor Who*." As we'll explain in Volume VII, this is a significant factor in the new version's success. Given a choice between pretending that everything up to 1989 was some kind of preamble to the "real" series (or dismissing the new ones for being the work of a bunch of forty-somethings trying to recapture their fading youth) and calling the new one "Welsh", we'll stick with the latter.

65 The present author of this book has taught the children of such people, and has become used to being called "Mr Ood". He doesn't look anything like Zoidberg, however.

66 A controversial but intriguing possibility is that the corpus callosum, the linkage between cerebral hemispheres, has developed since we started doing this.

67 Typically, they were trying something that legitimate SF authors had done better half a century before, and acting like they'd invented something radically new and exciting. Check out the use of typography in the names of characters in Alfred Bester's *The Demolished Man* to see how it should be done. The exclamation-mark thing is derived from the Bantu language of southern Africa and is a glottal click. It's terribly Aaronovitch-y and right on, but tends to make everyone sound like they've got hiccoughs. Hip young rock band *!!!* failed to make an impact with their debut album a couple of years back, because nobody could file it alphabetically or ask for it in record shops without sounding like a dolphin.

68 All right, we'll buy this as a running gag for X4.2, "The Fires of Pompeii", but was the nuclear power station in X1.11, "Boom Town" really called 'Lupus Malus'?

69 Fans of long silly names will know that there's at least one Welsh railway station worth mentioning at this point: In Anglesey, an island off the north of Wales there's a place called Llanfairpwllgwyngyllgogerychwyrndrobwllllan tysiliogogogoch. See, suddenly the Jagrafess' full name doesn't seem so challenging.

Generations of British schoolkids have tried to learn how to say this and show off, making it more remarkable when Jane Fonda uses it as the secret password in *Barbarella*. Of course, there are lots of Welsh place-names with "Llanfair" at the start - see 10.5, "The Green Death" - but the locals just call this place "Llanfair PG" and have done with it.

70 About six weeks earlier, BBC viewers saw an episode entitled "The Baddies", wherein Our Inept Heroes battle evil android duplicates of themselves, as constructed by Patrick Troughton. The fight resembles both 7.1, "Spearhead from Space" and 13.4, "The Android Invasion", but played for laughs and actually slightly more scary. The number of people who appeared in both *The Goodies* and *Doctor Who* is smaller than it seems once you start totting it up, but the cultural-reference cross-over is immense. If you've read *all* the **Where Does This Come From?** items in this book, you should get a lot of the jokes, although Moira Anderson will remain a mystery. To be honest, we never understood her appeal ourselves.

71 See also 11.2, "Invasion of the Dinosaurs" in connection with the stand-out Goodies episode, "Kitten Kong". If UNIT *is* in the same world that has the Scoutfinder General and a world shortage of string leading to vest-piracy, it would explains the presence of a Radio 1 DJ being an unwelcome intrusion to a mayday call. The *real* surprise, though, is that it's neither Tony Blackburn nor *The Archers*.

72 Barry Letts spent ages in his radio scripts in the 1990s clarifying this line, believing that as neutrons are, well, neutral, they can't have a polarity. Of course they can't but any atomic physicist, indeed anyone who knows basic English, will tell you that a *flow* of neutrons can have a direction. At least one real-life French physicist has asked why the translator was so amused by this concept.

73 Most ancient cultures have someone coming out of the sea to teach them how to write. The Egyptians have Thoth, who swam from the West; a lot of those "Did God Come From A Flying Saucer To Teach Us Cricket?" books of the early 70s claimed he was an Atlantean. In China, a turtle-man gave the world the hexagrams of the I Ching (see 18.5, "Warriors' Gate"), but the God of Literacy - Wen-Chang (see, um, 14.6, "The Talons of Weng Chiang") - has a dwarvish sidekick, Kui-Xing, who arrived on the head of a turtle and oversees exams and bureaucracy.

74 Err... not wishing to get all fan-fictionish here, but wouldn't Shura and / or Daleks blowing up Sir Reg and his house-guests result in a war that ends with the Master putting into place whatever plan he intended to follow the previous World Peace Conference being disrupted by Thunderbolt and panto dragons (8.2, "The Mind of Evil")? The Dalek timeline is notable for the absence of any hint of the Master. With all the continuity references in stories of this period, it's a remarkable omission.

75 We have to mention this somewhere: just as one rogue Time Agent from the fifty-first century picks up the name of a serving officer who died shortly before the Agent's arrival and became "Captain Jack Harkness", so we have to worry that the boss of HMS *Seasprite*, Captain John Hart, will be the victim of identity-theft when someone completely and utterly unlike Spike from *Buffy* turns up in Cardiff.

76 Horribly bland piece, theme from a horribly bland TV series called *Owen MD* which had Nigel Stock - Professor Hayter in 19.7, "Time-Flight" - in a misguided coals-to-Newcastle attempt to make a Welsh *Doctor Finlay's Casebook*. A lot of *Who* personnel paid the rent by working on this negligible show.

77 We're really keeping our fingers crossed for this to be returned to the archives for use as a DVD extra. *Television Club* is fondly remembered, especially the one on Pop Music that has been frequently plundered by nostalgia-show compilers for amusing clips of its presenter, Dave Freeland, responding with more than usual enthusiasm to Slade performing *Cum On Feel the Noize*. After this apparent seizure he is accused of needing pop music "like a drug", and his reaction didn't go as far above the heads of the nation's eight-year-olds as they might have hoped. All anyone can remember of the episode "Putting On a Show", which is like the Sea Devil version of *Doctor Who Confidential*, is that John Friedlander, the monster mask-maker, made remarkably little sense. Apart from the content's obvious appeal, this is well-remembered because the BBC took account of the way different schools took Half-Term breaks on different weeks by repeating the entire week's schools TV output. As Schools' TV would have been the only thing on at that hour of the day other than the test-card, far more people saw it.

78 American readers will need to be told that this isn't *quite* the same thing as a trailer-park. Although the mobile homes are laid out in rows in both cases, the object of a caravan site is to provide low-cost holidays for people who don't want the whole Holiday Camp experience - see 4.7, "The Macra Terror". More than anything else this shows the British attitude to holidays; if you're used to having everything laid on, or are accustomed to pitching a tent where you want to be and doing absolutely everything for yourself, caravan parks can be the most depressing places on Earth. But if you embrace the sheer strangeness of this limbo existence, they magically become marginally less miserable than being stuck in traffic for six days. This is holidaying for people who assume that it's going to be wet and everything interesting will be shut.

79 The most common reaction to the last two episodes of *Torchwood* Series One - to a *lot* of *Torchwood* stories, actually - was "What do you have to do to get fired?" The Torchwood crew certainly seem to shoot at each other a lot, when they're not putting Earth in danger through stunts like dating a Cyberman and releasing plagues to prove a point.

80 But compare this with X1.11, "Boom Town", in which Jack spends a whole day in Cardiff with the TARDIS right on top of where we later discover the Hub was built. We know this, because the "invisibility" of the Hub's secret exit uses the fact that the TARDIS was there when the Time Rift was re-opened. And we later discover that Jack's been working for them for a while, to get to meet the Doctor again next time he refuels. So either two Jacks were in central Cardiff that day (with a third asleep in the fridge since 1901; *Torchwood* 2.13, "Exit Wounds") or the later one made a point to leave town for a bit. (Not implausible, but he'd need to take his colleagues along, lest the the earlier Jack have baffling conversations with strangers who claim to work for him.

81 Annoying children's entertainers who gave Russell T Davies an early break. What's odd is that BBC1 repeated the 2004 series of *Chucklevision* on Thursdays in November / December 2006, meaning we'd get a new *Torchwood* on cable channel BBC3 on Sundays, then a terrestrial showing on BBC2 on Wednesdays, and *then* a *Chucklevision* episode with almost exactly the same premise on Thursdays. Sometimes, as with *Torchwood* 1.5, "Small Worlds" and the Chuckle Brothers episode about Garden Gnomes, the kid's version was actually creepier. The "Countrycide" analogue, where cannibals put them in a cooking pot, is only marginally more offensive and rather more plausible. One or two duplications would be amusing, but six weeks running looks suspicious. Then they announced that for Christmas 2007, they were doing a stage-show where they go hunting for ghosts...

82 We say "most viewers", but the abrupt slump in the ratings alerts us to something significant: this is the Pertwee story that practically nobody in the UK, even within fandom, remembered being shown until the novelisation came out several years later. Amongst fans, the majority of stories (good bad or atrocious) have some kind of anecdote as to what we were doing when watching... but not this one. It seems that no matter how high the ratings - or how low - the ones that got repeated whilst Pertwee was still in office are the ones that stuck, certainly amongst the British Public at large.

And this makes us ask: does the public memory require a second coating, like varnishing a fence? Maybe if Ky had been given the real *aide-memoire,* a Weetabix Card of his very own, things would have been different.

83 British readers under thirty only know him as a freelance curmudgeon on the exasperating *Grumpy Old Men* (half an hour of ageing minor celebrities mouthing off about the new coins being too fiddly, kids today don't know they're born, when I were a lad shoes were rationed so you only got one each...) and overseas readers might not know him at all. We'll begin by saying that in 1972 he went from being a session keyboardist (Bowie's *Hunky Dory*, Cat Stevens' "Morning Has Broken", the theme from *Ask Aspel*) to being the quintessential 70 Prog-rock oaf. As a member of Yes, he compensated for keyboards not being very visually exciting by dressing as a wizard and waving his magic hat and tinfoil batwing cloak during the month-long solos. Then he *became* a solo and went a bit nuts, producing pompous concept albums that turned into ludicrous stage-shows. It got into a bit of an arms-race with Emerson, Lake and Palmer (op cit) and Genesis - the front-man of the latter, Peter Gabriel, vied to outdo Wakeman's preposterous costumes and ponced about on stage dressed as a marigold or with giant papier-mache genitalia. This is why Punk happened.

84 Although it got proposed every so often. The nearest it came was in 1928, when the Mayor of Cardiff wanted legal sanction against the sailors and their children. *Torchwood* is only the latest manifestation of this city's xenophobia.

85 Just as in the 1930s, when literature had made the whole palaver of Empire a subject for regret and the cause of domestic angst, Hollywood filled India with Americans running the place for us. *Lives of a Bengal Lancer*, one of Hitler's favourite films, starred Gary Cooper because the producers thought an Englishman doing exciting Imperial

things in the Raj would be implausible for American audiences. Similarly, Errol Flynn was in *Gunga Din* and *Kim*. Raj-westerns and their post-war African counterparts are expressly to suit American idea of themselves as defending liberty while the British are stuffy, effete and yet, some-how, running a brutal and rapacious Empire.

86   Aye, ye ken: the bagpipes got to Number One, keeping Judy Collins' version - a bigger hit overseas - well away, and inadvertently inspiring the climax to *Star Trek II: The Wrath of Khan*. It also made *Top of the Pops* look odder than ever.

87   Not that it hadn't happened before; the film *The Brain Eaters* (1958) cheerfully recycled Shostakovich's Fifth Symphony but passed it off as the work of one "Tom Jonson". Why they did this - when US law wouldn't have allowed a plagiarism suit from a Soviet citizen - is a mystery, moreso when you look at all the other films that have (putting it delicately) "borrowed" his music with-out asking. *Stargate* is the climax of the Stalingrad Symphony to ten decimal places. Similarly, Ralph Vaughn Williams couldn't have foreseen that the opening of his Sixth Symphony was to become known to millions of fans of *The Two Ronnies* as the theme for "The Phantom Raspberry Blower", nor that by this stage it had become a classic of stock-music used for any melodramatic occur-rence in cheap serials. Kubrick, at least, sort of expected you to know the music and pick up on its associations.

88   This gives us an excuse to settle another thing a lot of British readers of a certain vintage have written in to ask: the theme from *Picture Box* was one of theirs, a track entitled *Manège*, which gets scarier in the bits we didn't hear. Other read-ers will have to accept that we were all dragged out of classrooms to wherever the school TV set was located, and forced to watch a series with a scary theme and an even scarier presenter in a shirt scarier than both combined, who introduced short films of various degrees of worthiness and mind-bending hallucinatory qualities. Lotte Reineger and Norman MacLaren's animations fea-tured prominently, a fact we appreciate rather more now. Those albums were on CD once, but good luck tracking them down now.

89   If you don't know, these were devices that had a bank of tape-loops with play-heads arranged as a keyboard, so you can play a chord of flutes or whatever - the intro to *Strawberry Fields Forever* is the most famous example. The fun came when the flute-sounds were replaced by other noises.

90   That album came at the last possible point where tape-splice techniques and monophonic synthesizers could happily coexist and owes more to the Radiophonic Workshop's 60s output than is commonly acknowledged. The montage of voic-es or cash-registers could be Delia Derbyshire's radio theme tunes. If you think it's coincidence, put on the earlier album *Meddle*, find "One of These Days" and wait two and a half minutes.

91   One of the most noticeable features about the selections on side one of the album *BBC Radiophonic Workshop - 21 Years* (not available on CD as yet) is that the whole of the BBC wanted something from them. As the production-line nature of this developed in the mid-60s, some-thing becomes apparent about the use of appro-priate found sound. Milking cows needs a sound-track? Use the suction devices as a bass-riff. A let-ters section for a radio show? Doorbells. The har-monics of whatever they sourced the basic "instruments" from didn't change as the sped-up or slowed-down versions of the original recorded sound shifted pitch. A piece for BBC Radio Sheffield, played on steel cutlery, sounds more melancholy than an ice-cream van for this reason. It's a jaunty little piece in C, but something's wrong.

In a conventionally recorded-piece that was played on an instrument made of forks of various sizes (look, it might have happened; John Cage had a lot of fans with money), the melodic line would be the same, but the relationship of the harmonics to every other instrument's sounds would be different to what the Workshop pro-duced. A sampled fork-twang would also lack the piquancy in the higher registers, as it's the lower harmonics being brought up into audible registers that do the damage, and a sample on 16 bit recording would miss those. This gives a lot of these pieces a bittersweet timbre that the com-posers know how to exploit through years of prac-tice. The next generation of Workshop employees never quite get to learn this but develop other skills. If you didn't know, the first emulator - the Fairlight CMI - was developed by someone who was such a fan that he gave one of the first production models to the Workshop around their 25th Anniversary in 1983.

92 Really, it was only about one in twenty and we soon learned to keep quiet about it.

93 We await George Lucas' next attempt to make us buy films we've already got in a dozen formats, wherein all Hayden Christiansen's dialogue is redubbed by Dave Prowse in Pigbinese.

94 You will have noticed a "strange British early 70s Horror film" theme in this story's background notes, which is inevitable for any disquisition on life in the UK in the Pertwee era. Most of the same anxieties and images you'll find in *Doctor Who* - especially in this period - are mined and sexed-up by Hammer Films and their rivals, and the "arms race" between these and what the major studios have been resorting to just to keep audiences leads to some downright bizarre phenomena, often using the same actors. Check out *Vampire Circus*. It's a bit like 18.1, "The Leisure Hive", but kinky and with a plot instead of technobabble. Or *Death Line*, which we mentioned under 5.5, "The Web of Fear" - you might know it as *Raw Meat*, by the way - which accidentally conveys exactly how it felt to be in Britain during the Three Day Week. As for *The Legend of the Seven Golden Vampires*...

95 An earlier edition of this book, and a piece in *DWM* by their "cultural" writer "Philip MacDonald", claims that this is the same character as in *Julius Caesar* who goes on about the Ides of March. But in truth, this guy is an Egyptian who tells Charmian the entire plot in code in Act I scene I, then tells Antony - director, star and co-adaptor Charlton Heston (him again) - that it's a good time to distance himself from Caesar. Paul Cornell committed a similar error in *Timewyrm: Revelation*. What's really galling is that the relationship between Cleopatra and her doting servant Charmian is obviously where Sloman lifted the whole Galleia / Lakis business. So this means that there is not, in fact, a role played by both Pertwee and Delgado, although the latter was cast in Carol Reed's film *The Running Man* as "Spanish Doctor", which suggests to those raised on 1970s

superhero comics the sort of set-up like the Mexican version of Batman.

96 Here we should remind readers that the first assertive feminist *moment* in the Pertwee era was in 7.2, "Doctor Who and the Silurians", when Pertwee himself intervened to have Caroline John given a boiler-suit and tin hat rather than the scripted idea of Liz going spelunking in a miniskirt and heels.

97 Levene's ability to pull girls apparently caused a lot of resentment, especially for a frustrated actor chum of his called Anthony Hopkins. Allegedly.

98 Tragically, the name "Wessex University" has come back to haunt us in the hilariously naff *Bonekickers*. It's possible that this might have been forgotten by the time this book sees print, but we shouldn't let the BBC off the hook for attempting to make an archaeology-action show that was like *Primeval* without the dinosaurs. Many of the guilty parties were connected with the BBC Wales *Doctor Who*, so we shall doubtless return to this in a later volume.

99 This sort of thing was clearly in the air. Watch, if you think you can handle it, John Boorman's extraordinary contribution to the early 70s odd SF flick canon, *Zardoz*, wherein a parody of the Wizard of Oz flies around Ireland in a giant stone Blake head. People reluctant to admit they haven't read as much as they pretend call this sort of thing "pretentious" and "wilfully obscure", but it's really rather too obvious.

100 Vedic Sanskrit has it as a spiritual throat-clearing, to precede prayers by purging the individual of Pride or Ambition and meaning something like "Hail" or "Amen". Puranic Hinduism uses it to denote their Holy Trinity, Vishnu, Shiva and Brahma, and is thus connected with the cycle of creation, destruction and preservation-through-meditation / dance / willpower. Saying the word can liberate a spirit from the material body. For the Advaita school, it represents three-into-one (oho!) and the breakdown of the boundary between knower and what is to be known. (Aha! We doubt that Bob 'n' Dave knew this, however.) The Upanishads claim that contemplation of this syllable - which they take to represent and in

some ways *be* a state of non-existence - will cleanse the essence of the person chanting it, allowing true freedom after death. All agree that the word is in and of itself powerful (not least because of the breath control it requires to get it *exactly* right). Which of these Professor Wagg intended in the TV Movie (27.0) is unclear.

101 Black holes are the maximum-entropy objects par excellence. Eventually it was worked out that the entropy of a black hole is 1/4 the area of the event horizon, if you're interested. If you're not, then you probably won't want to know how they reconciled this with the Law of the Conservation of Energy. It's easy: the mass / energy is on a one-way trip, but never gets there. The nearer it gets to this hypothetical hole in the Universe, the slower time goes. It's Xeno's paradox to the rescue! These days Hawking suggests the cosmos *in toto*, all the hypothetical add-on extras, parallel universes and D-branes and whatever, can be treated as a whole and thus Conservation still applies. Not everyone buys this, though.

102 Russell T Davies turned 10 the day before "Planet of the Daleks" episode four aired. See how this works?

103 Between 1965 and 1975, the UK singles sales were higher than those of the US. To even break into the Top 50 required selling more in a week than the Spice Girls did at the peak of their popularity and getting into the Top 20 (which was the only chart regularly published) needed sales in excess of what Kylie shifts in a year. Essentially, anything even moderately successful then was more popular than almost anything now. The Top 20 listings for the first three Doctors are therefore a more accurate barometer of what the intended audience liked than any other, and omitting this listing from Volumes I and II was a grave error. If you've been downloading... we mean, *borrowing* the suggested hits, you'll have a handle on early 70s Britain in ways that textbooks or documentaries either get wrong on purpose or don't think to include. Nothing quite replaces having been here at the time, but this will at least help get you asking the right questions.

British popular culture is bigger on the inside than it is on the outside, and even a five-year slice through the Top 20 provides a number of possible narratives. With the sheer volume of material out there, it's tempting to go for pre-packaged sources, but these of necessity leave out any inconvenient details that don't chime with whatever story they're trying to tell. That caveat about trusting any one source includes this book, obviously, but our story is one *about* the details that got forgotten. Great or grotty, this music is what Joe Public wanted then. We've aimed to include tracks that couldn't have been hits even a month earlier or later among the alleged "classics". If you can find video footage, ideally from *ToTP* or its "grown-up" equivalent, *The Old Grey Whistle Test,* so much the better.

In addition to the **What Was In The Charts?** listings and others mentioned along the way, we suggest three records / clips to sum up the era: *Leader of the Gang* by G*ry Gl*tt*r is pretty much a given, if you can find it these days. But before starting the first story we recommend CCS's version of *Whole Lotta Love*, a section of which is *the* theme for *Top of the Pops* the way the Tom Baker "tunnel" and Derbyshire version of the theme is *the* title-sequence for *Doctor Who*. (YouTube currently has a couple of extraordinarily pungent examples of the *ToTP* titles using this, from 29th of April, 1971, and 15th of November, 1973, including some amusingly inept dancing and bewildering juxtapositions in the charts [Gerry Monroe and the Plastic Ono Band, Bob Dylan and Alvin Stardust...]. We've also managed to source clips for all but two of the songs selected, although a couple are frustratingly static.) Then at the end of "Planet of the Spiders", we suggest the music that just misses it but sums up the valedictory feel of post-Glam: "Saturday Gigs", Mott the Hoople's farewell single. It seems to be about the Pertwee era more than about themselves. But remember, this is only the start...

104 It's not, as is usually stated, the 1977 *Morecambe and Wise* Christmas Special (see 9.1, "Day of the Daleks"). That comes in at No. 11, just ahead of an edition of *Sale of the Century* - see 26.3, "The Curse of Fenric" - and just below the Mike Yarwood Christmas show, screened just ten minutes before Eric and Ernie's '77 festive bash.

105 For benefit of overseas readers, we should mention that Westlife were one of about 150 identical boy-bands in the charts five years ago. You'd be hard-put to find anyone who can remember more than three of their singles, even their fans.

106 It's interesting to note that two sitcoms commissioned at the same time - long before any inkling that Israel was going to be attacked - treated this theme differently. *Whatever Happened to the Likely Lads* was a sequel to a 60s hit and showed one of the two main characters settling down with a mortgage, long hair and a wife who was keen to escape the working-class past of Newcastle. The other lead, returning to Britain after six years in the Army, watched the demolition of his old neighbourhoods and the "poncy" Southern values invading his old home town with undisguised dismay. We're meant to side with the latter, as the melancholy theme song suggests: "Tomorrow's almost over / today went by so fast / is the only thing to look forward to / the past?"

Starting at almost the same time was a vehicle for Jon Pertwee's *Navy Lark* co-star Leslie Phillips, *Casanova 73*, wherein the suave ladykiller attempted to keep up with the times and was amusingly in denial about being too old for this sort of thing. It was a sort of pre-watershed version of the *Confessions* films - if you don't know, don't bother to ask, there's a book to be written there. Whilst many middle-aged men could *just* about get away with early 70s male fashions - look at Pertwee off-set - the need to squeeze into hipsters was literally a bind for a lot of others. Phillips' caddish behaviour was suddenly out of keeping with the public taste, so his show was never repeated, whereas BBC2 still occasionally airs Bob and Terry's misadventures in Newcastle. (See 21.4, "Resurrection of the Daleks" for more on Rodney Bewes.)

107 Sadly, this book is written by the kind of person who knows these things. Anne-Marie David was Luxemburg's second consecutive winner, which is why they couldn't afford to hold the 1974 contest; Abba won it in Brighton. She sang the dreary "You Will Recognise Yourself" and beat the abysmal but funny Cliff Richard effort "Power to All Our Friends" by six points. Chelsea won the first Cup Final to go to a replay. When Thursday's replay ended, they'd beaten the plucky underdogs Leeds United (led by Billy Bremner, a scot for whom the word "feisty", in its original and current meaning, might have been invented), hence drivel such as *Blue Is The Colour* making the charts.

Miss Grenada, Jennifer Hosten, won the Miss World competition, but Bob Hope's attempt to announce this was was marred by a group of Women's Libbers chucking flour-bombs at him. South Africa fielded two contestants, one of each race ("Miss Africa, South" is a period phrase to warm the heart), so a Caribbean girl winning against the hotly-tipped Sweden was doubly amusing. BobHope pops up again as one of the guests on Earl Mountbatten's *This Is Your Life*, shown just two years before the last Viceroy of India was blown up by the IRA.

108 Like the one we all had in the school library by Willy Ley, seen in the titles of *Napoleon Dynamite* - see "The Wheel in Space" (5.7).

109 There's a whole social history connected to this, but we don't feel up to it right now. Suffice it to say that the "Cockerel" involved is the logo of Tottenham Hotspur FC. They attract bad records, as the *oeuvre* of Chas 'n' Dave proves. If you don't know about Chas 'n' Dave, you'll definitely not thank us for introducing you to their work.

110 *Moonbase 3* has as good a claim as anything else to be considered to be the first "adult" *Doctor Who* spin-off. Apart from Letts producing, Dicks script-editing, Dudley Simpson doing the music and an awful lot of the same designers and other ancillary staff, the series' entire ethos is like a gloomier *Who*.

It's set in 2003, when Europe has the "other" base, after the yanks and the commies - both presented as rather naïve and arrogant - and nothing rules it out as belonging to the same (sorry about this) "universe" as the ostensibly near-future UNIT stories like "The Ambassadors of Death". The one thing everyone who's seen it remarks on is that every single episode ends with a suicide... save for the last one, where they think that Earth's been destroyed and opt to leave some record of who the human race were before doing a Jonestown to avoid a slow lingering death from suffocation. They're rescued by BBC Radio coming through and the happy discovery that it wasn't a nuclear war after all, just a bit of fog. The idea that the sound of Ed "Stewpot" Stewart would restore someone's will to live is, to say the least, unusual.

James Burke acted as scientific advisor, and the attention to detail on the minutiae made it all the more annoying that the big things were so crashingly wrong that a nine-year-old (the one who grew up and wrote this book, at least) could spot most of them. The ratings started off healthy (it was shown in the slot vacated by *The Brothers* - see Volume VI for Colin Baker and Kate O'Mara - on Sundays at 7.20), but took a steep nose-dive. Letts was reported to be less than pleased when the long-lost tapes were rediscovered in the early 90s, and the series released on VHS. To be honest, it was less disappointing than *Doomwatch*, and the idea that the US and Soviet bases would be better-resourced and less under the cosh when it came to justifying their existence rings true today, even if there isn't a Soviet Union any more.

The show's basic theme, that a harsh environment requires everyone to drop petty "issues" and concentrate on keeping everyone else alive, is a healthy corrective to the near-magical technological solutions to everyday problems presented in *Star Trek*. It was simultaneously much more like real space-stations would be like and closer to the overall *Doctor Who* approach to SF. Compared to a lot of proposed or actual new series thrust at us in the wake of the 2005 series, something similar to *Moonbase 3* would be worth a try now. If nothing else it's got more laughs than *Hyperdrive*, albeit mainly for Ralph Bates' ow-you-say, atrocious fronsh ox-hent.

111 His typically wild and widescreen book *The Weapon Shops of Isher* has one of these musing to his colleague, in a manner resembling nothing so much as the prologue to *It's a Wonderful Life*, about humanity's potential. It ends with the memorable line, "Surely this is the race that shall rule the Sevagram." The trouble is, nobody in the entire book has ever *mentioned* a Sevagram. In a bid to end with a zoom out and a gasp-inducing vertiginous change of scale, he merely makes everyone go back and check to find if a page has fallen out. Incidentally, a Sevagram is a real thing - and if you look it up you'll find a surprising and probably accidental connection with a major critic of British imperialism...

112 Dick Seaton gets to the end of the second book and realises that Uranium might be a better power-source than copper. By this time his arch-rival Blacky Duquesne has gone from being Dick Dastardly to Ming the Merciless. It's hard to read his dialogue without imagining Anthony Ainley saying those lines. Worth a look just so you get all the jokes in Harry Harrison's *Star Smashers of the Galaxy Rangers*. See the essay with "Planet of the Daleks" for more in this vein.

113 For benefit of non-UK residents, he was the British soldier who helped establish the dominance of the East India Company, and aided in the creation of British India. Traditionally remembered as "Clive of India", he was hardly the heroic figure pre-War textbooks said he was. See the opening chapter of David Whitaker's 1965 novelisation *Doctor Who and the Crusaders* for an example of how he used to be discussed.

114 If you don't know where the term comes from, it's a song about the British resolve to, supposedly, "save" the Crimea from Russian expansionism. The pretext was defending the Greeks from an attempt to co-opt all Orthodox worship under Tsar Alexander, which he really was doing but only to get his hand on some Black Sea ports and start naval expansion into the Mediterranean and grab Suez. In fact - as all but the most blind or cynical British analysts admitted - the whole point was, as the song had it, "The Bear shall not have Constantinople." With typically Victorian doublethink, the chorus began "Oh we don't want to fight but, by Jingo, if we do / We've got the men, we've got the ships, we've got the money too". The whole affair was squalid and nobody comes out of it particularly well, so we've chosen to remember it as either knitwear or a prime example of what happens when you let inbred aristocrats run an army.

115 This might seem at first like the paradox of slums in London when the Empire was at its height. However, the various Education Acts made it possible to get out of these, especially once suburbs and public transport began, and one of the great ironies of World War I was that fewer young men were lost to the conflict than during the previous four year period when millions had emigrated to Dominions and Colonies. The restrictions on travel overseas caused by Kaiser Bill's torpedoes, plus the inevitable spike in the birth rate after a war, arrested a downward population trend.

116 Not as difficult as one might think. At least two associates of Mad Norwegian Press, back in the days when they had no programme guides, links to fandom or Internet at their disposal, didn't notice that an episode was missing from the Public Television broadcasts. Episode Three is fairly self-contained, and the "join" between the

surrounding episodes is no more awkward than a lot of the PBS compilations.

117 We'd better clarify: a "classic serial" was the official designation for an adapted book made to go out either at Sunday teatime or in a special high-profile slot, not a label attached years later. Americans might know some of these from Public Television showings as *Masterpiece Theatre*, but for us they were never labelled as such on screen or in the *Radio Times*. They were just shown on the understanding that if it was Sunday and there was a version of a Dickens or a Robert Louis Stevenson novel, it was probably by the same team that did the one last year or six months ago. Some of these found relatively unknown books and launched them onto the British viewers - few if any of us had read *Anne of Green Gables* before 1972's version. The ones that *weren't* family-friendly got either Wednesday at 9.00pm on BBC2 or Sunday after bedtime - *I, Claudius* was repeated on BBC1 after the BBC2 broadcast, and viewership increased unexpectedly.

By the late 70s, the family ones were a well-oiled machine and run by a team consisting of producer Terrance Dicks and script editor / director Barry Letts, with a few other familiar names cropping up here and there.

118 Sorry to get snarky, but one does have to wonder at times. In particular, we can't help but note how *A Teaspoon and an Open Mind* makes a stab at resolving the Hartnell titles controversy - see **What Are These Stories Really Called?** under 3.2, "Mission to the Unknown" - by telling us in its first footnote that the first episode was simply called *Doctor Who - Episode One*. Incidentally, don't bother looking for an entry on (say) telebiogenesis in this book, as the whole thing suspiciously looks like it's just notes on items the author has heard are mentioned in *Doctor Who*, as culled from Wikipedia and Carl Sagan books but slightly reworded.

119 It's a fizzy orange liquid that propels the Lensmen through ultra-space. British readers are even now thinking: "Made in Scotland from Girders." American readers will have to imagine a mix of syrup and root beer that's been advertised since the 1930s as having properties akin to Popeye's spinach. It's called "Irn Bru", but don't let that put you off.

120 Anyone who owns an original copy of the book might also like to consider the illustration on page 58, which appears to show a giant security guard playing with a Jon Pertwee action figure. Page 36 shows someone being subjected to "The Ghosts of N-Space".

121 With groundbreaking, never-heard-before electronic sounds by Dave Vorhaus that are oddly familiar to anyone who's seen - and listened to - episode one of 6.2, "The Mind Robber". See 7.4, "Inferno" for why.

122 Not all animals; the ones with souls almost as good as ours, like lions and donkeys, turn into bees. Check out the illustration on the tins of Tate and Lyle's Golden Syrup, if you don't believe it: it comes with a quotation from the Old Testament, where Samson proclaims "out of strength came sweetness".

123 1973 was the boom year for packets of dried brown things. If you had a lot of money there was Vesta packet curry (with the authentic Indian flavour of dried peas and monosodium glutamate) but for everyone else there was packet soup. Children tried to say the slogan *Chef square-shaped soups show how a good soup should be* but ate Knorr soup instead. It tasted almost identical to Vesta Chow Mein. Then there was Batchelor's Savoury Rice, which tasted of burnt Marmite. We could go on like this for ages, and often do if you let us.

124 Unlike the US release, the single was the uncut album version, allegedly because nobody at the BBC knew what "giving head" meant. Yeah, right: more likely nobody was going to be the first to *admit* to knowing...

125 Katy and Christopher Biggins play the children of a thinly-disguised Mary Whitehouse - see Volume IV - whose organisation is one of four who've funded a movie on condition that it's wholesome. One of the other donors wants something moderately smutty, and another wants real hardcore stuff. (By 70s comedy standards, this was only a notch above the stuff they cut out of US transmissions of *The Benny Hill Show*, but showed at primetime here.) It also stars Roy Kinnear and a load of comedy / character actors you don't expect to see in this sort of thing, but

that was the British Film Industry circa 1975 for you. The idea that *Star Wars* began filming in the same sound-stage that was still being used for the end of *Confessions of a Taxi Driver* is hilarious.

126 Still going strong and available to watch on the BBC Wales website. If you can get to see this, and have never heard Welsh before, you are in for a disorientating experience. Non-British readers might like to contemplate that the break-out star, Ioan Gruffudd, was in this show for seven years before *Hornblower* made him famous elsewhere. Bear this in mind when watching him as Mr Fantastic in the *Fantastic Four* movies.

127 Poulson sued people who said he was a crook. Nothing was proved, and his gifts to clients were generous but not outrageous. But this meant that when a play with a thinly disguised version of the architect was adapted for television, it had to be kept on ice until Poulson died. By the time *Our Friends in the North* reached the screen, the whole project became an epic. It also meant that promising youngsters Christopher Eccleston and Daniel Craig were the right age for career-making casting. Even if these two *weren't* in it, we'd recommend a look at this series to get some idea of how it felt to be in Britain in the period that the *About Time* books cover.

128 As many of you have pointed out, we completely forgot the most obvious reference to real-life politics in 70s *Who*: in *Terry Nation's Dalek Special* (Target, 1979). There was a reprint of a story, "The Secret Invasion", first published in *The Evening News* in late 1974. This is, amazingly, the first original fiction - i.e. not a novelisation of a televised adventure, not that it was especially inspired - published by Target books. In this, children were begged to save London from the Skaorine horde by Prime Minister Harold Wilson and Home Secretary Roy Jenkins. Needless to say, the real hero of the hour was one "Major Tarrant".

129 Anyone who doubts that *Dawson's Creek* is a suitable US analogue for *Doctor Who* should note that the characters seem to speak Pip and Jane Baker's idea of natural teenage dialogue.)

130 This means that the tapes for each episode must have been driven to Cardiff every week. Wouldn't it be funny if the much-sought-after colour version of "Invasion of the Dinosaurs" Part One was right under the new production team's noses...

131 Some have wondered if it's supposed to echo "Galilee", but apart from the old word for a hodge-podge ("Gallimaufry") it also sounds enough like "Galfredus", the alternative name for Geoffrey of Monmouth to be interesting. The proposal Holmes wrote had Linx identifying the Doctor as one of the tribe of "Galfreg". Galfredus is the main source for a lot of what was thought to be historical "fact" in the late middle ages - such as the life of Arthur, the founding of "Troynovaunt" (London) by the grandson of Aeneas, and thus a link with Troy *and* Rome and the giants Gog and Magog (see 16.3, "The Stones of Blood"). If the Doctor knew Bede and Shakespeare, he probably knew Geoffrey.

132 Now you're all trying to imagine "Genesis of the Daleks" with Fulton McKay as the Doctor, Michelle Dotrice as Sarah and an archer in woolly long-johns instead of Harry. Stop it at once.

133 As this book won't see the light of day until after *Primeawful* Series Two airs in the US, we can get away with pointing out that the big plot twist is that the temporal anomalies are caused by crazed eco-protesters. As the cliffhanger to the Series One was the Gordon Ramsay-like hero metaphorically treading on a butterfly and erasing his love-interest from history (a move that helped to ditch some annoying characters without recasting), we can assume that the show-makers hold the belief that viewers will regard this as a blindingly original turn of events.

134 At time of writing, the Restoration Team that handles the *Doctor Who* DVDs seems to have ruled against including CGI dinos as an option when this story sees release, on the grounds that *Primeval* spent *huge* sums of cash to produce entirely unconvincing dinosaurs, only just better than the ones that the BBC made in 1974 at a fraction of the cost. More to the point, the worst effects in "Dinos" are the ones with humans CSO'd into the shot, so it would take vastly more time and effort to rejig these than just to make new electronic lizards. So it becomes a question of whether the viewer wants ridiculous-looking puppet dinosaurs or ridiculous-looking CGI

dinosaurs, and the former is assuredly cheaper. The Restoration Team is, at least, hopeful that they can recolourise episode one.

135 It's unseemly to gloat, but the announcement that *Star Trek: Enterprise* was getting a mercy-killing just as they had *finally* started making some interesting storylines came the same weekend as we heard that BBC Wales was making a new series of defunct 60s kid's show *Doctor Who*. Anyone who didn't know that *Primeval's* Hannah Spearitt was in 1999's attempt to do *The Monkees* - the same S-Club 7 who made one of the most self-conscious pop-group-Vs-evil-manager films since *Slade in Flame* - probably thinks Billie Piper's most famous for her acting.

136 It's theoretically possible to re-create late-70s Royal Shakespeare Company productions using poseable action figures. Similarly, the one good thing about the BBC *Robin Hood* they're showing in the Saturday teatime slot that should by rights belong to *us* is that there's a Keith Allen doll, so you can remake *Shallow Grave* as a Punch and Judy show.

137 Seriously, this seems to have been the idea all along. Now you're all thinking of Squidward from *Spongebob Squarepants*.

138 It's the curious incident of the Royal Hunting Beast that didn't bark in the night... all those other guidebooks who claim that this and the other Peladon yarn are plundered from *Star Trek* and specifically the episode "Journey to Babel" should have tried to account for why the detail of the ginger-pig-men having their dilithium robbed out by smugglers, which was the ostensible reason for Spock's dad to be framed for killing one of the ginger-pig-men, isn't mentioned here. It's so amazingly obvious a plot, Terrance Dicks would have leapt on it in his hurry to rewrite this story into submission. In fact, its absence makes the storyline of "The Monster of Peladon" almost so cumbersome that you could make a case that someone was trying very hard indeed to avoid nicking anything from that *Trek* segment, or indeed "The Cloud Miners". (An episode so trite in its handling of industrial relations, Ettis and Gebek seem to have sprung from the pages of Zola's *Germinale* by comparison.)
The point is that anyone making up a story like

this from scratch would almost inevitably play up on the Gold Rush aspect of the story and have Trisilicate-smugglers - from the same author of 4.1, "The Smugglers", no less - so this is suspicious by its absence. It's a strange bit of logic, to think that if they don't mention something from *Star Trek*, ergo it's a rip-off of *Star Trek*.

139 The Woman With The Purple Dress is a figure in fan folklore whose reputation rests on her apparently not appearing after the Ice Warriors arrive. In fact she's lurking in the final episode, but not obviously. The various theories include her being a fiendishly-disguised Martian, a very annoying person whose horrible dress was the real reason the Ice Warriors invaded, one of many vengeful future incarnations of Susan who narrowly missed getting her own back for being dumped with the Scottish pig-farmer (just one of several regenerations who supposedly pop up throughout the series) and even the Peladonian Simon Bolivar, who was the *real* liberator of her people while the Doctor was getting his rocks off beating up a few miners. In *The New Adventures* sequel *Legacy*, in which Gary Russell namechecks half of fandom, she's named as Lianna and survives being blown up along with Queen Thalira... only to be impaled with a spear in such a way as to pin the crime on the Doctor and a talking hamster. The hamster is personally named after one of the *Doctor Who Adventures* staff, and his species owes to one of the people who went to Seville dressed as Shockeye - see 22.4, "The Two Doctors".

140 A road-safety campaign that has all the hallmarks of having had too many educational psychologists on the committee. Even if Pertwee could pronounce the letter "S", it would have been daft. We quote the ad directly, but imagine it in his voice for maximum comic effect:
"First find a safe place and Stop. Stand on the Pavement, near the kerb, Look for traffic and listen. If there is no traffic Near, walk straight across the road. Keep looking and listening for traffic while you cross. SPLINK!" Need we add that any Americans following this advice should be aware that "pavement" is what we have at the side of roads, the paved bit you call "sidewalks"? Mysteriously the campaign was tried again, in a Pertwee-less animated version where a cartoon of *Play School* presenter Derek Griffiths formed the

letters with his body - something the *real* Griffiths could have done cheaper and more memorably. Now go back and read our comments on Dave Prowse under 9.5, "The Time Monster". It's a miracle any of us survived to be nostalgic without his help.

141 Regularly enough, it must be said, by the mid-80s for Kate Bush to assume the record-buying public would recognise a sample from it at the start of *The Hounds of Love*. It was Mr Meek - one of those character actors you always thought would turn up in *Doctor Who* some time. Just in case this seems circumstantial, the full-length UK release edition, what we'd call a Director's Cut, has a trip to Stonehenge and a lot more of the séance and rural magicking, as per "The Daemons".

142 As far as we can work out, his apparent knowledge of future events is largely down to Tommy having a little chat off-camera. It might be the case that, as with the Watcher, Cho-Je is able to brief K'anpo on the events leading up to the regeneration, in which case Cho-Je knows everything up to Old K'anpo's apparent death. If this is the case, he can't know about the Great One's destruction. If, on the other hand, he's now so attuned to the universe that he knows all future events, then he has the destruction of great chunks of the universe when Logopolis is destroyed *and* the Time War on his conscience, all as a consequence of holding back and letting the Doctor learn from his mistakes. Shanti.

143 It's his only *official* chart entry, but listen carefully to the Boilerhouse Mix of "Can I Kick It?" by A Tribe Called Quest. He's been sampled doing one of his voices, saying "Mnyerr... you can" and "Then kindly do so at once" at various stages, at least on early versions before lawyers got involved. In the era of Rave, circa 1987-1992, Pertwee-sampling was something of a growth industry - especially "The Daemons" - but this is the only one to make it into the Top 20.

144 Even Freema Agyeman is too burly to wear it without ripping the seams - X4.5, "The Poison Sky".

145 The scene where they dump the hand-Doctor in Norway was to have him being given a bit of magic coral to grow his own TARDIS from, with Donna-as-Doctor suggesting a clever way of doing it in under a century that neither of the suited Doctors could have thought of. But evidently, this scene was long and annoying enough already.

146 A famous cut scene carries this to ludicrous extremes, with Smith dressing and humming "Robert de Niro's Waiting" by Bananarama and "Gimme Gimme Gimme" by Abba. With the Master's similar taste in music revealed a few episodes later, it seems that a lot of hen-parties occurred on Gallifrey.

147 They're obviously attempting to evoke a Northern-style Working Men's Club of the type still in business then, recreated on telly in the series *The Wheeltappers' and Shunters' Social Club*. This probably explains why such ancient and dreadful acts were permitted to reach our screens via *Doctor Who*, but the signs are that Letts hasn't actually been to one, so the whole style is of a more sedate and less smoke-fillled Variety theatre of the kind that television killed off. If they'd been watching this dire comic on telly, the 'streaker' joke would have dated this to six months either side of the story's first broadcast. But in the club circuit, gags such as this have a half-life of decades - trust us on this, they're still doing one-liners about punks with safety pins in their ears and unbroadcastably racist material, with a best-before date some time before Decimal money.

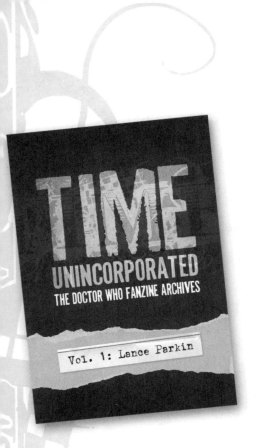

TIME
UNINCORPORATED
THE DOCTOR WHO FANZINE ARCHIVES

Vol. 1: Lance Parkin

Out Now... In *Time, Unincorporated*, the best commentary from a range of *Doctor Who* fanzines are collected and here made available to a wider audience. In spirit, this series picks up the torch from Virgin's *Licence Denied* collection (1997), concentrating some of the most insightful and strange writings on *Who* into a single source.

Volume 1 collects 15 years of *Doctor Who*-related essays and articles by novelist Lance Parkin. The cornerstone of this edition is a year-by-year analysis of *Doctor Who* that Parkin wrote for the series' 40th Anniversary, as well as a myriad of Parkin's articles and columns from the fanzines *Enlightenment* and *Matrix*. Also included: Parkin's original pitch for the celebrated Doctor Who novel *The Infinity Doctors* (1998), his extensive advice on the art of writing and more.

ISBN: 978-1935234012
Retail Price: $19.95

mad norwegian press

www.madnorwegian.com
1150 46th St, Des Moines, IA 50311 . madnorwegian@gmail.com

TIME UNINCORPORATED

THE DOCTOR WHO FANZINE ARCHIVES

Vol. 2: Classic Series CORNUCOPIA

Coming in 2009...

Time, Unincorporated 2 collects a broad cross-section of *Doctor Who* fanzine material, from such publications as *Enlightenment*, *Tides of Time*, *Burnt Toast*, *Fazed*, *The Whostorian*, *Dark Circus* and more. The authors of these pieces include such venerable *Doctor Who* writers as Paul Magrs and Matt Jones.

Also included are a number of essays on classic *Doctor Who* that were written exclusively for this volume, from such writers as Kate Orman, Simon Guerrier, Dave Owen and more.

All told, *Time, Unincorporated 2* delivers some of the most varied fanzine writings of years past - with added benefit from several original pieces written today.

ISBN: 978-1935234029
Retail Price: $19.95

mad norwegian press

www.madnorwegian.com
1150 46th St, Des Moines, IA 50311 . madnorwegian@gmail.com

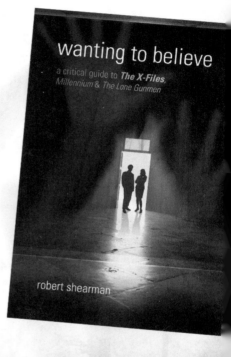

MORE DIGRESSIONS
PETER DAVID

A new collection of 'But I Digress' columns

FOREWORD BY HARLAN ELLISON

Out Now... The first compilation of its kind in 15 years, *More Digressions* collects about 100 essays from Peter David's long-running *But I Digress* column (as published in the pages of *Comics Buyer's Guide*). For this entirely new collection, David has personally selected *But I Digress* pieces written from 2001 to the present day, and also included many personal reflections and historical notes.

Topics covered in this collection include Peter's thoughts on comic book movies, his pleasing and sometimes less-than pleasing interactions with fandom, his take on the business aspects of the comic-book industry, his anecdotes about getting married and having children, his advocacy of free speech and much more.

More Digressions features a new foreword by the legendary Harlan Ellison, and sports a cover by J.K. Woodward (*Fallen Angel*) that highlights some of David's comic-book creations.

ISBN: 978-1935234005
Retail Price: $24.95

www.madnorwegian.com

mad norwegian press

1150 46th St
Des Moines, IA 50311
madnorwegian@gmail.com

who made all this ?

2008 saw the fortieth anniversary of the first time that **Tat Wood** proclaimed that *Doctor Who* wasn't as good as it used to be. During the period covered by this book, he was ferried between two of the more peculiar post-War New Towns (note caps) and got what seems now to be a freakish education.

This explains many things: his extraordinary recall of the era's ephemera - why else would correcting this book take three times longer than writing it? - his impatience with the slovenly nostaliga-shows that blur it all into Raleigh Choppers, Spangles and power cuts; his belief that *Gravity's Rainbow* is the most realistic book ever written (despite initial perplexity that Zippy, Bungle and George weren't in it) and his belief that the previous line was funny.

He has read an awful lot of books, including a lot of awful books. He stays up late to watch the kinds of television nobody else bothers with, but is often working when the things everyone else likes are on. Let's not get started on his record collection. And yes, he really *is* like that in real life...

Favourite story in this book: "Carnival of Monsters". Least favourite: "The Monster of Peladon".

Mad Norwegian Press

Publisher / Series Editor
Lars Pearson

Senior Editor / Design Manager
Christa Dickson

Cover Art
Steve Johnson

Senior Editor (AT3)
Lance Parkin

Associate Editors
For AT3: Robert Smith?, Michael D. Thomas;
For MNP: Joshua Wilson

Technical Support
Marc Eby

The publisher wishes to thank... Tat Wood and Lawrence Miles, for their tenacity in opening up new avenues of thought on *Doctor Who*; Daniel O'Mahony; Bill Albert, Jeremy Bement and everyone at the Iowa *Doctor Who* fan club; Brandon and Kelli Griffis; Jim Boyd; Lynne Thomas; and that nice lady who sends me newspaper articles.

1150 46th Street
Des Moines, Iowa 50311
madnorwegian@gmail.com
www.madnorwegian.com